REX STOUT

SEVEN COMPLETE NERO WOLFE NOVELS

About the Author

Rex Stout is a well-known mystery writer, most famous for his stories about Nero Wolfe and his able assistant, Archie Goodwin. Born in 1886 in Noblesville, Indiana, Stout was one of nine children and an avid reader—by the age of ten he had read more than a thousand books and was the Kansas State spelling champion.

In his adult years Stout held a long series of odd jobs, including a time in the navy during which he served as a yeoman on Theodore Roosevelt's yacht. He wrote his first book, *How Like a God,* in 1929, but his first mystery, *Fer-de-Lance,* was not published until 1934, after serialization in the *Saturday Evening Post.*

Stout was politically active and served as chairman of the Writers' War Board during World War II. Like his creation Nero Wolfe, Stout was a dedicated gardener and grew prize-winning strawberries as well as vegetables in his garden, often spending a large part of his day there. He died in 1975 at age eighty-nine.

REX STOUT

SEVEN COMPLETE NERO WOLFE NOVELS

The Silent Speaker

Might as Well Be Dead

If Death Ever Slept

3 at Wolfe's Door

Gambit

Please Pass the Guilt

A Family Affair

Avenel Books · New York

This Omnibus edition was previously published
in separate volumes under the titles:
The Silent Speaker copyright MCMXLVI by Rex Stout
Might as Well Be Dead copyright © MCMLVI by Rex Stout
If Death Ever Slept copyright © MCMLVII by Rex Stout
3 at Wolfe's Door copyright © MCMLX by Rex Stout
Gambit copyright © MCMLXII by Rex Stout
Please Pass the Guilt copyright © MCMLXXIII by Rex Stout
A Family Affair copyright © MCMLXXV by Rex Stout

This 1983 edition is published by Avenel Books,
distributed by Crown Publishers, Inc., by arrangement with
The Viking Press (Viking Penguin, Inc.)

Manufactured in the United States of America

Library of Congress Cataloging in Publication Data

Stout, Rex, 1886–1975.
  Rex Stout Seven complete Nero Wolfe novels.

  Contents: Three at Wolfe's door—Might as well
be dead—Silent speaker—[etc.]
  1. Detective and mystery stories, American.
I. Title.   II. Title: Seven complete Nero Wolfe
novels.   III. Title: 7 complete Nero Wolfe novels.
PS3537.T733A6   1983   813'.52   83-2808
ISBN 0-517-412497

h g f e d c b a

CONTENTS

The Silent Speaker

The characters in this book are imaginary, and resemblances to them, if any, borne by actual persons or corpses are accidental and in some cases deplorable.

1

SEATED in his giant's chair behind his desk in his office, leaning back with his eyes half closed, Nero Wolfe muttered at me:

"It is an interesting fact that the members of the National Industrial Association who were at that dinner last evening represent, in the aggregate, assets of something like thirty billion dollars."

I slid the checkbook into place on top of the stack, closed the door of the safe, twirled the knob, and yawned on the way back to my desk.

"Yes, sir," I agreed with him. "It is also an interesting fact that the prehistoric Mound Builders left more traces of their work in Ohio than in any other state. In my boyhood days—"

"Shut up," Wolfe muttered.

I let it pass without any feeling of resentment, first because it was going on midnight and I was sleepy, and second because it was conceivable that there might be some connection between his interesting fact and our previous conversation, and that was not true of mine. We had been discussing the bank balance, the reserve against taxes, expectations as to bills and burdens, one of which was my salary, and related matters. The exchequer had not swung for the third strike, but neither had it knocked the ball out of the park.

After I had yawned three more times Wolfe spoke suddenly and decisively.

"Archie. Your notebook. Here are directions for tomorrow."

In two minutes he had me wide awake. When he had finished and I went upstairs to bed, the program for the morning was so active in my head that I tossed and turned for a full thirty seconds before sleep came.

2

THAT was a Wednesday toward the end of the warmest March in the history of New York. Thursday it was more of the same, and I didn't even take a topcoat when I left the house on West Thirty-fifth Street and went to the garage for the car. I was fully armed, prepared for all contingencies. In my wallet was a supply of engraved cards reading:

```
                           ARCHIE GOODWIN

              With Nero Wolfe
              922 West 35th Street              PRoctor 5-5000
```

And in the breast pocket of my coat, along with the routine cargo, was a special item just manufactured by me on the typewriter. It was on a printed Memo form, and, after stating that it was FOR Nero Wolfe and FROM Archie Goodwin, it went on:

> Okay from Inspector Cramer for inspection of the room at
> the Waldorf. Will report later by phone.

At the right of the typing, scribbled in ink, also my work and worthy of admiration, were the initials LTC.

Since I had got an early start and the office of the Homicide Squad on Twentieth Street was less than a mile downtown, it was only a little after nine-thirty when I was admitted to an inside room and took a chair at the end of a crummy old desk. The man in the swivel chair, frowning at papers, had a big round red face, half-hidden gray eyes, and delicate little ears that stayed close to his skull. As I sat down he transferred the frown to me and grunted:

"I'm busy as hell." His eyes focused three inches below my chin. "What do you think it is, Easter?"

"I know of no law," I said stiffly, "against a man's buying a new shirt and tie. Anyhow, I'm in disguise as a detective. Sure you're busy, and I won't waste your time. I want to ask a favor, a big favor. Not for me, I'm quite aware that if I were trapped in a burning building you would yell for gasoline to toss on the flames, but on behalf of Nero Wolfe. He wants permission for me to inspect that room at the Waldorf where Cheney Boone was murdered Tuesday evening. Also maybe to take pictures."

Inspector Cramer stared at me, not at my new tie. "For God's sake," he said finally in bitter disgust. "As if this case wasn't enough of a mess already. All it needed to make it a carnival was Nero Wolfe, and by God here he is." He worked his jaw, regarding me sourly. "Who's your client?"

I shook my head. "I have no information about any client. As far as I know it's just Mr. Wolfe's scientific curiosity. He's interested in crime—"

"You heard me, who's your client?"

"No, sir," I said regretfully. "Rip me open, remove my heart for the laboratory, and you'll find inscribed on it—"

"Beat it," he grated, and dug into his papers.

I stood up. "Certainly, Inspector, I know you're busy. But Mr. Wolfe would greatly appreciate it if you'll give me permission to inspect—"

"Nuts." He didn't look up. "You don't need any permission to inspect and you know damn well you don't. We're all through up there and it's public premises. If what you're after is authority, it's the first time Wolfe ever bothered to ask for authority to do anything he wanted to do, and if I had time I'd try to figure out what the catch is, but I'm too busy. Beat it."

"Gosh," I said in a discouraged tone, starting for the door. "Suspicious. Always suspicious. What a way to live."

3

IN appearance, dress, and manner, Johnny Darst was about as far as you could get from the average idea of a hotel dick. He might have been taken for a vice-president of a trust company or a golf club steward. In a little room, more a cubbyhole than a room in size, he stood watching me dead-pan while I looked over the topography, the angles, and the furniture, which consisted of a small table, a mirror, and a few chairs. Since Johnny was not a sap I didn't even try to give him the impression that I was doing something abstruse.

"What are you really after?" he asked gently.

"Nothing whatever," I told him. "I work for Nero Wolfe just as you work for the Waldorf, and he sent me here to take a look and here I am. The carpet's been changed?"

He nodded. "There was a little blood, not much, and the cops took some things."

"According to the paper there are four of these rooms, two on each side of the stage."

He nodded again. "Used as dressing rooms and resting rooms for performers. Not that you could call Cheney Boone a performer. He wanted a place to look over his speech and they sent him in here to be alone. The Grand Ballroom of the Waldorf is the best equipped—"

"Sure," I said warmly. "You bet it is. They ought to pay you extra. Well, I'm a thousand times obliged."

"Got all you want?"

"Yep, I guess I've solved it."

"I could show you the exact spot where he was going to stand to deliver his speech if he had still been alive."

"Thanks a lot, but if I find I need that I'll come back."

He went with me down in the elevator and to the entrance, both of us understanding that the only private detectives hotels enjoy having around are the ones they hire. At the door he asked casually:

"Who's Wolfe working for?"

"There is never," I told him, "any question about that. He is working first, last, and all the time for Wolfe. Come to think of it, so am I. Boy, am I loyal."

4

IT was a quarter to eleven when I parked the car in Foley Square, entered the United States Court House, and took the elevator.

There were a dozen or more FBI men with whom Wolfe and I had had dealings during the war, when he was doing chores for the government and I was in G-2. It had been decided that for the present purpose G. G. Spero, being approximately three per cent less tightlipped than the others, was the man, so it was to him I sent my card. In no time at all a clean efficient girl took me to a clean efficient room, and a clean efficient face, belonging to G. G. Spero of the FBI, was confronting me. We chinned a couple of minutes and then he asked heartily:

"Well, Major, what can we do for you?"

"Two little things," I replied. First, quit calling me Major. I'm out of uniform, and besides, it stimulates my inferiority complex because I should have been a colonel. Second is a request from Nero Wolfe, sort of confidential. Of course he could have sent me to the Chief, or phoned him, but he didn't want to bother him about it. It's a little question about the Boone murder case. We've been told that the FBI is mixing in, and of course you don't ordinarily touch a local murder. Mr. Wolfe would like to know if there is something about the FBI angle that would make it undesirable for a private detective to take any interest."

Spero was still trying to look cordial, but training and habit were too much for him. He started to drum on the desk, realized what he was doing, and jerked his hand away. FBI men do not drum on desks.

"The Boone case," he said.

"That's right. The Cheney Boone case."

"Yes, certainly. Putting aside, for the moment, the FBI angle, what would Mr. Wolfe's angle be?"

He went at me and kept after me from forty different directions. I left half an hour later with what I had expected to leave with, nothing. The reliance on his three per cent under par in lip tightness was not for the sake of what he might tell me, but what he might tell about me.

5

THE last number on the program proved to be the most complicated, chiefly because I was dealing with total strangers. I didn't know a soul connected with the National Industrial Association, and so had to start from scratch. The whole atmosphere, from the moment I entered the offices on the thirtieth floor of a building on Forty-first Street, made a bad impression on me. The reception room was too big, they had spent too much money on rugs, upholstery had been carried to extremes, and the girl at the desk, though not a bad specimen from the standpoint of design, had been connected up with a tube running from a refrigerating unit. She was so obviously congealed for good that there wasn't the slightest temptation to start thawing her out. With females between twenty and thirty, meeting a certain standard in contour and coloring, I do not believe in being distant, but I was with that one as I handed her a card and said I wanted to see Hattie Harding.

The hurdles I had to make, you might have thought Hattie Harding was the goddess of a temple and this was it, instead of merely the Assistant Director of Public Relations for the NIA, but I finally made the last jump and was taken in to her. Even she had space, rugs, and upholstery. Personally, she had quality, but the kind that arouses one or two of my most dangerous instincts, and I do not mean what some may think I mean. She was somewhere between twenty-six and forty-eight, tall, well put together, well dressed, and had skeptical, competent dark eyes which informed you with the first glance that they knew everything in the world.

"This is a pleasure," she declared, giving me a firm and not cold handshake. "To meet *the* Archie Goodwin, coming direct from *the* Nero Wolfe. Really a great pleasure. At least, I suppose you do? Come direct, I mean?"

I concealed my feelings. "On a beeline, Miss Harding. As the bee from the flower."

She laughed competently. "What! Not to the flower?"

I laughed back. We were chums. "I guess that's nearer the truth, at that, because I admit I've come to get a load of nectar. For Nero Wolfe. He thinks he needs a list of the members of the NIA who were at that dinner at the Waldorf Tuesday evening, and sent me here to get it. He has a copy of the printed list, but he needs to know who is on it, that didn't come and who came that isn't on it. What do you think of my syntax?"

She didn't answer that, and she was through laughing. She asked, not as chum to chum, "Why don't we sit down?"

She moved toward a couple of chairs near a window, but I pretended not to notice and marched across to one for visitors at the end of her desk, so she would have to take her desk chair. The Memo from me to Wolfe, initialed for Inspector Cramer by me, was now in the side pocket of my coat, destined to be left on the floor of Miss Harding's office, and with the corner of her desk between us the operation would be simple.

"This is very interesting," she declared. "What does Mr. Wolfe want the list for?"

"Being honest," I smiled at her, "I can but tell you an honest lie. He wants to ask them for their autographs."

"I'm honest too," she smiled back. "Look, Mr. Goodwin. You understand of course that this affair is in the highest degree inconvenient for my employers. Our guest of the evening, our main speaker, the Director of the Bureau of Price Regulation, murdered right there just as the dinner was starting. I am in a perfectly terrible spot. Even if for the past ten years this office has done the best public relations job on record, which I am not claiming for it, all its efforts may have been destroyed by what happened there in ten seconds. There is no —"

"How do you know it happpened in ten seconds?"

She blinked at me. "Why — it must — the way —"

"Not proven," I said conversationally. "He was hit four times on the head with the monkey wrench. Of course the blows could all have been struck within ten seconds. Or the murderer could have hit him once and knocked him unconscious, rested a while and then hit him again, rested some more and hit him the third —"

"What are you doing?" she snapped. "Just trying to see how objectionable you can be?"

"No. I'm demonstrating what a murder investigation is like. If you made that remark to the police, that it happened in ten seconds, you'd never hear the last of it. With me it goes in one ear and out the other, and anyhow I'm not interested, since I'm here only to get what Mr. Wolfe sent me for, and we'd greatly appreciate it if you would give us that list."

I was all set for quite a speech, but stopped on seeing her put both hands to her face, and I was thinking my lord she's going to weep with despair at the untimely end of public relations, but all she did was press the heels of her palms against her eyes and keep them there. It was the perfect moment to drop the Memo on the rug, so I did.

She kept her hands pressed to her eyes long enough for me to drop a whole flock of memos, but when she finally removed them the eyes still looked competent.

"I'm sorry," she said, "but I haven't slept for two nights and I'm a wreck. I'll have to ask you to go. There's to be another conference in Mr. Erskine's office about this awful business, it starts in ten minutes and I'll have to do myself for it, and anyway you know perfectly well I couldn't give you that list without approval from higher up, and besides if Mr. Wolfe is as intimate with the police as people say, why can't he get it from them? Talk about your syntax, look at the way I'm talking. Only one thing you might tell me, I sincerely hope you will, who has engaged Mr. Wolfe to work on this?"

I shook my head and got upright. "I'm in the same fix you are, Miss Harding. I can't do anything important, like answering a plain simple question, without approval from higher up. How about a bargain? I'll ask Mr. Wolfe if I may answer your question, and you ask Mr. Erskine if you may give me the list. Good luck at your conference."

We shook hands, and I crossed the rugs to the door without lingering, not caring to have her find the Memo in time to pick it up and hand it to me.

The midtown midday traffic being what it was, the short trip to West Thirty-fifth Street was a crawl all the way. I parked in front of the old stone house, owned by Nero Wolfe, that had been my home for over ten years, mounted the stoop, and tried to get myself in with my key, but found that the bolt was in and had to ring the bell. Fritz Brenner, cook, housekeeper, and groom of the chambers, came and opened up, and, informing him that the chances looked good for getting paid Saturday, I went down the hall to the office. Wolfe was seated behind his desk, reading a book. That was the only spot where he was ever really comfortable. There were other chairs in the house that had been made to order, for width and depth, with a guaranty for up to five hundred pounds — one in his room, one in the kitchen, one in the dining room, one in the plant rooms on the roof where the orchids were kept, and one there in the office, over by the two-foot globe and the bookshelves — but it was the one at his desk that nearly always got it, night and day.

As usual, he didn't lift an eye when I entered. Also as usual, I paid no attention to whether he was paying attention.

"The hooks are baited," I told him. "Probably at this very moment the radio stations are announcing that Nero Wolfe, the greatest living private detective when he feels like working, which isn't often, is wrapping up the Boone case. Shall I turn it on?"

He finished a paragraph, dog-eared a page, and put the book down. "No," he said. "It's time for lunch." He eyed me. "You must have been uncommonly transparent. Mr. Cramer has phoned. Mr. Travis of the FBI has phoned. Mr. Rohde of the Waldorf has phoned. It seemed likely that one or more of them would be coming here, so I had Fritz bolt the door."

That was all for the moment, or rather for the hour or more, since Fritz entered to announce lunch, which that day happened to consist of corn cakes with breaded fresh pork tenderloin, followed by corn cakes with a hot sauce of tomatoes and cheese, followed by corn cakes with honey. Fritz's timing with corn cakes was superb. At the precise instant, for example, that one of us finished with his eleventh, here came the twelfth straight from the griddle, and so on.

6

I called it Operation Payroll. That name for the preliminary project, the horning-in campaign, was not, I admit, strictly accurate. In addition to the salaries of Fritz Brenner, Charley the cleaning man, Theodore Horstmann the orchid tender, and me, the treasury had to provide for other items too numerous to mention. But on the principle of putting first things first, I called it Operation Payroll.

It was Friday morning before we caught the fish we were after. All that happened Thursday afternoon was a couple of unannounced visits, one from Cramer and one from G. G. Spero, and Wolfe had told me not to let them in, so they went away without crossing the sill. To show how sure I felt that the fish would sooner or later bite, I took the trouble Thursday afternoon and evening to get up a typed report of the Boone case as I knew it, from newspaper accounts and a talk I had had Wednesday with Sergeant Purley Stebbins. I've just read that report over again and decided not to copy it all down here but only hit the high spots.

Cheney Boone, Director of the government's Bureau of Price Regulation, had been invited to make the main speech at a dinner of the National Industrial Association on Tuesday evening at the Grand Ballroom of the Waldorf-Astoria. He had arrived at ten minutes to seven, before the fourteen hundred guests had gone to their tables, while everyone was still milling around drinking and talking. Taken to the reception room reserved for guests of honor, which as usual was filled with over a hundred people, most of whom weren't supposed to be there, Boone, after drinking a cocktail and undergoing a quantity of greetings and introductions, had asked for a private spot where he could look over his speech, and had been taken to a small room just off the stage. His wife, who had come with him to the dinner, had stayed in the reception room. His niece, Nina Boone, had gone along to the private spot to help with the speech if required, but he had almost immediately sent her back to the reception room to get herself another cocktail and she had remained there.

Shortly after Boone and his niece had departed for the murder room, as the papers called it, Phoebe Gunther had showed up. Miss Gunther was Boone's confidential secretary, and she had with her two can openers, two monkey wrenches, two shirts (men's), two fountain pens, and a baby carriage. These were to be used as exhibits by Boone for illustrating points in his speech, and Miss Gunther wanted to get them to him at once, so she was escorted to the murder room, the escort, a member of the NIA, wheeling the baby carriage, which contained the other items, to the astonished amusement of the multitude as they passed through. Miss Gunther remained with Boone only a couple of minutes, delivering the exhibits, and then returned to the reception room for a cocktail. She reported that Boone had said he wanted to be alone.

At seven-thirty everybody in the reception room was herded out to the ballroom, to find their places on the dais and at the tables, where the fourteen hundred were settling down and the waiters were ready to hurl themselves into the fray. About seven forty-five Mr. Alger Kates arrived. He was from the Research Department of the BPR, and he had some last-minute statistics which were to be used in Boone's speech. He came to the dais looking for Boone, and Mr. Frank Thomas Erskine, the President of NIA, had told a waiter to show him where Boone was. The waiter had led him through the door to backstage and pointed to the door of the murder room.

Alger Kates had discovered the body. It was on the floor, the head battered with one of the monkey wrenches, which was lying near by. The implication of what Kates did next had been hinted at in some newspapers, and openly stated in others; namely, that no BPR man would trust any NIA man in connection with anything whatever, including murder. Anyhow, instead of returning to the ballroom and the dais to impart the news, Kates had looked around backstage until he found a phone, called the hotel manager, and told him to come at once and bring all the policemen he could find.

By Thursday evening, forty-eight hours after the event, something like a thousand other details had been accumulated, as for instance that nothing but smudges were found on the handle of the monkey wrench, no identifiable prints, and so forth and so forth, but that was the main picture as it had been painted when I was typing my report.

7

FRIDAY we got the bite. Since Wolfe spends every morning from nine to eleven up in the plant rooms, I was in the office alone when the call came. The call took the regular routine in this Land of the Secretary.

"Miss Harding calling Mr. Wolfe. Put Mr. Wolfe on, please."

If I put it all down it would take half a page to get me, not Mr. Wolfe, just me, connected with Miss Harding. Anyhow I made it, and got the idea across that Wolfe was engaged with orchids and I would have to do. She wanted to know how soon Wolfe could get up there to see Mr. Erskine, and I explained that he seldom left the house for any purpose whatever, and never merely on business.

"I know that!" she snapped. She must have missed another night's sleep. "But this is *Mr. Erskine!*"

I knew we had him now, so I snooted her. "To you," I agreed, "he is all of that. To Mr. Wolfe he is nothing but a pest. Mr. Wolfe hates to work, even at home."

Instructed to hold the wire, I did so, for about ten minutes. Finally her voice came again:

"Mr. Goodwin?"

"Still here. Older and wiser, but still here."

"Mr. Erskine will be at Mr. Wolfe's office at four-thirty this afternoon."

I was getting exasperated. "Listen, Public Relations," I demanded, "why don't you simplify it by connecting me with this Erskine? If he comes at four-thirty he'll wait an hour and a half. Mr. Wolfe's hours with orchids are from nine to eleven in the morning and from four to six in the afternoon, and nothing short of murder—I mean nothing—has ever changed it or ever will."

"That's ridiculous!"

"Sure it is. So is this ring-around-the-rosy method for a man communicating with another man, but I stand for it."

"Hold the wire."

I never got connected with Erskine, that was too much to expect, but in spite of everything we finally completed an arrangement, fighting our way through the obstacles, so that when Wolfe came downstairs at eleven o'clock I was able to announce to him:

"Mr. Frank Thomas Erskine, President of the National Industrial Association, with outriders, will be here at ten minutes past three."

"Satisfactory, Archie," he muttered.

Frankly, I wish I could make my heart quit doing an extra thump when Wolfe says satisfactory, Archie. It's childish.

8

WHEN the doorbell rang that afternoon right on the dot at three-ten and I left my chair to answer it, I remarked to Wolfe:

"These people are apt to be the kind that you often walk out on or, even worse, tell me to eject. It may be necessary to control yourself. Remember the payroll. There is much at stake. Remember Fritz, Theodore, Charley, and me."

He didn't even grunt.

The catch was above expectations, for in the delegation of four we got not one Erskine but two. Father and son. Father was maybe sixty and struck me as not imposing. He was tall and bony and narrow, wearing a dark blue ready-made that didn't fit, and didn't have false teeth but talked as if he had. He handled the introductions, first himself and then the others. Son was named Edward Frank and addressed as Ed. The other two, certified as members of the NIA Executive Committee, were Mr. Breslow and Mr. Winterhoff. Breslow looked as if he had been born flushed with anger and would die, when the time came, in character. If it had not been beneath the dignity of a member of the NIA Executive Committee, Winterhoff could have snagged a fee posing as a Man of Distinction for a whiskey ad. He even had the little gray mustache.

As for Son, not yet Ed to me, who was about my age, I reserved judgment because he apparently had a hangover and that is no time to file a man away. Unquestionably he had a headache. His suit had cost at least three times as much as Father's.

When I had got them distributed on chairs, with Father on the red leather number near the end of Wolfe's desk, at his elbow a small table just the right size for resting a checkbook on while writing in it, Father spoke:

"This may be time wasted for us, Mr. Wolfe. It seemed impossible to get any satisfactory information on the telephone. Have you been engaged by anyone to investigate this matter?"

Wolfe lifted a brow a sixteenth of an inch. "What matter, Mr. Erskine?"

"Uh—this—the death of Cheney Boone."

Wolfe considered. "Let me put it this way. I have agreed to nothing and accepted no fee. I am committed to no interest."

"In a case of murder," Breslow sputtered angrily, "there is only one interest, the interest of justice."

"Oh, for God's sake," son Ed growled.

Father's eyes moved. "If necessary," he said emphatically, "the rest of you can leave and I'll do this alone." He returned to Wolfe. "What opinion have you formed about it?"

"Opinions, from experts, cost money."

"We'll pay you for it."

"A reasonable amount," Winterhoff put in. His voice was heavy and flat. He couldn't have been cast as a Man of Distinction with a sound-track.

"It wouldn't be worth even that," Wolfe said, "unless it were expert, and it wouldn't be expert unless I did some work. I haven't decided whether I shall go that far. I don't like to work."

"Who has consulted you?" Father wanted to know.

"Now sir, really." Wolfe wiggled a finger at him. "It is indiscreet of you to ask, and I would be a blatherskite to answer. Did you come here with the notion of hiring me?"

"Well—" Erskine hesitated. "That has been discussed as a possibility."

"For you gentlemen as individuals, or on behalf of the National Industrial Association?"

"It was discussed as an Association matter."

Wolfe shook his head. "I would advise strongly against it. You might be wasting your money."

"Why? Aren't you a good investigator?"

"I am the best. But the situation is obvious. What you are concerned about is the reputation and standing of your Association. In the public mind the trial has already been held and the verdict rendered. Everyone knows that your Association was bitterly hostile to the Bureau of Price Regulation, to Mr. Boone, and to his policies. Nine people out of ten are confident that they know who murdered Mr. Boone. It was the National Industrial Association." Wolfe's eyes came to me. "Archie. What was it the man at the bank said?"

"Oh, just that gag that's going around. That NIA stands for Not Innocent Atall."

"But that's preposterous!"

"Certainly," Wolfe agreed, "but there it is. The NIA has been convicted and sentence has been pronounced. The only possible way of getting that verdict reversed would be to find the murderer and convict him. Even if it turned out that the murderer was a member of the NIA, the result would be the same; the interest and the odium would be transferred to the individual, if not altogether, at least to a great extent, and nothing else would transfer any of it."

They looked at one another. Winterhoff nodded glooomily and Breslow kept his lips compressed so as not to explode. Ed Erskine glared at Wolfe as if that was where his headache had come from.

"You say," Father told Wolfe, "that the public has convicted the NIA. But so have the police. So has the FBI. They are acting exactly like the Gestapo. The members of such an old and respectable organization as the NIA might be supposed to have some rights and privileges. Do you know what the police are doing? In addition to everything else, do you know that they are actually communicating with the police in every city in the United States? Asking them to get a signed statement from local citizens who were in New York at that dinner and have returned home?"

"Indeed," Wolfe said politely. "But I imagine the local police will furnish paper and ink."

"What?" Father stared at him.

"What the hell has that got to do with it?" Son wanted to know.

Wolfe skipped it and observed, "The deuce of it is that the probability that the police will catch the murderer seems somewhat thin. Not having studied the case thoroughly, I can't qualify as an expert on it, but I must say it looks doubtful. Three days and nights have passed. That's why I advise against your hiring me. I admit it would be worth almost any amount to your Association to have the murderer exposed, even if he proved to be one of you four gentlemen, but I would tackle the job, if at all, only with the greatest reluctance. I'm sorry you had your trip down here for nothing. —Archie?"

The implication being that I should show them what good manners we had by taking them to the front door, I stood up. They didn't. Instead they exchanged glances.

Winterhoff said to Erskine, "I would go ahead, Frank."

Breslow demanded, "What else can we do?"

Ed growled, "Oh, God, I wish he was alive again. That was better than this."

I sat down.

Erskine said, "We are businessmen, Mr. Wolfe. We understand that you can't guarantee anything. But if we persuade you to undertake this matter, exactly what would you engage to do?"

It took them nearly ten minutes to persuade him, and they all looked relieved, even Ed, when he finally gave in. It was more or less understood that the clinching argument was Breslow's, that they must not let justice down. Unfortunately, since the NIA had a voucher system, the check-writing table did not get used. As a substitute I typed a letter, dictated by Wolfe, and Erskine signed it. The retainer was to be ten thousand dollars, and the ultimate charge, including expenses, was left open. They certainly were on the ropes.

"Now," Erskine said, handing me back my fountain pen, "I suppose we had better tell you all we know about it."

Wolfe shook his head, "Not right now. I have to get my mind adjusted to this confounded mess. It would be better for you to return this evening, say at nine o'clock."

They all protested. Winterhoff said he had an appointment he couldn't break.

"As you please, sir. If it is more important than this. We must get to work without delay." Wolfe turned to me: "Archie, your notebook. A telegram. 'You are invited to join in a discussion of the Boone murder at the office of Nero Wolfe at nine o'clock this evening Friday March twenty-ninth.' Sign it with my name. Send it at once to Mr. Cramer, Mr. Spero, Mr. Kates, Miss Gunther, Mrs. Boone, Miss Nina Boone, Mr. Rohde, and perhaps to others, we'll see later. —Will you gentlemen be here?"

"My God," Ed grumbled, "with that mob, why don't you hold it in the Grand Ballroom at the Waldorf?"

"It seems to me," Erskine said in a grieved tone, "that this is a mistake. The first principle —"

"I," Wolfe said, in a tone used by NIA men only to people whose names were never on the letterhead, "am handling the investigation."

I started banging the typewriter, and since the telegrams were urgent, and since Wolfe took long walks only in emergencies, Fritz was sent for to escort them to the door. All I was typing was the text of the telegram and a list of the names and addresses, because the phone was the quickest way to send them. Some of the addresses were a problem. Wolfe was leaning back in his chair with his eyes closed, not to be bothered about trivialities, so I called Lon Cohen on the city desk at the Gazette and got the addresses from him. He knew everything. They had come up from Washington for the big speech that was never delivered and had not gone back. Mrs. Boone and the niece were at the Waldorf, Alger Kates was staying with friends on Eleventh Street, and Phoebe Gunther, who had been Boone's confidential secretary, had a room-and-bath on East Fifty-fifth Street.

When I had that job done I asked Wolfe who else he wanted to invite. He said no one. I stood up and stretched, and looked at him.

"I presume," I observed, "that the rest is merely routine collection of evidence. Ed Erskine has calluses on his hands. Will that help?"

"Confound it." He sighed clear down. "I was going to finish that book this evening. Now this infernal mishmash."

He heaved the bulk forward and rang for beer.

I, standing at the cabinet filing the germination records that Theodore had brought down from the plant rooms, was compelled to admit that he had earned my admiration. Not for his conception of the idea of digging up a paying customer; that was merely following precedent in times of drought. Not for the method he had adopted for the digging; I could have thought that up myself. Not for the execution, his handling of the NIA delegation; that was an obvious variation of the old hard-to-get finesse. Not for the gall of those telegrams; admiring Wolfe's gall would be like admiring ice at the North Pole or green leaves in a tropical jungle. No. What I admired was his common sense. He wanted to get a look at those people. What do you do when you want to get a look at a man? You get your hat and go where he is. But what if the idea of getting your hat and going outdoors is abhorrent to you? You ask the man to come where you are. What makes you think he'll come? That was where the common sense entered. Take Inspector Cramer. Why would he, the head of the Homicide Squad, come? Because he didn't know how long Wolfe had been on the case or how deep he was in it, and therefore he couldn't afford to stay away.

At four sharp Wolfe had downed the last of his beer and taken the elevator up to the plant rooms. I finished the filing and gathered up miscellaneous loose ends around the office, expecting to be otherwise engaged for at least a day or two, and then settled down at my desk with a stack of newspaper clippings to make sure I hadn't missed anything important in my typed summary of the Boone situation. I was deep in that when the doorbell rang, and I went to the front and opened up, and found confronting me a vacuum cleaner salesman. Or anyhow he should have been. He had that bright, friendly, uninhibited look. But some of the details didn't fit, as for example his clothes, which were the kind I would begin buying when my rich uncle died.

"Hello!" he said cheerfully. "I'll bet you're Archie Goodwin. You came to see Miss Harding yesterday. She told me about you. Aren't you Archie Goodwin?"

"Yep," I said. It was the easiest way out. If I had said no or tried to evade he would have cornered me sooner or later.

"I thought so." He was gratified. "May I come in? I'd like to see Mr. Wolfe. I'm Don O'Neill, but of course that doesn't mean anything to you. I'm president of O'Neill and Warder, Incorporated, and a member of that godforsaken conglomeration of antiques, the NIA. I was Chairman of the Dinner Committee for that affair we had at the Waldorf the other evening. I guess I'll never live that one down. Chairman of a Dinner Committee, and let the main speaker get murdered!"

Of course my reaction was that I had got along fairly well for something like thirty years without knowing Don O'Neill and saw no reason for a change in policy, but my personal feelings could not be permitted to dominate. So I let him in and steered him to the office and into a chair before I even explained that he would have to wait half an hour because Wolfe was engaged. For a brief moment he seemed irritated, but he realized instantly that that was no way to sell vacuum cleaners and said sure, that was all right, he didn't mind waiting.

He was delighted with the office and got up and went around looking. Books—what a selection! The big globe was marvelous, just what he had always wanted and never took the trouble to get one, now he would . . .

Wolfe entered, saw him, and gave me a dirty look. It was true that I was supposed to inform him in advance of any waiting caller and never let him come in cold like that, but it was ten to one that if I had told him about O'Neill he would have refused to see him and had me invite him for the nine o'clock party, and I saw no necessity for another three-hour rest for Wolfe's brains. He was so sore that he pretended he didn't believe in shaking hands, acknowledged the introduction with a nod that wouldn't have spilled a drop if he had had a jar of water on his head, sat down and regarded the visitor unsympathetically, and asked curtly:

"Well, sir?"

O'Neill wasn't at all taken aback. He said, "I was admiring your office."

"Thank you. But I assume that wasn't what you came for."

"Oh, no. Being the Chairman of that Dinner Committee, I'm in the middle of this thing whether I like it or not—this business of Boone's murder. I wouldn't say I'm involved, that's too strong a word—make it concerned. I'm certainly concerned."

"Has anyone suggested that you are involved?"

"Suggested?" O'Neill looked surprised. "That's putting it mildly. The police are taking the position that everyone connected with the NIA is involved. That's why I claim that the line the Executive Committee is taking is sentimental and unrealistic. Don't get me wrong, Mr. Wolfe." He took time out for a friendly glance at me, to include me in the Society of United Citizens for Not Getting Don O'Neill Wrong. "I am one of the most progressive members of the NIA. I was a Willkie man. But this idea of co-operating with the police the way they're acting, and even spending our own money to investigate, that's unrealistic. We ought to say to the police, all right, there's been a murder, and as good citizens we hope you catch the guilty man, but we had nothing to do with it and it's none of our business."

"And tell them to quit bothering you."

"That's right. That's exactly right." O'Neill was pleased to find a kindred spirit. "I was at the office when they came back an hour ago with the news that they had engaged you to investigate. I want to make it plain that I am not doing anything underhanded. I don't work that way. We had another argument, and I told them I was coming to see you."

"Admirable." Wolfe's eyes were open, which meant that he was bored and was getting nothing out of it. Either that, or he was refusing to turn on the brain until nine o'clock. "For the purpose of persuading me to call it off?"

"Oh, no. I saw that was hopeless. You wouldn't do that. Would you?"

"I'm afraid not without some excellent reason. As Mr. Breslow put it, the interest of justice is paramount. That was his position. Mine is that I need the money. Then what did you come for?"

O'Neill grinned at me, as if to say, your boss is really a card, isn't he? He shifted the grin intact to Wolfe. "I'm glad to see you stick to the point. With me you need to, the way I go floundering around. What brought me down here, frankly, was a sense of responsibility as Chairman of the Dinner Committee. I've seen a copy of the letter Frank Erskine gave you, but I didn't hear the conversation you had, and ten thousand dollars as a retainer on a straight inquiry job is away above the clouds. I hire detectives in my business, things like labor relations and so on, and I know what detectives get, so naturally the question occurs to me, is it really a straight inquiry job? I asked Erskine point-blank, have you hired Wolfe to protect the NIA members by — uh — getting attention shifted to other directions, and he said no. But I know Frank Erskine, and I wasn't satisfied, and I told him so. The trouble with me is I've got a conscience and a sense of responsibility. So I came to ask you."

Wolfe's lips twitched, but whether with amusement or fierce indignation I couldn't tell. The way he takes an insult never depends on the insult but on how he happens to be feeling. At the peak of one of his lazy spells he wouldn't have exerted himself to bat an eyelash even if someone accused him of specializing in divorce evidence.

His lips twitched. "I also say no, Mr. O'Neill. But I'm afraid that won't help you much. What if Mr. Erskine and I are both lying? I don't see what you can do about it, short of going to the police and charging us with obstructing justice, but then you don't like the police either. You're really in a pickle. We have invited some people to meet here this evening at nine o'clock and talk it over. Why don't you come and keep an eye on us?"

"Oh, I'm coming. I told Erskine and the others I'm coming."

"Good. Then we won't keep you now. — Archie?"

It wasn't as simple as that. O'Neill was by no means ready to go, on account of his sense of responsibility. But we finally got him out without resorting to physical violence. After wrangling him to the stoop, I returned to the office and asked Wolfe:

"Exactly what did he really come here for? Of course he killed Boone, I understand that, but why did he waste his time and mine —"

"You let him in," Wolfe said icily. "You did not notify me. You seem to forget —"

"Oh, well," I broke in cheerfully, "it all helps in studying human nature. I helped get him out, didn't I? Now we have work to do, getting ready for the party. How many will there be, around twelve not counting us?"

I got busy on the chair problem. There were six there in the office, and the divan would hold four comfortably, except that in a murder case three days old you don't often find four people connected with it who are still in a frame of mind to sit together on the same piece of furniture. It would be better to have plenty of chairs, so I brought five more in from the front room, the one facing on the street, and scattered them around, not in rows, which would have been too stiff, but sort of staggered and informal. Big as the room was, it made it look pretty crowded. I backed against the wall and surveyed it with a frown.

"What it needs," I remarked, "is a woman's touch."

"Bah," Wolfe growled.

9

AT a quarter past ten Wolfe was leaning back in his chair with his eyes half closed, taking them in. They had been at it for over an hour.

There were thirteen of them. Thanks to my foresight with the seating arrangements, there had been no infighting. The NIA contingent was at the side of the room farthest from my desk, the side toward the hall door, with Erskine in the red leather chair. There were six of them: the four who had formed the afternoon delegation, including Winterhoff, who had had an appointment he couldn't break, Hattie Harding, and Don O'Neill.

On my side of the room were the BPR's, four in number: Mrs. Boone the widow, Nina the niece, Alger Kates, and a gate-crasher named Solomon Dexter. Dexter was around fifty, under rather than over, looked like a cross between a statesman and a lumberjack, and was the ex-Deputy Director, now for twenty-four hours Acting Director, of the Bureau of Price Regulation. He had come, he told Wolfe, ex officio.

In between the two hostile armies were the neutrals or referees: Spero of the FBI, and Inspector Cramer and Sergeant Purley Stebbins. I had explained to Cramer that I was aware that he rated the red leather chair, but that he was needed in the middle. By a quarter past ten he was about as mad as I had ever seen him, because he had long ago caught on that Wolfe was starting from scratch and had arranged the gathering for the purpose of taking in, not giving out.

There had been one puny attempt to disrupt my seating plans. Mrs. Boone and the niece had come early, before nine, and since there is nothing wrong with my eyesight I had without the slightest hesitation put the niece in the chair—one of the yellow ones from the front room—nearest to mine. When Ed Erskine arrived, alone, a little later I assigned him to a seat on the NIA side, only to discover, after attending to a couple of other customers, that he had bounced across and was in my chair talking to the niece. I went over and told him:

"This side is for the Capulets. Would you mind sitting where I put you?"

He twisted his neck and lifted his chin to get me, and his focusing was not good. It was obvious that he had been applying the theory of acquired immunity to his hangover. I want to be fair, he was not pie-eyed, but neither was he in danger of desiccating.

He asked me, "Huh? Why?"

"Besides," I said, "this is my chair and I work here. Let's not make an issue of it."

He shrugged it off and moved. I addressed Nina Boone courteously: "You run into all sorts of strangers in a detective's office."

"I suppose you do," she said. Not a deep remark, nothing specially penetrating about it, but I smiled at her to show I appreciated her taking the trouble to make it when under a strain. She had dark hair and eyes, and was keeping her chin firm.

From the moment, right at the beginning, that Wolfe had announced that he had been retained by the NIA, the BPR's had been suspicious and antagonistic. Of course everyone who reads a newspaper or listens to the radio, which includes me, knew that the NIA hated Cheney Boone and all he stood for, and had done everything possible to get him tossed to the wolves, and also knew that the BPR would gladly have seen the atom bomb tested by bunching the NIA crowd on an island and dropping one on them, but I hadn't realized how it sizzled until that evening in Wolfe's office. Of course there were two fresh elements in it then: the fact that Cheney Boone had been murdered, at an NIA dinner of all places, and the prospect that some person or persons either would or wouldn't get arrested, tried, convicted, and electrocuted.

By a quarter past ten a good many points, both trivial and important, had been touched on. On opportunity, the BPR position was that everyone in the reception room, and probably many others, had known that Boone was in the room near the stage, the murder room, while the NIA claimed that not more than four or five people, besides the BPR's who were there, knew it. The truth was that there was no way of finding out who had known and who hadn't.

Neither hotel employees nor anyone else had heard any noise from the murder room, or seen anybody enter or leave it other than those whose presence there was known and acknowledged.

No one was eliminated on account of age, size, or sex. While a young male athlete can swing a monkey wrench harder and faster than an old female bridge player, either could have struck the blows that killed Boone. There had been no sign of a struggle. Any one of the blows, from behind, could have stunned him or killed him. G. G. Spero of the FBI joined in the discussion of this point, and replied to a crack from Erskine by stating that it was not a function of the FBI to investigate local murders, but that since Boone had been killed while performing his duty as a government official, the Department of Justice had a legitimate interest in the matter and was acting on a request for co-operation from the New York police.

One interesting development was that it was hard to see how Boone had got killed unless he did it himself, because everybody had alibis. Meaning by everybody not merely those present in Wolfe's office — there being no special reason to suppose that the murderer was there with us — but all of the fourteen or fifteen hundred at the dinner. The time involved was about half an hour, between seven-fifteen, when Phoebe Gunther left the baby carriage and its contents, including the monkey wrenches, with Boone in the room, and around seven forty-five, when Alger Kates discovered the body. The police had gone to town on that, and everybody had been with somebody else, especially those in the reception room. But the hitch was that all the alibis were either mutual NIA's or mutual BPR's. Strange to say, no NIA could alibi a BPR, or vice versa. Even Mrs. Boone, the widow, for instance—no NIA was quite positive that she had not left the reception room during that period or that she had gone straight from there to the dais in the ballroom. The BPR's were equally unpositive about Frank Thomas Erskine, the NIA president.

There was no evidence that the purpose had been to keep Boone from delivering that particular speech. The speech had been typical Boone, pulling no punches, but had exposed or threatened no particular individual, neither in the advance text distributed to the press nor in the last-minute changes and additions. Nothing in it pointed to a murderer.

The first brand-new ingredient for me, of which nothing had been reported in the papers, was introduced by accident by Mrs. Boone. The only person invited to our party who hadn't come was Phoebe Gunther, Boone's confidential secretary. Her name had of course been mentioned several times during the first hour or so, but it was Mrs. Boone who put the spotlight on it. I had the notion that she did it deliberately. She had not up to that moment got any of my major attention. She was mature and filled-out, though not actually fat and by no means run to seed, and she had been shortchanged as to nose.

Wolfe had doubled back to the question of Cheney Boone's arrival at the Waldorf, and Cramer, who was by then in a frame of mind to get it over with and disperse, had said sarcastically, "I'll send you a copy of my notes. Meanwhile Goodwin can take this down. Five of them—Boone and his wife, Nina Boone, Phoebe Gunther, and Alger Kates—were to take the one o'clock train from Washington to New York, but Boone got caught in an emergency conference and couldn't make it. The other four came on the train, and when they reached New York Mrs. Boone went to the Waldorf, where rooms had been engaged, and the other three went to the BPR New York office. Boone came on a plane that landed at LaGuardia Field at six-five, went to the hotel and up to the room where his wife was. By that time the niece was there too, and the three of them went together down to the ballroom floor. They went straight to the reception room. Boone had no hat or coat to check, and he hung onto a little leather case he had with him."

"That was the case," Mrs. Boone put in, "that Miss Gunther says she forgot about and left on a window sill."

I looked at the widow reproachfully. That was the first sign of a split in the BPR ranks, and it sounded ominous, with the nasty emphasis she put on says. To make it worse, Hattie Harding of the NIA immediately picked it up:

"And Miss Gunther is absolutely wrong, because four different people saw that case in her hand as she left the reception room!"

Solomon Dexter snorted. "It's amazing what—"

"Please, sir." Wolfe wiggled a finger at him. "What was this case? A brief case? A vanity case?"

"No." Cramer was helping out again. "It was a little leather case like a doctor's, and it contained cylinders from a dictating machine. Miss Gunther has described it to me. When she took that baby carriage and other stuff to him Tuesday evening, to the room where he was killed, he told her the conference in Washington had ended earlier than he expected, and he had gone to his office and spent an hour dictating before he took the plane to New York. He had the cylinders with him in that case for her to transcribe. She took it to the reception room when she went back there for a cocktail, and left it there on a window sill. That's the last of it."

"So she says," Mrs. Boone repeated.

Dexter glared at her. "Nonsense!"

"Did you," Hattie Harding demanded, "see the case in her hand when she left the reception room?"

All eyes went to the widow. She moved hers and got the picture. One word would be enough. She was either a traitor or she wasn't. Confronted with that alternative, it didn't take her long to decide. She met Hattie Harding's gaze and said distinctly:

"No."

Everybody breathed. Wolfe asked Cramer:

"What was on the cylinders, letters? What?"

"Miss Gunther doesn't know. Boone didn't tell her. No one in Washington knows."

"The conference that ended earlier than Boone expected, what was it about?"

Cramer shook his head.

"Who was it with?"

Cramer shook his head again. G. G. Spero offered, "We've been working on that in Washington. We can't trace any conference. We don't know where Boone was for about two hours, from one to three. The best lead is that the head NIA man in Washington had been wanting to see him, to discuss his speech, but he denies —"

Breslow exploded. "By God," he blurted, "there it is! It's always an NIA man! That's damned silly, Spero, and don't forget where FBI salaries come from! They come from taxpayers!"

From that point on the mud was flying more or less constantly. It wasn't on account of any encouragement from Wolfe. He told Breslow:

"The constant reference to your Association is unfortunate from your standpoint, sir, but it can't be helped. A murder investigation invariably centers on people with motives. You heard Mr. Cramer, early in this discussion, say that a thorough inquiry has disclosed no evidence of personal enemies. But you cannot deny that Mr. Boone had many enemies, earned by his activities as a government official, and that a large number of them were members of the NIA."

Winterhoff asked, "A question, Mr. Wolfe, it is always an enemy who kills a man?"

"Answer it yourself," Wolfe told him. "Obviously that's what you asked it for."

"Well, it certainly isn't always an enemy," Winterhoff declared. "For an illustration, you couldn't say that Mr. Dexter here was Boone's enemy, quite the contrary, they were friends. But if Mr. Dexter had been filled with ambition to become the Director of the Bureau of Price Regulation — and that's what he is at this moment — he might conceivaby have taken steps to make the office vacant. Incidentally, he would also have placed under grave suspicion the members of an organization he mortally hates — which also has happened."

Solomon Dexter was smiling at him, not a loving smile. "Are you prefer-
ring a charge, Mr. Winterhoff?"

"Not all all." The other met his gaze. "As I said, merely an illustration."

"Because I could mention one little difficulty. I was in Washington until
eleven o'clock Tuesday evening. You'll have to get around that somehow."

"Nevertheless," Frank Thomas Erskine said firmly and judicially, "Mr.
Winterhoff has made an obvious point."

"One of several," Breslow asserted. "There are others. We all know what
they are, so why not out with them? The talk about Boone and his secretary,
Phoebe Gunther, has been going on for months, and whether Mrs. Boone
was going to get a divorce or not. And lately a reason, a mighty good reason
from Phoebe Gunther's standpoint, why Boone had to have a divorce no
matter how his wife felt about it. What about it, Inspector, when you're
dealing with a murder don't you think it's legitimate to take an interest in
things like that?"

Alger Kates stood up and announced in a trembling voice: "I want to
protest that this is utterly despicable and beyond the bounds of common
decency!"

His face was white and he stayed on his feet. I had not supposed he had it
in him. He was the BPR research man who had taken some up-to-the-
minute statistics to the Waldorf to be used in Boone's speech and had
discovered the body. If my attention had been directed to him on the subway and I had been asked to guess what he did for a living, I would have
said, "Research man." He was that to a T, in size, complexion, age, and
chest measurement. But the way he rose to protest—apparently he led the
BPR, as there represented, in spunk. I grinned at him.

From the reaction he got you might have thought that what the NIA
hated and feared most about the BPR was its research. They all howled at
him. I caught the gist of only two of their remarks, one from Breslow to the
effect that he had only said what everyone was saying, and the wind-up from
Don O'Neill, in the accents of The Boss:

"You can keep out of this, Kates! Sit down and shut up!"

That seemed to me to be overdoing it a little, since he wasn't paying
Kates's wages; and then Erskine, twisting around in the red leather chair to
face the research man, told him cuttingly:

"Since you didn't regard the President of the NIA as a fit person to bring
the news to, you are hardly acceptable as a judge of common decency."

So, I thought, that's why they're jumping on him, because he told the
hotel manager instead of them. He should have had more sense than to hurt
their feelings like that. Erskine wasn't through with him, but was going on:

"Surely, Mr. Kates, you are aware that personal emotions, such as jealousy, revenge, or frustration, often result in violence, and therefore they are
proper matters of inquiry when a murder has been committed. It would be
proper to ask you, for example, whether it is true that you wanted to marry
Boone's niece, and you were aware that Boone opposed it and intended to
prevent—"

"Why, you big liar!" Nina Boone cried.

"Whether it is proper or not," Kates said in a high thin voice that was still
trembling, "it certainly is not proper for you to ask me anything whatever. If
I were asked that by the police, I would reply that part of it is true and part

of it isn't. There are at least two hundred men in the BPR organization who wanted, and it is a reasonable assumption that they still want, to marry Mr. Boone's niece. I was not under the impression that Mr. Boone was having anything to say about it one way or another, and, knowing Miss Boone as I do, not intimately but fairly well, I doubt it." Kates moved not his eyes, but his head, to change his target. "I would like to ask Mr. Wolfe, who has admitted that he is in the pay of the NIA, if we were invited here for a typical NIA inquisition."

"And I," Solomon Dexter put in, his voice sounding like a train in a tunnel in contrast to Kates's, "would like to inform you, Mr. Wolfe, that you are by no means the only detective in the employ of the NIA. For nearly a year executives and other BPR personnel have been followed by detectives, and their whole lives have been thoroughly explored in an effort to get something on them. I don't know whether you have taken part in those operations —"

More bedlam from the NIA, taking the form chiefly, as near as I could get it, of indignant denials. At that point, if it hadn't been for my seating arrangements, the two armies would probably have made contact. Wolfe was looking exasperated, but making no effort to stop it, possibly aware that it would take more energy than he wished to spend. What quieted them was Inspector Cramer getting to his feet and showing a palm, officially.

"*I* would like," he barked, "before going, to say three things. First, Mr. Dexter, I can assure you that Wolfe has not helped to tail your personnel or explore their lives, because there's not enough money in that kind of work. Second, Mr. Erskine and you other gentlemen, the police are aware that jealousy and things like that are often behind a murder, and we are not apt to forget it. Third, Mr. Kates, I have known Wolfe for twenty years, and I can tell you why you were invited here this evening. We were invited because he wanted to learn all he could as quick as he could, without leaving his chair and without Goodwin's buying gas and wearing out his tires. I don't know about the rest of you, but I was a sucker to come."

He turned. "Come on, Sergeant. You coming, Spero?"

Of course that ended it. The BPR didn't want any more anyhow, and though the NIA, or part of it, showed an inclination to stay and make suggestions, Wolfe used his veto power on that. With everyone out of their chairs, Ed Erskine crossed the lines again and tried another approach on Nina, but it appeared, from where I stood, that she disposed of that without even opening her mouth. I did much better, in spite of my being associated with Wolfe, who was in the pay of the NIA. When I told her that it was impossible to get a taxi in that part of town and offered to drive her and her aunt to their hotel, she said:

"Mr. Dexter is taking us."

A frank, friendly statement, and I appreciated it.

But after they had all gone and Wolfe and I were alone in the office, it appeared that I wouldn't have been able to go through with it even if she had accepted. I remarked to Wolfe:

"Too bad Cramer bolixed it up like that. If we had been able to keep them here a while, say two weeks, we might have got started somewhere. Too bad."

"It was not too bad," he said testily.

"Oh." I gestured, and sat down. "Okay, then it was a screaming success. Of all our guests, which do you think was the most interesting?"

To my surprise, he answered, "The most interesting was Miss Gunther."

"Yeah? Because?"

"Because she didn't come. You have her address."

"Sure. I sent the telegram —"

"Go and bring her here."

I stared at him, looked at my wrist, and stared at him again. "It is now twenty minutes past eleven."

He nodded. "The streets are less dangerous at night, with the reduced traffic."

"I won't argue." I stood up. "You are in the pay of the NIA, and I am in the pay of you. So it goes."

10

I took an assortment of keys along, to simplify things in case 611 East Fifty-fifth Street proved to be an old-fashioned walk-up with a locked entrance door, but instead of that it was one of the twelve-story beehives with an awning and hired men. I stepped down the broad hall to the elevator, went in, and said casually:

"Gunther."

Without even glancing at me, the pilot finished a yawn and called out, "Hey, Sam! For Gunther!"

The doorman, whom I had by-passed, appeared and looked in at me. "I'll phone up," he said, "but it's a waste of time. What's your name and what paper are you from?"

Ordinarily I like to save butter, but under the circumstances, with no ceiling on expenses, I saw no reason why he shouldn't be in the pay of the NIA too. So I left the elevator and walked down the hall with him, and when we got to the switchboard I spread a ten-dollar bill thereon, saying:

"I'm not on a paper. I sell sea shells."

He shook his head and started manipulations at the board. I put a hand on his arm and told him, "You didn't let me finish. That was papa. Here's mamma." I deployed another ten. "But I warn you they have no children."

He only shook his head again and flipped a lever. I was shocked speechless. I have had a lot to do with doormen, and I am certainly able to spot one too honest to accept twenty bucks for practically nothing, and that was not it. His principles didn't even approach as high a standard as that, and he was being pure from some other motive. I emerged from the shock when I heard him telling the receiver:

"He says he sells sea shells."

"The name," I said, "is Archie Goodwin, and I was sent by Mr. Nero Wolfe."

He repeated it to the receiver, and in a moment hung up and turned to me with a look of surprise. "She says go on up. Nine H." He accompanied me toward the elevator. "About papa and mamma, I've changed my mind, in case you still feel—"

"I was kidding you," I told him. "They really have got children. This is little Horace." I handed him two bits and went in and commanded the pilot, "Nine H."

It is not my custom to make personal remarks to young women during the first five minutes after meeting them, and if I violated it this time it was only because the remark popped out of me involuntarily. When I pushed the button and she opened the door and said good evening, and I agreed and removed my hat and stepped inside, the ceiling light right above her was shining on her hair, and what popped out was:

"Golden Bantam."

"Yes," she said, "that's what I dye it with."

I was already understanding, from the first ten seconds, what motive it was that the doorman was being pure from. Her pictures in the papers had been just nothing compared with this. After we had disposed of my hat and coat she preceded me into the room, and from the middle of it turned her head to say:

"You know Mr. Kates."

I thought it had popped out of her as my remark had popped out of me, but then I saw him, rising to his feet from a chair in a corner where the light was dim.

"Hello," I said.

"Good evening," he piped.

"Sit down." Phoebe Gunther straightened a corner of a rug with the toe of a little red slipper. "Mr. Kates came to tell me what happened at your party this evening. Will you have some Scotch? Rye? Bourbon? Gin? Cola?"

"No, thanks." I was getting my internal skull fixtures jerked back into place.

"Well." She sat on a couch against a nest of cushions. "Did you come to see what color my hair is or was there someting else?"

"I'm sorry to bust in on you and Mr. Kates."

"That's all right. Isn't it, Al?"

"It is not all right," Alger Kates said, without hesitation, in his thin voice stretched tight but extremely distinct, "with me. It would be folly to trust him at all or to believe anything he says. As I told you, he is in the pay of the NIA."

"So you did." Miss Gunther was relaxing among the cushions. "But since we know enough not to trust him, all we have to do is to be a little smarter than he is in order to get more out of him than he gets out of us." She looked at me, and seemed to be smiling, but I had already discovered that her face was so versatile, especially her mouth, that it would be better not to jump to conclusions. She told me, possibly smiling, "I have a theory about Mr. Kates. He talks the way people talked before he was born, therefore he must read old-fashioned novels. I wouldn't suppose a research man would read novels at all. What would you suppose?"

"I don't discuss people who don't trust me," I said politely. "And I don't think you are."

"Are what?"

"Smarter than me. I admit you're prettier, but I doubt if you're smarter. I was spelling champion of Zanesville, Ohio, at the age of twelve."

"Spell snoop."

"That's just childish." I glared at her. "I don't imagine you're hinting that catching people who commit crimes is work to be ashamed of, since you're smart, so if what you have in mind is my coming here, why didn't you tell the doorman—"

I stopped short because she was possibly laughing at me. I quit glaring, but went on looking at her, which was a bad policy because that was what was interfering with my mental processes.

"Okay," I said curtly, "you got a poke in and made me blink. Round One for you. Round Two. Your Mr. Kates may be as loyal as What's-his-name, the boy that stood on the burning deck, but he's a sap. Nero Wolfe is tricky, that I admit, but the idea that he would cover a murderer because he happened to belong to something out of the alphabet that signed checks is plain loony. Look at the record and show me where he ever accepted a substitute, no matter who said it was just as good. Here's a free tip: if you think or know a BPR man did it, and don't want him caught, bounce me out immediately and keep as far away from Wolfe as you can get. If you think an NIA man did it and you'd like to help, put on some shoes and get your hat and coat and come to his office with me. As far as I'm concerned you don't need to bother about the hat." I looked at Kates. "If you did it yourself, with some motive not to be mentioned for the sake of common decency, you'd better come along and confess and get it over with."

"I told you!" Kates told her triumphantly. "See how he led up to that?"

"Don't be silly." Miss Gunther, annoyed, looked at him. "I'll explain it to you. Finding that I am smarter than he is, he decided to pick on you, and he certainly got documentation for his statement that you're a sap. In fact, you'd better be going. Leave him to me. I may see you at the office tomorrow."

Kates shook his head bravely and firmly. "No!" he insisted. "He'll go on that way! I'm not going to—"

He continued, but there's no more use my putting it down than there was his saying it, for the hostess had got up, crossed to a table, and picked up his hat and coat. It seemed to me that in some respects she must have been unsatisfactory as a confidential secretary. A man's secretary is always moving around, taking and bringing papers, ushering in callers and out again, sitting down and standing up, and if there is a constant temptation to watch how she moves it is hard to get any work done.

Kates lost the argument, of course. Within two minutes the door had closed behind him and Miss Gunther was back on the couch among the cushions. Meanwhile I had been doing my best to concentrate, so when she possibly smiled at me and told me to go ahead and teach her the multiplication table, I arose and asked if I might use her phone.

Her brows went up. "What am I supposed to do? Ask who you want to call?"

"No, just say yes."

"Yes. It's right over—"

"I see it, thanks."

It was on a little table against a wall, with a stool there, and I pulled out the stool and sat with my back to her and dialed. After only one buzz in my ear, because Wolfe hates to hear bells ring, I got a hello and spoke:

"Mr. Wolfe? Archie. I'm up here with Miss Gunther in her apartment, and I don't believe it's a good plan to bring her down there as you suggested. In the first place she's extremely smart, but that's not it. She's the one I've been dreaming about the past ten years, remember what I've told you? I don't mean she's beautiful, that's merely a matter of taste, I only mean she is exactly what I have had in mind. Therefore it will be much better to let me handle her. She began by making a monkey of me, but that was because I was suffering from shock. It may take a week or a month or even a year, because it is very difficult to keep your mind on your work under these circumstances, but you can count on me. You go on to bed and I'll get in touch with you in the morning."

I arose from the stool and turned to face the couch, but she wasn't there. She was, instead, over toward the door, in a dark blue coat with a fox collar, standing in front of a mirror, adjusting a dark blue contraption on her head.

She glanced at me. "All right, come on."

"Come on where?"

"Don't be demure." She turned from the mirror. "You worked hard trying to figure out a way of getting me down to Nero Wolfe's office, and you did a good job. I'll give you Round Two. Some day we'll play the rubber. Right now I'm taking on Nero Wolfe, so it will have to be postponed. I'm glad you don't think I'm beautiful. Nothing irritates a woman more than to be thought beautiful."

I had my coat on and she had the door open. The bag under her arm was the same dark blue material as the hat. On the way to the elevator I explained, "I didn't say I didn't think you were beautiful. I said—"

"I heard what you said. It stabbed me clear through. Even from a stranger who may also be my enemy, it hurt. I'm vain and that's that. Because it just happens that I can't see straight and I do think I'm beautiful."

"So do—" I began, but just in time I saw the corner of her mouth moving and bit it off. I am telling this straight. If anyone thinks I was muffing everything she sent my way I won't argue, but I would like to point out that I was right there with her, looking at her and listening to her, and the hell of it was that she was beautiful.

Driving down to Thirty-fifth Street, she kept the atmosphere as neighborly as if I had never been within ten miles of the NIA. Entering the house, we found the office uninhabited, so I left her there and went to find Wolfe. He was in the kitchen, deep in a conference with Fritz regarding the next day's culinary program, and I sat on a stool, thinking over the latest development, Gunther by name, until they were finished. Wolfe finally acknowledged my presence.

"Is she here?"

"Yep. She sure is. Straighten your tie and comb your hair."

11

IT was a quarter past two in the morning when Wolfe glanced at the wall clock, sighed, and said, "Very well, Miss Gunther, I am ready to fulfill my part of the bargain. It was agreed that after you had answered my questions I would answer yours. Go ahead."

I hadn't been distracted much by gazing at beauty because, having been told to get it in the notebook verbatim, my eyes had been busy elsewhere. It was fifty-four pages. Wolfe had been in one of his looking-under-every-stone moods, and the stuff on some of the pages had no more to do with Boone's murder, from where I sat, than Washington crossing the Delaware.

Some of it might conceivably help. First and foremost, of course, was her own itinerary for last Tuesday. She knew nothing about the conference which had prevented Boone from leaving Washington on the train with the others, and admitted that that was surprising, since she was his confidential secretary and was supposed to know everything and usually did. Arriving in New York, she had gone with Alger Kates and Nina Boone to the BPR New York office, where Kates had gone into the statistical section, and she and Nina had helped department heads to collect props to be used as illustrations of points in the speech. There had been a large collection of all sorts of things, from toothpicks to typewriters, and it wasn't until after six o'clock that the final selection had been made: two can openers, two monkey wrenches, two shirts, two fountain pens, and a baby carriage; and the data on them assembled. One of the men had conveyed them to the street for her and found a taxi, and she had headed for the Waldorf, Nina having gone previously. A bellboy had helped her get the props to the ballroom floor and the reception room. There she learned that Boone had asked for privacy to go over his speech, and an NIA man, General Erskine, had taken her to the room, to be known before long as the murder room.

Wolfe asked, "*General* Erskine?"

"Yes," she said. "Ed Erskine, the son of the NIA President."

I snorted.

"He was a B.G.," she said. "One of the youngest generals in the Air Force."

"Do you know him well?"

"No, I had only seen him once or twice and had never met him. But naturally I hate him." At that moment there was no question about it; she was not smiling. "I hate everybody connected with the NIA."

"Naturally. Go ahead."

Ed Erskine had wheeled the baby carriage to the door of the room and left her there, and she had not stayed with Boone more than two or three minutes. The police had spent hours on those two or three minutes, since they were the last that anyone except the murderer had spent with Boone alive. Wolfe spent two pages of my notebook. Boone had been concentrated and tense, even more than usual, which was not remarkable under the circumstances. He had jerked the shirts and monkey wrenches out of the baby carriage and put them on the table, glanced at the data, reminded Miss Gunther that she was to follow a copy of the speech as he talked and take notes of any deviation he made from the text; and then had handed her the leather case and told her to get. She had returned to the reception room and had two cocktails, two quick ones because she felt she needed them, and then had joined the exodus to the ballroom and had found table number eight, the one near the dais reserved for BPR people. She was eating her fruit cocktail when she remembered about the leather case, and that she had left it on the window sill in the reception room. She said nothing about it because she didn't want to confess her carelessness, and just as she was starting to excuse herself to Mrs. Boone and leave the table, Frank Thomas Erskine, on the dais, had spoken into the microphone:

"Ladies and gentlemen, I regret the necessity of giving you this news, this abruptly, but I must explain why no one can be allowed to leave this room . . ."

It was an hour later when she finally got to the reception room, and the leather case was gone.

Boone had told her the case contained cylinders he had dictated in his Washington office that afternoon, and that was all she knew. It wasn't remarkable that he hadn't told her what the dictation was about, because he seldom did. Since he used other stenographers for all routine stuff, it was understood that any cylinders he turned over to her personally were important and probably confidential. There were twelve such cases in use in Boone's office, each holding ten cylinders, and they were constantly going back and forth among him and her and other stenographers, since Boone had done nearly all of his dictating on the machine. They were numbered, stamped on top, and this one had been number four. The machine that Boone had used was the Stenophone.

Miss Gunther admitted that she had made a mistake. She had not mentioned the missing case to anyone until Wednesday morning, when the police had asked her what had been in the leather case which she had had with her when she came to the reception room for a cocktail. Some NIA louse had of course told the police about it. She had told the police that she had been ashamed to confess her negligence, and anyway her silence had done no harm, since the case could have had no connection with the murder.

"Four people," Wolfe murmured, "say that you took the case with you from the reception room to the ballroom."

Phoebe Gunther nodded, unimpressed. She was drinking Bourbon and water and smoking a cigarette. "You believe them or you believe me. It wouldn't surprise me if four of that kind of people said they looked through the keyhole and saw me kill Mr. Boone. Or even forty."

"You mean NIA people. But Mrs. Boone isn't one."

"No," Phoebe agreed. She lifted her shoulders, kept them up a second, and let them down. "Mr. Kates told me what she said. Mrs. Boone doesn't like me. Yet — I rather doubt if that's true — I think maybe she does like me, but she hated having her husband depend on me. You notice she didn't actually lie about it; she didn't say she saw me have the case when I left the reception room."

"What did Mr. Boone depend on you for?"

"To do what he told me to."

"Of course." Wolfe was merely murmuring. "But what did he get from you? Intelligent obedience? Loyalty? Comfortable companionship? Happiness? Ecstasy?"

"Oh, for the lord's sake." She looked mildly disgusted. "You sound like a congressman's wife. What he got was first-class work. I'm not saying that during the two years I worked for Mr. Boone I was always fresh out of ecstasy, but I never took it to the office with me, and anyway I was saving it up until I met Mr. Goodwin." She gestured. "You've been reading old-fashioned novels too. If you want to know whether I was on terms of sinful intimacy with Mr. Boone, the answer is no. For one thing, he was too busy, and so was I, and anyhow he didn't strike me that way. I merely worshiped him."

"You did?"

"Yes, I did." She gave the impression that she meant it. "He was irritable and he expected too much, he was overweight and he had dandruff, and he nearly drove me crazy trying to keep his schedule under control, but he was honest clear through and the best man in Washington, and he was up against the dirtiest gang of pigs and chiselers on earth. So since I was born weak-minded to begin with, I merely worshiped him, but where he was getting ecstasy I really don't know."

That would seem to cover the ecstasy angle. It was around that point, as I filled page after page in my notebook, that I took a sounding on how much of it I believed, and when I found my credibility gauge mounting up into the nineties and still ascending, I disqualified myself for bias.

She had a definite opinion about the murder. She doubted if any number of NIA members were in cahoots on it, probably not even two of them, because they were too cagey to conspire to commit a murder that would be a nation-wide sensation. Her idea was that some one member had done it himself or hired it done, and it had to be one whose interests had been so damaged or threatened by Boone that he was willing to disregard the black eye the NIA would get. She accepted Wolfe's theory that it was now desirable, from the standpoint of the NIA, that the murderer be caught.

"Then doesn't it follow," Wolfe asked, "that you and the BPR would prefer not to have him caught?"

"It may follow," she admitted. "But I'm afraid that personally I'm not that logical, so I don't feel that way."

"Because you worshiped Mr. Boone? That's understandable. But in that case, why didn't you accept my invitation to come and discuss it last evening?"

She either had it ready or didn't need to get it ready. "Because I didn't feel like it. I was tired and I didn't know who would be here. Between the police and the FBI, I have answered a thousand questions a thousand times each and I needed a rest."

"But you came with Mr. Goodwin."

"Certainly. Any girl who needed a rest would go anywhere with Mr. Goodwin, because she wouldn't have to use her mind." She didn't even toss me a glance, but went on, "However, I didn't intend to stay all night, and it's after two, and what about my turn?"

That was when Wolfe looked at the clock and sighed and told her to go ahead.

She shifted in the chair to change pressure, took a couple of sips from her glass and put it down, leaned her head back against the red leather, getting a very nice effect, and asked as if it didn't matter much one way or the other:

"Who approached you from the NIA, what did they say, what have you agreed to do, and how much are they paying you?"

Wolfe was so startled he almost blinked at her. "Oh, no, Miss Gunther, nothing like that."

"Why not?" she demanded. "Then it wasn't a bargain at all."

He considered, realizing what he had let himself in for. "Very well," he said, "let's see. Mr. Erskine and his son, and Mr. Breslow and Mr. Winterhoff came to see me. Later Mr. O'Neill also came. They said many things, but the upshot was that they hired me to investigate. I have agreed to do so and to attempt to catch the murderer. What—"

"No matter who it is?"

"Yes. Don't interrupt. What they pay will depend on the expenses incurred and what I decide to charge. It will be adequate. I don't like the NIA. I'm an anarchist."

He had decided to make the best of it by being whimsical. She ignored that.

"Did they try to persuade you that the murderer is not an NIA member?"

"No."

"Did you get the impression that they suspect any particular person?"

"No."

"Do you think one of the five who came to see you committed the murder?"

"No."

"Do you mean you are satisfied that none of them did commit it?"

"No."

She made a gesture. "This is silly. You aren't playing fair. You say nothing but no."

"I'm answering your questions. And so far I haven't told you a lie. I doubt if you could say as much."

"Why, what did I tell you that wasn't true?"

"I have no idea. Not yet. I will have. Go ahead."

I broke in, to Wolfe. "Excuse me, but I have no precedent for this, you being grilled by a murder suspect. Am I supposed to take it down?"

He ignored me and repeated to her, "Go ahead. Mr. Goodwin was merely making an opportunity to call you a murder suspect."

She was concentrating and also ignored me. "Do you think," she asked, "that the use of the monkey wrench, which no one could have known would be there, proves that the murder was unpremeditated?"

"No."

"Why not?"

"Because the murderer could have come armed, have seen the wrench, and decided to use it instead."

"But it might have been unpremeditated?"

"Yes."

"Has any NIA man said anything to you that indicated that he or any of them might know who took that leather case or what happened to it?"

"No."

"Or where it is now?"

"No."

"Have you any idea who the murderer is?"

"No."

"Why did you send Mr. Goodwin after me? Why me, instead of—oh, anyone?"

"Because you had stayed away and I wanted to find out why."

She stopped, sat erect, sipped at her glass again, draining it, and brushed her hair back.

"This is a lot of nonsense," she said emphatically. "I could go on asking you questions for hours, and how would I know that a single thing you told me was the truth? For instance, I would give I don't know what for that case. You say that as far as you know no one knows what happened to it or where it is, and it may be in this room right now, there in your desk." She looked at the glass, saw it was empty, and put it down on the check-writing table.

Wolfe nodded. "That is always the difficulty. I was under the same handicap with you."

"But I have nothing to lie about!"

"Pfui. Everybody has something to lie about. Go ahead."

"No." She stood up and saw to her skirt. "It's perfectly useless. I'll go home and go to bed. Look at me. Do I look like a played-out hag?"

That startled him again. His attitude toward women was such that they rarely asked him what they looked like.

He muttered, "No."

"But I am," she declared. "That's the way it always affects me. The tireder I get the less I look it. Tuesday I got the hardest blow I ever got in my life, and since then I haven't had a decent night's sleep, and look at me." She turned to me. "Would you mind showing me which way to go for a taxi?"

"I'll run you up," I told her. "I have to put the car away anyhow."

She told Wolfe good night, and we got our things on and went out and climbed in. She let her head fall back against the cushion and closed her eyes for a second, then opened them, straightened up, and flashed a glance at me.

"So you took Nero Wolfe on," I remarked, as to a comparative stranger.

"Don't be aloof," she said. She reached to put her fingers around my arm, three inches below the shoulder, and press. "Don't pay any attention to that. It doesn't mean anything. Once in a while I like to feel a man's arm, that's all."

"Okay, I'm a man."

"So I suspected."

"When this is all over I'd be glad to teach you how to play pool or look up words in the dictionary."

"Thanks." I thought she shivered. "When this is all over."

When we stopped for a light in the upper Forties she said, "You know, I believe I'm going to be hysterical. But don't pay any attention to that either."

I looked at her, and there certainly wasn't any sign of it in her voice or her face. I never saw anyone act less hysterical. When I pulled up at the curb at her address, she hopped out before I could move and stuck her hand in.

"Good night. Or what is the protocol? Does a detective shake hands with one of the suspects?"

"Sure." We shook. It fitted nicely. "To get her off her guard."

She disappeared inside, probably to give the doorman a brief glance on her way to the elevator, to strengthen his motive.

When I got back home, after putting the car away, and stopped in the office to make sure the safe was locked, there was a scribbled note lying on my desk:

> Archie: Do not communicate further with Miss Gunther
> except on my order. A woman who is not a fool is dan-
> gerous. I don't like this case and shall decide tomorrow
> whether to abandon it and refund the retainer. In the
> morning get Panzer and Gore here. NW

Which gave me a rough idea of the state of confusion he was in, the way the note contradicted itself. Saul Panzer's rate was thirty bucks a day, and Bill Gore's was twenty, not to mention expenses, and his committing himself to such an outlay was absolute proof that there would be no retainer refund. He was merely appealing for my sympathy because he had taken on such a hard job. I went up two flights to my room, glancing at the door of his as I passed it on the first landing, and noting that the little red light was on, showing that he had flipped the switch for the alarm connection.

12

I realized all the more how hard the job was likely to be when, the next morning after Wolfe came down from the plant rooms at eleven o'clock, I heard him giving Saul Panzer and Bill Gore their instructions.

To anyone seeing him but not knowing him, Saul Panzer was nothing but a little guy with a big nose who never quite caught up with his shaving. To the few who knew him, Wolfe and me for instance, those details meant nothing. He was the one free-lance operative in New York who, year in and year out, always had at least ten times more jobs offered him than he had the time or inclination to take. He never turned Wolfe down if he could possibly help it. That morning he sat with his old brown cap on his knee, taking no notes because he never had to, while Wolfe described the situation and told him to spend as many hours or days at the Waldorf as might be necessary, milking and gathering eggs. He was to cover everything and everybody.

Bill Gore was full size and unpolished, and one glance at the top of his head showed that he was doomed. He would be bald in another five years. His immediate objective was the NIA office, where he was to compile certain lists and records. Erskine had been phoned to and had promised cooperation.

After they had departed I asked Wolfe, "Is it really as bad as that?"

He frowned at me. "As bad as what?"

"You know darned well what. Fifty dollars a day for the dregs. Where is there any genius in that?"

"Genius?" His frown became a scowl. "What can genius do with this confounded free-for-all? A thousand people, all with motive and opportunity, and the means at hand! Why the devil I ever let you persuade me —"

"No, sir," I said loudly and firmly. "Don't try it! When I saw how tough this was going to be, and then when I read that note you left for me last night, it was obvious you would try to blame it on me. Nothing doing. I admit I didn't know how desperate it was until I heard you telling Saul and Bill to dive into the holes the cops have already cleaned out. You don't have to admit you're licked. You can wriggle out. I'll draw a check to the NIA for their ten thousand, and you can dictate a letter to them saying that on account of having caught the mumps, or perhaps it would be better —"

"Shut up," he growled. "How can I return money I haven't received?"

"But you have. The check was in the morning mail and I've deposited it."

"Good God. It's in the bank?"

"Yes, sir."

He pushed the button, savagely, for beer. He was as close to being in a panic as I remembered seeing him.

"So you have nothing," I said without mercy. "Nothing whatever?"

"Certainly I have something."

"Yeah? What?"

"Something Mr. O'Neill said yesterday afternoon. Something very peculiar."

"What?"

He shook his head. "Not for you. I'll put Saul or Bill on it tomorrow."

I didn't believe a word of it. For ten minutes I went over in my mind everything I remembered Don O'Neill saying, and then believed it less than ever.

All day Saturday he had no jobs for me connected with the Boone case, not even a phone call to make. The calls all came the other way, and there were plenty of those. Most of them, from newspapers and Cramer's office and so on, were nothing but blah. Two of them were merely comic relief:

Winterhoff, the Man of Distinction, phoned around noon. He wanted something for his money right away. The cops were after him. Many hours of questioning about fourteen people had got it settled that it was he who had suggested the little room near the stage for Boone's privacy and had escorted him there, and he was being harassed. He had explained that his knowledge of the room had come from his participation in previous affairs on those premises, but they weren't satisfied. He wanted Wolfe to certify to his innocence and instruct the police to let him alone. His order wasn't filled.

Just before lunch there was a call from a man with an educated voice who said his name was Adamson, of counsel for the NIA. His tone implied that he wasn't very crazy about Wolfe's being hired anyway, and he wanted practically everything, including a daily report of all activities, operations, conversations, contacts, and intentions. He insisted on speaking to Wolfe, which was a mistake on his part, because if he had been willing to talk with me I might at least have treated him with common courtesy.

Another thing the NIA wanted the very day we got their retainer check was something we couldn't have furnished even if we had felt like it. This request was brought by their Hattie Harding in person, in the middle of the afternoon, just after Wolfe went up to the orchids. I took her to the office and we sat on the couch. She was still well put together and well dressed, and her eyes were still competent, but the strain was telling on her. She looked much nearer forty-eight than twenty-six.

She had come to yell for help, though she didn't put it that way. To hear her tell it, there was hell to pay from coast to coast and the end of the world was expected any minute. Public Relations was on its last legs. Hundreds of telegrams were pouring into the NIA office, from members and friends all over the country, telling of newspaper editorials, of resolutions passed by Chambers of Commerce and all sorts of clubs and groups, and of talk in the street. Even—this was stricly off the record—eleven resignations had been received from members, one a member of the Board of Directors. Something had to be done.

I asked what.

Something, she said.

"Like catching the murderer?"

"That, of course." She seemed to regard that as a mere detail. "But something to stop this insane hullabaloo. Perhaps a statement signed by a hundred prominent citizens. Or telegrams urging sermons tomorrow—to-morrow is Sunday—"

"Are you suggesting that Mr. Wolfe should send telegrams to fifty thousand preachers and priests and rabbis?"

"No, of course not." Her hands fluttered. "But something—something—"

"Listen, P.R." I patted her on the knee to quiet her. "You are stricken, I appreciate that. But the NIA seems to think this is a department store. Who you want is not Nero Wolfe but Russell Birdwell or Eddie Bernays. This is a specialty shop. All we're going to do is catch the murderer."

"Oh, my God," she said. Then she added, "I doubt it."

"Doubt what?" I stared at her. "That we're going to catch him?"

"Yes. That anyone is."

"Why?"

"I just doubt it." She met my gaze, competently. Then her eyes changed. "Look, this is off the record?"

"Sure, you and me. And my boss, but he never tells anybody anything."

"I'm fed up." She worked her jaw like man, no lip trembling. "I'm going to quit and get a job sewing on buttons. The day anyone catches the murderer of Cheney Boone, finds him and proves it on him, it will rain up instead of down. In fact it will—"

I nodded encouragingly. "What else will it do?"

She abruptly got to her feet. "I'm talking too much."

"Oh, no, not enough. You've just started. Sit down."

"No, thank you." Her eyes were competent again. "You're the first man I've collapsed in front of for a long, long time. For heaven's sake, don't get the idea that I know secrets and try to dig them out of me. It's just that this thing is more than I can handle and I've lost my head. Don't bother to let me out."

She went.

When Wolfe came down to the office at six o'clock I reported the conversation in full. At first he decided not to be interested, then changed his mind. He wanted my opinion and I gave it to him, that I doubted if she knew anything that would help much, and even if she did she was through collapsing in front of me, but he might have a go at her.

He grunted. "Archie. You are transparent. What you mean is that you don't want to bother with her, and you don't want to bother with her because Miss Gunther has got you fidgeting."

I said coldly, "I don't fidget."

"Miss Gunther has got you on a string."

Usually I stay right with him when he takes that line, but there was no telling how far he might go in the case of Phoebe Gunther and I didn't want to resign in the middle of a murder job, so I cut it off by going to the front door for the evening papers.

We get two of each, to avoid friction, and I handed him his share and sat at my desk with mine. I looked at the *Gazette* first, and on the front page saw headlines that looked like news. It was. Mrs. Boone had got something in the mail.

One detail that I believe I haven't mentioned before was Boone's wallet. I haven't mentioned it because its being taken by the murderer provided no new angle on the crime or the motive, since he hadn't carried money in it. His money had been in a billfold in his hip pocket and hadn't been touched. He had carried the wallet in the breast pocket of his coat and used it for miscellaneous papers and cards, and it had not been found on the body, and therefore it was presumed that the murderer had taken it. The news in the *Gazette* was that Mrs. Boone had received an envelope in the mail that morning with her name and address printed on it with a lead pencil, and in it had been two objects that Boone had always carried in the wallet: his automobile license and a photograph of Mrs. Boone in her wedding dress. The *Gazette* article remarked that the sender must be both a sentimentalist and a realist; sentimental, because the photo was returned; realistic, because the auto license, which was still of use, had been returned, while Boone's operator's license, which he had also kept in the wallet, had not been. The *Gazette* writer was picturesque about it, saying that the operator's license had been canceled with a monkey wrench.

"Indeed," Wolfe said loud enough for me to hear. I saw that he was reading it too, and spoke:

"If the cops hadn't already been there and got it, and if Miss Gunther didn't have me on a string, I'd run up to see Mrs. Boone and get that envelope."

"Three or four men in a laboratory," Wolfe said, "will do everything to that envelope but split its atoms. Before long they'll be doing that too. But this is the first finger that has pointed in any direction at all."

"Sure," I agreed, "now it's a cinch. All we have to do is find out which of those one thousand four hundred and ninety-two people is both a sentimentalist and a realist, and we've got him."

We went back to our papers.

Nothing more before dinner. After the meal, which for me consisted chiefly of thin toast and liver pâté on account of the way Fritz makes the pâté, we had just got back to the office again, a little before nine, when a telegram came. I took it from the envelope and handed it to Wolfe, and after he had read it he passed it over to me. It ran:

> NERO WOLFE 919 WEST 35 NYC
> CIRCUMSTANCES MAKE IT IMPOSSIBLE TO CONTINUE
> SURVEILLANCE OF ONEILL BUT BELIEVE IT ESSENTIAL
> THIS BE DONE ALTHOUGH CAN GUARANTEE NOTHING
> BRESLOW

I put my brows up at Wolfe. He was looking at me with his eyes half open, which meant he was really looking.

"Perhaps," he said witheringly, "you will be good enough to tell me what other arrangements you have made for handling this case without my knowledge?"

I grinned at him. "No, sir. Not me. I was about to ask if you have put Breslow on the payroll and if so at how much, so I can enter it."

"You know nothing of this?"

"No. Don't you?"

"Get Mr. Breslow on the phone."

That wasn't so simple. We knew only that Breslow was a manufacturer of paper products from Denver, and that, having come to New York for the NIA meeting, he was staying on, as a member of the Executive Committee, to help hold the fort in the crisis. I knew Frank Thomas Erskine was at the Churchill and tried that, but he was out. Hattie Harding's number, which was in the phone book, gave me a don't answer signal. So I tried Lon Cohen again at the *Gazette*, which I should have done in the first place, and learned that Breslow was at the Strider-Weir. In another three minutes I had him and switched him to Wolfe, but kept myself connected.

He sounded on the phone just the way he looked, red-faced with anger.

"Yes, Wolfe? Have you got something? Well? Well?"

"I have a question to ask—"

"Yes? What is it?"

"I am about to ask it. That was why I had Mr. Goodwin learn your number, and call it and ask for you, so you could be on one end of the telephone and me on the other end, and then I could ask you this question. Tell me when you are ready, sir."

"I'm ready! Damn it, what is it?"

"Good. Here it is. About that telegram you sent me—"

"Telegram? What telegram? I haven't sent you any telegram!"

"You know nothing about a telegram to me?"

"No! Nothing whatever! What—"

"Then it's a mistake. They must have got the name wrong. I suspected as much. I was expecting one from a man named Bristow. I apologize, sir, for disturbing you. Good-by."

Breslow tried to prolong the agony, but between us we got him off.

"So," I remarked, "he didn't send it. If he did, and didn't want us to know it, why would he sign his name? Do we have it traced? Or do we save energy by assuming that whoever sent it knows about phone booths?"

"Confound it," Wolfe said bitterly. "Probably someone peddling herrings. But we can't afford to ignore it." He glanced at the wall clock, which said three minutes past nine. "Find out if Mr. O'Neill is at home. Just ask him — no. Let me have him."

The number of O'Neill's residence, an apartment on Park Avenue, was listed, and I got both it and him. Wolfe took it, and told him about the request from Adamson, the NIA lawyer, and fed him a long rigmarole about the inadvisability of written reports. O'Neill said he didn't care a hang about reports, written or otherwise, and they parted friends.

Wolfe considered a moment. "No. We'll let him go for tonight. You had better get him in the morning as he leaves. If we decide to keep it up we can get Orrie Cather."

13

TAILING as a solo job in New York can be almost anything, depending on the circumstances. You can wear out your brain and muscles in a strenuous ten-hour stretch, keeping contact only by using all the dodges on the list and inventing some more as you go along, and then lose him by some lousy little break that nothing and no one could have prevented. Or you can lose him the first five minutes, especially if he knows you're there. Or, also in the first five minutes, he can take to a chair somewhere, an office or a hotel room, and stay there all day, not giving a damn how bored you get.

So you never know, but what I fully expected was a long day of nothing, since it was Sunday. A little after eight in the morning I sat in a taxi which, headed downtown, was parked on Park Avenue in the Seventies, fifty paces north of the entrance to the apartment house where O'Neill lived. I would have given even money that I would still be there six hours later, or even twelve, though I admitted there was a fair chance of our going to church at eleven, or to a restaurant for two o'clock dinner. I couldn't even read the Sunday paper with any satisfaction because I had to keep my eye on the entrance. The taxi driver was my old stand-by Herb Aronson, but he had never seen O'Neill. As the time went by we discussed various kinds of matters, and he read aloud to me from the *Times*.

At ten o'clock we decided to get a bet down. Each of us would write on a slip of paper the time that we thought my man would stick his nose out, and the one that was furthest off would pay the other one a cent a minute for the time he missed it by. Herb was just handing me a scrap he tore from the *Times* for me to write my guess on when I saw Don O'Neill emerging to the sidewalk.

I told Herb, "Save it for next time. That's him."

Whatever O'Neill did, it would be awkward, because his doorman knew us by heart by that time. He had previously signaled to Herb for a customer, and Herb had turned him down. What O'Neill did was look toward us, with me keeping my face in a corner so he couldn't see it if his vision was good for that distance, and speak to the doorman, who shook his head. That was about as awkward as it could get, unless O'Neill had walked to us for a conference.

Herb told me out of the corner of his mouth, "Our strategy stinks. He takes a taxi and we ride his tail, and when he comes home the doorman tells him he's being followed."

"So what was I to do?" I demanded. "Disguise myself as a flower girl and stand at the corner selling daffodils? Next time you plan it. This whole tailing idea has got to be a joke. Start your engine. Anyhow, he'll never get home. We'll pinch him for murder before the day's out. Start your engine! He's getting transportation."

The doorman had been blowing his whistle, and a taxi on its way south had swerved and was stopping at the curb. The doorman opened the door and O'Neill got in, and the taxi slid away. Herb got into gear and we moved.

"This," Herb said, "is the acme. The absolute acme. Why don't we just pull up to him and ask where he's going?"

"Because," I said, "you don't know an acme when you see one. He has no reason at all to think we're following him unless he has been alerted, and in that case nothing would unalert him and we are lost. Keep back a little more—just enough not to let a light part us."

Herb did so, and manged the light stops as if his heart was in it. With the thin traffic of Sunday morning, there were only two of them before we got to Forty-sixth Street, where O'Neill's cab turned left. One block over, at Lexington Avenue, it turned right, and in another minute it had stopped at the entrance to Grand Central Station.

We were two cars behind. Herb swung to the right and braked, and I stepped out behind a parked car and grinned at him. "Didn't I tell you? He's hopping it. See you in court." As soon as O'Neill had paid his driver and started across the sidewalk I left cover.

I was still selling it short. What I would have settled for at that stage was a ride out to Greenwich to join a week-end party for some drinks and maybe poker. At any rate, O'Neill didn't seem to be in any doubt as to what he would settle for, for he marched down the long corridor and across the concourse of the station like a man with a destination. He gave no sign of suspecting that anyone had an eye on him. Where he finally wound up was not one of the train entrances, but the main parcel room on the upper level. I lingered at a distance, with a corner handy. There were several ahead of him and he waited his turn, then handed in a ticket, and in a minute or so was given an object.

Even from where I stood, about thirty feet off, the object looked as if it might be of interest. It was a little rectangular leather case. He grabbed it up and went. I was now somewhat less interested in keeping my presence undetected, but a lot more interested in not losing him, so I closed up some, and nearly stepped on his heels when he suddenly slowed up, almost to a stop, put the case inside his topcoat, got his arm snugly around it, and buttoned the coat. Then he went on. Instead of returning to the Lexington Avenue entrance he went up the ramp toward Forty-second Street, and when he got to the sidewalk turned left, to where the taxis stop in front of the Commodore Hotel. He still hadn't spotted me. After a short wait he snared a cab, opened the door and got in, and reached to pull the door shut.

I decided that would not do. It would have been nice to know what address he would give the driver if there were no interruptions, but that wasn't vital, where as if I lost contact with that leather case through the hazards of solo tailing I would have to get a job helping Hattie Harding sew on buttons. So I moved fast enough to use a hand to keep the door from closing and spoke:

"Hello there, Mr. O'Neill! Going uptown? Mind giving me a lift?"

I was on the seat beside him, and now, willing to do my share, pulled the door shut.

I am not belittling him when I say he was flustered. It would have flustered most men. And he did pretty well.

"Why, hello, Goodwin! Where did you come from? I'm—well, no, the fact is I'm not going uptown. I'm going downtown."

"Make up your mind," the driver growled through at us.

"It doesn't matter," I told O'Neill cheerfully. "I just want to ask you a couple of questions about that leather case that's under your coat." I said to the driver, "Go ahead. Turn south on Eighth."

The driver was glaring at me. "It's not your cab. What is this, a hard touch?"

"No," O'Neill told him. "It's all right. We're friends. Go ahead."

The cab moved. There was no conversation. We passed Vanderbilt and, after waiting for a light, were crossing Madison when O'Neill leaned forward to tell the driver:

"Turn north on Fifth Avenue."

The driver was too hurt to reply, but when we got to Fifth and had a green light he turned right. I said:

"All right if you want to, but I thought we would save time by going straight to Nero Wolfe's place. He will be even curiouser than I am about what's in that thing. Of course we shouldn't discuss it in this taxi, since the driver doesn't like us."

He leaned forward again and gave the driver his home address on Park Avenue. I thought that over for three blocks and voted against it. The only weapon I had on me was a penknife. Since I had been watching that entrance since eight o'clock it was unlikely that the NIA Executive Committee was assembled in O'Neill's apartment, but if they were, and especially if General Erskine was with them, it would require too much exertion on my part to walk out of there with that case. So I spoke to O'Neill in an undertone:

"Lookit. If he's a public-spirited citizen, and if he hears anything that gives him the idea this is connected with murder, he'll probably stop at the first cop he sees. Maybe that's what you want too, a cop. If so you will be glad to know that I don't like the idea of your apartment and if we go there I'll display a license to that doorman, put my arms around you, and make him call the Nineteenth Precinct, which is at 153 East Sixty-seventh Street, Rhinelander four, one-four-four-five. That would create a hubbub. Why not get rid of this eavesdropper and talk it over on a bench in the sunshine? Also I saw the look in your eye and don't try it. I'm more than twenty years younger than you and I do exercises every morning."

He relinquished the expression of a tiger about to leap and leaned forward to tell the driver:

"Stop here."

Although I doubted if he carried shooters, I didn't want him fooling around his pockets, so I settled with the meter myself. We were at Sixty-ninth Street. After the cab had rolled off we crossed the avenue, walked to one of the benches against the wall enclosing Central Park, and sat down. He was keeping his left arm hooked tight around the object under his coat.

I said, "One easy way would be for me to take a look at it, inside and out. If it contains only black market butter, God bless you."

He turned sideways to regard me as man to man. "I'll tell you, Goodwin." He was choosing his words. "I'm not going to try a lot of stuff like indignation about your following me and that kind of stuff." I thought he wasn't choosing very well, repeating himself, but I was too polite to interrupt. "But I can explain how I happen to have this case, absolutely innocently — absolutely! And I don't know any more than you do about what's in it — I have no idea!"

"Let's look and see."

"No." He was firm. "As far as you know, it's my property —"

"But is it?"

"As far as you know it is, and I have a right to examine it privately. I mean a moral right, I admit I can't put it on the ground of legal right because you have offered to refer it to the police and this is of course legally correct. But I do have the moral right. You first suggested that we should go with it to Nero Wolfe. Do you think the police would approve of that?"

"No, but he would."

"I don't doubt it." O'Neill was in his stride now, earnest and persuasive. "But you see, neither of us actually wants to go to the police. Actually our interests coincide. It's merely a question of procedure. Look at it from your personal angle: what you want is to be able to go to your employer and say to him. 'You sent me to do a job, and I have done it, and here are the results,' and then deliver this leather case to him, and me right there with you if you want it that way. Isn't that what you want?"

"Sure. Let's go."

"We will go. I assure you, Goodwin, we will go." He was so sincere it was almost painful. "But does it matter exactly *when* we go? Now or four hours from now? Of course it doesn't! I have never broken a promise in my life. I am a businessman, and the whole basis of American business is integrity — absolute integrity. That brings us back to my moral rights in this matter. What I propose is this: I will go to my office, at 1270 Sixth Avenue. You will come there for me at three o'clock, or I will meet you anywhere you say, and I will have this leather case with me, and we will take it to Nero Wolfe."

"I don't —"

"Wait. Whatever my moral rights may be, if you extend me this courtesy you deserve to have it acknowledged and appreciated. When I meet you at three o'clock I will hand you one thousand dollars in currency as evidence of appreciation. A point I didn't mention: I will guarantee that Wolfe will know nothing about this four-hour delay. That will be easy to arrange. If I had the thousand dollars with me I would give it to you now. I have never broken a promise in my life."

I looked at my wrist and appealed to him, "Make it ten thousand."

He wasn't staggered, but only grieved, and he wasn't even grieved beyond endurance. "That's out of the question," he declared, but not in a tone to give offense. "Absolutely out of the question. One thousand is the limit."

I grinned at him. "It would be fun to see how far up I could get you, but it's ten minutes to eleven, so in ten minutes Mr. Wolfe will come down to his office and I don't like to keep him waiting. The trouble is it's Sunday and I never take bribes on Sunday. Forget it. Here are the alternatives: You and I and the object under your coat go now to Mr. Wolfe. Or give me the object and I take it to him, and you go for a walk or take a nap. Or I yell at the cop across the street and tell him to call the precinct, which I admit I like least, but you've got your moral rights. Heretofore I've been in no hurry, but now Mr. Wolfe will be downstairs, so I give you two minutes."

He wanted to try. "Four hours! That's all! I'll make it five thousand, and you come with me and I'll give it to you —"

"No. Forget it. Didn't I say it's Sunday? Come on, hand it over."

"I am not going to let this case out of my sight."

"Okay." I got up and crossed to the curb and stood so as to keep one eye out for a taxi and one on him. Before long I flagged an empty and it turned in to me and stopped. It had probably been years since Don O'Neill had done anything he disapproved of as strongly as he did of arising and walking to the cab and getting in, but he made it. I dropped beside him and gave the driver the address.

14

TEN hollow black cylinders, about three inches in diameter and six inches long, stood on end in two neat rows on Wolfe's desk. Beside them, with the lid open, was the case of good heavy leather, somewhat battered and scuffed. On the outside of the lid a big figure four was stamped. On its inside a label was pasted:

BUREAU OF PRICE REGULATION
POTOMAC BUILDING
WASHINGTON, D.C.

Before pasting in the label someone had typed on it in caps: OFFICE OF CHENEY BOONE, DIRECTOR.

I was at my desk and Wolfe was at his. Don O'Neill was walking up and down with his hands in his pants pockets. The atmosphere was not hail fellow well met. I had given Wolfe a full report, including O'Neill's last-minute offer to me of five grand, and Wolfe's self-esteem was such that he always regarded any attempt to buy me off as a personal affront, not to me but to him. I have often wondered who he would blame if I sold out once, himself or me.

He had repudiated without discussion O'Neill's claim to a moral right to hear what was on the cylinders before anyone else, and when O'Neill had seen it was hopeless the look on his face was such that I had decided to make sure and had given him a good frisking. He was not packing any tools, but that had not improved the atmosphere. The question then arose, how were we to make the cylinders perform? The next day, a business day, it would have been easy, but this was Sunday. It was O'Neill who solved the problem. The President of the Stenophone Company was a member of the NIA and O'Neill knew him. He lived in Jersey. O'Neill phoned him and, without disclosig any incriminating details, got him to phone the manager of his New York office and showroom, who lived in Brooklyn, and instruct him to go to the showroom, get a Stenophone and bring it to Wolfe's office. That was what we were sitting there waiting for — that is, Wolfe and I were sitting and O'Neill was walking.

"Mr. O'Neill." Wolfe opened his eyes enough to see. "That tramping back and forth is extremely irritating."

"I'm not going to leave this room," O'Neill declared without halting.

"Shall I tie him up?" I offered.

Wolfe, ignoring me, told O'Neill, "It will probably be another hour or more. What about your statement that you got possession of this thing innocently? Your word. Do you want to explain that now? How you got it innocently?"

"I'll explain it when I feel like it."

"Nonsense. I didn't take you for a nincompoop."

"Go to hell."

That always annoyed Wolfe. He said sharply. "Then you are a nincompoop. You have only two means of restraining Mr. Goodwin and me: your own physical prowess or an appeal to the police. The former is hopeless; Mr. Goodwin could fold you up and put you on a shelf. You obviously don't like the idea of the police, I can't imagine why, since you're innocent. So how do you like this: when that machine has arrived and we have learned how to run it and the manager has departed, Mr. Goodwin will carry you out and set you on the stoop, and come back in and shut the door. Then he and I will listen to the cylinders."

O'Neill stopped walking, took his hands from his pockets and put them flat on the desk to lean on them, and glowered at Wolfe.

"You won't do that!"

"I won't. Mr. Goodwin will."

"Damn you!" He held the pose long enough for five takes, then slowly straightened up. "What do you want?"

"I want to know where you got this thing."

"All right, I'll tell you. Last evening —"

"Excuse me. Archie. Your notebook. Go ahead, sir."

"Last evening around eight-thirty I got a phone call at home. It was a woman. She said her name was Dorothy Unger and she was a stenographer at the New York office of the Bureau of Price Regulation. She said she had made a bad mistake. She said that in an envelope addressed to me she had enclosed something that was supposed to be enclosed in a letter to someone else. She said that she had remembered about it after she got home, and that she might even lose her job if her boss found out about it. She asked me when I received the envelope to mail the enclosure to her at her home, and she gave me her address. I asked her what the enclosure was and she said it was a ticket for a parcel that had been checked at Grand Central Station. I asked her some more questions and told her I would do what she asked me to."

Wolfe put in, "Of course you phoned her back."

"I couldn't. She said she had no phone and was calling from a booth. This morning I received the envelope and the enclosure was —"

"This is Sunday," Wolfe snapped.

"Damn it, I know it's Sunday! It came special delivery. It contained a circular about price ceilings, and the enclosure. If it had been a weekday I would have communicated with the BPR office, but of course the office wasn't open." O'Neill gestured impatiently. "What does it matter what I would have done or what I thought? You know what I did do. Naturally, you know more about it than me, since you arranged the whole thing!"

"I see." Wolfe put up a brow. "You think I arranged it?"

"No." O'Neill leaned on the desk again. "I *know* you arranged it! What happened? Wasn't Goodwin right there? I admit I was dumb when I came here Friday. I was afraid you had agreed to frame Boone's murder on someone in the BPR, or at least someone outside the NIA. And already, you must have been, you were preparing to frame someone in the NIA! Me! No wonder you think I'm a nincompoop!"

He jerked erect, glared at Wolfe, turned to glare at me, went to the red leather chair and sat down, and said in a completely different voice, calm and controlled:

"But you'll find that I'm not a nincompoop."

"That point," Wolfe said, frowning at him, "is relatively unimportant. The envelope you received this morning special delivery — have you got it with you?"

"No."

"Where is it, at your home?"

"Yes."

"Telephone and tell someone to bring it here."

"No. I'm going to have some detective work done on that envelope and not by you."

"Then you won't hear what those cylinders have to say," Wolfe explained patiently. "Must I keep repeating that?"

This time O'Neill didn't try to argue. He used the phone on my desk, dialed, got his party, and told someone whom he called Honey to get the envelope as described from the top of his chiffonier and send it by messenger to Nero Wolfe's office. I was surprised. I would have made it five to one that there was no such envelope, and it was still even money with me that it would be gone from the chiffonier because it must have dropped to the floor and the maid thought it was trash.

When O'Neill was back in the red leather chair Wolfe said, "You're going to find it a little difficult to get anyone to believe that you suspect Mr.

Goodwin and me of arranging this. For if that's true, why didn't you insist on going to the police? He wanted to."

"He did not want to." O'Neill was keeping calm. "He merely threatened to."

"But the threat worked. Why did it work?"

"You know damn well why it worked. Because I wanted to hear what's on those cylinders."

"You did indeed. Up to five thousand dollars. Why?"

"Do I have to tell you why?"

"No. You don't have to. You know how it stands."

O'Neill gulped. He had probably swallowed "Go to hell" thirty times in thirty minutes. "Because I have reason to suppose, and so have you, that they are confidential dictation by Cheney Boone, and they may have something to do with what happened to him, and if so I want to know it."

Wolfe shook his head reproachfully. "You're inconsistent. Day before yesterday, sitting in that same chair, your attitude was that you of the NIA had nothing to do with it and it was none of your business. Another thing: you didn't try to bribe Mr. Goodwin to let you hear the cylinders. You tried to bribe him to give you four hours alone with them. Were you trying to scoop all of us — the police, the FBI, and me?"

"Yes, I was, if you want to call it scoop. I didn't trust you before, and now . . ."

Now, from his tone, we were something scraped off the under side of a bridge.

I could report it all, since it's still in the notebook, but it isn't worth it. Wolfe decided, apparently more to kill time than anything else, to put the microscope on the episode of the phone call from Dorothy Unger and the receipt of the envelope. He took O'Neill over it, back and forth and up and down, and O'Neill stayed with him, against his strongest instincts and inclinations, because he knew he had to if he wanted to hear those cylinders. I got so fed up with the repetitions that when the doorbell rang the interruption was welcome in more ways than one.

O'Neill sprang from his chair and came along to the front door. On the stoop was a middle-aged square-faced woman in a purple coat. He greeted her as Gretty, took the envelope she handed him, and thanked her.

Back in the office he let Wolfe and me handle it to look it over, but stayed close. It was a regulation BPR envelope, New York office, with his name and home address typed. Right in the corner, over the penalty clause, was a three-cent stamp, and a couple of inches to the left were five more three-cent stamps. Beneath them was printed by hand with a blue pencil: SPECIAL DELIVERY. Inside was a mimeographed BPR circular, dated March 27th, regarding price ceilings on a long list of copper and brass items.

When Wolfe handed it back to O'Neill and he stuck it in his pocket I remarked, "The post-office employees get more careless all the time. With that stamp in the corner canceled and the others not."

"What?" O'Neill got it from his pocket and glared at it. "What of it?"

"Nothing," Wolfe said shortly. "Mr. Goodwin likes to brag. It proves nothing.

I saw no reason why I shouldn't help to kill time, and I resent Wolfe's habit of making personal remarks in front of strangers, especially when he's an enemy, so I was opening my mouth to go on with it when the bell rang again. When I went to answer it O'Neill came along. You might have thought he was training for the job.

It was the Stenophone man. O'Neill did the honors, mentioning the president and apologizing for ruining his Sunday and so on, and I helped with the machine. It didn't amount to much, for O'Neill had explained on the phone that we didn't need a recorder. The chassis of the player had casters, and didn't weigh over sixty pounds anyhow. The Stenophone man wheeled it into the office, and was introduced to Wolfe, and in less than five minutes had us all instructed. Then, since he didn't seem disposed to linger, we let him go.

When I returned to the office after showing the visitor out, Wolfe sent me a certain type of glance to alert me and said:

"Now, Archie, if you'll get Mr. O'Neill's hat and coat, please. He is leaving."

O'Neill stared at him a second and then laughed, or at least made a noise. It was the first downright ugly noise he had made.

Just to try him for size I took two quick steps toward him. He took three quick steps back. I stopped and grinned at him. He tried to look at both Wolfe and me at once.

"So that's how it is," he said, extremely ugly. "You think you can double-cross Don O'Neill. You'd better not."

"Pfui." Wolfe wiggled a finger at him. "I have given you no assurance that you would be permitted to hear these things. It would be manifestly improper to permit an official of the NIA to listen to confidential dictation of the Director of the BPR, even after the Director has been murdered. Besides, you're inconsistent again. A while ago you said you didn't trust me. That could only have been because you considered me untrustworthy. Now you profess to be shocked to find that I am untrustworthy. Utterly inconsistent." The finger wiggled again. "Well, sir? Do you prefer to be self-propelled?"

"I'm not leaving this room."

"Archie?"

I moved to him. This time he didn't budge. From the look on his face, if he had had anything at all useful on him he would have used it. I took him by the arm and said, "Come on, come with Archie. You must weigh a hundred and eighty. I don't want to carry you."

He started a right for my jaw, or at least it seemed that that was what he thought he was doing, but it was too slow to hit anything that wasn't nailed down. Ignoring it, I started to spin him to attack from the rear, and the son of a gun hauled off and kicked me. He tried to kick high and got my knee. I am not claiming that it hurt much, but I do not like kickers. So I plugged him, with my left because it was handiest, on his soft neck just below the ear, and he teetered over against the bookshelves. I supposed that would explain things to him, but he teetered right back and tried another kick, so I used the right with more in it, also to the neck for the sake of knuckles, and he teetered again and tumbled.

I told Wolfe to buzz Fritz to open the door, saw that Fritz was already there, took my fallen foe by the ankles, and dragged him across to the hall, down the hall to the door, and on out to the stoop. Fritz handed me his coat and hat and I dropped them on him, re-entered the hall, and shut the door.

In the office I asked Wolfe, "Is he on the Executive Committee too, or was he just Chairman of the Dinner Committee? I was trying to remember while I was dragging him."

"I dislike commotion," Wolfe said peevishly. "I didn't tell you to hit him."

"He tried to kick me. He did kick me. Next time you do it."

Wolfe shuddered. "Start that machine going."

15

IT took more than an hour altogether to run off the ten cylinders, not counting time out for lunch.

I started the first one at the speed recommended by our instructor, but it had been going only a few seconds when Wolfe told me to slow it down. Having heard Cheney Boone on the radio I had expected this to sound about the same, but although there was enough similarity to recognize his voice, this seemed to be pitched higher and the words were more distinct. The first one began:

"Six-seventy-nine. Personal. Dear Mr. Pritchard. Thank you very much for your letter but I have decided not to get a Chesapeake retriever but to try an Irish setter. I have nothing against Chesapeakes and there is no good reason for my decision except the unpredictable vagary of the human mind. Sincerely. Six-eighty. Dear Mrs. Ambruster. I do indeed remember that pleasant day and evening in St. Louis last fall and I deeply regret my inability to be present at the spring meeting of your fine organization. The next time I get to St. Louis I shall certainly get in touch with you. The material you request will be sent you without delay, and if it fails to arrive promptly be sure to let me know. With best regards and best wishes for the success of your meeting. Sincerely. Six-eight-one. Memo—no, make it a letter to all regional directors. By name to each. Please return to this office immediately the advance copies of the press release for March 25th regarding household appliances. That release has been canceled and will not be sent out. Paragraph. The premature disclosure of some of the contents of that release by a press association has again raised the question whether advance copies of releases should be sent to regional offices. You are requested to investigate without delay, in your office, the handling of the advance copies of the release in question, and make a full report of the results directly to me. I shall expect this report to reach me not later than March 28th. Sincerely. Six-eight-two. Dear Mr. Maspero. Thank you very much for your letter of the 16th, and I assure you that its contents will be regarded as confidential. That of course would be impossible if your information were susceptible of use in a legal action that could be undertaken by me in the performance of my duty, but I am fully aware of the difficulties involved in any attempt . . ."

That one went on long enough to fill at least two full pages single-spaced, leaving room on that cylinder only for two more letters and an interoffice memo. When it reached the end I removed it and returned it to its place in the row, and picked up number two, remarking meanwhile:

"I suppose you noticed that Boone apparently sent his letters by rocket and the regional directors were expected to be streaks of lightning."

Wolfe nodded gloomily. "We've been sniggled." He leaned forward to look at his desk calendar. "He couldn't possibly have dictated that the afternoon of the day he was killed, March 26th. He told the regional directors to investigate and get a report to him by March 28th. Since it was to go to all regional directors, the West Coast was included. Even granting the speed of air mail, and allowing only one day for their investigations, which seems meager, that must have been dictated not later than March 23rd, and probably several days earlier."

He sighed deep. "Confound it. I was hoping —" He compressed his lips and frowned at the leather case. "That woman said four, didn't she?"

"Do you mean Miss Gunther?"

"Who the devil do you think I mean?"

"I think you mean Miss Phoebe Gunther. If so, yes. She said there were twelve of those cases, and the one Boone gave her in the murder room had the number four stamped on top, and he told her it contained cylinders he had dictated in his Washington office that afternoon. So it looks as if someone has been playing button button. Are we too discouraged to go on or would we care to hear number two?"

"Go ahead."

I proceeded with the concert. Lunch intervened at the end of the sixth movement, and after a leisurely but not especially gay meal we returned to the office and finished them up. There was nothing spectacular anywhere in the lot, though some of them contained matter that was certainly confidential; and considered as clues that might help solve a murder, I wouldn't have paid a dime for them. In four others besides number one there was evidence, some of it conclusive, that they had been dictated earlier than March 26th.

I couldn't blame Wolfe for being depressed. In addition to all the other complications, there were at least eight possible explanations of how leather case number four happened, when found, to contain cylinders dictated prior to the day of the murder, the simplest of all being that Boone himself had picked up the wrong case when he left his Washington office that afternoon. Not to mention the basic question, for which I didn't have even a guess, let alone an answer: were the cylinders only a side show or were they part of the main performance?

Leaning back in his chair digesting, Wolfe was, to an unaccustomed eye though not to mine, sound asleep. He didn't stir as I wheeled the machine out of the way, over to a corner. Then, as I went to his desk and started to return the cylinders to their nests in the case, his lids opened to make a slit.

He shook his head. "You'd better run them off again and make a transcription of them. Three carbons." He glanced at the wall clock. "I'll be going upstairs in thirty-five minutes. Do it then."

"Yes, sir." I was grim. "I expected this."

"You did? I didn't."

"I don't mean I expected the cylinders to be antiques. I expected this typewriting job. That's the level this case seems to have descended to."

"Don't badger me. I was an ass to undertake it. I have more Cattleyas than I have room for, and I could have sold five hundred of them for twelve thousand dollars." He let his eyes come half open. "When you have finished transcribing these things, take them down to Mr. Cramer and tell him how we got them."

"Tell him everything?"

"Yes. But before you go to him do another typing job. Your notebook. Send this letter to everyone who was here Friday evening." He frowned for words, and in a moment dictated, "'Since you were good enough to come to my office at my invitation Friday evening, and since you were present when it was intimated that Miss Gunther's statement that she had left the leather case on the window sill of the reception room might not deserve credence, I am writing to inform you of a development that occurred to-day. Paragraph. Mr. Don O'Neill received in the mail a ticket for a parcel that had been checked at Grand Central Station. The parcel proved to be the leather case in question, with the figure four stamped on the lid as described by Miss Gunther. However, most of the cylinders it contained were obviously dictated by Mr. Boone prior to March 26th. I send you this information in justice to Miss Gunther.'"

"That all?" I inquired.

"Yes."

"Cramer will throw a fit."

"No doubt. Mail them before you go to him, and take a him a carbon. Then bring Miss Gunther here."

"Her? Phoebe Gunther?"

"Yes."

"That's dangerous. Isn't it too risky to trust me with her?"

"Yes. But I want to see her."

"Okay, it's on you."

16

TWO hours and more of back-breaking drudgery. Ten whole cylinders. Three carbons. Not only that, it was new to me and I had to adjust the speed about twenty times before I got the knack of it. When I finally got it finished and the sheets collated, I gave the original to Wolfe, who was back in the office by that time, placed the first two carbons in the safe, and folded the third carbon and stuck it in my pocket. Then there were the dozen letters to be typed and envelopes for same. As Wolfe signed them he folded and inserted them, and even sealed the envelopes. Sometimes he has bursts of feverish energy that are uncontrollable. By that time it was the dinner hour, but I decided not to dawdle through a meal in the dining room with Wolfe and made a quickie of it in the kitchen.

I had phoned the Homicide Squad office to make sure that Cramer would be on hand, to avoid having to deal with Lieutenant Rowcliffe, whose murder I hoped to help investigate some day, and had also called Phoebe Gunther's apartment to make a date but got no answer. Getting the car from the garage, I went first to Eighth Avenue to drop the letters in the post office and then headed south for Twentieth Street.

After I had been in with Cramer ten minutes he said, "This sounds like something. I'll be damned."

After another twenty minutes he said, "This sounds like something. I'll be damned."

That, of course, showed clear as day where he stood—up to his hips in a swamp. If he had been anywhere near dry ground, or even in sight of some, he would have waved his prerogative in front of my nose and cussed Wolfe and me up one side and down the other for withholding evidence for nine hours and fourteen minutes and so forth, including threats, growls, and warnings. Instead of which, at one point it looked as if he might abandon all restraint and thank me. Obviously he was desperate.

When I left Cramer I still had the carbon of the transcription in my pocket, because it was not intended for him. If I was to take Phoebe Gunther to Wolfe it was desirable that I get her before Cramer did, and it seemed likely that he would want to know exactly what was on those cylinders before he started a roundup. So I had kept it sketchy and hadn't told him that a transcription had been made.

Also I wasted no time getting to Fifty-fifth Street.

The doorman phoned up, gave me another look of surprise when he turned to tell me I would be received, and called an okay to the elevator. Up at Nine H, Phoebe opened the door and allowed me to enter. I put my coat and hat on a chair and followed her into the room, and there was Alger Kates over in the corner where the light was dim.

I will not deny that I am often forthright, but I would put up an argument if anyone called me crude. Yet, at sight of Kates there again, I said

50

what I said. I suppose it could be interpreted different ways. I do not concede that Phoebe Gunther had me fidgeting on a string, but the fact remains that I stared at Alger Kates and demanded:

"Do you live here?"

He stared back and replied, "If it's any of your business, yes, I do."

"Sit down, Mr. Goodwin." Phoebe possibly smiled. She got against the cushions on the couch. "I'll straighten it out. Mr. Kates does live here, when he's in New York. His wife keeps this apartment because she can't stand Washington. Right now she's in Florida. I couldn't get a hotel room, so Mr. Kates is staying with friends on Eleventh Street and letting me sleep here. Does that clear me? And him?"

Naturally I felt foolish. "I'll take it up," I said, "with the Housing Administration and see what I can do. Meanwhile I may be in a hurry, depending on how urgent Inspector Cramer feels. When I phoned you about an hour ago there was no answer."

She reached for a cigarette. "Why, do I need clearance on that too? I was out for a bite to eat."

"Has Cramer's office called since you returned?"

"No." She was frowning. "Does he want me? What for?"

"He either wants you now or he soon will." It was in the line of duty to keep my eyes fastened to her, to get her reaction. "I just took him that case of cylinders that you left on a window sill Tuesday evening."

I do not believe there was any menace in my tone. I don't know where it would have come from, as I did not at that time regard myself as a menace to Miss Gunther. But Alger Kates suddenly stood up, as if I had brandished a monkey wrench at her. He immediately sat down again. She kept her seat, but stopped her cigarette abruptly on its way to her lips, and the muscles of her neck stiffened.

"That case? With the cylinders in it?"

"Yes, ma'am."

"Did you—what's on them?"

"Well, that's a long story—"

"Where did you find it?"

"That's another long story. We've got to step on it, because Cramer has it now, and he may send for you any minute, or come to see you, or he may wait until he has listened to the cylinders. Anyhow, Mr. Wolfe wants to see you first, and since it was me—"

"Then you don't know what's on them?"

Kates had left his dim corner and moved across to the end of the couch, and was standing there in an attitude of readiness to repel the enemy. I ignored him and told her:

"Sure, I know. So does Mr. Wolfe. We got a machine and ran them off. They're interesting but not helpful. Their outstanding feature is that they weren't dictated on Tuesday, but before that—some of them a week or more. I'll tell—"

"But that's impossible!"

"Nope. Possible and true. I'll—"

"How do you know?"

"Dates and things. Absolutely." I stood up. "I'm getting restless. As I say,

Mr. Wolfe wants to see you first. With Cramer there's no telling, especially when he's hanging on by his fingernails, so let's go. Kates can come along to protect you if you want him to. I've got a transcription of the cylinders in my pocket and you can look at it on the way, and I'll tell—"

A bell rang. Having, though from the outside, heard it ring twice previously, I knew what it was.

I thought goddam it. I asked her in a whisper, "You expecting anybody?"

She shook her head, and the look in her eyes, straight at mine, said plainly that I could name the tune. But of course it was hopeless. Whoever had got by the doorman had also got information. Even so, there's nothing like trying, so I put a finger to my lips and stood there looking at them—at least I gave Kates a glance. His expression said belligerently, I'm not doing this for you, mister. We had held the tableau maybe ten seconds when a voice I knew well, the voice of Sergeant Purley Stebbins, came loud and irritated through the door:

"Come on, Goodwin, what the hell!"

I marched across and opened up. He came in past me rudely, took off his hat, and began to try to pretend he was a gentleman.

"Good afternoon, Miss Gunther. Good afternoon, Mr. Kates." He looked at her. "Inspector Cramer would be much obliged if you'd let me drive you down to his office. He's got some things there he wants you to look at. He told me to tell you they're Stenophone cylinders."

I was at his side. "You come right to the point, don't you, Purley, huh?"

"Oh," he said, pivoting his big fine empty head, "you still here? I supposed you was gone. The Inspector will be glad to know I ran into you."

"Nuts." I dropped him. "Of course you know, Miss Gunther, that you may do as you please. Some people think that when a city employee comes to take them somewhere they have to go. that's a fallacy, unless he has a document, which he hasn't."

"Is that true?" she asked me.

"Yes. That's true."

She had stood up when Purley entered. Now she moved across right to me, facing me, and stood looking up to meet my eyes. It wasn't much of a slant, because her eyes were only about five inches below mine, and therefore it wasn't a strain for either of us.

"You know," she said, "you have a way of suggesting things that appeal to me. With all I know about cops and their attitude toward people with power and position and money, and with the little I know about you, even if your boss has been hired by the NIA, I almost think I would let you hold my purse if I had to fix my garter. So you decide for me. I'll go with you to see Mr. Wolfe, or I'll go with this oversize sergeant, whichever you say."

Whereupon I made a mistake. It isn't so much that I regret it because it was a mistake, since I believe in having my share of everything on my way through life, including mistakes. The trouble was, as I now admit, that I did it not for my sake, or for Wolfe's, or for the good of the job, but for her. I would have loved to escort her down to my car with Purley traipsing along behind growling. Wolfe liked nothing better than to rile Cramer. But I knew if I took her to Wolfe's house Purley would camp outside, and after Wolfe finished with her she would either go on downtown for a night of it, or she would refuse to go, and she would certainly never hear the last of that. So I made the mistake because I thought Miss Gunther should have some sleep. Since she had told me herself that the tireder she got the better she looked, and there I was looking at her, it was evident that she was about all in.

So I said, "I deeply appreciate your confidence, which I deserve. You hold onto the purse while I fix the garter. For the present, I hate to say it, but it would be better to accept Cramer's invitation. I'll be seeing you."

Twenty minutes later I walked into the office and told Wolfe:

"Purley Stebbins arrived at Miss Gunther's before I could get her away, and she likes him better than she does me. She is now down at Twentieth Street."

So not only had I made a mistake, but also I was lying to the boss.

17

MONDAY would fill a book if I let it, and so would any other day, I suppose, if you put it all in.

First thing in the morning Wolfe provided evidence of how we were doing, or rather not doing, by having Saul Panzer and Bill Gore sent up to his room during the breakfast hour for private instructions. That was one of his established dodges for trying to keep me from needling him. The theory was that if I contributed any remarks about inertia or age beginning to tell or anything like that, he could shut me up by intimating that he was working like a demon supervising Saul and Bill, and they were gathering in the sheaves. Also that it wouldn't be safe to let me in on the secret because I couldn't control my face. One reason that got my goat was that I knew that he knew it wasn't true.

The sheaves they had so far delivered had not relieved the famine. The armful of words, typed, printed and mimeographed, that Bill Gore had brought in from the NIA would have kept the *Time* and *Life* research staff out of mischief for a week, and that was about all it was good for. Saul Panzer's report on his week-end at the Waldorf was what you would expect, no man whose initials were not A.G. could have done better, but all it added up to was that no hair of a murderer's head was to be found on the premises. What Wolfe was continuing to shell out fifty bucks a day for was, as I say, presumably none of my business.

Public Relations had tottered to its feet again, taken a deep breath, and let out a battle cry. There was a full page ad in the *Times,* signed by the National Industrial Association, warning us that the Bureau of Price Regulation, after depriving us of our shirts and pants, was all set to peel off our hides. While there was no mention of homicide, the implication was that since it was still necessary for the NIA to save the country from the vicious deep-laid plots of the BPR, it was silly to imagine that it had had any hand in the bumping off of Cheney Boone. As strategy, the hitch in it was that it would work only with those who already agreed with the NIA regarding who or what had got the shirts and pants.

One of my Monday problems was to get my outgoing phone calls made, on account of so many coming in the other direction. I started bright and early after Phoebe Gunther and never did get her. First, from the Fifty-fifth Street apartment, I got no answer. At nine-thirty I tried the BPR office and was told she hadn't arrived, and no one seemed to know whether she was expected. At ten-thirty I was informed that she was there, but was in with Mr. Dexter and would I call later. Twice later, before noon, she was still with Mr. Dexter. At twelve-thirty she had gone to lunch; my message for her to call me had been given to her. At one-thirty she wasn't back yet. At two o'clock the word was that she wouldn't be back, and no one that I got to knew where she was. That may all sound as if I am a pushover for a runaround, but I had two strikes on me all the way. Apparently there was nobody at the BPR, from switchboard girls to the Regional Director, who didn't know that Nero Wolfe, as Alger Kates put it, was in the pay of the NIA, and they reacted accordingly. When I made an attempt to get connected with Dorothy Unger, the stenographer who had phoned Don O'Neill Saturday evening to ask him to mail her the parcel check which she had enclosed in his envelope by mistake, I couldn't even find anyone who would even admit he had ever heard of her.

What I got for my money on phone calls that day was enough to send Tel & Tel to a new low. On incoming calls the score was no better. In addition to the usual routine on a big case, like newspaper boys wanting a ringside seat in case Nero Wolfe was winding up for another fast one, there was all kinds of client trouble on account of the letters Wolfe had sent about finding the cylinders. The ad in the *Times* may have indicated that the NIA was a united front, but the phone calls didn't. Each one had a different slant. Winterhoff's line was that the assumption in the letter that the manner of finding the cylinders vindicated Miss Gunther was unjustified; that on the contrary it reinforced the suspicion that Miss Gunther was lying about it, since the parcel check had been mailed to Don O'Neill in a BPR envelope. Breslow, of course, was angry, so much so that he phoned twice, once in the morning and once in the afternoon. What had him sore this time was that we had spread the news about the cylinders. In the interests of justice we should have kept it to ourselves and the cops. He accused us of trying to make an impression on the Executive Committee, of trying to show that we were earning our money, and that was a hell of a note; we should have only two things in mind: the apprehension of the criminal and the proof of his guilt.

Even the Erskine family was divided. Frank Thomas Erskine, the father, had no complaint or criticism. He simply wanted something: namely, the full text of what was on the cylinders. He didn't get indignant but he was utterly astonished. To him the situation was plain. Wolfe was doing a paid job for the NIA, and any information he got in the performance of that job was the property of the NIA, and any attempt to exclude them from possession of their property was felonious, malevolent, and naughty. He insisted as long as he thought there was any chance, and then quit without any indications of hard feelings.

The son, Ed, was the shortest and funniest. All the others had demanded to talk to Wolfe, not just me, but he said it didn't matter, I would do fine, all he wanted was to ask a question. I said shoot, and he asked this, "How good is the evidence that O'Neill got the parcel check the way he says he did, in the mail?" I said that all we had, besides a look at the envelope, was O'Neill's say-so, but that of course the police were checking it and he'd better ask them. He said much obliged and hung up.

All day I kept expecting a call from Don O'Neill, but there wasn't a peep out of him.

The general impression I got was that the Executive Committee had better call a meeting and decide on policy.

The day went, and dusk came, and I turned on lights. Just before dinner I tried Fifty-fifth Street, but no Phoebe Gunther. The meal took even longer than usual, which is to be expected when Wolfe is completely at a loss. He uses up energy keeping thoughts out and trying to keep me quiet, and that makes him eat more. After dinner, back in the office, I tried Fifty-fifth Street once more, with the same result. I was stretched out on the couch, trying to work out an attack that would make Wolfe explode into some kind of action, when the bell rang and I went to the front door and swung it wide open without a preliminary peek through the glass. As far as I was concerned anybody at all would have been welcome, even Breslow, just for a friendly chat.

Two men stepped in. I told them to hang up their things and went to the office door and announced:

"Inspector Cramer and Mr. Solomon Dexter."

Wolfe sighed and muttered, "Bring them in."

18

SOLOMON DEXTER was a blurter. I suppose, as Acting Director of BPR, he had enough to make him blurt, what with this and that, including things like Congress in an election year and the NIA ad in the morning *Times*, not to mention the unsolved murder of his predecessor, but still Wolfe does not like blurters. So he listened with a frown when, after brief greetings and with no preamble, Dexter blurted:

"I don't understand it at all! I've checked on you with the FBI and the Army, and they give you a clean bill and speak of you very highly! And here you are tied up with the dirtiest bunch of liars and cutthroats in existence! What the hell is the idea?"

"Your nerves are on edge," Wolfe said.

He blurted some more. "What have my nerves got to do with it? The blackest crime in the history of this country, with that unscrupulous gang behind it, and any man, any man whatever, who ties himself up—"

"Please!" Wolfe snapped. "Don't shout at me like that. You're excited. Justifiably excited perhaps, but Mr. Cramer shouldn't have brought you in here until you had cooled off." His eyes moved. "What does he want, Mr. Cramer? Does he want something?"

"Yeah," Cramer growled. "He thinks you fixed that stunt about the cylinders. So it would look as if the BPR had them all the time and tried to plant them on the NIA."

"Pfui. Do you think so too?"

"I do not. You would have done a better job of it."

Wolfe's eyes moved again. "If that's what you want, Mr. Dexter, to ask me if I arranged some flummery about those cylinders, the answer is I didn't. Anything else?"

Dexter had taken a handkerchief from his pocket and was mopping his face. I hadn't noticed any moisture on him, and it was cool out, and we keep the room at seventy, but apparently he felt that there was something to mop. That was probably the lumberjack in him. He dropped his hand to his thigh, clutching the handkerchief, and looked at Wolfe as if he were trying to remember the next line of the script.

"There is no one," he said, "by the name of Dorothy Unger employed by the BPR, either in New York or Washington."

"Good heavens." Wolfe was exasperated. "Of course there isn't."

"What do you mean of course there isn't?"

"I mean it's obvious there wouldn't be. Whoever contrived that hocus-pocus about the parcel check, whether Mr. O'Neill himself or someone else, certainly Dorothy Unger had to be invented."

"You ought to know," Dexter asserted savagely.

"Nonsense." Wolfe moved a finger to brush him away. "Mr. Dexter. If you're going to sit there and boil with suspicion you might as well leave. You accuse me of being 'tied up' with miscreants. I am 'tied up' with no one. I have engaged to do a specific job, find a murderer and get enough evidence to convict him. If you have any—"

"How far have you got?" Cramer interrupted.

"Well." Wolfe smirked. He is most intolerable when he smirks. "Further than you, or you wouldn't be here."

"Yeah," Cramer said sarcastically. "Here the other evening, I didn't quite understand why you didn't pick him out and let me take him."

"Neither did I," Wolfe agreed. "For one moment I thought I might, when one of them said something extraordinary, but I was unable—"

"Who said what?"

Wolfe shook his head. "I'm having it looked into." His tone implied that the 82nd Airborne was at it from coast to coast. He shifted to one of mild reproach. "You broke it up and chased them out. If you had acted like an adult investigator instead of an ill-tempered child I might have got somewhere."

"Oh, sure. I bitched it for you. I'd do anything to square it, anything you say. Why don't you ask me to get them all in here again, right now?"

"An excellent idea." Wolfe nearly sat up straight, he was so overcome with enthusiasm. "Excellent. I do ask it. Use Mr. Goodwin's phone."

"By God!" Cramer stared. "You thought I meant it?"

"*I* mean it," Wolfe asserted. "You wouldn't be here if you weren't desperate. You wouldn't be desperate if you could think of any more questions to ask anyone. That's what you came to me for, to get ideas for more questions. Get those people here, and I'll see what I can do."

"Who the hell does this man think he is?" Dexter demanded of Cramer.

Cramer, scowling at Wolfe, didn't reply. After some seconds he arose and, without any alteration in the scowl, came to my desk. By the time he arrived I had lifted the receiver and started to dial Watkins 9-8242. He took it, sat on the corner of the desk, and went on scowling.

"Horowitz? Inspector Cramer, talking from Nero Wolfe's office. Give me Lieutenant Rowcliffe. George? No, what do you expect, I just got here. Anything from on high? Yeah. Yeah? File it under C for crap. No. You've got a list of the people who were here at Wolfe's Friday evening. Get some help on the phones and call all of them and tell them to come to Wolfe's office immediately. I know that, but *tell* them. You'd better include Phoebe Gunther. Wait a minute."

He turned to Wolfe. "Anyone else?" Wolfe shook his head and Cramer resumed:

"That's all. Send Stebbins here right away. Wherever they are, find them and get them here. Send men out if you have to. Yeah, I know, all right, they raise hell, what's the difference how I lose my job if I lose it? Wolfe says I'm desperate, and you know Wolfe, he reads faces. Step on it."

Cramer went back to the red leather chair, sat, pulled out a cigar and sank his teeth in it, and rasped, "There. I never thought I'd come to this."

"Frankly," Wolfe muttered, "I was surprised to see you. With what Mr. Goodwin and I furnished you yesterday I would have guessed you were making headway."

"Sure," Cramer chewed the cigar. "Headway in the thickest damn fog I ever saw. That was a big help, what you and Goodwin furnished. In the first place —"

"Excuse me," Dexter put in. He stood up. "I have some phone calls to make."

"If they're private," I told him, "there's a phone upstairs you can use."

"No, thanks." He looked at me impolitely. "I'll go and find a booth." He started out, halted to say over his shoulder that he would be back in half an hour, and went. I moseyed to the hall to see that he didn't stumble on the sill, and after the door had closed behind him returned to the office. Cramer was talking:

" . . . and we're worse off than we were before. Zeros all the way across. If you care for any details, take your pick."

Wolfe grunted. "The photograph and car license mailed to Mrs. Boone. The envelope. Will you have some beer?"

"Yes, I will. Fingerprints, all the routine, nothing. Mailed midtown Friday eight P.M. How would you like to check sales of envelopes in the five-and-dimes?"

"Archie might try it." It was a sign we were all good friends when Wolfe, speaking to Cramer, called me Archie. Usually it was Mr. Goodwin. "What about those cylinders?"

"They were dictated by Boone on March 19th and typed by Miss Gunther on the 20th. The carbons are in Washington and the FBI has checked them. Miss Gunther can't understand it, except on the assumption that Boone picked up the wrong case when he left his office Tuesday afternoon, and she says he didn't often make mistakes like that. But if that was it the case containing the cylinders he dictated Tuesday afternoon ought to be still in his office in Washington, and it isn't. No sign of it. There's one other possibility. We've asked everyone concerned not to leave the city, but on Thursday the BPR asked permission for Miss Gunther to go to Washington on urgent business, and we let her go. She flew down and back. She had a suitcase with her."

Wolfe shuddered. The idea of people getting on airplanes voluntarily was too much for him. He flashed a glance at Cramer. "I see you have eliminated nothing. Was Miss Gunther alone on her trip?"

"She went down alone. Dexter and two other BPR men came back with her."

"She has no difficulty explaining her movements?"

"She has no difficulty explaining anything. That young woman has no difficulty explaining period."

Wolfe nodded. "I believe Archie agrees with you." The beer had arrived, escorted by Fritz, and he was pouring. "I suppose you've had a talk with Mr. O'Neill."

"A talk?" Cramer raised his hands, one of them holding a glass of beer. "Saint Agnes! Have I had a talk with that bird!"

"Yes, he talks. As Archie told you, he was curious about what was on those cylinders."

"He still is." Cramer had half emptied his glass and hung onto it. "The damn fool thought he could keep that envelope. He wanted to have a private dick, not you, investigate it, so he said." He drank again. "Now there's an example of what this case is like. Would you want a better lead than one envelope like that? BPR stock, special delivery, one stamp canceled and the others not, typewritten address? Shall I tell you in detail what we've done, including trying a thousand typewriters?"

"I think not."

"I think not too. It would only take all night to tell you. The goddam post office says it's too bad they can't help us, but with all the new girls they've got, stamps canceled, stamps not canceled, you never can tell." Cramer emptied the bottle into the glass. "You heard that crack I made to Rowcliffe about my losing my job."

"That?" Wolfe waved it away.

"Yeah, I know," Cramer agreed, "I've made it before. It's a habit. All inspectors tell their wives every evening that they'll probably be captains tomorrow. But this time I don't know. From the standpoint of a Homicide Squad inspector, an atom bomb would be a baby firecracker compared to this damn thing. The Commissioner has got St. Vitus's Dance. The D.A. is trying to pretend his turn doesn't come until it's time to panel a jury. The

Mayor is having nightmares, and he must have got it in a dream that if there wasn't any Homicide Squad there wouldn't be any murders, at least not any involving bigtime citizens. So it's all my fault. I mustn't get tough with refined people who have got to the point where they employ tax experts to make sure they're not cheating the government. On the other hand, I must realize that public sentiment absolutely demands that the murderer of Cheney Boone shall not go unpunished. It's six days since it happened, and here by God I sit beefing to you."

He drank his glass empty, put it down, and used the back of his hand for a napkin. "That's the situation, my fat friend, as Charlie McCarthy said to Herbert Hoover. Look what I'm doing, letting you take the wheel is what it amounts to, at least long enough for you to run me in a ditch if you happen to need to. I know damn well that no client of yours has ever been convicted of murder, and in this case your clients—"

"No man is my client," Wolfe interposed. "My client is an association. An association can't commit murder."

"Maybe not. Even so, I know how you work. If you thought it was necessary, in the interest of your client—I guess here he comes or here it comes."

The doorbell had rung. I went to answer it, and found that Cramer's guess was right. This first arrival was a piece of our client, in the person of Hattie Harding. She seemed out of breath. There in the hall she gripped my arm and wanted to know:

"What is it? Have they—what is it?"

I used the hand of my other arm to pat her shoulder. "No, no, calm down. You're all tense. We've decided to have these affairs twice a week, that's all."

I took her to the office and put her to helping me with chairs.

From then on they dribbled in, one by one. Purley Stebbins arrived and apologized to his boss for not making it quicker, and took him aside to explain something. G. G. Spero of the FBI was third and Mrs. Boone fourth. Along about the middle Solomon Dexter returned and, finding the red leather chair unoccupied at the moment, copped it for himself. The Erskine family came separately, a quarter of an hour apart, and so did Breslow and Winterhoff. On the whole, as I let them in, they returned my greeting as a fellow member of the human race, one world or none, but there were two exceptions. Don O'Neill looked straight through me and conveyed the impression that if I touched his coat it would have to be sent to the cleaners, so I let him put it on the rack himself. Alger Kates acted as if I was paid to do the job, so no embraces were called for. Nina Boone, who came late, smiled at me. I didn't imagine it; she smiled right at me. To repay her, I saw to it that she got the same position she had had before, the chair next to mine.

I had to hand it to the Police Department as inviters. It was ten-forty, just an hour and ten minutes since Cramer had phoned Rowcliffe to get up a party. I stood and looked them over, checking off, and then turned to Wolfe and told him:

"It's the same as last time. Miss Gunther just doesn't like crowds. They're all here except her."

Wolfe moved his eyes over the assemblage, slowly from right to left and back again, like a man trying to make up his mind which shirt to buy. They were all seated, divided into two camps as before, except that Winterhoff and Erskine the father were standing over by the globe talking in undertones. From the standpoint of gaiety the party was a dud before it ever started. One second there would be a buzz of conversation, and the next second dead silence; then that would get on someone's nerves and the buzz would start again. A photographer could have taken a shot of that collection of faces and called it I Wonder Who's Kissing Her Now.

Cramer came to my desk and used the phone and then told Wolfe, leaning over to him, "They got Miss Gunther at her apartment over an hour ago, and she said she'd come immediately."

Wolfe shrugged. "We won't wait. Go ahead."

Cramer turned to face the guests, cleared his throat, and raised his voice:

"Ladies and gentlemen!" There was instant silence. "I want you to understand why you were asked to come here, and exactly what's going on. I suppose you read the papers. According to the papers, at least some of them, the police are finding this case too hot to handle on account of the people involved, and they're laying down on the job. I think every single person here knows how much truth there is in that. I guess all of you feel, or nearly all of you, that you're being pestered and persecuted on account of something that you had nothing to do with. The newspapers have their angle, and you have yours. I suppose it was an inconvenience to all of you to come here this evening, but you've got to face it that there's no way out of it, and you've got to blame that inconvenience not on the police or anybody else except one person, the person who killed Cheney Boone. I'm not saying that person is in this room. I admit I don't know. He may be a thousand miles from here —"

"Is that," Breslow barked, "what you got us here to listen to? We've heard all that before!"

"Yeah, I know you have." Cramer was trying not to sound sour. "We didn't get you here to listen to me. I am now turning this over to Mr. Wolfe, and he will proceed, after I say two things. First, you got the request to come here from my office, but from here on it is not official. I am responsible for getting you here and that's all. As far as I'm concerned you can all get up and go if you feel like it. Second, some of you may feel that this is improper because Mr. Wolfe has been engaged to work on this case by the National Industrial Association. That may be so. All I can say is, if you feel that way you can stay here and keep that in mind, or you can leave. Suit yourselves."

He looked around. Nobody moved or spoke. Cramer waited ten seconds and then turned and nodded at Wolfe.

Wolfe heaved a deep sigh and opened up with a barely audible murmur:

"One thing Mr. Cramer mentioned, the inconvenience you people are being forced to endure, requires a little comment. I ask your forbearance while I make it. It is only by that kind of sacrifice on the part of persons, sometimes many persons, who are themselves wholly blameless —"

I hated to disturb his flow, because I knew from long experience that at least he was really working. He had resolved to get something out of that bunch if he had to keep them there all night. But there was no help for it, on account of the expression on Fritz's face. A movement out in the hall had caught my eye, and Fritz was standing there, four feet back from the door to the office, which was standing open, staring wide-eyed at me. When he saw I was looking at him he beckoned to me to come, and the thought popped into my mind that, with guests present and Wolfe making an oration, that was precisely how Fritz would act if the house was on fire. The whole throng was between him and me, and I circled around behind them for my exit. Wolfe kept on talking. As soon as I made the hall I closed the door behind me and asked Fritz:

"Something biting you?"

"It's—it's—" He stopped and set his teeth on his lip. Wolfe had been trying to train Fritz for twenty years not to get excited. He tried again: "Come and I'll show you."

He dived for the kitchen and I followed, thinking it was some culinary calamity that he couldn't bear up under alone, but he went to the door of the back stairs, the steps that led down to what we called the basement, though it was only three feet below the street level. Fritz slept down there in the room that faced the street. There was an exit through a little hall to the front; first a heavy door out to a tiny vestibule which was underneath the stoop, and then an iron gate, a grill, leading to a paved areaway from which five steps mounted to the sidewalk. It was in the tiny vestibule that Fritz stopped and I bumped into him.

He pointed down. "Look." He put his hand on the gate and gave it a little shake. "I came to see if the gate was locked, the way I always do."

There was an object huddled on the concrete of the areaway, up against the gate, so that the gate couldn't be opened without pushing the object aside. I squatted to peer. The light there was dim, since the nearest street lamp was on the other side of the stoop, thirty paces away, but I could see well enough to tell what the object was, though not for certain who it was.

"What the hell did you bring me here for?" I demanded, pushing past Fritz to re-enter the basement. "Come with me."

He was at my heels as I mounted the stairs. In the kitchen I detoured to jerk open a drawer and get a flashlight, and then went down the main hall to the front door, out to the stoop and down to the sidewalk, and down the five steps to the areaway. There, on the same side of the gate as the object, I squatted again and switched on the flashlight. Fritz was beside me, bending over.

"Shall I—" His voice was shaking and he had to start again. "Shall I hold the light?"

I told him gruffly, "Shut up, goddam it."

After half a minute I straightened up, told him, "You stay right here," and headed for the stoop. Fritz had pulled the front door shut, and when I found myself fumbling to get the key in the hole I stood erect to take a deep breath and that stopped the fumbling. I went down the hall to the kitchen, to the phone there, and dialed the number of Dr. Vollmer, who lived down the street only half a block away. There were six buzzes before he answered.

"Doc? Archie Goodwin. Got your clothes on? Good. Get here as fast as you can. There's a woman lying in our areaway, by the gate to the basement, been hit on the head, and I think she's dead. There'll be cops on it, so don't shift her more than you have to. Right now? Okay."

I took another breath, filling my chest, then took Fritz's pad and pencil and wrote:

Phoebe Gunther is in our areaway dead. Hit on the head.
Have phoned Vollmer.

I tore off the sheet and went to the office. I suppose I had been gone six
minutes, not more, and Wolfe was still doing a monologue, with thirteen
pairs of eyes riveted on him. I sidled around to the right, got to his desk, and
handed him the note. He got it at a glance, gave it a longer glance, flashed
one at me, and spoke without any perceptible change in tone or manner:

"Mr. Cramer. If you please. Mr. Goodwin has a message for you and Mr.
Stebbins. Will you go with him to the hall?"

Cramer and Stebbins got up. As we went out Wolfe's voice was resuming
behind us:

"Now the question that confronts us is whether it is credible, under the
circumstances as we know them . . ."

19

THIRTY minutes past midnight was about the peak. At that moment I was
alone in my room, two flights up, sitting in the chair by the window,
drinking a glass of milk, or at least holding one in my hand. I do not
ordinarily hunt for a cave in the middle of the biggest excitement and the
most intense action, but this seemed to hit me in a new spot or something,
and anyhow there I was, trying to arrange my mind. Or maybe my feelings.
All I knew was that something inside of me needed a little arranging. I had
just completed a tour of the battlefield, and at that hour the disposition of
forces was as follows:

Fritz was in the kitchen making sandwiches and coffee, and Mrs. Boone
was there helping him.

Seven of the invited guests were scattered around the front room, with
two homicide dicks keeping them company. They were not telling funny
stories, not even Ed Erskine and Nina Boone, was were on the same sofa.

Lieutenant Rowcliffe and an underling with a notebook were in the spare
bedroom, on the same floor as mine, having a conversation with Hattie
Harding, the Public Relations Queen.

Inspector Cramer, Sergeant Stebbins, and a couple of others were in the
dining room firing questions at Alger Kates.

The four-star brass was in the office. Wolfe was seated behind his desk,
the Police Commissioner was likewise at my desk, the District Attorney was
in the red leather chair, and Travis and Spero of the FBI made a circle of it.
That was where the high strategy would come from, if and when any came.

Another dick was in the kitchen, presumably to see that Mrs. Boone
didn't jump out a window and Fritz didn't dust arsenic on the sandwiches.
Others were in the halls, in the basement, all over; and still others kept

coming and going from outdoors, reporting to, or getting orders from, Cramer or the Commissioner or the District Attorney.

Newspapermen had at one time infiltrated behind the lines, but they were now on the other side of the threshold. Out there the floodlights hadn't been removed, and some miscellaneous city employees were still poking around, but most of the scientists, including the photographers, had departed. In spite of that the crowd, as I could see from the window near which my chair was placed, was bigger than ever. The house was only a five-minute taxi ride or a fifteen-minute walk from Times Square, and the news of a spectacular break in the Boone case had got to the theater crowds. The little party Wolfe had asked Cramer to arrange had developed into more than he had bargained for.

A piece of 1/2-inch iron pipe, sixteen inches long, had been found lying on the concrete paving of the areaway. Phoebe Gunther had been hit on the head with it four times. Dr. Vollmer had certified her dead on arrival. She had also received bruises in falling, one on her cheek and mouth, presumably from the stoop, where she had been struck, to the areaway. The scientists had got that far before they removed the body.

I had been sitting in my room twenty minutes when I noticed that I hadn't drunk any milk, but I hadn't spilled any from the glass.

20

My intention was to go back downstairs and re-enter the turmoil when the microscope came. It was expected by some that the microscope would do the job, and it seemed to me quite likely.

I had myself been rinsed out, by Wolfe and Cramer working as a team, which alone made the case unique. But the circumstances made me a key man. The working assumption was that Phoebe had come and mounted the stoop, and that the murderer had either come with her, or joined her near or on the stoop, and had struck her before she had pushed the bell button, stunning her and knocking her off the stoop into the areaway. He had then run down into the areaway and hit her three times more to make sure she was finished, and shoved the body up against the gate, where it could not be seen by anyone on the stoop without leaning over and stretching your neck, and wasn't likely to be seen from the sidewalk on account of the dimness of the light. Then, of course, the murderer might have gone home and to bed, but the assumption was that he had remounted the stoop and pushed the button, and I had let him in and taken his hat and coat.

That put me within ten feet of them, and maybe less, at the moment it happened, and if by chance I had pulled the curtain on the glass panel aside at that moment I would have seen it. It also had me greeting the murderer within a few seconds after he had finished, and, as I admitted to Wolfe and Cramer, I had observed each arriving face with both eyes to discover how

they were getting along under the strain. That was another reason I had
gone up to my room, to look back on those faces. It didn't seem possible
that I couldn't pick the one, or at least the two or three most probable ones,
whose owner had just a minute previously been smashing Phoebe's skull
with an iron pipe. Well, I couldn't. They had all been the opposite of
carefree, showing it one way or another, and so what? Wolfe had sighed at
me, and Cramer had growled like a frustrated lion, but that was the best I
could do.

Naturally I had been asked to make up a list showing the order of arrivals
and the approximate intervals between, and had been glad to oblige. I
hadn't punched a time clock for them, but I was willing to certify my list as
pretty accurate. They had all come singly. The idea was that if any two of
them had arrived close together, say within two minutes or less of each
other, the one that entered the house first could be marked as improbable.
But not the one that came in second, because the murderer, having finished,
and hearing footsteps or a taxi approaching, could have flattened himself
against the gate in that dark corner, waited until the arriver had mounted
the stoop and been admitted, and then immediately ascended the stoop
himself to ring the bell. Anyhow, such close calculation wasn't required,
since, as my memory had it, none of the intervals had been less than three
minutes.

Of course the position on the list meant nothing. As far as opportunity
was concerned, there was no difference between Hattie Harding, who came
first, and Nina Boone, who came last.

All the guests had been questioned at least once, each separately, and it
was probable that repeat performances would go on all night if the microscope didn't live up to expectations. Since they had all already been put
through it, over and over, about the Boone murder, the askers had hard
going. The questions had to be about what had happened there that evening, and what was there to ask? There was no such thing as an alibi. Each
one had been on the stoop alone between nine-fifty and ten-forty, and
during that period Pheobe Gunther had arrived and been killed. About all
you could ask anybody was this, "Did you ring the bell as soon as you
mounted the stoop? Did you kill Phoebe Gunther first?" If he said Phoebe
Gunther wasn't there, and he pushed the button and was admitted by Mr.
Goodwin, what did you ask next? Naturally you wanted to know whether he
came by car or taxi, or on foot from a bus or subway, and where did that get
you?

Very neat management, I told myself, sitting by the window in my room.
Fully as neat as any I remembered. Very neat, the dirty deadly bastard.

I have said that the assumption was that the murderer had remounted
the stoop and entered the house, but perhaps I should have said one of the
assumptions. The NIA had another one, originated by Winterhoff, which
had been made a part of the record. In the questioning marathon Winterhoff had come toward the end. His story had three main ingredients:

    1. He (Winterhoff, the Man of Distinction) always had
shoe soles made of a composition which was almost as
quiet as rubber, and therefore made little noise when he
walked.

2. He disapproved of tossing trash, including cigarette butts, in the street, and never did so himself.

3. He lived on East End Avenue. His wife and daughters were using the car and chauffeur that evening. He never used taxis if he could help it, because of the revolutionary attitude of the drivers during the present shortage of cabs. So when the phone call had come requesting his presence at Wolfe's office, he had taken a Second Avenue bus down to Thirty-fifth Street, and walked crosstown.

Well. Approaching Wolfe's house from the east, on his silent soles, he had stopped about eighty feet short of his destination because he was stuck with a cigarette butt and noticed an ashcan standing inside the railing of an areaway. He went down the steps to the can and killed the butt therein, and, reascending the steps, was barely back to the sidewalk when he saw a man dart out from behind a stoop, out of an areaway, and dash off in the other direction, toward the river. He had gone on to Wolfe's house, and had noted that it was that areaway, probably, that the man had darted from, but he had not gone so far as to lean over the stoop's low parapet to peer into the areaway. The best he could do on the darting and dashing man was that he had worn dark clothes and had been neither a giant nor a midget.

And by gosh, there had been corroboration. Of the thousand more or less dicks who had been dispatched on errands, two had been sent up the street to check. In half an hour they had returned and reported that there was an ashcan in an areaway exactly twenty-four paces east of Wolfe's stoop. Not only that, there was a cigarette butt on top of the ashes, and its condition, and certain telltale streaks on the inside of the can, about one inch below its rim, made it probably that the butt had been killed by rubbing it against the inside of the can. Not only *that*, they had the butt with them.

Winterhoff had not lied. He had stopped to kill a butt in an ashcan, and he was a good judge of distances. Unfortunately, it was impossible to corroborate the part about the darting and dashing man because he had disappeared during the two hours that had elapsed.

How much Wolfe or Cramer had bought of it, I didn't know. I wasn't even sure how well I liked it, but I had been below normal since I had flashed the light on Phoebe Gunther's face.

Cramer, hearing it from Rowcliffe, who had questioned Winterhoff, had merely grunted, but that had apparently been because at the moment he had his mind on something else. Some scientist, I never knew which one, had just made the suggestion about the microscope. Cramer lost no time on that. He gave orders that Erskine and Dexter, who were elsewhere being questioned, should be returned immediately to the front room, and had then gone there himself, accompanied by Purley and me, stood facing the assemblage and got their attention, which took no effort at all, and had begun a speech:

"Please listen to this closely so you'll know what I'm asking. The piece of—"

Breslow blurted. "This is outrageous! We've all answered questions! We've let ourselves be searched! We've told everything we know! We—"

Cramer told a dick in a loud and hard voice, "Go and stand by him and if he doesn't keep his trap shut, shut it."

The dick moved. Breslow stopped blurting. Cramer said:

"I've had enough injured innocence for one night." He was as sore and savage as I had ever seen him. "For six days I've been handling you people as tender as babies, because I had to because you're such important people, but now it's different. On killing Boone all of you might have been innocent, but now I know one of you isn't. One of you killed that woman, and it's a fair guess that the same one killed Boone. I—"

"Excuse me, Inspector." Frank Thomas Erskine was sharp, by no means apologetic, but neither was he outraged. "You've made a statement that you may regret. What about the man seen by Mr. Winterhoff running from the areaway—"

"Yeah, I've heard about him." Cramer was conceding nothing. "For the present I stick to my statement. I add to it that the Police Commissioner has just confirmed my belief that I'm in charge here, at the scene of a murder with those present detained, and the more time you waste bellyaching the longer you'll stay. Your families have been notified where you are and why. One of you thinks he can have me sent up for twenty years because I won't let him phone all his friends and lawyers. Okay. He don't phone."

Cramer made a face at them, at least it looked like it to me, and growled, "Do you understand the situation?"

Nobody answered. He went on, "Here's what I came in here to say. The piece of pipe she was killed with has been examined for fingerprints. We haven't found any that are any good. The galvanizing was rough to begin with, and it's a used piece of pipe, very old, and the galvanizing is flaking off, and there are blotches of stuff, paint and other matter, more or less all over it. We figure that anybody grasping that pipe hard enough to crack a skull with it would almost certainly get particles of stuff in the creases of his hands. I don't mean flakes you could see, I mean particles too small to be visible, and you wouldn't get them all out of the creases just by rubbing your palms on your clothes. The examination would have to be made with a microscope. I don't want to take all of you down to the laboratory, so I'm having a microscope brought here. I am requesting all of you to permit this examination of your hands, and also of your gloves and handkerchiefs."

Mrs. Boone spoke up, "But, Inspector, I've washed my hands. I went to the kitchen to help make sandwiches, and of course I washed my hands."

"That's too bad," Cramer growled. "We can still try it. Some of those particles might not come out of the creases even with washing. You can give your answers, yes or no, to Sergeant Stebbins. I'm busy."

He marched out and returned to the dining room. It was at that point that I felt I needed some arranging inside, and went to the office and told Wolfe I would be in my room if he wanted me. I stayed there over half an hour. It was one A.M. when the microscope came. Police cars were coming and going all the time, and it was by accident that, through my window, I saw a man get out of one carrying a large box. I gulped the rest of the milk and returned downstairs.

21

I might as well have stayed put, because that was where the hand inspecting was done, my bedroom. The laboratory man wanted a quiet spot, and there was still activity everywhere else except Wolfe's room, which, by his instructions, was not to be entered. So the customers, one by one, had to climb the two flights. The apparatus, with its special light plugged in, was set up on my table. There were five of us in the room: the two experts, the dick who brought and took the customers, the current customer, and me sitting on the edge of the bed.

I was there partly because it was my room and I didn't care for the idea of abandoning it to a gang of strangers, and partly because I was stubborn and still couldn't understand why I was unable to pick the face, as I had greeted them at the door, of the one who had just finished killing Phoebe. That was the reason I might have bid as high as a nickel for Winterhoff's man in dark clothes darting and dashing. I wanted another good look at them. I had a feeling, of which I wouldn't have told Wolfe, that if I looked straight at the face of the person who had killed Phoebe, I would know it. It was an entirely new slant on crime detection, especially for me, but I had it. So I sat on the edge of my bed and looked straight at faces while the experts looked at hands.

First, Nina Boone. Pale, tired, and nervous.

Second, Don O'Neill. Resentful, impatient, and curious. Eyes bloodshot.

Third, Hattie Harding. Saggy and very jittery. Eyes nothing like as competent as they had been four days earlier in her office.

Fourth, Winterhoff. Distinguished, sweaty, and worried stiff.

Fifth, Father Erskine. Tense and determined.

Sixth, Alger Kates. Grim and about ready to cry. Eyes backing into his head.

Seventh, Mrs. Boone. Everything coming loose but trying to hang on. The tiredest of all.

Eighth, Solomon Dexter. Sort of swollen, with bags under the eyes. Not worried, but extremely resolute.

Ninth, Breslow. Lips tight with fury and eyes like a mad pig. He was the only one who stared back at me instead of at his own hand, under the light and the lens.

Tenth, Ed Erskine. Sarcastic, skeptical, and hangover all gone. About as worried as a pigeon in the park.

There had been no exclamations of delighted discovery from the experts, any more than from me. They had spoken to the customers, to instruct them about holding still and shifting position when required, and had exchanged brief comments in undertones, and that was all. They had tweezers and pillboxes and other paraphernalia handy, but had made no use of it. When the last one, Ed Erskine, had been escorted out, I asked them:

"Any soap?"

The one without much chin replied, "We report to the Inspector."

"Goodness gracious," I said enviously. "It must be wonderful to be connected with the Police Department, with all the secrets. Why do you think Cramer let me come up and sit here and watch? To keep my mind a blank?"

"No doubt," the other one, the one with a jaw, said primly, "the Inspector will inform you of our findings. Go down and report, Phillips."

I was beginning to get restless, so, deciding to leave my room to its fate temporarily, I followed Phillips downstairs. If it was a weird experience for me, all these aliens trampling all over the house as if they owned it, I could imagine what the effect must be on Wolfe. Phillips trotted into the dining room, but Cramer wasn't among those present, and I steered him into the office. Wolfe was at his desk, and the P.C., the D.A., and the two FBI's were still there, all with their eyes on Cramer, who stood talking to them. He stopped at sight of Phillips.

"Well?"

"On the microscope examination of hands the results are negative, Inspector."

"The hell they are. Another big rousing achievement. Tell Stebbins to get all gloves and handkerchiefs from their persons and send them up to you. Including the ladies' bags. Tell him to tag everything. Also from their overcoat pockets — no, send up coats and hats and all, and you see what's in the pockets. For God's sake don't mix anything up."

"Yes, sir." Phillips turned and went.

Not seeing how any good could come of staring straight at the faces of gloves and handkerchiefs, I crossed over to the Police Commissioner and addressed him:

"If you don't mind, this is my chair."

He looked startled, opened his mouth, shut it again, and moved to another seat. I sat down where I belonged. Cramer talked:

"You can do it if you can get away with it, but you know what the law is. Our jurisdiction extends to the limits of the premises occupied by the deceased provided it was the scene of the crime, but not otherwise. We can —"

"That's not the law," the D.A. snapped.

"You mean it's not statute. But it's accepted custom and it's what the courts stand for, so it's law for me. You wanted my opinion, and that's it. I won't be responsible for continued occupation of the apartment Miss Gunther was staying in, and not by my men anyway because I can't spare them. The tenant of the apartment is Kates. Three good searchers have spent an hour and a half there and haven't found anything. I'm willing to let them keep at it all night, or at least until we turn Kates loose, if and when we're through here, but any order for continued occupancy and keeping Kates out" — he looked at the P.C. —" will have to come from you, sir, or," he looked at the D.A., "from you."

Travis of the FBI put in, "I'd advise against it."

"This," the D.A. said stiffly, "is a local problem."

They went on. I started kicking my left ankle with my right foot, and vice versa. Wolfe was leaning back in his chair with his eyes closed, and I was pleased to note that his opinion of high strategy was apparently the same as mine. The P.C., the D.A., and the FBI, not to mention the head of the

Homicide Squad, debating where Alger Kates was going to sleep, when he got a chance to sleep, and that after three cops had had the apartment all to themselves long enough to saw all the legs off the chairs and glue them back on. It developed that it was the D.A. who was plugging for continued occupancy. I decided to enter the conversation just for the hell of it and was considering which side to be on when the phone rang.

It was from Washington, for FBI Travis, and he came to my desk to take it. The others stopped talking and looked at him. On his part it was mostly listening. When he had finished he shoved the phone back and turned to announce:

"This has some bearing on what we've been discussing. Our men and the Washington police have completed their search of Miss Gunther's apartment in Washington — one large room, bath, and kitchenette. In a hatbox on a shelf in a closet they found nine Stenophone cylinders —"

"Confound it!" Wolfe burst out. "Nine?" He was as indignant and irritated as if he had been served a veal cutlet with an egg perched on it. Everyone stared at him.

"Nine," said Travis curtly. He was justifiably annoyed at having his scene stolen. "Nine Stenophone cylinders. A BPR man was with them, and they are now at the BPR office running them off and making a transcription." He looked coldly at Wolfe. "What's wrong with nine?"

"For you," Wolfe said offensively, "apparently nothing. For me, nine is no better than none. I want ten."

"That's a damn shame. I apologize. They should have found ten." Having demolished Wolfe, he reported to the others, "They'll call again as soon as they get something we might use."

"Then they won't call," Wolfe declared, and shut his eyes again, leaving the discussion of the new development to the others. He was certainly being objectionable, and it wasn't hard to guess why. The howling insolence of committing a murder on his own stoop would alone have been enough, but in addition to that his house was filled from top to bottom with uninvited guests and he was absolutely powerless. That was dead against his policy, his practice, and his personality. Seeing that he was really in a bad way, and thinking it might be a good plan for him to keep himself at least partially informed of what was going on, since he was supposed to have an interest in the outcome, I went to the kitchen to get some beer for him. Evidently he was in too bad a humor even to remember to send for beer, since there were no signs of any.

Fritz and about a dozen assorted dicks were there drinking coffee. I told them:

"You sure are cluttering up the place, but I don't blame you. It isn't often that members of the lower clahsses get a chance to drink coffee made by Fritz Brenner."

There was a subdued, but close to unanimous, concert of Bronx cheers. One said, "Goodwin the gentleman. One, two, three, laugh."

Another said, "Hey, you know everything. What's the lowdown on this NIA-BPR stuff? Is it a feud or not?"

I was putting six bottles and six glasses on a tray, with Fritz's help. "I'm glad to explain," I said generously. "The NIA and the BPR are in one respect exactly like the glorious PD, or Police Department. They have esprit de corps. Repeat it after me—no, don't bother. That is a French term, the language spoken by Frenchmen, the people who live in France, the literal translation of which is 'spirit of the body.' In our language we have no precise equivalent—"

The cheers had begun again, and the tray was ready, so I left them. Fritz came to the hall with me, closed the kitchen door, held my sleeve, and told my ear:

"Archie, this is awful. I just want to say I know how awful it is for you. Mr. Wolfe told me when I took up his breakfast this morning that you had formed a passion for Miss Gunther and she had you wound around her finger. She was a beautiful girl, very beautiful. This is awful, what happened here."

I said, "Go to hell," jerked my arm to free my sleeve, and took a step. Then I turned to him and said, "All I meant was, this is a hell of a night and it will take you a week to clean up the joint. Go back and finish that lesson in French I was giving them."

In the office they were as before. I peddled beer around, making three sales to outsiders, leaving three bottles for Wolfe, which was about as I had calculated, went back to the kitchen and got myself a sandwich and a glass of milk, and returned to my desk with them. The strategy council was going on and on, with Wolfe still aloof in spite of the beer. The sandwich made me hungry and I went and got two more. Long after they were gone the council was still chewing the fat.

They were handicapped, of course, by continual interruptions, both by phone and by personal appearances. One of the phone calls was for Travis from Washington, and when he was through with it his face displayed no triumph. The nine cylinders had all been listened to, and there was nothing for us to bite on. They contained plenty of evidence that they had been dictated by Boone at his Washington office on Tuesday afternoon, but no evidence at all that would help to uncover a murderer. The BPR was trying to hang onto the transcriptions, but the Washington FBI promised to send a copy to Travis, and he agreed to let Cramer see it.

"So," Travis said aggressively, daring us to hint that we were no better off than before, "that proves that Miss Gunther was lying about them. She had them all the time."

"Nine." Wolfe grunted in disgust. "Pfui."

That was his only contribution to their discussion of the cylinders.

It was five minutes past three Tuesday morning when Phillips, the expert with less than his share of chin, entered the office with objects in his hands. In his right was a gray topcoat, and in his left was a silk scarf with stripes of dark brown and terra cotta. It was obvious that even an expert is capable of having feelings. His face showed plainly that he had something.

He looked at Wolfe and me and asked, "Do I report here, Inspector?"

"Go ahead!" Cramer was impatient. "What is it?"

"This scarf was in the right-hand pocket of this coat. It was folded as it is now. Unfolding one fold exposes about forty square inches of its surface. On that surface are between fifteen and twenty particles of matter which in our opinion came from that piece of pipe. That is our opinion. Laboratory tests—"

"Sure." Cramer's eyes were gleaming. "You can test from hell to breakfast. You've got a microscope up there, and you know what I want right now. Is it good enough to act on, or isn't it?"

"Yes, sir, it is. We made sure before—"

"Whose coat is it?"

"The tag says Alger Kates."

"Yeah," I agreed. "That's Kates's coat."

22

SINCE they were a strategy council, naturally they didn't send for Kates immediately. They had to decide on strategy first—whether to circle him and get him tangled, or slide it into him gently, or just hit him on the head with it. What they really had to decide was who was going to handle it; that would determine the method, and they started to wrangle about it. The point was, as it always is when you've got a crusher like that scarf in his pocket, which way of using it was most likely to crumble him and get a confession? They hadn't been going long when Travis interposed:

"With all this top authority present, and me not in it officially anyhow, I hesitate to make a suggestion."

"So what is it?" the D.A. asked tartly.

"I would suggest Mr. Wolfe for it. I have seen him operate, and if it means anything I freely admit that he is my superior at it."

"Suits me," Cramer said at once.

The other two looked at each other. Neither liked what he was looking at, and neither liked Travis's suggestion, so simultaneously they said nothing.

"Okay," Cramer said, "let's go. Where do you want the coat and scarf, Wolfe, in sight?"

Wolfe half opened his eyes. "What is this gentleman's name?"

"Oh. Phillips. Mr. Wolfe, Mr. Phillips."

"How do you do, sir. Give the coat to Mr. Goodwin. Archie, put it behind the cushions on the couch. Give me the scarf, please."

Phillips had handed me the coat without hesitation, but now he balked. He looked at Cramer. "This is vital evidence. If those particles get brushed off and scattered . . ."

"I'm not a ninny," Wolfe snapped.

"Let him have it," Cramer said.

Phillips hated to do it. He might have been a mother instructed to entrust her newborn infant to a shady character. But he handed it over.

"Thank you, sir. All right, Mr. Cramer, get him in here."

Cramer went, taking Phillips with him. In a moment he was back, without Phillips and with Alger Kates. We all gazed at Kates as he stepped across and took the chair indicated by Cramer, facing Wolfe, but it didn't visibly disconcert him. He looked to me as he had up in my room, as if he might bust out crying any minute, but there was no evidence that he had done so. After he had sat down all I had was his profile.

"You and I have hardly spoken, have we, Mr. Kates?" Wolfe asked.

Kates's tongue came out to wet his lips and went back in again. "Enough to satisfy—" he began, but his thin voice threatened to become only a squeak, and he stopped for a second and then started over. "Enough to satisfy me."

"But my dear sir." Wolfe was gently reproachful. "I don't believe we've exchanged a word."

Kates did not unbend. "Haven't we?" he asked.

"No, sir. The devil of it is that I can't honestly say that I don't sympath-ize with your attitude. If I were in your position, innocently or not, I would feel the same. I don't like people piling questions on me, and in fact I don't tolerate it." Wolfe let his eyes open another millimeter. "By the way, I am now, momentarily, official. These gentlemen in authority have deputized me to talk with you. As you doubtless know, that doesn't mean that you *must* tolerate it. If you tried to leave this house before they let you go, you would be arrested as a material witness and taken somewhere, but you can't be compelled to take part in a conversation if you are determined not to. What do you say? Shall we talk?"

"I'm listening," Kates said.

"I know you are. Why?"

"Because, if I don't, the inference will be made that I'm frightened, and the further inference will be made that I am guilty of something that I am trying to conceal."

"Good. Then we understand each other." Wolfe sounded as if he were grateful for a major concession. With casual unhurried movement he brought the scarf out from beneath the rim of the desk, where he had been holding it in his hand, and put it down on the blotter. Then he cocked his head at Kates as if trying to decide where to begin. From where I sat, having Kates's profile, I couldn't tell whether he even gave the scarf a glance. Certainly he didn't turn pale or exhibit any hand-clenching or tremors of the limbs.

"On the two occasions," Wolfe said, "that Mr. Goodwin went to Fifty-fifth Street to see Miss Gunther, you were there. Were you a close friend of hers?"

"Not a close personal friend, no. In the past six months, since I've been doing confidential research directly under Mr. Boone, I've seen her fre-quently in connection with the work."

"Yet she was staying in your apartment."

Kates looked at Cramer. "You people have gone over this with me a dozen times."

Cramer nodded. "That's the way it goes, son. This'll make thirteen."

Kates returned to Wolfe. "The present housing shortage makes it ex-tremely difficult, and often impossible, to get a room in a hotel. Miss Gunther could have used her position and connections to get a room, but that is against BPR policy, and also she didn't do things like that. A bed in a friend's apartment was available to me, and my wife was away. I offered the use of my apartment to Miss Gunther coming up on the plane from Wash-ington, and she accepted."

"Had she ever stayed there before?"

"No."

"You had seen her frequently for six months. What did you think of her?"

"I thought well of her."

"Did you admire her?"

"Yes. As a colleague."

"Did she dress well?"

"I never noticed particularly—no, that isn't true." Kates's voice zoomed for a squeak again and he used the controls. "If you think these questions are important and you want full and truthful answers. Considering Miss Gunther's striking appearance and her voluptuous figure, I thought she dressed extremely well for one in her position."

If Phoebe was here, I thought, she'd tell him he talks like an old-fashioned novel.

"Then," Wolfe said, "you did notice what she wore. In that case, when did you last see her wearing this scarf?" He used a thumb to indicate it.

Kates leaned forward to look at it. "I don't remember ever seeing her wear that. I never did." He settled back.

"That's strange." Wolfe was frowning. "This is important, Mr. Kates. Are you sure?"

Kates leaned forward again, saying, "Let me see it," and reached a hand for it.

Wolfe's hand was there before his, closing on it. "No," Wolfe said, "this will be an exhibit in a murder trial and therefore should not be handled indiscriminately." He stretched an arm to give Kates a closer look. Kates peered at it a moment, then leaned back and shook his head.

"I've never seen it before," he declared. "On Miss Gunther or anybody else."

"That's a disappointment," Wolfe said regretfully. "However, it doesn't exhaust the possibilities. You might have seen it before and now not recognize it because your previous view of it was in a dim light, for instance on the stoop of this house at night. I suggest that for your consideration, because clinging to this scarf are many tiny particles which came from the piece of pipe, showing that the scarf was used as a protection in clutching the pipe, and also because the scarf was found in the pocket of your overcoat."

Kates blinked at him. "Whose overcoat?"

"Yours. Get it, Archie." I went for it, and stood beside Kates, holding it by the collar, hanging full length. Wolfe asked, "That's your coat, isn't it?"

Kates sat and stared at the coat. Then he arose, turned his back on Wolfe, and called at the top of his voice, "Mr. Dexter! *Mr. Dexter! Come in here!*"

"Cut it out." Cramer was up and had him by the arm on the other side. "Cut out the yelling! What do you want Dexter for?"

"Then get him in here. If you want me to stop yelling, get him in here." Kates's voice was trembling. "I told him something like this would happen! I told Phoebe to have nothing to do with Nero Wolfe! I told her not to come here tonight! I—"

Cramer pounced. "When did you tell her not to come here tonight? When?"

Kates didn't answer. He realized his arm was being gripped, looked down at Cramer's hand gripping it, and said, "Let go of me. Let go!" Cramer did so. Kates walked across to a chair against the wall, sat on it, and clamped his jaw. He was breaking off relations.

I said to Cramer, "If you want it, I was there when Rowcliffe was questioning him. He said he was at his friend's apartment on Eleventh Street, where he's staying, and Miss Gunther phoned to say she had just been told to come here and wanted to know if he had been told too, and he said yes but he wasn't coming and he tried to persuade her not to come, and when she said she was going to he decided to come too. I know you're busy, but if you don't read reports you throw wild punches."

I turned to include them all. "And if you want my opinion, with no fee, that's not Miss Gunther's scarf because it's not her style. She wouldn't have worn that thing. And it doesn't belong to Kates. Look at him. Gray suit, gray topcoat. Also a gray hat. I've never seen him in anything but gray, and if he was still speaking to us you could ask him."

Cramer strode to the door which connected with the front room, opened it a crack, and commanded, "Stebbins! Come in here."

Purley came at once. Cramer told him, "Takes Kates to the dining room. Bring the others in here one at a time, and as we finish with them take them to the dining room."

Purley went with Kates, who didn't seem reluctant to go. In a moment another dick entered with Mrs. Boone. She wasn't invited to sit down. Cramer met her in the middle of the room, displayed the scarf, told her to take a good look at it but not to touch it, and then asked if she had ever seen it before. She said she hadn't, and that was all. She was led out and Frank Thomas Erskine was led in, and the performance was repeated. There were four more negatives, and then it was Winterhoff's turn.

With Winterhoff, Cramer didn't have to finish his speech. He showed the scarf and started, "Mr. Winterhoff, please look—"

"Where did you get that?" Winterhoff demanded, reaching for it. "That's my scarf!"

"Oh." Cramer backed up a step with it. "That's what we've been trying to find out. Did you wear it here tonight, or have it in your pocket?"

"Neither one. I didn't have it. That's the one that was stolen from me last week."

"Where and when last week?"

"Right here. When I was here Friday evening."

"Here at Wolfe's house?"

"Yes."

"You wore it here?"

"Yes."

"When you found it was gone, who helped you look for it? Who did you complain to?"

"I didn't—what's this all about? Who had it? Where did you get it?"

"I'll explain in a minute. I'm asking now, who did you complain to?"

"I didn't complain to anybody. I didn't notice it was gone until I got home. If—"

"You mentioned it to no one at all?"

"I didn't mention it here. I didn't know it was gone. I must have mentioned it to my wife—of course I did, I remember. But I have—"

"Did you phone here the next day to ask about it?"

"No, I didn't!" Winterhoff had been forcing himself to submit to the pressure. Now he was through. "Why would I? I've got two dozen scarves! And I insist that—"

"Okay, insist." Cramer was calm but bitter. "Since it's your scarf and you've been questioned about it, it is proper to tell you that there is evidence, good evidence, that it was wrapped around the pipe that Miss Gunther was killed with. Have you any comment?"

Winterhoff's face was moist with sweat, but it had already been that way up in my room when they were examining his hands. It was interesting that the sweat didn't seem to make him look any less distinguished, but it did detract some when he goggled, as he now did at Cramer. It occurred to me that his best friend ought to warn him not to goggle.

He finally spoke. "What's the evidence?"

"Particles from the pipe found on the scarf. Many of them, at one spot."

"Where did you find it?"

"In an overcoat pocket."

"Whose coat?"

Cramer shook his head. "You're not entitled to that. I'd like to ask you not to do any broadcasting on this, but of course you will." He turned to the dick. "Take him to the dining room and tell Stebbins not to bring any more in."

Winterhoff had things to say, but he was shooed out. When the door was closed behind him and the dick, Cramer sat down and put his palms on his knees, pulled in a deep breath, and expelled it noisily.

"Jee—zuss—Christ," he remarked.

23

THERE was a long silence. I looked at the wall clock. It said two minutes to four. I looked at my wrist watch. It said one minute to four. In spite of the discrepancy it seemed safe to conclude that it would soon be four o'clock. From beyond the closed doors to the front room and the hall came faint suggestions of little noises, just enough to keep reminding us that silence wouldn't do. Every little noise seemed to be saying, come on, it's getting late, work it out. The atmosphere there in the office struck me as both discouraged and discouraging. Some buoyancy and backbone were needed.

"Well," I said brightly, "we've taken a big step forward. We have eliminated Winterhoff's darting and dashing man. I am prepared to go on the stand and swear that he didn't dash into the hall."

That got a rise out of nobody, which showed the pathetic condition they were in. All that happened was that the D.A. looked at me as if I reminded him of someone who hadn't voted for him.

The P.C. spoke. "Winterhoff is a damned liar. He didn't see a man running away from that stoop. He made that up."

"For God's sake," the D.A. burst out ferociously, "we're not after a liar! We're after a murderer!"

"I would like," Wolfe muttered sulkily, "to go to bed. It's four o'clock and you're stuck."

"Oh, we are." Cramer glowered at him. "*We're* stuck. The way you put it. I suppose *you're* not stuck?"

"Me? No, Mr. Cramer. No indeed. But I'm tired and sleepy."

That might have led to violence if there hadn't been an interruption. There was a knock on the door and a dick entered, approached Cramer, and reported:

"We've got two more taxi drivers, the two that brought Mrs. Boone and O'Neill. I thought you might want to see them, Inspector. One is named —"

He stopped on account of Cramer's aspect. "This," Cramer said, "will make you a Deputy Chief Inspector. Easy." He pointed to the door. "Out that way and find someone to tell it to." The dick, looking frustrated, turned and went. Cramer said to anyone who cared to listen, "My God. Taxi drivers!"

The P.C. said, "We'll have to let them go."

"Yes, sir," Cramer agreed. "I know we will. Get 'em in here, Archie."

So that was the state of mind the Inspector was in. As I proceeded to obey his command I tried to remember another occasion on which he had called me Archie, and couldn't, in all the years I had known him. Of course after he had got some sleep and had a shower he would feel differently about it, but I put it away for some fitting moment in the future to remind him that he had called me Archie. Meanwhile Purley and I, with plenty of assistance, herded everybody from the front room and dining room into the office.

The strategy council had left their chairs and collected at the far end of Wolfe's desk, standing. The guests took seats. The city employees, over a dozen of them, scattered around the room and stood looking as alert and intelligent as the facts of the case would permit, under the eye of the big boss, the P.C. himself.

Cramer, on his feet confronting them, spoke:

"We're letting you people go home. But before you go, this is the situation. The microscopic examination of your hands didn't show anything. But the microscope got results. On a scarf that was in a pocket of one of your overcoats, hanging in the hall, particles from the pipe were found. The scarf was unquestionably used by the murderer to keep his hand from contact with the pipe. Therefore —"

"Whose coat was it in?" Breslow blurted.

Cramer shook his head. "I'm not going to tell you whose coat it was or who the scarf belongs to, and I think it would be better if the owners didn't tell, because it would be sure to get to the papers, and you know what the papers —"

"No, you don't," Alger Kates piped up. "That would suit your plans, you and Nero Wolfe and the NIA, but you're not going to put any gag on me! It was my coat! And I've never seen the scarf before! This is the most —"

"That's enough, Kates," Solomon Dexter rumbled at him.

"Okay." Cramer did not sound displeased. "So it was found in Mr. Kates's coat, and he says he never saw the scarf before. That—"

"The scarf," Winterhoff interposed, his voice heavier and flatter than ever, "belongs to me. It was stolen from my overcoat in this house last Friday night. I haven't seen it since, until you showed it to me here. Since you have permitted Kates to make insinuations about the plans of the NIA—"

"No," Cramer said curtly, "that's out. I'm not interested in insinuations. If you people want to carry on your quarrel you can hire a hall. What I want to say is this, that some hours ago I said that one of you killed Miss Gunther, and Mr. Erskine objected. Now there's no room for objection. Now there's no doubt about it. We could take you all down and book you as material witnesses. But being who you are, within a few hours you'd all be out on bail. So we're letting you go home, including the one who committed a murder here tonight, because we don't know which one it is. We intend to find out. Meanwhile, you may be expected to be called on or sent for any time, day or night. You are not to leave the city, even for an hour, without permission. Your movements may or may not be kept under observation. That's up to us, and no protests about it will get you anywhere."

Cramer scanned the faces. "Police cars will take you home. You can go now, but one last word. This isn't going to let up. It's bad for all of you, and it will go on being bad until the murderer is caught. So if any of you knows anything that will help, the worst mistake you can make is not to let us have it. Stay now and tell us. The Police Commissioner and the District Attorney and I are right here and you can talk with any of us."

His invitation wasn't accepted, at least not on the terms as stated. The Erskine family lingered to exchange words with the D.A., Winterhoff had a point to make with the P.C., Mrs. Boone got Travis of the FBI, whom she apparently knew, to one side, Breslow had something to say to Wolfe, and Dexter confronted Cramer with questions. But before long they had all departed, and it didn't appear that anything useful had been contributed to the cause.

Wolfe braced his palms against the rim of his desk, pushed his chair back, and got to his feet.

Cramer, on the contrary, sat down. "Go to bed if you want to," he said grimly, "but I'm having a talk with Goodwin." Already it was Goodwin again. "I want to know who besides Kates had a chance to put that scarf in his coat."

"Nonsense." Wolfe was peevish. "With an ordinary person that might be necessary, but Mr. Goodwin is trained, competent, reliable, and moderately intelligent. If he could help on that he would have told us so. Merely ask him a question. I'll ask him myself. —Archie. Is your suspicion directed at anyone putting the scarf in the coat, or can you eliminate anyone as totally without opportunity?"

"No sir twice," I told him. "I've thought about it and gone over all of them. I was moving in and out between bell rings, and so were most of them. The trouble is the door to the front room was standing open, and so was the door from the front room to the hall."

Cramer grunted. "I'd give two bits to know how you would have answered that question if you had been alone with Wolfe, and how you will answer it."

"If that's how you feel about it," I said, "you might as well skip it. My resistance to torture is strongest at dawn, which it is now, and how are you going to drag the truth out of me?"

"I could use a nap," G. G. Spero said, and he got the votes.

But what with packing the scarf in a box as if it had been a museum piece, which incidentally it now is, and collecting papers and miscellaneous items, it was practically five o'clock before they were finally out.

The house was ours again. Wolfe started for the elevator. I still had to make the rounds to see what was missing and to make sure there were no public servants sleeping under the furniture. I called to Wolfe:

"Instructions for the morning, sir?"

"Yes!" he called back. "Let me alone!"

24

FROM there on I had a feeling that I was out of it. As it turned out, the feeling was not entirely justified, but anyhow I had it.

What Wolfe tells me, and what he doesn't tell me, never depends, as far as I can make out, on the relevant circumstances. It depends on what he had to eat at the last meal, what he is going to have to eat at the next meal, the kind of shirt and tie I am wearing, how well my shoes are shined, and so forth. He does not like purple. Once Lily Rowan gave me a dozen Sulka shirts, with stripes of assorted colors and shades. I happened to put on the purple one the day we started on the Chesterton-Best case, the guy that burgled his own house and shot a week-end guest in the belly. Wolfe took one look at the shirt and clammed up on me. Just for spite I wore the shirt a week, and I never did know what was going on, or who was which, until Wolfe had it all wrapped up, and even then I had to get most of the details from the newspapers and Dora Chesterton, with whom I had struck up an acquaintance. Dora had a way of—no, I'll save that for my autobiography.

The feeling that I was out of it had foundation in fact. Tuesday morning Wolfe breakfasted at the usual hour—my deduction from this evidence, that Fritz took up his tray, loaded, at eight o'clock, and brought it down empty at ten minutes to nine. On it was a note instructing me to tell Saul Panzer and Bill Gore, when they phoned in, to report at the office at eleven o'clock, and furthermore to arrange for Del Bascom, head of the Bascom Detective Agency, also to be present. They were all there waiting for him when he came down from the plant rooms, and he chased me out. I was sent to the roof to help Theodore cross-pollinate. When I went back down at lunch time Wolfe told me that envelopes from Bascom were to reach him unopened.

"Hah," I said. "Reports? Big operations?"

"Yes." He grimaced. "Twenty men. One of them may be worth his salt."

There went another five hundred bucks a day up the flue. At that rate the NIA retainer wouldn't last long.

"Do you want me to move to a hotel?" I inquired. "So I won't hear anything unfit for my ears?"

He didn't bother to answer. He never let himself get upset just before a meal if he could help it.

I could not, of course, be really blackballed, no matter what whim had struck him. For one thing, I had been among those present, and was therefore in demand. Friends on papers, especially Lon Cohen of the *Gazette*, thought I ought to tell them exactly who would be arrested and when and where. And Tuesday afternoon Inspector Cramer decided there was work to be done on me and invited me to Twentieth Street. He and three others did the honors. What was eating him was logic. To this effect: The NIA was Wolfe's client. Therefore, if I had seen any NIA person lingering unnecessarily in the neighborhood of Kate's overcoat as it hung in the hall, I would have reported it to Wolfe but not to anyone else. So far so good. Perfectly sound. But then Cramer went on to assume that with two hours of questions, back-tracking, leap-frogging, and ambushing, he and his bunch could squeeze it out of me, which was droll. Add to that, that there was nothing in me to squeeze, and it became quaint. Anyhow, they tried hard.

It appeared that Wolfe too thought I might still have uses. When he came down to the office at six o'clock he got into his chair, rang for beer, sat for a quarter of an hour, and then said:

"Archie."

It caught me in the middle of a yawn. After that was attended to I said: "Yeah."

He was frowning at me. "You've been with me a long time now."

"Yeah. How shall we do it? Shall I resign, or shall you fire me, or shall we just call it off by mutual consent?"

He skipped that. "I have noted, perhaps in more detail than you think, your talents and capacities. You are an excellent observer, not in any respect an utter fool, completely intrepid, and too conceited to be seduced into perfidy."

"Good for me. I could use a raise. The cost of living has incr—"

"You eat and sleep here, and because you are young and vain you spend too much for your clothes." He gestured with a finger. "We can discuss that some other time. What I have in mind is a quality in you which I don't at all understand but which I know you have. Its frequent result is a willingness on the part of young women to spend time in your company."

"It's the perfume I use. From Brooks Brothers. They call it Stag at Eve." I regarded him suspiciously. "You're leading up to something. You've done the leading up. What's the something?"

"Find out how willing you can make Miss Boone, as quickly as possible."

I stared. "You know," I said reproachfully, "I didn't know that kind of a thought ever got within a million miles of you. Make Miss Boone? If you can think it you can do it. Make her yourself."

"I am speaking," he said coldly, "of an investigating operation by gaining her confidence."

"That way it sounds even worse." I continued to stare. "However, let's put the best possible construction on it. Do you want me to worm a confession out of her that she murdered her uncle and Miss Gunther? No, thanks."

"Nonsense. You know perfectly well what I want."

"Tell me anyway. What do you want?"

"I want information on these points. The extent of her personal or social contacts, if any, with anyone connected with the NIA, especially those who were here last night. The same for Mrs. Boone, her aunt. Also, how intimate was she with Miss Gunther, what did they think of each other, and how much did she see of Miss Gunther the past week? That would do to start. If developments warrant it, you can then get more specific. Why don't you telephone her now?"

"It seems legitimate," I conceded, "up to the point where we get specific, and that can wait. But do you mean to say you think one of those NIA specimens is it?"

"Why not? Why shouldn't he be?"

"It's so damn obvious."

"Bah. Nothing is obvious in itself. Obviousness is subjective. Three pursuers learn that a fugitive boarded a train for Philadelphia. To the first pursuer it's obvious that the fugitive has gone to Philadelphia. To the second pursuer it's obvious that he left the train at Newark and has gone somewhere else. To the third pursuer, who knows how clever the fugitive is, it's obvious that he didn't leave the train at Newark, because that would be too obvious, but stayed on it and went to Philadelphia. Subtlety chases the obvious up a never-ending spiral and never quite catches it. Do you know Miss Boone's telephone number?"

I might have suspected him of sending me outdoors to play, to keep me out of mischief, but for the fact that it was a nuisance for him to have me out of the house, since he either had to answer the phone himself or let Fritz interrupt his other duties to attend to both the phone and the doorbell. So I granted his good faith, at least tentatively, and swiveled my chair to dial the Waldorf's number, and asked for Mrs. Boone's room. The room answered with a male voice that I didn't recognize, and after giving my name, and waiting longer than seemed called for, I had Nina.

"This is Nina Boone. Is this Mr. Goodwin of Nero Wolfe's office? Did I get that right?"

"Yep. In the pay of the NIA. Thank you for coming to the phone."

"Why — you're welcome. Did you — want something?"

"Certainly I did, but forget it. I'm not calling about what I want or wanted, or could easily want. I'm calling about something somebody else wants, because I was asked to, only in my opinion he's cuckoo. You realize the position I'm in. I can't call you up and say this is Archie Goodwin and I just drew ten bucks from the savings bank and how about using it to buy dinner for two at that Brazilian restaurant on Fifty-second Street? What's the difference whether that's what I want to do or not, as long as I can't? Am I keeping you from something important?"

"No . . . I have a minute. What is it that somebody else wants?"

"I'll come to that. So all I can say is, this is Archie Goodwin snooping for the NIA, and I would like to use some NIA expense money to buy you a dinner at that Brazilian restaurant on Fifty-second Street, with the understanding that it is strictly business and I am not to be trusted. To give you an idea how tricky I am, some people look under the bed at night, but I look *in* the bed, to make sure I'm not already there laying for me. Is the minute up?"

"You sound really dangerous. Is that what somebody else wanted you to do, kid me into having dinner with you?"

"The dinner part was my idea. It popped out when I heard your voice again. As for somebody else — you appreciate that working on this thing I'm thrown in with all sorts of people, not only Nero Wolfe, who is — well, he can't help it, he's what he is — but also the police, the FBI, the District Attorney's outfit — all kinds. What would you say if I told you that one of them told me to call you and ask where Ed Erskine is?"

"Ed Erskine?" She was flabbergasted. "Ask me where Ed Erskine is?"

"That's right."

"I'd say he was out of his mind."

"So would I. So that's settled. Now before we hang up, to leave no loose ends hanging, maybe you'd better answer my own personally conducted question, about the dinner. How do you usually say no? Blunt? Or do you zigzag to avoid hurting people's feelings?"

"Oh, I'm blunt."

"All right, wait till I brace myself. Shoot."

"I couldn't go tonight, no matter how tricky you are. I'm eating here with my aunt in her room."

"Then supper later. Or breakfast. Lunch. Lunch tomorrow at one?"

There was a pause. "What kind of a place is this Brazilian restaurant?"

"Okay, out of the way, and good food."

"But . . . whenever I go on the street —"

"I know. That's how it is. Leave by the Forty-ninth Street entrance. I'll be there at the curb with a dark blue Wethersill sedan. I'll be right there from twelve-fifty on. You can trust me to be there, but beyond that, remember, be on your guard."

"I may be a little late."

"I should hope so. You look perfectly normal to me. And please don't, five or ten years from now, try to tell me that I said you look average. I didn't say average, I said normal. See you tomorrow."

As I pushed the phone back I had a notion that a gleam of self-congratulation might be visible in my eyes, so I didn't turn immediately to face Wolfe but found papers on my desk that needed attention. After a moment he muttered:

"This evening would have been better."

I counted to ten. Then, still without turning, I said distinctly, "My dear sir, try getting her to meet you any time whatever, even at Tiffany's to try things on."

He chuckled. Before long he chuckled again. Finding that irritating, I went up to my room and kept busy until dinnertime straightening up. Fritz and Charley hadn't been able to get up that high on account of the condition of the rest of the house, and while the microscope experts had been neat and apparently respectable, I thought a spot inventory wouldn't do any harm.

Toward the end of dinner, with the salad and cheese, a little controversy arose. I wanted to have our coffee there in the dining room and then go straight up to bed, and Wolfe, while admitting that he too needed sleep, wanted the coffee in the office as usual. He got arbitrary about it, and just as an object lesson I sat tight. He went to the office and I stayed in the dining room. When I was through I went to the kitchen and told Fritz:

"I'm sorry you had that extra trouble, serving coffee in two places, but he has got to learn how to compromise. You heard me offer to split the difference and drink it in the hall."

"It was no trouble at all," Fritz said graciously. "I understand, Archie. I understand why you're being erratic. There goes the doorbell."

It was a temptation to let the damn thing ring. I needed sleep. So did Wolfe, and all I had to do was flip the switch there on the kitchen wall to stop the bell ringing. But I didn't flip it. I said to Fritz, "Justice. The public weal. Duty, goddam it," and went to the front and pulled the door open.

25

THE guy standing there said, "Good evening. I would like to see Mr. Wolfe."

I had never seen him before. He was around fifty, medium-sized, with thin straight lips and the kind of eyes that play poker for blood. The first tenth of a second I thought he was one of Bascom's men, and then saw that his clothes ruled that out. They were quiet and conservative and must have had at least three try-ons. I told him:

"I'll see if he's in. Your name, please?"

"John Smith."

"Oh. What do you want to see him about, Mr. Jones?"

"Private and urgent business."

"Can you be more specific?"

"I can to him, yes."

"Good. Sit down and read a magazine."

I shut the door on him, clear shut, and went to the office and told Wolfe:

"Mr. John Smith, which he must have got out of a book, looks like a banker who would gladly lend you a dime on a cupful of diamonds. I left him on the stoop, but don't worry about him being insulted because he has no feelings. Please don't ask me to find out what he wants because it might take hours."

Wolfe grunted. "What is your opinion?"

"None at all. I am not being permitted to know where we're at. The natural impulse is to kick him off the stoop. I'll say this for him, he's not an errand boy."

"Bring him in."

I did so. In spite of his obnoxious qualities and of his keeping us up, I put him in the red leather chair because that had him facing both of us. He was not a lounger. He sat up straight, with his fingers intertwined in his lap, and told Wolfe:

"I gave the name of John Smith because my name is of no significance. I am merely an errand boy."

Starting off by contradicting me. He went on:

"This is a confidential matter and I must speak with you privately."

Wolfe shook his head. "Mr. Goodwin is my confidential assistant. His ears are mine. Go ahead."

"No." Smith's tone implied, and that settles it. "I have to be alone with you."

"Bah." Wolfe pointed to a picture of the Washington Monument, on the wall fifteen feet to his left. "Do you see that picture? It is actually a perforated panel. If Mr. Goodwin is sent from the room he will go to an alcove around the corner of the hall, across from the kitchen door, open the panel on that side, invisible to us, and watch us and listen to us. The objection to that is that he would be standing up. He might as well stay here sitting down."

Without batting an eye, Smith stood up. "Then you and I will go to the hall."

"No we won't. —Archie. Mr. Smith wants his hat and coat."

I arose and moved. When I was halfway across the room Smith sat down again. I whirled, returned to my base, and did likewise.

"Well, sir?" Wolfe demanded.

"We have somebody," Smith said, in what was apparently the only tone he ever used, "for the Boone and Gunther murders."

"We? Somebody?"

Smith untangled his fingers, raised a hand to scratch the side of his nose, dropped the hand, and retwined the fingers. "Of course," he said, "death is always a tragedy. It causes grief and suffering and often hardship. That cannot be avoided. But in this case, the deaths of these two people, it has already caused widespread injury to many thousands of innocent persons and created a situation that amounts to gross injustice. As you know, as we all know, there are elements in this country that seek to undermine the very foundations of our society. Death is serving them —*has* served them well. The very backbone of our free democratic system —composed of our most public-spirited citizens, our outstanding businessmen who keep things going for us —is in great and real peril. The source of that peril was an event —now two events —which may have resulted either from the merest chance or from deep and calculated malice. From the standpoint of the common welfare those two events were in themselves unimportant. But overwhelmingly —"

"Excuse me." Wolfe wiggled a finger at him. "I used to make speeches myself. The way I would put it, you're talking about the nation-wide reaction against the National Industrial Association on account of the murders. Is that correct?"

"Yes. I am emphasizing the contrast between the trivial character of the events in themselves and the enormous harm —"

"Please. You've made that point. Go on to the next one. But first tell me, do you represent the NIA?"

"No. I represent, actually, the founding fathers of this country. I represent the best and most fundamental interests of the American people. I—"

"All right. Your next point?"

Smith untwined his fingers again. This time it was the chin that needed scratching. When that was finished he proceeded, "The existing situation is intolerable. It is playing directly into the hands of the most dangerous and subversive groups and doctrines. No price would be too high to pay for ending it, and ending it at the earliest possible moment. The man who performed that service would deserve well of his country. He would earn the gratitude of his fellow citizens, and, naturally, especially of those who are being made to suffer under this unjust odium."

"In other words," Wolfe suggested, "he ought to be paid something."

"He *would* be paid something."

"Then it's too bad I'm already engaged. I like being paid."

"There would be no conflict. The objectives are identical."

Wolfe frowned. "You know, Mr. Smith," he said admiringly, "I like the way you started this. You said it all, except certain details, in your first short sentence. Who are you and where do you come from?"

"That," Smith declared, "is stupid. You're not stupid. You can learn who I am, of course, if you want to take the time and trouble. But there are seven respectable—*very* respectable—men and women with whom I am playing bridge this evening. After a dinner party. Which accounts for the whole evening, from seven o'clock on."

"That should cover it adequately. Eight against two."

"Yes, it really should," Smith agreed. He untangled his fingers once more, but not to scratch. He reached to his side coat pocket and pulled out a package wrapped neatly in white paper and fastened with Scotch tape. It was big enough to be tight in his pocket and he had to use both hands. "As you say," he remarked, "there are certain details. The amount involved is three hundred thousand dollars. I have one third of it here."

I gave it a look and decided it couldn't all be in hundreds. There must have been some five-hundreds and grands.

One of Wolfe's brows went up. "Since you're playing bridge this evening, and since you came here on the assumption that I'm a blackguard, isn't that a little foolhardy? Mr. Goodwin, as I told you, is my confidential assistant. What if he took that away from you and put it in the safe and saw you to the sidewalk?"

For the first time the expression on Smith's face changed, but the little crease that showed in his forehead didn't look like apprehension. "Perhaps," he said, and there was no change in his voice, "you're stupid after all, though I doubt it. We know your record and your character. There isn't the slightest assumption that you're a blackguard. You are being given an opportunity to perform a service—"

"No," Wolfe said positively. "We've had that."

"Very well. But that's the truth. If you ask why you're being paid so large a sum to perform it, here are the reasons. First, everybody knows that you get exorbitant fees for everything you do. Second, from the standpoint of the people who are paying you, the rapidly accumulating public disfavor, which is totally undeserved, is costing them or will cost them, directly or indirectly, hundreds of millions. Three hundred thousand dollars is a mere nothing. Third, you will have expenses, and they may be large. Fourth, we are aware of the difficulties involved, and I tell you frankly that we know of no one except you who can reasonably be expected to solve them. There is no assumption whatever that you're a blackguard. That remark was completely uncalled for."

"Then perhaps I misunderstood the sentence you started with." Wolfe's eyes were straight at him. "Didn't you say you have somebody for the Boone and Gunther murders?"

"Yes." Smith's eyes were straight back at him.

"Who have you?"

"The word 'have' was a little inexact. It might have been better to say we have somebody to suggest."

"Who?"

"Either Solomon Dexter or Alger Kates. We would prefer Dexter but Kates would do. We would be in a position to co-operate on certain aspects of the evidence. After your plans are made I'll confer with you on that. The other two hundred thousand, by the way, would not be contingent on conviction. You couldn't possibly guarantee that. Another third would be paid on indictment, and the last third on the opening day of the trial. The effect of indictment and trial would be sufficient, if not wholly satisfactory."

"Are you a lawyer, Mr. Smith?"

"Yes."

"Wouldn't you pay more for Dexter than for Kates? You should. He's the Acting Director of the Bureau of Price Regulation. It would be worth more to you."

"No. We made the amount large, even exorbitant, to exclude any bargaining." Smith tapped the pacakge with his finger. "This is probably a record."

"Good heavens, no." Wolfe was mildly indignant, as if it had been intimated that his schooling had stopped at about the sixth grade. "There was Teapot Dome. I could rattle off eight, ten, a dozen instances. Alyattes of Lydia got the weight of ten panthers in gold. Richelieu paid D'Effiat a hundred thousand livres in one lump — the equivalent, at a minimum, of two million dollars today. No, Mr. Smith, don't flatter yourself that you're making a record. Considering what you're bidding for, you're a piker."

Smith was not impressed. "In cash," he said. "For you its equivalent, paid by check, would be around two million."

"That's right," Wolfe agreed, being reasonable. "Naturally that had occurred to me. I'm not pretending you're being niggardly." He sighed. "I'm no fonder of haggling than you are. But I may as well say it, there's an insuperable objection."

Smith blinked. I caught him at it. "What is it?"

"Your choice of targets. To begin with, they're too obvious, but the chief obstacle would be motive. It takes a good motive for a murder, and a really tiptop one for two murders. With either Mr. Dexter or Mr. Kates I'm afraid it simply couldn't be done, and I'll have to say definitely that I won't try it. You have generously implied that I'm not a jackass, but I would be, if I undertook to get either Mr. Dexter or Mr. Kates indicted and tried, let alone convicted." Wolfe looked and sounded inflexible. "No, sir. But you might find someone who would at least attempt it. How about Mr. Bascom, of the Bascom Detective Agency? He's a good man."

"I have told you," Smith said, "that you'll get co-operation on evidence."

"No. The absence of adequate motive would make it impossible in spite of evidence, which would have to be circumstantial. Besides, considering the probable source of any evidence you would be able to produce, and since it would be directed against a BPR man, it would be suspect anyhow. You see that."

"Not necessarily."

"Oh, yes. Inevitably."

"No." Smith's face stayed exactly as before, though he had made a major decision, to show a card. He turned the card over without a flicker. "I'll give you an example. If the taxi driver who brought Dexter here testified that he saw him concealing a piece of iron pipe under his coat, with a scarf wrapped around it, that evidence wouldn't be suspect."

"Perhaps not," Wolfe conceded. "Have you got the taxi driver?"

"No. I was merely giving you an example. How could we go after the taxi driver, or anyone else, before we have come to an agreement on the — on a name?"

"You couldn't, of course. Have you any other examples?"

Smith shook his head. That was one way in which he resembled Wolfe. He didn't see any sense in using a hundred ergs when fifty would do the job. Wolfe's average on head-shaking was around an eighth of an inch to the right and the same distance to the left, and if you had attached a meter to Smith you would have got about the same result. However, Wolfe was still more economical on physical energy. He weighed twice as much as Smith, and therefore his expenditure per pound of matter, which is the only fair way to judge, was much lower.

"You're getting a little ahead," Smith stated. "I said we would confer on aspects of evidence after your plans are made. You will make plans only after you have accepted the offer. Do I understand that you've accepted it?"

"You do not. Not as described. I decline it."

Smith took it like a gentleman. He said nothing. After some long seconds of saying nothing, he swallowed, and that was his first sign of weakness. Evidently he was throwing in his hand and was ready for another deal. When, after another period of silence, he swallowed again, there was no question about it.

"There is another possibility," he said, "that would not be open to the objections you have made. Don O'Neill."

"M-m-m-m," Wolfe remarked.

"He also came in a taxicab. The motive is plain and in fact already established, since it is the motive that has already been accepted, wrongly and maliciously, all over the country. He would not serve the purpose as satisfactorily as Dexter or Kates, but it would transfer the public resentment from an institution or group to an individual; and that would change the picture completely."

"M-m-m-m."

"Also, evidence would not be suspect on account of its source."

"M-m-m-m."

"And therefore the scope of the evidence could be substantially widened. For example, it might be possible to introduce the testimony of a person or persons who saw, here in your hall, O'Neill putting the scarf into the pocket of Kates's overcoat. I understand that Goodwin, your confidential assistant, was there throughout—"

"No," Wolfe said curtly.

"He doesn't mean I wasn't there," I assured Smith with a friendly grin. "Only that I've already been too damn positive about it. You should have come sooner. I would have been glad to discuss terms. When O'Neill tried to buy me it was Sunday, and I can't be bribed on Sunday—"

His eyes darted at me and through me. "What did O'Neill want you to do?"

I shook my head. Probably a thousand ergs. "That wouldn't be fair. Would you want me to tell him what you wanted me to do?"

He was strongly tempted to insist, there was no doubt about his thirst for knowledge, but his belief in the conservation of energy, coupled with the opinion he had formed of me, won the day. He gave it up without another try and returned to Wolfe.

"Even if Goodwin couldn't give it," he said, "there is still a good chance of testimony to that effect being available."

"Not from Mr. Breslow," Wolfe declared. "He would be a wretched witness. Mr. Winterhoff would do fairly well. Mr. Erskine Senior would be admirable. Young Mr. Erskine—I don't know, I rather doubt it. Miss Harding would be the best of all. Could you get her?"

"You're going too fast again."

"Not at all. Fast? Such details are of the greatest importance."

"I know they are. *After* you are committed. Are you accepting my suggestion about O'Neill?"

"Well." Wolfe leaned back, opened his eyes to a wider slit, and brought his finger tips together at the apex of his central bulk. "I'll tell you, Mr. Smith. The best way to put it, I think, is in the form of a message, or rather messages, for Mr. Erskine. Tell Mr. Erskine—"

"I'm not representing Erskine. I have mentioned no names."

"No? I though I heard you mention Mr. O'Neill, and Mr. Dexter and Mr. Kates. However, the difficulty is this, that the police or the FBI may find that tenth cylinder at any moment, and in all likelihood that would make fools of all of us."

"Not if we have—"

"Please, sir. You have talked. Let me talk. On the hypothesis that you may run across Mr. Erskine. Tell him that I am grateful for this suggestion regarding the size of the fee I may ask for without shocking him. I'll remember it when I make out my bill. Tell him that I appreciate his effort to pay the fee in a way that would keep it off my income tax report, but that form of skulduggery doesn't appeal to me. It's a matter of taste, and I happen not to like that. Tell him that I am fully aware that every minute counts; I know that the death of Miss Gunther has increased the public resentment to an unprecedented outburst of fury; I read the editorial in today's *Wall Street Journal*; I heard Raymond Swing on the radio this evening; I know what's happening."

Wolfe opened his eyes still wider. "Especially tell him this. If this idiotic

flimflam is persisted in there will probably be the devil to pay and I'll be
helpless, but I'll send in a bill just the same, and I'll collect it. I am now
convinced that he is either a murderer or a simpleton, and possibly both.
He is not, thank God, my client. As for you — no, I won't bother. As you say,
you are merely an errand boy, and I suppose a reputable lawyer, of the
highest standing. Therefore you are a sworn officer of the law. Pfui! — Archie. Mr. Smith is going."

He had indeed left his chair and was upright. But he wasn't quite going.
He said, in precisely the same tone he had used at the door when telling me
he would like to see Mr. Wolfe:

"I would like to know whether I can count on this being treated as
confidential. I merely want to know what to expect."

"You're a simpleton too," Wolfe snapped. "What's the difference whether
I say yes or no — to you? I don't even know your name. Wouldn't I do as I
please?"

"You think —" Smith said, and didn't finish it. Probably the sentence as
conceived might have betrayed a trace of some emotion, like sizzling rage
for instance, and that wasn't to be permitted under any circumstances. So I
don't think it is exaggerating to say that he was rendered speechless. He
stayed that way clear out to the stoop, not even telling me good night.

By the time I got back to the office Wolfe had already rung for beer. I
knew that by deduction when Fritz entered almost immediately with the
tray. I blocked him off and told him:

"Mr. Wolfe has changed his mind. Take it back. It's after ten o'clock, he
had only two hours' sleep last night, and he's going to bed. So are you and
either me or I or both."

Wolfe said nothing and made no sign, so Fritz beat it with the tray.

"It reminds me," I remarked, "of that old picture, there was one in our
dining room out in Ohio, of the people in the sleigh throwing the baby out
to the wolves that were chasing them. That may not strictly apply to Dexter
or Kates, but it certainly does to O'Neill. Esprit de corps my eye. Good
God, he was the Chairman of the Dinner Committee. I used to worry about
that picture. One way of looking at it, it was heartless to toss out the baby,
but on the other hand if they hadn't, the wolves would eventually have got
the whole works, baby, horses and all. Of course the man could have
jumped out himself, or the woman could. I remember I decided that if it
was me I would kiss the woman and baby good-by and then jump. I was
eight years old at the time, a minor, and I don't regard myself as still
committed to that. What do you think of the lousy bastards, anyhow?"

"They're in a panic." Wolfe stood up and pulled his vest down, and
maneuvered himself into motion toward the door. "They're desperate. Good
night, Archie." From the threshold he rumbled, without turning, "For that
matter, so am I."

26

THE next day, Wednesday, here came the envelopes from Bascom. There were four in the morning mail, three in the one o'clock delivery (as I was later informed for bookkeeping purposes, since I was not there at the time), and in late afternoon nine more arrived by messenger. At that time I hadn't the slightest idea what line the Bascom battalion was advancing on, nor did I know what Saul Panzer and Bill Gore were doing, since their telephoned reports were taken by Wolfe, with me instructed to disconnect. The Bascom envelopes were delivered to Wolfe unopened, as ordered.

I was being entrusted with nothing but the little chores, as for example a phone call I was told to make to the Stenophone Company to ask them to deliver a machine to us on a daily rental basis — one equipped with a loud-speaker, like the one the manager had brought us on Sunday and sent for on Monday. They weren't very affable about it and I had to be persuasive to get a promise of immediate delivery. I followed instructions and got the promise, though it was clear over my head, since we had nothing to play on it. An hour later the machine came and I stuck it in a corner.

The only other Wednesday morning activity in which I had a share was a phone call to Frank Thomas Erskine. I was told to make it, and did so, informing Erskine that expenses were skyrocketing and we wanted a check for another twenty thousand at his early convenience. He took that as a mere routine detail and came back at me for an appointment with Wolfe at eleven o'clock, which was made.

The most noteworthy thing about that was that when they — Breslow, Winterhoff, Hattie Harding, and the two Erskines — arrived, sharp at eleven, they had Don O'Neill with them! That was a fair indication that they had not come to take up where John Smith had left off, since Smith's central idea had been to frame O'Neill for a pair of murders, unless they were prepared to sweeten it up with an offer of a signed confession by O'Neill in triplicate, one copy for our files, and I felt that I knew O'Neill too well to expect anything like that, since he had tried to kick me.

Erskine brought the check with him. They stayed over an hour, and it was hard to guess why they had bothered to come, unless it was to show us in the flesh how harassed they were. No comment remotely touching on the errand of John Smith was made by anyone, including Wolfe. Half of their hour was used up in trying to get from Wolfe some kind of a progress report, which meant it was wasted, and they spent most of the other half in an attempt to pry a prognosis out of him. Twenty-four hours? Forty-eight? Three days? For God's sake, when? Erskine stated categorically that each additional day's delay meant untold damage to the most vital interests of the Republic and the American people.

"You're breaking my heart, Pop," young Erskine said sarcastically.

"Shut up!" his father barked at him.

They scratched and pulled hair right in front of us. The pressure was too much for them, and the NIA was no longer an united front. I sat and looked them over, having in mind Smith's offer of testimony regarding the placing of the scarf in Kates's overcoat pocket, and came to the conclusion that it might be had from any one of them with respect to any other of them, with the possible exception of Erskine vs. Erskine, and even that was not unthinkable. Their only constructive contribution was the announcement that the next day, Thursday, over two hundred morning and evening papers in a hundred towns and cities would run a full page ad offering a reward of one hundred thousand dollars to anyone furnishing information leading to the arrest and trial of the murderer of either Cheney Boone or Phoebe Gunther, or both.

"There should be a healthy reaction to that, don't you think?" Erskine asked plaintively but not too hopefully.

I missed Wolfe's answer, and the rest of it, because I was leaving at that moment, on my way upstairs to run a comb through my hair and maybe wash my hands. I barely had time enough to get the car and be parked at the Forty-ninth Street entrance of the Waldorf at twelve-fifty, and since once in a million years a girl is early instead of late I didn't want to take a chance.

27

NINA BOONE showed up at fourteen minutes past one, which was par and therefore called for no comment one way or the other. I met her as she emerged, steered her to where I was parked just west of the entrance, and opened the door. She climbed in. I turned to observe, and, as I expected, there one was, looking left and right. He was not an acquaintance and I didn't know his name, but I had seen him around. I crossed to him and said:

"I'm Archie Goodwin, Nero Wolfe's handy man. If you'd been on her heels you'd have seen her get in my car there. I can't ask you to ride with us because I'm working on her, but here's some choices. I'll wait till you get a taxi, and I'll bet you a fin if I lose you in less than ten minutes; or I'll grease you to miss the trail right here. Two bits. Fifteen cents now and the other dime when I see a copy of your report. If—"

"I've been told," he said, "that there are only two ways to deal with you. One is to shoot you, and this is too public. The other—give me the fifteen cents."

"Okay." I fished for three nickels and handed them to him. "It's on the NIA. Actually I don't care. We're going to Ribeiro's, the Brazilian restaurant on Fifty-second Street."

I went and got in the car beside my victim, started the engine, and rolled.

A corner table in the side room at Ribeiro's is a good place to talk. The food is no great treat to one who gets fed by Fritz Brenner three times a day, but it goes down all right, there is no music, and you can wave a fork in any direction without stabbing anybody except your own companion.

"I don't believe," Nina said after we had ordered, "that anyone has recognized me. Anyhow no one is staring at me. I guess all obscure people think it would be wonderful to be a celebrity and have people look at you and point you out in restaurants and places. I know I did. Now I simply can't stand it. It makes me want to scream at them. Of course I might not feel that way if my picture had been in the papers because I was a movie star or because I had done something worth while — you know, remarkable."

So, I thought, she wanted someone besides Aunt Luella to talk to. Okay, let her talk.

"And yet," I told her, "you must have had your share of staring before this happened. You're not actually unsightly."

"No?" She didn't try to smile. "How do you know? The way I look now."

I inspected her. "It's a bad time to judge," I admitted. "Your eyes are puffy and you've been clamping your jaw so much that your chin juts. But still there's enough to go by for an estimate. The cheekbone curve is very nice, and the temples and forehead are way above the average. The hair, of course, has not been affected at all. Seeing you from behind on the sidewalk, one man out of three would walk faster to get a look at you from the side or the front."

"Oh? And the other two?"

"My lord," I protested, "what do you want for nothing? One out of three is tremendous. I was piling it on, merely because your hair happens to appeal to me and I might go so far as to break into a trot."

"Then next time I'll sit with my back to you." She moved her hand to her lap to make room for the waiter. "I've been wanting to ask you, and you've got to tell me, who was it that told you to ask me where Ed Erskine was?"

"Not yet. My rule with a girl is to spend the first fifteen minutes discussing her looks. There's always a chance I'll say something that appeals to her, and then it's smooth sailing. Besides, it wouldn't be in good taste to start working on you while we're eating. I'm supposed to drag everything out of you, so that's what I'll have to do, but I shouldn't start on it until the coffee, and by that time, if I'm any good, I'll have you in a frame of mind to let me even copy down your Social Security number."

"I would hate to miss that." She did try to smile. "It would be interesting to see you do it. But I promised my aunt I'd be back at the hotel by two-thirty — and by the way, I promised to bring you with me. Will you come?"

My brows went up. "To see Mrs. Boone?"

"Yes."

"She wants to see me?"

"Yes. Maybe only for fifteen minutes to discuss her looks. She didn't say."

"With girls over fifty, five is enough."

"She's not over fifty. She's forty-three."

"Five is still enough. But if we only have till two-thirty I'm afraid we'd better start without taking time to break down your resistance. How do you feel? Have you noticed any inclination to melt or relax or put your head on my shoulder?"

"Not the slightest." Her tone carried conviction. "The only impulse I've had was to pull your hair."

"Then it'll be a wonder," I said regretfully, "if you loosen up enough to tell me what size shoes you wear. However we'll see, as soon as he gets through serving. You haven't finished your cocktail."

She did so. The waiter gave us each a steaming plate of shrimps, cooked with cheese and covered with a spicy sauce, and individual bowls of salad on which he had just sprinkled a thin dressing. Nina spreared a shrimp with her fork, decided it was too hot to go in whole, halved it, and conveyed a portion to her mouth. She was in no mood for tasting food, but she tasted that, and immediately got some more on her fork.

"I like this," she said. "Go on and drag things out of me."

I finished chewing my second shrimp and swallowed it. "My technique is a little unusual," I told her. "For instance, not only are all ten of you people being followed around, to see what you're up to now, but also your pasts are being drained through cheesecloth. How do you like this cheese?"

"I like it. I love it."

"Good. We'll come here often. There are probably a hundred men—no, more than that, I forgot how important this case is—investigating your people's pasts, to find out, for example, if Mrs. Boone was having secret trysts with Frank Thomas Erskine on the boardwalk at Atlantic City, or if you and Breslow are champing at the bit until he can get his wife to give him a divorce. That takes time and money, and my technique is different. I prefer to ask you and settle it. Are you?"

"Am I what? Champing?"

"At the bit."

"No, I'm champing shrimps."

I swallowed another one. "You see," I explained, "they're all up a stump, including Nero Wolfe. They're not trying to make it more complicated just for the hell of it. The most satisfactory way out of it, the way that would please nearly everybody most, including the investigators themselves, would be the simplest way, namely that one of those six NIA people killed Cheney Boone for the obvious motive, and then killed Phoebe Gunther for some related reason. But the trouble is that if that's how it was, how are you ever going to find out which one of the six did it, let alone prove it? Apparently not a chance in a billion. The New York police and the FBI have been working on it over a week now, giving it all they've got, and where are they? Tailing you!"

"Well." She herded cheese and sauce with her fork. "You're buying me a lunch."

"Certainly, and I'm telling you why, aside from your hair and other personal details. We're all sunk unless we can find a new angle. I came to you because there's a possibility that you know something about such an angle without realizing it. Naturally I'm assuming that you want the murderer found and punished. Otherwise—"

"I do. Of course I do."

"Then suppose we try the direct approach and see how it sounds. Did you know any of these NIA birds personally?"

"No."

"None of those six?"

"No."

"How about any NIA people at all? There were around fifteen hundred of them at that dinner."

"This seems perfectly silly."

"Then let's get it over with. Did you?"

"Maybe a few—or rather, their sons and daughters. I graduated from Smith a year ago, and you meet a lot of people. But if we went back over every minute of it, every word of every conversation, we wouldn't find anything remotely resembling an angle."

"You don't think it would do me any good to probe?"

"No." She glanced at her wrist watch. "Anyway, we haven't time."

"Okay. We can go back to it. How about your aunt? Those trysts with Erskine. Did she have trysts?"

Nina made a noise which, under the circumstances, was a fair substitute for a laugh. "Ask her. Maybe that's what she wants to see you about. If all the pasts are being investigated as you say they are, I should think it would be established by now that Aunt Luella was utterly and exclusively devoted to my uncle, and to everything he did and everything he stood for."

I shook my head. "You don't get it. That's just the point. To illustrate: what if Boone learned something in Washington that Tuesday afternoon about something Winterhoff had done, or something that made him decide to take a certain step affecting Winterhoff's line of business, and what if he told his wife about it when he saw her in their hotel room (which you might also have heard since you were there too), and what if Mrs. Boone happened to know Winterhoff, not for trysting purposes but just knew him, and what if later, in the reception room, she was talking with Winterhoff during her third cocktail, and what if unintentionally she gave him an idea of what was up? That's what I mean by a new angle. I could invent a thousand of them just as I invented that one, but what is needed is one that really happened. So I'm asking about your aunt's circle of acquaintance. Is that malevolent?"

She had been making steady progress with the shrimps, which had now cooled off enough to permit it. "No," she admitted, "but you'd better ask her. All I can tell you is about me."

"Sure. You're virtuous and noble. It shows in your chin. The herald angels sing. A in deportment."

"What do you want?" she demanded. "Do you want me to tell you I saw my aunt sneaking into a corner with Winterhoff or with any of those apes and whispering to him? Well, I didn't. And if I had—" She stopped.

"If you had would you tell me?"

"No. In spite of the fact that in my opinion my aunt is a pain in the neck."

"You don't like her?"

"No. I don't like her and I disapprove of her and I regard her as a grotesque relic. That's spread all over my past, but it's strictly personal."

"You don't go so far as to accept Breslow's suggestion that Mrs. Boone killed her husband on account of jealousy of Phoebe Gunther, and later, at Wolfe's house, finished up?"

"No, does anybody?"

"I couldn't say." Having disposed of the last shrimp, I started on the salad. "I don't. But it does seem to be a sound idea that Mrs. Boone was jealous of Phoebe Gunther."

"Certainly she was. There are several thousand girls and women working for the BPR, and she was jealous of all of them."

"Yeah. Chiefly on account of her nose, of course. But Phoebe Gunther wasn't just one of thousands. Wasn't she special?"

"She was indeed." Nina flashed me a quick glance which I failed to interpret. "She was extremely special."

"Was she going to do anything as trite as having a baby?"

"Oh, good lord." Nina pulled her salad over. "You pick up all the crumbs, don't you?"

"Was she?"

"No. And my aunt had just as little reason to be jealous of her as of anybody else. Her idea that my uncle had wolf in him was simply silly."

"How well did you know Miss Gunther?"

"I knew her pretty well. Not intimately."

"Did you like her?"

"I — yes, I guess I liked her. I certainly admired her. Of course I envied her. I would have liked to have her job, but I wasn't foolish enough to think I could fill it. I'm too young for one thing, but that's only part of it, she wasn't such a lot older than me. She did field work for a year or so and made the best record in the whole organization, and then she was brought to the main office and before long she was on the inside of everything. Usually when an organization like that gets a new Director he does a great deal of shifting around, but when my uncle was appointed there wasn't any shifting of Phoebe except that she got a raise in pay. If she had been ten years older and a man she would have been made Director when my uncle — died."

"How old was she?"

"Twenty-seven."

"Did you know her before you went to work for the BPR?"

"No, but I met her the first day I went there, because my uncle asked her to keep an eye on me."

"Did she do so?"

"In a way she did, yes, as much as she had time for. She was very important and very busy. She had BPR fever."

"Yeah?" I stopped a forkload of salad on its way to my mouth. "Bad?"

"One of the most severe cases on record."

"What were the main symptoms?"

"It varies with character and temperament. In its simplest form, a firm belief that whatever the BPR does is right. There are all kinds of complications, from bitter and undying hatred of the NIA to a messianic yen to educate the young, depending on whether you are primarily a do-gooder or a fighter."

"Have you got it?"

"Certainly I have, but not in its acute form. With me it was mostly a personal matter. I was very fond of my uncle." Her chin threatened to get out of control for a moment, and she paused to attend to that and then explained, "I never had a father, to know him, and I loved Uncle Cheney. I don't really know an awful lot about it, but I loved my uncle."

"Which complications did Phoebe have?"

"All of them." The chin was all right again. "But she was a born fighter. I don't know how much the enemies of the BPR, for instance the heads of the NIA, really knew about the insides of it, but if their intelligence was any good they must have known about Phoebe. She was actually more dangerous to them than my uncle was. I've heard my uncle say that. A political shake-up might have got him out, but as long as she was there it wouldn't have mattered much."

"That's a big help," I grumbled, "I don't think. It gives precisely the same motive, to the same people, for her as for him. If you call that a new angle . . ."

"I don't call it anything. You asked me."

"So I did. How about dessert?"

"I don't think so."

"You'd better. You're going to have to help me out with your aunt maybe all afternoon, and that will take extra energy since you don't like her. A good number here is walnut pudding with cinnamon."

She conceded that it was a good idea and I passed it on to the waiter. While our table was being cleared and we were waiting for the pudding and coffee, we continued on the subject of Phoebe Gunther, with no revelations coming out of it, startling or otherwise. I introduced the detail of the missing tenth cylinder, and Nina snorted at the suggestion that Phoebe might have had concealed relations with some NIA individual and had ditched the cylinder because it implicated him or might have. I gave her that and asked how about the possibility that the cylinder implicated Solomon Dexter or Alger Kates. What was wrong with that?

With her spoon in her hand ready to start on the pudding, she shook her head positively. She said it was loony. To suppose that Dexter would have done anything to hurt Boone, thereby hurting the BPR also, was absurd. "Besides, he was in Washington. He didn't get to New York until late that night, when he was sent for. As for Mr. Kates, good heavens, look at him! He's just an adding machine!"

"He is in a pig's eye. He's sinister."

She gaped. "Alger Kates sinister!"

"Anyhow, mysterious. Down at Wolfe's house that evening Erskine accused him of killing your uncle because he wanted to marry you and your uncle opposed it, and Kates let it stand that he did want to marry you, along with two hundred other lovesick BPR's, and then later that same evening I learn that he already has a wife who is at present in Florida. A married adding machine does not covet another lovely maiden."

"Puh. He was merely being gallant or polite."

"An adding machine is not gallant. Another thing, where does the dough come from to send his wife to Florida at the present rates and keep her there until the end of March?"

"Really." Nina stopped eating pudding. "No matter what Nero Wolfe charges the NIA, you're certainly trying your best to earn it! You'd just love to clear them completely — and it looks as if you don't care how you do it! Perhaps Mrs. Kates won some money at a church bingo. You ought to check on that!"

I grinned at her. "When your face is flushed like that it makes me feel like refusing to take any part of my salary in NIA money. Some day I'll tell you

how wrong you are to suspect us of wanting to frame one of your heroes like
Dexter or Kates." I glanced at my wrist. "You just have time to finish your
cigarette and coffee. — What is it, Carlos?"

"Telephone, Mr. Goodwin. The middle booth."

I had a notion to tell him to say I had gone, because I had a natural
suspicion that it was the creature I had bribed with three nickels merely
wanting to know how much longer we were going to be in there, but I
thought better of it and excused myself, since there was one other person
who knew where I was.

It proved to be the other person.

"Goodwin talking."

"Archie. Get down here at once."

"What for?"

"Without delay!"

"But listen. We're just leaving to see Mrs. Boone. I've got her to agree to
see me. I'll put her through a —"

"I said get down here."

There was no use arguing. He sounded as if six tigers were crouching
before him, lashing their tails, ready to spring. I went back to the table and
told Nina that our afternoon was ruined.

28

HAVING delivered Nina at the Waldorf entrance, with my pet bribee on our
tail in a taxi, and having crowded the lights and the congested traffic down
and across to West Thirty-fifth Street, I was relieved to see, as I reached my
destination and braked to a stop at the curb, that the house wasn't on fire.
There were only two foreign items visible: a police car parked smack in front
of the address, and a man on the stoop. He was seated on the top step,
hunched over, looking gloomy and obstinate.

This one I knew by name, one Quayle. He was on his feet by the time I
had mounted the steps, and accosted me with what was meant to be
cordiality.

"Hello, Goodwin! This is a piece of luck. Don't anybody ever answer the
bell here when you're away? I'll just go in with you."

"Unexpected pleasure," I told him, and used my key, turned the knob,
and pushed. The door opened two inches and stopped. The chain bolt was
on, as it often was during my absence. My finger went to the button and
executed my private ring. In a minute Fritz's step came down the hall and
he spoke to me through the crack.

"Archie, that's a policeman. Mr. Wolfe doesn't —"

"Of course he doesn't. Take off the bolt. Then keep your eye on us. This
officer eagerly performing his duty might lose his balance and fall down the

stoop, and I may need you as a witness that I didn't push him. He must be twice my age."

"You witty son of a bitch," Quayle said sadly, and sat down on the step again. I entered, marched down the hall to the office, and saw Wolfe there alone behind his desk, sitting up straight as a ramrod, his lips pressed together in a thin straight line, his eyes wide open, his hands resting on the desk before him with the fingers curved ready for a throat.

His eyes darted at me. "What the devil took you so long?"

"Now just a minute," I soothed him. "Aware that you were having a fit, I made it as fast as I could in the traffic. Is it a pinch?"

"It is insufferable. Who is Inspector Ash?"

"Ash? You remember him. He was a captain under Cramer from 1938 to '43. Now in charge of Homicide in Queens. Tall guy, face all bones, plastic eyes, very incorruptible and no sense of humor. Why, what has he done?"

"Is the car in good condition?"

"Certainly. Why?"

"I want you to drive me to Police Headquarters."

"My God." So it was something not only serious, but drastic. Leaving the house, getting in the car, incurring all the outdoor risks, visiting a policeman; and besides all that, which was unheard of, almost certainly standing up the orchids for the regular four o'clock date. I dropped onto a chair, speechless, and gawked at him.

"Luckily," Wolfe said, "when that man arrived the door was bolted. He told Fritz that he had come to take me to see Inspector Ash. When Fritz gave him the proper reply he displayed a warrant for me as a material witness regarding the murder of Miss Gunther. He pushed the warrant in through the crack in the door and Fritz pushed it out again and closed the door, and through the glass panel, saw him walk toward the corner, presumably to telephone, since he left his car there in front of my house."

"That alone," I remarked, "leaving his car in front of your house, shows the kind of man he is. It's not even his car. It belongs to the city."

Wolfe didn't even hear me. "I called Inspector Cramer's office and was told he was not available. I finally succeeded in reaching some person who spoke in behalf of Inspector Ash, and was told that the man they had sent here had reported by telephone, and that unless I admitted him, accepted service of the warrant, and went with him, a search warrant would be sent without delay. I then, with great difficulty, got to the Police Commissioner. He has no guts. He tried to be evasive. He made what he called a concession, stating that I could come to his office instead of Inspector Ash's. I told him that only by using physical force could I be transported in any vehicle not driven by you, and he said they would wait for me until half-past three but no longer. An ultimatum with a time limit. He also said that Mr. Cramer has been removed from the Boone-Gunther case and relieved of his command and has been replaced by Inspector Ash. That's the situation. It is unacceptable."

I was staring incredulously. "Cramer got the boot?"

"So Mr. What's-his-name said."

"Who, Hombert? The Commissioner?"

"Yes. Confound it, must I repeat the whole thing for you?"

"For God's sake, don't. Try to relax. I'll be damned. They got Cramer." I looked at the clock. "It's five past three, and that ultimatum has probably got narrow margins. You hold it a minute and try to think of something pleasant."

I went to the front and pulled the curtain aside for a look through the glass, and saw that Quayle had acquired a colleague. The pair were sitting on the stoop with their backs to me. I opened the door and inquired affably:

"What's the program now?"

Quayle twisted around. "We've got another paper. Which we'll show when the time comes. The kind of law that opens all doors from the mightiest to the humblest."

"To be shown when? Three-thirty?"

"Go suck a pickle."

"Aw, tell him," the colleague growled. "What do you expect to get out of it, fame?"

"He's witty," Quayle said petulantly. He twisted back to me. "At three-thirty we phone in again for the word."

"That's more like it," I declared approvingly. "And what happens if I emerge with a large object resembling Nero Wolfe and wedge him into my car and drive off? Do you flash your first paper and interfere?"

"No. We follow you if it's straight to Centre Street. If you try detouring by way of Yonkers that's different."

"Okay. I'm accepting your word of honor. If you forget what you said and try to grab him I'll complain to the Board of Health. He's sick."

"What with?"

"Sitzenlust. Chronic. The opposite of wanderlust. You wouldn't want to jeopardize a human life, would you?"

"Yes."

Satisfied, I closed the door and returned to the office and told Wolfe, "All set. In spite of our having outriders I'm game either for Centre Street or for a dash for Canada, however you feel. You can tell me after we're in the car."

He started to get erect, his lips compressed tighter than ever.

29

"YOU are not an attorney," Inspector Ash declared in an insulting tone, though the statement was certainly not an insult in itself. "Nothing that has been said or written to you by anyone whatever has the status of a privileged communication."

It was not a convention as I had expected. Besides Wolfe and me the only ones present were Ash, Police Commissioner Hombert, and District Attorney Skinner, which left Hombert's spacious and well-furnished corner office looking practically uninhabited, even considering that Wolfe counted for three. At least he was not undergoing downright physical hardship, since there had been found available a chair large enough to accommodate his beam without excessive squeezing.

But he was conceding nothing. "That remark," he told Ash in his most objectionable tone, "is childish. Suppose I have been told something that I don't want you to know about. Would I admit the fact and then refuse to tell you about it on the ground that it was a privileged communication? Pfui! Suppose you kept after me. I would simply tell you a string of lies and then what?"

Ash was smiling. His plastic eyes had the effect of reflecting all the light that came at them from the four big windows, as if their surfaces could neither absorb light nor give it out.

"The trouble with you, Wolfe," he said curtly, "is that you've been spoiled by my predecessor, Inspector Cramer. He didn't know how to handle you. You had him buffaloed. With me in charge you'll see a big difference. A month from now or a year from now you may still have a license and you may not. It depends on how you behave." He tapped his chest with his forefinger. "You know me. You may remember how far you got with that Boeddiker case over in Queens."

"I never started. I quit. And your abominable handling gave the prosecutor insufficient evidence to convict a murderer whose guilt was manifest. Mr. Ash, you are both a numskull and a hooligan."

"So you're going to try it on me." Ash was still smiling. "Maybe I won't give you even a month. I don't see why—"

"That will do for that," Hombert broke in.

"Yes, sir," Ash said respectfully. "I only wanted—"

"I don't give a damn what you only wanted. We're in one hell of a fix, and that's all I'm interested in. If you want to ride Wolfe on this case go as far as you like, but save the rest till later. It was your idea that Wolfe was holding out and it was time to put the screws on him. Go ahead. I'm all for that."

"Yes, sir." Ash had quit smiling to look stern. "I only know this, that in every case I've ever heard of where Wolfe horned in and got within smelling distance of money he has always managed to get something that no one else gets, and he always hangs onto it until it suits his convenience to let go."

"You're quite correct, Inspector," District Attorney Skinner said dryly. "You might add that when he does let go the result is usually disastrous for some lawbreaker."

"Yes?" Ash demanded. "And is that a reason for letting him call the tune for the Police Department and your office?"

"I would like to ask," Wolfe put in, "if I was hauled down here to listen to a discussion of my own career and character. This babbling is frivolous."

Ash was getting stirred up. He glared. "You were hauled down here," he rasped, "to tell us what you know, and everything you know, about these crimes. You say I'm a numskull. I don't say you're a numskull, far from it, here's my opinion of you in one short sentence. I wouldn't be surprised if you know something that gives you a good clear idea of who it was that killed Cheney Boone and the Gunther woman."

"Certainly I do. So do you."

They made movements and noises. I grinned around at them, nonchalant, to convey the impression that there was nothing to get excited about, because I had the conviction that Wolfe was overplaying it beyond

all reason just to get even with them and it might have undesirable consequences. His romantic nature often led him to excesses like that, and once
he got started it was hard to stop him, the stopping being one of my
functions. Before their exclamations and head-jerkings were finished I
stepped in.

"He doesn't mean," I explained hastily, "that we've got the murderer
down in our car. There are details to be attended to."

Hombert's and Skinner's movements had been limited to minor muscular
reactions, but Ash had left his chair and strode masterfully to within two
feet of Wolfe, where he stopped short to gaze down at him. He stood with his
hands behind his back, which was effective in a way, but it would have been
an improvement if he had remembered that in the classic Napoleon stance
the arms are folded.

"You either mean it," he said like a menace, "or you don't. If it's a bluff
you'll eat it. If it isn't, for once in your life you're going to be opened up."
His bony head swiveled to Hombert. "Let me take him, sir. Here in your
office it might be embarrassing."

"Imbecile," Wolfe muttered. "Hopeless imbecile." He applied the levers
and got himself to his feet. "I had reluctantly accepted the necessity of a
long and fruitless discussion of a singularly difficult problem, but this is
farcical. Take me home, Archie."

"No you don't," Ash said, even more a menace. He reached and gripped
Wolfe's arm. "You're under arrest, my man. This time you—"

I was aware that Wolfe could move without delay when he had to, and,
knowing what his attitude was toward anybody's hand touching him, I had
prepared myself for motion when I saw Ash grab his arm, but the speed and
precision with which he slapped Ash on the side of his jaw were a real
surprise, not only to me but to Ash himself. Ash didn't even know it was
coming until it was there, a healthy open-palm smack with a satisfactory
sound effect. Simultaneously Ash's eyes glittered and his left fist started,
and I propelled myself up and forward. The emergency was too split-second
to permit anything fancy, so I simply inserted myself in between, and Ash's
left collided with my right shoulder before it had any momentum to speak
of. With great presence of mind I didn't even bend an elbow, merely staying
there as a barrier; but Wolfe, who claims constantly to detest a hubbub,
said through his teeth:

"Hit him, Archie. Knock him down."

By that time Hombert was there and Skinner was hovering. Seeing that
they were voting against bloodshed, and not caring to be tossed in the coop
for manhandling an inspector, I backed away. Wolfe glared at me and said,
still through his teeth:

"I am under arrest. You are not. Telephone Mr. Parker to arrange for bail
immed—"

"Goodwin is staying right here." Ash's eyes were really nasty. I had never
had an impulse to send him a birthday greeting card, but I was surprised to
learn how mean he was. "Or rather you're both going with me—"

"Now listen." Skinner had his hands spread out patting air, like a pleader
calming a mob. "This is ridiculous. We all want—"

"Am I under arrest?"

"Oh, forget that! Technically, I suppose—"

"Then I am. You can all go to the devil." Wolfe went back to the big chair and sat down. "Mr. Goodwin will telephone our lawyer. If you want me out of here send for someone to carry me. If you want me to discuss anything with you, if you want a word out of me, vacate those warrants and get rid of Mr. Ash. He jars me."

"I'll take him," Ash snapped. "He struck an officer."

Skinner and Hombert looked at each other. Then they looked at Wolfe, then at me, and then at each other again. Skinner shook his head emphatically. Hombert regarded Wolfe once more and then turned his gaze on Ash.

"Inspector," he said, "I think you had better leave this to the District Attorney and me. You haven't been in charge of this case long enough to — uh—digest the situation, and while I consented to your proposal to get Wolfe down here, I doubt if you're sufficiently aware of—uh—all the aspects. I have described to you the sources of the strongest pressure to take Inspector Cramer off of the case, which meant also removing him from his command, and therefore it is worth considering that Wolfe's client is the National Industrial Association. Whether we want to consider it or not, we have to. You'd better return to your office, give the reports further study, and continue operations. Altogether, at this moment, there are nearly four hundred men working on this case. That's enough of a job for one man."

Ash's jaw was working and his eyes were still glittering. "It's up to you, sir," he said with an effort. "As I told you, and as you already knew, Wolfe has been getting away with murder for years. If you want him to get away with calling one of your subordinates an imbecile and physically assaulting him, in your own office . . ."

"At the moment I don't care a damn who gets away with what." Hombert was a little exasperated. "I care about just one thing, getting this case solved, and if that doesn't happen soon I may not have any subordinates. Get back on the job and phone me if there's anything new."

"Yes, sir." Ash crossed to Wolfe, who was seated, until their toes touched. "Some day," he promised, "I'll help you lose some weight." Then he strode out of the room.

I returned to my chair. Skinner had already returned to his. Hombert stood looking at the door that had closed behind the Inspector, ran his fingers through his hair, shook his head slowly a few times, moved to his own chair behind his desk, sat, and lifted a receiver from its cradle. In a moment he spoke into the transmitter:

"Bailey? Have that warrant for the arrest of Nero Wolfe as a material witness vacated. Right away. No, just cancel it. Send me —"

"*And* the search warrant," I put in.

"Also the search warrant for Nero Wolfe's house. No, cancel that too. Send the papers to me."

He hung up and turned to Wolfe. "All right, you got away with it. Now what do you know?"

Wolfe sighed deep. A casual glance at his bulk might have given the impression that he was placid again, but to my experienced eye, seeing that he was tapping the arm of his chair with his middle finger, it was evident that there was still plenty of turmoil.

"First," he muttered, "I would like to learn something. Why was Mr. Cramer demoted and disgraced?"

"He wasn't."

"Nonsense. Whatever you want to call it, why?"

"Officially, for a change of scene. Off the record, because he lost his head, considering who the people are that are involved, and took on a bigger load than the Department could handle. Whether you like it or not, there's such a thing as a sense of proportion. You cannot treat some people like a bunch of waterfront hoodlums."

"Who brought the pressure?"

"It came from everywhere. I've never seen anything like it. I'm giving no names. Anyhow, that wasn't the only reason. Cramer was muffing it. For the first time since I've known him he got tangled up. Here at a conference yesterday morning he couldn't even discuss the problem intelligently. He had got his mind fixed on one aspect of it, one little thing, and that was all he could think of or talk about—that missing cylinder, the tenth cylinder that may or may not have been in the leather case Boone gave to Miss Gunther just before he was murdered."

"Mr. Cramer was concentrating on that?"

"Yes. He had fifty men looking for it, and he wanted to assign another fifty to it."

"And that was one of your reasons for removing him?"

"Yes. Actually the main reason."

Wolfe grunted. "Hah. Then you're an imbecile too. I didn't know Mr. Cramer had it in him to see that. This doubles my admiration and respect for him. Finding that cylinder, if not our only chance, is beyond all comparison our best one. If it is never found the odds are big that we'll never get the murderer."

A loud disgusted snort came from Skinner. "That's you all right, Wolfe! I suspected it was only fireworks. You said you've already got him."

"I said nothing of the sort."

"You said you know who it is."

"No." Wolfe was truculent. Having been aroused to the point of committing assault and battery, he had by no means calmed down again. "I said I know something that gives me a good clear idea of the murderer's identity, and I also said that you people know it too. You know many things that I don't know. Don't try to pretend that I bulldozed you into ejecting Mr. Ash and releasing me from custody by conveying the impression that I am prepared to name the culprit and supply the evidence. I am not."

Hombert and Skinner looked at each other. There was silence.

"You impervious bastard," Skinner said, but wasting no energy on it.

"In effect, then," Hombert said resentfully, "you are saying that you have nothing to tell us, that you have nothing to offer, that you can't help us any."

"I'm helping all I can. I am paying a man twenty dollars a day to explore the possibility that Miss Gunther broke that cylinder into little pieces and put it in the rubbish receptacle in her apartment in Washington. That's going to an extreme, because I doubt if she destroyed it. I think she expected to use it some day."

Hombert shifted impatiently in his chair as if the idea of hunting for a lousy cylinder, possibly broken anyhow, only irritated him. "Suppose," he said, "you tell us what it is we all know that gives you a good clear idea of who the murderer is, including the who. Off the record."

"It isn't any one thing."

"I don't care if it's a dozen things. I'll try to remember them. What are they?"

Wolfe shook his head. "No, sir."

"Why not?"

"Because of your idiotic treatment of Mr. Cramer. If it seemed to make sense to you, and I believe it would, you would pass it on to Mr. Ash, and heaven knows what he would do. He might even, by pure chance, do something that would result in his solving the case, and I would stop short of nothing to prevent that outcome." Wolfe's middle finger started tapping again. "Help Mr. Ash to a triumph? God forbid!" He frowned at Hombert. "Besides, I've already given you the best advice I've got. Find that cylinder. Put a hundred men on it, a thousand. Find it!"

"We're not neglecting the damn cylinder. How about this, do you think Miss Gunther knew who killed Boone?"

"Certainly she did."

Skinner broke in. "Naturally you'd like that," he said pessimistically, "since it would eliminate your clients. If Miss Gunther knew who it was, and it was an NIA man, she would have handed it to us on a platter. So if she did know, it was and is one of the other four — Dexter or Kates or one of the Boone women."

"Not at all," Wolfe contradicted him.

"But damn it, of course!"

"No." Wolfe sighed. "You're missing the whole point. What has been the outstanding fact about this case for a whole week now? What was its peculiar characteristic? This, that the public, the people, had immediately brought the case to trial as usual, without even waiting for an arrest, and instead of the customary prolonged disagreement and dissension regarding various suspects, they reached an immediate verdict. Almost unanimously they convicted — this was the peculiar fact — not an individual, but an organization. The verdict was that the National Industrial Association had murdered Cheney Boone. Now what if you were Miss Gunther and knew who had killed Boone? No matter how you knew, that's another question; the point is that you knew. I think she did know. Let's suppose she knew it was young Mr. Erskine. Would she have exposed him? No. She was devoted to the interests of her own organization, the BPR. She saw the rising tide of resentment and indignation against the NIA, constantly increasing in force and intensity. She saw that it might result, if sustained long enough, in completely discrediting the NIA and its purposes, policies, and objectives. She was intelligent enough to calculate that if an individual, no matter who, were arrested for the murder with good evidence, most of the resentment against the NIA would be diverted away from it as an organization."

Wolfe sighed again. "What would she do? If she had evidence that pointed to Mr. Erskine, or to anyone else, she would suppress it; but she wouldn't destroy it, for she wouldn't want the murderer eventually to escape his punishment. She would put it where it wouldn't be found, but where she could retrieve it and produce it when the time came, when the NIA had been sufficiently damaged. It is not even necessary to assume loyalty to the BPR as her dominating motive. Suppose it was personal devotion to Mr. Boone and a desire to avenge him. The best possible revenge, the perfect revenge, would be to use his death and the manner of it for the discomfiture and the destruction of the organization which had hated him and tried to thwart him. In my opinion Miss Gunther was capable of that. She was a remarkable young woman. But she made the mistake of permitting the murderer to learn that she knew who he was, how is still another question, and that she paid for."

Wolfe raised his hand and let it fall. "However, note this. Her own death served her purpose too. In the past two days the wave of anger against the NIA has increased tremendously. It is going deep into the feeling of the people, and soon it will be impossible to dredge it out again. She was a remarkable woman. No, Mr. Skinner, Miss Gunther's knowing the identity of the murderer would not eliminate my clients. Besides, no man is my client, and no men are. My checks come from the National Industrial Association, which, having no soul, could not possibly commit a murder."

Wolfe cocked an eye at Hombert. "Speaking of checks. You have seen the NIA advertisement offering a reward of one hundred thousand dollars. You might let your men know that whoever finds the missing cylinder will get that reward."

"Yes?" Hombert was skeptical. "You're as bad as Cramer. What makes you so damn sure about that cylinder? Have you got it in your pocket?"

"No. If I had!"

"What makes you so sure about it?"

"Well. I can't put it in a sentence."

"We've got all the time there is."

"Didn't Mr. Cramer explain it to you?"

"Forget Cramer. He's out of it."

"Which is nothing to your credit, sir." Wolfe rearranged his pressures and angles, shifting the mass to get the center of gravity exactly right for maximum comfort. An unaccustomed chair always presented him with a complicated engineering problem. "You really want me to go into this?"

"Yes."

"Mr. Skinner?"

"Yes."

"All right, I will." Wolfe closed his eyes. "It was apparent from the beginning that Miss Gunther was lying about the leather case. Mr. Cramer knew that, of course. Four people stated that they saw her leaving the reception room with it, people who couldn't possibly have been aware, at the time, that its contents had anything to do with the murder — unless they were all involved in a murder conspiracy, which is preposterous — and therefore had no valid reason for mendacity. Also, Mrs. Boone was barely able to stop herself short of accusing Miss Gunther of falsehood, and Mrs. Boone was at the same table with her in the ballroom. So Miss Gunther was lying. You see that."

"Keep right on," Skinner growled.

"I intend to. Why did she lie about the case and pretend that it had disappeared? Obviously because she didn't want the text of the cylinders, one or more of them, to become known. Why didn't she? Not merely because it contained confidential BPR information or intent. Such a text, as she knew, could safely have been entrusted to FBI ears, but she audaciously and jauntily suppressed it. She did that because something in it pointed definitely and unmistakably to the murderer of Mr. Boone. She—"

"No," Hombert objected. "That's out. She lied about the case before she could have known that. She told us Wednesday morning, the morning after Boone was killed, about leaving the case on the window sill in the reception room, before she had had an opportunity to listen to what was on the cylinders. So she couldn't have known that."

"Yes she could."

"She could tell what was on those cylinders without having access to a Stenophone machine?"

"Certainly. At least one of them. Mr. Boone told her what was on it when he gave her the leather case Tuesday evening, in the room there where he was soon to die. She lied about that too; naturally she had to. She lied about it to me, most convincingly, in my office Friday evening. I should have warned her then that she was being foolhardy to the point of impudence, but I didn't. I would have wasted my breath. Caution with respect to personal peril was not in her makeup—as the event proved. If it had been, she would not have permitted a man whom she knew to be capable of murder get close to her, alone, on the stoop of my house."

Wolfe shook his head, his eyes still closed. "She was really extraordinary. It would be interesting to know where she concealed the case, containing the cylinders, up to Thursday afternoon. It would have been too risky to hide it in Mr. Kates's apartment, which might have been searched by the police at any moment. Possibly she checked it in the Grand Central parcel room, though that seems a little banal for her. At any rate, she had it with her in her suitcase when she went to Washington Thursday afternoon, with Mr. Dexter and with your permission."

"Cramer's permission," Hombert grumbled.

Wolfe ignored it. "I would like to emphasize," he said with his voice up a little, "that none of this is conjecture except unimportant details of chronology and method. In Washington Miss Gunther went to her office, listened to the cylinders, and learned which one bore the message that Mr. Boone had told her about. Doubtless she wanted to know exactly what it said, but also she wanted to simplify her problem. It isn't easy to conceal an object the size of that case from an army of expert searchers. She wanted to reduce it to one little cylinder. Another thing, she had contrived a plot. She took the nine eliminated cylinders to her Washington apartment and hid them casually in a hatbox on a closet shelf. She also took ten other cylinders that had been previously used which were there in her office, put them in the leather case, brought it with her when she returned to New York, and checked it in the Grand Central parcel room.

"That was in preparation for her plot, and she probably would have proceeded with it the next day, using the police for the mystification, if it hadn't been for that invitation I sent around for a discussion at my office. She decided to wait for developments. Why she ignored my invitation I don't know, and I shall intrude no guesses. That same evening, Friday, Mr. Goodwin went after her and brought her to my office. She had made a profound impression on him, and she struck me as being of uncommon quality. Evidently her opinion of us was less flattering. She formed the idea that we were more vulnerable to guile than the police; and the next day, Saturday, after she had mailed the parcel room check to Mr. O'Neill and made the phone call to him, giving the name of Dorothy Unger, she sent me a telegram, signing Mr. Breslow's name to it, conveying the notion that observation of Mr. O'Neill's movements might be profitable. We validated her appraisal of us. Mr. Goodwin was at Mr. O'Neill's address bright and early Sunday morning, as Miss Gunther intended him to be. When Mr. O'Neill emerged he was followed, and you know what happened."

"I don't understand," Skinner interposed, "why O'Neill was such an easy sucker for that Dorothy Unger phone call. Didn't the damn fool suspect a plant? Or is he a damn fool or something else?"

Wolfe shook his head. "Now you're asking for more than I've got. Mr. O'Neill is a headstrong and bumptious man, which may account for it; and we know that he was irresistibly tempted to learn what was on those cylinders, whether because he had killed Mr. Boone or for some other reason is yet to be discovered. Presumably Miss Gunther knew what might be expected of him. Anyhow her plot was moderately successful. It kept us all in that side alley for a day or two, it further jumbled the matter of the cylinders and the leather case, and it was one more involvement of an NIA man, without, however, the undesirable result—undesirable for Miss Gunther— of exposing him as the murderer. She was saving that—the disclosure of the murderer's identity and the evidence she had—for the time that would best suit her purpose."

"You've got pictures of all this," Skinner said sarcastically. "Why didn't you call her on the phone or get her in your office and lecture her on the duties of a citizen?"

"It was impractical. She was dead."

"Oh? Then you didn't know it all until after she had been killed?"

"Certainly not. How the devil could I? Some of it, yes, it doesn't matter how much. But when word came from Washington that they had found in Miss Gunther's apartment, perfunctorily concealed, nine of the cylinders Mr. Boone had dictated the afternoon of his death—nine, not ten—there was the whole story. There was no other acceptable explanation. All questions became paltry and pointless except the one question: where is the tenth cylinder?"

"Wherever you start a sentence," Hombert complained grouchily, "it always ends on that goddam cylinder!"

Wolfe opened his eyes enough to pick Hombert out. "You try doing a sentence that makes any sense and leave the cylinder out."

Skinner demanded, "What if she threw it in the river?"

"She didn't."

"Why not?"

"I've already told you. Because she intended to use it, when the time came, to get the murderer punished."

"What if you're making your first and only mistake and she *did* throw it in the river?"

"Drag the river. All the rivers she could reach."

"Don't be whimsical. Answer my question."

Wolfe's shoulders went perceptibly up and down. "In that case we would be licked. We'd never get him."

"I think," Hombert said pointedly, "that it is conceivable that you would like to sell a bill of goods. I don't say you're a barefaced liar."

"I don't say I'm not, Mr. Hombert. We all take those chances when we exchange words with other people. So I might as well go home—"

"Wait a minute," Skinner snapped. "Do you mean that as an expert investigator you advise abandoning all lines of inquiry except the search for that cylinder?"

"I shouldn't think so." Wolfe frowned, considering. "Especially not with a thousand men or more at your disposal. Of course I don't know what has been done and what hasn't, but I know how such things go and I doubt if much has been overlooked in a case of this importance, knowing Mr. Cramer as I do. For instance, that piece of iron pipe; I suppose every possible effort has been made to discover where it came from. The matter of arrivals at my house Monday evening has of course been explored with every resource and ingenuity. The tenants of all the buildings in my block on both sides of the street have naturally been interviewed, on the slim chance, unlikely in that quiet neighborhood, that somebody saw or heard something. The question of opportunity alone, the evening of the dinner at the Waldorf, must have kept a dozen men busy for a week, and perhaps you're still working on it. Inquiries regarding relationships, both open and concealed, the checking and rechecking of Mr. Dexter's alibi—these and a thousand other details have unquestionably been competently and thoroughly attended to."

Wolfe wiggled a finger. "And where are you? So sunk in a bog of futility and bewilderment that you resort to such monkey tricks as ditching Mr. Cramer, replacing him with a buffoon like Mr. Ash, and swearing out a warrant for my arrest! Over a long period I have become familiar with the abilities and performances of the New York police, and I never expected to see the day when the inspector heading the Homicide Squad would try to solve a difficult murder case by dragging me off to a cell, attacking my person, putting me in handcuffs, and threatening me with mayhem!"

"That's a slight exaggeration. This is not a cell, and I don't—"

"He intended to," Wolfe asserted grimly. "He would have. Very well. You have asked my advice. I would continue, within reason, all lines of inquiry that have already been started, and initiate any others that offer any promise whatever, because no matter what the cylinder gives you—if and when you find it—you will almost certainly need all available scraps of support and corroboration. But the main chance, the only real hope, is the cylinder. I suggest you try this. You both met Miss Gunther? Good. Sit down and shut your eyes and imagine it is last Thursday afternoon, and you are Miss Gunther, sitting in your office in the BPR headquarters in Washington. You have decided what you are going to do with the leather case and the nine eliminated cylinders; forget all that. In your hand is *the* cylinder, and the question is what to do with it. Here's what you're after: you want to preserve it against any risk of damage, you want it easily accessible should you need it on short notice, and you want to be certain that no matter how many people look for it, or who, with whatever persistence and ingenuity, it will not be found."

Wolfe looked from one to the other. "There's your little problem, Miss Gunther. Anything so simple, for example, as concealing it there in the BPR office is not even to be considered. Something far above that, something really fine, must be conceived. Your own apartment would be merely ridiculous; you show that you are quite aware of that by disposing of the other nine cylinders as you do. Perhaps the apartment of a friend or colleague you can trust? This is murder; this is of the utmost gravity and of ultimate importance; would you trust any other human being that far? You are ready now to leave, to go to your apartment first and then take a plane to New York. You will probably be in New York some days. Do you take the cylinder with you or leave it in Washington? If so, where? Where? Where?"

Wolfe flipped a hand. "There's your question, gentlemen. Answer it the way Miss Gunther finally answered it, and your worries are ended." He stood up. "I am spending a thousand dollars a day trying to learn how Miss Gunther answered it." He was multiplying by two and it wasn't his money he was spending, but at least it wasn't a barefaced lie. "Come, Archie. I want to go home."

They didn't want him to go, even then, which was the best demonstration to date of the pitiable condition they were in. They certainly were stymied, flummoxed, and stripped to the bone. Wolfe magnanimously accommodated them by composing a few more well-constructed sentences, properly furnished with subjects, predicates, and subordinate clauses, none of which meant a damn thing, and then marched from the room with me bringing up the rear. He had postponed his exit, I noticed, until after a clerk had entered to deliver some papers to Hombert's desk, which had occurred just as Wolfe was telling the P.C. and D.A. to shut their eyes and pretend they were Miss Gunther.

Driving back home he sat in the back seat, as usual, clutching the toggle, because of his theory that when — not if and when, just when — the car took a whim to dart aside and smash into some immovable object, your chances in back, hopeless as they were, were slightly better than in front. On the way down to Centre Street I had, on request, given him a sketch of my session with Nina Boone, and now, going home, I filled in the gaps. I couldn't tell whether it contained any morsel that he considered nutritious, because my back was to him and his face wasn't in my line of vision in the mirror, and also because the emotions that being in a moving vehicle aroused in him were too overwhelming to leave any room for minor reactions.

As Fritz let us in and we entered the hall and I attended to hat and coat disposal, Wolfe looked almost good-humored. He had beaten a rap and was home safe, and it was only six o'clock, time for beer. But Fritz spoiled it at once by telling us that we had a visitor waiting in the office. Wolfe scowled at him and demanded in a ferocious whisper:

"Who is it?"

"Mrs. Cheney Boone."

"Good heavens. That hysterical gammer?"

Which was absolutely unfair. Mrs. Boone had been in the house just twice, both times under anything but tranquil circumstances, and I hadn't seen the faintest indication of hysteria.

30

I had made a close and prolonged study of Wolfe's attitude toward women. The basic fact about a woman that seemed to irritate him was that she was a woman; the long record showed not a single exception; but from there on the documentation was cockeyed. If woman as woman grated on him you would suppose that the most womany details would be the worst for him, but time and again I have known him to have a chair placed for a female so that his desk would not obstruct his view of her legs, and the answer can't be that his interest is professional and he reads character from legs, because the older and dumpier she is the less he cares where she sits. It is a very complex question and some day I'm going to take a whole chapter for it. Another little detail: he is much more sensitive to women's noses than he is to men's. I have never been able to detect that extremes or unorthodoxies in men's noses have any effect on him, but in women's they do. Above all he doesn't like a pug, or in fact a pronounced incurve anywhere along the bridge.

Mrs. Boone had a pug, and it was much too small for the surroundings. I saw him looking at it as he leaned back in his chair. So he told her in a gruff and inhospitable tone, barely not boorish:

"I have ten minutes to spare, madam."

Entirely aside from the nose she looked terrible. She had had a go at her compact, but apparently with complete indifference to the result, and anyway it would have been a job for a makeup artist. She was simply all shot and her face had quit trying to do any pretending about it.

"Naturally," she said, in a voice that was holding up much better than the face, "you're wondering why I'm here."

"Naturally," Wolfe agreed.

"I mean why I came to see you, since you're on the other side. It's because I phoned my cousin this morning and he told me about you."

"I am not," Wolfe said curtly, "on the other side or any side. I have undertaken to catch a murderer. Do I know your cousin?"

She nodded. "General Carpenter. That was my maiden name. He is my first cousin. He's in a hospital after an operation, or he would have come to help me when my husband was killed. He told me not to believe anything you said but to do whatever you told me to do. He said that you have your own private set of rules, and that if you are working on a case of murder the only one that can really rely on you is the murderer. Since you know my cousin, you know what he meant. I'm used to him."

She stopped, looked at me and back at Wolfe, and used her handkerchief on her lower lip and at the corners, which didn't improve things any. When her hand went back to her lap it was gripping the handkerchief as if it was afraid that someone was planning to snatch it.

"And?" Wolfe prompted her.

"So I came to see you to get some advice. Or maybe I ought to say make up my mind whether I want to ask your advice. I have to get some from somebody, and I don't know —" She looked at me again, returned to Wolfe, and made a gesture with the hand that wasn't guarding the handkerchief. "Do I have to tell you why I prefer not to go to someone in the FBI or the police?"

"You are under no compulsion, madam, to tell me anything at all. You've already been talking three or four minutes."

"I know. My cousin warned me that you would be incredibly rude. — Then I might as well come right out and say that I think I am responsible for the death of Phoebe Gunther."

"That's an uncomfortable thought," muttered Wolfe. "Where did you get it?"

"That's what I want to tell you, and I suppose I'm really going to or I wouldn't have come here, but while I was sitting here waiting I got up to leave a dozen times and then sat down again. I don't know what to do and last night I thought I was going crazy. I always depended on my husband to make important decisions. I don't want to tell the police or the FBI because I may have committed some kind of a crime, I don't know. But it seems silly to tell you on account of the way my husband felt about the NIA, and of course I feel the same way about them, and you're working for them, you're on their side. I suppose I ought to go to a lawyer, and I know lots of lawyers, but there doesn't seem to be one I could tell this to. They all seem to do all the talking and I never understand what they're saying."

That should have softened Wolfe up. He did get a little more receptive, taking the trouble to repeat that he wasn't on any side. "For me," he stated, "this is not a private feud, whatever it may be for others. What was the crime you committed?"

"I don't know—if it was one."

"What did you do?"

"I didn't do anything. That's the trouble. What happened was that Miss Gunther told me what she was doing and I promised her I wouldn't tell anyone and I didn't, and I have a feeling—"

She stopped. In a moment she went on, "That isn't true, I haven't just got a feeling. I'm sure."

"Sure of what?"

"I'm sure that if I had told the police what she told me she wouldn't have been killed. But I didn't tell, because she explained that what she was doing was helping the BPR and hurting the NIA, and that was what my husband would have wanted more than anything else." The widow was staring at Wolfe's face as if she were trying to see inside. "And she was perfectly correct. I'm still making up my mind whether to tell you about it. In spite of what you say, there's my husband's side and there's the other side, and you're working for the NIA. After I talked with my cousin I thought I'd come and see what you sounded like."

"What do I sound like?"

"I don't know." Her hand fluttered vaguely. "I really don't know."

Wolfe frowned at her in silence, then heaved a sigh and turned to me. "Archie."

"Yes, sir?"

"Your notebook. Take a letter. To be mailed this evening so it will be delivered in the morning. To the National Industrial Association, attention Mr. Frank Thomas Erskine.

"Gentlemen: The course events have taken obliges me to inform you that it will be impossible for me to continue to act in your behalf with regard to the investigation of the murders of Mr. Cheney Boone and Miss Phoebe Gunther. Therefore I enclose herewith my check for thirty thousand dollars, returning the retainer you have paid me and ending my association with you in this matter. Sincerely."

I made the last scratch and looked at him. "Do I draw the check?"

"Certainly. You can't enclose it if it hasn't been drawn." Wolfe's eyes moved to the visitor. "There, Mrs. Boone, that should have some effect on your reluctance. Even accepting your point of view, that I was on the other side, now I am not. What did Miss Gunther tell you she was doing?"

The widow was gazing at him. "Thirty thousand dollars?" she asked incredulously.

"Yes." Wolfe was smirking. "A substantial sum."

"But was that all the NIA was paying you? Just *thirty thousand?* I supposed it was twenty times that! They have hundreds of millions—billions!"

"It was only the retainer," Wolfe said testily. The smirk was gone. "Anyway, I am now a neutral. What did Miss Gunther tell you?"

"But now—but now you're not getting anything at all!" Mrs. Boone was utterly bewildered. "My cousin told me that during the war you worked hard for the government for nothing, but that you charge private people outrageous prices. I ought to tell you—if you don't know—that I can't afford to pay you anything outrageous. I could—" She hesitated. "I could give you a check for a hundred dollars."

"I don't want a check." Wolfe was exasperated. "If I can't have a client in this case without being accused of taking sides in a sanguinary vendetta, I don't want a client. Confound it, what did Miss Gunther tell you?"

Mrs. Boone looked at me, and I had the uncomfortable feeling that she was trying to find some sort of resemblance to her dead husband, he being gone and therefore no longer available for important decisions. I thought it might possibly help if I nodded at her reassuringly, so I did so. Whether that broke the tie or not I don't know, but something did, for she spoke to Wolfe:

"She knew who killed my husband. My husband told her something that day when he gave her the leather case, and she knew from that, and also he had dictated something on one of those cylinders that told about it, so the cylinder was evidence, and she had it. She was keeping it and she intended to give it to the police, but she was waiting until the talk and the rumors and the public feeling had done as much damage as possible to the NIA. She told me about it because I went to her and told her I knew she wasn't telling the truth about that leather case, I knew she had had it with her at the table in the dining room, and I wasn't going to keep still about it any longer. She told me what she was doing so I wouldn't tell the police about the case."

"When was that? What day?"

She thought a moment, the crease deepening in her forehead, and then shook her head uncertainly. "The days," she said. "The days are all mixed up."

"Of course they are, Mrs. Boone. It was Friday evening when you were here with the others the first time, when you almost spoke up about it and changed your mind. Was it before that, or after?"

"It was after. It was the next day."

"Then it was Saturday. Another thing that will help you to place it, Saturday morning you received an envelope in the mail containing your wedding picture and automobile license. Do you remember that? It was the same day?"

She nodded with assurance. "Yes, of course it was. Because I spoke of that, and she said she had written a letter to him—to the man who killed my husband—she knew my husband had always carried the wedding picture in the wallet that was missing—he had carried it for over twenty years—twenty-three years—"

The widow's voice got away from her. She gave it up and gulped, sat without trying to go on, and gulped again. If she lost control completely and started noises and tears there was no telling what Wolfe would do. He might even have tried to act human, which would have been an awful strain on all of us. So I told her gruffly:

"Okay, Mrs. Boone, take your time. Whenever you get ready, what did she write a letter to the murderer for? To tell him to send you the wedding picture?"

She nodded and got enough voice back to mumble, "Yes."

"Indeed," Wolfe said to help out.

The widow nodded again. "She told me that she knew I would want that picture, and she wrote him to say that she knew about him and he must send it to me."

"What else did she write him?"

"I don't know. That's all she told me about it."

"But she told you who he was."

"No, she didn't." Mrs. Boone halted again for a moment, still getting her voice back into place. "She said she wouldn't tell me that, because it would be too much to expect me not to show that I knew. She said I didn't need to worry about his not being punished, there would be no doubt about that, and besides it would be dangerous for me to know. That's where I now think I did wrong—that's why I said I'm responsible for her death. If it would have been dangerous for me it was dangerous for her, especially after she wrote him that letter. I should have made her tell the police about it, and if she wouldn't do it I should have broken my promise to her and told the police myself. Then she wouldn't have been killed. Anyway she said she thought she was breaking a law, withholding information and concealing evidence, so I have that on my mind too, helping her break a law."

"You can stop worrying about that, at least," Wolfe assured her. "I mean the lawbreaking. That part of it's all right. Or it will be, as soon as you tell me, and I tell the police, where Miss Gunther put the cylinder."

"But I can't. That's another thing. I don't know. She didn't tell me."

Wolfe's eyes had popped wide open. "Nonsense!" he said rudely. "Of course she told you!"

"She did not. That's one reason I came to see you. She said I didn't need to worry about the man who killed my husband being punished. But if that's the only evidence . . ."

Wolfe's eyes had gone shut again. There was a long silence. Mrs. Boone looked at me, possibly still in search of a resemblance, but whatever she was looking for her expression gave no indication that she was finding it. Finally she spoke to Wolfe again:

"So you see why I need advice . . ."

His lids went up enough to make slits. In his place I would at least have been grateful for all the corroboration of the guesses I had made, but apparently he was too overcome by his failure to learn where the cylinder was.

"I regret, madam," he said, without any noticeable tremor of regret or anything like it, "that I can't be of any help to you. There is nothing I can do. All I can give you is what you said you came for, advice, and you are welcome to that. Mr. Goodwin will drive you back to your hotel. Arriving there, telephone the police immediately that you have information for them. When they come, tell them everything you have told me, and answer their questions as long as you can stand it. You need have no fear of being regarded as guilty of lawbreaking. I agree with you that if you had broken your promise to Miss Gunther she would probably not have been killed, but it was she who asked you for the promise, so the responsibility is hers. Besides, she can afford it; it is astonishing, the burden of responsibility that dead people can bear up under. Dismiss that from your mind too if you can." He was on his feet. "Good afternoon, madam."

So I did get to drive a female Boone home from our office, though not Nina. Since it appeared that she had given us all she had and was therefore of no further immediate interest, I didn't even bother to discover whether anyone was on her tail and confined myself to the duties of a chauffeur. She didn't seem to care about conversing, which simplified matters. I delivered her safely at the Waldorf entrance and headed back downtown. Aside from the attention to driving, which was automatic, there was no point in trying to put my mind on my work, since I was being left out in the cold and therefore had no work, so I let it drift to Phoebe Gunther. I went back to the times I had been with her, how she had talked and acted, with my present knowledge of what she had been doing, and decided she had been utterly all right. I have an inclination to pick flaws, especially where young women are concerned, but on this occasion I didn't have the list started by the time I got back home.

Wolfe was drinking beer, as I observed when I stepped inside the office door merely to tell him:

"I'll be upstairs. I always like to wash my hands after I've been with certain kinds of policemen, meaning Inspector Ash, and I've —"

"Come in here. That letter and check. We'd better get that done."

I gawked. "What, to the NIA?"

"Yes."

"My God, you don't mean you're actually going to send it?"

"Certainly. Didn't I tell that woman I would? Wasn't it with that understanding that she told me things?"

I sat down at my desk and regarded him piercingly. "This," I said sternly, "is not being eccentric. This is plain loony. What about Operation Payroll? And where did you suddenly get a scruple? And anyway, she didn't tell you the one thing you wanted to know." I abruptly got respectful. "I regret to report, sir, that the checkbook is lost."

He grunted. "Draw the check and type the letter. At once." He pointed to a stack of envelopes on his desk. "Then you can go through these reports from Mr. Bascom's office. They just came by messenger."

"But with no client—shall I phone Bascom to call it off?"

"Certainly not."

I went to the safe for the checkbook. As I filled out the stub I remarked, "Statistics show that forty-two and three-tenths per cent of all geniuses go crazy sooner or later."

He had no comment. He merely drank beer and sat. Now that I was to be permitted to know what Bascom's men were doing, he wouldn't even co-operate enough to slit open the envelopes. Whatever it was it must be good, since he evidently intended to go on paying for it with his own dough. I pounded the typewriter keys in a daze. When I put the check and letter before him to be signed I said plaintively:

"Excuse me for mentioning it, but a century from Mrs. Boone would have helped. That seems to be more our speed. She said she could afford it."

He used the blotter. "You'd better take this to the post office. I suspect the evening collection from that box doesn't get made sometimes."

So I had some more chauffeuring to do. It was only a ten-minute walk to the post office on Ninth Avenue and back, but I was in no mood for walking. I only like to walk when I can see some future ahead of me. Returning, I put the car in the garage, since the evening would obviously be a complete blank.

Wolfe was still in the office, outwardly perfectly normal. He glanced at me, then at the clock, and back at me.

"Sit down a moment, Archie. You'll have plenty of time to wash before dinner. Dr. Vollmer is coming to see us later, and you need some instructions."

At least his mind was still functioning enough to send for a doctor.

31

DOC VOLLMER was due to arrive at ten o'clock. At five minutes to ten the stage was set, up in Wolfe's bedroom. I was in Wolfe's own chair by the reading lamp, with a magazine. Wolfe was in bed. Wolfe in bed was always a remarkable sight, accustomed to it as I was. First the low footboard, of streaky anselmo—yellowish with sweeping dark brown streaks—then the black silk coverlet, next the wide expanse of yellow pajama top, and last the flesh of the face. In my opinion Wolfe was quite aware that black and yellow are a flashy combination, and he used it deliberately just to prove that no

matter how showy the scene was he could dominate it. I have often thought
that I would like to see him try it with pink and green. The rest of the
room—rugs and furniture and curtains—was okay, big and comfortable
and all right to be in.

Doc Vollmer, admitted downstairs by Fritz and knowing his way around
the house, came up the one flight alone and walked into the room, the door
standing open. He was carrying his toolbox. He had a round face and round
ears, and two or three years had passed since he had given up any attempt
to stand with his belly in and his chest out. I told him hello and shook
hands, and then he went to the bedside with a friendly greeting and his
hand extended.

Wolfe twisted his neck to peer at the offered hand, grunted skeptically,
and muttered, "No, thank you. What's the ceiling on it? I don't want any."

Standing at the footboard, I began hastily, "I should have explained—"
but Wolfe broke in, thundering at Vollmer, "Do you want to pay two dollars
a pound for butter? Fifty cents for shoestrings? A dollar for a bottle of beer?
Twenty dollars for one orchid, one ordinary half-wilted Laeliocattleya?
Well, confound it, answer me!" Then he quit thundering and started
muttering.

Vollmer lowered himself to the edge of a chair, put his toolbox on the
floor, blinked several times at Wolfe, and then at me.

I said, "I don't know whether it's the willies or what."

Wolfe said, "You accuse me of getting you here under false pretenses. You
accuse me of wanting to borrow money from you. Just because I ask you to
lend me five dollars until the beginning of the next war, you accuse me!" He
shook a warning finger in the direction of Vollmer's round astonished face.
"Let me tell you, sir, you will be next! I admit that I am finished; I am
finally driven to this extremity. They have done for me; they have broken
me; they are still after me." His voice rose to thunder again. "And you, you
incomparable fool, you think to escape! Archie tells me you are masquerad-
ing as a doctor. Bah! They'll take your clothes off! They'll examine every
inch of your skin, as they did mine! They'll find the mark!" He let his head
fall back on the pillow, closed his eyes, and resumed muttering.

Vollmer looked at me with a gleam in his eyes and inquired, "Who wrote
his script for him?"

Managing somehow to control the muscles around my mouth, I shook
my head despairingly. "He's been like this for several hours, ever since I
brought him back home."

"Oh, he's been out of the house?"

"Yes. From three-fifteen til six o'clock. Under arrest."

Vollmer turned to Wolfe. "Well," he said decisively. "The first thing is to
get some nurses. Where's the phone? Either that or take him to a hospital."

"That's the ticket," I agreed. "It's urgent. We must act."

Wolfe's eyes came open. "Nurses?" he asked contemptuously. "Pfui.
Aren't you a physician? Don't you know a nervous breakdown when you see
one?"

"Yes," Vollmer said emphatically.

"What's the matter with it?"

"It doesn't seem to be—uh, typical."

"Faulty observation," Wolfe snapped. "Or a defect in your training. Specifically, it's a persecution complex."

"Who's doing the persecuting?"

Wolfe shut his eyes. "I feel it coming on again. Tell him, Archie."

I met Vollmer's gaze. "Look, Doc, the situation is serious. As you know, he was investigating the Boone-Gunther murders for the NIA. The high command didn't like the way Inspector Cramer was handling it and booted him, and replaced him with a baboon by the name of Ash."

"I know. It was in the evening paper."

"Yeah. In tomorrow's evening paper you'll learn that Nero Wolfe has returned the NIA retainer and quit."

"For God's sake, why?"

"I'm telling you. Ash's personal attitude toward Wolfe is such that he would rather slice his wrists than slash his throat because it would prolong the agony. Today he got a material witness warrant and Wolfe had to go to Centre Street, me taking him. Hombert had the warrant killed, for various reasons, but the main one was that Wolfe was working for the NIA, and if the NIA gets offended any worse than it is now it will probably fire the Mayor and everyone else and declare New York a monarchy. But. Wolfe no sooner gets home than he breaks off relations with the NIA. They'll get his letter, with check enclosed, in the morning mail. Whereupon hell will pop open. What the NIA will do we don't know and maybe we don't care — I should say maybe Wolfe doesn't care. But we know damn well what the cops will do. First, with Wolfe no longer sleeping with the NIA, that motive for tenderness will be gone. Second, they know that Wolfe has never yet had a murderer for a client, and they know what a job it is to pry him loose from money, especially thirty thousand bucks and up, and they will therefore deduce that one of the NIA boys is guilty, and the Wolfe knows it and knows who it is."

"Who is it?"

I shook my head. "I don't know, and since Wolfe's a raving lunatic you can't ask him. With that setup, it's a cinch to read the future. The wagon will be at the door ready for him, with the papers all in order, any time after ten o'clock, possibly earlier. It's a shame to disappoint them, but all I can do is meet them with another kind of paper, signed by a reputable physician, certifying that in Wolfe's present condition it would be dangerous either to move him from his bed or to permit anyone to converse with him."

I waved a hand. "That's how it stands. Five years ago, the time Wolfe did you a little favor when that crook — what was his name? Griffin — tried to frame you on a malpractice suit, and you told Wolfe if he ever wanted anything all he had to do was ask for it, I warned you you might regret it some day. Brother, this is the day."

Vollmer was rubbing his chin. He didn't really look reluctant, merely thoughtful. He looked at Wolfe, saying nothing, and then returned to me and spoke:

"Naturally I have an uncontrollable itch to ask a lot of questions. This is absolutely fascinating. I suppose the questions wouldn't be answered?"

"I'm afraid not. Not by me anyhow, because I don't know the answers. You might try the patient."

"How long will the certificate have to function?"

"I have no idea. Damn it, I tell you I'm ignorant."

"If he's bad enough to prohibit visitors I'll have to insist on calling on him at least twice a day. And to make it good there ought to be nurses."

"No," I said firmly. "I grant there ought to be, but he would run a fever. Nurses are out. As for you, call as often as you want to. I may get lonely. And make that certificate as strong as they come. Say it would kill him if anybody whose name begins with A even looked at him."

"It will be so worded as to serve its purpose. I'll bring it over in ten minutes or so." Vollmer stood up with his toolbox in his hand. "I did say that time, though, that Wolfe would get anything *he* asked for." He looked at Wolfe. "It would be gratifying just to hear you ask me for something. How about it?"

Wolfe groaned. "They come in hordes," he said distinctly, but in a phony voice. "In chariots with spiked wheels, waving the insolent banners of inflation! Five dollars for a pound of corned beef! Ten dollars for a squab! Sixty cents —"

"I'd better be going," Vollmer said, and moved.

32

I didn't get lonely during the two and a half days — Thursday, Friday, and part of Saturday — that the certificate worked. Newspapermen, cops, FBI's, NIA's — they all appreciated that I was holding the fort under trying circumstances and did their best to keep my mind occupied so I wouldn't fret. If ordinarily I earn twice as much as I get, which is a conservative estimate, during those sixty-some hours it was ten times as much at a minimum.

Throughout the siege Wolfe stayed put in his room, with the door locked and one of the keys in my pocket and one in Fritz's. Keeping away from the office, dining room, and kitchen for that length of time was of course a hardship, but the real sacrifice, the one that hurt, was giving up his two-a-day trips to the plant rooms. I had to bully him into it, explaining that if a surprise detachment shoved a search warrant at me I might or might not be able to get him back into bed in time, and besides, Theodore slept out, and while he was no traitor he might inadvertently spill it that his afflicted employer did not seem to be goofy among the orchids. For the same reason I refused to let Theodore come down to the bedroom for consultations. I told Wolfe Thursday or Friday, I forget which:

"You're putting on an act. Okay. Applause. Since it requires you to be out of circulation that leaves it strictly up to me and I make the rules. I am already handicapped enough by not knowing one single goddam thing about what you're up to. We had a —"

"Nonsense," he growled. "You know all about it. I have twenty men looking for that cylinder. Nothing can be done without that cylinder. It must be found and it will be. I simply prefer to wait here in my room instead of in jail."

"Nuts." I was upset because I had just spent a hot half hour with another NIA delegation down in the office. "Why did you have to break with the NIA before you went to bed to wait? Granting that one of them did it and you know all about it, which everybody is now sure of but you'll have to show me, that was no reason to return their money in order to keep from having a murderer for a client, because you said yourself that no man was your client, the NIA was. Why in the name of God did you return their dough? And if this cylinder gag is not merely a stall, if it's really it and all the it there is, as you say, what if it never is found? What are you going to do, stay in bed the rest of your life, with Doc Vollmer renewing the certificate on a monthly basis?"

"It will be found," he said meekly. "It was not destroyed, it exists, and therefore it will be found."

I stared at him suspiciously, shrugged, and beat it. When he gets meek it is absolutely no use. I went back to the office and sat and scowled at the Stenophone machine standing over in a corner. My chief reason for admitting that Wolfe really meant what he said about the cylinder was that we were paying a dollar a day rent for that machine.

Not the only reason, however. Bill Gore and twenty Bascom men were actually looking for the cylinder, no question about it. I had been instructed to read the reports before taking them up to Wolfe, and they were quite a chapter in the history of hunting. Bill Gore and another guy were working on all of Phoebe Gunther's friends and even acquaintances in Washington, and two others were doing likewise in New York. Three were flying all over the country, to places where she knew people, on the theory that she might have mailed the cylinder to one of them, though that seemed like a bum theory if, as Wolfe had said, she had wanted to have it easily accessible on short notice. His figure of a grand a day hadn't been so far out after all. One had learned that she had gone to a beauty parlor that Friday afternoon in New York, and he had turned it inside out. Three had started working on parcel rooms everywhere, but had discovered that parcel rooms were being worked by the police and the FBI, armed with authority, so they had switched to another field. They were trying to find out or guess all the routes she had taken on foot and were spending their days on the sidewalks, keeping their eyes peeled for something, anything — a window box with dirt in it, for instance — where she might have made a cache. The rest of them were trying this and that. Friday evening, to take my mind off my troubles, I tried to figure out some possible spot that they were missing. I kept at it an hour, with no result. They were certainly covering the territory.

There were unquestionably twenty-one expensive men on the cylinder chase, but what stuck in my craw was Saul Panzer. No matter what you had on the program Saul rated star billing, and he was not among the twenty-one at all. As far as I was allowed to know he was not displaying the slightest interest in any cylinder. Every couple of hours he phoned in, I didn't know from where, and I obeyed instructions to connect him with Wolfe's bedside extension and keep off the line. Also he made two personal appearances — one at breakfast time Thursday morning and one late Friday afternoon — and each time he spent a quarter of an hour alone with Wolfe and then departed. By that time I was so damn cylinder-conscious that I was inclined to suspect Saul of being engaged in equipping a factory in a Brooklyn basement so we could roll our own.

As the siege continued, my clashes wth Wolfe increased both in frequency and in range. One, Thursday afternoon, concerned Inspector Cramer. Wolfe buzzed me on the house phone and told me he wished to have a telephone conversation with Cramer, so would I please dig him up. I flatly refused. My point was that no matter how bitter Cramer might be, or how intensely he might desire to spray Ash with concentrated DDT, he was still a cop, and was therefore not be trusted with any evidence, as for instance Wolfe's voice sounding natural and making sense, that would tend to cast doubt on Doc Vollmer's certificate. Wolfe finally settled for my getting the dope on Cramer's whereabouts and availability, and that proved to be easy. Lon Cohen told me he had taken a two weeks' leave of absence, for sulking, and when I dialed the number of Cramer's home he answered the phone himself. He kept the conversation brief and to the point, and when I had hung up I got Wolfe on the house phone and told him:

"Cramer's on leave of absence and is staying home licking his wounds, possibly bedridden. He wouldn't say. Anyhow, he can be reached there any time, but he is not affable. I have a notion to send Doc Vollmer to see him."

"Good. Come up here. I'm having trouble with this window again."

"Damn it, you stay in bed and keep away from the windows!"

One feature of the play was that I was not supposed to deny entry to any legitimate caller. That was to convey the impression that our household was not churlish, far from it, but merely stricken with misfortune. Although newspapermen and various other assorted prospectors kept me hopping, the worst nuisances were the NIA and the cops. Around ten Thursday morning Frank Thomas Erskine phoned. He wanted Wolfe but of course didn't get him. I did my best to make the situation clear, but I might as well have tried to explain to a man dying of thirst that the water was being saved to do the laundry with. Less than an hour later here they came, all six of them — the two Erskines, Winterhoff, Breslow, O'Neill, and Hattie Harding. I was courteous, took them to the office, gave them seats, and told them that a talk with Wolfe was positively not on the agenda.

They seemed to be under the impression, judging from their attitudes and tones, that I was not a fellow being but a cockroach. At times it was a little difficult to keep up with them, because they were all full of ideas and words to express them and no one acted as chairman to grant the floor and prevent overlapping. Their main gripes were, first, that it was an act of treachery and betrayal for Wolfe to return their money; second, that if he did it because he was sick he should have said so in his letter; third, that he should immediately and publicly announce his sickness in order to stop the widespread and growing rumor that he broke with the NIA because he got hold of conclusive evidence that the NIA had committed murder; fourth, that if he did have evidence of an NIA man's guilt they wanted to know who and what it was within five minutes; fifth, that they didn't believe he was sick; sixth, who was the doctor; seventh, if he was sick how soon would he be well; eighth, did I realize that in the two days and three nights that had passed since the second murder, Phoebe Gunther's, the damage to the NIA had become incalculable and irretrievable; ninth, fifty or sixty lawyers were of the opinion that Wolfe's abandoning the case without notice would vastly increase the damage and was therefore actionable; tenth, eleventh and twelfth, and so on.

Through the years I have seen a lot of sore, frantic, and distressed people in that office, but this aggregation of specimens was second to none. As far as I could see the common calamity had united them again and the danger of an indiscriminate framing bee had been averted. At one point their unanimous longing to confront Wolfe reached such proportions that Breslow, O'Neill, and young Erskine actually made for the stairs and started up, but when I yelled after them, above the uproar, that the door was locked and if they busted it in Wolfe would probably shoot them dead, they faltered, about-faced, and came back for some more of me.

I made one mistake. Like a simp I told them I would keep a continual eye on Wolfe on the chance of his having a lucid interval, and if one arrived and the doctor permitted I would notify Erskine and he could saddle up and gallop down for an interview. I should have foreseen that not only would they keep the phone humming day and night to ask how about some lucidity, but also they would take turns appearing in person, in singles, pairs, and trios, to sit in the office and wait for some. Which they did. Friday some of them were there half the time, and Saturday morning they started in again. As far as their damn money was concerned, I did at least thirty thousand dollars' worth of entertaining.

After their first visit, Thursday morning, I went up and reported in full to Wolfe, adding that I had not seen fit to inform them that he was keeping the cylinder hounds on the job at his own expense. Wolfe only muttered:

"It doesn't matter. They'll learn it when the time comes."

"Yeah. The scientific name for the disease you've got is acute malignant optimism."

As for the cops, I was instructed by Wolfe to try to prevent an avalanche by volunteering information without delay, and therefore had phoned the Commissioner's office at eight-thirty Thursday morning, before any mail could have been opened up at the NIA office. Hombert hadn't arrived yet, nor had his secretary, but I described the situation to some gook and asked him to pass it on. An hour later Hombert himself called, and the conversation was almost verbatim what it would have been if I had written it down before it took place. He said he was sorry Wolfe had collapsed under the strain, and that the police official who would shortly be calling to see him would be instructed to conduct himself diplomatically and considerately. When I explained that it was doctor's orders that no one at all should see him, not even an insurance salesman, Hombert got brusque and wanted Vollmer's full name and address, which I obligingly furnished. He wanted to know if I had told the press that Wolfe was off the case, and I said no, and he said his office would attend to that to make sure they got it straight. Then he said that Wolfe's action, dropping his client, put it beyond argument that he knew the identity of the murderer, and was probably in possession of evidence against him, and since I was Wolfe's confidential assistant it was to be presumed that I shared the knowledge and the possession, and I was of course aware of the personal risk incurred by failing to communicate such information to the police immediately. I satisfied him on that point, I don't think. Anyhow I was telling the truth, and since I'm not very good at telling the truth I couldn't very well expect him to believe me.

In less than half an hour Lieutenant Rowcliffe and a detective sergeant showed up and I conducted them into the office. Rowcliffe read Doc Vollmer's certificate thoroughly, three times, and I offered to type a copy for him to take along for further study. He was keeping himself under restraint, since it was obvious that thunder and lightning would be wasted. He tried to insist that it wouldn't hurt a bit for him to tiptoe into Wolfe's room just for a compassionate look at a prostrated fellow citizen, and indeed a professional colleague, but I explained that much as the idea appealed to me I didn't dare because Doc Vollmer would never forgive me. He said he understood my position perfectly, and how about my getting wise to myself and spilling some beans? I was, I told him, fresh out of beans. He came about as close to believing me as Hombert had, but there was nothing he could do about it short of taking me downtown and using a piece of hose on me, and Rowcliffe knew me almost as well as he disliked me, so that didn't strike him as feasible.

When they departed Rowcliffe climbed in the police car and rolled away, and the sergeant began strolling up and down the sidewalk in front of the house. That was sensible. There was no point in hiring a window across the street or some similar subtlety, since they knew that we knew there would be a constant eye on our door. From there on we had a sentry out front right up to the end.

I never did understand why they didn't try quicker and harder to break it up, but I suspect it was on account of friction between Inspector Ash and the high command. Later, after it was all over, I tried to find out from Purley Stebbins what had gone on, but Purley never was willing to contribute more than a couple of grunts, probably because the Ash regime was something he wanted to erase from memory. Doc Vollmer got more of it than I did. He kept me informed when he came to pay visits to his patient. The first one, Thursday morning, I escorted him up to the bedroom, but when Wolfe started to enjoy himself by pointing a shaking finger at the wall and declaring that big black worms covered with dollar signs were crawling down from the ceiling, we both got out of there. Thereafter Vollmer never went near the patient, merely staying in the office chinning with me long enough to make it a call for the benefit of the sidewalk sentry. The police were pestering him, but he was getting a kick out of it. Thursday morning Rowcliffe had called on him right after leaving me, and that afternoon a police doctor had come to his office to get information about Wolfe on a professional level. Friday morning Ash himself had showed up, and twenty minutes with Ash had made Vollmer more enthusiastic than ever about the favor he was doing Wolfe. Later Friday afternoon another police doctor had come and had put Vollmer over some high hurdles. When Vollmer dropped in that evening he was, for the first time, not completely cocky about it.

Saturday noon the blow fell — the one I had been expecting ever since the charade started, and the one Vollmer was leery about. It landed via the telephone, a call from Rowcliffe at twenty past twelve. I was alone in the office when the bell rang, and I was even more alone when it was over and I hung up. I took the stairs two at a time, unlocked Wolfe's door, entered, and announced:

"Okay, Pagliaccio, luck is with us at last. You are booked for the big time. An eminent neurologist named Green, hired by the City of New York and equipped with a court order, will arrive to give you an audition at a quarter to six." I glared down at him and demanded, "Now what? If you try to bull it through I resign as of sixteen minutes to six."

"So." Wolfe closed his book with a finger in it. "This is what we've been fearing." He made the book do the split on the black coverlet. "Why must it be today? Why the devil did you agree on an hour?"

"Because I had to! Who do you think I am, Joshua? They wanted to make it right now, and I did the best I could. I told them your doctor had to be present and he couldn't make it until after dinner this evening, nine o'clock. They said it had to be before six o'clock and they wouldn't take no. Damn it, I got an extra five hours and I had to fight for it!"

"Quit yelling at me." His head went back to the pillow. "Go back downstairs. I'm going to have to think."

I stood my ground. "Do you actually mean you haven't got it figured out what to do? When I've warned you it would come any minute ever since Thursday morning?"

"Archie. Get out of here. How can I put my mind on it with you standing there bellowing?"

"Very well. I'll be in the office. Call me when you get around to it."

I went out, shut the door and locked it, and descended. In the office the phone was ringing. It was only Winterhoff, inquiring after my employer's health.

33

I try, as I go along, not to leave anything essential out of this record, and, since I'm telling it, I regard my own state of mind at various stages as one of the essentials. But for that two hours on Saturday, from twelve-thirty to two-thirty, my state of mind was really not fit to be recorded for family reading. I have a vague recollection that I ate lunch twice, though Fritz politely insists that he doesn't remember it that way. He says that Wolfe's lunch was completely normal as far as he knows — tray taken upstairs full at one o'clock and brought down empty an hour later — and that nothing struck him as abnormal except that Wolfe was too preoccupied to compliment him on the omelet.

What made me use up a month's supply of profanity in a measly two hours was not that all I could see ahead was ignominious surrender. That was a hard dose but by no means fatal. The hell of it was, as I saw it, that we were being bombed out of a position that no one but a maniac would ever

have occupied in the first place. I had a right to assume, now that I was
reading the reports from Bill Gore and Bascom's men, that I knew exactly
what was going on in every sector except the one that was occupied by Saul
Panzer, and it was impossible to imagine what Saul could be doing that
could justify, let alone necessitate, the gaudy and spectacular stunt Wolfe
was indulging in. When Saul phoned in at two o'clock I had a notion to
tackle him and try to open him up, but I knew it would be hopeless and put
him through to the bedroom. On any list of temptations I have resisted,
that one goes first. I was tingling from head to foot with the desire to listen
in. But a part of the understanding between Wolfe and me is that I never
violate instructions except when circumstances unknown to him, as interpreted by my best judgment, require it, and I couldn't kid myself that that
applied here. My instructions were that Saul Panzer was out of bounds for
me until further notice, and I put the thing on the cradle and walked up and
down with my hands in my pockets.

Other phone calls came, it doesn't matter what, and I did violate another
instruction, the one to receive any and all callers. Circumstances certainly
justified that. I was in the kitchen helping Fritz sharpen knives, I suppose
on the principle that in times of crisis we instinctively seek the companionship of fellow creatures, when the bell rang and I went to the front door,
fingered the curtain aside for a peak, and saw Breslow. I opened the door a
crack and barked through at him:

"No admittance this is a house of mourning beat it!"

I banged the door and started back to the kitchen, but didn't make it.
Passing the foot of the stairs I became aware of sound and movement, and
stopping to look up I saw what was making it. Wolfe, covered with nothing
but the eight yards of yellow silk it took to make him a suit of pajamas, was
descending. I goggled at him. If nothing else, it was unprecedented for him
to move vertically except with the elevator.

"How did you get out?" I demanded.

"Fritz gave me a key." He came on down, and I noted that at least he had
put his slippers on. He commanded me, "Get Fritz and Theodore in the
office at once."

I had never before seen him outside his room in deshabille. It was obviously an extreme emergency. I swung the kitchen door open and spoke to
Fritz and then went to the office, buzzed the plant rooms on the house
phone, and told Theodore to make it snappy. By the time Theodore trotted
down and in, Wolfe was seated behind his desk and Fritz and I were
standing by.

"How are you, Theodore? I haven't seen you for three days."

"I'm all right, thank you, sir. I've missed you."

"No doubt." Wolfe's glance went from him to Fritz, then to me, and he
said slowly and clearly, "I am a brainless booby."

"Yes, sir," I said cordially.

He frowned. "So are you, Archie. Neither of us has any right, henceforth,
to pretend possession of the mental processes of an anthropoid. I include
you because you heard what I said to Mr. Hombert and Mr. Skinner. You
have read the reports from Mr. Bascom's men. You know what's going on.
And by heaven, it hasn't occurred to you that Miss Gunther was alone in
this office for a good three minutes, nearer four or five, when you brought

her here that evening! And it occurred to me only just now! Pfui! And I have dared for nearly thirty years to exercise my right to vote!" He snorted. "I have the brain of a mollusk!"

"Yeah." I was staring at him. I remembered, of course, that when I had brought Phoebe that Friday night I had left her in the office and gone to the kitchen to get him. "So you think —"

"No. I am through pretending to think. This makes it untenable. —Fritz and Theodore, a young woman was in here alone four minutes. She had, in her pocket or her bag, an object she wanted to hide — a black cylinder three inches in diameter and six inches long. She didn't know how much time she would have; someone might enter any moment. On the assumption that she hid it in this room, find it. Knowing the quality of her mind, I think it likely that she hid it in my desk. I'll look there myself."

He shoved his chair back and dived to pull open a bottom drawer. I was at my own desk, also opening drawers. Fritz asked me, "What do we do, divide it in sections?"

"Divide hell," I told him over my shoulder. "Just start looking."

Fritz went to the couch and began removing cushions. Theodore chose, for his first guess, the two vases on top of the filing cabinet which at that season contained pussy willows. There was no more conversation; we were too busy. I can't give a detailed report of the part of the search conducted by Fritz and Theodore because I was too intent on my own part of it; all I had for them was occasional glances to see what they were covering; but I kept an eye on Wolfe because I shared his opinion of the quality of Phoebe's mind and it would have been like her to pick Wolfe's own desk for it provided she found a drawer which looked as if its contents were not often disturbed. But he drew a blank. As I was opening the back of the radio cabinet, which could be got at without moving the cabinet, he slid his chair back into position, got comfortable in it, muttered, "Confound that woman," and surveyed us like a field commander directing his troops in action.

Fritz's voice came, "Is this it, Mr. Wolfe?"

He was kneeling on the rug in front of the longest section of bookshelves, and stacked beside him were a dozen volumes of the bound *Lindenia,* with a big gap showing on the bottom shelf, which was only a few inches above the floor. He was extending a hand with an object in it at which one glance was enough.

"Ideal," Wolfe said approvingly. "She was really extraordinary. Give it to Archie. Archie, roll that machine out. Theodore, I'll be with you in the potting room possibly later today, certainly tomorrow morning at the usual hour. Fritz, I congratulate you; you tried the bottom shelf first, which was sensible."

Fritz was beaming as he handed me the cylinder and turned to go, with Theodore following him.

"Well," I remarked as I plugged the machine in and inserted the cylinder, "this may do it. Or it may not."

"Start it," Wolfe growled. He was tapping on an arm of his chair with a finger. "What's the matter? Won't it go?"

"Certainly it will go. Don't hurry me. I'm nervous and I have the brain of a — I forget what. Mollusk."

I flipped the switch and sat down. The voice of Cheney Boone came to our ears, unmistakably the same voice we had heard on the other ten cylinders. For five minutes neither of us moved a muscle. I stared at the grill of the loud-speaker attachment, and Wolfe leaned back with his eyes closed. When it came to the end I reached and turned the switch.

Wolfe sighed clear to the bottom, opened his eyes, and straightened up.

"Our literature needs some revision," he declared. "For example, 'dead men tell no tales.' Mr. Boone is dead. Mr. Boone is silent. But he speaks."

"Yep." I grinned at him. "The silent speaker. Science is wonderful, but I know one guy who won't think so, goddam him. Shall I go get him?"

"No. We can arrange this, I think, by telephone. You have Mr. Cramer's number?"

"Sure."

"Good. But first get Saul. You'll find him at Manhattan five, three-two-three-two."

34

BY ten minutes to four our guests had all arrived and were collected in the office. One of them was an old friend and enemy: Inspector Cramer. One was an ex-client: Don O'Neill. One was merely a recent acquaintance: Alger Kates. The fourth was a complete stranger: Henry A. Warder, Vice-President and Treasurer of O'Neill and Warder, Incorporated. Don O'Neill's vice. Saul Panzer, who had retired to a chair over in the corner behind the globe, was of course not regarded as a guest but as one of the family.

Cramer was in the red leather chair, watching Wolfe like a hawk. O'Neill, entering and catching sight of his Vice-President, who had arrived before him, had immediately hit the ceiling, and then had just as immediately thought better of it, clamped his mouth shut, and congealed. The vice, Henry A. Warder, who was both broad and tall, built like a concrete buttress, looked as if he could use some buttressing himself. He was the only one whose demeanor suggested that smelling salts might be called for, being obviously scared silly. Alger Kates had not spoken a word to anyone, not a word, not even when I let him in. His basic attitude was that of a Sunday School teacher in a den of thieves.

Wolfe had clothes on for the first time since Wednesday evening. He sat and did a circle with his eyes, taking them in, and spoke:

"This is going to be disagreeable, gentlemen, for all three of you, so let's make it as brief as we can. I'll do my share. The quickest way is to begin by letting you listen to a Stenophone cylinder, but first I must tell you where I got it. It was found in this room an hour ago, behind the books" —he pointed —"on that bottom shelf. Miss Gunther placed it there, hid it there, when she came to see me Friday evening a week ago—a week ago last evening."

"She wasn't here," O'Neill rasped. "She didn't come."

Wolfe regarded him without affection. "So you don't want this to be brief."

"You're damn right I do! The briefer the better!"

"Then don't interrupt. Naturally everything I'm saying is not only true but provable, or I wouldn't be saying it. Miss Gunther came that evening, brought by Mr. Goodwin, after the others left, and happened to be alone in this room for several minutes. That I did not remember that sooner and search the room was inexcusable. It was an appalling failure of an intellect which has sometimes been known to function satisfactorily.

"However." He made a brusque gesture. "That is between me and the universe. We shall now listen to that cylinder, which was dictated by Mr. Boone his last afternoon at his office in Washington. Do not, I beg you, interrupt it. Archie, turn it on."

There were murmurs as I flipped the switch. Then Cheney Boone, the silent speaker, had the floor:

> Miss Gunther, this is for no one but you and me. Make sure of that. One carbon only, for your locked file, and deliver the original to me.
>
> I have just had a talk in a hotel room with Henry A. Warder, Vice-President and Treasurer of O'Neill and Warder. He is the man who has been trying to reach me through you and refusing to give his name. He finally got me directly, at home, and I made this appointment with him, for today, March 26th. He told me the following —

Warder catapulted out of his chair and started for the machine, screaming, "Stop it!"

It would be more in keeping with his size and appearance to say that he roared or blared, but it literally was a scream. Having anticipated some such demonstration, I had placed the machine at the end of my desk, only four feet from me, and therefore had no difficulty intercepting the attack. I planted myself in Warder's line of approach, reached back of me to turn the switch, and spoke firmly:

"Nothing stirring. Back up and sit down." From my coat pocket I produced an automatic and let it be seen. "All three of you are going to like it less and less as it goes along. If you get a simultaneous idea and try to act on it, I'll wing you and it will be a pleasure."

"That was under a pledge of confidence!" Warder was trembling from head to foot. "Boone promised —"

"Can it!" Cramer had left his chair and was beside Warder. He asked me, "They haven't been gone over, have they?"

"They're not gunmen," Wolfe snapped. "They merely club people on the head — or one of them does."

Cramer paid no attention to him. He started with Warder, gave him a quick but thorough frisking, motioned him back, and said to O'Neill, "Stand up." O'Neill didn't move. Cramer barked at him, "Do you want to get lifted?" O'Neill stood up and did some fancy breathing while Cramer's expert hands went over him. When it was Alger Kates's turn no pressure was required. He looked dazed but not even resentful. Cramer, through with him and empty-handed, moved across to the machine and stood with a hand resting on its frame. He growled at me:

"Go ahead, Goodwin."

Not being a Stenophone expert and not wanting to damage the cylinder, I started it over at the beginning. Soon it was at the point where it had been interrupted:

> He told me the following. Warder has known for several months that the president of his company, Don O'Neill, has been paying a member of the BPR staff for confidential information. He did not discover it by accident or any secret investigation. O'Neill has not only admitted it, but bragged about it, and Warder, as Treasurer, has been obliged to supply corporation funds for the purpose through a special account. He has done so under protest. I repeat that this is Warder's story, but I am inclined to believe it as he tells it because he came to me voluntarily. It will have to be checked with the FBI to find out if they have had any lead in the direction of O'Neill and Warder and specifically Warder, but the FBI must not be given any hint of Warder's communicating with me. I had to give him my pledge on that before he would say a word, and the pledge must be kept absolutely. I'll talk this over with you tomorrow, but I have a hunch — you know how I have hunches — that I want to get it on a cylinder without delay.

Cramer made a little noise that was part snort and part sneeze, and three pairs of eyes went to him as if in irritation at his interfering with a fascinating performance. I didn't mind so much because I had heard it before. What I was interested in was the audience.

> Warder said that to his knowledge the payments began last September and that the total paid to date is sixteen thousand five hundred dollars. The reason he gave for coming to me is that he is a man of principle, so he put it, and he violently disapproves of bribery, especially bribery of government officials. He was not in a position to take a firm stand with O'Neill because O'Neill owns over sixty per cent of the corporation's stock and Warder owns less than ten per cent, and O'Neill could and would throw him out. That can easily be checked. Warder was extremely nervous and apprehensive. My impression is that his story is straight, that his coming to me was the result of his conscience gnawing at him, but there is a chance that his real motive is to build a fire under O'Neill, for undisclosed reasons. He swore that his only purpose was to acquaint me with the facts so I can put a stop to it by getting rid of my corrupted subordinate, and that is substantiated by his

exacting a pledge beforehand that makes it impossible for us to touch O'Neill in the matter.

This will be a surprise to you — I know it was to me — that the man O'Neill has bought is Kates, Alger Kates. You know what I have thought of Kates, and, so far as I know, you have thought the same. Warder claims he doesn't know exactly what O'Neill has got for his money, but that isn't important. We know what Kates has been in a position to sell — as much as any man in the organization outside of the very top ranks — and our only safe assumption is that he has given it all to O'Neill and that O'Neill has passed it on to the whole rotten NIA gang. I don't need to tell you how sick I am about it. For a miserable sixteen thousand dollars. I don't think I would mind quite so much being betrayed by a first-class snake for something up in the millions, but this just makes me sick. I thought Kates was a modest little man with his heart in his work and in our objectives and purposes. I have no idea what he wanted the money for and I don't care. I haven't decided how to handle it. The best way would be to put the FBI on him and catch him with O'Neill, but I don't know whether my pledge to Warder would permit that. I'll think it over and we'll discuss it tomorrow. If I were face to face with Kates right now I don't think I could control myself. Actually I don't ever want to see him again. This has gone pretty deep and if he entered this room now I think I'd get my fingers around his throat and choke him to death. You know me. That's the way I talk.

The important thing is not Kates himself, but what this shows. It shows that it is simply insanity for me to put complete trust in anybody, anyone whatever except Dexter and you, and we must install a much better system of checks immediately. To some extent we can continue to let the FBI handle it, but we must reinforce that with a setup and personnel that will work directly under us. I want you to think it over for tomorrow's discussion, to which no one will be invited but Dexter. The way it strikes me now, you'll have to take this over and drop everything else. That will leave me in a hole, but this is vitally important. Think it over. I have to appear before the Senate Committee in the morning, so I'll take this to New York and give it to you, and you can run it off while I'm up on the Hill, and we'll get at it as early in the afternoon as possible.

The voice stopped and was replaced by a faint sizzling purr, and I reached to flip the switch.

There was complete dead silence.

Wolfe broke it. "What about it, Mr. Kates?" he asked in a tone of innocent curiosity. "When you entered that room, taking Mr. Boone material for his speech, and he found himself face to face with you, did he get his fingers around your throat and try to choke you?"

"No," Kates squeaked. He sounded indignant, but that may have been only because squeaks often do.

O'Neill commanded him: "You keep out of this, Kates! Keep your mouth shut!"

Wolfe chuckled. "That's marvelous, Mr. O'Neill. It really is. Almost verbatim. That first evening here you admonished him, word for word, 'You can keep out of this, Kates! Sit down and shut up!' It was not very intelligent of you, since it sounded precisely like a high-handed man ordering an employee around, as indeed it was. It led to my having a good man spend three days trying to find a link between you and Mr. Kates, but you had been too circumspect." His eyes darted back to Kates. "I asked about Mr. Boone's choking you because apparently he had it in mind, and also because it suggests a possible line for you — self-defense. A good lawyer might do something with it — but then of course there's Miss Gunther. I doubt if a jury could be persuaded that she too tried to choke you, there on my stoop. By the way, there's one detail I'm curious about. Miss Gunther told Mrs. Boone that she wrote a letter to the murderer, telling him that he must return that wedding picture. I don't believe it. I don't think Miss Gunther would have put anything like that in writing. I think she got the picture and the automobile license from you and mailed them to Mrs. Boone herself. Didn't she?"

For reply Alger Kates put on one of the strangest performances I have ever seen, and I have seen plenty. He squeaked, and this time there was no question about the indignation, not at Wolfe but at Inspector Cramer. He was trembling with indignation, up on his feet, a retake in every way of the dramatic moment when he had accused Breslow of going beyond the bounds of common decency. He squeaked, "The police were utterly incompetent! They should have found out where that piece of pipe came from in a few hours! They never did! It came from a pile of rubbish in a basement hall in the building on Forty-first Street where the NIA offices are!"

"For Christ's sake," Cramer rumbled. "Listen to him! He's sore!"

"He's a fool," O'Neill said righteously, apparently addressing the Stenophone. "He's a contemptible fool. I certainly never suspected him of murder." He turned to look straight at Kates. "Good God, I never thought you were capable of that!"

"Neither did I," Kates squeaked. He had stopped trembling and was standing straight, holding himself stiff. "Not before it happened. After it happened I understood myself better. I wasn't as much of a fool as Phoebe was. She should have known it then, what I was capable of. I did. She wouldn't even promise not to tell or to destroy that cylinder. She wouldn't even promise!" He kept his unblinking eyes on O'Neill. "I should have killed you too, that same evening. I could have. You were afraid of me. You're afraid of me right now! Neither of them was afraid of me, but you are! You say you never suspected me of murder when you knew all about it!"

O'Neill started a remark, but Cramer squelched him and asked Kates, "How did he know all about it?"

"I told him." If Kates's squeak was as painful to perform as it was to listen to he was certainly being hurt. "Or rather I didn't have to tell him. He arranged to meet me —"

"That's a lie," O'Neill said coldly and precisely. "Now you're lying."

"Okay, let him finish it." Cramer kept at Kates, "When was that?"

"The next day, Wednesday. Wednesday afternoon. We met that evening."

"Where?"

"On Second Avenue between Fifty-third and Fifty-fourth. We talked there on the sidewalk. He gave me some money and told me that if anything happened, if I was arrested, he would furnish whatever I needed. He was afraid of me then. He kept watching me, watching my hands."

"How long were you together?"

"Ten minutes. My estimate would be ten minutes."

"What time was it?"

"Ten o'clock. We were to meet at ten o'clock and I was on time, but he was late about fifteen minutes because he said he had to make sure he wasn't being followed. I don't think an intelligent man should have any trouble about that."

Wolfe broke in. "Mr. Cramer. Isn't this a waste of time? You're going to have to go all over it again downtown, with a stenographer. He seems to be ready to cooperate."

"He is ready," O'Neill put in, "to get himself electrocuted and to make all the trouble he can for other people with his damn lies."

"I wouldn't worry too much about that if I were you." Wolfe regarded O'Neill with a glint in his eyes. "He is at least more of a philosopher than you are. Bad as he is, he has the grace to accept the inevitable with a show of decorum. You, on the contrary, try to wiggle. From the glances you have been directing at Mr. Warder, I suspect you have no clear idea of where you're at. You should be making up with him. You're going to need him to look after the business while you're away."

"I'm seeing this through. I'm not going away."

"Oh, but you are. You're going to jail. At least that seems —" Wolfe turned abruptly to the Vice-President. "What about it, Mr. Warder? Are you going to try to discredit this message from the dead? Are you going to repudiate or distort your interview with Mr. Boone and have a jury vote you a liar? Or are you going to show that you have some sense?"

Warder no longer looked scared, and when he spoke he showed no inclination to scream. "I am going," he said in a firm and virtuous voice, "to tell the truth."

"Did Mr. Boone tell the truth on that cylinder?"

"Yes. He did."

Wolfe's eyes flashed back to O'Neill. "There you are, sir. Bribery is a felony. You're going to need Mr. Warder. The other matter, complicity in murder as an accessory after the fact — that all depends, mostly on your lawyer. From here on the lawyers take over. — Mr. Cramer. Get them out of here, won't you? I'm tired of looking at them." He shifted to me. "Archie, pack up that cylinder. Mr. Cramer will want to take it along."

Cramer, moving, addressed me: "Hold it, Goodwin, while I use the phone," so I sat facing the audience, with the automatic in my hand in case someone had an attack of nerves, while he dialed his number and conversed. I was interested to hear that his objective was not the Homicide

Squad office, where Ash had been installed, nor even the Chief Inspector, but Hombert himself. Cramer did occasionally show signs of having more brain than a mollusk.

"Commissioner Hombert? Inspector Cramer. Yes, sir. No, I'm calling from Nero Wolfe's office. No, sir, I'm not trying to horn in, but if you'll let me . . . Yes, sir, I'm quite aware it would be a breach of discipline, but if you'll just listen a minute—certainly I'm here with Wolfe, I didn't break in, and I've got the man, I've got the evidence, and I've got a confession. That's exactly what I'm telling you, and I'm neither drunk nor crazy. Send—wait a minute, hold it."

Wolfe was making frantic gestures.

"What do you want?" Cramer growled.

"Tell him," Wolfe commanded, "to keep that confounded doctor away from here."

Cramer resumed. "All right, Commissioner, Send up—oh, nothing, just Wolfe raving something about a doctor. Were you sending him a doctor? He don't need one and in my opinion never will. Send three cars and six men to Wolfe's address. No, I don't, but I'm bringing three of them down. You'll see when I get there. Yes, sir, I'm telling you, the case is finished, all sewed up and no gaps worth mentioning. Sure, I'll bring them straight to you . . ."

He hung up.

"You won't have to put handcuffs on me, will you?" Alger Kates squeaked.

"I want to phone my lawyer," O'Neill said in a frozen voice.

Warder just sat.

35

SKIPPING a thousand or so minor details over the weekend, such as the eminent neurologist Green—no one having bothered to stop him—showing up promptly at a quarter to six, only a few minutes after Cramer had left with his catch, and being informed, in spite of his court order, that the deal was off, I bounce to Monday morning. Wolfe, coming down from the plant rooms at eleven o'clock, knew that he would have a visitor, Cramer having phoned for an appointment, and when he entered the office the Inspector was there in the red leather chair. Beside him on the floor was a misshapen object covered with green florist's paper which he had refused to let me relieve him of. After greetings had been exchanged and Wolfe had got himself comfortable, Cramer said he supposed that Wolfe had seen in the paper that Kates had signed a full and detailed confession to both murders.

Wolfe nodded. "A foolish and inadequate man, that Mr. Kates. But not intellectually to be despised. One item of his performance might even be called brilliant."

"Sure. I would say more than one. Do you mean his leaving that scarf in his own pocket instead of slipping it into somebody else's?"

"Yes, sir. That was noteworthy."

"He's noteworthy all right," Cramer agreed. "In fact he's in a class by himself. There was one thing he wouldn't talk about or sign any statement about, and what do you suppose it was, something that would help put him in the chair? Nope. We couldn't get anything out of him about what he wanted the money for, and when we asked if it was his wife, trips to Florida and so forth, he stuck his chin out and said as if we was worms, 'We'll leave my wife out of this, you will not mention my wife again.' She got here yesterday afternoon and he won't see her. I think he thinks she's too holy to be dragged in."

"Indeed."

"Indeed yes. But on the part that will do for him he was perfectly willing to oblige. For instance, with Boone there at the hotel. He entered the room and handed Boone some papers, and Boone threw it at him, what he had found out, and then told him to beat it and turned his back on him, and Kates picked up the monkey wrench and gave it to him. Kates tells us exactly what Boone said and what he said, and then carefully reads it over to be sure we got it down right. The same way with Phoebe Gunther here on your stoop. He wants the story straight. He wants it distinctly understood that he didn't arrange to meet her and come here with her, when she phoned him, he merely waited in an areaway across the street until he saw her coming and then joined her and mounted the stoop with her. The pipe was up his sleeve with the scarf already wrapped around it. Three days before that, the first time they were here, when he swiped the scarf out of Winterhoff's pocket, he didn't know then what he would be using it for, he only thought there might be some way of planting it somewhere to involve Winterhoff—an NIA man."

"Naturally." Wolfe was contributing to the conversation just to be polite. "Anything to keep eyes away from him. Wasted effort, since my eye was already on him."

"It was?" Cramer sounded skeptical. "What put it there?"

"Mostly two things. First, of course, that command Mr. O'Neill gave him here Friday evening, indubitably a command to one from whom he had reason to expect obedience. Second, and much more important, the wedding picture mailed to Mrs. Boone. Granted that there are men capable of that gesture, assuredly none of the five NIA men whom I had met had it in them. Miss Harding was obviously too cold-blooded to indulge in any such act of grace. Mr. Dexter's alibi had been tested and stood. Mrs. Boone and her niece were manifestly not to be suspected, not by me. There remained only Miss Gunther and Mr. Kates. Miss Gunther might conceivably have killed Mr. Boone, but not herself with a piece of pipe; and she was the only one of them who could without painful strain on probability be considered responsible for the return of the wedding picture. Then where did she get it? From the murderer. By name, from whom? As a logical and workable conjecture, Mr. Kates."

Wolfe fluttered a hand. "All that was mere phamtom-chasing. What was needed was evidence—and all the time here it was, on that bookshelf in my office. That, I confess, is a bitter pill to swallow. Will you have some beer?"

"No, thanks, I guess I won't." Cramer seemed to be nervous or uneasy or something. He looked at the clock and slid to the edge of the chair. "I've got to be going. I just dropped in." He elevated to his feet and shook his pants legs down. "I've got a hell of a busy day. I suppose you've heard that I'm back at my desk at Twentieth Street. Inspector Ash has been moved to Richmond. Staten Island."

"Yes, sir. I congratulate you."

"Much obliged. So with me back at the old stand you'll have to continue to watch your step. Try pulling any fast ones and I'll still be on your neck."

"I wouldn't dream of trying to pull a fast one."

"Okay. Just so we understand each other." Cramer started for the door. I called after him:

"Hey, your package!"

He said over his shoulder, barely halting, "Oh, I forgot, that's for you, Wolfe, hope you like it," and was on his way. Judging from the time it took him to get on out and slam the door behind him, he must have double-quicked.

I went over and lifted the package from the floor, put it on Wolfe's desk, and tore the green paper off, exposing the contents to view. The pot was a glazed sickening green. The dirt was just dirt. The plant was in fair condition, but there were only two flowers on it. I stared at it in awe.

"By God," I said when I could speak, "he brought you an orchid."

"Brassocattleya thorntoni," Wolfe purred. "Handsome."

"Nuts," I said realistically. "You've got a thousand better ones. Shall I throw it out?"

"Certainly not. Take it up to Theodore." Wolfe wiggled a finger at me. "Archie. One of your most serious defects is that you have no sentiment."

"No?" I grinned at him. "You'd be surprised. At this very moment one is almost choking me — namely, gratitude for our good luck at having Cramer back, obnoxious as he is. With Ash there life wouldn't have been worth living."

Wolfe snorted. "Luck!"

36

SOONER or later I had to make it plain to him that I was not a halfwit. I was waiting for a fitting moment, and it came that same day, Monday afternoon, about an hour after lunch, when we received a phone call from Frank Thomas Erskine. He was permitted to speak to Wolfe, and I listened in at my desk.

The gist of it was that a check for one hundred thousand dollars would be mailed to Wolfe that afternoon, which would seem to be enough gist for one little phone call. The rest was just trivial. The NIA deeply appreciated what Wolfe had done for it and was utterly unable to understand why he had returned its money. It was paying him the full amount of the reward at once, as offered in its advertisement, in advance of the fulfillment of the specified conditions, because of its gratitude and its confidence in him, and also because Kates's signed confession made the fulfillment of the conditions inevitable. It would be glad to pay an additional amount for expenses incurred if Wolfe would say how much. It had discussed the matter with Inspector Cramer, and Cramer had disavowed any claim to any part of the reward and insisted that it all belonged to Wolfe.

It was a nice phone call.

Wolfe said to me with a smirk, "That's satisfactory and businesslike. Paying the reward without delay."

I leered at him. "Yeah? Little does Mr. Erskine know."

"Little does he know what? What's wrong now?"

I threw one knee over the other and settled back. The time had come. "There are," I stated, "several ways of doing this. One would be to put a hunk of butter in your mouth and see if it melted. I prefer my way, which is just to tell you. Or I should say ask you, since I'll put it in the form of questions, only I'll supply the answers myself."

"What the devil are you talking about?"

"No, the questions originate with me. Number one: when did you find the cylinder? Saturday afternoon, when you waddled in here in your pajamas, belittling your brains? Not a chance. You knew where it was all the time, at least for three or four days. You found it either Tuesday morning, while I was down at Cramer's office being wrung out, or Wednesday while I was up having lunch with Nina Boone. I lean to Tuesday, but I admit it may have been Wednesday."

"You shouldn't," Wolfe murmured, "leave things teetering like that."

"Please don't interrupt me. Number two: why, if you knew where the cylinder was, did you pester Mrs. Boone to tell you? Because you wanted to make sure she *didn't* know. If she had known she might have told the cops before you decided to let loose, and the reward would have gone to her, or anyway not to you. And since Phoebe Gunther had told her a lot she might have told her that too. Also, it was part of your general plan to spread the impression that you didn't know where the cylinder was and would give an arm and several teeth to find it."

"That was actually the impression," Wolfe murmured.

"It was indeed. I could back all this up with various miscellaneous items, for instance your sending for the Stenophone Wednesday morning, which is the chief reason I lean to Tuesday, but let's go on to number three: what was the big idea? When you found the cylinder why didn't you say so? Because you let your personal opinions interfere with your professional actions, which reminds me I must do some reading up on ethics. Because your opinion of the NIA coincides roughly with some other people's, including my own, but that's beside the point, and you knew the stink about the murders was raising cain with the NIA, and you wanted to prolong it as much as possible. To accomplish that you even went to the length of letting yourself be locked in your room for three days, but there I admit another factor enters, your love of art for art's sake. You'll do anything to put on a good show, provided you get top billing."

"How long is this going on?"

"I'm about through. Number four, why did you drop the client and return the dough, is easy. There's always a chance that you may change your mind some day and decide you want to go to heaven, and a plain unadulterated double cross would rule it out. So you couldn't very well have kept the NIA's money, and gone on having it for a client, while you were doing your damnedest to push it off a cliff. Here, however, is where I get cynical. What if no reward had been publicly offered? Would you have put on the show just the same? I express no opinion, but boy, I have one. Another thing about ethics — exactly what is the difference between having a client and taking a fee, and accepting a reward?"

"Nonsense. The reward was advertised to a hundred million people and the terms stated. It was to be paid to whoever earned it. I earned it."

"Okay, I merely mention the point. I don't question your going to heaven if you decide you want in. Incidentally, you are not absolutely watertight. If Saul Panzer was put under oath and asked what he did from Wednesday to Saturday, and he replied that he kept in touch with Henry A. Warder to make sure that Warder could be had when needed, and then if you were asked where you got the idea that you might need Henry A. Warder, mightn't you have a little trouble shooting the answer? Not that it will happen, knowing Saul as I do. — Well. Let's see. I guess that's about all. I just wanted you to know that I resent your making contemptuous remarks about your brain."

Wolfe grunted. There was a silence. Then his eyes opened half way and he rumbled:

"You've left one thing out."

"What?"

"A possible secondary motive. Or even a primary one. Taking all that you have said as hypothesis — since of course it is inadmissible as fact — look back at me last Tuesday, six days ago, when — by hypothesis — I found the cylinder. What actually would have taken precedence in my mind?"

"I've been telling you. Not what would have, what did."

"But you left one thing out. Miss Gunther."

"What about her?"

"She was dead. As you know, I detest waste. She had displayed remarkable tenacity, audacity, and even imagination, in using the murder of Mr. Boone for a purpose he would have desired, approved, and applauded. In the middle of it she was herself murdered. Surely she deserved not to have her murder wasted. She deserved to get something out of it. I found myself — by hypothesis — in an ideal position to see that that was taken care of. That's what you left out."

I stared at him. "Then I've got a hypothesis too. If that was it, either primary or secondary, to hell with ethics."

Might as Well Be Dead

1

MOST of the people who come to see Nero Wolfe by appointment, especially from as far away as Nebraska, show some sign of being in trouble, but that one didn't. With his clear unwrinkled skin and alert brown eyes and thin straight mouth, he didn't even look his age. I knew his age, sixty-one. When a telegram had come from James R. Herold, Omaha, Nebraska, asking for an appointment Monday afternoon, of course I had checked on him. He was sole owner of the Herold Hardware Company, wholesale, a highly respected citizen, and rated at over half a million — a perfect prospect for a worthy fee if he had real trouble. Seeing him had been a letdown. From his looks, he might merely be after a testimonial for a gadget to trim orchid plants. He had settled back comfortably in the red leather chair.

"I guess," he said, "I'd better tell you why I picked you."

"As you please," Wolfe muttered from behind his desk. For half an hour after lunch he never gets above a mutter unless he has to.

Herold crossed his legs. "It's about my son. I want to find my son. About a month ago I put ads in the New York papers, and I contacted the New York police, and — What's the matter?"

"Nothing. Go on."

It was not nothing. Wolfe had made a face. I, at my desk, could have told Herold that unless his problem smelled like real money he might as well quit right there. One man who had made "contact" a verb in that office had paid an extra thousand bucks for the privilege, though he hadn't known it.

Herold looked doubtful; then his face cleared. "Oh. You don't like poking in a police matter, but that's all right. I've been keeping after the Missing Persons Bureau, a Lieutenant Murphy, and I've run some more newspaper ads in the Personals, but they've got no results at all, and my wife was getting impatient about it, so I phoned Lieutenant Murphy from Omaha and told him I wanted to hire a private detective agency and asked him to recommend one. He said he couldn't do that, but I can be pretty determined when I want to, and he gave me your name. He said that on a job like finding a missing person you yourself wouldn't be much because you were too fat and lazy, but that you had two men, one named Archie Goodwin and one named Saul Panzer, who were tops for that kind of work. So I wired you for an appointment."

Wolfe made the noise he uses for a chuckle, and moved a finger to indicate me. "This is Mr. Goodwin. Tell him about it."

"He's in your employ, isn't he?"

"Yes. My confidential assistant."

"Then I'll tell you. I like to deal with principals. My son Paul is my only son — I have two daughters. When he graduated from college, the University of Nebraska, I took him into my business, wholesale hardware. That was in nineteen forty-five, eleven years ago. He had been a little wild in college, but I thought he would settle into the harness, but he didn't. He stole twenty-six thousand dollars of the firm's money, and I kicked him out." His straight thin mouth tightened a little. "Out of the business and out of the house. He left Omaha and I never saw him again. I didn't want to see him, but now I do and my wife does. One month ago, on March eighth, I learned that he didn't take that money. I learned who did, and it has been proven beyond all doubt. That's being attended to, the thief is being taken care of, and now I want to find my son." He got a large envelope from his pocket, took things from it, and left his chair. "That's a picture of him, taken in June nineteen forty-five, the latest one I have." He handed me one too. "Here are six copies of it, and of course I can get more." He returned to the chair and sat. "He got a raw deal and I want to make it square with him. I have nothing to apologize for, because at the time there was good evidence that he had taken the money, but now I know he didn't and I've got to find him. My wife is very impatient about it."

The picture was of a round-cheeked kid in a mortarboard and gown, with a dimple in his chin. No visible resemblance to his father. As for the father, he certainly wasn't being maudlin. You could say he was bearing up well in the circumstances, or you could say he was plain cold fish. I preferred the latter.

Wolfe dropped the picture on the desk top. "Evidently," he muttered, "you think he's in New York. Why?"

"Because every year my wife and daughters have been getting cards from him on their birthdays — you know, those birthday cards. I suspected all along that my wife was corresponding with him, but she says not. She admits she would have, but he never gave her an address. He never wrote her except the cards, and they were all postmarked New York."

"When did the last one come?"

"November nineteenth, less than five months ago. My daughter Marjorie's birthday. Postmarked New York like the others."

"Anything else? Has anyone ever seen him here?"

"Not that I know of."

"Have the police made any progress?"

"No. None whatever. I'm not complaining; I guess they've tried; but of course in a great city like this they've got their hands full of problems and I'm only one. I'm pretty sure he came straight to New York from Omaha, by train, back eleven years ago, but I haven't been able to verify it. The police had several men on it for a week, or they said they had, but now I think they've only got one, and I agree with my wife that I've got to do something. I've been neglecting my business."

"That will never do," Wolfe said dryly. Apparently he favored the cold-fish slant too. "And no results from the newspaper advertisements?"

"No. I got letters from five detective agencies offering to help me — of course the replies were to a box number — and quite a few, at least two dozen, from crackpots and impostors. The police investigated all of them, and they were all duds."

"How were the advertisements worded?"

"I wrote them myself. They were all alike." Herold got a big leather wallet from his breast pocket, fished in it, and extracted a clipping. He twisted in his chair to get better light from a window, and read:

> Paul Herold, who left Omaha, Nebraska, in 1945, will learn something to his advantage by communicating with his father immediately. It has been learned that a mistake was made. Also anyone who sees this ad and knows anything of the said Paul Herold's whereabouts, either now or at any time during the past ten years, is requested to communicate and a proper reward will be given.
>
> X904 Times.

"I ran that in five New York papers." He returned the clipping to the wallet and the wallet to the pocket. "Thirty times altogether. Money wasted. I don't mind spending money, but I hate to waste it."

Wolfe grunted. "You might waste it on me — or on Mr. Goodwin and Mr. Panzer. Your son may have changed his name on arrival in New York — indeed, that seems likely, since neither the police nor the advertisements have found any trace of him. Do you know if he took luggage with him when he left Omaha?"

"Yes, he took all his clothes and some personal things. He had a trunk and a suitcase and a bag."

"Were his initials on any of it?"

"His initials?" Herold frowned. "Why — Oh, yes. They were on the trunk and the suitcase, presents from his mother. My wife. Why?"

"Just PH, or a middle initial?"

"He had no middle name. Just PH. Why?"

"Because if he changed his name he probably found it convenient to keep the PH. Initials on luggage have dictated ten thousand aliases. Even so, Mr. Herold, assuming that PH, it is a knotty and toilsome job, for we must also assume that your son prefers not to be found, since the advertisements failed to flush him. I suggest that you let him be."

"You mean quit looking for him?"

"Yes."

"I can't. My wife, and my daughters — Anyway, I won't. Right is right. I've got to find him."

"And you want to hire me?"

"Yes. You and Goodwin and Panzer."

"Then I must inform you that it may take months, the expenses will be considerable, the amount of my bill will not be contingent on success, and I charge big fees."

"I know you do. Lieutenant Murphy told me." Herold looked more like a man in trouble than when he came in. "But I can call you off at any time."

"Certainly."

"All right." He took a breath. "You want a retainer."

"As an advance for expenses. More important, I want all the information you can give me." Wolfe's head turned. "Archie, your notebook."

I already had it out.

An hour later, after the client had left and Wolfe had gone up to the plant rooms for his afternoon session with Theodore and the orchids, I put the check for three thousand dollars in the safe and then got at the typewriter to transcribe my notes. When I was done, I had five pages of assorted facts, one or two of which might possibly be useful. Paul Herold had a three-inch scar on his left leg, on the inside of the knee, from a boyhood accident. That might help if we found him with his pants down. It had made him 4F and kept him out of war. His mother had called him Poosie. He had liked girls, and had for a time concentrated on one at college named Arline Macy, but had not been hooked, and so far as was known had communicated with none after heading east. He had majored in Social Science, but on that his father had been a little vague. He had taken violin lessons for two years and then sold the violin for twenty bucks, and got hell for it. He had tried for football in spite of his bum knee, but didn't make the team, and in baseball had played left field for two innings against Kansas in 1944. No other sports to speak of. Smoke and drink, not to excess. Gambling, not to the client's knowledge. He had always pushed some on his allowance, but there had been nothing involving dishonesty or other moral turpitude before the blow-up.

And so on and so forth. It didn't look very promising. Evidence of some sort of dedication, such as a love for animals that hop or a determination to be President of the United States, might have helped a little, but it wasn't there. If his father had really known him, which I doubted, he had been just an ordinary kid who had had a rotten piece of luck, and now it was anybody's guess what he had turned into. I decided that I didn't appreciate the plug Lieutenant Murphy of the Missing Persons Bureau had given me, along with Saul Panzer. Any member of the NYPD, from Commissioner Skinner on down, would have given a day's pay, after taxes, to see Nero Wolfe stub his toe, and it seemed likely that Murphy, after spending a month on it, had figured that this was a fine prospect. I went to the kitchen and told Fritz we had taken on a job that would last two years and would be a washout

Fritz smiled and shook his head. "No washouts in this house," he said positively. "Not with Mr. Wolfe and you both here." He got a plastic container from the refrigerator, took it to the table, and removed the lid.

"Hey," I protested, "we had shad roe for lunch! Again for dinner?"

"My dear Archie." He was superior, to me, only about food. "They were merely saute, with a simple little sauce, only chives and chervil. These will be *en casserole*, with anchovy butter made by me. The sheets of larding will be rubbed with five herbs. With the cream to cover will be an onion and three other herbs, to be removed before serving. The roe season is short, and Mr. Wolfe could enjoy it three times a day. You can go to Al's place on Tenth Avenue and enjoy a ham on rye with coleslaw." He shuddered.

It developed into an argument, but I avoided getting out on a limb, not wanting to have to drop off into Al's place. We were still at it when, at six o'clock, I heard the elevator bringing Wolfe down from the plant rooms, and after winding it up with no hard feelings I left Fritz to his sheets of larding and went back to the office.

Wolfe was standing over by the bookshelves, looking at the globe, which was even bigger around than he was, checking to make sure that Omaha, Nebraska, was where it always had been. That done, he crossed over to his desk, and around it, and lowered his colossal corpus into his custom-made chair.

He cocked his head to survey the Feraghan, which covered all the central expanse, 14 x 26. "It's April," he said, "and that rug's dirty. I must remind Fritz to send it to be cleaned and put the others down."

"Yeah," I agreed, looking down at him. "But for a topic for discussion that won't last long. If you want to avoid discussing Paul Herold start something with some body to it, like the Middle East."

He grunted. "I don't have to avoid it. According to Lieutenant Murphy, that's for you and Saul. Have you reached Saul?"

"Yes. We're going to disguise ourselves as recruiting officers for the Salvation Army. He starts at the Battery and works north, and I start at Van Cortlandt Park and work south. We'll meet at Grant's Tomb on Christmas Eve and compare notes, and then start in on Brooklyn. Have you anything better to suggest?"

"I'm afraid not." He sighed, deep. "It may be hopeless. Has that Lieutenant Murphy any special reason to bear me a grudge?"

"It doesn't have to be special. He's a cop, that's enough."

"I suppose so." He shut his eyes, and in a moment opened them again. "I should have declined the job. Almost certainly he has never been known in New York as Paul Herold. That picture is eleven years old. What does he look like now? It's highly probable that he doesn't want to be found, and, if so, he has been put on the alert by the advertisements. The police are well qualified for the task of locating a missing person, and if after a full month they — Get Lieutenant Murphy on the phone."

I went to my desk and dialed CA 6-2000, finally persuaded a sergeant that only Murphy would do, and, when I had him, signaled to Wolfe. I stayed on.

"Lieutenant Murphy? This is Nero Wolfe. A man named James R. Herold, of Omaha, Nebraska, called on me this afternoon to engage me to find his son Paul. He said you had given him my name. He also said your bureau has been conducting a search for his son for about a month. Is that correct?"

"That's correct. Did you take the job?"

"Yes."

"Fine. Good luck, Mr. Wolfe."

"Thank you. May I ask, did you make any progress?"

"None whatever. All we got was dead ends."

"Did your search go beyond your set routine?"

"That depends on what you call routine. It was a clear-cut case and the boy had had a rough deal, and you could say we made a special effort. I've still got a good man on it. If you want to send Goodwin down with a letter from Herold we'll be glad to show him the reports."

"Thank you. You have no suggestions?"

"I'm afraid not. Good luck."

Wolfe didn't thank him again. We hung up.

"Swell," I said. "He thinks he's handed you a gazookis. The hell of it is, he's probably right. So where do we start?"

"Not at the Battery," Wolfe growled.

"Okay, but where? It may even be worse than we think. What if Paul framed himself for the theft of the twenty-six grand so as to have an excuse to get away from father? Having met father, I would buy that. And seeing the ad asking him to communicate with father — not mentioning mother or sisters, just father — and saying a mistake was made, what does he do? He either beats it to Peru or the Middle East — there's the Middle East again — or he goes and buys himself a set of whiskers. That's an idea; we can check on all sales of whiskers in the last month, and if we find —"

"Shut up. It *is* an idea."

I stared. "My God, it's not that desperate. I was merely trying to stir your blood up and get your brain started, as usual, and if you —"

"I said shut up. Is it too late to get an advertisement into tomorrow's papers?"

"The *Gazette*, no. The *Times*, maybe."

"Your notebook."

Even if he had suddenly gone batty, I was on his payroll. I went to my desk, got the notebook, turned to a fresh page, and took my pen.

"Not in the classified columns," he said. "A display two columns wide and three inches high. Headed 'To P.H.' in large boldface, with periods after the P and H. Then this text, in smaller type: 'Your innocence is known and the injustice done you is regretted.'" He paused. "Change the 'regretted' to 'deplored.' Resume: 'Do not let bitterness prevent righting of a wrong'" Pause again. "'No unwelcome contact will be urged upon you, but your help is needed to expose the true culprit. I engage to honor your reluctance to resume any tie you have renounced.'"

He pursed his lips a moment, then nodded. "That will do. Followed by my name and address and phone number."

"Why not mention mother?" I asked.

"We don't know how he feels toward his mother."

"He sent her birthday cards."

"By what impulse? Do you know?"

"No."

"Then it would be risky. We can safely assume only two emotions for him: resentment of the wrong done him, and a desire to avenge it. If he lacks those he is less or more than human, and we'll never find him. I am aware, of course, that this is a random shot at an invisible target and a hit would be a prodigy. Have you other suggestions?"

I said no and swiveled the typewriter to me.

2

AT any given moment there are probably 38,437 people in the metropolitan area who have been unjustly accused of something, or think they have, and

66 of them have the initials P.H. One-half of the 66, or 33, saw that ad, and one-third of the 33, or 11, answered it — three of them by writing letters, six by phoning, and two by calling in person at the old brownstone house on West 35th Street, Manhattan, which Wolfe owns, inhabits, and dominates except when I decide that he has gone too far.

The first reaction was not from a P.H. but a L.C. — Lon Cohen of the *Gazette*. He phoned Tuesday morning and asked what the line was on the Hays case. I said we had no line on any Hays case, and he said nuts.

He went on. "Wolfe runs an ad telling P.H. he knows he's innocent, but you have no line? Come on, come on. After all the favors I've done you? All I ask is —"

I cut him off. "Wrong number. But I should have known, and so should Mr. Wolfe. We do read the papers, so we know a guy named Peter Hays is on trial for murder. Not our P.H. But it could be a damn nuisance. I hope to God he doesn't see the ad."

"Okay. You're sitting on it, and when Wolfe's sitting on something it's being sat on good. But when you're ready to loosen up, think of me. My name is Damon, Pythias."

Since there was no use trying to convince him, I skipped it. I didn't buzz Wolfe, who was up in the plant rooms for his morning exercise, to ride him for not remembering there was a P.H. being tried for murder, because I should have remembered it myself.

The other P.H.'s kept me busy, off and on, most of the day. One named Phillip Horgan was no problem, because he came in person and one look was enough. He was somewhat older than our client. The other one who came in person, while we were at lunch, was tougher. His name was Perry Hettinger and he refused to believe the ad wasn't aimed at him. By the time I got rid of him and returned to the dining room Wolfe had cleaned up the kidney pie and I got no second helping.

The phone calls were more complicated, since I couldn't see the callers. I eliminated three of them through appropriate and prolonged conversation, but the other three had to have a look, so I made appointments to see them; and since I had to stick around I phoned Saul Panzer, who came and got one of the pictures father had left and went to keep the apppointments. It was an insult to Saul to give him such a kindergarten assignment, considering that he is the best operative alive and rates sixty bucks a day, but the client had asked for him and it was the client's dough.

The complication of the P.H.'s being on trial for murder was as big a nuisance as I expected, and then some. All the papers phoned, including the *Times*, and two of them sent journalists to the door, where I chatted with them on the threshold. Around noon there was a phone call from Sergeant Purley Stebbins of Homicide. He wanted to speak to Wolfe, and I said Mr. Wolfe was engaged, which he was. He was working on a crossword puzzle by Ximenes in the London *Observer*. I asked Purley if I could help him.

"You never have yet," he rumbled. "But neither has Wolfe. But when he runs a display ad telling a man on trial for murder that he knows he's innocent and he wants to expose the true culprit, we want to know what he's trying to pull and we're going to. If he won't tell me on the phone I'll be there in ten minutes."

"I'll be glad to save you the trip," I assured him. "Tell you what. You wouldn't believe me anyway, so call Lieutenant Murphy at the Missing Persons Bureau. He'll tell you all about it."

"What kind of a gag is this?"

"No gag. I wouldn't dare to trifle with an officer of the law. Call Murphy. If he doesn't satisfy you come and have lunch with us. Peruvian melon, kidney pie, endive with Martinique dressing —"

It clicked and he was gone. I turned and told Wolfe it would be nice if we could always get Stebbins off our neck as easy as that. He frowned a while at the London *Observer* and then raised his head.

"Archie."

"Yes, sir."

"That trial, that Peter Hays, started about two weeks ago."

"Right."

"The *Times* had his picture. Get it."

I grinned at him. "Wouldn't that be something? It popped into my head too, the possibility, when Lon phoned, but I remembered the pictures of him — the *Gazette* and *Daily News*, all of them, and crossed it off. But it won't hurt to look."

One of my sixteen thousand duties is keeping a five-week file of the *Times* in a cupboard below the bookshelves. I went and slid the door open and squatted, and before long I had it, on the seventeenth page of the issue of March 27. I gave it a look and went and handed it to Wolfe, and from a drawer of my desk got the picture of Paul Herold in mortarboard and gown, and handed him that too. He held them side by side and scowled at them, and I circled around to his elbow to help. The newspaper shot wasn't any too good, but even so, if they were the same P.H. he had changed a lot in eleven years. His round cheeks had caved in, his nose had shrunk, his lips were thinner, and his chin had bulged.

"No," Wolfe said. "Well?"

"Unanimous," I agreed. "That would have been a hell of a spot to find him. Is it worth going to the courtroom for a look?"

"I doubt it. Anyway, not today. You're needed here."

But that only postponed the agony for a few hours. That afternoon, after various journalists had been dealt with, and some of the P.H.'s, and Saul had been sent to keep the appointments, we had a visitor. Just three minutes after Wolfe had left the office for his daily four-to-six conference with the orchids, the doorbell rang and I answered it. On the stoop was a middle-aged guy who would need a shave by sundown, in a sloppy charcoal topcoat and a classy new black homburg. He could have been a P.H., but not a journalist. He said he would like a word with Mr. Nero Wolfe. I said Mr. Wolfe was engaged, told him my name and station, and asked if I could be of any service. He said he didn't know.

He looked at his wristwatch. "I haven't much time," he said, looking harassed. "My name is Albert Freyer, counselor-at-law." He took a leather case from his pocket, got a card from it, and handed it to me. "I am attorney for Peter Hays, who is on trial for first-degree murder. I'm keeping my cab waiting because the jury is out and I must be at hand. Do you know anything about the advertisement Nero Wolfe put in today's papers, 'To P.H.'?"

"Yes I know all about it."

"I didn't see it until an hour ago. I didn't want to phone about it. I want to ask Nero Wolfe a question. It is being assumed that the advertisement was addressed to my client, Peter Hays. I want to ask him straight, was it?"

"I can answer that. It wasn't. Mr. Wolfe had never heard of Peter Hays, except in the newspaper accounts of his trial."

"You will vouch for that?"

"I do vouch for it."

"Well." He looked gotten. "I was hoping — No matter. Who is the P.H. the advertisement was addressed to?"

"A man whose initials are known to us but his name is not."

"What was the injustice mentioned in the ad? The wrong to be righted?"

"A theft that took place eleven years ago."

"I see." He looked at his wrist. "I have no time. I would like to give you a message for Mr. Wolfe. I admit the possibility of coincidence, but it is not unreasonable to suspect that it may be a publicity stunt. If so, it may work damage to my client, and it may be actionable. I'll want to look into the matter further when time permits. Will you tell him that?"

"Sure. If you can spare twenty seconds more tell me something. Where was Peter Hays born, where did he spend his boyhood, and where did he go to college?"

Having half turned, he swiveled his head to me. "Why do you want to know?"

"I can stand it not to. Call it curiosity. I read the papers. I answered six questions for you, why not answer three for me?"

"Because I can't. I don't know." He was turning to go.

I persisted. "Do you mean that? You're defending him on a murder charge, and you don't know that much about him?" He was starting down the seven steps of the stoop. I asked his back, "Where's his family?"

He turned his head to say, "He has no family," and went. He climbed into the waiting taxi and banged the door, and the taxi rolled away from the curb. I went back in, to the office, and buzzed the plant rooms on the house phone.

"Yes?" Wolfe hates to be disturbed up there.

"We had company. A lawyer named Albert Freyer. He's Peter Hay's attorney, and he doesn't know where Hays was born and brought up or what college he went to, and he says Hays has no family. I'm switching my vote. I think it's worth the trip, and the client will pay the cab fare. I'm leaving now."

"No."

"That's just a reflex. Yes."

"Very well. Tell Fritz."

The gook. I always did tell Fritz. I went to the kitchen and did so, returned to the office and put things away and locked the safe, fixed the phone to ring in the kitchen, and got my hat and coat from the rack in the hall. Fritz was there to put the chain bolt on the door.

After habits get automatic you're no longer aware of them. One day years ago a tail had picked me up when I left the house on an errand, without my knowing it, and what he learned from my movements during the next hour had cost us an extra week, and our client an extra several thousand dollars, solving a big and important case. For a couple of months after that experience I never went out on a business errand without making a point of checking my rear, and by that time it had become automatic, and I've done it ever since without thinking of it. That Tuesday afternoon, heading for Ninth Avenue, I suppose I glanced back when I had gone about fifty paces, since that's the routine, but if so I saw nothing. But in another fifty paces, when I glanced back again automatically, something clicked and shot to the upper level and I was aware of it. What had caused the click was the sight of a guy some forty yards behind, headed my way, who hadn't been there before. I stopped, turned, and stood, facing him. He hesitated, took a piece of paper from his pocket, peered at it, and started studying the fronts of houses to his right and left. Almost anything would have been better than that, even tying his shoestring, since his sudden appearance had to mean either that he had popped out of an areaway to follow me or that he had emerged from one of the houses on his own affairs; and if the latter, why stop to glom the numbers of the houses next door?

So I had a tail. But if I tackled him on the spot, with nothing but logic to go on, he would merely tell me to go soak my head. I could lead him into a situation where I would have more than logic, but that would take time, and Freyer had said the jury was out, and I was in a hurry. I decided I could spare a couple of minutes and stood and looked at him. He was middle-sized, in a tan raglan and a brown snap-brim, with a thin, narrow face and a pointed nose. At the end of the first minute he got embarrassed and mounted the stoop of the nearest house, which was the residence and office of Doc Vollmer, and pushed the button. The door was opened by Helen Grant, Doc's secretary. He exchanged a few words with her turned away without touching his hat, descended to the sidewalk, mounted the stoop of the house next door, and pushed the button. My two minutes were up, and anyway that was enough, so I beat it to Ninth Avenue without bothering to look back, flagged a taxi, and told the driver Centre and Pearl Streets.

At that time of day the courthouse corridors were full of lawyers, clients, witnesses, jurors, friends, enemies, relatives, fixers, bloodsuckers, politicians, and citizens. Having consulted a city employee below, I left the elevator at the third floor and dodged my way down the hall and around a corner to Part XIX, expecting no difficulty about getting in, since the Hays case was no headliner, merely run-of-the-mill.

There certainly was no difficulty. The courtroom was practically empty — no judge, no jury, and even no clerk or stenographer. And no Peter Hays. Eight or nine people altogether were scattered around on the benches. I went and consulted the officer at the door, and was told that the jury was still out and he had no idea when it would be in. I found a phone booth and made two calls: one to Fritz, to tell him I might be home for dinner and I might not, and one to Doc Vollmer's number. Helen Grant answered.

"Listen, little blessing," I asked her, "do you love me?"

"No. And I never will."

"Good. I'm afraid to ask favors of girls who love me, and I want one from you. Fifty minutes ago a man in a tan coat rang your bell and you opened the door. What did he want?"

"My lord!" She was indignant. "Next thing you'll be tapping our phone! If you think you're going to drag me into one of your messes!"

"No mess and no dragging. Did he try to sell you some heroin?"

"He did not. He asked if a man named Arthur Holcomb lived here, and I said no, and he asked if I knew where he lived, and I said no again. That was all. What is this, Archie?"

"Nothing. Cross it off. I'll tell you when I see you if you still want to know. As for not loving me, you're just whistling in the dark. Tell me good-by."

"Good-by forever!"

So he had been a tail. A man looking for Arthur Holcomb wouldn't need to pop or slink suddenly from an areaway. There was no profit in guessing, but as I went back down the corridor naturally I wondered whether and how and why he was connected with P.H. and if so, which one.

As I approached the door of Part XIX I saw activity. People were going in. I got to the elbow of the officer and asked him if the jury was coming, and he said, "Don't ask me, mister. Word gets around fast here, but not to me. Move along." I entered the courtroom and stepped aside to be out of the traffic lane, and was surveying the scene when a voice at my shoulder pronounced my name. I turned, and there was Albert Freyer. His expression was not cordial.

"So you never heard of Peter Hays," he said through his teeth. "Well, you're going to hear of me."

My having no reply ready didn't matter, for he didn't wait for one. He walked down the center aisle with a companion, passed through the gate, and took a seat at the counselors table. I followed and chose a spot in the third row on the left, the side where the defendant would enter. The clerk and stenographer were at their desks, and Assistant District Attorney Mandelbaum, who had once been given a bigger dose by Wolfe than he could swallow, was at another table in the enclosure, with his briefcase in front of him and a junior at his side. People were straggling down the aisle, and I had my neck twisted for a look at them, with a vague idea of seeing the man in the tan coat who wanted to find Arthur Holcomb, when there was a sudden murmur and faces turned left, and so did mine. The defendant was being escorted in.

I have good eyes and I used them as he crossed to a chair directly behind Albert Freyer. I only had about four seconds, for when he was seated, with his back to me, my eyes were of no use, since the picture of Paul Herold, in mortarboard and gown, had given nothing to go by but the face. So I shut my eyes to concentrate. He was and he wasn't. He could be, but. Looking at the two pictures side by side with Wolfe, I would have made it thirty to one that he wasn't. Now two to one, or maybe even money, and I would take either end. I had to press down with my fanny to keep from bobbing up and marching through the gate for a full-face close-up.

The jury was filing in, but I hardly noticed. The courtroom preliminaries leading up to the moment when a jury is going to tell a man where he stands on the big one will give any spectator either a tingle in the spine or a lump of lead in his stomach, but not that time for me. My mind was occupied, and I was staring at the back of the defendant's head, trying to make him turn around. When the officer gave the order to rise for the entrance of the judge, the others were all on their feet before I came to. The judge sat and told us to do likewise, and we obeyed. I could tell you what the clerk said, and the question the judge asked the foreman, and the questions the clerk asked the foreman, since that is court routine, but I didn't actually hear it. I was back on my target.

The first words I actually heard came from the foreman. "We find the defendant guilty as charged, of murder in the first degree."

A noise went around, a mixture of gasps and murmurs, and a woman behind me tittered, or it sounded like it. I kept on my target, and it was well that I did. He rose and turned square around, all in one quick movement, and sent his eyes around the courtroom — searching, defiant eyes — and they flashed across me. Then the guard had his elbow and he was pulled around and down, and Albert Freyer got up to ask that the jury be polled.

At such a moment the audience is supposed to keep their seats and make no disturbance, but I had a call. Lowering my head and pressing my palm to my mouth as if I might or might not manage to hold it in, I got up and sidestepped to the aisle, and double-quicked to the rear and on out. Waiting for one of the slow-motion elevators didn't fit my mood, so I took to the stairs. Out on the sidewalk there were several citizens strung along on the lookout for taxis, so I went south a block, soon got one, climbed in, and gave the hackie the address.

The timing was close to perfect. It was 5:58 when, in response to my ring, Fritz came and released the chain bolt and let me in. In two minutes Wolfe would be down from the plant rooms. Fritz followed me to the office to report, the chief item being that Saul had phoned to say that he had seen the three P.H.'s and none of them was it. Wolfe entered, went to his desk, and sat, and Fritz left.

Wolfe looked up at me. "Well?"

"No, sir." I said emphatically. "I am not well. I am under the impression that Paul Herold, alias Peter Hays, has just been convicted of first-degree murder."

His lips tightened. He released them. "How strong an impression? Sit down. You know I don't like to stretch my neck."

I went to my chair and swiveled to face him. "I was breaking it gently. It's not an impression, it's a fact. Do you want details?"

"Relevant ones, yes."

"Then the first one first. When I left here a tail picked me up. Also a fact, not an impression. I didn't have time to tease him along and corner him, so I passed it. He didn't follow me downtown — not that that matters."

Wolfe grunted. "Next."

"When I got to the courtroom the jury was still out, but they soon came in. I was up front, in the third row. When the defendant was brought in he passed within twenty feet of me and I had a good look, but it was brief and it was mostly three-quarters and profile. I wasn't sure. I would have settled for tossing a coin. When he sat, his back was to me. But when the foreman announced the verdict he stood up and turned around to survey the audience, and what he was doing, or wanting to do, was to tell somebody to go to hell. I got his full face, and for that instant there was something in it, a kind of cocky something, that made it absolutely the face of that kid in the picture. Put a flattop and a kimono on him and take eleven years off, and he was Paul Herold. I got up and left. And by the way, another detail. That lawyer, Albert Freyer, I told him in effect that we weren't interested in Peter

Hays, and he saw me in the courtroom and snarled at me and said we'd hear from him."

Wolfe sat and regarded me. He heaved a sigh. "Confound it. But our only engagement was to find him. Can we inform Mr. Herold that we have done so?"

"No. I'm sure, but not that sure. We tell him his son has been convicted of murder, and he comes from Omaha to take a look at him through the bars, and says no. That would be nice. Lieutenant Murphy expected to get a grin out of this but that wouldn't be a grin, it would be a horse laugh. Not to mention what I would get from you. Nothing doing."

"Are you suggesting that we're stalemated?"

"Not at all. The best thing would be for you to see him and talk with him and decide it yourself, but since you refuse to run errands outside the house, and since he is in no condition to drop in for a chat, I suppose it's up to me — I mean the errand. Getting me in to him is your part."

He was frowning. "You have your gifts, Archie. I have always admired your resourcefulness when faced by barriers."

"Yeah, so have I. But I have my limitations, and this is it. I was considering it in the taxi on the way home. Cramer or Stebbins or Mandelbaum, or anyone else on the public payroll, would have to know what for, and they would tell Murphy and he would take over, and if he *is* Paul Herold, who would have found him? Murphy. It calls for better gifts than mine. Yours."

He grunted. He rang for beer. "Full report, please. All you saw and heard in the courtroom."

I obliged. That didn't take long. When I finished, with my emergency exit as the clerk was polling the jury, he asked for the *Times*'s report of the trial, and I went to the cupboard and got it — all issues from March 27 to date. He started at the beginning, and, since I thought I might as well bone up on it myself, I started at the end and went backward. He had reached April 2, and I had worked back to April 4, and there would soon have been a collision but for an interruption. The doorbell rang. I went to the hall, and seeing, through the one-way glass panel of the front door, a sloppy charcoal topcoat and a black homburg that I had already seen twice that day, I recrossed the sill to the office and told Wolfe, "He kept his word. Albert Freyer."

His brows went up. "Let him in," he growled.

3

THE counselor-at-law hadn't had a shave, but it must be admitted that the circumstances called for allowances. I suppose he thought he was flattening somebody when, convoyed to the office and introduced, he didn't extend a hand, but if so he was wrong. Wolfe is not a handshaker.

When Freyer had got lowered into the red leather chair Wolfe swiveled to face him and said affably, "Mr. Goodwin has told me about you, and about the adverse verdict on your client. Regrettable."

"Did he tell you you would hear from me?"

"Yes, he mentioned that."

"All right, here I am." Freyer wasn't appreciating the big, comfortable chair; he was using only the front half of it, his palms on his knees. "Goodwin told me your ad in today's papers had no connection with my client, Peter Hays. He said you had never heard of him. I didn't believe him. And less than an hour later he appears in the courtroom where my client was on trial. That certainly calls for an explanation, and I want it. I am convinced that my client is innocent. I am convinced that he is the victim of a diabolical frame-up. I don't say that your ad was a part of the plot, I admit I don't see how it could have been since it appeared on the day the case went to the jury, but I intend to —"

"Mr. Freyer." Wolfe was showing him a palm. "If you please. I can simplify this for you."

"You can't simplify it until you explain it to my satisfaction."

"I know that. That's was I am prepared to do something I have rarely done, and should never do except under compulsion. It is now compelled by extraordinary circumstances. I'm going to tell you what a client of mine has told me. Of course you're a member of the New York bar?"

"Certainly."

"And you are attorney-of-record for Peter Hays?"

"Yes."

"Then I'm going to tell you something in confidence."

Freyer's eyes narrowed. "I will not be bound in confidence in any matter affecting my client's interests."

"I wouldn't expect you to. The only bond will be your respect for another man's privacy. The interests of your client and my client may or may not intersect. If they do we'll consider the matter; if they don't, I shall rely on your discretion. This is the genesis of that advertisement."

He told him. He didn't report our long session with James R. Herold verbatim, but neither did he skimp it. When he was through, Freyer had a clear and complete picture of where we stood up to four o'clock that afternoon, when Freyer had rung our doorbell. The lawyer was a good listener and had interrupted only a couple of times, once to get a point straight and once to ask to see the picture of Paul Herold.

"Before I go on," Wolfe said, "I invite vertification. Of course Mr. Goodwin's corroboration would have no validity for you, but you may inspect his transcription of the notes he made, five typewritten pages. Or you can phone Lieutenant Murphy, provided you don't tell him who you are. On that of course, I am at your mercy. At this juncture I don't want him to start investigating a possible connection between your P.H. and my P.H."

"Verification can wait," Freyer conceded. "You would be a fool to invent such a tale, and I'm quite aware that you're not a fool." He had backed up in the chair and got more comfortable. "Finish it up."

"There's not much more. When you told Mr. Goodwin that your client's background was unknown to you and that he had no family, he decided he had better have a look at Peter Hays, and he went to the courtroom for that purpose. His first glimpse of him, when he was brought into court, left him uncertain; but when, upon hearing the verdict, your client rose and turned to face the crowd, his face had a quite different expression. It had, or Mr. Goodwin thought it had, an almost conclusive resemblance to the picture of the youthful Paul Herold. When you asked to see the picture, I asked you to wait. Now I ask you to look at it. Archie?"

I got one from the drawer and went and handed it to Freyer. He studied it a while, shut his eyes, opened them again, and studied it some more. "It could be," he conceded. "It could easily be." He looked at it some more. "Or it couldn't." He looked at me. "What was it about his face when he turned to look at the crowd?"

"There was life in it. There was—uh—spirit. As I told Mr. Wolfe, he was telling someone to go to hell, or ready to."

Freyer shook his head. "I've never seen him like that, with any life in him. The first time I saw him he said he might as well be dead. He had nothing but despair, and he never has had."

"I take it," Wolfe said, "that as far as you know he *could* be Paul Herold. You know nothing of his background or connections that precludes it?"

"No." The lawyer considered it. "No, I don't. He has refused to disclose his background, and he says he has no living relatives. That was one of the things against him with the District Attorney—not evidential, of course, but you know how that is."

Wolfe nodded. "Now, do you wish to verify my account?"

"No. I accept it. As I said, you're not a fool."

"Then let's consider the situation. I would like to ask two questions."

"Go ahead."

"Is your client in a position to pay adequately for your services?"

"No, he isn't. Adequately, no. That is no secret. I took the case at the request of a friend—the head of the advertising agency he works for—or worked for. All his associates at the agency like him and speak well of him, and so do others—all his friends and acquaintances I have had contact with. I could have had dozens of character witnesses if that would have helped any. But in addition to the prison bars he has erected his own barrier to shut the world out—even his best friends."

"Then if he is Paul Herold it seems desirable to establish that fact. My client is a man of substantial means. I am not trying to stir your cupidity, but the laborer is worthy of his hire. If you're convinced of your client's innocence you will want to appeal, and that's expensive. My second question: will you undertake to resolve our doubt? Will you find out, the sooner the better, whether your P.H. is my P.H.?"

"Well." Freyer put his elbows on the chair arms and flattened his palms together. "I don't know. He's a very difficult man. He wouldn't take the stand. I wanted him to, but he wouldn't. I don't know how I'd go about this. He would resent it, I'm sure of that, after the attitude he has taken to my questions about his background, and it might become impossible for me to continue to represent him." Abruptly he leaned forward and his eyes gleamed. "And I want to represent him! I'm convinced he was framed, and there's still a chance of proving it!"

"Then if you will permit a suggestion"—Wolfe was practically purring—"do you agree that it's desirable to learn if he is Paul Herold?"

"Certainly. You say your client is in Omaha?"

"Yes. He returned last night."

"Wire him to come back. When he comes tell him how it stands, and I'll arrange somehow for him to see my client."

Wolfe shook his head. "That won't do. If I find that it is his son who has been convicted of murder of course I'll have to tell him, but I will not tell him that it *may* be his son who has been convicted of murder and ask him to resolve the matter. If it is not his son, what am I? A bungler. But for my suggestion: if you'll arrange for Mr. Goodwin to see him and speak with him, that will do it."

"How?" The lawyer frowned. "Goodwin has already seen him."

"I said 'and speak with him.'" Wolfe turned. "Archie. How long would you need with him to give us a firm conclusion?"

"Alone?"

"Yes. I suppose a guard would be present."

"I don't mind guards. Five minutes might do it. Make it ten."

Wolfe went back to Freyer. "You don't know Mr. Goodwin, but I do. And he will manage it so that no resentment will bounce to you. He is remarkably adroit at drawing resentment to himself to divert it from me or one of my clients. You can tell the District Attorney that he is investigating some aspect of the case for you; and as for your client, you can safely leave that to Mr. Goodwin." He glanced up at the wall clock. "It could be done this evening. Now. I invite you to dine with me here. The sooner it's settled the better, both for you and for me."

But Freyer wouldn't buy that. His main objection was that it would be difficult to get access to his convicted client at that time of day even for himself, but also he wanted to think it over. It would have to wait until morning. When Wolfe sees that a point has to be conceded he manages not to be grumpy about it, and the conference ended much more sociably than it had begun. I went to the hall with Freyer and got his coat from the rack and helped him on with it, and let him out.

Back in the office, Wolfe was trying not to look smug. As I took the picture of Paul Herold from his desk to return it to the drawer, he remarked, "I confess his coming was opportune, but after your encounter with him in the courtroom it was to be expected."

"Uh-huh." I closed the drawer. "You planned it that way. Your gifts. It might backfire on you if his thinking it over includes a phone call to Omaha or even one to the Missing Persons Bureau. However, I admit you did the best you could, even inviting him to dinner. As you know, I have a date this evening, and now I can keep it."

So he dined alone, and I was only half an hour late joining the gathering at Lily Rowan's table at the Flamingo Club. We followed the usual routine, deciding after a couple of hours that the dance floor was too crowded and moving to Lily's penthouse, where we could do our own crowding. Getting home around three o'clock, I went to the office and switched a light on for a glance at my desk, where Wolfe leaves a note if there is something that needs early-morning attention, found it bare, and mounted the two flights to my room.

For me par in bed is eight full hours, but of course I have to make exceptions, and Wednesday morning I entered the kitchen at nine-thirty, only half awake but with my hair brushed and my clothes on, greeted Fritz with forced cheerfulness, got my orange juice, which I take at room temperature, from the table, and had just swallowed a gulp when the phone rang. I answered it there, and had Albert Freyer's voice in my ear. He said he had arranged it and I was to meet him in the City Prison visitors' room at ten-thirty. I said I wanted to be alone with his client, and he said he understood that but he had to be there to identify me and vouch for me.

I hung up and turned to Fritz. "I'm being pushed, damn it. Can I have two cakes in a hurry? Forget the sausage, just the cakes and honey and coffee."

He protested, but he moved. "It's a bad way to start a day, Archie, cramming your breakfast down."

I told him I was well aware of it and buzzed the plant rooms on the house phone to tell Wolfe.

4

I wasn't exactly alone. Ten feet to my right a woman sat on a wooden chair just like mine, staring through the holes of the steel lattice at a man on the other side. By bending an ear I could have caught what the man was saying, but I didn't try because I assumed she was as much in favor of privacy as I was. Ten feet to my left a man on another chair like mine was also staring through the lattice, at a lad who wasn't as old as Paul Herold had been when the picture was taken. I couldn't help hearing what he was saying, and apparently he didn't give a damn. The boy across the lattice from him was looking bored. There were three or four cops around, and the one who had brought me in was standing back near the wall, also looking bored.

During the formalities of getting passed in, which had been handled by Freyer, I had been told that I would be allowed fifteen minutes, and I was about to leave my chair to tell the cop that I hoped he wouldn't start timing me until the prisoner arrived, when a door opened in the wall on the other side of the lattice and there he was, with a guard behind his elbow. The guard steered him across to a chair opposite me and then backed up to the wall, some five paces. The convict sat on the edge of the chair and blinked through the holes at me.

"I don't know you," he said. "Who are you?"

At that moment, with his pale hollow cheeks and his dead eyes and his lips so thin he almost didn't have any, he looked a lot more than eleven years away from the kid in the flattop.

I hadn't decided how to open up because I do better if I wait until I have a man's face to choose words. I had a captive audience, of course, but that wouldn't help if he clammed up on me. I tried to get his eyes, but the damn lattice was in the way.

"My name is Goodwin," I told him. "Archie Goodwin. Have you ever heard of a private detective named Nero Wolfe?"

"Yes, I've heard of him. What do you want?" His voice was hollower than his cheeks and deader than his eyes.

"I work for Mr. Wolfe. Day before yesterday your father, James R. Herold, came to his office and hired him to find you. He said he had learned that you didn't steal that money eleven years ago, and he wanted to make it square with you. The way things stand that may not mean much to you, but there it is."

Considering the circumstances, he did pretty well. His jaw sagged for a second, but he jerked it up, and his voice was just the same when he said, "I don't know what you're talking about. My name is Peter Hays."

I nodded at him. "I knew you'd say that, of course. I'm sorry, Mr. Herold, but it won't work. The trouble is that Mr. Wolfe needs money, and he uses part of it to pay my salary. So we're going to inform your father that we have found you, and of course he'll be coming to see you. The reason I'm here, we thought it was only fair to let you know about it before he comes."

"I haven't got any father." His jaw was stiff now, and it affected his voice. "You're wrong. You've made a mistake. If he comes I won't see him!"

I shook my head. "Let's keep our voices down. What about the scar on your left leg on the inside of the knee? It's no go, Mr. Herold. Perhaps you can refuse to see your father — I don't know how much say they give a man in your situation — but he'll certainly come when we notify him. By the way, if we had had any doubt at all of your identity you have just settled it, the way you said if he comes you won't see him. Why should you get excited about it if he's not your father? If we've made a mistake the easiest way to prove it is to let him come and take a look at you. We didn't engage to persuade you to see him; our job was just to find you, and we've done that, and if —"

I stopped because he started to shake. I could have got up and left, since my mission was accomplished, but Freyer wouldn't like it if I put his client in a state of collapse and just walked out on him, and after all Freyer had got me in. So I stuck. There was a counter on both sides to keep us away from the lattice, and he had his fists on his, rubbing it with little jerks.

"Hang on," I told him. "I'm going. We thought you ought to know."

"Wait." He stopped shaking. "Will you wait?"

"Sure."

He took his fists off the counter, and his head thrust forward. "I can't see you very well. Listen to me, for God's sake. For God's sake don't tell him. You don't know what he's like."

"Well, I've met him."

"And my mother and sisters, they'll know. I think they believed I was framed on stealing that money, I think they believed me, but he didn't, and now I've been framed again. For God's sake don't tell him. This time it's all over, I'm going to die, and I might as well be dead now, and it's not fair for me to have this too. I don't want them to know. My God, don't you see how it is?"

"Yeah, I see how it is." I was wishing I had gone.

"Then promise me you won't tell him. You look like a decent guy. If I've got to die for something I didn't do, all right, I can't do anything about that, but not this too. I know I'm not saying this right, I know I'm not myself, but if you only—"

I didn't know why he stopped, because, listening to him, I didn't hear the cop approaching from behind. There was a tap on my shoulder and the cop's voice.

"Time's up."

I arose.

"Promise me!" Paul Herold demanded.

"I can't," I told him, and turned and walked out.

Freyer was waiting for me in the visitors' rooom. I don't carry a mirror, so I don't know how my face looked when I joined him, but when we had left the building and were on the sidewalk, he asked, "It didn't work?"

"You can't always tell by my expression," I said. "Ask the people I play poker with. But if you don't mind I'll save it for Mr. Wolfe, since he pays my salary. Coming along?"

Evidently he was. I'll hand it to him that he could take a hint. In the taxi, when I turned my head to the window to study the scenery as we rolled along, he made no attempt to start a conversation. But he overdid it a little. When we stopped at the curb in front of the old brownstone, he spoke.

"If you want a word with Wolfe first I'll wait out here."

I laughed. "No, come on in and I'll find you some earmuffs."

I preceded him up the stoop and pushed the button, and Fritz let us in, and we put our hats and coats on the rack and went down the hall to the office. Wolfe, at his desk pouring beer, shot me a glance, greeted Freyer, and asked if he would like some beer. The lawyer declined and took the red leather chair without waiting for an invitation.

I stood and told Wolfe, "I saw him and talked with him. Instead of a yes or no, I'd like to give you a verbatim report. Do you want Mr. Freyer to hear it?"

Wolfe lifted his glass from the tray. "Is there any reason why he shouldn't?"

"No, sir."

"Then go ahead."

I didn't ham it, but I gave them all the words, which was no strain, since the only difference between me and a tape recorder is that a tape recorder can't lie. I lie to Wolfe only on matters that are none of his business, and this was his business. As I say, I didn't ham it, but I thought they ought to have a clear picture, so I described Paul Herold's condition—his stiff jaw, his shaking, his trying to shove his fists through the counter, and the look in his eyes when he said it wasn't fair for him to have this too. I admit one thing: I made the report standing up so I could put my fists on Wolfe's desk to show how Paul Herold's had looked on the counter. When I was through I slid the chair out from my desk and sat.

"If you still want a firm conclusion," I said, "it is yes."

Wolfe put his glass down, took in air clear to his belly button, and shut his eyes.

Freyer was shaking his head with his jaw set. "I've never had a case like it," he said, apparently to himself, "and I never want another one." He looked at Wolfe. "What are you going to do? You can't just shut your eyes on it."

"They're my eyes," Wolfe muttered, keeping them closed. In a moment he opened them. "Archie. That's why you wanted Mr. Freyer to hear your report, to make it even more difficult."

I lifted my shoulders and dropped them. "No argument."

"Then send Mr. Herold a telegram, saying merely that we have found his son, alive and well, here in New York. That was our job. Presumably he will come."

Freyer made a noise and came forward in his chair. I looked at Wolfe, swallowed, and spoke.

"You do it. I've got a sore finger. Just dial Western Union, WO two-seven-one-one-one."

He laughed. A stranger would have called it a snort, but I know his different snorts. He laughed some more.

"It's fairly funny," I said, "but have you heard the one about the centipede in the shoe store?"

Freyer said positively, "I think we should discuss it."

Wolfe nodded. "I agree. I was merely forcing Mr. Goodwin to reveal his position." He looked at me. "You prefer to wire Mr. Herold that I have decided I don't like the job?"

"If those are the only alternatives, yes. As he said, he might as well be dead. He's practically a corpse, and I don't have to rob corpses to eat and neither do you."

"Your presentment is faulty," Wolfe objected. "No robbery is contemplated. However I am quite willing to consider other alternatives. The decision, of course, is mine. Mr. Herold gave me the job of finding his son, and it is wholly in my discretion whether to inform him that the job is done."

He stopped to drink some beer. Freyer said, "As the son's attorney, I have some voice in the matter."

Wolfe put the glass down and passed his tongue over his lips. "No, sir. Not on this specific question. However, though you have no voice you certainly have an interest, and it deserves to be weighed. We'll look at it first. Those two alteratives, telling my client that his son is found, or telling him that I withdraw from my job, call them A and B. If A, my surmise is that you would be through. He would come to see his son, and survey the situation, and decide whether to finance an appeal. If he decided no, that would end it. If he decided yes, he would probably also decide that you had mishandled the case and he would hire another lawyer. I base that on the impression I got of him. Archie?"

"Right." I was emphatic.

Wolfe returned to Freyer "And if B, you'd be left where you are now. How much would an appeal cost?"

"That depends. A lot of investigation would be required. As a minimum, twenty thousand dollars. To fight it through to the end, using every expedient, a lot more."

"Your client can't furnish it?"

"No."

"Can you?"

"No."

"Then B is no better for you than A. Now what about me? A should be quite simple and satisfactory. I've done a job and I collect my fee. But not only must I pay my bills, I must also sustain my self-esteem. That man, your client, has been wounded in his very bowels, and to add insult to his injury as a mere mercenary would be a wanton act. I can't afford it. Even if I must gainsay Rochefoucauld, who wrote that we should only affect compassion, and carefully avoid having any."

He picked up his glass, emptied it, and put it down. "Won't you have some beer? Or something else?"

"No, thank you. I never drink before cocktail time."

"Coffee? Milk? Water?"

"No, thanks."

"Very well. As for *B*, I can't afford that either. I've done what I was hired to do, and I intend to be paid. And I have another reason for rejecting *B*. It would preclude my taking any further interest in this affair, and I don't like that. You said yesterday that you are convinced that your client is innocent. I can't say that I am likewise convinced, but I strongly suspect that you're right. With reason."

He paused because we were both staring and he loves to make people stare.

"With reason?" Freyer demanded. "What reason?"

Satisfied with the stares, he resumed. "When Mr. Goodwin left here yesterday afteroon to go to look at your client, a man followed him. Why? It's barely possible that it was someone bearing a grudge on account of some former activity of ours, but highly unlikely. It would be puerile for such a person to merely follow Mr. Goodwin when he left the house. He must be somehow connected with a present activity, and we are engaged in none at the moment except Mr. Herold's job. Was Mr. Herold checking on us? Absurd. The obvious probability is that my advertisement was responsible. Many people—newspapers, the police, you youself—had assumed that it was directed at Peter Hays and others might well have done so. One, let us say, named X. X wants to know why I declare Peter Hays to be innocent, but does not come, or phone, to ask me; and he wants to know what I am doing about it. What other devices he may have resorted to, I don't know; but one of them was to come, or send someone, to stand post near my house."

Wolfe turned a hand over. "How account for so intense and furtive a curiosity? If the murder for whch Peter Hays was on trial was what it appeared to be—a simple and common-place act of passion—who could be so inquisitive and also so stealthy? Then it wasn't so simple. You said yesterday that you were convinced that your client was the victim of a diabolical frame-up. If you're correct, no wonder a man was sent to watch my house when I announced, on the last day of his trial, that he was known to be innocent—as was assumed. And it is with reason that I suspect that there is someone, somewhere, who felt himself threatened by my announcement. That doesn't convince me that your client is innocent, but it poses a question that needs an answer."

Freyer turned to me. "Who followed you?"

I told him I didn't know, and told him why, and described the tail.

He said the description suggested no one to him and went back to Wolfe. "Then you reject *A* and *B* for both of us. Is there a *C?*"

"I think there is," Wolfe declared. "You want to appeal. Can you take preliminary steps for an appeal without committing yourself to any substantial outlay for thirty days?"

"Yes. Easily."

"Very well. You want to appeal and I want to collect my fee. I warned my client that the search might take months. I shall tell him merely that I am working on his problem, as I shall be. You will give me all the information you have, all of it, and I'll investigate. In thirty days—much less, I hope—I'll know where we stand. If it is hopeless there will be nothing for it but *A* or *B*, and that decision can wait. If it is promising we'll proceed. If and when we get evidence that will clear your client, my client will be informed and he will foot the bill. Your client may not like it but he'll have to lump it; and anyway, I doubt if he would really rather die in the electric chair than face his father again, especially since he will be under no burden of guilt, either of theft or of murder. I make this proposal not as a paragon, but only as a procedure less repugnant than either *A* or *B*. Well, sir?"

The lawyer was squinting at him. "You say you'll investigate. Who will pay for that?"

"I will. That's the rub. I'll hope to get it back."

"But if you don't?"

"Then I don't."

"There should be a written agreement."

"There won't be. I take the risk of failure; you'll have to take the risk of my depravity." Wolfe's voice suddenly became a bellow. "Confound it, it is your client who has been convicted of murder, not mine!"

Freyer was startled, as well he might be. Wolfe can bellow. "I meant no offense," he said mildly. "I had no thought of depravity. As you say, the risk is yours. I accept your proposal. Now what?"

Wolfe glanced up at the wall clock and settled back in his chair. A full hour till lunchtime. "Now," he said, "I want all the facts. I've read the newspaper accounts, but I want them from you."

5

PETER HAYS had been convicted of killing the husband of the woman he loved, on the evening of January 3, by shooting him in the side of the head, above the left ear, with a Marley .38. I might as well account for things as I go along, but I can't account for the Marley because it had been taken by a burglar from a house in Poughkeepsie in 1947 and hadn't been seen in public since. The prosecution hadn't explained how Peter Hays had got hold of it, so you can't expect me to.

The victim, Michael M. Molloy, forty-three, a real-estate broker, had lived with his wife, no children, in a four-room apartment on the top floor, the fifth, of a remodeled tenement on East 52nd Street. There was no other apartment on the floor. At 9:18 P.M. on January 3 a man had phoned police headquarters and said he had just heard a shot fired on one of the upper floors of the house next door. He gave the address of the house next door, 171 East 52nd Street, but hung up without giving his name, and he had never been located, though of course the adjoining houses had been canvassed. At 9:23 a cop from a prowl car had entered the building. When he got to the top floor, after trying two floors below and drawing blanks, he found the door standing open and entered. Two men were inside, one alive and one dead. The dead one, Molloy, was on the living-room floor. The live one, Peter Hays, with his hat and topcoat on, had apparently been about to leave, and when the cop had stopped him he had tried to tear away and had to be subdued. When he was under control the cop had frisked him and found the Marley .38 in his topcoat pocket.

All that had been in the papers. Also:

Peter Hays was a copywriter. He had been with the same advertising agency, one of the big ones, for eight years, and that was as far back as he went. His record and reputation were clean, with no high or low spots. Unmarried, he had lived for the past three years in an RBK — room, bath and kitchenette — on West 63rd Street. He played tennis, went to shows and movies, got along all right with people, had a canary in his room, owned five suits of clothes, four pairs of shoes, and three hats, and had no car. A key to the street door of 171 East 52nd Street had been found on his key ring. The remodeled building had a do-it-yourself elevator, and there was no doorman.

The District Attorney's office, the personnel of Homicide West, all the newspapers, and millions of citizens, were good and sore at Peter Hays because he wasn't playing the game. The DA and cops couldn't check his version of what had happened, and the papers couldn't have it analyzed by experts, and the citizens couldn't get into arguments about it, because he supplied no version. From the time he had been arrested until the verdict came, he had refused to supply anything at all. He had finally, urged by his lawyer, answered one question put by the DA in a private interview: had he shot Molloy? No. But why and when had he gone to the apartment? What were his relations with Molloy and with his wife? Why was a key to that building on his key ring? Why did he have the Marley .38 in his pocket? No reply. Nor to a thousand other questions.

Other people had been more chatty, some of them on the witness stand. The Molloy's daily maid had seen Mrs. Molloy and the defendant in close embrace on three different occasions during the past six months, but she had not told Mr. Molloy because she liked Mrs. Molloy and it was none of her business. Even so, Mr. Molloy must have been told something by somebody, or seen or heard something, because the maid had heard him telling her off and had seen him twisting her arm until she collapsed. A private detective, hired by Molloy late in November, had seen Mrs. Molloy and Peter Hays meet at a restaurant for lunch four times, but nothing juicier. There were others, but those were the outstanding items.

The prosecution's main attraction, though not its mainstay, had been the widow, Selma Molloy. She was twenty-nine, fourteen years younger than her husband, and was photogenic, judging from the pictures the papers had run. Her turn on the witness stand had sparked a debate. The Assistant DA had claimed the right to ask her certain questions because she was a hostile witness, and the judge had refused to allow the claim. For example, the ADA had tried to ask her, "Was Peter Hays your lover?" but he had to settle for "What were the relations between you and Peter Hays?"

She said she liked Peter Hays very much. She said she regarded him as a good friend, and she had affection for him, and believed he had affection for her. The relations between them could not properly be called misconduct. As for the relations between her and her husband, she had begun to feel less than a year after their marriage, which had taken place three years ago, that the marriage had been a mistake. She should have known it would be, since for a year before their marriage she had worked for Molloy as his secretary, and she should have known what kind of man he was. The prosecutor had fired at her, "Do you think he was the kind of man who should be murdered?" and Freyer had objected and been sustained, and the prosecutor had asked, "What kind of man was he?" Freyer had objected to that too as calling for an opinion on the part of the witness, and that had started another debate. It was brought out, specifically, that he had falsely accused her of infidelity, had physically mistreated her, had abused her in the presence of others, and had refused to let her get a divorce.

She had seen Peter Hays at a New Year's Eve party three days before the murder, and had not seen him since until she entered the courtroom that day. She had spoken with him on the telephone on January 1 and again on January 2, but she couldn't remember the details of the conversations, only that nothing noteworthy had been said. The evening of January 3 a woman friend had phoned around seven-thirty to say that she had an extra ticket for a show and invited her to come, and she had accepted. When she got home, around midnight, there were policemen in her apartment and she was told the news.

Freyer had not cross-examined her. One of the hundred or so details of privileged communications between a lawyer and a client furnished us by Freyer explained that. He had promised Peter Hays he wouldn't.

Wolfe snorted, not his laughing snort. "Isn't it," he inquired, "a function of counsel to determine the strategy and tactics of defense?"

"When he can, yes." Freyer, who had spent three-quarters of an hour reviewing the testimony and answering questions about it, had lubricated himself with a glass of water. "Not with this client. I've said he is difficult. Mrs. Molloy was the prosecution's last witness. I had five, and none of them helped any. Do you want to discuss them?"

"No." Wolfe looked at the wall clock. Twenty minutes to lunch. "I've read the newspaper accounts. I would like to know why you're convinced of his innocence."

"Well—it's a combination of things. His expressions, his tones of voice, his reactions to my questions and suggestions, some questions he has asked me—many things. But there was one specific thing. During my first talk with him, the day after he was arrested, I got the idea that he had refused to answer any of their questions because he wanted to protect Mrs. Molloy— either from being accused of the murder, or of complicity, or merely from harassment. At our second talk I got a little further with him. I told him that exchanges between a lawyer and his client were privileged and their disclosure could not be compelled, and that if he continued to withhold vital information from me I would have to retire from the case. He asked what would happen if I did retire and he engaged no other counsel, and I said the court would appoint counsel to defend him; that on a capital charge he would have to be represented by counsel. He asked if anything he told me would have to come out at the trial, and I said not without his consent."

The water glass had been refilled and he took a sip. "Then he told me some things, and more later. He said that on the evening of January third he had been in his apartment, alone, and had just turned on the radio for the nine-o'clock news when the phone rang. He answered it, and a man's voice said, 'Pete Hays? This is a friend. I just left the Molloys, and Mike was starting to beat her up. Do you hear me?' He said yes and started to ask a question, but the man hung up. He grabbed his hat and coat and ran, took a taxi across the park, used his key on the street door, took the elevator to the fifth floor, found the door of the Molloy apartment ajar, and went in. Molloy was lying there. He looked through the apartment and found no one. He went back to Molloy and decided he was dead. A gun was on a chair against the wall, fifteen feet from the body. He picked it up and put it in his pocket, and was looking around to see if there was anything else when he heard footsteps in the hall. He thought he would hide, then thought he wouldn't, and as he started for the door the policeman entered. That was his story. This is the first time anyone has heard it but me. I could have traced the cab, but why spend money on it? It could have happened just as he said, with only one difference, that Molloy was alive when he arrived."

Wolfe grunted. "Then I don't suppose that convinced you of his innocence."

"Certainly not. I'll come to that. To clean up as I go along: when I had him talking I asked why he had the key, and he said that on taking Mrs. Molloy home from the New Year's Eve party he had taken her key to open the door for her and had carelessly neglected to return it to her. Probably not true."

"Nor material. The problem is murder, not the devices of gallantry. What else?"

"I told him that it was obvious that he was deeply attached to Mrs. Molloy and was trying to protect her. His rushing to her on getting the anonymous phone call, his putting the gun in his pocket, his refusal to talk to the police, not only made that conclusive but also strongly indicated that he believed, or suspected, that she had killed her husband. He didn't admit it, but he didn't deny it, and for myself I was sure of it — provided he hadn't killed him himself. I told him that his refusal to divulge matters even to his attorney was understandable as long as he held that suspicion, but that now that Mrs. Molloy was definitely out of it I expected of him full and candid cooperation. She was completely in the clear, I said, because the woman and two men with whom she had attended the theater had stated that she had been with them constantly throughout the evening. I had a newspaper with me containing that news, and had him read it. He started to tremble, and the newspaper shook in his hands, and he called on God to bless me. I told him he needed God's blessing more than I did."

Freyer cleared his throat and took a gulp of water. "Then he read it again, more slowly, and his expression changed. He said that the woman and the men were old and close friends of Mrs. Molloy and would do anything for her. That if she had left the theater for part of the time they wouldn't hesitate to lie for her and say she hadn't. That there was no point in his spilling his guts—his phrase—unless it cleared him of the murder charge, and it probably wouldn't, and even if it did, then she would certainly be suspected and her alibi would be checked, and if it proved to be false she would be where he was then. I couldn't very well impeach his logic."

"No," Wolfe agreed.

"But I was convinced of his innocence. His almost hysterical relief on learning of her alibi, then the doubt creeping in, then his changing expression as he read the paper again and grasped the possibilities—if that was all counterfeit I should be disbarred for incompetence."

"Certainly I'm not competent to judge," Wolfe stated, "since I didn't see him. But since I have my own reason for not thinking it as simple as it seems I won't challenge yours. What else?"

"Nothing positive. Only negatives. I had to promise him I wouldn't cross-examine Mrs. Molloy, or quit the case, and I didn't want to quit. I had to accept his refusal to take the witness stand. If he had been framed the key question was the identity of the man who had made the phone call that made him dash to the Molloy apartment, but he said he had spent hours trying to connect the voice with someone he knew, and couldn't. The voice had been hoarse and guttural and presumably disguised, and he couldn't even guess.

"Two other negatives. He knew of no one who bore him enough ill will to frame him for murder, and he knew of no one who might have wanted Molloy out of the way. In fact he knows very little about Molloy—if he is to be believed, and I think he is. Of course the ideal suspect would be a man who coveted Mrs. Molloy and schemed to remove both her husband and Peter Hays at one stroke, but he is sure there is no such man. On these matters, and others, I have had no better luck with Mrs. Molloy."

"You have talked with her?"

"Three times. Once briefly and twice at length. She wanted me to arrange for her to see Peter, but he refused to permit it. She wouldn't tell me much about her relations with Peter, and there was no point in pressing her; I knew all I needed to know about that. I spent most of my time with her asking about her husband's activities and associates—everything about him. It had become apparent that I couldn't possibly get my client acquitted unless I found a likely candidate to replace him. She told me all she could, in fact she told me a lot, but there was a drag on her, and it wasn't hard to guess what the drag was. She thought Peter had killed her husband. The poor woman was pathetic; she kept asking me questions about the gun. It was obvious how her mind was working. She was willing to accept it that Peter had acted in a fit of passion, but if it had happened that way, how account for his having the gun with him? I asked her if there was any chance that the gun had been her husband's, there in the apartment, and she was sure there wasn't. When I told her that Peter had denied his guilt, and that I believed him, and why, she just stared at me. I asked her if she had in fact been continuously with her companions at the theater that evening, and she said yes, but her mind wasn't on that, it was on Peter. I honestly think she was trying to decide whether I really believed him or was only pretending to. As for what she told me about her husband, I didn't have the funds for a proper investigation —"

He stopped because Fritz had entered and was standing there. Fritz spoke. "Luncheon is ready, sir."

Wolfe got up. "If you'll join us, Mr. Freyer? There'll be enough to go around. Chicken livers and mushrooms in white wine. Rice cakes. Another place, Fritz."

6

AT four o'clock that afternoon I left the house, bound for 171 East 52nd Street, to keep an appointment, made for me by Freyer, with Mrs. Michael M. Molloy.

After lunch we had returned to the office and taken up where we had left off. Freyer had phoned his office to send us the complete file on the case, and it had arrived and been pawed over. I had summoned Saul Panzer, Fred Durkin, Orrie Cather, and Johnny Keems to report to the office at six o'clock. They were our four main standbys, and they would call for a daily outlay of $160, not counting expenses. If it lasted a month, 30 times $160 equals 4800, so Wolfe's self-esteem might come high if he found he couldn't deliver.

Nothing had come of any of the leads suggested by what Mrs. Molloy had told Freyer about her deceased husband, and no wonder, since they had been investigated only by a clerk in Freyer's office and a sawbuck squirt supplied by the Harland Ide Detective Agency. I will concede that they had dug up some relevant facts: Molloy had had a two-room office in a twenty-story hive on 46th Street near Madison Avenue, and it said on the door MICHAEL M. MOLLOY, REAL ESTATE. His staff had consisted of a secretary and an errand boy. His rent had been paid for January, which was commendable, since January 1 had been a holiday and he had died on the third. If he had left a will, it had not turned up. He had been a fight fan and an ice-hockey fan. During the last six months of his life he had taken his current secretary, whose name was Delia Brandt, to dinner at a restaurant two or three times a week, but the clerk and the squirt hadn't got any deeper into that.

Mrs. Molloy hadn't been very helpful about his business affairs. She said that during her tenure as his secretary he had apparently transacted most of his business outside the office, and she had never known much about it. He had opened his own mail, which hadn't been heavy, and she had written only ten or twelve letters a week for him, and less than half of them had been on business matters. Her chief function had been to answer the phone and take messages when he was absent, and he had been absent most of the time. Apparently he had been interested almost exclusively in rural properties; as far as she knew, he had never had a hand in any New York City real-estate transactions. She had no idea what his income was, or his assets.

As for people who might have had a motive for killing him, she had supplied the name of four men with whom he had been on bad terms, and they had been looked into, but none of them seemed very promising. One of them had merely got sore because Molloy had refused to pay on a bet the terms of which had been disputed, and the others weren't much better. It had to be a guy who had not only croaked Molloy but had also gone to a lot of trouble to see that someone else got hooked for it, specifically Peter Hays, and that called for a real character.

In the taxi on my way uptown, if someone had hopped in and offered me ten to one that we had grabbed the short end of the stick, I would have passed. I will ride my luck on occasion, but I like to pick the occasion.

Number 171 East 52nd Street was an old walk-up which had had a thorough job of upgrading, inside and out, along with the houses on either side. They had all been painted an elegant gray, one with yellow trim, one with blue, and one with green. In the vestibule I pushed the button at the top of the row, marked MOLLOY, took the receiver from the hook and put it to my ear, and in a moment was asked who it was. I gave my name, and, when the latch clicked, pushed the door open, entered, and took the do-it-yourself elevator to the fifth floor. Emerging, I took a look around, noting where the stairs were. After all, this was the scene of the crime, and I was a detective. Hearing my name called, I turned. She was standing in the doorway.

She was only eight steps away, and by the time I reached her I had made a decision which sometimes, with one female or another, may take me hours or even days. I wanted no part of her. The reason I wanted no part was that just one look had made it plain that if I permitted myself to want a part it would be extremely difficult to keep from going on and wanting the whole; and that was highly inadvisable in the circumstances. For one thing, it wouldn't have been fair to P.H., handicapped as he was. This would have to be strictly business, not only outwardly but inwardly. I admit I smiled at her as she moved aside to let me enter, but it was merely a professional smile.

The room she led me into, after I put my coat and hat on a chair in the foyer, was a large and attractive living room with three windows. It was the room that P.H. had entered to find a corpse — if you're on our side. The rugs and furniture had been selected by her. Don't ask me how I know that; I was there and saw them, and saw her with them. She went to a chair over near a window, and, invited, I moved one around to face her. She said that Mr. Freyer had told her on the phone that he was consulting with Nero Wolfe, and that Mr. Wolfe wanted to send his assistant, Mr. Goodwin, to have a talk with her, and that was all she knew. She did not add, "What do you want?"

"I don't know exactly how to begin," I told her, "because we have different opinions on a very important point. Mr. Freyer and Mr. Wolfe and I all think Peter Hays didn't kill your husband, and you think he did."

She jerked her chin up. "Why do you say that?"

"Because there's no use beating around the bush. You think it because there's nothing else for you to think, and anyhow you're not really thinking. You've been hit so hard that you're too numb to think. We're not. Our minds are free and we're trying to use them. But we'd like to be sure on one point: if we prove we're right, if we get him cleared—I don't say it looks very hopeful, but if we do—would you like that or wouldn't you?"

"Oh!" she cried. Her jaw loosened. She said, "Oh," again, but it was only a whisper.

"I'll call that a yes," I said. "Then just forget our difference of opinion, because opinions don't count anyway. Mr. Freyer spent five hours with Nero Wolfe today, and Mr. Wolfe is going to try to find evidence that will clear Peter Hays. He has seen reports of your conversations with Freyer, but they didn't help any. Since you were Molloy's secretary for a year and his wife for three years, Mr. Wolfe thinks it likely—or, say, possible—that at some time you saw or heard something that would help. Remember he is assuming that someone else killed Molloy. He thinks it's very improbable that a situation existed which resulted in Molloy's murder, and that he never said or did anything in your presence that had a bearing on it."

She shook her head, not at me but at fate. "If he did," she said, "I didn't know it."

"Of course you didn't. If you had you would have told Freyer. Mr. Wolfe wants to try to dig it up. He couldn't ask you to come to his office so he could start the digging himself, because he has to spend two hours every afternoon playing with orchids, and at six o'clock he has a conference scheduled with four of his men who are going to be given other assignments—on this case. So he sent me to start in with you. I'll tell you how it works by giving you an example. Once I saw him spend eight hours questioning a young woman about everything and nothing. She wasn't suspected of anything; he was merely hoping to get some little fact that would give him a start. At the end of eight hours he got it: she had once seen a newspaper with a piece cut out of the front page. With that fact for a start, he got proof that a man had committed a murder. That's how it works. We'll start at the beginning, when you were Molloy's secretary, and I'll ask questions. We'll keep at it as long as you can stand it."

"It seems—" Her hand fluttered. I caught myself noticing how nice her hands were, and had to remind myself that that had all been decided. She said, "It seems so empty. I mean I'm empty."

"You're not really empty, you're full. When and where did you first meet Molloy?"

"That was four years ago," she said. "The way you—what you want to try—wouldn't it be better to start later? If there was a situation, the way you say, it would have been more recent, wouldn't it?"

"You never know, Mrs. Molloy." It seemed stiff to be calling her Mrs. Molloy. She fully deserved to be called Selma. "Anyhow, I have my instructions from Mr. Wolfe—and by the way, I skipped something. I was to tell you how simple it could have been. Say I decided to kill Molloy and frame Peter Hays for it. The drugstore on the corner is perfectly placed for me. Having learned that you are out for the evening and Molloy is alone in the apartment, at nine o'clock I phone Peter Hays from the booth in the drugstore and tell me—Freyer has told you what Peter says I told him. Then I cross the street to this house, am admitted by Molloy, shoot him, leave the gun here on a chair, knowing it can't be traced, go back down to the street, watch the entrance from a nearby spot until I see Hays arrive in a taxi and enter the building, return to the drugstore, and phone the police that a shot has just been fired on the top floor of One-seventy-one East Fifty-second Street. You couldn't ask for anything simpler than that."

She was squinting at me, concentrating. It gave the corners of her eyes a little upturn. "I see," she said. "Then you're not just —" She stopped.

"Just playing games? No. We really mean it. Settle back and relax a little. When and where did you first meet Molloy?"

She interlaced her fingers. No relaxing. "I wanted another job. I was modeling and didn't like it, and I knew shorthand. An agency sent me to his office, and he hired me."

"Had you ever heard of him before?"

"No."

"What did he pay you?"

"I started at sixty, and in about two months he raised it to seventy."

"When did he begin to show a personal interest in you?"

"Why — almost right away. The second week he asked me to have dinner with him. I didn't accept, and I liked the way he took it. He knew how to be nice when he wanted to. He always was nice to me until after we were married."

"Exactly what were your duties? I know what you told Freyer, but we're going to fill in."

"There weren't many duties, really — I mean there wasn't much work. I opened the office in the morning — usually he didn't come until around eleven o'clock. I wrote his letters, but that didn't amount to much, and answered the phone, and did the filing, what there was of it. He opened the mail himself."

"Did you keep his books?"

"I don't think he had any books. I never saw any."

"Did you draw his checks?"

"I didn't at first, but later he asked me to sometimes."

"Where did he keep his checkbook?"

"In a drawer of his desk that he kept locked. There wasn't any safe in the office."

"Did you do any personal chores for him? Like getting prizefight tickets or buying neckties?"

"No. Or very seldom. He did things like that himself."

"Had he ever been married before?"

"No. He said he hadn't."

"Did you go to prizefights with him?"

"Sometimes I did, not often. I didn't like them. And later, the last two years, we didn't go places together much."

"Let's stick to the first year, while you were working for him. Were there many callers at the office?"

"Not many, no. Many days there weren't any."

"How many in an average week, would you say?"

"Perhaps —" She thought. "I don't know, perhaps eight or nine. Maybe a dozen."

"Take the first week you were there. You were new then and noticing things. How many callers were there the first week, and who were they?"

She opened her eyes at me. Wide open, they were quite different from when they were squinting. I merely noted that fact professionally. "But Mr. Goodwin," she said, "that's impossible. It was four years ago!"

I nodded. "That's just a warm-up. Before we're through you'll be remembering lots of things you would have thought impossible, and most of them will be irrelevant and immaterial. I hope not all of them. Try it. Callers the first week."

We kept at it for nearly two hours, and she did her best. She enjoyed none of it, and some of it was really painful, when we were on the latter part of the year, the period when she was cottoning to Molloy, or thought she was, and was making up her mind to marry him. She would have preferred to let the incidents of that period stay where they were, down in the cellar. I won't say it hurt me as much as it did her, since with me it was strictly business, but it was no picnic. Finally she said she didn't think she could go on, and I said we had barely started.

"Then tomorrow?" she asked. "I don't know why, but this seems to be tougher than it was with the police and the District Attorney. That seems strange, since they were enemies and you're a friend — you are a friend, aren't you?"

It was a trap, and I dodged it. "I want what you want," I told her.

"I know you do, but I just can't go on. Tomorrow?"

"Sure. Tomorrow morning. But I'll have some other errands, so it will have to be with Mr. Wolfe. Could you be at his office at eleven o'clock?"

"I suppose I could, but I'd rather go on with you."

"He's not so bad. If he growls just ignore it. He'll dig up something quicker than I would, in order to get rid of you. He doesn't appreciate women, and I do." I got out a card and handed it to her. "There's the address. Tomorrow at eleven?"

She said yes, and got up to see me to the door, but I told her that with a friend it wasn't necessary.

7

WHEN I got back to 35th Street it was half-past six and the conference was in full swing.

I was pleased to see that Saul Panzer was in the red leather chair. Unquestionably Johnny Keems had made a go for it, and Wolfe himself must have shooed him off. Johnny, who at one time, under delusions of grandeur, had decided my job would look better on him or he would look better on it, no matter which, but had found it necessary to abandon the idea, was a pretty good operative but had to be handled. Fred Durkin, big and burly and bald, knows exactly what he can expect of his brains and what he can't, which is more than you can say for a lot of people with a bigger supply. Orrie Cather is smart, both in action and in appearance. As for Saul Panzer, I thoroughly approve of his preference for free-lancing, since if he decided he wanted my job he would get it or anybody else's.

Saul, as I say, was in the red leather chair, and the others had three of the yellow ones in a row facing Wolfe's desk. I got greetings and returned them, and circled around to my place. Wolfe remarked that he hadn't expected me so early.

"I tired her out," I told him. "Her heart was willing but her mind was weak. She'll be here at eleven in the morning. Do you want it now?"

"If you got anything promising."

"I don't know whether I did or not. We were at it nearly two hours, and mostly it was just stirring up the dust, but there were a couple of things, maybe three, that you might want to hear. One day in the fall of nineteen fifty-two, she thinks it was October, a man called at the office, and there was a row that developed into combat. She heard a crash and went in, and the caller was flat on the floor. Molloy told her he would handle it, and she returned to the other room, and pretty soon the caller came out on his feet and left. She doesn't know his name, and she didn't hear what the row was about because the door between the rooms was shut."

Wolfe grunted. "I hope we're not reduced to that. And?"

"This one was earlier. In the early summer. For a period of about two weeks a woman phoned the office nearly every day. If Molloy was out she left word for him to call Janet. If Molloy was in and took the call he told her he couldn't discuss the matter on the phone and rang off. Then the calls stopped and Janet was never heard from again."

"Does Mrs. Molloy know what she wanted to discuss?"

"No. She never listened in. She wouldn't."

He sent me a sharp glance. "Are you bewitched again?"

"Yes, sir. It took four seconds, even before she spoke. From now on you'll pay me but I'll really be working for her. I want her to be happy. When that's attended to I'll go off to some island and mope." Orrie Cather laughed, and Johnny Keems tittered. I ignored them and went on. "The third thing was in February or March nineteen-fifty-three, not long before they were married. Molloy phoned around noon and said he had expected to come to the office but couldn't make it. His ticket for a hockey game that night was in a drawer of his desk, and he asked her to get it and send it to him by messenger at a downtown restaurant. He said it was in a small blue envelope in the drawer. She went to the drawer and found the envelope, and noticed that it had been through the mail and slit open. Inside there were two things: the hockey ticket and a blue slip of paper, which she glanced at. It was a bill from the Metropolitan Safe Deposit Company for rent of a safe-deposit box, made out to Richard Randall. It caught her eye because she had once thought she might marry a man named Randall but had decided not to. She put it back in the envelope, which was addressed to Richard Randall, but if she noticed the address she has forgotten it. She had forgotten the whole incident until we dug it up."

"At least," Wolfe said, "if it's worth a question we know where to ask it. Anything else?"

"I don't think so. Unless you want the works."

"Not now." He turned to the others. "Now that you've heard Archie, you gentlemen are up to date. Have you any more questions?"

Johnny Keems cleared his throat. "One thing. I don't get the idea of Hays being innocent. I only know what I read in the papers, but it certainly didn't take the jury very long."

"You'll have to take that from me." Wolfe was brusque. You have to be brusque with Johnny. He turned to me. "I've explained the situation to them in some detail, but I have not mentioned our client's name or the nature of his interest. We'll keep that to ourselves. Any more questions?"

There were none.

"Then we'll proceed to assignments. Archie, what about phone booths in the neighborhood?"

"The drugstore that Freyer mentioned is the nearest place with a booth. I didn't look around much."

He went to Durkin. "Fred, you will try that. The phone call to Peter Hays, at nine o'clock, was probably made from nearby, and the one to the police, at nine-eighteen, had to be made as quickly as possible after Peter Hays was seen entering the building. The hope is of course forlorn, since more than three months have passed, but you can try it. The drugstore seems the likeliest, but cover the neighborhood. If both phone calls were made from the same place, it's possible you can jog someone's memory. Start this evening, at once. The calls were made in the evening. Any questions?"

"No, sir. I've got it." Fred never takes his eyes off of Wolfe. I think he's expecting him to sprout either a horn or a halo, I'm not sure which, and doesn't want to miss it. "Shall I go now?"

"No, you might as well stay till we're through." Wolfe went to Cather. "Orrie, you will look into Molloy's business operations and associates and his financial standing. Mr. Freyer will see you at his office at ten in the morning. He'll give you whatever information he has, and you will start with that. Getting access to Molloy's records and papers will be rather complicated."

"If he kept books," I said, "they weren't in his office. At least Mrs. Molloy never saw them, and there was no safe."

"Indeed." Wolfe's brows went up. "A real-estage brokerage business and no books? I think, Archie, I'd better have a full report on the dust you stirred up." He returned to Orrie. "Since Molloy died intestate, as far as is known, his widow's rights are paramount in such matters as access to his records and papers, but they should be exercised as legal procedure provides. Mr. Freyer says that Mrs. Molloy has no attorney, and I'm going to suggest to her that she retain Mr. Parker. Mr. Freyer thinks it inadvisable to suggest him, and I agree. If Molloy kept no records in his office you will first have to find them. Any questions?"

Orrie shook his head. "Not now. I may have after I've talked with Freyer. If I do I'll phone you."

Wolfe made a face. Except in emergencies the boys never call between nine and eleven in the morning or four and six in the afternoon, when he is up in the plant rooms, but even so the damn phone rings when he's deep in a book or working a crossword or busy in the kitchen with Fritz, and he hates it. He went to Keems.

"Johnny, Archie will give you names and addresses. Mr. Thomas L. Irwin and Mr. and Mrs. Jerome Arkoff. They were Mrs. Molloy's companions at the theater; it was Mrs. Arkoff who phoned Mrs. Molloy that she had an extra ticket and invited her to join them. That may have no significance; X may merely have been awaiting an opportunity and grasped it; but he must have known that Mrs. Molloy would be out for the evening, and it is worth inquiry. Two investigators looked into it for Mr. Freyer, but they were extraordinarily clumsy, judging by their reports. If you get any hint that the invitation to Mrs. Molloy was designed, confer with me at once. I have known you to overstrain your talents."

"When?" Johnny demanded.

Wolfe shook his head. "Some other time. Will you communicate with me if you find cause for suspicion?"

"Sure. If you say so."

"I do say so." Wolfe turned to Saul Panzer. "For you, Saul, I had something in mind, but it can wait. It may be worth the trouble to learn why Molloy had in his possession an envelope addressed to Richard Randall, containing a bill for rental of a safe-deposit box, even though it was more than three years ago. If it were a simple matter to get information from the staff of a safe-deposit company about a customer I wouldn't waste you on it, but I know it isn't. Any questions?"

"Maybe a suggestion," Saul offered. "Archie might phone Lon Cohen at the *Gazette* and ask him to give me a good print of a picture of Molloy. That would be better than a newspaper reproduction."

The other three exchanged glances. They were all good operatives, and it would have been interesting to know, as a check on their talents, whether they had all caught the possibility as quickly as Saul had that Molloy had himself been Richard Randall. There was no point in asking them, since they would all have said yes.

"That will be done," Wolfe told him. "Anything else?"

"No, sir."

Wolfe came to me. "Archie. You've gone through Mr. Freyer's file and seen the report on Miss Delia Brandt, Molloy's secretary at the time of his death. You know where to find her."

"Right."

"Please do so. If she has anything we can use, get it. Since you are working for Mrs. Molloy you may need her approval. If so, get that."

Saul smiled. Orrie laughed. Johnny tittered. Fred grinned.

8

I joined Wolfe in the dining room at seven-fifteen as usual, and sat at table, but I didn't really dine because I had an eight-thirty date down in the Village and had to rush it some. Par for Wolfe from clams to cheese is an hour and a half.

Dating Delia Brandt hadn't been any strain on my talents. I had got her on the phone at the first try, given her my own name and occupation, and told her I had been asked by a client to see her and find out if she could supply enough material on Michael M. Molloy, her late employer, for a magazine article under her by-line, to be ghosted by the client. The proceeds would be split. After a few questions she said she would be willing to consider it and would be at home to me at eight-thirty. So I hurried a little with the roast duckling and left Wolfe alone with the salad.

It wouldn't have hurt the house at 43 Arbor Street any to get the same treatment as the one at 171 East 52nd. The outside could have used some paint, and a do-it-yourself elevator would have been a big improvement on the narrow, dingy wooden stairs. Three flights up, she was not waiting on the threshold to greet me, and, finding no button to push, I tapped on the door. From the time it took her you might have thought she had to traverse a spacious reception hall, but when the door opened the room was right there. I spoke.

"My name's Goodwin. I phoned."

"Oh," she said, "of course. I had forgotten, Come in."

It was one of those rooms that call for expert dodging to get anywhere. God knows why the piano bench was smack in the main traffic lane, and He also knows why there was a piano bench at all, since there was no piano. Anyway it was handy for my hat and coat. She crossed to a couch and invited me to sit, and since there was no chair nearby I perched on the couch too, twisting around to face her.

"I really had forgotten," she said apologetically. "My mind must have been soaring around." She waved a hand to show how a mind soars.

She was young, well shaped and well kept, well dressed and well shod, with a soft, clear skin and bright brown eyes, and well-cut fine brown hair, but a mind that soared. . . .

"Didn't you say you were a detective?" she asked. "Something about a magazine?"

"That's right," I told her. "This editor thinks he'd like to try a new slant on a murder. There have been thousands of pieces about murderers. He thinks he might use one called 'The Last Month of a Murdered Man' or 'The Last Year of a Murdered Man.' By his secretary."

"Oh, not my name?"

"Sure, your name too. And, now that I've seen you, a good big picture of you. I wouldn't mind having one myself."

"Now don't get personal."

It was hard to believe, the contrast between what my eyes saw and my ears heard. Any man would have been glad to walk down a theater aisle with her, but there would have to be an understanding that she would keep her mouth shut.

"I'll try not to," I assured her. "I can always turn my back. The idea is this: you'll tell me things about Mr. Molloy, what he said and did and how he acted, and I'll report to the editor, and if he thinks there's an article in it he'll come and talk with you. How's that?"

"Well, it couldn't be called 'The Last Year of a Murdered Man.' It would have to be called 'The Last Ten Months of a Murdered Man' because I only worked for him ten months."

"Okay, that's even better. Now. I understand —"

"How many days are there in ten months?"

"It depends on the months. Roughly three hundred."

"We could call it 'The Last Three Hundred Days of a Murdered Man.'"

"A good idea. I understand that occasionally you had dinner with Molloy at a restaurant. Was it —"

"Who told you that?"

I had three choices: get up and go, strangle her, or sit on her. "Look, Miss Brandt. I'm being paid by the hour and I've got to earn it. Was it to discuss business matters or was it social?"

She smiled, which made her even prettier. "Oh, that was just social. He never talked about business to me. It had got so he didn't want to have dinner with his wife, and he hated to eat alone. I'd love to put that in. I know some people think I allowed him liberties, but I never did."

"Did he try to take liberties?"

"Oh, of course. Married men always do. That's because with their wives it's not a liberty any more."

"Yeah, that's why I never married. Did he —"

"Oh, aren't you married?"

But you've had enough of her. So had I, but I was on duty, and I stuck with it for three solid hours. I had to go through another ordeal, about halfway through. We were thirsty, and she went to the kitchenette for liquid, and came back with a bottle of ginger ale, a bottle of gin, and two glasses with one cube of ice in each. I apologized, said I had ulcers, and asked for milk. She said she didn't have any, and I asked for water. I will go beyond the call of duty in a pinch, but I wouldn't drink gin and ginger ale to get the lowdown on Lizzie Borden. It was bad enough to sit there and watch her sipping away at it.

In the taxi on my way downtown to keep the date, I had felt some slight compunction at imposing on a poor working girl with a phony approach. In the taxi on my way home, having told her I would let her know if the editor still liked the idea, my conscience was sound asleep. If a conscience could snore, it probably would have.

Wolfe, who rarely turns in before midnight, was at his desk, reading *A Secret Understanding* by Merle Miller. He didn't look up when I entered, so I went to the safe for the expense book and entered the amounts I had given the hired help for expenses, a hundred bucks for each, put the book back and closed the safe and locked it, and cleared up my desk. I refuse to meet a cluttered desk in the morning.

Then I stood up and looked down at him. "Excuse me. Anything from Fred or Johnny that needs attention?"

He finished a paragraph and looked up. "No. Fred called at eleven and reported no progress. Johnny didn't call."

"Shall I save mine for morning?"

"No. That woman will be here. Did you get anything?"

"I don't know." I sat. "She's either a featherbrain or a damn good imitation. She starts every other sentence with 'Oh.' You'd walk out on her in three minutes. She drinks four parts ginger ale and one part gin."

"No."

"Yes."

"Good heavens. Did you?"

"No. But I had to watch her. Two items. One day last October a button on his coat was loose and she offered to sew it on for him. While she was doing so some papers fell out of the pocket and when she picked them up she glanced at them. So she says; papers can fall out of pockets or they can be taken out. Anyhow, she was looking at one of the papers which was a list of names and figures when he suddenly entered from his room, snatched the paper from her, and gave her hell. He slapped her, but that's off the record because she doesn't want it to be in the article, and besides he apologized and bought her champagne at dinner that evening. She says he was so mad he turned white."

"And the names and figures?"

"I hoped you would ask that. She can't remember. She thinks the figures were amounts of money, but she's not sure."

"Hardly a bonanza."

"No, sir. Neither is the other item, but it's more recent. One day between Christmas and New Year's he asked her how she would like to take a trip to South America with him. He had to go on business and would need a secretary. I should mention that he had been trying to take liberties and she hadn't allowed it. She liked the idea of a trip to South America, but, knowing that what are liberties up here are just a matter of course down there, she told him she'd think it over. He said there wouldn't be much time for thinking it over because the business matters wouldn't wait. He also said they were confidential matters and made her promise she wouldn't mention the proposed trip to anyone. She put him off and hadn't said yes or no by January third, the day he died. So she says. I think she said yes. She is not a good liar. I didn't mention that her mind soars."

"Soars where?"

I waved a hand. "Just soars. You would enjoy her."

"No doubt." He looked up at the clock. Past midnight. "Has she a job?"

"Oh, yes. With an import firm downtown. Apparently no connection."

"Very well." He pushed his chair back, yawned, and got up. "Johnny should have reported. Confound him, he's too set on a master stroke."

"Instructions for morning?"

"No. I'll need you here for developments. If any. Good night."

He went, to the elevator, and I went, to the stairs. Up in my room, undressing, I decided to dream of Selma Molloy — something like her being trapped in a blazing building, at an upper window, afraid to jump for the firemen's net. I would march up, wave the firemen aside, stretch my arms, and down she would come, light as a feather, into my embrace. The light as a feather part was important, since otherwise there might have been some bones broken. I didn't consider this reneging on my decision, because you can't hold a man responsible for his dreams. But I didn't follow through on it. No dreams at all. In the morning I didn't even remember that I had been going to dream, but I never do remember anything in the morning until I have washed and showered and shaved and dressed and made my way down to the kitchen. With the orange juice the fog begins to lift, and with the coffee it's all clear. It's a good thing Wolfe breakfasts in his room, on a tray taken up by Fritz, and then goes up to the plant rooms. If we met before breakfast he would have fired me or I would have quit long ago.

Thursday started busy and kept it up. There were three letters from
P.H.'s, answers to the ad, in the morning mail, and I had to answer them.
There was a phone call from Omaha, from James R. Herold. His wife was
impatient. I told him we had five men working on the case, including Saul
Panzer and me, and we would report as soon as there was anything worth
reporting. Fred Durkin came in person to confer. He had visited five estab-
lishments with phone booths within two blocks of the 52nd Street house,
and had found no one who remembered anything about any user of the
phone around nine o'clock on January 3. The soda jerk who had been on
duty at the drugstore that evening had left and gone somewhere in Jersey.
Should Fred find him? I told him yes and wished him luck.

Orrie Cather phoned from Freyer's office to ask if we had arranged with
Mrs. Molloy to hire a lawyer to establish her position legally, and I told him
no, that would be done when she came to see Wolfe.

Lon Cohen of the *Gazette* phoned and said he had a riddle for me. It goes
like this, he said. "Archie Goodwin tells me on Tuesday that he and Nero
Wolfe aren't interested in the Hays murder trial. The P.H. in Wolfe's ad is a
different person, no connection. But Wednesday evening I get a note from
Goodwin asking me to give the bearer, Saul Panzer, a good clear print of a
picture of Michael M. Molloy. Here's the riddle: what's the difference between Archie Goodwin and a double-breasted liar?"

I couldn't blame him, but neither could I straighten him out. I told him
the note Saul had brought him must have been a forgery, and promised to
give him a front-page spread as soon as we had one.

Selma Molloy came on the dot at eleven. I let her in and took her coat, a
quiet gray plaid, in the hall, and was putting it on a hanger when the
elevator bumped to a stop and Wolfe emerged. He stopped, facing her,
inclined his head nearly an inch when I pronounced her name, turned, and
made for the office, and I convoyed her in and to the red leather chair. He
sat and leveled his eyes at her, trying not to scowl. He hates to work, and
this would probably be not only an all-day session, but all day with a
woman. Then he had an idea. His head turned and he spoke.

"Archie. Since I'm a stranger to Mrs. Molloy, and you are not, it might be
better for you to tell her about the legal situation regarding her husband's
estate."

She looked at me. In her apartment she had sat with her back to a
window, and here she was facing one, but the stronger light gave me no
reason to lower my guard.

She squinted at me. "His estate? I thought you wanted to go on from
yesterday."

"We do," I assured her. "By the way, I told you I wouldn't be here, but my
program was changed. The estate thing is a part of the investigation. We
want access to Molloy's records and papers, and since no will has been
found the widow has a right to them, and you're the widow. Of course you
can let us look at anything that's in the apartment, but there should be some
legal steps — for instance, you should be named as administrator."

"But I don't want to be administrator. I don't want anything to do with
his estate. I might have wanted some of the furniture, if —" She let it hang.
She shook her head. "I don't want anything."

"What about cash for your current expenses?"

"I wondered about that yesterday, after you had gone." Her eyes were meeting mine, straight. "Whether Nero Wolfe was expecting me to pay him."

"He isn't." I looked at Wolfe, and his head moved left, just perceptibly, and back. So we were still keeping our client under our hat. I met her eyes again. "Our interest in the case developed through a conversation with Mr. Freyer, and all we expect from you is information. I asked about cash only because there must be some in your husband's estate."

"If there is I don't want it. I have some savings of my own, enough to go along on a while. I just don't know what I'm going to do." She pinned her lower lip with her teeth, and after a moment released it. "I don't know what I'm going to do, but I don't want to be his administrator or have anything to do with it. I should have left him long ago, but I had married him with my eyes open and my silly pride—"

"Okay, but it might help if we could take a look at his papers. For instance, his checkbook. Miss Brandt tells me that the furniture in the office was sold, and that before it was taken away some man went through the desks and removed the contents. Do you know about that?"

"Yes, that was a friend of mine—and he had been a friend of my husband's—Tom Irwin. He said the office should be closed up and I asked him to attend to it."

"What happened to the stuff he took?"

"He brought it to the apartment. It's there now, in three cartons. I've never looked at it."

"I would like to. You'll be here with Mr. Wolfe for quite a while. I could go up to the apartment and do it now if you're willing to let me have the key."

Without the slightest hesitation she said, "Of course," and opened her handbag. It didn't put her down a notch in my book—her being so trustful with a comparative stranger. All it meant was that with her P.H. convicted of murder she didn't give a damn about anything at all, and besides, I was the comparative stranger. Glancing at Wolfe and getting a nod, I went to her and took the keys, told her I would let her know if I found anything helpful and would give her a receipt for anything I brought away, and headed for the hall. I had just taken my topcoat from the rack when the doorbell rang, and a look through the one-way glass showed me Saul Panzer out on the stoop. Putting the coat back, I opened up.

There are things about Saul I don't understand and never will. For instance, the old cap he always wears. If I wore that cap while tailing a subject I'd be spotted in the first block. If I wore it while calling on people for information they would suspect I was cuckoo or quaint and draw the curtains. But Saul never gets spotted unless he wants to, and for extracting material from people's insides nothing can equal him except a stomach pump. While he was hanging up his coat and sticking the cap in its pocket I stepped to the office door to tell Wolfe, and Wolfe said to bring him in. He came, and I followed him.

"Yes?" Wolfe inquired.

Saul, standing, shot a glance at the red leather chair and said, "A report."

"Go ahead. Mrs. Molloy's interest runs with ours. Mrs. Molloy, this is Mr. Panzer."

She asked him how he did and he bowed. That's another thing about him, his bow; it's as bad as his cap. He sat down on the nearest yellow chair, knowing that Wolfe wants people at eye level, and reported.

"Two employees of the Metropolitan Safe Deposit Company identified a picture of Michael M. Molloy. They say it's a picture of Richard Randall, a renter of a box there. I didn't tell them it was Molloy, but I think one of them suspects it. I didn't try to find out what size the box is or when he first rented it or any other details, because I thought I'd better get instructions. If they get stirred up enough to look into it and decide that one of their boxes was probably rented under another name by a man who has been murdered, they'll notify the District Attorney. I don't know the law, I don't know what rights the DA has after he has got a conviction, since he couldn't be looking for evidence, but I thought you might want to get to the box first."

"I do," Wolfe declared. "How good is the identification?"

"I'd bank on it. I'm satisfied. Do you want to know just how it went?"

"No. Not if you're satisfied. How much are they already stirred up?"

"I think not much. I was pretty careful. I doubt if either of them will go upstairs with it, but they might, and I thought you might want to move."

"I do." Wolfe turned. "Mrs. Molloy. Do you know what this is about?"

"Yes, I think so." She looked at me. "Isn't it what I told you yesterday, the envelope and slip of paper when I was looking for the hockey ticket?"

"That's it," I told her.

"And you've found out already that my husband was Richard Randall?"

"We have," Wolfe said, "and that changes the situation. We must find out what is in that box as soon as possible, and to do so we must, first, demonstrate that Randall was Molloy, and, second, establish your right to access. Since in handling his safe-deposit box a man certainly makes fingerprints, the first presents no technical problem, but it must wait upon the second. When you said, madam, that you would have nothing to do with your husband's estate, I understood and respected your attitude. Rationally it could not be defended, but emotionally it was formidable; and when feeling takes over sense is impotent. Now it's different. We must see the contents of that box, and we can get to it only through you. You will have to assert your rights as the widow and take control of the estate. The law can crawl and usually does, but in an emergency it can — What are you shaking your head for?"

"I've told you. I won't do that."

Hearing her tone, and seeing her eyes and her jaw, he started to glare but decided it wouldn't work. So he turned to me. "Archie."

I did the glaring, at him, and then toned the glare down as I transferred it to her. "Mrs. Molloy," I said, "Mr. Wolfe is a genius, but geniuses have their weak spots, and one of his is that he pretends to believe that attractive young women can refuse me nothing. It comes in handy when an attractive young woman says no to something he wants, because it's an excuse for passing the buck to me, which he just did. I don't know what to do with it and he can't expect me to — he just said himself that when feeling takes over sense is impotent, so what good will it do to try to reason with you? But may I ask you a question?"

She said yes.

"Suppose no good grounds for a retrial or an appeal are found, and the sentence is carried out, and Peter Hays dies in the electric chair, and some time later, when a court gets around to it, that safe-deposit box is opened and it contains something that starts an investigation and leads to evidence that someone else committed the murder. What would your feeling be then?"

She had her lip pinned again, and had to release it to say, "I don't think that's a fair question."

"Why not? All I did was suppose, and it wasn't inconceivable. That box may be empty, but it *could* contain what I said. I think the trouble is that you don't believe there is any evidence, in that safe-deposit box or anywhere else, that will clear Peter Hays, because he's guilty, so why should you do something you don't want to do?"

"That's not true! It's not true!"

"You know damn well it's true."

Her head went down, forward, and her hands came up to cover her face. Wolfe glowered at me. From that room he has walked out on a lot of different people, but when a woman goes to pieces he doesn't walk out, he runs. I shook my head at him. I didn't think Selma Molloy was going to slip the bit.

She didn't. When she finally raised her head her eyes met mine and she said calmly, "Listen, Mr. Goodwin. Didn't I help all I could yesterday and didn't I come today? You know I did. But how can I claim any rights as Mike Molloy's widow when for two years I bitterly regretted I was his wife? Don't you see it's impossible? Isn't there some other way? Can't I ask for someone else to be administrator and he can have rights?"

"I don't know," I told her. "That's a legal question."

"Get Mr. Parker," Wolfe snapped.

I turned and pulled the phone to me and dialed. Since Nathaniel Parker had answered some ten thousand legal questions for us over the years I didn't have to look up the number. While I was getting him Saul Panzer asked Wolfe if he should leave, and was told to wait until there was some place for him to leave for. When I had Parker, Wolfe took his phone.

I had to admire his performance. He would have liked to tell Parker that we were being obstructed by a perverse and capricious female, but with her sitting there that would have been inadvisable, so he merely said that for reasons of her own the widow refused to assert her claims, and put the legal problem. From there on his part was mostly grunts.

When he hung up he turned to the female. "Mr. Parker says it's complicated, and since it's urgent he wants to ask you some questions. He will be here in twenty minutes. He says it will expedite matters if you will decide whom you would like to suggest as administrator. Have you anyone in mind?"

"Why—no." She frowned. She looked at me, and back at him. "Could it be Mr. Goodwin?"

"My dear madam." Wolfe was exasperated. "Use your faculties. You met Mr. Goodwin yesterday for the first time, in his capacity as a private investigator. It would be highly inappropriate, and the court would find it so. It should be someone you know well, and trust. What about the man who closed the office and took the cartons to your apartment? Thomas Irwin."

"I don't think —" She considered it. "I don't think I'd want to ask him to do this. His wife wouldn't like it. But I wouldn't mind asking Pat Degan. He might say no, but I could ask him."

"Who is he?"

"Patrick A. Degan. He's the head of the Mechanics Alliance Welfare Association. His office isn't far from here, on Thirty-ninth Street. I could call him now."

"How long have you known him?"

"Three years, since I was married. He was a friend of my husband's, but he always — I mean, he really is my friend, I'm sure he is. Shall I call him? What will I say?"

"Tell him you wish to request a favor of him, and ask him to come here. Now, if possible. If he asks questions tell him you would rather not discuss it on the phone. And I venture a suggestion, in case he comes and consents to act. Legal services will be required, and he may want to name the lawyer to be engaged to perform them. I urge you not to agree. From a legal standpoint it will be your interests the lawyer will represent, whether you wish to renounce them or not, and it will be proper and desirable for you to choose him."

"Why can't I choose the lawyer he names?"

"Because I wouldn't trust him. Because I suspect Mr. Degan of having killed your husband."

She goggled at him. "You suspect Pat Degan? You never heard of him until just now!"

Wolfe nodded. "I made it sensational. Purposely. I suspect each and all of your husband's associates, as I must until I have reason to discriminate, and Mr. Degan is one of them. I advise you not to let him name the lawyer. If you are at a loss to choose one, I suggest Nathaniel Parker, who will be here shortly. I have dealt with him many years, and I recommend him without reservation. As for trusting me, either you believe that I am earnestly seeking an end you desire or it is folly for you to be here at all."

It was a good pitch, but it didn't do the job — not completely. She looked at me, looking the question instead of asking it.

I gave her a strictly professional smile. "Parker is as good as they come, Mrs. Molloy."

"All right, then." She arose. "May I use the phone?"

9

SINCE Patrick A. Degan was the first suspect we had laid eyes on, unless you want to count Albert Freyer or Delia Brandt, naturally I gave him some attention, and I had plenty of opportunity during the hour that the conference lasted. In appearance I wouldn't have called him sinister — a medium-sized specimen in his early forties with a fair start on a paunch, round face, wide nose, and dark brown eyes that moved quickly and often. He greeted Selma Molloy as a friend, taking her hand in both of his, but not as one who had been bewitched by her into shooting her husband and framing her P.H. for it. I had him mostly in profile during the conference, since he was on a yellow chair facing Wolfe, with Nathaniel Parker on another one between Degan and me. After making the phone call, Mrs. Molloy had returned to the red leather chair. Saul Panzer had retired to one in the rear, over by the bookshelves.

When the situation had been explained to Degan by Mrs. Molloy and she had asked the favor, he wasted five minutes trying to get her to change her mind. When he saw that was no go, he said he would be willing to do what she wanted provided it was legally feasible, and on that point he would have to consult his lawyer. She said of course he would want to ask his lawyer about it, but her lawyer, Mr. Parker, was right there and would explain how it could be done. Not bad for a girl who wasn't using her faculties. Degan turned his quick brown eyes on Parker, polite but not enthusiastic. Parker cleared his throat and started in. That was the first he had heard that he was Mrs. Molloy's counsel, since he had had only a minute or two with us before Degan arrived, but he didn't raise the point.

From there on it got highly technical, and I had a notion, rejected as unprofessional, to give Mrs. Molloy's faculties a recess by taking her up to the plant rooms and showing her the orchids. Anyone sufficiently interested can call Parker at his office, Phoenix 5-2382, and get the details. What it boiled down to was that there were three different ways of handling it, but one would be much too slow, and which of the other two was preferable? Degan made two phone calls to his lawyer, and finally they got it settled. Parker would start the ball rolling immediately, and Degan agreed to be available for an appearance before a judge on short notice. Parker thought we might get a look at the inside of the safe-deposit box by Monday, and possibly sooner. He was just getting up to go when the phone rang and I answered it.

It was Sergeant Purley Stebbins of Homicide West. He told me some news, and I asked a few questions, and when he asked me a question I decided I didn't know the answer and asked him to hold the wire. Covering the transmitter, I turned to Wolfe.

"Stebbins. At eleven-forty-eight last night a man was hit by a car on Riverside Drive in the Nineties, and killed. The body has been identified as that of John Joseph Keems. About an hour ago the car that hit him was found parked on upper Broadway, and it's hot. It was stolen last night from where it was parked on Ninety-second Street. The fact that it was a stolen car makes Purley think it may have been premeditated murder, possibly in connection with a case Keems was working on, and, knowing that Johnny Keems often does jobs for you, he asks if he was working for you last night. I told him you sometimes hire an operative without telling me, and I'd ask you. I'm asking you."

"Tell him I'm engaged and you'll call him back."

I did so, hung up, and swiveled. Wolfe's lips were tight, his eyes were half closed, and his temple was twitching. He met my eyes and demanded, "You knew him. How much chance is there that he would have let a car kill him by inadvertence?"

"Practically none. Not Johnny Keems."

Wolfe's head turned. "Saul?"

"No, sir." Saul had got to his feet while I was reporting to Wolfe. "Of course it could happen, but I agree with Archie."

Wolfe's head turned more, to the left. "Mrs. Molloy, if Mr. Goodwin was correct when he said that you believe there can be no evidence that will clear Peter Hays, this bitter pill for me is not so bitter for you. Not only can there be such evidence, there will be. Johnny Keems was working for me last night, on this case, and he was murdered. That settles it. You have been told that I thought it likely that Peter Hays is innocent; now I know he is."

His head jerked right. "Mr. Parker, the urgency is now pressing. I beg you to move with all possible speed. Well?"

I wouldn't say that Parker moved with all possible speed, but he moved. He made for the hall and was gone.

Degan, lifted from his chair by Wolfe's tone and manner, had a question. "Do you realize what you're saying?"

"Yes, sir, I do. Why? Do you challenge it?"

"No, I don't challenge it, but you're worked up and I wondered if you realized that you were practically promising Mrs. Molloy that Peter Hays will be cleared. What if you're giving her false hopes? What if you can't make good on it? I think I have the right to ask, as an old friend of hers."

"Perhaps you have." Wolfe nodded at him. "I concede it. It's a stratagem, Mr. Degan, directed at myself. By committing myself to Mrs. Molloy, before witnesses, I add to other incentives that of preserving my self-conceit. If the risk of failure is grave for her it is also grave for me."

"You didn't have to make it so damned positive." Degan went to Mrs. Molloy and put a hand on her shoulder. "I hope to God he's right, Selma. It's certainly rough on you. Anything more I can do?"

She said no and thanked him, and I went to the hall to let him out. Back in the office, Saul had moved back to a seat up front, presumably by invitation, and Wolfe was lecturing Mrs. Molloy.

". . . and I'll answer your question, but only on condition that henceforth you confide in no one. You are to tell no one anything you may learn of my surmises or plans. If I suspected Mr. Degan, as I did and do, I now have better reason to suspect other friends of yours. Do you accept the condition?"

"I'll accept anything that will help," she declared. "All I asked was what he was doing—the man that was killed."

"And I want to tell you because you may be of help, but first I must be assured that you will trust no one. You will repeat nothing and reveal nothing."

"All right. I promise."

Regarding her, he rubbed the end of his nose with a finger tip. It was a dilemma that had confronted him many times over the years. There were very few men whose tongues he had ever been willing to rely on, and no women at all, but she might have facts he needed and he had to risk it. So he did.

"Mr. Keems left here shortly after seven o'clock last evening with specific instructions, to see the three people who were with you at the theater the evening of January third. He was to learn — What's the matter?"

Her chin had jerked up and her lips had parted. "You might have told me that you suspect me too. I suppose you did, when you said you suspect all of my husband's associates."

"Nonsense. His target was not your alibi. He was to learn all the circumstances of the invitation you got to use an extra theater ticket. That was what got you away from your apartment for the evening. Whoever went there to kill your husband certainly knew you were safely out of the way; and not only that, he may have arranged for your absence. That was what Mr. Keems was after. He had the names and addresses of Mr. Irwin and Mr. and Mrs. Arkoff, and he was to report to me at once if he got any hint that the invitation to you was designed. He didn't report, but he must have got a hint, or someone thought he did; and it must have been a betraying hint, since to suppress it someone stole an automobile and killed him with it. That is not palpable, but it's highly probable, and it's my assumption until it's discredited."

"But then — " She shook her head. "I just don't believe — Did he see them? Who did he see?"

"I don't know. As I say, he didn't report. We'll find out. I want all you can tell me about that invitation. It came from Mrs. Arkoff?"

"Yes. She phoned me."

"When?"

"At half-past seven. I told all about it on the — at the trial."

"I know you did, but I want it first-hand. What did she say?"

"She said that she and Jerry — her husband — had asked Tom and Fanny Irwin to dinner and a show, and she and Jerry were at the restaurant, and Tom had just phoned that Fanny had a headache and couldn't come and he would meet them in the theater lobby, and Rita — that's Mrs. Arkoff — she asked me to come, and I said I would."

"Did you go to the restaurant?"

"No, there wasn't time, and I had to dress. I met them at the theater."

"At what time?"

"Half-past eight."

"They were there?"

"Rita and Jerry were. We waited a few minutes for Tom, and then Rita and I went on it and Jerry waited in the lobby for Tom. Rita told him to leave the ticket at the box office, but he said no, he had told him they'd meet him in the lobby. Rita and I went on in because we didn't want to miss the curtain. It was Julie Harris in *The Lark*."

"How soon did the men join you?"

"It was quite a while. Almost the end of the first act."

"When does the first act end?"

"I don't know. It's rather long."

Wolfe's head moved. "You've seen that play, Archie?"

"Yes, sir. I would say a quarter to ten, maybe twenty to."

"Have you seen it, Saul?"

"Yes sir. Twenty to ten."

"You know that?"

"Yes, sir. Just my habit of noticing things."

"Don't disparage it. The more you put in a brain, the more it will hold — if you have one. How long would it take to get from One-seventy-one East Fifty-Second Street to that theater?"

"After nine o'clock?"

"Yes."

"With luck, if you were in a hurry, eight minutes. That would be a minimum. From that up to fifteen."

Wolfe turned. "Mrs. Molloy, I wonder that you haven't considered the possible signficance of this. The anonymous call to the police, saying that a shot had been heard, was at nine-eighteen. The police arrived at nine-twenty-three. Even if he waited to see them arrive, and he probably didn't, he could have reached the theater before the first act ended. Didn't that occur to you."

She was squinting at him. "If I understand you — you mean didn't it occur to me that Jerry or Tom might have killed Mike?"

"Obviously. Didn't it?"

"No!" She made it a little louder than it had to be, and I hoped Wolfe understood that she was raising her voice not at him, but at herself. It hadn't occurred to her because the minute she had learned, on getting home that January night, that her husband had been found with a bullet in his head, and that P.H., with a gun in his pocket, had tried to force his way out, she thought she knew what had happened, and it had settled in her like a lump of lead. But she wasn't going to tell Wolf that. She told him instead, "There was no reason for Jerry to kill him. Or Tom. Why? And they had been in the bar across the street. Tom came not long after Rita and I went in, and said he needed a drink, and they went and had one."

"Which one of them told you that?"

"Both of them. They told Rita and me, and we said they must have had more than one."

Wolfe grunted. "Go back a little. Wouldn't it have been the natural thing for Mr. Arkoff to leave the ticket at the box office instead of waiting in the lobby?"

"Not the way it was. Rita didn't ask him to leave it at the box office, she told him to, and he doesn't like to have her tell him to do things. So she does." She came forward in the chair. "Listen, Mr. Wolfe," she said earnestly. "If that man getting killed, if that means what you think it does, I don't care what happens to anybody. I haven't been caring what happened to me, I've just been feeling I might as well be dead, and I'm certainly not going to start worrying about other people, not even my best friends. But I think this is no use. Even if they lied about being in the bar, neither of them had any *reason!*"

"We'll see about that," he told her. "Someone had reason to fear Johnny Keems enough to kill him." He glanced up at the clock. "Luncheon will be ready in seven minutes. You'll join us? You too, Saul. Afterward you'll stay here to be on hand if Mr. Parker needs you. And Mrs. Molloy, you'll stay too and tell me everything you know about your friends, and you'll invite them to join us here at six o'clock."

"But I can't!" she protested. "How can I? Now?"

"You said you weren't going to worry about them. Yesterday morning

Peter Hays, talking with Mr. Goodwin, used the same words you have just used. He said he might as well be dead. I intend that both of you—"

"Oh!" she cried, to me. "You saw him? What did he say?"

"I was only with him a few minutes," I told her. "Except that he might as well be dead, not much. He can tell you himself when we finish this job." I went to Wolfe. "I've got to call Purley. What do I tell him?"

He pinched his nose. He has an idea that pinching his nose makes his sense of smell keener, and a faint aroma of cheese dumplings was coming to us from the kitchen. "Tell him that Mr. Keems was working for me last evening, investigating a confidential matter, but I don't know whom he had seen just prior to his death; and that we'll inform him if and when we get information that might be useful. I want to speak with those people before he does."

As I turned to dial, Fritz entered to announce lunch.

10

NOT long ago I got a letter from a woman who had read some of my accounts of Nero Wolfe's activities, asking me why I was down on marriage. She said she was twenty-three years old and was thinking of having a go at it herself. I wrote her that as far as I knew there was absolutely nothing wrong with marriage; the trouble was the way people handled it, and I gave her a couple of examples. The examples I used were Mr. and Mrs. Jerome Arkoff and Mr. and Mrs. Thomas L. Irwin, though I didn't mention their names, and I had got my material from what I saw and heard in the first five minutes after they arrived at Wolfe's place that Thursday at six o'clock.

They all arrived together, and there was a little bustle in the hall, getting their things off and disposed of. That was finished and I was ready to herd them down the hall and into the office when Rita Arkoff touched her husband's elbow, pointed to a chair against the wall, and told him. "Your hat, Jerry. Hang it up."

No wonder he hadn't left the ticket at the box office. Before he could react normally, like making a face at her or telling her to go to hell, I got the hat myself and put it on the rack, and we proceeded to the office, where the Irwins immediately contributed their share. I had the chairs spaced comfortably to give everyone elbow room, but Tom Irwin pushed his close to his wife's, sat, and took her hand in his and held onto it. I am not by any means against holding hands, in wedded bliss or unwedded, but only if both hands want to, and Fanny Irwin's didn't. She didn't actually try to pull it away, but she sure would have liked to. I hope the examples I gave her will keep my twenty-three-year-old correspondent from developing into an order-giver or a one-way hand-holder, but leave it to her, she'll find some kind of monkey wrench to toss into the machinery, and if she doesn't her husband will.

However, I'm getting ahead of myself. Before six o'clock came, and brought the two couples, there were other happenings. My lunch was interrupted twice. Fred Durkin phoned to say that he had seen the soda jerk who have moved to Jersey, and got nothing, and had worn out his welcome at all places with phone booths within two blocks of 171 East 52nd Street. I told him to come in. Orrie Cather phoned to ask if we had an administrator yet, and I told him also to come in. They arrived before we finished lunch, and, back in the office, Wolfe told them about Johnny Keems.

They agreed with Saul and me that the odds were big that the car that had hit enough of him to kill him had been not careless but careful. They hadn't had much love for him, but they had worked a lot with him. As Fred Durkin said, "Lots of worse guys are still walking around." Orrie Cather said, "Yes, and one of them has got something coming." No one mentioned that until he got it they had better keep an eye out when crossing a street, but they were all thinking it.

They were given errands. Saul was to go to Parker's office to be at hand. Orrie, armed with Selma Molloy's keys, was to go to her apartment and inspect the contents of the three cartons. Fred, supplied by Mrs. Molloy with descriptions of Jerome Arkoff and Tom Irwin, was to go to the Longacre Theatre and the bar across the street and see if he could find someone who could remember as far back as January 3. Fred was getting the scraps.

When they had gone Wolfe tackled Mrs. Molloy again, to get the lowdown on her friends. Using the phone in the kitchen while he was busy with the staff, she had asked them to come to Wolfe's office at six o'clock. I don't know what she had told them, since she couldn't very well say that Wolfe wanted to find out which one of them had killed Mike Molloy, but anyhow they had said they would come. I had suggested that she could tell them that Wolfe was working with Freyer and was trying to find some grounds for an appeal, and probably she did.

Of course Wolfe had her cornered. If there was any chance of springing her P.H. she was all for it, but friends are friends, for people who are entitled to have any, until shown to be otherwise. If you want to take the word of one bewitched, she handled it very nicely. She stuck strictly to facts. For instance, she did not say that Fanny Irwin and Pat Degan were snatching a snuggle; she merely said that Rita Arkoff thought they were.

Jerome Arkoff, thirty-eight, a husky six-footer with a long solemn face, gray-blue eyes, a long nose, and big ears, according to the description she had given Fred Durkin, was a television producer, successful enough to have ulcers. She had met him through Rita, who had been a model when Selma was, and who had married Arkoff about the time Selma had quit modeling and gone to work for Molloy. Arkoff and Molloy had met through their wives' friendship, and there had been nothing special in their relations, either of harmony or of hostility. If there had been anything between them that could possibly have led to murder, Selma knew nothing of it. She conceded it was conceivable that Molloy and Rita had put horns on Arkoff without her ever suspecting it, and Arkoff had removed the blot by blotting out Molloy, but not that he had also framed Peter Hays. Arkoff had liked Peter Hays.

Thomas L. Irwin, forty, was slender, handsome, and dark-skinned, with a skimpy black mustache. He was an executive in a big printing company, in charge of sales. Selma had met him shortly after her marriage, about the same time she had met Patrick Degan. His company did printing for Degan's organization, the Mechanics Alliance Welfare Association, MAWA for short. Fanny Irwin called Degan "Mawa." Irwin and Molloy had got on each other's nerves and had had some fairly hot exchanges, but Selma had never seen any indication of serious enmity.

It was a thin crop. Wolfe poked all around, but the only real dirt he found was Rita Arkoff's suspicion about Fanny Irwin and Pat Degan, and that wasn't very promising. Even if it was true, and even if Irwin had been aware of it or suspected it, he could hardly have expected to relieve his feelings by killing Molloy. Wolfe abandoned it as fruitless and had gone back to the relationships among the men when a phone call came from Saul Panzer, from Parker's office. Some papers were ready for Mrs. Molloy to sign before a notary and would she please come at once. She left, and five minutes later it was four o'clock and Wolfe went up to the plant rooms.

With a couple of hours to go before company was expected, I would have liked to take a trip up to 52nd Street and help Orrie paw through the cartons, but I had been instructed to stay put, and it was just as well. There were phone calls — one from Lon Cohen, one from our client in Omaha, and one from Purley Stebbins, wanting to know if we had got a line on Johnny Keem's movements and contacts Wednesday evening. I told him no and he was skeptical. When the doorbell rang a little after five o'clock I expected to find Purley on the stoop, come to do a little snarling, but it was a stranger — a tall, slim, narrow-shouldered young man, looking very grim. When I opened the door he was going to push right in, but I was wider and heavier than he was. He announced aggressively, "I want to see Archie Goodwin."

"You are."

"I are what?"

"Seeing Archie Goodwin. Who am I seeing?"

"Oh, a wise guy."

We were off to a bad start, but we got it straightened out that he meant that I was a wise guy, not that I was seeing one; and after I had been informed that his name was William Lesser and he was a friend of Delia Brandt I let him in and took him to the office. When I offered him a chair he ignored it.

"You saw Miss Brandt last night," he said, daring me to try to crawl out of it.

"Right," I confessed.

"About a piece about Molloy for some magazine."

"Right."

"I want to know what she told you about her and Molloy."

I swiveled the chair at my desk and sat. "Not standing up," I told him. "It would take too long. And besides, I'd want — "

"Did she mention me?"

"Not that I remember. I'd want some kind of a reason. You don't look like a city detective. Are you her brother or uncle or lawyer or what?"

He had his fists on his hips. "If I was her brother my name wouldn't be Lesser, would it? I'm a friend of hers. I'm going to marry her."

I raised the brows. "Then you're off on the wrong foot, brother. A happy marriage must be based on mutual trust and understanding, so they say. Don't ask me what she told me about her and Molloy, ask her."

"I don't have to ask her. She told me."

"I see. If that's how it is you'd better sit down. When are you going to be married?"

The chair I had offered was right beside him. He looked at the seat of it as if he suspected tacks, looked back at me, and sat. "Listen," he said, "it's not the way you make it sound. I told her I was coming to see you. It's not that I don't trust her, it's having it come out in a magazine. Haven't I got a right to find out what's going to be printed about my wife and a man she used to work for?"

"You certainly have, but she's not your wife yet. When is the wedding?"

"Right away. We got the license today. Next week."

"Congratulations. You're a lucky man, Mr. Lesser. How long have you known her?"

"About a year. A little over. Now are you going to tell me what I asked?"

"I have no objection." I crossed my legs and leaned back. "This may ease your mind a little, the fact that the magazine wouldn't dream of printing anything Miss Brandt disapproved of, or anything her husband disapproved of. Invasion of privacy. And you've given me an idea. The article would be a lot better with some real love interest. You know what the slant is, the last ten months of a murder victim as seen by his secretary. Well, all the time she is working for him, and letting him take her out to dinner because she feels sorry for him, her heart is already in bond to another. She is deeply in love with a young man she intends to marry. That would make it a masterpiece — the contrast between the tragedy of the man who is going to die but doesn't know it, and the blush and promise of young love. Huh?"

"I guess so. What did she tell you?"

"Don't worry about that." I waved it away. "When it's written you and she can change anything you don't like, or take it out. When were you engaged?"

"Well — it was understood quite a while ago."

"Before the murder?"

"Formally engaged, no. Does that matter?"

"Maybe not. While she's being sorry for Molloy she can either be promised to another or just hoping she soon will be. It would be swell if we could work in some reference, a sort of minor key, to the murderer. We could call him that, since he's been convicted. Only I don't suppose you knew Peter Hays."

"No."

"Did you know about him? Did you know he was in love with Mrs. Molloy?"

"No. I never heard of him until he was arrested."

"It doesn't really matter. I thought perhaps Miss Brandt had mentioned him to you. Of course Molloy told her about him."

"How do you know he did? Did she say so?"

"I don't remember." I considered. "I'd have to look at my notes, and they're not here. Did she tell you about Molloy asking her to go to South America with him?"

"No, she didn't." Lesser was looking aggressive again. "I didn't come to tell you what she told me, I came to ask you what she told you."

"I know you did." I was sympathetic. "But you have my word that nothing will be printed that you don't like, and that's what you were concerned about. I can't tell you about my talk with Miss Brandt because I was working for a client and my report of that talk is his property. But I think—"

"Then you're not going to tell me."

"I'd like to, but I can't. But I think—"

He got up and walked out. From the back he looked even thinner than from the front. I went to the hall to be polite, but he already had his coat off the rack and was reaching for the doorknob. He banged the door shut behind him, and I returned to the office. The wall clock said twenty-five to six. Delia Brandt might have got home from work, or, since she had gone with Lesser to get their marriage license, she might have taken the day off. I got at the phone and dialed the number of her apartment. No answer.

I thought him over. There was one nice thing about him, he had had the makings of a motive, which was more than I could say for anyone else on the list. And he might easily have known enough about Peter Hays to get the idea of framing him for it. But how could he have arranged for Fanny Irwin to have a headache and stay home, and for Rita Arkoff to invite Selma Molloy to use the ticket? Even if that wasn't essential, if he was merely waiting for an opportunity to knock, how did he know it was knocking? How did he know Mrs. Molloy was away from the apartment and would stay away? It was worth looking for answers to those questions, because there was another nice thing about him: a wife cannot be summoned to testify against her husband.

I dialed Delia Brandt's number again, and got her.

"I've just heard a piece of news," I told her. "That you're going to be married. I'm calling to wish you luck, and happiness, and everything that goes with it."

"Oh, thank you! Thank you very much. Is Bill there with you?"

"No, he left a few minutes ago. A fine young man. It was a pleasure to meet him. Apparently he was a little worried about the magazine article, but I promised him he would have a chance to veto anything he didn't like. So you knew he was coming to see me?"

"Oh, sure. He said he wanted to, and I thought since he was going to be my husband it was only natural. Did you tell him everything—what did you tell him?"

It didn't look like paradise to me, him wanting to know what she had told me, and her wanting to know what I had told him, and they weren't even married yet. "Nothing much," I assured her. "Really nothing. After the promise I gave him it wasn't necessary. Oh, by the way, now that I have you on the phone, I missed one bet entirely last night. At the end of the article, a sort of climax, you ought to tell where you were and what you were doing the evening of January third. At the very minute Molloy was murdered, just after nine o'clock, if you remember. Do you?"

"Certainly I do. I was with Bill. We were dining and dancing at the Dixie Bower. We didn't leave until after midnight."

"That's wonderful. That will fit right in with an idea I had and told Bill about, how all the time you were trying to be nice to Molloy because you were sorry for him you were deeply in love with a young man who—"

She cut me off. "Oh, the bell's ringing! It must be Bill."

A little click and she was gone. It didn't matter much, since there was soon an interruption at my end. I had just hung up when the sound came of Wolfe's elevator descending, and he had just entered and was crossing to his desk when the doorbell rang and I had to go to the hall to receive the company. I have already told about that, about Rita Arkoff ordering her mate to hang up his hat, and about Tom Irwin moving his chair next to his wife's and holding her hand. But, looking back, I see that I haven't mentioned Selma Molloy. I could go back and insert her, but I don't care to cover up. I am not responsible for my subconscious, and if it arranged, without my knowing it, to leave Selma out because it didn't want you to know how it felt about her, that's its lookout. I now put her back in. Around five o'clock she had returned from her errand at Parker's office, and, at Wolfe's suggestion, had gone up to the plant rooms to look at the orchids. He had brought her down with him, and she was sitting in the red leather chair, after greeting her friends. Try again, subconscious.

11

THE exchange of greetings between Selma and the quartet had seemed a little cramped for old friends, but that might have been expected. After all, she was aiding and abetting a program that might lead to one of them getting charged with murder, and they had been invited by her to the office of a well-known private detective. When they had got seated she sent her eyes to Wolfe and kept them there. Their eyes were more interested in her than in Wolfe. I concentrated on them.

Selma's descriptions of Tom and Jerry had been adequate and accurate. Jerome Arkoff was big and broad, taller than me, and so solemn it must have hurt, but it could have been the ulcers that hurt. Tom Irwin, with his dark skin and thin little clipped mustache, looked more like a saxophone artist than a printing executive, even while holding his wife's hand. His wife, Fanny, was obviously not at her best, with her face giving the impression that she was trying not to give in to a raging headache, but even so she was no eyesore. Under favorable conditions she would have been very decorative. She was a blonde, and a headache is much harder on a blonde than on a brunette; some brunettes are actually improved by a mild one. This brunette, Rita Arkoff, didn't need one. There was a faint touch of snake hips in her walk, a faint suggestion of slant at the corners of her eyes, and a faint hint of a pout in the set of her well-tinted lips. But an order-giver . . .

Wolfe's eyes went from the Arkoffs on his left to the Irwins on his right. "I don't presume," he said, "to thank you for coming, since it was at Mrs. Molloy's request. She has told you what I'm after. Mr. Albert Freyer, counsel for Peter Hays, wishes to establish a basis for a retrial or an appeal, and I'm trying to help him. I assume you are all in sympathy with that?"

They exchanged glances. "Sure we are," Jerome Arkoff declared. "If you can find one. Is there any chance?"

"I think so." Wolfe was easy and relaxed. "Certain aspects have not been thoroughly investigated — not by the police because of the overwhelming evidence against Peter Hays, and not by Mr. Freyer because he lacked funds and facilities. They deserve —"

"Does he have funds now?" Tom Irwin asked. His voice didn't fit his physique. You would have expected a squeak, but it was a deep baritone.

"No. My interest has been engaged, no matter how, and I am indulging it. Those aspects deserve inquiry, and last evening I sent a man to look into one of them — a man named Johnny Keems, who worked for me intermittently. He was to learn if there was any possibility that on the evening the murder was committed, January third, the invitation to Mrs. Molloy to join a theater party had been designed with the purpose of getting her out of the way. Of course it didn't —"

"You sent that man?" Arkoff demanded.

His wife looked reproachfully at her friend. "Selma darling, really! You know perfectly well —"

"If you please!" Wolfe showed her a palm, and his tone sharpened. "Save your resentment for a need; I'm imputing no malignity to any of you. I was about to say, it didn't have to be designed, since the murderer may have merely seized an opportunity; and if it was designed, it didn't have to be one of you who designed it. You might have been quite unaware of it. That was what I sent Mr. Keems to find out, and he was to begin by seeing you, all four of you. First on his list was Mrs. Arkoff, since she had phoned the invitation to Mrs. Molloy." His eyes leveled at Rita. "Did he see you, madam?"

She started to answer, but her husband cut in. "Hold it, Rita." Apparently he could give orders too. He looked at Wolfe. "What's the big idea? If you sent him why don't you ask him? Why drag us down here? Did someone else send him?"

Wolfe nodded. He closed his eyes for a moment, and opened them, and nodded again. "A logical inference, Mr. Arkoff, but wrong. I sent him, but I can't ask him, because he's dead. On Riverside Drive in the Nineties, shortly before midnight last night, an automobile hit him and killed him. It's possible that it was an accident, but I don't think so. I think he was murdered. I think that, working on the assignment I had given him, he had uncovered something that was a mortal threat to someone. Therefore I must see the people he saw and find out what was said. Did he see you, Mrs. Arkoff?"

Her husband stopped her again. "This is different," he told Wolfe, and he looked and sounded different. "*If* he was murdered. What makes you think it wasn't an accident?"

Wolfe shook his head. "We won't go into that, Mr. Arkoff, and we don't have to because the police also suspect that it wasn't. A sergeant at the Homicide Bureau phoned me today to ask if Mr. Keems was working for me last night, and if so, what his assignment was and whom he had seen. Mr. Goodwin put him off —"

"He phoned again later," I put in.

"Yes? What did you tell him?"

"That we were trying to check and would let him know as soon as we had anything useful."

Wolfe went back to them. "I wanted to talk with you people myself first. I wanted to learn what you had told Mr. Keems, and whether he had uncovered anything that might have threatened one of you or someone else. I'll have —"

Fanny Irwin blurted, "He didn't uncover anything with me!" She had got her hand back from her husband's hold.

"Then that's what I'll learn, madam. I'll have to tell the police what he was to do and whom he was to see; that can't be postponed much longer; but it may make things easier for you if I can also tell them that I have talked with you — depending, of course, on what you tell me. Or would you prefer to save it for the police?"

"My God." Tom Irwin groaned. "This is a nice mess."

"And we can thank you for it," Arkoff told Wolfe. "Sicking your damn snoop on us." His head turned. "And you, Selma. You started it."

"Let Selma alone," Rita ordered him. "She's had a rough time and you can't blame her." She looked at Wolfe, and she wasn't pouting. "Let's go ahead and get it over with. Yes, your man saw me, at my apartment. He came when I was about ready to leave, to meet my husband for dinner. He said he was investigating the possibility of a new trial for Peter Hays. I thought he was after Selma's alibi and I told him he might as well save his breath because she was with me every minute, but it was the invitation he wanted to ask about. He asked when I first thought of asking Selma, and I said at the restaurant when Tom phoned and told me Fanny couldn't make it. He asked why I asked Selma instead of someone else, and I said because I liked her and enjoyed her company, and also because when Tom phoned I asked him if he wanted to suggest anyone and he suggested Selma. He asked if Tom gave any special reason for having Selma, and I said he didn't have to because I wanted her anyway. He was going to ask more, but I was late and I said that was all I knew anyhow. So that was all — no, he asked when he could see my husband, and I told him we'd be home around ten o'clock and he might see him then."

"Did he?"

"Yes. We got home a little after ten and he was waiting down in the lobby."

Wolfe's eyes moved. "Mr. Arkoff?"

Jerry hesitated, then shrugged. "I talked with him there in the lobby. I didn't take him upstairs because I had some scripts to go over. He asked me the same things he had asked my wife, but I couldn't tell him as much as she had because she had talked with Tom on the phone. I really couldn't tell him anything. He tried to be clever, asking trick questions about how it was decided to invite Mrs. Molloy, and finally I got fed up and told him to go peddle his papers."

"Did he say anything about having seen Mr. or Mrs. Irwin?"

"No. I don't think so. No."

"Then he left?"

"I suppose so. We left him in the lobby when we went to the elevator."

"You and your wife went up to your apartment?"

"Yes."

"What did you do the rest of the evening?"

Arkoff took a breath. "By God," he said, "if anyone had told me an hour ago that I was going to be asked where I was at the time of the murder I would have thought he was crazy."

"No doubt. It does often seem an impertinence. Where were you?"

"I was in my apartment, working with scripts until after midnight: My wife was in another room, and neither of us could have gone out without the other one knowing it. No one else was there."

"That seems conclusive. Certainly either conclusive or collusive." Wolfe's eyes went right. "Mr. Irwin, since Mr. Keems had been told that you had suggested Mrs. Molloy, I presume he sought you. Did he find you?"

From the expression on Tom Irwin's face, he needed a hand to hold. He opened his mouth and closed it again. "I'm not sure I like this," he said. "If I'm going to be questioned about a murder I think I'd rather be questioned by the police."

"Oh, for heaven's sake," his wife protested. "He won't bite you! Do what Rita did, get it over with!" She went to Wolfe. "Do you want me to tell it?"

"If you were present, madam."

"I was. That man—what was his name?"

"John Joseph Keems."

"It was nearly nine o'clock when he came, and we were just going out. We had promised to drop in at a party some friends were giving for somebody, and we would have been gone if my maid hadn't had to fix the lining of my wrap. He said the same thing he told Rita, about the possibility of a new trial for Peter Hays, and he asked my husband about the phone call to the restaurant. Rita has told you about that. Actually—"

"Did your husband's account of it agree with Mrs. Arkoff's?"

"Of course. Why wouldn't it? Actually, though, it was I who suggested asking Selma Molloy. While Tom was at the phone I told him to tell her to ask Selma because I could trust him with her. It was partly a joke, but I'm one of those jealous wives. Then he wanted to ask some more questions, I mean that man Keems, but by that time my wrap was ready and we had told him all we knew. That was all there was to it."

"Did your husband tell him that you had suggested asking Mrs. Molloy?"

"Yes, I'm pretty sure—Didn't you, Tom?"

"Yes."

"And you went to the party? How late did you stay?"

"Not late at all. It was a bore, and my husband was tired. We got home around eleven and went to bed. We sleep in the same room."

Wolfe started to make a face, realized he was doing it, and called it off. The idea of sleeping in the same room with anybody on earth, man or woman, was too much. "Then," he asked, "you had only that one brief talk with Mr. Keems? You didn't see him again?"

"No. How could we?"

"Did you see him again, Mr. Irwin?"

"No."

"Can you add anything to your wife's account of your talk with him?"

"No. That was all there was to it. I might add that our maid sleeps in, and she was there that night."

"Thank you. That should be helpful. I'll include it in my report to the police." Wolfe went back to the wife. "One little point, Mrs. Irwin. If you decided earlier in the day that you wouldn't be able to go to the theater that evening, you might have mentioned it to someone, for instance to some friend on the phone, and you might also have mentioned, partly as a joke, that you would suggest that Mrs. Molloy be asked in your place. Did anything like that happen?"

She shook her head. "No, it couldn't have, because I didn't decide not to go until just before my husband came home."

"Then your headache was a sudden attack?"

"I don't know what you would call sudden. I was lying down with it most of the afternoon, and taking emagrin, and I was hoping it would go away. But I had to give up."

"Do you have frequent headaches?"

Irwin burst out, "What the hell has that got to do with it?"

"Probably nothing," Wolfe conceded. "I'm fishing white water, Mr. Irwin, and am casting at random."

"It seems to me," Arkoff put in, "that you're fishing in dead water. Asking Mrs. Molloy didn't have to be designed at all. If Peter Hays didn't kill Molloy, if someone else did, of course it was somebody who knew him. He could have phoned Molloy and said he wanted to see him alone, and Molloy told him to come to the apartment, they would be alone there because Mrs. Molloy had gone to the theater. Why couldn't it have happened like that?"

"It could," Wolfe agreed. "Quite possible. The invitation to Mrs. Molloy was merely one of the aspects that deserved inquiry, and it might have been quickly eliminated. But not now. Now there is a question that must be answered: who killed Johnny Keems, and why?"

"Some damned fool. Some hit-and-run maniac."

"Possibly, but I don't believe it. I must be satisfied now, and so must the police, and even if you people are innocent of any complicity you can't escape harassment. I'll want to know more than I do now about the evening of January third, about what happened at the theater. I understand — Yes, Archie?"

"Before you leave last night," I said, "I have a question to ask them."

"Go ahead."

I leaned forward to have all their faces as they turned to me. "About Johnny Keems," I said. "Did he ask any of you anything about Bill Lesser?"

They had never heard the name before. You can't always go by the reaction to a sudden unexpected question, since some people are extremely good at handling their faces, but if that name meant anything to one or more of them they were better than good. They all looked blank and wanted to know who Bill Lesser was. Of course Wolfe would also have liked to know who he was but didn't say so. I told him that was all, and he resumed.

"I understand that Mrs. Molloy and Mrs. Arkoff went in to their seats before curtain time, and that Mr. Arkoff and Mr. Irwin joined them about an hour later, saying they had been in a bar across the street. Is that correct, Mr. Arkoff?"

Arkoff didn't care for that at all, and neither did Irwin. Their position was that their movements on the evening of January 3 had no significance unless it was assumed that one or both of them might have killed Molloy and framed Peter Hays, and that was absurd. Wolfe's position was that the police would ask him if he had questioned them about January 3, and if he said he had and they had balked, the police would want to know why.

Rita told her husband to quit arguing and get it over with, and that only made it worse, until she snapped at him, "What's so touchy about it? Weren't you just dosing up?"

He gave her a dirty look and then transferred it to Wolfe. "My wife and I," he said, "met Mrs. Molloy in the theater lobby at half-past eight. The ladies went on in and I waited in the lobby for Irwin. He came a few minutes later and said he wanted a drink, and he also said he didn't care much for plays about Joan of Arc. We went across the street and had a couple of drinks, and by the time we got in to our seats the first act was about over."

Wolfe's head turned. "You corroborate that, Mr. Irwin?"

"I do."

Wolfe turned a hand over. "So simple, gentlemen, Why all the pother? And with a new and quite persuasive detail, that Mr. Irwin doesn't care for plays about Joan of Arc — an inspired hoyden. To show you to what lengths an investigation can be carried, and sometimes has to be, a dozen men could make a tour of Mr. Irwin's friends and acquaintances and ask if they have ever heard him express an attitute toward Joan of Arc and plays about her. I doubt if I'll be driven to that extremity. Have you any questions?"

They hadn't, for him. Rita Arkoff got up and went to Selma, and Fanny Irwin joined them. The men did too, for a moment, and then headed for the hall, and I followed them. They got their coats on and stood and waited, and finally their women came, and I opened the door. As they moved out Rita was telling the men that she had asked Selma to come and eat with them, but she had said she wasn't up to it. "And no wonder," Rita was saying as I swung the door to.

When I re-entered the office Selma didn't look as if she were up to anything whatever, sitting with her shoulders slumped and her head sagging and her eyes closed. Wolfe was speaking, inviting her to stay for not only dinner but also the night. He said he wanted her at hand for consultation if occasion arose, but that wasn't it. She had brought word from Parker that the court formalities might be completed in the morning, and if so we might get to the safe-deposit box by noon. For that Mrs. Molloy would be needed, and Wolfe would never trust a woman to be where she was supposed to be when you wanted her. Therefore he was telling her how pleasant our south room was, directly under his, with a good bed and morning sunshine, but no sale, not even for dinner. She got to her feet, and I went to the hall with her.

"It's hopeless, isn't it," she said, not a question. I patted her shoulder professionaly and told her we had barely started.

In the office again, Wolfe demanded, "Who is Bill Lesser?"

I told him, reporting it verbatim, including my phone call to Delia Brandt, and explaining I had hoped to get a glimmer from one or more of the quartet at sound of the name. He wasn't very enthusiastic but admitted it was worth a look and said we would put Fred Durkin on it. I asked if I should phone Purley Stebbins, and he said no, it was too close to dinner-time and he wanted first to think over his talk with Mrs. Molloy's friends.

He heaved a sigh. "Confound it," he complained, "no gleam anywhere, no little fact that stings, no word that trips. I have no appetite!"

I snorted. "That's the least of my worries," I declared.

12

I never did phone Purley because I didn't have to.

Fred Durkin called during dinner and said he had had no better luck at the theater and the bar than at the phone-booth places, and I told him to come in, and he was there by the time we returned to the office with coffee. He had drawn nothing but blanks and I was glad we had a bone for him with a little meat on it. He was to do a take on William Lesser — address, occupation, and the trimmings — and specifically, had he been loose at 11:48 Wednesday night? That last seemed a waste of time and energy, since I had it entered that the Arkoffs and Irwins had never heard of him, but Wolfe wanted a little fact that stung and you never can tell. Just before Fred left Orrie Cather came.

Orrie brought a little package of items he had selected from the cartons in the Molloy apartment, and if they were the cream the milk must have been dishwater. He opened the package on my desk and we went through the treasure together, while Wolfe sat and read a book. There was a desk calendar with an entry on the leaf for January 2, *Call B,* and nothing else; a batch of South American travel folders; half a dozen books of matches from restaurants; a stack of carbon copies of letters, of which the most exciting was one to the Pearson Appliance Corporation telling them what he thought of their electric shaver; and more of the same.

"I don't believe it," I told Orrie. "You must have brought the wrong package."

"Honest to God," he swore. "Talk about drek, I never saw anything to equal it."

"Not even check stubs?"

"Not a stub."

I turned to Wolfe. "Mike Molloy was one of a kind. Meeting sudden death by violence in the prime of his manhood, as you would put it, he left in his office not a single item that would interest a crow, let alone a detective. Not even the phone number of his barber. No gleam anywhere."

"I wouldn't put it that way. Not 'prime of manhood.'"

"Okay. But unless he expected to get killed —"

The doorbell rang. I stepped to the door to the hall, switched on the stoop light, took a look, and turned.

"Cramer. Alone."

"Ah." Wolfe lifted his eyes from the book. "In the front room, Orrie, if you please? Take that stuff with you. When Mr. Cramer has passed through you might as well leave, and report in the morning."

I stood a moment until Orrie had gathered up the treasure and started for the door to the front room, and then went to the hall and opened up. Many a time, seeing the burly breadth and round red face of Inspector Cramer of Homicide there on the stoop, I had left the chain bolt on and spoken with him through the crack, but I now swung the door wide.

"Good evening," I said courteously.

"Hello, Goodwin. Wolfe in?"

That was a form of wit. He knew damn well Wolfe was in, since he was never out. If I had been feeling sociable I would have reciprocated by telling him no, Wolfe had gone skating at Rockefeller Center, but the haul Orrie had brought had been hard on my sense of humor, so I merely admitted him and took his coat. He didn't wait for escort to the office. By the time I got there he was already in the red leather chair and he and Wolfe were glaring at each other. They do that from force of habit. Which way they go from the glare, toward a friendly exchange of information or toward a savage exchange of insults, depends on the circumstances. That time Cramer's opening pass was mild enough. He merely remarked that Goodwin had told Sergeant Stebbins he would call him back and hadn't done so. Wolfe grunted and merely remarked that he didn't suppose Cramer had come in person for information which Mr. Goodwin could have given Mr. Stebbins on the phone.

"But he didn't," Cramer growled.

"He will now," Wolfe growled back. "Do you want him to?"

"No." Cramer got more comfortable. "I'm here now. There's more to it than Johnny Keems, but I'll take that first. What was he doing for you last night?"

"He was investigating a certain aspect of the murder of Michael M. Molloy on January third."

"The hell he was. I thought a murder investigation was finished when the murderer was tried and convicted."

Wolfe nodded. "It is. But not when an innocent man is tried and convicted."

It looked very much as if they were headed for insults. But before Cramer had one ready Wolfe went on. "You would ask, of course, if I have evidence to establish Peter Hays's innocence. No, I haven't. My reasons for thinking him innocent would not be admissible as evidence, and would have no weight for you. I intend to find the evidence if it exists, and Johnny Keems was looking for it last night."

Cramer's sharp gray eyes, surrounded by crinkles, were leveled at Wolfe's brown ones. He was not amused. On previous occasions, during a murder investigation, he had found Wolfe a thorn in his hide and a pain in his neck, but this was the first time it had ever happened after it had been wrapped up by a jury.

"I am familiar," he said, "with the evidence that convicted Hays. I collected it, or my men did."

"Pfui. It didn't have to be collected. It was there."

"Well, we picked it up. What aspect was Keems working on?"

"The invitation to Mrs. Molloy to go to the theater. On the chance that it was designed, to get her away from the apartment. His instructions were to see Mr. and Mrs. Arkoff and Mr. and Mrs. Irwin, and to report to me if he got any hint of suspicion. He didn't report, which was typical of him, and he paid for his disdain. However, I know that he saw those four, all of them. They were here this afternoon for more than an hour. He saw Mrs. Arkoff at her apartment shortly after eight o'clock, and returned two hours later and saw her and her husband. In between those two visits he saw Mr. and Mrs. Irwin at their apartment. Do you want to know what they say they told him?"

Cramer said he did, and Wolfe obliged. He gave him a full and fair report, including all essentials, unless you count as an essential his telling them that he wanted to talk with them before he told the police what Johnny Keems had been doing — and anyway Cramer could guess that for himself.

At the end he added a comment. "The inference is patent. Either one or more of them were lying, or Johnny saw someone besides them, or his death had no connection with his evening's work. I will accept the last only when I must, and apparently you will too or you wouldn't be here. Did the circumstances eliminate fortuity?"

"If you mean could it have been an accident, it's barely possible. It wasn't on the Drive proper, it was on one of those narrow side approaches to apartment houses. A man and woman were in a parked car a hundred feet away, waiting for someone. The car was going slow when it passed them, going up the lane. They saw Keems step into the lane from between two parked cars, and they think the driver of the car blinked his lights, but they're not sure. As the car approached Keems it slowed nearly to a stop, and then it took a sudden spurt and swerved straight at Keems, and that was it. It kept going and had turned a corner before the man and woman were out of their car. You know we found the car this morning parked on upper Broadway, and it was stolen?"

"Yes."

"So it doesn't look like fortuity. I must remember to use that in a report. You said it could be that one of them was lying, or more than one. What do you think?"

Wolfe puckered his lips. "It's hard to say. It can't very well be just one of them, since their alibis are all in pairs — the two men in the bar the evening of January third, and for last night man and wife at home together in both cases. Of course you know their addresses, since you collected the evidence against Peter Hays."

"They're in the file." Cramer's eyes came to me. "In the neighborhood, Goodwin?"

"Near enough," I told him. "The Arkoffs in the Eighties on Central Park West, and the Irwins in the Nineties on West End Avenue."

"Not that that's important. You understand, Wolfe, as far as I'm concerned the Hays case is closed. He's guilty as hell. You admit you have no evidence. It's Keems I'm interested in. If it was homicide, homicide is my business. That's what I'm after."

Wolfe's brows went up. "Do you want a suggestion?"

"I can always use a suggestion."

"Drop it. Charge Johnny Keem's death to accident and close the file. I suppose a routine search for the hit-and-run driver must be made, but confine it to that. Otherwise you'll find that the Hays case is open again, and that would be embarrassing. For all I know you may have already been faced with that difficulty and that's why you're here — for instance, through something found in Johnny Keem's pockets. Was there something?"

"No."

Wolfe's eyes were narrowed at him. "I am being completely candid with you, Mr. Cramer."

"So am I. Nothing was found on Keems but the usual items — keys, cigarettes, driving license, handkerchief, a little cash, pen and pencil. After what you tell me I'm surprised he didn't have a memo of those people's names and addresses. Didn't you give him one, Goodwin?"

"No. Johnny didn't believe in memos. He didn't even carry a notebook. He thought his memory was as good as mine, but it wasn't. Now it's no good at all."

He went back to Wolfe. "About your being completely candid, I didn't think I'd go into this, but I will. Tuesday's papers had an ad headed 'To P.H.' and signed by you. Tuesday noon Sergeant Stebbins phoned to ask Goodwin about it, and Goodwin told him to ask Lieutenant Murphy of the Missing Persons Bureau. What he learned from Murphy satisfied him, and me too, that your ad hadn't been directed at Peter Hays but at a man named Paul Herold, and we crossed it off as coincidence. But Wednesday morning, yesterday, Goodwin goes to the City Prison and has a talk with Peter Hays. News of that gets to Murphy, and he sees Hays and asks him if he is Paul Herold, and Hays says no. But here you are saying you think Hays is innocent and up to your neck in it hell for breakfast. If you had Keems investigating one aspect, how many men have you got on other aspects? You don't toss money around just to see it flutter in the breeze. So if you're being so goddamn candid, who's your client?"

Wolfe nodded. "That would interest you, naturally. I'm sorry, Mr. Cramer, I can't tell you. You can ask Mr. Albert Freyer, counsel for Peter Hays, and see if you have better luck."

"Nuts. Is Peter Hays Paul Herold?"

"He told Mr. Goodwin he is not. You say he told Lieutenant Murphy he is not. He should know."

"Then why are you on the warpath?"

"Because both my curiosity and cupidity have been aroused, and together they are potent. Believe me, Mr. Cramer, I have been candid to the limit of my discretion. Will you have some beer?"

"No. I'm going. I have to start somebody on these Arkoffs and Irwins."

"Then the Hayes case is open again. That is not a gibe, merely a fact. Can you spare me another minute? I would like to know exactly what was found in Johnny Keems's pockets."

"I've told you." Cramer got up. "The usual items."

"Yes, but I'd like a complete list. I would appreciate it, if you'll indulge me."

Cramer eyed him. He could never make up his mind whether Wolfe was really after something or was merely putting on an act. Thinking he might find out, he turned to me. "Get my office, Goodwin."

I swiveled and dialed, and when I had the number Cramer came to my desk and took it. I was supposing he would tell someone to get the list from the file and read it off to me, but no sir. That way I could have faked something, and who would trust Goodwin? He stayed at the phone, and when the list had been dug out and was called off to him he relayed it to me, item by item, and I wrote it down. As follows:

> Motor operator's license
> Social Security card
> Eastern Insurance Co. Identification card
> 2 tickets to baseball game for May 11th
> 3 letters in envelopes (personal matters)
> Newspaper clipping about fluorine in drinking water
> $22.16 in bills and coins
> Pack of cigarettes
> 2 books of matches
> 4 keys on a ring
> 1 handkerchief
> Ballpoint pen
> Pencil
> Pocket knife

I started to hand it to Wolfe, but Cramer reached and grabbed it. When he had finished studying it he returned it to me and I passed it to Wolfe, and Cramer asked him, "Well?"

"Thank you very much." Wolfe sounded as if he meant it. "One question: is it possible that something, some small article, was taken from his clothing before this list was made?"

"Possible, yes. Not very likely. The man and woman who saw it from the parked car are respectable and responsible citizens. The man went to where the body was lying, and the woman blew the horn, and an officer came in a couple of minutes. The officer was the first one to touch the body. Why? What's missing?"

"Money. Archie, how much did you give Johnny for expenses?"

"One hundred dollars."

"And presumably he had a little of his own. Of course, Mr. Cramer, I am not ass enough to suggest that you have a thief on your force, but that hundred dollars belonged to me, since Johnny Keems had possession of it as my agent. If by any chance it should turn up—"

"Goddam you, I ought to knock you through that wall," Cramer said through his teeth, and whirled and tramped out.

I waited until I heard the front door slam, then went to the hall and on to the one-way glass panel to see him cross the sidewalk and climb into his car. When I returned to the office Wolfe was sitting with his fingers interlaced at the apex of his central mound, trying not to look smug.

I stood and looked down at him. "I'll be damned," I said. "So you've got your little fact that stings. Next, who did he grease with it?"

He nodded. "Not too difficult, I should think. Apparently you share my assumption that he bribed somebody?"

"No question about it. Johnny wasn't perfect, but he came close to it about money. That hundred bucks was yours, and for him that was that." I sat down. "I'm glad to hear that it won't be difficult to find out who got it. I was afraid it might be."

"I think not—at least not to reach an assumption worth testing. Let us suppose it was you instead of Johnny. Having seen Mrs. Arkoff, you arrive at the Irwins' apartment and find them about ready to leave, being detained by a necessary repair to Mrs. Irwin's garment which is being made by the maid. Mostly they merely confirm what Mrs. Arkoff has already told you, but contribute one new detail: that the suggestion to invite Mrs. Molloy came originally from Mrs. Irwin. That is interesting, even provocative, and you want to pursue it, and try to, but by then the maid has the garment repaired and Mrs. Irwin puts it on, and they leave. You leave with them, of course, going down in the elevator with them, and they go off. There you are. You have seen three of them and have only one more on your list, it's a little after nine o'clock, and there is an hour to pass before you can see Mr. Arkoff. What do you do?"

"Nothing to it. As soon as the Irwins are out of sight I go back upstairs and see the maid."

"Would Johnny?"

"Absolutely."

"Then he did. Worth testing, surely."

"Yeah, it stings, all right. If that maid took your hundred bucks she'll take more." I looked at my wrist. "Ten minutes to eleven. Shall I give her a whirl now?"

"I think not. Mr. and Mrs. Irwin might be there."

"I can phone and find out."

"Do so."

I got the number from the book and dialed it, and after four whirrs a female voice told me hello.

I sent my voice through my nose. "May I speak to Mrs. Irwin, please?"

"This is Mrs. Irwin. Who is this?"

I cradled it gently, not to be rude, and turned. "Mrs. Irwin answered. I guess it will have to wait until morning. I'll call Mrs. Molloy first and get the maid's name. She probably knows it."

Wolfe nodded. "It will be ticklish, and it must not be botched."

"Right. I'll bring her here and take her to the basement and hold matches to her toes. I have a remark. Your asking Cramer for a list of the contents of Johnny's pockets, that was only par for a genius, but your bumping him off the trail by pretending you wanted your money back—I couldn't have done it better myself. Satisfactory. I hope I'm not flattering you."

"Not likely," he grumbled, and picked up his book.

13

THE maid's name was Ella Reyes. I got that from Selma Molloy on the phone at eight o'clock Friday morning, and also that she was around thirty years old, small and neat, the color of coffee with cream, and had been with the Irwins for about a year.

But I didn't get to tackle her. Relieving Fritz of the chore of taking Wolfe's breakfast tray up to his room, where, a mountain of yellow silk pajamas, he stood barefoot in the flood of sunshine near a window, I learned that he had shifted the line-up. Orrie Cather was to call on the man and woman who, sitting in a parked car, had seen the end of Johnny Keems. Their name and address was in the papers, as well as the fact that they agreed that the driver of the hit-and-run car had been a man, and that was about all. They had of course been questioned by old hands at it, but Wolfe wanted Orrie to get it direct.

Saul Panzer was to take the maid, write his own opening, and ad lib it from there. He was to be equipped with five hundred bucks from the safe, which, added to the C he already had, would make six hundred. A rosy prospect for Ella Reyes, since it would be tax-free. I was to be on call for the ceremony of opening the safe-deposit box, if and when it was scheduled. Wolfe was good enough to supply a reason for giving Saul the maid and me the ceremony. He said that if difficulties arose Mrs. Molloy would be more tractable with me present. Wit.

I was fiddling around the office when Wolfe came down from the plant rooms at eleven o'clock. Saul had arrived at nine and got a thorough briefing and five Cs, and departed, and Orrie had come and gone, to see the eyewitnesses. Parker phoned a little after ten, said he would probably get the court order before noon, and told me to stand by. I asked if I should alert Mrs. Molloy, and he said she wouldn't be needed, so I phoned her that she could relax.

Feeling that the situation called for a really cutting remark to the wit, I concocted a few, but none of them was sharp enough, so when he entered and crossed to his desk I merely said, "Mrs. Molloy isn't coming to the party. You have bewitched her. She admits she wouldn't stay last night because she was afraid to trust herself so close to you. She never wants to go anywhere any more unless you are there."

He grunted and picked up a catalogue that had come in the morning mail, and the phone rang. It was Parker. I was to meet him and Patrick Degan at the Metropolitan Safe Deposit Company at noon.

When I got there, on Madison Avenue in the Forties, five minutes early, I discovered that I hadn't exaggerated when I called it a party, and nobody was late. There were ten of us gathered down in the anteroom of the vaults: Parker, Degan; two officers of the safe deposit company; an attendant of the same; an Assistant District Attorney with a city dick, known to me, apparently as his bodyguard; a fingerprint scientist from the police laboratory, also known to me; a stranger in rimless cheaters whose identity I learned later; and me. Evidently opening a safe-deposit box outside of routine can be quite an affair. I wondered where the mayor was.

After the two MSDC officers had thoroughly studied a document Parker had handed them we were all escorted through the steel barrier and into a room, not any too big, with three chairs and a narrow table in its center. One of the MSDC officers went out and in a couple of minutes came back, carrying a metal box about twenty-four by eight by six, not normally, but with his fingertips hooked under the bottom edges at front and back. Before an appreciative audience he put it down, tenderly, on the table, and the fingerprint man took the stage, putting his case also on the table and opening it.

I wouldn't say that he stretched it purposely, playing to the gallery, but he sure did an all-out job. He was at it a good half-hour, covering top, sides, ends, and bottom, with dusters, brushes, flippers, magnifying glasses, camera and print records which came from a brief case carried by the Assistant DA. They should have furnished more chairs.

He handled his climax fine, putting all his paraphernalia back in his case and shutting it before he told us, "I identify six separate prints on the box as the same as those on the records marked Michael M. Molloy. Five other prints are probably the same but I wouldn't certify them. Some other prints may be."

Nobody applauded. Someone sighed, tired of standing up, Parker addressed the stranger with the rimless cheaters. "That meets the provisions of the order, doesn't it?"

"Yes," the stranger conceded, "but I think the expert should certify it in writing."

That started an argument. The expert was allergic to writing. He would maintain his conclusion orally, without reservation, before nine witnesses, but he wouldn't sign a statement until he had made a prolonged study in the laboratory of his photographs and Molloy's recorded prints, and had his findings verified by a colleague. That wasn't very logical, but they couldn't budge him. Finally the stranger said he would stand by his concession that the oral conclusion satisfied the order, and told the MSDC officer to give Parker the box and the key — the duplicate key which had been provided by the MSDC to open the compartment the box had been in. Parker said no, give them to Mr. Degan. But before Degan got them he had to sign a receipt for them.

"All right, open it," the Assistant DA told him.

Degan stood with a hand resting on the box and sent his quick brown eyes around the arc. "Not in public," he said, politely but firmly. "This was Mr. Molloy's box, and I represent his estate by a court order. If you will leave, please? Or if you prefer, I'll take it to another room."

Another argument, a free-for-all. They wanted to see the box opened, but in the end had to give up, when the Assistant DA reluctantly agreed with Parker that Degan's position was legally sound. He left the room, with his bodyguard, and the fingerprint scientist followed them. The two MSDC officers didn't like it at all, but with the law gone they had no choice, so out they went.

Degan looked at the stranger in rimless cheaters and demanded, "Well, sir?"

"I stay," the stranger declared. "I represent the New York State Tax Commission." He was close enough to the table to reach the box by stretching an arm.

"Death and taxes," Parker told Degan. "The laws of nature and the laws of man. You can't budge him. Close the door, Archie."

"Behind you," Degan said. He was looking at Parker. "As you go out."

Parker smiled at him. "Oh, come. Mr. Goodwin and I are not the public. We have a status and a legitimate interest. It was through us that you got that box."

"I know it." Degan kept his hand on it. "But I am now legally in charge of Molloy's estate, temporarily at least, and my only proper obligation is to the estate. You're a lawyer, Mr. Parker, you know that. Be reasonable! What do I actually know about what Nero Wolfe is after or what you're after? Only what you've told me. I don't say that I think you already know about something that's in this box, and that I'm afraid Goodwin will grab it and run, but I do say that it's my responsibility to run no risk of any kind in guarding the estate, and the fact that I got the responsibility through you has nothing to do with it. Isn't that reasonable?" It was an appeal.

"Yes," Parker said, "it's eminently reasonable. I can't challenge it, and I don't. But we're not going to leave. We're not going to grab anything, or even touch anything unless invited, but we're going to see what you find in that box. If you summon help and demand that we be put out I doubt if you'll be obeyed, under the circumstances. If we leave we all leave, and I shall go to Judge Rucker at once and complain that you refuse to open the box in the presence of the widow's counsel. I believe he would enjoin you from opening it at all, pending a hearing."

Degan picked up the box.

"Hold it," I told him. I stepped and closed the door and stepped back. "Mr. Parker has covered most of the ground, but he didn't mention what we'll do if you try moving to another room. That's my department. I'll stand with my back against the door." I moved. "Like this. I'm three inches taller than you and fifteen pounds heavier in spite of your belly, and with the box you'll only have one hand. Of course you can try, and I promise not to hurt you. Much."

He regarded me, not cordially, and breathed.

"This is a farce." Parker declared. He came and joined me with his back against the door. "Now. Now or never. Go ahead and open it. If Goodwin leaps for you I'll trip him. After all, I'm a member of the bar and an officer of the law."

Degan was a stubborn devil. Even then he took another twenty seconds to consider the situation, after which he moved to the far end of the table, facing us at a distance of twelve feet, put the box down, and lifted the lid. The tax man moved with him and was at his elbow. The raised lid obstructed our view, and the inside was not visible, except to him and the New York State Tax Commission. They stared at it a moment, then Degan put a hand in. When he withdrew it, it held a bundle of lettuce three inches thick, fastened with rubber bands. He inspected it all over, put it on the table beside the box, inserted his hand again, and took out another bundle. And others. Eight of them altogether.

He looked at us. "By God," he said, with a little shake in his voice, "I'm glad you fellows stayed. Come and look."

We accepted the invitation. The box was empty. The top bills on five of the bundles were Cs, on two of them fifties, and on the other one a twenty. They were used bills, held tight and compact by the rubber bands. They wouldn't run as healthy as new stuff, around 250 to the inch, but they were not hay.

"Quite a hoard," Parker said. "No wonder you're glad we stayed. If I had been here alone I would have been tempted myself."

Degan nodded, looking dazed. "I'll be damned. We'll have to count it. Will you help me count it?"

We obliged him. I moved the chairs up and we sat, Degan at the table end and Parker and I at either elbow, and started in. The tax man was right behind Degan's shoulder, bending over to breathe down the back of his neck. It took a long while because Degan wanted each bundle counted by all of us, which seemed reasonable, and one of the bundles of fifties had to be gone over six times to reach agreement. When we finished each bundle was topped with a slip of paper with the amount and our initials on it. On another slip Degan listed the amounts and got a total. $327,640.00.

If you don't believe it I'll spell it out. Three hundred and twenty-seven thousand, six hundred and forty berries.

Degan looked at Parker. "You expected this?"

"No. I had no expectations whatever."

He looked at me. "Did you?"

I shook my head. "Same here."

"I wonder. I wonder what Wolfe expected."

"You'd have to ask him."

"I would like to. Is he in his office?"

I looked at my wrist. "He will be for another fifteen minutes. Lunch at one-thirty on Friday."

"We might make it." He returned the bundles to the box, locked it, picked it up, and headed for the door, with the New York State Tax Commission practically stepping on his heels. Parker and I followed, and waited outside while he went with an attendant and the tax man to have the box slid into its niche and locked in, and when he rejoined us we mounted together to the street floor. There the tax man parted from us. Except for interested glances from a couple of guards we drew no attention inside, but the press was on the job. As we emerged to the sidewalk a journalist blocked our path and said the public wanted to know what had been found in Molloy's box, and when we refused to spill it he stayed right with us until we were in the taxi with the door shut.

The midtown traffic kept us from getting to the old brownstone before one-thirty, but since as far as I knew Patrick A. Degan was still a suspect I took him in along with Parker. Herding them into the office, I crossed the hall to the dining room and shut the door. Wolfe, in the big chair with arms, at the far end of the table, had just started operating on an eight-inch ring of ham and sweetbreads mousse.

"You brought visitors," he accused me.

"Yes, sir. Parker and Degan. I know you won't work with the feedbag on, but we found a third of a million dollars in used currency in the safe-deposit box, and Degan wants to ask you if you knew it was there. Shall they wait?"

"Have they eaten?"

"No."

Of course that wouldn't do. The thought of a hungry human, even a hungry murder suspect, even a hungry woman, in his house, is intolerable. So we had luncheon guests. They and I split the mousse that was waiting for me, and while we finished it Fritz manufactured a celery and mushroom omelet. Wolfe tells me there was a man in Marseilles who made a better omelet than Fritz, but I don't believe it. The guests protested that the mousse was all they wanted, but I noticed that the omelet was cleaned up, though I admit Wolfe took a portion just to taste.

Leaving the dining room, I gave Wolfe a sign, and, letting Parker conduct Degan to the office, he and I went to the kitchen, and I reported on the ceremony of opening the box. He listened with a scowl, but not for me. He hates to stand up right after a meal, and he hates to sit down in the kitchen because the stools and chairs aren't fit to sit on — for him.

When I was through he demanded, "How sure are you that the box contained nothing but the money?"

"Dead sure. My eyes were glued to him, and they're good eyes. Not a chance."

"Confound it," he muttered.

"My God," I complained, "you're hard to satisfy. Three hundred and twenty-seven thou —"

"But only that. It's suggestive, of course, but that's all. When a man is involved in a circumstance pressing enough to cause his murder he must leave a relic of it somewhere, and I had hoped it was in that box. Very well. I want to sit down."

He marched to the office, and I followed.

Parker had let Degan have the red leather chair, and Degan had lit a cigar, so Wolfe's nose twitched as he got his bulk adjusted in his chair.

"You gentlemen doubtless have your engagements," he said, "so I apologize for keeping you so long, but I never discuss business at the table. Mr. Goodwin has told me what you found in that box. A substantial nest egg. You have a question for me, Mr. Degan?"

"A couple," Degan said, "but first I must thank you for the lunch. The best omelet I ever ate!"

"I'll tell Mr. Brenner. It will please him. And the question?"

"Well." He blew smoke, straight at his host. "Partly it's just plain curiosity. Were you expected to find a large sum of money in the box?"

"No. I had no specific expectation. I was hoping to find something that would forward the job I'm on, as I told you yesterday, but I had no idea what it might be."

"Okay." Degan gestured with the cigar. "I'm not a suspicious man, Mr. Wolfe, anyone who knows me will tell you that, but now I've got this responsibility. The thought would have occurred to anybody, finding that fortune in that box, what if you knew it was there or thought it was? And now that it's been found, what if you are figuring that a sizable share of it will be used to pay you for this job you're doing?"

Wolfe grunted. "Surely that's a question for me to ask, not answer. What if I am?"

"Then you are."

"I haven't said so. But what if I am?"

"I don't know. I don't know what to say." Degan took a puff, and this time blew it at Parker. "Frankly, I'm sorry I agreed to this. I did it for a friend who has had a tough break, Selma Molloy, and I wish I hadn't. I'm on a spot. I know she's all for the job you're doing, trying to find grounds for a new trial for Peter Hays, and I am too, personally, so you might think I'd be willing to commit the estate to pay for your services and expenses, but the hell of it is that she says she won't take the estate or any part of it. That didn't matter when there were no visible assets to speak of, but now it does. It will go to someone eventually, relatives always turn up when there's a pile in it, and what will they say if I've paid you some of it? You see my problem." He took a puff.

"I do indeed." Wolfe's lips were slightly twisted—one of his smiles. "But you asked the wrong question. Instead of asking *what* if I am you should have asked *if* I am. The answer is no. I shall not demand, or accept if offered, anything from that trove."

"You won't? You mean that?"

"I do."

"Then why didn't you say so?"

"I have said so." Wolfe's lips straightened. "And now that I have answered your questions, I beg you to reciprocate. You knew Mr. Molloy for some years. Have you any knowledge of the source of that money?"

"No. I was absolutely amazed when I saw it."

"Please bear with me. I don't challenge you, I'm merely trying to stimulate you. You were intimate with him?"

"Intimate? I wouldn't say intimate. He was one of my friends, and I did a little business with him from time to time."

"What kind of business?"

"I bought advice from him now and then." Degan reached to break cigar ash into the tray. "In connection with investments of my organization. He was an expert on certain areas of the real-estate market."

"But you didn't pay him enough to supply an appreciable fraction of that fortune in the box."

"My God, no. On an average, maybe two or three thousand a year."

"Was that the main source of Molloy's income, supplying investment advice regarding real estate?"

"I couldn't say. It may have been, but he did some brokerage and I think he did a little operating on his own. I never heard him say much about his affairs. He had a close mouth."

Wolfe cocked his head. "I appeal to you, Mr. Degan. You had a problem and I relieved you of it. Now I have one. I want to know where that money came from. Surely, in your long association with Mr. Molloy, both business and social, he must have said or done something that would furnish a hint of activities which netted him a third of a million dollars. Surely he did, and if it meant nothing to you at the time, it might now if you recall it. I ask you to make the effort. If, as you said, you wish me success in my efforts on behalf of Mrs. Molloy, I think my request is justified. Don't you agree?"

"Yes, I do." Degan looked at his watch and arose. "I'm late for an appointment. I'll put my mind on it and let you know if I remember anything." He turned, and turned back. "I know a few people who had dealings with Molloy. Do you want me to ask them?"

"Yes indeed. I would appreciate it."

"I suppose you'll ask Mrs. Molloy yourself."

Wolfe said he would, and Degan went. Returning to the office after seeing him out, I stopped at the sill because Parker was on his feet, set to go. He told me not to bother, but I like to be there when the gate of Wolfe's castle opens to the world, so I got his coat from the rack and held it for him.

In the office, Wolfe was having a burst of energy. He had left his chair to get the ashtray Degan had used and was on his way to the door of the bathroom in the corner, to dump it. When he reappeared I asked him, "Nothing from Saul or Fred or Orrie?"

He returned the tray to its place, sat, rang for beer, two short and one long, and roared at me, "No!"

When a hippopotamus is peevish it's a lot of peeve. I should have brought a bundle of Cs for him to play with, and told him so.

14

HOW much Wolfe likes to show the orchids to people depends on who it is. Gushers he can stand, and even jostlers. The only ones he can't bear are those who pretend they can tell a P. stuartiana from a P. schilleriana but can't. And there is an ironclad rule that except for Fritz and me, and of course Theodore, who is there all the time, no one goes to the plant rooms for any other purpose than to look at orchids.

Since he refuses to interrupt his two daily turns up there for a trip down to the office, no matter who or what, there have been some predicaments over the years. Once I chased a woman who was part gazelle clear to the top of the second flight before I caught her. The rule hasn't been broken more than half a dozen times altogether, and that afternoon was one of them.

He was in no better mood at four o'clock than an hour earlier. Fred Durkin had come with a report on William Lesser. He was twenty-five years old, lived with his parents on Washington Heights, had been to Korea, was a salesman for a soft-drink distributor, and had never been in jail. No discoverable connection with the Arkoffs or Irwins. No one who had heard him announce that a man named Molloy was going to cart his girl off to South American and he intended to prevent it. No one who knew he had a gun. And more negatives. Wolfe asked Fred if he wanted to try Delia Brandt, disguised as the editor who wanted the magazine article, and Fred said no. As I said before, Fred knows what he can expect of his brains and what he can't. He was told to go and dig some more at Lesser, and went.

Orrie Cather, who came while Fred was there, also drew a blank. The man and woman who had seen the car hit Johnny Keems were no help at all. They were sure the driver had been a man, but whether he was broad or narrow, light or dark, big or little, or with or without a clipped mustache, they couldn't say. Wolfe phoned Patrick Degan at his office and got eight names and addresses from him, friends and associates of Molloy who might furnish some hint of where the pile had come from, and told Orrie to make the rounds.

No word from Saul Panzer.

At half-past four I went to answer the doorbell, and there was the predicament on the stoop. I didn't know it was the predicament; I thought it was just our client, James R. Herold of Omaha, coming for a progress report; so I swung the door wide and welcomed him and took his things and ushered him to the office and moved a chair so he would be facing me. I told him on the way that Wolfe wouldn't be available until six o'clock but I was at his service. I admit that with the light from the window on his face I should have guessed he hadn't come merely for a report. He looked, as he hadn't before, like a man in trouble. His thin straight mouth was now tight and drawn, and his eyes were more dead than alive. He spoke. "I'd rather see Wolfe but I guess you'll do. I want to pay him to date, the expenses. I'd like to have an itemized account. Lieutenant Murphy has found my son, and I've seen him. I won't object if you want to add a small fee to the expenses."

At least I know a predicament when it pushes my nose in. When a man as pigheaded as Wolfe has ironclad rules he's stuck with them. If I went upstairs to him and broke the news there wasn't a chance. He would tell me to tell Herold that he would like to discuss the matter and would be down at six o'clock; and it was ten to one, from the look on Herold's face and the tone of his voice, that he wouldn't wait. He would say we could mail him a bill and get up and go.

So I stood up. "About the fee," I said, "I wouldn't want to decide that. That's up to Mr. Wolfe. Come along and we'll see what he says. This way."

I used the elevator instead of the stairs because the noise it made would notify Wolfe that something drastic was happening. Pushing the button to bring it down, entering with the ex-client, and pushing the button marked R for roof, my mind wasn't on the predicament at all, it was on Murphy. If I had had him there I wouldn't have said a word. I wouldn't have bothered with words. As we stopped at the top and the door slid open I told Herold, "I'll lead the way, if you don't mind."

It's hard to believe anyone could go along those aisles without seeing the array of color at all, but my mind was on Murphy. I don't know where Herold's was. Wolfe wasn't in the first room, the cool one, nor in the second, the medium, nor in the third, the tropical, and I went on through to the potting room. He was with Theodore at the bench, and turned to glare at us with a pot in one hand and a bunch of sphagnum in the other. With no greeting for the man who, in his ignorance, he thought was still his client, he barked at me, "Why this intrusion?"

"To report," I said, "Mr. Herold just came, and I told him you were engaged and took him to the office, and this is what he said. Quote." I recited Herold's little speech verbatim, and ended, "Unquote."

He had several choices. The rule that nobody came to the roof except to look at orchids had already been broken, by me. He could break the other one by going down to the office with us, or he could tell Herold that he would join him in the office at six o'clock, or he could throw the pot at me. He chose none of them. He turned his back on us, put the pot on the bench, tossed the sphagnum aside, got a trowelful of the charcoal and osmundine mixture from the tub, and dumped it into the pot. He reached for another pot and repeated the operation. And another. When six pots had been prepared he turned around and spoke.

"You have a record of the expenses, Archie."

"Yes, sir."

"Invoice them, including the commitments for today, and add the fee. The fee is fifty thousand dollars."

He turned to the bench and picked up a pot. I said, "Yes, sir," turned to go, and told Herold, "Okay, he's the boss."

"He's not my boss." He was staring at Wolfe's back, which is an eyeful. "You don't mean that. That's ridiculous!" No reaction. He took a step and raised his voice. "You haven't earned any fee at all! Lieutenant Murphy phoned me last night, and I took a plane, and he arranged for me to see my son. Do you even know where he is? If you do, why didn't you tell me?"

Wolfe turned and said quietly, "Yes, I know where he is. I suspect you, Mr. Herold."

"*You* suspect *me*? Of what?"

"Of chicanery. Mr. Murphy has his own credit and glory to consider, and so couldn't be expected to toot my horn, but I do not believe he made no mention of the part I've played. He's not an utter fool. I think you came here aware that I have earned a fee and conceived a shoddy stratagem to minimize it. The fee is fifty thousand dollars."

"I won't pay it!"

"Yes, you will." Wolfe made a face. "I don't run from contention, sir, but this sort of squabble is extremely distasteful. I'll tell you briefly how it will go. I'll render my bill, you'll refuse to pay it, and I'll sue you. By the time the action goes to trial I shall be armed with evidence that I not only found your son, which is what you hired me to do, but that I also freed him from a charge of murder by proving his innocence. Actually I doubt if you'll let it go to trial. You'll settle."

Herold looked around, saw a big comfortable chair, moved to it, and sat. Presumably he had had a tough day.

"That's my chair," Wolfe snapped. He can snap. "There are stools."

Three sound reasons: one, he didn't like Mr. Herold; two, he wanted to squash him; and three, if it went on he might want the chair himself. If Herold got to his feet and stayed on them he was still a contender; if he stayed in the chair he was cornered; if he took to a stool he was licked. He went to a stool and got on it. He spoke, not squabbling.

"Did you say you can prove his innocence?"

"No. Not now. But I expect to." Wolfe propped the back of his lap against the bench. "Mr. Goodwin saw him and talked with him Wednesday morning, day before yesterday, and established that he is your son. He didn't want you to be notified. That's an understatement. Did you speak with him today?"

"I saw him. He wouldn't speak to me. He denied me. His mother is coming."

That was some improvement. Before it had been only "my wife." Now it was "his mother." One big unhappy family.

He went on. "I didn't want her to, but she's coming. I don't know whether he'll speak to her or not. He hasn't just been arrested, he's been convicted, and the District Attorney says there can't be any question about it. What makes you think he's innocent?"

"I don't think it, I know it. One of my men has been killed—and I haven't earned a fee? Pfui. You'll know about it when the time comes."

"I want to know about it now."

"My dear sir." Wolfe was scornful. "You have fired me. We are adversaries in a lawsuit, or soon will be. Mr. Goodwin will conduct you downstairs." He turned, picked up a pot, and got a trowelful of the charcoal-osmundine mixture. That, by the way, was fake. You don't put that mixture in a pot until you have covered the bottom with crock.

From his perch on the stool Herold had him more in profile than full-face. He watched for four pots and then spoke. "I haven't fired you. I didn't know what the situation was. I don't now, and I want to."

Wolfe asked, not turning, "You want me to go on?"

"Yes. His mother is coming."

"Very well. Archie, take Mr. Herold to the office and tell him about it. Omit our inference from the contents of Johnny's pockets. We can't risk Mr. Cramer's meddling in that for the present."

I asked, "Give him everything else?"

"You might as well."

Getting down off the stool, Herold tripped on his own toe and nearly fell. To give him footwork practice I took him back down by way of the stairs.

He wasn't much impressed by my outline of the situation, but he had probably had all the impressions he had room for in one day. The guy was in shock. However, when he left we were still hired. He gave me the name of his hotel, and I said we would report any developments. At the door I told him it wouldn't be a good idea for his wife to come to see Wolfe, because when Wolfe was deep in a case he was apt to forget his manners. I didn't add that he was also apt to forget his manners when he wasn't deep in a case.

Alone again, I had a notion to try a few phone calls. In discussing an assignment for Orrie we had considered my tail—the party in a tan raglan and a brown snap-brim who had started to stalk me Tuesday afternoon when I left the house to go to the courtroom for a look at Peter Hays. Since there had been no sign of him since, the assumption was that somebody's curiosity had been aroused by the newspaper ad and he had lost interest after the jury had settled Hays's hash. We had decided it would be useless to put Orrie on it, since there was nowhere to start, but it wouldn't do any harm for me to phone a few of the agencies I was acquainted with and chat a little. The chance was slim that one of them had been hired to put a man on me, and slimmer still that they would spill it to me, but things do sometimes slip out in a friendly conversation, and I might as well be trying it as merely sitting on my fanny. I considered it, and decided to hit Del Bascom first, and was just starting to dial when two interruptions came at once. Wolfe came down from the plant rooms and Saul Panzer arrived.

Saul's face will never tell you a damn thing when he's playing poker with you, or playing anything else that calls for cover, but he's not so careful with it when he doesn't have to be, and at sight of it as I let him in I knew he had something hot.

Wolfe knew it too, and he was on edge. As Saul was turning a chair around he demanded, "Well?"

Saul sat. "From the beginning?"

"Yes."

"I phoned the apartment at nine-thirty-two and a woman answered and I asked to speak to Ella Reyes. She asked who I was and I said a Social Security investigator. She asked what I wanted with Ella Reyes and I said there was apparently a mix-up in names and I wanted to check. She said she wasn't there, and she wasn't sure when she would be, and I thanked her. So already it had a twist. A maid who sleeps in wasn't there and it wasn't known when she would be. I went to the apartment house and identified myself to the doorman."

You should hear Saul identifying himself. What he meant was that after three minutes with the doorman they were on such good terms that he was allowed to take the elevator without a phone call to announce him. It's no good trying to imitate him; I've tried it.

"I went up to Apartment Twelve-B, and Mrs. Irwin came to the door. I told her I had another errand in the neighborhood and dropped in to see Ella Reyes. She said she wasn't there and still didn't know when she would be. I pressed a little, but of course I couldn't overdo it. I said the mix-up had to do with addresses, and maybe she could straighten it out, and asked if her Ella Reyes had another address, perhaps her family's address, at Two-nineteen East One-hundred-and-twelfth Street. She said not that she knew of, that her Ella Reyes' family lived on East One-hundred-and-thirty-seventh Street. I asked if she could give me the number, and she went to another room and came back and said it was Three-oh-six East One-hundred-and-thirty-seventh Street."

Saul looked at me. "Do you want to note that, Archie?" I did so and he resumed. "I went down and asked the doorman if he had noticed Mrs. Irwin's maid going out this morning, and he said no, and he hadn't noticed her coming in either. He said Thursday was her night out and she always came in at eight o'clock Friday morning and he hadn't seen her. He asked the elevator man, and he hadn't seen her either. So I went to Three-oh-six East One-hundred-and-thirty-seventh Street. It's a dump, a cold-water walk-up. I saw Ella Reyes' mother. I was as careful as possible, but it's hard to be careful enough with those people. Anyway, I got it that Ella always came home Thursday nights and she hadn't showed up. Mrs. Reyes had been wanting to go to a phone and call Mrs. Irwin, but she was afraid Ella might be doing something she wouldn't want her employer to know about. She didn't say that, but that's what it was.

"I spent the rest of the day floundering around. Back at the Irwins' address the doorman told me that Ella Reyes had left as usual at six o'clock yesterday, alone. Mrs. Reyes had given me the names of a couple of Ella's friends, and I saw them, and they gave me more names. Nobody had seen her or heard from her. I phoned Mrs. Irwin twice during the afternoon, and I phoned headquarters once an hour to ask about accidents, of course not mentioning Ella Reyes. My last call to headquarters, at five o'clock, I was told that the body of a woman had been found behind a pile of lumber on the Harlem River bank near One-hundred-and-fortieth Street, with nothing on it to identify it. The body was on its way to the morgue. I went there, but the body hadn't arrived yet. When it came I looked at it, and it fits Mrs. Molloy's description of Ella Reyes—around thirty, small and neat, coffee with cream. Only the head wasn't neat. The back of the skull was smashed. I just came from there."

I stood up, realized that that didn't help matters any, and sat down. Wolfe took a long deep breath through his nose, and let it out through his mouth.

"I needn't ask," he said, "if you communicated your surmise."

"No sir. Of course not. A surmise isn't enough."

"No. What time does the morgue close?"

That's one way I know he's a genius. Only a genius would dare to ask such a question after functioning as a private detective for more than twenty years right there in Manhattan, and specializing in murder. The hell of it was, he really didn't know.

"It doesn't close," Saul said.

"Then we can proceed. Archie. Call Mrs. Molloy and ask her to meet you there."

"Nothing doing," I said firmly. "There are very few women I would ask to meet me at the morgue, and Mrs. Molloy is not one of them. Anyway, her phone may be tapped. This sonofabitch probably taps lines in between murders to pass the time. I'll go and get her."

"Then go."

I went.

15

I sat on a chair facing her. I had accepted the offer of a chair because on the way uptown in the taxi I had made a decision which would prolong my stay a little. She was wearing a light-weight woolen dress, lemon-colored, which could have been Dacron or something, but I prefer wool.

"When I first saw you," I told her, "fifty hours ago, I might have bet you one to twenty that Peter Hays would get clear. Now it's the other way around. I'll bet you twenty to one."

She squinted at me, giving the corners of her eyes the little upturn, and her mouth worked. "You're just bucking me up," she said.

"No, I'm not, but I admit it's a lead. We need your help. You remember I phoned you this morning to get the name of Mrs. Irwin's maid and a description of her. A body of a woman with a battered skull was found today behind a lumber pile on One-hundred-and-fortieth Street, and it is now in the morgue. We think it's Ella Reyes but we're not sure, and we need to know. I'm going to take you down there to look. It's your turn."

She sat and regarded me without blinking. I sat and waited. Finally she blinked.

"All right," she said, "I'll go. Now?"

No shivers or shudders, no squeals, or screams, no string of questions. I admit the circumstances were very favorable, since one thing was so heavy on her mind that there was no room for anything else.

"Now it is," I told her. "But you'll pack a bag for a night or two and we'll take it along. You'll stay at Wolfe's house until this thing is over."

She shook her head. "I won't do that. I told you yesterday. I have to be alone. I can't be with people and eat with people."

"You don't have to. You can have your meals in your room, and it's a nice room. I'm not asking you, lady, I'm telling you. Fifty hours ago I had to swallow hard to keep from having personal feelings about you, and I don't want to do it again, as I would have to if *you* were found with your skull battered. I'm perfectly willing to help get your guy out to you alive, but not to your corpse. This specimen has killed Molloy, and Johnny Keems, and now Ella Reyes. I don't know his reason for killing her, but he might have as good a one for killing you, or think he had, and he's not going to. Go pack a bag, and step on it. We're in a hurry."

I'll be damned if she didn't start to reach out a hand to me and then jerk it back. The instinct of a woman never to pass up an advantage probably goes back to when we had tails. But she jerked it back.

She stood up. "I think this is foolish," she said, "but I don't want to die now." She left me.

Another improvement. It hadn't been long since she had said she might as well be dead. She reappeared shortly with a hat and jacket on and carrying a brown leather suitcase. I took the case, and we were off.

To save time I intended to explain the program en route in the taxi, but I didn't get to. After I had told the hackie, "City Mortuary, Four hundred East Twenty-ninth," and he had given us a second look, and we had started to roll, she said she wanted to ask me a question and I told her to shoot.

She moved closer to me to get her mouth six inches from my ear, and asked, "Why did Peter try to get away with the gun in his pocket?"

"You really don't know," I said.

"No, I—How could I know?"

"You might have figured it out. He thought your fingerprints were on the gun and he wanted to ditch it."

She stared. Her face was so close I couldn't see it. "But how could—Oh, no! He couldn't think that! He couldn't!"

"If you want to keep this private, tone it down. Why couldn't he? You could. Sauce for the goose and sauce for the gander. You are now inclined to change your mind, but you have been worked on. He hasn't been in touch as you have, so I suppose he still thinks it. Why shouldn't he?"

"Peter thinks I killed Mike?"

"Of course. Since he knows he didn't. Goose is right."

She gripped my arm with both hands. "Mr. Goodwin, I want to see him. I've *got* to see him *now!*"

"You will, but not where we're going and not now. And for God's sake don't crumple on me at this point. Steady the nerves and stiffen the spine. You've got a job to do. I should have stalled and saved it for later, but you asked me."

So when the cab stopped at the curb in front of the morgue I hadn't briefed her, and, not caring to share it with the hackie, I told him to wait, with the suitcase as collateral, helped her out, and walked her down to the corner and back. Uncertain of the condition of her wits after the jolt I had given her, I made darned sure she had the idea before going inside.

Since I was known there, I had considered sending her in alone, but decided not to risk it. In the outer room I told the sergeant at the desk, whose name was Donovan, that my companion wanted to view the body of the woman which had been found behind a lumber pile. He put an eye on Mrs. Molloy.

"What's her name?"

"Skip it. She's a citizen and pays her taxes."

He shook his head. "It's a rule, Goodwin, and you know it. Give me a name."

"Mrs. Alice Bolt, Churchill Hotel."

"Okay. Who does she think it is?"

But that, as I knew, was not a rule, so I didn't oblige. After a brief wait an attendant who was new to me took us through the gate and along the corridor to the same room where Wolfe had once placed two old dinars on the eyes of Marko Vukcic's corpse. Another corpse was now stretched out on the long table under the strong light, with its lower two-thirds covered with a sheet. At the head an assistant medical examiner whom I had met before was busy with tools. As we approached he told me hello, suspended operations, and backed up a step. Selma had her fingers around my arm, not for support, but as part of the program. The head of the object was on its side, and Selma stooped for a good view at a distance of twenty inches. In four seconds she straightened up and squeezed my arm, two little squeezes.

"No," she said.

It wasn't in the script that she was to hang onto my arm during our exit, but she did, out to the corridor and all the way to the gate and on through. In the outer corridor I broke contact to cross to the desk and tell Donovan that Mrs. Bolt had made no identification, and he said that was too bad.

On the sidewalk I stopped her before we got in earshot of the hackie and asked, "How sure are you?"

"I'm positive," she said. "It's her."

Crossing town on 34th Street can be a crawl, but not at that time of day. Selma leaned back with her eyes closed all the way. She had had three severe bumps within the hour: learning that her P.H. thought she had killed her husband, taking it that he hadn't, and viewing a corpse. She could use a recess.

So when we arrived at the old brownstone I took her up the stoop and in, told her to follow me, and, with the suitcase, mounted one flight to the

South Room. It was too late for sunshine, but it's a nice room even without it. I turned on the lights, put the suitcase on the rack, and went to the bathroom to check towels and soap and glasses. She sank into a chair. I told her about the two phones, house and outside, said Fritz would be up with a tray, and left her.

Wolfe was in the dining room, staving off starvation, with Saul Panzer doing likewise, and Fritz was standing there.

"We have a house guest," I told them. "Mrs. Molloy. With luggage. I showed her how to bolt the door. She doesn't feel like eating with people, so I suppose she'll have to get a tray."

They discussed it. The dinner dish was braised pork filets with spiced wine, and they hoped she would like it. If she didn't, what? It was eight o'clock, and I was hungry, so I left it to them and went to the kitchen and dished up a plate for myself. By the time I returned the tray problem had been solved, and I took my place, picked up my knife and fork, and cut into a filet.

I spoke. "I was just thinking, as I dished this pork, about the best diet for a ballplayer. I suppose it depends on the player. Take a guy like Campanella, who probably has to regulate his intake—"

"Confound you, Archie."

"What?" I raised my brows. "No business talk at the table is your rule, not mine. But to change the subject, just for conversation, the study of the human face under stress is absolutely fascinating. Take, for instance, a woman's face I was studying just half an hour ago. She was looking at a corpse and recognizing it as having belonged to a person she knew, but she didn't want two bystanders to know that she recognized it. She wanted to keep her face deadpan, but under the circumstances it was difficult."

"That must have been interesting," Saul said. "You say she recognized it?"

"Oh, sure, no question about it. But you gentlemen continue the conversation. I'm hungry." I forked a bite of filet to my mouth.

It was a tough day for rules. Still another one got a dent when, the dessert having been disposed of, we went to the office for coffee, but that happened fairly often.

I reported, in detail as usual, but not in full. Certain passages of my talk with Mrs. Molloy were not material, and neither was the fact that she had started to put out a hand to me and jerked it back. We discussed the situation and the outlook. The obvious point of attack was Mr. and Mrs. Thomas L. Irwin, but the question was how to attack. If they denied any knowledge of the reason for their maid's absence, and if, told that she had been murdered, they denied knowledge of that too, what then? Saul and I did most of the talking. Wolfe sat and listened, or maybe he didn't listen.

But the only point in keeping the identity of the corpse to ourselves was to have first call on the Irwins and Arkoffs, and if we weren't going to call we might as well let the cops take over. Of course they were already giving the lumber pile and surroundings the full routine, and putting them on to the Irwins and Arkoffs wouldn't help that any, but someone who knew what the medical examiner gave as the time of death should at least ask them where they were between this hour and that hour Thursday night. That was only common politeness.

When Fritz came to bring beer and reported that Mrs. Molloy had said she liked the pork very much but had eaten only one small piece of it, Wolfe told me to go and see if she was comfortable. When I went up I found that she hadn't bolted the door. I knocked and got a call to enter, and did so. She was on her feet, apparently doing nothing. I told her that if she didn't care for the books on the shelf there were a lot more downstairs, and asked if she wanted some magazines or anything else. While I was speaking the door-bell rang downstairs, but with Saul there I skipped it. She said she didn't want anything; she was going to bed and try to sleep.

"I hope you know," she added, "that I realize how wonderful you are. And how much I appreciate all you're doing. And I hope you won't think I'm just a silly goose when I ask if I can see Peter tomorrow. I want to."

"I suppose you could," I said. "Freyer might manage it. But you shouldn't."

"Why not?"

"Because you're the widow of the man he's still convicted of murdering. Because there would be a steel lattice between you with guards present. Because he would hate it. He still thinks you killed Molloy, and that would be a hell of a place to try to talk him out of it. Go to bed and sleep on it."

She was looking at me. She certainly could look straight at you. "All right," she said. She extended a hand. "Good night."

I took the hand in a professional clasp, left the room, pulling the door shut as I went, and went back down to the office to find Inspector Cramer sitting in the red leather chair and Purley Stebbins on one of the yellow ones, beside Saul Panzer.

16

As I circled around Saul and Purley to get to my desk Cramer was speaking.

" . . . and I'm fed up! At one o'clock yesterday afternoon Stebbins phoned and told Goodwin about Johnny Keems and asked him if Keems was working for you, and Goodwin said he would have to ask you and would call back. He didn't. At four-thirty Stebbins phoned again, and Goodwin stalled him again. At nine-thirty last evening I came to see you, and you know what you told me. Among other things —"

"Please, Mr. Cramer," Wolfe might have been gently but firmly stopping a talky brat. "You don't need to recapitulate. I know what has happened and what was said."

"Yeah, I don't doubt it. All right, I'll move to today. At five-forty-two this afternoon Saul Panzer is waiting at the morgue to view a body when it arrives, and he views it, and beats it. At seven-twenty Goodwin shows up at the morgue to view the same body, and has a woman with him, and he says they can't identify it and goes off with the woman. He gives her name as

Mrs. Alice Bolt — Mrs. Ben Bolt, I suppose — and her address as the
Churchill Hotel. There is no Mrs. Bolt registered at the Churchill. So you're
up to your goddam tricks again. You not only held out on us about Keems
for eight hours yesterday, you held out on me last night, and I'm fed up.
Facts connected with a homicide in my jurisdiction belong to me, and I
want them."

Wolfe shook his head. "I didn't hold out on you last night, Mr. Cramer."

"Like hell you didn't!"

"No, sir. I was at pains to give you all the facts I had, except one,
perhaps — that despite Peter Hays's denial we had concluded he is Paul
Herold. But you took care of that, characteristically. Knowing, as you did,
that James R. Herold was my client, you notified him that you thought you
had found his son and asked him to come and verify it, omitting the courtesy of even telling me you had done so, let alone consulting me in advance.
Considering how you handle facts I give you, it's a wonder I ever give you
any at all."

"Nuts. I didn't notify James R. Herold. Lieutenant Murphy did."

"After you had told him of your talk with me." Wolfe flipped a hand to
push it aside. "However, as I say, I gave you all the facts I had relevent to
your concern. I reported what had been told me by Mr. and Mrs. Arkoff
and Mr. and Mrs. Irwin. And I made a point of calling to your attention a
most significant fact — more than significant, provocative — the contents of
Johnny Keems's pockets. You knew, because I told you, these things: that
Keems left here at seven-thirty Wednesday evening to see the Arkoffs and
Irwins, with a hundred dollars in his pocket for expenses; that during his
questioning of the Irwins their maid had been present, and the questioning
had been cut short by the Irwins' departure; and that only twenty-two
dollars and sixteen cents had been found on his body. I gave you the facts, as
of course I should, but it was not incumbent on me to give you my
inference."

"What inference?"

"That Keems had spent the hundred dollars in pursuance of his mission,
that the most likely form of expenditure had been a bribe, and that a
probable recipient of the bribe was the Irwins' maid. Mr. Goodwin got the
maid's name, and a description of her, from Mrs. Molloy, and Mr. Panzer
went to see her and couldn't find her. He spent the day at it and was finally
successful. He found her at the morgue, though the identification was only
tentative until Mrs. Molloy verified it."

"That's not what Goodwin told Donovan. He said she couldn't make an
identification."

"Certainly. She was in no condition to be pestered. Your colleagues would
have kept at her all night. I might as well save you the trouble of a foray on
her apartment. She is in this house, upstairs asleep, and is not to be
disturbed."

"But she identified that body?"

"Yes. Positively. As Miss Ella Reyes, the Irwins' maid."

Cramer looked at Stebbins, and Stebbins returned it. Cramer took a cigar
from his pocket, rolled it between his palms, and stuck it in his mouth,
setting his teeth in it. I have never seen him light one. He looked at Stebbins
again, but the sergeant had his eyes at Wolfe.

"I realize," Wolfe said, "that this is a blow for you and you'll have to absorb it. It is now next to certain that an innocent man stands convicted of murder on evidence picked up by your staff, and that's not a pleasant dose —"

"It's far from certain."

"Oh, come, Mr. Cramer. You're not an ass, so don't talk like one. Keems was working on the Molloy murder, and he was killed. He made a contact with Ella Reyes, and she was killed — and by the way, what money was found on her, if any?"

Cramer took a moment to answer, because he would have preferred not to. But the newspaper boys probably already had it. Even so, he didn't answer, he asked, and not Wolfe, but me.

"Goodwin, the hundred you gave Keems. What was it?"

"Five used tens and ten used fives. Some people don't like new ones." His sharp gray eyes moved. "Was that it, Purley?"

"Yes, sir. No purse or handbag was found. There was a wad in her stocking, ten fives and five tens."

Wolfe grunted. "They belong to me. And speaking of money, here's another point. I suppose you know that I learned that Molloy had rented a safe-deposit box under an alias, and a man named Patrick A. Degan was appointed administrator of the estate, and in that capacity was given access to the box. The safe-deposit company had to have a key made. When Mr. Degan opened the box, with Mr. Goodwin and Mr. Parker present, it was found to contain three hundred and twenty-seven thousand, six hundred and forty dollars in currency. But —"

"I didn't know *that*."

"Mr. Degan will doubtless confirm it for you. But the point is, where is Molloy's key to that box? Almost certainly he carried it on his person. Was it found on his corpse?"

"Not that I remember." Cramer looked at Stebbins. "Purley?"

Stebbins shook his head.

"And Peter Hays, caught, as you thought, red-handed. Did he have it?"

"I don't think so. Purley?"

"No, sir. He had keys, but none for a safe-deposit box."

Wolfe snorted. "Then consider the high degree of probability that Molloy was carrying the key and the certainty that it was not found on him or on Peter Hays. Where was it? Who took it? Is it still far from certain, Mr. Cramer?"

Cramer put the cigar in his mouth, chewed on it, and took it out again. "I don't know," he rasped, "and neither do you, but you sure have stirred up one hell of a mess. I'm surprised I didn't find those people here — the Arkoffs and Irwins. That must be why you were saving the identification, to have a crack at them before I did. I'm surprised I didn't find you staging one of your goddam inquests. Are they on the way?"

"No. Mr. Goodwin and Mr. Panzer and I were discussing the situation. I don't stage an inquest, as you call it, until I am properly equipped. Obviously the question is, where did Keems go and whom did he see after he talked with the maid? The easiest assumption is that he stayed at the Irwins' apartment until they came home, but there is nothing to support it, and that sort of inquiry is not my métier. It is too laborious and too in-

conclusive, as you well know. Of course your men will now question the
doorman and elevator man, but even if they say that Keems went up again
shortly after he left Wednesday night with the Irwins, and didn't come
down until after the Irwins returned, what if the Irwins simply deny that he
was there when they came home — deny that they ever saw or heard of him
again after they left?"

Wolfe gestured. "However, I am not deprecating such inquiry — checking
of alibis and all the long and intricate routine — only I have neither the men
nor the temper for it, and you have. For it you need no suggestions from me.
If, for example, there is discoverable evidence that Keems returned to the
Arkoffs' apartment after talking with Ella Reyes, you'll discover it, and
you're welcome to. I'm quite willing for you to finish the job. Since you
don't want two unsolved homicides on your record you'll use all your skills
and resources to solve them, and when you do you will inevitably clear Peter
Hays. I've done my share."

"Yeah. By getting two people murdered."

"Nonsense. That's childish, Mr. Cramer, and you know it."

Stebbins made a noise, and Cramer asked him, "You got a question,
Purley?"

"Not exactly a question," Purley rumbled. He was always a little hoarser
than normal in Wolfe's presence, from the strain of controlling his impulses.
Or rather, one impulse, the one to find out how many clips it would take to
make Wolfe incapable of speech. He continued. "Only I don't believe it,
that Wolfe's laying off. I never saw him lay off yet. He's got something he's
holding onto, and when we've got the edges trimmed by doing all the work
that he's too good for he'll spring it. Why has he got that Molloy woman
here? You remember the time we got a warrant and searched the whole
damn house, and up in the plant rooms he had a woman stretched out in a
box covered with moss or something and he was spraying it with water,
which we found out later. I can go up and bring her down, or we can both go
up. Goodwin won't try stopping an officer of the law, and if he —"

He stopped and was on his feet, but I had already buzzed the South
Room on the house phone and in a second was speaking.

"Archie Goodwin, Mrs. Molloy. Bolt your door, quick. Step on it. I'll hold
on."

"It's already bolted. What —"

"Fine. Sorry to bother you, but a character named Stebbins, a sort of a
cop, is having trouble with his brain, and I thought he might go up and try
to annoy you. Forget it, but don't unbolt the door for anybody but me until
further notice."

I hung up and swiveled. "Sit down, Sergeant. Would you like a glass of
water?"

The cord at the side of his big neck was tight. "We're in the house," he
told Cramer, hoarser than ever, "and they're obstructing justice. She recognized a corpse and denied it. She's a fugitive. To hell with the bolt."

He knew better, but he was upset. Cramer ignored him and demanded of
Wolfe, "What does Mrs. Molloy know that you don't want me to know?"

"Nothing whatever, to my knowledge." Wolfe was unruffled. "Nor do I.
She is my guest. It would be vain to submit her to your importunity even if
you requested it civilly, and Mr. Stebbins should by now know the folly of

trying to bully me. If you wish the identification confirmed, why not Mr. or Mrs. Irwin or a member of Ella Reyes' family? The address is—Saul?"

"Three-oh-six East One-hundred-and-thirty-seventh Street."

Purley got out his notebook and wrote. Cramer threw the chewed cigar at my wastebasket, missing as usual, and stood up. "This may be the time," he said darkly, "or it may not. The time will come." He marched out, and Purley followed. I left it to Saul to see them out, thinking that as Purley passed by at the door he might accidentally get his fist in my eye and I might accidentally get my toe on his rump, and that would only complicate matters.

When Saul came back in, Wolfe was leaning back with his eyes closed and I was picking up Cramer's cigar. He asked me if there was a program for him, and I said no.

"Sit down," I told him. "There soon will be. As you know, Mr. Wolfe thinks better with his eyes shut."

The eyes opened. "I'm not thinking. There's nothing to think about. There is no program."

That's what I was afraid of. "That's too bad," I said sympathetically. "Of course if Johnny was still around it would be worse because you would have five of us to think up errands for instead of only four."

He snorted. "That's bootless, Archie. I'm quite aware that Johnny was in my service when he died, and his disregard of instructions didn't lift my onus. By no means. But Mr. Cramer and his army are at it now, and you would be lost in the stampede. The conviction of Peter Hays is going to be undone, and he knows it. He picked up the evidence that doomed him; now let him pick up the evidence that clears him."

"If he does. What if he doesn't?"

"Then we'll see. Don't badger me. Go up and let Mrs. Molloy thank you properly for your intrepidity in saving her from annoyance. First rumple your hair as evidence of the fracas." Suddenly he roared, "Do you think I enjoy sitting here while that bull smashes through to the wretch I have goaded into two murders?"

I said distinctly, "I think you enjoy sitting here."

Saul asked sociably, "How about some pinochle, Archie?"

17

WE didn't play pinochle for three nights and two days, but we might as well have. Friday night, Saturday, Saturday night, Sunday, and Sunday night.

It was not a vacuum. Things happened. Albert Freyer spent an hour with Wolfe Saturday morning, got a full report on the situation, and walked out on air. He even approved of letting the cops take it from there, since it was a cinch they couldn't nail the killer of Johnny Keems and Ella Reyes without unnailing Peter Hays. James R. Herold phoned twice a day, and Sunday afternoon came in person and brought his wife along. She taught me once more that you should never seal your verdict until the facts are in. I was sure she would be a little rooster-pecked specimen, and she was little, but in the first three minutes it became clear that at pecking time she went on the theory that it was more blessed to give than to receive. I won't say that I reversed the field on him entirely, but I understood him better. If and when he mentioned again that his wife was getting impatient I would know where my sympathy belonged if I had any to spare. Also he brought her after four o'clock, when he knew Wolfe would be up in the plant rooms, which was both intelligent and prudent. I made out fairly well with her, and when they left we still had a client.

Patrick A. Degan phoned Saturday morning and came for a talk at six o'clock. Apparently his main concern was to find out from Selma Molloy what her attitude was toward the $327,640.00, and he tried to persuade her that she would be a sap to pass it up, but he took the opportunity to discuss other developments with Wolfe and me. It had got in the paper, the *Gazette*, that Nero Wolfe's assistant, Archie Goodwin, had been at the morgue to look at the body of Ella Reyes, and that therefore there was probably some connection between her and Johnny Keems, though the police refused to say so, and Degan wanted to know. The interview ended on a sour note when Wolfe commented that it was natural for Degan to show an interest in that detail, since Ella Reyes had been Mrs. Irwin's maid and Degan was on familiar terms with Mrs. Irwin. When that warmed Degan up under the collar, Wolfe tried to explain that the word "familiar" implied undue intimacy only when it was intended to, and that he had given no reason for inferring such an intention, but Degan hadn't cooled off much when he left.

Since we wanted to keep informed fully and promptly on the progress of Cramer and his army, and therefore had to be on speaking terms, we graciously permitted Sergeant Stebbins an audience with Mrs. Molloy Saturday afternoon, and he was with her three hours, and Fritz served refreshments. We were pleased to hear later, from her, that Purley had spent a good third of the time on various aspects of the death of her husband, such as possible motives for Arkoff or Irwin to want him removed. The Molloy case had definitely been taken off the shelf. From the questions Purley asked it was evident that no one had been eliminated and no one had been treed. When I asked him, as he departed, if they were getting warm, he was so impolite that I knew the temperature had gone down rather than up.

Saturday evening Selma ate with us in the dining room, and Sunday at one she joined us again for chicken fricassee with dumplings, Methodist style. Fritz is not a Methodist, but his dumplings are plenty good enough for angels.

Saul Panzer and Orrie Cather spent the two days visiting with former friends of Molloy's, spreading out from the list Patrick Degan had supplied, and concentrating on digging up a hint of the source of the third of a million in the safe-deposit box. Saul thought he might have found one Sunday morning, but it petered out. Fred Durkin plugged away at William Lesser and got enough material to fill three magazines, but none of it showed a remote connection with either the Arkoffs or Irwins, and that was essential. However, Fred got results, of a kind. Sunday afternoon, while I was down in the basement with Selma, teaching her how to handle a billiard cue, the doorbell rang, and I went up to find Fritz conversing through the crack permitted by the chain bolt, with Delia's Bill. It was my first contact with a suspect for many hours, and I felt like greeting him with a cordial hand-shake, but he wasn't having any. He was twice as grim as he had been before. In the office he stood with his fists on his hips and read the riot act. He had found out who the guy was going around asking about him, and that he worked for Nero Wolfe, and so did I, and the guff about the maga-zine article had been a blind, and he damn well wanted to know. It was rather confused the way he put it, and not clear at all exactly what he wanted to know, but I got the general idea. He was sore.

Neither of us got any satisfaction out of it. For him, I wouldn't apologize or promise to lock Wolfe and myself up for kidding Delia Brandt and damaging his reputation; and for me, he wasn't answering questions. He wasn't even hearing questions. He wouldn't even tell me when they were going to be married. I finally eased him to the hall and along to the door and on out, and went back to the basement to resume the billiard lesson.

Late that evening, Sunday, Inspector Cramer turned up, and when, after he got his big broad behind deposited in the red leather chair, Wolfe invited him to have some beer and he accepted, I knew he didn't have to be asked how they were making out. They weren't. He takes Wolfe's beer only when he wants it understood that he's only human and should be treated accord-ingly. He tried to be tactful because he had no club to use, but what it amounted to was that he had got nowhere at all after two nights and two days, and he wanted the fact or facts that Wolfe was reserving for future use.

Wolfe didn't have any, and said so. But that didn't satisfy Cramer, and never will, on account of certain past occasions, so it ended with him bouncing up, his glass still half full of beer, and tramping out.

When I returned from closing the door after him I told Wolfe cheerfully, "Forget it, he's just tired. In the morning he'll be back on the job, full of whatever he's full of. In a month or so he'll pick up a trail, and by August he'll have it wrapped up. Of course by that time Peter Hayes will be elec-trocuted, but what the hell, they can apologize to his father and mother and two sis —"

"Shut up, Archie."

"Yes, sir. If I wasn't afraid to leave Mrs. Molloy alone here with you I'd resign. This job is too dull. In fact, it doesn't seem to be a job."

"It will be." He took in air down to his waist, or where it would have been if he had one. When it was out he muttered, "It will have to be. When you become insufferable something has to be done. Have Saul and Fred and Orrie here at eight in the morning."

I locked the safe, made my desk neat, and went up to my room to call the boys from there, leaving him sitting behind his desk, an ideal model for an oversized martyr.

In a way he has spoiled me. Some of the spectacular charades he has thought up have led me to expect too much, and it was something of a letdown Monday morning when I learned what the program was. Nothing but another treasure hunt, and not even a safe-deposit box. I admit that it did the trick, but at the time it struck me as a damned small mouse to come out of so big a mountain.

I had made sacrifices, having rolled out early enough to finish my breakfast by the time Saul and Fred and Orrie arrived at eight, only to find that it hadn't been necessary when Wolfe told me on the house phone to bring them up at a quarter to nine. When the time came I led the way up the two flights and found his door standing open, and we entered. He was seated at the table near a window, his breakfast gone, but still with coffee, with the morning *Times* propped on the reading rack. He greeted the staff and asked me if there was any news, and I said no, I had phoned Stebbins and he had not bitten my ear off only because you can't bite over the wire.

He took a sip of coffee and put the cup down. "Then we'll have to try. You will go, all four, to Mrs. Molloy's apartment, and search it, covering every inch. Take probes for the upholstery and whatever tools may be required. The devil of it is you won't know what you're looking for."

"Then how will we know when we find it?"

"You won't, with any certainty. But we know that a situation existed which led to Molloy's murder; that he had cached a large sum of money in a safe-deposit box under an alias; that he was contemplating departure from the country; and that exhaustive inquiry among his friends and associates has disclosed no hint of where the money came from or when or how he got it. Further, there was no such hint found on his person, or among the papers taken from his office, or in his apartment, or in the safe-deposit box. I don't believe it. I do not believe that no such hint exists. As I said to Archie on Friday, when a man is involved in a circumstance pressing enough to cause his murder he must leave a relic of it somewhere, and I had hoped it was in that box. When it wasn't I should have persisted, but other matters intervened—for one thing, a woman got killed."

He took a sip of coffee. "We want that relic. It could be a portfolio, a notebook, a single slip of paper. It could be some object other than a record on paper, though I have no idea what. There are of course numberless places he could have left it—with some friend, checked at a hotel or other public place—but first we'll try his apartment, since it is as likely as any and is accessible. Regarding each article you see and touch you must ask yourselves, 'Could this possibly be it?' Archie, you will explain the matter to Mrs. Molloy, ask if she wishes to accompany you, and if not get her permission and the key. That's all, gentlemen. I don't ask if you have any questions, since I wouldn't know the answers to them. Archie, leave the phone number on my desk, in case I need to get you."

We went. I turned off one flight down. I knew she was up, since Fritz had delivered her breakfast tray. By then I was on sufficiently familiar terms with her—the word "familiar" implying no undue intimacy—to have a private knock, 2-1-2, and I used it and was told to enter. She was in a dressing gown or house gown or negligee or dishabille—anyway, it was soft and long and loose and lemon-colored—and without make-up. Without lipstick her mouth was even better than with. A habit of observation of minor details is an absolute must for a detective. We exchanged good mornings and I told her there had been no developments worth mentioning, but there was a program. When I explained it she said she didn't believe there could be anything in the apartment she didn't know about, but I reminded her that she hadn't even bothered to open the cartons that had come from the office, and asked if she had got rid of Molloy's clothing and other effects.

She said no, she hadn't felt like touching them, and nothing had been taken away. I told her the search would be extremely thorough, and she said she didn't mind. I asked if she wanted to go along, and she said no.

"You'll think I'm crazy," she said, "after my not wanting to come here, but now I never want to enter that door again. I guess that was one thing that was wrong with me — I should have got out of there."

I told her that the only thing that had been wrong with her was that she thought Peter Hays had killed Molloy, whereas now she didn't, got the keys from her, went downstairs, where the hired help was waiting for me in the hall, put the phone number on Wolfe's desk, told Fritz where we were going, and left. Saul and Fred had assembled a kit of tools from the cupboard in the office where we kept an assortment of everything from keys to jimmies.

If I described every detail of our performance in the Molloy apartment that day between 9:35 A.M. and 3:10 P.M. you might get some useful pointers on how to look for a lost diamond or postage stamp, but if you haven't lost a diamond or a postage stamp it wouldn't interest you. When we got through we knew a lot of things: that Molloy had hoarded old razor blades in a cardboard box in his dresser; that someone had once upon a time burned a little hole in the under side of a chair cushion, probably with a cigarette, and at a later time someone had stuffed a piece of lemon peel in the hole, God knew why; that there were three loose tiles in the bathroom wall and a loose board in the living-room floor; that Mrs. Molloy had three girdles, liked pale yellow underwear and white nighties, used four different shades of nylons, and kept no letters except those from a sister who lived in Arkansas; that apparently there were no unpaid bills other than one for $3.84 from a laundry; that none of the pieces of furniture had hollow legs; that if a jar of granulated sugar slips from your hand and spills you have a problem; and a thousand others. Saul and I together went over every scrap of the contents of the three cartons, already inspected by Orrie.

It would be misleading to say we found nothing whatever. We found two empty drawers. They were the two top drawers, one on each side, of a desk against the wall of what Molloy might have called his den. None of the six keys Selma had given me fitted their locks, which were good ones, Wetherbys, and Saul had to work on them with the assortment in the kit. The drawers were as empty as the day they were built, and had presumably been locked from force of habit.

At 3:10 P.M. I used the phone there in the apartment and told Wolfe the bad news, including the empty drawers. Orrie said to tell him that never had so many searched so long for so little, but it didn't appeal to me. Wolfe told me to tell Fred and Orrie that was all for the day and to bring Saul in with me. After making a tour to verify that we were leaving things as we had found them, we moved out. Down on the sidewalk we parted, Fred and Orrie heading for the corner to get a drink to drown the disappointment, and Saul and I, with the kit of tools, flagging a taxi. It wasn't a cheerful ride. If the best the genius could do was start us combing the metropolitan area, including Jersey and Long Island, for a relic that might not exist, the future wasn't very bright.

But he had something a little more specific. We had barely crossed the sill to the office when he blurted at me, "About that Delia Brandt. About Molloy's proposal to her of a trip to South America. You said last Wednesday that she told you she had put him off, but you thought she lied. Why did you think she lied?"

I stood. "The way she said it, the way she looked, the way she answered questions about it. And just her. I had formed an opinion of her."

"Have you changed your opinion? Since she is going to marry William Lesser?"

"Hell no. She couldn't go to South America with a dead man, and evidently, from Fred's reports, she was playing Lesser all the time on an option. If Lesser found out what the score was and decided to take—"

"That's not my target. If Molloy was preparing to decamp and take that girl with him, and if she had agreed to go, he might have entrusted certain objects to her care—for example, some of the objects he removed from the empty drawers you found. Is it fantastic to assume that he left them in her apartment for safekeeping pending departure?"

"No, not fantastic. I wouldn't trust her with a subway token, but apparently his opinion of her wasn't the same flavor as mine. It's quite possible."

"Then you and Saul will go and search her apartment. Now."

When Wolfe gets desperate he is absolutely fearless. He will expose me to the risk of a five-year stretch up the river without batting an eye. That's okay, since I am old enough to vote and can always say no, but that time he was inviting another party too, so I turned to look at Saul. He merely asked, "Will she be there?"

"If she's working, probably not until around five-thirty, maybe later. If she's there I might be able to take her out to buy champagne, but then you'd have to do the work. Shall I phone?"

"You might as well."

I went to my desk and dialed the number, waited through fifteen whirrs, hung up, and swiveled. "No answer. If you like the idea, we won't want the kit, just some of the keys. The door downstairs has a Manson lock, old style. The one to her apartment is a Wyatt. You know more about them than I do."

Saul brought the kit to my desk and opened it, selected four strings of keys and dropped them in his pocket, and closed the kit. While he was doing that I went to the cupboard and got two pairs of rubber gloves.

"I must remind you," Wolfe said as we started out, "that prudence is no shame to valor. I shall not evade my responsibility as accessory."

"Much obliged," I thanked him. "If we're caught we'll say you begged us not to."

We went to Ninth Avenue for a taxi, and on the way downtown discussed modus operandi. Not that it needed much discussion. Dismissing the cab on Christopher Street, we walked on to Arbor Street, rounded the corner, and continued to Number 43. Nobody had painted it in the five days since I had seen it. We entered the vestibule, and I pushed the button marked Brandt. Getting no click, I pushed it again, and, after another wait, a third time.

"Okay," I told Saul, and stepped to the outer door, which was standing open, for an outlook. Arbor Street is not Fifth Avenue, and only two boys and a woman with a dog had passed by when Saul told my back, "Come on in." It had taken him about a minute and a half. We entered.

He preceded me up the narrow dingy stairs, the idea being that we would do a quick once-over and then I would stand guard outside, at the head of the stairs, while he dug deeper. As we reached the top of the third flight he had a string of keys in his hand, ready to tackle the Wyatt, but I remembered that prudence is no shame to valor and went to the door first and knocked. I waited, knocked louder, got no response, and stepped aside for Saul. The Wyatt took longer than the one downstairs, perhaps three minutes. When he got it he pushed the door open. Since I was supposed to be in command, the proper thing would have been for him to let me go in first, but he crossed the threshold, saying, "Jumping Jesus."

I was at his elbow, staring with him. At my former visit it had been one of those rooms that call for expert dodging to get anywhere. Now it would have taken more than dodging. The piano bench was still where it belonged, in the center of the main traffic lane, and the other pieces of furniture were more or less in place, but otherwise it was a first-rate mess. Cushions had been ripped open and the stuffing pulled out and scattered around; books and magazines were off their shelves and helter-skelter on the floor; flowerpots had been dumped and dropped; and the general effect was about what you would get if you turned a room over to a dozen orangoutangs and told them to enjoy themselves.

"He didn't leave it as neat as we —" I started to comment, and stopped. Saul had spotted it too, and we moved together, on past the piano bench. It was Delia Brandt, on the floor near the couch where I had sat with her. She was on her face, her legs stretched out. I squatted on one side and Saul on the other, but one feel of her bare forearm was enough to show that no tests were necessary. She had been dead at least twelve hours and probably longer. We didn't look for a wound because that wasn't necessary either. A cord as thick as a clothesline was tight around her neck.

We got erect and I stepped through the clutter to a doorway, the door standing open, for a look at the bedroom, while Saul went and closed the door to the hall. The bedroom was even worse, with the bed torn apart, the innards of the mattress all over, and clothing and other objects sprayed around. A glance in the bathroom showed that it had not been neglected. Back in the living room, Saul was standing looking down at her.

"He killed her," he said, "before he started looking. Stuff from cushions on top of her."

"Yeah, so I noticed. He worked the bedroom and closets too, so there's nothing left for us except one thing. She's got her clothes on. Either he found it or something scared him out or what he was after was too bulky to be on her."

"The clothes women wear nowadays he wouldn't have to take them off. Why the gloves? Going to rake through the leavings?"

"No. Put them on." I handed him a pair, and started pulling mine on. "We'll try the one thing he left. Unless you've got a date."

"You don't make prints on clothes."

"You don't make prints on anything with gloves on." I got my knife from my pocket, opened it, squatted, slipped two fingers under the neck of the blouse, and slit it down to the waist. Saul, squatting on the other side, unzipped the skirt and moved to the feet to take the hem and pull the skirt off. I told him to look at the shoes, which were house sandals, tied on, and he did so, removing them and tossing them aside. The slip was as simple as the blouse. I cut the straps and slit it down the back from top to bottom and pushed it to either side. The pants were simple too; I got my fingers inside under the hips, and Saul worked them down and off. The girdle was slower, since I didn't care to scratch the skin. Saul squatted on the other side again and helped me keep it lifted enough to slit it and leave her intact.

"She's good and cold," he said.

"Yeah. Stuff the edges under and we'll roll her over to you."

He did so, and with one hand under a hip and the other under a shoulder I rolled her, and Saul eased her as she came, and she was on her back. That way, face up, it was something else. The face of a girl who was strangled to death twelve or fourteen hours ago is not a girl's face. Saul covered it with what was left of a cushion and then helped me finish the operation. There was nothing between the blouse and the slip, and nothing between the slip and the girdle, and nothing between the girdle and the skin, but when I lifted the brassiere and she was naked, there it was, fastened between the breasts with tape. A key. I pulled it loose, pulled the tape off, gave it a look, said, "Grand Central locker, out quick" went to the bedroom for a blanket, and came back and covered her. Saul was at the door, peeling his gloves off, and I had mine off by the time I joined him. He used one of his to turn the doorknob, and, in the hall, to pull the door shut. The spring lock clicked and we made for the stairs.

We saw no one on the way down, but as we stepped out to the sidewalk a man turned in, evidently a tenant, as he gave us a glance. However, he was two seconds too late to be able to swear that we had been inside the house. When we had turned the corner and were on Christopher Street, Saul asked, "Walking for our health?"

"I could use some health after that," I told him. "I suppose it doesn't matter how you do it if you do it, but some ways seem worse than others. At Seventh Avenue we'll split. One of us will take the subway and shuttle to Grand Central, and the other will phone Centre Street and go and report to Wolfe. Which do you prefer?"

"I'll take Grand Central."

"Okay." I handed him the locker key. "But it's possible there's an eye on it, no telling whose. You'd better give me the keys and gloves."

He transferred them to my pocket as we walked. At Seventh Avenue he went for the subway stairs and I entered the cigar store at the corner, found the phone booth, dialed SP 7-3100, and, when I got a voice, whined into the transmitter, high and thin, "Name and address, Delia Brandt, B-R-A-N-D-T, Forty-three Arbor Street, Manhattan, Got it?"

"Yes. What—"

"I'm telling you. I think she's dead. In her apartment. You'd better hurry." I hung up, heard the rattle, felt in the coin-return cup to see if the machine had swallowed the wrong way because you never know, departed, and got a taxi.

When I got out in front of the old brownstone it was a quarter to five, precisely one hour since Wolfe had told us he wouldn't evade his responsibility as accessory. With the chain bolt on as usual during my absence, Fritz had to come to let me in, and after one glance at my face he said, "Ah."

"Right," I told him. "Ah it is. But I don't want you to be an accessory too, so if they ask you how I looked say just like always, debonair."

In the office I put the gloves and strings of keys away and then went to my desk and buzzed the plant rooms. He must have been hard at work, for it took him a while to answer.

"Yes?"

"Sorry to disturb you, but I thought you ought to know that it's more serious than breaking and entering. It's also disturbing a body in a death by violence. Her apartment looked as if a hurricane had hit it, and she was on the floor, dead and cold. Strangled. We took her clothes off and found a key to a Grand Central checking locker taped to her skin, and took it and left. I phoned the police from a booth, and Saul has gone to Grand Central to see what's in the locker. He should be here in about twenty minutes."

"When did she die?"

"More than twelve hours ago. That's the best I can do."

"What time was William Lesser here yesterday?"

"Four-forty."

Silence. Then: "There is nothing to say or do until we learn what is in the locker. If it is merely another fortune in currency — but speculation is idle. Whatever it is, you and Saul will examine it."

I choked the temptation to ask if he wanted us to bring it up to the plant rooms. He would have had to say no, and to pile that on top of the news of another corpse would have been hitting him when he was down. But I had no ironclad rules between me and normal conduct, so when he hung up I went out to the stoop to wait for Saul. I even went down the seven steps to the sidewalk. Two neighborhood kids who were playing catch on the pavement stopped, stepped onto the opposite curb, and stood watching me. That house and its occupants had been centers of attraction, either sinister or merely mysterious, I wasn't sure which, ever since a boy named Pete Drossos had been let in by me for a conference with Wolfe and had got murdered the next day. By the time I looked at my wristwatch the tenth time the situation was a little strained, with them standing there staring at me, and I was about ready to retreat to an inside post behind the glass panel when a taxi came rolling up and stopped at the curb, and Saul climbed out, after paying the driver, with a medium-sized black leather suitcase dangling in his hand. Letting him have the honor of delivering the bacon, I followed him up the steps and on in. He took it to the office and put it on a chair.

At a glance it had been manhandled. The lock had been pried open, not by an expert, and it was held shut only by the catches at the ends. I asked Saul, "Do you want to tell me or shall I tell you?"

"You tell me."

"Glad to. Wolfe guessed right. Molloy had it stowed in her apartment, and after his death, maybe right away or maybe only yesterday, she busted it open and took a look." I hefted it. "Another deduction: she didn't clean it out. Because if she had why should she stash it in a locker and tape the key to her hide, and also because it's not empty. Wolfe says we're to examine it, but first, I think, for prints."

I went to the cupboard and got things and we set to work. We weren't as expert as the scientist had been with the safe-deposit box, but when we got through we had an assortment of photographs marked with locations that were nothing to be ashamed of. Of course they were only for future refer-

ence, since we had no samples of anybody for comparison. After putting
them in envelopes and putting things away, we placed the suitcase on my
desk and opened it.

It was about two-thirds full of a mixed collection. There were shirts and
ties, probably his favorites that he couldn't bear to leave, a pair of slippers,
six tubes of Cremasine for shaving, two suits of pajamas, socks, and handkerchiefs, and other miscellaneous personal items. Stacking them on the
desk, we came to a bulging leather briefcase. It should have been dusted for
prints too, but we were too warm to wait, and I lifted it out, opened it, and
extracted the contents.

It wasn't a relic, it was a whole museum. Saul pulled a chair up beside
mine, and we went through it together. I won't describe the items, or even
list them, because it would take too long and also because it was Wolfe who
had guessed where they were and he should have the pleasure of showing
them. We had just reached the bottom of the pile when six o'clock brought
Wolfe down from the plant rooms. He started for his desk, veered to come to
mine, and glared down at the haberdashery.

"That's just packing," I told him. I tapped the pile of papers. "Here it is.
Enough relics to choke a camel."

He picked it up and circled around his desk to his chair and started in.
Saul and I put the rest of the stuff back in the suitcase and closed it, and
then sat and watched. For ten minutes the only sounds were rustlings of the
papers and Wofle's occasional grunts. He had nearly reached the bottom of
the stack when the phone rang and I answered it.

"Nero Wolfe's office, Archie Good—"

"This is Stebbins. About a woman named Brandt, Delia Brandt. When
did you see her last?"

"Hold it a second while I sneeze." I covered the transmitter and turned.
"Stebbins asking about Delia Brandt, if you're interested." Wolfe frowned,
hesitated, took his phone, and put it to his ear. I uncovered the transmitter
and sneezed at it and then spoke.

"I hope I'm not going to have a cold. The last one I had—"

"Quit stalling," he snarled. "I asked you a question."

"I know you did, and you ought to know better by this time. If there's any
good reason, or even a poor one, why I should answer questions about a
woman named Delia Brandt, what is it?"

"Her body has been found in her apartment. Murdered. Your name and
address are on the memo page in her phone book, the last entry. When did
you see her last?"

"My God. She's dead?"

"Yeah. When you're murdered you're dead. Quit stalling."

"I'm not stalling. If I didn't react you might think I killed her myself.
The first and last time I saw her was last Wednesday evening around nine-
thirty, at her apartment. We were collecting background on Molloy, and she
was his secretary for ten months, up to the time he died. I had a brief talk
with her on the phone late Thursday afternoon. That's all."

"You were just collecting background?"

"Right."

"We'd like to have you come and tell us what you collected. Now."

"Where are you?"

"At Homicide West. I just got here with a man named William Lesser. When did you see him last?"

"Give me a reason. I always need a reason."

"Yeah, I know. He came to Delia Brandt's apartment twenty minutes ago and found us there. He says he had a date with her. He also says he thinks you killed her. Is that a good enough reason? When did you see him last?"

I never got to answer that. Wolfe's voice broke in.

"Mr. Stebbins, this is Nero Wolfe. I would like to speak with Mr. Cramer."

"He's busy." I swear Purley got hoarser the instant he heard Wolfe. "We want Goodwin down here."

"Not until I have spoken with Mr. Cramer."

Silence; then: "Hold it. I'll see."

We waited. I looked at Wolfe, but it was one-way because his eyes were closed. He opened them only when Cramer's voice came.

"You there, Wolfe? Cramer. What do you want?"

"I want to expose a murderer, and I'm ready to. If you wish to be present, bring Mr. and—"

"I'm coming there right now!"

"No. I have to study some documents. You wouldn't get in. Come at nine o'clock, and bring Mr. and Mrs. Irwin and Mr. and Mrs. Arkoff—and you may as well bring Mr. Lesser. He deserves to be in the audience. The others must be. Nine o'clock."

"Goddam it, I want to know—"

"You will, but not now. I have work to do."

He cradled his phone, and I followed suit. He spoke. "Archie, phone Mr. Freyer, Mr. Degan, and Mr. Herold. If he wishes to bring his wife he may. For this sort of thing the bigger the audience the better. And inform Mrs. Molloy."

"Mrs. Molloy won't be here."

"She is here."

"I mean she won't be in the audience, not if Herold is. She doesn't know Peter Hays is Paul Herold, and let him tell her if and when he wants to. Anyway she doesn't want to be with people, and you don't need her."

"Very well." He leered at me. He may have thought it was a tender glance of sympathy, but I call it a leer. "It is understood, of course, that you were not there today. If an explanation of how I got this material is required I'll supply it."

"Then that's all for me?" Saul asked.

"No. You'll be at his elbow. He has degenerated into a maniac. If you'll dine with us? Now I must digest this stuff."

He went back to the pile of papers.

18

THE host was late to the party, but it wasn't his fault. I wasn't present at the private argument Cramer insisted on having with Wolfe in the dining room, being busy elsewhere, but as I passed in the hall, admitting guests as

they arrived, I could hear their voices through the closed door. Since the
door to the office was soundproofed and I kept it shut, they weren't audible
in there.

The red leather chair was of course reserved for Inspector Cramer, and
Purley Stebbins was on one nearby against the wall, facing the gathering.
Jerome and Rita Arkoff and Tom and Fanny Irwin were in the front row,
where Saul and I had spaced the chairs, but Irwin had moved his close to
his wife's — not, however, taking her hand to hold. Mr. and Mrs. Herold and
Albert Freyer were grouped over by the globe, off apart. Back of the Arkoffs
and Irwins were William Lesser and Patrick Degan, and between them and
slightly to the rear was Saul Panzer. That way the path from me to Degan
was unobstructed and Saul was only an arm's length from him.

It was a quarter past nine, and the silence, broken only by a mutter here
and there, was getting pretty heavy when the door opened and Wolfe and
Cramer entered. Wolfe crossed to his desk and sat, but Cramer stood to
make a speech.

"I want you to understand," he told them, "that this is not an official
inquiry. Five of you came here at my request, but that's all it was, a request.
Sergeant Stebbins and I are here as observers, and we take no responsibility
for anything Nero Wolfe says or does. As it stands now, you can walk out
whenever you feel like it."

"This is a little irregular, isn't it, Inspector?" Arkoff asked.

"I said you can walk out," Cramer told him. He stood a moment, turned
and sat, and scowled at Wolfe.

Wolfe was taking them in. "I'm going to begin," he said conversationally,
"by reporting a coincidence, though it is unessential. It is unessential, but
not irrelevant. Reading the *Times* at breakfast this morning, I noticed a
Washington dispatch on page one." He picked up a newspaper from his
desk. "If you'll indulge me I'll read some of it:

> "A total disclosure law requiring all private welfare and
> pension plans to open books to governmental inspection
> was recommended today by a Senate subcommittee. The
> proposal was based on a two-year study that disclosed
> practices ranging from sloppy bookkeeping to a $900,000
> embezzlement.
>
> "The funds have grown to the point, the committee said,
> that they now provide benefits to 29,000,000 workers and
> to 46,000,000 dependents of these workers. Assets of the
> pension funds alone now total about 25 billion dollars, it
> was said.
>
> "The Senate group, headed by Senator Paul H. Douglas,
> Democrat of Illinois, said: 'While the great majority of
> welfare and pension programs are being responsibly and
> honestly administered, the rights and equities of the bene-
> ficiaries in many instances are being dangerously ignored.
> In other cases, the funds of the programs are being dissi-
> pated and at times become the hunting ground of the
> unscrupulous.'"

Wolfe put the paper down. "It goes on, but that will do. I read it for the record and because it juxtaposed two things: the word 'welfare' and large sums of money. For a solid week I had been trying to find a hint to start me on the trail of the man who killed Michael Molloy — and subsequently Johnny Keems and Ella Reyes — enough of one at least to stir my pulse, to no avail. This, if not a flare, was at least a spark. Patrick Degan was the head of an organization called the Mechanics Alliance Welfare Association, and a large sum of money had been found in a safe-deposit box Molloy had rented under an assumed name."

He pushed the newspaper aside. "That faint hint, patiently and persistently pursued, might eventually have led me to the truth, but luckily it wasn't needed. I have here in my drawer a sheaf of papers which contain evidence of these facts: that from nineteen-fifty-one to nineteen-fifty-five Molloy made purchases of small pieces of land in various parts of the country; that their value, and the amounts of money he had to put up, were negligible; that in each case the purchaser of record was some 'camp' — examples are the Wide World Children's Camp and the Blue Sky Children's Camp; that these camps, twenty-eight in all, borrowed a total of nearly two million dollars from Mr. Degan's organization on mortgages; that Molloy's share of the loot was one-fourth and Degan's share three-fourths, from which each had presumably to meet certain expenses; and that the date of the last such loan on mortgage was October seventeenth, nineteen-fifty-five. I can supply many details, but those are the essentials. Do you wish to comment, Mr. Degan?"

Of course all eyes were on him, but his were only for Wolfe. "No," he said, "except that it's outrageous and libelous and I'll get your hide. Produce your sheaf of papers."

Wolfe shook his head. "The District Attorney will produce them when the time comes. But I'll humor your curiosity. When Molloy decided to leave the country with his loot, alarmed by the Senate investigation, and to take his secretary, Delia Brandt, with him, he stowed his records in a suitcase and left it in Delia Brandt's apartment. That is suggestive, since prudence would have dictated their destruction. It suggests that he foresaw some future function for them, and the most likely one would have been to escape penalty for himself by supplying evidence against you. No doubt you foresaw that too, and that's why you killed him. Do you wish to comment?"

"No. Go ahead and hang yourself."

"Wait a minute," Cramer snapped. "I want to see those papers."

"Not now. By agreement I have an hour without interruption."

"Where did you get them?"

"Listen and you'll know." Wolfe returned to Degan. "The best conjecture is that you knew Molloy had those records, some in your writing, and you knew or suspected he was preparing to decamp. If you demanded that he give them to you or destroy them in your presence, he refused. After you killed him you had no time to search the apartment, but enough to go through his clothing, and it must have been a relief to find the key to the safe-deposit box, since that was the most likely repository of the records — but it was a qualified relief, since you didn't dare to use the key. If you still have it, and almost certainly you have, it can be found and will be a damaging bit of evidence. You now have another, as the administrator of

Molloy's estate, but surely the safe-deposit company can distinguish between the original and the duplicate they had to have made—and by the
way, what would you have done if, opening the box in the presence of Mr.
Goodwin and Mr. Parker, you had found the records in it? Had you decided
on a course?"

Degan didn't reply. "Get on," Cramer rasped. "Where did you get them?"

Wolfe ignored him. "However, they weren't there. Another question: how
did you dare to kill him when you didn't know where they were? But I'll
venture to answer that myself. By getting Peter Hays there and giving the
police an obvious culprit, you insured plenty of time and opportunity for
searching the apartment as an old friend of Mrs. Molloy's. She is not
present to inform us, but that can wait."

"Where is she?" Cramer demanded.

Ignored again. "You must admit, Mr. Degan, that luck was with you. For
instance, the safe-deposit box. You had the key, but even if you had known
the name Molloy had used in renting it, and you probably didn't, you
wouldn't have dared to try to get at it. Then fortune intervened, represented
by me. I got you access to the box. But in spite of that good fortune you
weren't much better off, for the records weren't there, and until you found
them you were in great jeopardy. What did you do? I wouldn't mind paying
you the compliment of supposing that you conceived the notion that Molloy
had cached the records in Delia Brandt's apartment, and you approached
her, but I doubt if you deserve it. It is far more likely that she approached
you; that, having decided to marry William Lesser, she wanted to get rid of
Molloy's suitcase, still in her apartment; that before doing so she forced it
open and inspected its contents, that if items such as passports and steamship or airplane tickets were there she destroyed them; that she examined
the sheaf of papers and from them learned that there was a large sum of
money somewhere and that you had been involved with Molloy in extensive
and lucrative transactions and probably knew where the money was. She
was not without cunning. Before approaching you she took the suitcase,
with the records in it, to Grand Central Terminal and put it in a checking
locker. Then she saw you, told you what she knew and what she had, and
demanded the money."

"That's a lie!" William Lesser blurted.

Wolfe's eyes darted to him. "Then what did she do? Since you know?"

"I don't know, but I know she wouldn't do that! It's a lie!"

"Then let me finish it. A lie, like a truth, should reach its destination.
And that, Mr. Degan, was where luck caught up with you. You couldn't give
her the money from the safe-deposit box, but even if you gave her a part of
your share of the loot and she surrendered the records to you, you couldn't
empty her brain of what she knew, and as long as she lived she would be a
threat. So last night you went to her apartment, ostensibly, I presume, to
give her the money and get the records, but actually to kill her, and you did
so. I don't know—*Saul!*"

I wouldn't say that Saul slipped up. Sitting between Lesser and Degan,
naturally he was concentrating on Degan, and Lesser gave no warning. He
just lunged, right across Saul's knees, either to grab Degan or hit him, or
maybe both. By the time I got there Saul had his coattail, jerking him off,
Degan was sitting on the floor, and Purley Stebbins was on the way. But

Purley, who has his points, wasn't interested in Lesser, leaving him to Saul. He got his big paws on Degan's arm, helped him up, and helped him down again onto the chair, while Saul and I bulldozed Lesser to the couch. When we were placed again it was an improvement: Stebbins on one side of Degan and Saul on the other, and Lesser on the sidelines. Cramer, who had stood to watch the operation, sat down.

Wolfe resumed. "I was saying, Mr. Degan, that I don't know whether you searched her apartment for the records, but naturally — Did he, Mr. Cramer?"

"Someone did," Cramer growled. "Good. I'm stopping this right here. I want to see those records and I want to know how you got them."

Wolfe looked at the wall clock. "I still have thirty-eight minutes of my hour. If you interpose authority of course you have it. But I have your word. Is it garbage?"

Cramer's face got redder, and his jaw worked. "Go ahead."

"I should think so." Wolfe returned to Degan. "You did search, naturally, without success. You weren't looking for something as small as a key, but even if you had been you still wouldn't have found it, for it was destined for me. How it reached me is a detail Mr. Cramer may discuss with me later if he still thinks it worth while; all that concerns you is that I received it, and sent Mr. Panzer with it to Grand Central, and he returned with the suitcase. From it I got the sheaf of papers now in my drawer. I was inspecting them when Mr. Cramer phoned me shortly after six o'clock, and I arranged with him for this meeting. That's all, Mr. Degan."

Wolfe's eyes went left, and his voice lifted and sharpened. "Now for you, Mrs. Irwin. I wonder if you know how deep your hole is?"

"Don't say anything, Fanny." Irwin stood up. "We're going. Come on, Fanny." He took her shoulder and she came up to her feet.

"I think not," Wolfe said. "I quote Mr. Cramer: 'As it stands now, you can walk out whenever you feel like it.' But the standing has been altered. Archie, to the door. Mr. Cramer, I'll use restraint if necessary."

Cramer didn't hesitate. He was gruff. "I think you'd better stay and hear it out, Mr. Irwin."

"I refuse to, Inspector. I'm not going to sit here while he insults and bullies my wife."

"Then you can stand. Stay at the door, Goodwin. No one leaves this room until I say so. That's official. All right, Wolfe. God help you if you haven't got it."

Wolfe looked at her. "You might as well sit down, Mrs. Irwin. That's better. You already know most of what I'm going to tell you, perhaps all. Last Wednesday evening a man named Keems, in my employ, called at your apartment and spoke with you and your husband. You were leaving for a party and cut the interview short. Keems left the building with you, but soon he went back to your apartment and talked with your maid, Ella Reyes, and gave her a hundred dollars in cash. In return she gave him information. She told him that on January third you complained of no headache until late in the afternoon, immediately after you received a phone call from Patrick Degan. She may even —"

"That isn't true." Fanny Irwin had to squeeze it out.

"If you mean she didn't tell him that, I admit I can't prove it, since

Johnny Keems and Ella Reyes are both dead. If you mean that didn't happen, I don't believe you. She may even have also told him that she heard the phone conversation on an extension, and that Mr. Degan told you to withdraw from the theater party that evening, giving a headache as an excuse, and to suggest that Mrs. Molloy be invited in your stead."

"You know what you're saying," Jerome Arkoff said darkly.

"I do," Wolfe told Mrs. Irwin, not him. "I am charging you with complicity in the murder of Michael Molloy, and, by extension, of Johnny Keems and Ella Reyes and Delia Brandt. With that information from your maid, Keems, ignoring the instructions I had given him, sought out Degan. Degan, seeing that he was in great and imminent peril, acted promptly and effectively. On some pretext, probably of taking Keems to interview some other person, he had Keems wait for him at a place not frequented at that time of night while he went for his car; and instead of going for his car he stole one, drove it to the appointed place, and killed Keems with it."

Wolfe's head moved. "Do you wish to challenge that detail, Mr. Degan? Have you an alibi for that night?"

"I'm listening," Degan said, louder than necessary. "And don't forget others are listening too."

"I won't." Wolfe returned to Fanny Irwin. "But Degan had learned from Keems the source of his information, and Ella Reyes was almost as great a menace as Keems had been. Whether he communicated with her directly or through you, I don't know. He arranged to meet her, and killed her, and put the body where it was not found until somewhat later, taking her handbag to delay identification. By then he was no better than a maniac, and when, two or three days afterward, he was confronted with still another threat, this time from Delia Brandt, qualms, either of conscience or of trepidation, bothered him not at all. But I wonder about you. You felt no qualms? You feel none?"

"Don't say anything," her husband told her. He had her hand.

"I'm not sure that's good advice," Wolfe said. "There are certainly people present who would question it. If you'll turn your head, madam, to your right and rear, there by the big globe—the man on the left and the woman beside him—they are the parents of Peter Hays, who has been convicted of a murder you helped to commit. The other man is also deeply interested; he is Peter Hays's counsel. Now if you'll turn your head the other way. The man on the couch, who lost control of himself a few minutes ago, is—or was—the fiancé of Delia Brandt. They were to be married—tomorrow, Mr. Lesser?"

No reply.

Wolfe didn't press him. "And standing at the door is Archie Goodwin, and on Mr. Degan's left is Saul Panzer. They were friends and colleagues of Johnny Keems—and I myself knew Keems for some years and had esteem for him. I'm sorry I can't present to you any of the friends or family of Ella Reyes; you knew her better than anyone else here."

"What the hell good does this do?" Jerome Arkoff demanded.

Wolfe ignored it. "The point is this, Mrs. Irwin. Mr. Degan is done for. I have this sheaf of papers in my drawer. The key for the safe-deposit box which he took from Molloy's body will almost certainly be found in Degan's possession. There are other items—for example, when Mr. Goodwin left this house last Tuesday a man followed him, and that man will be found and will tell who engaged him. I'll stake my reputation that it was Degan. Now that we know that Degan killed those four people, the evidence will pile up. Fingerprints in Delia Brandt's apartment, his movements Wednesday night and Thursday night and Sunday night, an examination of the books of his organization; it will be overwhelming."

"What do you want of me?" she asked. They were her first words since he had called her a murderer.

"I want you to consider your position. Your husband advises you to say nothing, but he should consider it too. You are clearly open to a charge as accessory to murder. If you think you must not admit that Degan phoned you on January third, and suggested that you withdraw from the theater party and that Mrs. Molloy be asked in your stead, you are wrong. Such an admission would injure you only if it carried the implication that you knew why Degan wanted Mrs. Molloy away from her apartment—knew it either when he made the suggestion or afterward. And such an implication is not inherent. It is even implausible, since Degan wouldn't want to disclose his intention to commit murder. He could have told you merely that he wanted a private conversation with you and asked you to make an opportunity for that evening, and his suggestion of Mrs. Molloy could have been offhand. If so, it is unwise and dangerous for you to keep silent, for silence can carry implications too. If Degan merely wanted an opportunity to discuss some private matter—"

"That was it!" she said, for all to hear.

Her husband let go of her hand.

Jerome Arkoff croaked, "Don't be a goddam fool, Tom! This is for keeps!"

Rita sang out, "Go on, Fanny! Spit it out!"

Fanny offered both hands to her husband, and he took them. She gave him her eyes too. "You know me, Tom. You know I'm yours. He just said he had to see me, he had to tell me something. He came to the apartment, but now I see, because he didn't come until nearly ten—"

Degan went for her. Of course it was a convulsion rather than a calculated movement. It couldn't very well have been calculated, since Saul and Purley were right there beside him, and since, even if he got his hands on her and somehow managed to finish her, it wouldn't have helped his prospects any. It was as Wolf had said, after killing four people he was no better than a maniac, and, hearing her blurting out her contribution to his doom, he acted like one. He never touched her. Saul and Purley had him and jerked him back, and those two together are enough for any maniac.

Irwin was on his feet. So were the Arkoffs, and so was Cramer. Albert Freyer went loping over to my desk and reached for the phone.

Wolfe was speaking. "I'm through, Mr. Cramer. Twelve minutes short of my hour."

They didn't need me for a minute or two. I opened the door to the hall and went upstairs to report to Mrs. Molloy. She had it coming to her if anyone did. And from her room I could chase Freyer off the phone and call Lon Cohen at the *Gazette* and give him some news.

19

A few days later Cramer dropped in at six o'clock and called me Archie when I let him in. After getting settled in the red leather chair, accepting beer, and exchanging some news and views with Wolfe, he stated, not aggressively, "The District Attorney wants to know where and how you got the key to the locker. I wouldn't mind knowing myself."

"I think you would," Wolfe declared.

"Would what?"

"Would mind. It would only ruffle you to no purpose. If the District Attorney persists, and I tell him it came to me in the mail and the envelope has been destroyed, or that Archie found it on the sidewalk, what then? He has the murderer, and you delivered him. I doubt if you will persist."

He didn't.

The problem of the fee, which had to be settled as soon as Peter Hays had been turned loose, was a little more complicated. Having mentioned to James R. Herold, while under a strain, the sum of fifty thousand dollars, Wolfe wanted to stick to it, but fifty grand and expenses seemed pretty steep for a week's work, and besides, he was already in the 80% bracket. He solved it very neatly, arranging for Herold to donate a check for $16,666.67 to Johnny Keems's widow and one for the same amount to Ella Reyes' mother. That left $16,666.66, plus expenses, for Wolfe, and makes a monkey out of people who call him greedy, since he got only $16,666.66 instead of $16,666.67. And P.H., after he got from under, finally conceded that his father and mother were his parents, though the announcement of the wedding in the *Times* had it Peter Hays, and the *Times* is always right.

They were married a month or so after Patrick A. Degan had been convicted of first-degree murder, and a couple of weeks later they called at the office. I wouldn't have recognized P.H. as the guy I had seen that April day through the steel lattice. He looked comparatively human and even acted human. I want to be fair, but I also want to report accurately, and the fact is that he didn't impress me as any particular treat. When they got up to go Selma Hays moved to the corner of Wolfe's desk and said she had to kiss him. She said she doubted if he wanted to be kissed, but she simply had to.

Wolfe shook his head. "Let us forgo it. You wouldn't enjoy it and neither would I. Kiss Mr. Goodwin instead; that will be more to the point."

I was right there. She turned to me, and for a second she thought she was going to, and so did I. But as pink started to show in her cheeks she drew back, and I said something, I forget what. That girl has sense. Some risks are just too big to take.

238

If Death Ever Slept

1

IT would not be strictly true to say that Wolfe and I were not speaking that Monday morning in May.

We had certainly spoken the night before. Getting home — home being the old brownstone on West 35th Street owned by Wolfe, and occupied by him and Fritz and Theodore and me — around two a.m., I had been surprised to find him still up, at his desk in the office, reading a book. From the look he gave me as I entered, it was plain that something was eating him, but as I crossed to the safe to check that it was locked for the night I was supposing that he had been riled by the book, when he snapped at my back, "Where have you been?"

I turned. "Now really," I said. "On what ground?"

He was glaring. "I should have asked, where have you *not* been. Miss Rowan has telephoned five times, first shortly after eight o'clock, last half an hour ago. If I had gone to bed she wouldn't have let me sleep. As you know, Fritz was out for the evening."

"Hasn't he come home?"

"Yes, but he must be up to get breakfast and I didn't want him pestered. You said you were going to the Flamingo Club with Miss Rowan. You didn't. She telephoned five times. So I, not you, have spent the evening with her, and I haven't enjoyed it. Is that sufficient ground?"

"No, sir." I was at his desk, looking down at him. "Not for demanding to know where I've been. Shall we try it over? I'll go out and come in again, and you'll say you don't like to be interrupted when you're reading and you wish I had let you know I intended to teach Miss Rowan a lesson but no doubt I have a good explanation, and I'll say I'm sorry but when I left here I didn't know she would need a lesson. I only knew it when I took the elevator up to her penthouse and found that there were people there whom she knows I don't like. So I beat it. Where I went is irrelevant, but if you insist I can give you a number to call and ask for Mrs. Schrebenwelder. If her husband answers, disguise your voice and say —"

"Pfui. You could have phoned."

Of course that left him wide open. He was merely being childish, since my phoning to tell him I had changed my program for the evening wouldn't have kept Lily Rowan from interrupting his reading. I admit it isn't noble to jab a man when his arms are hanging, but having just taught Lily a lesson I thought I might as well teach him one too, and did so. I may have been a little too enthusiastic. Anyway, when I left to go up to bed we didn't say good night.

But it wouldn't be true to say that we were not speaking Monday morning. When he came down from the plant rooms at eleven o'clock I said good morning distinctly, and he muttered it as he crossed to his desk. By the time Otis Jarrell arrived at noon, by appointment, we had exchanged at least twenty words, maybe more. I remember that at one point he asked what the bank balance was and I told him. But the air was frosty, and when I answered the doorbell and ushered Otis Jarrell into the office, and to the red leather chair at the end of Wolfe's desk, Wolfe practically beamed at him as he inquired, "Well, sir, what is your problem?"

For him that was gushing. It was for my benefit. The idea was to show me that he was actually in the best of humor, nothing wrong with him at all, that if his manner with me was somewhat reserved it was only because I had been very difficult, and it was a pleasure, by contrast, to make contact with a fellow being who would appreciate amenities.

He was aware that the fellow being, Otis Jarrell, had at least one point in his favor: he was rated upwards of thirty million dollars. Checking on him, as I do when it's feasible on everyone who makes an appointment to see Nero Wolfe, I had learned, in addition to that important item, that he listed himself in *Who's Who* as "capitalist," which seemed a little vague; that he maintained no office outside of his home, on Fifth Avenue in the Seventies; that he was fifty-three years old; that (this through a phone call to Lon Cohen of the *Gazette*) he had a reputation as a tough operator who could smell a chance for a squeeze play in his sleep; and that he had never been in jail.

He didn't look tough, he looked flabby, but of course that's no sign. The toughest guy I ever ran into had cheeks that needed a brassiere. Jarrell's weren't that bad, but they were starting to sag. And although the tailor who had been paid three hundred bucks, or maybe four hundred, for making his brown shadow-striped suit had done his best, the pants had a problem with a ridge of surplus flesh when he sat.

But that wasn't the problem that had brought the capitalist to Nero Wolfe. With his sharp brown eyes leveled at Wolfe's big face, he said, "I want to hire you on a confidential matter. Absolutely confidential. I know your reputation or I wouldn't be here, and your man's, Goodwin's, too. Before I tell you what it is I want your word that you'll take it on and keep it to yourselves, both of you."

"My dear sir." Wolfe, still needing to show me that he was perfectly willing to have sociable intercourse with one who deserved it, was indulgent. "You can't expect me to commit myself to a job without knowing what it is. You say you know my reputation; then you are satisfied of my discretion or you wouldn't have come. Short of complicity in a felony, I can keep a secret even if I'm not working on it. So can Mr. Goodwin."

Jarrell's eyes moved, darted, and met mine. I looked discreet.

He went back to Wolfe. "This may help." His hand went to a pocket and came out again with a brown envelope. From it he extracted a bundle of engravings held by a paper band. He tossed the bundle onto Wolfe's desk, looked around for a wastebasket, saw none, and dropped the envelope on the floor. "There's ten thousand dollars for a retainer. If I gave you a check it might be known, possibly by someone I don't want to know it. It will be charged to expense without your name appearing. I don't need a receipt."

It was a little raw, but there is always human nature, and net without taxes instead of net after taxes certainly has its attractions. I thought I saw two of Wolfe's fingers twitch a little, but the state of our relations may have influenced me.

"I prefer," he said dryly, "to give a receipt for anything I accept. What do you want me to do?"

Jarrell opened his mouth, closed it, made a decision, and spoke. "I want you to get a snake out of my house. Out of my family." He made fists. "My daughter-in-law. My son's wife. It must be absolutely confidential. I want you to get evidence of things she has done, things I know damn well she has done, and she will have to go!" He defisted to gesture. "You get the proof and I'll know what to do with it! My son will divorce her. He'll have to. All I need —"

Wolfe stopped him. "If you please, Mr. Jarrell. You'll have to go elsewhere. I don't deal with marital afflictions."

"It's not marital. She's my daughter-in-law."

"You spoke of divorce. Divorce is assuredly marital. You want evidence that will effect divorce." Wolfe straightened a finger to point at the bundle of bills. "With that inducement you should get it, if it exists — or even if it doesn't."

Jarrell shook his head. "You've got it wrong. Wait till I tell you about her. She's a snake. She's not a good wife, I'm sure she's two-timing my son, that's true, but that's only part of it. She's cheating me too. I'll have to explain how I operate. My office is at my home; I keep a secretary and a stenographer there. They live there. Also my wife, and my son and his wife, and my daugher, and my wife's brother. I buy and sell. I buy and sell anything from a barn full of horses to a corporation full of red ink. What I have is cash on hand, plenty of it, and everybody knows it from Rome to Honolulu, so I don't need much of an office. If you know anyone who needs money and has sommething that is worth money, refer him to me."

"I shall." Wolfe was still demonstrating, to me, so he was patient. "About your daugher-in-law?"

"This is about her. Three times in the past year I've had deals ruined by people who must have had information of my plans. I think they got that information through her. I don't know exactly how she got it — that's part of the job I want you to do — but on one of the deals the man who got in ahead of me, a man named Brigham, Corey Brigham — I'm sure she's playing with him, but I can't prove it. I want to prove it. If you want to call that a marital affliction, all right, but it's not my marital affliction. My marital affliction is named Trella, and I can handle her myself. Another thing, my daughter-in-law is turning my home into a madhouse, or trying to. She wants to take over. She's damned slick about it, but that's what she's after. I want her out of there."

"Then eject her. Isn't it your house?"

"It's not a house, it's an apartment. Penthouse. Duplex. Twenty rooms. I own it. If I eject her my son will go too, and I want him with me. That's another thing, she's getting between him and me, and I can't stop it. I tell you she's a snake. You said with that inducement" —he gestured at the bundle of bills — "I should get evidence for a divorce, but you don't know her. She's as slick as grease. The kind of man you were suggesting—one of that kind would never get her. It will take a man of your quality, your ability." He shot a glance at me. "And Archie Goodwin's. As I said, I know Goodwin's reputation too. As a matter of fact, I had a specific suggestion about Goodwin in my mind when I came here. Do you want to hear it?"

"I doubt if it's worth the trouble. What you're after is divorce evidence."

"I told you what I'm after, a snake. About Goodwin, I said I have a secretary, but I haven't. I fired him a week ago. One of those deals I got hooked on, the most recent one, I suspected him of leaking information on it to a certain party, and I fired him. So that—"

"I though you suspected your daughter-in-law."

"I did. I do. You can't say a man can't suspect two different people at once, not you. So that job is vacant. What was in my mind, why can't Goodwin take it? He would be right there, living under the same roof with her. He can size her up, there'll be plenty of opportunities—she'll see to that if he doesn't. My secretary had his meals with us, so of course Goodwin will. It occurred to me that that would be the best and quickest way, at least to start. If you're not tied up with something he could come today. Right now."

I didn't like him, but I was feeling sorry for him. A man of my broad sympathies must make allowances. If she was as slick a snake as he thought she was, and he should have been a good judge of slickness, he was out of luck. Of course the idea that Wolfe would consider getting along without me at hand, to be called on for anything from typing a letter to repelling an invasion force, was ludicrous. It was hard enough to get away for week ends. Add to that Wolfe's rule against spouse-snooping, and where was he?

So I was feeling sorry for him when I heard Wolfe say, "You realize, Mr. Jarrell, that there could be no commitment as to how long he would stay there. I might need him."

"Yes, certainly. I realize that."

"And the job itself, the nominal job. Isn't there a danger that it would be apparent that he isn't qualified for it?"

"No, none whatever. Not even to Miss Kent, my stenographer. No secretary I hired would know how I operate until I broke him in. But there's a detail to consider, the name. Of course his name is not as widely known as yours, but it is known. He'll have to use another name."

I had recovered enough to risk my voice. Unquestionably Wolfe had figured that, taken by surprise, I would raise a squawk, giving him an out, and equally unquestionably he was damned well going to be disappointed. I admit that after the jolt he had given me I was relieved when my voice came out perfectly okay. "About the name, Mr. Jarrell." I was talking to him, not to Wolfe. "Of course I'll have to take some luggage, quite a lot since I may stay indefinitely, and mine has my initials on it. The usual problem. A.G. Let's see. How about Abe Goldstein?"

Jarrell, regarding me, screwed his lips. "I don't think so. No. I've got nothing against Jews, especially when they need money, but you don't look it. No."

"Well, I'll try again. I suppose you're right, I ought to look it. How about Adonis Guilfoyle?"

He laughed. It started with a cackle, then he threw his head back and roared. It tapered off to another cackle before he spoke.

"One thing about me, I've got a sense of humor. I could appreciate you, Goodwin, don't think I couldn't. We'll get along. You'd better let me try. A. Alan? That's all right. G. Green? Why not? Alan Green."

"Okay." I arose. "It hasn't got much flavor, but it'll do. It will take me a little while to pack, fifteen or twenty minutes." I moved.

"Archie! Sit down."

The round was mine, against big odds. He owned the house and everything in it except the furniture in my bedroom. He was the boss and paid my salary. He weighed nearly a hundred pounds more than my 178. The chair I had just got up from had cost $139.95; the one he was sitting in, oversized and custom-made of Brazilian Mauro, had come to $650.00. We were both licensed private detectives, but he was a genius and I was merely an operative. He, with or without Fritz to help, could turn out a dish of *Couronne de Canard au Riz à la Normande* without batting an eye; I had to concentrate to poach an egg. He had ten thousand orchids in his plant rooms on the roof; I had one African violet on my windowsill, and it wasn't feeling well. Etc.

But he was yelling uncle. He had counted on getting a squawk out of me, and now he was stuck, and he would have to eat crow instead of *Couronne de Canard au Riz à la Normande* if he wanted to get unstuck.

I faced him and inquired pleasantly, "Why, don't you like Alan Green?"

"Pfui. I haven't instructed you to comply with Mr. Jarrell's suggestion."

"No, but you indicated plainly that you intended to. Very plainly."

"I intended to confer with you."

"Yes, sir. We're conferring. Points to consider: would you like to improve on Alan Green, and would it be better for me to get a thorough briefing here, and get it in my notebook, before going up there? I think maybe it would."

"Then—" He swallowed it. What had started for his tongue was probably, "Then you persist in this pigheaded perversity," or something stronger, but he knew darned well he had asked for it, and there was company present. You may be thinking that the bundle of bills was also present, but I doubt if that was a factor. I have heard him turn down more than a few husbands, and more than a few wives, who had offered bigger bundles than that one if he would get them out of bliss that had gone sour. No. He knew he had lost the round, and knew that I knew it, but he wasn't going to admit it in front of a stranger.

"Very well," he said. He pushed his chair back, got up, and told

Jarrell, "You will excuse me. Mr. Goodwin will know what information he needs." He circled around the red leather chair and marched out.

I sat at my desk, got notebook and pen, and swiveled to the client. "First," I said, "all the names, please."

2

I can't undertake to make you feel at home in that Fifth Avenue duplex penthouse because I never completely got the hang of it myself. By the third day I decided that two different architects had worked on it simultaneously and hadn't been on speaking terms. Jarrell had said it had twenty rooms, but I think it had seventeen or nineteen or twenty-one or twenty-three. I never made it twenty. And it wasn't duplex, it was triplex. The butler, Steck, the housekeeper, Mrs. Latham, and the two maids, Rose and Freda, slept on the floor below, which didn't count. The cook and the chauffeur slept out.

Having got it in my notebook, along with ten pages of other items, that Wyman, the son, and Lois, the daughter, were Jarrell's children by his first wife, who had died long ago, I had supposed that there were so many variations in taste among the rooms because Jarrell and the first wife and the current marital affliction, Trella, had all had a hand at it, but was set right on the second day by Roger Foote, Trella's brother. It was decorators. At least eight decorators had been involved. Whenever Jarrell decided he didn't like the way a room looked he called in a decorator, never one he had used before, to try something else. That added to the confusion the architects had contributed. The living room, about the right size for badminton, which they called the lounge because some decorator had told them to, was blacksmith modern — black iron frames for chairs and sofas and mirrors, black iron and white tile around the fireplace, black iron and glass tables; and the dining room, on the other side of an arch, was Moorish or something. The arch itself was in a hell of a fix, a very bad case of split personality. The side terrace outside the dining room was also Moorish, I guess, with mosaic tubs and boxes and table tops. It was on the first floor, which was ten stories up. The big front terrace, with access from both the reception hall and the lounge, was Dupont frontier. The tables were redwood slabs and the chairs were chromium with webbed plastic seats. A dozen pink dogwoods in bloom, in big wooden tubs, were scattered around on Monday, the day I arrived, but when I went to the lounge at cocktail time on Wednesday they had disappeared and been replaced by rhododendrons covered with buds. I was reminded of the crack George Kaufman made once to Moss Hart — "That just shows what God could do if only he had money."

Jarrell's office, which was called the library, was also on the first floor, in the rear. When I arrived, with him, Monday afternoon, he had taken me straight there after turning my luggage over to Steck, the butler. It was a big square room with windows in only one wall, and no decorator had had a go at it. There were three desks, big, medium, and small. The big desk had four phones, red, yellow, white, and black; the medium one had three, red, white, and black; and the small one had two, white and black. All of one wall was occupied by a battery of steel filing cabinets as tall as me. Another was covered by shelves to the ceiling, crammed with books and magazines; I found later that they were all strictly business, everything from *Profits in Oysters* to *North American Corporation Directory* for the past twenty years. The other wall had three doors, two big safes, a table with current magazines — also business — and a refrigerator.

Jarrell had led me across to the small desk, which was the size of mine at home, and said, "Nora, this is Alan Green, my secretary. You'll have to help me show him the ropes."

Nora Kent, seated at the desk, tilted her head back to aim a pair of gray eyes at me. Her age, forty-seven, was recorded in my notebook, but she didn't look it, even with the gray showing in her soft brown hair. But the notebook also said that she was competent, trustworthy, and nobody's fool, and she looked that. She had been with Jarrell twenty-two years. There was something about the way she offered a hand that gave me the feeling it would be more appropriate to kiss it than to grip it, but she reciprocated the clasp firmly though briefly.

She spoke. "Consider me at your service, Mr. Green." The gray eyes went to Jarrell. "Mr. Clay has called three times. Toledo operator seven-nineteen wants you, a Mr. William R. Bowen. From Mrs. Jarrell, there will be three guests at dinner; the names are on your desk, also a telegram. Where do you want me to start with Mr. Green?"

"There's no hurry. Let him get his breath." Jarrell pointed to the medium-sized desk, off to the right. "That's yours, Green. Now you know your way here, and I'll be busy with Nora for a while. I told Steck — here he is." The door had opened and the butler was there. "Steck, before you show Mr. Green to his room take him around. We don't want him getting lost. Have you told Mrs. Jarrell he's here?"

"Yes, sir."

Jarrell was at his desk. "Don't come back, Green. I'll be busy. Get your bearings. Cocktails in the lounge at six-thirty."

Steck moved aside for me to pass, pulled the door shut as he backed out, said, "This way, sir," and started down the corridor a mile a minute. I called to him, "Hold it, Steck," and he braked and turned.

"You look harassed," I told him. He did. He was an inch taller than me, but thinner. His pale sad face was so long and narrow that he looked taller than he was. His black tie was a little crooked. I added, "You must have things to do."

"Yes, sir, certainly, I have duties."

"Sure. Just show me my room."

"Mr. Jarrell said to take you around, sir."

"You can do that later, if you can work it in. At the moment I need a room. I want to gargle."

"Yes, sir. This way, sir."

I followed him down the corridor and around a corner to an elevator. I

asked if there were stairs and was told that there were three, one off the
lounge, one in the corridor, and one for service in the rear. Also three
elevators. The one we were in was gold-plated, or possibly solid. On the
upper floor we went left, then right, and near the end of the hall he
opened a door and bowed me in. He followed, to tell me about the
phones. A ring would be for the green one, from the outside world. A
buzz would be for the black one, from somewhere inside, for instance
from Mr. Jarrell. I would use that one to get Steck when I was ready to
be taken around. I thanked him out.

The room was twelve by sixteen, two windows with venetians, a little
frilly but not bad, mostly blue and lemon-yellow except the rugs, which
were tan with dark brown stripes. The bed was okay, and so was the
bathroom. Under ordinary circumstances I would have used the green
phone to ring Wolfe and report arrival, but I skipped it, not wanting to
rub it in. After unpacking, taking my time, deciding not to shave, washing my hands, and straightening my tie, I got out my notebook, sat by a
window, and turned to the list of names:

> Mrs. Otis Jarrell (Trella)
> Lois Jarrell, daughter by first wife
> Wyman Jarrell, son by ditto
> Mrs. Wyman Jarrell (Susan)
> Roger Foote, Trella's brother
> Nora Kent, stenographer
> James L. Eber, ex-secretary
> Corey Brigham, friend of family who queered deal

The last two didn't live there, but it seemed likely that they would
need attention if I was going to get anywhere, which was doubtful. If
Susan was really a snake, and if the only way to earn a fee was to get her
bounced out of the house and the family, leaving her husband behind, it
would take a lot of doing. My wrist watch said there was still forty minutes before cocktail time. I returned the notebook to my bag, the small
one, which contained a few personal items not appropriate for Alan
Green, locked the bag, left the room, found the stairs, and descended to
the lower floor.

It would be inaccurate to say I got lost five times in the next quarter of
an hour, since you can't get lost when you have no destination, but I
certainly got confused. Neither of the architects had had any use for a
straightaway, but they had had conflicting ideas on how to handle turns
and corners. When I found myself passing an open door for the third
time, recognizing it by the view it gave of a corner of a grand piano, and
the blah of a radio or TV, with no notion of how I got there, I decided to
call it off and make for the front terrace, but a voice came through to my
back. "Is that you, Wy?"

I backtracked and stepped through into what, as I learned later, they
called the studio.

"I'm Alan Green," I said. "Finding my way around."

She was on a couch, stetched out from the waist down, with her upper
half propped against cushions. Since she was too old for either Lois or

Susan, though by no means aged, she must be Trella, the marital affliction. There was a shade too much of her around the middle and above
the neck—say six or eight pounds. She was a blue-eyed blonde, and her
face had probably been worthy of notice before she had buried the bones
too deep by thickening the stucco. What showed below the skirt hem of
her blue dress—from the knees on down—was still worthy of notice.
While I noticed it she was reaching for a remote-control gadget, which
was there beside her, to turn off the TV.

She took me in. "Secretary," she said.

"Yes, ma'am," I acknowledged. "Just hired by your husband—if
you're Mrs. Otis Jarrell."

"You don't look like a secretary."

"I know, it's a handicap." I smiled at her. She invited smiles. "I try to
act like one."

She put up a hand to pat a yawn—a soft little hand. "Damn it, I'm
still half asleep. Television is better than a pill, don't you think so?" She
patted the couch. "Come and sit down. What made you think I'm Mrs.
Otis Jarrell?"

I stayed put. "To begin with, you're here. You couldn't be Miss Lois
Jarrell because you must be married. You couldn't be Mrs. Wyman Jarrell because I've got the impression that my employer feels a little cool
about his daughter-in-law and it seemed unlikely he would feel cool
about you."

"Where did you get the impression?"

"From him. When he told me not to discuss his business affairs with
anyone, including members of the family, I thought he put some emphasis on his daugher-in-law."

"Why must I be married?"

I smiled again. "You'll have to pardon me because you asked. Seeing
you, and knowing what men like, I couldn't believe that you were still at
large."

"Very nice." She was smiling back. "*Very* nice. My God, I don't have to
pardon you for that. You don't talk like a secretary, either." She pushed
the remote control gadget aside. "Sit down. Do you like leg of lamb?"

I felt that a little braking was required. It was all very well to get on a
friendly basis with the mistress of the house as soon as possible, since
that might be useful in trapping the snake, and the smiling and sit-
downing was very nice, but her concern about feeding the new secretary
right after only three minutes with him was going too far too quick.
Since I didn't look like a secretary or talk like one, I though I had better
at least act like one, and I was facing up to it when help came.

There were footsteps in the corridor and a man entered. Three steps in
he stopped short, at sight of me. He turned to her. "Oh. I don't need to
wake you."

"Not today, Wy. This is your father's new secretary. Green. Alan
Green. We were getting acquainted."

"Oh." He went to her, leaned over, and kissed her on the lips. It didn't
strike me as a typical filial operation, but of course she wasn't his
mother. He straightened up. "You don't look as sleepy as usual. Your
eyes don't look sleepy. You've had a drink."

"No, I haven't." She was smiling at him. She gestured at me. "He woke me up. We're going to like him."

"Are we?" He turned, moved, and extended a hand. "I'm Wyman Jerrell."

He was two inches shorter than me and two inches narrower across the shoulders. He had his father's brown eyes, but the rest of him came from somebody else, particularly his tight little ears and thin straight nose. There were three deep creases down the middle of his brow, which at his age, twenty-seven, seemed precocious. He was going on. "I'll be talking with you, I suppose, but that's up to my father. I'll be seeing you." He turned his back on me.

I headed for the door, was told by Mrs. Jarrell there would be cocktails in the lounge at six-thirty, halted to thank her, and left. As I moved down the corridor toward the front a female in uniform came around a corner and leered at me as she approached. Taken by surprise, I leered back. Evidently, I thought, this gang doesn't stand on formality. I was told later by somebody that Freda had been born with a leer, but I never went into it with Freda.

I had stepped out to the front terrace for a moment during my tour, so had already met the dogwoods and glanced around the layout of red-wood slabs and chrome and plastic, and now I crossed to the parapet for a look down at Fifth Avenue and across to the park. The sun was smack in my eyes, and I put a hand up to shade them for a view of a squirrel perched on a limb high in a tree, and was in that pose when a voice came from behind.

"Who are you, Sitting Bull?"

I pivoted. A girl all in white with bare tanned arms and a bare tanned throat down to the start of the curves and a tanned face with dimples and greenish brown eyes and a pony tail was coming. If you are thinking that is too much to take in with a quick glance, I am a detective and a trained observer. I had time not only to take her in but also to think, Good Lord, if that's Susan and she's a snake I'm going to take up herpetology, if that's the word, and I can look it up.

She was still five steps off when I spoke. "Me good Indian. Me good friend white man, only you're not a man and you're not white. I was looking at a squirrel. My name is Alan Green. I am the new secretary, hired today. I was told to get my bearings and have been trying to. I have met your husband."

"Not *my* husband, you haven't. I'm a spinster named Lois. Do you like squirrels?"

"It depends. A squirrel with integrity and charm, with no bad habits, a squirrel who votes right, who can be counted on in a pinch, I like *that* squirrel." At close quarters they weren't what I would call dimples, just little cheek dips that caught shadows if the light angle was right. "I hope I don't sound fussy."

"Come here a minute." She led me off to the right, put a hand on the tiled top of the parapet, and with the other pointed across the avenue. "See that tree? See the one I mean?"

"The one that lost an arm."

"That's it. One day in March a squirrel was skipping around on it, up near the top. I was nine years old. My father had given my brother a rifle for his birthday. I went and got the rifle and loaded it, and came out and stood here, right at this spot, and waited until the squirrel stopped to rest, and shot it. It tumbled off. On the way down it bumped against limbs twice. I yelled for Wy, my brother, and he came and I showed it to him, there on the ground not moving, and he —but the rest doesn't matter. With anyone I might possibly fall in love with I like to start off by telling him the worst thing I ever did, and anyway you brought it up by saying you were looking at a squirrel. Now you know the worst, unless you think it's worse that several years later I wrote a poem called 'Requiem for a Rodent.' It was published in my school paper."

"Certainly it's worse. Running it down by calling it a rodent, even though it was one."

She nodded. "I've suspected it myself. Some day I'll get analyzed and find out." She waved it away, into the future. "Where did you ever get the idea of being a secretary?"

"In a dream. Years ago. In the dream I was the secretary of a wealthy pirate. His beautiful daughter was standing on the edge of a cliff shooting at a gopher, which is a rodent, down on the prairie, and when she hit it she felt so sorry for it that she jumped off the cliff. I was down below and caught her, saving her life, and it ended romantically. So I became a secretary."

Her brows were lifted, opening her eyes as wide as they would go. "I can't imagine how a pirate's daughter happened to be standing on a cliff on top of a prairie. You must have been dreaming."

No man could stop a conversation as dead in its tracks as that. It takes a woman. But at least she had the decency to start up another one. With her eyes back to normal, she cocked her head a little to the side and said, "You know, I'm bothered. I'm sure I've seen you before somewhere, and I can't remember where, and I always remember people. Where was it? Have you forgotten too?"

I had known that might come from one or more of them. My picture hadn't been in the papers as often as the president of Egypt's, or even Nero Wolfe's, and the latest had been nearly a year ago, but I had known it might happen. I grinned at her. I hadn't been grinning in any published picture. One thing, it gave me a chance to recover the ball she had taken away from me.

I shook my head. "I wouldn't forget. I only forget faces I don't care to remember. The only way I can account for it, you must have seen me in a dream."

She laughed. "All right, now we're even. I wish I could remember. Of course I may have seen you in a theater or restaurant, but if that's it and I do remember I won't tell you, because it would puff you up. Only you'll need puffing up after you've been here a while. He's my dear father, but he must be terrible to work for. I don't see —Hi, Roger. Have you met Alan Green? Dad's new secretary. Roger Foote."

I had turned. Trella's brother bore as little resemblance to her as Wyman Jarrell did to his father. He was big and broad and brawny, with no stuffing at all between the skin and the bones of his big wide face. If his size and setup hadn't warned me I might have got some knuckles crushed by his big paw; as it was, I gave as good as I got and it was a draw.

"Muscle man," he said. "My congratulations. Trust the filly to arch her neck at you. Ten to one she told you about the squirrel."

"Roger," Lois told me, "is horsy. He nearly went to the Kentucky Derby. He even owned a horse once, but it sprang a leak. No Pimlico today, Roger?"

"No, my angel. I could have got there, but I might never have got back. Your father has told Western Union not to deliver collect telegrams from me. Not to mention collect phone calls." He switched to me. "Do you suppose you're going to stick it?"

"I couldn't say, Mr. Foote. I've only been here two hours. Why, is it rough going?"

"It's worse than rough. Even if you're not a panhandler like me. My brother-in-law is made of iron. They could have used him to make that godawful stuff in the lounge, and I wish they had. Look at the Derby. I was on Iron Liege, or would have been if I had had it. I could have made myself independent for a week or more. You get the connection. You would think a man made of iron would stake me for a go on Iron Liege? No." He lifted a hand to look at it, saw it was empty, and dropped it. "I must have left my drink inside. You're not thirsty?"

"I am," Lois declared. "You, Mr. Green? Or Alan. We make free with the secretary." She moved. "Come along."

I followed them into the lounge, and across to a portable bar where Otis Jarrell, with a stranger at each elbow, a man and a woman, was stirring a pitcher of Martinis. The man was a wiry little specimen, black-eyed and black-haired, very neat in charcoal, with a jacket that flared at the waist. The woman, half a head taller, had red hair that was either natural or not, a milk-white face, and a jaw. Jarrell introduced me, but I didn't get their names until later: Mr. and Mrs. Herman Dietz. They weren't interested in the new secretary. Roger Foote moved to the other side of the bar and produced a Bloody Mary for Lois, a scotch and water for me, and a double bourbon with no accessories for himself.

I took a healthy sip and looked around. Wyman, the son, and Nora Kent, the stenographer, were standing over near the fireplace, which had no fire, presumably talking business. Not far off Trella was relaxed in a big soft chair, looking up at a man who was perched on one of the arms.

Lois' voice came up to my ear. "You've met my stepmother, haven't you?"

I told her yes, but not the man, and she said he was Corey Brigham, and was going to add something but decided not to. I was surprised to see him there, since he was on my list as the guy who had spoiled a deal, but the guests had been invited by her, not him. Or maybe not. Possibly Jarrell had suggested it, counting on bringing me home with him and wanting me to meet him. From a distance he was no special treat. Leaning over Trella with a well-trained smile, he had all the earmarks of a middle-aged million-dollar smoothie who would slip a head waiter twenty bucks and tip a hackie a dime. I was taking him in, filing him under unfinished business, when he lifted his head and turned it left, and I turned mine to see what had got his attention.

The snake had entered the room.

3

OF course it could have been that she planned it that way, that she waited until everyone else was there to make her entrance, and then, floating in, deliberately underplayed it. But also it could have been that she didn't like crowds, even family crowds, and put it off as long as she could, and then, having to go through with it, made herself as small and quiet as possible. I reserved my opinion, without prejudice — or rather, with two prejudices striking a balance. The attraction of the snake theory was that she had to be one if we were going to fill our client's order. The counterattraction was that I didn't like the client and wouldn't have minded seeing him stub his toe. So my mind was open as I watched her move across toward the fireplace, to where her husband was talking with Nora Kent. There was nothing reptilian about the way she moved. It might be said that she glided, but she didn't slither. She was slender, not tall, with a small oval face. Her husband kissed her on the cheek, then headed for the bar, presumably to get her a drink.

Trella called my name, Alan, making free with the secretary, and I went over to her and was introduced to Corey Brigham. When she patted the vacant arm of the chair and told me to sit I did so, thinking it safer there than it had been in the studio, and Brigham got up and left. She said I hadn't answered her question about leg of lamb, and she wanted to know. It seemed possible that I had got her wrong, that her idea was merely to function as a helpmate and see to it that the hired help liked the grub — but no. She might have asked it, but she didn't; she cooed it. I may not know as much about women as Wolfe pretends he thinks I do, but I know a coo when I hear it.

While giving her due attention as my hostess and my boss's wife, I was observing a phenomenon from the corner of my eye. When Wyman returned to Susan with her drink, Roger Foote was there. Also Corey Brigham was wandering over to them, and in a couple of minutes there went Herman Dietz. So four of the six males present were gathered around Susan, but as far as I could see she hadn't bent a finger or slanted an eye to get them there. Jarrell was still at the bar with Dietz's redheaded wife. Lois and Nora Kent had stepped out to the terrace.

Apparently Trella had seen what the corner of my eye was doing, for she said, "You have to be closer to appreciate her. She blurs at a distance."

"Her? Who?"

She patted my arm. "Now now. I don't mind, I'm used to it. Susan. My stepdaughter-in-law. Go and put an oar in."

"She seems to have a full crew. Anyway, I haven't met her."

"You haven't? That won't do." She turned and sang out, "Susan! Come here."

She was obeyed instantly. The circle opened to make room, and Susan crossed to us. "Yes, Trella?"

"I want to present Mr. Green. Alan. He has taken Jim's place. He has met everyone but you, and that didn't seem fair."

I took the offered hand and felt it warm and firm for the fifth of a second she let me have it. Her face *had* blurred at a distance. Even close up none of her features took your eye; you only saw the whole, the little oval face.

"Welcome to our aerie, Mr. Green," she said. Her voice was low, and was shy or coy or wary or demure, depending on your attitude. I had no attitude, and didn't intend to have one until I could give reasons. All I would have conceded on the spot was that she didn't hiss like a cobra or rattle like a rattler. As for her being the only one of the bunch to bid me welcome, that was sociable and kindhearted, but it would seem that she might have left that to the lady of the house. I thanked her for it anyway. She glanced at Trella, apparently uncertain whether to let it go at that or stay for a chat, murmured something polite, and moved away.

"I think it's in her bones," Trella said. "Or maybe her blood. Anyhow it's nothing you can see or hear. Some kind of hypnotism, but I think she can turn it on and off. Did you feel anything?"

"I'm a secretary, Mrs. Jarrell. Secretaries don't feel."

"The hell they don't. Jim Eber did. Of course you've barely met her and you may be immune."

Trella was telling me about a book on hypnotism she had read when Steck came to tell her dinner was ready.

It was uneven, five women and six men, and I was put between Lois and Roger Foote. There were several features deserving comment. The stenographer not only ate with the family, she sat next to Jarrell. The housekeeper, Mrs. Latham, helped serve. I had always thought a housekeeper was above it. Roger Foote, who had had enough to drink, ate like a truck driver — no, cut that — like a panhandler. The talk was spotty, mostly neighbor-to-neighbor, except when Corey Brigham sounded off about the Eisenhower budget. The leg of lamb was first-rate, not up to Fritz's, but good. I noticed Trella noticing me the second time around. The salad was soggy. I'm not an expert on wine, but I doubted if it deserved the remarks it got from Herman Dietz.

As we were passing through the Moorish arch — half-Moorish, anyway — to return to the lounge for coffee, Trella asked me if I played bridge, and Jerrell heard her.

"Not tonight," he said. "I need him. I won't be here tomorrow. You've got enough."

"Not without Nora. You know Susan doesn't play."

"I don't need Nora. You can have her."

If Susan had played, and if I could have swung it to be at her table, I would have been sorry to miss it. Perhaps you don't know all there is to know about a woman after watching her at an evening of bridge, but you should know more than when you sat down. By the time we were through with coffee they had chosen partners and Steck had the tables ready. I had wondered if Susan would go off to her pit, but apparently not. When Jerrell and I left she was out on the terrace.

He led the way through the reception hall, across a Kirman twice as big as my room at home—I have a Kirman there, paid for by me, 8′4″ x 3′2″—down the corridor, and around a couple of corners, to the door of the library. Taking a key fold from a pocket, he selected one, used it, and pushed the door open; and light came at us, so sudden and so strong that it made me blink. I may also have jumped.

He laughed, closing the key fold. "That's my idea." He pointed above the door. "See the clock? Anyone coming in, his picture is taken, and the clock shows the time. Not only that, it goes by closed circuit to the Horland Protective Agency, only three blocks away. A man there saw us come in just now. There's a switch at my desk and when we're in here we turn it off—Nora or I. I've got them at the doors of the apartment too, front and back. By the way, I'll give you keys. With this I don't have to wonder about keys—for instance, Jim Eber could have had duplicates made. I don't give a damn if he did. What do you think of it?"

"Very neat. Expensive, but neat. I ought to mention, if someone at Horland's saw me come in with you, he may know me, by sight anyway. A lot of them do. Does that matter?"

"I doubt it." He had turned on lights and gone to his desk. "I'll call them. Damn it, I could have come in first and switched it off. I'll call them. Sit down. Have a cigar?"

It was the cigar he had lit in the lounge after dinner that had warned me to keep my eyes on the road. I don't smoke them myself, but I admit that the finest tobacco smell you can get is a whiff from the lit end of a fine Havana, and when the box had been passed I had noticed that they were Portanagas. But I had not enjoyed the whiff I had got from the one Jerrell had lit. In fact, I had snorted it out. That was bad. When you can't stand the smell of a Portanaga because a client is smoking it, watch out or you'll be giving him the short end of the stick, which is unethical. Anyway, I saved him three bucks by not taking one.

He leaned back, let smoke float out of his mouth, and inquired, "What impression did you get?"

I looked judicious. "Not much of any. I only spoke a few words with her. Your suggestion that I get the others talking about her, especially your wife and your wife's brother—there has been no opportunity for that, and there won't be while they're playing cards. I think I ought to cultivate Corey Brigham."

He nodded. "You saw how it was there before dinner."

"Sure. Also Foote and Dietz, not to mention your son. Your wife thinks she hypnotizes them."

"You don't know what my wife thinks. You only know what she says she thinks. Then you discussed her with my wife?"

"Not at any length. I don't quite see when I'm going to discuss her at length with any of them. I don't see how this is going to work. As your secretary I should be spending my day in here with you and Miss Kent, and if they spend the evening at bridge?"

"I know." He tapped ash off in a tray. "You won't have to spend tomorrow in here. I'm taking a morning plane to Toledo, and I don't know when I'll be back. Actually my secretary has damn little to do when I'm not here. Nora knows everything, and I'll tell her to forget about you until I return. As I told you this afternoon, I'm certain that everybody here, every damn one of them, knows things about my daughter-in-law that I don't know. Even my daughter. Even Nora." His eyes were leveled at me. "It's up to you. I've told you about my wife, she'll talk your head off, but anything she tells you may or may not be so. Do you dance?"

"Yes."

"Are you a good dancer?"

"Yes."

"Lois likes to dance, but she's particular. Take her out tomorrow evening. Has Roger hit you for a loan yet?"

"No. I haven't been alone with him."

"That wouldn't stop him. When he does, let him have fifty or a hundred. Give him the impression that you stand in well with me — even let him think you have something on me. Buy my wife some flowers — nothing elaborate, as long as it's something she thinks you paid for. She loves to have men buy things for her. You might take her to lunch, to Rusterman's, and tip high. When a man tips high she takes it as a personal compliment."

I wanted to move my chair back a little to get less of his cigar, but vetoed it. "I don't object to the program personally," I said, "but I do professionally. That's a hell of a schedule for a secretary. They're not halfwits."

"That doesn't matter." He flipped it off with the cigar. "Let them all think you have something on me — let them think anything they want to. The point is that the house is mine and the money is mine, and whatever I stand for they'll accept whether they understand it or not. The only exception to that is my daughter-in-law, and that's what you're here for. She's making a horse's ass out of my son, and she's getting him away from me, and she's sticking a finger in my affairs. I'm making you a proposition. The day she's out of here, with my son staying, you get ten thousand dollars in cash, in addition to any fee Nero Wolfe charges. The day a divorce settles it, with my son still staying, you get fifty thousand. You personally. That will be in addition to any expenses you incur, over and above Wolfe's fee and expenses."

I said that no man can stop a conversation the way a woman can, but I must admit that Otis Jarrell had made a darned good stab at it. I also admit I was flattered. Obviously he had gone to Wolfe just to get me, to get me there in his library so he could offer me sixty grand and expenses to frame his daughter-in-law, who probably wasn't a snake at all. If she had been, his itch to get rid of her would have been legitimate, and he could have left it as a job for Wolfe and just let me earn my salary.

It sure was flattering. "That's quite a proposition," I said, "but there's a hitch. I work for Mr. Wolfe. He pays me."

"You'll still be working for him. I only want you to do what I hired him to do. He'll get his fee."

That was an insult to my intelligence. He didn't have to make it so damned plain. It would have been a pleasure to square my shoulders and lift my chin and tell him to take back his gold and go climb a tree, and that would have been the simplest way out, but there were drawbacks.

For one thing, it was barely possible that she really was a snake and no framing would be required. For another, if she wasn't a snake, and if he was determined to frame her, she needed to know it and deserved to know it, but he was still Wolfe's client, and all I had was what he had said to me with no witnesses present. For still another, there was the ten grand in Wolfe's safe, not mine to spurn. For one more if we need it, I have my full share of curiosity.

I tightened my face to look uncomfortable. "I guess," I said, "I'll have to tell Mr. Wolfe about your proposition. I think I will. I've got to protect myself."

"Against what?" he demanded.

"Well . . . for instance, you might talk in your sleep."

He laughed. "I like you, Goodwin. I knew we'd get along. This is just you and me, and you don't need protection any more than I do. You know your way around and so do I. What do you want now for expenses? Five thousand? Ten?"

"Nothing. Let it ride and we'll see." I loosened the face. "I'm not accepting your proposition, Mr. Jarrell. I'm not even considering it. If I ever found myself feeling like accepting it, I'd meet you somewhere that I was sure wasn't wired for sound. After all, Horland's Protective Agency might be listening in right now."

He laughed again. "You *are* cagey."

"Not cagey, I just don't want my hair mussed. Do you want me to go on with the program? As you suggested?"

"Certainly I do. I think we understand each other, Goodwin." He put a fist on the desk. "I'll tell you this, since you probably know it anyway. I'd give a million dollars cash any minute to get rid of that woman for good and call it a bargain. That doesn't mean you can play me for a sucker. I'll pay for what I get, but not for what I don't get. Any arrangements you make, I want to know who with and for exactly what and how much."

"You will. Have you any more suggestions?"

He didn't have, at least nothing specific. Even after propositioning, as it looked to me, an out-and-out frame, he still thought, or pretended to, that I might raise some dust by cultivating the inmates. He tried to insist on an advance for expenses, but I said no, I would ask for it if and when needed. I was surprised that he didn't refer again to my notion that I might have to tell Wolfe about his proposition; apparently he was taking it for granted that I would take my bread buttered on both sides if the butter was thick enough. He was sure we understood each other, but I wasn't. I wasn't sure of anything. Before I went he gave me two keys, one for the front door and one for the library. He said he had to make a phone call, and I said I was going out for a walk. He said I could use the phone there, or in my room, and I said that wasn't it, I always took a little walk in the evening. Maybe we understood each other at that, up to a point.

I went to the front vestibule, took the private elevator down, nodded at the sentinel in the lobby—not the one who had been there when I arrived— walked east to Madison, found a phone booth, and dialed a number.

After one buzz a voice was in my ear. "Nero Wolfe's residence, Orville Cather speaking."

I was stunned. It took me a full second to recover. Then I spoke, through my nose. "This is the city mortuary. We have a body here, a young man with classic Grecian features who jumped off Brooklyn Bridge. Papers in his wallet identify him as Archie Goodwin and his address—"

"Toss it back in the river," Orrie said. "What good is it? It never was much good anyway."

"Okay," I said, not through my nose. "Now I know. May I please speak to Mr. Wolfe?"

"I'll see. He's reading a book. Hold it."

I did so, and in a moment got a growl. "Yes?"

"I went for a walk and am in a booth. Reporting: the bed is good and the food is edible. I have met the family and they are not mine, except possibly the daughter, Lois. She shot a squirrel and wrote a poem about it. I'm glad you've got Orrie in to answer the phone and do the chores because that may simplify matters. You can stop my salary as of now. Jarrell has offered me sixty grand and expenses, me personally, to get the goods on his daughter-in-law and bounce her. I think his idea is that the goods are to be handmade, by me, but he didn't say so in so many words. If it takes me twelve weeks that will be five grand a week, so my salary would be peanuts and you can forget it. I'll get it in cash, no tax to pay, and then I'll probably marry Lois. Oh yes, you'll get your fee too."

"How much of this is flummery?"

"None of the facts. The facts are straight. I am reporting."

"Then he's either a nincompoop or a scalawag or both."

"Probably but not necessarily. He said he would give a million dollars to get rid of her and consider it a bargain. So it's just possible he has merely got an itch he can't reach and is temporarily nuts. I'm giving him the benefit of the doubt because he's your client."

"And yours."

"No, sir. I didn't accept. I declined an advance for expenses. I turned him down, but with a manner and a tone of voice that sort of left it hanging. He thinks I'm just being cagey. What I think, I think he expects me to fix up a stew that will boil her alive, but I have been known to think wrong. I admit it's conceivable that she has it coming to her. One thing, she attracts men without apparently trying to. If a woman gathers them around by working a come-on, that's okay, they have a choice, they can play or not as they please. But when they come just because she's there, with no invitation visible to the naked eye, and I have good eyes, look out. She may not be a snake, in fact she may be an angel, but angels can be more dangerous than snakes and usually are. I can stick around and try to tag her, or you can return the ten grand and cross it off. Which?"

He grunted. "Mr. Jarrell has taken me for a donkey."

"And me for a goop. Our pride is hurt. He ought to pay for the privilege, one way or another. I'll keep you informed of developments, if any."

"Very well."

"Please remind Orrie that the bottom drawer of my desk is personal and there's nothing in it he needs."

He said he would, and even said good night before he hung up. I bought a picture postcard at the rack, and a stamp, addressed the card to Fritz, and wrote on it, "Having wonderful time. Wish you were here. Archie," went and found a mailbox and dropped the card in, and returned to the barracks.

In the tenth-floor vestibule I gave my key a try, found that it worked, and was dazzled by no flash of light as I entered, so the thing hadn't been turned on for the night. As I crossed the reception hall I was thinking that the security setup wasn't as foolproof as Jarrell thought, until I saw that Steck had appeared from around a corner for a look at me. He certainly had his duties.

I went to him and spoke. "Mr. Jarrell gave me a key."

"Yes, sir."

"Is he around?"

"In the library, sir, I think."

"They're playing cards?"

"Yes, sir."

"If you're not tied up I cordially invite you to my room for some gin. I mean gin rummy."

He batted an eye. "Thank you, sir, but I have duties."

"Some other time. Is Mrs. Wyman Jarrell on the terrace?"

"I think not, sir. I think she is in the studio."

"Is that on this floor?"

"Yes, sir. The main corridor, on the right. Where you were with Mrs. Jarrell this afternoon."

Now how the hell did he know that? Also, was it proper for a butler to let me know he knew it? I suspected not. I suspected that my gin invitation, if it hadn't actually crashed the sound barrier, had made a dent in it. I headed for the corridor and for the rear, and will claim no credit for spotting the door because it was standing open and voices were emerging. Entering, I was in semi-darkness. The only light came from the corridor and the television screen, which showed the emcee and the panel members of "Show Your Slip." The voices were theirs. Turning, I saw her, dimly, in a chair.

"Do you mind if I join you?" I asked.

"Of course not," she said, barely loud enough. That was all she said. I moved to a chair to her left, and sat.

I have no TV favorites, because most of the programs seem to be intended for either the under-brained or the over-brained and I come in between, but if I had, "Show Your Slip" wouldn't be one of them. If it's one of yours, you can assume you have more brains that I have, and what I assume is my own affair. I admit I didn't give it my full attention that evening because I was conscious of Susan there within arm's reach, and was keeping myself receptive for any sinister influences that might be oozing from her, or angelic ones either. I felt none. All that got to me was a faint trace of a perfume that reminded me of the one Lily Rowan uses, but it wasn't quite the same.

When the windup commercial started she reached to the chair on her other side, to the control, and the sound stopped and the picture went. That made it still darker. The pale blur of her face turned to me. "What channel do you want, Mr. Green?"

"None particularly. Mr Jarrell finished with me, and the others were playing cards, and I heard it going and came in. Whatever you want."

"I was just passing the time. There's nothing I care for at ten-thirty."

"Then let's skip it. Do you mind if we have a little light?"

"Of course not."

I went to the wall switch at the door, flipped it, and returned to the chair, and her little oval face was no longer merely a pale blur. I had the impression that she was trying to produce a smile for me and couldn't quite make it.

"I don't want to intrude," I said. "If I'm in the way—"

"Not at all." Her low voice, shy or coy or wary or demure, made you feel that there should be more of it, and that when there was you would like to be present to hear it. "Since you'll be living here it will be nice to get acquainted with you. I was wondering what you are like, and now you can tell me."

"I doubt it. I've been wondering about it myself and can't decide."

The smile got through. "So to begin with, you're witty. What else? Do you go to church?"

"No. Should I?"

"I don't know because I don't know you yet. I don't go as often as I should. I noticed you didn't eat any salad at dinner. Don't you like salad?"

"Yes."

"Aha!" A tiny flash came and went in her eyes. "So you're frank too. You didn't like *that* salad. I have been wanting to speak to my mother-in-law about it, but I haven't dared. I think I'm doing pretty well. You're witty, and you're frank. What do you think about when you're alone with nothing to do?"

"Let's see. I've got to make it both frank and witty. I think about the best and quickest way to do what I would be doing if I were doing something."

She nodded. "A silly question deserves a silly answer. I guess it was witty too, so that's all right. I would love to be witty—you know, to sparkle. Do you suppose you could teach me how?"

"Now look," I protested, "how could I answer that? It makes three assumptions—that I'm witty, that you're not, and that you have something to learn from me. That's more than I can handle. Try one with only one assumption."

"I'm sorry," she said. "I didn't realize. But I do think you could teach me—Oh!" She looked at her wrist watch. "I forgot!" She got up—floated up—and was looking down at me. "I must make a phone call. I'm sorry if I annoyed you, Mr. Green. Next time, you ask questions." She glided to the door and was gone.

I'll tell you exactly how it was. I wasn't aware that I had moved until I found myself halfway to the door and taking another step. Then I stopped, and told myself, I will be damned, you might think she had me on a chain. I looked back at the chair I had left; I had covered a good ten feet before I had realized I was being pulled.

I went and stood in the doorway and considered the situation. I started with a basic fact: she was a little female squirt. Okay. She hadn't fed me a potion. She hadn't stuck a needle in me. She hadn't used any magic words, far from it. She hadn't touched me. But I had come to that room with the idea of opening her up for inspection, and had ended by springing up automatically to follow her out of the room like a lapdog, and the worst of it was I didn't know why. I am perfectly willing to be attracted by a woman and to enjoy the consequences, but I want to know what's going on. I am not willing to be pulled by a string without seeing the string. Not only that; my interest in this particular specimen was supposed to be strictly professional.

I had an impulse to go to the library and tell Jarrell he was absolutely right, she was a snake. I had another impulse to go find her and tell her something. I didn't know what, but tell her. I had another one, to pack up and go home and tell Wolfe we were up against a witch and what we needed was a stake to burn her at. None of them seemed to be what the situation called for, so I found the stairs and went up to bed.

4

BY Wednesday night, forty-eight hours later, various things had happened, but if I had made any progress I didn't know it.

Tuesday I took Trella to lunch at Rusterman's. That was a little risky, since I was well known there, but I phoned Felix that I was working on a case incognito and told him to pass the word that I mustn't be recognized. When we arrived, though, I was sorry I hadn't picked another restaurant. Evidently everybody, from the doorman on up to Felix, knew Mrs. Jarrell too, and I couldn't blame them for being curious when, working on a case incognito, I turned up with an old and valued customer. They handled it pretty well, except that when Bruno brought my check he put a pencil down beside it. A waiter supplies a pencil only when he knows the check is going to be signed and that your credit is good. I ignored it, hoping that Trella was ignoring it too, and when Bruno brought the change from my twenty I waved it away, hoping he wouldn't think I was setting a precedent.

She had said one thing that I thought worth filing. I had brought Susan's name into the conversation by saying that perhaps I should apologize for being indiscreet the day before, when I had mentioned the impression I had got that Jarrell felt cool about his daughter-in-law, and she said that if I wanted to apologize, all right, but not for being indiscreet, for being wrong. She said her husband wasn't cool about Susan, he was hot. I said okay, then I would switch from cool to hot and apologize for that. Hot about what?

"What do you think?" Her blue eyes widened. "About her. She slapped him. Oh, for God's sake, quit trying to look innocent! Your first day as his secretary, and spending the morning on the terrace with Lois and taking me to Rusterman's for lunch! Secretary!"

"But he's away. He said to mark time."

"He'll get a report from Nora when he comes back, and you know it. I'm not a fool, Alan, really I'm not. I might be fairly bright if I wasn't so damn lazy. You probably know more about my husband than I do. So quit looking innocent."

"I have to look innocent, I'm his secretary. So does Steck, he's his butler. As for what I know, I didn't know Susan had slapped him. Were you there?"

"Nobody was there. I don't mean slapped him with her hand, she wouldn't do that. I don't know how she did it, probably just by looking at him. She can look a man on or look him off, either way. I wouldn't have thought any woman could look *him* off, I'd think she'd need a hatpin or a red-hot poker, but that was before I had met her. Before she moved in. Has she given you a sign yet?"

"No." I didn't know whether I was lying or not. "I'm not sure I'm up with you. If I am, I'm innocent enough to be shocked. Susan is his son's wife."

"Well. What of it?"

"It seems a little undignified. He's not an ape."

She reached to pat the back of my hand. "I must have been wrong about you. Look innocent all you want to. Certainly he's an ape. Everybody knows that. Since I'm in walking distance I might as well do a little shopping. Would you care to come along?"

I declined with thanks.

On my way uptown, walking the thirty blocks to stretch my legs, I had to decide whether to give Wolfe a ring or not. If I did, and reported the development, that Trella said our client had made a pass at his daughter-in-law and had been looked off, and that therefore it seemed possible he had hired Wolfe and tried to suborn me only to cure an acute case of pique, I would certainly be instructed to pack and come home; and I preferred to hang on a while, at least long enough to expose myself to Susan once more and see how it affected my pulse and respiration. And if I rang Wolfe and didn't report the development, I had nothing to say, so I saved a dime.

Mrs. Wyman Jarrell was out, Steck said, and so was Miss Jarrell. He also said that Mr. Foote had asked to be informed when I returned, and I said all right, inform him. Thinking it proper to make an appearance at my desk before nightfall, I left my hat and topcoat in the closet around the corner and went to the library. Nora Kent was at Jarrell's desk, using the red phone, and I moseyed over to the battery of filing cabinets and pulled out a drawer at random. The first folder was marked PAPER PRODUCTION BRAZIL, and I took it out for a look.

I was fingering through it when Nora's voice came at my back. "Did you want something, Mr. Green?"

I turned. "Nothing special. It would be nice to do something useful. If the secretary should be acquainted with these files I think I could manage it in two or three years."

"Oh, it won't take you that long. When Mr. Jarrell gets back he'll get you started."

"That's polite, and I appreciate it. You might have just told me to keep hands off." I replaced the folder and closed the drawer. "Can I help with anything? Like emptying a wastebasket or changing a desk blotter?"

"No, thank you. It would be a little presumptuous of me to tell you to keep hands off since Mr. Jarrell has given you a key."

"So it would. I take it back. Have you heard from him?"

"Yes, he phoned about an hour ago. He'll return tomorrow, probably soon after noon."

There was something about her, her tone and manner, that wasn't just right. Not that it didn't fit a stenographer speaking to a secretary; of course I had caught on that calling her a stenographer was like calling Willie Mays a bat boy. I can't very well tell you what it was, since I didn't know. I only felt that there was something between her and me, one-way, that I wasn't on to. I was thinking a little more conversation might give me an idea, when a phone buzzed.

She lifted the receiver of the black one, spoke and listened briefly, and turned to me. "For you. Mr. Foote."

I went and took it. "Hello, Roger?" I call panhandlers by their first names. "Alan."

"You're a hell of a secretary. Where have you been all day?"

"Out and around. I'm here now."

"So I hear. I understand you're a gin player. Would you care to win a roll? Since Old Ironsides is away and you're not needed."

"Sure, why not? Where?"

"My room. Come on up. From your room turn right, first left, and I'll be at my door."

"Right." I hung up, told Nora I would be glad to run an errand if she had one, was assured that she hadn't, and left. So, I thought, Roger was on pumping terms with the butler. It was unlikely that Steck had volunteered the information that I had invited him to a friendly game.

Foote's room was somewhat larger than mine, with three windows, and it was all his. The chairs were green leather, and the size and shape of one of them, over by a window, would have been approved even by Wolfe. Fastened to the walls with Scotch Tape were pictures of horses, mostly in color, scores of them, all sizes. The biggest one was Native Dancer, from the side, with his head turned to see the camera.

"Not one," Roger said, "that hasn't carried my money. Muscle. Beautiful. Beautiful! When I open my eyes in the morning there they are. Something to wake up to. That's all any man can expect, something to wake up to. You agree?"

I did.

I had supposed, naturally, that the idea would be something like a quarter a point, maybe more, and that if he won I would pay, and if I won he would owe me. But no, it was purely social, a cent a point. Either he gambled only on the beautiful muscles, or he was stringing me along, or he merely wanted to establish relations for future use. He was a damn good gin player. He could talk about anything, and did, and at the same time remember every discard and every pickup. I won 92 cents, but only because I got most of the breaks.

At one point I took advantage of something he had said. "That reminds me," I told him, "of a remark I overheard today. What do you think of a man who makes a pass at his son's wife?"

He was dealing. His hand stopped for an instant and then flipped me a card. "Who made the remark?"

"I'd rather not say. I wasn't eavesdropping, but I happened to hear it."

"Any names mentioned?"

"Certainly."

He picked up his hand. "Your name's Alfred?"

"Alan."

"I forget names. People's. Not horses'. I'll tell you, Alan. For what I think about my brother-in-law's attitude on money and his wife's brother, come to me any time. Beyond that I'm no authority. Anyone who thinks he ought to be shot, they can shoot him. No flowers. Not from me. Your play."

That didn't tell me much. When, at six o'clock, I said I had to wash and change for a date with Lois, and he totaled the score, fast and accurate, he turned it around for me to check. "At the moment," he said, "I haven't got ninety-two cents, but you can make it ninety-two dollars. More. Peach Fuzz in the fifth at Jamaica Thursday will be eight to one. With sixty dollars I could put forty on his nose. Three hundred and twenty, and half to you. And ninety-two cents."

I told him it sounded very attractive and I'd let him know tomorrow. Since Jarrell had said to let him have fifty or a hundred I could have dished it out then and there, but if I did he probably wouldn't be around tomorrow, and there was an off chance that I would want him for something. He took it like a gentleman, no shoving.

When, that morning on the terrace, I had proposed dinner and dance to Lois, I had mentioned the Flamingo Club, but the experience at Ruster-man's with Trella had shown me it wouldn't be advisable. So I asked her if she would mind making it Colonna's in the Village, where there was a good band and no one knew me, at least not by name, and we weren't apt to run into any of my friends. For a second she did mind, but then decided it would be fun to try one she had never been to.

Jarrell had said she was particular about her dancing partners, and she had a right to be. The rhythm was clear through her, not just from her hips down, and she was right with me in everything we tried. To give her as good as she gave I had to put the mind away entirely and let the body take over, and the result was that when midnight came, and time for champagne, I hadn't made a single stab at the project I was supposed to be working on. As the waiter was pouring I was thinking, What the hell, a detective has to get the subject feeling intimate before he can expect her to discuss intimate matters, and three more numbers ought to do it. Actually I never did get it started. It just happened that when we returned to the table again and finished the champagne, she lifted her glass with the last thimbleful, said, "To life and death," and tossed it down. She put the glass on the table and added, "If death ever slept."

"I'm with you," I said, putting my empty glass next to hers, "or I guess I am. What does it mean?"

"I don't know. I ought to, since I wrote it myself. It's from that poem I wrote. The last five lines go:

> "Or a rodent kept
> High and free on the twig of a tree,
> Or a girl who wept
> A bitter tear for the death so near,
> If death ever slept!"

"I'm sorry," I said. "I like the sound of it, but I'm still not sure what it means."

"Neither am I. That's why I'm sure it's a poem. Susan understands it, or says she does. She says there's one thing wrong with it, that instead of 'a bitter tear' it ought to be 'a welcome tear.' I don't like it. Do you?"

"I like 'bitter' better. Is Susan strong on poems?"

"I don't really know. I don't understand her any better than I understand that poem. I think she's strong on Susan, but of course she's my sister-in-law and her bedroom is bigger than mine, and I'm fond of my brother when I'm not fighting with him, so I probably hate her. I'll find out when I get analyzed."

I nodded. "That'll do it. I noticed last evening the males all gathered around except your father. Apparently he didn't even see her."

"He saw her all right. If he doesn't see a woman it's because she's not there. Do you know what a satyr is?"

"More or less."

"Look it up in the dictionary. I did once. I don't believe my father is a satyr because half the time his mind is on something else — making more money. He's just a tomcat. What's that they're starting? 'Mocajuba?'"

It was. I got up and circled the table to pull her chair back.

To be fair to Wednesday, it's true that it was more productive than Tuesday, but that's not saying I got any farther along. It added one more to my circle of acquaintances. That was in the morning, just before noon. Having turned in around two and stayed in bed for my preferred minimum of eight hours, as I went downstairs I was thinking that breakfast would probably be a problem, but headed for the dining room anyway just to see, and in half a minute there was Steck with orange juice. I said that and coffee would hold me until lunch, but no, sir. In ten minutes he brought toast and bacon and three poached eggs and two kinds of jam and a pot of coffee. That attended to, in company with the morning *Times*, I went to the library and spent half an hour not chatting with Nora Kent. She was there, and I was willing to converse, but she either had things to do or made things to do, so after a while I gave up and departed. She did say that Jarrell's plane would be due at La Guardia at 3:05 p.m.

Strolling along the corridor toward the front and seeing that my watch said 11:56, I thought I might as well stop in at the studio for the twelve-o'clock news. The door was closed, and I opened it and entered, but two steps in I stopped. It was inhabited. Susan was in a chair, and standing facing her was a stranger, a man in a dark gray suit with a jaw that looked determined in profile. Evidently he had been too occupied to hear the door opening, for he didn't wheel to me until I had taken the two steps.

"Sorry," I said, "I'm just cruising," and was going, but Susan spoke.

"Don't go, Mr. Green. This is Jim Eber. Jim, this is Alan Green. You know he — I mentioned him."

My predecessor was still occupied, but not too much to lift a hand. I took it, and found that his muscles weren't interested. He spoke, not as if he wanted to. "I dropped in to see Mr. Jarrell, but he's away. Nothing important, just a little matter. How do you like the job?"

"I'd like it fine if it were all like the first two days. When Mr. Jarrell gets back, I don't know. I can try. Maybe you could give me some pointers."

"Pointers?"

You might have thought it was a word I had just made up. Obviously his mind wasn't on his vocabulary or on me; it was working on something, and not on getting his job back or I would have been a factor.

"Some other time," I said. "Sorry I interrupted."

"I was just going," he said, and, with his jaw set, marched past me and on out.

"Oh dear," Susan said.

I looked down at her. "I don't suppose there's anything I can help with?"

"No, thank you." She shook her head and her little oval face came up. Then she left the chair. "Do you mind? But of course you don't — only I don't want to be rude. I want to think something over."

I said something polite and she went. Eber had closed the door behind him and I opened it for her. She made for the rear and turned a corner, and in a moment I heard the elevator. With that settled, that she hadn't set out after Eber, I turned on the radio and got the tail end of the newscast.

That was the new acquaintance. The only other contribution that Wednesday made worth mentioning came six hours later, and though, as I said, it got me no farther along, it did add a new element to the situation. Before reporting it I should also mention my brief exchange with Wyman. I was in the lounge with a magazine when he appeared, stepped out to the terrace, came back in, and approached.

"You're not overworked, are you?" he asked.

There are several possible ways of asking that, running from the sneer to the brotherly smile. His was about in the middle. I might have replied, "Neither are you," but didn't. He was too skinny, and too handicapped by his tight little ears and thin straight nose, to make a good target, and besides, he thought he was trying. He had produced two shows on Broadway, and while one had folded after three days, the other had run nearly a month. Also his father had told me that in spite of the venomous influence of the snake he was still trying to teach him the technique of making money grow.

So I humored him. "No," I said.

The creases in his brow deepened. "You're not very talkative, either."

"You're wrong there. When I get started I can talk your head off. For example. An hour ago I went into the studio to catch the newscast, and a man was there speaking with your wife, and she introduced me to him. It was Jim Eber. I'm wondering if he's trying to get his job back, and if so, whether he'll succeed. I left a good job to come here, and I don't want to find myself out on a limb. I don't want to ask your wife about it, and I'd appreciate it if you would ask her and let me know."

His lips had tightened, and he had become aware of it and had loosened them. "When was this? An hour ago?"

"Right. Just before noon."

"Were they talking about the—uh, about the job?"

"I don't know. I didn't know they were there and I opened the door and went in. I thought he might have said something that would show if he's trying to get it back."

"Maybe he did."

"Will you ask her?"

"Yes. I'll ask her."

"I'll appreciate it a lot."

"I'll ask her." He turned, and turned back. "It's lunch time. You're joining us?"

I said I was.

There were only five of us at the table—Trella, Susan, Wyman, Roger, and Alan. Lois didn't show, and Nora lunched from a tray in the library. When, afterward, Roger invited me up to his room, I thought the two hours before Jarrell arrived might as well be spent with him as with anyone. He won $2.43, and I deducted 92 cents and paid him $1.51. Wanting to save him the trouble of bringing up the Peach Fuzz project, I brought it up myself and told him the sixty bucks would be available that evening after dinner.

I was in the library with Nora when Jarrell returned, shortly after four o'clock. He breezed in, tossed his bag under a table, told Nora, "Get Clay," and went to his desk. Apparently I wasn't there. I sat and listened to his end of three phone conversations which I would have paid closer attention to if my name had been Alan Green. I did attend, with both ears, when I heard Nora, reporting on events during his absence, tell him that Jim Eber had called that morning.

His head jerked to her. "Called? Phoned?"

"No, he came. He got some papers he had left in his desk. He said that was what he came for. That was all. I looked at the papers; they were personal. Then he was with Susan in the studio; I don't know whether it was by appointment or not. Mr. Green was there with them when he left."

Evidently everybody knew everything around there. The fact that Eber had been there had been mentioned at the lunch table, but Nora hadn't been present. Of course any of the others might have told her, including Steck.

Jarrell snapped at me, "You were with them?"

I nodded. "Only briefly. I was going to turn on the radio for the news, and opened the door and went in. Your daughter-in-law introduced me to him and that was about all. He said he was just going, and he went."

He opened his mouth and closed it again. Questions he might have asked Archie Goodwin could not properly be asked Alan Green with the stenographer there. He turned to her. "What else did he want? Besides the papers."

"Nothing. That was all, except that he thought you would be here and wanted to see you. That's what he said."

He licked his lips, shot me a glance, and turned back to her. "All right, hand me the mail."

She got it from a drawer of her desk and took it to him. If you think it would have been natural for it to be on his desk waiting for him you're quite right, but in that case it would have been exposed to the view of the new secretary, and that wouldn't do. After sticking around a while longer I asked Jarrell if I was wanted, was told not until after dinner, and left them and went up to my room.

I can't tell you the exact minute that Jarrell came dashing in, yelling at me, but I can come close. It was a quarter to six when I decided to shower and shave before going down to the lounge for cocktails, and my par for that operation when I'm not pressed is half an hour, and I was pulling on my pants when the door flew open and he was there yapping, "Come on!" Seeing me, he was off down the hall, yapping again, "Come on!" It seemed that the occasion was informal enough not to demand socks and shoes, so I merely got my shirttail in, and fastened my belt and closed my zipper en route. I could hear him bounding down the stairs, and made for them and on down, and turned the corner just as he reached the library door. As I came up he tried the knob and then stood and stared at it.

"It's locked," he said.

"Why not?" I asked. "What's wrong?"

"Horland's phoned. He said the signal flashed and the screen showed the door opening and a blanket or rug coming in. He's sending a man. There's somebody in there. There must be."

"Then open the door."

"Horland's said to wait till his man got here."

"Nuts. I will." Then I realized I couldn't. My key, along with my other belongings, was up on the dresser. "Give me your key."

He got out his key fold and handed it to me, and I picked one and stuck it in the slot. "It's just possible," I said, "that we'll be rushed. Move over." He did so. I got behind the jamb, turned the key and the knob, pushed on the door with my bare toes, and it swung open. Nothing happened. I said, "Stay here," and stepped inside. Nothing and no one. I went and took a look, behind desks, around corners of cabinets and shelves, in the closet, and in the bathroom. I was going to call to him to come on in when the sound came of footsteps pounding down the corridor, and I reached the door in time to see the reinforcement arrive — a middle-aged athlete in a gray uniform. He wasn't one that I knew. He was panting, and he had a gun in his hand.

"At ease," I commanded. "False alarm. Apparently. What's this about a blanket or a rug?"

"It's not a false alarm," Jarrell said. "I turned the switch on myself when I left, and the light didn't flash when you opened the door. Someone went in and turned the switch off. What was it you saw?"

Horland's didn't answer. He was looking at the floor at our feet. "By God, that's it," he said. He pointed. "That's it right there."

"What the hell are you talking about?" Jarrell blurted.

"That rug. That's what came in. The signal flashed and I looked at the screen, and in came that rug, hanging straight down, that was all I could see. Then it was gone, and in about two seconds the screen was dead. You get it? Someone came in holding that rug in front of him, and went and turned the switch off, and when he came out he put the rug back here where he got it. That's how I know he's not still in there; if he was, the rug wouldn't be here." He sounded as pleased as if he had just done a job of brain work that would be hard to match.

Thinking a little pruning wouldn't hurt him, I asked, "How do you know it was this rug?"

"Why, the pattern. The squares, the lines crossing. I saw it."

"It might be one of a pair. He might be in there now, in the closet or the bathroom."

"Oh." He squared his shoulders. "Stand aside."

"Don't bother, I looked. He's gone. He didn't stay long." I turned to Jarrell. "You might try the switch. Go and turn it on and we'll enter."

He did so. After he was in I shut the door, and when he called to us I pushed it open, and the blaze of light came. I swung the door shut, and the light went, and we crossed to his desk.

"After you saw it on the screen, the rug coming in," I asked Horland's, "how long was it before you phoned here?"

"Right away. No time at all. I didn't phone, the other man did, I told him to."

"How long did it take the call to get through?"

"It got through right away. I was putting on my cap and jacket and getting my gun, and I wasn't wasting any time, and he had Mr. Jarrell when I left."

"Then say thirty seconds. Make it a minute, not to skimp. Even two minutes. You answered the phone in your room, Mr. Jarrell?"

"Yes."

"How long were you on the phone?"

"Only long enough for him to tell me what had happened. Not more than a minute."

"And you came on the run immediately? Only stopping at my door on the way?"

"You're damn right I did."

"Then add another minute. That makes four minutes from the time the rug came in to the time we got here, and probably less, and he was gone. So he didn't have time for much more than turning off the switch."

"We ought to find out who it was," Horland's said. "While it's hot."

He certainly worked his brain, that bird. Obviously it had been a member of the household, and how and when to find out who it was was strictly a family affair. Jarrell didn't bother to tell him so. He merely gave him a chore, to unlock and open the door of a metal box that was set in the wall facing the entrance. Its door had a round hole for the lens to see through, and inside was the camera. Horland's took the camera out, extracted the film and put in a new one, returned the camera and locked the door, and departed.

Jarrell regarded me. "You realize it could have been anybody. We may know more when we see the picture. But with that rug in front of her, she could have held it up high with her hands not showing, nothing at all showing, and you couldn't tell."

"Yes," I agreed, "she could. Anybody could. One pronoun is as good as another. As I said, she didn't have time for much more than turning off the switch, but you might look around. Is any little item missing?"

He moved his head from side to side, got up, went and tried the knobs of the safes, crossed to the battery of cabinets and pulled at the handles of the drawers in the two end tiers, which had locks on them, went and opened the top drawer of Nora Kent's desk and took a look, and then came back to his own desk and opened the top drawer of it. His face changed immediately. He pulled the drawer wide open, moved things around, and pushed it shut. He looked at me.

"Don't tell me," I said. "Let me guess."

He took a breath. "I keep a gun in there, a Bowdoin thirty-eight. It's gone. It was there this afternoon."

"Loaded?"

"Yes."

"Whoever got it knew you had it. He—I beg your pardon—she came straight to the desk, turned off the switch, grabbed the gun, and ran. That's all there was time for."

"Yes."

"Horland's was right about one thing. If you want to find out who it was, the sooner the better, while it's hot. The best way would be to get them all in here, now, and go to it."

"What good would that do?" His hands were fists. "I know who it was. So do you."

"I do not." I shook my head. "Look, Mr. Jarrell. Suspecting her of cheating your son and diddling you, without any evidence, that's your privilege. But saying that I know she came in here and took a loaded gun, when I don't, that is not your privilege. Of course you have a permit for it?"

"Certainly."

"The law says when a gun is stolen it must be reported. It's a misdemeanor not to. Do you want to report it?"

"Good God, no." The fists relaxed. "How about this? I'll get her in here, and Wyman too, and I'll keep them here while you go up and search their room. You know how to search a room."

One of two things, I thought. Either he is sure it was her, for some reason or no reason, or he took it himself and planted it in her room. "No good," I declared. "If she took it, the last place she would hide it would be in her room. I could find it, of course, in a couple of days, or much quicker if I got help in, but what if it turned up in one of the tubs on the terrace? You'd have the gun back, that's true, if that's what you want."

"You know damn well what I want."

"Yes, I ought to, but that's not the point now, or not the whole point. Anyone going to all that trouble and risk to get hold of a gun, he must — I beg your pardon — she must intend to use it for something. I doubt if it's to shoot a squirrel. It might even be to shoot you. I would resent that while I'm employed as your secretary. I advise you to get them in here and let me ask questions. Even better, take them all down to Mr. Wolfe and let him ask questions."

"No."

"You won't?"

"No."

"Then what?"

"I don't know. I'll see. I'll have to think." He looked at his wrist. "They're in the lounge." He stood up. "I'll see."

"Okay." I stood up. "I'd rather not appear barefooted. I'll go up and put on my shoes and socks."

As I said before, that added a new element to the situation.

5

WHEN Nero Wolfe came down from the plant rooms at six o'clock Thursday afternoon I was at my desk in the office, waiting for him. Growling a greeting, if you can call it that, as he crossed to his chair, he lowered his bulk and got it properly disposed, rested his elbows on the chair arms, and glared at me:

"Well?"

I had swiveled to him. "To begin with," I said, "as I told you on the phone, I'm not asking you to exert yourself if you'd rather not. I can hang on up there if it takes all summer, and with Orrie here you certainly don't need me. Only I didn't want you to have a client shot from under you with no warning from me. By the way, where is Orrie?"

"He stepped out. Who is going to shoot Mr. Jarrell?"

"I don't know. I don't even know he's going to be the target. Do you care to hear about it?"

"Go ahead."

I did so. Giving him only a sketchy outline of my encounters and experiences up to 6:15 p.m. Wednesday, when Jarrell had opened my door and yelled at me to come on, from there I made it more detailed. I reported verbatim my conversation with Jarrell after Horland's had gone.

Wolfe grunted. "The man's an ass. Every one of those people would profit by his death. They need a demonstration, or one of them does. He should have corralled them and called in the police to find the gun."

"Yeah. He's sure his daughter-in-law took it, or pretends he is. As I said on the phone Monday night, he may have an itch he can't reach and is not accountable. He could have pulled the rug act himself, answered the phone call from Horland's there in the library, raced upstairs to get me, and raced down again. He could have taken the gun earlier. I prefer it that way, since in that case there will probably be no bullets flying, but I admit it's not likely. He is not a nitwit."

"What has been done?"

"Nothing, actually. After dinner we played bridge, two tables—Trella, Lois, Nora, Jarrell, Wyman, Roger Foote, Corey Brigham, me. Incidentally, when I finally got down to the lounge before dinner Brigham was there with them, and I learned from Steck that he had come early, shortly after six o'clock, so I suppose it could have been him that got the gun, provided he had a key to the library. It was around midnight when we quit, and—"

"You didn't include the daughter-in-law."

"Haven't I mentioned that she doesn't play bridge? She doesn't. And we went to bed. Today I saw four of them at breakfast—Jarrell, Wyman, Lois, and Nora—but not much of anybody since, except Susan and Trella at lunch. Jarrell mentioned at lunch that he would be out all afternoon, business appointments. At two-thirty, when I went around looking for company, they were all out. Of course Roger had gone to Jamaica, with the sixty bucks I gave him—by the way, I haven't entered that on the expense account. At three o'clock I went for a walk and phoned you, and when I got back there was still nobody at home except Nora, and she is no—oh, I forgot. The pictures."

"Pictures?"

"Sure, from the camera. A Horland's man brought them while I was out phoning you, and when I got back Nora had them. She wasn't sure whether she should let me look at them, but I was. That woman sure plays them close to her chin; I don't know now whether Jarrell had told her about the rug affair or not. If not, she must have wondered what the pictures were all about. There were three of them; the camera takes one every two seconds until the door is shut. They all showed the rug broadside, coming straight in. He must have kicked the door shut. That rug is seven by three, so it could have been a tall man holding the top edge a little above the top of his head, or it could have been a short woman holding it as high as she could reach. At the bottom the rug was just touching the floor. At the top its edge was turned back, hiding the hands. I was going to bring the pictures along to show you, but would have had to shoot Nora to get away with them. Jarrell wasn't back when I left at five-thirty."

I turned a hand over. "That's it. Any instructions?"

He made a face. "How the devil can I have instructions?"

"You might. For instance, instruct me to take Lois out tonight. Or take Trella to lunch tomorrow. Or stick around until Sunday and take Susan to church."

"Pfui. Give me a plain answer for once. How likely is it that you'll accomplish anything up there?"

"One in a million, if you mean fairly soon. Give me until Thanksgiving and I might show you something. However, there's one little teaser. It's name is Eber, James L. Eber. He was upset about something when I found him in the studio with Susan, and so was she. Wyman was upset when I told him Eber had been there. When it was mentioned at the lunch table Roger was upset, and maybe one or two of the others. Jarrell was upset when Nora told him about it. And it was only an hour or so later that the gun was taken. There might be something to be pried out of Eber. I've been prying for three days without breaking off a splinter, and as a last resort he might have one loose. He just might have something interesting to say to the guy who took his job."

He grunted. "I doubt if any of those people has anything interesting to say to anyone."

I said I did too but that Eber should have a chance and I would go and give him one after dinner.

Orrie Cather dined with us. I went upstairs two flights to tell my room hello, and when I went back down Orrie was there, and we had time to exchange some friendly insults before Fritz announced dinner. The main dish was shad roe with créole sauce. Shad roe is all right, and Fritz's créole sauce is one of his best, but the point is that with that item Fritz always serves bread triangles fried in anchovy butter; and since he had known four hours ago that I would be there, and he was aware of my attitude toward bread triangles fried in anchovy butter, he had proceeded beyond the call of duty. Again I passed up a salad, but only because there wasn't room for it.

Back in the office, with coffee, Orrie, who had been told that I was going on an errand, asked if I needed any help, and I said I hoped not. When he saw me getting a ring of keys from a drawer he said I might need a lookout, and I repeated that I hoped not. When he saw me getting a shoulder holster and a gun from another drawer he said I might need a loader, and I told him he ought to know better, that if six wasn't enough what I would need would be a meat basket to bring me home in.

I had no reason to think there would be any occasion for the gun, but ever since Jarrell had opened the drawer and found his gone I had felt unfurnished. A man who — I beg your pardon — a woman who steals a loaded gun deserves to be treated with respect. As for the keys, they were routine equipment when calling on a stranger who might have useful information and who might or might not be home. There would probably be no occasion for them either, but I dislike waiting in dark halls with nothing to sit on.

The address, which I got from my notebook, on 49th Street between Second and Third Avenues, was above the door of an old five-story building that was long past its glory if it had ever had any. In the vestibule, I found EBER in the middle of the row of names, and pushed the button. No click. I pushed it five times, with waits in between, before giving up. I certainly wasn't going to do my waiting there, if any, and the old Manson lock was no problem, so I got out the keys, selected one, and in less than a minute was inside. If the position of his name in the row was correct he was two flights up, and he was — or his name was, on the jamb of a door in the rear, with a button beside it. When I pushed the button I could hear the ring inside.

I was in the dark hall with nothing to sit on that I don't like to wait in. Since there might be some information inside, in some form or other, that I could get more easily with him not there, I was sorry I hadn't brought

Orrie along, because with a lookout there would have been nothing to it, but in three minutes I was glad I hadn't. That was how long it took me to decide to go on in, to get the lock worked, to enter, to see him sprawled on the floor, and to check that he was dead. Then I was glad Orrie hadn't come.

He was backside up, so I didn't have to disturb him in order to see the hole in the back of his head, a little below the center. When I spread the hair it looked about the right size for a .38, but I wasn't under oath. Standing up, I looked around, all the way around. There was no gun in sight, and it couldn't very well be under him. I didn't have to sniff to get the smell of powder, but there were no open windows, so it would take a while to go.

I stood and considered. Had I been seen by anybody who might identify me later? Possibly, but I doubted it. Certainly by no one inside, or even in the vestibule. Was it worth the risk to give the dump a good going over to see what I could find? Maybe; but I had no gloves, and everything there would be tried for prints; and it would be embarrassing if someone came before I left. Had I touched anything besides his hair? You can touch something without knowing it — the top of a table, for instance, as you cross a room. I decided I hadn't.

It was a pity that I had to wipe the doorknob and the surface around the keyhole outside, since there might be prints there that Homicide could use, but there was no help for it. I did it thoroughly but quickly. I hadn't liked the idea of hanging around the hall before, and I liked it much less now. At the top of the stairs I listened three seconds, and, descending, did the same on the next landing. My luck held, and I was down, out to the sidewalk, and on my way without anyone to notice me. I was thinking that items of routine that become automatic through habit, though they are usually wasted, can be very useful — for instance, my having the taxi drop me at 49th Street and Third Avenue instead of taking me to the address. Now, not caring to have anything at all to do with a taxi on the East Side, I walked crosstown all the way to Ninth Avenue before flagging one. I needed a little walk anyway, to jolt my brain back into place. It had been 8:57 when I had stood up after looking at the hole in Jim Eber's head. It was 9:28 when the taxi pulled up at the curb in front of the old brownstone on West 35th Street.

When I entered the office Orrie was in one of the yellow chairs over by the big globe, with a magazine. I noted that with approval, since it showed that he fully appreciated the fact that my desk was mine. At sight of me Wolfe, behind his desk with a book, dropped his eyes back to the page. I hadn't been gone long enough to get much of a splinter.

I tossed my hat on my desk and sat. "I have a comment to make about the weather," I said, "privately. Orrie hates to hear the weather mentioned. Don't you, Orrie?"

"I sure do." He got up, closing the magazine. "I can't stand it. If you touch on anything you think I'd be interested in, whistle." He went, closing the door behind him.

Wolfe was scowling at me. "What is it now?"

"A vital statistic. Ringing James L. Eber's bell several times and getting no reaction, and finding the door was locked, I used a key and entered. He was on the floor face down in the middle of the room, with a bullet hole in the back of his head which could have been made by a thirty-eight. He was cooling off, but not cold. I would say, not for quotation, that he had been dead from three to seven hours. As you know, that depends. I did no investigating because I didn't care to stay. I don't think I was seen entering or leaving."

Wolfe's lips had tightened until he practically didn't have any. "Preposterous," he said distinctly.

"What is?" I demanded. "It's not preposterous that he's dead, with that hole in his skull."

"This whole affair. You shouldn't have gone there in the first place."

"Maybe not. You suggested it."

"I did not suggest it. I raised difficulties."

I crossed my legs. "If you want to try to settle that now," I said, "okay, but you know how things like that drag on, and I need instructions. I should have called headquarters and told them where to find something interesting, but didn't, because I thought you might possibly have a notion."

"I have no notion and don't intend to have one," Wolfe said.

"Then I'll call. From a booth. They say they can't trace a local dial call, but there might be a miracle. Next, do I get back up there quick, I mean to Jarrell's, and if so what's my line?"

"I said I have no notion. Why should you go back there at all?"

I uncrossed my legs. "Look," I said, "you might as well come on down. I could go back just to return his ten grand and tell him we're bowing out, if that's what you want, but it's not quite so simple and you know it. When the cops learn that Eber was Jarrell's secretary and got fired, they'll be there asking questions. If they learn that Jarrell hired you and you sent me to take his place—don't growl at me, they'll think you sent me no matter what you think—you know what will happen, they'll be on our necks. Even if they don't learn that, we have a problem. We know that a thirty-eight revolver was taken from Jarrell's desk yesterday afternoon, and we know that Eber was there yesterday morning and it made a stir, and if and when we also know that the bullet that killed him came from a thirty-eight, what do we do, file it and forget it?"

He grunted. "There is no obligation to report what may be merely a coincidence. If Mr. Jarrell's gun is found and it is established that Eber was killed by a bullet from it, that will be different."

"Meanwhile we ignore the coincidence?"

"We don't proclaim it."

"Then I assume we keep the ten grand and Jarrell is still your client. If he turns out to be a murderer, what the hell, many lawyers' clients are murderers. And I'm back where I started, I need instructions. I'll have to go—"

The phone rang. I swiveled and got it, and I noticed that Wolfe reached for his too, which he rarely does unless I give him a sign.

"Nero Wolfe's residence, Archie Goodwin speaking."

"Where the hell are you? This is Jarrell."

"You know what number you dialed, Mr. Jarrell. I'm with Mr. Wolfe, reporting and getting instructions about your job."

"I've got instructions for you myself. Nora says you left at five-thirty. You've been gone over four hours. How soon can you be here?"

"Oh, say in an hour."

"I'll be in the library."

He hung up. I cradled it and turned.

"He reminds me of you a little," I said—just an interesting fact, nothing personal. "I was about to say, I'll have to go back up there and I need to know what for. Just hang around or try to start something? For instance, it would be a cinch to put the bee on Jarrell. You couldn't ask for a better setup for blackmail. I tell him that if he makes a sizable contribution in cash, say half a million, we'll regard the stolen gun as a coincidence and forget it. If he doesn't, we'll feel that we must report it. Of course I'll have to wait until the news is out about Eber, but if—"

"Shut up."

"Yes, sir."

He eyed me. "You understand the situation. You have expounded it."

"Yes, sir."

"This may or may not affect the job you undertook for Mr. Jarrell—don't interrupt me—very well, that *we* undertook. Murder sometimes creates only ripples, but more frequently high seas. Assuredly you are not going back there to take women to lunch at Rusterman's or to taverns to dance. I offer no complaint for what has been done; I will concede that we blundered into this mess by a collaboration in mulishness; but if it was Mr. Jarrell's gun that was used to kill Eber, and it isn't too fanciful to suppose that it was, we are in it willy-nilly, and we should emerge, if not with profit, at least without discomfiture. That is our joint concern. You ask if you should start something up there. I doubt if you'll need to; something has already started. It is most unlikely that the murder had no connection with that hive of predators and parasites. I can't tell you how to proceed because you'll have to wait on events. You will be guided by your intelligence and experience, and report to me as the occasion dictates. Mr. Jarrell said he has instructions for you. Have you any notion what they'll be?"

"Not a glimmer."

"Then we can't anticipate them. You will call police headquarters?"

"Yes, on my way."

"That will expedite matters. Otherwise there's no telling when the body would be found."

I was on my feet. "If you phone me there," I told him, "keep it decent. He has four phones on his desk, and I suspect two of them."

"I won't phone you. You'll phone me."

"Okay," I said, and went.

6

PASSING the gantlet of the steely eyes of the lobby sentinel, mounting in the private elevator, and using my key in the tenth-floor vestibule, I found that the electronic security apparatus hadn't been switched on yet. Steck appeared, of course, and said that Mr. Jarrell would like to see me in the library. The eye I gave him was a different eye from what it had been. It could even have been Steck who had worked the rug trick to get hold of a gun. He had his duties, but he might have managed to squeeze it in.

Hearing voices in the lounge, I crossed the reception hall to glance in, and saw Trella, Nora, and Roger Foote at a card table.

Roger looked up and called to me. "Pinochle! Come and take a hand!"

"Sorry, I can't. Mr. Jarrell wants me."

"Come when you're through! Peach Fuzz ran a beautiful race! Beautiful! Five lengths back at the turn and only a head behind at the finish! Beautiful!"

A really fine loser, I was thinking as I headed for the corridor. You don't often meet that kind of sporting spirit. Beautiful!

The door of the library was standing open. Entering, I closed it. Jarrell, over by the files with one of the drawers open, barked at me, "Be with you in a minute," and I went to the chair at an end of his desk. A Portanaga with an inch of ash intact was there on a tray, and the smell told me it was still alive, so it couldn't have been more than ninety seconds since he left his desk to go to the files. That's the advantage of being a detective with a trained mind; you collect all kinds of useless facts without even trying.

He came and sat, picked up the cigar and tapped the ash off, and took a couple of puffs. He spoke. "Why did you go to see Wolfe?"

"He pays my salary. He likes to know what he's getting for it. Also I had told him on the phone about your gun disappearing, and he wanted to ask me about it."

"Did you have to tell him about that?"

"I thought I'd better. You're his client, and he doesn't like to have his clients shot, and if somebody used the gun to kill you with and I hadn't told him about it he would have been annoyed. Besides, I thought he might want to make a suggestion."

"Did he make one?"

"Not a suggestion exactly. He made a comment. He said you're an ass. He said you should have corralled everybody and got the cops in to find the gun."

"Did you tell him I'm convinced that my daughter-in-law took it?"

"Sure. But even if she did, and if she intends to use it on you, that would still be the best way to handle it. It would get the gun back, and it would notify her that you haven't got a hole in your head and don't intend to have one."

He showed no reaction to my mentioning a hole in the head. "It was you who said we'd probably find it in a tub on the terrace."

"I didn't say probably, but what if I did? We'd have the gun. You said on the phone you've got instructions for me. About looking for it?"

"No, not that." He took a pull on the cigar, removed it, and let the smoke float out. "I don't remember just how much I've told you about Corey Brigham."

"Not much. No details. That he's an old friend of yours — no, you didn't use the word friend — that he got in ahead of you on a deal, and that you think your daughter-in-law was responsible. I've been a little surprised to see him around."

"I want him around. I want him to think I've accepted his explanation and that I don't suspect anything. The deal was about a shipping company. I found out about a claim that could be made against it, and I was all set to buy the claim and then put the screws on, and when I was ready to close in I found that Brigham was there ahead of me. He said he had got next to it through somebody else, that he didn't know I was after it, but he's a damn liar. There wasn't anybody else. The only source was mine, and I had it clamped tight. He got it through information that was in this room, and he got it from my daughter-in-law."

"That raises questions," I told him. "I don't have to ask why Susan gave it to him because I already know your answer to that. She gives things to men, including her — uh, favors, because that's what she's like. But how did she get it?"

"She got my gun yesterday, didn't she?"

"I don't know and neither do you. Anyhow, how many times has that rug walked in here?"

"Not any. That was a new one. But she knows how to find a way to get anything she wants. She could have got it from Jim Eber. Or from my son. Or she could have been in here with my son when Nora and I weren't here, and sent him out for something, and got it herself. God only knows what else she got. Most of my operations are based on some kind of inside information, and a lot of it is on paper, it has to be, and I'm afraid to leave anything important in here any more. Goddamn it, she has to go!"

He pulled at the cigar, found it was out, and dropped it in the tray. "There's another aspect. I stood to clear a million on that deal, probably more. So Brigham did instead of me, and she got her share of it. She gives things to men, including her favors if you want to call it that, but all the time her main object is herself. She got her share. That's what I've got instructions about. See if you can find it. She's got it salted away somewhere and maybe you can find it. Maybe you can get a lead to it through Brigham. Get next to him. He's a goddamn snob, but he won't be snooty to my secretary if you handle him right. Another possibility is Jim Eber. Get next to him too. You met him yesterday. I don't know just what your approach will be, but you should be able to work that out yourself. And don't forget our deal — yours and mine. Ten thousand the day she's out of here, with my son staying, and fifty thousand more when the divorce papers are signed."

I had been wondering if he had forgotten about that. I was also wondering if he figured that later, remembering that he had told me Thursday night to get next to Jim Eber, I would regard that as evidence that he hadn't been aware that Eber was no longer approachable.

I reminded him that it takes two to make a deal and that I hadn't accepted his offer, but he waved that away as not worth discussing. His suggestion that I cultivate Eber made it relevant for me to ask questions about him, and I did so, but while some of the answers I got might have been helpful for getting to know him better, none of them shed any light on the most important fact about him, that he was dead. He had been with Jarrell five years, was unmarried, was a Presbyterian but didn't work at it, played golf on Sunday, was fair to good at bridge, and so on. I also collected some data on Corey Brigham.

When Jarrell finished with me and I went, leaving him at his desk, I stood outside for a moment, on the rug that walked like a man, or woman, debating whether to go and join the pinochle players, to observe them from the new angle I now had on the whole bunch, or to go for a walk and call Wolfe to tell him what Jarrell's instructions had been. It was a draw, so I decided to do neither and went upstairs to bed.

I slept all right, I always sleep, but woke up at seven o'clock. I turned over and shut my eyes again, but nothing doing. I was awake. It was a damn nuisance. I would have liked to get up and dress and go down to the studio and hear the eight o'clock news. It had been exactly ten-thirty when I had phoned headquarters to tell them, in falsetto, that they had better take a look at a certain apartment at a certain number on 49th Street, and by now the news would be out and I wanted to hear it. But on Tuesday I had appeared for breakfast at 9:25, on Wednesday at 10:15, and on Thursday at 9:20, and if I shattered precedent by showing before eight, making for the radio, and announcing what I had heard to anyone available — and it would be remarkable not to announce it — someone might have wondered how come. So when my eyes wouldn't stay closed no matter which side I tried, I lay on my back and let them stay open, hoping they liked the ceiling. They didn't. They kept turning — up, down, right, left. I got the impression that they were trying to turn clear over to see inside. When I found myself wondering what would happen if they actually made it I decided that had gone far enough, kicked the sheet off, and got up.

I took my time in the shower, and shaving, and putting cuff links in a clean shirt, and other details; and history repeated itself. I was pulling on my pants, getting the second leg through, when there was a knock at the door, and nothing timid about it. I called out, "Who is it?", and for reply the door opened, and Jarrell walked in.

I spoke. "Good morning. Come some time when I've got my shoes on."

He had closed his door. "This can't wait. Jim Eber is dead. They found his body in his apartment. Murdered. Shot."

I stared, not overdoing it. "For God's sake. When?"

"I got it on the radio — the eight o'clock news. They found him last night. He was shot in the head, in the back. That's all it said. It didn't mention that he worked for me." He went to a chair, the big one by the window, and sat. "I want to discuss it with you."

I had put my shoes and clean socks by that chair, intending to sit there to put them on. Going to get them, taking another chair, pulling my pants leg up, and starting a sock on, I said, "If they don't already know he worked for you they soon will, you realize that."

"Certainly I realize it. They may phone, or come, any minute. That's what I want to discuss."

I picked up the other sock. "All right, discuss. Shoot."

"You know what a murder investigation is like, Goodwin. You know that better than I do."

"Yeah. It's no fun."

"It certainly isn't. Of course they may already have a line on somebody, they may even have the man that did it, there was nothing on the radio about that. But if they haven't, and if they don't get him soon, you know what it will be like. They'll dig everywhere as deep as they can. He was with me five years, and he lived here. They'll want to know everything about him, and it's mostly here they'll expect to get it."

I was tying a shoelace. "Yeah, they have no respect for privacy, when it's murder."

He nodded. "I know they haven't. And I know the best way to handle it is to tell them anything they want to know, within reason. If they think I'm holding out that will only make it worse, I appreciate that. One thing I want to discuss with you, they'll ask why I fired Eber, and what do I say?"

I had my shoes on now and was on equal terms. Conferring in bare feet with a man who is properly shod may not put you at a disadvantage, but it seems to. It may be because he could step on your toes. With mine now protected, I said, "Just tell them why you fired him. That you suspected him of leaking business secrets."

He shook his head. "If I do that they'll want details — what secrets he leaked and who to, all that. That would take them onto ground where I don't want them. I would rather tell them that Eber was getting careless, he seemed to be losing interest, and I decided to let him go. No matter who else they ask, nobody could contradict that, not even Nora, except one person. You. If they ask you, you can simply say that you don't know much about it, that you understand that I was dissatisfied with Eber but you don't know why. Can't you?"

I was frowning at him. "This must have given you quite a jolt, Mr. Jarrell. You'd better snap out of it. Two of Mr. Wolfe's oldest and dearest enemies, and mine, are Inspector Cramer and Sergeant Stebbins of Homicide. The minute they catch sight of me and learn that I'm here under another name in Eber's job, the sparks will start flying. No matter what reason you give them for firing him they won't believe you. They won't believe me. They won't believe anybody. The theory they'll like best will be that you decided that Eber had to be shot and got me in as a technical consultant. That may be stretching it a little, but it gives you an idea."

"Good God." He was stunned. "Of course."

"So I can't simply say I don't know much about it."

"Good God no. My mind wasn't working." He leaned forward at me. "Look, Goodwin. The other thing I was going to ask, I was going to ask you to say nothing about what happened Wednesday — about my gun being taken. I'm not afraid that gun was used to shoot Eber, that's not it, it may not have been that caliber, but when they come here on a murder investigation you know how it will be if they find out that my gun was stolen just the day before. And if it was that caliber it will be a hundred times worse. So I was going to ask you not to mention it. Nobody else knows about it. Horland's man doesn't. He left before I found it was gone."

"I told you I told Mr. Wolfe."

"They don't have to get Wolfe."

"Maybe they don't have to but they will, as soon as they see me. I'll tell you, Mr. Jarrell, it seems to me you're still jolted. You're not thinking straight. The way you feel about your daughter-in-law, this may be right in your lap. You want to sink her so bad you can taste it. You hired Mr. Wolfe and gave him ten thousand dollars for a retainer, and then offered me another sixty thousand. If you tell Inspector Cramer all about it — only

Cramer, not Stebbins or Rowcliff or any of his gang, and not some squirt of an assistant district attorney—and tell him about the gun, and he starts digging at it and comes up with proof that Susan shot Eber, what better could you ask? You said you knew Susan took the gun, and if so she wanted to use it on someone, and why not Eber? And if you're afraid Cramer might botch it, keep Mr. Wolfe on the job. He loves to see to it that Cramer doesn't botch something."

"No," he said positively.

"Why not? You'll soon know if Eber was shot with a thirty-eight. I can find out about that for you within an hour, as soon as I get some breakfast. Why not?"

"I won't have them—I won't do it. No. You know damn well I won't. I won't tell the police about my personal affairs and have them spread all over. I don't want you or Wolfe telling them, either. I see now that my idea wouldn't work, that if they find out you're here in Eber's place there'll be hell to pay. So they won't find out. You won't be here, and you'd better leave right now because they might come any minute. If they want to know where my new secretary is I'll take care of that. He has only been here four days and knew nothing about Eber. You'd better leave now."

"And go where?"

"Where you belong, damn it!" He gestured, a hand out. "You'll have to make allowances for me, Goodwin. I've had a jolt, certainly I have. If you're not here and if I account for the absence of my new secretary, they'll never get to you or Wolfe either. Tell Wolfe I'm still his client and I'll get in touch with him. He said he was discreet. Tell him there's no limit to what his discretion may be worth to me."

He left the chair. "As for you, no limit with you too. I'm a tough operator, but I pay for what I get. Go on, get your necktie on. Leave your stuff here, that won't matter, you can get it later. We understand each other, don't we?"

"If we don't we will."

"I like you, Goodwin. Get going."

I moved. He stood and watched me while I got my tie and jacket on, gathered a few items and put them in the small bag, and closed the bag. When I glanced back as I turned the corner at the end of the hall, he was standing in front of the door of my room. I was disappointed not to see Steck in the corridor or reception hall; he must have had morning duties somewhere. Outside, I crossed the avenue, flagged a taxi headed downtown, and at a quarter past nine was mounting the stoop of the old brownstone. Wolfe would be up in the plant rooms for his morning session, from nine to eleven, with the orchids.

The chain bolt was on, so I had to ring, and it was Orrie Cather who opened up. He extended a hand. "Take your bag, sir?"

I let him take it, strode down the hall to the kitchen, and pushed the door. Fritz, at the sink, turned. "Archie! A pleasure! You're back?"

"I'm back for breakfast, anyhow. My God, I'm empty! No orange juice even. One dozen pancakes, please."

I did eat seven.

7

I was in the office, refreshed and refueled, in time to get the ten o'clock news. It didn't add much to what Jarrell had heard two hours earlier, and nothing that I didn't already know.

Orrie, at ease on the couch, inquired, "Did it help any? I'm ignorant, so I have to ask. What's hot, the budget?"

"Yeah, I'm underwriting it. I'm also writing a book on criminology and researching it. Excuse me, I'm busy."

I dialed a number I didn't have to look up, the *Gazette,* asked for Lon Cohen's extension, and in a minute had him.

"Lon? Archie. I'm col—"

"I'm busy."

"So am I. I'm collecting data for a book. What did you shoot James L. Eber with, an arquebus?"

"No, my arquebus is in hock. I used a flintlock. What is it to you?"

"I'm just curious. If you'll satisfy my curiosity I'll satisfy yours some day. Have they found the bullet?"

Lon is a fine guy and good poker player, but he has the occupational disease of all journalists: before he'll answer a question he has to ask one. So he did. "Has Wolfe got a thumb in it already?"

"Not a thumb, a foot. No, he hasn't, not for the record. If and when, you first as usual. Have they found the bullet?"

"Yes. It just came in. A thirty-eight, that's all so far. Who is Wolfe's client?"

"J. Edgar Hoover. Have they arrested anybody?"

"No. My God, give 'em time to sweep up and sit down and think. It was only twelve hours ago. I've been thinking ever since I heard your voice just now. What I think, I think it was you who called headquarters last night and told them to go and look, and I'm sore. You should have called me first."

"I should, at that. Next time. Have they or you or anyone got any kind of a lead?"

"To the murderer, no. So far the most interesting item is that up to a couple of weeks ago he was working for a guy named Otis Jarrell, you know who he is—*by God!* It was him you phoned me the other day to get dope on!"

"Sure it was. That's one reason—"

"Is Jarrell Wolfe's client?"

"For the present, as far as you're concerned, Wolfe has no client. I was saying, that's one reason I'm calling now. I thought you might remember I had asked about him, and I wanted to tell you not to trust your memory until further notice. Just go ahead and gather the news and serve the public. You may possibly hear from me some day."

"Come on up here. I'll buy you a lunch."

"I can't make it, Lon. Sorry. Don't use any wooden bullets."

As I pushed the phone back Orrie asked, "What's an arquebus?"

"Figure it out yourself. A combination of an ark and a bus. Amphibian."

"Then don't." He sat up. "If I'm not supposed to be in on whatever you think you're doing, okay, but I have a right to know what an arquebus is. Do you want me out of here?"

I told him no, I could think better with him there for contrast.

But he got bounced when Wolfe came down at eleven o'clock. From the kitchen I had buzzed the plant rooms on the house phone to tell him I was there, so he wasn't surprised to see me. He went to his desk, glanced at the morning mail, which was skimpy, straightened his desk blotter, and focused on me. "Well?"

"In my opinion," I said, "the time has come for a complete report."

His eyes went over my shoulder to the couch. "If we need you on this, Orrie, you will get all the required information. That can wait."

"Yes, sir." Orrie got up and went.

When the door had closed behind him I spoke. "I called Lon Cohen. The bullet that killed Eber is a thirty-eight. Jarrell didn't know that when he entered my room this morning, knocking but not waiting for an invitation. He only knew what he had heard on the radio at eight o'clock, and I suppose you heard it too. Even so, he badly needed a tranquilizer. When I report in full you'll know what he said. It ended with his telling me to beat it quick before the cops arrived. He said to tell you he's still your client and he'll get in touch with you, and there's no limit to what your discretion may be worth to him. Me too. My discretion is as good as yours. Now that I know it was a thirty-eight, I have only two alternatives. Either I go down to Homicide and open the bag, or I give you the whole works from the beginning, words and music, and you listen, and then put your mind on it. If I get tossed in the coop for withholding evidence you can't operate anyhow, with me not here to supervise, so you might as well be with me."

"Pfui. As I said last night, there is no obligation to report what may be merely a coincidence." He sighed. "However, I concede that I'll have to listen. As for putting my mind on it, we'll see. Go ahead."

It took me two hours. I will not say that I gave him every word that had been pronounced in my hearing since Monday afternoon, four days back, but I came close to it. I left out some of Tuesday evening at Colonna's with Lois; things that are said between dances, when the band is good and your partner is better than good, are apt to be irrelevant and off key in a working detective's report. Aside from that I didn't miss much, and nothing of any importance, and neither did he. If he listens at all, he listens. The only interruptions were the two bottles of beer he rang for, brought by Fritz — both, of course, for Wolfe. The last half hour he was leaning back in his chair with his eyes closed, but that didn't mean he wasn't getting it.

I stood up and stretched and sat down again. "So what it amounts to is that we are to sit it out, nothing to do but eat and sleep, and name our figure."

"Not an intolerable lot, Archie. The figure you suggested last evening was half a million."

"Yes, sir. I've decided that Billy Graham wouldn't approve. Say that the chance is one in ten that one of them killed Eber. I think it's at least fifty-

fifty, but even if it's only one in ten I pass. So do you. You have to. You know darned well it's one of two things. One is to call it off with Jarrell, back clear out, and hand it over to Cramer. He would appreciate it."

He made a face. His eyes opened. "What's the other?"

"You go to work."

"At what? Investigating the murder of Mr. Eber? No one has hired me to."

I grinned at him. "No good. You call it quibbling, I call it dodging. The murder is in only because one of them might have done it, with Jarrell's gun. The question is, do we tell Cramer about the gun. We would rather not. The client would rather not. The only way out, if we're not going to tell Cramer, is to find out if one of them killed Eber — not to satisfy a judge and jury, just to satisfy us. If they didn't, to hell with Cramer. If they did, we go on from there. The only way to find out is for you to go to work, and the only way for you to get to work is for me to phone Jarrell and tell him to have them there, all of them, at six o'clock today. What's wrong with that?"

"You would," he growled.

"Yes, sir. Of course there's a complication: me. To them I'm Alan Green, so I can't be here as Archie Goodwin, but that's easy. Orrie can be Archie Goodwin, at my desk, and I'll be Alan Green. Since I was in on the discovery that the gun was gone, I should be present." I looked up at the wall clock. "Lunch in eight minutes. I should phone Jarrell now."

I made it slow motion, taking ten seconds to swivel, pull the phone over, lift the receiver, and start dialing, to give him plenty of time to stop me. He didn't. How could he, after my invincible logic? Nor did he move to take his phone.

Then a voice was in my ear. "Mr. Otis Jarrell's office."

It wasn't Nora, but a male, and I thought I knew what male. I said I was Alan Green and wanted to speak to Mr. Jarrell, and in a moment had him.

"Yes, Green?"

I kept my voice down. "Is anyone else on?"

"No."

"You're sure?"

"Yes."

"Was that Wyman answering?"

"Yes."

"He's there in the office with you?"

"Yes."

"Then you'd better let me do the talking and stick to yes and no. I'm here with Mr. Wolfe. Do you know that the bullet that killed Eber is a thirty-eight?"

"No."

"Well, it is. Have you had any callers?"

"Yes."

"Anything drastic?"

"No."

"Ring me later and tell me about it if you want to. I'm calling for Mr. Wolfe. Now that we know it was a thirty-eight, he thinks I should tell the police about your gun. It could be a question of withholding evidence. He feels strongly about it, but he is willing to postpone it, on one condition.

The condition is that you have everybody in this office at six o'clock today so he can question them. By everybody he means you, your wife, Wyman, Susan, Lois, Nora Kent, Roger Foote, and Corey Brigham. I'll be here as Alan Green, your secretary. Another man will be at my desk as Archie Goodwin."

"I don't see how —"

"Hold it. I know you're biting nails, but hold it. You can tell them that Mr. Wolfe will explain why this conference is necessary, and he will. Have you told any of them about your gun being taken?"

"No."

"Don't. He will. He'll explain that when you learned that Eber had been shot with a thirty-eight — that should be on the air by now, and it will be in the early afternoon papers — you were concerned, naturally, and you hired him to investigate, and he insisted on seeing all of you. I know you've got objections. You'll have to swallow them, but if you want help on it get rid of Wyman and Nora and call me back. If you don't call back we'll be expecting you, all of you, here at six o'clock."

"No. I'll call back."

"Sure, glad to have you."

I hung up, turned, and told Wolfe, "You heard all of it except his noes and yeses. Satisfactory?"

"No," he said, but that was just reflex.

I'll say one thing for Wolfe, he hates to have anyone else's meal interrupted almost as much as his own. One of the standing rules in that house is that when we are at table, and nothing really hot is on, Fritz answers the phone in the kitchen, and if it seems urgent I go and get it. There may be something or somebody Wolfe would leave the table for, but I don't know what or who.

That day Fritz was passing a platter of what Wolfe calls hedgehog omelet, which tastes a lot better than it sounds, when the phone rang, and I told Fritz not to bother and went to the office. It was Jarrell calling back, and he had a lot of words besides yes and no. I permitted him to let off steam until it occurred to me that the omelet would be either cold or shriveled, and then told him firmly that it was either bring them or else. Back at the table, I found that the omelet had had no chance to either cool or shrivel, not with Orrie there to help Wolfe with it. I did get a bite.

We had just started on the avocado, whipped with sugar and lime juice and green chartreuse, when the doorbell rang. During meals Fritz was supposed to get that too, but I thought Jarrell might have rushed down to use more words face to face, so I got up and went to the hall for a look through the one-way glass panel in the front door. Having looked, I returned to the dining room and told Wolfe, "One's here already. The stenographer. Nora Kent."

He swallowed avocado. "Nonsense. You said six o'clock."

"Yes, sir. She must be on her own." The bell rang again. "And she wants in." I aimed a thumb at Orrie. "Archie Goodwin here can take her to the office and shut the door."

"Confound it." He was going to have to work sooner than expected. To Orrie: "You are Archie Goodwin."

"Yes, sir," Orrie said. "It's a comedown, but I'll try. Do I know her?"

"No. You have never seen or heard of her." The bell rang again. "Take her to the office and come and finish your lunch."

He went. He closed the door, but the office was just across the hall, and it might startle her if she heard Alan Green's voice as she went by, so I used my mouth for an avocado depot only. Sounds came faintly, since the walls and doors on that floor are all soundproofed.

When Orrie entered he shut the door, returned to his place, picked up hs spoon, and spoke. "You didn't say to rub it in that I'm Archie Goodwin, and she didn't ask, so I didn't mention it. She said her name was Nora Kent, and she wants to see Mr. Wolfe. How long am I going to be Archie Goodwin?"

I put in. "Mr. Wolfe never talks business at the table, you know that, Orrie. You haven't been told yet, but you were going to be me at a party later on, and now you can practice. Just sit at my desk and look astute. I'll have my eye on you. I'll be at the hole — unless Mr. Wolfe has other plans."

"No," Wolfe muttered. "I have no plans."

The hole, ten inches square, was at eye level in the wall twelve feet to the right of Wolfe's desk. On the office side it was covered by what appeared to be just a pretty picture of a waterfall. On the other side, in a wing of the hall across from the kitchen, it was covered by nothing, and you could not only see through but also hear through. My longest stretch there was one night when we had four people in the front room waiting for Wolfe to show up (he was in the kitchen chinning with Fritz), and we were expecting and hoping that one of them would sneak into the office to get something from a drawer of Wolfe's desk, and we wanted to know which one. That time I stood there at that hole more than three hours, and the door from the front room never opened.

This time it was much less than three hours. Orrie waited to open the door to the office until I was around the corner to the wing, so I saw his performance when they went in. As Goodwin he was barely adequate introducing Wolfe to her, hamming it up, I thought; and crossing to my desk and sitting, he was entirely out of character, no grace or flair at all. I would have to rehearse him before six o'clock came. I had a good view of him and Nora, but could get Wolfe, in profile, only by sticking my nose into the hole and pressing my forehead against the upper edge.

WOLFE: I'm sorry you had to wait, Miss Kent. It is *Miss* Kent?

NORA: Yes. I am employed by Mr. Otis Jarrell. His stenographer. I believe you know him.

WOLFE: There is no taboo on beliefs, or shouldn't be. The right to believe will be the last to go. Proceed.

NORA: You do know Mr. Jarrell?

WOLFE: My dear madam. I have rights too — for instance, the right to decline inquisition by a stranger. You are not here by appointment.

(That was meant to cut. If it did, no blood showed.)

NORA: There wasn't time to make one. I had to see you at once. I had to ask you why you sent your confidential assistant, Archie Goodwin, to take a job with Mr. Jarrell as his secretary.

WOLFE: I wasn't aware that I had done so. Archie, did I send you to take a job as Mr. Jarrell's secretary?

ORRIE: No, sir, not that I remember.

NORA (with no glance at Orrie): He's not Archie Goodwin. I knew Archie Goodwin the minute I saw him, Monday afternoon. I keep a scrapbook, Mr. Wolfe, a personal scrapbook. Among the things I put in it are pictures of people who have done things that I admire. There are three pictures of you, two from newspapers and one from a magazine, put in at different times, and one of Archie Goodwin. It was in the *Gazette* last year when you caught that murderer — you remember — Patrick Degan. I knew him the minute I saw him, and after I looked in my scrapbook there was no question about it.

(Orrie was looking straight at the pretty picture of the waterfall, at me though he couldn't see me, with blood in his eye, and I couldn't blame him. He had been given to understand that the part was a cinch, that he wouldn't have to do or say anything to avert suspicion because she wouldn't have any. And there he was, a monkey. I couldn't blame him.)

WOLFE (not visibly fazed, but also a monkey): I am flattered, Miss Kent, to be in your scrapbook. No doubt Mr. Goodwin is also flattered, though he might challenge your taste in having three pictures of me and only one of him. It will save —

NORA: Why did you send him there?

WOLFE: If you please. It will save time, and also breath, to proceed on an assumption, without prejudice. Obviously you're convinced that Mr. Goodwin took a job as Mr. Jarrell's secretary, and that I sent him, and it would be futile to try to talk you out of it. So we'll assume you're right. I don't concede it, but I'm willing to assume it for the sake of discussion. What about it?

NORA: I *am* right! You know it!

WOLFE: No. You may have it as an assumption, but not as a fact. What difference does it make? Let's get on. Did Mr. Goodwin take the job under his own name?

NORA: Certainly not. You know he didn't. Mr. Jarrell introduced him to me as Alan Green.

WOLFE: Did you tell Mr. Jarrell that that wasn't his real name? That you recognized him as Archie Goodwin?

NORA: No.

WOLFE: Why not?

NORA: Because I wasn't sure what the situation was. I thought that Mr. Jarrell might have hired you to do something and he knew who Green was, but he didn't want me to know or anyone else. I thought in that case I had better keep it to myself. But now it's different. Now I think that someone else may have hired you, someone who wanted to know something about Mr. Jarrell's affairs, and you arranged somehow for Goodwin to take that job, and Mr. Jarrell doesn't know who he is.

WOLFE: You didn't have to come to me to settle that. Ask Mr. Jarrell. Have you?

NORA: No. I told you why. And then — there are reasons . . .

WOLFE: There often are. If none are at hand we contrive some. A moment ago you said, "But now it's different." What changed it?

NORA: You know what changed it. Murder. The murder of Jim Eber. Archie Goodwin has told you all about it.

WOLFE: I'm willing to include that in the assumption. I think, madam, you had better tell me why you came here and what you want—still, of course, on our assumption.

(I said Monday afternoon that she didn't look her age, forty-seven. She did now. Her gray eyes were just as sharp and competent, and she kept her shoulders just as straight, but she seemed to have creases and wrinkles I hadn't observed before. Of course it could have been the light angle, or possibly it was looking through the waterfall.)

NORA: If we're assuming that I'm right, that man (indicating Orrie) can't be Archie Goodwin, and I don't know who he is. I haven't got *his* picture in my scrapbook. I'll tell *you* why I came.

WOLFE: That's reasonable, certainly. Archie, I'm afraid you'll have to leave us.

(Poor Orrie. As Orrie Cather he had been chased twice, and now he was chased as Archie Goodwin. His only hope now was to be cast as Nero Wolfe. When he was out and the door shut Nora spoke.)

NORA: All right, I'll tell you. Right after lunch today I went on an errand, and when I got back Mr. Jarrell told me that the bullet that killed Jim Eber was a thirty-eight. That was all he told me, just that. But I knew why he told me, it was because his own gun is a thirty-eight. He has always kept it in a drawer of his desk. I saw it there Wednesday afternoon. But it wasn't there Thursday morning, yesterday, and it hasn't been there since. Mr. Jarrell hasn't asked me about it, he hasn't mentioned it. I don't know—

WOLFE: Haven't you mentioned it?

(Orrie was at my elbow.)

NORA: No. If I mentioned it, and he had taken it himself, he would think I was prying into matters that don't concern me. I don't know whether he took it himself or not. But yesterday afternoon a man from Horland's Protective Agency delivered some pictures that must have been taken by the camera that works automatically when the door of the library is opened. The clock above the door said sixteen minutes past six. The pictures showed the door opening and a rug coming in—just the rug, flat, held up perpendicular, hanging straight down. Of course there was someone behind it. Archie Goodwin looked at the pictures, and of course he has told you all about it.

WOLFE: On our assumption, yes.

NORA: The camera must have taken them the day before, at sixteen minutes past six Wednesday afternoon. At that hour I am always up in my room, washing and changing, getting ready to go to the lounge for cocktails. So is everyone else, nearly always. So there it is, take it altogether. On Monday Archie Goodwin comes as the new secretary under another name. Thursday morning Mr. Jarrell's gun is gone. Thursday afternoon the pictures come, taken at a time when I was up in my room alone. Friday morning, today, the news comes that Jim Eber has been murdered, shot. Also this morning Archie Goodwin isn't there, and Mr. Jarrell says he has sent him on a trip. And this afternoon Mr. Jarrell tells me that Jim was shot with a thirty-eight.

(The gray eyes were steady and cold. I had the feeling that if they aimed my way they would see me right through the picture, though I knew they couldn't.)

NORA: I'm not frightened, Mr. Wolfe. I don't scare easily. And I know you wouldn't deliberately conspire to have me accused of murder, and neither would Archie Goodwin. But all those things together, I wasn't going to just wait and see what happened. It wouldn't have helped any to say all this to Mr. Jarrell. I know all about his business affairs, but this is his personal life, his family, and I don't count. I'd rather not have him know I came to you, but I don't really care. I've worked long enough anyhow. Was Archie Goodwin there because Mr. Jarrell hired you, or was it someone else?

WOLFE: Even granting the assumption, I can't tell you that.

NORA: I suppose not. But he's not there today, so you may be through. In the twenty-two years I have been with Mr. Jarrell I have had many opportunities, especially the past ten years, and my net worth today, personally, is something over a million dollars. I know you charge high fees, but I could afford it. I said I'm not frightened, and I'm not, but something is going to happen to somebody, I'm sure of that, and I don't want it to happen to me. I want you to see that it doesn't. I'll pay you a retainer, of course, whatever you say. I believe the phrase is "to protect my interests."

WOLFE: I'm sorry, Miss Kent, but I must decline.

NORA: Why?

WOLFE: I've undertaken a job for Mr. Jarrell. He has —

NORA: Then he did hire you! Then he knew it was Archie Goodwin!

WOLFE: No. That remains only an assumption. He has engaged me to conduct a conference for him. On the telephone today. He feels that the situation calls for an experienced investigator, and at six o'clock, three hours from now, he will come here and bring seven people with him — his family, and a man named Brigham, and you. That is, if you care to come. Evidently you are in no mood to trot when he whistles.

NORA: He phoned you today?

WOLFE: Yes.

NORA: You were already working for him. You sent Archie Goodwin up there.

WOLFE: You have a right, madam, to your beliefs, but I beg you not to be tiresome with them. If you join us at six o'clock, and I advise you to, you should know that the Mr. Goodwin who scurried from this room at your behest will be here, at his desk, and Alan Green, Mr. Jarrell's secretary, will also be present. The others, the members of Mr. Jarrell's family, unlike you, will probably be satisfied that those two men know who they are. Will you gain anything by raising the question?

NORA: No. I see. No. But I don't — then Mr. Jarrell doesn't know either?

WOLFE: Don't get tangled in your own assumption. If you wish to revise it after the conference by all means do so. And now I ask you to reciprocate. I have an assumption too. We have accepted yours as a basis for discussion, now let us accept mine. Mine is that none of the people who will be present at the conference fired the shot that killed Mr. Eber. What do you think of it?

(The gray eyes narrowed.)

NORA: You can't expect me to discuss that. I am employed by Mr. Jarrell.

WOLFE: Then we'll turn it around. We'll assume the contrary and take them in turn. Start with Mr. Jarrell himself. He took his own gun, with that hocus-pocus, and shot Eber with it. What do you say to that?

NORA: I don't say anything.

(She stood up.)

NORA: I know you're a clever man, Mr. Wolfe. That's why your picture is in my scrapbook. I may not be as clever as you are, but I'm not an utter fool.

(She started off, and, halfway to the door, turned.)

NORA: I'll be here at six o'clock if Mr. Jarrell tells me to.

She went. I whispered to Orrie, "Go let her out, Archie." He whispered back, "Let her out yourself, Alan." The result was that she let herself out. When I heard the front door close I left the wing and made it to the front in time to see her, through the one-way glass panel, going down the stoop. When she had reached the sidewalk safely I went to the office.

Wolfe was forward in his chair, his palms on his desk. Orrie was at my desk, in my chair, at ease. I stood and looked down at Wolfe.

"First," I said, "Who is whom?"

He grunted. "Confound that woman. When you were introduced to her Monday afternoon I suppose you were looking at her. And you saw no sign that she had recognized you?"

"No, sir. A woman who has it in her to collar a million bucks knows how to hide her feelings. Besides, I thought it was only women under thirty who put my picture in scrapbooks. Then the program will be as scheduled?"

"Yes. Have you a reason for changing it?"

"No, sir. You're in for it. Please excuse me a minute." I pivoted to Orrie. "You'll be me at six o'clock, I can't help that, but you're not me now."

Down went my hands, like twin snakes striking, and I had his ankles. With a healthy jerk he was out of my chair, and I kept him coming, and going, until he was flat on his back on the rug, six feet away. By the time he had bounced up I was sitting. I may or may not know how to deal with a murderer, but I know how to handle an impostor.

8

I made a crack, I remember, about Susan's entrance in the lounge Monday evening, after everyone else was there, as to whether or not she had planned it that way. My own entrance in Wolfe's office that Friday afternoon, after everyone else was there, was planned that way all right. There were two reasons: first, I didn't want to have to chat with the first arrivals, whoever they would be, while waiting for the others; and second, I didn't want to see Orrie being Archie Goodwin as he let them in and escorted them to the office. So at five-forty, leaving the furnishing of the refreshment table to Fritz and Orrie, I left the house and went across the street to the tailor shop, from where there was a good view of our stoop.

The first to show were Lois and Nora Kent and Roger Foote, in a taxi. Nora paid the hackie, which was only fair since she could afford it, and anyway, she probably put it on the expense account. Transportation to and from a conference to discuss whether anyone present is a murderer is probably tax deductible. The next customer was also in a taxi—Corey Brigham, alone. Then came Wyman and Susan in a yellow Jaguar, with him driving. He had to go nearly to Tenth Avenue to find a place to park, and they walked back. Then came a wait. It was 6:10 when a black Rolls Royce town car rolled to the curb and Jarrell and Trella got out. I hadn't grown impatient, having myself waited for Trella twenty-five minutes on Tuesday, bound for lunch at Rusterman's. As soon as they were inside I crossed the street and pushed the button. Archie Goodwin let me in and steered me to the office. He was passable.

He had followed instructions on seating. The bad thing about it was that I had four of them in profile and couldn't see the others' faces at all, but we couldn't very well give the secretary a seat of honor confronting the audience. Of course Jarrell had the red leather chair, and in the front row of yellow chairs were Lois, Trella, Wyman, and Susan. The family. Behind them were Alan Green, Roger Foote, Nora Kent, and Corey Brigham. At least I had Lois right in front of me. She wasn't as eye-catching from the back as from the front, but it was pleasant.

When Wolfe entered he accepted Jarrell's offer of a hand, got behind his desk, stood while Jarrell pronounced our names, inclined his head an eighth of an inch, and sat.

Jarrell spoke. "They all know that this is about Eber, and I've hired you, and that's all. I've told them it's a conference, a family conference, and it's off the record."

"Then I should clarify it." Wolfe cleared his throat. "If by 'off the record' you mean that I am pledged to divulge nothing that is said, I must dissent. I'm not a lawyer and cannot receive a privileged communication. If you mean that this proceeding is confidential and none of it will be disclosed except under constraint of law, if it ever applies, that's correct."

"Don't shuffle, Wolfe. I'm your client."

"Only if we understand each other." Wolfe's eyes went left to right and back again. "Then that's understood. I believe none of you know about the disappearance of Mr. Jarrell's gun. You have to know that. Since his secretary, Mr. Green, was present when its absence was discovered, I'll ask him to tell you. Mr. Green?"

I had known that would come, but not that he would pick on me first. Their heads were turned to me. Lois twisted clear around in her chair, and her face was only arm's length away. I reported. Not as I had reported to Wolfe, no dialogue, but all the main action, from the time Jarrell had dashed into my room until we left the library. I had their faces.

The face that left me first was Trella's. She turned it to her husband and protested. "You might have told us, Otis!"

Corey Brigham asked me, "Has the gun been found?" Then he went to Jarrell too. "Has it?"

Wolfe took over. "No, it has not been found. It has not been looked for. In my opinion Mr. Jarrell should have had a search made at once, calling in the police if necessary, but it must be allowed that it was a difficult situation for him. By the way, Mr. Green, did you get the impression that Mr. Jarrell suspected anyone in particular?"

I hoped I got him right. Since he had asked it he wanted it answered, but

he hadn't asked what Jarrell had said, only if I had got an impression. I
gave him what I thought he wanted. "Yes, I did. I might have been wrong,
but I had the feeling that he thought he knew who had taken it. It was—"

"Goddamn it," Jarrell blurted, "you knew what I thought! I didn't think,
I knew! If it's out let it come all the way out!" He aimed a finger at Susan.
"You took it!"

Dead silence. They didn't look at Susan, they looked at him, all except
Roger Foote, next to me. He kept his eyes on Wolfe, possibly deciding
whether to place a bet on him.

The silence was broken by Wyman. He didn't blurt, he merely said,
"That won't get you anywhere, Dad, not unless you've got proof. Have you
got any?" He turned, feeling Susan's hand on his arm, and told her, "Take it
easy, Sue." He was adding something, but Wolfe's voice drowned it.

"That point should be settled, Mr. Jarrell. Do you have proof?"

"No. Proof for you, no. I don't need any."

"Then you'd better confine your charge to the family circle. Broadcast, it
would be actionable." His head turned to the others. "We'll ignore Mr. Jarrell's
specification of the culprit, since he has no proof. Ignoring that, this is the
situation: When Mr. Jarrell learned this afternoon that Mr. Eber had been
killed with a gun of the same caliber as his, which had been taken from a drawer
of his desk, he was concerned, and no wonder, since Eber had been in his
employ five years, had lived in his house, had recently been discharged, had
visited his house on Wednesday, the day the gun was taken, and had been killed
the next day. He decided to consult me. I told him that his position was
precarious and possibly perilous; that his safest course was to report the
disappearance of his gun, with all the circumstances, to the police; that, with a
murder investigation under way it was sure to transpire eventually, unless the
murderer was soon discovered elsewhere; and that, now that I knew about it, I
would myself have to report it, for my own protection, if the possibility that his
gun had been used became a probability. Obviously, the best way out would be
to establish that it was not his gun that killed Eber, and that can easily be done."

"How?" Brigham demanded.

"With an if, Mr. Brigham, or two of them. It can be established if it is
true, and if the gun is available. Barring the servants, one of you took Mr.
Jarrell's gun. Surrender it. Tell me where to find it. I'll fire a bullet from it,
and I'll arrange for that bullet to be compared with the one that killed Eber.
That will settle it. If the markings on the bullets don't match, the gun is
innocent and I have no information for the police. Per contra, if they do
match, I must inform the police immediately, and give them the gun, and
all of you are in a pickle." He upturned both palms. "It's that simple."

Jarrell snapped at his daughter-in-law, "Where is it, Susan?"

"No," Wolfe snapped back at him, "that won't do. You have admitted you
have no proof. I am conducting this conference at your request, and I won't
have you bungling it. These people, including you, are jointly in jeopardy,
at least of severe harassment, and I insist on making the appeal to
them jointly." His eyes went right and left. "I appeal to all of you. Mrs.
Wyman Jarrell." Pause. "Mr. Wyman Jarrell." Pause. "Mrs. Otis Jarrell."
Pause. "Miss Jarrell." Pause. "Mr. Green." Pause. "Mr. Foote." Pause. "Miss
Kent." Pause. "Mr. Brigham."

Lois twisted around in her chair to face me. "He's good at remembering names, isn't he?" she asked. Then she made two words, four syllables, with her lips, without sound. I am not an accomplished lip reader, but there was no mistaking that. The words were "Archie Goodwin."

I was arranging my face to indicate that I hadn't caught it when Corey Brigham spoke. "I don't quite see why I have been included." His well-trained smile was on display. "It's an honor, naturally, to be considered in the Jarrell family circle, but as a candidate for taking Jarrell's gun I'm afraid I don't qualify."

"You were there, Mr. Brigham. Perhaps I haven't made it clear, or Mr. Green didn't. The photograph, taken automatically when the door opened, showed the clock above the door at sixteen minutes past six. You were a dinner guest that evening, Wednesday, and you arrived shortly after six and were in the lounge."

"I see." The smile stayed on. "And I rushed back to the library and worked the great rug trick. How did I get in?"

"Presumably, with a key. The door was intact."

"I have no key to the library."

Wolfe nodded. "Possession of a key to that room would be one of the many points to be explored in a laborious and prolonged inquiry, if it should come to that. Meanwhile you cannot be slighted. You're all on equal terms, if we ignore Mr. Jarrell's specification without evidence, and I do."

Roger Foote's voice boomed suddenly, louder than necessary. "I've got a question." There were little spots of color beneath the cheekbones of his big wide face — at least there was one on the side I could see. "What about this new secretary, this Alan Green? We don't know anything about him, anyway I don't. Do you? Did he know Eber?"

My pal. My pet panhandler. I had lent the big bum sixty bucks, my money as far as he knew, and this was what I got for it. Of course, Peach Fuzz hadn't won. He added a footnote. "He had a key to the library, didn't he?"

"Yes, Mr. Foote, he did." Wolfe conceded. "I don't know much about him and may have to know more before this matter is settled. One thing I do know, he says he was in his room alone at a quarter past six Wednesday afternoon, when the gun was taken. So was Mr. Jarrell, by his account. Mr. Green has told you of Mr. Jarrell's coming for him, and what followed. Mr. Brigham was in the lounge. Where were you, Mr. Foote?"

"Where was I when?"

"I thought I had made it plain. At a quarter past six Wednesday afternoon."

"I was on my way back from Jamaica, and I got home — no. No, that was yesterday, Thursday. I must have been in my room, shaving. I always shave around then."

"You say 'must have been.' Were you?"

"Yes."

"Was anyone with you?"

"No. I'm not Louis the Fourteenth. I don't get an audience in to watch me shave."

Wolfe nodded. "That's out of fashion." His eyes went to Trella. "Mrs. Jarrell, we might as well get this covered. Do you remember where you were at that hour on Wednesday?"

"I know where I am at that hour every day—nearly every day, except week ends." I could see one of her ears, but not her face. "I was in the studio looking at television. At half past six I went to the lounge."

"You're sure you were there on Wednesday?"

"I certainly am."

"What time did you go to the studio?"

"A little before six. Five or ten minutes before."

"You remained there continuously until six-thirty?"

"Yes."

"I believe the studio is on the main corridor. Did you see anyone passing by in either direction?"

"No, the door was closed. And what do you take me for? Would I tell you if I had?"

"I don't know, madam; but unless we find that gun you may meet importunity that will make me a model of amenity by comparison." His eyes went past Wyman to Susan. "Mrs. Jarrell? If you please."

She replied at once, her voice down as usual, but firm and distinct. "I was in my room with my husband. We were there together, from about a quarter to six, for about an hour. Then we went down to the lounge together."

"You confirm that, Mr. Jarrell?"

"I do." Wyman was emphatic.

"You're sure it was Wednesday?"

"I am."

Wolfe's eyes went left and were apparently straight at me, but I was on a line with Lois, who was just in front. "Miss Jarrell?"

"I think I'm it," she said. "I don't know exactly where I was at a quarter past six. I was out, and I got home about six o'clock, and I wanted to ask my father something and went to the library, but the door was locked. Then I went to the kitchen to look for Mrs. Latham, but she wasn't there, and I found her in the dining room and asked her to iron a dress for me. I was tired and I started for the lounge to get a quick one, but I saw Mr. Brigham in there and I didn't feel like company, so I skipped it and went up to my room to change. If I had had a key to the library, and if I had thought of the rug stunt, I might have gone there in between and got the gun, but I didn't. Anyway, I hate guns. I think the rug stunt was absolutely dreamy." She twisted around. "Don't you, Ar—Al—Alan?"

A marvelous girl. So playful. If I ever got her on a dance floor again I'd walk on her toes. She twisted back again when Wolfe asked a question.

"What time was it when you saw Mr. Brigham in the lounge? As near as you can make it."

She shook her head. "Not a chance. If it were someone I'm rather warm on, for instance Mr. Green, I'd say it was exactly sixteen minutes after six, and he would say he saw me looking in and he looked at his watch, and we'd both be out of it, but I'm not warm on Mr. Brigham. So I won't even try to guess."

"This isn't a parlor game, Lois," her father snapped. "This may be serious."

"It is already, Dad. It sounds darned serious to me. You notice I told him all I could. Didn't I, Mr. Wolfe?"

"Yes, Miss Jarrell. Thank you. Will you oblige us, Miss Kent?"

I was wondering if Nora would rip it. Not that it would have been fatal, but if she had announced that the new secretary was Archie Goodwin, that Wolfe was a damn liar when he gave them to understand that he had had no finger in the Jarrell pie until that afternoon, and that therefore they had better start the questions going the other way, it would have made things a little complicated.

She didn't. Speaking as a competent and loyal stenographer, she merely said, "On Wednesday Mr. Jarrell and I left the library together at six o'clock, as usual, locking the door. We took the elevator upstairs together and parted in the hall. I went to my room to wash and change, and stayed there until half past six, or a minute or two before that, perhaps twenty-eight minutes after six, and then I went down to the lounge."

Wolfe leaned back, clasped his fingers at the highest point of his central mound, took in a bushel of air and let it out, and grumbled, "I may have gone about this wrong. Of course one of you has lied."

"You're damn right," Jarrell said, "and I know which one."

"If Susan lied," Roger objected, "so did Wyman. What about this Green?"

I would walk on his toes too, some day when I could get around to it.

"It was a mistake," Wolfe declared, "to get you all on record regarding your whereabouts at that hour. Now you are all committed, including the one who took the gun, and he will be more reluctant than ever to speak. It would be pointless to hammer at you now; indeed, I doubt if hammering would have helped in any case. The time for hammering was Wednesday afternoon, the moment Mr. Jarrell found that the gun was gone. Then there had been no murder, with its menace of an inexorable inquisition."

He looked them over. "So here we are. You know how it stands. I said that I shall have to inform the police if the possibility that Mr. Jarrell's gun was used to kill Mr. Eber becomes a probability. It is nearer a probability, in my mind, now than it was an hour ago—now that all of you have denied taking the gun, for one of you did take it."

His eyes went over them again. "When I speak to a man, or a woman, I like to look at him, but I speak now to the one who took the gun, and I can't look at him because I don't know who he is. So, speaking to him, I close my eyes." He closed them. "If you knew where the gun is, and it is innocent, all you have to do is let it reappear. You need not expose yourself. Merely put it somewhere in sight, where it will soon be seen. If it does not appear soon I shall be compelled to make one of two assumptions."

He raised a finger, his eyes still closed. "One. That it is no longer in your possession and is not accessible. If it left your possession before Eber was killed it may have been used to kill him, and the police will have to be informed. If it left your possession after he was killed and you know it wasn't used to kill him—and, as I said, that can be demonstrated—you will then have to expose yourself, but that will be a trifle since it will establish the innocence of the gun. I don't suppose Mr. Jarrell will prosecute for theft."

Another finger went up. "Two. My alternative assumption will be that you killed Eber. In that case you certainly will not produce the gun even if it is still available to you; and every hour that I delay telling the police what I know is a disservice to the law you and I live under."

He opened his eyes. "There it is, ladies and gentlemen. As you see, it is exigent. There is nothing more to say at the moment. I shall await notice that the gun has been found, the sooner the better. The conference is ended, except for one of you. Mr. Foote has suggested that the record of the man who took Mr. Eber's place, Mr. Alan Green, should be looked into, and I agree. Mr. Green, you will please remain. For the rest of you, that is all for the present. I should apologize for a default in hospitality. That refreshment table is equipped and I should have invited you. I do so now. Archie?"

Orrie Archie Cather Goodwin said, "I asked them, Mr. Wolfe," and got up and headed for the table. Roger Foote was there as soon as he was, so the bourbon would get a ride. Thinking it might be expected that my nerves needed a bracer, since my record was going to be probed, I went and asked Mr. Goodwin for some scotch and water. The others had left their chairs, but apparently not for refreshment. Jarrell and Trella were standing at Wolfe's desk, conversing with him, and Corey Brigham stood behind them, kibitzing. Nora Kent stood at the end of the couch, sending her sharp gray eyes around. Seeing that Wyman and Susan were going, I caught Orrie's eye and he made for the hall to let them out. I took a sip of refreshment, stepped over to Roger Foote, and told him, "Many thanks for the plug."

"Nothing personal. It just occurred to me. What do I know about you? Nothing. Neither does anybody else." He went to the table and reached for the bourbon bottle.

I had been considering whether I should tackle Lois or let bad enough alone, and was saved the trouble when she called to me and I went to her, over by the big globe.

"We pretend we're looking at the globe," she said. "That's called covering. I just wanted to tell you that the minute I saw that character, when he let us in, I remembered. One thing I've got to ask, does my father know who you are?"

She was pointing to Venezuela on the globe, and I was looking at her hand, which I knew was nice to hold to music. Obviously there was no chance of bulling it; she knew; and there wasn't time to take Wolfe's line with Nora and set it up as an assumption. So I turned the globe and pointed to Madagascar.

"Yes," I said, "he knows."

"Because," she said, "he may not be the flower of knighthood, but he's my father, and besides, he pays my bills. You wouldn't string me, would you?"

"I'd love to string you, but not on this. Your father knew I was Archie Goodwin when he took me to his place Monday afternoon. When he wants you and the others to know I suppose he'll tell you."

"He never tells me anything." She pointed to Ceylon. "If there was anything I wanted to blackmail you for, this would be wonderful, but if I ever do yearn for anything from you I would want it to pour out, just gush out from an uncontrollable passion. I wouldn't meet you halfway, because that wouldn't be maidenly, but I wouldn't run. It's too bad —"

"You coming, Lois?"

It was Roger Foote, with Nora beside him. Lois said the globe was the biggest one she had ever seen and she hated to leave it, and Roger said he would buy her one, what with I don't know, and they went. I stayed with the globe. Jarrell and Trella were still with Wolfe, but Corey Brigham had gone. Then they left too, ignoring me, and while Orrie was in the hall seeing them out I went and sat on one of the yellow chairs, the one Susan had occupied.

I cringed. "Very well, sir," I said, "you want my record. I was born in the maternity ward of the Ohio State Penitentiary on Christmas Eve, Eighteen sixty-five. After they branded me I was taken —"

"Shut up."

"Yes, sir." I got up and went to my own chair as Orrie appeared. "Do you want my opinion?"

"No."

"You're quite welcome. One will get you twenty that the gun will not be found."

He grunted.

I replied, "Lois has remembered who I am, and I had to tell her that her father knows. She won't spread it. One will get you thirty that the gun will not be found."

He grunted.

I replied, "To be practical about it, the only real question is how soon we call Cramer, and I'm involved in that as much as you are. One will get you fifty that the gun will not be found."

He grunted.

9

AT nine-thirty Saturday morning, having breakfasted with Lois and Susan and Wyman, more or less — more or less, because we hadn't synchronized — I made a tour of the lower floor of the duplex, all except the library and the kitchen. It wasn't a search; I didn't look under cushions or in drawers. Wolfe's suggestion had been to put the gun at some spot where it would soon be seen, so I just covered the territory and used my eyes. I certainly didn't expect to see it, having offered odds of fifty to one, and so wasn't disappointed.

There was no good reason why I shouldn't have slept in my own bed Friday night, but Wolfe had told Jarrell (with Trella there) that he would send his secretary back to him as soon as he was through asking him about his past. I hadn't really minded, since even a fifty-to-one shot has been known to deliver, and if one of them sneaked the gun out into the open that very evening it would be a pleasure to be the one to discover it, or even to be there when someone else discovered it. So I made a tour before I went up to bed.

My second tour, Saturday morning, was more thorough, and when, having completed it, I entered the reception hall on my way to the front door, Steck was there.

He spoke. "Could I help you, sir? Were you looking for something?"

I regarded him. What if he was a loyal and devoted old retainer? What if he had been afraid his master was in a state of mind where he might plug somebody, and had pinched the gun to remove temptation? Should I take him up to my room for a confidential talk? Should I take him down to Wolfe? It would make a horse laugh if we unloaded to Cramer, and our client and his family were put through the wringer, and it turned out that the gun had been under Steck's mattress all the time. I regarded him, decided that it would have to be referred to a genius like Wolfe, and told him that I was beyond help, I was just fidgety, but thanked him all the same. When he saw I was going out he opened the door for me, trying not to look relieved.

Whenever possible I go out every morning, some time between nine and eleven, when Wolfe is up in the plant rooms, to loosen up my legs and get a lungful of exhaust fumes, but it wasn't just through force of habit that I was headed outdoors. An assistant district attorney, probably accompanied by a dick, was coming to see Jarrell at eleven o'clock, to get more facts about James L. Eber, deceased, and I had agreed that it was just as well for me to be off the premises.

Walking the thirty blocks to the *Gazette* building, I dropped in to ask Lon Cohen if the Giants were going to move to San Francisco. I also asked him for the latest dope on the Eber murder, and he asked me who Wolfe's client was. Neither of us got much satisfaction. As far as he knew, the cops were making a strenuous effort to turn up a lead and serve the cause of justice, and as far as I knew, Wolfe was fresh out of clients but if and when I had anything good enough for the front page I would let him know. From there, having loosened up my legs, I took a taxi to 35th Street.

Wolfe had come down from the plant rooms and was at his desk, dictating to Orrie, at my desk. They took time out to greet me, which I appreciated, from two busy men with important matters to attend to like writing to Lewis Hewitt to tell him that a cross of Cochlioda noezliana with Odontoglossum armainvillierense was going to bloom and inviting him to come and look at it. Not having had my usual forty minutes with the morning *Times* at breakfast, I got it from the rack and went to the couch, and had finished the front-page headlines and the sports pages when the doorbell rang. The man seated at my desk should have answered it, but he was being told by Wolfe how to spell a word which should have been no problem, so I went.

One glance through the panel, at a husky specimen in a gray suit, a pair of broad shoulders, and a big red face, was sufficient. I went and put the chain bolt on, opened the door to the two inches allowed by the chain, and spoke through the crack. "Good morning. I haven't seen you for months. You're looking fine."

"Come on, Goodwin, open up."

"I'd like to, but you know how it is. Mr. Wolfe is engaged, teaching a man how to spell. What do I tell him?"

"Tell him I want to know why he changed your name to Alan Green and got you a job as secretary to Otis Jarrell."

"I've been wondering about that myself. Make yourself comfortable while I go ask him. Of course if he doesn't know, there's no point in your bothering to come in."

Leaving the door open to the chain, not to be rude, I went to the office and crossed to Wolfe's desk. "Sorry to interrupt, but Inspector Cramer wants to know why you changed my name to Alan Green and got me a job as secretary to Otis Jarrell. Shall I tell him?"

He scowled at me. "How did he find out? That Jarrell girl?"

"No. I don't know. If you have to blame it on a woman, take Nora Kent, but I doubt it."

"Confound it. Bring him in."

I returned to the front, removed the chain, and swung the door open. "He's delighted that you've come. So am I."

He may not have caught the last three words, as he had tossed his hat on the bench and was halfway down the hall. By the time I had closed the door and made it back to the office he was at the red leather chair. Orrie wasn't visible. He hadn't come to the hall, so Wolfe must have sent him to the front room. That door was closed. I went to my chair and was myself again.

Cramer, seated, was speaking. "Do you want me to repeat it? What I told Goodwin?"

"That shouldn't be necessary." Wolfe, having swiveled to face him, was civil but not soapy. "But I am curious, naturally, as to how you got the information. Has Mr. Goodwin been under surveillance?"

"No, but a certain address on Fifth Avenue has been, since eight o'clock this morning. When Goodwin was seen coming out, at a quarter to ten, and recognized, and it was learned from the man in the lobby that the man who had just gone out was named Alan Green and he was Otis Jarrell's secretary, and it was reported to me, I wasn't just curious. If I had just been curious I would have had Sergeant Stebbins phone you. I've come myself."

"I commend your zeal, Mr. Cramer. And it's pleasant to see you again, but I'm afraid my wits are a little dull this morning. You must bear with me. I didn't know that taking a job under an alias is an offense against society and therefore a proper subject for police inquiry. And by you? The head of the Homicide Squad?"

"I ought to be able to bear with you, I've had enough practice. But by God, it's just about all I —" He stopped abruptly, got a cigar from a pocket, rolled it between his palms, stuck it in his mouth, and clamped his teeth on it. He never lit one. The mere sight of Wolfe, and the sound of his voice, with the memories they recalled, had stirred his blood, and it needed calming down.

He took the cigar from his mouth. "You're bad enough," he said, under control, "when you're not sarcastic. When you are, you're the hardest man to take in my jurisdiction. Do you know that a man named Eber was shot, murdered, in his apartment on Forty-ninth Street Thursday afteroon? Day before yesterday?"

"Yes, I know that."

"Do you know that for five years he had been Otis Jarrell's secretary and had recently been fired?"

"Yes, I know that too. Permit me to comment that this seems a little silly. I read newspapers."

"Okay, but it's in the picture, and you want the picture. According to information received, Goodwin's first appearance at Jarrell's place was on Monday afternoon, three days before Eber was killed. Jarrell told the man in the lobby that his name was Alan Green and that he was going to live there. And he has been. Living there." His head jerked to me. "That right, Goodwin?"

"Right," I admitted.

"You've been there since Monday, under an assumed name, as Jarrell's secretary?"

"Right—with time out for errands. I'm not there now."

"You're damn right you're not. You're not there now because you knew someone was coming from the DA's office to see Jarrell and you didn't want to be around. Right?"

"Fifth Amendment."

"Nuts. That's for Reds and racketeers, not for clowns like you." He jerked back to Wolfe, decided his blood needed calming again, stuck the cigar in his mouth, and chewed on it.

He removed it. "That's the picture, Wolfe" he said. "We've got no lead that's worth a damn on who killed Eber. Naturally our best source on his background and his associates has been Jarrell and the others at his place. Eber not only worked there, he lived there. We've got a lot of facts about him, but nothing with a motive for murder good enough to fasten on. We're just about ready to decide we're not going to get anywhere with Jarrell and that bunch and we'd better concentrate on other possibilities, and then this. Goodwin. Goodwin and you."

His eyes narrowed, then he realized that was the wrong attitude and opened them. "Now it's different. If a man like Otis Jarrell hires you for something so important that you're even willing to get along without Goodwin so he can go and stay there under an assumed name, with a job as Jarrell's secretary, and if the man who formerly had the job gets murdered three days later, do you expect me to believe there's no connection?"

"I'm not sure I follow you, Mr. Cramer. Connection between what?"

"Like hell you don't follow me! Between whatever Jarrell hired you for and the murder!"

Wolfe nodded. "I assumed you meant that, but I am wary of assumptions. You should be too. You are assuming that Mr. Jarrell hired me. Have you grounds for that? Isn't it possible that someone else hired me, and I imposed Mr. Goodwin on Mr. Jarrell's household to get information for my client?"

That settled it. Ever since I had opened the door a crack and got Cramer's message for Wolfe, I had been thinking that Wolfe would probaby decide that the cat was too scratchy to hang onto, and would let Cramer take it, but not now. Jarrell's gun would not be mentioned. The temptation to teach Cramer to be wary of assumptions had been irresistible.

Cramer was staring. "By God," he said. "Who's your client? No. I'd never pry that out of you. But you can tell me this: was Eber your client?"

"No, sir."

"Then is it Jarrell or isn't it? Is Jarrell your client?"

Wolfe was having a picnic. "Mr. Cramer. I am aware that if I have information relevant to the crime you're investigating I am bound to give it to you; but its relevance may be established, not by your whim or conjecture, but by an acceptable process of reason. Since you don't know what information I have, and I do, you can't apply that process and it must be left to me. My conclusion is that I have nothing to tell you. I have answered your one question that was clearly relevant, whether Mr. Eber was my client. You will of course ask Mr. Jarrell if he is my client, telling him his secretary is my confidential assistant, Archie Goodwin; I can't prevent that. I'm sorry you gave yourself the trouble of coming, but your time hasn't been entirely wasted; you have learned that I wasn't working for Mr. Eber."

Cramer looked at me, probaby because, for one thing, if he had gone on looking at Wolfe he would have had to get his hands on him, and for another, there was the question whether I might possibly disagree with the conclusion Wolfe had reached through an acceptable process of reason. I met his look with a friendly grin which I hoped wouldn't strike him as sarcastic.

He put the cigar in his mouth and closed his teeth on it, got up, risked another look at Wolfe, not prolonged, turned, and tramped out. I stayed put long enough for him to make it down the hall, then went to see if he had been sore enough to try the old Finnegan on us. He hadn't; he was out, pulling the door shut as he went.

As I stepped back into the office Wolfe snapped at me, "Get Mr. Jarrell."

"The assistant DA is probably still with him."

"No matter, get him."

I went to my desk, dialed, got Nora Kent, and told her that Mr. Wolfe wished to speak to Mr. Jarrell. She said he was engaged and would call back, and I said the sooner the better because it was urgent. Say two minutes. It wasn't much more than that before the ring came, and Jarrell was on, and Wolfe got at his phone. I stayed at mine.

Jarrell said he had gone to another phone because two men from the district attorney's office were with him, and Wolfe asked, "Have they mentioned Mr. Goodwin or me?"

"No, why should they?"

"They might have. Inspector Cramer of the Homicide Squad was here and just left. The entrance to your address is under surveillance and Mr. Goodwin was recognized when he came out this morning, and it has been learned that he has been there as your secretary since Monday, with Alan Green as his name. Mr. Goodwin told you what would happen if that were disclosed, and it has happened. I gave Mr. Cramer no information whatever except that Mr. Eber was not my client. Of course you —"

"Did you tell him what I hired you for?"

"You're not listening. I said I gave him no information whatever. I didn't even tell him that you hired me, let alone what for. Of course they'll be at you immediately, since they know about Mr. Goodwin. I suggest that you reflect on the situation with care. Whatever you tell them, do not fail to inform me at once. If you admit that you hired me —"

"What the hell, I've got to admit it! You say they know about Goodwin!"

"So they do. But I mentioned to Mr. Cramer the possibility that someone else hired me to send Goodwin there to spy on you. Merely as a possibility. Please understand that I told him nothing."

"I see." Silence. "I'll be damned." Silence. "I'll have to think it over and decide what to say."

"You will indeed. It will probably be best for you to tell them that you hired me on a personal and confidential matter, and leave it at that. But on

one point, between you and me, there must be no ambiguity. I am free to
disclose what I know about your gun, and its disappearance, at any moment that I think it necessary or desirable. You understand that."

"That's not the way you put it. You said you'd have to report it if the
possibility that my gun was used to kill Eber became a probability."

"Yes, but the decision rests with me. I am risking embarrassment and so
is Mr. Goodwin. We don't want to lose our licenses. It would have been
prudent to tell Mr. Cramer when he was here, but he provoked me."

He hung up and glared at me as if I had done the provoking.

I hung up and glared back. "License my eye," I told him. "We're risking
eating on the State of New York for one to ten years with time off for good
behavior."

"Do you challenge me?" He demanded. "You were present. You have a
tongue, heaven knows. Would you have loosened it if I hadn't been here?"

"No," I admitted. "He goes against the grain. He has bad manners. He
lacks polish. Look at you for contrast. You are courteous, gracious, tactful,
eager to please. What now? I left up there to be out of the way when
company came, but now they're on to me. Do I go back?"

He said no, not until we heard further from Jarrell, and I went to the
front room to tell Orrie to come and get on with the day's work, and then
returned to the couch and the *Times*.

10

THE other day I looked up "moot" in the dictionary. The murderer of
James L. Eber had just been convicted, and, discussing it, Wolfe and I had
got onto the question of whether or not a life would have been saved if he
had told Cramer that Saturday morning about Jarrell's gun, and he had
said it was moot, and, though I thought I knew the word well enough, I
went to the dictionary to check. In spite of the fact that I had taken a
position just to give the discussion some spirit, I had to agree with him on
that. It was moot all right, and it still is.

The thirty hours from noon Saturday until six o'clock Sunday afternoon
were not without events, since even a yawn is an event, but nobody seemed
to be getting anywhere, least of all me. Sooon after lunch Saturday, at
Wolfe's table with him and Orrie, Jarrell phoned to tell us the score.
Cramer had gone straight there from our place to join the gathering in the
library. Presumably he hadn't started barking, since even an inspector
doesn't bark at an Otis Jarrell unless he has to, but he had had questions to
which he intended to get answers. Actually he had got only one answered:
had Jarrell hired Nero Wolfe to do something? Yes. Plus its rider: had
Archie Goodwin, alias Alan Green, come as Jarrell's secretary to do the
something Wolfe had been hired for, or to help do it? Yes. That was all.
Jarrell had told them that the something was a personal and confidential

matter, with no bearing on their investigation, and that therefore they could forget it.

It was a cinch Cramer wouldn't forget it, but evidently he decided that for the present he might as well lump it, for there wasn't a peep out of him during those thirty hours.

I could see no point in Alan Green's getting back into the picture, and apparently Jarrell couldn't either, for he also reported that Alan Green was no more. He was telling the family, and also Corey Brigham, who I was and why, but was leaving the why vague. He had engaged the services of Nero Wolfe on a business matter, and Wolfe had sent me there to collect some facts he needed. He was also telling them I wouldn't be back, but on that Wolfe balked. I was going back, and I was staying until further notice. When Jarrell asked what for, Wolfe said to collect facts. When Jarrell asked what facts, Wolfe said facts that he needed. Jarrell, knowing that if I wasn't let in he would soon be letting Cramer in to ask about a gun, had to take it. When Wolfe had hung up and pushed his phone back I had asked him to give me a list of the facts he needed.

"How the devil can I," he demanded, "when I don't know what they are? If something happens I want you there, and with you there it's more likely to happen. Now that they know who you are, you are a threat, a pinch at their nerves, at least for one of them, and he may be impelled to act."

Since it was May it might have been expected that at least some of them would be leaving town for what was left of the week end, and they probably would have if their nerves weren't being pinched. Perhaps Jarrell had told them to stick around, anyway, they were all at the dinner table Saturday. Their attitude toward me, with my own name back, varied. Roger Foote thought it was a hell of a good joke, his asking Wolfe to investigate my past; he couldn't get over it, and didn't. Trella not only couldn't see the joke; she couldn't see me. Her cooing days were over as far as I was concerned. Wyman didn't visibly react one way or another. Susan went out of her way to indicate that she still regarded me as human. In the lounge at cocktail time she actually came up to me as I was mixing a Bloody Mary for Lois, and said she hoped she wouldn't forget and call me Mr. Green.

"I'm afraid," she added, almost smiling, "that my brain should have more cells. It put you and that name, Alan Green, in a cell together, and now it doesn't know what to do."

I told her it didn't matter what she called me as long as it began with G. I hadn't forgotten that she was supposed to be a snake, or that she had been the only one to bid me welcome, or that she had pulled me halfway across a room on an invisible string. That hadn't happened again, but once was enough. I didn't have her tagged yet, not by any means. As a matter of fact, I was a little surprised to see her and Wyman still there, since Jarrell had accused her of swiping his gun before witnesses. Maybe, I thought, they were staying on just to get that detail settled. Her little mouth in her little oval face could have found it hard to smile, not because it was shy but because it was stubborn.

I had supposed there would be bridge after dinner, but no. Jarrell and Trella had tickets for a show, and Wyman and Susan for another show. Nora Kent was going out, destination unspecified. Roger Foote suggested gin for an hour or so, saying that he had to turn in early because he was going to

get up at six in the morning to go to Belmont. I asked what for, since there
was no racing on Sunday, and he said he had to go and look at the horses.
Declining his gin invitation, I approached Lois. There was no point in my
staying in for the evening, since there would be no one there to have their
nerves pinched except Roger, and he was soon going to bed, so I told Lois
that now that my name was changed it would be both possible and agreea-
ble to take her to the Flamingo Club. She may have had no plans because
her week end had been upset, or she may have had plans but took pity on
me, or my charm may simply have been too much for her. Anyhow, we went,
and got home around two o'clock.

On Sunday it looked at first as if I might do fairly well as a threat. Four of
them were at breakfast with me — Wyman, Susan, Lois, and Nora. Jarrell
had already had his and gone out somewhere, Roger had gone to look at
horses, and I gathered that Trella wasn't up yet. But the future didn't look
promising. Nora was going to church and then to the Picasso show at the
Modern Museum, apparently to spend the day. Susan was going to church.
Wyman went to the side terrace with an armload of Sunday papers. So
when Lois said she was going for a walk I said I was too and which way
should I head, away from her or with her? She said we could try with and
see how it worked. I found that she wouldn't walk in the park, probably on
account of squirrels, so we kept to the avenues, Madison and Park. After
half an hour she took a taxi to go have lunch with friends, not named. I was
invited to come along, but thought I had better go and see if there was
anyone around to be threatened. On the way back I phoned Wolfe to tell
him what had happened: nothing. In the reception hall, Steck told me
Jarrell wanted me in the library.

He thought he had news, but I wasn't impressed. He had spent an hour
at the Penguin Club with an old friend, or at least an old acquaintance,
Police Commissioner Kelly, and had been assured that while the district
attorney and the police would do their utmost to bring the murderer of
Jarrell's former secretary to the bar of justice, there would be no officious
prying into Jarrell's private affairs. Respectable citizens deserved to be
treated with respect, and would be. Jarrell said he was going to ring Wolfe
to tell him about it, and I said that would be fine. I didn't add that Wolfe
would be even less impressed than I was. Officious prying would be no
name for it if and when they learned about Jarrell's gun.

Having bought a newspaper of my own on the way back, I went to the
lounge with it, finding no one there, and caught up with the world, including the latest non-news on the Eber murder. There was no mention of the
startling fact that Otis Jarrell's new secretary had turned out to be no other
than Nero Wolfe's man Friday, Saturday, Sunday, Monday, Tuesday,
Wednesday, and Thursday, the celebrated detective, Archie Goodwin. Evidently Cramer and the DA weren't going to give us any free publicity until
and unless we were involved in murder, a typical small-minded attitude of
small men, and it was up to Wolfe's public-relations department, namely
me, to do something about it; and besides, I owed Lon Cohen a bone. So I
went up to my room and phoned him, and wished I hadn't, since he tried to
insist on a hunk of meat with it. I had no sooner hung up than a ring called
me to the green phone. It was Assistant District Attorney Mandelbaum,
who invited me to appear at his office at three o'clock that afternoon for a

little informal chat. I told him I would be delighted, and went down to get some oats, having been informed by Steck that lunch would be at one-thirty.

Lunch wasn't very gay, since there were only three of them there — Jarrell, Wyman, and Susan. Susan said maybe thirty words altogether, as for instance, "Will you have cream, Mr. Goodwin?" When I announced that I would have to leave at two-thirty for an appointment at the district attorney's office, thinking that might pinch a nerve, Wyman merely used a thumb and forefinger to pinch his thin straight nose, whether or not meant as a vulgar insult I couldn't say, and Susan merely said that she supposed talking with an assistant district attorney was nothing for a detective but she would be frightened out of her wits. Jarrell said nothing then, but when we left the table he took me aside and wanted to know. I told him that since the police commissioner had promised that there would be no officious prying into his private affairs there was no problem. I would just tell Mandelbaum that I was part of Mr. Jarrell's private affairs and therefore a clam.

Which I did. Having stopped on the way to phone Wolfe because he always likes to know where I am, I was a little late, arriving in the anteroom at 3:02 p.m., and then I was kept waiting exactly one hour and seventeen minutes. Taken in to Mandelbaum at 4:19, I was in no mood to tell him anything whatever except that he was a little balder and a little plumper than when I had last seen him, but he surprised me. I had expected him to try to bulldoze me, or sugar me, into spilling something about my assignment at Jarrell's, but he didn't touch on that at all. Apparently Jarrell's session with the commissioner had had some effect. After apologizing for keeping me waiting, Mandelbaum wanted to know what I had seen and heard when I entered the studio at noon on Wednesday and found James L. Eber there with Mrs. Wyman Jarrell. Also whether I had seen Eber with anyone else or had heard anyone say anything about him.

Since that was about Eber and his movements and contacts the day before he was killed, I couldn't very well say that I concluded by an acceptable process of reasoning that it was irrelevant, so I obliged. I even gave him verbatim the words that had passed among Eber and Susan and me. He spent some time trying to get me to remember other words, comments that had been made in my hearing about Eber and his appearance there that day, but on that I passed. I had heard a few, chiefly at the lunch table, and had reported them to Wolfe, but none of them had indicated any desire or intention to kill him, and I saw no point in supplying them for the record.

It was for the record. A stenographer was present, and after Mandelbaum finished with me I had another wait while a statement was typed for me to sign. Reading it, I could find nothing that needed changing, so I signed it "Archie Goodwin, alias Alan Green." I thought that might as well be on record too.

Back at my threatening base at twenty minutes to six, I found that bridge was under way in the lounge, but only one table: Jarrell, Trella, Wyman, and Nora. Steck informed me, when asked, that neither Lois nor Roger had returned, and that Mrs. Wyman Jarrell was in the studio. Proceeding down the corridor and finding the studio door open, I entered.

The only light was from the corridor and the television screen. Susan was in the same chair as before, in the same spot. Since she was concentrating on the screen, with the discussion panel, "We're Asking You," it wasn't much of a setup from a professional standpoint, but personally it might be interesting. The conditions were precisely the same as formerly, and I wanted to see. If I felt another trance coming on I could make a dash for the door and safety. Not to cut her view of the screen, I circled behind her chair and took the one on the other side.

I would have liked to look at her, her profile, instead of the screen, giving her magic every chance, but she might have misunderstood, so I kept my eyes on "We're Asking You" clear to the end. I didn't learn much. They were asking what to do about extra-bright children, and since I didn't have any and intended to stay as far away as I could from those I had seen and heard on TV and in the movies, I wasn't concerned.

When they got it settled and the commercial started Susan turned to me. "Shall I leave it on for the news?"

"Sure, might as well, I haven't heard the baseball scores."

I never did hear them, not on that TV set. It was Bill Brundage, the one who has the trick of rolling his eyes up, pretending he's looking for a word, when it's right there in front of him and everybody knows it. I listened with one ear while he gave us the latest on the budget, Secretary Dulles, a couple of Senatorial investigations, and so forth, and then suddenly he got both ears.

"The body of Corey Brigham, well-known socialite and man-about-town, was found this afternoon in a car parked on Thirty-ninth Street near Seventh Avenue. According to the police, he had been shot in the chest. The body was on the floor of the car in front of the rear seat, covered with a rug. It was discovered when a boy saw the toe of a shoe at the edge of the rug and notified a policeman. The windows of the car were closed and there was no gun in the car. Mr. Corey Brigham lived at the Churchill Towers. He was a bachelor and was a familiar figure in society circles and in the amusement world."

Susan's fingers had gripped my arm, with more muscle than I would have guessed she had. Apparently just realizing it, she took her hand back and said, "I beg your pardon." Her voice was low, as always, and Bill Brundage was talking, but I caught it, and that's what she said. I reached across her lap to the chair on the other side and flipped the switch on the control box.

"Corey Brigham?" she said. "He said Corey Brigham, didn't he?"

"He certainly did." I got up, went to the door, turned on lights, and came back. "I'm going to tell Mr. Jarrell. Do you want to come?"

"What?" Her face tilted up. It was shocked. "Oh, of course, tell them. You tell them."

Evidently she wasn't coming, so I left her. Going along the corridor I was thinking that the news might not be news to one of them. It was even possible that it hadn't been news to Susan. At the card table in the lounge they were in the middle of a hand, and I went and stood by until the last trick was raked in.

"I wasted my queen, damn it," Jarrell said. He turned to me. "Anything new, Goodwin?"

"Not from the district attorney," I told him. "Just routine, about the last time I saw Jim Eber — and for me the only time. Now he'll be asking about the last time I saw Corey Brigham. You too. All of you."

I had three of their faces: Jarrell, Trella, and Wyman. Nora was shuffling.

None of them told me anything. There was no point in prolonging it, so I went on. "Something new on TV just now. The body of Corey Brigham has been found in a parked car. Shot. Murdered."

Jarrell said, "Good God. No!" Nora stopped shuffling and her head jerked to me. Trella's blue eyes stretched at me. Wyman said, "You wouldn't be pulling a gag, would you?"

"No gag. Your wife was there, I mean in the studio. She heard it."

Wyman shoved his chair back and was up and gone. Jarrell demanded, "Found in a car? Whose car?"

"I don't know. For what I do know I'll give you the broadcast verbatim. I'm good at that." I did so, not trying to copy Bill Brundage's delivery, just his words. At the end I added, "Now you know all I know."

Trella spoke. "You said he was murdered. That didn't say murder. He might have shot himself."

I shook my head. "No gun in the car."

"Anyway," Nora said, "he wouldn't have got under a rug. If Corey Brigham was going to shoot himself he would do it in the dining room of the Penguin Club." It wasn't as mean as it reads; she was merely stating a fact.

"He had no family," Trella said. "I guess we were his closest friends. Shouldn't you do something, Otis?"

"You don't need me," I said. "I'm sorry I had to break up your game." To Jarrell: "I'll be with Mr. Wolfe, in case."

"No." He was emphatic. "I want you here."

"You'll soon be too busy here to bother with me. First your former secretary, and now your friend Brigham. I'm afraid that calls for officious prying, and I'd rather not be in the way."

I moved, and I didn't mosey. I was surprised that someone hadn't already come, since they had got sufficiently interested in the Jarrells to collect miscellaneous facts and the collection must have included the name of Corey Brigham. The one who came might be Lieutenant Rowcliff—it was his kind of errand; and while I liked nothing better than twisting Rowcliff's ear, I wasn't in the humor for it at the moment. I wanted a word with Wolfe before twisting anybody's ear, even Rowcliff's. So I didn't mosey, leaving the premises, crossing the avenue, and getting a taxi headed downtown.

When I entered the office Wolfe was there alone, no Orrie on Sunday, and one glance at him was enough. He had a book in his hand, with a finger inserted to keep his place, but he wasn't reading, and a good caption for a picture of the face he turned to me would have been *The Gathering Storm*.

"So," I said, crossing to his desk, "I see I don't bring news. You've already heard it."

"I have," he growled. "Where were you?"

"Watching television with Susan. We heard it together. I notified Jarrell and his wife and Wyman and Nora Kent. Lois and Roger Foote weren't there. Nobody screamed. Then I beat it to come and get instructions. If I had stayed I wouldn't have known whether the time has come to let the cat out or not. Do you?"

"No."

"Do you mean you don't know or the time hasn't come?"

"Both."

I swiveled my chair around and sat. "That's impossible. If I said a thing like that you'd say I had a screw loose, only you never use that expression. I'll put it in its simplest terms. Do you wish to speak to Cramer?"

"No. I'll speak to Mr. Cramer only when it is requisite."

The gathering storm had cleared some. "Archie. I'm glad you came. I confess I needed you, to say no to. Now that I have said it, I can read." He opened the book. "I will speak to no one on the phone, and no one will enter my door, until I have more facts." His eyes went to the book and he was reading.

I was glad he was glad I had come, but I wasn't glad, if I make myself clear. I might as well have stayed up there and twisted Rowcliff's ear.

11

I slept in my own bed that night for the first time in nearly a week.

That was a very interesting period, Sunday evening and part of Monday. I suppose you noticed what Wolfe said, that he would see no one and hear no one until he had more facts. Exactly how he thought he would get facts, under the conditions he imposed, seeing or hearing no one, I couldn't say. Maybe by ESP or holding a séance. However, by noon on Monday it had become evident that he hadn't meant it that way. What he had really meant was that he wanted no facts. If he had seen a fact coming he would have shut his eyes, and if he had heard one coming he would have stuck fingers in his ears.

So it was a very interesting period. There he was, a practicing private detective with no other source of income except selling a few orchid plants now and then, with a retainer of ten grand in cash in the safe, with a multi-millionaire client with a bad itch, with a fine fat fee in prospect if he got a move on and did some first-class detecting; and he was afraid to stay in the same room with me for fear I would tell him something. He wouldn't talk with Jarrell on the phone. He wouldn't turn on the radio or television. I even suspected that he didn't read the *Times* Monday morning, though I can't swear to that because he reads the *Times* at breakfast, which is taken up to his room by Fritz on a tray. He was a human ostrich with his head stuck in the sand, in spite of the fact that he resembles an ostrich in physique less than any other human I know of with the possible exception of Jackie Gleason.

All there was to it, he was in a panic. He was scared stiff that any minute a fact might come bouncing in that would force him to send me down to Cramer bearing gifts, and there was practically nothing on earth he wouldn't rather do, even eating ice cream with cantaloupe or putting horseradish on oysters.

I understood how he felt, and I even sympathized with him. On the phone with Jarrell, both Sunday evening and Monday morning, I did my

best to string him along, telling him that Wolfe was sitting tight, which he
was, God knows, and explaining why it was better for me to be out of the
way, at least temporarily. It wasn't too bad. Lieutenant Rowcliff had called
on the Jarrell family, as I had expected, but hadn't been too nasty about the
coincidence that two of Jarrell's associates, his former secretary and a close
friend, had got it within a week. He had been nasty, of course — Rowcliff
would be nasty to Saint Peter if he ever got near him; but he hadn't actually
snarled.

But although I sympathized with Wolfe, I'm not a genius like him, and if
I was sliding into a hole too deep to crawl out of I wanted to know about it
in time to get a haircut and have my pants pressed before my appearance in
the line-up. Of the half a dozen possible facts that could send me over the
edge there was one in particular that I wanted very much to get a line on,
but it wasn't around. None of the newscasts mentioned it, Sunday night or
Monday morning. It wasn't in the Monday morning papers. Lon Cohen
didn't have it. There were four guys — one at headquarters, one on the DA's
staff, and two on Homicide — for whom I had done favors in the past, who
could have had it and who might have obliged me, but with two murders in
the stew it was too risky to ask them.

So I was still factless when, ten minutes before noon, the phone rang and
I got an invitation to call at the DA's office at my earliest convenience. Wolfe
was still up in the plant rooms. He always came down at eleven o'clock, but
hadn't shown that morning — for fear, as I said, that I would tell him
something. I buzzed him on the house phone to tell him where I was going,
went out and walked to Ninth Avenue, and took a taxi to Leonard Street.

That time I was kept waiting only a few minutes before I was taken in to
Mandelbaum. He was polite, as usual, getting to his feet to shake hands. I
was only a private detective, true, but as far as he knew I had committed
neither a felony nor a misdemeanor, and the only way an assistant DA can
get the "assistant" removed from his title is to have it voted off, making it
DA, and I was a voter. The chair for me at the end of his desk was of course
placed so I was facing a window.

What he wanted from me was the same as before, things I had seen and
heard at Jarrell's place, but this time concentrating on Corey Brigham
instead of James L. Eber. I had to concede that that had now become
relevant, and there was more ground to cover since Brigham had been there
for dinner and bridge on Monday, and again on Wednesday, and also I
might have heard comments about him at other times. Mandelbaum was
patient, and thorough, and didn't try to be tricky. He did double back a lot,
but doubling back has been routine for so many centuries that you can't call
it a trick. I didn't mention one of my contacts with Brigham, the conference
at Wolfe's office Friday afternoon, and to my surprise he didn't either. I
would have thought they would have dug that up by now, but apparently
not.

After he told the stenographer to go and type the statement, and she
went, I stood up. "It will take her quite a while," I said. "I have to run a
couple of errands, and I'll drop in later and sign it. If you don't mind."

"Quite all right. Certainly. If you make it today. Say by five o'clock."

"Oh, sure." I turned to go, and turned back, and grinned at him. "By the way, you may have noticed that I didn't live up to my reputation for wisecracks."

"Yes, I noticed that. Maybe you're running out."

"I hope not. I'll do better next time. I guess my mind was too busy with something I had just heard—about the bullets."

"What bullets?"

"Why, the two bullets. Haven't you got that yet? That the bullet that killed Eber and the one that killed Brigham were fired by the same gun?"

"I thought that was—" He stopped. "Where did you hear that?"

I gave him another grin. "I know, it's being saved. Don't worry, I won't slip it out—I may not even tell Mr. Wolfe. But it won't keep long, it's too hot. The guy who told me, it was burning his tongue, and he knows me."

"Who was it? Who told you?"

"I *think* it was Commissioner Kelly. There's a wisecrack, I seem to be recovering. I suppose I shouldn't have mentioned it. Sorry. I'll be in to sign the statement before five." I was going. He called after me, wanting to know who had told me, but I said I couldn't remember, and went.

So the fact was a fact, and I had it. I hadn't risked anything. If it had turned out not to be a fact, and his reaction would have shown it, it could have been that someone had been stringing me, and of course I wouldn't have remembered who. Okay, I had it. If Wolfe had known what I was bringing home with me he would probably have locked himself in his room and not answered the phone, and I would have had to yell through the door.

He had just sat down to lunch—red snapper filets baked in butter and lemon juice and almonds—so I had to hold it. Even without the rule that business was taboo at the table, I wouldn't have had the heart to ruin his meal. But I still might want time to get a haircut and have my pants pressed, so as soon as we had crossed to the office and coffee had been poured I spoke. "I hate to bring it up right after lunch, but I think you ought to know. We're out of the frying pan. We're in the fire. At least that is my opinion."

He usually takes three little sips of coffee at its hottest before putting the cup down, but that time, knowing my tones of voice, he took only two. "Opinion?"

"Yes, sir. It may be only that because it's an inference. For more than an hour Mandelbaum asked me what I had seen and heard from, by, to, and about Corey Brigham. I said I'd drop in later to sign the statement, got up to go, and said something. So you can form your own opinion, I'll give it to you."

I did so. His frown at the start was a double-breasted scowl at the end. He said nothing, he just scowled. It isn't often that his feelings are too strong for words.

"If you want to," I said, "you can be sore at me for fishing it up. If I hadn't worked that on him it would have been another day, possibly two, before you had to face it. But you can be sore and use your mind at the same time, I've seen you, and it looks to me as if a mind is needed. I'm assuming that your opinion is the same as mine."

He snorted. "Opinion? Bah. He might as well have certified it."

"Yes, sir."

"He's a simpleton. He should have known you were gulling him."

"Yes, sir. You can be sore at him."

"Soreness won't help. Nor will it help to use my mind — supposing that I have one. This is disaster. There is only one forlorn issue to raise: whether we should verify it before we act, and if so how."

"If you had been there I doubt if you would think it was necessary. If you could have seen his face when he said 'I thought that was —' and chopped it off."

"No doubt. He's a simpleton."

He flattened his palms on his desk and stared into space. That didn't look promising. It didn't mean he was using his mind; when he uses his mind he leans back and closes his eyes, and when he's hard at it his lips go in and out. So he wasn't working. He was merely getting set to swallow a pill that would taste bad even after it was down and dissolved. It took him a full three minutes.

Then he transferred his palms to the chair arms and spoke. "Very well. Your notebook. A letter to Mr. Jarrell, to be delivered at once by messenger. It might be best to take it yourself, to make sure he gets it without delay."

He took a breath. "Dear Mr. Jarrell. I enclose herewith my check for ten thousand dollars, returning the retainer you paid me in that amount for which I gave you a receipt. My outlay for expenses has not been large and I shall not bill you.

"Paragraph. A circumstance has transpired which makes it necessary for me to report to the proper authority some of the information I have acquired while acting on your behalf, particularly the disappearance of your Bowdoin thirty-eight revolver. Not being at liberty to specify the circumstance, I will say only that it compels me to take this step in spite of my strong inclination against it. I shall take it later this afternoon, after you have received this letter and the enclosure.

"Paragraph. I assume, naturally, that in this situation you will no longer desire my services and that our association ceases forthwith. In the unlikely event that you —"

He stopped short and I raised my eyes from the notebook. His lips were clamped tight and a muscle at the side of his neck was twitching. He was having a fit.

"No," he said. "I will not. Tear it up."

I hadn't cared much for it myself. I put the pen down, ripped two pages from the notebook, tore them across three times, and dropped them in the wastebasket.

"Get Mr. Cramer," he said.

I cared for that even less. Apparently he had decided it was too ticklish to wait even a few hours and was going to let go even before notifying the client. Of course that wasn't unethical, with two murders sizzling, but it was rather unindomitable. I would have liked to take a stand, but in the first place he was in no mood for one of my stands, and in the second place the only alternative was the letter to Jarrell and that had been torn up. So I got Cramer, who, judging from his tone, was in a mood too. He told Wolfe he could give him a minute.

"That may do," Wolfe said. "You may remember our conversation Saturday. Day before yesterday."

"Yeah, I remember it. What about it?"

"I said then that if I have reason to think I have information relevant to the crime you're investigating I am bound to give it to you. I now suspect that I have such information but I want to make sure. To do so I must proceed on the basis of knowledge that has come to me in a peculiar manner and I don't know if I can rely on it. Mr. Goodwin has learned, or thinks he has, that the markings on the bullet which killed Corey Brigham have been compared with those on the bullet which killed James L. Eber, and that they are identical. I can proceed to verify my suspicion only if I accept that as established, and I decided to consult you. Do you advise me to proceed?"

"By God," Cramer said.

"I'm afraid," Wolfe objected, "that I need something more explicit."

"Go to hell and get it there," Cramer advised. "I know where Goodwin got it, from that damn fool at Leonard Street. He wanted us to find out who had leaked it to Goodwin, and we wanted to know exactly what Goodwin had said, and he told us, and we told him if he wanted to know who leaked it to Goodwin just look in a mirror. And now you've got the gall to ask me to verify it. By God. If you've got relevant information about a murder you know where it belongs."

"I do indeed. And I'll soon know whether I have it or not if I proceed on the basis of Mr. Goodwin's news. If and when I have it you'll get it without undue delay. Do you advise me to proceed?"

"Look, Wolfe. Are you listening?"

"Yes, I'm listening."

"Okay, you want my advice. Here it is. Get the written permission of the police commissioner and the mayor too, and then proceed all you want to."

He hung up.

I did too, and swiveled, and spoke. "So that's settled. It was the same gun. And in spite of it, Jarrell's private affairs are still private, or we'd be downtown right now, both of us, and wouldn't get home for dinner. By the way, I apologize. I thought you were going to cough it up."

"I am, confound it. I'll have to. But not until I get the satisfaction of a gesture. Get Mr. Jarrell."

"Where he can talk?"

"Yes."

That took a little doing. Nora Kent answered and said he was on another phone, long distance, and also someone was with him and I told her to have him call Wolfe for a private conversation as soon as possible. While we waited Wolfe looked around for something to take his mind off his misery, settled on the big globe, and got up and walked over to it. Presumably he was picking a spot to head for, some remote island or one of the poles, if he decided to lam. When the phone rang and I told him it was Jarrell he took his time getting to it.

"Mr. Jarrell? I have in my hand a letter which Mr. Goodwin has just typed, dictated by me, which I intended to send you at once by messenger, but on second thought I'm going to read it to you first. Here it is."

He read it. My notes were in the wastebasket, but my memory is good too, and not a word was changed. It was just as he had dictated it. He even finished the last sentence, which he had left hanging: "'In the unlikely event that you wish me to continue to act for you, let me know at once. Sincerely.' That's the letter. It occurs to me —"

"You can't do that! What's the circumstance?"

"No, sir. As I said in the letter, I'm not at liberty to reveal it, at least not in a letter, and certainly not on the telephone. But it occurs —"

"Get this straight, Wolfe. If you give anybody information about my private affairs that you got working for me in a confidential capacity, you'll be sorry for it as long as you live!"

"I'm already sorry. I'm sorry I ever saw you, Mr. Jarrell. Let me finish, please. It occurs to me that there is a chance, however slim, that a reason can be found for ignoring the circumstance. I doubt it, but I'm willing to try. When I dictated the letter I intended to ask Mr. Cramer to visit me here at six o'clock, three hours from now. I'll postpone it on one condition, that you come at that hour and bring with you everyone who was here on Friday —except Mr. Brigham, who is dead —with the —"

"What for? What good will that do?"

"If you'll let me finish. With the understanding that you stay, all of you, until I am ready to adjourn, and that I will insist on answers to any questions I ask. I can't compel answers, but I can insist, and I may learn more from refusals to answer than from the answers I get. That's the condition. Will you come?"

"What do you want to ask about? They have already told you they didn't take my gun!"

"And you have told me that you know your daughter-in-law took it. Anyway, one of them lied, and I told them so. You'll know what I want to ask about when you hear me. Will you come?"

He balked for another five minutes, among other things demanding to know what the circumstance was that had made Wolfe write the letter, but only because he was used to being at the other end of the whip and it was a new experience for him. He had no choice and he knew it.

Wolfe hung up, shook his head like a bull trying to chase a fly, and rang for beer.

12

WOLFE started it off with a bang. He surveyed them with the air of a judge about to impose a stiff one, and spoke, in a tone that was meant to be offensive and succeeded.

"There is nothing to be crafty about so I won't try. When you were here on Friday my main purpose was to learn which of you had taken Mr. Jarrell's gun; today it is to learn which of you used it to kill Mr. Eber and Mr. Brigham. I am convinced that one of you did. First I'll —Don't interrupt me!"

He glared at Jarrell, but it was more the voice than the glare that stopped Jarrell with only two words out. Wolfe doesn't often bellow, and almost never at anyone but Cramer or me, but when he does he means it. Having corked the client, who was in the red leather chair, he gave the others the glare. In front were Susan, Wyman, Trella, and Lois, as before. With Brigham no longer available and me back where I belonged, there were only two in the rear, Nora Kent and Roger Foote.

"I will not be interrupted." It was as positive as the bellow, though not so loud. "I have no more patience for you people—including you, Mr. Jarrell. Especially you. First I'll explain why I am convinced that one of you is a murderer. To do so I'll have to disclose a fact that the police have discovered but are keeping to themselves. If they learn that I've told you about it and are annoyed, then they'll be annoyed. I am past regard for trivialities. The fact is that the bullets that killed Eber and Brigham came from the same gun. That, Mr. Jarrell, is the circumstance I spoke of on the phone."

"How do—"

"Don't interrupt. The technical basis of the fact is of course a comparison of the bullets in the police laboratory. How I learned it is not material. So much for the fact; now for my conclusion from it. The bullets are thirty-eights; the gun that was taken from Mr. Jarrell's desk was a thirty-eight. On Friday I appealed to all of you to help me find Mr. Jarrell's gun, and told you how, if it was innocent, it could be recovered with no stigma for anyone. Surely, if it was innocent, one of you would have acted on that appeal, but you didn't, and it was therefore a permissible conjecture that the gun had been used to kill Eber but only a conjecture. Now it is no longer a conjecture; it has reached that status of a reasonable assumption. For Brigham was killed by a bullet from the gun that killed Eber, and those two men were both closely associated with you people. Eber lived with you for five years, and Brigham was in your familiar circle. Not only that, they were both concerned in the matter which I was hired to investigate one week ago today, the matter which took Mr. Goodwin there—"

"That'll do! You know what—"

"Don't interrupt!" It was close to a bellow again. "The matter which took Mr. Goodwin there under another name. I need not unfold that mattter; enough that it was both grave and exigent, and that both Eber and Brigham were involved in it. So consider a hypothesis: that those two men were killed by some outsider with his own private motive, and it is merely a chain of coincidences that they were both in your circle, that the gun was the same caliber as Mr. Jarrell's, that Mr. Jarrell's gun was taken by one of you the day before Eber was killed , and that in spite of my appeal the gun has not been found. If you can swallow that hypothesis, I can't. I reject it, and I conclude that one of you is a murderer. That is our starting point."

"Just a minute." It was Wyman. His thin nose looked thinner, and the deep creases in his brow looked deeper. "That may be your starting point, but it's not mine. Your man Goodwin was there. What for? All this racket about a stolen gun—what if he took it? That's your kind of stunt, and his too, and of course my father was in on it. That's *my* starting point."

Wolfe didn't waste a bellow on him. He merely shook his head. "No, sir. Apparently you don't know what you're here for. You're here to give me a chance to wriggle out of a predicament. I am desperate. I dislike acting under compulsion in any case, and I abominate being obliged to divulge information about a client's affairs that I have received in confidence. The starting point is my conclusion that one of you is a murderer, not to go on from there to identify the culprit and expose him — that isn't what I was hired for — but to show you the fix I'm in. What I desperately need is not sanction for my conclusion, but plausible ground for rejecting it. I want to impeach it. As for your notion that Mr. Goodwin took the gun, in a stratagem devised by me with your father's knowledge, that is mere drivel and is no credit to your wit. If it had happened that way I would be in no predicament at all; I would produce the gun myself, demonstrate its innocence, and have a good night's sleep."

"If death ever slept," Lois blurted.

Their heads all turned to her. Not, probably, that they expected her to supply anything helpful; they were glad to have an excuse to take their eyes off Wolfe and relieve the strain. They hadn't been exchanging glances. Apparently no one felt like meeting other eyes.

"That's all," Lois said. "What are you all looking at me for? That just came out."

The heads went back to Wolfe. Trella asked, "Am I dumb? Or did you say you want us to prove you're wrong?"

"That's one way of putting it, Mrs. Jarrell. Yes."

"How do we prove it?"

Wolfe nodded. "That's the difficulty. I don't expect you to prove a negative. The simplest way would be to produce the gun, but I've abandoned hope of that. I don't intend to go through the dreary routine of inquiry on opportunity; that would take all night, and checking your answers would take an army a week, and I have no army. But I have gathered from the public reports that Eber died between two o'clock and six o'clock Thursday afternoon, and Brigham died between ten o'clock Sunday morning and three o'clock that afternoon, so it may be possible to exclude one or more of you. Has anyone an alibi for either of those periods?"

"You've stretched the periods," Roger Foote declared. "It's three to five Thursday and eleven to two Sunday."

"I gave the extremes, Mr. Foote. The extremes are the safest. You seem well informed."

"My God, I ought to be. The cops."

"No doubt. You'll soon see much more of them if we don't discredit my conclusion."

"You can start by excluding me," Otis Jarrell said. "Thursday afternoon I had business appointments, three of them, and got home a little before six. Sunday —"

"Were the appointments all at the same place?"

"No. One downtown and two midtown. Sunday morning I was with the police commissioner at the Penguin Club for an hour, from ten-thirty to eleven-thirty, went straight home, was in my library until lunch time at one-thirty, returned to the library and was there until five o'clock. So you can exclude me."

"Pfui." Wolfe was disgusted. "You can't be as fatuous as you sound, Mr. Jarrell. Your Thursday is hopeless, and your Sunday isn't much better. Not only were you loose between the Penguin Club and your home, but what about the library? Were you alone there?"

"Most of the time, yes. But if I had gone out I would have been seen."

"Nonsense. Is there a rear entrance to your premises?"

"There's a service entrance."

"Then it isn't even worth discussing. A man with your talents and your money, resolved on murder, could certainly devise a way of getting down to the ground without exposure." Wolfe's head moved. "When I invited exclusion by alibis I didn't mean to court inanities. Can any of you furnish invulnerable proof that you must be eliminated for either of those periods?"

"On Sunday," Roger Foote said, "I went to Belmont to look at horses. I got there at nine o'clock and didn't leave until after five."

"With company? Continuously?"

"No. I was always in sight of somebody, but a lot of different people."

"Then you're no better off than Mr. Jarrell. Does anyone else want to try, now that you know the requirements?"

Apparently nobody did. Wyman and Susan, who were holding hands, looked at each other but said nothing. Trella turned around to look at her brother and muttered something I didn't catch. Lois just sat, and so did Jarrell.

Then Nora Kent spoke. "I want to say something, Mr. Wolfe."

"Go ahead, Miss Kent. You can't make it any worse."

"I'd like to make it better — for me. If you're making an exception of me you haven't said so, and I think you should. I think you should tell them that I came to see you Friday afternoon and what I said."

"You tell them. I'll listen."

But she kept focused on him. "I came right after lunch on Friday. I told you that I had recognized the new secretary as Archie Goodwin as soon as I saw him, and I asked why you had sent him, and whether Mr. Jarrell had hired you or someone else had. I told you that the murder of Jim Eber had made me think I had better try to find out what the situation was. I told you I had discovered that Mr. Jarrell's gun was missing from the drawer of his desk, and that I had just found out that the caliber of the bullet that killed Jim Eber was the same as Mr. Jarrell's gun. I told you that I wasn't frightened, but I didn't want to just wait and see what happened, and I wanted to hire you to protect my interests and pay you a retainer. Is that correct?"

"It is indeed, madam. And well reported. And?"

"And I wanted Mr. Jarrell to know. I wanted them all to know. And I wanted to be sure that you hadn't forgotten."

"You may be. And?"

"And I wanted it on the record. I don't think they're going to discredit your conclusion. I think you're going to tell the police about the gun, and I know what will happen then. I would appreciate it if you'll tell them that I came to see you Friday and what I said. I'll tell them myself, of course, but I wish you would. I'm not frightened, but —"

Jarrell had been controlling himself. Now he exploded. "Damn you, Nora! You saw Wolfe Friday, three days ago? And didn't tell me?"

She sent the gray eyes at him. "Don't yell at me, Mr. Jarrell. I won't have you yelling at me, not even now. Will you tell the police, Mr. Wolfe?"

"I will if I see them, Miss Kent, and I agree with you, reluctantly, that I'm probably going to." He took in the audience. "There is a third period, a brief one, which I haven't mentioned, because we covered it on Friday — from six to six-thirty Wednesday afternoon, when the gun was taken. None of you was excluded from that, either, not even Mr. Brigham, but he is now." He went to Jarrell. "I bring that up, sir, because you stated explicitly that your daughter-in-law took the gun, but you admitted that you had no proof. Have you any now?"

"No. Proof that you would accept, no."

"Have you proof that anyone would accept?"

"Certainly he hasn't." It was Wyman. He was looking, not at Wolfe, but at his father. But he said "he," not "you," though he was looking at him. "And now it's a little too much. Now it may not be just taking a gun, it may be killing two men with it. Of course he has no proof. He hates her, that's all. He wants to smear her. He made passes at her, he kept it up for a year, and she wouldn't let him touch her, and so he hates her. That's all there is to it."

Wolfe made a face. "Mrs. Jarrell. You heard what your husband said?"

Susan nodded, just perceptibly. "Yes, I heard."

"Is is true?"

"Yes. I don't want —" She closed her mouth and opened it again. "Yes, it's true."

Wolfe's head jerked left. "Mr. Jarrell. Did you make improper advances to your son's wife?"

"No!"

Wyman looked straight at his father and said distinctly, "You're a liar."

"Oh, my God," Trella said. "This is fine. This is wonderful."

If I know any man who doesn't need feeling sorry for it's Nero Wolfe, but I came close to it then. After all the trouble he had taken to get them there to help him out of his predicament, they had turned his office into a laundromat for washing dirty linen.

He turned and snapped at me, "Archie, draw a check to Mr. Jarrell for ten thousand dollars." As I got up and went to the safe for the checkbook he snapped at them, "Then it's hopeless. I was afraid it would be, but it was worth trying. I admit I made the effort chiefly for the sake of my own self-esteem, but also I felt that you deserved this last chance, at least some of you. Now you're all in for it, and one of you is doomed. Mr. Jarrell, you don't want me any more, and heaven knows I don't want you. Some of Mr. Goodwin's things are up there in the room he occupied, and he'll send or go for them. The check, Archie?"

I gave it to him, he signed it, and I went to hand it to Jarrell. I had to go to the far side of the red leather chair to keep from being bumped by Wolfe, who was on his way out and who needs plenty of room whether at rest or in motion. Jarrell was saying something, but Wolfe ignored it and kept going.

They left in a bunch, not a lively bunch. I accompanied them to the hall, and opened the door, but no one paid any attention to me except Lois, who offered a hand and frowned at me — not a hostile frown, but the kind you use instead of a smile when you are out of smiles for reasons beyond your control. I frowned back to show that there was no hard feeling as far as she was concerned.

I watched them down the stoop to the sidewalk through the one-way glass panel, and when I got back to the office Wolfe was there behind his desk. As I crossed to mine he growled at me, "Get Mr. Cramer."

"You're riled," I told him. "It might be a good idea to count ten first."

"No. Get him."

I sat and dialed WA 9-8241, Manhattan Homicide West, asked for Inspector Cramer, and got Sergeant Purley Stebbins. He said Cramer was in conference downtown and not approachable. I asked how soon he would be, and Purley said he didn't know and what did I want.

Wolfe got impatient and picked up his receiver. "Mr. Stebbins? Nero Wolfe. Please tell Mr. Cramer that I shall greatly appreciate it if he will call on me this evening at half past nine — or, failing that, as soon as his convenience will permit. Tell him I have important information for him regarding the Eber and Brigham murders. . . . No, I'm sorry, but it must be Mr. Cramer. . . . I know you are, but if you come without Mr. Cramer you will not be admitted. With him you will be welcome. . . . As soon as he can make it, then."

As I hung up I spoke. "One thing, anyhow, there is no longer —"

I stopped becase I had turned and seen that he had leaned back and shut his eyes, and his lips had started to go in and out. He was certainly desperate. It was only fifteen minutes until dinner time.

13

I would say that Inspector Cramer and Sergeant Stebbins weigh about the same, around one-ninety, and little or none of it is fat on either of them, so you would suppose their figures would pretty well match, but they don't. Cramer's flesh is tightweave and Stebbins' is loose-weave. On Cramer's hands the skin follows the line of the bones, whereas on Stebbins' hands you have to take the bones for granted, and presumably they are like that all over, though I have never played with them on the beach and so can't swear to it. I'm not sure which of them would be the toughest to tangle with, but some day I may find out, even if they are officers of the law.

That was not the day, that Monday evening. They were there by invitation, to get a handout, and after greeting Wolfe and sitting — Cramer in the red leather chair and Purley near him, against the wall, on a yelllow one — they wore expressions that were almost neighborly. Almost. Cramer even tried to be jovial. He asked Wolfe how he was making out with his acceptable process of reason.

"Not at all," Wolfe said. He had swiveled to face them and wasn't trying to look or sound cordial. "My reason has ceased to function. It has been swamped in a deluge of circumstance. My phone call, to tell you that I have information for you, was dictated not by reason but by misfortune. I am sunk and I am sour. I just returned a retainer of ten thousand dollars to a client. Otis Jarrell. I have no client."

You might have expected Cramer's keen gray eyes to show a gleam of glee, but they didn't. He would swallow anything that Wolfe offered only after sending it to the laboratory for the works. "That's too bad," he rumbled. "Bad for you but good for me. I can always use information. About Eber and Brigham, you said."

Wolfe nodded. "I've had it for some time, but it was only today, a few hours ago, that I was forced to acknowledge the obligation to disclose it. It concerns an event that occurred at Mr. Jarrell's home last Wednesday, witnessed by Mr. Goodwin, who reported it to me. Before I tell you about it I need answers to a question or two. I understand that you learned from Mr. Jarrell that he had hired me for a job, and that it was on that job that Mr. Goodwin went there as his secretary under another name. I also understand that he declines to tell you what the job was, on the ground that it was personal and confidential and has no relation to your inquiry; and that the police commissioner and the district attorney have accepted his position. That you have been obliged to concur is obvious, since you haven't been pestering Mr. Goodwin and me. Is that correct?"

"It's correct that I haven't been pestering you. The rest, what you understand, I can't help what you understand."

"But you don't challenge it. I understand that too. I only wanted to make it clear why I intend to tell you nothing about the job Mr. Jarrell hired me for, though he is no longer my client. I assume that the police commissioner and the district attorney wouldn't want me to, and I don't care to offend them. Another question, before I—yes, Mr. Stebbins?"

Purley hadn't said a word. He had merely snarled a little. He set his jaw.

Wolfe resumed to Cramer. "Another question. It's possible that my piece of information is bootless because your attention is elsewhere. If so, I prefer not to disclose it. Have you arrested anyone for either murder?"

"No."

"Have you passable grounds for suspicion of anyone outside of the Jarrell family?"

"No."

"Now a multiple question which can be resolved into one. I need to know if any discovered fact, not published, renders my information pointless. Was someone, presumably the murderer, not yet identified, seen entering or leaving the building where Eber lived on Thursday afternoon? The same for Brigham. According to published accounts, it is assumed that someone was with him in the back seat of his car, which was parked at some spot not under observation, that the someone shot him, covered the body with the rug, drove the car to Thirty-ninth Street near Seventh Avenue, from where the subway was easily and quickly accessible, parked the car, and decamped. Is that still the assumption? Has anyone been found who saw the car, either en route or while being parked, and can describe the driver? To resolve them into one: Have you any promising basis for inquiry that has not been published?"

Cramer grunted. "You don't want much, do you? You'd better have something. The answer to the question is no. Now let's hear it."

"When I'm ready. I am merely taking every advisable precaution. My information carries the strong probability that the two murders were committed by Otis Jarrell, his wife, Wyman Jarrell, his wife, Lois Jarrell, Nora Kent, or Roger Foote. Or two or more of them in conspiracy. So another question. Do you know anything that removes any of those people from suspicion?"

"No." Cramer's eyes had narrowed. "So that's what it's like. No wonder you got from under. No wonder you gave him back his retainer. Let's have it."

"When I'm ready," Wolfe repeated. "I want something in return. I want a cushion for my chagrin. You will be more than satisfied with what I give you, and you will not begrudge me a crumb of satisfaction for myself. After I give you my information I want some from you. I want a complete report of the movements of the seven people I named, and I want the report to cover a considerable period: from two o'clock Thursday afternoon to three o'clock Sunday afternoon. I want to know everywhere they went, with an indication of what has been verified by your staff and what has not. I'm not asking for—"

"Save it," Cramer rasped. "You asking! You're in a hell of a position to ask. You've been withholding material evidence, and it's got too hot for you and you've got to let go. Okay, let go!"

He might not have spoken as far as Wolfe was concerned. He took up where he left off. "I'm not asking for much. You already have some of that and will now be getting the rest of it, and all you need to do is let Mr. Goodwin copy the reports of their movements. That will reveal no departmental secrets, and that's all I want. I'm not haggling. If you refuse my request you'll get what you came for anyway; I have no choice. I make the request in advance only because as soon as I give you the information you'll be leaving. You'll have urgent business and you wouldn't wait to hear me. Will you oblige me?"

"I'll see. I'll consider it. Come on, spill it."

Wolfe turned to me. "Archie?"

Since I had been instructed I didn't have to ask him what to spill. I was to tell the truth, the whole truth, and nothing but the truth about the gun, and that was all. I did so, beginning with Jarrell dashing into my room at 6:20 Wednesday afternoon, and ending twenty-four hours later in Wolfe's office, with my report to him. When I finished Purley was on the edge of his chair, his jaw clamped, looking holes through me. Cramer was looking at Wolfe.

"Goddamn you," he said. "Four days. You've had this four days."

"Goodwin's had it five days," Purley said.

"Yeah." Cramer transferred to me. "Okay, go on."

I shook my head. "I'm through."

"Like hell you're through. You'll be surprised. If you—"

"Mr. Cramer," Wolfe cut in. "Now that you have it, use it. Railing at us won't help any. If you think a charge of obstructing justice will hold, get a warrant, but I advise against it. I think you'd regret it. As soon as the possibility became a probability I acted. And when it was merely a possibility I explored it. I had them all here, on Friday, including Mr. Brigham, and told them that the gun must be produced. Yesterday, when the news came about Brigham, it was touch and go. Today, when Mr. Goodwin learned about the bullets, it became highly probable, but I felt that I owed my client at least a gesture, and I had them here again. It was fruitless. I repaid Mr. Jarrell's retainer, dismissed them, and phoned you. I will not be squawked at. I have endured enough. Either get a warrant, or forget me and go to work on it."

"Four days," Cramer said. "When I think what we've been doing those four days. What are you hanging onto? What else have you got? Which one was it?"

"No, sir. If I had known that I would have called you here, not to give it up but to deliver a murderer. I would have been exalted, not mortified. I haven't the slightest notion."

"It was Jarrell himself. It was Jarrell, and he was your client, and you cut him loose, but you wouldn't deliver him on account of your goddamn pride."

Wolfe turned. "Archie. How much cash is in the safe?"

"Thirty-seven hundred dollars in the reserve and around two hundred in petty."

"Bring me three thousand."

I went and opened the door of the safe, unlocked the cash drawer and opened it, counted three grand from the reserve stack, and stepped to Wolfe's desk and handed it to him. With it in his fist he faced Cramer.

"The wager is that when this is over and the facts are known you will acknowledge that at this hour, Monday evening, I had no inkling of the identity of the murderer, except that I had surmised that it was one of the seven people I have named, and I have told you that. Three thousand dollars to three dollars. One thousand to one. You have three dollars? Mr. Stebbins can hold the stakes."

Cramer looked at Stebbins. Purley grunted. Cramer looked at me. I grinned and said, "For God's sake grab it. A thousand to one? Give me that odds and I'll bet you I did it myself."

"That's not as funny as you think it is, Goodwin. You could have." Cramer looked at Wolfe. "You know I know you. You know I never yet saw you open a bag and shake it out without hanging onto a corner that had something in it you were saving for yourself. If you're backing clear out, if you've got no client and no fee in sight, why do you want the reports on their movements from two o'clock Thursday to three o'clock Sunday?"

"To exercise my brain." Wolfe put the stack of bills on the desk and put a paperweight—a chunk of jade that a woman had once used to crack her husband's skull—on top. "It needs it, heaven knows. As I said, I want a crumb of satisfaction for myself. Do you believe in words of honor?"

"I do when the honor is there."

"Am I a man of honor?"

Cramer's eyes widened. He was flabbergasted. He started to answer and stopped. He had to consider. "You may be, at that," he allowed. "You're tricky, you're foxy, you're the best liar I know, but if anybody asked me to name something you had done that was dishonorable I'd have to think."

"Very well, think."

"Skip it. Say you're a man of honor. What about it?"

"Regarding the reports I have asked for, to exercise my brain on. I give you my word of honor that I have no knowledge, withheld from you, which can be applied to those reports; that when I inspect them I'll have no relevant facts that you don't have."

"That *sounds* good." Cramer stood up. "I was going home, and now this. I've heard you sound good before. Who's at my desk, Purley? Rowcliff?"

"Yes, sir." Stebbins was up too.

"Okay, let's get started. Come on, Goodwin, get your hat if you've got one big enough."

I knew that was coming. It would probably go on all night, and my style would be cramped because if they got exasperated Wolfe wouldn't get the reports to exercise his brain on. I didn't even remark that I didn't wear a hat when I went slumming.

14

THAT was twenty minutes past ten Monday night. At six o'clock Wednesday afternoon, when Wolfe came down from the plant rooms, I had just finished typing the last of the time-tables and had them ready for him.

It had taken that long to fill his order, for three reasons. First, the city and county employes hadn't got started on the trails of the Jarrells until Tuesday morning, and each of the subjects was given two sittings before Cramer got the results. Second, Cramer didn't decide until Wednesday noon that he would let Wolfe have it, though I had known darned well he would, since it included nothing he wanted to save, and since he was curious to see what Wolfe wanted with it. And third, after I had been given permission to look at a selected collection of the reports, it took quite a job of digging to get what Wolfe wanted, not to mention my own contributions and the typing after I got home.

I can't tell you what Wolfe did Tuesday and Wednesday because I wasn't there to see, but if you assume that he did nothing whatever I won't argue — that is, nothing but eat, sleep, read, drink beer, and play with orchids. As for me, I was busy. Monday night they kept me at 20th Street — Rowcliff and a Sergeant Coffey — until four o'clock in the morning, going over it back and forth and across and up and down, and when they got through they knew every bit as much as Cramer and Stebbins had already known when they took me down. Rowcliff could not believe that he wasn't smart enough to maneuver me into leaking what I was at Jarrell's for, and I didn't dare to make it clear to him in words he would understand for fear he might see to it that Wolfe didn't get what he wanted for brain exercise. So daylight was trying to break through at my windows when I turned in.

And Tuesday at noon, when I had just started on my fourth griddle cake and my second cup of coffee, the phone rang to tell me that I would be welcome at the DA's office in twenty minutes. I made it in forty, and was there five solid hours, one of them with the DA himself present, and at the end they knew everything that Rowcliff did. There was one little spot where the chances looked good for my getting booked as a material witness, but I bumped through it without having to yell for help.

My intention was, if and when I left Leonard Street a free man, to stop in at Homicide West to see if Cramer had decided to let me look at the reports, but I was interrupted. After finally being dismissed by Mandelbaum, as I was on my way down the hall from his room to the front, a door on the right opened and one of the three best dancers I had ever stepped with came out. Seeing me, she stopped.

"Oh," she said. "Hello."

An assistant DA named Riley, having opened the door for her, was there shutting it. He saw me, thought he would say something, decided not to, and closed the door. The look Lois was giving me was not an invitation to dance, far from it.

"So," she said, "you've made it nice for us, you and your fat boss."

"Then don't speak to me," I told her. "Give me an icy stare and flounce out. As for making it nice for you, wrong address. We held on till the last possible tenth of a second."

"Hooray for you. Our hero." We were moving down the hall. "Where are you bound for?"

"Home, with a stopover."

We were in the anteroom, with people there on chairs. She waited until we were in the outer hall to say, "I think I want to ask you something. If we go where we can get a drink, by the time we get there I'll know."

I looked at my wrist. Ten minutes to six. We no longer had a client to be billed for expenses, but there was a chance she would contribute something useful for the timetables, and besides, looking at her was a pleasant change after the five hours I had just spent. So I said I'd be glad to buy her a drink whether she decided to ask me something or not.

I took her to Mohan's, which was in walking distance around the corner, found an empty booth at the far end, and ordered. When the drinks came she took a sip of her Bloody Mary, made a face, took a bigger sip, and put the glass down.

"I've decided to ask you," she said. "I ought to wait until I've had a couple because my nerves have gone back on me. When I saw you there in the hall my knees were shaking."

"After you saw me or before?"

"They were already shaking. I knew I'd have to tell about it, I knew that yesterday, but I was afraid nobody would believe me. That's what I want to ask you, I want you to back me up and then they'll have to believe me. You see, I know that nobody used my father's gun to kill Jim Eber and Corey Brigham. I want you to say you were with me when I threw it in the river."

I raised my brows. "That's quite a want. God knows what you might have wanted if you waited till you had a couple. You threw your father's gun in the river?"

"Yes." She was making her eyes meet mine. "Yes, I did."

"When?"

"Thursday morning. That's how I know nobody could have used it, because Jim was killed Thursday afternoon. I got it the day before, Wednesday, you know how I got it, going in with that rug held up in front of me. I hid it—"

"How did you open the library door?"

"I had a key. Jim Eber let me have a duplicate made from his—about a year ago. Jim was rather warm on me for a while. I hid the gun in my room, under the mattress. Then I was afraid Dad might have the whole place searched and it would be found, so I got rid of it. Don't you want to know why I took it?"

"Sure, that would help."

"I took it because I was afraid something might happen. I knew how Dad felt about Susan, and I knew it was getting worse every day between him and Wyman, and I knew he had a gun in his drawer, and I hate guns anyway. I didn't think any one thing—I didn't think he would shoot Susan or Wyman would shoot him—I just thought something might happen. So Thursday morning I put it in my bag and went and got my car, and drove up the West Side Highway and onto George Washington Bridge, and stopped on the bridge and threw the gun in the river."

She finished the drink and put the glass down. "Naturally I never intended to tell anybody. Friday morning, when the news came that Jim Eber had been shot, it never occurred to me that that had anything to do with Dad's gun. How could it, when I knew Dad's gun was in the river? Then that afternoon at Nero Wolfe's office I saw how wrong I was. What he suggested, that whoever took the gun should put it out in sight somewhere, naturally I would have done that if I could—but I was afraid that if I told what I had done no one would believe me. It would sound like I was just trying to explain it away. Could I have a refill?"

I caught the waiter's eye and gave him the sign.

She carried on. "Then Sunday, the news about Corey Brigham—of course that made it worse. And then yesterday, with Nero Wolfe again—you know how that was. And all day today, detectives and district attorneys with all of us—they were there all morning, and we have been at the district attorney's office all afternoon, in separate rooms. Now I have to tell about it, I know that, but I don't think they'll believe me. I'm sure they won't. But they will if you say you went with me and saw me throw it in the river."

The waiter was coming with the refills, and I waited until he had gone.

"You left out something," I told her. "You left out about hiring a crew of divers to search the river bottom and offering a trip to Hollywood and ten thousand dollars in cash to the one who found the gun."

She surveyed me. "Are you being droll?"

"Not very. But that would give it color and would stand up just as well. Since you've been answering questions all day, I suppose you have accounted for your movements Thursday morning. What did you tell them?"

She nodded. "I'll have to admit I lied, I know that. I told them that after breakfast I was on the terrace until about half past eleven, and then I went shopping, and then I went to lunch on the *Bolivar*. Now I'll have to admit I didn't go shopping."

"Where did you tell them you went?"

"To three shoe shops."

"Did you name the shops?"

"Yes. They asked. Zussman's, and Yorio's, and Weeden's."

"Did you buy any shoes?"

"Yes, I—" She chopped it off. "Of course not, if I wasn't there. How could I?"

I shook my head at her. "Drink up. What was the name of the girl who hung onto the clapper so the bell couldn't ring, or was it a boy?"

"Damn it, don't be droll!"

"I'm not. You are. Beyond remarking that they'll check at those three shops, and that if you tried that mess on them they'd find that you didn't get your car from the garage that morning, there's no point in listing the dozen or so other holes. I should be sore at you for thinking I could be sap enough to play with you, but you meant well, and it's a tough trick to be both noble and nimble. So drink up and forget it — unless you want to tell me who *did* take the gun. Do you know?"

"Of course I don't!"

"Just protecting the whole bunch, including Nora?"

"I'm not protecting anybody! I just want this awful business to stop!" She touched my hand with fingertips. "Archie. So I made a mess of it, but it wouldn't be a mess if you would help me work it out. We could have done it Wednesday night. We didn't take my car, we took a taxi — or we walked to the East River and threw it in. Won't you help me?"

And there you are. What if I had lost sight of basic facts? The circumstances had been favorable. When I first saw her Monday afternoon on the terrace, as she approached with the sun full on her, I had realized that no alterations were needed anywhere, from the top of her head clear down to her toes. Talking with her, I had realized that she was fine company. At Colonna's Tuesday evening I had realized that she was good to be close to. Not to mention that by the time I was too old to provide properly for the family her father would have died and left her a mint. What if I had lost my head, made a supreme effort, rushed her off her feet, and wrapped her up? I would now be stuck with a female who got so rattled in a pinch that she thought she could sidetrack a murder investigation with a plant so half-baked it was pathetic. There you are.

But she meant well, so I let her down easy, paid for the drinks without entering it on my expense pad, helped her into a taxi, and had no hard feelings as I took another one, to 20th Street.

Nothing doing on the reports. Neither Cramer nor Stebbins was around, and all Rowcliff had for me was a glassy eye.

As I said, Cramer didn't shake loose until noon the next day, Wednesday. I lunched on sandwiches and milk at a desk he let me use, digging out what was wanted, got home with it at four o'clock and got at the typewriter, and had just finished and was putting the original and a carbon on Wolfe's desk when he came down from the plant rooms. He got arranged in his chair, picked up the original, and started his brain exercise. I give it here, from the original from the Jarrell file, not for you to exercise your brain — unless you insist on it — but for the record.

May 29, 1957
AG for NW

JARRELL TIMETABLES

(Mostly from police reports, but some from AG is included. Comments are AG's. Some items have been firmly verified by police, some partly verified, some not yet verified at all. Too complicated to try to distinguish among them, but can supply information on items considered important from my notes. OJ is Otis Jarrell, TJ is his wife, WJ is Wyman Jarrell, SJ is his wife, LJ is Lois Jarrell, NK is Nora Kent, RF is Roger Foote, AG is either Alan Green or Archie Goodwin, depending.)

OTIS JARRELL

Thursday

9:30 breakfast with WJ, LJ, NK, AG, then in library until lunch at 1:30 with TJ, SJ, & AG. Left at 2:30 for three business appointments: (1) Continental Trust Co., 287 Madison Ave., (2) Lawrence H. Eggers, 630 5th Ave., (3) Paul Abramowitz, 250 Park Ave. Exact times on these being checked. Got home at 6:00, went to his room. AT 6:30 cocktails and dinner, then to library; AG joins him there at 10:35 p.m. Bed.

Friday

8:15 to AG's room to tell him Eber killed. 8:45 breakfast. 9:30 gathers everyone in library for conference about Eber. At 11:00 Lieut. Rowcliff comes, stays an hour, NK is present. Stays in library with WJ & NK; at 1:22 phone call comes from AG; at 1:40 calls AG, is told to bring everyone to NW office at 6:00. 1:45 lunch with SJ, LJ, & RF, tells them to be at NW office at 6:00. After lunch phones WJ and Corey Brigham to tell them. Phones Clarinda Day's & leaves word for TJ to call him. She does so at 3:00 & he tells her about NW summons. Phones district attorney, whom he knows, & has friendly talk about Eber. 5:00 RF comes to library, asks for $335, doesn't get it. 5:30 is ready to leave for NW, waits til 5:50 for TJ to be ready. 6:10 arrives NW, leaves 7:10; home, dinner, long famly discussion of situation, bed.

Saturday

8:30 breakfast with NK. Has everyone told to stand by because asst. DA coming at 11:00. 9:15 Herman Dietz comes on busines matter, leaves at 9:45. 10:00 tells AG to make himself scarce because asst. DA coming. 10:10 WJ comes in for talk. 11:00 Mandelbaum arrives with dick stenographer; 11:15 everybody is called in, except that TJ doesn't make it until 11:45. 12:05 Cramer joins them, having just left NW. 1:35 Mandelbaum and Cramer leave. All lunch together except NK. 2:45 phones DA, can't get him. Phones Police Commissioner Kelly & arranges to meet him at Penguin Club at 10:30 Sunday. 3:40 leaves to meet WJ at Metropolitan Athletic Club for talk. 5:40 they go home together for early dinner. 8:10 to theater with TJ.

Sunday

9:00 breakfast. 10:10 leaves for Penguin Club for date with Police Commissioner Kelly, with him until 11:30, goes home & to library. 12:00 AG comes in and stays 10 minutes. 1:30 lunch with WJ, SJ, & AG. 2:30 to 5:00 in library, then bridge with TJ, WJ, & NK. At 6:10 AG comes to announce Corey Brigham's death.

TRELLA JARRELL

Thursday

Up at noon, coffee on terrace. 1:30 lunch with OJ, SJ, & AG. 2:30 to Clarinda Day's. 3:45 shopping, information about where & when confused & incomplete & being checked. 6:00 home to change for cocktails & dinner. After dinner, pinochle with RF & NK.

Friday

9:30 goes to family conference in library in negligee, returns to bed, up at noon, eats big breakfast. 1:15 goes to park, arrives 2:30 at Clarinda Day's, gets message to call OJ, does so at 3:00. 4:00 to 5:00 looks at cats in two pet shops, gets home at 5:15, ready to leave for NW at 5:50. From there on with others as under OJ.

Saturday

Told at 11:05 to come to library to join party with asst. DA, makes it at 11:45. 1:35 lunch with others. 2:30 to Clarinda Days'. 3:45 to movie at Duke's Screen Box on Park Avenue. 5:30 home to dress for early dinner. 8:10 to theater with OJ.

Sunday

Up at noon, big breakfast again. On terrace with papers. 2:00 went to park, back at 3:00, went to studio to watch television, is wakened by WJ at 5:00 for bridge with OJ, WJ, & NK. At 6:10 AG announces Corey Brigham's death.

WYMAN JARRELL

Thursday

9:30 breakfast with OJ, LJ, NK, & AG. 10:30 to 12:15, on terrace reading play in manuscript. 2:45 arrives at Sardi's and has lunch with three men to discuss financing of play he may produce (two of them have verified it). 2:45 to 4:30, auditions for casting play at Drew Theatre. 4:35 to 6:30, at Metropolitan Athletic Club, watching handball & drinking. 6:45 meets Susan at Sardi's, dinner, theater, home, bed.

Friday

9:30 family conference in library, then breakfast. Reads papers, waits around with SJ until Rowcliff has come & gone. In library with OJ & NK until 1:22, when phone call comes from AG; leaves, cashes check at bank, then to his office in Paramount Bldg. Lunch at Sardi's with same three men as on Thursday. 3:00 back to his office, gets call from OJ telling him to be at NW office at 6:00. Gets call from SJ. 3:45 SJ comes for him in Jaguar, they drive up to Briscoll's in Westchester for a drink, then back to town, arriving NW at 5:56. From there on with others as under OJ.

Saturday

9:10 breakfast with SJ, LJ, & AG. 10:10 in library with OJ until 11:00, when asst. DA arrives. 1:35 lunch with others. 3:00 meets Corey Brigham at Churchill men's bar, with him until 3:50. 4:00 to 5:40 with OJ at Metropolitan Athletic Club; they go home together, arriving at 6:00 for early dinner. 8:15 to theater with SJ.

Sunday

10:00 breakfast with SJ, LJ, NK, & AG. Reads papers and does crossword puzzles until 1:30 lunch with OJ, SJ, & AG. 2:40 leaves for Drew Theatre to hear auditions. 4:40 leaves theater, gets home at 5:00, goes to studio and wakes TJ, bridge with OJ, TJ, & NK. At 6:10 AG announces Corey Brigham's death.

SUSAN JARRELL

Thursday

10:30 breakfast alone. To Masson's, jeweler, 52nd & 5th Ave., to leave watch. Walks to park & in park, then home at 1:30 for lunch with OJ, TJ, & AG. 2:45 back to Masson's to get watch; buys stockings at Merrihew's, 58th & Madison. Arrives Clarinda Day's at 4:00, leaves at 6:30, meets WJ at Sardi's at 6:45. Dinner, theater, home, bed.

Friday

9:30 family conference in library, then breakfast. Waits around with WJ until Rowcliff has come & gone. 12:10 goes to Abingdon's, florist at 65th & Madison, to order plants for terrace. Back home. 1:45 lunch with OJ, LJ, & RF, is told to be at NW office at 6:00. Rings WJ's office three times, gets him at 3:20, gets Jaguar and goes for him. Rest of day & evening, corroborates WJ.

Saturday

9:10 breakfast with WJ, LJ, & AG. On terrace until 11:15, joins party in library with asst. DA. 1:35 lunch with others. 2:45 goes to Abingdon's to look at plants. Home at 3:45, in room until 4:40, leaves, arrives Clarinda Day's 5:05, leaves at 6:15, is late at home for early dinner. 8:15 to theater with WJ.

Sunday

10:00 breakfast with WJ, LJ, NK, & AG. 10:30 leaves for St. Thomas Church, 53rd & 5th Ave. After church walks home, arriving at 1:15. 1:30 lunch with OJ, WJ, & AG. Reads papers, looks at television, goes to room and takes nap, back to television at 5:30, is there with AG at 6:00 when news comes about Corey Brigham.

LOIS JARRELL

Thursday

9:30 breakfast with OJ, WJ, NK, & AG. 10:15 to 11:30 on terrace reading. 11:45 to 1:00 buying shoes at three shops: Zussman's, Yorio's, and Weeden's. Bought seven pairs altogether, not liking to go barefoot. 1:15 lunch at party on steamship *Bolivar* at dock in Hudson River. 3:00 got car from garage & drove to Net Club in Riverdale, tennis until 6:00. Home at 6:35 to change. Left at 7:30 for dinner and dancing with a group at Flamingo Club; wish I had been there.

Friday

Up at 7:00 for breakfast & ride on a horse in park. Home just in time for family conference in library at 9:30. Drives to net Club for an hour of tennis, home at 1:15. 1:45 lunch with OJ, SJ, & RF, is told to be at NW office at 6:00. 3:00 to Evangeline's, 49th Street near Madison, to try on clothes. Home at 5:20, leaves at 5:30 with RF & NK to taxi to NW. From there on with others as under OJ.

Saturday

Up at 7:00 to ride in park, back for breakfast at 9:10 with WJ, SJ, & AG. Cancels tennis date because of party in library with asst. DA at 11:15. 1:35 lunch with others. 2:30 takes nap in her room. 4:15 goes for walk, goes to Abingdon's & cancels Susan's order for plants for terrace. Home at 5:45, dresses for early dinner. 8:20 goes with AG to Flamingo Club, home at 2:00 a.m.

Sunday

10:00 breakfast with WJ, SJ, NK, & AG. Goes for walk with AG, at 11:30 takes taxi to apartment of friends named Buchanan, 185 East River Drive, goes with them to Net Club for lunch, tennis, drinks. Home at 6:40, learns about Corey Brigham.

NORA KENT

Thursday

9:30 breakfast with OJ, WJ, LJ, & AG. Library all morning, lunch alone there, remains there alone until OJ returns at 6:00. After cocktails & dinner, pinochle with TJ & RF.

Friday

8:45 breakfast. 9:30 family conference in library. 11:00 with OJ when Rowcliff comes. Lunches in library, learns caliber of bullet that killed Eber, leaves at 1:45 to go to see NW.

Home at 3:10, in library until 5:30, leaves with LJ & RF to go to the meeting at NW. From there on with others as under OJ.

Saturday

8:30 breakfast with OJ, then with him to library. 10:10 WJ comes for talk with OJ & she is told to beat it. In her room until 11:15, when she joins party in library with asst. DA. 1:35 lunch with others. 2:30 back to library with OJ; he leaves at 3:40. 3:45 gets phone call from Abingdon's about plants; she goes and cancels orders given by both SJ & LJ. Goes shopping, buys various personal items not specified. 5:45 gets home, dresses for early dinner. 7:50 leaves for meeting of Professional Women's League at Vassar Club, 58th Street. Home at 11:10.

Sunday

10:00 breakfast with WJ, SJ, LJ, & AG. 10:50 goes to church at 5th Ave. Presbyterian, 55th St. Lunch at Borgner's on 6th Ave., then to Picasso show at Modern Museum, 53rd St. Home at 5:00 for bridge with OJ, TJ, & WJ. At 6:10 AG announces Corey Brigham's death.

ROGER FOOTE

Thursday

7:00 breakfast alone. To Jamaica race track, loses $60 I lent him, home at 6:00. After cocktails and dinner, pinochle with TJ & NK.

Friday

9:30 family conference in library, then breakfast. On terrace & in his room until 1:45, then lunch with OJ, SJ, & LJ, is told to be at NW office at 6:00. 2:50 leaves to go to 49th Street to see if he can get into Eber's apartment to look for a record, if any, of the fact that he owed Eber $335. No luck, apartment sealed. Calls on a lawyer he knows, unnamed, to find out where he stands. Gets home at 5:00, goes to library to try to borrow $335 from OJ, is turned down. 5:30 leaves with LJ & NK for NW office.

Saturday

10:15 breakfast alone. 11:15 joins party with asst. DA in library. 1:35 lunch with others. 2:45 goes to Mitchell's Riding Academy on West 108th Street to look at a horse. 3:45 returns home and plays solitaire in his room until time for early dinner. After dinner invites AG to play gin, AG declines. Goes to bed at 9:00.

Sunday

7:00 breakfast alone. To Belmont race track to look at horses. Home at 7:00 p.m., learns about Corey Brigham. Has given police details of his day at Belmont, but they are too confused & complicated to be worth copying.

15

AT a quarter past ten Thursday morning, Memorial Day, I arrived at Jamaica race track to start the damnedest four days of detecting, or non-detecting, that I have ever put in.

After Wolfe had picked up the timetables, at six o'clock Wednesday, he had read them in twenty minutes, and then had gone over them for more than an hour, until dinner time. Back in the office after dinner, he had asked a few dozen assorted questions. What did I know about Mr. and Mrs. Herman Dietz? Practically nothing. Had Trella Jarrell's hour in the park from two o'clock to three on Sunday been checked? No, and probably it never would be. If I wanted to leave a revolver in Central Park where I was reasonably certain it wouldn't be discovered for three days, but where I could get it when I wanted it, where would I hide it? I made three suggestions, none of them any good, and said I'd have to think it over. Who was Clarinda Day? She was a woman who ran an establishment on 48th Street just off Fifth Avenue where women could get almost anything done that occurred to them — to their hair, their faces, their necks, their busts, their waists, their hips, their legs, their knees, their calves, their ankles — and where they could sweat, freeze, rest, or exercise forty-two different ways. Her customers ran all the way from stenographers to multi-millionairesses.

Did Nora Kent have keys to all the files in Jarrell's library and the combination to the safes? Don't know. Had a thorough search been made of the Jarrell duplex? Yes; a regiment of experts, with Jarrell's permission, had spent all day Tuesday at it. Including the library? Yes, with Jarrell present. Who had told me so? Purley Stebbins. Where was the Metropolitan Athletic Club? Central Park South, 59th Street. How long would it take to get from where the steamship *Bolivar* was docked to Eber's apartment on 49th Street? Between ten and thirty minutes, depending on traffic. Average, say eighteen minutes. How difficult would it have been for Nora Kent to get from the library to the street, and, later, back in again, without being observed? With luck, using the service entrance, fairly simple. Without luck, impossible.

Etc.

At ten-thirty Wolfe leaned back and said, "Instructions."

"Yes, sir."

"Before you go to bed get Saul, Fred, and Orrie, and ask them to be here at eleven in the morning."

"Yes, sir."

"Tomorrow is a holiday. I don't suppose Miss Bonner will be at her office. If possible, get her tonight and ask her to breakfast with me at eight."

I looked at him. He meant business, though what business I couldn't say. Add his opinion of women to his opinion of other detectives, and you get his opinion of female detectives. Circumstances had compelled him to use Dol

Bonner a year or so back, but now he was asking for it, and even inviting her to breakfast. Fritz would be on needles.

"I have her home number," I told him, "and I'll try, but she may already be gone for the long week end. If so, is it urgent enough to dig her out?"

"Yes. I want her. Now for you. You will go early in the morning to Jamaica race track and—"

"No racing at Jamaica now. It's closed."

"What about Belmont?"

"Open. Big day tomorrow."

"Then we'll see. You will act on this hypothesis: that Roger Foote took Jarrell's gun and hid it in his room or elsewhere on the premises. Thursday afternoon he shot Eber with it. Since he intended to say he had spent the day at Jamaica, he went there so as to be seen, and he hid the gun somewhere there. To speculate as to why he hid it instead of disposing of it is pointless; we know he did hide it because it was used again on Sunday. Either he hid it at Jamaica or, having made an appearance there, he went to Belmont and hid it there. In either case, on Sunday he went and retrieved it, returned to New York, met Brigham by appointment, and killed him. Acting on that hypothesis, your job is to learn where he left the gun from Thursday to Sunday, and you may start either at Jamaica or at Belmont. It's barely possible you'll even find the gun. He may have thought he might have further use for it and went back and hid it again in the same place after killing Brigham. He didn't get home Sunday until seven o'clock."

I said—not an objection, just a fact—"Of course he had all of New York City too."

"I know, but that's hopeless. He had to go to Jamaica on Thursday and to Belmont on Sunday, to be seen, and since we know he was there we'll look there. We know little or nothing of his movements in New York City; we know of no place particulary available to him where he could hide a gun and count on getting it again. First explore the possibilities at Jamaica and Belmont."

I explored them for four straight days, equipped with five hundred bucks in small bills from cash reserve and eight pictures of Roger Foote, procured early Thursday morning from the files at the *Gazette*. I went to Jamaica first because Belmont would have such a mob on the holiday that I would merely have got trampled.

Meanwhile, throughout the four days, Wolfe presumably had the gang busy working on other hypotheses—including Dol Bonner—though he never told me who was after what, except that I gathered Saul Panzer was on Otis Jarrell himself. That was a compliment to the former client, since Saul's rate was sixty bucks a day and expenses and he was worth at least five times that. Fred Durkin was good but no Saul Panzer. Orrie Cather, whom you have seen at my desk, was yes and no. On some tricks he was unbeatable, but on others not so hot. As for Dol Bonner, I didn't know much about her first-hand, but the word around was that if you had to have a female dick she was it. She had her own office and a staff—with one of which, Sally Colt, I was acquainted.

By Sunday night I knew enough about Jamaica and Belmont, especially Belmont, to write a book, with enough left over for ten magazine articles. I knew four owners, nine trainers, seventeen stable boys, five jockeys, thirteen touts, twenty-eight miscellaneous characters, one lamb, three dogs, and six cats, to speak to. I had aroused the suspicions of two track dicks and become close friends with one. I had seen two hundred and forty-seven girls it would have been fun to talk to but was too busy. I had seen about the same number of spots where a gun could be hid, but could find no one who had seen Roger Foote near any of them. None of them held a gun at the time I called, nor could I detect any trace of oil or other evidence that a gun had been there. One of them, a hole in a tree the other side of the backstretch, was so ideal that I was tempted to hide my own gun in it. Another good place would have been the bottom of a rack outside Gallant Man's stall, but there were too many eagle eyes around. Peach Fuzz wasn't there.

Sunday night I told Wolfe there was nothing left to explore unless he wanted me to start looking in horses' mouths, and he said he would have new instructions in the morning.

But he never gave them to me, for a little after ten on Monday a call came inviting me to visit the DA's office, and, after buzzing Wolfe in the plant rooms to tell him where to find me, I went. After thirty minutes with Mandelbaum and a dick I knew one thing, that the several hundred city and county employes working on the case had got exactly as far as I had at Jamaica and Belmont. After another thirty minutes I knew another thing, that the police commissioner and the district attorney had decided it had become necessary to find out what I was doing at Jarrell's under an assumed name, no matter how Jarrell felt about it. I said I wanted to phone Mr. Wolfe and was told that all the phones were busy. At noon I was taken in to the DA himself and had forty minutes with him that did neither of us any good. At one o'clock I was allowed to take my pick of ham or turkey in a sandwich; no corned beef. I insisted on milk and got it. At two-thirty I decided it had gone far enough and was walking out, but was stopped. Held as a material witness. Then, of course, they had to let me make a phone call, and within ten minutes there was a call for Mandelbaum from Nathaniel Parker, who is Wolfe's lawyer when Wolfe is driven to the extremity of using one.

I didn't get locked up at all. The DA had another try at me and then sent me into another room with a dick named O'Leary, and in two hours I won $3.12 from him at gin. I was perfectly willing to give him a chance to get it back, but someone came and took me to Mandelbaum's room, and Nathaniel Parker was there. As I shook hands with him Mandelbaum warned me not to leave the jurisdiction, and I said I wanted it in writing, and he said to go to hell, and I said I didn't know that was in the jurisdiction, and Parker steered me out.

Down on the sidewalk I asked him, "How high am I priced this time?"

"No bail, Archie. No warrant. I persuaded Mandelbaum that the circumstances didn't call for it, and promised that you will be available when needed."

I was a little disappointed because being out on bail is good for the ego. It gives you a sense of importance, of being wanted; it makes you feel that people care. However, I didn't reproach Parker; he had acted for the best. We took a taxi together uptown, but he said he had a dinner appointment and didn't get out when we reached the old brownstone on West 35th Street. So I thanked him for the rescue and the lift. As I crossed the sidewalk to the stoop my wrist watch said 6:23.

Wolfe, at his desk reading a book, lifted his eyes to grunt a greeting and returned them to the book. I went to my desk to see if there were any memos for me, found none, sat, and inquired, "Anything happen?"

He said no, without looking up.

"Parker said to give you his regards. I am not under bail. He talked Mandelbaum out of it."

He grunted.

"They've decided that Jarrell's private affairs are no longer private. They'll be after you any time, in the morning at the latest. Do you want a report?"

He said no, without looking up.

"Any instructions?"

He lifted his eyes, said, "I'm reading, Archie," and lowered them back to the book.

The best thing to throw at him would have been the typewriter, but I didn't own it. Next best would have been the telephone, but I didn't own that, either, and the cord wasn't long enough. I got up and left, mounted the two flights to my room, showered, decided not to shave, put on a clean shirt and a lighter suit, and was sewing buttons on pajamas when Fritz called up that dinner was ready.

It was at the table that I caught on that something was up. Wolfe wasn't being crusty because the outlook was dark; he was being smug because he had tasted blood, or was expecting to. He always enjoyed his food, whether in spite of circumstances or in harmony with them, and after ten thousand meals with him I knew all the shades. The way he spread pâté on a cracker, the way he picked up the knife to slice the filet of beef in aspic, the way he used his fork on the salad, the way he made his choice from the cheese platter — no question about it, he had something or somebody by the tail, or at least the tail was in sight.

I was thinking that when we were back in the office with coffee he might think it was time to let me have a taste too, but no. After taking three sips he picked up his book. That was a little too much, and I was deciding whether to go after him head on or take him from the flank, when the doorbell rang and I went to answer it. In view of Wolfe's behavior I wouldn't have been surprised if it had been the whole gang, all seven of them, with a joint confession in triplicate signed and ready to deliver, but it was merely a middle-aged man in a light brown suit and no hat whom I had never seen before.

When I opened the door he spoke before I did. "Is this Nero Wolfe's house?"

"Right."

"Are you Archie Goodwin?"

"Right again."

"Okay." He extended a hand with a little package. "This is for Nero Wolfe."

I took it and he turned and was going. I told him to wait, but he called over his shoulder, "No receipt," and kept going. I looked at the package. It was the size of a box of kitchen matches, wrapped in brown paper, fastened with Scotch Tape, and if it bore any name or address it was in invisible ink.

I shut the door and returned to the office and told Wolfe, "The man who handed me this said it was for you, but I don't know how he knew. There's no name on it. It doesn't tick. Shall I open it under water?"

"As you please. It's hardly large enough to be dangerous."

That seemed optimistic, remembering the size of the capsule that had once exploded in that office inside a metal percolator, blowing the percolator lid at the wall, missing Wolfe's head by an inch. However, I could stand it if he could. I got out my knife to cut the tape, removed the paper wrapping, and disclosed a cardboard box with no label. Putting it on the desk midway between us, which was only fair, I eased the lid off. Cotton. I lifted the cotton, and there was more cotton, with an object resting in its center. Bending over for a close-up, I straightened and announced, "A thirty-eight bullet. Isn't that interesting?"

"Extremely." He reached for the box and gave it a look. "Very interesting. You're sure it's a thirty-eight?"

"Yes, sir. Quite a coincidence."

"It is indeed." He put the box down. "Who brought it?"

"A stranger. Too bad I didn't invite him in."

"Yes. Of course there are various possibilities — among them, that some prankster sent it."

"Yeah. So I toss it in the wastebasket?"

"I don't think so. There is at least one other possibility that can't be ignored. You've had a long day and I dislike asking it, but you might take it to Mr. Cramer, tell him how we got it, and suggest that it be compared with the bullets that killed Mr. Eber and Mr. Brigham."

"Uh-huh. In time, say in a week or so, that might have occurred to me myself. My mind's not as quick as yours." I replaced the top layer of cotton and put the lid on. "I'd better take the wrapping paper too. If the bullet matches, and it just might, he'll want it. Incidentally, he'll want me too. If I take him a thirty-eight bullet, with that suggestion, and with that story of how we got it, I'll have to shoot my way out if you want to see me again tonight."

"The devil." He was frowning. "You're quite right. That won't do." He thought a moment. "Your notebook. A letter to Mr. Cramer."

I got at my desk and took notebook and pen.

He dictated: "Dear Mr. Cramer. I send you herewith a package which was delivered at my door a few minutes ago. It bore no name or address, but the messenger told Mr. Goodwin it was for me and departed. It contains a bullet which Mr. Goodwin says is a thirty-eight. Doubtless it is merely a piece of tomfoolery, but I thought it best to send it to you. You may think it worth while to have the bullet compared with those that killed Mr. Eber and Mr. Brigham. Then discard it. Don't bother to return it. Sincerely."

"By mail?" I asked.

"No. Take it, please. Immediately. Hand it in and return at once."

"Glad to." I pulled the typewriter around.

16

THAT Monday night may not have been the worst night Fritz ever spent, for he has had some tough ones, but it was bad enough. When I had got back after delivering the package at 20th Street, a little after ten o'clock, Wolfe had called him to the office.

"Some instructions, Fritz."

"Yes, sir."

"Archie and I will go up to bed shortly, but we are not here and will not be here. You will answer the phone. You do not know where we are or when we will return. You do not know exactly when we left. You may be bully ragged, by Mr. Cramer or others, but you will maintain that position. You will take messages if any are given, to be delivered to us when we return. You will ignore the doorbell. You will open no outside door, stoop or basement or back, under any circumstances whatever. If you do, a search warrant may be thrust at you and the house will be overrun. A contingency might arise that will make you consider it necessary to disturb Archie or me, but I think not and hope not. Bring my breakfast an hour early, at seven o'clock. Archie will have his at seven also. I shall be sorry if you fail of a proper night's sleep, but it can't be helped. You can take a nap tomorrow."

"Yes, sir." Fritz swallowed. "If there is danger, may I suggest—" He stopped and started over. "I know you are reluctant to leave the house, that is understood, but there are times when it is better to leave a house, at least for a short time. Especially in your profession." He looked at me. "You know that, Archie."

Wolfe reassured him, "No, Fritz, there is no danger. On the contrary, this is the preamble to triumph. You understand the instructions?"

He said he did, but he wasn't happy. For years he had been expecting the day to come when Wolfe would be dragged out of the house in handcuffs, not to mention me, and he was against it. He gave me a reproachful look, which God knows I didn't deserve, and left, and Wolfe and I, not being there anyway, went up to bed.

Seven o'clock is much too early a breakfast hour unless you're a bird or a bird watcher, but I made it to the kitchen by 7:08. My glass of orange juice was there, but Fritz wasn't, and the phone was ringing. It was a temptation to take it and see how well I could imitate Fritz's voice, but I let it ring. By the time Fritz came it had given up. I told him he must have been late taking Wolfe's breakfast tray up, and he said no, he had got it there on the dot at seven, but had stayed to report on the night.

While I dealt with toast, bacon, fresh strawberry omelet, and coffee, he reported to me, referring to notes. The first call from Lieutenant Rowcliff had come at 11:32, and he had been so emphatic that Fritz had hung up on him. The second had been at 11:54, less emphatic but stubborner. At 12:21 Cramer had called, and had got both personal and technical, explaining the penalities that could be imposed on a man, Fritz for instance, for complicity in withholding evidence and obstructing justice in a murder investigation. At 12:56 the doorbell had started to ring, and at 1:03 pounding on the front door had begun. From 1:14 to a little after six peace had reigned, but at 6:09 Cramer had phoned, and at 6:27 the doorbell had started up again, and through the one-way glass panel Sergeant Stebbins had been visible. He had kept at it for five minutes and was now in a police car with a colleague out at the curb.

I got up, went to the front door for a look, came back, requested more toast, and poured more coffee. "He's still there," I told Fritz, "and there's one danger. As you know, Mr. Wolfe can't bear the idea of a hungry man in his house, and while Stebbins isn't actually in the house he's there in front and wants to be, and he looks hungry. If Mr. Wolfe sees him and suspects he hasn't had breakfast there'll be hell to pay. Could I borrow a little wild thyme honey?"

I was on the last bite of toast and honey and the last inch of coffee when the sound of Wolfe's elevator came, and by the time I was through swallowing and got to the office he was there behind his desk. We said good morning.

"So," I said, "it wasn't a prankster."

"Apparently not." With the edge of a blotter he was flipping from his desk pad dust that wasn't there. "Get Mr. Cramer."

I got at the phone and dialed, and soon had him, and Wolfe took it. I held my receiver an inch from my ear, expecting a blast, but it had gone beyond that. Cramer's voice was merely hoarse with fury.

"Where are you?" he demanded.

"I'm on an errand, no matter where. I'm calling to ask about the bullet I sent you. Does it match the others?"

"You know damn well it does. You knew it when you sent it. This is the rawest —"

"No. I suspected it, but I didn't know it. That was what I had to know before I divulged where it came from. That was why I arranged to keep its source anonymous until I knew. I would like to have it explicitly. Was the bullet I sent you fired from the same gun as those that killed Eber and Brigham?"

"By God." Cramer knew darned well he shouldn't use profanity on the phone, so he must have been upset. "You arranged! I'll arrange you! I'll arrange for you to —"

"Mr. Cramer! This is ridiculous. I'm supplying the solution of an extremely bothersome case, and you sputter at me. If you must sputter, wait until you have the facts. Will you please answer my question?"

"The answer is yes."

"Then I'm ready to deliver the murderer and the weapon, but there is the matter of procedure to consider. I can invite the district attorney to my house and give him the weapon and two excellent witnesses, and let him get the culprit. Or I can do that with you. I don't like either of those because I have been at considerable expense and I have earned a fee, and I want to be paid, and there is plenty of money in that family. I want the family to know what I have done, and how, and the most effective and impressive way to inform them is to have them present when I produce the weapon and identify the murderer. If I invite them they won't come. You can bring them.

If you'll—please let me finish. If you'll have them at my house at eleven
o'clock, all of them, I'll be there to receive you, and you'll get all you need
and more. Three hours from now. I hope you'll oblige me because I like
dealing with you better than with the district attorney."

"I ought to appreciate that," Cramer said, hoarser than ever. "You're
home now. You've been home all night. You knew damn well the bullet
would match, and you knew as soon as we checked it we'd be on you, and
you didn't want to be bothered until morning so you could spring this on
me. In half an hour we'll have a search warrant for your house, and we'll
have warrants for you and Goodwin as material witnesses."

"Indeed. Then forgive me if I ring off. I have a call to make."

"Yeah. You would. By God, you would. I let you have those reports and
this is what I get for it. Who do you want there?"

"The five people named Jarrell, and Miss Kent and Mr. Foote. At eleven
o'clock."

"Sure, I know. Until eleven you'll be up with your goddamn orchids. We
mustn't interfere with that."

He hung up. So did we.

"You know," I said, "I think the orchids irritate him. I've noticed it
before. Maybe you should get rid of them. Do I answer the phone now?"

"Yes. Miss Bonner and Saul and Fred and Orrie are going to call between
nine and nine-thirty. Tell them to come at eleven. If the Jarrells are to be
properly impressed they should see all of them."

"Okay. But it wouldn't hurt if I knew in advance which one to keep an
eye on. I know darned well it's not Roger Foote."

He looked up at the wall clock. "It's early. Very well."

17

I had turned over the doorman-and-usher job to Saul and Orrie because I
was otherwise engaged. Cramer, with Stebbins, had arrived twenty minutes
early and insisted on seeing Wolfe, and I had taken them to the dining room
and stayed to keep them company. They didn't want my company, they
wanted Wolfe's, but I told them that if they climbed three flights to the
plant rooms they would find the door locked. I offered to pass the time by
telling them the story about the chorus girl and the anteater, but it didn't
seem to appeal to them.

When Wolfe opened the dining-room door and said, "Good morning,
gentlemen," and Cramer told him to come in and shut the door, a wrangle
seemed unavoidable, but Wolfe avoided it by saying, "In the office, please,"
and turning and going. Cramer and Stebbins followed, and I brought up
the rear.

On the three previous occasions that Otis Jarrell had been in that office
he had had the seat of honor, the red leather chair, but this time Saul,

following instructions, had kept it for Inspector Cramer, and the ex-client was in the front row of the audience with his wife, his son, and his daughter-in-law. Behind them were Lois, Nora Kent, Roger Foote, and Saul Panzer. On the couch, at my back when I got to my desk, were Sally Colt, of Dol Bonner's staff, and Fred Durkin and Orrie Cather. Purley Stebbins' chair was where he always put it himself if we didn't, against the wall at arm's length from Cramer.

Actually, for that particular party, the red leather chair was not the seat of honor. The seat of honor was one of the yellow chairs which had been placed at the other end of Wolfe's desk, on his right, and in it was Dol Bonner, a very attractive sight for a female dick, with her home-grown long black lashes making a curling canopy for her caramel-colored eyes. I had warned Fritz she would be there. She had once been invited to dine at the table he cooks for, and he suspects every woman who ever crosses the threshold of wanting to take over his kitchen, not to mention the rest of the house.

Inspector Cramer, standing, faced the audience and spoke. "Nero Wolfe is going to say something and you can listen along with me. You're here on police orders, so I want to make one thing clear. Any questions Wolfe asks you are his questions and not mine. Answer them or not as you please. Wolfe is not acting for the police or speaking for the police."

"I have nothing to ask, Mr. Cramer," Wolfe said. "Not a single question. I have only to report and expound."

"All right, go ahead." Cramer sat down.

"What I wish to report," Wolfe told the audience, "is how I found the weapon that killed two men, and how its finding revealed the identity of the killer. After you people left here on Monday, eight days ago, and after I had given Mr. Cramer the information I had told you I would give him, I was without a client and had no assigned function in this affair. But my curiosity was alive, my self-esteem was involved, and I wanted to be paid for the time I had spent and the ignominy I had endured. I resolved to pursue the matter."

He cleared his throat. "You people were no longer available to me for inquiry. You were through with me. I had neither the personnel nor the facilities for the various lines of routine investigation, and besides, the police were seeing to that. But there was one established fact that offered possibilities: the bullets that killed Eber and Brigham had been fired by the same gun. Assuming that they had also been fired by the same person, obviously the gun had been in his possession from Thursday afternoon, when Eber was killed, to Sunday afternoon, when Brigham was killed — or at least it had been kept where he could get it again. Where had it been kept?"

His eyes went to Cramer and back to them. "Mr. Cramer obliged me by permitting Mr. Goodwin access to the reports of your movements during that period. I was and am deeply appreciative of his cooperation; it would be churlish to suppose that he let me learn the contents of the reports only because he wanted to know what I was going to do with them. Here they are."

With a forefinger he tapped papers on his desk. "Here they are, as typed by Mr. Goodwin. I inspected and analyzed them. It was possible, of course, that the gun had been kept somewhere on the premises where you all live, but I thought it extremely unlikely. At any moment the police, learning of the disappearance of Mr. Jarrell's gun, might search the place—as they did eventually, one week ago today. It was highly probable that the gun had been kept somewhere else, and I proceeded on that theory."

"So did I," Cramer rasped.

Wolfe nodded. "No doubt. But for you it was only one of many lines of inquiry, whereas it was all I had. And not only was it near-certainty that the gun had been kept in some available spot from Thursday afternoon to Sunday afternoon, but also there was a chance that it had been returned to that spot after Brigham was killed and was still there. On Sunday, when he left the car on Thirty-ninth Street, the murderer had the gun and had to dispose of it somehow. If he put it somewhere, anywhere, where it might be found, there was the risk that it *would* be found and would be identified both as Mr. Jarrell's gun and as the gun the bullets had come from. If he put it somewhere it would *not* be found—for instance, at the bottom of the river— he might be seen, and besides, time was probably pressing. So it was quite possible that he had returned it, at the first opportunity, if not immediately, to the place where he had kept it for three days. Therefore my quest was for a spot not merely where the gun had been kept for the three days, but where it might still be."

He took a breath. "So I analyzed the timetables. They offered various suggestions, some promising, some far-fetched. To explore them I needed help, and I called on Mr. Saul Panzer, who is seated there beside Mr. Foote; on Mr. Fred Durkin, on the couch; on Mr. Orville Cather, on the couch beside Mr. Durkin; on Miss Theodolinda Bonner, here at my right; and on Miss Sally Colt, Miss Bonner's assistant, on the couch beside Mr. Durkin."

"Get on with it," Cramer growled.

Wolfe ignored him. "I won't detail all their explorations, but some deserve brief mention. They were all severely handicapped by the holiday and the long week end. Mr. Goodwin spent four days at the Jamaica and Belmont race tracks. Mr. Panzer traced Mr. Jarrell's movements on the Thursday when Eber was killed with extraordinary industry and acumen. Mr. Durkin performed with perseverance and ingenuity at the Metropolitan Athletic Club. Mr. Cather found three different people who had seen Mrs. Otis Jarrell in Central Park on the Sunday when Brigham was killed. But it was Miss Bonner and Miss Colt who had both ability and luck. Miss Bonner, produce the gun, please?"

Dol Bonner opened her bag, took out a revolver, said, "It's loaded," and put it on Wolfe's desk. Cramer came breezing around the front of the desk, nearly tripping on Wyman's foot, spouting as he came, and Purley Stebbins was up too. Dol Bonner told Cramer, "I tried it for prints, Inspector. There were no good ones. Look out, it's loaded."

"You loaded it?"

"No. It held two cases and four cartridges when I found it. I fired one cartridge, and that left—"

"You fired it?"

"Mr. Cramer," Wolfe said sharply. "How could we learn if it was the guilty gun without firing it? Let me finish and you can have all day."

I opened a drawer of my desk, got a heavy manila envelope, and handed it to Cramer. He picked the gun up by the trigger guard, put it in the envelope, circled Wolfe's desk to hand the envelope to Purley, said, "Go ahead and finish," and sat.

Wolfe asked, "What did you do after you found the gun, Miss Bonner?"

"Miss Colt was with me. We phoned you and got instructions and followed them. We went to my office and filed a nick in the barrel of the gun so we could identify it. We then went to my apartment, turned on the radio as loud as it would go, fired a bullet into some cushions, got the bullet, put it in a box with cotton, wrapped the box in paper, and sent it to you by messenger."

"When did you find the gun?"

"At ten minutes after six yesterday afternoon."

"Has it been continuously in your possession since then?"

"It has. Every minute. I slept with it under my pillow."

"Was Miss Colt with you when you found it?"

"Yes."

"Where did you find it?"

"In a locker on the fourth floor at Clarinda Day's on Forty-eighth Street."

Trella Jarrell let out a king-size gasp. Eyes went to her and she coverd her mouth with both hands.

Wolfe went on. "Was the locker locked?"

"Yes."

"Did you break it open?"

"No. I used a key."

"I won't ask you how you got the key. You may be asked in court, but this is not a court. Was the locker one of a series?"

"Yes. There ar four rows of private lockers on that floor, with twenty lockers to a row. Clarinda Day's customers put their clothes and belongings in them while they are doing exercises or getting massages. Some of them keep changes of clothing or other articles in them."

"You said private lockers. Is each locker confined to a single customer?"

"Yes. The customer has the only key, except that I suppose the management has a master key. The key I used—but I'm not to tell that now?"

"It isn't necessary. You may tell it on the witness stand. As you know, what you did is actionable, but since you discovered a weapon that was used in two murders I doubt if you will suffer any penalty. Instead, you should be rewarded and probably will be. Do you know which of Clarinda Day's customers the locker belonged to? The one you found the gun in."

"Yes. Mrs. Wyman Jarrell. Her name was on it. It also had other articles in it, and among them were letters in envelopes addressed to her."

No gasp from anyone. No anything, until Otis Jarrell muttered, barely loud enough to hear, "The snake, the snake."

Wolfe's eyes were at Susan. "Mrs. Jarrell. Do you wish to offer an explanation of how the gun got into your locker?"

Naturally, knowing what was coming, I had been watching her little oval face from a corner of my eye, and she was only four feet from me, and I swear there hadn't been a flicker. As she met Wolfe's eyes her lip muscles moved a little as if they were trying to manage a smile, but I had seen them do that before. And when she spoke it was the same voice, low, and shy or coy or wary or demure, depending on your attitude.

"I can't explain it," she said, "because I don't know. But you can't think I

took it that day, that Wednesday, because I told you about that. I was
upstairs in my room, and my husband was with me. Weren't you, Wy?"

She would probably have skipped that if she had turned for a good look at
his face before asking it. He was paralyzed, staring at Wolfe with his jaw
hanging. He looked incapable of speech, but a kind of idiot mumble came
out, "I was taking a shower, a long shower, I always take a long shower."

You might think, when a man is hit so hard with the realization that his
wife is a murderess that he lets something out which will help to sink her, he
would at least give it some tone, some quality. That's a hell of a speech in a
crisis like that: "I was taking a shower, a long shower, I always take a long
shower."

As Wolfe would say, pfui.

18

As it turned out, when Otis Jarrell's private affairs, at least some of them,
became public, it was out of his own mouth on the witness stand. While it is
true that evidence of motive is not legally essential in a murder case, it helps
a lot, and for that the DA had to have Jarrell. The theory was that Susan
had worked on Jim Eber and got information from him, specifically about
the claim on the shipping company, and passed it along to Corey Brigham,
who had acted on it. After Eber was fired he had learned about Brigham's
clean-up on the deal, suspected he had been fired because Jarrell thought he
had given the information to Brigham, remembered he had told Susan
about it, suspected her of telling Brigham, and told her, probably just before
I entered the studio that day, that he was going to tell Jarrell. To support the
theory Jarrell was needed, though they had other items, the strongest one
being that they found two hundred thousand dollars in cash in a safe-
deposit box Susan had rented about that time, and she couldn't remember
where she had got it.

Brigham's death was out of it as far as the trial was concerned, since she
was being tried for Eber, but the theory was that he had suspected her of
killing Eber and had told her so, and take your pick. Either he had disapproved of murder so strongly that he was going to pass it on, or he wanted
something for not passing it on—possibly the two hundred grand back,
possibly something more personal.

None of the rest of them was called to testify by either side. The defense
put neither Susan nor Wyman on, and that probably hurt. Susan's having a
key to the library was no problem, since her husband had one and she slept
in the same room with him. As for whether they'll ever get her to the chair,
you'll have to watch the papers. The jury convicted her of the big one, with
no recommendation, but to get a woman actually in that seat, especially a
young one with a little oval face, takes a lot of doing.

Wolfe took Jarrell's money, a check this time, and a very attractive one, and that's all right, he earned it. But that was all he wanted from that specimen, or me either. He said it for both of us the day after Susan was indicted, when Jarrell phoned to say he was going to mail a check for a certain amount and would that be satisfactory, and when Wolfe said it would Jarrell went on: "And I was right, Wolfe. She's a snake. You didn't believe me the day I came to hire you, and neither did Goodwin, but now you know I was right, and that gives me a lot of satisfaction. She's a snake."

"No, sir." Wolfe was curt. "I do not know you were right. She is a murderess, a hellcat, and a wretch, but you have furnished no evidence that she is a snake. I still do not believe you. I will be glad to get the check."

He hung up and so did I.

3 at Wolfe's Door

Contents

Poison à la Carte

1

I slanted my eyes down to meet her big brown ones, which were slanted up. "No," I said, "I'm neither a producer nor an agent. My name's Archie Goodwin, and I'm here because I'm a friend of the cook. My reason for wanting it is purely personal."

"I know," she said, "it's my dimples. Men often swoon."

I shook my head. "It's your earrings. They remind me of a girl I once loved in vain. Perhaps if I get to know you well enough — who can tell?"

"Not me," she declared. "Let me alone. I'm nervous, and I don't want to spill the soup. The name is Nora Jaret, without an H, and the number is Stanhope five, six-six-two-one. The earrings were a present from Sir Laurence Olivier. I was sitting on his knee."

I wrote the number down in my notebook, thanked her, and looked around. Most of the collection of attractive young females were gathered in an alcove between two cupboards, but one was over by a table watching Felix stir something in a bowl. Her profile was fine and her hair was the color of corn silk just before it starts to turn. I crossed to her, and when she turned her head I spoke. "Good evening, Miss — Miss?"

"Annis," she said. "Carol Annis."

I wrote it down, and told her my name. "I am not blunt by nature," I said, "but you're busy, or soon will be, and there isn't time to talk up to it. I was standing watching you, and all of a sudden I had an impulse to ask you for your phone number, and I'm no good at fighting impulses. Now that you're close up it's even stronger, and I guess we'll have to humor it."

But I may be giving a wrong impression. Actually I had no special hankering that Tuesday evening for new telephone numbers; I was doing it for Fritz. But that could give a wrong impression too, so I'll have to explain.

One day in February, Lewis Hewitt, the millionaire and orchid fancier for whom Nero Wolfe had once handled a tough problem, had told Wolfe that the Ten for Aristology wanted Fritz Brenner to cook their annual dinner, to be given as usual on April first, Brillat-Savarin's birthday. When Wolfe said he had never heard of the Ten for Aristology, and Hewitt explained that it was a group of ten men pursuing the ideal of perfection in food and drink, and he was one of them, Wolfe had swiveled to the dictionary on its stand at a corner of his desk, and after consulting it had declared that "aristology" meant the science of dining, and therefore the Ten were witlings, since

347

dining was not a science but an art. After a long argument Hewitt had admitted he was licked and had agreed that the name should be changed, and Wolfe had given him permission to ask Fritz to cook the dinner.

In fact Wolfe was pleased, though of course he wouldn't say so. It took a big slice of his income as a private detective to pay Fritz Brenner, chef and housekeeper in the old brownstone on West 35th Street — about the same as the slice that came to me as his assistant detective and man Friday, Saturday, Sunday, Monday, Tuesday, Wednesday, and Thursday — not to mention what it took to supply the kitchen with the raw materials of Fritz's productions. Since I am also the bookkeeper, I can certify that for the year 1957 the kitchen and Fritz cost only slightly less than the plant rooms on the roof bulging with orchids. So when Hewitt made it clear that the Ten, though they might be dubs at picking names, were true and trustworthy gourmets, that the dinner would be at the home of Benjamin Schriver, the shipping magnate, who wrote a letter to the *Times* every year on September first denouncing the use of horseradish on oysters, and that the cook would have a free hand on the menu and the Ten would furnish whatever he desired, Wolfe pushed a button to summon Fritz. There was a little hitch when Fritz refused to commit himself until he had seen the Schriver kitchen, but Hewitt settled that by escorting him out front to his Heron town car and driving him down to Eleventh Street to inspect the kitchen.

That's where I was that Tuesday evening, April first, collecting phone numbers: in the kitchen of the four-story Schriver house on Eleventh Street west of Fifth Avenue. Wolfe and I had been invited by Schriver, and though Wolfe dislikes eating with strangers and thinks that more than six at table spoils a meal, he knew Fritz's feelings would be hurt if he didn't go; and besides, if he stayed home who would cook his dinner? Even so, he would probably have balked if he had learned of one detail which Fritz and I knew about but had carefully kept from him: that the table was to be served by twelve young women, one for each guest.

When Hewitt had told me that, I had protested that I wouldn't be responsible for Wolfe's conduct when the orgy got under way, that he would certainly stamp out of the house when the girls started to squeal. Good lord, Hewitt said, nothing like that; that wasn't the idea at all. It was merely that the Ten had gone to ancient Greece not only for their name but also for other precedents. Hebe, the goddess of youth, had been cupbearer to the gods, so it was the custom of the Ten for Aristology to be waited on by maidens in appropriate dress. When I asked where they got the maidens he said through a theatrical agency, and added that at that time of year there were always hundreds of young actresses out of a job glad to grab a chance to make fifty bucks, with a good meal thrown in, by spending an evening carrying food, one plate at a time. Originally they had hired experienced waitresses from an agency, but they had tripped on their *stolas*.

Wolfe and I had arrived at seven on the dot, and after we had met our host and the rest of the Ten, and had sampled oysters and our choice of five white wines, I had made my way to the kitchen to see how Fritz was making out. He was tasting from a pot on the range, with no more sign of fluster than if he had been at home getting dinner for Wolfe and me. Felix and Zoltan, from Rusterman's, were there to help, so I didn't ask if I was needed.

And there were the Hebes, cupbearers to the gods, twelve of them, in their stolas, deep rich purple, flowing garments to their ankles. Very nice. It gave me an idea. Fritz likes to pretend that he has reason to believe that no damsel is safe within a mile of me, which doesn't make sense since you can't tell much about them a mile off, and I thought it would do him good to see me operate at close quarters. Also it was a challenge and an interesting sociological experiment. The first two had been a cinch: one named Fern Faber, so she said, a tall self-made blonde with a wide lazy mouth, and Nora Jaret with the big brown eyes and dimples. Now I was after this Carol Annis with hair like corn silk.

"I have no sense of humor," she said, and turned back to watch Felix stir.

I stuck. "That's a different kind of humor and an impulse like mine isn't funny. It hurts. Maybe I can guess it. Is it Hebe one, oh-oh-oh-oh?"

No reply.

"Apparently not. Plato two, three-four-five-six?"

She said, without turning her head, "It's listed. Gorham eight, three-two-one-seven." Her head jerked to me. "Please?" It jerked back again.

It rather sounded as if she meant please go away, not please ring her as soon as possible, but I wrote it down anyway, for the record, and moved off. The rest of them were still grouped in the alcove, and I crossed over. The deep purple of the stolas was a good contrast for their pretty young faces topped by nine different colors and styles of hairdos. As I came up the chatter stopped and the faces turned to me.

"At ease," I told them. "I have no official standing. I am merely one of the guests, invited because I'm a friend of the cook, and I have a personal problem. I would prefer to discuss it with each of you separately and privately, but since there isn't time for that I am—"

"I know who you are," one declared. "You're a detective and you work for Nero Wolfe. You're Archie Goodwin."

She was a redhead with milky skin. "I don't deny it," I told her, "but I'm not here professionally. I don't ask if I've met you because if I had I wouldn't have forgot—"

"You haven't met me. I've seen you and I've seen your picture. You like yourself. Don't you?"

"Certainly. I string along with the majority. We'll take a vote. How many of you like yourselves? Raise your hands."

A hand went up with a bare arm shooting out of the purple folds, then two more, then the rest of them, including the redhead.

"Okay," I said, "that's settled. Unanimous. My problem is that I decided to look you over and ask the most absolutely irresistibly beautiful and fascinating one of the bunch for her phone number, and I'm stalled. You are all it. In beauty and fascination you are all far beyond the wildest dreams of any poet, and I'm not a poet. So obviously I'm in a fix. How can I possibly pick on one of you, any one, when—"

"Nuts." It was the redhead. "Me, of course. Peggy Choate. Argyle two, three-three-four-eight. Don't call before noon."

"That's not fair," a throaty voice objected. It came from one who looked a little too old for Hebe, and just a shade too plump. It went on, "Do I call you Archie?"

"Sure, that's my name."

"All right, Archie, have your eyes examined." She lifted an arm, baring it, to touch the shoulder of one beside her. "We admit we're all beautiful, but we're not in the same class as Helen Iacono. Look at her!"

I was doing so, and I must say that the throaty voice had a point. Helen Iacono, with deep dark eyes, dark velvet skin, and wavy silky hair darker than either skin or eyes, was unquestionably rare and special. Her lips were parted enough to show the gleam of white teeth, but she wasn't laughing. She wasn't reacting at all, which was remarkable for an actress.

"It may be," I conceded, "that I am so dazzled by the collective radiance that I am blind to the glory of any single star. Perhaps I'm a poet after all, I sound like one. My feeling that I must have the phone numbers of *all* of you is certainly no reflection on Helen Iacono. I admit that that will not completely solve the problem, for tomorrow I must face the question which one to call first. If I feel as I do right now I would have to dial all the numbers simultaneously, and that's impossible. I hope to heaven it doesn't end in a stalemate. What if I can never decide which one to call first? What if it drives me mad? Or what if I gradually sink—"

I turned to see who was tugging at my sleeve. It was Benjamin Schriver, the host, with a grin on his ruddy round face. He said, "I hate to interrupt your speech, but perhaps you can finish it later. We're ready to sit. Will you join us?"

2

THE dining room, on the same floor as the kitchen, three feet or so below street level, would have been too gloomy for my taste if most of the dark wood paneling hadn't been covered with pictures of geese, pheasants, fish, fruit, vegetables, and other assorted edible objects; and also it helped that the tablecloth was white as snow, the wineglasses, seven of them at each place, glistened in the soft light from above, and the polished silver shone. In the center was a low gilt bowl, or maybe gold, two feet long, filled with clusters of Phalaenopsis Aphrodite, donated by Wolfe, cut by him that afternoon from some of his most treasured plants.

As he sat he was scowling at them, but the scowl was not for the orchids; it was for the chair, which, though a little fancy, was perfectly okay for you or me but not for his seventh of a ton. His fundament lapped over at both sides. He erased the scowl when Schriver, at the end of the table, complimented him on the flowers, and Hewitt, across from him, said he had never seen Phalaenopsis better grown, and the others joined in the chorus, all but the aristologist who sat between Wolfe and me. He was a Wall Street character and a well-known theatrical angel named Vincent Pyle, and was living up to his reputation as an original by wearing a dinner jacket, with tie to match, which looked black until you had the light at a certain slant andthen you saw that it was green. He eyed the orchids with his head cocked and his mouth puckered, and said, "I don't care for flowers with spots and streaks. They're messy."

I thought, but didn't say, Okay, drop dead. If I had known that that was what he was going to do in about three hours I might not even have thought it. He got a rise, not from Wolfe or me, or Schriver or Hewitt, but from three others who thought flowers with spot and streaks were wonderful: Adrian Dart, the actor who had turned down an offer of a million a week, more or less, from Hollywood; Emil Kreis, Chairman of the Board of Codex Press, book publishers; and Harvey M. Leacraft, corporation lawyer.

Actually, cupbearers was what the Hebes were not. The wines, beginning with the Montrachet with the first course, were poured by Felix; but the girls delivered the food, with different routines for different items. The first course, put on individual plates in the kitchen, with each girl bringing in a plate for her aristologist, was small *blinis* sprinkled with chopped chives, piled with caviar, and topped with sour cream — the point, as far as Fritz was concerned, being that he had made the blinis, starting on them at eleven that morning, and also the sour cream, starting on that Sunday evening. Fritz's sour cream is very special, but Vincent Pyle had to get in a crack. After he had downed all of his blinis he remarked, loud enough to carry around the table, "A new idea, putting sand in. Clever. Good for chickens, since they need grit."

The man on my left, Emil Kreis, the publisher, muttered at my ear, "Ignore him. He backed three flops this season."

The girls, who had been coached by Fritz and Felix that afternoon, handled the green turtle soup without a splash. When they had brought in the soup plates Felix brought the bowl, and each girl ladled from it as Felix held it by the plate. I asked Pyle cordially, "Any sand?" but he said no, it was delicious, and cleaned it up.

I was relieved when I saw that the girls wouldn't dish the fish — flounders poached in dry white wine, with a mussel-and-mushroom sauce that was one of Fritz's specialties. Felix did the dishing at a side table, and the girls merely carried. With the first taste of the sauce there were murmurs of appreciation, and Adrian Dart, the actor, across from Wolfe, sang out, "Superb!" They were making various noises of satisfaction, and Leacraft, the lawyer, was asking Wolfe if Fritz would be willing to give him the recipe, when Pyle, on my right, made a face and dropped his fork on his plate with a clatter. I thought he was putting on an act, and still thought so when his head drooped and I heard him gnash his teeth, but then his shoulders sagged and he clapped a hand to his mouth, and that seemed to be overdoing it. Two or three of them said something, and he pushed his chair back, got to his feet, said, "You must excuse me, I'm sorry," and headed for the door to the hall. Schriver arose and followed him out. The others exchanged words and glances.

Hewitt said, "A damn shame, but I'm going to finish this," and used his fork. Someone asked if Pyle had a bad heart, and someone else said no. They all resumed with the flounder, and the conversation, but the spirit wasn't the same.

When, at a signal from Felix, the maidens started removing the plates, Lewis Hewitt got up and left the room, came back in a couple of minutes, sat, and raised his voice. "Vincent is in considerable pain, and a doctor has come. There is nothing we can do, and Ben wishes us to proceed. He will rejoin us when — when he can."

"What is it?" someone asked.

Hewitt said the doctor didn't know. Zoltan entered bearing an enormous covered platter, and the Hebes gathered at the side table, and Felix lifted the cover and began serving the roast pheasant, which had been larded with strips of pork soaked for twenty hours in Tokay, and then — but no. What's the use? The annual dinner of the Ten for Aristology was a flop. Since for years I have been eating three meals a day cooked by Fritz Brenner I would like to show my appreciation by getting in print some idea of what he can do in the way of victuals, but it won't do here. Sure, the pheasant was good enough for gods if there had been any around, and so was the suckling pig, and the salad, with a dressing which Fritz calls Devil's Rain, and the chestnut croquettes, and the

cheese—only the one kind, made in New Jersey by a man named Bill
Thompson under Fritz's supervision; and they were all eaten, more or less. But
Hewitt left the room three more times and the last time was gone a good ten
minutes, and Schriver didn't rejoin the party at all, and while the salad was
being served Emil Kreis went out and didn't come back.

When, as coffee and brandy were being poured and cigars and cigarettes
passed, Hewitt left his chair for the fifth time, Nero Wolfe got up and followed
him out. I lit a cigar just to be doing something, and tried to be sociable by
giving an ear to a story Adrian Dart was telling, but by the time I finished my
coffee I was getting fidgety. By the glower that had been deepening on Wolfe's
face for the past hour I knew he was boiling, and when he's like that, especially
away from home, there's no telling about him. He might even have had the idea
of aiming the glower at Vincent Pyle for ruining Fritz's meal. So I put what was
left of the cigar in a tray, arose, and headed for the door, and was halfway to it
when here he came, still glowering.

"Come with me," he snapped, and kept going.

The way to the kitchen from the dining room was through a pantry, twenty feet
long, with counters and shelves and cupboards on both sides. Wolfe marched
through with me behind. In the kitchen the twelve maidens were scattered around
on chairs and stools at tables and counters, eating. A woman was busy at a sink.
Zoltan was busy at a refrigerator. Fritz, who was pouring a glass of wine,
presumably for himself, turned as Wolfe entered and put the bottle down.

Wolfe went to him, stood, and spoke. "Fritz. I offer my apologies. I permitted
Mr. Hewitt to cajole you. I should have known better. I beg your pardon."

Fritz gestured with his free hand, the wineglass steady in the other. "But it
is not to pardon, only to regret. The man got sick, that's a pity, only not from
my cooking. I assure you."

"You don't need to. Not from your cooking as it left you, but as it reached him. I
repeat that I am culpable, but I won't dwell on that now; it can wait. There is an
aspect that is exigent." Wolfe turned. "Archie. Are those women all here?"

I had to cover more than half a circle to count them, scattered as they were.
"Yes, sir, all present. Twelve."

"Collect them. They can stand"—he pointed to the alcove—"over there.
And bring Felix."

It was hard to believe. They were eating; and for him to interrupt a man, or
even a woman, at a meal, was unheard of. Not even me. Only in an extreme
emergency had he ever asked me to quit food before I was through. Boiling was
no name for it. Without even bothering to raise a brow, I turned and called out,
"I'm sorry, ladies, but if Mr. Wolfe says it's urgent that settles it. Over there,
please? All of you." Then I went through the pantry corridor, pushed the two-
way door, caught Felix's eye, and wiggled a beckoning finger at him, and he
came. By the time we got to the kitchen the girls had left the chairs and stools
and were gathering at the alcove, but not with enthusiasm. There were
mutterings, and some dirty looks for me as I approached with Felix. Wolfe
came, with Zoltan, and stood, tight-lipped, surveying them.

"I remind you," he said, "that the first course you brought to the table was
caviar on blinis topped with sour cream. The portion served to Mr. Vincent Pyle,
and eaten by him, contained arsenic. Mr. Pyle is in bed upstairs, attended by
three doctors, and will probably die within an hour. I am speaking—"

He stopped to glare at them. They were reacting, or acting, no matter which.

There were gasps and exclamations, and one of them clutched her throat, and another, baring her arms, clapped her palms to her ears. When the glare had restored order Wolfe went on, "You will please keep quiet and listen. I am speaking of conclusions formed by me. My conclusion that Mr. Pyle ate arsenic is based on the symptoms: burning throat, faintness, intense burning pain in the stomach, dry mouth, cool skin, vomiting. My conclusion that the arsenic was in the first course is based, first, on the amount of time it takes arsenic to act; second, on the fact that it is highly unlikely it could have been put in the soup or the fish; and third, that Mr. Pyle complained of sand in the cream or caviar. I admit the possibility that one or both of my conclusions will be proven wrong, but I regard it as remote and I am acting on them." His head turned. "Fritz. Tell me about the caviar from the moment it was put on the individual plates. Who did that?"

I had once told Fritz that I could imagine no circumstances in which he would look really unhappy, but now I wouldn't have to try. He was biting his lips, first the lower and then the upper. He began, "I must assure you—"

"I need no assurance from you, Fritz. Who put it on the plates?"

"Zoltan and I did." He pointed. "At that table."

"And left them there? They were taken from that table by the women?"

"Yes, sir."

"Each woman took one plate?"

"Yes, sir. I mean, they were told to. I was at the range."

Zoltan spoke up. "I watched them, Mr. Wolfe. They each took one plate. And believe me, nobody put any arsenic—"

"Please, Zoltan, I add another conclusion: that no one put arsenic in one of the portions and then left to chance which one of the guests would get it. Surely the poisoner intended it to reach a certain one—either Mr. Pyle, or, as an alternative, some other one and it went to Mr. Pyle by mishap. In any case, it was the portion Pyle ate that was poisoned, and whether he got it by design or by mischance is for the moment irrelevant." His eyes were at the girls. "Which one of you took that plate to Mr. Pyle?"

No reply. No sound, no movement.

Wolfe grunted. "Pfui. If you didn't know his name, you do now. The man who left during the fish course and who is now dying. Who served him?"

No reply; and I had to hand it to them that no pair of eyes left Wolfe to fasten on Peggy Choate, the redhead. Mine did. "What the heck," I said. "Speak up, Miss Choate."

"I didn't!" she cried.

"That's silly. Of course you did. Twenty people can swear to it. I looked right at you while you were dishing his soup. And when you brought the fish—"

"But I didn't take him that first thing! He already had some! I didn't!"

Wolfe took over. "Your name is Choate?"

"Yes." Her chin was up. "Peggy Choate."

"You deny that you served the plate of caviar, the first course, to Mr. Pyle?"

"I certainly do."

"But you were supposed to? You were assigned to him?"

"Yes. I took the plate from the table there and went in with it, and started to him, and then I saw that he had some, and I thought I had made a mistake. We hadn't seen the guests. That man"—she pointed to Felix—"had shown us which chair our guest would sit in, and mine was the second from the right on this side as I went in, but that one had already been served, and I thought someone else had made a mistake or I was mixed up. Anyway, I saw that the man next to him, on his right, hadn't been served, and I gave it to him. That was you. I gave it to you."

"Indeed." Wolfe was frowning at her. "Who was assigned to me?"

That wasn't put on. He actually didn't know. He had never looked at her. He had been irritated that females were serving, and besides, he hates to twist his neck. Of course I could have told him, but Helen Iacono said, "I was."

"Your name, please?"

"Helen Iacono." She had a rich contralto that went fine with the deep dark eyes and dark velvet skin and wavy silky hair.

"Did you bring me the first course?"

"No. When I went in I saw Peggy serving you, and a man on the left next to the end didn't have any, so I gave it to him."

"Do you know his name?"

"I do," Nora Jaret said. "From the card. He was mine." Her big brown eyes were straight at Wolfe. "His name is Kreis. He had his when I got there. I was going to take it back to the kitchen, but then I thought, someone had stage fright but I haven't, and I gave it to the man at the end."

"Which end?"

"The left end. Mr. Schriver. He came and spoke to us this afternoon."

She was corroborated by Carol Annis, the one with hair like corn silk who had no sense of humor. "That's right," she said. "I saw her. I was going to stop her, but she had already put the plate down, so I went around to the other side of the table with it when I saw that Adrian Dart didn't have any. I didn't mind because it was him."

"You were assigned to Mr. Schriver?"

"Yes. I served him the other courses, until he left."

It was turning into a ring-around-a-rosy, but the squat was bound to come. All Wolfe had to do was get to one who couldn't claim a delivery, and that would tag her. I was rather hoping it wouldn't be the next one, for the girl with the throaty voice had been Adrian Dart's, and she had called me Archie and had given Helen Iacono a nice tribute. Would she claim she had served Dart herself?

No. She answered without being asked. "My name is Lucy Morgan," she said, "and I had Adrian Dart, and Carol got to him before I did. There was only one place that didn't have one, on Dart's left, the next but one, and I took it there. I don't know his name."

I supplied it. "Hewitt. Mr. Lewis Hewitt." A better name for it than ring-around-a-rosy would have been passing-the-buck. I looked at Fern Faber, the tall self-made blonde with a wide lazy mouth who had been my first stop on my phone-number tour. "It's your turn, Miss Faber," I told her. "You had Mr. Hewitt. Yes?"

"I sure did." Her voice was pitched so high it threatened to squeak.

"But you didn't take him his caviar?"

"I sure didn't."

"Then who did you take it to?"

"Nobody."

I looked at Wolfe. His eyes were narrowed at her. "What did you do with it, Miss Faber?"

"I didn't do anything with it. There wasn't any."

"Nonsense. There are twelve of you, and there were twelve at the table, and each got a portion. How can you say there wasn't any?"

"Because there wasn't. I was in the john fixing my hair, and when I came back in she was taking the last one from the table, and when I asked where mine was he said he didn't know, and I went to the dining room and they all had some."

"Who was taking the last one from the table?"

She pointed to Lucy Morgan. "Her."

"Whom did you ask where your was?"

She pointed to Zoltan. "Him."

Wolfe turned. "Zoltan?"

"Yes, sir. I mean, yes, sir, she asked where hers was. I had turned away when the last one was taken. I don't mean I know where she had been, just that she asked me that. I asked Fritz if I should go in and see if they were one short and he said no, Felix was there and would see to it."

Wolfe went back to Fern Faber. "Where is that room where you were fixing your hair?"

She pointed toward the pantry. "In there."

"The door's around the corner," Felix said.

"How long were you in there?"

"My God, I don't know, do you think I timed it? When Archie Goodwin was talking to us, and Mr. Schriver came and said they were going to start, I went pretty soon after that."

Wolfe's head jerked to me. "So that's where you were. I might have known there were young women around. Supposing that Miss Faber went to fix her hair shortly after you left — say three minutes — how long was she at it, if the last plate had been taken from the table when she returned to the kitchen?"

I gave it a thought. "Fifteen to twenty minutes."

He growled at her, "What was wrong with your hair?"

"I didn't say anything was wrong with it." She was getting riled. "Look, Mister, do you want all the details?"

"No." Wolfe surveyed them for a moment, not amiably, took in enough air to fill all his middle — say two bushels — let it out again, turned his back on them, saw the glass of wine Fritz had left on a table, went and picked it up, smelled it, and stood gazing at it. The girls started to make noises, and, hearing them, he put the glass down and came back.

"You're in a pickle," he said. "So am I. You heard me apologize to Mr. Brenner and avow my responsibility for his undertaking to cook that meal. When, upstairs, I saw that Mr. Pyle would die, and reached the conclusions I told you of, I felt myself under compulsion to expose the culprit. I am committed. When I came down here I thought it would be a simple matter to learn who had served poisoned food to Mr. Pyle, but I was wrong. It's obvious now that I have to deal with one who is not only resourceful and ingenious, but also quick-witted and audacious. While I was closing in on her just now, as I thought, inexorably approaching the point where she would either have to contradict one of you or deny that she had served the first course to anyone, she was fleering at me inwardly, and with reason, for her coup had worked. She had slipped through my fingers, and —"

"But she didn't!" It came from one of them whose name I didn't have. "She said she didn't serve anybody!"

Wolfe shook his head. "No. Not Miss Faber. She is the only one who is eliminated. She says she was absent from this room during the entire period when the plates were being taken from the table, and she wouldn't dare to say that if she had in fact been here and taken a plate and carried it in to Mr. Pyle. She would certainly have been seen by some of you."

He shook his head again. "Not her. But it could have been any other one of you. You — I speak now to that one, still to be identified — you must have extraordinary faith in your attendant godling, even allowing for your craft. For you took great risks. You took a plate from the table — not the first probably, but one of the first — and on your way to the dining room you put arsenic in the cream. That wasn't difficult; you might even have done it without stopping if you had the arsenic in a paper spill. You could get rid of the spill later, perhaps in the room which Miss Faber calls a john. You took the plate to Mr. Pyle, came back here immediately, got another plate, took it to the dining room, and gave it to one who had not been served. I am not guessing; it had to be like that. It was a remarkably adroit strategem, but you can't possibly be impregnable."

He turned to Zoltan. "You say you watched as the plates were taken, and each of them took only one. Did one of them come back and take another?"

Zoltan looked fully as unhappy as Fritz. "I'm thinking, Mr. Wolfe. I can try to think, but I'm afraid it won't help. I didn't look at their faces, and they're all dressed alike. I guess I didn't watch very close."

"Fritz?"

"No, sir. I was at the range."

"Then try this, Zoltan. Who were the first ones to take plates — the first three or four?"

Zoltan slowly shook his head. "I'm afraid it's no good, Mr. Wolfe. I could try to think, but I couldn't be sure." He moved his eyes right to left and back again, at the girls. "I tell you, I wasn't looking at their faces." He extended his hands, palms up. "You will consider, Mr. Wolfe, I was not thinking of poison. I was only seeing that the plates were carried properly. Was I thinking which one has got arsenic? No."

"I took the first plate," a girl blurted — another whose name I didn't know. "I took it in and gave it to the man in my chair, the one at the left corner at the other side of the table, and I stayed there. I never left the dining room."

"Your name, please?"

"Marjorie Quinn."

"Thank you. Now the second plate. Who took it?"

Apparently nobody. Wolfe gave them ten seconds, his eyes moving to take them all in, his lips tight. "I advise you," he said, "to jog your memories, in case it becomes necessary to establish the order in which you took the plates by dragging it out of you. I hope it won't come to that." His head turned. "Felix, I have neglected you purposely, to give you time to reflect. You were in the dining room. My expectation was that after I had learned who had served the first course to Mr. Pyle you would corroborate it, but now that there is nothing for you to corroborate I must look to you for the fact itself. I must ask you to point her out."

In a way Wolfe was Felix's boss. When Wolfe's oldest and dearest friend, Marko Vukcic, who had owned Rusterman's restaurant, had died, his will had left the restaurant to members of the staff in trust, with Wolfe as the trustee, and Felix was the maître d'hôtel. With that job at the best restaurant in New York, naturally Felix was both bland and commanding, but now he was neither. If he felt the way he looked, he was miserable.

"I can't."

"Pfui! You, trained as you are to see everything?"

"That is true, Mr. Wolfe. I knew you would ask me this, but I can't. I can only explain. The young woman who just spoke, Marjorie Quinn, was the first one in with a plate, as she said. She did not say that as she served it one of the blinis slid off onto the table, but it did. As I sprang toward her she was actually about to pick it up with her fingers, and I jerked her away and put it back on the plate with a fork, and I gave her a look. Anyway, I was not myself. Having women as waiters was bad enough, and not only that, they were without experience. When I recovered command of myself I saw the red-haired one, Choate, standing back of Mr. Pyle, to whom she had been assigned, with a plate in her hand, and I saw that he had already been served. As I moved forward she stepped to the right and served the plate to you. The operation was completely upset, and I was helpless. The dark-skinned one, Iacono, who was assigned to you, served Mr. Kreis, and the —"

"If you please." Wolfe was curt. "I have heard them, and so have you. I have always found you worthy of trust, but it's possible that in your exalted position, maître d'hôtel at Rusterman's, you would rather dodge than get involved in a poisoning. Are you dodging, Felix?"

"Good God, Mr. Wolfe, I *am* involved!"

"Very well. I saw that woman spill the blini and start her fingers for it, and I saw you retrieve it. Yes, you're involved, but not as I am." He turned to me. "Archie. You are commonly my first resort, but now you are my last. You sat next to Mr. Pyle. Who put that plate before him?"

Of course I knew that was coming, but I hadn't been beating my brain because there was no use. I said merely but positively, "No." He glared at me and I added, "That's all, just no, but like Felix I can explain. First, I would have had to turn around to see her face, and that's bad table manners. Second, I was watching Felix rescue the blini. Third, there was an argument going on about flowers with spots and streaks, and I was listening to it and so were you. I didn't even see her arm."

Wolfe stood and breathed. He shut his eyes and opened them again, and breathed some more. "Incredible," he muttered. "The wretch had incredible luck."

"I'm going home," Fern Faber said. "I'm tired."

"So am I," another one said, and was moving, but Wolfe's eyes pinned her. "I advise you not to," he said. "It is true that Miss Faber is eliminated as the culprit, and also Miss Quinn, since she was under surveillance by Felix while Mr. Pyle was being served, but I advise even them to stay. When Mr. Pyle dies the doctors will certainly summon the police, and it would be well for all of you to be here when they arrive. I had hoped to be able to present them with an exposed murderer. Confound it! There is still a chance. Archie, come with me. Fritz, Felix, Zoltan, remain with these women. If one or more of them insist on leaving do not detain them by force, but have the names and the times of departure. If they want to eat feed them. I'll be —"

"I'm going home," Fern Faber said stubbornly.

"Very well, go. You'll be got out of bed by a policeman before the night's out. I'll be in the dining room, Fritz. Come, Archie."

He went and I followed, along the pantry corridor and through the two-way door. On the way I glanced at my wrist watch: ten past eleven. I rather expected to find the dining room empty, but it wasn't. Seven of them were still there, the only ones missing being Schriver and Hewitt, who were probably upstairs. The air was heavy with cigar smoke. All of them but Adrian Dart were at the table with their chairs pushed back at various angles, with brandy glasses and cigars. Dart was standing with his back to a picture of honkers on the wing, holding forth. As we entered he stopped and heads turned.

Emil Kreis spoke. "Oh, there you are. I was coming to the kitchen but didn't want to butt in. Schriver asked me to apologize to Fritz Brenner. Our custom is to ask the chef to join us with champagne, which is barbarous but gay, but of course in the circumstances . . ." He let it hang, and added, "Shall I explain to him? Or will you?"

"I will." Wolfe went to the end of the table and sat. He had been on his feet for nearly two hours — all very well for his twice-a-day sessions in the plant rooms, but not elsewhere. He looked around. "Mr. Pyle is still alive?"

"We hope so," one said. "We sincerely hope so."

"I ought to be home in bed," another said. "I have a hard day tomorrow. But it doesn't seem . . ." He took a puff on his cigar.

Emil Kreis reached for the brandy bottle. "There's been no word since I came down." He looked at his wrist. "Nearly an hour ago. I suppose I should go up. It's so damned unpleasant." He poured brandy.

"Terrible," one said. "Absolutely terrible. I understand you were asking which one of the girls brought him the caviar. Kreis says you asked him."

Wolfe nodded. "I also asked Mr. Schriver and Mr. Hewitt. And Mr. Goodwin and Mr. Brenner, and the two men who came to help at my request. And the women themselves. After more than an hour with them I am still at fault. I have discovered the artifice the culprit used, but not her identity."

"Aren't you a bit premature?" Leacraft, the lawyer, asked. "There may be no culprit. An acute and severe gastric disturbance may be caused —"

"Nonsense. I am too provoked for civility, Mr. Leacraft. The symptoms are typical of arsenic, and you heard Mr. Pyle complain of sand, but that's not all. I said I have discovered the artifice. None of them will admit serving him the first course. The one assigned to him found he had already been served and served me instead. There is indeed a culprit. She put arsenic in the cream *en passant*, served it to Mr. Pyle, returned to the kitchen for another portion, and came and served it to someone else. That is established."

"But then," the lawyer objected, "one of them served no one. How could that be?"

"I am not a tyro at inquiry, Mr. Leacraft. I'll ravel it for you later if you want, but now I want to get on. It is no conjecture that poison was given to Mr. Pyle by the woman who brought him the caviar; it is a fact. By a remarkable combination of cunning and luck she has so far eluded identification, and I am appealing to you. All of you. I ask you to close your eyes and recall the scene. We are here at table, discussing the orchids — the spots and streaks. The woman serving that place" — he pointed — "lets a blini slip from the plate and Felix retrieves it. It helps to close your eyes. Just about then a woman enters with a plate, goes to Mr. Pyle, and puts it before him. I appeal to you: which one?"

Emil Kreis shook his head. "I told you upstairs, I don't know. I didn't see her. Or if I did, it didn't register."

Adrian Dart, the actor, stood with his eyes closed, his chin up, and his arms folded, a fine pose for concentration. The others, even Leacraft, had their eyes closed too, but of course they couldn't hold a candle to Dart. After a long moment the eyes began to open and heads to shake.

"It's gone," Dart said in his rich musical baritone. "I must have seen it, since I sat across from him, but it's gone. Utterly."

"I didn't see it," another said. "I simply didn't see it."

"I have a vague feeling," another said, "but it's too damn vague. No."

They made it unanimous. No dice.

Wolfe put his palms on the table. "Then I'm in for it," he said grimly. "I am your guest, gentlemen, and would not be offensive, but I am to blame that Fritz Brenner was enticed to this deplorable fiasco. If Mr. Pyle dies, as he surely will—"

The door opened and Benjamin Schriver entered. Then Lewis Hewitt, and then the familiar burly frame of Sergeant Purley Stebbins of Manhattan Homicide West.

Schriver crossed to the table and spoke. "Vincent is dead. Half an hour ago. Doctor Jameson called the police. He thinks that it is practically certain—"

"Hold it," Purley growled at his elbow. "I'll handle it if you don't mind."

"My God," Adrian Dart groaned, and shuddered magnificently.

That was the last I heard of the affair from an aristologist.

3

"I did not!" Inspector Cramer roared. "Quit twisting my words around! I didn't charge you with complicity! I merely said you're concealing something, and what the hell is that to scrape your neck? You always do!"

It was a quarter to two Wednesday afternoon. We were in the office on the first floor of the old brownstone on West 35th Street—Wolfe in his oversized chair at his desk, I at my desk, and Cramer in the red leather chair. The daily schedule was messed beyond repair. When we had finally got home, at five o'clock in the morning, Wolfe had told Fritz to forget about breakfast until further notice, and had sent me up to the plant rooms to leave a note for Theodore saying that he would not appear at nine in the morning and perhaps not at all. It had been not at all. At half past eleven he had buzzed on the house phone to tell Fritz to bring up the breakfast tray with four eggs and ten slices of bacon instead of two and five, and it was past one o'clock when the sounds came of his elevator and then his footsteps in the hall, heading for the office.

If you think a problem child is tough, try handling a problem elephant. He is plenty knotty even when he is himself, and that day he was really special.

After looking through the mail, glancing at his desk calendar, and signing three checks I had put on his desk, he had snapped at me, "A fine prospect. Dealing with them singly would be interminable. Will you have them all here at six o'clock?"

I kept calm. I merely asked, "All of whom?"

"You know quite well. Those women."

I still kept calm. "I should think ten of them would be enough. You said yourself that two of them can be crossed off."

"I need them all. Those two can help establish the order in which the plates were taken."

I held on. I too was short on sleep, shorter even than he, and I didn't feel up to a fracas. "I have a suggestion," I said. "I suggest that you postpone operations until your wires are connected again. Counting up to five hundred might help. You know damn well that all twelve of them will spend the afternoon either at the District Attorney's office or receiving official callers at their homes — probably most of them at the DA's office. And probably they'll spend the evening there too. Do you want some aspirin?"

"I want *them*," he growled.

I could have left him to grope back to normal on his own and gone up to my room for a nap, but after all he pays my salary. So I picked up a sheet of paper I had typed and got up and handed it to him. It read:

	Assigned to	Served
Peggy Choate	Pyle	Wolfe
Helen Iacono	Wolfe	Kreis
Nora Jaret	Kreis	Schriver
Carol Annis	Schriver	Dart
Lucy Morgan	Dart	Hewitt
Fern Faber	Hewitt	No one

"Fern Faber's out," I said, "and I realize it doesn't have to be one of those five, even though Lucy Morgan took the last plate. Possibly one or two others took plates after Peggy Choate did, and served the men they were assigned to. But it seems —"

I stopped because he had crumpled it and dropped it in the wastebasket. "I heard them," he growled. "My faculties, including my memory, are not impaired. I am merely ruffled beyond the bounds of tolerance."

For him that was an abject apology, and a sign that he was beginning to regain control. But a few minutes later, when the bell rang, and after a look through the one-way glass panel of the front door I told him it was Cramer, and he said to admit him, and Cramer marched in and planted his fanny on the red leather chair and opened up with an impolite remark about concealing facts connected with a murder, Wolfe had cut loose; and Cramer asked him what the hell was that to scrape his neck, which was a new one to me but sounded somewhat vulgar for an inspector. He had probably picked it up from some hoodlum.

Ruffling Cramer beyond the bounds of tolerance did Wolfe good. He leaned back in his chair. "Everyone conceals something," he said placidly. "Or at least omits something, if only because to include everything is impossible. During those wearisome hours, nearly six of them, I answered all questions, and so did Mr. Goodwin. Indeed, I thought we were helpful. I thought we had cleared away some rubble."

"Yeah." Cramer wasn't grateful. His big pink face was always a little pinker than normal, not with pleasure, when he was tackling Wolfe. "You had witnessed the commission of a murder, and you didn't notify —"

"It wasn't a murder until he died."

"All right, a felony. You not only failed to report it, you —"

"That a felony had been committed was my conclusion. Others present disagreed with me. Only a few minutes before Mr. Stebbins entered the room Mr. Leacraft, a member of the bar and therefore himself an officer of the law, challenged my conclusion."

"You should have reported it. You're a licensed detective. Also you started an investigation, questioning the suspects —"

"Only to test my conclusion. I would have been a ninny to report it before learning —"

"Damn it," Cramer barked, "will you let me finish a sentence? Just one?"

Wolfe's shoulders went up an eighth of an inch and down again. "Certainly, if it has import. I am not baiting you, Mr. Cramer. But I have already replied to these imputations, to you and Mr. Stebbins and an assistant district attorney. I did not wrongly delay reporting a crime, and I did not usurp the function of the police. Very well, finish a sentence."

"You knew Pyle was dying. You said so."

"Also my own conclusion. The doctors were still trying to save him."

Cramer took a breath. He looked at me, saw nothing inspiring, and returned to Wolfe. "I'll tell you why I'm here. Those three men — the cook, the man that helped him, and the man in the dining room — Fritz Brenner, Felix Courbet, and Zoltan Mahany — were all supplied by you. All close to you. I want to know about them, or at least two of them. I might as well leave Fritz out of it. In the first place, it's hard to believe that Zoltan doesn't know who took the first two or three plates or whether one of them came back for a second one, and it's also hard to believe that Felix doesn't know who served Pyle."

"It is indeed," Wolfe agreed. "They are highly trained men. But they have been questioned."

"They sure have. It's also hard to believe that Goodwin didn't see who served Pyle. He sees everything."

"Mr. Goodwin is present. Discuss it with him."

"I have. Now I want to ask your opinion of a theory. I know yours, and I don't reject it, but there are alternatives. First a fact. In a metal trash container in the kitchen — not a garbage pail — we found a roll of paper, ordinary white paper that had been rolled into a tube, held with tape, smaller at one end. The laboratory has found particles of arsenic inside. The only two fingerprints on it that are any good are Zoltan's. He says he saw it on the kitchen floor under a table some time after the meal had started, he can't say exactly when, and he picked it up and dropped it in the container, and his prints are on it because he pinched it to see if there was anything in it."

Wolfe nodded. "As I surmised. A paper spill."

"Yeah. I don't say it kills your theory. She could have shaken it into the cream without leaving prints, and she certainly wouldn't have dropped it on the floor if there was any chance it had her prints. But it *has* got Zoltan's.

What's wrong with the theory that Zoltan poisoned one of the portions and saw that it was taken by a certain one? I'll answer that myself. There are two things wrong with it. First, Zoltan claims he didn't know which guest any of the girls were assigned to. But Felix knew, and they could have been in collusion. Second, the girls all deny that Zoltan indicated which plate they were to take, but you know how that is. He could have done it without her knowing it. What else is wrong with it?"

"It's not only untenable, it's egregious," Wolfe declared. "Why, in that case, did one of them come back for another plate?"

"She was confused. Nervous. Dumb."

"Bosh. Why doesn't she admit it?"

"Scared."

"I don't believe it. I questioned them before you did." Wolfe waved it away. "Tommyrot, and you know it. My theory is not a theory; it is a reasoned conviction. I hope it is being acted on. I suggested to Mr. Stebbins that he examine their garments to see if some kind of pocket had been made in one of them. She had to have it readily available."

"He did. They all had pockets. The laboratory has found no trace of arsenic." Cramer uncrossed his legs. "We're following up your theory all right; we might even have hit on it ourselves in a week or two. But I wanted to ask you about those men. You know them."

"I do, yes. But I do not answer for them. They may have a dozen murders on their souls, but they had nothing to do with the death of Mr. Pyle. If you are following up my theory—my conviction, rather—I suppose you have learned the order in which the women took the plates."

Cramer shook his head. "We have not, and I doubt if we will. All we have is a bunch of contradictions. You had them good and scared before we got to them. We do have the last five, starting with Peggy Choate, who found that Pyle had been served and gave it to you, and then—but you know them. You got that yourself."

"No. I got those five, but not that they were the last. There might have been others in between."

"There weren't. It's pretty well settled that those five were the last. After Peggy Choate the last four plates were taken by Helen Iacono, Nora Jaret, Carol Annis, and Lucy Morgan. Then that Fern Faber, who had been in the can, but there was no plate for her. It's the order in which they took them before that, the first seven, that we can't pry out of them—except the first one, that Marjorie Quinn. You couldn't either."

Wolfe turned a palm up. "I was interrupted."

"You were not. You left them there in a huddle, scared stiff, and went to the dining room to start in on the men. Your own private murder investigation, and to hell with the law. I was surprised to see Goodwin here when I rang the bell just now. I supposed you'd have him out running errands like calling at the agency they got the girls from. Or getting a line on Pyle to find a connection between him and one of them. Unless you're no longer interested?"

"I'm interested willy-nilly," Wolfe declared. "As I told the assistant district attorney, it is on my score that a man was poisoned in food prepared by Fritz Brenner. But I do not send Mr. Goodwin on fruitless errands. He is one and you have dozens, and if anything is to be learned at the agency or by inquiry into Mr. Pyle's associations your army will dig it up. They're already at it, of course, but if they had started a trail you wouldn't be here. If I send Mr. Goodwin—"

The doorbell rang and I got up and went to the hall. At the rear the door to the kitchen swung open part way and Fritz poked his head through, saw me, and withdrew. Turning to the front for a look through the panel, I saw that I had exaggerated when I told Wolfe that all twelve of them would be otherwise engaged. At least one wasn't. There on the stoop was Helen Iacono.

4

IT had sounded to me as if Cramer had about said his say and would soon be moving along, and if he bumped into Helen Iacono in the hall she might be too embarrassed to give me her phone number, if that was what she had come for, so as I opened the door I pressed a finger to my lips and *sshh*ed at her, and then crooked the finger to motion her in. Her deep dark eyes looked a little startled, but she stepped across the sill, and I shut the door, turned, opened the first door on the left, to the front room, motioned to her to enter, followed, and closed the door.

"What's the matter?" she whispered.

"Nothing now," I told her. "This is soundproofed. There's a police inspector in the office with Mr. Wolfe and I thought you might have had enough of cops for a while. Of course if you want to meet him—"

"I don't. I want to see Nero Wolfe."

"Okay, I'll tell him as soon as the cop goes. Have a seat. It shouldn't be long."

There is a connecting door between the front room and the office, but I went through the hall, and here came Cramer. He was marching by without even the courtesy of a grunt, but I stepped to the front to let him out, and then went to the office and told Wolfe, "I've got one of them in the front room. Helen Iacono, the tawny-skinned Hebe who had you but gave her caviar to Kreis. Shall I keep her while I get the rest of them?"

He made a face. "What does she want?"

"To see you."

He took a breath. "Confound it. Bring her in."

I went and opened the connecting door, told her to come, and escorted her across to the red leather chair. She was more ornamental in it than Cramer, but not nearly as impressive as she had been at first sight. She was puffy around the eyes and her skin had lost some glow. She told Wolfe she hadn't had any sleep. She said she had just left the District Attorney's office, and if she went home her mother would be at her again, and her brothers and sisters would come home from school and make noise, and anyway she had decided she had to see Wolfe. Her mother was old-fashioned and didn't want her to be an actress. It was beginning to sound as if what she was after was a place to take a nap, but then Wolfe got a word in.

He said drily, "I don't suppose, Miss Iacono, you came to consult me about your career."

"Oh, no. I came because you're a detective and you're very clever and I'm afraid. I'm afraid they'll find out something I did, and if they do I won't have any career. My parents won't let me even if I'm still alive. I nearly gave it away already when they were asking me questions. So I decided to tell you about it and then if you'll help me I'll help you. If you promise to keep my secret."

"I can't promise to keep a secret if it is a guilty one — if it is a confession of a crime or knowledge of one."

"It isn't."

"Then you have my promise, and Mr. Goodwin's. We have kept many secrets."

"All right. I stabbed Vincent Pyle with a knife and got blood on me."

I stared. For half a second I thought she meant that he hadn't died of poison at all, that she had sneaked upstairs and stuck a knife in him, which seemed unlikely since the doctors would probably have found the hole.

Apparently she wasn't going on, and Wolfe spoke. "Ordinarily, Miss Iacono, stabbing a man is considered a crime. When and where did this happen?"

"It wasn't a crime because it was in self-defense." Her rich contralto was as composed as if she had been telling us the multiplication table. Evidently she saved the inflections for her career. She was continuing. "It happened in January, about three months ago. Of course I knew about him, everybody in show business does. I don't know if it's true that he backs shows just so he can get girls, but it might as well be. There's a lot of talk about the girls he gets, but nobody really knows because he was always very careful about it. Some of the girls have talked but he never did. I don't mean just taking them out, I mean the last ditch. We say that on Broadway. You know what I mean?"

"I can surmise."

"Sometimes we say the last stitch, but it means the same thing. Early last winter he began on me. Of course I knew about his reputation, but he was backing *Jack in the Pulpit* and they were about to start casting, and I didn't know it was going to be a flop, and if a girl expects to have a career she has to be sociable. I went out with him a few times, dinner and dancing and so forth, and then he asked me to his apartment, and I went. He cooked the dinner himself—I said he was very careful. Didn't I?"

"Yes."

"Well, he was. It's a penthouse on Madison Avenue, but no one else was there. I let him kiss me. I figure it like this, an actress gets kissed all the time on the stage and the screen and TV, and what's the difference? I went to his apartment three times and there was no real trouble, but the fourth time, that was in January, he turned into a beast right before my eyes, and I had to do something, and I grabbed a knife from the table and stabbed him with it. I got blood on my dress, and when I got home I tried to get it out but it left a stain. It cost forty-six dollars."

"But Mr. Pyle recovered."

"Oh, yes. I saw him a few times after that, I mean just by accident, but he barely spoke and so did I. I don't think he ever told anyone about it, but what if he did? What if the police find out about it?"

Wolfe grunted. "That would be regrettable, certainly. You would be pestered even more than you are now. But if you have been candid with me you are not in mortal jeopardy. The police are not simpletons. You wouldn't be arrested for murdering Mr. Pyle last night, let alone convicted, merely because you stabbed him in self-defense last January."

"Of course I wouldn't," she agreed. "That's not it. It's my mother and father. They'd find out about it because they would ask them questions, and if I'm going to have a career I would have to leave home and my family, and I don't want to. Don't you see?" She came forward in the chair. "But if they find out right away who did it, who poisoned him, that would end it and I'd be all right. Only I'm afraid they won't find out right away, but I think you could if I help you, and you said last night that you're committed. I can't offer to help the police because they'd wonder why."

"I see." Wolfe's eyes were narrowed at her. "How do you propose to help me?"

"Well, I figure it like this." She was on the edge of the chair. "The way you explained it last night, one of the girls poisoned him. She was one of the first ones to take a plate in, and then she came back and got another one. I don't quite understand why she did that, but you do, so all right. But if she came back for another plate that took a little time, and she must have been one of the last ones, and the police have got it worked out who were the last five. I know that because of the questions they asked this last time. So it was Peggy Choate or Nora Jaret or Carol Annis or Lucy Morgan."

"Or you."

"No, it wasn't me." Just matter-of-fact. "So it was one of them. And she didn't poison him just for nothing, did she? You'd have to have a very good reason to poison a man, I know I would. So all we have to do is find out which one had a good reason, and that's where I can help. I don't know Lucy Morgan, but I know Carol a little, and I know Nora and Peggy even better. And now we're in this together, and I can pretend I want to talk about it. I can talk about him because I had to tell the police I went out with him a few times, because I was seen with him and they'd find out, so I thought I'd better tell them. Dozens of girls went out with him, but he was so careful that nobody knows which ones went to the last ditch except the ones that talked. And I can find out which one of those four girls had a reason, and tell you, and that will end it."

I was congratulating myself that I hadn't got her phone number; and if I had got it, I would have crossed it off without a pang. I don't say that a girl must have true nobility of character before I'll buy her a lunch, but you have to draw the line somewhere. Thinking that Wolfe might be disgusted enough to put into words the way I felt, I horned in. "I have a suggestion, Miss Iacono. You could bring them here, all four of them, and let Mr. Wolfe talk it over with them. As you say, he's very clever."

She looked doubtful. "I don't believe that's a good idea. I think they'd be more apt to say things to me, just one at a time. Don't you think so, Mr. Wolfe?"

"You know them better than I do," he muttered. He was controlling himself.

"And then," she said, "when we find out which one had a reason, and we tell the police, I can say that I saw her going back to the kitchen for another plate. Of course just where I saw her, where she was and where I was, that will depend on who she is. I saw you, Mr. Wolfe, when I said you could if I helped you, I saw the look on your face. You didn't think a twenty-year-old girl could help, did you?"

He had my sympathy. Of course what he would have liked to say was that it might well be that a twenty-year-old hellcat could help, but that wouldn't have been tactful.

"I may have been a little skeptical," he conceded. "And it's possible that you're over-simplifying the problem. We have to consider all the factors. Take one: her plan must have been not only premeditated but also thoroughly rigged, since she had the poison ready. So she must have known that Mr. Pyle would be one of the guests. Did she?"

"Oh, yes. We all did. Mr. Buchman at the agency showed us a list of them and told us who they were, only of course he didn't have to tell us who Vincent Pyle was. That was about a month ago, so she had plenty of time to get the poison. Is that arsenic very hard to get?"

"Not at all. It is in common use for many purposes. That is of course one of the police lines of inquiry, but she knew it would be and she is no bungler. Another point: when Mr. Pyle saw her there, serving food, wouldn't he have been on his guard?"

"But he didn't see her. They didn't see any of us before. She came up behind him and gave him that plate. Of course he saw her afterwards, but he had already eaten it."

Wolfe persisted. "But then? He was in agony, but he was conscious and could speak. Why didn't he denounce her?"

She gestured impatiently. "I guess you're not as clever as you're supposed to be. He didn't know she had done it. When he saw her she was serving another man, and —"

"What other man?"

"I don't know. How do I know? Only it wasn't you, because I served you. And anyway, maybe he didn't know she wanted to kill him. Of course she had a good reason, I know that, but maybe he didn't know she felt like that. A man doesn't know how a girl feels — anyhow, some girls. Look at me. He didn't know I would never dream of going to the last ditch. He thought I would give up my honor and my virtue just to get a part in that play he was backing, and anyhow it was a flop." She gestured again. "I thought you wanted to get her. All you do is make objections."

Wolfe rubbed the side of his nose. "I do want to get her, Miss Iacono. I intend to. But like Mr. Pyle, though from a different motive, I am very careful. I can't afford to botch it. I fully appreciate your offer to help. You didn't like Mr. Goodwin's suggestion that you get them here in a body for discussion with me, and you may be right. But I don't like your plan, for you to approach them singly and try to pump them. Our quarry is a malign and crafty harpy, and I will not be a party to your peril. I propose an alternative. Arrange for Mr. Goodwin to see them, together with you. Being a trained investigator, he knows how to beguile, and the peril, if any, will be his. If they are not available at the moment, arrange it for this evening — but not here. Perhaps one of them has a suitable apartment, or if not, a private room at some restaurant would do. At my expense, of course. Will you?"

It was her turn to make objections, and she had several. But when Wolfe met them, and made it plain that he would accept her as a colleague only if she accepted his alternative, she finally gave in. She would phone to let me know how she was making out with the arrangements. From her manner, when she got up to go, you might have thought she had been shopping for some little item, say a handbag, and had graciously deferred to the opinion of the clerk. After I graciously escorted her out and saw her descend the seven steps from the stoop to the sidewalk, I returned to the office and found Wolfe sitting with his eyes closed and his fists planted on the chair arms.

"Even money," I said.

"On what?" he growled.

"On her against the field. She knows damn well who had a good reason and exactly what it was. It was getting too hot for comfort and she decided that the best way to duck was to wish it on some dear friend."

His eyes opened. "She would, certainly. A woman whose conscience has no sting will stop at nothing. But why come to me? Why didn't she cook her own stew and serve it to the police?"

"I don't know, but for a guess she was afraid the cops would get too curious and find out how she had saved her honor and her virtue and tell her mother and father, and father would spank her. Shall I also guess why you proposed your alternative instead of having her bring them here for you?"

"She wouldn't. She said so."

"Of course she would, if you had insisted. That's your guess. Mine is that you're not desperate enough yet to take on five females in a bunch. When you told me to bring the whole dozen you knew darned well it couldn't be done, not even by me. Okay, I want instructions."

"Later," he muttered, and closed his eyes.

5

IT was on the fourth floor of an old walk-up in the West Nineties near Amsterdam Avenue. I don't know what it had in the way of a kitchen or bedroom — or bedrooms — because the only room I saw was the one we were sitting in. It was medium-sized, and the couch and chairs and rugs had a homey look, the kind of homeyness that furniture gets by being used by a lot of different people for fifty or sixty years. The chair I was on had a wobbly leg, but that's no problem if you keep it in mind and make no sudden shifts. I was more concerned about the spidery little stand at my elbow on which my glass of milk was perched. I can always drink milk and had preferred it to Bubble-Pagne, registered trademark, a dime a bottle, which they were having. It was ten o'clock Wednesday evening.

The hostesses were the redhead with milky skin, Peggy Choate, and the one with big brown eyes and dimples, Nora Jaret, who shared the apartment. Carol Annis, with the fine profile and the corn-silk hair, had been there when Helen Iacono and I arrived, bring Lucy Morgan and her throaty voice after detouring our taxi to pick her up at a street corner. They were a very attractive collection, though of course not as decorative as they had been in their ankle-length purple stolas. Girls always look better in uniforms or costumes. Take nurses or elevator girls or Miss Honeydew at a melon festival.

I was now calling her Helen, not that I felt like it, but in the detective business you have to be sociable, of course preserving your honor and virtue. In the taxi, before picking up Lucy Morgan, she told me she had been thinking it over and she doubted if it would be possible to find out which one of them had a good reason to kill Pyle, or thought she had, because Pyle had been so very careful when he had a girl come to his penthouse. The only way would be to get one of them to open up, and Helen doubted if she could get her to, since she would be practically confessing murder, and she was sure I couldn't. So the best way would be for Helen and me, after spending an evening with them, to talk it over and decide which one was the most likely, and then she would tell Wolfe she had seen her going back to the kitchen and bringing another plate, and Wolfe would tell the police, and that would do it.

No, I didn't feel like calling her Helen. I would just as soon have been too far away from her to call her at all.

Helen's declared object in arranging the party — declared to them — was to find out from me what Nero Wolfe and the cops had done and were doing, so they would know where they stood. Helen was sure I would loosen up, she had told them, because she had been to see me and found me very nice and sympathetic. So the hostesses were making it sort of festive and intimate by serving Bubble-Pagne, though I preferred milk. I had a suspicion that at least one of them, Lucy Morgan, would have preferred whisky or gin or rum or vodka, and maybe they all would, but that might have made me suspect that they were not just a bunch of wholesome, hard-working artists.

They didn't look festive. I wouldn't say that they were haggard, but much of the bloom was off. And they hadn't bought Helen's plug for me that I was nice and sympathetic. They were absolutely skeptical, sizing me up with sidewise looks, especially Carol Annis, who sat cross-legged on the couch with her head cocked. It was she who asked me, after a few remarks had been made about how awful it had been and still was, how well I knew the chef and the other man in the kitchen. I told her she could forget Fritz. He was completely above suspicion, and anyway he had been at the range while the plates were taken. As for Zoltan, I said that though I had known him a long while we were not intimate, but that was irrelevant because, granting that he had known which guest each girl would serve, if he poisoned one of the portions and saw that a certain girl got it, why did she or some other girl come back for another plate?

"There's no proof that she did," Carol declared. "Nobody saw her."

"Nobody *noticed* her." I wasn't aggressive; I was supposed to be nice and sympathetic. "She wouldn't have been noticed leaving the dining room because the attention of the girls who were in there was on Felix and Marjorie Quinn, who had spilled a blini, and the men wouldn't notice her. The only place she would have been noticed was in the corridor through the pantry, and if she met another girl there she could have stopped and been patting her hair or something. Anyhow, one of you must have gone back for a second plate, because when Fern Faber went for hers there wasn't any."

"Why do you say one of us?" Nora demanded. "If you mean one of us here. There were twelve."

"I do mean one of you here, but I'm not saying it, I'm just quoting the police. They think it was one of you here because you were the last five."

"How do you know what they think?"

"I'm not at liberty to say. But I do."

"I know what I think," Carol asserted. She had uncrossed her legs and slid forward on the couch to get her toes to the floor. "I think it was Zoltan. I read in the *Gazette* that he's a chef at Rusterman's, and Nero Wolfe is the trustee and so he's the boss there, and I think Zoltan hated him for some reason and tried to poison him, but he gave the poisoned plate to the wrong girl. Nero Wolfe sat right next to Pyle."

There was no point in telling her that she was simply ignoring the fact that one of them had gone back for a second helping, so I just said, "Nobody can stop you thinking. But I doubt very much if the police would buy that."

"What would they buy?" Peggy asked.

My personal feelings about Peggy were mixed. For, she had recognized me and named me. Against, she had accused me of liking myself. "Anything that would fit," I told her. "As I said, they think it was one of you five that went back for more, and therefore they have to think that one of you gave the poison to Pyle, because what other possible reason could you have had for serving another portion? They wouldn't buy anything that didn't fit into that. That's what rules out everybody else, including Zoltan." I looked at Carol. "I'm sorry, Miss Annis, but that's how it is."

"They're a bunch of dopes," Lucy Morgan stated. "They get an idea and then they haven't got room for another one." She was on the floor with her legs stretched out, her back against the couch. "I agree with Carol, there's no proof that any of us went back for another plate. That Zoltan said he didn't see anyone come back. Didn't he?"

"He did. He still does."

"Then he's a dope too. And he said no one took two plates. Didn't he?"

"Right. He still does."

"Then how do they know which one he's wrong about? We were all nervous, you know that. Maybe one of us took two plates instead of one, and when she got to the dining room there she was with an extra, and she got rid of it by giving it to some guest that didn't have any."

"Then why didn't she say so?" I asked.

"Because she was scared. The way Nero Wolfe came at us was enough to scare anybody. And now she won't say so because she has signed a statement and she's even more scared."

I shook my head. "I'm sorry, but if you analyze that you'll see that it won't do. It's very tricky. You can do it the way I did this afternoon. Take twenty-four little pieces of paper, and on twelve of them write the names of the guests, and arrange them as they sat at the table. On the other twelve pieces write the name of the twelve girls. Then try to manipulate the twelve girl pieces so that one of them either took in two plates at once, and did not give either of them to Pyle, or went back for a second plate, and did not give either the first one or the second one to Pyle. It can't be done. For if either of those things happened there wouldn't have been one mix-up, there would have been two. Since there was only one mix-up, Pyle couldn't possibly have been served by a girl who neither brought in two plates at once nor went back for a second one. So the idea that a girl *innocently* brought in two plates is out."

"I don't believe it," Nora said flatly.

"It's not a question of believing." I was still sympathetic. "You might as well say you don't believe two plus two is four. I'll show you. May I have some paper? Any old kind."

She went to a table and brought some, and I took my pen and wrote the twenty-four names, spacing them, and tore the paper into twenty-four pieces.

Then I knelt on a rug and arranged the twelve guest pieces in a rectangle as they had sat at table — not that that mattered, since they could have been in a straight line or a circle, but it was plainer that way. The girls gathered around. Nora knelt facing me, Lucy rolled over closer and propped on her elbows, Carol came and squatted beside me, Peggy plopped down at the other side, and Helen stood back of Nora.

"Okay," I said, "show me." I took "Quinn" and put it back of "Leacraft." "There's no argument about that, Marjorie Quinn brought the first plate and gave it to Leacraft. Remember there was just one mix-up, started by Peggy when she saw Pyle had been served and gave hers to Nero Wolfe. Try having any girl bring in a second plate — or bring in two at once if you still think that might have happened — without either serving Pyle or starting a second mix-up."

My memory has had a long stiff training under the strains and pressures Wolfe has put on it, but I wouldn't undertake to report all the combinations they tried, huddled around me on the floor, even if I thought you cared. They stuck to it for half an hour or more. The more persistent was Peggy Choate, the redhead. After the others had given up she stayed with it, frowning and biting her lip, propped first on one hand and then the other. Finally she said, "Nuts," stretched an arm to make a jumble of all the pieces of paper, guests and girls, got up, and returned to her chair. I did likewise.

"It's just a trick," said Carol Annis, perched on the couch again.

"I still don't believe it," Nora Jaret declared. "I do not believe that one of us deliberately poisoned a man — one of us sitting here." Her big brown eyes were at me. "Good lord, look at us! Point at her! Point her out! I dare you to!"

That, of course, was what I was there for — not exactly to point her out, but at least to get a hint. I had had a vague idea that one might come from watching them maneuver the pieces of paper, but it hadn't. Nor from anything any of them had said. I had been expecting Helen Iacono to introduce the subject of Vincent Pyle's *modus operandi* with girls, but apparently she had decided it was up to me. She hadn't spoken more than twenty words since we arrived.

"If I could point her out," I said, "I wouldn't be bothering the rest of you. Neither would the cops if *they* could point her out. Sooner or later, of course, they will, but it begins to look as if they'll have to get at it from the other end. Motive. They'll have to find out which one of you had a motive, and they will — sooner or later — and on that maybe I can help. I don't mean help them, I mean help you — not the one who killed him, the rest of you. That thought occurred to me after I learned that Helen Iacono had admitted that she had gone out with Pyle a few times last winter. What if she had said she hadn't? When the police found out she had lied, and they would have, she would have been in for it. It wouldn't have proved she had killed him, but the going would have been mighty rough. I understand that the rest of you have all denied that you ever had anything to do with Pyle. Is that right? Miss Annis?"

"Certainly." Her chin was up. "Of course I had met him. Everybody in show business has. Once when he came backstage at the Coronet, and once at a party somewhere, and one other time but I don't remember where."

"Miss Morgan?"

She was smiling at me, a crooked smile. "Do you call this helping us?" she demanded.

"It might lead to that after I know how you stand. After all, the cops have your statement."

She shrugged. "I've been around longer than Carol, so I had seen him to speak to more than she had. Once I danced with him at the Flamingo, two years ago. That was the closest I had ever been to him."

"Miss Choate?"

"I never had the honor. I only came to New York last fall. From Montana. He had been pointed out to me from a distance, but he never chased me."

"Miss Jaret?"

"He was Broadway," she said. "I'm TV."

"Don't the twain ever meet?"

"Oh, sure. All the time at Sardi's. That's the only place I ever saw the great Pyle, and I wasn't with him."

I started to cross my legs, but the wobbly chair leg reacted, and I thought better of it. "So there you are," I said, "you're all committed. If one of you poisoned him, and though I hate to say it I don't see any way out of that, that one is lying. But if any of the others are lying, if you saw more of him than you admit, you had better get from under quick. If you don't want to tell the cops tell me, tell me now, and I'll pass it on and say I wormed it out of you. Believe me, you'll regret it if you don't."

"Archie Goodwin, a girl's best friend," Lucy said. "My bosom pal."

No one else said anything.

"Actually," I asserted, "I *am* your friend, all of you but one. I have a friendly feeling for all pretty girls, especially those who work, and I admire and respect you for being willing to make an honest fifty bucks by coming there yesterday to carry plates of grub to a bunch of finickers. I *am* your friend, Lucy, if you're not the murderer, and if you are no one is."

I leaned forward, forgetting the wobbly chair leg, but it didn't object. It was about time to put a crimp in Helen's personal project. "Another thing. It's quite possible that one of you *did* see her returning to the kitchen for another plate, and you haven't said so because you don't want to squeal on her. If so, spill it now. The longer this hangs on the hotter it will get. When it gets so the pressure is too much for you and you decide you have got to tell it, it will be too late. Tomorrow may be too late. If you go to the cops with it tomorrow they probably won't believe you; they'll figure that you did it yourself and you're trying to squirm out. If you don't want to tell me here and now, in front of her, come with me down to Nero Wolfe's office and we'll talk it over."

They were exchanging glances, and they were not friendly glances. When I had arrived probably not one of them, excluding the murderer, had believed that a poisoner was present, but now they all did, or at least they thought she might be; and when that feeling takes hold it's good-by to friendliness. It would have been convenient if I could have detected fear in one of the glances, but fear and suspicion and uneasiness are too much alike on faces to tell them apart.

"You *are* a help," Carol Annis said bitterly. "Now you've got us hating each other. Now everybody suspects everybody."

I had quit being nice and sympathetic. "It's about time," I told her. I glanced at my wrist. "It's not midnight yet. If I've made you all realize that this is no Broadway production, or TV either, and the longer the pay-off is postponed the tougher it will be for everybody, I *have* helped." I stood up. "Let's go. I don't say Mr. Wolfe can do it by just snapping his fingers, but he might surprise you. He has often surprised me."

"All right," Nora said. She arose. "Come on. This is getting too damn painful. Come on."

I don't pretend that that was what I had been heading for. I admit that I had just been carried along by my tongue. If I arrived with that gang at midnight and Wolfe had gone to bed, he would almost certainly refuse to play. Even if he were still up, he might refuse to work, just to teach me a lesson, since I had not stuck to my instructions. Those thoughts were at me as Peggy Choate bounced up and Carol Annis started to leave the couch.

But they were wasted. That tussle with Wolfe never came off. A door at the end of the room which had been standing ajar suddenly swung open, and there in its frame was a two-legged figure with shoulders almost as broad as the doorway, and I was squinting at Sergeant Purley Stebbins of Manhattan Homicide West. He moved forward, croaking, "I'm surprised at you, Goodwin. These ladies ought to get some sleep."

6

OF course I was a monkey. If it had been Stebbins who had made a monkey of me I suppose I would have leaped for a window and dived through. Hitting the pavement from a fourth-story window should be enough to finish a monkey, and life wouldn't be worth living if I had been bamboozled by Purley Stebbins. But obviously it hadn't been him; it had been Peggy Choate or Nora Jaret, or both; Purley had merely accepted an invitation to come and listen in.

So I kept my face. To say I was jaunty would be stretching it, but I didn't scream or tear my hair. "Greetings," I said heartily. "And welcome. I've been wondering why you didn't join us instead of skulking in there in the dark."

"I'll bet you have." He had come to arm's length and stopped. He turned. "You can relax, ladies." Back to me: "You're under arrest for obstructing justice. Come along."

"In a minute. You've got all night." I moved my head. "Of course Peggy and Nora knew this hero was in there, but I'd—"

"I said come along!" he barked.

"And I said in a minute. I intend to ask a couple of questions. I wouldn't dream of resisting arrest, but I've got leg cramp from kneeling too long and if you're in a hurry you'll have to carry me." I moved my eyes. "I'd like to know if you all knew. Did you, Miss Iacono?"

"Of course not."

"Miss Morgan?"

"No."

"Miss Annis?"

"No, I didn't, but I think you did." She tossed her head and the corn silk fluttered. "That was contemptible. Saying you wanted to help us, so we would talk, with a policeman listening."

"And then he arrests me?"

"That's just an act."

"I wish it were. Ask your friends Peggy and Nora if I knew — only I suppose you wouldn't believe them. *They* knew, and they didn't tell you. You'd better all think over everything you said. Okay, Sergeant, the leg cramp's gone."

He actually started a hand for my elbow, but I was moving and it wasn't there. I opened the door to the hall. Of course he had me go first down the three flights; no cop in his senses would descend stairs in front of a dangerous criminal in custody. When we emerged to the sidewalk and he told me to turn left I asked him, "Why not cuffs?"

"Clown if you want to," he croaked.

He flagged a taxi on Amsterdam Avenue, and when we were in and rolling I spoke. "I've been thinking, about laws and liberties and so on. Take false arrest, for instance. And take obstructing justice. If a man is arrested for obstructing justice, and it turns out that he didn't obstruct any justice, does that make the arrest false? I wish I knew more about law. I guess I'll have to ask a lawyer. Nathaniel Parker would know."

It was the mention of Parker, the lawyer Wolfe uses when the occasion calls for one, that got him. He had seen Parker in action.

"They heard you," he said, "and I heard you, and I took some notes. You interfered in a homicide investigation. You quoted the police to them, you said so. You told them what the police think, and what they're doing and are going to do. You played a game with them with those pieces of paper to show them exactly how it figures. You tried to get them to tell you things instead of telling the police, and you were going to take them to Nero Wolfe so he could pry it out of them. And you haven't even got the excuse that Wolfe is representing a client. He hasn't got a client."

"Wrong. He has."

"Like hell he has. Name her."

"Not her, him. Fritz Brenner. He is seeing red because food cooked by him was poisoned and killed a man. It's convenient to have the client living right in the house. You admit that a licensed detective has a right to investigate on behalf of a client."

"I admit nothing."

"That's sensible," I said approvingly. "You shouldn't. When you're on the stand, being sued for false arrest, it would be bad to have it thrown up to you, and it would be two against one because the hackie could testify. Can you hear us, driver?"

"Sure I can hear you," he sang out. "It's very interesting."

"So watch your tongue," I told Purley. "You could get hooked for a year's pay. As for quoting the police, I merely said that they think it was one of those five, and when Cramer told Mr. Wolfe that he didn't say it was confidential. As for telling them what the police think, same comment. As for playing the game with them, why not? As for trying to get them to tell me things, I won't comment on that at all because I don't want to be rude. That must have been a slip of the tongue. If you ask me why I didn't balk there at the apartment and bring up these points then and there, what was the use? You had spoiled

the party. They wouldn't have come downtown with me. Also I am saving a
buck of Mr. Wolfe's money, since you had arrested me and therefore the taxi
fare is on the city of New York. Am I still under arrest?"

"You're damn right you are."

"That may be ill-advised. You heard him, driver?"

"Sure I heard him."

"Good. Try to remember it."

We were on Ninth Avenue, stopped at Forty-second Street for a light. When
the light changed and we moved, Purley told the hackie to pull over to the
curb, and he obeyed. At that time of night there were plenty of gaps. Purley
took something from a pocket and showed it to the hackie, and said, "Go get
yourself a Coke and come back in ten minutes," and he climbed out and went.
Purley turned his head to glare at me.

"I'll pay for the Coke," I offered.

He ignored it. "Lieutenant Rowcliff," he said, "is expecting us at Twentieth
Street."

"Fine. Even under arrest, one will get you five that I can make him start
stuttering in ten minutes."

"You're not under arrest."

I leaned forward to look at the meter. "Ninety cents. From here on we'll
split it."

"Goddamn it, quit clowning! If you think I'm crawling you're wrong. I just
don't see any percentage in it. If I deliver you in custody I know damn well
what you'll do. You'll clam up. We won't get a peep out of you, and in the
morning you'll make a phone call and Parker will come. What will that get
us?"

I could have said, "A suit for false arrest," but it wouldn't have been
diplomatic, so I made it, "Only the pleasure of my company."

There was one point of resemblance between Purley and Carol Annis, just
one: no sense of humor. "But," he said, "Lieutenant Rowcliff is expecting you,
and you're a material witness in a homicide case, and you were up there
working on the suspects."

"You could arrest me as a material witness," I suggested helpfully.

He uttered a word that I was glad the hackie wasn't there to hear, and
added, "You'd clam up and in the morning you'd be out on bail. I know it's
after midnight, but the lieutenant is expecting you."

He's a proud man, Purley is, and I wouldn't go so far as to say that he has
nothing to be proud of. He's not a bad cop, as cops go. It was a temptation to
keep him dangling for a while, to see how long it would take him to bring
himself to the point of coming right out and asking for it, but it was late and I
needed some sleep.

"You realize," I said, "that it's a waste of time and energy. You can tell him
everything we said, and if he tries to go into other aspects with me I'll only
start making cracks and he'll start stuttering. It's perfectly useless."

"Yeah, I know, but—"

"But the lieutenant expects me."

He nodded. "It was Nora Jaret told about it, and he sent me. The inspector
wasn't around."

"Okay. In the interest of justice. I'll give him an hour. That's understood?
Exactly one hour."

"It's not understood with me." He was emphatic. "When we get there you're his and he's welcome to you. I don't know if he can stand you for an hour."

7

AT noon the next day, Thursday, Fritz stood at the end of Wolfe's desk, consulting with him on a major point of policy: whether to switch to another source of supply for water cress. The quality had been below par, which for them means perfection, for nearly a week. I was at my desk, yawning. It had been after two o'clock when I got home from my chat with Lieutenant Rowcliff, and with nine hours' sleep in two nights I was way behind.

The hour since Wolfe had come down at eleven o'clock from his morning session with the orchids had been spent, most of it, by me reporting and Wolfe listening. My visit with Rowcliff needed only a couple of sentences, since the only detail of any importance was that it had taken me eight minutes to get him stuttering, but Wolfe wanted my conversation with the girls verbatim, and also my impressions and conclusions. I told him my basic conclusion was that the only way she could be nailed, barring a stroke of luck, would be by a few dozen men sticking to the routine — her getting the poison and her connection with Pyle.

"And," I added, "her connection with Pyle may be hopeless. In fact, it probably is. If it's Helen Iacono, what she told us is no help. If what she told us is true she had no reason to kill him, and if it isn't true how are you going to prove it? If it's one of the others she is certainly no halfwit, and there may be absolutely nothing to link her up. Being very careful with visitors to your penthouse is fine as long as you're alive, but it has its drawbacks if one of them feeds you arsenic. It may save her neck."

He was regarding me without enthusiasm. "You are saying in effect that it must be left to the police. I don't have a few dozen men. I can expose her only by a stroke of luck."

"Right. Or a stroke of genius. That's your department. I make no conclusions about genius."

"Then why the devil were you going to bring them to me at midnight? Don't answer. I know. To badger me."

"No, sir. I told you. I had got nowhere with them. I had got them looking at each other out of the corners of their eyes, but that was all. I kept on talking, and suddenly I heard myself inviting them to come home with me. I was giving them the excuse that I wanted them to discuss it with you, but that may have been just a cover for certain instincts that a man is entitled to. They are very attractive girls — all but one."

"Which one?"

"I don't know. That's what we're working on."

He probably would have harped on it if Fritz hadn't entered to present the water-cress problem. As they wrestled with it, dealing with it from all angles, I swiveled my back to them so I could do my yawning in private. Finally they got it settled, deciding to give the present source one more week and then switch if the quality didn't improve; and then I heard Fritz say, "There's another matter, sir. Felix phoned me this morning. He and Zoltan would like an appointment with you after lunch, and I would like to be present. They suggested half past two, if that will suit your convenience."

"What is it?" Wolfe demanded. "Something wrong at the restaurant?"

"No, sir. Concerning the misfortune of Tuesday evening."

"What about it?"

"It would be better for them to tell you. It is their concern."

I swiveled for a view of Fritz's face. Had Felix and Zoltan been holding out on us? Fritz's expression didn't tell me, but it did tell Wolfe something: that it would be unwise for him to insist on knowing the nature of Felix's and Zoltan's concern because Fritz had said all he intended to. There is no one more obliging than Fritz, but also there is no one more immovable when he has taken a stand. So Wolfe merely said that half past two would be convenient. When Fritz had left I offered to go to the kitchen and see if I could pry it out of him, but Wolfe said no, apparently it wasn't urgent.

As it turned out, it wasn't. Wolfe and I were still in the dining room, with coffee, when the doorbell rang at 2:25 and Fritz answered it, and when we crossed the hall to the office Felix was in the red leather chair, Zoltan was in one of the yellow ones, and Fritz was standing. Fritz had removed his apron and put on a jacket, which was quite proper. People do not attend business conferences in aprons.

When we had exchanged greetings, and Fritz had been told to sit down and had done so, and Wolfe and I had gone to our desks, Felix spoke. "You won't mind, Mr. Wolfe, if I ask a question? Before I say why we requested an appointment?"

Wolfe told him no, go ahead.

"Because," Felix said, "we would like to know this first. We are under the impression that the police are making no progress. They haven't said so, they tell us nothing, but we have the impression. Is it true?"

"It was true at two o'clock this morning, twelve hours ago. They may have learned something by now, but I doubt it."

"Do you think they will soon make progress? That they will soon be successful?"

"I don't know. I can only conjecture. Archie thinks that unless they have a stroke of luck the inquiry will be long and laborious, and even then may fail. I'm inclined to agree with him."

Felix nodded. "That is what we fear—Zoltan and I and others at the restaurant. It is causing a most regrettable atmosphere. A few of our most desirable patrons make jokes, but most of them do not, and some of them do not come. We do not blame them. For the maître d'hôtel and one of our chefs to assist at a dinner where a guest is served poison—that is not pleasant. If the—"

"Confound it, Felix! I have avowed my responsibility. I have apologized. Are you here for the gloomy satisfaction of reproaching me?"

"No, sir." He was shocked. "Of course not. We came to say that if the poisoner is not soon discovered, and then the affair will be forgotten, the effect on the restaurant may be serious. And if the police are making no progress that may happen, so we appeal to you. We wish to engage your professional services. We know that with you there would be no question. You would solve it quickly and completely. We know it wouldn't be proper to pay you from restaurant funds, since you are the trustee, so we'll pay you with our own money. There was a meeting of the staff last night, and all will contribute, in a proper ratio. We appeal to you."

Zoltan stretched out a hand, arm's length. "We appeal to you," he said.

"Pfui," Wolfe grunted.

He had my sympathy. Not only was their matter-of-fact confidence in his prowess highly flattering, but also their appealing instead of demanding, since he had got them into it, was extremely touching. But a man with a long-standing reputation for being hard and blunt simply can't afford the softer feelings, no matter what the provocation. It called for great self-control.

Felix and Zoltan exchanged looks. "He said 'pfui,'" Zoltan told Felix. "I heard him," Felix snapped. "I have ears."

Fritz spoke. "I wished to be present," he said, "so I could add my appeal to theirs. I offered to contribute, but they said no."

Wolfe took them in, his eyes going right to left and back again. "This is preposterous," he declared. "I said 'pfui' not in disgust but in astonishment. I am solely to blame for this mess, but you offer to pay me to clean it up. Preposterous! You should know that I have already bestirred myself. Archie?"

"Yes, sir. At least you have bestirred me."

He skipped it. "And," he told them, "your coming is opportune. Before lunch I was sitting here considering the situation, and I concluded that the only way to manage the affair with dispatch is to get the wretch to betray herself; and I conceived a plan. For it I need your cooperation. Yours, Zoltan. Your help is essential. Will you give it? I appeal to you."

Zoltan upturned his palms and raised his shoulders. "But yes! But how?"

"It is complicated. Also it will require great dexterity and aplomb. How are you on the telephone? Some people are not themselves, not entirely at ease, when they are phoning. A few are even discomfited. Are you?"

"No." He reflected. "I don't think so. No."

"If you are it won't work. The plan requires that you telephone five of those women this afternoon. You will call first Miss Iacono, tell her who you are, and ask her to meet you somewhere—in some obscure restaurant. You will say that on Tuesday evening, when you told me that you had not seen one of them return for a second plate, you were upset and flustered by what had happened, and later, when the police questioned you, you were afraid to contradict yourself and tell the truth. But now that the notoriety is harming the restaurant you feel that you may have to reveal the fact that you did see her return for a second plate, but that before—"

"But I didn't!" Zoltan cried. "I told—"

"*Tais-toi!*" Felix snapped at him.

Wolfe resumed. "—but that before you do so you wish to discuss it with her. You will say that one reason you have kept silent is that you have been unable to believe that anyone as attractive and charming as she is could be guilty of such a crime. A parenthesis. I should have said at the beginning that you must not try to parrot my words. I am giving you only the substance; the words must be your own, those you would naturally use. You understand that?"

"Yes, sir." Zoltan's hands were clasped tight.

"So don't try to memorize my words. Your purpose is to get her to agree to meet you. She will of course assume that you intend to blackmail her, but you will not say so. You will try to give her the impression, in everything you say and in your tone of voice, that you will not demand money from her, but will expect her favors. In short, that you desire her. I can't tell you how to convey that impression; I must leave that to you. The only requisite is that she must be convinced that if she refuses to meet you, you will go at once to the police and tell them the truth."

"Then you know," Zoltan said. "Then she is guilty."

"Not at all. I haven't the slightest idea who is guilty. When you have finished with her you will phone the other four and repeat the performance — Miss Choate, Miss Annis, Miss—"

"My God, Mr. Wolfe! That's impossible!"

"Not impossible, merely difficult. You alone can do it, for they know your voice. I considered having Archie do it, imitating your voice, but it would be too risky. You said you would help, but there's no use trying it if the bare idea appalls you. Will you undertake it?"

"I don't . . . I would . . ."

"He will," Felix said. "He is like that. He only needs to swallow it. He will do well. But I must ask, can he be expected to get them all to agree to meet him? The guilty one, yes, but the others?"

"Certainly not. There is much to discuss and arrange. The innocent ones will react variously according to their tempers. One or more of them will probably inform the police, and I must provide for that contingency with Mr. Cramer." To Zoltan: "Since it is possible that one of the innocent ones will agree to meet you, for some unimaginable reason, you will have to give them different hours for the appointments. There are many details to settle, but that is mere routine. The key is you. You must of course rehearse, and into a telephone transmitter. There are several stations on the house phone. You will go to Archie's room and speak from there. We will listen at the other stations: Archie in the plant rooms, I in my room, Fritz in the kitchen, and Felix here. Archie will handle the other end of the conversation; he is much better qualified than I to improvise the responses of young women. Do you want me to repeat the substance of what you are to say before rehearsal?"

Zoltan opened his mouth and closed it again. "Yes," he said.

8

SERGEANT Purley Stebbins shifted his fanny for the nth time in two hours. "She's not coming," he muttered. "It's nearly eight o'clock." His chair was about half big enough for his personal dimensions.

We were squeezed in a corner of the kitchen of John Piotti's little restaurant on 14th Street between Second and Third Avenues. On the midget table between us were two notebooks, his and mine, and a small metal case. Of the three cords extending from the case, the two in front went to the earphones we had on, and the one at the back ran down the wall, through the floor, along the basement ceiling toward the front, back up through the floor, and on through a table top, where it was connected to a microphone hidden in a bowl of artificial flowers. The installation, a rush order, had cost Wolfe $191.67. Permission to have it made had cost him nothing because he had once got John Piotti out of a difficulty and hadn't soaked him beyond reason.

"We'll have to hang on," I said. "You never can tell with a redhead."

The exposed page of my notebook was blank, but Purley had written on his. As follows:

Helen Iacono	6:00 p.m.
Peggy Choate	7:30 p.m.
Carol Annis	9:00 p.m.
Lucy Morgan	10:30 p.m.
Nora Jaret	12:00 p.m.

It was in my head. If I had had to write it down I would certainly have made one "p.m." do, but policeman are trained to do things right.

"Anyhow," Purley said, "we know damn well who it is."

"Don't count your poisoners," I said, "before they're hatched." It was pretty feeble, but I was tired and still short on sleep.

I hoped to heaven he was right, since otherwise the operation was a flop. So far everything had been fine. After half an hour of rehearsing Zóltan had been wonderful. He had made the five calls from the extension in my room, and when he was through I told him his name should be in lights on a Broadway marquee. The toughest job had been getting Inspector Cramer to agree to Wolfe's terms, but he had no good answer to Wolfe's argument that if he insisted on changing the rules Zoltan wouldn't play. So Purley was in the kitchen with me, Cramer was with Wolfe in the office, prepared to stay for dinner, Zoltan was at the restaurant table with the hidden mike, and two homicide dicks, one male and one female, were at another table twenty feet away. One of the most elaborate charades Wolfe had ever staged.

Purley was right when he said we knew who it was, but I was right too — she hadn't been hatched yet. The reactions to Zoltan's calls had settled it. Helen Iacono had been indignant and after a couple of minutes had hung up on him, and had immediately phoned the District Attorney's office. Peggy Choate had let him finish his spiel and then called him a liar, but she had not said definitely that she wouldn't meet him, and the DA or police hadn't heard from her. Carol Annis, after he had spoken his lines, had used only ten words: "Where can I meet you?" and, after he had told her where and when: "All right, I'll be there." Lucy Morgan had coaxed him along, trying to get him to fill it all in on the phone, had finally said she would keep the appointment, and then had rushed downtown and rung our doorbell, told me her tale, demanded that I accompany her to the rendezvous, and insisted on seeing Wolfe. I had to promise to go to get rid of her. Nora Jaret had called him assorted names, from liar on up, or on down, and had told him she had a friend listening in on an extension, which was almost certainly a lie. Neither we nor the law had had a peep from her.

So it was Carol Annis with the corn-silk hair, that was plain enough, but there was no salt on her tail. If she was really smart and really tough she might decide to sit tight and not come, figuring that when they came at her with Zoltan's story she would say he was either mistaken or lying, and we would be up a stump. If she was dumb and only fairly tough she might scram.

Of course they would find her and haul her back, but if she said Zoltan was lying and she had run because she thought she was being framed, again we would be up a stump. But if she was both smart and tough but not quite enough of either, she would turn up at nine o'clock and join Zoltan. From there on it would be up to him, but that had been rehearsed too, and after his performance on the phone I thought he would deliver.

At half past eight Purley said, "She's not coming," and removed his earphone.

"I never thought she would," I said. The "she" was of course Peggy Choate, whose hour had been seven-thirty. "I said you never can tell with a redhead merely to make conversation."

Purley signaled to Piotti, who had been hovering around most of the time, and he brought us a pot of coffee and two fresh cups. The minutes were snails, barely moving. When we had emptied the cups I poured more. At 8:48 Purley put his earphone back on. At 8:56 I asked, "Shall I do a count-down?"

"You'd clown in the hot seat," he muttered, so hoarse that it was barely words. He always gets hoarser as the tension grows; that's the only sign.

It was four minutes past nine when the phone brought me the sound of a chair scraping, then faintly Zoltan's voice saying good evening, and then a female voice, but I couldn't get the words.

"Not loud enough," Purley whispered hoarsely.

"Shut up." I had my pen out. "They're standing up."

There came the sound of chairs scraping, and other little sounds, and then:

ZOLTAN: Will you have a drink?

CAROL: No. I don't want anything.

ZOLTAN: Won't you eat something?

CAROL: I don't feel . . . maybe I will.

Purley and I exchanged glances. That was promising. That sounded as if we might get more than conversation.

ANOTHER FEMALE VOICE, BELONGING TO MRS. PIOTTI: We have good Osso Buco, madame. Very good. A specialty.

CAROL: No, not meat.

ZOLTAN: A sweet perhaps?

CAROL: No.

ZOLTAN: It is more friendly if we eat. The spaghetti with anchovy sauce is excellent. I had some.

CAROL: You had some?

I bit my lip, but he handled it fine.

ZOLTAN: I've been here half an hour, I wanted so much to see you. I thought I should order something, and I tried that. I might even eat another portion.

CAROL: You should know good food. All right.

MRS. PIOTTI: Two spaghetti anchovy. Wine? A very good Chianti?

CAROL: No. Coffee.

Pause.

ZOLTAN: You are more lovely without a veil, but the veil is good too. It makes me want to see behind it. Of course I —

CAROL: You have seen behind it, Mr. Mahany.

ZOLTAN: Ah! You know my name?

CAROL: It was in the paper.

ZOLTAN: I am not sorry that you know it, I want you to know my name, but it will be nicer if you call me Zoltan.

CAROL: I might some day. It will depend. I certainly won't call you Zoltan if you go on thinking what you said on the phone. You're mistaken, Mr. Mahany. You didn't see me go back for another plate, because I didn't. I can't believe you would tell a vicious lie about me, so I just think you're mistaken.

Mrs. Piotti, in the kitchen for the spaghetti, came to the corner to stoop and hiss into my free ear, "She's wearing a veil."

ZOLTAN: I am not mistaken, my dear. That is useless. I know. How could I be mistaken when the first moment I saw you I felt . . . but I will not try to tell you how I felt. If any of the others had come and taken another plate I would have stopped her, but not you. Before you I was dumb. So it is useless.

Needing only one hand for my pen, I used the free one to blow a kiss to Purley.

CAROL: I see. So you're sure.

ZOLTAN: I am, my dear. Very sure.

CAROL: But you haven't told the police.

ZOLTAN: Of course not. As I told you.

CAROL: Have you told Nero Wolfe or Archie Goodwin?

ZOLTAN: I have told no one. How could I tell anyone? Mr. Wolfe is sure that the one who returned for another plate is the one who killed that man, gave him poison, and Mr. Wolfe is always right. So it is terrible for me. Could I tell anyone that I know you killed a man? You? How could I? That is why I had to see you, to talk with you. If you weren't wearing that veil I could look into your beautiful eyes. I think I know what I would see there. I would see suffering and sorrow. I saw that in your eyes Tuesday evening. I know he made you suffer. I know you wouldn't kill a man unless you had to. That is why—

The voice stopped. That was understandable, since Mrs. Piotti had gone through the door with the spaghetti and coffee and had had time to reach their table. Assorted sounds came as she served them. Purley muttered, "He's overdoing it," and I muttered back, "No. He's perfect." Piotti came over and stood looking down at my notebook. It wasn't until after Mrs. Piotti was back in the kitchen that Carol's voice came.

CAROL: That's why I am wearing the veil, Zoltan, because I know it's in my eyes. You're right. I had to. He did make me suffer. He ruined my life.

ZOLTAN: No, my dear. Your life is not ruined. No! No matter what he did. Was he . . . did he . . .

I was biting my lip again. Why didn't he give them the signal? The food had been served and presumably they were eating. He had been told that it would be pointless to try to get her to give him any details of her relations with Pyle, since they would almost certainly be lies. Why didn't he give the signal? Her voice was coming:

CAROL: He promised to marry me. I'm only twenty-two years old, Zoltan. I didn't think I would ever let a man touch me again, but the way you . . . I don't know. I'm glad you know I killed him because it will be better now, to know that somebody knows. To know that *you* know. Yes, I had to kill him, I *had* to, because if I didn't I would have had to kill myself. Some day I may tell you what a fool I was, how I — Oh!

ZOLTAN: What? What's the matter?

Carol: My bag. I left it in my car. Out front. And I didn't lock the car. A blue Plymouth hardtop. Would you . . . I'll go. . . .

Zoltan: I'll get it.

The sound came of his chair scraping, then faintly his footsteps, and then silence. But the silence was broken in ten seconds, whereas it would have taken him at least a minute to go for the purse and return. What broke it was a male voice saying, "I'm an officer of the law, Miss Annis," and a noise from Carol. Purley, shedding his earphone, jumped up and went, and I followed, notebook in hand.

It was quite a tableau. The male dick stood with a hand on Carol's shoulder. Carol sat stiff, her chin up, staring straight ahead. The female dick, not much older than Carol, stood facing her from across the table, holding with both hands, at breast level, a plate of spaghetti. She spoke to Purley. "She put something in it and then stuck something in her dress. I saw her in my mirror."

I moved in. After all, I was in charge, under the terms Cramer had agreed to. "Thank you, Miss Annis," I said. "You were a help. On a signal from Zoltan they were going to start a commotion to give him an excuse to leave the table, but you saved them the trouble. I thought you'd like to know. Come on, Zoltan. All over. According to plan."

He had entered and stopped three paces off, a blue handbag under his arm. As he moved toward us Purley put out a hand. "I'll take that."

9

CRAMER was in the red leather chair. Carol Annis was in a yellow one facing Wolfe's desk, with Purley on one side of her and his female colleague on the other. The male colleague had been sent to the laboratory with the plate of spaghetti and a roll of paper that had been fished from inside Carol's dress. Fritz, Felix, and Zoltan were on the couch near the end of my desk.

"I will not pretend, Miss Annis," Wolfe was saying. "One reason that I persuaded Mr. Cramer to have you brought here first on your way to limbo was that I needed to appease my rancor. You had injured and humiliated not only me, but also one of my most valued friends, Fritz Brenner, and two other men whom I esteem, and I had arranged the situation that gave you your opportunity; and I wished them to witness your own humiliation, contrived by me, in my presence."

"That's enough of that," Cramer growled.

Wolfe ignored him. "I admit the puerility of that reason, Miss Annis, but in candor I wanted to acknowledge it. A better reason was that I wished to ask you a few questions. You took such prodigious risks that it is hard to believe in your sanity, and it would give me no satisfaction to work vengeance on a madwoman. What would you have done if Felix's eyes had been on you when you entered with the plate of poison and went to Mr. Pyle? Or if, when you returned to the kitchen for a second plate, Zoltan had challenged you? What would you have done?"

No answer. Apparently she was holding her gaze straight at Wolfe, but from my angle it was hard to tell because she still had the veil on. Asked by Cramer to remove it, she had refused. When the female dick had extracted the roll of paper from inside Carol's dress she had asked Cramer if she should pull the veil off and Cramer had said no. No rough stuff.

There was no question about Wolfe's gaze at her. He was forward in his chair, his palms flat on his desk. He persisted. "Will you answer me, Miss Annis?"

She wouldn't.

"Are you a lunatic, Miss Annis?"

She wasn't saying.

Wolfe's head jerked to me. "Is she deranged, Archie?"

That was unnecessary. When we're alone I don't particularly mind his insinuations that I presume to be an authority on women, but there was company present. I gave him a look and snapped, "No comment."

He returned to her. "Then that must wait. I leave to the police such matters as your procurement of the poison and your relations with Mr. Pyle, mentioning only that you cannot deny possession of arsenic, since you used it a second time this evening. It will unquestionably be found in the spaghetti and in the roll of paper you concealed in your dress; and so, manifestly, if you are mad you are also ruthless and malevolent. You may have been intolerably provoked by Mr. Pyle, but not by Zoltan. He presented himself not as a nemesis or a leech, but as a bewitched and befuddled champion. He offered his homage and compassion, making no demands, and your counter-offer was death. I would myself—"

"You lie," Carol said. It was her first word. "And he lied. He was going to lie about me. He didn't see me go back for a second plate, but he was going to say he did. And you lie. He did make demands. He threatened me."

Wolfe's brows went up. "Then you haven't been told?"

"Told what?"

"That you were overheard. That is the other question I had for you. I have no apology for contriving the trap, but you deserve to know you are in its jaws. All that you and Zoltan said was heard by two men at the other end of a wire in another room, and they recorded it—Mr. Stebbins of the police, now seated at your left, and Mr. Goodwin."

"You lie," she said.

"No, Miss Annis. This isn't the trap; it has already sprung. You have it, Mr. Stebbins?"

Purley nodded. He hates to answer questions from Wolfe.

"Archie?"

"Yes, sir."

"Did Zoltan threaten her or make demands?"

"No, sir. He followed instructions."

He returned to Carol. "Now you know. I wanted to make sure of that. To finish, since you may have had a just and weighty grievance against Mr. Pyle, I would myself prefer to see you made to account for your attempt to kill Zoltan, but that is not in my discretion. In any case, my rancor is appeased, and I hold—"

"That's enough," Cramer blurted, leaving his chair. "I didn't agree to let you preach at her all night. Bring her along, Sergeant."

As Purley arose a voice came. "May I say something?" It was Fritz. Heads turned as he left the couch and moved, detouring around Zoltan's feet and Purley's bulk to get to Carol, and turning to stand looking down at her.

"On account of what Mr. Wolfe said," he told her. "He said you injured me, and that is true. It is also true that I wanted him to find you. I can't speak for Felix, and you tried to kill Zoltan and I can't speak for him, but I can speak for myself. I forgive you."

"You lie," Carol said.

Method Three for Murder

1

WHEN I first set eyes on Mira Holt, as I opened the front door and she was coming up the seven steps to the stoop, she was a problem, though only a minor one compared to what followed.

At the moment I was unemployed. During the year, I have worked for Nero Wolfe and lived under his roof, I have quit and been fired about the same number of times, say thirty or forty. Mostly we have been merely letting off steam, but sometimes we have meant it, more or less, and that Monday evening in September I was really fed up. The main dish at dinner had been pork stewed in beer, which both Wolfe and Fritz know I can get along without, and we had left the dining room and crossed the hall to the office, and Fritz had brought coffee and Wolfe had poured it, and I had said, "By the way, I told Anderson I'd phone and confirm his appointment for tomorrow morning."

And Wolfe had said, "No. Cancel it." He picked up the book he was on, John Gunther's *Inside Russia Today*.

I sat in my working chair and looked across his desk at him. Since he weighs a seventh of a ton he always looks big, but when he's being obnoxious he looks even bigger. "Do you suppose it's possible," I asked, "that that pork has a bloating effect?"

"No indeed," he said, and opened the book.

If I had been a camel and the book had been a straw you could have heard my spine crack. He knew darned well he shouldn't have opened it until we had finished with coffee. I put my cup down. "I am aware," I said, "that you are sitting pretty. The bank balance is fat enough for months of paying Fritz and Theodore and me, and buying pork and beer in car lots, and adding more orchids to the ten thousand you've already got. I'll even grant that a private detective has a right to refuse to take a case with or without a reason. But as I told you before dinner, this Anderson is known to me, and he asked me as a personal favor to get him fifteen minutes with you, and I told him to come at eleven o'clock tomorrow morning. If you're determined not to work because your tax bracket is already too high, okay, all you have to do is tell him no. He'll be here at eleven."

He was holding the book open and his eyes were on it, but he spoke. "You know quite well, Archie, that I must be consulted on appointments. Did you owe this man a favor?"

"I do now that he asked for one and I said yes."

"Did you owe him one before?"

"No."

"Then you are committed but I am not. Since I wouldn't take the job it would waste his time and mine. Phone him not to come. Tell him I have other engagements."

So I quit. I admit that on some other occasions my quitting had been merely a threat, to jolt him into seeing reason, but not that time. When a mule plants its feet a certain way there's no use trying to budge it. I swiveled, got my memo pad, wrote on it, yanked the sheet off, got up and crossed to his desk, and handed him the sheet.

"That's Anderson's number," I told him. "If you're too busy to phone him not to come, Fritz can. I'm through. I'll stay with friends tonight and come tomorrow for my stuff."

His eyes had left the book to glare at me. "Pfui," he said.

"I agree," I said. "Absolutely." I turned and marched out. I do not say that as I got my hat from the rack in the hall my course was clearly mapped for the next twenty years, or even twenty hours. Wolfe owned the house but not everything in it, for the furniture in my room on the third floor had been bought and paid for by me. That would have to wait until I found a place to move it to, but I would get my clothes and other items tomorrow, and would I come for them before eleven o'clock and learn from Fritz whether a visitor named Anderson was expected, or would it be better strategy to come in the afternoon and learn if Anderson had been admitted and given his fifteen minutes? Facing that problem as I pulled the door open, I was immediately confronted by another one. A female was coming up the seven steps to the stoop.

2

I couldn't greet her and ask her business, since it was a cinch she would say she wanted to see Nero Wolfe and I couldn't carry on with a job I no longer held by returning to the office to ask Wolfe if he would receive a caller. Anyway I wouldn't. I couldn't step aside and let her enter by the door I had opened with no questions asked, since there was a possibility that she was one of the various people who had it in for Wolfe, and while I might have considered shooting him myself I didn't want to get him plugged by a total stranger. So I crossed the sill, pulled the door shut, sidestepped to pass her, and was starting down the steps when my sleeve was caught and jerked.

"Hey," she said, "aren't you Archie Goodwin?"

My eyes slanted down to hers. "You're guessing," I said.

"I am not. I've seen you at the Flamingo. You're not very polite, shutting the door in my face." She spoke in jerks, as if she wasn't sure she had enough breath. "I want to see Nero Wolfe."

"This is his house. Ring the bell."

"But I want to see you too. Let me in. Take me in."

My eyes had adjusted enough to the poor light to see that she was young,

attractive, and hyped. She had on a cap with a beak. In normal circumstances it would have been a pleasure to escort her into the front room and
go and badger Wolfe into seeing her, but as things stood I didn't even
consider it. "I'm sorry," I said, "but I don't work here any more. I just quit.
I am now on my way to bum a bed for the night. You'll have to ring the bell,
but I should warn you that in Mr. Wolfe's present mood there's not a
chance. You might as well skip it. If your trouble is urgent you ought to—"

"I'm not in trouble."

"Good. You're lucky."

She touched my sleeve. "I don't believe it. That you've quit."

"I do. Would I say so if I hadn't? Running the risk that you're a journalist
and tomorrow there will be a front-page spread, 'Archie Goodwin, the
famous private detective, has severed his connection with Nero Wolfe, also a
detective, and it is thought—'"

"Shut up!" She was close to me, gripping my arm. She let loose and
backed up a step. "I beg your pardon. I seem to be . . . you think Nero Wolfe
wouldn't see me?"

"I don't think. I know."

"Anyway I want to see you too. For what I want I guess you would be
better than him. I want some advice—no, not advice exactly, I want to
consult you. I'll pay cash, fifty dollars. Can't we go inside?"

Naturally I was uplifted. Since I had left Wolfe, and since there was no
other outfit in New York I would work for, my only possible program was to
set up for myself, and before I even got down to the sidewalk here was a
pretty girl offering me fifty bucks just for consultation.

"I'm afraid not," I told her, "since I no longer belong here. If that's your
taxi waiting that will do fine, especially with the driver gone." A glance had
shown me that there was no one behind the wheel of the cab at the curb.
Probably, having been told to wait for her, he had beat it to Al's diner at the
corner of Tenth Avenue, which was popular with hackies.

She shook her head. "I don't—" she began, and let it hang. She glanced
around. "Why not here? It shouldn't take very long—I just want you to
help me win a bet." She moved, descended two steps, and sat on the landing, swaying a little as she bent. "Have a seat."

We were still on Wolfe's premises, but he rarely used the outdoors part,
and after she paid me I could slip a buck under the door for rent. I sat down
beside her, not crowding. I had often sat there watching the neighborhood
kids at stoop ball.

"Do I pay in advance?" she asked.

"No thanks, I'll trust you. What's the bet about?"

"Well . . ." She was squinting at me in the dim light. "I had an argument
with a friend of mine. She said there were ninety-three women cab drivers in
New York, and she thought it was dangerous because sometimes things
happen in cabs that it takes a man to handle, and I said things like that can
happen anywhere just as well as in cabs, and we had an argument, and she
bet me fifty dollars she could prove that something dangerous could happen
in a cab that couldn't happen anywhere else. She thought up some things,
but I made her admit they could happen other places too, and then she said
what if a woman cab driver left her empty cab to go into a building for
something, and when she came back there was a dead woman in the cab?

She claimed that won the bet, and the trouble was I didn't know enough about what you're supposed to do when you find a dead body. That's what I want you to tell me. I'm sure she's wrong. And I'll pay you the fifty dollars."

I was squinting back at her. "You don't look it," I stated.

"I don't look what?"

"Loony. Two things. First, the same thing could happen if she were driving a private car instead of a cab, and why didn't you tell her that? Second, where's the danger? She merely finds a phone and notifies the police. It would be a nuisance, but you said dangerous."

"Oh. Of course." She bit her lip. "I left something out. It's not her cab. She has a friend who is a cab driver, and she wanted to see what driving a cab was like, and her friend let her take it. So she can't notify the police because her friend broke some law when she let her take the cab, and she broke one too, driving a cab without a license, so it wouldn't have been the same if she had been driving a private car. And the only way I can win the bet is to prove that it wouldn't be dangerous. She doesn't know how the dead woman got in the cab or anything about it. All she has to do is get the body out of the cab, but that might be dangerous unless she did it just right, and that's what I want you to tell me so I won't make some awful mistake — I mean when I tell my friend why it wouldn't be dangerous. Things like where would she go to — to take it out of the cab, and would she have to wait until late at night, and how would she make sure there were no traces left in the cab." She bit her lip again, and her fingers were curled to make fists. "Things like that."

"I see." I had stopped squinting. "What's your name?"

She shook her head. "You don't have to know. I'm just consulting you." She stuck her fingers in the pocket of her jacket, a grayish number with pointed lapels that had seen wear, came out with a purse, and opened it.

I reached to snap it shut. "That can wait. I certainly wouldn't take your money without knowing your name. Of course you can make one up."

"Why should I?" She gestured. "All right. My name is Mira Holt. Mira with an I." She opened the purse again.

"Hold it," I told her. "A couple of questions. The dead woman she finds in the cab — does she recognize her?"

"No, how could she?"

"She could if she knew her when she was alive."

"She didn't."

"Good. That helps. You say she left her empty cab to go into a building for something. For what?"

"Oh, just anything. I don't know. That doesn't matter."

"It might, but if you don't know you can't tell me. I want to make it clear, Miss Holt, that I accept without question all that you *have* told me. Since I am a trained detective I am chronically suspicious, but you are so frank and intelligent and pleasing to look at that I wouldn't dream of doubting you. A man who was sap enough to size you up wrong might even suspect you of feeding him a phony, and go and take a look in that taxi, but not me. I don't even ask you where the driver is, because I assume he has gone to the corner for a ham on rye and a cuppa coffee. In short, I trust you fully. That's understood?"

Her lips were tight. She was probably frowning, but the beak of her cap screened her brow. "I guess so." She wasn't at all sure. "But maybe — if that's how you feel — maybe it would be better just to —"

"No. It's better like this. Much better. About this situation your friend thought up and claims she won the bet, it has many aspects. You say you didn't know enough about what you're supposed to do when you find a dead body. First and foremost, you're supposed to notify the police immediately. That goes for everybody, but it's a must for a private detective — me, for instance — if he wants to keep his license. Is that clear?"

"Yes." She nodded. "I see."

"Also you're not supposed to touch the body or anything near it. Also you're not supposed to leave it unguarded, but that's not so important because you may have to in order to call a cop. As for your idea that all she has to do is get the body out of the cab, and where would she go to ditch it, and would she have to wait until late at night, and so on, I admit it has possibilities and I could make a lot of practical suggestions. But you have to show that it could be done without danger, and that's too big an order. That's what licks you. Forget it. However, your friend hasn't won the bet. She was to produce a situation showing that a woman cab driver runs special risks as a hackie, and in this case the danger comes from the fact that she was *not* driving the cab. So your friend —"

"That's no help. You know very well —"

"Shut up. I beg your pardon."

Her fingers were curled into fists again. "You said you could make some practical suggestions."

"I was carried away. The idea of disposing of a dead body is fascinating as long as it's only an idea. By the way, I took one thing for granted that I shouldn't have — that your friend specified that the woman had died by violence. If she could have died of natural causes —"

"No. She had been stabbed. There was a knife, the handle of a knife. . . ."

"Then it's impossible. A hackie letting someone else drive his cab is a misdemeanor, and so is driving a cab without a license, but driving off with a dead body with a knife sticking in it, and dumping it somewhere, and not reporting it — that's a felony. Good for at least a year and probably more."

She opened a fist to grip my arm, leaning to me. "But not if she did it right! Not if no one ever knew! I told you one thing wrong — she *did* — *recognize her! She did* know her when she was alive! So she can't —"

"Hold it," I growled. "Give me some money quick. Pay me. A dollar bill, five — don't sit and stare. See that police car? If it goes on by — no, it's stopping — pay me!"

She was going to panic. She started up, but my hand on her shoulder stopped her and held her down. She opened the purse and took out folded bills without fumbling, and I took them and put them in my pocket. "Staring is okay," I told her, not too loud. "People stare at police cars. Stay put and keep your mouth shut. I'm going to take a look. Naturally I'm curious."

That was perfectly true. I *was* curious. The prowl car had stopped alongside the taxi, and a cop, not the one who was driving, had got out and circled around to the door of the taxi on his side and was opening it as I reached the sidewalk. When you have a reputation for cheek you should live up to it, so I crossed to the door on my side and pulled it open. The seat was empty, but in front of it was a spread of brown canvas held up by whatever was under it. The cop, lifting a corner of the canvas, snarled at me, "Back up, you," and I retreated half a step, but he hadn't said to close the door, so I had a good view when he pulled the canvas off. More light would have helped, but there was enough to see that it was a woman, or had been, and that the knife whose handle was perpendicular to her ribs was all the way in.

"My God," I said with feeling.

"Shut that door!" the cop barked. "No, don't touch it!"

"I already have."

"I saw you. Beat it! No! What's your name?"

"Goodwin. Archie Goodwin. This is Nero Wolfe's house, and—"

"I know it is. And I know about you. Is this your cab?"

"Certainly not. I'm not a hackie."

"I know you're not. I mean—" He stopped. Apparently he had realized that the function of a prowl cop on finding a corpse is not to argue with onlookers. His head jerked around. "Climb out, Bill. DOA. I'll call in." The cop behind the wheel wriggled out, and the one in command wriggled in, and I mounted the stoop and sat down beside my client, noting that she had removed the cap and apparently had stashed it.

I kept my voice low, though it wasn't necessary since the cop was talking on his radio. "In about eight minutes," I said, "experts will begin arriving. They will not be strangers to me. Since as far as I know you merely came to get me to tell you how to win a bet, when they start asking questions I'll be glad to answer them if you want to leave it to me. I've had practice answering questions."

She was gripping my arm again. "You looked in. You saw—"

"Shut up, and I don't beg your pardon. You talk too much. Even if I still lived and worked here we wouldn't go inside because it wouldn't be natural, with cops in a prowl car finding a corpse in a taxi parked at the curb—oh, I haven't mentioned that, that there's a dead woman in the taxi. I mention it now because naturally I would, and naturally I would stick around to watch developments. I'm talking to keep you from talking, since naturally we would talk. Not only have I had practice answering questions, but I know some of the rules. There are only three methods that are any good in the long run. You have strong fingers."

"I'm sorry." Her grip relaxed a little, but she held on. "What are the three methods?"

"One. Button your lip. Answer nothing whatever. Two. Tell the truth straight through. The works. Three. Tell a simple basic lie with no trimmings, and stick to it. If you try a fancy lie, or a mixture of truth and lies, or part of the truth but try to save some, you're sunk. Of course I'm just talking to pass the time. In the present situation, as far as I know, there is no reason why you shouldn't just tell the truth."

"You said to leave it to you."

"Yes, but they won't. There are very few people in their jurisdiction they wouldn't rather leave it to than me, on account of certain—here they come. We can stop talking. Naturally we would watch."

An official car I had seen before rolled to a stop behind the prowl car, and Inspector Cramer of Homicide West climbed out.

3

IF you are surprised that an inspector had come in response to a report that a corpse had been found, I wasn't. The report had of course given the location, in front of 918 West 35th Street, and that address held memories, most of them sour, for the personnel at Homicide West, from Cramer down. A violent death that was in any way connected with Nero Wolfe made them itch, and presumably the report had included the item that Archie Goodwin was present and had stuck his nose in.

My client and I watched the routine activities from our grandstand seat. They were swift, efficient, and thorough. Traffic was detoured at the corner of Ninth Avenue. A section of the street and sidewalk was roped off to enclose the taxi. Floodlights were focused on the taxi and surroundings. A photographer took shots from various angles. Pedestrians from both directions were shunted across the street, where a crowd gathered behind the rope. Some twenty city employees, in uniform and out, were on the scene in less than half an hour after the cop had made the radio call — five of them known to me by name and four others by sight. The second floodlight had just been turned on when Cramer came around the front of the taxi, crossed to the steps and mounted the first three, and faced me. Since I was sitting, that made our eyes level.

"All right," he said. "Let's go in. I might as well have you and Wolfe together, and this woman too. That may simplify it. Open the door."

"On the contrary," I said, not moving, "it would complicate it. Mr. Wolfe is in the office reading a book and knows nothing of all the excitement, and cares less. If I went in and told him you wanted to see him, and what about, you know what he would say and so do I. Nothing doing."

"Who came here in that taxi?"

"I don't know. I know nothing whatever about the taxi. When I came out it was there at the curb."

"When did you come out?"

"Twenty minutes past nine."

"Why did you come out?"

"To find a place to spend the night. I have quit my job, so if you're determined to see Mr. Wolfe you'll have to ring the bell."

"You're telling me you've *quit*?"

"Right. I don't work here any more."

"By God. I thought you and Wolfe had tried all the wrinkles there are but this is a new one. Do you expect me to buy it?"

"It's not a wrinkle. I meant it. I wouldn't sign a pledge never to sleep here again, that depends on Mr. Wolfe's handling of a certain problem, but when I left the house I meant it. The problem has no connection with that taxi or what's in it."

"Did this woman leave the house with you?"

"No. When I opened the door, coming out, she was coming up the stoop.

She said she wanted to see Nero Wolfe, and when I told her I no longer
worked for him, and anyway he probably wouldn't see her, she said she
guessed that for what she wanted I would be better than him. She offered to
pay me fifty dollars for consultation on how to win a bet she had made, and
we sat here to consult. We had been here fifteen or twenty minutes when the
prowl car came along and stopped by the taxi, which had been standing
there when I left the house, and naturally I was curious and went to take a
look. The cop asked me my name and I told him. When he went to his radio
to report I came back to my client, but we didn't do much consulting on
account of the commotion. That's the crop."

"Had you ever seen this woman before?"

"No."

"What was the bet she wanted to consult about?"

"That's her affair. She's here. Ask her."

"Did she come in that taxi?"

"Not to my knowledge. Ask her."

"Did you see her get out of the taxi?"

"No. She was halfway up the stoop when I opened the door."

"Did you see anyone get out of the taxi? Or near it?"

"No."

"What's her name?"

"Ask her."

His head moved. "Is your name Judith Bram?"

That was no news for me, since my view through the open door had
included the framed picture of the hackie and her name. As well as I had
been able to tell in the dim light, the picture was not of my client.

"No," she said.

"What is it?"

"Mira Holt. Mira with an I." Her voice was clear and steady.

"Did you drive that taxi here?"

"No."

"Did you come here in it?"

"No."

So she had picked method three, a simple basic lie.

"Did you have an appointment to see Nero Wolfe?"

"No."

"Where do you live?"

"Seven-fourteen East Eighty-first Street."

"What is your occupation?"

"Modeling. Mostly fashion modeling."

"Are you married?"

"Yes, but I don't live with my husband."

"What's your husband's name?"

She opened her mouth and closed it again. "Waldo Kearns. I use my own
name."

"Are you divorced?"

"No."

"Was that taxi here when you arrived?"

"I don't know. I didn't notice, but I suppose it was because it didn't come
after we sat down."

"How did you come here?"

"I don't think that matters."

"I'll decide if it matters. How did you come?"

She shook her head. "No. For instance, if somebody drove me here or near here, you would ask him, and I might not want you to. No."

So she also knew what "no trimmings" meant.

"I advise you," Cramer advised her, "to tell me how you came."

"I would rather not."

"What was the bet you wanted to consult about?"

"That doesn't matter either. It was a private bet with a friend."

Her head turned. "You're a detective, Mr. Goodwin, so you ought to know, do I have to tell him about my private affairs just because I was sitting here with you?"

"Of course not," I assured her. "Not unless he shows some connection between your private affairs and his public affairs, and he hasn't. It's entirely up to you whether—"

"What the devil is all this?" Nero Wolfe bellowed.

I twisted around and so did my client. The door was wide open and he was standing on the threshold, his bulk towering above us. "What's going on?" he demanded.

Since I was merely an ex-employee and Cramer was an inspector I thought it fitting to let him reply, but he didn't. Apparently he was too flabbergasted at seeing Wolfe actually stick his nose outdoors. Wolfe advanced a step. "Archie. I asked a question."

I had stood up. "Yes, sir, I heard you. Miss Holt, this is Mr. Wolfe. Miss Mira Holt. When I left the house she was coming up the steps. I had never seen her before. When I told her I was no longer in your employ she said I would be better than you and asked to consult me. She has paid me. We sat down to confer. There was an empty taxi parked at the curb, no driver in it. A police car came along and stopped, and a cop found a dead body, female, in the taxi under a piece of canvas. I was there looking in when he removed the canvas. I came back up the stoop to sit with my client. We recessed our conference to watch the proceedings. Officers arrived promptly, including Inspector Cramer. When he got around to it he came and questioned us. I knew nothing about the taxi or its contents and said so. She told him she had not driven the taxi here and hadn't come in it. She gave him her name and address and occupation, but refused to answer questions about her private affairs—for instance, what she was consulting me about. I was telling her that was entirely up to her when you appeared."

Wolfe grunted. "Why didn't you bring Miss Holt inside?"

"Because it's not my house. Or my office."

"Nonsense. There is the front room. If you wish to stand on ceremony, I invite you to use it for consultation with your client. Sitting here in this hubbub is absurd. Have you any further information for Mr. Cramer?"

"No."

"Have you, Miss Holt?"

She was on her feet beside me. "I didn't have any," she said. "I haven't got any."

"Then get away from this turmoil. Come in."

Cramer found his tongue. "Just a minute." He had come on up to the stoop and was at my elbow, focused on Wolfe. "This is all very neat. Too damn neat. Goodwin says he quit his job. Did he?"

"Yes."

"Why?"

"Pfui. That's egregious, Mr. Cramer, and you know it."

"Did it have anything to do with Miss Holt or what she was coming to consult about?"

"No."

"Or with the fact that a taxi was parked at your door with a dead body in it?"

"No."

"Did you know Miss Holt was coming?"

"No. Nor, patently, did Mr. Goodwin."

"Did you know the taxi was out here?"

"No. I am bearing with you, sir. You persist beyond reason. If Mr. Goodwin or I were involved in the circumstance that brought you here or Miss Holt, would he have sat here with her, supine, awaiting your assault? You know him and you know me. Come, Archie. Bring your client." He turned.

I told Cramer, "I'll be glad to type up statements and bring them down," touched Mira Holt's arm, and followed her inside, Wolfe having preceded us.

When I had shut the door and the lock had clicked Wolfe spoke. "Since there's no telephone in the front room and you may have occasion to use one, perhaps the office would be better. I will go to my room."

"Thank you," I said politely. "But it might be still better for us to leave the back way. You may not want us here when I explain the situation. Miss Holt drove that taxi here. A friend of hers named Judith Bram is one of the ninety-three female hackies in New York, and she let Miss Holt take her cab—or maybe Miss Holt took it without Miss Bram's knowledge. She left—"

"No," Mira said. "Judy let me take it."

"Possible," I conceded. "You're a pretty good liar. Let me finish. She left it, empty, in front of a building and went in the building for something, and when she came back there was a dead body in it, a woman, with a knife between its ribs. Either it was covered with a canvas, or she—"

"I covered it," Mira said. "It was under that panel by the driver's seat."

"She's level-headed," I told Wolfe. "Somewhat. She couldn't notify the police, because not only had she and her friend violated the law, but also she had recognized the dead woman. She knew her. She decided to come and consult you and me. I met her on the stoop. She told me a cockeyed tale about a bet she had made with a friend which I'll skip. I said *somewhat* level-headed. I let her see that I knew she was feeding me soap but kept her from blurting it out. So I told Cramer no lies, but she did, and did a good job. But the lies won't keep long. It's barely possible that Judith Bram will deny that she let someone take her cab, but sooner or later—"

"I tried to phone her," Mira said, "but she didn't answer. I was going to tell her to say that someone stole it."

"Quit interrupting me. Did you ever hear of fingerprints? Did you see them working on that cab? So I have a client who is in a double-breasted jam. I'll know more about it after she tells me things. The point is, did she kill that woman? If I thought she did I would bow out quick — I would already have bowed out because it would have been hopeless. But she didn't. One will get you ten that she didn't. If she had —"

That interruption wasn't words; it was her lips against mine and her palms covering my ears. If she had been Wolfe's client I would have shoved her off quick, since that sort of demonstration only ruffles him, but she was mine and there was no point in hurting her feelings. I even patted her shoulder. When she was through I resumed.

"If she had killed her she would not have driven here with the corpse for a passenger to tell you, or even me, a goofy tale about a bet with a friend. Not a chance. She would have dumped the corpse somewhere. Make it twenty to one. Add to that my observation of her while we sat there on the stoop, and it's thirty to one. Therefore I am keeping the fee she paid me, and I'm — by the way." I reached in my pocket for the bills she had given me, unfolded them, and counted. Three twenties, three tens, and a five. Returning two twenties and a ten to my pocket, I offered her the rest. "Your change. I'm keeping fifty."

She hesitated, then took it. "I'll pay you more. Of course. What are you going to do?"

"I'll know better after you answer some questions. One that shouldn't wait: what did you do with the cap?"

"I have it." She patted her front.

"Good." I returned to Wolfe. "So we'll be going. Thank you again for your offer of hospitality, but Cramer may be ringing the bell any minute. We'll go out the rear, Miss Holt. This way."

"No." Wolfe snapped it. "This is preposterous. Give me half of that fifty dollars."

I raised a brow. "For what?"

"To pay me. You have helped me with many problems; surely I can help you with one. I am not being quixotic. I do not accept your headstrong decision that our long association has ended, but even if it has, your repute is inextricably involved with mine. Your client is in a pickle. I have never tried to do a job without your help; why should you try to do one without mine?"

I wanted to grin at him, but he might have misunderstood. "Okay," I said, and got a twenty from the pocket where I had put the fee, and a five from my wallet, and handed them to him. He took them, turned, and headed for the office, and Mira and I followed.

4

WHERE to sit was a delicate question — not for Wolfe, who of course went to his oversized custom-built chair behind his desk, nor for the client, since Wolfe wiggled a finger to indicate the red leather chair that would put her facing him, but for me. The desk at right angles to Wolfe's was no longer mine. I had a hand on one of the yellow chairs, to move it up, when Wolfe growled, "Confound it, don't be frivolous. We have a job to do."

I went and sat where I had belonged, and asked him, "Do I proceed?"

"Certainly."

I looked at her. In good light, with the cap off, she was very lookable, even in a pickle. "I would like," I said, "to be corroborated. Did you kill that woman?"

"No. *No!*"

"Okay. Out with it. This time, method two, the truth. Judith Bram is a friend of yours?"

"Yes."

"Did she let you take her cab?"

"Yes."

"Why?"

"I asked her to."

"Why did you ask her to?"

"Because . . . it's a long story."

"Make it as short as you can. We may not have much time."

She was on the edge of the chair, which would have held two of her. "I have known Judy three years. She was a model too, but she didn't like it. She's very unconventional. She had money she had inherited, and she bought a cab and a license about a year ago. She cruises when she feels like it, but she has some regular customers who think it's chic to ride in a cab with a girl driver, and my husband is one of them. He often—"

"Your husband?" Wolfe demanded. "*Miss* Holt?"

"They don't live together," I told him. "Not divorced, but she uses her own name. Fashion model. Go ahead but keep it short."

She obeyed. "My husband's name is Waldo Kearns. He paints pictures but doesn't sell any. He has money. He often calls Judy to take him somewhere, and he called last night when I was with her and told her to come for him at eight o'clock this evening, and I asked Judy to let me go instead of her. I have been trying to see him for months, to have a talk with him, and he refuses to see me. He doesn't answer my letters. I want a divorce and he doesn't. I think the reason he doesn't is that—"

"Skip it. Get on."

"Well . . . Judy said I could take the cab, and today at seven o'clock I went to her place and she brought it from the garage, and she gave me her cap and jacket, and I drove it to—"

"Where is her place?"

"Bowdoin Street. Number seventeen. In the Village."

"I know. You got in the cab there?"

"Yes. I drove it to Ferrell Street. It's west of Varick, below—"

"I know where it is."

"Then you know it's a dead end. Close to the end is an alley that goes between walls to a little house. That's my husband's. I lived there with him about a year ago. I got there a little before eight, and turned around and parked in front of the alley. Judy had said she always waited for him there. He didn't come. I didn't want to go to the house, because as soon as he saw me he would shut the door on me, but when he hadn't come at half past eight I got out and went—"

"You're sure of the time?"

"Yes. I looked at my watch. Of course."

"What does it say now?"

She lifted her wrist. "Two minutes after eleven."

"Right. You went through the alley?"

"Yes, to the house. There's a brass knocker on the door, no bell. I knocked with it, but nobody came. I knocked several times. I could hear the radio or television going inside, I could just barely hear it, so I knocked loud. He couldn't have recognized me through a window because it was too dark and I had the cap pulled down. Of course it could have been Morton, his man as he calls him, playing the radio, but I don't think so because he would have heard the knocker and come to the door. I finally gave up and went back to the cab, and as I was getting in I saw her. At first I thought it was a trick he had played, but when I looked closer I saw the knife, and then I recognized her, and she was dead. If I hadn't turned around and gripped the wheel as hard as I could I think I would have fainted. I never have fainted. I sat there—"

"Who was it?"

"It was Phoebe Arden. She was the reason my husband didn't want a divorce. I'm sure she was, or anyway one of the reasons. I think he thought that as long as he was still married to me she couldn't expect him to marry her, and neither could anyone else. But I wasn't thinking about that while I sat there, I was thinking what to do. I knew the right thing was to call the police, but I was driving Judy's cab, and, what was worse, I would have to admit I knew who she was, and they would find out about her and my husband. I don't know how long I sat there."

"It must have been quite a while. You left the cab to go to the house at eight-thirty. How long were you gone?"

"I don't know. I knocked several times, and looked in at the windows, and then knocked some more." She considered. "At least ten minutes."

"Then you were back at the cab at eight-forty, and from there to here wouldn't take more than ten minutes, and you got here at nine-twenty. Did you sit there half an hour?"

"No. I decided to get her—to get it out of the cab. I found that canvas under the panel. I thought the best place would be somewhere along the river front, and I drove there but didn't see a good place, and men tried to stop me twice, and once when I stopped for a light a man opened the door and when I told him I was making a delivery he almost climbed in anyway. Then I thought I would just leave the cab somewhere, anywhere, and I went to a phone booth to call Judy and tell her to say the cab had been stolen, but there was no answer. Then I thought of Nero Wolfe and you, and I drove here. I didn't have much time to make that up about the bet, just on my way here. I knew it wasn't good while I was telling it."

"So did I." I was frowning at her. "I want you to realize one thing. I believe you when you say you didn't kill her, but it doesn't follow that I swallow you whole. For instance, the divorce situation. If the fact is that your husband wanted one so he could marry Phoebe Arden, and you balked, that would make it different."

"No." She was frowning back. "I've told you the truth, every word. I lied to you out there, but if I lied to you now I'd be a fool."

"You sure would. How good a friend of yours is Judy Bram?"

"She's my best friend. She's a little wild, but I like her. I love her."

"Are you sure she rates it?"

"Yes."

"You'd better cross your fingers." I turned to Wolfe. "Since you're helping on this, and I fully appreciate it, our minds should meet. Do you accept it that she didn't kill her?"

"As a working hypothesis, yes."

"Then isn't it likely that she was killed by someone who knew that Miss Holt would be driving the cab? Since Kearns didn't show, taking her away from the cab, and the radio or television was on in the house?"

"Likely, but far from certain. It could have been impromptu. Or the embarrassment could have been meant for Miss Bram, not for Miss Holt."

I returned to Mira. "How close are Judy Bram and your husband?"

"Close?" The frown was getting chronic. "They aren't close. If you mean intimate, I doubt if Judy has ever allowed any man to be intimate. My husband may have tried. I suppose he has."

"Could Judy have had any reason to kill Phoebe Arden?"

"Good lord, no."

"Isn't it possible that Judy, unknown to you, had got an idea that she would like to break the ice with your husband, and Phoebe Arden was in the way?"

"I suppose it is, if you want to say that anything is possible, but I don't believe it."

"You heard what I asked Mr. Wolfe and what he answered. I still like it that whoever killed her knew that you were going to drive the cab there. It's certainly possible that Judy Bram told someone."

"Yes, it's possible, but I don't believe it. Judy wouldn't. She just wouldn't."

"It's also possible that you told someone. Did you?"

Her lips twitched. Twice. Two seconds. "No," she said.

"You're lying. I haven't time to be polite. You're lying. Whom did you tell?"

"I'm not going to say. The person I told couldn't possibly have . . . have done anything. Some things are *not* possible."

"Who was it?"

"No, Mr. Goodwin. Really."

I got the twenty and ten from my pocket and a twenty from my wallet, got up, and went to her. "Here's your fifty bucks," I said. "Count me out. You can leave the back way."

"But I tell you he couldn't!"

"Then he won't get hurt. I won't bite him. But I've got to know everything you do or it's no good."

Her lips twitched again. "You would really do that? Just give me up?"

"I sure would. I will. With regrets and best wishes."

She breathed. "I phoned a friend of mine last evening and told him. His name is Gilbert Irving."

"Is he more than a friend?"

"No. He is married and so am I. We're friends, that's all."

"Does he know your husband?"

"Yes. They've known each other for years, but they've never been close."

"Did he know Phoebe Arden?"

"He had met her. He didn't *know* her."

"Why did you tell him about your plan to drive the cab?"

"Because I wanted to know what he thought of it. He is very—a very intelligent man."

"What did he think of it?"

"He thought it was foolish. Not foolish exactly, useless. He thought my husband would refuse to listen to me. Honestly, Mr. Goodwin, this *is* foolish. There is absolutely no—"

The doorbell rang. I had taken three steps before I remembered that I no longer worked there; then, not wishing to be frivolous, I continued to the hall and took a look through the one-way glass panel of the front door. A man and a woman were there on the stoop. A glance was enough to recognize Inspector Cramer, but it took closer inspection for the woman, and I moved down the hall. Even then I wasn't positive, since the light had been dim on the picture of the female hackie in the taxi, but I was sure enough. It was Judith Bram.

5

IT was up to me, since it was my case and Wolfe was merely helping, but he had many times asked for my opinion and it wouldn't hurt to reciprocate, so I stepped to the office door and said, "Cramer and Judy Bram. Shall I—"

"Judy!" Mira cried. "She's here?"

I ignored her. "Shall I scoot with Miss Holt and leave them to you?"

He closed his eyes. In three seconds he opened them. "I would say no. The decision is yours."

"Then we stick. I want to meet Judy anyhow. Sit tight, Miss Holt. Never drop a simple basic lie until it drops you."

As I turned the bell rang again. I went to the front, put the chain bolt on, opened the door the two inches the chain allowed, and spoke through the crack. "Do you want me, Inspector?"

"I want in. Open up."

"Glad to for you, but not for strangers. Who is the lady?"

"Her name is Judith Bram. She's the owner and driver—"

"I want to see Mira Holt!" the lady said, meaning it. "Open the door!"

I removed the chain, but didn't have to swing the door because she saved me the trouble. She came with it and darted down the hall. Seeing that Cramer, after her, would brush me, I stiffened to make the brush a bump, and he wobbled and lost a step, giving me time to shut the door and reach the office at his heels. When we entered Judy was sitting on the arm of the red leather chair with her arm across Mira's shoulders, jabbering. Cramer grabbed her arm and barked at her, but she ignored him.

"—and I said yes, the cab might have still been there in front when you left, but I was sure you wouldn't take it, and anyway—"

Cramer yanked her up and around, and as she came she swung with her free hand and smacked him in the face. There was too much of him to be staggered by it, but the sound effect was fine. She jerked loose and glared at him. Her big, brown, well-spaced eyes were ideal for glaring. I had a feeling that I had seen her before, but I hadn't. It was just an old memory: a seventh-grade classmate out in Ohio whom I had been impelled to kiss, and she had socked me on the ear with her arithmetic. She is now married, with five children.

"That's not advisable, Miss Bram," Cramer stated. "Striking a police officer." He moved, got a yellow chair, and swung it around. "Here. Sit down."

"I'll sit where I please." She perched again on the red leather arm. "Is it advisable for a police officer to manhandle a citizen? When I got a hack license I informed myself about laws. Am I under arrest?"

"No."

"Then don't touch me." Her head swung around. "You're Nero Wolfe? You're even bigger." She didn't say bigger than what. "I'm Judy Bram. Are you representing my friend Mira Holt?"

His eyes on her were half closed. " 'Representing' is not the word, Miss Bram. I'm a detective, not a lawyer. Miss Holt has hired Mr. Goodwin, and he has hired me as his assistant. You call her your friend. Are you her friend?"

"Yes. And I want to know. She left my place around half past seven, and about an hour later I went out to keep a date. I had left my cab out front and it wasn't there, but I supposed—"

"Hold it," Cramer snapped. He was on the yellow chair, and I was at my desk. "I'll do the talking—"

She merely raised her voice. "—I supposed a man from the garage had come and got it, I have that arrangement—"

"Shut up!" Cramer roared. "Or I'll shut you up!"

"How?" she asked.

It was a question. He had several choices: clamp his paw on her mouth, or pick her up and carry her out, or call in a couple of big strong men from out front, or hit her with a blunt instrument, or shoot her. All had drawbacks.

"Permit me," Wolfe said. "I suggest, Mr. Cramer, that you have bungled it. The notion of suddenly confronting Miss Holt with Miss Bram was of course tempting, but your appraisal of Miss Bram's temperament was faulty. Now you're stuck. You won't get the contradictions you're after. Miss Holt would be a simpleton to supply particulars until she knows what Miss Bram has said. As you well know, that does not necessarily imply culpability for either of them."

Cramer rasped, "You're telling Miss Holt not to answer any questions."

"Am I? If so, unwittingly. Now, of course, you have made it plain. It would appear that you have only two alternatives: either let Miss Bram finish her account, or remove her."

"There's a third one I like better. I'll remove Miss Holt." Cramer got up. "Come on, Miss Holt. I'm taking you down for questioning in connection with the murder of Phoebe Arden."

"Is she under arrest?" Judy demanded.

"No. But if she doesn't talk she will be. As a material witness."

"Can he do that, Mr. Wolfe?"

"Yes."

"Without a warrant?"

"In the circumstances, yes."

"Come on, Miss Holt," Cramer growled.

I was sitting with my jaw set. Wolfe would rather miss a meal than let Cramer or any other cop take a client of his from that office into custody, and over the years I had seen and heard him pull some fancy maneuvers to prevent it. But this was my client, and he wasn't batting an eye. I admit that it would have had to be something extra fancy, and it was up to me, not him, but I had split the fee with him. So I sat with my jaw set while Mira left the chair and Judy jabbered and Cramer touched Mira's arm and they headed for the door. Then I came to, scribbled on my memo pad — formerly my memo pad — tore the sheet off, and made for the hall. Cramer had his hand on the knob.

"Here's the phone number," I told her. "Twenty-four-hour service. Don't forget method three."

She took the slip, said, "I won't," and crossed the sill, with Cramer right behind. I noted that the floodlights and the taxi were still there before I shut the door.

Back in the office, Wolfe was leaning back with his eyes closed and Judy Bram was standing scowling at him. She switched the scowl to me and demanded, "Why don't you put him to bed?"

"Too heavy. How many people did you tell that Mira was going to drive your cab to her husband's house?"

She eyed me, straight, for two breaths, then went to the red leather chair and sat. I took the yellow one, to be closer.

"I thought you were working for her," she said.

"I am."

"You don't sound like it. She didn't drive my cab."

I shook my head. "Come on down. Would I be working for her if she hadn't opened up? You told her yesterday that Kearns had phoned you to call for him at eight o'clock today, and she asked you to let her go instead of you. She wanted to have a talk with him about a divorce. How many people did you tell about it?"

"Nobody. If she opened up what's the rest of it?"

"Ask her when you see her. Did you kill Phoebe Arden?"

From the flash in her eye she would have smacked me if I had been close enough. "Oh, for God's sake," she said. "Get a club. Drag me by the hair."

"Later maybe." I leaned to her. "Look, Miss Bram. Give your temperament a rest and use your brain. I am working for Mira Holt. I know exactly where she was and what she did, every minute, from seven o'clock this evening on, but I'm not going to tell you. Of course you know that the dead body of a woman named Phoebe Arden was found in your cab. I am certain that Mira didn't kill her, but she is probably going to be charged. I am not certain that the murderer tried to get her tagged for it, but it looks like it. I would be a fathead to tell the murderer about her movements. Wouldn't I? Answer with your brain."

"Yes." She was meeting my eyes.

"Okay. Give me one good reason why I should cross you off. One you would accept if you were in my place. Mira has, naturally, but why should I?"

"Because there's not the slightest—" She stopped. "No. You don't know that. All right. But don't try twisting my arm. I know some tricks."

"I'll keep my distance if you will. Did you kill Phoebe Arden?"

"No."

"Do you know who did?"

"No."

"Have you any suspicions? Any ideas?"

"Yes. Or I would have if I knew anything—where and when it happened. Did Phoebe come out to the cab with Waldo Kearns?"

"No. Kearns didn't show up. Mira never saw him."

"But Phoebe came?"

"Not alive. When Mira saw her she was dead. In the cab."

"Then my idea is Waldo. The sophisticated ape. You know, you're not any too bright. If I killed her in my own cab while Mira was driving it, I already know everything you do and more. Why not tell me?"

I looked at Wolfe, who had opened his eyes off and on. He grunted. "You told her to use her brain," he muttered.

I returned to Judy. "You certainly would know this: Mira got there before eight o'clock and parked in front. When Kearns hadn't showed at eight-thirty she went to the house and spent ten minutes knocking and looking in windows. When she returned to the cab the dead body was in it. She never saw Kearns."

"But my God." Her brows were up. She turned her hands over. "All she had to do was dump it out!"

"She hasn't got your temperament. She—"

"She drove *here* with it? To consult with *you*?"

"She might have done worse. In fact, she tried to. She phoned *you*, and got no answer. What's your idea about Kearns?"

"He killed Phoebe."

"Then that's settled. Why?"

"I don't know. He tried to shake her and she hung on. Or she cheated on him. Or she had a bad cold and he was afraid he would catch it. He put the body in the cab to fix Mira. He hates her because she told him the truth about himself once."

"Did you know Phoebe well? Who and what was she?"

"Well enough. She was a widow at thirty, roaming around. I might have killed her, at that. About a year ago she started scattering remarks about me, and I broke her neck. Almost. She spent a week in a hospital."

"Did it cure her? I mean of remark-scattering?"

"Yes."

"We might as well finish with you. You told Mr. Wolfe Mira left your place around half past seven and about an hour later you went out to keep a date. So you might have left at a quarter after eight."

"I might, but I didn't. I walked to Mitchell Hall on Fourteenth Street to make a speech at a cab driver's meeting, and I got there at five minutes to nine. After the meeting I walked back home, and two cops were there waiting for me. They were dumb enough to ask me first where my cab was, and I said I supposed it was in the garage. When they said no, it was parked on Thirty-fifth Street, and asked me to come and identify it, naturally I went. I also identified a dead body, which they hadn't mentioned. Is that Inspector Cramer dumb?"

"No."

"I thought not. When he asked me if I knew Mira Holt of course I said yes, and when he asked when I last saw her I told him. Since I had no idea what had happened I thought that was safest, but I said I hadn't told her she could take the cab and I knew she wouldn't take it without asking me. Does that finish with me?"

"It's a good start. How well do you know Gilbert Irving?"

That fazed her. Her mouth opened and she gawked with her big, brown, well-spaced eyes. "Are my ears working?" she demanded. "Did you say Gilbert Irving?"

"That's right."

"Who let him in?"

"Mira mentioned him. How well do you know him?"

"Too well. I dream about a lion standing on a rock about to spring at me, and I suspect it's him. If my subconscious is yearning for him it had better go soak its head, because first he's married and his wife has claws, and second, when he looks at Mira or hears her voice he has to lean against something to keep from trembling. Did she tell you that?"

"No. Who is he? What does he do?"

"Something in Wall Street, but he doesn't look it. Why did Mira mention him?"

"Because I made her. She phoned him last evening and told him she was going to drive your cab and why. She wanted to know what he thought of it. I want to know what motive he might have for killing Phoebe Arden."

She opened her mouth to reply, then decided to laugh instead. It was a real laugh, no giggle.

I raised a brow. "Your subconscious taking over?" I inquired.

"No." She sobered. "I couldn't help it. It struck me, of course Gil killed her. He couldn't bear the thought of Mira's husband being unfaithful to her, it was an insult to her womanhood, so he killed Phoebe. Do you blame me for laughing?"

"No. I'll laugh too when I get around to it. Does anything else strike you? A motive for him you wouldn't laugh at?"

"Of course not. It's ridiculous. You're just floundering around. Have you finished with me?"

I looked at Wolfe. His eyes were closed. "For now, yes," I told her, "unless Mr. Wolfe thinks I skipped something."

"How can he? You can talk in your sleep, but you can't think." She stood up. "What are you going to do?"

"Find a murderer and stick pins in him. Or her."

"Not sitting here you aren't. Don't bother, I know the way out. Why don't you go and tackle Wally Kearns? I'll go with you."

"Thanks, I'll manage."

"Where did he take Mira?"

"Either to Homicide West, two-thirty West Twentieth, or to the District Attorney's office, one-fifty-five Leonard. Try Twentieth Street first."

"I will." She turned and was off. I followed, to let her out, but she was a fast walker and I would have had to trot to catch up. When I reached the door she had it open. I stepped out to the stoop and watched her descend to the sidewalk and turn west. The floodlights and ropes and police cars were gone, and so was Judy's cab. My wrist watch said five minutes past midnight as I went in and shut the door. I returned to the office and found Wolfe on his feet with his eyes open.

"I assumed," I said, "that if you wanted something from her I hadn't got you would say so."

"Naturally."

"Have you any comments?"

"No. It's bedtime."

"Yeah. Since you're with me on this, which I appreciate, perhaps I'd better sleep here. If you don't mind."

"Certainly. You own your bed. I have a suggestion. I presume you intend to have a look at that place in the morning, and to see Mr. Kearns. It might be well for me to see him too."

"I agree. Thank you for suggesting it. If they haven't got him downtown I'll have him here at eleven o'clock." I made it eleven because that was his earliest hour for an appointment, when he came down from his two-hour session up in the plant rooms with the orchids.

"Make it a quarter past eleven," he said. "I will be engaged until then with Mr. Anderson."

I opened my mouth and closed it again. "Didn't you phone him not to come?"

"On the contrary, I phoned him to come. On reflection I saw that I had been hasty. In my employ, as my agent, you had made a commitment, and I was bound by it. I should not have repudiated it. I should have honored it, and then dismissed you if I considered your disregard of the rules intolerable."

"I see. I can understand that you'd rather fire me than have me quit."

"I said 'if.' "

I lifted my shoulders and dropped them. "It's a little complicated. If I have quit you can't fire me. If I haven't quit I am still on your payroll, and it would be unethical for me to have Miss Holt as my client. It would also be wrong for you to accept pay from me for helping with the kind of work you are paying me to do. If you return the twenty-five to me and I return the fifty to Miss Holt, I will be deserting an innocent fellow being in a jam whom I have accepted as a client, and that would be inexcusable. It looks to me as if we have got ourselves in a fix that is absolutely hopeless, and I can't see —"

"Confound it," he roared, "go to bed!" and marched out.

6

BY 8:15 Tuesday morning I was pretty well convinced that Mira Holt was in the coop, since I had got it from three different sources. At 7:20 Judy Bram phoned to say that Mira was under arrest and what was I going to do. I said it wouldn't be practical to tell a suspect my plans, and she hung up on me. At 7:40 Lon Cohen of the *Gazette* phoned to ask if it was true that I had quit my job with Nero Wolfe, and if so what was I doing there, and was Mira Holt my client, and if so what was she doing in the can, and had she killed Phoebe Arden or not. Since Lon had often been useful and might be again, I explained fully, off the record, why I couldn't explain. And at eight o'clock the radio said that Mira Holt was being held as a material witness in the murder of Phoebe Arden.

Neither Lon nor the radio supplied any items that helped, nor did the morning papers. The *Star* had a picture of the taxi parked in front of Wolfe's house, but I had seen that for myself. It also had a description of the clothes Phoebe Arden had died in, but what I needed was a description of the clothes the murderer had killed in. And it gave the specifications of the knife — an ordinary kitchen knife with a five-inch blade and a plastic handle — but if the answer was going to come from any routine operation like tracing the knife or lifting prints from the handle, it would be Cramer's army who would get it, not me.

I made one phone call, to Anderson, to ask him to postpone his appointment because Wolfe was busy on a case, and he said sure, it wasn't urgent; and, since Fritz takes Wolfe's breakfast to his room and I seldom see him before he comes down to the office at eleven, I put a note on his desk. I wanted to make another call, to Nathaniel Parker, the lawyer, but vetoed it. For getting Mira out on bail he would have charged about ten times what she had paid me, and there was no big hurry. It would teach her not to drive a hack without a license.

At a quarter past eight I left the house and went to Ninth Avenue for a taxi, and at half past I dismissed it at the corner of Carmine and Ferrell, and walked down Ferrell Street to its dead end. There were only two alternatives for what had happened during the period — call it ten minutes — when Mira had been away from the cab: either the murderer, having already killed Phoebe Arden, had carried or dragged the body to the cab and hoisted it in, or he had got in the cab with her and killed her there. I preferred the latter, since you can walk to a cab with a live woman in much less time than you can carry her to it dead, and also since, even in a secluded spot like that and even after dark, there is much less risk of being noticed. But in either case they had to come from some place nearby.

The first place to consider was Kearns' house, but it only took five minutes to cross it off. The alley that led to it was walled on both sides, Mira had been parked at its mouth, and there was no other way to get from the house to the street. On the left of the alley was a walled-in lumber yard, and on the right was a dingy old two-story warehouse. On inspection neither of them seemed an ideal spot for cover, but across the street was a beaut. It was an open lot cluttered with blocks of stone scattered and piled around, some rough and some chiseled and polished. A whole company could have hid there, let alone one murderer and one victim. As you know, I was already on record that Mira hadn't killed her, but it was nice to see that stoneyard. If there had been no place to hide in easy distance . . . Three men were there, two discussing a stone and one chiseling, but they wouldn't be there at eight in the evening. I recrossed the street and entered the alley, and walked through.

By gum, Kearns had a garden, a sizable patch, say forty by sixty, with flowers in bloom and a little pool with a fountain, and a flag-stone path leading to the door of a two-story brick house painted white. I hadn't known there was anything like it in Manhattan and I thought I knew Manhattan. A man in a gray shirt and blue jeans was kneeling among the flowers, and half way up the path I stopped and asked him, "Are you Waldo Kearns?"

"Do I look it?" he demanded.

"Yes and no. Are you Morton?"

"That's my name. What's yours?"

"Goodwin." I headed for the house, but he called, "Nobody there," and I turned.

"Where's Mr. Kearns?"

"I don't know. He went out a while ago."

"When will he be back?"

"I couldn't say."

I looked disappointed. "I should have phoned. I want to buy a picture. I came last evening around half past eight and knocked, but nothing doing. I knocked loud because I heard the radio or TV going."

"It was the TV. I was watching it. I heard you knock. I don't open the door at night when he's not here. There's some tough ones around this neighborhood."

"I don't blame you. I suppose I just missed him. What time did he leave last evening?"

"What difference does it make when he left if he wasn't here?"

Perfectly logical, not only for him but for me. If Kearns hadn't been there when Mira arrived in the cab it didn't matter when he had left. I would have liked to ask Morton one more question, whether anyone had left with him, but from the look in his eye he would have used some more logic on me, so I skipped it, said I'd try again, and went.

There was no use hanging around because if Kearns had gone to call at the District Attorney's office by request, which was highly probable, there was no telling when he would be back. I had got Gilbert Irving's business address from the phone book, on Wall Street, but there was no use going there at that early hour. However, I had also got his home address, on East 78th Street, and I might catch him before he left, so I hoofed it along Ferrell Street back to civilization and flagged a taxi.

It was 9:15 when I climbed out in front of the number on 78th Street, a tenement palace with a marquee and a doorman. In the lobby another uniformed sentry sprang into action, and I told him, "Mr. Gilbert Irving. Tell him a friend of Miss Holt." He went and used a phone, returned and said, "Fourteen B," and watched me like a hawk as I walked to the elevator and entered. When I got out at the fourteenth floor the elevator man stood and watched until I had pushed the button and the door had opened and I had been invited in.

The inviter was no maid or butler. She might have passed for a maid in uniform, but not in the long, flowing, patterned-silk number which she probably called a breakfast gown. Without any suggestions about my hat she said, "This way, please," and led me across the hall, through an arch into a room half as big as Kearns' garden, and over to chairs near a corner. She sat on one of them and indicated another for me.

I stood. "Perhaps the man downstairs didn't understand me," I suggested. "I asked for Mr. Irving."

"I know," she said. "He isn't here. I am his wife. We are friends of Miss Holt, and we're disturbed about the terrible — about her difficulty. You're a friend of hers?" Her voice was a surprise because it didn't fit. She was slender and not very tall, with a round little face and a little curved mouth, but her deep strong voice was what you would expect from a female sergeant. Nothing about her suggested the claws Judy Bram had mentioned, but they could have been drawn in.

"A new friend," I said. "I've known her twelve hours. If you've read the morning paper you may have noted that she was sitting on the stoop of Nero Wolfe's house with a man named Archie Goodwin when a cop found the body in the taxi. I'm Goodwin, and she has hired me to find out things."

She adjusted the gown to cover a leg better. "According to the radio she has hired Nero Wolfe. She was arrested in his house."

"That's a technical point. We're both working on it. I'm seeing people who might have some information, and Mr. Irving is on my list. Is he at his office?"

"I suppose so. He left earlier than usual." The leg was safe, no exposure above the ankle, but she adjusted the gown again. "What kind of information? Perhaps I could help?"

I couldn't very well ask if her husband had told her that Mira had told him she was going to drive Judy's cab. But she wanted to help. I sat down. "Almost anything might be useful, Mrs. Irving. Were you and your husband also friends of Phoebe Arden?"

"I was. My husband knew her, of course, but you couldn't say they were friends."

"Were they enemies?"

"Oh, no. It was just that they didn't hit it off."

"When did you see her last?"

"Four days ago, last Friday, at a cocktail party at Waldo Kearns' house. I was thinking about it when you came. She was so gay. She was a gay person."

"You hadn't seen her since?"

"No." She was going to add something, but checked it.

It was so obvious that I asked, "But you had heard from her? A letter or a phone call?"

"How did you know that?" she demanded.

"I didn't. Most detective work is guessing. Was it a letter?"

"No." She hesitated. "I would like to help, Mr. Goodwin, but I doubt if it's important, and I certainly don't want any notoriety."

"Of course not, Mrs. Irving." I was sympathetic. "If you mean, if you tell me something will I tell the police, absolutely not. They have arrested my client."

"Well." She crossed her legs, glancing down to see that nothing was revealed. "I phoned Phoebe yesterday afternoon. My husband and I had tickets for the theater last evening, but about three o'clock he phoned me that a business associate from the West Coast had arrived unexpectedly, and he had to take him to dinner. So I phoned Phoebe and we arranged to meet at Morsini's at a quarter to seven for dinner and then go to the theater. I was there on time, but she didn't come. At a quarter past seven I called her number, but there was no answer. I don't like to eat alone at a place like Morsini's, so I waited a little longer and then left word for her and went to Schrafft's. She didn't come. I thought she might come to the theater, the Majestic, and I waited in the lobby until after nine, and then I left a ticket for her at the box office and went in. I would tell the police about it if I thought it was important, but it doesn't really *tell* anything except that she was at home when I phoned around three o'clock. Does it?"

"Sure it does. Did she agree definitely to meet you at Morsini's or was it tentative?"

"It was definite. Quite definite."

"Then it was certainly something that happened after three o'clock that kept her from meeting you. It was probably something that happened after six-thirty or she would have phoned you—if she was still alive. Have you any idea at all what it might have been?"

"None whatever. I can't guess."

"Have you any ideas about who might have killed her?"

"No. I can't guess that either."

"Do you think Mira Holt killed her?"

"Good heavens, no. Not Mira. Even if she had—"

"Even if she had what?"

"Nothing. Mira wouldn't kill anybody. They don't think that, do they?"

Over the years at least a thousand people have asked me what the police think, and I appreciate the compliment though I rarely deserve it. Life would be much simpler if I always knew what the police think at any given moment. It's hard enough to know what I think. After another ten minutes with her I decided that I thought that Mrs. Irving had nothing more to contribute, so I thanked her and departed. She came with me to the hall, and even picked up my hat from the chair where I had dropped it. I had yet to get a glimpse of her legs.

It was ten minutes to ten when I emerged to the sidewalk and turned left for Lexington Avenue and the subway, and a quarter past when I entered the marble lobby of a towering beehive on Wall Street and consulted the building directory. Gilbert Irving's firm had the whole thirtieth floor, and I found the proper bank of elevators, entered one, and was hoisted straight up three hundred feet for nothing. In a paneled chamber with a thick conservative carpet a handsome conservative creature at a desk bigger than Wolfe's told me in a voice like silk that Mr. Irving was not in and that she knew not when he would arrive or where he was. If I cared to wait?

I didn't. I left, got myself dropped back down the three hundred feet, and went to another subway, this time the west side; and, leaving at Christopher, walked to Ferrell Street and on to its dead end and through the allley. Morton, still at work in the garden, greeted me with reserve but not coldly, said Kearns had not returned and there had been no word from him, and, as I was turning to go, suddenly stood up and asked, "Did you say you wanted to *buy* a picture?"

I said that was my idea but naturally I wanted to see it first, left him wagging his head, walked the length of Ferrell Street the fourth time that day, found a taxi, and gave the driver the address whch might or might not still be mine. As we turned into 35th Street from Eighth Avenue, at five minutes past eleven, there was another taxi just ahead of us, and it stopped at the curb in front of the brownstone. I handed my driver a bill, hopped out, and had mounted the stoop by the time the man from the other cab had crossed the sidewalk. I had never seen him or a picture of him, or heard him described, but I knew him. I don't know whether it was his floppy black hat or shoestring tie, or neat little ears or face like a squirrel, but I knew him. I had the door open when he reached the stoop.

"I would like to see Mr. Nero Wolfe," he said. "I'm Waldo Kearns."

7

SINCE Wolfe had suggested that I should bring Kearns there so we could look at him together, I would just as soon have let him think that I had filled the order, but of course that wouldn't do. So when, having taken the floppy black hat and put it on the shelf in the hall, I escorted him to the office and pronounced his name, I added, "I met Mr. Kearns out front. He arrived just as I did."

Wolfe, behind his desk, had been pouring beer when we entered. He put the bottle down. "Then you haven't talked with him?"

"No, sir."

He turned to Kearns, in the red leather chair. "Will you have beer, sir?"

"Heavens, no." Kearns was emphatic. "I didn't come for amenities. My business is urgent. I am extremely displeased with the counsel you have given my wife. You must have hypnotized her. She refuses to see me. She refuses to accept the services of my lawyer, even to arrange bail for her. I demand an explanation. I intend to hold you to account for alienating the affection of my wife."

"Affections," Wolfe said.

"What?"

"Affections. In that context the plural is used." He lifted the glass and drank, and licked his lips.

Kearns stared at him. "I didn't come here," he said, "to have my grammar corrected."

"Not grammar. Diction."

Kearns pounded the chair arm. "What have you to say?"

"It would be futile for me to say anything whatever until you have re-gained your senses, if you have any. If you think your wife had affection for you until she met me twelve hours ago, you're an ass. If you know she hadn't your threat is fatuous. In either case what can you expect but contempt?"

"I expect an explanation! I expect the truth! I expect you to tell me why my wife refuses to see me!"

"I can't tell you what I don't know. I don't even know that she has, since in your present state I question the accuracy of your reporting. When and where did she refuse?"

"This morning. Just now, in the District Attorney's office. She won't even talk to my lawyer. She told him she was waiting to hear from you and Goodwin." His head jerked to me. "You're Goodwin?"

I admitted it. His head jerked back. "It's humiliating! It's degrading! My wife under arrest! Mrs. Waldo Kearns in jail! Dishonor to my name and to me! And you're to blame!"

Wolfe took a breath. "I doubt if it's worth the trouble," he said, "but I'm willing to try. I presume what you're after is an account of our conversation with your wife last evening. I might consider supplying it, but first I would have to be satisfied of your *bona fides*. Will you answer some questions?"

"It depends on what they are."

"Probably you have already answered them, to the police. Has your wife wanted a divorce and have you refused to consent?"

"Yes. I regard the marriage contract as a sacred covenant."

"Have you refused to discuss it with her in recent months?"

"The police didn't ask me that."

"I ask it. I need to establish not only your *bona fides*, Mr. Kearns, but also your wife's. It shouldn't embarrass you to answer that."

"I doesn't embarrass me. You can't embarrass me. It would have been useless to discuss it with her since I wouldn't consider it."

"So you wouldn't see her?"

"Naturally. That was all she would talk about."

"Have you been contributing to her support since she left you?"

"She didn't leave me. We agreed to try living separately. She wouldn't let me contribute to her support. I offered to. I wanted to."

"The police certainly asked you if you killed Phoebe Arden. Did you?"

"No. Why in God's name would I kill her?"

"I don't know. Miss Judith Bram suggested that she may have had a bad cold and you were afraid you would catch it, but that seems farfetched. By the way—"

"Judy? Judy Bram said that? I don't believe it!"

"But she did. In this room last evening, in the chair you now occupy. She also called you a sophisticated ape."

"You're lying!"

"No. I'm not above lying, or below it, but the truth will do now. Also—"

"You're lying. You've never seen Judy Bram. You're merely repeating something my wife said."

"That's interesting, Mr. Kearns, and even suggestive. You are willing to believe that your wife called you a sophisticated ape, but not that Miss Bram did. When I do lie I try not to be clumsy. Miss Bram was here last evening, with Mr. Goodwin and me, for half an hour or more and that brings me to a ticklish point. I must ask you about a detail that the police don't know about. Certainly they asked about your movements last evening, but they didn't know that you had arranged with Judith Bram to call for you in her cab at eight o'clock. Unless you told them?"

Kearns sat still, and for him it is worth mentioning. With many people sitting still is nothing remarkable, but with him it was. His sitting, like his face, reminded me of a squirrel; he kept moving or twitching something—a hand, a shoulder, a foot, even his head. Now he was motionless all over.

"Say that again," he commanded.

Wolfe obeyed. "Have you told the police that you had arranged with Miss Bram to call for you in her cab at eight o'clock last evening?"

"No. Why should I tell them something that isn't true?"

"You shouldn't, ideally, but people often do. I do occasionally. However, that's irrelevant, since it would have been the truth. Evidently Miss Bram hasn't told the police, but she told me. I mention it to ensure that you'll tell *me* the truth when you recount your movements last evening."

"If she told you that she lied."

"Oh, come, Mr. Kearns." Wolfe was disgusted. "It is established that her cab stood at the mouth of the alley leading to your house for more than half an hour, having come at your bidding. If you omitted that detail in your statement to the police I may have to supply it. Haven't you spoken with Miss Bram since?"

"No." He was still motionless. "Her phone doesn't answer. She's not at home. I went there." He passed his tongue across his lower lip. I admit I have never seen a squirrel do that. "I couldn't tell the police her cab was there last evening because I didn't know it was. I wasn't there."

"Where were you? Consider that I know you had ordered the cab for eight o'clock and hadn't canceled the order."

"I've told the police where I was."

"Then your memory has been jogged."

"It didn't need jogging. I was at the studio of a man named Prosch, Carl Prosch. I went there to meet Miss Arden and look at a picture she was going to buy. I got there at a quarter to eight and left at nine o'clock. She hadn't come, and—"

"If you please. Miss Phoebe Arden?"

"Yes. She phoned me at half past seven and said she had about decided to buy a painting, a still life, from Prosch, and was going to his studio to look at it again, and asked me to meet her there to help her decide. I was a little surprised because she knows what I think of daubers like Prosch, but I said I would go. His studio is on Carmine Street, in walking distance from my house, and I walked. She hadn't arrived, and I had only been there two or three minutes when she phoned and asked to speak to me. She said she had been delayed and would get there as soon as she could, and asked me to wait for her. My thought was that I would wait until midnight rather than have her buy a still life by Prosch, but I didn't say so. I didn't wait until midnight, but I waited until nine o'clock. I discussed painting with Prosch a while, until he became insufferable, and then went down to the street and waited there. She never came. I walked back home."

Wolfe grunted. "Can there be any doubt that it was Miss Arden on the phone? Both times?"

"Not the slightest. I couldn't possibly mistake her voice."

"What time was it when you left Mr. Prosch and went down to the street?"

"About half past eight. I told the police I couldn't be exact about that, but I could about when I started home. It was exactly nine o'clock." Kearns' hands moved. Back to normal. "Now I'll hear what you have to say."

"In a moment. Miss Bram was to come at eight o'clock. Why didn't you phone her?"

"Because I thought I would be back. Probably a little late, but she would wait. I didn't phone her after Miss Arden phoned that she was delayed because she would be gone."

"Where was she to drive you?"

"To Long Island. A party. What does that matter?" He was himself again. "You talk now, and I want the truth!"

Wolfe picked up his glass, emptied it, and put it down. "Possibly you are entitled to it, Mr. Kearns. Unquestionably a man of your standing would feel keenly the ignominy of having a wife in jail—the woman to whom you have given your name, though she doesn't use it. You may know that she came to this house at twenty minutes past nine last evening."

"I know nothing. I told you she won't see me."

. "So you did. She arrived just as Mr. Goodwin was leaving the house on an errand and they met on the stoop. No doubt you know that Mr. Goodwin is permanently in my employ as my confidential assistant—permanently, that is, in the sense that neither of us has any present intention of ending it or changing its terms."

Kearns was fidgeting again. I was not. He spoke. "The paper said he had left your employ. It didn't say on account of my wife, but of course it was."

"Bosh." Wolfe's head turned. "Archie?"

"Bosh," I agreed. "The idea of quitting on account of Miss Holt never entered my head."

Kearns hit the chair arm. "Mrs. Kearns!"

"Okay," I conceded. "Mrs. Waldo Kearns."

"So," Wolfe said, "your wife's first contact was with Mr. Goodwin. They sat on the stoop and talked. You know, of course, that Miss Bram's cab was there at the curb with Miss Arden's body in it."

"Yes. What did my wife say?"

"I'll come to that. Police came along in a car and discovered the body, and reported it, and soon there was an army. A policeman named Cramer talked with Mr. Goodwin and your wife, I went to the door and invited them to enter—not Mr. Cramer—and they did so. We talked for half an hour or so, when Mr. Cramer came with Miss Bram, and they were admitted. Mr. Cramer, annoyed by the loquacity of Miss Bram, and wishing to speak with your wife privately, took her away. You demanded the truth, sir, and you have it. I add one item, also true: since your wife had engaged Mr. Goodwin's services, and through him mine also, what she told us was confidential and can't be divulged. Now for—"

Kearns bounced out of the chair, and as he did so the doorbell rang. Since a man who might have stuck a knife in a woman might be capable of other forms of violence, I was going to leave it to Fritz, but Wolfe shot me a glance and I went to the hall for a look. On the stoop was a tall guy with a bony face and a strong jaw. Behind me Kearns was yapping but had drawn no weapon. I went to the front and opened the door.

"To see Mr. Wolfe," he said. "My name is Gilbert Irving."

The temptation was too strong. Only twelve hours ago I had seen a confrontation backfire for Cramer, when he had brought Judy Bram in to face Mira, but this time the temperament was already in the office, having a fit, and it would be interesting to see the reaction, and possibly helpful. So I told him to come in, took his Homburg and put it on the shelf beside the floppy black number, and steered him to the office.

Kearns was still on his feet yapping, but when Wolfe's eyes left him to direct a scowl at me he turned his head. I ignored the scowl. I had disregarded another rule by bringing in a visitor without consulting Wolfe, but as far as I was concerned Mira was still my client and it was my case. I merely pronounced names. "Mr. Gilbert Irving. Mr. Wolfe."

The reaction was interesting enough, though not helpful, since it was no news that Kearns and Irving were not pals. Perhaps Kearns didn't actually spit at him because it could have been merely that moisture came out with his snort. Two words followed immediately. "You bastard!"

Irving must have had lessons or practice, or both. His uppercut, with his right, was swift and sure, and had power. He caught Kearns right on the button and sent him straight up a good six inches before he swayed against the corner of Wolfe's desk.

8

TO do him justice, Kearns handled it as well as could be expected, even better. He surprised me. He didn't utter a peep. The desk saved him from going down. He stayed propped against it for three seconds, straightened with his hand on it for support, moved his head backward and forward twice, decided his neck was still together, and moved. His first few steps were wobbly, but by the time he reached the door to the hall they were steadier, and he made the turn okay. I went to the hall and stood, as he got his hat from the shelf and let himself out, pulling the door shut without banging it, and re-entered the office as Irving was saying, "I should beg your pardon. I do. I'm sorry."

"You were provoked." Wolfe told him. He gestured at the red leather chair. "Be seated."

"Hold it." I was there. "I guess I should beg your pardon, Mr. Irving, for not telling you he was here, and now I must beg it again. I have to tell Mr. Wolfe something that can't wait. It won't take long." I went and opened the door to the front room. "If you'll step in here."

He didn't like the idea. "My business is pressing," he said.

"So is mine. If you please?"

"Your name is Archie Goodwin?"

"Yes."

He hesitated a second, and then came, and crossed the sill, and I closed the door. Since it and the wall were soundproofed, I didn't have to lower my voice to tell Wolfe, "I want to report. I saw his wife."

"Indeed. Will a summary do?"

"No." I sat. "It will for one detail, that eighty feet from where the cab was parked there is a stoneyard that would be perfect cover, you couldn't ask for better, but you must have my talk with Mrs. Irving verbatim."

"Go ahead."

I did so, starting with a description of her. It had been years since he had first told me that when I described a man he must see him and hear him, and I had learned the trick long ago. I also knew how to report conversations word for word — much longer ones than the little chat I had had with Mrs. Irving.

When I had finished he asked one question. "Was she lying?"

"I wouldn't bet either way. If so she is good. If it was a mixture I'd hate to have to sort it out."

"Very well." He closed his eyes. In a moment they opened. "Bring him."

I went and opened the door to the front room and told him to come, and he entered, crossed to the red leather chair, sat, and aimed his eyes at Wolfe. "I should explain," he said, "that I am here as a friend of Miss Mira Holt, but she didn't send me."

Wolfe nodded. "She mentioned your name last evening. She said you are an intelligent man."

"I'm afraid she flatters me." Evidently it was normal for him to sit still. "I have come to you for information, but I can't pretend I have any special right to it. I can only tell you why I want it. When I learned on the radio this morning that Miss Holt was in custody I started downtown to see her, to offer my help, but on the way I decided that it wouldn't be advisable because it might be misconstrued, since I am merely a friend. So I called on my lawyer instead. His name is John H. Darby. I explained the situation and asked him to see Miss Holt, and he arranged to see her and has talked with her, but she won't tell him anything. She even refused to authorize him to arrange bail for her. She says that Archie Goodwin and Nero Wolfe are representing her, and she will say nothing and do nothing without their advice."

I touched my lips with a fingertip, the lips that Mira had kissed. I was blowing the kiss back to her. Not only had she put my name first, but also she had improved on my suggestion by combining method three and method one. She was a client in a thousand. She had even turned down two offers to spring her.

"I'm not a lawyer," Wolfe said, "and neither is Mr. Goodwin."

"I'm aware of that. But you seem to have hypnotized Miss Holt. With no offense intended, I must ask, are you acting in her interest or in Waldo Kearns'?"

Wolfe grunted. "Hers. She hired us."

I put in, "You and Kearns agree. He thinks we hypnotized her too. Nuts."

He regarded me. "I prefer to deal with Mr. Wolfe. This is his office."

"You're dealing with both of us," Wolfe told him. "Professionally we are indiscrete. What information do you want?"

"I want to know why you are taking no steps to get her released and what action you intend to take in her interest. I also want you to advise her to accept the services of my lawyer. He is highly qualified."

Wolfe rested his palms on the chair arms. "You should know better, Mr. Irving; you're a man of affairs. Before I gave you an inch, let alone the mile you ask for, I would have to be satisfied that your interest runs with hers."

"Damn it, I'm her friend! Didn't she say I am? You said she mentioned me."

"She could be mistaken." Wolfe shook his head. "No. For instance, I don't even know what you have told the police."

"Nothing. They haven't asked me anything. Why should they?"

"Then you haven't told them that Miss Holt told you on the phone Sunday evening that she was going to drive Judith Bram's cab?"

It got him. He stared. He looked at me and back at Wolfe. "No," he said. "Even if she had, would I tell the police?"

"Do you deny that she did?"

"I neither deny it nor affirm it."

Wolfe upturned a palm. "How the devil can you expect candor from me? Do you want me to suspect that Miss Holt lied when she told us of that phone call?"

"When did she tell you?"

"Last evening. Here. Not under hypnosis."

He considered. "All right. She told me that."

"And whom did you tell?"

"No one."

"You're certain?"

"Of course I'm certain."

"Then it won't be easy to satisfy me. Assuming that Miss Holt fulfilled her intention and took the cab, and arrived with it at Mr. Kearns' address at eight o'clock, and combining that assumption with the fact that at twenty minutes past nine the cab was standing in front of my house with a dead body in it, where are you? Miss Bram states that she told no one of the arrangement. Miss Holt states that she told no one but you. Is it any wonder that I ask where you are? And, specifically, where you were last evening from eight o'clock on?"

"I see." Irving took a breath, and another. "It's utterly preposterous. You actually suspect me of being involved in the murder of Phoebe Arden."

"I do indeed."

"But it's preposterous! I had no concern whatever with Miss Arden. She meant nothing to me. Not only that, apparently whoever killed her managed to get Miss Holt involved — either managed it or permitted it. Would I do that?" He made his hands fists and raised them, shook them. "Damn it, I have to know what happened! You know. Miss Holt told you. I have to know!"

"There are things *I* have to know," Wolfe said drily. "I mentioned one: your movements last evening. We have it from your wife, but I prefer it from you. That's the rule, and a good one: get the best available evidence."

Irving was staring again. "My wife? You have seen my wife?"

"Mr. Goodwin has. He called at your home this morning to see you, and you had gone. Your wife wished to be helpful. You know, of course, what she told him."

"Did she tell him—" He stopped and started over "Did she tell him about a phone call she made yesterday afternoon?"

Wolfe nodded. "And one she received. She received one from you and made one to Miss Arden."

Irving inclined his head forward to look at his right hand. Its fingers bent, slowly, to make a fist. Apparently something about the operation was unsatisfactory, for he repeated it several times, gazing at it. At length his head came up. "My lawyer wouldn't like this," he said, "but I'm going to tell you something. I have to if I expect you to tell me anything. If I told you what I told my wife you would check it, and it won't check. I know Miss Holt drove Judy Bram's cab there last evening. I know she got there at five minutes to eight and left at ten minutes to nine. I saw her."

"Indeed. Where were you?"

"I was in a cab parked on Carmine Street, around the corner from Ferrell Street. I suppose you know what her purpose was in driving Judy's cab?"

"Yes. To talk with her husband."

"I had tried to persuade her not to. Did she tell you that?"

"Yes."

"I didn't like it. There isn't much that Kearns isn't capable of. I don't mean violence; just some trick like getting her out of the cab and going off with it. I decided to be there, and I phoned my wife that I would have to spend the evening with a business associate. I was afraid if I took my car Miss Holt might recognize it, so I got a taxi with a driver I know. Carmine Street is one-way, and we parked where we would be ready to follow when she came out of Ferrell Street. We were there when she arrived, at five minutes to eight. When she came back, nearly an hour later, she was alone. There was no one in the cab. I supposed Kearns had refused to let her drive him, and I was glad of it."

"What then?"

"I went to my club. If you want to check I'll give you the cab driver's name and address. I rang Judy Bram's number, and I rang Miss Holt's number three or four times, but there was no answer. I supposed they were out somewhere together. And this morning I heard the radio and saw the paper." He breathed. "I hope to heaven I won't have to regret telling you this. If it contradicts anything she told you she's right and I'm wrong. I could be lying, you know, for my own protection."

I was thinking, if so you're an expert.

Wolfe's eyes, at him, were half closed. "It was dark. How could you know there was no one in the cab?"

"There's a light at that corner. I have good eyes and so has the driver. She was going slow, for the turn."

"You didn't follow her?"

"No. There was no point in following her if Kearns wasn't with her."

"What would you say if I told you that Miss Holt saw you in your parked taxi as she drove by?"

"I wouldn't believe it. When she drove by arriving I was flat on the seat. It was dark but I didn't risk her seeing me. When she left she didn't drive by. Carmine Street is one-way."

Wolfe leaned back and shut his eyes, and his lips began to work. Irving started to say something, and I snapped at him, "Hold it." Wolfe pushed his lips out and pulled them in, out and in, out and in . . . He was earning the twenty-five bucks I had paid him. I had no idea how, but when he starts that lip operation the sparks are flying inside his skull.

Irving tried again. "But I want—"

"Hold it."

"But I don't—"

"Shut up!"

He sat regarding me, not warmly.

Wolfe opened his eyes and straightened. "Mr. Irving." He was curt. "You will get what you came here for, but not forthwith. Possibly within the hour, probably somewhat later. Tell me where I can reach you, or you may—"

"Damn it, no! I want—"

"If you please. Confound it, I've been yelped at enough today. Or you may wait here. That room has comfortable chairs—or one at least. Mr. Goodwin and I have work to do."

"I don't intend—"

"Your intentions have no interest or point. Where can we reach you?"

Irving looked at me and saw nothing hopeful. He arose. "I'll wait here," he said, and headed for the front room.

9

HAVING turned my head to see that Irving shut the door, I turned it back again. "Fine," I said. "We're going to work."

"I'm a dunce," he said. "So are you."

"It's possible," I conceded. "Can you prove it?"

"It's manifest. Why did that policeman stop his car to look inside that cab?"

"Cops do. That's what a prowl car is for. They saw it parked with the hackie gone, and while that's nothing strange they thought it was worth a look. Also it was parked in front of your house. He knew it was your house. He said so."

"Nevertheless, we are dunces not to have questioned it. I want to know if that policeman had been prompted. At once."

"It's a point," I admitted. "The papers haven't mentioned it. I doubt if Cramer would—"

"No."

"I could try Lon Cohen."

"Do so."

I swiveled and dialed the *Gazette* number and got Lon. Wolfe lifted his receiver to listen in. I told Lon I wanted something for nothing. He said I always did and usually got it, but if what I was after this time was an ad under "Situations Wanted" I would have to pay.

"That was just a dirty rumor," I said. "I am permanently in Mr. Wolfe's employ—permanently, that is, in the sense that I may still be here tomorrow. On our present job we're shy a detail. If you'll supply it I'll give you something for the front page if and when. We don't know whether the cop who stopped to uncover Phoebe Arden's body in the taxi had been steered or was just nosy. Do you?"

"Yes, but I'm not supposed to. The DA is saving it. He may release it this afternoon. If he does I'll call you."

"We need it now. Not for publication, and we wouldn't dream of quoting you. We're just curious."

"I'll bet you are. I wish I got paid as much for being curious as Wolfe does. Okay. It was a dialed phone call to Canal six, two thousand. Probably a man, but it could have been a woman trying to sound like a man or the reverse. It said there was a taxi standing in front of nine-eighteen West Thirty-Fifth Street with a dead woman in it. As you know, that address has been heard from before. The sergeant radioed a prowl car."

"Has the call been traced?"

"How? Modern improvements. But you'd better ask the DA."

"A good idea. I will. Many thanks and I won't forget the front page." I hung up and swiveled. "I'll be damned. Where can we buy dunce caps? For a passerby to see it he would have had to open the door and lift the canvas."

Wolfe's lips were tight. "We should have done that hours ago."

"Lon may not have known hours ago."

"True. Even so. Get Mr. Cramer."

I swiveled and dialed. It wasn't as simple as getting Lon Cohen had been. Cramer was in conference and couldn't be disturbed. I was hacking away at it when Wolfe took his phone and said, "This is Nero Wolfe. I have something that will not wait. Ask Mr. Cramer if he prefers that I deal with the District Attorney."

In two minutes there was a bark. "What do you want?"

"Mr. Cramer?" He knew darned well it was.

"Yes. I'm busy."

"So am I. Is it true that Miss Holt refuses to talk without advice from Mr. Goodwin or me?"

"Yes it is, and I was just telling Stebbins to get Goodwin down here. And then I'm going —"

"If you please. Mr. Goodwin and I have decided that it is now desirable for Miss Holt to answer any questions you care to ask — or that it will be after we have had a brief talk with her. Since I must be present and I transact business only in my own office, it will be pointless for you to send for him. If you want her to talk bring her here."

"You're too late, Wolfe. I don't need her to tell me that she drove that cab to your address. I already know it. Her prints are on the steering wheel and the door, and other places. You're too late."

"Has she admitted it?"

"No, but she will."

"I doubt it. She's rather inflexible. I regret having called you to the phone to no purpose. May I make a request? Don't keep Mr. Goodwin longer than necessary. I am about to conclude a matter in which he has an interest and would like him present. I wanted Miss Holt here too, but since I'm too late I'll have to manage without her."

Silence. Prolonged.

"Are you there, Mr. Cramer?"

"Yes. So you're going to conclude a matter."

"I am. Soon afterwards Miss Holt and Mr. Goodwin and I will talk not by your sufferance but at our will."

"Are you saying that you know who killed Phoebe Arden?"

" 'Know' implies certitude. I have formed a conclusion and intend to verify it. It shouldn't take long. But I'm keeping you. Could you do without Mr. Goodwin until, say, four o'clock? It's half past twelve. By then we should have finished."

Another silence, not quite so long. "I'll be there in fifteen minutes," Cramer said.

"With Miss Holt?"

"Yes."

"Satisfactory. But not in fifteen minutes. I must get Judith Bram and Waldo Kearns. Do you know where they are?"

"Kearns is at his home. He said he would be if we wanted him again. Judith Bram is here. I'll bring her along, and I'll send for Kearns. Now."

"No. People have to eat. Will you lunch with us? And Miss Holt?"

"I will not. Did you ever skip a meal in your life?"

"Many times when I was younger, by necessity. Then I suggest that you arrive with Miss Holt at two o'clock, and arrange for Miss Bram and Mr. Kearns to come at two-thirty. Will that be convenient?"

"By God. *Convenient!*"

A click. He was off. We hung up. I said, "Probably Irving eats too."

"Yes. Bring him."

I went and got him. He marched to Wolfe's desk and demanded, "Well?"

Wolfe's head slanted back. "I forgot, sir, when I said possibly within the hour, that lunch would interfere. It will be a little longer. I have spoken with Inspector Cramer, and he will arrive with Miss Holt at two o'clock. We shall expect you and your wife to join us at two-thirty."

His jaw was working. "Miss Holt will be here?"

"Yes."

"Why my wife?"

"Because she has something to contribute. As you know, she had an appointment with Miss Arden which Miss Arden did not keep. That will be germane."

"Germane to what?"

"To our discussion."

"I don't want a discussion. I certainly don't want one with a police inspector. I told you what I want."

"And you'll get it, sir, but the method and manner are in my discretion. I give you my assurance without qualification that I am acting solely in the interest of Miss Holt, that I expect to free her of any suspicion of complicity in the murder of Phoebe Arden, and that I shall not disclose what you have told me of your movements last evening without your prior permission. Confound it, do I owe you anything?"

"No." His jaw was still working. "I'd rather not bring my wife."

"We'll need her. If you prefer, I'll arrange for Inspector Cramer to send for her."

"No." He breathed. He looked at me and back to Wolfe. "All right. We'll be here." He wheeled and went.

10

FIVE of the yellow chairs were in place facing Wolfe's desk, three in front and two behind, and Mira was in the one nearest to Cramer. I had intended the one at my end for her, but Cramer had vetoed it, and since she was his prisoner I hadn't insisted. Of course he was in the red leather chair, and the uninvited guest he had brought along, Sergeant Purley Stebbins, was seated at his right, with his broad, burly shoulders touching the wall.

Mira looked fine, considering. Her eyes were a little heavy and the lids were swollen, and her jacket could have stood washing and ironing, and the corners of her mouth pointed down, but I thought she looked fine. Wolfe, seated behind his desk, was glowering at her, but the glower wasn't meant for her. It was merely that he had had to tell Fritz to advance the lunch hour fifteen minutes, and then had had to hurry through the corn fritters and sausage cakes and wild-thyme honey from Greece and cheese and blackberry pie with not enough time to enjoy it properly.

"Was it bad?" he asked her.

"Not too bad," she said. "I didn't get too much sleep. The worst was when the morning passed and I didn't hear from you." Her head turned. "Or you, Mr. Goodwin."

I nodded. "I was busy earning my fee. I wasn't worried about you because you had promised you wouldn't forget method three."

"I kept my promise."

"I know you did. I'll buy you a drink any time you're thirsty."

"Get on," Cramer growled.

"Have you been told," Wolfe asked her, "that others will join us shortly?"

"No," she said. "Here? Who?"

"Miss Bram, Mr. Kearns, and Mr. and Mrs. Gilbert Irving."

Her eyes widened. "Why Mr. and Mrs. Irving?"

"That will appear after they arrive. I thought you should know that they're coming. They'll soon be here, and we have two points to cover. First I need a question answered. When you drove away from Ferrell Street last evening, and meandered in search of a place to dispose of the corpse—don't interrupt me—and finally drove here, did you at any time suspect that you were being followed by another car?"

Her mouth was hanging open. "But you—" she stammered. Her head jerked to me. "Did you know he was—what good did it do to keep my promise?"

"A lot," I told her. "Yes, I knew he was. Everything is under control. Believe me, I would rather lose an arm than lose the right to ask you to promise me something. We know what we're doing. Shall I repeat the question?"

"But—"

"No buts. Leave it to us. Shall I repeat the question?"

"Yes."

I did so, omitting the "don't interrupt me."

"No," she said.

"Proceed," Wolfe told me.

I knew it would have been better to have her closer. She was six yards away. "This one is more complicated and more important. During that drive, from Ferrell Street to here, are you certain that another car was *not* following you? There are various ways of making sure of that. Did you use any of them?"

"No. I never thought of that. I was looking for a place—"

"I know you were. All we want is this: if I told you that a car was following you, all the way, what would you say?"

"I would want to know who it was."

I wanted to go and pat her on the head, but it might have been misconstrued. "Okay," I said. "That's one point. The other one is simple. Tell Inspector Cramer what you told us last night, including the phone call to

Gilbert Irving to tell him that you were going to drive Judy's cab." I looked at my wrist. "You only have fifteen minutes, so reel it off."

"I won't," she said. "Not until you tell me why you're doing this."

"Then I'll tell him. You'll know why after the others get here. I'll tell you this: someone tried to frame you for murder and this is payday. Anyway there's not much left, now that the inspector knows you drove the cab here with the corpse in it. Would we have spilled that if we didn't have a good hold? Go ahead."

Wolfe put in, "Don't interrupt with questions, Mr. Cramer. They can wait. Yes, Miss Holt?"

She still didn't like it, not a bit, but she delivered, starting with Sunday evening. She left gaps. She didn't say that Judy had given her permission to take the cab, merely that she had taken it, and she didn't mention the phone call to Irving; but since I had already mentioned it that didn't matter. The main thing was what had happened after she got to Ferrell Street with the cab, and she covered that completely; and when she got to where she and I had sat on the stoop and talked, Cramer began cutting in with questions. I will not say that he was more interested in tagging me for obstructing justice than he was in solving a murder case, since I don't like to brag, but it sounded like it. He was firing away at her, and Sergeant Stebbins was scrawling in his notebook, when the doorbell rang and I went to answer it. It was Waldo Kearns. When I took him to the office he went to Mira, without so much as a glance for the three men, and put out a hand.

"My dear wife," he said.

"Don't be ridiculous," Mira said.

I can't report whether he handled that as well as he had handled the uppercut by Irving because the bell rang again and I had to leave them, to admit Judy Bram. She had an escort, a Homicide dick I only knew by sight, and he thought he was going to enter with her and I didn't, and while we were discussing it she slipped in and left it to us. We were still chatting when a taxi stopped out front and Mr. and Mrs. Irving got out and headed for the steps. The dick had to give them room to pass, and I was able to shut the door on him without flattening his nose. Since it was quite possible that Irving's appearance would start something I entered the office on their heels.

Nothing happened. Mira merely shot him a glance and he returned it. Kearns didn't even glance at him. The newcomers stood while Wolfe pronounced their names for Cramer and Stebbins and told them who Cramer and Stebbins were, and then went to the two chairs still vacant, the two nearest my desk. Mrs. Irving took the one in front, with Judy between her and Mira, and her husband took the one back of her, which put him only a long arm's length from Waldo Kearns.

As Wolfe's eyes moved from right to left, stopping at Mira, and back again, Cramer spoke. "You understand that this is not an official inquiry. Sergeant Stebbins and I are looking on. You also understand that Mira Holt is under arrest as a material witness. If she had been charged with murder she wouldn't be here."

"Why isn't she out on bail?" Judy Bram demanded. "I want to know why—"

"That will do," Wolfe snapped. "You're here to listen, Miss Bram, and if you don't hold your tongue Mr. Goodwin will drag you out. If necessary Mr. Stebbins will help."

"But why—"

"No! One more word and out you go."

She set her teeth on her lip and glared at him. He glared back, decided she was squelched, and left her.

"I am acting," he said, "jointly with Mr. Goodwin, on behalf of Miss Holt. At our persuasion she has just told Mr. Cramer of her movements last evening. I'll sketch them briefly. Shortly after seven-thirty she took Miss Bram's cab and drove it to Ferrell Street and parked at the mouth of the alley leading to Mr. Kearns' house. She expected him to appear but he didn't. At eight-thirty she left the cab, went through the alley to the house, knocked several times, and looked in windows. Getting no response, she returned to the cab, having been gone about ten minutes. There was a dead body in the cab, a woman, and she recognized her. It was Phoebe Arden. I will not—"

"You fat fool!" Judy blurted. "You're a fine—"

"Archie!" he commanded.

I stood up. She clamped her teeth on her lip. I sat down.

"I will not," Wolfe said, "go into her thought processes, but confine myself to her actions. She covered the body with a piece of canvas and drove away. Her intention was to dispose of her cargo in some likely spot, and she drove around in search of one, but found none. I omit details—for instance, that she rang the number of Miss Bram from a phone booth and got no answer. She decided she must have counsel, drove to my house, met Mr. Goodwin on the stoop, and gave him a rigmarole about a bet she had made. Since he is vulnerable to the attractions of personable young women, he swallowed it."

I swallowed *that*. I had to, with Cramer sitting there.

"Now," Wolfe said, "a crucial fact. I learned it myself less than three hours ago. Only a few minutes after Miss Holt and Mr. Goodwin met on the stoop someone phoned police headquarters to say that a taxi standing in front of this address had a dead woman in it. That is—"

"Where did you get that?" Cramer demanded.

Wolfe snorted. "Pfui. Not from you or Mr. Stebbins. That is proof, to me conclusive, that the murderer of Phoebe Arden had no wish or need for her to die. Phoebe Arden was killed only because her corpse was needed as a tool for the destruction of another person—a design so cold-blooded and malign that even I am impressed. Whether she was killed in the cab, or at a nearby spot and the body taken to the cab, is immaterial. The former is more likely, and I assume it. What did the murderer do? He, or she—we lack a neuter pronoun—he entered the cab with Phoebe Arden the moment Miss Holt disappeared in the alley, coming from their hiding place in the stoneyard across the street. Having stabbed his victim—or rather his tool—he walked up Ferrell Street and around the corner to where his car was parked on Carmine Street. Before going to his car he stood near the corner to see if Miss Holt, on returning to the cab, removed the body before driving away. If she had, he would have found a booth and phoned police headquarters immediately."

Cramer growled, "What if Kearns had come out with Miss Holt?"

"He knew he wouldn't. I'll come to that. You are assuming that Kearns was not the murderer."

"I am assuming nothing."

"That's prudent. When Miss Holt turned the cab into Carmine Street and drove on, he followed her. He followed her throughout her search for a place to get rid of the corpse, and on to her final destination, this house. Some of my particulars are assumption or conjecture, but not this one. He must have done so, for when she stopped here he drove on by, found a phone booth, and made the call to the police. The only other possible source of the call was a passerby who had seen the corpse in the cab as it stood at the curb, and a passerby couldn't have seen it without opening the door and lifting the canvas." His eyes went to Cramer. "Of course that hadn't escaped you."

Cramer grunted.

Wolfe turned a hand over. "If his objective was the death of Phoebe Arden, why didn't he kill her in the stoneyard — they must have been there, since there is no other concealment near — and leave her there? Of if he did kill her there, which is highly unlikely, why did he carry or drag the body to the cab? And why, his objective reached, did he follow the cab in its wanderings and at the first opportunity call the police? I concede the possibility that he had a double objective, to destroy both Miss Arden and Miss Holt, but if so Miss Holt must have been his main target. To kill Miss Arden, once he had her in the stoneyard with a weapon at hand, was simple and involved little risk; to use her body as a tool for the destruction of Miss Holt was a complicated and daring operation, and the risks were great. I am convinced that he had a single objective, to destroy Miss Holt."

"Then why?" Cramer demanded. "Why didn't he kill *her*?"

"I can only conjecture, but it is based on logic. Because it was known that he had reason to wish Miss Holt dead, and no matter how ingenious his plan and adroit its execution, he would have been suspected and probably brought to account. I have misstated it. That's what he did. He devised a plan so ingenious that he thought he would be safe."

Purley Stebbins got up, circled around the red leather chair, and stood at Waldo Kearns' elbow.

"No, Mr. Stebbins," Wolfe said. "Our poor substitute for a neuter pronoun is misleading. I'll abandon it. If you want to guard a murderer stand by Mrs. Irving."

Knowing that was coming any second, I had my eye on her. She was only four feet from me. She didn't move a muscle, but her husband did. He put a hand to his forehead and squeezed. I could see his knuckles go white. Mira's eyes stayed fixed on Wolfe, but Judy and Kearns turned to look at Mrs. Irving. Stebbins did too, but he didn't move.

Cramer spoke. "Who is Mrs. Irving?"

"She is present, sir."

"I know she is. Who is she?"

"She is the wife of the man whom Miss Holt called on the phone Sunday evening to tell him that she was going to take Miss Bram's cab, and why. Mr. Irving has stated that he told no one of that call. Either he lied or his wife eavesdropped. Mr. Irving. Might your wife have overheard that conversation on an extension?"

Irving's hand left his forehead. He lowered it slowly until it touched his knee. I had him in profile. A muscle at the side of his neck was twitching. "To say that she might," he said slowly and precisely, as if he only had so many words and didn't want to waste any, "isn't saying that she did. You have made a shocking accusation. I hope—" He stopped, leaving it to anybody's guess what he hoped for. He blurted, "Ask her!"

"I shall. Did you, madam?"

"No." Her deep, strong voice needed more breath behind it. "Your accusation is not only shocking, it's absurd. I told Mr. Goodwin what I did last evening. Hasn't he told you?"

"He has. You told him that your husband had been prevented by a business emergency from keeping a dinner and theater engagement with you, and you had phoned Phoebe Arden to go in his stead, and she agreed. When she didn't appear at the restaurant you rang her number and got no answer, and then went to another restaurant to eat alone, presumably one where you are not known and plausibly would not be remembered. After waiting for her at the theater until after nine o'clock you left a ticket for her at the box office and went in to your seat. That sounds impressive, but actually it leaves you free for the period that counts, from half past seven until well after nine o'clock. Incidentally, it was a mistake to volunteer that account of your movements, so detailed and precise. When Mr. Goodwin reported it to me I marked you down as worthy of attention."

"I wasn't free at all," she said. "I told Mr. Goodwin I wanted to help, and—"

"Don't talk," her husband commanded the back of her head. "Let him talk." To Wolfe: "Unless you're through?"

"By no means. I'll put it directly to you, madam. This is how you really spent those hours. You did phone Phoebe Arden yesterday afternoon, but not to ask her to join you at dinner and the theater. You told her of Miss Holt's plan to drive Miss Bram's cab in an effort to have a talk with her husband, and you proposed a prank. Miss Arden would arrange that Mr. Kearns would fail to appear, and if he didn't, Miss Holt would certainly leave the cab to go to his house to inquire. Whereupon you and Miss Arden, from your concealment in the neighboring stoneyard, would go and enter the cab, and when Miss Holt returned she would find you there, to her discomfiture and even consternation."

"You can't prove any of this," Cramer growled.

"No one ever can, since Miss Arden is dead." Wolfe's eyes didn't leave Mrs. Irving. He went on, "I didn't know Miss Arden, so I can't say whether she agreed to your proposal from mere caprice or from an animus for Miss Holt, but she did agree, and went to her doom. The program went as planned, without a hitch. No doubt Miss Arden herself devised the stratagem by which Mr. Kearns was removed from the scene. But at this point I must confess that my case is not flawless. Certainly you would not have been so witless as to let anyone have a hand in your deadly prank—either a cab driver or your private chauffeur. Do you drive a car?"

"Don't answer," Irving commanded her.

"Yes, she does," Judy Bram said, louder than necessary.

"Thank you, Miss Bram. Apparently you *can* speak to the point. Then you and Miss Arden went in your car, and parked it on Carmine Street—away from the corner in the direction Miss Holt would take when, leaving, she made the turn from Ferrell Street. You walked to the stoneyard and chose your hiding spot, and when Miss Holt left the cab you went and entered it. It is noteworthy that at that point you were committed to nothing but a prank. If Miss Holt had suddenly returned, or if anyone had come close enough to observe, you would merely have abandoned your true objective — a disappointment, but no disaster. As it was, you struck. I am not a moralizer, but I permit myself the comment that in my experience your performance is without parallel for ruthlessness and savagery. It appears that Miss Arden was not merely no enemy of yours; she was your friend. She must have been, to join with you in your impish prank; but you needed her corpse for a tool to gratify your mortal hatred for Miss Holt. That was —"

"Her hatred for Miss Holt," Cramer said. "You assume that too?"

"No indeed. That is established. Miss Bram. Speaking of Gilbert Irving, you said that when he looks at Miss Holt or hears her voice he has to lean against something to keep from trembling. You didn't specify the emotion that so affects him. Is it repugnance?"

"No. It's love. He wants her."

"Was his wife aware of it?"

"Yes. Lots of people were. You only had to see him look at her."

"That is not true," Irving said. "I am merely Miss Holt's friend, that's all, and I hope she is mine."

Judy's eyes darted at him and returned to Wolfe. "He's only being a husband because he thinks he has to. He's being a gentleman. A gentleman doesn't betray his wife. I was wrong about you. I shouldn't have called you a fat fool. I didn't know —"

Cramer cut in, to Wolfe. "All right, if that isn't established it can be. But it's about all that's established. There's damn little you can prove. Do you expect me to charge a woman with murder on your guess?"

You don't often hear a sergeant disagree with an inspector in public, but Purley Stebbins — no, I used the wrong word. Not hear, see. Purley didn't say a word. All he did was leave his post at Kearns' elbow and circle around Irving to stand beside Mrs. Irving, between her and Judy Bram. Probably it didn't occur to him that he was disagreeing with his superior; he merely didn't like the possibility of Mrs. Irving's getting a knife from her handbag and sticking it in Judy's ribs.

"There's nothing at all I can prove," Wolfe said. "I have merely exposed the naked truth; it is for you, not me, to drape it and arm it with the evidence the law requires. For that you are well equipped; surely you need no suggestions from me; but, item, did Mrs. Irving get her car from the garage yesterday evening? What for? If to drive to a restaurant and then to a theater, in itself unlikely, where did she park it? Item, the knife. If she conceived her prank only after her husband phoned to cancel their engagement, which is highly probable, she hadn't time to contrive an elaborate and prudent plan for getting a weapon. She either bought one at a convenient shop, or she took one from her own kitchen; and if the latter her cook or maid will have missed it and can identify it. Her biggest mistake, of course, was leaving the knife in the body, even with the handle wiped clean; but she was in a hurry to leave, she was afraid blood would spurt on her, and she was confident that she would never be suspected of killing her good friend Phoebe Arden. Other items—"

Mrs. Irving was up, and as she arose her husband did too, and grabbed her arm from behind. He wasn't seizing a murderer; he was being a gentleman and stopping his wife from betraying herself. She jerked loose, but then Purley Stebbins had her other arm in his big paw.

"Take it easy," Purley said. "Just take it easy."

Mira's head dropped and her hands came up to cover her face, and she started to shake. Judy Bram put a hand on her shoulder and said, "Go right ahead, Mi, don't mind us. You've got it coming." Waldo Kearns was sitting still, perfectly still. I got up and went to the kitchen, to the extension, and dialed the *Gazette* number. I thought I ought to be as good at keeping a promise as Mira had been.

11

YESTERDAY I drove Mira and Judy to Idlewild, where Mira was to board a plane for Reno. Judy and I had tossed a coin to decide whether the trip would be made in the Heron sedan which Wolfe owns and I drive, or in Judy's cab, and I had won. On the way back I remarked that I supposed Kearns had agreed to accept service for a Reno divorce because now it wouldn't leave him free to marry Phoebe Arden.

"No," Judy said. "Because his wife was a witness in a murder trial and that wouldn't do."

A little later I remarked that I supposed she had stopped dreaming about a lion standing on a rock about to spring on her.

"No," she said. "Only now I'm not sure who it is. It could even be you."

A little later I remarked that if the state of New York carried out its program for Mrs. Irving, who was in the death house at Sing Sing, I supposed Mira would get back from Reno just in time for a wedding.

"No," Judy said. "They'll wait at least a year. Gil Irving will always be a gentleman."

Three supposes and all wrong. And still men keep on marrying women.

The Rodeo Murder

1

CAL BARROW was standing at the tail end of the horse with his arm extended and his fingers wrapped around the strands of the rope that was looped over the horn of the cowboy saddle. His gray-blue eyes — as much of them as the half-closed lids left in view — were straight at me. His voice was low and easy, and noise from the group out front was coming through the open door, but I have good ears.

"Nothing to start a stampede," he said. "I just wanted to ask you how I go about taking some hide off a toad in this town." To give it as it actually sounded I would have to make it, "Ah jist wanted to ask yuh how Ah go about takin' some hide off a toad," but that's too complicated, and from here on I'll leave the sound effects to you if you want to bother.

I was sliding my fingertips up and down on the polished stirrup strap so that observers, if any, would assume that we were discussing the saddle. "I suppose," I said, "it's a two-legged toad." Then, as brown-haired cowgirl named Nan Karlin, in a pink silk shirt open at the throat and regulation Levis, came through the arch and headed for the door to the terrace, lifting the heels of her fancy boots to navigate the Kashan rug that had set Lily Rowan back fourteen thousand bucks, I raised my voice a little so she wouldn't have to strain her ears if she was curious. "Sure," I said, rubbing the leather, "you could work it limber, but why don't they make it limber?"

But I may be confusing you, since a Kashan carpet with a garden pattern in seven colors is no place for a horse to stand, so I had better explain. The horse was a sawhorse. The saddle was to go to the winner in a roping contest that was to start in an hour. The Kashan, 19 × 34, was on the floor of the living room of Lily Rowan's penthouse, which was on the roof of a ten-story building on 63rd Street between Madison and Park Avenues, Manhattan. The time was three o'clock Monday afternoon. The group out on the terrace had just gone there for coffee after leaving the dining room, where the high point of the meal had been two dozen young blue grouse which had come from Montana on man-made wings, their own having stopped working. As we had moseyed through the living room on our way to the terrace Cal Barrow had got me aside to say he wanted to ask me something private, and we had detoured to inspect the saddle.

When Nan Karlin had passed and was outside, Cal Barrow didn't have to lower his voice again because he hadn't raised it. "Yeah, two legs," he

said. (Make it "laigs.") "I got to ask somebody that knows this town and I
was thinking this bozo Goodwin is the one to ask, he's in the detective
business here and he ought to know. And my friend Harvey Greve tells me
you're okay. I'm calling you Archie, am I?"

"So it was agreed at the table. First names all around."

"Suits me." He let go of the rope and gripped the edge of the cantle. "So
I'll ask you. I'm a little worked up. Out where I live I wouldn't have to ask
nobody, but here I'm no better'n a dogie. I been to Calgary and Pendleton,
but I never come East before for this blowout. Huh. World Series Rodeo.
From what I see so far you can have it."

He made it "roe-day-oh" with the accent on the "day." I nodded. "Madison Square Garden has no sky. But about this toad. We're supposed to go
out with them for coffee. How much of his hide do you need?"

"I'll take a fair-sized patch." There was a glint in his eye. "Enough so he'll
have to lick it till it gets a scab. The trouble is this blamed blowout, I don't
want to stink it up my first time here, if it wasn't for that I'd just handle it.
I'd get him to provoke me."

"Hasn't he already provoked you?"

"Yeah, but I'm leaving that out. I was thinking you might even like to
show him and me something. Have you got a car?"

I said I had.

"Then when we get through here you might like to take him and me to
show us some nice little spot like on the river bank. There must be a spot
somewhere. It would be better if you was there anyhow because if I kinda
lost control and got too rough you could stop me. When I'm worked up I
might get my teeth on the bit."

"Or I could stop him if necessary."

The glint showed again. "I guess you don't mean that. I wouldn't like to
think you mean that."

I grinned at him, Archie to Cal. "What the hell, how do I know? You
haven't named him. What if it's Mel Fox? He's bigger than you are, and
Saturday night at the Garden I saw him bulldog a steer in twenty-three
seconds. It took you thirty-one."

"My steer was meaner. Mel said so himself. Anyway it's not him. It's
Wade Eisler."

My brows went up. Wade Eisler couldn't bulldog a milk cow in twenty-
three hours, but he had rounded up ten million dollars, more or less, and he
was the chief backer of the World Series Rodeo. If it got out that one of the
cowboy contestants had taken a piece of his hide it would indeed stink it up,
and it was no wonder that Cal Barrow wanted a nice little spot on a river
bank. I not only raised my brows; I puckered my lips.

"Ouch," I said. "You'd better let it lay, at least for a week, until the
rodeo's over and the prizes awarded."

"No, sir. I sure would like to, but I got to get it done. Today. I don't
rightly know how I held off when I got here and saw him here. It would be a
real big favor, Mr. Goodwin. Here in your town. Will you do it?"

I was beginning to like him. Especially I liked his not shoving by over-
working the "Archie." He was a little younger than me, but not much, so it
wasn't respect for age; he just wasn't a fudger.

"How did he provoke you?" I asked.

"That's private. Didn't I say I'm leaving that out?"

"Yes, but I can leave it out too. I don't say I'll play if you tell me, but I certainly won't if you don't. Whether I play or not, you can count on me to leave it out—or keep it in. As a private detective I get lots of practice keeping things in."

The gray-blue eyes were glued on me. "You won't tell anyone?"

"Right."

"Whether you help me or not?"

"Right."

"He got a lady to go to his place last night by telling her he was having a party, and when they got there there wasn't any party, and he tried to handle her. Did you see the scratch on his cheek?"

"Yes, I noticed it."

"She's not very big, but she's plenty active. All she got was a little skin off her ear when her head hit a corner of a table."

"I noticed that too."

"So I figure he's due to lose a bigger—" He stopped short. He slapped the saddle. "Now, damn it, that's me every time. Now you know who she is. I was going to leave that out."

"I'll keep it in. She told you about it?"

"Yes, sir, she did. This morning."

"Did she tell anyone else?"

"No, sir, she wouldn't. I got no brand on her, nobody has, but maybe some day when she quiets down a little and I've got my own corral . . . You've seen her on a bronc."

I nodded. "I sure have. I was looking forward to seeing her off of one, closer up, but now of course I'll keep my distance. I don't want to lose any hide."

His hand left the saddle. "I guess you just say things. I got no claim. I'm a friend of hers and she knows it, that's all. A couple of years ago I was wrangling dudes down in Arizona and she was snapping sheets at the hotel, and we kinda made out together and I guess I come in handy now and then. I don't mind coming in handy as long as I can look ahead. Right now I'm a friend of hers and that suits me fine. She might be surprised to know how I—"

His eyes left me and I turned. Nero Wolfe was there, entering from the terrace. Somehow he always looks bigger away from home, I suppose because my eyes are so used to fitting his dimensions into the interiors of the old brownstone on West 35th. There he was, a mountain coming at us. As he approached he spoke. "If I may interrupt?" He allowed two seconds for objections, got none, and went on. "My apologies, Mr. Barrow." To me: "I have thanked Miss Rowan for a memorable meal and explained to her. To watch the performance I would have to stretch across that parapet and I am not built for it. If you drive me home now you can be back before four o'clock."

I glanced at my wrist. Ten after three. "More people are coming, and Lily has told them you'll be here. They'll be disappointed."

"Pfui. I have nothing to contribute to this frolic."

I wasn't surprised; in fact, I had been expecting it. He had got what he came for, so why stick around? What had brought him was the grouse.

When, two years back, I had returned from a month's visit to Lily Rowan on a ranch she had bought in Montana, (where, incidentally, I had met Harvey Greve, Cal Barrow's friend), the only detail of my trip that had really interested Wolfe was one of the meals I described. At that time of year, late August, the young blue grouse are around ten weeks old and their main item of diet has been mountain huckleberries, and I had told Wolfe they were tastier than any bird Fritz had ever cooked, even quail or wood-cock. Of course, since they're protected by law, they can cost up to five dollars a bite if you get caught.

Lily Rowan doesn't treat laws as her father did while he was piling up the seventeen million dollars he left her, but she can take them or leave them. So when she learned that Harvey Greve was coming to New York for the rodeo, and she decided to throw a party for some of the cast, and she thought it would be nice to feed them young blue grouse, the law was merely a hurdle to hop over. Since I'm a friend of hers and she knows it, that will do for that. I will add only a brief report of a scene in the office on the ground floor of the old brownstone. It was Wednesday noon. Wolfe, at his desk, was reading the *Times*. I, at my desk, finished a phone call, hung up, and swiveled.

"That's interesting," I said. "That was Lily Rowan. As I told you, I'm going to a roping contest at her place Monday afternoon. A cowboy is going to ride a horse along Sixty-third Street, and other cowboys are going to try to rope him from the terrace of her penthouse, a hundred feet up. Never done before. First prize will be a saddle with silver trimmings."

He grunted. "Interesting?"

"Not that. That's just games. But a few of them are coming earlier for lunch, at one o'clock, and I'm invited, and she just had a phone call from Montana. Twenty young blue grouse, maybe more, will arrive by plane Saturday afternoon, and Felix is going to come and cook them. I'm glad I'm going. It's too bad you and Lily don't get along—ever since she squirted perfume on you."

He put the paper down to glare. "She didn't squirt perfume on me."

I flipped a hand. "It was her perfume."

He picked up the paper, pretended to read a paragraph, and dropped it again. He passed his tongue over his lips. "I have no animus for Miss Rowan. But I will not solicit an invitation."

"Of course not. You wouldn't stoop. I don't—"

"But you may ask if I would accept one."

"Would you?"

"Yes."

"Good. She asked me to invite you, but I was afraid you'd decline and I'd hate to hurt her feelings. I'll tell her." I reached for the phone.

I report that incident so you'll understand why he got up and left after coffee. I not only wasn't surprised when he came and interrupted Cal Barrow and me, I was pleased, because Lily had bet me a sawbuck he wouldn't stay for coffee. Leaving him there with Cal, I went to the terrace.

In the early fall Lily's front terrace is usually sporting annual flowers along the parapet and by the wall of the penthouse, and a few evergreens in tubs scattered around, but for that day the parapet was bare, and instead of the evergreens, which would have interfered with rope whirling, there were clumps of sagebrush two feet high in pots. The sagebrush had come by rail, not by air, but even so the part of Lily that had ordered it and paid for it is not my part. That will be no news to her when she reads this.

I glanced around. Lily was in a group seated to the right, with Wade Eisler on one side and Mel Fox on the other. In dash she wasn't up to the two cowgirls there, Nan Karlin in her pink silk shirt and Anna Casado, dark-skinned with black hair and black eyes, in her yellow one, but she was the hostess and not in competition. In situtations that called for dash she had plenty. The other four were standing by the parapet at the left — Roger Dunning, the rodeo promoter, not in costume; his wife Ellen, former cowgirl, also not in costume; Harvey Greve in his brown shirt and red neck rag and corduroy pants and boots; and Laura Jay. Having Laura Jay in profile, I could see the bandage on her ear through the strands of her hair, which was exactly the color of the thyme honey that Wolf gets from Greece. At the dinner table she had told me that a horse had jerked his head around and the bit had bruised her, but now I knew different.

Stepping across to tell Lily I was leaving but would be back in time for the show, I took a side glance at Wade Eisler's plump, round face. The scratch, which began an inch below his left eye and slanted down nearly to the corner of his mouth, hadn't gone very deep and it had had some fifteen hours to calm down by Cal Barrow's account, but it didn't improve his looks any, and there was ample room for improvement. He was one of those New York characters that get talked about and he had quite a reputation as a smooth operator, but he certainly hadn't been smooth last night — according to Laura Jay as relayed by Cal Barrow. The cave-man approach to courtship may have its points if that's the best you can do, but if I ever tried it I would have more sense than to pick a girl who could rope and tie a frisky calf in less than a minute.

After telling Lily I would be back in time for the show and was looking forward to collecting the sawbuck, I returned to the living room. Wolfe and Cal were admiring the saddle. I told Cal I would think it over and let him know, went to the foyer and got Wolfe's hat and stick, followed him down the flight of stairs to the tenth floor, and rang for the elevator. We walked the two blocks to the parking lot where I had left the Heron sedan, which Wolfe had paid for but I had selected. Of course a taxi would have been simpler, but he hates things on wheels. To ride in a strange vehicle with a stranger driving would be foolhardy; with me at the wheel in a car of my choice it is merely imprudent.

Stopped by a red light on Park Avenue in the Fifties, I turned my head to say, "I'm taking the car back because I may need it. I may do a little errand for one of the cowboys. If so I probably won't be home for dinner."

"A professional errand?"

"No. Personal."

He grunted. "You have the afternoon, as agreed. If the errand is personal it is not my concern. But, knowing you as I do, I trust it is innocuous."

"So do I." The light changed and I fed gas.

2

IT was ten minutes to four when I got back to the parking lot on 63rd Street. Walking wast, I crossed Park Avenue and stopped for a look. Five cops were visible. One was talking to the driver of a car who wanted to turn the corner, two were standing at the curb talking, and two were holding off an assortment of pedestrians who wanted to get closer to three mounted cowboys. The cowboys were being spoken to by a man on foot, not in costume. As I moved to proceed one of the cops at the curb blocked me and spoke. "Do you live in this block, sir?"

I told him no, I was going to Miss Lily Rowan's party, and he let me pass. The New York Police Department likes to grant reasonable requests from citizens, especially when the request comes from a woman whose father was a Tammany district leader for thirty years. There were no parked cars on that side of the street, but twenty paces short of the building entrance a truck with cameras was hugging the curb, and there was another one farther on, near Madison Avenue.

When I had left with Wolfe Lily had had nine guests; now she had twenty or more. Three of the new arrivals were cowboys, making six with Cal Barrow, Harvey Greve, and Mel Fox; the rest were civilians. They were all on the terrace. The civilians were at the parapet, half at one end and half at the other, leaving the parapet clear for thirty feet in the middle. The cowboys, their ten-gallon hats on their heads and their ropes in their hands, were lined up facing a tall skinny man in a brown suit. At the man's elbow was Roger Dunning, the promoter. The man was speaking.

". . . and that's the way it's going to be. I'm the judge and what I say goes. I repeat that Greve hasn't done any practicing, and neither has Barrow or Fox. I have Miss Rowan's word for that, and I don't think you want to call her a liar. I've told you the order, but you don't move in until I call your name. Remember what I said, if you take a tumble off a bronc it's four feet down; here it's a hundred feet down and you won't get up and walk. Once again, *no hooligan stuff.* There's not supposed to be any pedestrians on this side of the street from four o'clock to five, but if one comes out of a house and one of you drops a loop on him you won't sleep in a hotel room tonight. We're here to have some fun, but don't get funny." He looked at his watch. "Time to go. Fox, get—"

"I want to say something," Roger Dunning said.

"Sorry, Roger, no time. We promised to start on the dot. Fox, get set. The rest of you scatter."

He went to the parapet, to the left, and picked up a green flag on a stick that was there on a chair. Mel Fox stepped to the middle of the clear stretch, straddled the parapet, and started his noose going. The others went right and left to find spots in the lines of guests. I found a spot on the right that happened to be between Laura Jay and Anna Casado. Leaning over to get a view of the street, I saw I was blocking Laura Jay and drew in a little. The three mounted cowboys and the man I had seen talking to them were grouped on the pavement halfway to Park Avenue. The judge stuck his arm out with the green flag and dipped it, the man down with the mounted cowboys said something, and one of the ponies was off on the jump, heading down the middle of the lane between the curb on our side and the parked cars on the other. Mel Fox, leaning out from his hips, moved his whirling loop back a little, and then brought it forward and let it go. When it reached bottom it was a little too far out and the cowboy on the pony was twenty feet ahead of it. The instant it touched the pavement Fox started hauling it in; he had thirty seconds until the flag started number two. He had it up and a noose going in less than that, but the judge went by his watch. The flag dipped, and here came the second one. That was a little better; the rope touched the pony's rump, but it was too far in. Fox hauled in again, shifted his straddle a little, and started another whirl. That time he nearly made it. Anna Casado, on my left, let out a squeal as the rope, descending smoothly in a perfect circle, brushed the edge of the cowboy's hat. The audience clapped, and a man in a window across the street shouted "Bravo!" Fox retrieved his rope, taking his time, dismounted from the parapet, said something I didn't catch because of other voices, and moved off as the judge called out, "Vince!"

A chunky little youngster in a purple shirt, Levis, and working boots mounted the parapet. Saturday night I had seen him stick it out bareback on one of the roughest broncs I had ever seen—not speaking as an expert. He wasn't so hot on a parapet. On his first try his loop turned straight up, which could have been an air current, on his second it draped over a parked car across the street, and on his third it hit the asphalt ten feet ahead of the pony.

Harvey Greve was next. Naturally I was rooting for him, since he had done me a lot of favors during the month I had spent at Lily's ranch. Lily called something to him from the other end of the parapet, and he gave her a nod as he threw his leg over and started his loop. His first throw was terrible; the noose buckled and flipped before it was halfway down. His second was absolutely perfect; it centered around the cowboy like a smoke ring around a fingertip, and Harvey timed the jerk just right and had him. A yell came from the audience as the cowboy tightened the reins and the pony braked, skidding on the asphalt. He loosened the loop with one hand and passed it over his head, and as soon as it was free the judge sang out "Thirty seconds!" and Harvey started hauling in. His third throw sailed down round and flat, but it was too late by ten feet.

As the judge called Barrow's name and Cal stepped to the parapet, Laura Jay, on my right, muttered, "He shouldn't try it." She was probably muttering to herself, but my ear was right there and I turned my head and asked her why. "Somebody stole his rope," she said.

"Stole it? When? How?"

"He don't know. It was in the closet with his hat and it was gone. We looked all around. He's using the one that was on that saddle and it's new and stiff, and he shouldn't—"

She stopped and I jerked my head around. The flag had dipped and the target was coming. Considering that he was using a strange rope, and a new one, Cal didn't do so bad. His loops kept their shape clear down, but the first one was short, the second was wide, and the third hit bottom before the pony got there. Neither of the last two ropers, one named Lopez and the other Holcomb, did as well. When Holcomb's third noose curled on the curb below us the judge called, "Second round starts in two minutes! Everybody stay put!"

There were to be three rounds, giving each contestant a total of nine tries. Roger Dunning was stationed near the judge, with a pad of paper and a pen in his hand, to keep score in case the decision had to be made on form and how close they came, but since Harvey Greve had got one that wouldn't be necessary.

In the second round Fox got a rider and Lopez got a pony. In the third round Holcomb got a rider and Harvey got his second one. The winner and first world champion rope-dropper or drop-roper from one hundred feet up: Harvey Greve! He took the congratulations and the riding from the other competitors with the grin I knew so well, and when he got kissed by a friend of Lily's who was starring in a hit on Broadway and knew how to kiss both on stage and off, his face was nearly as pink as Nan Karlin's shirt. Anna Casado broke off a branch of sagebrush and stuck it under his hatband. Lily herded us into the living room, where we gathered around the sawhorse, and Roger Dunning was starting a presentation speech when Cal Barrow stopped him.

"Wait a minute, this goes with it," Cal said, and went and hung the rope on the horn. He turned and sent the blue-gray eyes right and then left. "I don't want to start no fuss right now, but when I find out who took mine I'll want to know." He moved to the rear of the crowd, and Dunning put his hand on the seat of the saddle. Dunning had a long and narrow bony face with a scar at the side of his jaw.

"This is a happy occasion," he said. "Thank God nothing happened like one of you falling off. I wanted to have a net down—"

"Louder!" Mel Fox called.

"You're just sore because you didn't win," Dunning told him. "I wanted to have a net below but they wouldn't. This magnificent saddle with genuine silver rivets and studs was handmade by Morrison, and I don't have to tell you what that means. It was donated by Miss Lily Rowan, and I want to thank her for her generosity and hospitality on behalf of everybody concerned. I now declare Harvey Greve the undisputed winner of the first and only roping contest ever held in a Park Avenue penthouse—anyway just outside the penthouse and we could see Park Avenue—and I award him the prize, this magnificent saddle donated by Miss Lily Rowan. Here it is, Harvey. It's all yours."

Applause and cheers. Someone called "Speech!" and others took it up, as Harvey went and flattened his palm on the sudadero. He faced the audience. "I tell you," he said, "if I tried to make a speech you'd take this saddle away from me. The only time I make a speech is when a cayuse gets from under me and that's no kind for here. You all know that was just luck out there, but I'm mighty glad I won because I sure had my eye on this saddle. The lady that kissed me, I didn't mind that atall, but I been working for Miss Lily Rowan for more'n three years and she never kissed me yet and this is her last chance."

They let out a whoop, and Lily ran to him, put her hands on his shoulders, and planted one on each cheek, and he went pink again. Two men in white jackets came through the arch, with trays loaded with glasses of champagne. In the alcove a man at the piano and two with fiddles started "Home on the Range." Lily had asked me a week ago what I thought of having the rug up and trying some barn dancing, and I had told her I doubted if many of the cowboys and girls would know how, and none of the others would. Better just let the East meet the West.

The best way to drink champagne, for me anyhow, is to gulp the first glass as a primer and sip from there on. Lily was busy being a hostess, so I waited to go and touch glasses with her until I had taken a couple of sips from my second. "Doggone it," I told her, "I'd a brung my rope and give it a whirl if I'd a known you was goin' tuh kiss the winner." She said, "Huh. If I ever kissed you in front of an audience the women would scream and the men would faint."

I moved around a while, being sociable, and wound up on a chair by a clump of sagebrush on the terrace, between Laura Jay and a civilian. Since I knew him well and didn't like him much, I didn't apologize for horning in. I asked her if Cal had found his rope, and she said she didn't think so, she hadn't seen him for the last half hour.

"Neither have I," I said. "He doesn't seem to be around. I wanted to ask him if he'd found it. I haven't seen Wade Eisler either. Have you?"

Her eyes met mine straight. "No. Why?"

"No special reason. I suppose you know I'm in the detective business."

"I know. You're with Nero Wolfe."

"I work for him. I'm not here on business, I'm a friend of Miss Rowan's, but I'm in the habit of noticing things, and I didn't see Wade Eisler at the parapet while they were roping, and I haven't seen him since. I know you better than I do the others, except Harvey Greve, because I sat next to you at lunch, so I just thought I'd ask."

"Don't ask me. Ask Miss Rowan."

"Oh, it's not that important. But I'm curious about Cal's rope. I don't see why—"

Cal Barrow was there. He had come from the rear and was suddenly there in front of me. He spoke, in his low easy voice. "Can I see you a minute, Archie?"

"Where have *you* been?" Laura demanded.

"I been around."

I stood up. "Find your rope?"

"I want to show you. You stay hitched, Laura." She had started up. "You hear me?" It was a command, and from her stare I guessed it was the first one he had ever given her. "Come along, Archie," he said, and moved.

He led me around the corner of the penthouse. On that side the terrace is only six feet wide, but in the rear there is space enough for a badminton court and then some. The tubs of evergreens that had been removed from the front were there, and Cal went on past them to the door of a shack which Lily used for storage. The grouse had been hung there Saturday afternoon. He opened the door and entered, and when I was in shut the door. The only light came from two small windows at the far end, so it was half dark coming in from broad daylight, and Cal said, "Look out, don't step on him."

I turned and reached for the light switch and flipped it, turned back, and stood and looked down at Wade Eisler. As I moved and squatted Cal said, "No use taking his pulse. He's dead."

He was. Thoroughly. The protruding tongue was purple and so were the lips and most of the face. The staring eyes were wide open. The rope had been wound around his throat so many times, a dozen or more, that his chin was pushed up. The rest of the rope was piled on his chest.

"That's my rope," Cal said. "I was looking for it and I found it. I was going to take it but I thought I better not."

"You thought right." I was on my feet. I faced him and got his eyes. "Did you do it?"

"No, sir."

I looked at my wrist: twelve minutes to six. "I'd like to believe you," I said, "and until further notice I do. The last I saw you in there you were taking a glass of champagne. More than half an hour ago. I haven't seen you since. That's a long time."

"I been hunting my rope. When I drank that one glass I asked Miss Rowan if she minded if I looked and she said no. We had already looked inside and out front. Then when I come in here and found him I sat on that box a while to think it over. I decided the best thing was to get you."

"Wasn't this door locked?"

"No, sir. It was shut but it wasn't locked."

That was possible. It was often left unlocked in the daytime. I looked around. The room held all kinds of stuff—stacks of luggage, chairs, card tables, old magazines on shelves—but at the front, where we were, there was a clear space. Everything seemed to be in place; there was no sign that Eisler had put up a fight, and you wouldn't suppose a man would stand with his hands in his pockets while someone got a noose around his neck and pulled it tight. If he had been conked first, what with? I stepped on a rack against the wall on the left and put a hand out, but pulled it back. One of those three-foot stainless-steel rods, for staking plants, would have been just the thing, and the one on top was lying across the others. If I had had gloves and a glass with me, and there had been no rush, and Cal hadn't been there with his eyes boring at me, I would have given it a look.

I opened the door, using my handkerchief for the knob, and stepped out. There were six windows in the rear of the penthouse, but except for the two near the far corner, which belonged to the maid's room and bathroom, their view of the shack and the approach to it was blocked by the evergreens. That had been a break for the murderer; there had certainly been someone in the kitchen. I went back inside, shut the door, and told Cal, "Here's how it is. I have to get the cops here before anyone leaves if I want to keep my license. I don't owe Wade Eisler anything, but this will be a sweet mess for Miss Rowan and I'm a friend of hers, so I'm curious. When did you first miss the rope?"

He opened his mouth and closed it again. He shook his head. "I guess I made a mistake," he said. "I should have took that rope off and found it somewhere else."

"You should like hell. It would have been a cinch for the police lab to prove it had been around his neck. When did you first miss it?"

"But I had told you about last night and how I was worked up and you had promised to keep it in, and I figured I couldn't expect you to be square with me if I wasn't square with you, so I went and got you. Now the way you take it, I don't know."

"For God's sake." I wasn't as disgusted as I sounded. "What did you think, I'd bring you a bottle of champagne? Wait till you see how the cops take it. When did you first miss the rope?"

"I don't know just what time. It was a while after you left, maybe twenty minutes. With people coming and putting things in that closet I thought I'd get it and hang onto it."

"Had you put it in the closet yourself?"

"Yeah. On the shelf with my hat on top. The hat was there but the rope was gone."

"Did you tell someone right away?"

"I looked all over the closet and then I told Laura and she told Miss Rowan. Miss Rowan asked everybody and she helped Laura and me look some, but people started coming."

"At the time you missed the rope had anybody already come? Was anyone here besides those who ate lunch with us?"

"No, sir."

"You're sure?"

"I'm sure enough to put a no on it. They ain't much a man can be dead sure of. It might be someone came I didn't see, but I was right there and I'd have to—"

"Save it." I glanced at my watch: five minutes to six. "At the time you missed the rope where was Wade Eisler?"

"I don't know."

"When did you see him last?"

"I can't say exactly. I wasn't riding herd on him."

"Did you see him after you missed the rope? Take a second. This is important. Take ten.

"He screwed up his lips and shut his eyes. He took the full ten seconds. His eyes opened. "No, sir, I didn't."

"Sure enough to put a no on it?"

"I already did."

"Okay. Do you know if anyone else was worked up about Wade Eisler?"

"I wouldn't say worked up. I guess nobody wanted him for a pet."

"As it looks now, someone who ate lunch with us killed him. Have you any idea who?"

"No, sir. I don't expect to have none."

"That's noble. Don't be *too* noble. There's plenty more, but it will have to wait. If I leave you here while I go in and tell Miss Rowan and call the cops will you stay put and keep your hands off of that rope?"

"No, sir. I'm going to see Laura. I'm going to tell her if they ask her anything she better leave it out about last night."

"You are not." I was emphatic. "You've got no brand on her, you said so. You may think you know how she'll take a going-over by experts, but you don't. Every move anybody makes from now on will get on the record, and if you go and call her away from that baboon she's sitting with, what does she say and what do you say when they ask you why? She'll either leave it out or she won't, and you'll only make it worse if you tell her to. If you won't promise you'll stick here I'll just open the door and yell for Miss Rowan, and she can call the cops."

His jaw was working. "You said you believed me."

"I do. If I change my mind I'll let you know first. What you told me and what you asked me to do, I said I'd keep it in and I will, provided you do too. We were discussing the saddle. Well?"

"I figure to keep everything in. But if I could just tell her—"

"No. She probably won't spill it, but if she does and says she told you about it that won't break any bones. You left it out because you didn't want to cause her trouble. Everybody leaves things out when cops ask questions. Do I yell for Miss Rowan?"

"No. I'll stay hitched."

"Come outside and stand at the door. You've already touched the knob twice and that's enough. If anyone comes keep them off." Using my handkerchief again, I opened the door. He stepped out and I pulled the door shut as I crossed the sill. "Be seeing you," I said, and went.

I entered at the rear and glanced in at the kitchen on the chance that Lily was there. No. Nor the living room. The piano and fiddles were playing "These Fences Don't Belong." I found her on the terrace, caught her eye and gave her a sign, and she came. I headed for the dining room, and when she had followed me in I closed the door.

"One question," I said. "That's all there's time for. When did you last see Wade Eisler?"

She cocked her head and crinkled her eyes, remembering. I have mentioned a part of her that wasn't mine; this was a part of her that was mine. No what or why; I had asked her a question and she was digging up the answer. She took longer than Cal had. "It was soon after you left," she said. "He put his cup down and I asked him if he wanted more coffee and he said no. Someone did want some and the pot was nearly empty and I went to the kitchen for more. Felix and Robert were arguing about when the champagne should be put on ice, and I sent Freda to the terrace with the coffee and stayed there to calm them down. Who's worrying about Wade Eisler?"

"Nobody. How long did you stay in the kitchen?"

"Oh, ten minutes. Felix can be difficult."

"Eisler wasn't there when you went back?"

"I didn't notice. They had scattered. Some of them were in the living room. Then Laura Jay told me Cal Barrow's rope was gone and I helped them look, and then people came."

"When did you notice that Eisler wasn't around?"

"Some time later. Roger Dunning wanted someone to meet him and asked me where he was. I didn't know and didn't care. I supposed he had left without bothering to thank me for the meal. He would." She tossed her head. "That's four questions. What's the point?"

"Cal Barrow was looking for his rope and found Eisler's body on the floor of the shack with the rope around his neck. He came and got me. He's there guarding the door. Will you phone the police or do you want me to?" I glanced at my wrist: four minutes after six. "It's already been sixteen minutes since I saw him and that's enough."

"No," she said.

"Yes," I said.

"Wade Eisler hung himself?"

"No. He's not hanging, he's on the floor. Also after the noose was pulled tight the rope was wound around his neck a dozen times. He didn't do that."

"But how could—who would—*no!*"

"Yes. It would be me to hand you something like this, but at that I'm glad it is. I mean since it happened I'm glad I'm here. Do you want me to phone?"

She swallowed. "No, I will. It's my house." She touched my sleeve. "I'm *damn* glad you're here."

"Spring seven, three one hundred. I'll repeat that number: Spring seven—"

"You clown! All right, I needed it, that helped. I'll phone from the bedroom."

She moved, but I stopped her. "Do you want me to collect the guests and tell them the cops are coming?"

"Oh my God. Here in my house—but of course that's routine. That's etiquette—when you're having a party and someone finds a body you collect the guests and make an announcement and say you hope they'll come again and—"

"You're babbling."

"So I am." She went, and I had to step to get to the door ahead of her.

Since a prowl car was certainly in the neighborhood there wasn't much time, and I went to the terrace and sang out, "Everybody inside! Don't walk, run! Inside, everybody!" I entered the living room and mounted a chair. I wanted to see their faces. You seldom get anything helpful from faces, especially when there are more than twenty of them, but you always think you might. Those already inside approached, and those coming from the terrace joined them. I turned to the musicians and patted the air, and they broke off. Mel Fox said in a champagne-loud voice, "She's gone and got a saddle for me." Laughter. When you've been drinking champagne for an hour laughing comes easy.

I raised a hand and waggled it. "I've got bad news," I said. "I'm sorry, but here it is. A dead body has been found on the premises. The body of Wade Eisler. I have seen it. He was murdered. Miss Rowan is notifying the police and they will soon be here. She asked me to tell you. Of course nobody will leave."

What broke the silence was not a gasp but a giggle, from Nan Karlin. Then Roger Dunning demanded, "Where is he?" and Laura Jay moved, darting to the door to the terrace and on out, and the faces I had wanted to see turned away as Lily appeared through the arch.

She came on. She raised her voice. "All right, I got you here and we're in for it. I don't go much by rules, but now I need one. What does the perfect hostess do when a guest murders another guest? I suppose I ought to apologize, but that doesn't seem . . ."

I had stepped down from the chair. It wasn't up to me to welcome the cops, it was Lily's house and she was there, and anyway it would only be a pair from a prowl car. The homicide specialists would come later. Circling the crowd, I made for a door at the other side of the room, passed through, and was in what Lily called the kennel because a guest's dog had once misused the rug there. There were book shelves, and a desk and safe and typewriter, and a phone. I went to the phone and dialed a number I could have dialed with my eyes shut. Since Wolfe's afternoon session up in the plant rooms with the orchids was from four to six, he would have gone down to the office and would answer it himself.

He did. "Yes?"

"Me. Calling from the library in Miss Rowan's apartment. Regarding Wade Eisler. The one with a pudgy face and a scratch on his cheek. I gathered from your expression when he called you Nero that you thought him objectionable."

"I did. I do."

"So did somebody else. His body has been found in a storage room here on the roof. Strangled with a rope. The police are on the way. I'm calling to say that I have no idea when I'll be home, and I thought you ought to know that you'll probably be hearing from Cramer. A man getting croaked a few hours after he ate lunch with you—try telling Cramer you know nothing about it."

"I shall. What do you know about it?"

"The same as you. Nothing."

"It's a confounded nuisance, but it was worth it. The grouse was superb. Give Miss Rowan my respects."

I said I would.

The kennel had a door to the side hall, and I left that way, went to the side terrace, and headed for the shack. As I expected, Cal was not alone. He stood with his back against the door, his arms folded. Laura Jay was against him, gripping his wrists, her head tilted back, talking fast in a voice so low I caught no words. I called sharply, "Break it up!" She whirled on a heel and a toe, her eyes daring me to come any closer. I went closer. "You damn fool," I said, reaching her. "Snap out of it. Beat it! Get!"

"She thinks I killed him," Cal said. "I been trying to tell her, but she won't—"

What stopped him was her hands pressed against his mouth. He got her wrists and pulled them away. "He knows about it," he said. "I told him."

"Cal! You didn't! You mustn't—"

I got her elbow and jerked her around. "If you want to make it good," I said, "put your arms around his neck and moan. When I poke you in the ribs that'll mean a cop's coming and you'll moan louder and then turn and let out a scream, and when he's close enough, say ten feet, you leap at him and start clawing his face. That'll distract him and Cal can run to the terrace and jump off. Have you got anything at all in your skull besides air? What do you say when they ask you why you dashed out to find Cal when I announced the news? That you wanted to be the first to congratulate him?"

Her teeth were clamped on her lip. She unclamped them. She twisted her neck to look at Cal, twisted back to look at me, and moved. One slow step, and then she was off, and just in time. As she passed the first evergreen the sound came of the back door of the penthouse closing, and heavy feet, and I turned to greet the company. It was a harness bull.

3

EVEN when I get my full ration of sleep, eight hours, I don't break through my personal morning fog until I have emptied my coffee cup, and when the eight is cut to five by events beyond my control, as it was that night, I have to grope my way to the bathroom. After getting home at five in the morning, and leaving a note for Fritz saying I would be down for breakfast at 10:45, I had set the alarm for ten o'clock. That had seemed sensible, but the trouble with an alarm clock is that what seems sensible when you set it seems absurd when it goes off. Before prying my eyes open I stayed flat a while, trying to find an alternative, and had to give up when I was conscious enough to realize that Wolfe would come down from the plant rooms at eleven. Forty minutes later I descended the two flights to the ground floor, entered the kitchen, told Fritz good morning, got my orange juice from the refrigerator, and sat at the table where my copy of the *Times* was on the rack. Fritz, who is as well acquainted with my morning fog as I am and never tries to talk through it, uncovered the sausage and lit the fire under the griddle for cakes.

The murder of Wade Eisler with a lasso at the penthouse of Lily Rowan rated the front page even in the *Times*. There was no news in it for me, nothing that I didn't already know, after the five hours I had spent at the scene of the crime with Homicide personnel, three hours at the District Attorney's office, and three hours back at the penthouse with Lily, at her request. Cal Barrow was in custody as a material witness. The District Attorney couldn't say if he would be released in time for the Tuesday-evening rodeo performance. Archie Goodwin had told a *Times* reporter that he had not been at the penthouse in his professional capacity; he and Nero Wolfe had merely been guests. The police didn't know what the motive had been, or weren't telling. Wade Eisler, a bachelor, had been a well-known figure in sporting and theatrical circles. The *Times* didn't say that he had had a chronic and broad-minded taste for young women, but the tabloids certainly would. And so forth.

I was spreading honey on the third griddle cake when the sounds came of the elevator jolting to a stop and then Wolfe's footsteps in the hall crossing to the office. He wouldn't expect to find me there, since Fritz would have told him of my note when he took his breakfast tray up, so I took my time with the cake and honey and poured more coffee. As I was taking a sip the doorbell rang and I got up and went to the hall for a look. Through the one-way glass in the front door I saw a big broad frame and a big pink face that was all too familiar. The hall on the ground floor of the old brownstone is long and wide, with the walnut clothes rack, the elevator, the stairs, and the door to the dining room on one side, the doors to the front room and the office on the other, and the kitchen in the rear. I stepped to the office door, which was standing open, and said, "Good morning. Cramer."

Wolfe, in his oversized chair behind his desk, turned his head to scowl at me. "Good morning. I told him on the phone last evening that I have no information for him."

I had had two cups of coffee and the fog was gone. "Then I'll tell him to try next door."

"No." His lips tightened. "Confound him. That will only convince him that I'm hiding something. Let him in."

I went to the front, opened the door, and inquired, "Good lord, don't you ever sleep?"

I will never get to see Inspector Cramer at the top of his form, the form that has kept him in charge of Homicide for twenty years, because when I see him I am there and that throws him off. It's only partly me; it's chiefly that I make him think of Wolfe, and thinking of Wolfe is too much for him. When he has us together his face gets pinker and his voice gets gruffer, as it did that morning. He sat in the red leather chair near the end of Wolfe's desk, leaning forward, his elbows planted on the chair arms. He spoke. "I came to ask one question, why were you there yesterday? You told me on the phone last night that you went there to eat grouse, and Goodwin said the same. It's in his signed statement. Nuts. You could have had him bring the grouse here and had Fritz cook it."

Wolfe grunted. "When you are invited to someone's table to taste a rare bird you accept or decline. You don't ask that the bird be sent to you — unless you're a king."

"Which you think you are. You're named after one."

"I am not. Nero Claudius Caesar was an emperor, not a king, and I wasn't named after him. I was named after a mountain."

"Which you are. I still want to know why you were there with that bunch. You never leave your house on business, so it wasn't for a client. You went with Goodwin because he asked you to. Why did he ask you to? Why did you sit next to Wade Eisler at lunch? Why did Goodwin have a private talk with one of them, Cal Barrow, just before he drove you home? Why did Barrow go to him when he found the body? Why did Goodwin wait twenty minutes before he had Miss Rowan report it?"

Wolfe was leaning back, his eyes half closed, being patient. "You had Mr. Goodwin at your disposal all night. Weren't those points covered?"

Cramer snorted. "They were covered, all right. He knows how to cover. I'm not saying he knew or you knew Eisler's number was up. I don't say you know who did it or why. I do say there was some kind of trouble and Miss Rowan was involved in it, or at least she knew about it, and that's why Goodwin got you to go. You told me last night that you know nothing whatever about any of those people except Miss Rowan, and that your knowledge of her is superficial. I don't believe it."

"Mr. Cramer." Wolfe's eyes opened. "I lie only for advantage, never merely for convenience."

I cut in. "Excuse me." I was at my desk, at right angles to Wolfe's. Cramer turned to me. "I'd like to help if I can," I told him, "on account of Miss Rowan. I was backstage at the rodeo twice last week, and it's barely possible I heard or saw something that would open a crack. It would depend on how it stands. I know you're holding Cal Barrow. Has he been charged?"

"No. Material witness. It was his rope and he found the body."

"I am not concerned," Wolfe growled, "but I remark that that would rather justify holding the others."

"We haven't got your brains," Cramer growled back. To me: "What did you hear and see backstage at the rodeo?"

"I might remember something if I knew more about it. I know Eisler wasn't there when I returned at four o'clock, but I don't know who saw him last or when. Is everybody out except the ones who were there for lunch?"

"Yes. He was there when Miss Rowan left to go to the kitchen for coffee. That was at three-twenty, eight minutes after you left, as close as we can get it. No one remembers seeing him after that, so they say. No one noticed him leave the terrace, so they say. He got up from the lunch table at five minutes to three. He emptied his coffee cup at three-twenty. The stomach contents say that he died within twenty minutes of that. None of the other guests came until a quarter to four. So there's three cowboys: Harvey Greve, Cal Barrow, and Mel Fox. There's three cowgirls: Anna Casado, Nan Karlin, and Laura Jay. There's Roger Dunning and his wife. You and Wolf weren't there. Miss Rowan was, but if you saw or heard anything that points at her you wouldn't remember it. Was she at the rodeo with you?"

"I don't remember. Skip it. You've got it down to twenty minutes, from three-twenty to three-forty. Wasn't anyone else missed during that period?"

"Not by anybody who says so. That's the hell of it. Nobody liked Eisler. Not a single one of them would give a bent nickle to see the murderer caught. Some of them might give a good nickel to see him get away with it. This might make you remember something you saw or heard: Sunday night he took a woman to his apartment; and it could have been one of the cowgirls. We haven't got a good description of her, but the fingerprint men are there now. Were you at the Garden Sunday night?"

I shook my head. "Wednesday and Saturday. What about prints in the shack?"

"None that are any good."

"Last night I mentioned that a steel rod in a rack was crosswise."

"Yeah. We might have noticed it ourselves in time. It had been wiped. He had been hit in the back of the head with it. You can read about it in the evening paper. Do you want to come down and look at it?"

"You don't have to take that tone." I was hurt. "I said I'd like to help and I meant it. You need help, you're up a stump, or you wouldn't be here. As for what I heard and saw at the rodeo, I didn't know there was going to be a murder. I'll have to sort it out. I'll see if I can dig up anything and let you know. I thought you might —"

"Why, goddam you!" He was on his feet. "String *me* along? I know damn well you know something! I'll see that you choke on it!" He took a step. "For the record, Goodwin. Have you knowledge of any facts that would help to identify the murderer of Wade Eisler?"

"No."

To Wolfe: "Have you?"

"No, sir."

"Have you any involvement of any kind with any of those people?"

"No, sir."

"Wait a minute," I put in. "To avoid a possible future misunderstanding." I got my case from my pocket, took out a slip of paper, and displayed it to

Wolfe. "This is a check for five thousand dollars, payable to you, signed by Lily Rowan."

"What's it for?" he demanded. "She owes me nothing."

"She wants to. It's a retainer. She asked me to go back to her place after they finished with me at the DA's office last night, and I did so. She didn't like Wade Eisler any better than the next one, but two things were biting her. First, he was killed at her house by someone she had invited there. She calls that an abuse of hospitality and she thought you would. Don't you?"

"Yes."

"No argument there. Second, the daughter of District Attorney Bowen is a friend of hers. They were at school together. She has known Bowen for years. He has been a guest both at her apartment and her place in the country. And at midnight last night an assistant DA phoned her and told her to be at his office in the Criminal Courts Building at ten o'clock this morning, and she phoned Bowen, and he said he couldn't allow his personal friendships to interfere with the functions of his staff. She then phoned the assistant DA and told him she would call him today and tell him what time it would be convenient for her to see him at her apartment."

"There's too many like her," Cramer muttered.

"But she has a point," I objected. "She had told you all she knew and answered your questions and signed a statement, and why ten o'clock?" To Wolfe: "Anyway, here's her check. She wants you to get the murderer before the police do, and let her phone the DA and tell him to come for him — or she and I will deliver him to the DA's office, either way. Of course I told her you wouldn't take the job on those terms, but you might possibly consider investigating the abuse of hospitality by one of her guests. I also told her you charge high fees, but she already knew that. I bring this up now because you just told Cramer you're not involved, and if you take this retainer you *will* be involved. I told Miss Rowan you probably wouldn't take it because you're already in the ninety-per-cent bracket for the year and you hate to work."

He was glowering at me. He knew that I knew he wouldn't turn it down with Cramer there. "It will be a costly gratification of a pique," he said.

"I told her so. She can afford it."

"Her reason for hiring me is the most capricious in my experience. But I have not only eaten her bread and salt, I have eaten her grouse. I am in her debt. Mr. Cramer. I change my answer to your last question. I do have an involvement. My other answer holds. I have no information for you."

Cramer's jaw was clamped. "You know the law," he said, and wheeled and headed for the door.

When a visitor leaves the office it is my custom to precede him to the hall and the front door to let him out; but when it's Cramer and he's striding out in a huff I would have to hop on it to get ahead of him, which would be undignified, so I just follow to see that he doesn't take our hats from the shelf and tramp on them. When I emerged from the office Cramer was halfway down the hall, and after one glance I did hop on it. Out on the stoop, reaching a finger to the bell button, was Laura Jay.

I can outhop Cramer any day, but he was too far ahead and was opening the door when I reached it. Not wanting to give him an excuse to take me downtown, I didn't bump him. I braked. He said, "Good morning, Miss Jay. Come in."

I got Laura's eye and said, "Inspector Cramer is just leaving."

"I'm in no hurry," Cramer said, and backed up a step to give her room. "Come in, Miss Jay."

I saw it coming in her eyes — that is, I saw something was coming. They were at Cramer, not at me, but I saw the sudden sharp gleam of an idea, and then she acted on it. She came in all right, on the jump, through the air straight at Cramer, hands first reaching for his face. By instinct he should have jerked back, but experience is better than instinct. He ducked below her hands and came up against her with his arms around her, clamping her to him, leaving her nothing to paw but air. I got her wrists from the rear, pulled them to me, and crossed her arms behind her back.

"Okay," I said, "you can unwrap."

Cramer slipped his arms from under hers and backed away. "All right, Miss Jay," he said. "What's the idea?"

She tried to twist her head around. "Let me go," she demanded. "You're breaking my arm."

"Will you behave yourself?"

"Yes."

As I let go she started to tremble, but then she stiffened, pulling her shoulders back. "I guess I lost my head," she told Cramer. "I didn't expect to see you here. I do that sometimes, I just lose my head."

"It's a bad habit, Miss Jay. What time is your appointment with Nero Wolfe?"

"I haven't got an appointment."

"What do you want to see him about?"

"I don't want to see him. I came to see Archie Goodwin."

"What about?"

Before she could answer a voice came from behind Cramer. "Now what?" Wolfe was there, at the door to the office.

Cramer ignored him. "To see Goodwin about what?" he demanded.

"I think I know," I said. "It's a personal matter. Strictly personal."

"That's it," Laura said. "It's personal."

Cramer looked at me, and back to her. Of course the question was, if he took us downtown and turned us over to a couple of experts could they pry it out of us? He voted no. He spoke to me. "You heard me tell Wolfe he knows the law. So do you," and marched to the door, opened it, and was gone.

"Well?" Wolfe demanded.

I tried the door to make sure it was shut, and turned. "Miss Jay came to see me. I'll take her in the front room."

"No. The office." He turned and headed for the kitchen.

I allowed myself an inside grin. Thanks to my having produced the check with Lily's offer of a job in Cramer's presence, he was actually working. When Laura and I had entered the office he would emerge from the kitchen and station himself at the hole. On the office side the hole was covered by a picture of a waterfall, on the wall at eye level to the right of Wolfe's desk. On the other side, in a little alcove at the end of the hall, it was covered by a

sliding panel, and with the panel pushed aside you could not only hear but
also see through the waterfall. I had once stood there for three hours with a
notebook, recording a conversation Wolfe was having with an embezzler.

Laura retrieved her handbag, a big gray leather one, from the floor where
it had dropped when she went for Cramer, and I escorted her to the office,
took her jacket and put it on the couch, moved a chair for her to face my
desk, swiveled my chair around, and sat. I looked at her. She was a wreck. I
wouldn't have known her, especially since I had previously seen her all
rigged out, and now she was in a plain gray dress with a black belt. Her
cheeks sagged, her hair straggled, and her eyes were red and puffed. You
wouldn't suppose a dashing cowgirl could get into such a state.

"First," I said, "why? Why did you go for him?"

She swallowed. "I just lost my head." She swallowed again. "I ought to
thank you for helping me, when he asked what I came to see you for. I didn't
know what to say."

"You're welcome. What do you say if I ask you?"

"I came to find out something. To find out if you told them what Cal told
you yesterday. I know you must have because they've arrested him."

I shook my head. "They're holding him as a material witness because it
was his rope and he found the body. I promised Cal I wouldn't repeat what
he told me, and I haven't. If I did they'd have a motive for him, they
couldn't ask for better, and they'd charge him with murder."

"You haven't told them? You swear you haven't?"

"I only swear on the witness stand and I'm not there yet. I have told no
one, but I am now faced with a problem. Miss Rowan has hired Nero Wolfe
to investigate the murder, and he will ask me for a full report of what
happened there yesterday. I can't tell him what Cal told me because of my
promise to Cal, and I'll have to tell him I am leaving something out, which
he won't like. If Cal were available I would get his permission to tell Mr.
Wolfe, but he isn't."

"Then you haven't even told Nero Wolfe?"

"No."

"Will you promise me you won't tell the police? That you'll never tell
them no matter what happens?"

"Certainly not." I eyed her. "Use your head if you've found it again. Their
charging Cal with murder doesn't depend only on me. They have found out
that Eisler took a woman to his apartment Sunday night and they're going
over it for fingerprints. If they find some of yours, and if they learn that you
and Cal are good friends, as they will, he's in for it, and I would be a damn
fool to wait till they get me on the stand under oath."

I turned a palm up. "You see, one trouble is, you and me talking, that you
think Cal killed him and I know he didn't. You should be ashamed of
yourself. You have known him two years and I only met him last week, but I
know him better than you do. I can be fooled and have been, but when he
got me aside yesterday and asked me how to go about taking some hide off a
toad he was not getting set to commit a murder, and the murder of Wade
Eisler was premeditated by whoever took Cal's rope. Not to mention how he
looked and talked when he showed me the body. If I thought there was a
chance that Cal killed him I wouldn't leave anything out when I report to
Mr. Wolfe. But I can't promise to hang onto it no matter what happens."

"You can if you will," she said. "I don't think Cal killed him. I know he didn't. I did."

My eyes widened. "You did what? Killed Eisler?"

"Yes." She swallowed. "Don't you see how it is? Of course I've got to tell them I killed him, but when they arrest me Cal will say he killed him because I told him about Sunday night. But I'll say I *didn't* tell him about Sunday night, and it will be my word against his, and they'll think he's just trying to protect me. So it *does* depend on you. You've got to promise you won't tell them what Cal told you yesterday. Because I killed him, and why should you protect me? Why should you care what happens to me if I killed a man?"

I regarded her. "You know," I said, "at least you've answered my question, why you went for Cramer. You wanted to plant the idea that you're a holy terror. That wasn't so dumb, in fact it was half bright, but now listen to you. You might possibly sell it to the cops that you killed him, at least you could ball them up a while, but not me. When I went to the shack yesterday and found you there with Cal, the first thing he said was that you thought he had killed him. And now you—"

"Cal was wrong. How could I think he had killed him when I knew I had?"

"Nuts. I not only heard what he said, I saw his face, and I saw yours. You still think Cal killed him and you're acting like a half-wit."

Her head went down, her hands went up to cover her face, and she squeezed her breasts with her elbows. Her shoulders shook.

I sharpened my voice. "The very worst thing you could do would be to try telling the cops that you killed him. It would take them about ten minutes to trip you up, and then where would Cal be? But maybe you should tell them about Sunday night, but of course not that you told Cal about it. If they find your fingerprints in Eisler's apartment you'll have to account for them, and it will be better to give them the account before they ask for it. That won't be difficult; just tell them what happened."

"They won't find my fingerprints," she said, or I thought she did. Her voice was muffled by her hands, still over her face.

"Did you say they won't find your fingerprints?" I asked.

"Yes. I'm sure they won't."

I gawked at her. It wasn't so much the words as the tone—or not the tone, muffled as it was, but something. Call it a crazy hunch, and you never know exactly what starts a hunch. It was so wild that I almost skipped it, but it never pays to pass a hunch. "You can't be sure," I said. "You must have touched something. I've been to a party in that apartment. When you entered did you stop in the hall with the marble statues?"

"No. He . . . we went on through."

"To the living room. You stopped there?"

"Yes."

"Did he take you across to look at the birds in the cages? He always does. The cages are stainless steel, perfect for prints. Did you touch any of them?"

"No, I'm sure I didn't." She had dropped her hands and lifted her head.

"How close did you go to them?"

"Why . . . not very close. I'm sure I didn't touch them."

"So am I. I am also sure that you're a damn liar. There are no marble statues or bird cages in Eisler's apartment. You have never been there. What kind of a double-breasted fool are you, anyway? Do you go around telling lies just for the hell of it?"

Naturally I expected an effect, but not the one I got. She straightened up in her chair and gave me a straight look, direct and steady.

"I'm not a liar," she said. "I'm not a fool either, except about Cal Barrow. The kind of a life I've had a girl gets an attitude about men, or anyway I did. No monkey business. Keep your fences up and your cinch tight. Then I met Cal and I took another look, and after a while I guess you would say I was in love with him, but whatever you call it I know how I felt. I thought I knew how he felt too, but he never mentioned it, and of course I didn't. I only saw him now and then, he was mostly up north, and when I came to New York for this rodeo here he was. I thought he was glad to see me, and I let him know I was glad to see him, but still he didn't mention it, and when two weeks went by and pretty soon we would scatter I was trying to decide to mention it myself, and then Sunday night Nan told me about Wade Eisler, how he had —"

"Nan Karlin?"

"Yes. He had told her he was having a party at his apartment, and she went with him, and when they got there there wasn't any party, and he got rough, and she got rough too, and she got away."

"She told you this Sunday night?"

"Yes, when she got back to the hotel she came to my room. It's next to hers. Then there was this ear." She lifted a hand to push her hair back over her left ear. "I'm telling you the whole thing. I got careless with a bronc Sunday night and got bruised by a buckle, and I didn't want to admit to Cal that I didn't know how to keep clear around a horse. So when we met for breakfast yesterday morning I told him — you know what I told him. I guess I thought when he heard that, how a man had tried to bulldog me, he would see that it was time to mention something. I know I was a damn fool, I said I'm a fool when it comes to Cal Barrow, but I guess I don't know him as well as I thought I did. He never goes looking for trouble. I thought he would just ride herd on me, and that would be all right, I wanted him to. I never dreamt he would kill him."

"He didn't. How many times do I have to tell you he didn't? Who else did Nan tell about it?"

"She was going to tell Roger, Roger Dunning. She asked me if I thought she should tell Roger, and I said yes, because he had asked us to go easy with Eisler, not to sweat him unless we had to, so I thought he ought to know. Nan said she would tell him right away."

"Who else did she tell?"

"I guess not anybody. She made me promise not to tell Mel."

"Mel Fox?"

"Yes. She and Mel are going to tie up, and she was afraid he might do something. I'm sure she didn't tell him."

"Did you tell him?"

"Of course not. I promised Nan I wouldn't."

"Well." I lifted my hands and dropped them. "You're about the rarest specimen I've ever come across. I know something about geniuses, I work for one, but you're something new, an anti-genius. It wouldn't do any good to try to tell you—"

The phone rang, and I swiveled my chair around to get it. It was Lon Cohen of the *Gazette*. He wanted to know how much I would take for an exclusive on who roped Wade Eisler and why, and I told him I did and when I typed my confession I would make an extra carbon for him but at the moment I was busy.

As I reached to cradle the receiver Wolfe's voice sounded behind me, not loud but clear enough though it was coming through the waterfall that covered the hole. "Archie, don't move. Don't turn around. She has taken a gun from her bag and is pointing it at you. Miss Jay. Your purpose is clear. With Mr. Goodwin dead there will be no one to disclose what you told Mr. Barrow at breakfast yesterday but Mr. Barrow himself, and you will deny it. You will of course be doomed since you can't hope to escape the due penalty for killing Mr. Goodwin, but you accept it in order to save Mr. Barrow from the doom you think you have contrived for him. A desperate expedient but a passable one; but it's no good now because I have heard you. You can't kill me too; you don't know where I am. Drop the gun. I will add that Mr. Goodwin has worked with me many years; I know him well; and I accept his conclusion that Mr. Barrow did not kill Wade Eisler. He is not easily gulled. Drop the gun."

I had stayed put, but it wasn't easy. Of course tingles were chasing up and down my spine, but worse than that I felt so damned silly, sitting there with my back to her while Wolfe made his speech. When he stopped it was too much. I swiveled. Her hand with the gun was resting on her knee, and she was staring at it, apparently wondering how it got there. I got up and took it, an old snub-nosed Graber, and flipped the cylinder. Fully loaded.

As I jiggled the cartridges out Wolf entered from the hall. As he approached he spoke. "Archie. Does Mr. Barrow cherish this woman?"

"Sure he does. This could even key him up to mentioning it."

"Heaven help him." He glared down at her. "Madam, you are the most dangerous of living creatures. However, here you are, and I may need you." He turned his head and roared, "Fritz!" Fritz must have been in the hall; he appeared immediately. "This is Miss Laura Jay," Wolfe told him. "Show her to the south room, and when lunch is ready take her a tray."

"I'm going," Laura said. "I'm going to—I'm going."

"No. You'd be up to some mischief within the hour. I am going to expose a murderer, and I have accepted Mr. Goodwin's conclusion that it will not be Mr. Barrow, and you will probably be needed. This is Mr. Fritz Brenner. Go with him."

"But I must—"

"Confound it, will you go? Mr. Cramer would like to know why you came to see Mr. Goodwin. Do you want me to ring him and tell him?"

She went. I got her jacket from the couch and handed it to Fritz, and he convoyed her out and to the elevator. Wolfe commanded me, "Get Mr. Dunning," and went to his desk and sat. I put the Graber and the cartridges in a drawer, looked in the book for the number of the Paragon Hotel, got at the phone, and dialed. The girl said Dunning's room didn't answer, and I asked her to have him paged. When he couldn't be found I left a message, and tried Madison Square Garden, and finally got him.

Wolfe took his phone. I stayed on mine. "Mr. Dunning? This is Nero Wolfe. We met yesterday at the home of Miss Lily Rowan. Miss Rowan has hired me to investigate what she calls an abuse of her hospitality — the death by violence of one of her guests — and I would like to see you. If you will please come to my office, say at a quarter past two?"

"I can't, Dunning said. "Impossible. Anyway, I've told the police everything I know. I suppose Miss Rowan has a right to hire you if she wants to, but I don't see why . . . anyhow, I can't. It's a nightmare, this is, a nightmare, but we're going to have a performance tonight if I live that long."

"Murder hatches nightmares. Did you tell the police about Miss Karlin's visit to Mr. Eisler's apartment Sunday night?"

Silence. Five seconds.

"Did you?"

"I don't know what you're talking about."

"That won't do, Mr. Dunning. I can ask the police that question if I must, but I would rather not. I would prefer to discuss it with you, and with Miss Karlin and Mr. Fox. If you will please be here with them at a quarter past two? A yes or no will be sufficient. It might be unwise to discuss it on the phone."

Another silence. Six seconds.

"I'll be there."

"With Miss Karlin and Mr. Fox?"

"Yes."

"Good. I'll expect you." He hung up and looked at me. "Archie. Will that woman try climbing out a window?"

"No. She's hooked."

"Very well." He looked up at the wall clock. "Lunch in forty minutes. Report."

4

WHEN the company arrived I wasn't there to let them in. They came five minutes early, at ten after two, and I was upstairs with Laura Jay. The south room is two flights up, on the same floor as my room, in the rear, above Wolfe's room. I left the lunch table before Wolf finished his coffee, and mounted the two flights, partly to make sure she was still there, partly to see if she had eaten anything from the tray Fritz had taken up, and partly to tell her that Nan and Mel and Roger Dunning were expected and if Wolfe wanted her to join the party later I would either come and get her or send Fritz for her. All three purposes were served. She was there, standing at a window, the sun setting fire to her honey-colored hair. There was only one Creole fritter left on the plate and no salad in the bowl. I had expected her to insist on going down with me instead of waiting for a summons, but she didn't. Just for curiosity I asked her if she had intended to pull the trigger as soon as I hung up or wait until I turned around, and she said I ought to know she wouldn't shoot a man in the back.

When I descended to the office they were there — Roger Dunning in the red leather chair, and Nan Karlin and Mel Fox in two of the yellow ones facing Wolfe's desk. When I entered and circled around them I got no glances; they were too intent on Wolfe, who was speaking.

". . . and the source of my information is not important. If you persist in your denial you will merely be postponing your embarrassment. The police have learned, not from me, that Eisler took a woman to his apartment Sunday night, and they are going over it for fingerprints. Almost certainly they will find some of yours, Miss Karlin, and Mr. Goodwin has told me that all of you permitted them to take samples last evening. You're in a pickle. If you refuse to discuss it with me I advise you to tell the police about it at once, before they confront you with it."

Nan turned her head to look at Mel, and I had her full-face. Even without her pink silk shirt and Levis and boots, in a blouse and skirt and pumps, she would have been spotted by any New Yorker as an alien. The skin of a girl's face doesn't get that deep tone from week ends at the beach or even a two weeks' go-now-pay-later trip to Bermuda.

Mel Fox, meeting her look, said, "What the hell."

Nan went back to Wolfe. "Laura told you," she said. "Laura Jay. She's the only one that knew about it except Roger Dunning and he didn't."

"He *says* he didn't," Mel said. His eyes went to Dunning. "You wouldn't be letting out anybody's cinch, would you, Roger?"

"Of course not," Dunning said. It came out a little squeaky, and he cleared his throat. His narrow, bony face was just a sliver. I have noticed over and over that under strain a fat face gets fatter and a long face gets longer. He asked Wolfe, "Did I tell you?"

"No." To Nan: "You say that Miss Jay and Mr. Dunning are the only ones who knew about it. When did you tell them?"

"Sunday night when I got back to the hotel. Laura's room is next to mine and I went in and told her. I thought I ought to tell Roger and so did she, and when I went to my room I phoned him and he came and I told him."

"Why him? Are you on terms of intimacy with him?"

"With *him*? Good lord. Him?"

"The question arises. It is conceivable that he was so provoked by the outrage that he decided to kill Eisler, moved perhaps by an unavowed passion. Is it not?"

"Look at him," Nan said.

We did so. With no desire to slander him, it must be admitted that he didn't look like a man apt to burn with passion, avowed or unavowed.

"I never killed a man yet," he said. "Why Nan told me, she thought she ought to and she was absolutely right. It was partly my fault she had gone with Eisler to his apartment, I had asked the girls to let him have a little rope as long as he didn't get too frisky, I knew they could take care of themselves, and Nan wanted to tell me that if he ever came near her again she would give him worse than a scratch, and I couldn't blame her."

"Why did you ask them to give him rope?"

"Well." Dunning licked his lips. "In a way I was hog-tied. If Eisler hadn't put up the money we wouldn't have made it to New York this year, or anyhow it wouldn't have been easy. I didn't know much about him when I first signed up with him except that he had the money. Anyhow he was all right except with the girls, and I didn't know he was that kind. I knew if he didn't pull up there might be trouble, but I figured it wouldn't do any good to tell him so. What could I do? I couldn't fence him out. When Nan told me about Sunday night I thought that might stop him, it might show him that a girl that can handle a bronc can handle his kind."

"Did you tell him that?"

"No, I didn't. I hoped I wouldn't have to. But I decided I would keep my eyes open. Up there yesterday when I noticed he wasn't on the terrace I looked around for him some, inside and outside. When I couldn't find him and I saw all the girls were there I thought he had up and gone, and that suited me fine."

"What time was that? When you looked around and couldn't find him."

Dunning shook his head. "I can't make it close. The police wanted me to and I did the best I could, but all I can say, it wasn't long after Miss Rowan went in for some more coffee — maybe three minutes, maybe more than that. Then when I went back in after looking outside Cal Barrow said his rope was gone and he was looking for it, and I wondered if Eisler had took it but I couldn't guess why."

"How many people did you tell about Miss Karlin's experience at Eisler's apartment?"

"How many?" Dunning frowned. "No people at all. What good would that do?"

"You told no one?"

"No."

"And you haven't told the police?"

"No." He licked his lips. "I figured it would just sick them on Nan, and I couldn't see any sense in that. What you asked her about her and me, there's nothing to that, she's just one of the girls, but I know her pretty well and she wouldn't kill a man just because he had pawed at her. I'd like to ask you a question. You say Miss Rowan has hired you to investigate?"

"Yes."

"You weren't there when it happened, and neither was Goodwin. Is that right?"

"Yes."

"But Miss Rowan was, and she hires you. She's paying you. So you're not going to investigate *her*, naturally. I got the idea there yesterday that she didn't like Eisler any too well. I don't suppose you're interested in that? I suppose you think it has to be one of us, the boys and girls and me?"

Wolfe grunted. He turned his head. "Archie. I haven't asked you. Did Miss Rowan kill Mr. Eisler?"

"No, sir."

"Then that's settled. Mr. Dunning, obviously it was one of you. By the way, Miss Karlin, I haven't asked you: did you kill Mr. Eisler?"

"No."

"Mr. Fox. Did you?"

"No."

"When did you first learn of Miss Karlin's visit to Eisler's apartment Sunday night?"

"Today. Two hours ago. Roger told me after you phoned him. If I'd knew about it Sunday night or yesterday morning Eisler wouldn't of got killed there yesterday because he wouldn't of been there. He would of been in bed or maybe in the hospital."

"Then it's a pity you didn't know."

"Yeah. Roger told me because you told him to bring me along, he didn't know why and I don't either, but I can make a guess. You're a friend of Harvey Greve's."

"Mr. Goodwin is."

"Yeah. So Harvey tells him things. He tells him about Nan and me, that we're fixing to get hitched, which we are, and you—"

"Not Harvey," Nan said. "Laura. Laura told him. Because they've arrested Cal."

"All right, maybe Laura." Mel stayed at Wolfe. "So that looks like a good setup. Eisler went after my girls and I killed him. So you tell Roger to bring me along. I understand you're about as slick as they come, you can bend a loop around a corner, but let's see you try. Here's Roger says he didn't tell anybody about Nan going there. Here's Nan says she didn't tell anybody but Laura and Roger. So I didn't know about it unless Eisler told me himself, and that don't seem practical, and he's dead. So here I am and it's your move."

"You did know about it!"

It was Laura Jay's voice and it came from the waterfall that covered the hole, which was only a couple of arms' lengths from Roger Dunning, and he jerked around. I bounced up and started for the hall, but had got only halfway when here came Laura.

She went straight to Mel and stopped, facing him, and spoke. "You knew about it because I told you." She turned to Wolfe: "Yesterday. I told him yesterday morning. I thought he—"

She was interrupted. Nan flew at her and smacked her on the side of the head.

5

SOMEHOW when two women tie into each other it's harder to separate them than it is two men. It's not just that you don't want to hurt a woman if you can help it; they're actually more wriggly and you're more apt to get scratched or bit; and when it's two active cowgirls it's a real problem. However, I had help. Roger and Mel were closer than I was, and Roger had Laura's shoulders, and Mel had Nan around the waist, when I reached them. They yanked them apart, and I merely stepped in between. Laura wriggled free from Roger, but I was there. Mel had Nan wrapped up.

"Pfui," Wolfe said. "Miss Jay, your talent for turmoil is extraordinary. Archie, put her—"

"She's a liar," Nan said. She was panting a little, and her eyes were blazing. "I knew it was her. I knew she—"

"Hold it, Nan," Mel commanded her. His eyes were narrowed at Wolfe. "So you had it rigged good, huh? So you had her all primed, huh?"

"I did not." Wolfe was emphatic. "This is becoming farcical. You were right, up to a point, Miss Karlin. Miss Jay, concerned on account of Mr. Barrow, came to see Mr. Goodwin, to tell him of your experience at Eisler's apartment. She stated that you made her promise not to tell Mr. Fox, and that she had kept the promise. Thinking it well to have her at hand, I had her shown to a room upstairs and told her to stay there. Her abrupt entry surprised me as much as you. Miss Jay, did you tell Mr. Goodwin that you had not told Mr. Fox?"

"Yes." Laura's chin was up.

"But you now say you had?"

"Yes."

"Precisely where and when?"

"Yesterday morning at the hotel. In the lobby after breakfast."

"You had breakfast with Mr. Barrow. Was he present?"

"No. He went to buy some cigarettes, and I saw Mel there and went and told him."

"Look here, Laura," Mel said. "Look at me."

Her head came around, slowly, and she met his eyes straight.

"You know darned well that ain't so," he said. "This slicker talked you into it. He told you that was the way to get Cal out of trouble. Didn't he?"

"No."

"You mean you can stand there and look me in the eye and lie like that?"

"I don't know, Mel, I never tried."

"Listen, Laura," Roger Dunning said, to her back. "If it's on account of Cal, I don't think you have to. I've got a lawyer on it and he'll soon have him out on bail, thirty thousand dollars. He may be out already. They can't charge him with murder unless they can show some reason why he wanted to kill Eisler, and there wasn't any."

"It's not just her," Mel said. He had backed Nan up and moved in front of her. He turned to me. "You're slick too, huh?"

"Not very," I said. "I manage somehow."

"I bet you do. I bet you're pretty good at answering questions. What if I asked you where you was yesterday while someone was killing Eisler?"

"That's easy. I was driving a car. Driving Mr. Wolfe home and then back to Sixty-third Street."

"Was anybody else along?"

"Nope. Just us two."

"Did you see anybody on the way that knows you?"

"No."

"Did anybody here see you except Wolfe?"

"No, I didn't come in. I wanted to get back in time for the roping — I mean the contest, not roping Eisler. You're asking pretty good questions, but you'll hit the same snag with me as with Cal Barrow. You'll have to show some reason why I wanted to kill Eisler."

"Yeah. Or why Wolfe would want you to, the man you work for. Or why that Miss Rowan would, the woman that's hired him." He turned to Wolfe. "You better look out with this Laura Jay. She ain't cut out for a liar." He turned to Laura. "I'll be having a talk with you, Laura. Private." He turned to Roger Dunning. "This lawyer you got to get bail for Cal, is he any good?"

Roger's long narrow face was even longer. "I think he's all right. He seems to know his way around."

"I want to see him. Come on, Nan. You come along. We're not going to get—"

The doorbell rang. Mel had Nan under control, so I went. A glance through the glass of the front door showed me a hundred and ninety pounds of sergeant out on the stoop—Sergeant Purley Stebbins of Homicide. I proceeded, put the chain bolt on, opened the door to the two-inch crack the chain permitted, and said politely, "No clues today. Out of stock."

"Open up, Goodwin." Like a sergeant. "I want Nan Karlin."

"I don't blame you. She's a very attractive—"

"Can it. Open up. I've got a warrant for her and I know she's here."

There was no use making an issue of it, since there had probably been an eye on the house ever since Cramer left. As for the warrant, of course the prints she had left at Eisler's apartment had caught up with her. But Wolfe doesn't approve of cops' taking anyone in his house, no matter who. "What if you brought the wrong warrant?" I asked.

He got it from a pocket and stuck it through the crack, and I took it and looked it over. "Okay," I said, "but watch her, she might bite." Removing the chain, swinging the door open, and handing him the warrant as he crossed the sill, I followed him to the office. He didn't make a ceremony of it. He marched across to Nan, displayed the paper, and spoke. "Warrant to take you as a material witness in the murder of Wade Eisler. You're under arrest. Come along."

My concern was Laura. As like as not, she would blurt out that he should take Mel too because she had told him about it, so I lost no time getting to her, but she didn't utter a peep. She stood stiff, her teeth clamped on her lip. Wolfe let out a growl, but no words. Nan gripped Mel's arm. Mel took the warrant, read it through, and told Stebbins, "This don't say what for."

"Information received."

"Where you going to take her?"

"Ask the District Attorney's office."

"I'm getting a lawyer for her."

"Sure. Everybody ought to have a lawyer."

"I'm going along."

"Not with us. Come on, Miss Karlin."

Wolfe spoke. "Miss Karlin. You will of course be guided by your own judgment and discretion. I make no suggestion. I merely inform you that you are under no compulsion to speak until you have consulted an attorney."

Stebbins and Mel Fox both spoke at once. Stebbins said, "She didn't ask you anything." Mel said, "You goddam snake." Stebbins touched Nan's elbow and she moved. I stayed with Laura as they headed out, Nan and Stebbins in front and Mel and Roger following; seeing them go might touch her off. She still had her teeth on her lip. When I heard the front door close I went and took a look and came back.

I expected to find Wolfe scowling at her, but he wasn't. He was leaning back with his eyes closed and his lips moving. He was pushing out his lips, puckered, and then drawing them in—out and in, out and in. He only does that, and always does it, when he has found a crack somewhere, or thinks he

has, and is trying to see through. I am not supposed to interrupt the
process, so I crossed to my desk, but didn't sit, because Laura was still on
her feet, and a gentleman should not seat himself when a lady or a wildcat is
standing.

Wolfe opened his eyes. "Archie."

"Yes, sir."

"It would help to know whether Miss Jay had told Mr. Fox or not. Is
there any conceivable way of finding out?"

I raised a brow. If that was the crack he had been trying to see through he
was certainly hard up for cracks. "Not bare-handed," I said. "It would take
a scientist. I know where you can get one with a lie detector. Or you might
try a hypnotist."

"Pfui. Miss Jay, which is it now, now that Miss Karlin is in custody? Had
you told Mr. Fox?"

"Yes."

"Yesterday morning in the hotel lobby?"

"Yes."

"I suppose you understand what that will let you in for — or rather, I
suppose you don't. You will be —"

The phone rang. I got it. "Nero Wolfe's office, Archie Goodwin speaking."

"This is Cal, Archie. Do you know where Laura is?"

"I might have an idea. Where are you?"

"I'm at the hotel. I'm out on bail. They say she went out this morning
and she hasn't been back, and she's not at the Garden. I thought maybe she
might have been to see you."

"Hold the wire a minute. I'll go to another phone."

I got my memo pad, wrote on it, *Cal Barrow out on bail looking for Laura, get
him here & you can check her,* tore off the sheet, and handed it to Wolfe. He read
it and looked up at the clock. His afternoon date with the orchids was at
four.

"No," he said. "You can. Get her out of here. Of course you must see him
first."

I resumed at the phone. "I think I know where to find her. It's a little
complicated, and the best way —"

"Where is she?"

"I'll bring her. What's your room number?"

"Five-twenty-two. Where is she?"

"I'll have her there in half an hour, maybe less. Stay in your room."

I hung up and faced Laura. "That was Cal. He's out on bail and he wants
to see you. I'll take —"

"Cal! Where is he?"

"I'll take you to him, but I'm going to see him first. I don't ask you to
promise because you'd promise anything, but if you try any tricks I'll show
you a new way to handle a calf. Where's your jacket?"

"It's upstairs."

"Go get it. If I went for it you might not be here when I came back."

6

THE Paragon Hotel, around the corner from Eighth Avenue on 54th Street, not exactly a dump but by no means a Waldorf, is convenient for performers at the Garden — of course not including the stars. When Laura and I entered there were twenty or more cow-persons in the lobby, both male and female, some in costume and some not. We went to the elevator, and to my surprise she stuck to the program we agreed upon in the taxi, getting out at the fourth floor to go to her room. I stayed in, left at the fifth, found Room 522 and knocked on the door, and it opened before I was through knocking.

"Oh," Cal said. "Where is she?"

He was still in the same outfit he had worn yesterday — bright blue shirt, blue jeans and fancy boots. His face wasn't any fresher than his clothes.

"She's in her room," I said. "She wanted to fix her hair. Before she joins us I want to ask you something. Do I see a chair in there?"

"Why sure. Come on in and sit." He gave me room and I entered. There were two chairs, about all there was space for, what with the bed and chest of drawers and a little table. I took one. Cal stood and yawned, wide.

"Excuse me," he said. "I'm a little short on sleep."

"So am I. Some things have been happening, but Laura can tell you about them. Miss Rowan has hired Nero Wolfe to investigate, and he knows about what you told me yesterday. Laura can tell you how he found out. I haven't told the cops or anyone else."

He nodded. "I figured you hadn't or they would have asked me. I guess you've got your tongue in straight. I'm mighty glad. I guess I picked the right man to tell."

"Frankly, you could have done worse. Now you can tell me something else. Yesterday morning you met Laura downstairs and had breakfast with her. Remember?"

"Sure I remember."

"Mel Fox says that when you and Laura went into the lobby after breakfast you left her and went to the cigar counter to buy cigarettes, and he went and had a little talk with you. Remember that?"

"I don't seem to." He frowned. "I didn't buy no cigarettes. I got a carton here in my room. Mel must of got mixed up."

"I'd like to be sure about this, Cal. Go back to it, it was only yesterday. You and Laura had breakfast in the coffee shop?"

"Yes."

"Then you went into the lobby together. If you didn't leave her to buy cigarettes, maybe it was to buy a paper. The newsstand is —"

"Wait a minute. We didn't go into the lobby. We left the coffee shop by the street door. We went down to the Garden to look at some things."

"Then it might have been when you came back. You went into the lobby then."

"We didn't come back. When we left the Garden we went up to that Miss

457

Rowan's. I guess you might tell me why this is so particular. What does Mel say we talked about?"

"You'll know pretty soon. I had to be sure —"

There was a knock at the door, and he lost no time getting to it. It was Laura. She was running true to form. We had agreed on fifteen minutes, and it had been only ten. The reunion was mighty dramatic. Cal said, "Well, hello." Laura said, "Hello, Cal." He stood aside so she wouldn't have to brush against him as she entered. I arose and said, "You fudged a little but I expected you to." Cal shut the door and came and said, "Gosh, you look like you got throwed by a camel."

I took command. "Look," I told them, "when I leave you'll have all the time there is, but now I've got some talking to do and you can listen. Sit down."

"You've already talked," Laura said. "What did you tell him?"

"Nothing yet but I'm going to. If you don't want to listen I know who will — Inspector Cramer if I phone him and say I'm ready to unload. Sit down!"

Laura sat in the other chair. Cal sat on the edge of the bed. "I guess you got the drop on us, Archie," he said. "I hope you don't feel as mean as you sound."

"I don't feel mean at all." I sat. "I'm going to tell you a love story. I take valuable time to tell it because if I don't God only knows what Laura will be up to next. Yesterday she told you a colossal lie. Today she told me she killed Wade Eisler. Then she — shut up, both of you! Then she pointed a loaded gun at my back and would have plugged me if she hadn't been interrupted. Then she told another lie, trying to frame Mel Fox for the murder. That's —"

"No!" Laura cried. "That was the truth!"

"Nuts. You and Cal didn't go to the lobby after breakfast. You went to the Garden and from there to Miss Rowan's. You didn't tell Mel Fox what you said you did. You were framing him, or trying to."

"You're talking pretty fast," Cal said. "Maybe you'd better slow down and back it up a little. If you can. What was the lie she told me yesterday?"

"That she had gone to Eisler's apartment Sunday night. She hadn't. She has never been there. It was Nan Karlin that Eisler took there Sunday night, and Nan told Laura about it when she got back to the hotel. Laura told you *she* had been there for two reasons: she didn't want to admit she had been careless about a horse and got her ear bruised, and the real reason, she hoped it would make you realize it was time to break out the bridle. All for love. You are her dream man. She wants to hook you. She wants you to take her for better or for worse, and she has done her damnedest to make it worse."

"I didn't say that!" Laura cried.

"Not in those words. Was that why you told him that lie or wasn't it? Try telling the truth once."

"All right, it was!"

Cal stood up. "You might go and leave us alone awhile. You can come back."

"This is a respectable hotel. A gentleman isn't supposed to be in his room alone with a lady. I'll go pretty soon, after I fill in a little. Sit down. She came today and told me she killed Eisler because she thought you had—she still thinks so—and it was her fault and she wanted to take the rap. When I showed her that wouldn't work she took a gun from her bag—she had thoughtfully brought it along—when my back was turned, and got set to let me have it, the idea being that I was the only one who knew you had a motive. She can tell you why that didn't work either. Then—"

"She wouldn't of shot you," Cal said.

"The hell she wouldn't. Then Mel and Nan and Roger came, and she got another idea. She announced that she had told Mel about Nan going to Eisler's place Sunday night, the idea being to give Mel a motive for killing Eisler. She said she told him yesterday morning when you and she went to the lobby after breakfast and you went to buy cigarettes. I have now stepped on that one." I turned to Laura. "You'd better see Mel and tell him. Tell him you had a fit."

I returned to Cal. "Of course that's fairly thick, trying to dump a murder on a guy, but after all, she would have dumped it on herself if she could. She tried that first, so I admit I should make allowances. I'm telling you all this for three reasons: first, so you'll know what she's capable of and you'll head her off. No one else can. If she keeps on having ideas there'll be hell to pay and you'll probably do the paying. Second, I want you both to realize that whoever killed Eisler is going to get tagged, and the sooner the better. It's one of six people: Nan Karlin, Anna Casado, Harvey Greve, Mel Fox, and Roger Dunning and his wife. If you know of any reason, anything at all, why one of them might have wanted Eisler dead, I expect you to tell me and tell me now."

"You say Laura still thinks I killed him," Cal said.

"She may be losing her grip on that. After the way her other ideas have panned out she must be shaky on that one." I looked at her. "Make it hypothetical, Laura. If Cal didn't, who did?"

"I don't know."

"What about Harvey Greve? He's a friend of mine, but I'll overlook that if he's it. Could he have had a motive?"

"I don't know."

"What about Roger Dunning? Did Eisler make passes at his wife?"

"If he did I never saw him. Neither did anybody else. She's not—well, you saw her—why would he? With all the girls to paw at. She must be nearly fifty."

Ellen Dunning probably wasn't a day over forty, but I admit she was a little faded. I turned to Cal. "Your turn. If you didn't kill him who did?"

He shook his head. "You got me. Does it have to be one of them six?"

"Yes."

"Then I pass. I just couldn't guess."

"It will take more than a guess. My third reason for taking up your time, not to mention mine: I wanted to have another look at you and listen to you some more. You're the only one with a known motive, and I'm the one that knows it. Nero Wolfe has bought my conclusion that you're out, and I haven't told the cops, and if I'm wrong I'm sunk. Besides, Laura would have the laugh on me, and I'd hate that. Did you kill him?"

"I'll tell you, Archie." He was actually grinning at me, and there was nothing but me between him and a murder trial. "I wouldn't want her to have the laugh on me, either. And she won't."

"Okay." I got up. "For God's sake keep an eye on her. Do you know Harvey's room number?"

"Sure. He's down the hall, Five-thirty-one."

I went.

Knocking on the door of Room 531, first normal and then loud, got no result. I intended to see Harvey. He might be down in the lobby, and if he wasn't I would try the Garden. There was no hurry about getting back to the office, since it was only four-thirty and Wolfe wouldn't be down from the plant rooms until six. Taking the elevator down, I found that there were more people in the lobby than when I came. Moving around, I didn't see Harvey, but I saw a man I knew, standing over in a corner chinning with a couple of cowboys. It was Fred Durkin. Fred, a free-lance, was second-best of the three operatives whom Wolfe considers good enough to trust with errands when we need help on a job. I looked at my watch: 4:34. Nearly an hour and a half since I had left with Laura, time enough for Wolfe to get Fred on the phone, brief him, and put him to work. Had he? Of course it could be that Fred was there on a job for one of the agencies that used him, but that would have been quite a coincidence and I don't like coincidences.

That question would have to wait for an answer. Knowing that Harvey Greve liked a drink when one was handy, I crossed the lobby and entered the bar. The crowd there was smaller but noisier. No Harvey, but there were booths along the wall, and I strolled back for a look, and found him. He was in a booth, deep in conversation with a man. Neither of them saw me, and I went on by, circled and backtracked, returned to the lobby, and on out to the street.

The man with Harvey was Saul Panzer. Saul is not only the first-best of the three men Wolf uses for errands, he is the best operative south of the North Pole. That settled it. Fred could have been a coincidence, but not both of them. Wolfe had got busy on the phone the minute I was out of the house, or darned soon after. What had stung him? No answer. At Ninth Avenue I flagged a taxi. When I gave the hackie the number on West 35th Street, he said, "What a honor. Archie Goodwin in person. Your name in the paper again but no pitcher this time. Stranglin' a guy with a lasso right on Park Avenue, can you beat that? Whodunit?"

I'm all for fame, but I was too busy guessing to smirk.

The hackie had another honor coming. When the cab rolled to a stop in front of the old brownstone and I climbed out, a man appeared from behind a parked car and spoke to him. It was Sergeant Purley Stebbins. He said to the hackie, "Hold it, driver. Police." He said to me, "You're under arrest. I've got a warrant." He took a paper from a pocket and offered it.

He was enjoying it. He would have enjoyed even more to see me squirm, so I didn't. I didn't bother to look at the paper. "Information received?" I asked politely. "Or just on general principles?"

"The inspector will tell you. We'll use this cab. Get in."

I obeyed. He climbed in beside me and told the driver, "Two-thirty West Twentieth," and we rolled.

I chose to snub him. He was of course expecting me to try some appropriate cracks, so of course I didn't. I didn't open my trap from the time I climbed in the cab until he ushered me into the office of Inspector Cramer, which is on the third floor of the dingy old building that houses the precinct. I didn't open it even then. I waited until I was in a chair at the end of Cramer's desk, and he said, "I've been going over your statement, Goodwin, and I want to know more about your movements yesterday afternoon. The District Attorney does too, but I'll have a go at it first. You left with Wolfe, to drive him home, at twelve minutes after three. Right?"

I spoke. "It's all in my statement, and I answered a thousand questions, some of them a dozen times. That's enough. I am now clamming, unless and until you tell me why I am suddenly grabbed. If you think you dug up something, what?"

"That will develop as we go along. You left with Wolfe at three-twelve?"

I leaned back and yawned.

He regarded me. He looked up at Stebbins, who was standing. Stebbins said, "You know him. He hasn't said a word since I took him."

Cramer looked at me. "A woman phoned headquarters this afternoon and said she saw you there yesterday at half past three on the terrace in the rear of the penthouse. She was sure about the time. She didn't give her name. I don't have to tell you that if Wolfe came home in a taxi we'll find the driver. You left with him at three-twelve?"

"Thanks for the warning. What time did the woman phone?"

"Three-thirty-nine."

I looked at it. Laura and I had got to the hotel about twenty-five to four. The first thing on my program when I got loose would be to wring her neck and toss her in the river. "Okay," I said, "naturally you're curious. You say the DA is too, so it will be a long discussion. I'll talk after I make a phone call. May I use your phone?"

"In my hearing."

"Certainly, it's your phone."

He moved it across and I got it and dialed. Fritz answered and I asked him to buzz the plant rooms. After a wait Wolfe's voice came, cranky, as it always is when he is interrupted up there.

"Yes?"

"Me. I'm with Cramer in his office. When I got home Stebbins was waiting for me out front with a warrant. A woman, name unknown, phoned the police that she saw me at half past three yesterday afternoon on Miss Rowan's terrace. If you think you'll need me tomorrow you'd better get Parker. Of the two contradictory statements you sent me to check, the first one is true. Tell Fritz to save some of the veal knuckle for me. He can warm it over tomorrow."

"At half past three yesterday afternoon you were with me in the car."

"I know it, but they don't. Cramer would give a month's pay to prove I wasn't."

I hung up and sat back. "Where were we? Oh yes. I left with Mr. Wolfe at three-twelve. Next question?"

7

AT 10:39 Wednesday morning, standing at the curb on Leonard Street waiting for an empty taxi, I said to Nathaniel Parker, the lawyer, "It's a dirty insult. Did you say five *hundred?*"

He nodded. "It is rather a slap, isn't it? As your attorney, I could hardly suggest a higher figure. And of course the cost will be much—here comes one." He stepped off the curb and raised an arm to stop an approaching cab.

The insult, having my bail set at a measly five C's, one-sixtieth of Cal Barrow's, was merely an insult. The injuries were what I would some day, preferably that one, get even for. I had spent fourteen hours in a detention room with too much heat and not enough air; I had asked for corned-beef sandwiches and got ham and rubbery cheese; I had been asked the same questions over and over by four different county and city employees, none of whom had a sense of humor; I had been served lukewarm coffee in a paper thing that leaked; I had not been allowed to use the phone; I had been told three times to take a nap on a bumpy couch and had been roused for more questions just as I was fading out; and I had been asked to sign a statement that had four mistakes in content, three misspelled words, and five typographical errors. And at the end of it all, which must have cost the taxpayers at least a thousand bucks, counting overhead, they were exactly where they had been when they started.

After climbing out of the taxi in front of the old brownstone and thanking Parker for the lift, I mounted the stoop, let myself in, and headed for the office to tell Wolfe that I would be available as soon as I had showered, shaved, brush my teeth, cleaned my nails, brushed my hair, dressed, and had breakfast. It was five minutes past eleven, so he would be down from the plant rooms.

But he wasn't. The overgrown chair behind his desk was empty. Four of the yellow chairs were grouped in front of his desk, facing it, and Fritz was emerging from the front room carrying two more of them. On the couch at the far side at right angles to my desk two people sat holding hands—Cal Barrow and Laura Jay. As I entered Cal jerked his hand away and stood up.

"We came a little early," he said. "We thought you might tell us what's up."

"Roping contest," I said. "I run down the block and you snare me from the stoop. Orchids for prizes." I turned to Fritz. "There's a mermaid in the sink." I wheeled and went to the kitchen, and in a moment he came.

"Where is he?" I demanded.

"In his room with Saul and Fred. Your tie's crooked, Archie, and your—"

"I fell off a horse. Having a party?"

"Yes. Mr. Wolfe—"

"What time?"

"I was told they would come at half past eleven. The lady and gentleman on the couch—"

462

"Came early to hold hands. Excuse my manners, I spent the night with louts and it rubbed off on me. I've got to rinse it off. Could you possibly bring up toast and coffee in eight minutes?"

"Easy. Seven. Your orange juice is in the refrigerator." He went to the range.

I got the glass of juice from the refrigerator, got a spoon and stirred it, took a healthy sip, and headed for the hall and the stairs. One flight up the door of Wolfe's room was at the left, but I kept going and mounted another flight to my room, which was to the right, at the front of the house.

Ordinarily, what with my personal morning fog, it takes me around forty minutes to get rigged for the day, but that time I made it in thirty, with time out for the juice, toast and jam, and coffee. When Fritz came with the tray I asked him to tell Wolfe I was there, and he said he had done so on his way up, and Wolfe was pleased. I don't mean Wolfe said he was pleased; Fritz said he was. Fritz thinks he is a diplomat. At 11:42, cleaner and neater but not gayer, I went down to the office.

They were all there, all of Lily's Monday luncheon guests but Wade Eisler. Lily was in the red leather chair. Cal and Laura were still on the couch, but not holding hands. The other six were on the yellow chairs, Mel Fox, Nan Karlin, and Harvey Greve in front, and Roger Dunning, his wife, and Anna Casado in the rear. Saul Panzer and Fred Durkin were off at the side, over by the big globe.

Wolfe, at his desk, was speaking as I entered. He stopped to dart a glance at me. I halted and inquired politely, "Am I intruding?"

Lily said, "You look pretty spruce for a man who spent the night in jail."

Wolfe said, "I have told them why you were delayed. Now that you're here I'll proceed." As I circled around the company to get to my desk he went on, to them, "I repeat. I have been employed by Miss Rowan and am acting in her interest, but I am solely responsible for what I am about to say. If I defame I alone am liable; she is not. You are here at my invitation, but you came, of course, not to please me but to hear me. I won't keep you longer than I must."

"We have to be at the Garden by a quarter after one," Roger Dunning said. "The show starts at two."

"Yes, sir, I know." Wolfe's eyes went right and then left. "I think it likely that one of you won't be there. I am not prepared to say to one of you, 'You killed Wade Eisler and I can prove it,' but I can offer a suggestion. All of you had the opportunity and the means; you were there, the steel rod was there, the rope was there. None of you was eliminated with certainty by a check of your movements. I made no such check, but the police did, and at that sort of thing they are inimitable. So it was a question of motive, as it often is."

He pinched his nose with a thumb and forefinger, and I suppressed a grin. He is convinced that when a woman is present, let alone four of them, the air is tainted with perfume. Sometimes it is, naturally, but not then and there. I have a good nose and I hadn't smelled any on the cowgirls, and you have to get a good deal closer to Lily than Wolfe was to catch hers. But he pinched his nose.

He resumed. "From the viewpoint of the police two facts pointed to Mr. Barrow: it was his rope, and he found the body. Rather, it seemed to me, they pointed away from him, but let that pass. He had a motive, but no one knew it but Miss Jay and Mr. Goodwin. If the police had known it he would have been charged with murder. I learned of it only yesterday, and I ignored it because Mr. Goodwin told me to. He was convinced that Mr. Barrow was innocent, and he is not easy to convince. Mr. Barrow, you and I are in his debt — you because he saved you from a mortal hazard, and I because he saved me from wasting time and trouble on you."

"Yes, sir," Cal said. "That's not all I owe him." He looked at Laura, and for a second I thought he was going to take her hand in public, but he reined in.

"I also learned yesterday," Wolfe went on, "that Miss Karlin had had a motive, and, according to Miss Jay, that Mr. Fox had had one. But later Miss Jay recanted. Miss Jay, did you tell Mr. Fox of Miss Karlin's experience at Eisler's apartment?"

"No. I must have been—"

"The 'no' is enough. But you did phone the police yesterday that you saw Mr. Goodwin on Miss Rowan's terrace at half past three Monday afternoon?"

"What?" Laura stared. "I never phoned the police anything!"

"You must have. It is of no consequence now, but—"

"I phoned the police," Ellen Dunning said. "I phoned them and told them that because it was true, and I thought they ought to know."

"But you didn't identify yourself."

"No, I didn't. I was afraid to. I didn't know what they might do because I hadn't told about it before. But I thought they ought to know."

I wouldn't have dreamed that the day would ever come when I would owe Laura an apology.

"I doubt," Wolf said, "if you have earned their gratitude. Certainly not mine or Mr. Goodwin's. To go back to Mr. Fox — by the way, Miss Karlin, you were released on bail this morning?"

"Yes," Nan said.

"You were questioned at length?"

"I certainly was."

"Did they worm it out of you that you had told Mr. Fox of your visit to Eisler's apartment?"

"Of course not! I *hadn't* told him! He didn't know about it until yesterday!"

Wolfe's eyes moved. "Do you confirm that, Mr. Fox?"

"I sure do." Mel was on the edge of his chair, leaning forward, his elbows on his knees, his head tilted up. "If this is the suggestion you said you'd offer you can stick it somewhere."

"It isn't. I'm merely clearing away the brush. Even if you and Miss Karlin are lying, if she did tell you, it can't be proven. Therefore it is impossible to establish a motive for you. No, that is not my suggestion. I only—"

"Wait a minute," Roger Dunning blurted. "I've held off up to now, but I might have known I couldn't forever. I told Mel about it — about Nan going to Eisler's place and what he did."

"When?"

"I told him Sunday night. I thought he ought to know because I knew he—"

"You're a dirty liar. Get on your feet." Mel was on his. Dunning's chair was right behind his, and Mel had turned to face him.

"I'm sorry, Mel," Dunning said. "I'm damn sorry, but you can't expect—"

"On your feet!"

"That won't help any, Mel. That won't—"

Mel smacked him on the jaw with his open hand, his right, and his left was on the way to countersmack him at his head swayed, but Saul Panzer and Fred Durkin were there. I was up, but they were closer. They got his arms and backed him up and turned him, and Wolfe spoke.

"If you please, Mr. Fox. I'll deal with him. I know he's lying."

Mel squinted. "How the hell do *you* know he's lying?"

"I know a cornered rat when I see one. Move your chair and sit down. Saul, see if Mr. Dunning has a weapon. We don't need any melodrama."

Dunning was on his feet, focused on Wolfe. "You said Miss Rowan's not responsible," he said, louder than necessary. "You said you are." He turned to Lily. "You hired him. I advise you to fire him quick."

Lily looked at me. I shook my head. Fred moved behind Dunning and took his arms, and Saul went over him. Mel Fox moved his chair away and sat. Cal said something to Laura, and Anna Casado spoke to Harvey Greve. Saul turned and told Wolfe, "No gun." Dunning said to his wife, "Come on, Ellen, we're going." She reached and grabbed his sleeve.

Wolfe spoke. "You are not going, Mr. Dunning. When you do go you will be under escort. I repeat, I can't say to you, 'You killed Wade Eisler and I can prove it,' but I do say that the probability of your guilt is so great that I stake my reputation on it. I must confess that this is impetuous, but your motive couldn't be established without warning you; and I wished to gratify a caprice of my client, Miss Rowan, who invited me to her table for a memorable meal. She wants to deliver you to the District Attorney. Mr. Panzer and Mr. Durking will go along to give him some information they have gathered. You are going willy-nilly. Do you want to challenge me here and now?"

Dunning turned his head to see where his chair was, and sat. He pulled his shoulders up and lifted his chin. "What information?" he asked.

"I'll tell you its nature," Wolfe said. "I doubt if the District Attorney would want me to give you the particulars. But first, what fixed my attention on you? You did—something that you said when you were here yesterday morning. I didn't worm it out of you, you volunteered it, that on Monday at Miss Rowan's place you noticed that Mr. Eisler wasn't on the terrace, and you looked around for him, inside and outside. I asked you when, and you said—I quote you verbatim: 'It wasn't long after Miss Rowan went in for some more coffee—maybe three minutes, maybe more than that.' That was entirely too pat, Mr. Dunning. You were accounting for your absence in case it had been remarked by anyone, and more important, you were accounting for your appearance in the rear of the penthouse in case you had been observed. And you did it gratuitously; I hadn't asked for it."

"I said it because it was true." Dunning licked his lips.

"No doubt. But it suggested the question, what if, instead of looking for him, you were killing him? What if, having got the rope from the closet and concealed it under your jacket, you got Eisler to go with you to that shack on some pretext, or to meet you there? That attracted me. Of the persons there you were the only one whose absence during that period could be established; you yourself avowed it. But then the question, what impelled you? Had you had a cogent motive? To avenge his misconduct with Miss Karlin or with another woman or women?"

Wolf shook his head. "That seemed unlikly, though not impossible. More probably it had been some other factor of your relations with him. But when I put Mr. Panzer and Mr. Durkin on your trail I told them to explore all avenues, and they did so. They found no hint that you had a personal interest in any of the young women Mr. Eisler had pestered, but they gathered facts that were highly suggestive. By the way, a detail: on the phone last evening I asked Miss Rowan if you knew of that shack in the rear of the penthouse, and she said that you not only knew of it, you had been in it. You went there on Sunday to make sure that the terrace would be cleared of obstructions so the ropes could be manipulated, and she took you to the shack to see the grouse that were hanging there. Is that correct, Miss Rowan?"

Lily said yes. She didn't look happy. Since it was beginning to look as if she was going to get her money's worth, she should have been pleased, but she didn't look it.

"That's a lie," Dunning said. "I didn't know about that shack. I never saw it."

Wolfe nodded. "You're desperate. You knew I wouldn't arrange this gathering unless I had discovered something of consequence, so you start wriggling; you try to implicate Mr. Fox, your word against his, and you deny you knew of the shack, your word against Miss Rowan's. Indeed, you started wriggling yesterday, when you had your wife phone the police in an effort to implicate Mr. Goodwin. Probably you have learned that something has been taken from your hotel room. Have you inspected the contents of your suitcase since ten o'clock last evening? The old brown one in the closet that you keep locked?"

"No." Dunning swallowed. "Why should I?"

"I think you have. I have reason to believe that an envelope now in my safe came from that suitcase. I have examined its contents, and while they don't prove that you killed Wade Eisler they are highly suggestive of a possible motive. I said I'll tell you the nature of the information I have but not the particulars. However, you may have one detail." His head turned. "Mr. Greve. You told Mr. Panzer that in the past two years you have purchased some three hundred horses, two hundred steers and bulls, and a hundred and fifty calves, in behalf of Mr. Dunning. Is that correct?"

Harvey didn't look happy either. "That's about right," he said. "That's just rough figures."

"From how many different people did you buy them?"

"Maybe a hundred, maybe more. I scouted around."

"How did you pay for them?"

"Some I gave them a check, but mostly cash. They like cash."

"Your own checks?"

"Yes. Roger made deposits in my account, eight or ten thousand dollars at a time, and I paid out of that."

"Did Mr. Dunning tell you not to divulge the amounts you paid for the animals?"

Harvey screwed up his mouth. "I don't like this."

"Neither do I. I am earning a fee. You are exposing a man who made you a party to a swindle and who is almost certainly a murderer. Did he tell you not to divulge the amounts?"

"Yes, he did."

"Has anyone asked you to?"

"Yes. Wade Eisler. About ten days ago. I told him Roger had all the records and he'd have to ask him."

"Did you tell Mr. Dunning that Mr. Eisler had asked you?"

"Yes."

"That's a lie," Dunning said.

Wolfe nodded. "Again one person's word against yours. But I have the envelope, and I have the names of three other men who have made purchases for you under similar arrangements, and Mr. Durkin and Mr. Panzer have spoken with them. Two of them were asked for figures recently by Wade Eisler, as was Mr. Greve. I don't know how much you cheated Eisler out of, but from the contents of the envelope I surmise that it was many thousands." His head turned. "Saul and Fred, you will escort Mr. Dunning to the District Attorney's office and deliver the envelope and the information you have collected. Archie, get the envelope from the safe."

I moved. As I passed behind Dunning's chair he started up, but Saul's hand on one shoulder and Fred's on the other stopped him. As I opened the safe door Wolfe said, "Give it to Saul. Miss Rowan, do you want Mr. Goodwin to phone the District Attorney to expect you?"

I had never seen Lily so completely got. "Good lord," she said, "I didn't realize. You couldn't drag me. I wish I hadn't . . . No, I don't . . . but I didn't realize how—how *hard* it is."

"You're not going?"

"Of course not!"

"You, Mr. Greve? You might as well. If you don't you'll be sent for later."

"Then I'll go later." Harvey was on his feet. "We've got a show on." He looked at Cal and Mel. "What about it? Think you can handle a calf if I hold his tail?"

"But we can't," Nan Karlin said. "Just go and—we *can't!*"

"The hell we can't," Cal Barrow said. "Come on, Laura."

8

ONE snowy morning in January I got a letter from Cal Barrow.

> Dear Archie:
>
> You used them two dots like that when you wrote me on the typewriter so if you can I can. I read in the paper today about Roger Dunning getting convicted and Laura said I ought to write you and I said she ought to and she said did I want her writing letters to the man she should have married instead of me: and so it went. Remember when I said about that blowout I didn't want to stink it up, well it sure got stunk up. We are making out pretty well here in Texas but it is cold enough to freeze the tits on a steer if he had any. Laura says to give you her love but don't believe it. Best regards.
>
> Yours truly:
Cal

Gambit

1

AT twenty-seven minutes past eleven that Monday morning in February, Lincoln's Birthday, I opened the door between the office and the front room, entered, shut the door, and said, "Miss Blount is here."

Without turning his head Wolfe let out a growl, yanked out some more pages and dropped them on the fire, and demanded, "Who is Miss Blount?"

I tightened my lips and then parted them to say, "She is the daughter of Matthew Blount, president of the Blount Textile Corporation, who is in the coop charged with murder, and she has an appointment with you at eleven-thirty, as you know. If you're pretending you've forgotten, nuts. You knew you couldn't finish that operation in half an hour. Besides, how about the comments I have heard you make about book burners?"

"They are not relevant to this." He yanked out more pages. "I am a man, not a government or a committee of censors. Having paid forty-seven dollars and fifty cents for this book, and having examined it and found it subversive and intolerably offensive, I am destroying it." He dropped the pages on the fire. "I'm in no mood to listen to a woman. Ask her to come after lunch."

"I have also heard you comment about people who dodge appointments they have made."

Pause. More pages. Then: "Very well. Bring her here."

I returned to the office, shutting the door, crossed to the red leather chair near the end of Wolfe's desk where I had seated the caller, and faced her. She tilted her head back to look up at me. She was a brownie, not meaning a Girl Scout — small ears and a small nose, big brown eyes, a lot of brown hair, and a wide mouth that would have been all right with the corners turned up instead of down.

"I'd better explain," I told her. "Mr. Wolfe is in the middle of a fit. It's complicated. There's a fireplace in the front room, but it's never lit because he hates open fires. He says they stultify mental processes. But it's lit now because he's using it. He's seated in front of it, on a chair too small for him, tearing sheets out of a book and burning them. The book is the new edition, the third edition, of Webster's New International Dictionary, Unabridged, published by the G. & C. Merriam Company of Springfield, Massachusetts. He considers it subversive because it threatens the integrity of the English language. In the past week he has given me a thousand examples of its crimes. He says it is a deliberate attempt to murder the — I beg your pardon. I describe the situation at length because he told me to bring you in there, and it will be bad. Even if he hears what you say, his mental processes are stultified. Could you come back later? After lunch he may be human."

She was staring up at me. "He's burning up a *dictionary?*"

"Right. That's nothing. Once he burned up a cookbook because it said to remove the hide from a ham end before putting it in the pot with lima beans. Which he loves most, food or words, is a tossup."

"I don't want to come back." She stood up. "I want to see him now. I *must* see him now."

The trouble was, if I persuaded her to put it off she might not show again. When she had phoned for an appointment it had looked as if we were going to have Matthew Blount for a client, and, judging from the newspapers and the talk around town, he could use plenty of good detective work; and he could pay for it, even at Nero Wolfe's rates. So I didn't want to shoo her out, and also there was her face — not only the turned-down corners of her mouth, but the look in her eyes. There is trouble in the eyes of nearly everyone who comes to that office, but hers were close to desperate. If I eased her out she might go straight to some measly agency with no genius like Wolfe and no dog like me.

"Okay, but I told you," I said, and went to my desk for my notebook, stepped to the door to the front room, and opened it. She came, leaving her coat, pallid mink, on the back of the chair.

I moved up chairs for us, but with Wolfe so close to the fireplace I couldn't put her directly facing him. He rarely stands when a caller enters, and of course he didn't then, with the dictionary, the two-thirds of it that was left, on his lap. He dropped sheets on the fire, turned to look at her, and inquired, "Do you use 'infer' and 'imply' interchangeably, Miss Blount?"

She did fine. She said simply, "No."

"This book says you may. Pfui. I prefer not to interrupt this auto-da-fé. You wish to consult me?"

"Yes. About my father. He is in — he has been arrested for murder. Two weeks ago a man died, he was poisoned —"

"If you please. I read newspapers. Why do you come to me?"

"I know my father didn't do it and I want you to prove it."

"Indeed. Did you father send you?"

"No."

"Did his attorney, Mr. Kalmus?"

"No, nobody sent me. Nobody knows I'm here. I have twenty-two thousand dollars here in my bag." She patted it, brown leather with straps, on her lap. "I didn't have that much, but I sold some things. I can get more if I have to. My father and mother mustn't know I'm doing this, and neither must Dan Kalmus."

"Then it's impossible." Wolfe tore pages loose and dropped them on the fire. "Why must they not know?"

"Because they wouldn't let — they'd stop it. I'm sure my father would." She was gripping the bag. "Mr. Wolfe, I came to you because I had to. I knew I'd have to tell you things I shouldn't tell anybody. This is the first good thing I have ever done. That's the trouble with me, I never do anything bad and I never do anything good, so what's the use? And I'm twenty-two years old, that's why I brought twenty-two thousand dollars."

She patted the bag. "But I'm doing this. Dan Kalmus has been my father's lawyer for years, and he may be good at business things, but he's no good for this. I *know* he isn't; I've known him all my life. Last week I told him he should get you, get you to help, and he smiled at me and said no, he didn't like the way you work. He says he knows what he's doing and it will be all right, but it won't. I'm afraid; I'm scared clear through." She leaned forward. "Mr. Wolfe, my father will be convicted of *murder.*"

Wolfe grunted. He tore pages. "If your father wants to hire me I might consider it without his attorney's approval, but it would be difficult."

She was shaking her head. "He wouldn't. If Dan Kalmus said no, he wouldn't. And my mother wouldn't if my father said no. So it's just me. I can hire you, can't I?"

"Certainly not. Without the cooperation of your father and his attorney I couldn't move a finger." Wolfe tore pages with a little extra force. Twenty-two grand wouldn't break any record, but it would be a nice start on 1962.

"That's silly," Miss Blount said. "Of course your mental processes are stultified by the fire. Why I told Dan Kalmus to get you, and why I came, I thought you could do things that nobody else can do. You're supposed to be a wizard. Everyone says you are. Dan Kalmus himself said you're a wizard, but he doesn't want you taking over his case. That's what he said, 'my case.' It's not his case, it's my father's case!"

"Yes." Wolfe agreed, "your father's case, not yours. You must —"

"I'm making it mine! Didn't I say this is the first good thing I've ever done?" Leaning forward, she grabbed his wrist and jerked his hand away from the dictionary, and hung on to the wrist. "Does a wizard only do easy things? What if you're the only man on earth who can save my father from being convicted of a murder he didn't do? If there was something I could do that no one else on earth could do, I'd do it! You don't need my father or his attorney because I can tell you anything they can. I can tell you things they wouldn't, like that Dan Kalmus is in love with my mother. Dan Kalmus wouldn't, and my father couldn't because he doesn't know it, and he's in jail and I'm not!"

She turned loose the wrist, and Wolfe tore out pages and dropped them on the fire. He was scowling, not at the dictionary. She had hit exactly the right note, calling him a wizard and implying (not inferring) that he was the one and only — after mentioning what she had in her bag.

He turned the scowl on her. "You say you know he didn't do it. Is that merely an opinion seemly for a daughter or can you support it with evidence?"

"I haven't any evidence. All the evidence is against him. But it's not just an opinion. I *know* it. I know my father well enough to —"

"No." He snapped it. "That is cogent for you but not for me. You want to engage me, and pay me, to act on behalf of a man without his knowledge — a man who, in spite of his wealth and standing, has been charged with murder and locked up. The evidence must be strong. Your father wouldn't be my client; you would."

"All right, I will." She opened the bag.

"I said *would*. It's preposterous, but it is also tempting. I need to know — but first what Mr. Goodwin and I already know." His head turned. "Archie. What do we know?"

"The crop?" I asked. "Or the high lights?"

"Everything. Then we'll see if Miss Blount has anything to add."

"Well." I focused on the prospective client. "This is from the papers and some talk I've heard. If I'm wrong on anything don't try to remember until I'm through, stop me. The Gambit Club is a chess club with two floors in an old brick building on West Twelfth Street. It has about sixty members, business and professional men and a couple of bankers. As chess clubs go, it's choosy. Tuesday evening, January thirtieth, two weeks ago tomorrow, it had an affair. A man named Paul Jerin, twenty-six years old, not a member, was to play simultaneous blindfold games with twelve of the members.

"About Paul Jerin. I'm mixing the papers and the talk I've heard without separating them. He was a screwball. He had three sources of income: from writing verses and gags for greeting cards, from doing magic stunts at parties, and from shooting craps. Also he was hot at chess, but he only played chess for fun, no tournament stuff. You knew him. You met him — how long ago?"

"About a year. I met him at a party where he did tricks."

"And he cultivated you — or you cultivated him. I've heard it both ways — of course you realize there's a lot of talk, a thing like this. Learning that he played chess, you arranged for him to play a game with your father, at your home. Then he came again, and again. How often? I've heard different versions."

"He played chess with my father only three times. Three evenings. He said it was no fun because it was too easy. The last time he gave my father odds of a rook and beat him. That was months ago."

"But aside from chess you saw a lot of him. One version, you were going to marry him, but your father —"

"That's not true. I never dreamed of marrying him. And I didn't see a lot of him. The police have asked me about it, and I know exactly. In the last three months I saw him just five times, at parties, mostly dancing. He was a good dancer. No girl with any sense would have *married* him."

I nodded. "So much for talk. But you got your father to arrange that affair at the Gambit Club." We had to keep our voices up because of the noise Wolfe made tearing paper.

"They've asked me about that too," she said. "The way it happened, Paul suggested it to me, he said it would be fun to flatten their noses, and I told my father, but I didn't *get* him to do it. He said he thought two or three of the members could beat Paul with him playing blindfold, and he arranged it."

"Okay, he arranged it. Of course that's important. Did your father know that Paul always drank hot chocolate when he was playing chess?"

"Yes. Paul drank hot chocolate when he was doing almost anything."

"Then we'll tackle the affair of January thirtieth. It was stag. Men only."

"Yes."

"This is from the papers. I read murders in the papers, but with full attention only when we're in on it, so I may slip up. If I do, stop me. No one was there but club members, about forty of them, and Paul Jerin, and the steward, named Bernard Nash, and the cook, named Tony Laghi. In a big room on the ground floor there were twelve chess tables, in two rows, six tables in each row, ranged along the two long walls, and at each table a club member sat with his back to the wall. They were the players. That left room in the middle, the length of the room, for the other members to move around and watch the play. Right?"

"Yes."

"But four of the other members didn't just watch the play, they were messengers. Paul Jerin was in a smaller room to the rear of the house which one paper, I think the *Times*, said contains the best chess library in the country. He was sitting on a couch, and, after play started, he was alone in the room. The tables were designated by numbers, and each messenger served three tables. When play started a messenger went in to Jerin and told him the table —"

"Not when play started. A man playing blindfold has white at all the boards and makes the first move."

"I should think he'd need it. Anyway, whenever a member at one of the tables made a move the messenger serving that table went in to Jerin and told him the table number and the move, and Jerin told him his move in reply, and he went back out to the table and reported it. Right?"

"Yes."

"Okay, but I don't believe it. I have monkeyed with chess a little, enough to get the idea, and I do not believe that any man could carry twelve simultaneous games in his head without seeing the boards. I know men have done it, even twenty games, but I don't believe it."

Wolfe grunted. "One hundred and sixty-nine million, five hundred and eighteen thousand, eight hundred and twenty-nine, followed by twenty-one ciphers. The number of ways the first ten moves, both sides, may be played. A man who can play twelve simultaneous games blindfold is a *lusus naturae*. Merely a freak."

"Is that material?" I asked him.

"No."

I returned to Sally Blount. She had told me on the phone that her name was Sarah but everyone called her Sally and she preferred it. "Play was to start at eight-thirty," I said, "but it actually started at eight-forty, ten minutes late. From then on Jerin was alone in the library except when one of the messengers entered. I think I can name them. Charles W. Yerkes, banker. Daniel Kalmus, attorney-at-law. Ernst Hausman, wealthy retired broker, one of the founders of the club. Morton Farrow, a nephew of Mrs. Matthew Blount, your mother." I paused, shutting my eyes. I opened them. "I pass. I'm sure one of the papers said what your cousing Morton does for a living, but I can't recall it."

"He's in my fther's business." Her brows were up, making her eyes even bigger. "You must have a good memory, even without your full attention."

"My memory is so good I'm practically a freak, but we keep newspapers for two weeks and I admit I looked them over after you phoned. From here on you may know things that haven't been published. The police and the District Attorney always save some details. I know from the papers that your father played at Table Number Six. That the steward and the cook, Bernard Nash and Tony Laghi, were in the kitchen in the basement, down a flight. That shortly after play started a pot of hot chocolate was taken from the kitchen to Paul Jerin in the library, and he drank some, I don't know how much, and about half an hour later he told one of the messengers, Yerkes, the banker, that he didn't feel well, and at or about nine-thirty he told another messenger, Kalmus, the lawyer, that he couldn't go on; and Kalmus went and brought a doctor, one of the players — I don't know which table — named Victor Avery. Dr. Avery asked Jerin some questions and sent someone to a drug store on Sixth Avenue for something. By the time the medicine arrived Jerin was worse and the doctor dosed him. In another half an hour Jerin was even worse and they sent for an ambulance. He arrived at St. Vincent's Hospital in the ambulance, accompanied by Dr. Avery, at a quarter to eleven, and he died at twenty minutes past three. Later the Medical Examiner found arsenic in him. The *Times* didn't say how much, but the *Gazette* said seven grains. Any correction?"

"I don't know."

"Not published if the arsenic was in the chocolate. Was it?"

"I don't know."

"Also not published, the name of the person who took the chocolate from the kitchen up to the library. Do you know that?"

"Yes. My father did."

I gawked at her. Wolfe's hand stopped short on its way to the fire with pages. I spoke. "But your father was at Table Six, playing chess. Wasn't he?"

"Yes. But when he made his second move the messenger for that table, Mr. Hausman, wasn't there at the moment, and he got up and went to see if Paul had been supplied with chocolate. Table Six was at the end of the room next to the library. The chocolate hadn't been brought, and my father went down to the kitchen and got it."

"And took it up to Jerin himself?"

"Yes."

Wolfe shot a glance at her. I took a breath. "Of course I believe you, but how do you know?"

"My father told me. The next day. He wasn't arrested until Saturday — of course you know that. He told my mother and me exactly what happened. That's partly why I know he didn't do it, the way he told us about it, the way he took it for granted that we would know he didn't do it." Her eyes went to Wolfe. "You would say that's not cogent for you, but it certainly is for me. I *know.*"

"Okay," I said, "he delivered the chocolate. Putting it on a table by the couch Jerin was sitting on?"

"Yes. A tray, with the pot and a cup and saucer and a napkin."

"You say your father told you all about it. Did Jerin eat or drink anything besides the chocolate?"

"No. There was nothing else."

"Between the time your father took him the chocolate and the time he told Yerkes he didn't feel well, about half an hour, did anyone enter the library besides the messengers?"

"No. At least my father thought not, but he wasn't absolutely certain." She looked at Wolfe. "I can ask him. You said you couldn't move a finger without his cooperation, but I can get to see him and ask him anything you want me to. Of course without telling him it's for you."

No comment. He tore pages out.

I eyed her. "You said you don't know if the arsenic was in the chocolate. Didn't your father mention if there was any left in the pot and if it was kept for the police?"

"Yes, it was kept, but the pot was full."

"Full? Hadn't Jerin drunk any?"

"Yes, he had drunk a lot. When Mr. Yerkes told my father that Paul had told him he wasn't feeling well, my father went to the library. The pot had a little left in it, and the cup was half full. He took them down to the kitchen and rinsed them out. The cook and steward said nothing had been put in but milk and powdered chocolate and sugar. They had some more ready, and they filled the pot, and my father took it up to the library with a clean cup. Apparently Paul didn't drink any of that because the pot was still full."

I was staring at her, speechless. Wolfe wasn't staring, he was glaring. "Miss Blount," he said. "Either your father is an unexampled jackass, or he is innocent."

She nodded. "I know. I said I'd have to tell you things I shouldn't tell anybody. I've already told you Dan Kalmus is in love with my mother, and now this. I don't know whether my father has told the police about it. I suppose the cook and steward have, but maybe they haven't. But I had to tell you, I have to tell you everything I know, so you can decide what to do. Don't I?"

"Yes. I commend you. People seldom tell me everything they know. The cook and steward have of course told the police; no wonder your father has been charged with murder." Wolfe shut his eyes and tried leaning back, but it was no go in that chair. In the made-to-order oversized chair at his desk that was automatic when he wanted to consider something, leaning back and closing his eyes, and, finding that it wouldn't work, he let out a growl. He straightened up and demanded, "You have money in that bag?"

She opened it and took out a fat wad of bills with rubber bands around them. "Twenty-two thousand dollars," she said, and held it out to him.

He didn't take it. "You said you sold some things. What things? Yours?"

"Yes. I had some in my bank account, and I sold some jewelry."

"Your own jewelry?"

"Yes. Of course. How could I sell someone else's?"

"It has been done. Archie. Count it."

I extended a hand and she gave me the wad. As I removed the rubber bands and started counting, Wolfe tore out pages and dropped them on the fire. There wasn't much of the dictionary left, and, while I counted, five-hundreds and then C's, he tore and dropped. I counted it twice to make sure, and when I finished there was no more dictionary except the binding.

"Twenty-two grand," I said.

"Will this burn?" he asked.

"Sure; it's buckram. It may smell a little. You knew you were going to burn it when you bought it. Otherwise you would have ordered leather."

No response. He was bending forward, getting the binding satisfactorily placed. There was still enough fire, since Fritz had used wood as well as kindling. Watching the binding starting to curl, he spoke. "Take Miss Blount to the office and give her a receipt. I'll join you shortly."

2

TWENTY-TWO thousand dollars is not hay. Even after expenses and taxes it would make a healthy contribution to the upkeep of the old brownstone on West Thirty-fifth Street, owned by Wolfe, lived in and worked in by him, by Fritz Brenner, chef and housekeeper, and by me, and worked in by Theodore

Horstmann, who spent ten hours a day, and sometimes more, nursing the ten thousand orchids in the plant rooms at the top of the house. I once calculated the outgo per hour for a period of six months, but I won't mention the figure because the District Director of Internal Revenue might read this and tell one of his sniffers to compare it with the income tax report. As for the twenty-two grand, received in cash, he would find it included in income.

But when, at a quarter past one, I returned to the office after letting Sally Blount out and put the wad in the safe, I was by no means chipper. We had the wad with no string attached; Wolfe had made it clear that his only commitment was to give it a try, but it seemed more than likely that we were licked before we started, and that's hard to take for the ego of a wizard, not to mention a dog.

I had filled a dozen pages of my notebook with such items as: 1. As far as Sally knew, none of the four messengers, the only ones besides her father and the cook and steward who had been in reaching distance of the chocolate, had ever seen Paul Jerin before or had any connection with him; and if they had she would almost certainly have known because they were all in the Blounts' circle, one way or another, and she saw them fairly frequently. Ditto for Bernard Nash and Tony Laghi, the steward and cook, though she had never seen them.

2. The messengers. Charles W. Yerkes, the banker, had occasional social contacts with the Blounts. Blount was on the Board of Directors of Yerkes's bank. Yerkes enjoyed being in the same room with Mrs. Blount, Sally's mother, but so did lots of men. In my notes I included a parenthesis, a guess that Sally thought it would be just as well if men would take time out from looking at her mother to give her a glance now and then. That was a little odd, since Sally herself was no eyesore, but of course I hadn't seen her mother.

3. Morton Farrow, age thirty-one, was not a wizard, but wasn't aware of it. He drew a good salary from the Blount Textile Corporation only because he was Mrs. Blount's nephew, and thought he was underpaid. I'm translating what Sally told us, not quoting it.

4. Ernst Hausman, retired broker, a lifelong friend of Matthew Blount, was Sally's godfather. He was an unhappy man and would die unhappy because he would give ten million dollars to be able to play a chess master without odds and mate him, and there was no hope. He hadn't played a game with Blount for years because he suspected Blount of easing up on him. He had disapproved of the idea of having Paul Jerin come to the club and do his stunt; he thought no one but members should ever be allowed in. In short, a suffering snob.

5. Daniel Kalmus, the lawyer, had for years been counsel for Blount's corporation. Sally had some kind of strong feeling for him, but I wasn't sure what it was, and I'm still not sure, so I'll skip it. She had said that Yerkes was in his forties, and Hausman, her godfather, was over seventy, but she said definitely that Kalmus was fifty-one. If a twenty-two-year-old girl can rattle off the age of a man more than twice as old who is not a relative and with whom she isn't intimate, there's a reason. There were other indications, not only things she said but her tone and manner. I put it down that her not trusting Kalmus — she always said "Dan Kalmus," not "Mr. Kalmus" or just "Kalmus" — that her not trusting him to pull her father out of the hole was only partly because she thought he couldn't. The other part was a suspicion that even if he could, he wouldn't. If Blount were sent to the chair, or even sent up for life, Mrs. Blount might be available. Sally didn't say that, but she mentioned for the third time that Dan Kalmus was in love with her mother. Wolfe asked her, "Is your mother

in love with him?" and she said, "Good heavens, no. She's not in love with anyone — except of course my father."

6. So much for the messengers. Of the other items in my notebook I'll report only one, the only one that was material. If any container that had held arsenic had been found the newspapers didn't know about it, but that's the kind of detail the police and DA often save. When Wolfe asked Sally if she knew anything about it I held my breath. I wouldn't have been surprised if she had said yes, a bottle half full of arsenic trioxide had been found in her father's pocket. Why not? But she said that as far as she knew no container had been found. Dr. Avery, who was usually called on by her father or mother when a doctor was needed, had told her father two or three days after the affair, before Blount had been arrested, that after questioning and examining Jerin he had considered the possibility of poison and had looked around; he had even gone down to the kitchen; and he had found nothing. And four days ago, last Thursday, when Sally, after two sleepless nights, had gone to his office to get a prescription for a sedative, he had said that he had been told by an assistant DA that no container had ever been found, and now that Blount had been charged and was in custody he doubted if the police would try very hard to find one. The police hadn't been called in until after Jerin died, and Blount, who had walked to the hospital, only a couple of blocks from the Gambit Club, after the ambulance had taken Jerin, had had plenty of opportunity to ditch a small object if he had one he wanted to get rid of. Dr. Avery, convinced that his friend and patient Matthew Blount was innocent, had told Sally that someone must have had a container and disposed of it, and had advised her to tell Kalmus to hire a detective to try to find it. It was that advice from Dr. Avery that had given Sally the idea of coming to Nero Wolfe.

One item not in the notebook. At the end Wolfe told her that it was absurd to suppose that he could act without the knowledge of Kalmus and her father. He would have to see people. At the very least he would have to see the four men who had been messengers, and, since he never left the house on business, they would have to come to him, and Sally would have to bring them or send them. Inevitably Kalmus would hear about it and would tell Blount. Sally didn't like that. For a couple of minutes it had looked as if there was going to be an exchange, me handing her the wad and her giving me back the receipt, but after chewing on her lip for twenty seconds she decided to stick. She asked Wolfe who he wanted to see first, and he said we would let her know. She asked when, and he said he had no idea, he had to consider it.

At a quarter past one, when I returned to the office, not chipper, after letting her out, and put the wad in the safe, he was sitting straight, his mouth pressed so tight he had no lips, his palms flat on the desk pad, scowling at the door to the front room. It could have been either his farewell to the subversive dictionary or his greeting to a hopeless job, and it wouldn't help matters any to ask him which. As I swung the safe door shut, Fritz appeared to announce lunch, saw Wolfe's pose and expression, looked at me, found my face no better, said, "All right, you tell him," and went.

Of course business was out at the table, but Wolfe refuses to let anything whatever spoil a meal if the food is good, as it always is in that house, and he managed to pretend that life was sweet and the goose hung high. But when we finished the coffee, got up, and crossed the hall back to the office, he went to his desk, sat, rested fists on the chair arms, and demanded, "Did he do it?"

I raised a brow. If Sally herself had been suspected of murder I would have humored him, since I am supposed, by him, after an hour or so in the company of an attractive young woman, to be able to answer any question he wants to ask about her. But it was stretching it too far to assume that my insight extended to relatives I had never seen, even a father.

"Well," I said. "I admit that if there is anything to the idea of guilt by association there can also be innocence by association, but I recall that you once remarked to Lewis Hewitt that the transference —"

"Shut up!"

"Yes, sir."

"Why didn't you intervene? Why didn't you stop me?"

"My job is starting you, not stopping you."

"Pfui. Why in heaven's name did I consent? The money? Confound it, I'll take to a cave and eat roots and berries. Money!"

"Nuts are good too, and the bark of some trees, and for meat you could try bats. It was only partly the money. She said you can do things no one else on earth can do, so when it developed that prying Blount loose is obviously something that no one on earth can do you were stuck. Whether Blount did it or not is beside the point. You have to prove he didn't even if he did. Marvelous. By far your best case."

"Yours too. Ours. You didn't stop me." He reached to put a finger on the button and pressed it, two short and one long, the beer signal. That was bad. He never rings for beer until an hour after lunch, giving him half an hour or so before he is to leave for his four-to-six afternoon session with Theodore in the plant rooms. I went to my desk. Seated there, my back is to the door to the hall, but in the mirror before me I saw Fritz enter with the beer and stop two paces in to aim his eyes at me with a question in them. One of my two million functions, as Fritz knows, is to keep Wolfe from breaking his beer rules. So I swiveled and said, "Okay. He's taking to a cave, and I'm going along. This is a farewell fling."

Fritz stood. "That woman? Or the dictionary?"

"I don't want the beer," Wolfe said. "Take it back."

Fritz turned and went. Wolfe took in a bushel of air through his nose as far down as it would go, and let it out through his mouth. "I agree," he said. "Consideration of his guilt or innocence would be futile. Either we proceed on the assumption that he is innocent or we withdraw. Do you wish to get that stuff from the safe and go and return it to her?"

"No. We took it and let her go. You know damn well why I didn't try to stop you. It was too good to pass up — the chance of seeing you tackle one that was absolutely impossible."

"You're prepared to assume that Mr. Blount is innocent?"

"Hell, I have to. As you say."

"Then someone else is guilty. I begin by eliminating the cook and the steward."

"Good. That simplifies it. Why?"

"Look at it. The arsenic was in the chocolate. Therefore if either —"

"No. Not known. The only arsenic found was inside Jerin. The pot was full of fresh chocolate, no arsenic, the cup was clean, and no container was found. Not known."

"But it is." Usually Wolfe's tone had a trace of satisfaction when he corrected me, but that time he didn't bother. "After four days of investigation the District

Attorney charged Mr. Blount with murder. Blount couldn't possibly have given Jerin arsenic in any medium other than the chocolate. Before arresting him, the possibility that the arsenic had been administered in some other medium had to be eliminated beyond question, and at that sort of inquiry the police are highly competent. Certainly they have established that Jerin didn't swallow the arsenic before he arrived at the Gambit Club, and at the club he swallowed only the chocolate; otherwise they wouldn't have charged Blount."

"Check," I conceded. "The cook and steward?"

"This is not conclusive, only strongly probable. There they were in the kitchen, preparing the chocolate. One or both of them knew Mr. Jerin, had reason to wish him dead, knew he was coming to the club, and knew the chocolate was for him. Confine it to one. He puts arsenic in the chocolate. At the time he does so he doesn't know that Mr. Blount will come for it; he supposes that it will be taken to the library by himself or his colleague. He doesn't know that later Mr. Blount will bring the pot and cup down and rinse them out. He doesn't know that any club member has an animus toward Mr. Jerin—unless you think I should allow that?"

"No."

"He doesn't know if there will be an opportunity for anyone else to put something in the chocolate. He does know that the police will certainly discover his connection, whatever it is, with Jerin. But he puts arsenic in the chocolate?"

"No. At least we can save them for the last. Of course the cops have checked on them. With Blount and the cook and steward out, what you have left is the messengers. Unless someone sneaked in uninvited?"

He shook his head. "Mr. Blount told his daughter only that he thought not, he wasn't absolutely certain, but his table was near the door to the library. And it would have been foolhardy. Only the messengers were supposed to go in to Mr. Jerin, and anyone else entering would have been observed and noted. It would have been rash beyond sanity. I exclude it, tentatively. But there is one other possibility besides the messengers, Mr. Jerin himself. He had arsenic in a soluble capsule, put it in his mouth, and washed it down with the chocolate. Shall I deal with that?"

"No, thanks. I don't need help with that one. Deal with the messengers. I grant opportunity. He goes in to report a move, shutting the door. We assume that he shut the door on account of the noise made by the spectators moving around in the big room?"

"Yes."

"Right. He knows that another messenger may enter at any moment, but he only needs five seconds. The pot is there on the table. Jerin, on the couch, has his eyes closed, concentrating. He has the arsenic ready, say in a paper spill, and in it goes. He wouldn't have to stir it. Nothing to it. Shall I name him?"

"Yes indeed."

"Ernst Hausman, the chess fiend. He had been against inviting Jerin to come, but since he was there, there was his chance at a guy who could give odds of a rook to Blount, who could beat *him*. He would have liked to poison all the chess masters alive, beginning with the world champion, who I understand is a Russian."

"Botvinnik."

"Not only a *lusus naturae*, but also a Commie. I know of no case on record where that was the motive, killing a man because he played chess too well, but everything has to have a first. I am not blathering. Hausman may be off the rails."

Wolfe grunted. "Not may be. Is. If he would give a fortune to excel at chess. Then you dismiss the other three."

"I file them. Until I take a look at Hausman. The client says they had never seen Jerin, though they may have heard of him, from her. Of course we might cut a motive to fit the lawyer, Dan Kalmus. He's not really in love with her mother, he's in love with her. Being a married man, if he is, he has to hide his passion for a virgin, if she is, so when he's with the Blounts he ogles the mother as a cover. He has the impression that Sally has fallen for Paul Jerin, which could be true in spite of what she told you, and the thought of her holding hands with another man is unbearable, so he buys some arsenic."

"That's a little farfetched."

"Murder is usually farfetched. Would we settle for making Blount merely an accessory? We have to assume he didn't commit the murder, sure, but he could have suspected that Hausman or Kalmus had doctored the chocolate, so he took care of the pot and cup."

"No." Wolfe shook his head. "Our assumption is that Mr. Blount is not involved. He took the pot and cup, and emptied and cleaned them, because he thought that Jerin's indisposition might have been caused by something in the chocolate — as indeed it had been. A natural and proper action." He closed his eyes, but he didn't lean back, so he wasn't thinking, he was merely suffering. His lips twitched. After a dozen or so twitches he opened his eyes and spoke. "At least we have a free field. The police and District Attorney have Mr. Blount in custody and are committed; they have no interest in our targets except as witnesses, and of course they have signed statements from them. There will be no jostling." He looked up at the wall clock. "Mr. Cohen is in his office?"

"Sure."

"See him. Besides the published accounts we have information from only one source, Miss Blount, and we have no knowledge of either her competence or her veracity. Tell Mr. Cohen that I have engaged to inquire into certain aspects of this matter, and I need —"

"It'll be tough — I mean for him. He'll know that can mean only one thing, that you've been hired to get Blount out, and you think it can be done or you wouldn't have taken the job, and to expect him to sit on *that* — I don't know."

"I don't expect him to sit on it."

"He can print it?"

"Certainly. As I told Miss Blount, my intervention can't be kept secret, and the sooner the murderer knows of it the better. He may think it necessary to do something."

"Yeah. Of course if — no. I'll have to tie a string on my finger to remind me that Blount didn't do it." I got up. "If I don't tell Lon who hired you he'll assume it was Blount. Kalmus."

"Let him. You can't prescribe his assumptions."

"I wouldn't try. Any particular point or points?"

"No. *All* points."

I went to the hall, got my hat and coat from the rack, let myself out, and nearly got pushed off the stoop by a gust of the icy winter wind.

3

IN his own little room on the twentieth floor of the *Gazette* building, which had LON COHEN on the door but no title, two doors down the hall from the corner office of the publisher, Lon cradled the phone, one of three on his desk, turned to me, and said, "You may be in time for the twilight if it's a quickie. Front page?"

I slumped and crossed my legs, showing that there was plenty of time. I shook my head. "Not even the second section. I'm just looking for scraps that may not be fit to print. About Paul Jerin and the Gambit Club."

"You don't say." He ran a palm over his hair, which was almost black and slicked back and up over his sloping dome. I knew that gesture well, but had learned the hard way not to try to interpret it. He was next to the best of the poker players I spent one night a week with, the best being Saul Panzer, whom you will meet later on. He asked, "Doing research for a treatise on adult delinquency?"

"All I would need for that would be a mirror. Nero Wolfe is inquiring into certain aspects of the matter."

"Well well. Just for curiosity?"

"No. He has a client."

"The hell he has. For release when?"

"Oh, tomorrow."

"Who's the client?"

"I don't know. He won't tell me."

"I'll bet he won't." Lon leaned forward. "Now look, Archie. It's basic. In a newspaper sentences must always be active, never passive. You can't say 'Mr. Kaczynski was bitten by a woman today.' You must say 'Miss Mable Flum bit Mr. Kaczynski today.' The lead-off on this must be, 'Daniel Kalmus, attorney for Matthew Blount, has engaged Nero Wolfe to get evidence that Blount did not murder Paul Jerin.' Then further along mention the fact that Wolfe is the greatest detective this side of outer space and has never failed to deliver, with the invaluable assistance of the incomparable Archie Goodwin. That's the way to do it."

I was grinning at him. "I like it. Then the next day you could feature Kalmus's denial."

"Are you saying it's not Kalmus?"

"I'm not saying. What the hell, it's just as good, even better, leaving it open who hired him, hinting that you know but you're not telling. Next day they'll buy a million *Gazettes* to find out."

"Are you going to fill it in any? Now?"

"No. Not a word. Just that he's been hired and has been paid a retainer."

"Can we say we have it direct from you?"

"Sure."

He turned and got at a phone, the green one. It didn't take long, since he only had enough for one short paragraph. He hung up and turned to me. "Just in time. Now for tomorrow's follow-up. I don't expect words and music, but what's the slant that makes Wolfe think—"

"Whoa." I showed him a palm. "You've got the gall of a journalist. It's my turn. I want everything about everybody that you know or guess but haven't printed."

"That would take all night. First, off the record, does Wolfe actually expect to spring Blount?"

"Off the record, that's the idea." I had my notebook out. "Now. Have they found a container with arsenic in it?"

"I'll be damned." His head was cocked. "Does Wolfe know that Blount went down to the kitchen for the chocolate and took it up to Jerin?"

"Yes."

"Does he know that after Jerin had drunk most of the chocolate Blount took the cup and pot away and rinsed them out?"

"Yes."

"Does he know that Blount chased Jerin out of his apartment and told him to stay away from his daughter?"

"No. Do you?"

"I couldn't prove it, but the word is that the cops can. And one of our men got it—a good man, Al Proctor—he got it from a friend of Jerin's. Do you want to talk to Proctor?"

"No. What for? That would only help on a motive for Blount, and since Blount's innocent why waste time on it? Have they—"

"I *will* be damned. My God, Archie, this is hot! Come on, give! Off the record until you say the word. Have I ever fudged on you?"

"No, and you won't now. Skip it, Lon. Nothing doing. Have they found a container?"

He reached for a phone, sat a moment with his fingers on it, vetoed it, and settled back. "No," he said, "I don't think so. If they had I think one of our men would know."

"Did Jerin know or suspect he had been poisoned?"

"I don't know."

"*Gazette* men must have talked with men who were there."

"Sure, but the last four hours, at the hospital, only doctors and nurses were with him and they don't talk."

"At the club, Jerin didn't point to someone and say, 'You did this, you bastard'?"

"No. If he had, whom should he have pointed to?"

"I'll tell you later. Not today. Who went to the hospital? I know Dr. Avery went in the ambulance, and Blount went. Who else?"

"Three of the club members. One of them was Kalmus, the lawyer. I can get the names of the other two if you want them."

"Not unless it was Hausman or Yerkes or Farrow."

"It wasn't."

"Then don't bother. What's the talk in the trade? I've heard this and that, at the Flamingo and around, but I don't see much of journalists except you. What are they saying? Have they got angles?"

"None that you would like. Of course there were plenty of angles the first few days, but not since they took Blount. Now the big question is did Jerin lay Sally or didn't he. That wouldn't interest you."

"Not a particle. Then they all think Blount's wrapped up? No minority opinion?"

"None worth mentioning. That's why this from you, and Wolfe, is a bomb. Now there *will* be angles."

"Fine. So there's been no interest in anyone else since Blount was charged, but how about before that? The four messengers. Hausman, Yerkes, Farrow, Kalmus. You must have got quite a collection of facts you didn't print."

He eyed me exactly the way he eyed me when I took another look at my hole card, lifted one brow, and raised him the limit. "I'd give more than a nickel," he said, "I'd give a shiny new dime, to know which one of them you want to know about. Damn it, we could help. We have our share of beetle-brains, but also there's a couple of good men. At your service."

"Wonderful," I said. "Send me their names and phone numbers. Tell them not to call me, I'll call them. Now tell me about the messengers. Start with Kalmus."

He told me. Not only what he had in his head; he sent for the files. I filled eight pages of my notebook with the most useless-looking conglomeration of facts you could imagine. Of course you never know; Wolfe had once been able to crack a very hard nut only because Fred Durkin had reported that a certain boy had bought bubble gum at two different places, but there's no point in bothering to tell you that Yerkes had been a halfback at Yale or that Farrow had a habit of getting bounced out of night clubs. I'll keep it to a minimum:

Ernst Hausman, seventy-two, retired but still owner of a half interest in a big Wall Street firm, was a widower with no children, no friends (Blount didn't count?), and no dogs. His obsession with chess was common knowledge. Owned the finest collection of chessmen in the world, some two hundred sets, one of Imperial jade, white and green.

Morton Farrow, thirty-one, single, lived at the Blount apartment on Fifth Avenue (not mentioned by Sally). He was an assistant vice-president of the Blount Textiles Corporation. Had got a ticket for speeding the night of January thirtieth, the night of the affair at the Gambit Club.

Charles W. Yerkes, forty-four, senior vice-president of the Continental Bank and Trust Company, was married and had two children. At the age of twenty-six he had come out eleventh in a field of fourteen in the annual tournament for the United States chess championship, and had entered no tournament since.

Daniel Kalmus, fifty-one, prominent corporation lawyer, a partner in the firm of McKinney, Best, Kalmus, and Green, was a widower, with four children, all married. One of the club members had told a *Gazette* reporter that he had been surprised that Kalmus had been a messenger instead of playing, because he thought that Kalmus, the club's best player, could have beaten Jerin.

And so forth. While I was going through the files Lon made a couple of phone calls and received a couple, but he kept me in a corner of his eye. Presumably the idea was that if Wolfe was particularly interested in one of that quartet I might show it by a flicker of the eye or a twist of the lip. Not wanting to disappoint him, I eased a slip of paper out and slipped it up my cuff, and later, when I put the folders back on his desk, he asked, "Would you like a copy of the item in your sleeve?"

"All right, I tried," I said, and fingered it out and forked it over. All it had on it, scribbled in pencil, was *2/8 11:40 A.M. LC says MJN says too much chess AR.* I said, "If LC means Lon Cohen that may settle it."

"Go climb a tree." He dropped it in the wastebasket. "Anything else?"

"A few little details. What's Sally Blount like?"

"I thought Blount was out of it."

"He is, but she may have some facts we need, and it'll help to know what to expect when I see her. Is she a man-eater?"

"No. Of course she's still an angle with us, and presumably with the cops. With most girls of her age and class you'll find a little dirt, sometimes a lot, if you dig, but apparently not with her. She seems to be clean, which should be newsworthy but isn't. We have nothing on her, even with Paul Jerin, and I doubt if the cops have."

"College?"

"Bennington. Graduated last year."

"How about her mother? Of course she's not an angle, but she may have some facts too. Know anything about her?"

"I sure do. I've told my wife that she needn't wonder what I'll do if she dies. I'll get Anna Blount. I don't know how, but I'll get her."

"So you know her?"

"I've never met her, but I've seen her a few times, and once is enough. Don't ask me why. It's not just looks or the call of the glands. She's probably a witch and doesn't know it. If she knew it it would show, and that would spoil it. As you say, she's not an angle, but, with her husband arrested for murder, she's news, and it appears that I'm not the only one. She attracts. She pulls."

"And?"

"Apparently there is no and. Apparently she's clean too. It's hard to believe, but I'd like to believe it. As you know, I'm happily married, and my wife is healthy, and I hope she lives forever, but it's nice to know that such a one as Anna Blount is around just in case. I can't understand why I don't dream about her. What the hell, a man's dreams are private. If you see her be sure to tell me how you take it."

"Glad to." I rose. "I'm not thanking you this time because I gave more than I got."

"I want more. Damn it, Archie, just a little something for tomorrow?"

I told him he would get more if and when there was more, got my coat and hat from the other chair, and went.

I walked downtown. That would have been ideal for arranging my mind, my legs working, my lungs taking in plenty of good cold air, and a few snowflakes coming at me and then away from me, if there had been anything in my mind to arrange. Even worse, my mind was refusing to cooperate on the main point. I had bought the assumption that Matthew Blount was innocent, but my mind hadn't. It kept trying to call my attention to the known facts, which was subversive.

Headed south on Sixth Avenue, my watch said 4:30 as I approached Thirty-fifth Street, and instead of turning I continued downtown. Wolfe wouldn't come down from the plant rooms until six o'clock, and there was no point in going home just to sit at my desk and try to get my mind on something useful when there was nothing useful to get it on. So I kept going, clear to Twelfth Street, turned left, stopped half way down the long block, and focused on a four-story brick building, painted gray with green trim, across the street. A brass plate to the right of the door, nice and shiny, said GAMBIT CLUB. I crossed the street, entered the vestibule, tried the door, but it was locked, pushed the button, got a click, opened the door, and entered.

Of course I was just kidding my mind. There wasn't a chance in a million that I would get any new facts for it to switch to, but at least I could show it that I was in charge. There was a long rack in the hall, and, as I disposed of my coat and hat, a man appeared in an open doorway on the right and said, "Yes, sir?"

It was Bernard Nash, the steward. There had been a picture of him in the *Gazette*. He was tall and narrow with a long sad face. I said, "I'm checking something," and made for the doorway, but without giving me room to pass he asked, "Are you from the police?"

"No," I said, "I'm a gorilla. How often do you have to see a face?"

He would probably have asked to see my buzzer if I hadn't kept moving, and I brushed against him as I went through. It was the big room. Evidently the chess tables had been specially placed for the affair, for there were now more than a dozen — more like two dozen — and three of them were in use, with a couple of kibitzers at one. Halting only for a quick glance around, I headed for an open door at the rear end, followed by the steward. If Table Six, Blount's, had been in the row at the left wall, he had been sitting only ten feet from the door to the library.

The library was almost small enough to be called cozy, with four leather chairs, each with a reading light and a stand with an ashtray. Book shelves lined two walls and part of a third. In a corner was a chess table with a marble top, with yellow and brown marble for the squares, and the men spread around, not on their home squares. The *Gazette* had said that the men were of ivory and Kokcha lapis lazuli and they and the table had belonged to and been played with by Louis XIV, and that the men were kept in the position after the ninth move of Paul Morphy's most famous game, his defeat of the Duke of Brunswick and Count Isouard in Paris in 1858.

The couch was backed up to the left wall, but there was no table, just stands at the ends. I looked at Nash. "You've moved the table."

"Certainly." Since I was just a cop, so he thought, no "sir" was required. "We were told things could be moved."

"Yeah, the inspector would, with members in the high brackets. If it had been a dump he'd have kept it sealed for a month. Has your watch got a second hand?"

He glanced at his wrist. "Yes."

"All right, time me. I'm checking. I'm going down to the kitchen and coming right back. I'll time it too, but two watches are better than one. When I say 'go.'" I looked at my watch. "Go." I moved.

There were only two doors besides the one we had entered by, and one of them was to the hall, and near the other one, at the far end, was a little door that had to be to an old-fashioned dumb-waiter shaft. Crossing to it — not the dumb-waiter — I opened it and stepped through. There was a small landing and stairs down, narrow and steep. Descending, I was in the kitchen, larger than you would expect, and nothing old-fashioned about it.

Stainless steel and fluorescent lights. A round little bald guy in a white apron, perched on a stool with a magazine, squinted at me and muttered, "My God, another one."

"We keep the best till the last." I was brusque. "You're Laghi?"

"Call me Tony. Why not?"

"I don't know you well enough." I turned and mounted the stairs. In the library, Nash, who apparently hadn't moved, looked at his watch and said, "One minute and eighteen seconds."

I nodded. "Close enough. You said in your statement that when Blount went down the first time to get the chocolate he was in the kitchen about six minutes."

"That's wrong. I said about three minutes. If you don't — Oh. You're trying to — I see. I know what I said in my statement."

"Good. So do I." I went to the door to the big room, on through, and to the table where the game had a couple of kibitzers. Neither they nor the players gave me a glance as I arrived. More than half of the men were still on the board. One of Black's knights was attacked by a pawn, and I raised a brow when he picked up a rook to move it, but then I saw that the white pawn was pinned. Nash's voice came from behind my shoulder. "This man is a police officer, Mr. Carruthers." No eyes came to me, not an eye. White, evidently Mr. Carruthers, said without moving his head, "Don't interrupt, Nash. You know better."

A fascinating game if it fascinates you. With nothing better to do, I stuck with it for half an hour, deciding for both White and Black what the next move should be, and made a perfect record. Wrong every time. When Black moved a rook to where a knight could take it, but with a discovered check by a bishop which I hadn't seen, I conceded I would never be a Botvinnik or even a Paul Jerin and went to the hall for my hat and coat. The only words that had passed had been when White had pushed a pawn and Black had murmured, "I thought you would," and White had murmured, "Obvious."

It was snowing harder, but there were still twenty minutes before six o'clock, so I walked some more. As for my mind, I told it that it now had some new data to work on, since I had shown it the scene of the crime and had even established the vital fact that it took seventy-eight seconds to go down to the kitchen and back up, but it wasn't interested. Around Eighteenth Street I gave up and began to look at people going by. Girls are better looking in snowstorms, especially at night.

When I mounted the stoop of the old brownstone and used my key I found that the bolt wasn't on, so I didn't have to push the button for Fritz. Shaking the snow off my coat and hat before entering, putting them on the hall rack, and proceeding to the office, the only greeting I got was a sidewise glance. Wolfe was at his desk with his current book, *African Genesis,* by Robert Ardrey. Crossing to my desk, I sat and picked up the late edition of the *Gazette.* We have three copies delivered, one for Wolfe, one for Fritz, and one for me. It was on the front page, the first item under LATE BULLETINS.

Wolfe must have been on a long paragraph, for a full minute passed before he looked up and spoke.

"It's snowing?"

"Yes. And blowing some."

His eyes went back to his book. "I hate to interrupt," I said, "but I might forget to mention it later. I saw Lon Cohen. He got it in today, as you may have noticed."

"I haven't looked. Did you get anything useful?"

"Not useful to me. Possibly to you." I got my notebook from my pocket.

"Doubtful. You have a nose." He went back to his book.

I gave him time for another paragraph. "Also I went and had a look at the Gambit Club."

No comment.

"I know," I said, "that that book is extremely interesting. As you told me at lunch, it tells what happened in Africa a hundred thousand years ago, and I realize that that is more important than what is happening here now. My talk with Lon can wait, and all I did at the Gambit Club, besides taking a look at the couch Jerin sat on, was watch a game of chess, but you told Miss Blount you would let her know who you want to see first. If you expect her to get someone here this evening I ought to phone her now."

He grunted. "It isn't urgent. It's snowing."

"Yeah. It may clear up by the time the trial starts. Don't you think?"

"Confound it, don't badger me!"

So he was phutzing. Since one of my most important functions is needling him when his aversion to work takes control, it was up to me, but the trouble was my mind. Showing it the scene of the crime had accomplished nothing. If I couldn't sick it onto the job how could I expect to sick him? I got up and went to the kitchen to ask Fritz if there had been any phone calls, though I knew there hadn't, since there had been no note on my desk.

However, there were three calls in the next hour, before dinner, and two during dinner—the *Times*, the *Daily News*, and the *Post*, and two of the networks, CBS and NBC. With all of them I confirmed the item in the *Gazette* and told them we had nothing to add. The *News* was sore because I had given it to the *Gazette*, and of course the *Times* tried to insist on speaking with Wolfe. When the last trumpet sounds the *Times* will want to check with Gabriel himself, and for the next edition will try to get it confirmed by even Higher Authority.

I had returned to the dining room after dealing with CBS, to deal with my second helping of papaya custard, when the doorbell rang. During meals Fritz answers it. He came from the kitchen, went down the hall to the front, and in a minute came back, entered, and said, "Mr. Ernst Hausman. He said you would know the name."

Wolfe looked at me, not as at a friend or even a trusted assistant. "Archie. This is your doing."

I swallowed custard. "No, sir. Yours. The *Gazette*. I merely followed instructions. You said the murderer might think it necessary to do something, and here he is."

"Pfui. Through a blizzard?"

He really meant it. On a fine day he would venture out to risk his life in the traffic only on a strictly personal errand, and this was night and snow was falling. "He had to," I said. "With you on it he knew he was done for and he came to confess." I pushed my chair back and left it. A man coming without an appointment before we had had our coffee—he was capable of telling Fritz to tell him to come tomorrow morning.

"Okay, Fritz," I said, "I'll do it."

4

WE always have our after-dinner coffee in the office, mainly because the chair behind his desk is the only one that Wolfe can get his bulk really comfortable in, and of course the guest had to be invited to partake. He said he'd try it, he was very particular about coffee, and when Fritz put a cup on the stand by the red leather chair and was going to pour he said the cup was too small and told Fritz to bring a larger one. Ideal company. He must have been fun at dinner parties.

He didn't look his seventy-two years, and I had to admit he didn't look like a murderer, but murderers seldom do. One thing was sure, if he murdered at all he would use poison, because with a gun or knife or club he might get spots on his perfectly tailored three-hundred-dollar suit or his sixty-dollar shoes or his twenty-dollar tie, or soil his elegant little hands, or even spatter blood on his neat little face with its carefully barbered mustache.

He lifted the larger cup and took a sip. "Quite good," he conceded. He had a thin finicky voice. He took another sip. "Quite good." He looked around. "Good room. For a man in your line or work quite unexpected. That globe over there — I noticed it when I came in. What's its diameter? Three feet?"

"Thirty-two and three-eighths inches."

"The finest globe I ever saw. I'll give you a hundred dollars for it."

"I paid five hundred."

Hausman shook his head and sipped coffee. "Not worth it. Do you play chess?"

"Not now. I have played."

"How good were you?"

Wolfe put his cup down. "Mr. Hausman. Surely you didn't come through a snowstorm at night for this." He reached for the pot.

"Hardly." He showed his teeth. It wasn't a grin; it was simply that his lips suddenly parted enough for his teeth to show and then closed again. "But before I go into matters I have to be satisfied about you. I know you have a reputation, but that doesn't mean anything. How far can you be trusted?"

"That depends." Wolfe put the pot down. "I trust myself implicitly. Anyone else will do well to make certain of our understanding."

Hausman nodded. "That's always essential. But I mean — uh — suppose I hire you to do a job, how far can I depend on you?"

"If I commit myself, to the extent of my abilities. But this is fatuous. Do you hope to determine my quality by asking banal and offensive questions? You must know that a man can have only one invulnerable loyalty, loyalty to his own concept of the obligations of manhood. All other loyalties are merely deputies of that one."

"Hunh," Hausman said. "I'd like to play you a game of chess."

"Very well. I have no board or men. Pawn to Queen Four."

"Pawn to Queen Four."

"Pawn to Queen Bishop Four."

"Pawn to King Three."

"Knight to King Bishop Three."

"You mean Queen Bishop Three."

"No. King Bishop Three."

"But the Queen's Knight is a better move! All the books say so."

"That's why I didn't make it. I knew you would expect it and know the best answer to it."

Hausman's lips worked a little. "Then I can't go on. Not without a board." He picked up his cup, emptied it, and put it down. "You're sharp, aren't you?"

"I prefer 'adroit,' but yes."

"I have a job for you." He showed his teeth. "Who has hired you to work on that—uh—murder at the Gambit Club? Kalmus?"

"Ask him."

"I'm asking you."

"Mr. Hausman." Wolfe was patient. "First you inquired about my furniture and my habits, then about my probity, and now about my private affairs. Can't you contrive a question which deserves an answer?"

"You won't tell me who hired you?"

"Of course not."

"But someone did?"

"Yes."

"Then it must have been Kalmus. Or Anna—Mrs. Blount . . ." He took a moment to consider it. "No. Kalmus. He has had no experience with this kind of thing and no talent for it. I am Matthew Blount's oldest friend. I knew him as a boy. I am his daughter's godfather. So I am interested, deeply interested, in his—uh—welfare. And with Kalmus handling this there's no hope for him, no hope at all. Kalmus has hired you, but you're under his direction and control, and with him in charge there's no hope. He has paid you a retainer. How much?"

Wolfe's shoulders went up an eighth of an inch and down again. He looked at me with his brows raised, saying without words, "See what you let in?"

"Then you won't," Hausman said. "All right, that can wait. I want to hire you to do something that will get results. There will be no conflict of interest because this is in Matthew Blount's interest too. I'll pay you myself. I may get it back from Blount later, but that's no concern of yours. How much do you already know about what happened that night at the Gambit Club?"

"Enough, perhaps. If I lack needed information you can probably supply it."

"You know about the chocolate? That the police theory is that Blount poisoned that man by putting arsenic in the chocolate?"

"Yes."

"Then all we have to do is to prove that somebody else put arsenic in the chocolate. That would free Blount?"

"Yes."

"Then that's the thing to do. I thought of this last week, but I knew how Kalmus would react if I went to him with it, and I didn't want to do it myself because there are certain—uh—difficulties. Then today I saw that item in the paper about you. I asked you how far I can count on you because this has to be absolutely confidential. Would you do something that would free Blount without telling Kalmus, before or after?"

"If it were something I had engaged to do, yes."

"And without telling anyone else?"

"If I had made the engagement with that condition, yes."

"It will be with that condition." Hausman looked at me. "What's your name?"

"Archie Goodwin."

"Leave the room."

I put my coffee cup down. I seldom drink three cups, but the situation had got on my nerves hours ago, and that bozo wasn't helping any. "Anything to oblige a client," I said, "but you're not a client yet. If I left, I'd have to stand at the peephole to look and listen, and I'd rather sit."

He looked at Wolfe. "This is for you only."

"Then it's not for me. What's for me is categorically for Mr. Goodwin."

I thought for ten seconds Hausman was going to call it off, and so did he. He showed his teeth, and his lips stayed parted for a full ten seconds while his eyes went back and forth to Wolfe and me. Finally they settled on Wolfe, and he spoke. "I act on impulse. I came here on impulse. You said something about a man's loyalty to his concept of the obligations of manhood, and I owe this to Matthew Blount. I'm a hard man, Wolfe. If you or Goodwin cross me you'll regret it."

Wolfe grunted. "Then we must be at pains not to."

"You had better. No man has ever crossed me without regretting it. I want you to get proof that someone else put the arsenic in the chocolate. I'll tell you exactly how to do it. All you have to do is follow instructions. I have it planned to the last detail."

"Indeed." Wolfe leaned back. "Then it shouldn't be difficult. You say 'someone.' Any particular one?"

"Yes. His name is Bernard Nash. He's the steward of the Gambit Club. There was arsenic there in the kitchen. Isn't arsenic used to poison rats?"

"It has been. It can be."

"There was some there in the kitchen, and by mistake Nash put some in the chocolate. Perhaps instead of sugar. When I said I have it planned to the last detail I meant the basic details. You will arrange the minor details with Nash, of course without any mention of me—the kind of container the arsenic was in, where it was kept, how much he put in the chocolate—all such points. Also, of course, how and when he disposed of the container afterward. When Blount went down to the kitchen with the pot and cup and emptied them—do you know about that?"

"Yes."

"He told the steward and the cook that Jerin was ill and asked about the chocolate. After he left, with the fresh chocolate, Nash thought about it, and realized what he had done, and disposed of the container with arsenic in it. Isn't that plausible?"

"It's credible."

"Of course that will have to be carefully considered—how and where and when he disposed of the container. I realize that in a matter like this nothing can be overlooked, absolutely nothing. That's why I came to you. With your

experience, you know exactly what the police will do. You will know how to
arrange it so there will be no possibility of a slip. But on one point I'm going
to insist. Nash will have to retract what he has told the police — undoubt-
edly he has signed a statement — and he must have a good reason. The
reason will be that after Kalmus hired you, you saw Nash and questioned
him, and you forced him to admit what he had done. I insist on that. That
way there will be no indication that I have had a hand in it. Of course you
agree."

Wolfe was rubbing his nose with a finger tip. "I might, after talking with
Mr. Nash. Has he agreed?"

"Certainly not. But he will, with the inducement you'll offer. That won't
be the difficulty, getting him to do it; the difficulty will be arranging all the
little details so the police will be satisfied. That's up to you."

"What inducement will I offer?"

"That's up to you too. I'll pay you fifty thousand dollars, and you'll give
me a receipt for payment in full for services rendered. I think if you offer
Nash half that amount, twenty-five thousand, that will be ample. He has
personal difficulties and needs money badly. Only a month ago he appealed
to me for help. He wanted me to lend him fifteen thousand dollars, but I
would never have got it back. His wife is ill and needs a series of operations
and other expensive treatment, he's in debt on account of her, and he has
two sons in college, and two daughters. He has the stupid pride of a man
who can't afford pride. All you're asking him to do is admit he made a
mistake. A mistake isn't a crime. With twenty-five thousand dollars he
could get a good lawyer, and with a good lawyer he would probably get off.
Wouldn't he?"

Wolfe flipped a hand. "That would be his risk, not yours or mine. To our
risk we could not plead inadvertence. It's barely possible that I misunder-
stand you, and, as I said, we should be certain of our understanding. Have
you any evidence that Mr. Nash did in fact put arsenic in the chocolate?"

"No."

"Or any reason to suppose that he did?"

"Reason." Hausman showed his teeth. "Reason? No."

"Then our risk would be formidable. If Mr. Nash accepted the offer and
collaborated with me on contrivance of the details, naturally I would put
them in an affidavit for him to sign. Without such an affidavit we would
have nothing. And if he repudiated it later, we would have no defense to a
charge of subornation of perjury. No lawyer could get *us* off. We would —"

"Not us. You. Your share of the —"

"Pfui." Wolfe had straightened up. "Mr. Hausman. I do not say that I
would suborn perjury in no conceivable circumstances. But if I did so for
money, and if it became known, do you imagine I would refuse to disclose
who had paid me? Or that Mr. Goodwin would refuse to confirm it? To
show his appreciation for our cooperation, the judge might in his mercy
sentence us to five years instead of six. Or even four."

"It would be two against one, but a man of my standing —"

"Bah. Asked what you paid me fifty thousand dollars for, what would you
say?" Wolfe shook his head. "You said that you know my reputation but it
doesn't mean anything. Assuredly it doesn't to you, since, knowing it, you
come to me with this witless proposal. Why? You're not a nincompoop. It

invites conjecture. Are you concerned not for Mr. Blount, but for yourself? Did you put the arsenic in the chocolate, and does Mr. Nash know it or suspect it, and is this your devious—"

The phone rang. I swiveled and got it. "Nero Wolfe's residence, Archie Goodwin speaking."

"Mr. Goodwin, this is Sally Blount. I want to speak with Nero Wolfe."

"Hold the wire." I covered the receiver and turned. "That girl who came this morning about her jewelry."

He was frowning because he had had a speech interrupted. "What does she want?"

"You."

He tightened his lips, turned and glared at his phone, then reached for it. I put mine to my ear. "Yes, madam? This is Nero Wolfe."

"This is Sally Blount, Mr. Wolfe."

"Yes."

"I know you never go anywhere, but you have to. You *must*. You must come and talk with my mother. You didn't say you were going to put it in the paper."

"I didn't decide to until after you left. Your name wasn't mentioned."

"I know, but when my mother saw it she guessed. She didn't guess, she *knew*. She knew I had tried to persuade Dan Kalmus, and I had tried to persuade her too—didn't I tell you that?"

"No."

"I should have. Well, she knew, and I had to admit it, and you'll have to come and talk with her. Right away. *Now*."—

"No. Bring her here tomorrow morning."

"It has to be *now*. —She has phoned Dan Kalmus, and he may come, and . . . you *must!*"

"No. Out of the question. But if you apprehend—you are at home?"

"Yes."

"Mr. Goodwin will go. Shortly."

"It ought to be you! Surely you can—"

"No. Mr. Goodwin will be there within half an hour."

He hung up, but, since I was on, the line was still open and she was talking. I cut in. "Save it. Relax. Expect me in twenty minutes." I cradled the phone and left my chair. Wolfe had pushed the button, and, as I headed for the hall, Fritz appeared at the door.

"Come, Fritz," Wolfe said. "Take Archie's chair. Your memory may not match his, but it will serve."

"Yes, sir." As Fritz moved he winked at me, and as I passed him I winked back.

5

IN the marble lobby of the marble tenement on Fifth Avenue in the Seventies, I was expected. The man in uniform didn't even let me finish. When I said, "Name, Archie Goodwin, to see—," he broke in, "Yes, Mr. Goodwin," and showed me to the elevator. But he phoned while I was being lifted, for when I emerged on the sixteenth floor the client was there, standing in the doorway. She put a hand out, not as an offer to shake but asking for help. I took it with my right and gave it a pat with my left as I told her, "Nineteen minutes. Taxi drivers don't like snow."

Inside, in a foyer the size of Wolfe's office, after I had shed my hat and coat she led me through an arch and across a dozen yards of rug to a fireplace. On the way I took a glance around. Pictures, chairs, a piano in a corner, doodads on stands, potted plants on a rack that took up most of the far end, lamps here and there. The fireplace, where a fire was going, was three times as wide as the one Wolfe used for burning dictionaries.

"Sit down," Sally said. "I'll bring my mother, but I don't know what you're going to say to her. Do you?"

"Of course not. It depends. What's the pinch?"

"She says I must call it off—with Nero Wolfe. She's going to tell Dan Kalmus to tell my father, and I know what he'll say. I'm *sure* he will." She put finger tips on my arm. "I'm going to call you Archie."

"Good. I answer to it."

"I can't call him Nero, I don't think anybody could, but I can call you Archie, and I'm going to. This morning, did I say this is the first good thing I have ever done?"

"Yes."

"Well, it is, and I'm doing it, but I have to know somebody is with me. Really *with* me." Her fingers were around my arm. "Will you? Are you? Archie?"

My mind wasn't. It was still with the facts. But having it put to me straight like that, if I had tried hedging I wouldn't have been loyal to my concept of the obligations of manhood. It had to be either yes or no. "Okay," I said, "since it's the first good thing you've ever done I'm with you all the way. Anyhow, you're Nero Wolfe's client and I work for him, so everything fits. As for what I'll say to your mother, I'll decide that when I see her. If she's willing to—"

I stopped because her eyes left me. With her back to the fireplace, she had the room in view and I didn't. I turned. A woman had entered and was approaching. Sally spoke. "I was coming for you, mother. Mr. Wolfe couldn't come. This is Archie Goodwin."

I would have appreciated better light. The lamps were shaded and not close. As she came near the firelight played on her face, but that's tricky; one second she looked younger than her daughter, and the next, she was a hag. "You'll forgive me if I don't shake hands, Mr. Goodwin," she said. "I wouldn't mean it. Please sit down."

She didn't sit, she sank, into an armchair on the right. I took one at right angles to her and twisted to face her. Sally stood. I spoke. "Your daughter asked me what I was going to say to you, and I told her I didn't know. She has hired Nero Wolfe to do a job for her and I work for him. If I tell you anything about it, it will have to be with your daughter's consent. She's the client."

Her eyes were brown like Sally's, but not as big. "You're a private detective," she said.

"Right."

"It's grotesque." She shook her head. "A private detective telling me my daughter is his client and he can talk to me only with her consent. But of course it's all grotesque. My husband in jail charged with murder. He has a lawyer, a good one. My daughter can't hire a private detective without his approval. I have told her that, and now you must tell her. That's . . . isn't that wrong? It must be."

Taking her in, I was making allowances. When lots of men had enjoyed being in the same room with her (according to Sally), and when Lon Cohen had been bewitched by her on sight, the circumstances had been different. The strain of the past ten days had to be considered, and allowing for it, I conceded that I too might have enjoyed being in the same room with her. I suspected that she might even have what will pull three men out of five, that without knowing it she could give you the feeling that she knew absolutely nothing but understood everything. It's a rare gift. I once knew a woman in her sixties who — but Mrs. Blount had asked me a question. She had a long way to go to her sixties.

"That depends," I said. "If your daughter's over twenty-one and she pays Mr. Wolfe with her own money, who can say it's wrong?"

"I can. I'm her mother."

I nodded. "Sure, but that doesn't settle it, that just starts an argument. If by 'wrong' you mean illegal or unethical, the answer is no. Isn't it fairly simple, Mrs. Blount? Isn't it just a difference of opinion? Your daughter thinks the services of Nero Wolfe are needed, and you don't. Isn't that it?"

"No. I mean it's not just a difference of opinion."

"Then what is it?"

Her lips parted and closed again. Her eyes went to Sally and came back to me. "I don't know what my daughter has told you," she said.

I turned to Sally. "This isn't going to get us anywhere unless I have a free hand. Unless you turn me loose, no strings. Yes or no?"

"Yes," she said.

"I'm not a wizard, Sally."

"That's all right if you meant what you said about being with me."

"I did. Sit down."

"I'd rather stand."

I turned to Mrs. Blount. "Your daughter told Mr. Wolfe that her father thinks Dan Kalmus is competent to handle his defense, and you do too, but she doesn't; that Kalmus may be good on business matters but he is no good for this; and she is afraid that if it is left to Kalmus her father will be convicted of murder. So I still say it's a difference of opinion. Admitting that she may be wrong, it's her opinion, and it's her money. And even if she's wrong and Kalmus makes good, why all the fuss? She'll have the satisfaction of making a try, her father will be free, and Mr. Wolfe will collect a fee, so everyone will be happy. The only ground for objection is that Mr. Wolfe might mess it up and make it tougher instead of easier, and of course for him and me that's out. It would also be out for any one who knows his record."

She was slowly shaking her head, and I, looking at her, was getting a faint glimmer of the impression she had made on Lon Cohen. It didn't come from her eyes or from anything about her you could name, it simply came somehow from her to me, the idea that though she could explain nothing, she didn't have to; between her and me no explanation was needed. Of course that can come to a man from any woman he has fallen for, or is falling, but I wasn't falling for her, far from it, and yet I was distinctly feeling it. Probably a witch and didn't know it, Lon had said. A damned dangerous woman, whether she knew it or not.

She spoke. "It's not that, Mr. Goodwin."

Guessing what a woman means is usually the shortest way, but guessing that one wrong would have been risky, so I asked, "What's not what, Mrs. Blount?"

"Read this," she said, and extended a hand with a folded paper.

I took it and unfolded it. It was memo size, 4 × 6, good quality, with *from the desk of Daniel Kalmus* printed at the top. Written on it with a ball-point pen was this:

> Friday.
>
> My dearest — I send this by Dan. Tell Sally I know she means well, but I fully agree with Dan about her idea of hiring that detective, Nero Wolfe. I don't see how it could help and it isn't necessary. As Dan has told you, there is a certain fact known only to him and me which he will use at the right time and in the right way — a fact I haven't told even you. Don't worry, my dearest, don't worry, and tell Sally not to — Dan knows what he's doing. All my love,
>
> Your Matt

I read it twice, folded it, and handed it back to her. "I still say it's a difference of opinion. Of course you have shown that to your daughter?"

"Yes."

"Have you any idea what the fact is, the fact that your husband says is known only to him and Kalmus?"

"No."

I turned. "Have you, Sally?"

"No," she said.

"Not even a wild guess?"

"No."

"You see why this is wrong." Mrs. Blount said. "Mr. Kalmus has spoken with me on the phone, and he says that item in the paper has already done harm because everyone will think he has hired Nero Wolfe. So tomorrow the paper must say that it was a mistake, that no one has hired Nero Wolfe. Whatever my daughter has paid him, that doesn't matter, he can keep it."

I looked up at Sally, who was still standing. My mind, still harping on the facts, of course excluding the one known only to Kalmus and Blount, wanted to grab at the excuse to ditch the whole damn mess. If Kalmus already had a fact that would do the trick, that was that; and if he didn't, the chance that there was one somewhere and Wolfe and I could dig it up looked slimmer than ever. Of course we would have to return the twenty-two grand. Whenever Wolfe sent me on an errand without specific instructions the general instruction was that I was to use my intelligence guided by experience. I would have to go home and tell him that I had done so and had concluded that we should drop it. So I looked up at Sally. If she had been looking at me with any sign of doubt or funk I might have passed. But she had her big brown eyes aimed straight at her mother, no blinking, with her chin up and her lips tight. So I turned to Mrs. Blount and said, "All right, I admit it's not just a difference of opinion."

She nodded. "I was sure you would understand if I showed you that note from my husband."

I shook my head. "That's beside the point. The point is that your daughter has paid Mr. Wolfe twenty-two thousand dollars, and in order to—"

"I said he could keep it."

"He only keeps money he earns. In order to get that amount she cleaned out her bank account and sold her jewelry. A girl doesn't sell her jewelry just like that." I snapped my fingers. "I'm not telling you now what she told Mr. Wolfe, I'm telling you what I inferred from what she did tell him. She told him three times that Kalmus is in love with you. I inferred that she thinks her father will be convicted of murder not just because Kalmus is incompetent, but because with Blount convicted and set up either to the chair or for life, you would be loose. So if that's what—"

"Stop," she said. She was sitting straight, stiff, staring at me, frowning. "I'm not sure I understand. Are you saying that Mr. Kalmus *wants* my husband to be convicted?"

"No. I'm saying that I believe your daughter thinks he does. So she sold her jewelry. And she certainly deserves—"

"Stop." She was on her feet. She moved, across to her daughter, and gripped her arms. "Sally," she said, "my dear Sally. You can't think . . . you *can't!*"

"Yes I can," Sally said. "I do. You know he's in love with you. You know he would do anything, *anything,* to have you. Are you blind, mother? Are you *blind?* Do you actually not see how men look at you? How Dan Kalmus always looks at you? I was going . . . last week I was going to—"

A voice came booming. "Anybody home?"

I turned. A man had passed through the arch and was coming. Mrs. Blount said, raising her voice, "We're busy, Mort," but, not stopping, he said, "Maybe I can help," and, arriving kissed her on both cheeks. Sally had backed away. He turned for a look at me, started to say something, stopped, and looked some more. "You're Archie Goodwin," he said. "I've seen you around." He offered a hand. "I'm Mort Farrow. You may have seen me too, but I'm not a famous detective so I don't get pointed out." He wheeled to his aunt. "I had that dinner date, but I broke away as soon as I could. I thought something might be stirring when I heard about Nero Wolfe. Was it you, or Dan? Or Uncle Matt? Brief me, huh?"

A fine moment for a six-foot big-mouth to break in. If I had been his aunt or uncle and he had been living under my roof I would have trimmed him down to size long ago. But Anna Blount only said, no protest, "It was a mistake, Mort—about Nero Wolfe. I was explaining to Mr. Goodwin. I'll tell you about it later." Her eyes came to me. "So you see, Mr. Goodwin, it was just a—a mistake. A misunderstanding. I'm sorry, we regret it very much, and Mr. Kalmus will tell the newspaper. As for the money, please tell Nero Wolfe—"

She stopped, sending her eyes past me, and I turned. There had been a sound of a gong off somewhere, and through the arch I caught a glimpse of a maid's uniform passing in the foyer. In a moment a man's voice came, and in another moment the man appeared. He halted to dart a glance around, then came on, and Mrs. Blount took three steps to meet him. As he took her hand he said something so low I didn't catch it, and she said, "Mr. Wolfe didn't come, but Mr. Goodwin is here and I've been explaining to him." I hadn't sat down again after rising to shake with Morton Farrow, and so was on my feet when the newcomer, nodding to Sally and Farrow, faced me, extended a hand, and said, "I'm Dan Kalmus. In a case one of my partners tried a couple of years ago he had to cross-examine you and he hasn't forgotten it."

I might or might not have known him from the picture the *Gazette* had had. In the flesh he didn't have much flesh, just bones and skin—felt on his hand and seen on his jaw and cheeks. With no wrinkles or creases and his full share of hair with no gray, he didn't look the fifty-one years Sally had given him.

"I'm afraid I have," I said. "So he must have made a monkey of me."

"He did not. On the contrary." He was squinting at me. "Mrs. Blount says she has explained the situation to you, but can I add anything? Do you want to ask me anything?"

"Yes. What's the fact that is known only to you and Mr. Blount?"

His eyes widened for a second, then squinted again. "You know," he said, "that might be a good question if Wolfe were on the case. But since he isn't, since Mrs. Blount has explained it's out of order. You know?"

I decided to pass the buck to Sally, since it really depended on her. If she hung on with Kalmus present, after the fur I had started flying, that would settle it for good as far as I was concerned. "That would be a good answer," I said, "if Mr. Wolfe were out of the case. But as far as I know, he isn't. Let's ask Miss Blount, she hired him." I turned to her. "What about it? Do you want out?"

"No." It came out a croak, and she repeated it. "No."

"Do you want Mr. Wolfe to go on with it? And me?"

"Yes."

"Then I have a sugges—"

"Now come off it, Sally." Kalmus had turned to face her. "You stubborn little imp. If your dad were here—anyway he is, by proxy." He tapped his chest. "Me. It's an order, from him, by him, and for him. You can't disobey an order from your dad."

"Yes I can." She had drawn back when he stepped close. "I would even if he were here and told me himself. He trusts you and I don't."

"Nonsense. You're not qualified to judge my professional competence. You don't even—"

"It's not just your professional competence. I don't *trust* you. Tell him, Archie."

I told his back, "Miss Blount considers that if her father is convicted and sentenced you can make a set at his wife, and she thinks that that may be affecting your judgment. It was on account of that—"

He had whirled and pulled a fist back, his right, and was starting it for my face. Anna Blount made a grab for his arm and missed. The nephew took a step and stopped. I could have ducked and jabbed him in the kidney, but he was so slow it was simpler to sidestep and get his wrist as it came and give it a good twist. It hurt, but the damn fool started his left, and I jerked him around and as he went down to his knees I sent my eyes to Farrow, who had taken another step.

"I wouldn't," I said. "I'm probably in better condition and I've had more practice." I looked at Kalmus, who was scrambling up. "If you must hit somebody hit Miss Blount. I was merely telling you what she thinks. That's why she came to Nero Wolfe, and that's why she won't let go." I turned to her. "I was saying, I have a suggestion. It's not going to be very pleasant for you here. If you'd like to spend the night with some friend, and if you want to pack a bag, I'll be glad to take you. I'll wait downstairs. Of course if you prefer to stay here and take it —"

"No." She moved. "I'll pack a bag." She headed for the arch, and I followed. From behind, Mrs. Blount said something, but we kept going. In the foyer she said, "I won't be long. You'll wait?" I said I would, took my hat and coat, let myself out, and pushed the elevator button.

I put it at fifty-fifty, an even chance that either her mother or Kalmus, or both, would talk her out of leaving, and down in the lobby I considered alternatives. My watch said 10:41. I would give her half an hour, and then I would go back up, or I would go to a phone booth on Madison Avenue and ring her, or I would go home, report to Wolfe, and let him use *his* intelligence guided by experience. But she saved me the trouble of deciding. I had just looked at my watch and seen 10:53 when the elevator door closed, and in a couple of minutes it opened again, and there she was, in the pallid mink, with a matching turban, and luggage — not just an overnight bag, a medium-size brown leather suitcase.

Her face was glum but grim, with her jaw set. The hallman was coming for the suitcase, but I was there first. I asked him to get a taxi, and when he was outside I asked her if she had phoned someone, and she said no, she hadn't decided where to go. She was going on, but the hallman got a break on a snowy night. A cab pulled up at the curb outside, and I ushered her out, let the flunky put the luggage in with the driver, handed him a quarter, got in after the client, told the hackie the first stop would be the nearest phone booth, and we rolled. Sally started to say something, but I put a finger to my lips and shook my head. The hackie might not only know the address of Matthew Blount who was booked for murder, he might even have recognized his daughter from her picture in the paper, and there was no point in letting him in on the latest development. He turned right on Seventy-eighth Street, right again on Madison, and in a couple of blocks stopped in front of a drugstore.

I leaned forward to poke a dollar bill at him. "Here," I said, "go in and blow it. Aspirin, cigarettes, lipstick for your wife, whatever you need. We're going in conference. I'll come in for you, say ten minutes, maybe less."

"Can't," he said. "The law."

"Nuts. If a cop shows I'll tell him it's an emergency." I got out my card case and showed him my license. He gave it a look, said, "Oh. How-do-you-do," took the dollar, climbed out, and went.

Sally gave me her face. "I'm glad you did that," she blurted. "I'm *glad.*"

"Sure," I said, "I thought we could use a little privacy. Taxi drivers talk too much. Now if you've decided —"

"I don't mean that. I mean I'm glad you told my mother. And him. I wanted to, but I couldn't. Now they know. How did you know?"

"The deductive process. I'm a licensed detective, so I'm allowed to guess. Have you decided where you're going?"

"Yes, I'm going to a hotel — some little hotel. You know about hotels, don't you?"

"Yeah. But . . . haven't you any friends with an extra bed?"

"Of course I have. I was going to phone one, but then I thought what would I say? All of a sudden like this, eleven o'clock at night . . . I'd have to give some reason, and what could I say? With all the talk . . ." She shook her head. "I'm going to a hotel."

"Well." I gave it a look. "That might be even worse. You could use another name, but if someone spots you and the papers get onto it, talk about talk. Good headlines. BLOUNTS DAUGHTER FLEES HOME IN MIDDLE OF NIGHT. Also possibly that I escorted you. The hallman. I showed the cab driver my license."

"Oh. That would be awful." She eyed me. Silence. My hand was there on the seat between us, and she touched it. "It was your suggestion," she said.

"Ouch," I said. "But so it was. Okay. As you may know, I live where I work, in Nero Wolfe's house. There's a room above his on the third floor which we call the south room. It has a good bed, two windows, its own bath, hot and cold running water, a Kashan rug fifteen by eleven, and a bolt on the door. The best cook in New York, Fritz Brenner, would get your breakfast, which you could eat either from a tray in your room or in the kitchen with me. His sour milk griddlecakes are beyond any —"

"But I couldn't," she blurted. "I might have to stay . . . I don't know how long . . ."

"It's cheaper by the month. We'll take it out of the twenty-two grand. Anyway, you couldn't pay a hotel bill, you've even sold your jewelry. Of course you'll never live it down, shacking up with three unmarried men, and one of them a Frenchman, but you can't sleep in the park."

"You're making a joke of it, Archie. It's no joke."

"The hell it isn't. That a girl wearing a ten-thousand-dollar coat, with her own bed in a sixteen-room Fifth Avenue apartment, with a flock of friends so-called, with credit in any hotel in town, needs a safe place to sleep? Certainly it's a joke."

She tried to smile and nearly made it. "All right," she said. "Some day maybe I can laugh at it. All right."

I got out and headed for the drugstore to get the hackie.

6

AT a quarter past nine Tuesday morning, seated with Sally at the side table in the kitchen, I passed her the guava butter for her third griddlecake. I had told her the household morning routine when I had taken her and the suitcase up to the south room an hour after midnight — Wolfe, breakfast in his room at 8:15 from a tray taken up by Fritz, and to the plant room at nine o'clock for two hours with the orchids; and me, breakfast in the kitchen whenever I got down for it, no set time, and then, unless there was an outside errand, to the office for dusting, putting fresh water in the vase on Wolfe's desk, opening the mail, finishing with the morning *Times* if I hadn't done so at breakfast, and performing whatever chores were called for.

Wolfe had done pretty well, for him. He had been at his desk with *African Genesis* when I had entered with Sally at eleven-thirty, and at least he hadn't got up and marched out when I announced that we had a house guest. After a growl and a couple of deep breaths he had put his book down, and when I asked if he wanted just a summary or the whole crop, verbatim, he said verbatim. It's more satisfactory to report a lot of conversation in the presence of someone who was in on it, just as a kid named Archie, years ago out in Ohio, got a bigger kick climbing to the top of a tree if a girl was there watching. Or fifteen or twenty girls. When I was through and he had asked a few questions, he told the client about the caller we had had earlier in the evening, Ernst Hausman, her godfather — not verbatim, but the gist of it. The end of that was for me too, since the phone call from Sally had come just as Wolfe was conjecturing that Hausman had put the arsenic in the chocolate himself. He had not broken down and confessed. After a few rude remarks he had got up and gone.

Wolfe had had no instructions and no comments before going up to bed.

The *Times* had a two-inch paragraph on page twenty-seven, saying that Archie Goodwin had told a *Times* reporter that Nero Wolfe had been retained in connection with the Jerin murder case, but that Daniel Kalmus, Matthew Blount's attorney, had stated that he had not engaged Wolfe's services and he doubted if anyone had.

At breakfast Sally and I had decided a) that it was desirable for her mother to know where she was, b) that she would phone to tell her, c) that she would go out and around at will but would be in her room at eleven o'clock, in case Wolfe wanted her when he came down from the plant rooms, d) that she would help herself to any of the books on the shelves in the office except *African Genesis*, e) that she would not go along when I walked to the bank to deposit the twenty-two grand, and f) that she would join us in the dining room for lunch at 1:15.

I was at my desk at eleven o'clock when the sound came of the elevator, which Wolfe always uses and I never do. He entered, with the day's desk orchids as usual, said good morning, went and put the branch of Laelia gouldiana in the vase, sat, glanced through the morning mail, focused on me, and demanded, "Where is she?"

I swiveled. "In her room. Breakfast with me in the kitchen. Good table manners. She phoned her mother to tell her where she is, went to Eighth Avenue to buy facial tissues because she doesn't like the brand we have, returned, and took three books from the shelves with my permission. I have been to the bank."

He left his chair and went across to the shelves for a look. I doubt if he really could tell, from the vacant spaces among the twelve hundred or so books, which ones she had taken, but I wouldn't have bet on it either way. He went back to his desk, sat, narrowed his eyes at me, and spoke. "Not another coup for you. Not this time."

"Maybe not," I conceded. "But when Mrs. Blount said you could keep whatever her daughter had paid you it looked ticklish, so I spilled it. Or do you mean my telling Kalmus?"

"Neither one. I mean your bringing her here. You did it, of course, to press me. Pfui. Knowing I would sooner have a tiger in my house than a woman, you thought I would —"

"No, sir. Not guilty." I was emphatic. "I start pressing, or trying to, only when you're soldiering, and you've had this only twenty-four hours. I brought her because if she went to a hotel there was no telling what might happen. She might cave in. She might even lam. I told Mrs. Blount you only keep money you earn. It would be embarrassing not to have the client available to return the fee to when you decide you can't earn it. I admit you have stirred up some dust by having me toss it to Lon Cohen, you even got an offer of fifty grand from maybe the murderer, but what next? Hope for a better offer from one of the others?"

He made a face. "I'll speak with Miss Blount after lunch. I must first see them — Mr. Yerkes, Mr. Farrow, Dr. Avery, and, if possible, Mr. Kalmus. It may not be —"

"Avery wasn't a messenger."

"But he was at the hospital with Jerin until he died. He told Mr. Blount that even at the Gambit Club he had considered the possibility of poison and looked around; he had gone down to the ktichen. If there is any hope of getting —"

The doorbell rang. I rose and went to the hall for a look through the one-way glass panel in the front door, stepped back into the office, and said, "More dust. Cramer."

He grunted. "Why? He has *his* murderer."

"Yeah. Maybe for Miss Blount. To take her as an accessory."

"Pah. Bring him."

Going to the front, I took a couple of seconds to observe him through the one-way glass before opening the door. With Inspector Cramer of Homicide West there are signs I am familiar with — the set of his broad burly shoulders, the redness of his big round face, the angle of his old felt hat. When it's obvious, as it often is, that he intends to dingdong. I open the door a crack and say something with a point to it, such as, "A man's house is his castle." But that time he looked fairly human, so I swung the door wide and greeted him without prejudice, and, entering, he let me take his coat and hat, and even made a remark about the weather before proceeding to the office. You might have thought we had signed up for peaceful coexistence. In the office, of course he didn't offer Wolfe a hand, since he knows how he feels about shaking, but, as he lowered his big fanny onto the red leather chair, he said, "I suppose I should have phoned, but you're always here. I wish to God I could always be somewhere. What I want to ask, the Jerin case. Matthew Blount. According to the papers, you've been hired to work on it. According to Goodwin."

"Yes," Wolfe said.

"But according to Blount's attorney you *haven't* been hired. Who's right?"

"Possibly both of us." Wolfe turned a palm up. "Mr. Cramer. There are alternatives. Mr. Kalmus has hired me but prefers not to avow it, or Mr. Blount has hired me independently of his attorney, or someone else has hired me. In any case, I have been hired."

"By whom?"

"By someone with a legitimate interest."

"Who?"

"No."

"You're working on it?"

"Yes."

"You refuse to tell me who hired you?"

"Yes. That has no bearing on your performance of your duty or the demands of justice."

Cramer got a cigar from a pocket, rolled it between his palms, and stuck it in his mouth. Since he never lights one, the palm-rolling is irrelevant and immaterial. He looked at me, went back to Wolfe, and said, "I think I know you as well as anybody does, except maybe Goodwin. I don't believe Kalmus would hire you and then say he hadn't. What possible reason could he have to deny it? I don't believe Blount would hire you without his lawyer's approval. What the hell, if it was like that he'd get another lawyer. As for someone else, who? The wife or daughter or nephew wouldn't unless Blount and Kalmus approved, and neither would anyone else. I don't believe it. Nobody has hired you."

A corner of Wolfe's mouth was up. "Then why bother to pay me a call?"

"Because I know you. Because you may be on to something. You had Goodwin pass that to his friend Lon Cohen, that you had been hired, to start something that would result in your *being* hired and getting a fee. I don't know what you expected to start, I don't know why you played it like that instead of going to Kalmus with it, whatever you've got, but the point is that you've got something or you wouldn't have played it at all. You've got something that you think will get you a fat fee, and the only way to get a fat fee would be to spring Blount. So what have you got?"

Wolfe's brows were up. "You actually believe that, don't you?"

"You're damn right I do. I think you know something that you think will get Blount out, or at least that there's a good chance. Understand me, I don't object to your copping a fee. But if there's any reason to think Blount didn't murder Paul Jerin I want to know it. We got the evidence that put him in, and if there's anything wrong with it I have a *right* to know it. Do you have any kind of an idea that I would like to see an innocent man take a murder rap?"

"That you would like to, no."

"Well, I wouldn't." Cramer pointed the cigar at Wolfe and waggled it. "I'll be frank. Do you know that Blount went down to the kitchen for the chocolate and took it up to Jerin?"

"Yes."

"Do you know that when Jerin drank most of it and got sick Blount went and got the pot and cup and took them down to the kitchen and rinsed them out, and got fresh chocolate and took it up?"

"Yes."

"Then is he the biggest goddam fool on earth?"

"I haven't met him. Is he?"

"No. He's a very intelligent man. He's anything but a fool. And he's level-headed. Some men fixed like him, men of wealth and standing, have the idea that they can do anything they please, and get away with it, because they're above suspicion, but not him. He's not like that, not at all. So I took it easy — or rather, I didn't. It was hard to belive that such a man had put poison in the chocolate and took it to Jerin and then went and got the cup and pot and rinsed them out. I don't have to spell that out."

"No."

"So we covered it good, every angle. We eliminated the possibility that the arsenic had been in something else, not in the chocolate, and I mean eliminated. We established that no one besides Blount and those four men, the messengers, had entered that room, the library, after the chess games started, and the games had been going for about seven minutes when Blount went to see about the chocolate — and I mean established. So that left it absolutely that the arsenic had been put in the chocolate by one of seven men: the four messengers, the cook, the steward, and Blount. Okay. Which one of them, or which ones, had some kind of connection with Jerin? I put eleven of my men on that angle, and the District Attorney put eight from the Homicide Bureau. For that kind of job there are no better men anywhere. You know that."

"They're competent," Wolfe conceded.

"They're better than competent. We got Blount's connection right away, from Blount himself. Of course you know about that. The daughter."

"Yes."

"But we kept the nineteen men on the other six. In four days and nights they didn't get a smell. Even after the District Attorney decided it had to be Blount and charged him, I kept nine of my men on the others. A full week. Okay. You know how it is with negatives, you can't nail it down, but I'll bet a year's pay to one of the flowers in that vase that none of those six men had ever met Paul Jerin or had any connection with him or his."

"I won't risk the flower," Wolfe said.

"You won't?"

"No."

"Then do you think one of them happened to have arsenic with him and put it in the chocolate just because he didn't like the way Jerin played chess?"

"No."

"Then what kind of a game are *you* playing? What can you possibly have that makes you think you can spring Blount?"

"I haven't said I have anything."

"Nuts. Damn it, I *know* you!"

Wolfe cleared his throat. "Mr. Cramer. I admit that I know something you don't know about one aspect of this matter: I know who hired me and why. You have concluded that no one has hired me, that, having somehow learned of a circumstance not known to you, I am arranging to use it for my private gain. You're wrong; you are incomparably better acquainted than I am with all the circumstances — *all* of them — surrounding the death of Paul Jerin. But you don't believe me."

"I do not."

"Then there's nothing more to say. I'm sorry I have nothing for you because you have put me in your debt. You have just furnished me with a fact which suggests an entirely different approach to the problem. It will save me —"

"What fact?"

Wolfe shook his head. "No, sir. You wouldn't believe me. You wouldn't accept my interpretation of it. But I'm obliged to you, and I don't forget an obligation. If and when I learn something significant I'll stretch a point to share it with you as soon as may be. At present I have nothing to share."

"Like hell you haven't." Cramer got to his feet. He threw the cigar at my wastebasket, twelve feet away, and missed as usual. "One little point, Wolfe. Anyone has a right to hire you to investigate something, even a homicide. But if you haven't been hired, and I know damn well you haven't, if you're horning in on your own, that's different. And if you are in possession of information the law is entitled to—I don't have to tell *you*." He turned and marched out.

I got up and went to the hall, decided he wouldn't properly appreciate help with his coat, and stood and watched until he was out and the door was closed. Turning back to the office, I started, "So he gave you . . .", and stopped. Wolfe was leaning back with his eyes shut and his lips pushed out. He drew the lips in, then out again, in and out, in and out. I stood and regarded him. That is supposed to be a sign that he's hard at work, but I hadn't the dimmest idea what he was working on. If it was the fact Cramer had just furnished, which one? Running over them in my mind, I stood and waited. The lip exercise is not to be interrupted. I had decided it was going to take a while and was starting for my desk when he opened his eyes, straightened up, and issued a command: "Bring Miss Blount."

I obeyed. As I said, I don't use the elevator; I took the stairs, two flights. Finding the door of the south room closed, I knocked. I heard no footsteps, but in a moment the door opened. There had been no footsteps because she had no shoes on. "Mr. Wolfe wants you," I said. "With or without shoes, as you prefer."

"Has anything happened?"

Not knowing if he wanted her to know we had had a caller, I said, "He just did lip exercises, but of course you don't know how important that is. Don't bother with your lips and hair, he wouldn't know the difference."

Of course that was ignored. She went to the dresser to use comb and lipstick, then to the chair near a window to put on her shoes, and then came. You get a new angle on a figure when it precedes you down stairs; she had nice shoulders, and her neck curved into them with a good line. As we entered the office Wolfe was frowning at a corner of his desk, rubbing his nose with a finger tip, and we got no attention from him. Sally went to the red leather chair and, after sitting in silence for a full minute, said, "Good morning."

He moved the frown to her, blinked, and demanded, "Why did you take a volume of Voltaire?"

Her eyes widened. "Archie said I could take any book except the one you're reading."

"But why Voltaire?"

"No special reason. Just that I've never read him . . ."

"Unh," Wolfe said. "We'll discuss it at lunch. There has been a development. Did Archie tell—" He stopped short. He had thoughtlessly allowed himself to speak familiarly to a woman. He corrected it. "Did Mr. Goodwin tell you that a policeman has been here? Inspector Cramer?"

"No."

"He has. Uninvited and unexpected. He just left. Mr. Goodwin can tell you later why he came and what was said. What I must tell you, he gave me some information that changes the situation substantially. The police have established, for Mr. Cramer beyond question, three facts. One, that the arsenic was in the chocolate. Two, that no one had an opportunity to put it in the chocolate besides the cook, the steward, the four messengers, and your father. Three, that only your father could have had a motive. None of the other six — I quote Mr. Cramer — 'had ever met Paul Jerin or had any connection with him or his.' Though all —"

"I told you that. Didn't I?"

"Yes, but based only on your knowledge, which was deficient. Mr. Cramer's conclusions are based on a thorough and prolonged inquiry by an army of trained men. Though all three of those facts are important, the significant one is the third, that none of those six could have had a motive to kill Jerin. But Jerin was killed — with premeditation, since the arsenic was in hand. Do you play chess?"

"Not really. I know the moves. Do you mean you —"

"If you please. Do you know what a gambit is?"

"Why . . . vaguely . . ."

"It's an opening in which a player gives up a pawn or a piece to gain an advantage. The murder of Paul Jerin was a gambit. Jerin was the pawn or piece. The advantage the murderer gained was that your father was placed in mortal peril — a charge of murder and probable conviction. He had no animus for Jerin. Jerin wasn't the target, he was merely a pawn. The target was your father. You see how that alters the situation, how it affects the job you hired me for."

"I don't . . . I'm not sure . . ."

"You deserve candor, Miss Blount. Till half an hour ago the difficulties seemed all but insurmountable. To take the job and your money I had to assume your father's innocence, but to demonstrate it I had to find evidence that one of those six men had had sufficient motive to kill Jerin and had acted on it. And the three most telling points against your father — that he had taken the chocolate to Jerin, that he had taken the pot and cup and rinsed them, and that he knew Jerin and could plausibly have had a motive — those were merely accidental and had to be ignored. In candor, it seemed hopeless, and, conceiving nothing better for a start, I merely made a gesture; I had Mr. Goodwin arrange for a public notice that I had been hired."

"You didn't tell me you were going to."

"I seldom tell a client what I'm going to do. I tell you now because I need your help. That gesture brought Mr. Cramer, and he brought the fact that it would be fatuous to proceed on the assumption that one of the others had premeditated the murder of Paul Jerin. But, holding to my assumption that your father hadn't, one of the others must have. Why? Jerin was nothing to him, but he went there, with the poison, prepared to kill him, and he did; and what happened? A chain of circumstances pointed so clearly to your father as the culprit that he is in custody without bail, in grave jeopardy. By the operation of cause, calculated cause, and effect. The three most telling points against your father were not accidental; they were essential factors in the calculation. Is that clear?"

"I think . . . yes." She looked at me, and back at Wolfe. "You mean someone killed Paul because he knew they would think my father did it."

"I do. And if it was Mr. Kalmus he also knew he would be in a position, as your father's counsel, to protect his gain from his gambit."

"Yes." Her hands were clenched. "Of course."

"So I propose to proceed on that theory, that Jerin was merely a pawn in a gambit and the true target was your father. If I continue to assume your father's innocence, no other theory is tenable. That gives me a totally new situation, for I now have indications, if the theory is to hold—some facts and some surmises. We'll test them. To avoid verbal complexities I'll call the murderer Kalmus, though I may be slandering him."

He stuck a finger up. "The first fact. Kalmus knew that Jerin would drink or eat something during the game into which arsenic could be put. Preferably, he knew that Jerin would drink chocolate. Did he?"

Sally was frowning. "I don't know. He may have. He may have heard me mention it, or father may have told him. Paul always drank chocolate when he played chess with father."

"That will serve." Another finger. "The second fact. Kalmus knew what the arrangements were. He knew that Jerin would be alone in the library, and that he would be a messenger and so would have an opportunity to use the arsenic. Did he?"

"I don't know, but he must have. Father must have told all of them, the messengers."

Another finger. "The third fact. Kalmus knew that investigation would disclose an acceptable motive for your father. He knew of your association with Jerin and of your father's attitude toward it. Did he?"

"He knew I knew Paul, of course. But my father's attitude—if you mean he might have wanted to kill him, that's just silly. He thought he was—well, what you called him yourself, a freak."

"He disapproved of your associating with him?"

"He disapproved of my associating with various people. But he certainly didn't have any—"

"If you please." Wolfe snapped it. "This isn't a court, and I'm not a prosecutor trying to convict your father. I'm merely asking if Kalmus knew that inquiry would reveal circumstances that could be regarded as a possible motive for your father. I take it that he did. Yes?"

"Well . . . yes."

"That will do. So much for the facts. I call them facts because if one or more of them can be successfuly challenged my theory in untenable. Now the surmises, two of them. They can't be tested, merely stated. They are desirable but not essential. First, Kalmus knew that your father would himself take the chocolate to Jerin. Ideally, he suggested it, but I'll take less than the ideal. Second, when Mr. Yerkes brought word that Jerin was indisposed, Kalmus suggested to your father that it might be well to dispose of the pot and cup. Since Kalmus was a messenger, he had had opportunity to observe that Jerin had drunk most of the chocolate. And he ran no risk of arousing suspicion of his good faith. Since Jerin had been taken ill suddenly, it was a natural precaution to suggest. You said yesterday that your father told you and your mother exactly what had happened. Did he say that anyone had suggested that he see to the pot and cup?"

"No." Sally's fists were so tight I could see the white on her knuckles. "I don't believe it, Mr. Wolfe. I *can't* believe it. Of course Archie was right, I thought Dan Kalmus might want . . . I thought he wouldn't do everything he could, everything he ought to do . . . but now you're saying he killed Paul, he *planned* it, so my father would be arrested and convicted. I *can't* believe it!"

"You need not. As I said, I specified Kalmus only to avoid verbal complexities. It could have been one of the others—Hausman, Yerkes, Farrow—or even the cook or steward, though they are less probable. He must fit my three facts, and he should be eligible for my two surmises. Above all, he must meet the most obvious requirement, that he had a compelling reason to wish to ruin your father, to take his liberty if not his life. Does any of the others qualify? Hausman, Yerkes, Farrow, the cook, or steward?"

She shook her head. Her mouth opened and shut, but no words came.

"One of them might, of course, without your knowledge. But that was another reason for specifying Kalmus; you had yourself supplied a possible inducement for him. And now, with this theory, I must of course see him in any case. If he is guiltless and is proceeding on the assumption that the death of Jerin was the sole and final objective of the murderer, unless I intervene your father is doomed. It may be that the fact known only to Kalmus and your father, mentioned in the note to your mother which Mr. Goodwin read, is relevant, but speculation on that would be futile. I must see Mr. Kalmus, peccant or not, and for that I need your help." He swiveled. "Your notebook, Archie."

I got it, and my pen. "Shoot."

"Just a draft for Miss Blount. Any paper, no carbon. She will supply the salutation. I suppose my mother had told you that I am at Nero Wolfe's house, comma, and I am going to stay here until I am sure I have done all I can for my father. Period. Mr. Wolfe has a theory you should know about, comma, and you must come and talk with him tomorrow, comma, Wednesday. Period. He will be here all day and evening, comma, but is not available from nine to eleven in the morning and from four to six in the afternoon. Period. If you haven't come by noon Thursday I shall see a newspaper reporter and tell him why I came here and why I don't trust you to represent my father effectively."

He turned to her. "From you to Mr. Kalmus, handwritten. On my letterhead or plain paper, as you prefer. Mr. Goodwin will take it to his office after lunch."

"I won't," she said positively. "I couldn't tell a reporter that. I *couldn't*. I won't."

"Certainly you won't. You won't have to. He'll come."

"But if he doesn't?"

"He will. If he doesn't we'll try something else. Notify him that you have engaged an attorney to take legal steps to have him superseded as your father's counsel. I'm not a lawyer, but I know a good one, and the law has room for many stratagems." He flattened his palm on the desk. "Miss Blount. I shall see Mr. Kalmus, or quit. As you please."

"Not quit." She looked at me. "How does it . . . will you read it, Archie?"

I did so, including commas and periods.

She shook her head. "It's not like me. He'll know I didn't write it." She looked at Wolfe. "He'll know you did."

"Certainly he will. That is intended."

"Well." She took a breath. "But I won't tell any reporter, no matter what happens."

"That is *not* intended." Wolfe twisted his head to look up at the wall clock. "Before you write it, please make a phone call or two. Mr. Yerkes, Mr. Farrow, Dr. Avery. It's just as well I didn't see them before Mr. Cramer brought me that fact; it would have been wasted time and effort. Can you get them to come? At six'clock or, preferably, after dinner, say at nine-thirty. Either separately or together."

"I can try. What phone do I use? There isn't one in my room."

Wolfe's lips tightened. A woman saying casually "my room," meaning a room in his house, was hard to take. I told her she could use my phone and went to get another chair to sit on while I typed the letter to Kalmus for her to copy.

7

USUALLY I know exactly what Wolfe is doing while he's doing it, and why. I always know afterwards exactly what he did, and nearly always I know why. But I'm still not dead sure, months later, that I know why he had Sally phone those guys and get them to come that day. At the time I not only wasn't sure, I couldn't even guess. He hates to work. When I return from an errand on a case and sit down to report, and he knows he must listen and listen hard, from the look he gives me you might think I had put ketchup in his beer. When a caller enters the office, even if he expects to pry out of him some essential fact on a tough one, from the welcome he gets you might think he had come to examine the income tax reports for the past ten years.

So why ask Sally to get the people to work on both before and after dinner, before he had had a go at the most likely candidate? I didn't get it. I now believe that though he wasn't aware of it, he was grabbing at straws. He was pretending, not only to Sally and me but also to himself, that the new situation, resulting from the fact Cramer had brought, was just dandy because it gave him a new approach. But actually what it amounted to was that it was now extremely close to certain that none of the other candidates had had a shadow of a reason to kill Paul Jerin, and therefore it took either a mule or a sap to stick to the basic assumption that Blount hadn't. You can't sit and enjoy a book, even a fascinating one about what happened in Africa a hundred thousand years ago, while you're fighting off a suspicion that you're acting like a mule or a sap, so you tell your client to get people to come to take your mind off your misery. As I say, I'm not dead sure, but I suspect that was it.

Of course it's barely possible that even at that stage he had some vague notion in some corner of his skull of what had really happened that night at the Gambit Club, but I don't think so. In that case he would have — but I'd better save that.

However, there wasn't much work to the first interview, before dinner, with Morton Farrow. Yerkes, the banker, had told Sally he would come around nine-thirty, but the best she could get out of Avery, the doctor, was that he would try to make it some time during the evening. It had been decided after lunch, after I returned from taking the letter to Kalmus' office — in a steel-and-glass fifty-story hive in the financial district where his firm had a whole floor — that Sally would not appear, and before six o'clock came she went up to her room. Farrow had said he would arrive at six but was twenty minutes late. I left it to Fritz to admit him, thinking he would consider it improper for a famous detective to answer a doorbell.

When Fritz ushered him to the office he came across to me with his hand out. I took it and let it go, and he turned to Wolfe, but Wolfe, who is always prepared for it, had turned to the Webster's New International Dictionary, Second Edition, leather-bound, on the stand at his elbow, and was busy turning pages. Farrow stood and watched him for five seconds and then turned back to me and boomed, "Where's Sally?" I told him she was upstairs and might be down later, and indicated the red leather chair, and, when he was seated and it was safe, Wolfe closed the dictionary and swiveled.

"Good evening," he said. "I'm Nero Wolfe. You told Miss Blount you couldn't stay long."

Farrow nodded. "I've got a dinner date." Twice as loud as necessary. He glanced at his wrist. "I'll have to trot along in half an hour, but that should be enough. I couldn't make it by six, couldn't get away. With the big boss gone I've got my hands full. I was glad Sally called me. She said you wanted to see me, and I wanted to see you. I know her, and of course you don't. She's a good kid, and I'm all for her, but like everybody else she has kinks. Apparently she has sold you a bill of goods. I'm a salesman myself, a sales manager for a hundred-million-dollar corporation, but it depends on what you're selling. Sally just doesn't understand her mother, my aunt, and never will. Of course that's strictly a family matter, but she's brought it into this mess herself, she's sold you on it, and I've got to set you straight. She's got you believing that there's something between my aunt and Dan Kalmus. That's plain moonshine. Anybody who knows my Auntyanna — have you ever seen her?"

"No." Wolfe was regarding him without enthusiasm.

"If she wanted to she could have something not only with Kalmus but with about any man she wanted to pick. I'm her nephew, so you might think I'm prejudiced, but ask anyone. But it's wasted on her because she's strictly a one-man woman, and she's married to the man. Sally knows that, she can't help but know it, but you know how it is with daughters. Or do you?"

"No."

"It's always one way or the other, either the mother is jealous of the daughter or the daughter is jealous of the mother. It never fails. Give me ten minutes with any mother and daugher and I'll tell you how it stands, and with my Auntyanna and Sally I've had years. This idea of Sally's, the idea that Kalmus will cross up Uncle Matt so he can make a play for her mother, that's pure crap. She may even think her mother knows it or suspects it but pretends not to. Does she?"

"No."

"I'll bet she does. A daughter jealous of a mother can think anything. So to protect her father she comes and hires you, and what good does that do? The fact remains that he arranged it, Jerin being there at the club, and he took the chocolate to him, and he got the cup and pot and washed them out. You may be a great detective, but you can't change the facts."

Wolfe grunted. "Then you think Mr. Blount is guilty."

"Of course I don't. I'm his nephew. I only say you can't change the evidence."

"I can try to interpret it. Are you a chess player, Mr. Farrow?"

"I play *at* it. I'm all right the first three or four moves, any opening from the Ruy Lopez to the Caro-Kann, but I soon get lost. My uncle got me started at it because he thinks it develops the brain. I'm not so sure. Look at Bobby Fischer, the American champion. Has he *got* a brain? If I've developed enough to handle a hundred-million-dollar corporation, and that's what I've been doing for two weeks now, I don't think playing chess has helped me any. I'm cut out to be a top executive, not to sit and concentrate for half an hour and then push a pawn."

"I understand you didn't play one of the boards that evening, against Mr. Jerin."

"Hell no. He would have mated me in ten moves. I was one of the messengers. I was there in the library with Jerin, reporting a move from Table Ten, when Uncle Matt came up with the chocolate for him."

"On a tray. The pot, a cup and saucer, and a napkin."

"Yes."

"Did your uncle linger or did he leave at once, to return to the other room and his chessboard?"

"He didn't linger. He put the tray on the table and left. I've been over this several times with the police."

"Then you may oblige me in my attempt to interpret the evidence. It seems unlikely that Mr. Blount put arsenic in the chocolate while in the kitchen, since the steward and cook were there. He might have done it while mounting the stairs, which are steep and narrow, but it would have been awkward. He didn't do it after entering the library, for you were there and would have seen him, and after that he remained at his chessboard until word came that Jerin was ill. So his one opportunity was on the stairs, whereas each of the messengers had an opportunity each time he entered the library to report a move. Correct?"

"Not if I understand you." Farrow reversed his crossed legs. "Do you mean one of the messengers could have put the arsenic in the chocolate?"

"I do."

"With Jerin sitting right there? Right under his nose?"

"He might have closed his eyes to concentrate. I often do. Or he might have got up to pace the floor and turned his back."

"He might have, but he didn't. I went in there to report a move about thirty times, and he never moved from the couch, and his eyes were open. Anyway—of course you know who the messengers were, besides me?"

Wolfe nodded. "Mr. Yerkes, Mr. Kalmus, Mr. Hausman."

"Then how silly can you get? One of *them* poisoned the chocolate?"

"I'm examining the evidence. They had opportunity. You don't think it conceivable?"

"I certainly don't!"

"Indeed," Wolfe scratched his chin. "That leaves only the steward, Mr. Nash, and the cook, Mr. Laghi. Which one do you consider most likely?"

"Neither one." Farrow flipped a hand. "You realize I've been over all this, with the police and at the District Attorney's office. If there's any possible reason why Nash or Tony would have done it *I* don't know what it is, and the police would have dug it up."

"Then you exclude them?"

"If the cops do, I do."

"Then you're up a stump, Mr. Farrow. You've excluded everybody. No one put arsenic in the chocolate. Can you explan how it got into Mr. Jerin?"

"I don't have to. That's not up to me, it's up to the police." He uncrossed his legs. He looked at his watch. "All right, I came here to say something and I've said it. Before I leave I want to see my cousin. Where is she?"

Wolfe looked at me, putting it up to the supposed expert on women. It seemed to me that the situation called more for an expert on top executives, but I was for anything that might possibly give a gleam of light or hope, so I said I would ask her and got up and headed for the hall and the stairs. Mounting the two flights, I found that I wouldn't have to knock; she was there at the landing with her shoes on. Halting on the third step from the top, I asked her, "Could you hear?"

"I wasn't trying to," she said. "I was wanting to go down, but Mr. Wolfe said not to. Of course I could hear his voice. What does he say?"

"He's a psychologist. He says you have kinks. He says it's always one way or the other, either the mother is jealous of the daughter or the daughter is jealous of the mother, and a daughter jealous of a mother can think anything. He wants to see you before he goes; probably to straighten out a kink or two, and if you would like —"

"What does he say about Dan Kalmus?"

"That's one of your kinks. Your idea about Kalmus is pure crap. You may even —"

She moved. I had to either sidestep or get bumped, so I made room for her to get by, and had another look at the nice shoulders and the neck curve as I followed her down. As we entered the office Farrow twisted around in his chair and then arose, and apparently he intended to give her a cousinly kiss, but the look on her face stopped him. It certainly would have stopped me. He was starting, "Now look here, Sal, you —", but she stopped that also.

"You too," she said, with more scorch that I would have thought she had in her. "You would like it too, wouldn't you? You think she would have it all, she would own everything, and she would let you run it. You *would* think that, but you're wrong. You're always wrong. She would let *him* run it; that's what he's after, besides her. You're just a fool, a complete fool, you always have been."

She turned and went, to the door and on out. Farrow stood and gawked at her back, then wheeled to Wolfe, extended his hands, palms up, and waggled his head. "By God," he said, "there you are. Calling me a fool. What did I tell you? Calling *me* a fool!"

8

AT the dinner table, and with coffee in the office afterwards, Wolfe resumed on the subject he had started at lunch — Voltaire. The big question was, could a man be called great on account of the way he used words, even though he was a toady, a trimmer, a forger, and an intellectual fop. That had been dealt with at lunch, and Voltaire had come out fairly well except on the toady count. How could you call a man great who sought the company and the favors of dukes and duchesses, of Richelieu, of Frederick of Prussia? But it was at dinner and in the office that Voltaire really got it. What finally ruled him out was something that hadn't been mentioned at lunch at all: he had no palate and not much appetite. He was indifferent to food; he might even eat only once a day; and he drank next to nothing. All his life he was extremely skinny, and in his later years he was merely a skeleton. To call him a great man was absurd; strictly speaking, he wasn't a man at all, since he had no palate and a dried-up stomach. He was a remarkable word-assembly plant, but he wasn't a man, let alone a great one.

I suppose I shouldn't do this. I should either report Wolfe's table talk verbatim, and you could either enjoy it or skip it, or I shouldn't mention it. Usually I leave it out, but that evening I had a suspicion that I want to put in. Reporting to him on my visit to the Blount apartment, I had of course included a description of Kalmus: mostly bones and skin. I suspected that that was why Wolfe picked on Voltaire for both lunch and dinner, leading up to the climax. It wasn't much of a connection, but it was a connection, and it showed that he couldn't forget the fix he was in even at meals. That was my suspicion, and, if I was right, I didn't like it. It had never happened before. It had to mean that he was afraid that sooner or later he was going to have to eat something highly unpleasant for both his palate and his stomach — the assumption that Matthew Blount was innocent.

The coffee things were still there and he was still on Voltaire when Charles W. Yerkes came a little before nine-thirty. Another indication of Wolfe's state of mind was when the doorbell rang and Sally asked him if she should leave, and he raised his shoulders an eighth of an inch and said, "As you please." That wasn't him at all, and, as I went to the front to admit the caller, I had to arrange my face not to give him the impression that what we needed was sympathy and plenty of it.

Sally had stood when I went to answer the bell, and she met Yerkes at the office door. He took her offered hand in both of his, murmuring something, gave her hand a pat and let it go, and shot a glance to right and left as he entered. When Wolfe didn't extend a hand of course he didn't; he *was* a top executive. They exchanged nods as I pronounced names, and he waited until Sally was seated, in one of the yellow chairs I had moved up, to take the red leather one. As he sat he spoke, to her. "I came because I said I would, Sally, but I'm a little confused. After you phoned I called your mother, and apparently there's a . . . a misunderstanding. She seems to think you're making a mistake."

Sally nodded. "Did she tell you what I — why I'm here?"

"Only vaguely. Perhaps you'll tell me, so I'll know why *I'm* here." He was smiling at her, friendly but wanting to know. Cagey, but why not? A senior vice-president of a billion-dollar bank who is involved in a front-page murder case, even accidentally, isn't going to get involved any deeper if he can help it. Also he was good at chess.

"I *don't* think I'm making a mistake," Sally said. "The reason I'm here is . . . because I . . ." She let it hang, turned her head to look at me, and then looked at Wolfe. "Will you tell him, Mr. Wolfe?"

Wolfe was leaning back, his eyes at Yerkes. "I presume, sir, you're a man of discretion."

"I like to think I am." At Wolfe, the banker wasn't smiling. "I try to be"

"Good. The circumstances require it. It's merely a difference of opinion, but it would be unfortunate if it were made public at the moment. You may have seen an item in a newspaper yesterday that I have been engaged to inquire into the murder of Paul Jerin."

"It was called to my attention."

"It was Miss Blount who engaged me, against the advice of her father and his attorney, and her mother agrees with them. She offered me a sizable fee and I took it. Knowing that her father is in serious jeopardy, she fears that her counsel is not up to the emergency, and she has a high regard for my talents, possibly exaggerated. In making an inquiry I need to inquire, and you are one of those concerned in the matter. Mrs. Blount thinks her daughter has made a mistake in hiring me, but her daughter doesn't and I don't. My self-esteem rejects any supposition that I'll be a hindrance. I may conceivably hit upon a point that Mr. Kalmus would miss — not that I challenge his competence, though he decries mine. Have I made it clear — why Miss Blount asked you to come?"

"Not entirely. Of course I have been questioned by law officers, and by Mr. Kalmus, but I could contribute nothing useful." Yerkes's eyes went to Sally, shifting around ninety degrees while his head hardly moved at all. It's a good trick for a shoplifter or pickpocket because it helps on security, and it's probably also good at directors' meetings because it saves energy. He asked her, "Why do you think Dan isn't up to it, Sally? Any particular reason?"

Either Mrs. Blount hadn't mentioned the problem of jealous daughters or he was being discreet. Sally did all right. "No," she said, "not particular. I'm just . . . *afraid*."

"Well." His quick keen eyes went back to Wolfe. "Frankly, Wolfe, I'm inclined to agree with them. My bank doesn't happen to use Kalmus's firm, and neither do I personally, but he certainly is a reputable lawyer, and as far as I know an able one. What can you do that he can't do?"

"I won't know until I've done it." Wolfe straightened up. "Mr. Yerkes. Do you think Mr. Blount killed that man?"

"Of course not. Certainly not." But before he said it his eyes darted a glance at Sally, a dead give away. If he had really felt and meant that "of course not" why glance at her? Either he simply didn't mean it or he was an extremely smooth customer who knew more tricks than one and also knew more about the death of Paul Jerin than he was supposed to. He didn't add one of the old stand-bys, such as that he had known Blount for many years and he wouldn't kill a fly.

"Neither do I," Wolfe said, as if he did mean it. "But the factual evidence pointing to him is weighty and can't be impeached. You know that?"

"Yes."

"So I ignore it. There are other facts — for instance, that four other men, the four messengers, had opportunities to poison the chocolate, when they entered the library to report moves. I understand that on those occasions, some if not all, Jerin closed his eyes to concentrate. Is that true?"

"Yes. Usually he did, after the first three or four moves. He bent his head down and sometimes covered his eyes with his hands." Yerkes turned to the client. "You understand, Sally, my answering these questions doesn't mean that I'm siding with you against your father and mother. I'm not. But you have a right to your opinion, and I'm willing to oblige you within reason." Back to Wolfe. "And I agree that you're not likely to be a hindrance. I know something of your record. But Kalmus is quite aware that the four messengers had plenty of opportunities, including me. That's obvious. The question is, why would I? Why would any of them?"

Wolfe nodded. "That's the point. Take you. You had no animus for Mr. Jerin. But it's conceivable that you had, and still have, ill will toward Mr. Blount. And Jerin's death was only one of two dismal consequences of his drinking that chocolate, the other is that Blount is in deadly peril. Is that somehow pleasing to you, Mr. Yerkes? I have been hired to make an inquiry and I'm inquiring. Did you perhaps suggest to Blount that he should himself take the chocolate to Jerin?? Or, when you informed him that Jerin was unwell, did you suggest that he should attend to the pot and cup?"

The banker's eyes were narrowed, and his lips were tight. "I see," he said, low, so low that I barely got it, and I have good ears. "That's how you . . . I see." He nodded. "Very clever. Possibly more than clever. Kalmus may have it in mind too — I don't know. You asked me two questions — no, three. The answer is no to all of them. But you have certainly hit on a point. This makes it . . . hmmm . . . Hausman, Farrow, and Kalmus . . . hmmm. Of course I have no comment." He turned to Sally. "But I'm not so sure you made a mistake." Back to Wolfe. "I do understand you? You're saying that Jerin was merely a pawn to be sacrified in a deliberate plot to destroy Blount?"

"I'm suggesting it. It's my working hypothesis. Naturally you said no to my three questions; so would the other three. You would also say no if I asked you whether you have any knowledge of their relations with Blount that would be suggestive, and so would they. But a man's feeling toward another so intense that he is bent implacably on his ruin — such a feeling doesn't exist in a vacuum. It has discoverable roots, and I intend to find them. Or the feeling, intense feeling, might not be directed at Blount; it might be fastened on some desired object which only Blount's removal would render accessible. With Farrow, it might be control of an industrial empire, through his aunt; with Hausman, who is by nature fanatic, it might be some grotesque aspiration; with you or Kalmus, it might be Mrs. Blount. I intend —"

"Mrs. Blount's daughter is present, Wolfe."

"So she is. I'm only speculating at random. I didn't inject Mrs. Blount's name wantonly; Mr. Goodwin, who has seen her and who is qualified to judge, says that she might well unwittingly lead a man to defy the second prescription of the Tenth Commandment, thou shalt not covet thy neighbor's wife. But I am only speculating. I intend to find the roots. I haven't the legions of the law, but I have three good men available besides Mr. Goodwin, and there is no pressing urgency. Mr. Blount won't be brought to trial this week or month."

He was talking to hear himself, rambling on about vacuums and roots and quoting the Bible. He hadn't the faintest notion that Charles W. Yerkes had murdered Paul Jerin in order to erase Matthew Blount, nor did he expect to get any drop of useful information from that bimbo. Merely he would rather talk than try some other way of occupying his mind to keep it off of the fix he was in.

At that, he had a good listener. Yerkes wasn't missing a word. When Wolfe paused for breath he asked, "Have you suggested this working hypothesis to the District Attorney's office?"

Fine. A satisfactory answer to that, with a full explanation, would take a good three minutes. But Wolfe only said, "No, sir. They're satisfied with Mr. Blount. I am not."

Yerkes looked at Sally and then at me, but he wasn't seeing us; he was merely giving his eyes a change from Wolfe while he decided something. It took him some seconds, then he returned to Wolfe. "You realize," he said, "that for a senior officer of an important financial institution the publicity connected with an affair like this is . . . regrettable. Even a little . . . embarrassing. Of course it was proper and necessary for the police to see some of my friends and associates, to learn if I had had any kind of connection with that man Jerin, but it has been disagreeable. And now you, your men, private detectives, inquiring into my relations with Blount—that could be even more disagreeable, but I know I can't stop you. I admit your hypothesis is at least plausible. But I can save you some time and trouble, and perhaps make it less disagreeable for me."

He paused to swallow, it wasn't coming easy. "It is common knowledge in the banking world that before long a choice will be made for a new president of my bank, and that I will probably be named, but some of the directors, a minority, at present favor another man. Matthew Blount is one of that minority, but naturally since he is now . . . in the circumstances, he will not be able to attend the Board meeting next week. It wouldn't have taken much inquiry for you to learn this, hundreds of people know it, but I want to add that it has had no effect on my personal relations with Blount. It isn't that he's against me, it's only that he has greater obligations to the other man, and I understand it and so does he. I will *not* add that I didn't kill that man Jerin with the purpose of getting Blount charged with murder, I won't dignify anything so fantastic by denyiing it."

He rose. "I wish you luck with your hypothesis. The other three, Hausman and Farrow and Kalmus, are merely men I know, but Matthew Blount *is* my old and valued friend, and so is his wife." He moved, to Sally. "So are you, Sally, I think you should go home, that's where you belong at a time like this. I'm sure your father would want—"

The doorbell rang. I could have left it to Fritz, since he was still in the kitchen and it wasn't ten o'clock yet, but I had to go to the hall anyway to

see Yerkes out, so I went. There had been no picture in the papers of Victor
Avery, M.D., but if you're expecting an upper-bracket doctor to drop in and
you see on the stoop a middle-aged well-fed specimen in a conventional gray
overcoat, with scarf, and a dark gray homburg, when you open the door you
greet him politely, "Dr. Avery?"

As he removed the coat, with an assist from me, Yerkes came, followed by
Sally, and I observed that apparently Avery was just another man Yerkes
knew, not an old and valued friend; or it may have been only that Yerkes's
mind was too occupied for more than a word and a nod, and Avery's
attention was all for Sally. He took her hand and patted her arm and said,
"My *dear* child," and let the hand go only when they reached the office door.
When I joined them in the office after closing the door behind Yerkes, Avery
was in the red leather chair and speaking, telling Sally that he had turned a
matter over to an assistant so he could come. I noticed as I passed, looking
down at him, that he had just the right amount of gray in his hair to look
the part.

He turned to Wolfe. "There aren't many things I wouldn't do for Miss
Blount. In fact I feel responsible, since I brought her into the world. So I'm
here, at your disposal, though I don't know exactly what for. She told me on
the phone that she has employed you in her father's interest — professionally.
If that's correct — to call a detective a professional man?"

Wolfe nodded. "The dictionary would permit it."

"Good enough. Miss Blount also told me that you're acting independently of her father's attorney. That seems to me a little difficult, a little
awkward, but I'm not qualified to judge. The only profession I know anything about is medicine. She said you wanted to see me, and here I am. I
would go much farther, to see the devil himself, if it might be of assistance to
Miss Blount's father."

Wolfe grunted. "Do you think he killed Paul Jerin?"

"No. I do not." He didn't glance at Sally as Yerkes had.

"How long have you been a member of the Gambit Club?"

"Fifteen years."

"How well do you know Mr. Hausman?"

"Not well at all. I rarely see him except at the club. I see him once every
year on Matthew Blount's birthday. Mrs. Blount gives a party."

"How well do you know Mr. Yerkes?"

"Not much better than I know Hausman. Except at the club, only
casually."

"Mr. Farrow?"

"I know *him*, certainly. You know he is Mrs. Blount's nephew."

"Yes. Mr. Kalmus?"

"I have known him for years. Aside from our friendship, I attend him
professionally." Avery shifted in the chair, settling back. "Those four men
were the messengers, as of course you know."

"Of course. More of them later. First the event itself. I understand it was
Mr. Kalmus who summoned you to go to Mr. Jerin."

"That's right. But I knew before that that Jerin was indisposed, about
half an hour before, when Yerkes told Blount. I was at Table Five, next to
Blount, Table Six."

"It was then that Blount went to the library to take the pot and cup and clean them."

"That's right."

"Did Yerkes suggest to Blount that he do that?"

"I don't think so. If he did I didn't hear him."

"Did anyone else suggest it?"

"I don't think so, but I don't know. Yerkes was the messenger for our tables, and he had brought me Jerin's sixth move, and I was concentrating on my reply. I was trying the Albin Counter Gambit. Houghteling had used it against Dodge in 1905 and had mated him on the sixteenth move. But perhaps you don't play chess."

"I don't know that gambit." From Wolfe's tone, he didn't care to. "When you went in to Jerin, having been summoned by Kalmus, did you suspect poison at once?"

"Oh no, not at once. There was faintness, depression, and some nausea, and those symptoms can come from a variety of causes. It was only when he complained of intense thirst, and his mouth was dry, that I considered the possibility of poison, specifically arsenic, but the clinical picture of arsenical poisoning is by no means always the same. A a precaution I sent to a nearby drugstore for mustard, tinctura ferri chloridi, and magnesium oxide, and when they came I administered mustard water, but not the tincture. That's the official arsenic antidote, and it should be used only after gastric lavage and a test of the washings. Of course there was no equipment at the club for that, and, when the symptoms became more acute, I sent for an ambulance and he was taken to a hospital. St. Vincent's."

"You continued in attendance at the hospital?"

Avery nodded. "With members of the staff. They took over, actually."

"But you were present?"

"Yes. Until he died."

"At what point did he know he had been poisoned?"

"That's hard to say." Avery pursued his lips. "When I went to him he thought there had been something wrong with the chocolate, naturally, since he had taken nothing else, and of course anything swallowed by a man that makes him ill is toxic, but it was only after he had been at the hospital for some time that he voiced a suspicion that he had been poisoned deliberately. You asked when he *knew*. He never did know, but he suspected it."

"Did he name anyone? Accuse anyone?"

"I prefer not to say."

"Pfui. Did he name someone only in your hearing?"

"No."

"Did he name someone in the hearing of yourself and another?"

"Yes. Others."

"Then the police know about it, and presumably Mr. Kalmus. Why shouldn't I know?"

Avery turned, slowly, to look at Sally. "I haven't told you, Sally," he said, "nor your mother. But of course the police have been told—a doctor and two nurses were there and heard it. You asked me to come to see Wolfe, so I suppose you want him to know. Do you?"

"Yes," Sally said, "I want him to know everything."

Avery regarded her a moment, opened his mouth and closed it, turned to Wolfe, and said, "He named Blount."

"What did he say?"

"He said — these were his words: 'Where's that bastard Blount? He did this, he did it. Where is he? I want to see him. Where is the bastard?' Of course he was raving. It meant absolutely nothing. But he said it, and the police know it." Back to Sally: "Don't tell your mother. It wouldn't do any good, and it's hard enough for her without that."

Sally, staring at him, was shaking her head. "Why would he . . ." She looked at me, and I had to say something. "Nuts," I said. "He was off the rails." Having already swallowed a full-grown camel, though it was tough keeping it down, I wasn't going to strain at a gnat.

Wolfe, focused on Avery, asked, "Did he elaborate on that?"

"No. That was all"

"Or repeat it?"

"No."

"Was he questioned about it? By you or another?"

"No. He was not in a condition to be questioned."

"Then as information it has no value. To go back to the club. You said that when you went to him he thought there had been something wrong with the chocolate, and naturally you shared that suspicion. Did you make any inquiry?"

"Yes, but it was fruitless because none of the chocolate that he had taken was left. The pot and cup had been taken — but you know about that. I went down to the kitchen and questioned the cook and steward and looked around some. However, I didn't do the one thing I should have done, and I regret it; I regret it deeply. I should have asked Jerin if he had put anything in the chocolate that he had brought with him. At the time that possibility didn't occur to me, since he was saying there must have been something wrong with the chocolate as it was served. It only occurred to me later, two days later, when it developed that Blount was seriously suspected of deliberate murder. If I had been fully alert to the possibilities of the situation then and there, at the club, I would have questioned Jerin insistently. I would even have searched him, his pockets. I regret it deeply."

"Are you suggesting that he committed suicide? And then, at the point of death, accused Blount?"

"Not necessarily suicide. That's conceivable, but more likely, he put something in the chocolate which he believed to be innocuous but wasn't. It could have been some stimulant, either powder or liquid, or it could even have been some special form of sugar he fancied. And either by mistake or through the malign purpose of some other person, arsenic in one of its many forms had been substituted for the harmless substance. Of course it would have had to be in some kind of container, and I went to the club to search and inquire, but two days had passed and the police had already made a thorough inspection. The library had been put in order by the steward Tuesday night and the wastebasket emptied. I have been told by the police that there was no container on Jerin's person, but they don't really know, since he was undressed soon after his arrival at the hospital."

Wolfe grunted. "So all you have is a conjecture that can't be supported."

"I'm not so sure, and I'm sorry you say that." Avery was leaning forward.

"Your attitude is the same as Kalmus's when I made the suggestion to him. Kalmus is an able lawyer, a brilliant lawyer, but naturally his approach to any problem is the *legal* approach. You're right, my idea is no good if it can't be supported, but that's just the point, perhaps it *can* be supported, and that's why I wanted to tell you about it, because it's a job for a detective, not a lawyer. I won't try to tell *you* the dozen different ways it *might* be supported because that's your profession, not mine. But I'll say this, if I were a detective trying to get evidence that would clear Blount of the murder he has been charged with, which he didn't commit, or at least raise a strong enough doubt, I certainly wouldn't ignore this as a conjecture that can't be supported. I don't want to be importunate, but you realize I'm deeply concerned."

"Naturally." Wolfe was patient. "I concede that your suggestion is worth considering. It has the great merit that if it can be established it will clear not only Blount but also the others who had access to the chocolate—the four messengers. I said more of them later. A detective must consider them too. You have advanced a suggestion; now I offer one. One of those four men killed Jerin, not because of any malice toward him, but to destroy Blount. The malice was for Blount. That's why I asked how well you know them. If it can be shown—"

"Good lord." Avery was gawking. "That's tommyrot. You're not serious?"

"Why not? My suggestion is as worthy of consideration as yours and can be more easily investigated. Why is it tommyrot?"

"Why . . ." Avery turned his palms up. "Perhaps I should have said . . . implausible. To kill a man like that, deliberately, a man who means nothing to you, in an attempt to injure another man . . . I may be naïve for a man of my age and experience, but such depravity . . . it's hard for me to believe. I can't deny that it's conceivable."

"Then it's not tommyrot. But apparently it would be futile to ask if you have any knowledge or suspicion that would single out one of them."

"It certainly would." He was emphatic. "Even if I had any I wouldn't—" He stopped abruptly, looked at Sally, and returned to Wolfe. "No, that isn't true. If I had any such knowledge or suspicion I'd tell you. Have you any?"

Wolfe shook his head. "If I have I'm reserving it. I have spoken with three of them—Hausman, Farrow, and Yerkes—and I expect to see Kalmus tomorrow. They all profess belief in Blount's innocence, which is gratifying but not helpful. I not only profess it, I am commimtted to it, and whether through your suggestion or mine, or by some device not yet conceived, I intend to demonstrate it."

Hooray.

9

DANIEL KALMUS, counselor at law, arrived a little after noon Wednesday. It was a good thing he didn't put it off until after lunch, as some extra fine lamb kidneys, skewered to keep them open, doused in olive oil seasoned

with salt, pepper, thyme, dry mustard, and mace, broiled five-and-three —
five minutes on the skin side and three minutes on the cut side — and
brushed twice with deviled butter, would have been practically wasted. I
have said that Wolfe refuses to let anything whatever spoil a meal if the food
is good, but that day, if there had been no reaction whatever, not even a
phone call, to Sally's ultimatum to Kalmus, the kidneys would of course
have been chewed and swallowed, but they wouldn't have been appreciated.
They might as well have been served to Voltaire.

That was the first and only time Wolfe has given me instructions and then
canceled them, without anything having happened to change his mind.
While Sally and I were having breakfast, fresh-baked croissants and eggs
poached in red wine and bouillon, he buzzed me on the house phone from
his room and told me to call Saul Panzer, Fred Durkin, and Orrie Cather —
the three good men he had mentioned to Yerkes — and ask them to come at
six o'clock. That improved my appetite for breakfast. I hadn't the dimmest
notion what he was going to have them do, but it couldn't be just to ask
their opinion of Dr. Avery's suggestion, since together they came to twenty-
five bucks an hour. Then only ten minutes later he buzzed me again and
told me to skip it. Absolutely unheard of. If there's one thing he never does
it's toss and turn. A hell of a way to start a day.

When he came down to the office at eleven o'clock and saw the client
there, in a chair over by the filing cabinet, with the *Times*, he paused on the
way to his desk to scowl at her for a couple of seconds, acknowledged her
good morning with a curt nod, switched the scowl to me, went and put
orchids in the vase, sat, removed the paperweight, a chunk of petrified
wood, from the little pile of morning mail, and picked up the first item, a
letter from the president of a women's club in Montclair asking if and when
about a hundred of the members could come and look at the orchids. I had
considered withholding it and answering it myself, in view of his current
acute feeling about club members, but had decided that if I could take it he
could.

He looked through the mail, put the paperweight back on it, and looked
at me. "Any phone calls?"

He never asked that, knowing as he did that if there had been a call which
he would want or need to know about I would report it without being
asked. So I said, "Yes, sir. Lon Cohen wants to send a man to interview
Miss Blount."

"Why did you tell him she's here?"

"I didn't. You know damn well I didn't. She went for a walk and some
journalist probably saw her and tailed her. We can get Saul and Fred and
Orrie and have them find out."

"Archie, I am in no mood for raillery."

"Neither am I."

His eyes went to his client. "Miss Blount. When Mr. Kalmus comes you
will of course retire before he enters."

"I'd rather stay," she said. "I want to."

"No. Mr. Goodwin will tell you later what was said. You will please
withdraw."

She shook her head. "I'm going to stay." Not arguing, just stating a fact.

If he had been anything like normal he would have exploded, and if she had stuck to it he would have instructed me to carry her upstairs and lock her in. Instead, he merely glared at her, and then at me, removed the paperweight from the mail, picked up the top letter, and growled, "Your notebook, Archie."

In the next hour he dictated sixteen letters, only three of them in reply to items that had come in that morning. I still have the notebook, and it's quite an assortment. Though they all got typed, nine of them were never signed and mailed. They were all quite polite. One, to a boy in Wichita, Kansas, apologized for not answering his letter, received two weeks back, asking two pages of questions about detective work, but he didn't go so far as to answer the questions. He was in the middle of one to an orchid hunter in Ecuador when the doorbell rang; I stepped to the hall for a look, and turned to inform him, "Kalmus." It was ten minutes past noon.

Naturally I was curious to see how Sally would handle it, so when I ushered the caller to the office and he entered I was right behind. She stayed put, on the chair over by the cabinet looking straight at him, but obviously not intending to move or speak. He was going to her but stopped halfway, muttered at her, "You silly little goose," and about-faced. His eyes met Wolfe's at eight paces, and I pronounced names and indicated the red leather chair. Kalmus spoke. "So you got me here with a threat from a hysterical girl."

That wasn't so easy to meet, since Wolfe thinks that any calm and quiet woman is merely taking time out from her chronic hysteria, building up for the next outbreak. So he ignored it. "Since you *are* here," he said, with no heat, "you might as well be seated. Eyes at a level are equal. Of course that's why a judge's bench is elevated."

Kalmus went to the red leather chair, but he didn't settle in it; he just perched on the front half of the seat. "I want to make one thing clear,"he declared. "If you think you can force me to take you as a colleague in handling the defense of Matthew Blount, you're wrong. Anything I do or don't do, I'll decide it strictly on the only proper ground, is it in the interest of my client or isn't it. Also I want to say that I'm not surprised at the tactics you're using. It was partly because I know how you operate that I was against hiring you. I don't blame Miss Blount because she doesn't know any better. She doesn't know that coercion by threat partakes of the nature of blackmail, or that if she did what she threatened to do it would be libel. You can't deny that she wrote that letter at your direction."

Wolfe nodded. "I dictated it to Mr. Goodwin, he typed it, and she copied it." From his expression as he regarded the lawyer you might have thought he was merely trying to decide whether I had exaggerated about skin and bones. "As for blackmail, the only thing extorted is half an hour or so of your time. As for intent to libel, her defense would be the truth of the libel, but I concede that she couldn't possibly prove it. For you and me to discuss it would be pointless. She mistrusts your good faith as her father's counsel because she thinks you are capable of betraying him for your personal advantage, and of course you deny it. The quesion is moot and can't be resolved, so why waste time and words on it? What I would—"

"It's ridiculous! Childish nonsense!"

"That may be. You're the only one who knows the real answer, since it is inside you, your head and your heart. What I would like to discuss is the theory Miss Blount mentioned in her letter. It is based partly on a conclusion from established fact and partly on an assumption. The assumption is that Mr. Blount is innocent. The conclusion is that—"

"I know all about the theory."

Wolfe's brows went up. "Indeed?"

"Yes. If it's what you told Yerkes last evening. Is it?"

"It is."

"He told me about it this morning. Not on the phone—he came to my office. He was impressed by it, and so am I. I was impressed when it first entered my mind, a week ago, and when I told Blount about it he too was impressed. I didn't do what you have done—speak of it to those who may be vitally concerned—at least one of them may be. Have you also told Farrow and Hausman?"

Wolfe's brows were still up. "It had already occurred to you?"

"Certainly. It had to. If Blount didn't put arsenic in that chocolate, and he didn't, it had to be one of those three, and he had to have a reason. I don't have to tell you that when a crime is committed the first and last quesion is *cui bono*? And the only result of the murder of Jerin that could possibly have benefited one of the three was the arrest of Blount on a capital charge. Of course you include me on the list, and I don't. Is that why you told Yerkes? Because you think this idiotic idea of Miss Blount's points to me and he's out of it?"

"No. At present you seem the most likely, but none of them is out of it. I told Yerkes to get talk started. Not just talk about you and Mrs. Blount; even if Miss Blount's suspicion is valid you have probably been too discreet to give occasion for talk; talk about the other three and their relations with Blount. The success of any investigation depends mainly on talk, as of course you know." Wolfe turned a hand. "You may not need it. You have known all of them for years. You may already have an inkling, more than an inkling, and, combining it with the fact known only to you and Blount, you may have your case secure. If so you don't need me."

Kalmus put his hands on the chair arms to lever himself back on the seat, cocked his head, and closed his eyes to look at something inside. Facing the window beyond Wolfe's desk, he didn't look quite as bony as he had in the firelight in the Blount living room, but he looked older; he did have creases, slanting down from the corners of his mouth and nose.

His eyes opened. "I haven't got my case secure," he said.

"Hmmmm," Wolfe said.

"Not secure. That theory, it's obvious enough if Blount is innocent, but why are you so sure he is? I know why I am, but why are you?"

Wolfe shook his head. "You can't expect a candid answer to that, since we're not colleagues. But if I have no other ground there is this: if Blount is guilty I can't possibly earn the fee I have accepted from his daughter, and an unearned fee is like raw fish—it fills the stomach but is hard to digest. Therefore my client's father didn't kill that man."

"You happen to be right. He didn't."

"Good. It's gratifying to have concurrence from one who knows. It would be even more gratifying to be told *how* you know, but I can't expect you to tell me. Presumably it's the fact known only to you and Mr. Blount."

"That's partly it. Chiefly." Kalmus took a deep breath. "I'm going to ask you something. I'm going to see my client this afternoon. If I suggest to him that we engage you to investigate something, and he approves, will you do it? Investigate one particular matter under my direction?"

"I can't say. I doubt it. I would have to know first precisely what is to be investigated, and how much I would be restricted by the direction. You disapprove my tactics on principle."

"But they get results. If you were satisfied on those two points would you accept?"

"If there were no conflict of interest, if Miss Blount approved, and if it were stated in writing that Mr. Blount is my client, not you, yes. What would I investigate?"

"That will have to wait until I consult Blount. Will you be available this evening?"

"Yes. But I'll commit myself, if at all, only upon written request from Mr. Blount. I owe some deference to Miss Blount's opinion of your probity, right or wrong. She *is* my client. And what of your abrupt somersault regarding me?"

"It wasn't abrupt." Kalmus twisted in the chair to face Sally, started to say something, vetoed it, and returned to Wolfe. "The fact you've mentioned twice, the fact known only to Blount and me, required investigation — not the fact itself, but what it suggested. I thought I could handle it myself with the help of a couple of men in my office, but day before yesterday, Monday afternoon, I realized that it would take an expert investigator, and I decided to call on you. Then came that item in the paper, that you had been hired on behalf of Blount, and I thought you were trying to horn in, and my reaction to that was natural. But that evening Mrs. Blount phoned me that her daughter had hired you, so you weren't just trying to horn in, and when I went up there I intended to smooth it out and hire you myself, but you know what I ran into. That ridiculous idea of Miss Blount's. I admit I acted like a damn fool. It wasn't Goodwin's fault, or yours; it was hers."

He waved it away. "All right, that was stupid. Then yesterday that letter came, obviously drafted by you. I forced myself to look at it objectively, and I had to admit that from your viewpoint you were acting in the legitimate interest of the person who had hired you. And this morning when Yerkes came and told me what you said to him last evening, the theory that I already had myself, it was obvious that you weren't just making gestures to get a fee, you genuinely thought Blount was innocent. So I came here with the definite intention of engaging your services. It may not have sounded like it, the way I started off, but I still resented that letter and you can't blame me. I didn't do any abrupt somersault about you."

He got up and crossed over to Sally. "Where you got that fool notion," he said, "God only knows. If you have any sense at all you'll go home where you belong. Two different newspapers have phoned my office this morning to ask what you're doing at Nero Wolfe's house. For God's sake get some sense." He put out a hand, pulled it back, and wheeled to face Wolfe. "I'll see Blount this afternoon and you'll hear from me either this evening or tomorrow morning. He'll feel better if I tell him that you're sending his daughter home. Can I tell him that?"

"No, sir. I don't prescribe my clients' movements."

"Very well." He thought he was going to add something, decided he wasn't, and headed for the door. I followed him out, for the courtesies of the hall.

Back at the office door, I didn't enter because Sally was there on the sill. "Do you believe him?" she demanded. From her tone and expression it seemed likely that if I said yes I might get my face scratched, so I took her arm and turned her to escort her to the red leather chair, and darned if she didn't balk. She wasn't going to sit where it was still warm from Dan Kalmus. She jerked her arm away, stood at the corner of Wolfe's desk and demanded, "Do *you* believe him?"

"Confound it," Wolfe snapped, "sit down! My neck isn't rubber."

"But if you're going —"

"Sit down!"

She turned, saw I had moved up a chair, sat, and said, "You said I would have to approve. Well, I don't. Not under his direction."

Wolfe regarded her, not with enthusiasm. "He made one excellent suggestion," he declared. "That I send you home. But if I put you out you probably wouldn't go home, there's no telling where you'd go, and I need you. I need you now, and I may need you again at any moment. I neither believe him nor disbelieve him." He turned. "Archie?"

I was back at my desk. "Pass," I told him. "If he's a liar he's good. If he's straight Sally's a goof, and I told her Monday evening that I'm with her all the way, so I'm prejudiced. I pass."

He grunted. To her, "You heard me. I told him I would have to be satisfied about the direction. What do you want, Miss Blount? Did you hire me to discredit Mr. Kalmus or to clear your father?"

"Why . . . my father, of course."

"Then don't interfere. If there really is an important fact known only to Kalmus and your father I may soon learn what it is, before I commit myself to Kalmus, and then I'll decide what to do. He has by no means convinced me of his integrity, and I'm going to spend some of your money in an effort to verify or impeach your opinion of him. He is a widower?"

"Yes. His wife died ten years ago."

"He has children?"

She nodded. "Four. Two sons and two daughters. They've all married."

"Do any of them live with him? Or he with them?"

"No. He has an apartment on Thirty-eighth Street in a remodeled house that he owns. When the children got married and left he had it turned into apartments, one to a floor."

"Does he live alone?"

"Yes. He doesn't —"

"Yes is enough. Does he have servants? A servant?"

"Not to sleep in. A daily cleaning woman is all. He only eats breakfast —"

"If you please. Have you a key to his apartment?"

Her eyes widened. "Of course not. Why would I have a key?"

"I couldn't say. I merely ask." He turned. "Archie. Get Saul and Fred and Orrie. After lunch. Two-thirty if possible."

I swiveled and got the phone and dialed. Getting them in the middle of the day was doubtful, but Saul had an answering service, Fred had a wife, and for Orrie I had three different numbers, two of which were strictly his affair; and for Wolfe any and all of them would leave a job he happened to be on unless it was really hot.

I was at the phone off and on until lunchtime, and my meal was interrupted twice by call-backs from Fred and Orrie, but I wouldn't have minded if I had got no meal at all if necessary in order to get a ball rolling, though it did seem that Wolfe was piling it on. If all he had in mind was a tour of Kalmus's apartment, as was indicated by the questions he had asked Sally, why the platoon? Why not just send me? I had a suspicion and I didn't care for it. He wanted me around on account of Sally. With me not there to keep an eye on her, she might try to tell Fritz how to cook, or put tacks in Wolfe's bed, or change the furniture around. If that was it, if having her as a house guest meant that I would be sent on no errand if and when there was one, I was inclined to agree with Yerkes and Kalmus, at a time like this the place for her was home.

Bones were dwelt upon again at lunch, but not Voltaire's; these had been found in some gorge somewhere in Africa, and they proved that the chief difference between me and the galoots who put them there a million years ago was that I can use a typewriter; I *think* that was it. The kidneys were fully appreciated, and, as I was chewing my last one, Fritz stepped in after answering the doorbell to say that Mr. Panzer was there. If Sally hadn't been present he would of course have said Saul. By the time we finished with the salad and coffee Fred and Orrie had also come.

I had told them on the phone that Sally Blount would be present, and, when we entered the office and I introduced them to her, it was interesting, as it always is, to see how true they ran to form. Saul Panzer, five-feet-seven, 140 pounds, with a big nose and flat ears, not a good design for beauty, apparently looked casually in her direction only to be polite, but you could safely give a thousand to one that he had every little detail on her on file for good. Fred Durkin, five-feet-ten, 190 pounds, bald and burly, looked at her, then away, then back at her. He doesn't know he does that. Ever since the time, years ago, when he fell temporarily for a pretty little trick with ample apples, and his wife caught on, he doesn't trust himself with females under thirty. Orrie Cather, six-feet-flat, 180 pounds, good design from tip to toe, gave her a straight, honest, inquisitive, and acquisitive eye. He was born with the attitude toward all attractive women that a fisherman has toward all the trout in a stream, and has never seen any reason to change it.

Their three chairs lined up before Wolfe's desk didn't leave much space, and the red leather chair had had time to cool off from Kalmus, so Sally took it. Wolfe, after performing as usual with that trio, shaking hands with all of them because he wanted to with Saul, sat, moved his eyes left to right and back again, and spoke. "If it was troublesome for you to arrange to come I should thank you, and I do. I suppose you know what I'm concerned with—Matthew Blount, charged with the murder of Paul Jerin. You have just met his daughter. I won't describe the situation because for the present I have a single specific assignment for you. You probably know the name of Blount's lawyer: Daniel Kalmus."

Nods.

"There is reason to suspect that at some time prior to Tuesday evening, January thirtieth, he procured some arsenic somewhere; I have no slightest hint of where or how or when, but it was probably not more than a week or two before January thirtieth; it may well have been only a day or two. Note that I said 'reason to suspect'; that's all it is. Usually when I ask you to find something I have concluded that it exists; this time it's not a conclusion, merely a surmise. But you will spare no pains, and if you find it your fees will be doubled. Saul will be in charge and will direct you, but report here to Archie as usual."

He focused on Saul. "On such an operation you know how to proceed better than I do. I offer no suggestions. Evidence that he actually procured or possessed arsenic in some form would be most satisfactory, but even to establish that he had access to it would help substantially. Make no undue sacrifice to discretion; if he learns of your inquiries no harm will be done, for of course he has already taken all possible precautions. But you will exclude his doctor and his apartment. His doctor, Victor Avery, is his old and intimate friend; I have talked with him; and any approach to him or his office should be discussed with me beforehand. As for his apartment, it will be visited and inspected this evening by Archie, accompanied by Miss Blount. Miss Blount is an excellent source of information regarding his habits, haunts, associates — all about him. Get all you can from her first." He turned to her. "There are comfortable seats in the front room. If you please?"

She had fists again, her knuckles white. "But I told you . . . I just don't believe it . . ."

"You're not required to. I neither believe it nor reject it; I'm investigating. That's what you hired me for."

"You said I would go to his apartment with Archie. I *couldn't*."

"We'll consider that later. In talking with Mr. Panzer, Mr. Durkin and Mr. Cather, you need not disclose any matter which you wish to reserve. Mr. Goodwin will be with you." He turned. "Have your notebook, Archie."

I got it, arose, and headed for the door to the front room, and the trio got up and came, but stood aside at the door to let Sally go first. Ops appreciate a chance to be polite, they get so few. As I pulled the door shut a glance at Wolfe showed him reaching for *African Genesis*. Now that he was hard at work he could read again.

10

AT ten minutes past ten that evening Sally and I got out of a taxi at the corner of Park Avenue and Thirty-eighth Street, walked a block and a half east with a gusty winter wind at our backs shoving us along, stood at the curb, and looked across the street at the windows of the fourth floor, the top, of a brick house painted gray with green trim. Seeing no sign of light, we crossed over, entered the vestibule, and inspected the row of names and buttons on the panel, and I pushed the button marked Kalmus, expecting no response, since I had dialed his phone number only a quarter of an hour ago and got no answer. After a thirty-second wait I pushed the button at the bottom, marked SUPERINTENDENT, and as I did so Sally gripped my arm.

It had taken some persuading to get her to come — in fact, more than persuading, since she had held out until Wolfe explained that if I came alone I would have to bring an assortment of keys and tools, and even if one of the keys worked I could be nailed for breaking and entering. Naturally that did it, since she was faced with the prospect of me in the coop and her there at Wolfe's mercy. The arrangement was that if and when Kalmus came to see Wolfe that evening Sally and I would not be visible, and after Fritz had escorted him to the office and shut the door we would take off on our errand, and Wolfe would keep him until word came from me that we were through. Also, if he hadn't shown by ten o'clock and his phone didn't answer, we would go anyhow and risk getting interrupted. On that I had fudged a little and dialed his number at nine-fifty.

So there we were in the vestibule. There was no receiver on a hook, just a pair of little circular grills in the wall at chin level, and after a brief wait there was a crackle and then a voice: "Who is it?" Sally, still gripping my arm, spoke to the grill. "It's Sarah Blount. We want to see Mr. Kalmus. We rang his bell, but he didn't answer. Do you know where he is?"

"No, I don't."

"Well . . . we want to see him, but it's cold here in the vestibule. May we wait inside? Will you let us in?"

"I guess so. I'll be up in a minute."

I put my hand to the door and kept it there, but there was no click. A minute passed, and another, and still no click, and then the door opened. The man who opened it, a thin tall guy with a face as black as Jim Crow, made room for us to enter, and when we were in let it shut. I knew more about him, from Sally, than he did about me. His name was Dobbs, and he had been the butler when the Kalmus family had occupied the whole house.

He was frowning at Sally. "It's you all right, Miss Sarah," he said. "It's been so long since I saw you."

She nodded. "It certainly has. This is Mr. Goodwin. Mr. Dobbs, Archie."

I offered a hand, and he took it. Of course shaking hands with a butler is vulgar, but he wasn't a butler any more, he was a superintendent.

"You haven't changed any," Sally said. "Except your hair. All that gray." She was hating it, and I admit I couldn't blame her.

"You have," Dobbs said, "but that's natural. You're on the up, and I'm on the down. Will you permit me to say, I'm sorry about your father's trouble. I know it's going to come out all right, sure it will, but it's a big trouble." He looked at me and he had a good keen eye. "I know your name, you're a detective." Back to Sally. "I guess that's why you want to see Mr. Kalmus, your father's trouble."

"Yes, it is." For a moment I thought Sally was going to flunk it, but she got it out: "Could we wait for him in his apartment? Could you . . . would you . . . let us in? If we have to wait long . . . we have to see him tonight . . ."

"Of course." After all, she had sat on his knee, with a Kalmus daughter on the other knee, while he told them stories, before the gray came to his hair — a detail I got from Sally. He said, "Mr. Kalmus wouldn't want *you* waiting for him down here, that's sure," and headed for the open door of the do-it-yourself elevator. Entering after us, he pushed a button, the door closed, and we were lifted.

On the fourth floor the foyer was just a cell, four feet square, merely to provide walls for a door. Dobbs had taken a ring of keys from a pocket, but before he used one he pushed the button on the jamb and waited a full half a minute — in case Kalmus was in but had preferred not to answer our ring from downstairs. Evidently not. He used the key, opened the door, entered and flipped a wall switch, and there was light — plenty of it, though indirect, from troughs at the ceiling along two of the walls.

"There you are, Miss Sarah," he said. "It's not the way it used to be, is it?"

"No, it isn't, Dobbsy." She started a hand out but took it back. You don't shake the hand of a man you're tricking. But apparently it's all right to kiss him. Anyway, she did — a peck on the cheek — and said, "Did you hear that? Dobbsy!"

"You bet I heard it. You just bet I did." He bowed to her, and it could have been a butler bowing or an ambassador from somewhere in Africa. "I hope you don't have long to wait," he said, and went. When the door had closed behind him Sally flopped onto the nearest chair.

"My God," she groaned. "How awful. I didn't *want* to come. Will you hurry, Archie? Will you please hurry?"

I told her to relax, took my hat and coat off and dropped them on a chair, and glanced around. It was a big room, and by no means bare, and of course there would be a bedroom and a bath, and a kitchenette. Even if I had been after some specific object like a bottle of arsenous oxide it would have been a three-hour job if done right, and since I expected nothing so obvious but merely hoped for something, no matter what, that would open a crack to let in a little light, the whole night wouldn't be too much. Say it was a single piece of paper, a letter or a record of something; one item alone, the books in the shelves that lined the wall on the right, to the ceiling, would take hours. And Kalmus might show any second. I decided to have a look at the bedroom first and started for a door at the left, but on the way I caught something from the corner of my eye and stopped and turned. Then I moved.

It was Kalmus. He was on the floor in front of a couch, and the couch hid him from view until you passed the end of it. He was fully dressed, on his back with his legs straight out. After glancing at Sally and seeing that she was still on the chair, her head bent forward and her face covered by her hands, I squatted. His eyes were open, staring at the ceiling, the pupils dilated, his face was purple, his tongue was sticking out, and there was dried froth around his mouth and nose. With the froth dry there was no use trying for a pulse or breath. I poked a finger into a deep crease around his neck, felt something besides skin, and leaned closer for a look, forcing the crease open. It was cord, the kind used for Venetian blinds, with a knot under his left ear, and the surplus ends had been tucked under his shoulder. I told myself then and there to remember to ask the murderer, when we had him, if he had tucked the cord in consciously because he liked things neat, or if his mind had been occupied and he had done it without thinking. It was one of the most remarkable details I have ever seen or heard of about a death by violence. I was resisting the temptation to pull it out to see how much there was of it when there was a sound behind me, and I twisted around and sprang up. Sally was there, staring down, her mouth hanging open, and she was starting to sag as I reached her. Not wanting a faint to deal with, I picked her up, carried her to a chair at the other side of the room, put her in it, pushed her head forward, down to her knees, and kept my hand there, at the back of her nice neck. She was limp and there was no resistance, but she wasn't out. I knelt beside her, in case she went.

"So you were wrong," I said, "dead wrong. If you hadn't been wrong you wouldn't have come to Nero Wolfe, but to hell with that now. Do you hear me?"

No answer.

"Damn it, do you hear me?"

"Yes." It wasn't loud, but it was audible. "Is he dead?"

"Certainly he's dead. He —"

"How?"

"Strangled. There's a cord around his throat." I took my hand away, and her head started up, slow, and I stood up. "Do you think you can walk?"

"I don't . . . want to walk." Her head was up.

"That's too bad. Will I have to carry you down and put you in a cab?"

"Archie." Her head tilted back to look up at me. Her jaw started working, out of control, and she stopped to manage it. She made it, and asked, "He killed himself?"

"No. I'll be glad to help you straighten your mind out later but now I have things to do. He was murdered. I don't want you here when the cops come. I'd rather explain why we came and got Dobbs to let us in without your help. Do you want to spend the night answering questions?"

"No".

"Can you make it down and get a taxi? Mr. Wolfe will be expecting you. I'll phone him."

"I think . . . I'll go home."

"You will not. Absolutely not. Either you give me your word that you'll go straight back there or you stay here and take it. Well?"

"I don't want to stay."

"Will you go to Nero Wolfe and do what he says?"

"Yes."

"Okay. Can you stand? Can you walk?"

She could. I didn't help her. I went to the door and opened it, and she came, none too steady but she made it. Propping the door open with my foot, I reached for the elevator button and pushed it, and when it came and the door opened she entered and pushed the button, and the door closed. I went back in, crossed to a table in a corner where I had seen a phone, lifted the receiver, and dialed the number I knew best.

Wolfe's voice came: "Yes?" He never has answered the phone properly and never will.

"Me," I said. "In Kalmus's apartment. Everything worked fine as planned. Sally did all right, and Superintendent Dobbs brought us up and let us in and left. But Kalmus was here and still is. He's stretched out on the floor with a cord tight around his neck. He has started to cool off, but of course skinny ones cool faster. At a guess, he has been dead around three hours. He didn't tie the cord himself, and anyway the loose ends are neatly tucked under his shoulder."

Silence for five seconds, then: "Pfui."

"Yes, sir. I agree. I have bounced Sally, she just left, and, if she stays conscious and keeps her promise, she will be there in about ten minutes. I have a suggestion. Send her up to bed and have Doc Vollmer come. He may find that she needs a sedative and shouldn't see any callers, official or otherwise, until sometime tomorrow. I'll notify the law right away, since they'll learn from Dobbs what time he let us in. Have you any instructions?"

"No. Confound it."

"Yes, sir. Absolutely. I assume I don't tell the law what we had in mind when we came, since what was in our minds is none of their damn business. You wondered why Kalmus didn't show up this evening, and when I tried his number there was no answer, so we came to ask him. Will that do?"

"Yes. Must you stay?"

"Oh, no. I'm staying because I like it here. Tell Fritz I may be there for breakfast and I may not."

I hung up and took a couple of seconds to shake my head at the phone with my lips tight. Must I stay. Only a genius could ask such a damn fool question. Still shaking my head, I picked up the phone and dialed another number I knew: WA 9-8241. I dialed that instead of Headquarters because I preferred to tell Inspector Cramer himself, or at least Sergeant Purley Stebbins, if either of them was on duty.

11

A couple of electricians had installed a juke box inside my skull, and they were still there, testing it to see how many selections it could play simultaneously. About a dozen, apparently, judging from the noise. Also they were jumping up and down to find out how much vibration it could stand. Or maybe it wasn't a juke box, it was a band, and they were all jumping up and down. If I wanted to see which it was I would have to turn my eyes around to look inside, and in the effort to do that my lids came open, and there facing me was the clock on my bedstand. I quit trying to reverse my eyes and concentrated on the clock. Seventeen minutes past eleven. The noise was neither a juke box nor a band; it was the house phone buzzer. Someone somewhere had a finger on the button and was keeping it there. Nuts. I could stop it by reaching for the cord and yanking it loose. But it takes a hero to do something as sensible as that, and I wasn't awake enough to be a hero, so when I reached I got the phone instead of the cord, brought it to the neighborhood of my mouth, and said, "Now what?"

Wolfe's voice came: "I'm in the kitchen. What time did you get home?"

"Nine minutes to seven, and had three fingers of bourbon while I was fixing a bowl of milk toast. I intended to sleep through dinner. Why are you in the kitchen?"

"Mr. Cramer is in the office. Have you anything I should know?"

"Yes. Lieutenant Rowcliff's stutter is getting worse. Sergeant Stebbins has a bandage on the middle finger of his left hand, probably got bit by a pigeon he was trying to put salt on the tail of. An assistant DA named Schipple whom I never met before has amended the Constitution; a man is guilty until he proves he's innocent. That's all. In my answers to ten thousand questions and in the statement I signed there was nothing to affect your program if you have one. I didn't even admit in so many words that Sally is your client. As for Kalmus, he was hit on the back of the head, probably with a heavy metal ash tray that was there on the table, before the cord was tied around his throat. The cord was from one of the window blinds there in the room. The ME's on-the-spot guess was that he had been dead two to five hours. Where's Sally?"

"In the south room." (Even after three nights, not "in her room.") "Dr. Vollmer is attending. Before he dosed her last evening I told her why you went to that apartment — when she is asked. How soon can you be down?"

"Oh, six hours. What does Cramer want? He can't want me, he had me off and on all night. Does he want Sally?"

"I don't know. When he arrived I came to the kitchen and Fritz took him to the office. He may presume to quote something you said, even something in your statement, and you should be present. Can you be down in ten minutes?"

"Yes, but I won't. Twenty. Tell Fritz I would appreciate orange juice and coffee."

He said certainly and hung up, and I stretched out on my back and yawned good and wide before reaching to switch the electric blanket off. On my feet, before I closed the open window I stuck my head out for a whiff of winter air, which helped a little, enough to rouse me to the point where I could put my pants on right side front and my shoes on the right feet. More than that couldn't be expected. All night, in between sessions with dicks and the assistant DA, I had considered the situation with Kalmus out of it, and had decided that the best idea would be for the morning mail to bring a letter from Kalmus, telling why he had killed Jerin and saying that after his talk with Wolfe he knew it was all up, so he was bowing out. I might have gone to bed looking forward to the morning mail but for one thing. It wasn't positively inconceivable that he had tied the cord himself, but he simply could not have tucked the ends under his shoulder; he would have been too far gone.

By the time I got downstairs, in twenty minutes flat, my personal fog had cleared a little. In the kitchen, Wolfe, at the center table inspecting a string of dried mushrooms, put it down when I appeared, and moved. I said, "Orange juice," and he said Fritz would bring it, and I sidestepped to let him by, and followed him to the office. If Cramer, in the red leather chair, wished us a good morning he didn't say so. As we went to our desks he looked at his wrist watch, not just a glance but holding his cuff back with the other hand and staring, and as Wolfe sat he rasped, "Half an hour, by God. If you were the Mayor, but you're not."

"I offer no apology," Wolfe said, no hard feeling. "You had no appointment."

Cramer uttered a word that I omit, out of respect for his rank and his long and faithful public service. He was short on sleep too, and his eyes showed it. But he went on, "Appointment my ass. In the kitchen lapping up beer?"

His hand went to his inside breast pocket and came out with a piece of paper. "This is to you, but it was found on the body of a man who died by violence, so it's evidence and I'm keeping it. Shall I read it to you?"

Wolfe's shoulders went up an eighth of an inch. "As you please. I would return it."

"When?"

"As soon as Mr. Goodwin makes a copy of it."

Cramer looked at me. Apparently he decided that I would probably eat it, for he shook his head and said, "I'll read it." He unfolded the paper. "Printed at the top is 'From the desk of Daniel Kalmus.' It's dated yesterday, February 19, 1962. It says, written by hand, in ink: 'To Nero Wolfe: I hereby engage your professional services in my behalf and will pay you a reasonable fee plus necessary expenses. My attorney, Daniel Kalmus, will explain what I wish investigated, and you will work in collaboration with him and at his direction.' It's signed, 'Matthew Blount.'" He looked at me. "I see you've got it down."

"Sure," I said, and closed my notebook.

He returned the paper to his pocket. "All right," he told Wolfe, "I want to know. Monday you announced through Goodwin that you had been hired on behalf of Blount. Kalmus denied it. Tuesday you told me you had been hired but wouldn't say who had hired you. Wednesday, yesterday, Kalmus comes to you and, according to Goodwin, tells you that he wants to hire you but he has to get Blount's okay first. Last night Kalmus is murdered, and in his pocket is this note to you from Blount. I want to know and you're going to tell me. First, if you were hired Monday who hired you?"

Wolfe's brows went up. "Didn't Mr. Goodwin tell you?"

"You know damn well he didn't. He told us damn little. I wanted to hold him as a material witness, but the DA said no. Who hired you?"

"Isn't it obvious?" Wolfe turned a hand over. "Since she went there with Mr. Goodwin last evening, and I hadn't yet been engaged by Mr. Kalmus or Mr. Blount? Surely you can add two and two. Miss Blount, of course."

Cramer nodded. "Yeah, I can add. Now that you know I already know, you tell me. I also know she has been here since Monday night, and she's here now. I want to see her."

"She's under a doctor's care and you must have his permission. Dr. Edwin A. Voll—"

"Nuts. She discovered a dead body and left before the police arrived. Where is she, in the kitchen?"

"Mr. Goodwin discovered the body and you kept him all night." Wolfe turned to me. "Tell Miss Blount to bolt the door."

I swiveled to get the house phone, but Cramer roared, "Your goddam clowning!" and I swiveled back and grinned at him, and told Wolfe, "I hate to disturb her. If he starts upstairs there'll be time enough."

"That's the first thing you wanted to know," Wolfe told Cramer. "Miss Blount was and is my client. Now her father is too if I accept the engagement. Next?"

Cramer had his fingers curled over the chair arms, regaining control. He must have told himself many times over the years never to let Wolfe get him roaring, and here he had done it again. I expected him to get out a cigar and give it a massage, but Fritz saved him the trouble and expense by coming with my orange juice and coffee on a tray, and by the time he had put it on my desk and gone, and I had picked up the glass and taken a sip, Cramer had himself in hand.

He cleared his throat. "You remember," he said, a little hoarse, "that I said Tuesday I knew damn well you hadn't been hired. Okay, maybe I was wrong. But I also said that I thought you had got hold of something, some piece of information or evidence, that you thought would spring Blount, or at least might, and now I'm sure of it. It's a fair guess that you got it from the daughter. You used it to get Kalmus here. You told him what it was, or gave him a good hint, good enough so he told Blount and advised him to hire you, and Blount wrote you this note." He tapped his chest. "But Kalmus went ahead and did something with that piece of information himself without calling you in, and he got himself killed, and you learned about it or suspected it, and when Goodwin went there last night, taking the daughter along to get him in, he *expected* to find a corpse."

He paused for breath. "You and your goddam tricks. You probably *told* Kalmus to try something. I'd bet a dollar to a dime that you know who killed him. All right, you've jockeyed yourself into a fee, and Kalmus is dead, but your client is still in jail. Can you pry him loose or can't you? I'm not going to tell you for the twentieth time that if and when the DA thinks he can get you for obstructing justice by withholding evidence I'll do all I can to make it stick, and it looks as if this is it. Do I have to get a warrant for the arrest of Sarah Blount as a material witness?"

Wolfe, leaning back, took in air, all he had room for, which was plenty, and let it out. "Day before yesterday," he said, "I told you that you were incomparably better acquainted than I was with all the circumstances surrounding the death of Paul Jerin. That was true, and it still is, and it is equally true of the circumstances surrounding the death of Daniel Kalmus. You've had your army working at it for twelve hours, and I have merely read the morning paper. I have had no report from Mr. Goodwin. As for his expecting to find a corpse when he went there last night, at that time he was of the opinion, and so was I, that Kalmus had probably murdered Paul Jerin."

Cramer again uttered a word that I omit, the same one, and this time he added nothing.

"Not an opinion based on evidence," Wolfe said, "only on a suspicion held by a person I had spoken with, now of course discredited. You know Saul Panzer, Fred Durkin, and Orrie Cather."

"I ought to. What about them?"

"I hired them yesterday. Their assignment was to find evidence that Kalmus procured or possessed arsenic in some form prior to Tuesday evening, January thirtieth. When Mr. Panzer telephoned this morning I told him to drop it. Naturally."

Cramer was staring. "That's not your kind of lie. Three men would have to back it up."

"Nor ordinarily, I hope, my kind of truth — admission of error. Two hundred dollars of Miss Blount's money wasted."

Cramer still stared. "Kalmus was Blount's lawyer. You thought *he* had put arsenic in the chocolate? Why?"

"I considered that the most likely alternative. I reserve the *why*; as I said, it wasn't based on evidence. Now for the only alternatives left — Hausman,

Yerkes and Farrow—since Blount is excluded. Don't you too exclude him now? Your elaborate theory of my trickery was at fault, but one of its assumptions, that Kalmus was killed by the man who killed Jerin, is surely sound, and Blount is in jail. Should you keep him there?"

Cramer looked at me. I had the orange juice down and was on the second cup of coffee. "You lied in that statement," he said. "You said you went to Kalmus's place to find out if Blount had okayed hiring Wolfe, and what you really went for was to search it to try to find—" He cut it off short. "Oh, nuts." He got up. "This is the first time I ever left here," he told Wolfe, "thinking you may have grabbed a bear's tail and can't let go. You *may* have. If you actually thought at ten o'clock last night that Kalmus had killed Jerin where are you now? Who comes next? Huh?"

He turned and was on his way, but I stayed put, ready to whirl to the house phone. He just might make a dash for the stairs and the south room, and if I were in the hall it would be ticklish. You can bolt a door on a cop, but you can't touch him. But he turned right, to the front, and when the sound came of the door closing I stepped to the hall to see that he wasn't still inside, then returned to my desk, poured coffee, emptying the pot, and took a swallow. Wolfe had his arms folded and his eyes shut. I sat and drank coffee. The morning mail was there on my desk pad, mostly junk stuff as usual, and when my cup was empty, I started slitting it open.

Wolfe's voice came, a growl. "You had four hours sleep."

"I did not." I didn't turn. "It takes time to make milk toast and eat it. Do you want a report?"

"No."

I opened an envelope. "Here's another invitation to become a charter member of the National Foundation for the Control of Crime. Have you any instructions for me regarding crime?"

"I have a question. Can you see Mr. Blount today? Now?"

"I doubt it. No one can visit a man in for murder without bail but his lawyer and members of his immediate family, on a permit from the DA's office. The visiting hours are from six to eight P.M. He's your client, but you're not a lawyer. We can ask the DA's office for an exception and get turned down. Cramer might fix it as a special personal favor."

"Pfui."

"Check." I opened another envelope and removed the contents. "Weniger has a fresh batch of ready-mixed Berrichon cheese which is incredibly delicious. When we found Kalmus last night Sally's first idea was to go home to mother. Are you sure she's in her room?"

"No."

I turned. "No?"

"Fritz took a breakfast tray to her, and Dr. Vollmer came and saw her shortly before ten o'clock. I was in the plant rooms as usual, and he spoke to me on the house phone."

"She could have walked downstairs and on out."

"Yes. Go and see."

I swiveled, rose and headed for the hall. Naturally he was boiling, since she had given him a bum steer on Kalmus, but the one sure thing was that we had to reach Blount, and we had a member of his immediate family right there. Or we had had. On my way down I had noticed that her door was

closed and, mounting two steps at a time, I found that it still was. I was so
sure she had blown that my hand went to the knob without knocking, but I
told it no, and it swerved and rapped, somewhat louder than necessary; and
her voice came immediately: "Who is it?", and I opened the door and entered.

She was standing over by a window, and even with the light at her back, it
was apparent from a glance that she was twenty years older. Since Vollmer
had dosed her she must have slept, but she looked a lot worse than I felt
with my measly three hours. She had nothing to say, just stood facing me as
I approached. I stopped at two arms' length, eyed her, shook my head, and
said, "If you'll take some friendly advice, don't look in a mirror. What the
hell. You were wrong about him, but you didn't kill him. Fritz and I can
give you an airtight alibi. Inspector Cramer called and one of the things he
wanted was to see you, but Mr. Wolfe said no. When one of them does see
you, you can come clean with why we went there last night — to look for
something that might put it on Kalmus — but when they ask why we sus-
pectd him, as they will, just say you don't know, they'll have to ask Mr.
Wolfe or me. I came to tell you that and also to see if you were still here. I
thought you might have cleared out, gone home. I'm going on talking
because it may buck you up to hear the manly voice of one who is still with
you all the way in spite of your bobble on Kalmus. If and when you wish to
speak raise your hand. Speaking for myself, with only a professional interest, not personal, the silver lining makes up for the cloud. Cramer realizes
that if whoever killed Jerin also killed Kalmus, and that's better than even
money, he's got the wrong man in the coop. He'll hate to let go, and so will
the DA, but your father isn't just riffraff. A suit by him for false arrest would
be a lulu. Do you want to say something or shall I go on?"

"Archie," she said.

I nodded. "That's me. That's a good start. You're Sally Blount. Lunch in
an hour and a half."

"What will . . . what am I going to do?"

"Snap out of it, of course. You've had a hell of a jolt, and at least you're on
your feet, which is something. Fix your hair and get some lipstick on before
lunch. I think it very likely that Mr. Wolfe will ask you to go and see your
father this afternoon. A note written by him to Nero Wolfe, engaging his
services, was found in Kalmus's pocket, and naturally we want — "

The house phone buzzed. In that room it was on a table in a corner, and I
went and got it and said, "Me."

Wolfe's voice: "I'm in the kitchen. Is she there?"

"Yes. The worse for wear, but she's here."

She was standing there staring at me.

"Her mother is in the office and wishes to see her. Fritz will bring her up."

"Hold it!" I took two seconds. "No. I'll bring her down. Take it from your
expert on females, that's better. I'll explain why some day when you have an
hour to spare."

"I would prefer — "

"Sure you would. That's the only chair you really like. A little hardship
will be good for you."

I hung up and turned. I considered leading up to it, decided not to bother,
and said, "Your mother's downstairs and wants to see you. Lipstick?"

You never know. She might have collapsed, or screamed, or set her jaw and refused to budge, or anything. What she did was say "All right" and head for the door, and as I followed her out and down the two flights I was reminding myself of the one basic rule for experts on females: confine yourself absolutely to explaining why she did what she has already done because that will save the trouble of explaining why she didn't do what you said she would. I even forgot to notice the nice neck and curves into the shoulders.

Mrs. Blount was in the red leather chair. I suppose the tactful thing would have been for me to join Wolfe in the kitchen, but it was I who had spilled the beans at Sally's request, and I might be able to help with the sweeping up, so I went in part way and stood. Mrs. Blount got up, floated up, and took hold of Sally's arms. That woman unquestionably had witch in her; when she rose from a chair you got the impression that she had no need of muscles, it was some kind of automation that IBM never heard of. She didn't say anything, just took Sally's arms and looked, and damned if I didn't catch myself wishing I was Sally. They were close, nearly touching in front.

Sally's chin was up. "I'll say I'm sorry if you want me to," she said, "but I won't say I was wrong. Archie says I was, but I wasn't. He *was* in love with you, you *must* have known it. Lots of men are, you must know they are. Maybe I was wrong not trusting him about father, and if I was I would tell him I was sorry about that, but I can't now. Do you want me to tell *you* I'm sorry?"

Mrs. Blount was slowly shaking her head. "It doesn't matter," she said. "Of course we're both sorry."

"Yes, I suppose we are."

"Of course. I'm as sorry as you are that you hurt Dan like that. You hurt him terribly." She let go of Sally's arms. "About me, men being in love with me, there's nothing to say. You thought that years ago, you told me so, when you were just a child, and what can I say? You don't remember what I said then."

"Oh yes I do. You said love was really love only when it was returned. I never said you returned it. I never *thought* you did. Not even with Dan Kalmus. And what I did, coming to Nero Wolfe, and leaving that night, that had nothing to do with you, that was just for my father."

"I know it was. But—I'm your mother."

"I'd do it for you too. Mother, I *would.*"

"I believe you would. But I hope . . ." Mrs. Blount let it hang. She turned. "Mr. Goodwin, it seems to be your lot to hear our intimate affairs. That evening I didn't shake hands with you because I wouldn't mean it, but I would now." She extended a hand. "If you would."

I moved to take the hand. It was small and firm, and cold. "There's no longer a difference of opinion," I said. "Why not sit down?"

Sally had sat, and where, do you suppose? In the red leather chair. As I moved up one of the yellow ones for her mother I was thinking that jealousy wasn't enough, it was more complicated than that, but Mrs. Blount was speaking. "May I see Nero Wolfe? If he's not too busy?"

I said I'd see, and went. In the kitchen Wolfe was on the stool at the big table, drinking beer and watching Fritz peel shallots. He gave me a frown and asked, "They're bickering?"

"No sir. They're both sorry, but Sally copped the red leather chair. Mrs. Blount wants to see you if you're not too busy. She shook hands with me, so be prepared for physical contact with a woman."

Nothing doing. He said something to Fritz, left the stool, picked up the glass with one hand and the bottle with the other, proceeded to the office and on in, stopped three paces short of the yellow chair, said, "I'm Nero Wolfe, Mrs. Blount," bowed from the waist like an ambassador or a butler, went to his desk, put the glass and bottle down, sat, and asked Sally, "Should you be up? Dr. Vollmer said you need rest and quiet."

"I'm all right," she said. She didn't look it.

He turned to the mother. "You wanted me?"

She nodded. "Yes. My husband does. He wants you to come—he wants to see you. Today."

Wolfe grunted. "You have spoken with him?"

"No, but Mr. McKinney has. He's the senior partner in the law firm. He saw him this morning. My husband told him that he wouldn't—oh. Perhaps you don't know. Did Mr. Kalmus tell you, before he—did he tell you yesterday that my husband had written to you to engage your services?"

"No."

"He told me, on the phone yesterday afternoon. He said—"

"What time did he phone you?"

"About six o'clock. A little before six."

"Where did he phone from?"

"I don't know. He said he had told my husband that he thought you should be engaged to investigate something, and my husband had written to you. Then this morning—"

"Did Mr. Kalmus say what I was to investigate?"

"He didn't say *what*, just that it was something only he and my husband knew about. Then this morning Mr. McKinney went to see my husband, and—" She stopped, and smiled. It wasn't actually a smile, just a little twist of her lips that it took good eyes to see. "It isn't natural for me," she said, "saying 'my husband, my husband.' Since you're going to . . . I call him Matt. If I may?"

"As you please, madam."

"This morning Mr. McKinney went to see him, to tell him about Dan— Mr. Kalmus, and he said he wants to see you. He wouldn't tell Mr. McKinney what you are to investigate. Mr. McKinney is getting a permit for you from the District Attorney. He wanted to phone you, to ask you to come to see him, but I told him I would rather come to you. I . . . I insisted."

She didn't look like an insister or sound like one, but toughness is as toughness does, and there she was, no red in her eyes and no sag to her jaw, only a few hours after she had heard about Kalmus. But she wasn't cold, though her hand had been; you couldn't possibly look at her and call her cold.

Wolfe had his arms folded. "The permit will have to be for Mr. Goodwin," he said, "since I leave my house only on personal errands. But I need—"

"Matt told Mr. McKinney that he must see *you*."

"Outside this house Mr. Goodwin is me, in effect—if not my alter ego, my vicar. But I need some information from you. I presume it's your opinion that your husband did not kill Paul Jerin."

"Not in my opinion. Of course he didn't."

"Have you considered the alternatives?"

"Why . . . yes. Yes, I have."

"Eliminating the two men in the kitchen, the cook and the steward, and on that I accept the conclusion of the police and the District Attorney, one of the four men must have put the arsenic in the chocolate. The four messengers. You realize that?"

"Yes."

"That's manifest. But what was the motive? None of them had had any connection or association with Jerin. Therefore I concluded that the purpose was to injure your husband — indeed, to destroy him — and that purpose had apparently been attained. Yesterday my attention was centered on Mr. Kalmus as the most likely of the four. His objective was you. He wanted you, and your husband was in the way. When Mr. Goodwin —"

"That's absurd, Mr. Wolfe. *Absurd*."

He shook his head. "It still isn't absurd, now that I've seen you. For any man vulnerable to the lure of a woman, and most men are, you would be a singular temptation. Kalmus's death by violence has made the assumption of his guilt untenable, but it hasn't rendered it absurd. Now we have the other three — Hausman, Yerkes, and Farrow, your nephew. By the only acceptable hypothesis left to us, one of them killed both Jerin and Kalmus — Jerin to injure your husband, and Kalmus because he knew or suspected the truth and threatened exposure. When Mr. Goodwin sees your husband he may learn what it is that Kalmus knew, but you are here and I have questions for you; and if you hope to see your husband cleared you will answer with complete candor. Which of those three men had reason to destroy your husband?"

Her eyes were meeting his, straight. "None of them," she said. "Or if they did . . . no. It's impossible."

"Nothing is impossible in the relations between men and women. Your nephew, Morton Farrow. It has been suggested that he calculated that with your husband gone, through you he would be able to take control of the corporation. Is that impossible?"

"It certainly is. I wouldn't give my nephew control of anything whatever, and he knows it." Again the little twist of her lips. "He came to see you, didn't he?"

"Yes."

"Well."

Wolfe nodded. "Quite. But it's still possible that he miscalculated. Mr. Hausman?"

She made a little gesture. "Ernst Hausman is Matt's oldest friend. He is our daughter's godfather. He would do anything for Matt, anything. I'm absolutely sure."

"He's a dotard. Just short of demented. He came Monday evening to propose a scheme to extricate your husband unequaled, in my experience, for folly and fatuity. Either he's unhinged or he's exceptionally crafty, and if the latter you have been hoodwinked. Mr. Yerkes?"

She shook her head. "No."

"Your daughter got him to come here, and he told me himself of dissension with your husband. He wants to be president of his bank, and your husband favors another candidate."

She nodded. "I know. Matt has told me. Mr. Yerkes knows why and he doesn't resent it. It hasn't affected their friendship."

"Pfui. Are they paragons? But granting that, even a paragon is still a man. If it wasn't absurd to suppose that Mr. Kalmus coveted you, what about Mr. Yerkes? He has seen much of you, hasn't he?"

For five seconds I thought she wasn't going to reply. She sat stiff, her eyes level at him. Then she said, "Must you go out of your way to be offensive, Mr. Wolfe?"

"Nonsense," he snapped. "Offensive to whom? I suggest that you have a person and a personality capable of arousing desire; should that offend you? I suggest that Mr. Yerkes is not blind and has sensibility; should that offend him? We are not tittle-tattling, madam; we are considering your husband's fate. I asked for candor. How does Mr. Yerkes feel toward you?"

"We are friends." She stayed stiff. "But only because he and my husband are friends. My daughter has given you a wrong impression." She turned to the daughter, "I'm not blaming you, Sally, but you have." Back to Wolfe, "If you didn't mean to offend . . . very well. But I'm just what I am, a middle-aged woman, and what you suggest, I can't believe it. I certainly can't believe it of Charles Yerkes."

Obviously she meant every word. Lon Cohen had been right, she simply didn't know it. Wolfe's eyes were narrowed at her. The minute we were alone he would ask his expert on females for the low-down on her, and the expert was ready.

"Then we've wasted ten minutes," he said. He looked up at the wall clock. "What is to be done, what *can* be done, now depends on what Mr. Goodwin learns from your husband, and speculation on that would be idle. Can you reach Mr. McKinney now? To tell him that the permit must be for Mr. Goodwin?"

"Yes. At his office. He said he would be there."

"Do you know his number?"

She said she did, and floated up, and I vacated my chair for her; and she came and took it and dialed. My eyes went to Sally, and the look she gave me said as plain as words, *And now of course you've fallen for her too.* Which was a lie. I merely agreed with Wolfe that she had a person and a person-ality capable of arousing desire, a purely objective judgment.

12

AT a quarter to five that afternoon I was seated on a wooden chair at a wooden table, face to face with Matthew Blount, with my notebook on the table and my pen in my hand. After years of practice I had proved more than once that I could report verbatim, without notes, an hour-long three- or four-way conversation, but I was taking no chances with this one. Once before, six years back, I had been admitted to the hoosegow to confer with a man in for the big one, by name Paul Herold, alias Peter Hays, but that time there had been a grill between us, in a big room which contained other inmates and visitors. This time the room was small and we had no com-pany; the guard who had brought him was standing outside the glass door. Of course there were two reasons why the DA had let me come at an off hour and given us some privacy: one, Blount was a prominent citizen with plenty of prominent friends; and two, the murder of Kalmus had made him suspect that he had hold of the short end of the stick.

Matthew Blount, forty-seven, Harvard 1937, did not look as you would expect of a man who had been in the jug for twelve days on a murder rap. Not that he was chipper, but the skin of his well-arranged face, shaved that day, was smooth and clear, his hair had been trimmed within three or four days, his hands were perfectly clean and so were his nails, his custom-made jacket might have been pressed that morning, his shirt was on its first day, and he had a necktie on. He could have gone as was to Peacock Alley for a drink if he could have got past the guard at the door and on out.

It wasn't easy to persuade him that I was as good as Nero Wolfe. I explained that even if Wolfe had broken the one rule he never broke, and come, it wouldn't have made any difference, because as soon as he got home he would have told me everything that was worth telling.

"No, he wouldn't," Blount said. "He would have been bound to secrecy."

"Not a chance," I said. "No one has ever bound him to secrecy or ever will if it means leaving me out. He leaves me out only if and when *he* wants to. If he had come and you insisted that he keep it strictly to himself he would have walked out on you."

He shook his head. "I have told this to no one, not even my wife, because I was ashamed of it. I still am. Only Kalmus knew about it, and he's dead. I don't—oh. You're Archie Goodwin? You went there and found him, and my daughter was with you?"

"Right."

"Did my daughter—how was she?"

"She did fine. Three minutes after we found him she could leave on her own feet, alone, take the elevator down, and get a taxi. Your wife and daughter are both fine, as I told you, Mr. Blount. As soon as—"

"Forget the Mister."

"Sure. As soon as it had been arranged for me to get the permit to see you they left together, for home."

"I want a straight answer to a straight question. Did my wife tell Wolfe what it is that I want him to investigate?"

"No. She said she didn't know. She said no one knew—except Kalmus."

He nodded. "Then he kept his word. There aren't many men you can rely on absolutely. Dan Kalmus was one. And he's dead." He set his jaw. In a moment he went on, "This thing I'm ashamed of, I have told no one. McKinney wanted me to tell him this morning, he insisted, but I wouldn't. I didn't tell Kalmus, he knew all about it. From what he told me about Nero Wolfe, I decided he was the man to tell. Now you say I must tell you."

"Not you must. I only say that telling me is the same as telling Mr. Wolfe. I add this, that I will tell only him. Also I'll tell you what he would say if you tried to bind him to secrecy. He would say that the best protection for your secret would be his discretion, and that if a circumstance arose that made him think it necessary to disclose it he would first tell you. That's the best you'd get from him. From me, you get my word that I'll tell him and no one else in any circumstances whatever."

Our eyes were meeting, and he knew how to meet eyes. "Kalmus was my lawyer," he said.

"I know he was."

"Now I'll have to get another one, and I won't tell him, and I won't want you or Wolfe to tell him."

"Then we won't. What the hell, Blount, what is it? After all this—did you poison that chocolate yourself?"

"Yes. I did."

I stared. "*You* did?"

"Yes."

"Then no wonder." I put the pen in my pocket and closed the notebook, which I hadn't used. For this I preferred my memory to a notebook, which could be lost or even possibly taken from me on my way out. I demanded, "This is the fact known only to Kalmus and you that he was counting on to clear you?"

"Yes. I bitterly regret it and I'm bitterly ashamed of it. As you know, I made the arrangements for Jerin to come to the club. I arranged all the details. I knew he drank chocolate when he was playing chess, and I told the steward to have some prepared. I don't know, and I never will know, how in the name of God I conceived the idea of putting something in the chocolate that would befuddle him. I'm not a practical joker, I never have been. It may have been suggested by something somebody said, but if so I don't remember it, and anyway it was I who did it. It's even possible that I was prouder of my skill at chess than I thought I was and I had a sub-conscious resentment of a man who could give me odds of a rook and beat me. I hate to think I'm that petty, but damn it, I did it. I put something in the chocolate while I was taking it upstairs and stirred it with a pencil."

"Arsenic, to befuddle him?"

"It wasn't arsenic. It was poison, since anything toxic is a poison, but it wasn't arsenic. I didn't know exactly what it was until later, when I had it analyzed. Kalmus got it for me. I told him what I intended to do, as a precaution; there wasn't much risk of discovery, but I wanted to know if it would be criminally actionable. He said no, and he liked the idea, and that wasn't surprising because I thought he would, it was the kind of prank that would appeal to him. But he said I must be extremely careful of what I used, of course I knew that, and he offered to find out what would be best for the effect we wanted, and I asked him to get it, and he said he would. Which he did. He gave it to me that evening, that Tuesday evening, at the club. It was a two-ounce bottle, a liquid, and he told me to use about half of it. Which *I* did." He pointed a finger at me. "Listen, Goodwin. I don't want my wife or daughter ever to know what an incredible chump I was, in *any* circumstances."

"Yeah. I don't blame you. So of course you had to go for the chocolate and take it to him."

"Of course."

"And when Yerkes came and told you Jerin was sick you went and got the pot and cup and washed them out and brought fresh chocolate."

"Of course. I went to see him, and obviously he had had enough."

"Did you suspect then that there was something in the chocolate besides what you put in?"

"No, why should I? Kalmus had given me the bottle, and it had been in my pocket until I used it."

"When he got worse and Kalmus got Dr. Avery to go to him, didn't you suspect *then* that something else had been put in the chocolate by someone?"

"No. I didn't suspect that until two days later, Thursday. What I did suspect was that a mistake had been made in preparing the contents of the bottle. So did Kalmus. I began to suspect that when Jerin got so bad he had to be taken to the hospital, and on my way to the hospital—I walked, and I was alone—I hid the bottle, and later, on my way home—"

"Where did you hide it?"

"In a plant tub. In the areaway of one of the houses I passed there was a tub with an evergreen shrub, and I put the bottle in under the peat moss. When I left the hospital later, that was after Jerin died, I got it and took it home, and the next day I took it to a laboratory to have it analyzed. I got the report—"

"What laboratory?"

"The Ludlow Laboratories on Forty-third Street. I got the report on the analysis the next day, Thursday, and showed it to Kalmus. It was just what he had ordered, a very mild dilution of a mixture of chloral hydrate and carbon tetrachloride. It couldn't possibly have been fatal even if I had used all of it."

"No arsenic?"

"No, damn it, just what I said."

"Where's the report now?"

"In a locked drawer in my desk at my office, and the bottle too, with what's left in it."

"Well," I took a moment to look at it. "You didn't *suspect* that someone else had put arsenic in the chocolate, you *knew* it. Didn't you? Since you knew they had found arsenic in Jerin?"

"Of course I knew it."

"Did you have any idea who?"

"No."

"Have you any idea now?"

"Apparently it must have been one of four men, the four who acted as messengers, because they were the only ones who entered the library. That didn't seem possible because none of them could have had any reason. Then last week Kalmus had the idea that the purpose had been to get me—to get me where I am. But who? Of course not Kalmus, and which one of the other three could possibly have wanted to get me? They're my *friends*. One of them is my wife's nephew."

"Are you telling me you still have no idea which one it was?"

"I am."

I turned a hand over. "Look. Last night Kalmus was murdered, and almost certainly by the man who killed Jerin to get you. If so Kalmus had an idea, and a damn good one—too good. He tried to do something about it, which wasn't very bright since he had got you to hire Nero Wolfe, and he got slugged and strangled. He came yesterday afternoon and talked you into hiring Nero Wolfe, didn't he?"

"He didn't have to talk me into it. I didn't oppose it."

"But he talked, and he had some one man in mind. He must have. Didn't he say who?"

"No. He only said that he would have to tell Nero Wolfe about it, about

what I had put in the chocolate, because he had to have an expert investigator and Wolfe was the best. If he had any one man in mind he didn't say so.
He just—wait a minute. He did say one thing. He asked me if I didn't see
what might have happened, and I said no and asked him what he meant,
and he said he would tell me after he had discussed it with Wolfe. You think
he had a particular man in mind?"

"Of course he did."

"Who?"

That was one of the biggest temptations I have ever had to strangle. It
would have been highly satisfying to show the client then and there that
while Wolfe had the best brain he didn't have the only brain, not to mention
the additional pleasure of telling Wolfe what I had told the client. But I had
to skip it; there was one chance in a thousand that I was wrong, and I
needed to examine it for possible holes.

So I shook my head. "Search me," I said. "There may have been something in his apartment that would give a hint, but if so the cops have got it
now. I could go on asking you questions, plenty of them, but I've got what I
came for, the fact that was known only to Kalmus and you, and it's quite a
fact, and Kalmus would be alive now if he had waited to consult Nero Wolfe
instead of going ahead on his own." I picked up the notebook that had
nothing in it. "When Mr. Wolfe decides how to proceed he may let you know
and he may not. With you here it's complicated and it takes time." I rose
and got my hat and coat from a chair. "He can't consult with your lawyer
because even if you had one you wouldn't want him to know about this."

"But how will he—what will he do?"

"I don't know. That's for him. One thing sure, he'll do something, but
first he may send me back to you with questions. You may see me again
tomorrow." I stuck an arm in the coat.

He was on his feet. "My God," he said. "My whole—I'm completely in
the hands of a man I've never seen. Remember what I said, I'd rather stay
here a month, a year, than have my wife and daughter know what an utter
fool I was."

That was what was on his mind as we parted, with a handshake, but not
on mine. Was it possible that it was as simple as it looked? Wasn't there a
catch somewhere? As I went along the corridor, under escort, and on out to
the sidewalk, and flagged a taxi, I looked it over from every angle, and by
the time the taxi turned into Thirty-fifth Street I had decided that it was a
hundred to one on two conclusions: one, I knew exactly what had happened
that evening at the Gambit Club; and two, it would take a better man than
even Nero Wolfe to prove it. There was positively no crack anywhere to get a
wedge started.

But at least I could jostle him. Whatever he might have expected me to
bring back, if anything, he hadn't expected this. It was two minutes past six
as the taxi rolled to the curb in front of the old brownstone, so he would be
down from the plant rooms. I paid the hackie and got out, mounted the
stoop and used my key, put my hat and coat on the hall rack, and went to
the office. He was at his desk, opening a book with a blue binding; apparently *African Genesis* was finished. As I crossed to my desk he closed it. I put
the unused notebook in the drawer, sat and faced him, and said, "I can
name the man who killed Paul Jerin and Dan Kalmus."

"Flummery," he growled.

"No, sir. Any odds you name. But I prefer to see if you're as sharp as I am, so I'll just report, and I'll begin by giving you the jolt Blount gave me. He poisoned the chocolate."

"Pfui. Who killed Kalmus?"

"You'll soon know. Verbatim?"

"Yes."

I gave it to him, straight through. Usually he closes his eyes when I start a report and keeps them closed, but that time they opened when I asked Blount if he had poisoned the chocolate himself and he said yes, he did, and they didn't close again until Blount said the report and the bottle were in a drawer in his office desk. When I finished he opened them, cocked his head, and said, "No wonder you can name him."

"Yes, sir. I guess it's a tic. I have a question. Had this possibility occurred to you Tuesday noon when you had Sally phone and get them to come, including him?"

"No. How could it? It was the chocolate that made Jerin ill, indubitably. Now that is accounted for." He took a deep breath. "I am inexpressibly relieved. It has been all but intolerable, the strain of insulting my intelligence by forcing it to assume that one of them tampered with the chocolate when he entered to report a move, with Jerin there, and with the likelihood—no, certainty—that someone would interrupt at any instant. I knew it was egregious, and so did you. This is satisfactory, Archie." He breathed deep again. "An analeptic for my self-esteem. Has it any flaws?"

That showed how hard he had been taking it, asking me if it had any flaws instead of telling me. As I reported he had been so busy enjoying the feel of the pressure going that he hadn't concentrated, though he had got the main point.

"None that I can see," I said. "Of course his killing Kalmus is what settles it. With Kalmus and Blount out, and with your inexpressible relief that we can forget the other three messengers, what else is there? The arsenic got in him somehow. Of course there's plenty to guess about, for instance what Kalmus said or did that told him that Kalmus had figured it out, but that's not a flaw, it's only a gap. The only flaw I see is that there's no possible way you can ever prove that he killed Jerin. He's absolutely airtight. On Kalmus there may be a chance. He goes to Kalmus's apartment, maybe invited and expected, maybe not. Anyhow Kalmus lets him in, no doorman or hallman, and the elevator is do-it-yourself. He catches Kalmus off guard, knocks him out with the ash tray, gets the cord and uses it, and leaves. Fingerprints were no problem; they're no problem any more for anyone with an ounce of brains. The only chance would be if someone saw him enter or leave, and naturally the cops are working on that, though not with him in mind. In order to get motive you'd have to prove that he killed Jerin and Kalmus knew it or suspected it, and that's hopeless. As for his motive for killing Jerin, why not your theory, to get Blount because he wanted his wife. He had had more contacts with her person and personality than any of the others. As for taking some arsenic with him when he went to the club that night, that's easy. He knew what Blount was going to do because Kalmus had asked him what to use to get the effect Blount wanted. He would be the natural one for Kalmus to ask."

I nodded. "Perfect. Not a flaw except the one little detail that you and Homicide and the FBI all put together will never hang it on him. He was a sap to kill Kalmus because they might possibly tag him for that if they find someone who saw him enter or leave, and no matter how well Kalmus had it mapped, his killing Jerin, he couldn't possibly have had any evidence to back it up. There just couldn't be any. He could have told Kalmus to go soak his head."

Wolfe grunted. "An adequate exposition."

"I like it."

"Adequate as far as it goes. But granting that Kalmus had no evidence that would convince the police, even if he revealed the fact that Blount was determined to keep secret, his knowledge or suspicion presented another threat. What if he convinced Blount? Or, more to the point, Mrs. Blount?"

I raised a brow. "Yeah. Sure. That would have been a nuisance, no matter what happened to Blount. But while that may explain why he killed Kalmus, it doesn't alter the main—"

I stopped. He had leaned back and closed his eyes and started his lips going, out and in, out and in. As I said before, the lip exercise is not to be interrupted, and I crossed my legs and got comfortable for a two-minute wait, maybe three, glancing at my watch.

It was nearer thirty than three. Twenty-one minutes and ten seconds had passed when he opened his eyes and straightened up, setting a record. As always, I had exercised my mind by trying to decide where and what he was headed for, and as usual, I ended up with an assortment of possibilities, worth a dime a dozen. What he did that time was not in my assortment. No wonder he had taken a while to make up his mind; he had decided he had to call a woman on the phone.

"I must speak with Mrs. Blount," he said. "What's her number?"

I swiveled and reached for the phone, but he snapped, "No. The number. I'll dial it. You aren't here."

I turned. "Where am I?"

"I don't know. You have been dismissed, discharged by me for dereliction of duty immediately after you reported to me on your conversation with Mr. Blount. Don't leave the house. Don't answer the telephone or doorbell. Tell Fritz that if anyone asks for you, you have gone out—that's all he knows. I'll give you instructions after I have spoken with Mrs. Blount. What's her number?"

I told him, and sat and watched him dial it. As I said, that had not been in my assortment, getting fired just after I had brought him inexpressible relief.

13

THREE hours later, at twenty minutes to ten, I stood in the alcove at the end of the hall next to the kitchen, observing, through the hole in the wall, the cast that had been assembled for what I consider one of the best charades Wolfe has ever staged.

On the office side the hole is covered by a pretty picture of a waterfall on the wall five feet to the right of Wolfe's desk. On the alcove side it is covered by a metal panel at eye level which slides open without a hint of a noise, and, standing there, you find that the made-to-order waterfall is no obstruction to your view of the office or to your hearing. It wasn't quite as clear for either my eyes or my ears as if I had been inside seated at my desk, but I couldn't very well be there since I had been fired in disgrace, and besides, that chair won't hold two and Saul Panzer was in it.

At twenty minutes to ten Wolfe enterd, crossed to his desk, greeted them with three stingy nods—left, center, and right—and sat. All of them except Saul had come at the request of Mrs. Blount, after Wolfe's phone call to her. She had been put in the red leather chair by Saul, as instructed by me. In the front row of yellow chairs Sally was on the left, Ernst Hausman in the center, and Dr. Avery on the right, next to Saul at my desk. Behind them were Morton Farrow, the nephew, and Charles W. Yerkes, the banker.

Sally was the only one who had any idea what was up. Because she had had to be not only briefed, but rehearsed, thoroughly, she had come at seven-thirty and eaten dinner with me in the kitchen. In the kitchen for two reasons: so Wolfe could stick to his rule of no business at the table, and so Fritz could hear us. One of them might possibly ask Fritz some question when he admitted them, a question that must be answered right, and he had to know what to say. The one thing Sally didn't know was that I would be watching the performance through the hole. That was no part of it anyway; I was watching only to pass the time and to see and hear Wolfe tell a pack of lies; and Sally would probably have glanced so often at the picture of the waterfall that she might have attracted attention, and Wolfe wanted all the attention.

He was getting it, from seven pairs of eyes. "I don't thank you for coming," he told them, "because you came to oblige Mrs. Blount, not me, and because I am not in a mood to feel gratitude for anything whatever. As you all know, three days ago, Monday, I was hired by Miss Blount to act in the interest of her father. Yesterday he himself wrote me a note engaging my services, though I didn't learn of it until this morning. I am now compelled to make an extremely humiliating admission, and I felt that I should make it to all of you—you who because of your concern have been good enough to come to see me and answer my questions. True, one of you is twice a murderer, one of you killed both Paul Jerin and Daniel Kalmus, but I couldn't exclude him because I can't name him. I won't keep you long, I merely—"

"That's slander," Hausman blurted. "That's libel." His lips parted to show his teeth. "Unless you can prove it. Can you prove it?"

"No." I had Wolfe in profile and couldn't see his eyes. "Nor do I expect to. I am withdrawing from the case. I shall return to Miss Blount the fee she paid me. I have received none from her father."

I can't report the reactions of the others because I was focused on Sally. She did fine. She stared, and her mouth dropped open, and then she jumped up and cried, "But you can't! You *can't!* Where's Archie?" I could report on Mrs. Blount if there were anything to report, since her profile was almost on the line to Sally, but she didn't move or speak.

"Sit down," Wolfe commanded the former client. "Confound it, don't interrupt. This is the most galling moment of my long experience, and I don't want to prolong it. Mr. Goodwin is not here and he will never be here. I owe this —"

"Why? Where is he?"

"I don't know. Sit down! If you want him try Gehenna; if he isn't there he should be. I owe this to him." Wolfe's head turned to Mrs. Blount. "I force myself to face you, madam. I told you today that yesterday my attention was centered on Mr. Kalmus, but I didn't tell you what I had done about it. Yesterday afternoon I put four men to work. One of them is present, at the desk that was Mr. Goodwin's — Mr. Saul Panzer. Two of them were given certain errands pertaining to Mr. Kalmus. The other two, Mr. Panzer and Mr. Goodwin, were told to keep Mr. Kalmus under constant surveillance, dividing the hours. Late in the afternoon, by an unavoidable mischance, Mr. Panzer lost contact, and when he phoned to report it —" He turned. "What time, Saul?"

"Five-thirty-nine," Saul said.

Wolfe turned back. "Mr. Goodwin told him he would meet him at Mr. Kalmus's house and would take over for the evening. They met there a few minutes after six, and Mr. Panzer quit for the day, and Mr. Goodwin found a suitable post for watching the entrance to the house. Of course the one inviolable rule for such a job is that the surveillance must be constant. Otherwise —"

"But I don't understand." Mrs. Blount turned to Sally. "You went there with him — Mr. Goodwin. You told me you left at ten o'clock."

That had been deliberately invited. That point had to be covered. Not only did millions of people, all who read murder news in the papers, know that Sally and I had entered the house together, and when, but also Sally had told me that she had told her mother that she had eaten dinner with Wolfe and me Wednesday evening. We had considered briefing and rehearsing Mrs. Blount along with Sally, but had vetoed it as too risky. It wasn't at all certain that Mrs. Blount would play, and even if she would she might flub it. And the point had to be covered.

Sally handled it perfectly. "I know I did," she told her mother, not apologizing. "But I met him there. I didn't want to tell you I went alone, to meet him and get Dobbs to let him into Dan's apartment. I guess I — I was ashamed to. If he took me, if he made me go . . . that was different." She jerked her head to Wolfe. "Mr. Wolfe, where is he?"

Wolfe ignored her. "I was saying," he told Mrs. Blount, "that the surveillance must be constant, for otherwise its whole purpose may be nullified. Mr. Goodwin knew that, of course. But during the time he was at his post, or supposed to be, a man he should have recognized, since it was one of those now in this room, entered that house, and later he left it, and Mr. Goodwin did not see him. That was inexcusable nonfeasance, and this morning, when he returned from a night with the police and the District Attorney, I took him severely to task. But this afternoon, when he returned from his interview with your husband, I learned that it was worse than nonfeasance. He admitted that he had been absent from his post for nearly an hour. He refused to say where he had gone, but that was immaterial. If he had performed his duty, if he had not betrayed my trust, I would know who killed both Jerin and Kalmus, and I could complete the job both your daughter and your husband hired me for."

His head turned to the right and back to the left. "I would know which one of you is a treacherous friend and twice a murderer, and I could proceed with assurance. Now I can't proceed at all. As for Jerin, the chance of finding any cogent evidence is so remote that it's hopeless; and as for Kalmus, if any evidence exists it will be found by the normal police routine, not by me. So I am withdrawing. This is the greatest humiliation I have ever had to suffer, and I felt that all of you should hear me acknowledge it. I owed you that, but not more than that, and I'll leave." He pushed his chair back and rose. "As I said, I have discharged Goodwin, and I intend to see that he loses his license to function as a private detective. Pfui. He is not fit to function as anything whatever." He took a step. "Miss Blount, Mr. Panzer has a check for you, for the amount you paid me . . . Saul, give it to her." He headed for the door.

Again I can't report reactions, and certainly not words, for I was concentrating on the man I expected to be speaking with in an hour or so, Dr. Avery. He handled his act fully as well as Sally had handled hers. As Wolfe marched out he got up and went to Mrs. Blount and bent over her and spoke, but others were speaking too and I couldn't hear what he said; and when Hausman joined them he gave him place and a minute later went to Sally; and that was when I clamped my teeth, when Avery took hold of Sally's arm. She would pull back or tighten up when he touched her, but by gum she didn't and she managed her face as if she had been training it for years. Wonderful. Saul rescued her by coming with the check, and she could turn away to say she didn't want to take it, but she finally did, since that was in the script. As she was putting it in her bag I slid the panel shut and beat it to the kitchen. There was one chance in a million that when they left the office one of them would turn left instead of right, and round the corner to the alcove and bump into me, and that would have been regrettable. In the kitchen I went to the refrigerator for a carton of milk, and poured a glass. My part was to come, and I needed some support. Fritz was out in the hall to help Saul speed the parting guests.

I could hear the sounds of their going, including, twice, the closing of the front door, but I stayed put even after Fritz came and told me the coast was clear. A couple of minutes later Saul stepped in, stopped, and stared at me, and demanded, "What are you doing here? This is your day of infamy, and anyway I like my new job. Fritz, help me bounce him."

"Bah," I said. "I could take both of you with one hand. She did all right, huh?"

"She sure did. So did he."

"Why not? He's had plenty of practice. You were magnificent. The way you said *five-thirty-nine* — that was the high point." I went to the house phone and pushed the button for Wolfe's room, and his voice came: "Yes?"

"They're gone, and I'm off. Any changes?"

"No. Proceed."

"Okay. I'll try not to betray your trust again." I hung up, got my coat and hat from the chair where they were waiting and put them on, picked up my luggage, a packed bag also there waiting, told Saul he would hear from me soon, I hoped, and left by the back door. The subject might have turned his ankle going down the steps and be sitting out front rubbing it. The back door leads to the small yard where Fritz grows herbs, or tries to, and at the far end there is a bolted door in the eight-foot fence. Fritz came along to bolt the door after me. A narrow passage between two buildings takes you to Thirty-fourth Street. It was a quarter past ten when I climbed into a taxi and told the hackie the Talbott Hotel, where I had a reservation, and it was a quarter to eleven when, in Room 914, having let the bellhop hang up my coat and tipped him and told him good night, I went to the telephone and asked the switchboard to get a certain number.

One of the million little things you get on to that you'll probably never have any use for but you never know is how to tell the voice of an answering service filly from a maid or secretary. It would take a page to explain so I'll skip it. Since Dr. Avery was a bachelor there was no question of a wife or daughter. What I got was an answering service, and she said Dr. Avery wasn't available but she would be in touch with him later and did I care to leave a message. I did. I gave her my name and number and room number and said I had to speak with Avery as soon as possible on an extremely urgent matter.

Answering services are often a damned nuisance. If you ring a number and get no answer you can keep trying, but when you get an answering service all you can do is wait, and you don't know if your message will be relayed; and if you keep ringing back, say every ten minutes, she gets sore and you can give odds that it *won't* be relayed. That time, though, I had no kick coming. I had decided to start fidgeting at a quarter to twelve and to get the number again at midnight, so I was at ease in a chair with the *Gazette* when the phone rang at 11:20. I went and got it and told it hello.

"Who is this?" a voice demanded.

A question in that tone doesn't deserve an answer, so I said, "Who wants to know?"

"I'm Victor Avery. Are you Archie Goodwin?"

"Right. I need to be sure it's you, doctor, as much for your protection as for mine. You may remember that Tuesday evening you told Nero Wolfe the name of the gambit you used against Paul Jerin. What was it — the gambit?"

Brief silence. "The Albin Counter Gambit."

"Okay. Is there any chance that anyone is on an extension at your end?"

"No."

"I want to see you. It's a long story, and I'll just sketch it. I am no longer with Nero Wolfe. He fired me this afternoon. At six o'clock yesterday afternoon he sent me to put my eye on the entrance to Daniel Kalmus's house and keep it there. When I reported to him this morning, after spending the night with the cops, I told him that I had seen no one enter or leave that I recognized. This afternoon he tore into me and made me admit that I had been away from my post for about an hour. So he gave me the boot."

"That's unfortunate."

"Yeah. But the point is, I lied to him. I wasn't away from my post. I was right there all evening, and I did see someone I recognized, entering and leaving. That's what I want to discuss with you."

"Why with me?"

"Well, you've had a lot of experience giving people advice. Doctors get asked about all sorts of things. I think I can get my job back if I go to Mr. Wolfe and tell him the truth, and I want to know if you would advise me to do that. I can't put it off; if I do it at all I'll have to do it tomorrow. So I'll have to see you — say around noon? One o'clock?"

A longer silence. Then, and he managed his voice darned well: "I don't believe a word of this. It's some kind of clumsy trick. I'll have nothing to do with it."

"Okay. I'm sorry, but of course you'll be sorrier than I am. Good night and pleasant dreams."

I hung up, glanced at my watch, and went back to the chair and the paper. The only question was how long it would be. Half an hour? No. In exactly eighteen minutes the phone rang, and when I went and told it hello his voice came: "Goodwin?"

"Speaking. Who is this?"

"Victor Avery. On second thought I have decided I may be able to give you some good advice. Not at noon or one o'clock because I have appointments. The fact is, it would be difficult for me to make it before evening, around seven o'clock. The best place for a private conversation is in a car, and we can use mine. I'll pick you up at some convenient —"

"Save it," I cut in. It was time to get tough. "Do you think you're dealing with a cluck? Listen, and get it. There's a little restaurant, Piotti's, P-i-o-t-t-i, on Thirteenth Street just east of Second Avenue, downtown side. I'll be there, inside, expecting you, at one o'clock tomorrow. If you're not there by one-fifteen I'll go straight to Nero Wolfe. And I'll go anyway if you don't have with you one hundred thousand dollars in cash. Goodnight again."

"Wait! That's fantastic! I couldn't possibly get any such amount. And why should I?"

"Forget the rhetoric. Bring as much as you can, and don't make it peanuts, and maybe we can arrange about the rest. Now I'm going to bed and I don't like to be disturbed. You have it? Piotti, Thirteenth Street east of Second Avenue?"

"Yes."

"Better write it down."

I hung up, straightened, and had a good stretch and yawn. On the whole I thought I had done about as well as Sally, but of course my part wasn't finished. After another stretch I returned to the phone and asked the switchboard to get a number, and in a minute a voice came: "Nero Wolfe's residence, Saul Panzer speaking."

I falsettoed. "This is Liz Taylor. May I please speak to Archie?"

"Archie is out streetwalking, Miss Taylor. I'm just as good, in fact better."

I normalized. "You are like hell. All set. One o'clock at Piotti's. We'll have a busy morning. Meet me for breakfast at eight o'clock in the Talbott restaurant."

"No snags?"

"Not a snag. Like falling off a log. As I said to the subject, pleasant dreams."

Getting ready for bed, as I buttoned my pajama jacket it occurred to me that the character who had done such a neat job with Kalmus might be capable of something really fancy, so after bolting the door I put the table against it and a chair on top. The windows were absolutely inaccessible

without a rope down from the roof, and if he could manage that between
midnight and seven A.M. he was welcome to me.

14

AT ten minutes to one Friday afternoon I was seated at one of the small
tables along the right wall of Piotti's little restaurant, eating spaghetti with
anchovy sauce and sipping red wine — and not the wine you'll get if you go
there. Wolfe had once got John Piotti out of a difficulty and hadn't soaked
him, and one result was that whenever I dropped in for a plate of the best
spaghetti in New York I got, for sixty cents, a pint of the wine which John
reserved for himself and three or four favorite customers, and which was
somewhat better than what you paid eight bucks for at the Flamingo.
Another result had been that back in 1958 John had let us use his premises
for a setup for a trap, including running some wires through the cellar,
coming up through the floor in the kitchen at one end, and up to one of the
tables in the restaurant at the other end. That was the table I was sitting at.

That morning hadn't been as busy as I had expected, chiefly because the
wires running through the cellar were still there, intact, and when we tested
them they were as good as new. We didn't have to call in a technician at all.
For the kitchen end Saul brought the tape recorder from the cupboard in
Wolfe's kitchen, and for the restaurant end I bought the latest model midget
mike. That was the main cash outlay, $112.50 for the mike, a lot of lettuce for
a mike, but it had to be good and it had to fit into the bowl of artificial
flowers on the table. Of course the bowl had to be the same as those on the
other tables, and we had a devil of a time making a hole in the bottom for
the wires to come through. Against the risk that my table companion would
take it into his head to move the bowl and find himself pulling wires up
through a hole in the table, which would have stopped the show, we made
two smaller holes in the bottom of the bowl and screwed it to the table. So if
he tried to move it and it wouldn't budge I could say, "By golly, Piotti
doesn't let the customers walk out with anything, does he?"

Everything was in order by half past eleven, well before the lunch hour,
which is early in that neighborhood. Saul went to the kitchen, to stick there,
since it was just possible that the subject might come for a look around in
advance, and it wouldn't do for him to catch sight of the man who had
taken my job. I went to the Talbott, to learn if there were any messages for
me. There weren't. I phoned Wolfe that we were ready, and returned to
Piotti's at twelve-thirty. John had kept the table free, and I took it and
began on the spaghetti and wine. At ten minutes to one the tables were
pretty well filled with customers, and two of them were known to me. At the
next table in front of me, seated facing me, was Fred Durkin, and at the next
table but one back of me was Orrie Cather. I was facing the door. Very neat.

At four minutes to one Dr. Victor Avery entered, stopped three steps in,
saw my raised hand, and came. I took in a forkload of spaghetti while he
removed his coat and hat and hung them on the wall hooks, and I was

sipping wine as he sat. He looked more middle-aged than he had last night, more than middle-aged, and not so well-fed.

"The spaghetti here is something special," I said. "Better have some." He shook his head. "I'm not hungry."

"The wine is special too."

"I never drink during the day."

"Neither do I usually, but this is a special occasion." My eyes were on my plate, where I was twisting spaghetti onto my fork, and I raised them and aimed them at him. "How much did you bring?"

His hands were open on the table and his finger tips were working. "I came out of curiosity," he said. "What kind of a trick is this?" He was nothing like as good as he had been on the phone, but of course he had had a hard night.

I leaned to him. "Look," I said, "you'll just waste your breath dodging. I saw you go in Kalmus's house Wednesday and I saw you come out. Yesterday I asked—"

"What time did I go in? What time did I come out?"

"Nuts. Don't think I can't tell Nero Wolfe, and also the cops, and also a judge and jury when the time comes. If you want to try fixing up an alibi, you know the times as well as I do. This isn't a quiz show with you asking the questions. Yesterday I asked myself a question, could it have been you who killed Paul Jerin? Of course it could; when you mixed the mustard water you put arsenic in it. But the trouble was, Jerin had got sick before you went in to him, and that stopped me, until yesterday afternoon, when I learned *why* he got sick before you were called in. Not only that, I also learned that you knew he was going to get sick, so you brought some arsenic along because you knew you would have a chance to use it. So you *had* killed Jerin, and I knew why, or at least a damned good guess. Tuesday evening Nero Wolfe told you that the man who killed Jerin had no malice for him, he wanted to destroy Matthew Blount, and you said tommyrot, but you knew it wasn't, because you were the man who did it and that was your motive. Then when you learned that Kalmus had figured it out and was on to you, you went to his place and killed him, and I saw you coming and going. So how much did you bring?"

He had realized that his hands were out of control and had taken them from the table. "That's *all* tommyrot," he said. "Every word of it."

"Okay, then get up and walk out. Or ring the District Attorney's office and have them come and take me for attempted blackmail. The phone booth is in the rear. I promise to wait here for them."

He licked his lips. "That's what I ought to do," he said, "report you for attempted blackmail."

"Go ahead."

"But that would be—it would start—scandal. It would be very—disagreeable. Even if you saw me entering and leaving that house—you didn't, but even if you did—that wouldn't be proof that I killed Kalmus. It was after ten o'clock when you went up to his apartment and found the body. Someone had entered after I left—that is, it would have been after I left if I had been there. So your lie that you saw me enter and leave—it's not a very good lie. But if you—"

"Cut." I snapped it. "I'll listen to sense if you've got any, but not that crap. We'll settle that right now, yes or no, and if it's no *I* get up and walk out. To Nero Wolfe. Did you enter that house Wednesday, late afternoon or early evening, whichever you want to call it, or didn't you? Yes or no."

He licked his lips. "I'm not going to give you the satisfaction of coercing me into—"

I had pushed my chair back and was getting up. He put a hand out. "No," he said. "Sit down."

I bent over to him. "No?"

"I mean yes."

"Did you enter that house at that time Wednesday?"

"Yes. But I didn't kill Dan Kalmus."

I sat down and picked up my glass for a sip of wine. "I advise you to watch your step," I told him. "If I have to keep jumping up to make you talk sense it will attract attention. How much money did you bring?"

His hand went into his breast pocket but came out again empty. "You admit you're a blackmailer," he said.

"Sure. Birds of a feather, a murderer and a blackmailer."

"I am not a murderer. But if I refuse to be victimized and you do what you threaten to do I'll be involved in a scandal I can never live down. I'll be under a suspicion that will never be entirely removed. To prevent that I'm willing to—to submit. Under protest."

His hand went to the pocket again and this time got something, a slip of paper. He unfolded it, glanced at it, said, "Read that," and handed it to me. It was handwritten in ink:

> I hereby affirm, and will swear if necessary, that my statement to Dr. Victor Avery that I saw him enter the house of Daniel Kalmus on Wednesday, February 14, 1962, was untrue. I have never seen Dr. Victor Avery enter that house at any time. I write this and sign it of my own free will, not under duress.

I dropped it on the table and grinned at him. "You could frame it," I suggested.

"I have ten thousand dollars in cash," he said. "When you write that and sign it and give it to me, I'll hand it over."

"And the other ninety thousand?"

"That's fantastic. I couldn't possibly pay such a sum, and even if I had it . . . it's absurd. In addition to the ten thousand now, I'll guarantee to give you another twenty thousand within a week."

"I'll be damned. You actually have the gall to haggle."

"I'm not haggling. To me thirty thousand dollars is a fortune."

I regarded him. "You know," I said, "I admire your nerve, I really do. You're too much for me." I looked around, caught the eye of Mrs. Piotti, and signed to her, and she came. I asked her how much, and she said a dollar-forty, and I handed her two ones and told her to keep the change. Of course that was just for appearance's sake; I had given John fifty bucks and would give him more.

I shook my head at Avery. "Positively too much for me. We'll have to go and put it up to Mr. Wolfe."

He gawked. "What?"

"I said, put it up to Mr. Wolfe. This isn't my show, it's his, I only work for him. That last night, me being fired, that was just dressing. You'll have to come and do your haggling with him. He certainly won't settle for a measly thirty grand."

He was still gawking. "Nero Wolfe is behind this?"

"He sure is, and also in front of it." I shoved my chair back. "Okay, let's go."

"I will not."

"For God's sake." I leaned to him. "Dr. Avery, you are unquestionably the champion beetlebrain. Nero Wolfe has got you wrapped up and addressed straight to hell, and you sit there and babble *I will not*. Do you prefer hell or are you coming?" I picked up the slip of paper and pocketed it, rose, got my coat from the hook and put it on, got my hat, and headed for the door. As I passed the next table Fred Durkin, crammed with spaghetti and wine to his chin, got up and headed in the opposite direction, toward the kitchen. As I emerged to the sidewalk a gust of winter wind nearly took my hat, and as I clapped my hand on it here came Avery, his coat on his arm. When he tried to put the coat on, the wind tossed it around, so I helped him, and he thanked me. A murderer and a blackmailer, both with good manners.

Second Avenue was downtown, so we walked to Third for a taxi. When we had got one and were in and rolling I rather expected Avery to start a conversation, but he didn't. Not a word. I didn't look at him, but out of the corner of my eye I saw that his hand was working inside his overcoat pocket. If he had nerve he also had nerves.

Wolfe made more concessions during the five days of the Blount thing than he usually makes in a year. Ordinarily, at ten minutes to two, the hour at which Avery and I mounted the stoop of the old brownstone and entered, Wolfe is right in the middle of lunch, and I was expecting to have to entertain the guest in the office for at least half an hour while we waited. But as I learned later from Fritz, he had been told when he took up the breakfast tray that lunch would be at 12:45 sharp. To you that merely means that Wolfe had sense enough to change the schedule when it was called for, but to me it meant that at breakfast time he had taken it for granted that half an hour with Avery at Piotti's would be all I would need and I would have him at the office before two o'clock. It's nice to have your gifts recognized, but some day he'll take too much for granted.

So I had barely got the guest into the office and seated in the red leather chair when Wolfe entered. I went and shut the door. Saul and Fred and Orrie would soon be passing by on their way to the kitchen with the recorder and tape. As I returned to my desk Avery was blurting, "I'm here under protest, and if you think you and Goodwin—"

"Shut up!" It wasn't a roar, just the crack of a whip. Wolfe, seated, turned to me: "Was there any difficulty?"

"No, sir." I sat. "All okay. More than enough. To the question did he enter that house at that time Wednesday, a flat yes. He offered me ten thousand cash now and a guarantee of twenty grand more within a week if I would sign a statement that I hadn't seen him. He didn't—"

"That's a lie," Avery said.

So he hadn't started a conversation in the taxi because he had been too busy deciding on his line, and the line was to call me a liar and make Wolfe start from scratch. Not so dumb at that.

Wolfe leaned back and regarded him, not with hostility, merely as an object of interest. Of course he was just passing the time until the trio arrived. "A book could be written," he said, "on the varieties of conduct of men in a pickle. Men confronted with their doom. In nearly all cases the insuperable difficulty is that their mental processes are numbed by the emotional impact of the predicament. It is a fallacy to suppose that the best mind will deal most effectively with a crisis; if the emotion has asphyxiated the mind what good is it? Take you with Mr. Goodwin in that restaurant. Since you have succeeded in your profession you probably have a fairly capable mind, but you reacted like a nincompoop. You should either have defied him and prepared to fight it out, or, asking him to sign a document that would remove his threat, you should have met his demands in full; and you should have admitted nothing. Instead, you tried to dicker, and you made the one vital admission, that you had entered that house Wednesday evening. Indeed —"

"That's a lie." Apparently that was to be his verse and chorus. Not a bad idea if he had the guts to fight it out, but in that case he should get up and go.

The doorbell rang. I went and opened the door to the hall a crack. Fritz came from the kitchen and went to the front and opened up, and here came the trio, not stopping at the rack to take their coats off. Saul nodded at my face in the crack as he passed, and Orrie made the sign, a jerk with the tips of thumb and forefinger joined. When they had disappeared into the kitchen I swung the door wide, returned to my desk, and reached around behind it to flip a switch. That was all that was needed at my end.

Wolfe was talking. ". . . and perhaps that would have been your wisest course. After Mr. Goodwin had spoken with you from his hotel room last night, you knew you were in mortal danger, and you thought he was its sole agent. He alone had knowledge of the crucial fact; but for him, you had little to fear. Why didn't you kill him, at whatever hazard? You knew where he was and you had all night. Disguise yourself and bribe one of the hotel staff, any amount required, to get you into the room. Engage the room next to his, or above or below it, and go from window to window. A man in your plight should be able to scale a perpendicular wall of marble by force of will. Any normal will can overcome a mere difficulty; one made desperate by impending disaster should —"

The house phone buzzed. I took it and said, "Archie," and Saul's voice came: "All set."

"Right. I'll buzz you." I hung up and gave Wolfe a nod, and he nodded back and sat up.

"I'm boring you," he told Avery. "What you might have done is vinegar. What matters now is what you're going to do, and to consider that realistically you must hear something." He turned. "All right, Archie."

I pushed the button, three short, and swiveled to face Avery. In a moment there was a faint whirring sound from a grill at the wall back of my desk, where the loudspeaker was, then a few little crackles, then other noises, not loud, which could have been from a restaurant where people were moving and eating and talking, and then my voice:

"The spaghetti here is something special. Better have some."

After a slight pause another voice: "I'm not hungry."

"The wine is special too."

"I never drink during the day."

"Neither do I usually, but this is a special occasion. How much did you bring?"

"I came out of curiosity. What kind of a trick is this?"

"Look, you'll just waste your breath dodging. I saw you go in Kalmus's house Wednesday and I saw you come out. Yesterday I asked—"

"What time did I go in? What time did I come out?"

As Wolfe had said, a book could be written on the varieties of conduct of men in a pickle. At the sound of the first words, mine, Avery frowned at me. When his own voice came, "I'm not hungry," he twisted his neck to look around, right and then left. Then he clamped his teeth on his lip and sat frowning at me through my main spiel, and when he said, "That's all tommyrot, every word of it," he nodded in approval. But when I asked him did he enter that house at that time Wednesday and he said yes, he yawped "That's a lie!" and bounced up and started for me. I was on my feet by the time he arrived, but he had no idea of slugging or choking, he had no idea at all, he was merely reacting. I sidestepped only because I wanted to hand something to Wolfe—the slip of paper—and he was in the way. Wolfe took it and read it while all that came from the grill was the background restaurant noise when I had been reading it, and he dropped it on his desk just as I dropped it on the table and said, "You could frame it." Good timing. And Avery stopped reacting and acted. He lunged to get the slip of paper, but I beat him to it. I call your attention to Wolfe. If he had hung onto it he might have had the bother of warding off Avery, so he left it to me. More taking for granted. Avery grabbed my arm and I didn't jerk loose, thinking the poor goof might as well have the satisfaction of that much personal contact. He was gripping me with both hands, but when I told him, or the speaker did, that Wolfe had him wrapped up and addressed straight to hell, which I admit was a little corny, he let go and stood, his jaw set, looking down at Wolfe. I stepped to the end of my desk and reached around to the switch and turned it off, and when I faced around Saul and Fred and Orrie were there, in a group at the door.

"I thought it best," Wolfe told Avery, "to leave no loophole." He motioned at the group. "You saw the man on the left, Mr. Panzer, here last evening. He had the tape recorder in the kitchen. The others, Mr. Durkin and Mr. Cather, were at nearby tables in the restaurant while you and Mr. Goodwin conversed. There's no room for wriggling, doctor."

Avery took a couple of uncertain steps toward the group and stopped. Wolfe said, "Move aside, Saul. Don't block the door—if he wishes to leave."

Avery turned. "Five of you," he said. "*Five* of you." He came to the desk. "You said a tape recorder? It's on a tape?"

"Yes."

"I'll give you one hundred thousand dollars for it. In cash. Tomorrow morning. For the tape and that signed by Goodwin. You can't prove anything, I know that, but I don't . . . All right. Tomorrow morning."

Wolfe nodded. "You see? You tried to dicker with doom. Mr. Goodwin would have declined it, but you didn't know that, and if you had gone ready to meet his terms it would have been ticklish business getting any admission from you for the record. Now I can decline with unconcern. You're right, I can't prove anything, but I can earn my fee, and I can demonstrate to my client that I have earned it — by letting Mr. Blount and his wife and daughter listen to that tape."

"No," Avery said. "Never."

"But yes. Of course."

Avery's jaw was working. "How much do you want?"

Wolfe shook his head. "My self-esteem is the hitch. Quite possibly you are of more value to the world, to the society I am a member of, than Matthew Blount. If I held its interest paramount perhaps I should salvage you, but there's my ego. Like most of my fellow-beings, I like myself too well. I'll be insufferably smug as I sit and watch the Blount family listen to that tape. You had better go, doctor."

"I'm not going. How much will you take? How much?"

"Confound it, go."

"No! No! No!"

Wolfe turned. "Fred. Orrie. Archie and Saul have done a day's work. You have been merely spectators. Take him out."

They came, and, as they took his arms, Fred said gruffly, "Come on, what the hell." I would like to be able to record that he jerked away and marched out, but I'm reporting. He had to be propelled, and, as they hustled him to the door, he squawked, and as soon as they were in the hall Saul shut the door. Wolfe growled at me, "Without dignity a man is not a man. Get Mr. Cramer."

I thought it would have been more dignified to wait until Fred and Orrie returned to say he was out of the house, since he wouldn't want Cramer until he came down from the plant rooms at six o'clock, so there was no rush, but I obeyed. And had a time of it. Some character at Homicide wasn't going to relay me at all, even to Sergeant Stebbins, unless I told him everything about everything, and when he finally passed me on it was to Lieutenant Rowcliff. Of course that was a battle, and I won it only because I reminded him of an occasion a couple of years back when he had hung up on me and we had called the District Attorney, and Wolfe had given him something that Cramer would have liked to get first. So at last I got Cramer and gave Wolfe a nod, and he took his phone. I stayed on.

"This is Nero —"

"I know it is. I'm busy. What do you want?"

"You. Here at your earliest convenience. The man who killed Paul Jerin and Daniel Kalmus just left my house, and I —"

"*Left* your house?"

"Yes, and I —"

"Why did you let him go?"

You couldn't beat that for a compliment. Not how do you know he killed them, or this or that, but why did you let him go.

"Because he was repugnant," Wolfe said. "I put him out. I would like —"

"Who is he?"

"Confound it, stop interrupting. I would like to refer the matter to you. I have something here —"

"I want his name now!"

"No. When may I expect you?"

"You know damn well when you may expect me." He hung up.

I looked at my watch. Twenty to three. It was hard to believe. Another rule in danger, and this time the strictest of all. For years it had been to the plant rooms at four on the dot, no matter what, every day except Sunday, and he couldn't leave Cramer in the middle of the showdown. It had certainly got under his skin. As I swiveled to ask Fred and Orrie if any bones had been broken the phone rang, and I swiveled back and got it.

"Nero Wolfe's office, Archie Good—"

"It's Sally, Archie."

"Good morning. I mean good afternoon. We miss you. I was going to ring you as soon as I could fit it in. I've been kind of busy."

"Did you . . . was it . . ."

"I did and it was. Everything went according to plan. I'm glad to have met you and I want your autograph. If this is the first good thing you ever did you did it good. If you ever want a job as a blackmailer's moll give me a ring."

"But was it . . . did he . . ."

"He did exactly what he was expected to do. I'll tell you all about it, words and music, but not now. Everything's under control. Just sit tight for another twenty-four hours, maybe less. Of course say nothing to your mother—or to anyone."

"Of course not. But can't I . . . I could come . . ."

"Not now, we're busy. If you can't take it easy take it hard, but take it until I call you. Okay?"

"Okay." She hung up.

15

CRAMER, seated in the red leather chair, said, "Skip the buildup. What have you got?"

It was a family party, with Saul and Fred and Orrie in chairs lined up before Wolfe's desk, with refreshments. Fred had bourbon and water, and Saul and Orrie and I were sharing a bottle of champagne. Wolfe had beer. Cramer had nothing, though he had been invited.

Wolfe put his glass down and licked his lips. "It's a preamble, Mr. Cramer, not a buildup. It's necessary, and it will be brief. You may recollect an event that occurred four years ago in Piotti's restaurant on Thirteenth Street."

"I do. Sergeant Stebbins in the kitchen with Goodwin, with earphones."

"Yes. A similar event took place there today, with variations. Mr. Panzer was in the kitchen, with a tape recorder instead of earphones. Mr. Durkin and Mr. Cather were in the restaurant, at separate tables. At still another table was Mr. Goodwin, alone, and the bowl of hideous artificial flowers on that table contained a microphone. He had an appointment with Dr. Victor Avery. Shortly before one o'clock Dr. Avery entered the restaurant, went to the table where Mr. Goodwin was, and sat, and Mr. Piotti notified Mr. Panzer in the kitchen, and he started the tape recorder. You are now going to hear the playback. Have I described the circumstances sufficiently?"

"Yes."

"Have you any questions?"

"I'll hear it first."

Wolfe turned. "All right, Saul." Saul got up and left, taking a glass of champagne along. The speaker was already on. In a moment came the crackles and background noises, and then my voice:

"The spaghetti here is something special. Better have some."

There was no point in watching Cramer; he would sit with his eyes on Wolfe, his lips tight and his eyes narrowed, no matter what he heard. It was more interesting to watch Fred and Orrie, who hadn't heard it and knew next to nothing about it. They had turned on their chairs to face the grill. Fred assumed a deadpan, but broke into a broad grin when I told Avery to ring the DA's office. Orrie cocked his head critically, to judge a colleague's performance, and he glanced at me off and on to show that he appreciated the fine points. He smiled and nodded approvingly when I pried it out of Avery that Wolfe had him wrapped up and addressed straight to hell. Just jealous because he knew such a fine line was out of his class—followed by my exit line, "Do you prefer hell or are you coming?" Curtain.

Cramer pulled his feet back, not to get up. "By God," he said hoarsely. "Did he come? Here?"

"Yes. After he had heard the recording he offered me one hundred thousand dollars in cash, in the hearing of these four men, for the tape and the statement signed by Mr. Goodwin. . . . Give it to him, Archie."

I got the slip of paper from my pocket and went and handed it over. Cramer read it and looked up. "This is in his handwriting?"

"I don't know. Presumably."

He read it again, folded it, and stuck it in his pocket. "I have known you to pull some awful fancy ones. How fancy is this?"

"If by 'fancy' you mean specious, not at all. Knowing that Dr. Avery was twice a murderer, I determined to establish it. Since it was impossible—"

"When did you know it? Did you know it when—" Cramer chopped it and got up and made for me, and, knowing what he wanted, I left my chair and he sat. While he took the phone and dialed I helped myself to some champagne, and by the time I had the bottle back in the ice he had Sergeant Stebbins.

"Purley? I'm at Wolfe's. Get Dr. Victor Avery and bring him in and keep him until I get there. Go yourself. Don't stop for a warrant. Take him as a material witness in the Kalmus murder, and I mean take him. I want him there when I come—half an hour, maybe more."

He stood, gave me as sour a look as he had ever favored me with, returned to the red leather chair, gave Wolfe the same look if not worse, and said, "And when I go you and Goodwin are going with me. Who do you two baboons think you are? Goodwin told a barefaced lie and it's in his signed statement, and yesterday morning you told me I was better acquainted with all the circumstances surrounding the death of Kalmus than you were. How you expect to get away with—damn you, don't sit there with that curl on your lip! I'll wipe *that* off!"

"I'll save you the trouble," Wolfe said, no hard feeling. "Mr. Goodwin lied to Dr. Avery, not to you. He didn't have that house under surveillance Wednesday. As he told you, he arrived there shortly after ten o'clock, accompanied by Miss Blount, so he couldn't have seen the murderer enter or leave. We gulled Dr. Avery. Since it was impossible —"

That interruption wasn't by Cramer. Saul had entered with another bottle of champagne. Stopping three steps in and seeing that Wolfe was giving him the floor, he came and got the extra glass and filled it and handed it to Cramer, refilled Orrie's and mine and his own, put the bottle in the bucket, and sat. Cramer, who had accepted the glass without knowing it, spilled a little on his pants, glared at the glass in his hand as if demanding how it got there, moved it to his mouth, drained it in three gulps, and put it down on the stand.

He sent the glare at Wolfe. "I don't believe it," he said. "To make me swallow it, try telling me how you knew Avery had entered that house if Goodwin hadn't seen him. And knew he had killed Jerin. Let's hear you."

Wolfe nodded. "That's the point, of course. It's complicated."

"I'll bet it is. I'll try to understand it. Well?"

Wolfe leaned back. "It was an inference, not a conclusion from demonstrable evidence, for I had none. The inference had three legs. First, Blount had not killed Jerin. As you know, I had previously made that assumption, and the murder of Kalmus established it. Second, Jerin had not been killed by one of the messengers — Hausman, Yerkes, Farrow. I have already apologized to myself for my preposterous pretense that that was possible; I now apologize to you. With Jerin sitting there, the tray at his elbow, and with other messengers entering momentarily?"

He jerked a hand to brush it off. "Pfui. Third, only Avery was left. He had had an opportunity, as good as Blount's if not better; he had made a concoction, ostensibly mustard water, and administered it to Jerin. It was credible that he had had a motive; as recorded on that tape, Mr. Goodwin told him that he had had no malice for Jerin, his purpose was to destroy Blount. That can't be —"

"Why did he want to destroy Blount?"

"Because he wanted Blount's wife. That can't be established, since the only evidence for it is inside him, but neither can it be impeached. I presume you have spoken with Mrs. Blount?"

"Yes. Several times."

"Is it credible that she might provoke an appetite unwittingly?"

"Hell yes."

"Then motive is at least plausible. But granted opportunity and motive, two questions remain: why was Jerin taken ill so conveniently before Avery was called in to attend him, and why, again so conveniently, did Avery have arsenic on his person? Indeed, it was not until the answers to those two questions were supplied by Mr. Goodwin, after his conversation with Mr. Blount at the prison yesterday, that my attention was on Dr. Avery at all. There's a third question, did Dr. Avery know in advance that Jerin would be taken ill, but that's merely a part of the second one, and the answer is that he could have and almost certainly did. Kalmus had told him. That was what —"

"Come on," Cramer cut in. "Goodwin got that from Blount. He's in jail for murder. He's your client. He's not mine."

"I'll come to that. I'm telling you why I hit on Avery. That was what made Kalmus suspect him, and he made the mistake of undertaking to deal with him tête-à-tête — a mistake that cost him his life." Wolfe turned a palm up. "So there it was. When Mr. Goodwin reported on his talk with Mr. Blount, I was satisfied that Avery was the man, but I had no scrap of evidence and no hope of getting any. I say I was satisfied, but satisfaction isn't certainty, and only certainty would do. I decided to test it and made elaborate arrangements. I asked Mrs. Blount to get all of them here last evening — all of those involved, including Dr. Avery — and, when they were assembled, I announced that I had discharged Mr. Goodwin, who was not present, and that I was withdrawing from the case. I returned to Miss Blount the fee she had paid me. She was privy to the plan. I told them that I had discharged Mr. Goodwin for dereliction of duty; that he had had Kalmus's house under surveillance Wednesday evening and had deserted his post for an hour or more, and so had failed to see the murderer enter and leave."

"They don't know Goodwin," Cramer muttered, and I raised a brow at him.

"They do now," Wolfe said, "or I should say Avery does. From a hotel room he telephoned Avery, told him he had been discharged and why, told him he had *not* deserted his post, gave him to understand that he had seen him enter and leave Kalmus's house Wednesday evening, and told him to bring one hundred thousand dollars to a rendezvous at Piotti's restaurant. Of course Avery's reaction settled it. If, innocent or guilty, he had disdained the challenge, I would have been through. May I digress?"

Cramer grunted. "You always do."

"It's relevant but not material. I believe he would have disdained it if he had had nothing to fear but the law. He knew there was no conclusive evidence against him and that the prospect of getting any was remote; his having been seen entering and leaving the house wouldn't convict him of murder, even if Mr. Goodwin's word were credited. There could have been no motive for him to kill Kalmus unless he had killed Jerin, and the possibility of getting proof that he had killed Jerin was more than remote, it was non-existent. His compelling dread was not of the law, it was of Mrs. Blount. Would *she* believe Mr. Goodwin? Or, more to the point, would she disbelieve him? If she merely doubted, his purpose was defeated. It was not to be borne. He made the appointment with Mr. Goodwin and kept it. You have heard the result."

Wolfe folded his arms. "That's all, Mr. Cramer. You could legally get that tape only by a court order, but I won't stand on formality. Take it, with the understanding that I may arrange for Mr. and Mrs. Blount to hear it should that be necessary. Will Mr. Blount be released today or must he wait until tomorrow?"

"Like hell it's all." Cramer was trying not to explode. "We can't keep Blount, I give you that, and you're damn right I'll take the tape, and you heard me tell Stebbins to get Avery, but when I get him what have I got? As you said yourself, not a scrap of evidence. You got information that identified a murderer, and what did you do with it?"

"Nonsense." Wolfe was curt. "Just now you contemned that information as coming from a man in jail for murder and my client. Am I obliged to disclose information entrusted to me by a client for investigation in his interest?"

"It's not a—"

"I want an answer. Am I?"

"No. But you are now. You trap a murderer, and you let him listen to that tape, and you let him go, before you call me. *Now* you're obliged to give me the information, and I want it. What made Jerin sick? Was it in the chocolate? Who put it in? How did Avery know he would get sick? What did Kalmus know? Exactly what did Blount tell Goodwin? Well?"

Wolfe turned. "Archie. What was your commitment to Mr. Blount?"

I admit I was slightly keyed. I seldom drink champagne when on duty, to prevent dereliction. "Everything he told me," I said, "was in absolute confidence. There was no Bible handy, so I crossed my heart. If you pass it on to a cop, even an inspector, I'm sunk. Possibly Saul and Fred and Orrie combined can fill my shoes."

Wolfe turned to Cramer. "Mr. Goodwin is tipsy. But his commitment extends to me. I suggest that before you release Mr. Blount you ask him to give you the information he gave Mr. Goodwin, in confidence of course, and probably he will oblige you. You know very well—"

The phone rang, and I swiveled and got it. After the first two words of my phone formula a deep gritty voice interrupted, "I want Inspector Cramer," and I turned and told him, "For you. Stebbins."

In writing these reports I try not to give the impression that I think I can see through solid doors or around corners. If I had a hunch at a certain point, as I do now and then, I usually omit it because I can't expect you to take my word for it. But if Wolfe can break his rules I can break mine, and here goes one. When I handed Cramer the receiver I knew what he was going to hear. I didn't suspect, I knew. I suppose Purley's interrupting me, his tone of voice, his not asking if Cramer was there but just saying he wanted him—anyway, I knew, and I was even surer when Cramer said practically nothing, just listened, with only a couple of growls and a couple of questions. So it was no surprise when he cradled the phone and wheeled to Wolfe and croaked, "Damn you and your lousy tricks! *Goddam* you!"

"Mr. Cramer, if you—"

"Don't Mister me! You think you're a—I don't know what you think you are, but I know what I know you are! Avery stuck a gun in his mouth and blew the top of his head off. Go ahead and collect your fee. That will satisfy you, won't it? Are you satisfied?" He hit the desk with his fist. "*Are you?*"

Wolfe turned his head to look at the wall clock. Quarter past four. He would be late for his date with the orchids.

"Yes," he said politely, "I'm satisfied. You will be too when you cool off. You have been delivered from the ignominy of convicting an innocent man, and from the embarrassment of arresting a guilty man who couldn't be convicted."

Please Pass the Guilt

1

HE grunted—the low brief rumble that isn't meant to be heard—turned his head to dart a glance at me, and turned back to Dr. Vollmer, who was in the red leather chair facing the end of Wolfe's desk.

It wasn't just that he was being asked for a favor. If there was a man alive who could say no to a request for a favor easier than Nero Wolfe, I hadn't met him. The trouble was that it was Dr. Vollmer, whose house and office was only a few doors away, who had said he wanted one, and the favor score between him and us was close to a tie. So Wolfe was probably going to be stuck, and therefore the grunt.

Vollmer crossed his long, lean legs and rubbed his narrow, lean jaw with a knuckle. "It's really for a friend of mine," he said, "a man I would like to oblige. His name is Irwin Ostrow, a psychiatrist—not a Freudian. He's interested in a new approach to psychiatric therapy, and he's working at it. Crisis intervention, they call it. I'll have to explain how it works. It's based on—"

"First aid," Wolfe said. "Emotional tourniquet."

"How—you know about it?"

"I read. I read for various purposes, and one of them is to learn what my fellow beings are up to. There are several thousand emergency-treatment centers now operating in this country. The Detroit Psychiatric Institute has a Suicide Prevention Center. The crisis center at Grady Memorial Hospital in Atlanta is staffed by psychiatrists, nurses, social workers, lay therapists, and clergymen. The director of clinical psychiatry at San Francisco General Hospital has written and spoken at length about it. His name is Decker."

"What's his first name?"

"Barry."

Vollmer shook his head. "You know," he said, "you are the most improbable combination of ignorance and knowledge on earth. You don't know what a linebacker does. You don't know what a fugue is."

"I try to know what I need to know. I make sure to know what I want to know."

"What if it's unknowable?"

"Only philosphers and fools waste time on the unknowable. I am neither. What does Dr. Ostrow want to know?"

Vollmer slid back in the red leather chair, which was deep. "Well. I don't want to bore you with things you already know. If I do, stop me. The Washington Heights Crisis Clinic is on 178th Street, near Broadway. It's a storefront operation; people can just walk in, and they do. A woman who can't stop beating her two-year-old daughter. A man who keeps getting up in the middle of the night and going outdoors in his pajamas. Most of them are on the way to a mental hospital if they're not headed off quick, and the clinic — but you know all that. Eight days ago, a week ago yesterday, a young man came and told a nurse he needed help and she sent him to Irwin — Dr. Ostrow. He gave the nurse his name, Ronald Seaver."

Vollmer looked at me with his brows up. "I hope *they* don't have to go to a crisis clinic," I said, and turned to Wolfe. "One of your ignorance areas, baseball. Ron Swoboda is an outfielder and Tom Seaver is a pitcher. 'Ron Seaver' is obviously a phony, but it might help to know he's a Met fan, if a clue is needed."

"It is," Vollmer said. "Of course Irwin knew it was an alias, but people often do that their first visit. But he came back five days later, Saturday morning, and again the next day, Sunday, and he not only hasn't told his real name, he won't give any facts at all except what his crisis is. It's blood on his hands. His hands get covered with blood, not visible to anybody else, and he goes and washes them. The first time, ten days ago — no, twelve — it was in the middle of the night and he had to go to the bathroom and wash his hands. It happens any time, no pattern, day or night, but usually when he's alone. A nurse there says it's the Lady Macbeth syndrome. He says he knows of no event or experience that could have caused it, but Irwin is sure he's lying."

He turned a palm up. "So that's his crisis. Irwin says he really has one, a severe one; the possibility of a complete mental breakup is indicated. But they can't get through to him. One of Irwin's colleagues there is a woman, a lay therapist, who has had remarkable success with some tough ones, even catatonics, but after two hours with him — that was Sunday, day before yesterday, she told him he was wasting his time and theirs. Then she said she had alternative suggestions: either he could go to a surgeon and have his hands amputated, or he could go to a detective, perhaps Nero Wolfe, and try to dodge his questions. And do you know what he said? He said, 'I'll do that. I'll go to Nero Wolfe.'"

My brows were up. "He tried to," I said. "So that was Ron Seaver. He phoned yesterday around noon and said he wanted to come and pay Nero Wolfe a hundred dollars an hour to ask him questions. He wouldn't give his name and didn't mention bloody hands. Naturally I thought he was a nut and said no and hung up."

Vollmer nodded. "And he phoned Irwin and Irwin phoned me." To Wolfe: "Of course the hundred dollars an hour wouldn't tempt you, but I didn't come to tempt you, I came to ask a favor for a friend. You said you make sure to know what you want to know. Well, Dr. Ostrow thinks it's possible that this man *did* have blood on his hands, and he wants to know if he can and should be helped. I admit I do too. I've dealt with people in crises myself, any doctor has, but this is a new one to me."

Wolfe looked at the wall clock. Twenty minutes to seven. "Will you dine with us? Shad roe Creole. Fritz uses shallots instead of onion and no cayenne. Chablis, not sherry."

Vollmer smiled, broad. "Knowing how few people get invited to your table, I should beam. But I know it's only compasssion for my —"

"I am *not* compassionate."

"Hah. You think my meals are like the one Johnson described to Boswell: 'ill-killed, ill-dressed, ill-cooked, and ill-served,' and you feel sorry for me. Thank you, but I have things to do before I eat. If I could come tomorrow and bring that man . . ."

Wolfe made a face. "Not for dinner. I suppose he'll see Dr. Ostrow tomorrow, or telephone. If he does, tell him to come tomorrow evening at nine o'clock. There will be no fee. And no compassion."

2

THAT was Tuesday, the third of June. The next morning there was a little problem. When we haven't got a job or jobs going, I usually get out for a walk after breakfast, with or without an excuse like a trip to the bank, but that Wednesday I didn't. I don't know if I have ever mentioned that the three employes of the Midtown Home Service Corporation who come once a week are always male because Wolfe insists on it. That Wednesday Andy and Sam came at nine o'clock as usual, but they had a woman along, a husky coal-black female with shoulders nearly as broad as mine. Andy, who was white but broad-minded, explained that it was tougher than ever to get men, and repeated one of his favorite remarks, "Goddam it, TV men and carpet layers work in homes." He called the woman Lucile and started her on the dining room, across the hall from the office on the ground floor of the old brownstone. Of course Wolfe, up in the plant rooms on the roof for his morning session with the orchids, hadn't seen her. I went back to the kitchen, sat at my little breakfast table for my second cup of coffee, and told Fritz, "We'll tell him it's a man in disguise because he's wanted."

"There's batter for another cake, Archie."

"No, thanks. They're extra good, they always are, but I've had five. He's wanted for peddling pot. Or maybe acid."

"But his front? The *monts*?"

"Part of the disguise. King-size bra. Is this the Brazilian coffee?"

"No, Colombian. Of course you're just talking. If he sees her —" He threw his hands, and aimed his eyes, up.

"But he probably will. He often comes to the kitchen while you're giving them lunch." I sipped hot coffee. "I'll tell him when he comes down. Have your ear plugs in, he may let out a roar."

So I didn't go for a walk. Anything could happen; Lucile might know about the orchids and sneak up for a look. I was at my desk in the office when the sound of the elevator came at eleven o'clock, and when Wolfe entered and told me good morning and went to put a cluster of Acampe pachyglossa in the vase on his desk, I said, "There's an amendment to the by-laws. Andy is here with Sam and a woman, a black one named Lucile. She is now up in your room with Andy. He says that more and more men

think housework isn't manly, which is silly since Fritz and Theodore and I
work in your house and we're as manly as they come. It looks like a case of
circumstances beyond our control, but if you don't agree, control it."

He sat, got his nineteen stone (it looks better in stone than in pounds)
arranged in his made-to-order chair, glanced at his desk calendar, and
picked up the stack the mailman had brought. He looked at me. "Are there
female Black Panthers?"

"I'll look it up. If there are, Lucile isn't one. She would be a black mare,
Clydesdale or Percheron. She can pick up the vacuum cleaner with one finger."

"She is in my house by invitation. I'll have to speak with her, at least with
a nod and word."

But he didn't. He didn't go to the kitchen while they were there at lunch,
and Andy, who knew Wolfe's habits, kept their paths from crossing. Their
regular leaving time was four o'clock, but that was also the time for Wolfe's
afternoon turn in the plant rooms, and Andy waited until he was in the
elevator on his way up. With them gone, I relaxed. In view of Wolfe's basic
attitude on women, there's no telling what will happen when one is in that
house. I was making entries, from notes supplied by Theodore, on the
germination and performance cards, when Dr. Vollmer phoned to say that
Ronald Seaver would come at nine o'clock. The only preparation needed
took about six minutes — going to a cabinet for a fancy glass-and-metal jar
with the sharpened ends of a dozen pencils protruding at the top, and
placing it at a certain spot and a certain angle near the right edge of my
desk, and putting a certain plug in a certain hidden outlet.

He was nearly half an hour late. It was 9:23, and we had just finished
with after-dinner coffee in the office, when the doorbell rang and I went.
Going down the hall, what I saw on the stoop through the one-way glass
panel was commonplace for anyone who knows midtown Manhattan: a
junior executive, medium-sized, with a poorly designed face tired too
young, in a dark gray suit that had been cut to fit, no hat. I opened the door
and invited him in, and added as he entered, "If you had told me on the
phone you were Ron Seaver I would have asked you to come and discuss the
outlook."

He smiled — the kind of smile that comes quick and goes quicker — and
mumbled, "They're doing better."

I agreed and ushered him down the hall. In the office, he stopped about
three steps in and one foot backed up a little. I thought that at sight of Wolfe
he was deciding to call it off, and so did he, but when I indicated the red
leather chair, he came to Wolfe's desk, muttered something, and put out a
hand, and Wolfe said, "No, there's blood on it. Sit down."

He went to the red leather chair, sat, met Wolfe's eyes, and said, "If you
could see it, if *you* could actually *see* it."

As I went to my chair at my desk I glanced at the jar of pencils; it was in
position.

Wolfe nodded. "But I can't. If Dr. Vollmer has described the situation
accurately it must be assumed that you are either obtuse or deranged. In
your right mind, if you have one, you couldn't possibly expect the people at
the clinic to help you unless you supplied some facts. Are you going to tell
me your name?"

"No." It wasn't a mumble.

"Are you going to tell me anything at all? Where you live, where you work, where you have seen blood that other people saw or could have seen?"

"No." His jaw worked a little. "I explained to Dr. Ostrow that I couldn't. I knew that that clinic had done some remarkable things for people. I had been—I had heard about it. I thought it was just possible—I thought it was worth trying."

Wolfe turned to me. "How much did his suit cost?"

"Two hundred or more. Probably more. The shoes, at least forty."

How much would a magazine or newspaper pay him for an article about that clinic?"

"My god," Ronald Seaver blurted, "that's not—" He bit it off and clamped his jaw.

"It's merely one of the valid conjectures." Wolfe shook his head. I don't like to be imposed on, and I doubt if Dr. Ostrow does. The simplest way to learn if you are an impostor is to discover who and what you are. For Mr. Goodwin to follow you when you leave would take time and trouble, and it isn't necessary.—Archie?"

I picked up the jar and told Ronald Seaver, "Candid camera inside." I removed a couple of the pencils and held them up; they were only two-inch stubs. "Leaving room for the camera below. It now has eight shots of you. Tomorrow I'll show them to people I know—a newspaper man, a couple of cops—"

When you are sitting in a chair and a man comes at you, your first reaction depends on what he has in mind. If he has an idea of hurting you, with or without a weapon, you get on your feet fast. But if he merely intends to take something from you, for instance a jar of pencils, and if you have decided that you are stronger and quicker than he is, you merely pull your feet back. Actually he didn't even come close. He stopped three steps short, turned to Wolfe, and said, "You can't do that. Dr. Ostrow wouldn't permit it."

Wolfe nodded. "Of course he wouldn't, but this office is not in his jurisdiction. You have presumed to take an evening of my time, and I want to know why. Are you desperately in need of help, or are you playing some silly game? I'll soon know, probably tomorrow, depending on how long it takes Mr. Goodwin to get you identified from the photographs. I hope it won't be prolonged; I am merely doing a favor for a friend. Good evening, sir. I'll communicate with Dr. Ostrow, not with you."

With me it had been a tossup whether the guy was in some kind of bad jam or was merely on a complicated caper. His long, pointed nose, which didn't go well with his wide, square chin, had twitched a couple of times, but that didn't prove anything. Now, however, he gave evidence. His half-closed, unblinking eyes, steady at me, with a deep crease across his forehead, showed that something was really hurting.

"I don't believe it," he said, louder than necessary, since he was only two arm's lengths away.

Without letting my eyes leave him, I reached for the jar, which I had put back on my desk, stood, removed the top that held the pencil stubs, tilted the jar to show him what was inside, and said, "Autophoton, made in Japan. Electronic control. One will get you ten I'll have you tagged by sundown tomorrow."

His lips parted to let words out, but none came. His head turned to Wolfe, then back to me, and then he turned clear around and took a slow, short step, and another, and I thought he was heading out. But he veered to the right, toward the big globe near the book shelves, stopped halfway to it, and stood. Apparently he wanted his face to himself while he decided something. It took him a good two minutes, maybe three. He turned, got a leather case from his breast pocket, took things from it, selected one — a card — went to Wolfe's desk, and handed it to him. By the time Wolfe had given it a look, I was there, and he passed it to me. It was a New York driver's license: Kenneth Meer, 5 feet 11, age 32, 147 Clover Street, New York 10012.

"Saving you the trouble of asking quesions," he said, and extended a hand. I gave him the card and he put it back in the case and the case in his pocket; and he turned and went. Not slow short steps; he marched. I followed out to the hall, and when he had opened the front door and crossed the sill and pulled the door shut, not banging it, I went back to my desk, sat, cocked my head at Wolfe, and spoke:

"You told Doc Vollmer yesterday that you read to learn what your fellow beings are up to. Well?"

He scowled. "I have told you a dozen times that 'Doc' is an obnoxious vulgarism."

"I keep forgetting."

"Pfui. You never forget anything. It was deliberate. As for Kenneth Meer, there has been no picture of him in the *Times*. Has there been one in the *Gazette*?"

"No. His name several times, but no picture. Nor any report that he got blood on his hands, but of course he saw plenty. I suppose, since it's a favor for a friend, I'll have to see a couple of people and find out—"

"No. Get Dr. Vollmer."

"But shouldn't I—"

"No."

I swiveled and swung the phone around. Of Vollmer's three numbers, the most likely one at that hour was the unlisted one on the third floor of his house, and when I dialed it he answered himself. Wolfe got at his phone and I stayed on.

"Good evening, doctor. That man came, half an hour late, and has just left. He refused to give us any information, even his name, and we had to coerce him by a ruse with a concealed camera. Under constraint he identified himself by showing us his motor vehicle operator's license, and then departed without a word. His name has recently been in the news in connection with a murder, but only as one of those present at the scene; there has been no published indication that he is under suspicion or is likely to be. Do you want his name, for Dr. Ostrow?"

"Well." Silence for at least ten seconds. "You've got it by — uh — coercion?"

"Yes. As I said."

"Then I don't think—" Another silence, shorter. "I doubt if Irwin would want it. He never uses coercion. May I ask him and let you know?"

"Certainly."

"Do you intend — Are you interested in the murder? Professionally?"

"Only as a spectator. I am not involved and don't expect to be."

Vollmer thanked him for the favor, not enthusiastically, and they hung up. Wolfe looked at the wall clock—five past ten—and reached for his current book, *Grant Takes Command*, by Bruce Catton. I went to the hall and up the two flights to my room, to catch the last inning or two at Shea Stadium on television.

3

WE keep both the *Times* and the *Gazette* for three weeks, sometimes longer, and even if the bank balance had been at a record high I would probably have had another go at the accounts of the Odell murder just for curiosity, since I had now met one of the cast of characters. But we needed a job. In the past five months, the first five of 1969, we had had only six cases, and the fee had gone to five figures in only one of them—getting a damn fool out of a nasty mess with a bunch of smoothies he should have been on to at the first contact. So the checking account balance had lost a lot of weight, and to meet the upkeep of the old brownstone, including the weekly payroll for Theodore and Fritz and me, by about the middle of July Wolfe would have to turn some documents into cash, and that should be prevented if possible. So it wasn't just curiosity that sent me to the basement Thursday morning for old newspapers.

The murder was two weeks old, but what had happened, and how, had been plain and clear in the first reports and had not been substantially revised or amended. At 3:17 P.M. on Tuesday, May 20, a man named Peter J. Odell had entered a room on the sixth floor of the CAN building on West Fifty-fourth Street, pulled open the bottom drawer of a desk, and died instantly. The bomb that shredded him was so powerful that it not only blew the metal desk up to the ceiling but even buckled two of the walls. CAN stood for Contintental Air Network, which occupied the whole building, and Peter J. Odell had been its vice-president in charge of development. The room and desk were not his; they belonged to Amory Browning, the vice-president in charge of programming.

All right, that was what happened, but in addition to the main question, who had put the bomb in the drawer, there were others that had still not been answered, at least not for publication. It wasn't unheard of for a vice-president to enter another vice-president's room, but why had Odell opened that drawer? *That* drawer. It was known to enough people at CAN to get into both the *Times* and the *Gazette* that that drawer had rarely, possibly never, been opened by anyone but Browning himself because nothing was kept in it but a bottle or bottles of twelve-year-old Ten-Mile Creek bourbon. It had almost certainly been known to Odell.

No one had admitted seeing Odell enter Browning's room. Helen Lugos, Browning's secretary, whose room adjoined his, had been down the hall in a file room. Kenneth Meer, Browning's chief assistant, had been down on the ground floor in conference with some technicians. Browning himself had

been with Cass R. Abbott, the president of CAN, in his office — the corner
office on that floor. If anyone knew why Odell had gone to Browning's
room, he wasn't saying. So the answer to the question, Who put the bomb
in the drawer? depended partly on the answer to another question: Whom
did he expect to open the drawer?

Rereading the accounts in fifteen copies of the *Times* and fifteen of the
Gazette, I was impressed by how well I had absorbed the details of an event
we had not been involved in, and by nothing else. There was nothing to give
me a nudge on a start of what I had in mind. It was after eleven o'clock
when I finished, so Wolfe had come down from the plant rooms, and I went
up to the phone in my room to dial a number — the switchboard of the
Gazette. It was an afternoon paper and Lon Cohen's line was usually busy
from 10 A.M. to 4:20 P.M., but I finally got him. I told him I wanted thirty
seconds and he said I could have five.

"Then," I said, "I won't tell you about the steer that grew the
Chateaubriands that Felix is saving for us. Can you meet me at Rusterman's
at a quarter past six?"

"I can if I have to. Bringing what?"

"Just your tongue. And of course plenty of lettuce for later."

The "later" meant the poker game at Saul Panzer's apartment which
started at eight o'clock Thursday evenings. Lon made an appropriate retort
about lettuce and hung up, and I dialed another number I didn't have to
look up and got Felix, and told him that this time my request for the small
room upstairs was strictly personal, not on behalf of Wolfe, and that if he
was short on chateaubriands, tournedos would be fine. He asked what kind
of flowers would be preferred, and I said my guest would be a man from
whom I hoped to get some useful information, so instead of flowers, make it
four-leaf clovers for luck.

An announcement to Wolfe that I wouldn't be there for dinner was not
required, since I never was on Thursdays. Since his dinner time was 7:15, I
couldn't eat at his table and be at Saul's poker table at eight. I merely
mentioned casually, after we had finished with the morning mail, that I
would be leaving around a quarter to six, before he came down from the
plant rooms. I did not mention Kenneth Meer, and neither did he, but
around the middle of the afternoon Vollmer phoned to say that Dr. Ostrow
didn't want to know what Ronald Seaver's name was. Which of course was
a polite lie. Dr. Ostrow would certainly have liked to know the name, but
not from Wolfe if he had got it by a trick.

The small room upstairs at Rusterman's had many memories for me,
back to the days when Marko Vukcic was still alive and making it the best
restaurant in New York, with frequent meals with his old friend Nero Wolfe
helping to keep it the best. It was still better than good, as Lon Cohen
remarked that evening after his third spoonful of Germiny à l'Oseille, and
again after his second bite of Chateaubriand and his first sip of the claret.

With about his fourth sip he said, "I'd be enjoying this more — or less, I
don't know which — if I knew the price. Of course you want something, or
Nero Wolfe does. What?"

I swallowed meat. "Not Nero Wolfe. Me. He doesn't know about it and I
don't want him to. I need some facts. I spent two hours this morning
reading everything two great newspapers have printed about the murder of

Peter J. Odell and I still don't know enough for my personal satisfaction. I thought a chat with you might be helpful."

He squinted at me. "How straight is that? That Wolfe doesn't know you're feeding me."

"As straight as from a ten to an ace."

His eyes aimed about a foot above my head, as they often did when he was deciding whether to call or raise, stayed there while I buttered a bite of roll, and leveled down to mine. "Well, well," he said. "You could just put an ad in the *Gazette*. Of course with a box number since Wolfe mustn't know you're drumming."

Just looking at Lon you would never guess, from his neat little face and his slick black hair, how sharp he is. But people who know him know, including the publisher of the *Gazette*, which is why he has a room to himself two doors down the hall from the publisher's room.

I shook my head. "The kind of people I want to reach don't read *Gazette* ads. To be perfectly frank, I'm going stale and I need exercise. There must be plenty about that crowd that isn't fit to print. This room isn't bugged and neither am I. Have Cramer and the DA got a lead that they're saving?"

"No." He forked peas. "Almost certainly not. Of course the hitch is that they don't know who the bomb was intended for." He put the peas where he wanted them. "Probably no one does but the guy who planted it. It's reasonable to suppose it was meant for Browning, but after all it was Odell who got it. A fact is a fact. Did Browning plant it *for* Odell? He did have a motive."

"Good enough?"

"Apparently. Of course you know that Abbott is retiring the last of August and the board of directors was going to decide on his successor at a meeting scheduled for five o'clock that afternoon, and it would be either Browning or Odell. Odell certainly didn't plant the bomb for Browning and then open the drawer himself, but did Browning plant it and somehow get Odell to open it?"

I sipped claret. "Of course your best men are on it, or have been. What do they think?"

"They've quit thinking. All they have is guesses. Landry's guess is that Mrs. Browning put the bomb there for Helen Lugos, her husband's secretary, knowing, or thinking she knew, that Helen checked the bourbon supply every morning."

"Did she? Check the bourbon supply every morning?"

"I don't know and I doubt if Cramer does. Helen isn't speaking to reporters and it is said that she isn't wasting any words with the law. Also I don't know for sure that Helen and Browning were bedding, but Landry thinks he does. Ask Inspector Cramer, he may know. Another guess, Gahagan's, is that Odell was setting the bomb for Browning and fumbled it. He has been trying for a week to trace where and how Odell got the bomb. Perlman's guess is that Abbott did it because he thought they were going to pick Browning for the new president and he was for Odell. He has three theories on why Odell went to Browning's room and opened the drawer, none of them much good. Damiano's guess is that Helen Lugos did it, to get Browning, but he is no better than Perlman on why Odell horned in."

"Why would Helen want to get Browning?"

"Sex."

"That's not responsive."

"Certainly it's responsive. When sex comes in by the window, logic leaves by the door. When two people collaborate sexually, either one is capable of doing anything and nobody can be sure he knows why he did it. I think Damiano's guess is based on something a man named Meer, Kenneth Meer, told him. Meer is Browning's chief of staff. Damiano got him talking the day after it happened — they had been choir boys together at St. Andrew's — and Meer said that anyone who wanted to know how it happened should concentrate on Helen Lugos. Of course Damiano kept at him then, but Meer backed off. And as I said, Helen isn't doing any talking."

"Has Damiano told Inspector Cramer what Meer said?"

"Of course not. He didn't even tell us until a couple of days ago. He was hoping to earn a medal."

"Does anybody guess that Meer did it?"

"No one at the *Gazette* does. Naturally he has been considered, everybody has, but even for a wild guess you've got to have a motive. Meer certainly wouldn't have wanted to get Browning; if Browning is made president, Meer will be right up near the top. And how could he have got Odell to go to Browning's room and open that drawer? Of course guesses are a dime a dozen. If the bomb was intended for Browning, there are at least a dozen possible candidates. For instance, Madeline Odell, now the widow Odell. She had been expecting her husband to be the CAN president ever since she married him, twenty years ago, and it looked as if Browning was going to get it instead. Or Theodore Falk, the Wall Street Falk, old friend of the Odells and a member of the CAN board of directors. Of course he didn't do it himself, but millionaires don't have to do things themselves. Or Sylvia Venner. You know?"

I nodded. " 'The Big Town.' "

"Right. She had that program for two years and Browning bounced her. Now she does chores, and she hates Browning's guts. I could name more. Of course if the bomb was intended for Odell, there are candidates for that too, but for them there's the problem of getting Odell to enter that room and open that drawer."

I swallowed my last bite of Chateaubriand and pushed the button for Pierre. "You said Odell's wife had been expecting him to be president ever since she married him. Had she been doing anything about it?"

"Plenty. She inherited a big block of CAN stock from her father, Carl Hartig, along with a lot of oil wells and miscellaneous items, and she's been on the board of directors for ten years. She would probably have given half of her seventy or eighty million to have Browning removed from competition, but if she had known that bomb was in that drawer she would have made damn sure that her husband wouldn't go near that room that day. That's why she's not *my* guess — or anybody else's as far as I know."

"Seventy or eighty *million?*"

"At least that. She's really loaded."

"Huh. What kind of sauce do you want on your soufflé? Brandy ginger or mocha rum?"

"Mocha rum sounds better."

Pierre had come and was removing empty dishes. I told him what we would have and waited until he was gone to resume with Lon. You never know. Abbott or Browning or Madeline Odell might be one of Pierre's pet customers.

When at a quarter to eight, out on the sidewalk, we decided to walk the eleven blocks to Saul Panzer's instead of scouting for a taxi, I had collected around a hundred more facts and guesses, but it would be a waste of paper and ink to list them for you since none of them was any help to my program. Also I will not report on the course of events at the poker table, except to say that having a complicated operation on my mind was no help to my wallet. I lost sixty-eight bucks.

4

THE first problem was how to get to her, and the second one was what to say when I did. "Her" was of course Madeline Odell, the widow. She was almost certainly in the clear on the bomb, she had the best reason for wanting the bomber to be caught and nailed, and she had the biggest stack. It was those two problems trying to take over that had caused me to make three big mistakes and several smaller ones at the poker game, and cost me money. They did not keep me from getting a good eight hours' sleep, nothing ever does, and they didn't affect my appetite at breakfast, but I skipped things in the *Times* that I usually cover, and I guess I was short with Fritz. In the office I actually forgot to put fresh water in the vase on Wolfe's desk.

I still hadn't decided at lunchtime. Of course any one of a dozen dodges would have got me to her; no one is inaccessible if you put your mind on it; but then what? If possible the approach should lead naturally to the proposition. After lunch I went for a walk with a couple of unnecessary errands for an excuse, and didn't get back until after four o'clock, so Wolfe was up in the plant rooms and I had the office to myself. I swung the typewriter around and rolled paper in and gave it a try.

> *Dear Mrs. Odell: This is on Nero Wolfe's letterhead because I work for him and am writing it in his office, but it is strictly personal, from me, and Mr. Wolfe doesn't know I am writing you. I do so because I am an experienced professional detective and it hurts me to see or read about poor detective work, especially in an important case like the murder of your husband. Mr. Wolfe and I have of course followed the published accounts of the investigation, and yesterday he remarked to me that apparently the most crucial fact was being ignored, or at least not getting the priority it deserved, and I agreed with him. Such a criticism from him to the police or the District Attorney would probably have no effect, but it occurred to me this morning that it might have some effect if it came from you. If you wish to reach me the address and telephone number are above.*

I read it over twice and made five improvements: I took out "strictly" and "professional," changed "poor" to "inferior," "crucial" to "important," and "priority" to "attention." I read it again, changed "an important case like" to "such a vital case as," typed it on a letterhead with two carbons, signed it, and addressed an envelope to a number on East Sixty-third Street. I went to the kitchen to tell Fritz I was going out for air, and walked to the post office on Eighth Avenue.

Since it was a Friday afternoon in June, it was possible, even probable, that she wouldn't get it until Monday, and nothing would interfere with my weekend pleasures at Shea Stadium, but a little after eleven o'clock Saturday morning, when Wolfe was dictating a long letter to an orchid collector in Malaysia, the phone rang and I swiveled and took it.

"Nero Wolfe's office, Archie Goodwin speaking."

A businesslike female voice: "This is Mrs. Peter Odell's secretary. She has received your letter and wishes to speak to Mr. Wolfe."

Of course I had known that might happen, with Wolfe right there. "I'm sorry," I said, "but Mr. Wolfe isn't available and won't be until Monday. Anyway I made it clear that the letter was personal."

She covered the transmitter and I heard nothing. In a couple of minutes she was back: "Mr. Goodwin?"

"Here."

"Mrs. Odell wishes to see you. Will you be here promptly at three o'clock?"

One of my basic opinions is that people who take things for granted should be helped to a better understanding of democracy, and at three o'clock it would be about the fourth inning, but I hadn't been asked to write that letter. "Yes," I said, "I'll be there," and hung up, and swiveled.

"Someone using your name in vain," I told Wolfe. "People should read letters at least three times." I looked at my notebook. "The last I have is 'in spite of all the crosses hybridizers have tried.'"

It took another full page of the notebook.

My intention had been to get to Shea Stadium a little after one and enjoy a couple of hot dogs and a pint of milk while watching batting practice. Instead, I got to Sam's diner on Tenth Avenue a little after one and enjoyed rye bread and baked beans, two items that never appear at Wolfe's table, and then walked the nearly two miles from West Thirty-fifth Street to East Sixty-third. The people you see on midtown sidewalks Saturday afternoons are completely different from other days.

It was a five-story, forty-foot-wide stone mansion, between Fifth and Madison, and I was stopped at the entrance to the vestibule by a broad-shouldered husky with a Lathrop Protective Service badge on his buttoned-up jacket. Apparently after more than two weeks, pests — for instance, journalists — were still a problem, or Mrs. Odell thought they were. He said grimly, "Well, sir?"

I pronounced my name and said I was expected, and produced evidence of my identity from my card case. He entered the vesibule and pushed the button, and the door was opened by a woman in a neat gray uniform with a skirt that reached a good four inches below her knees who accepted my name without evidence. She crossed the marble floor to an intercom on a marble table and told it Mr. Goodwin was there, and in a couple of minutes there was the sound of an elevator about one-tenth as noisy as Wolfe's. A door at the far end of the large entrance hall slid open, and a woman stuck her head out and invited me to join her. We went up past two doors and stopped at the third, and she led me down the hall to an open door at the front and stood aside for me to enter.

It was a big room, the whole width of the house, and my sweeping glance saw desks, working chairs and easy chairs, two couches, oil paintings, filing cabinets, a color television — and my glance stopped there because a ball game was on, Ralph Kiner was talking, and his audience was a woman propped against a bank of cushions on an oversized couch. Even if it hadn't been her house I would have recognized her from pictures in the *Times* and *Gazette*: a face bulged in the middle by wide cheek bones, and a wide full-lipped mouth. Her loose, pale blue dress or robe or sack was zippered shut in front, top to bottom. I crossed over to her and asked politely, "What's the score?"

Her brown eyes darted to me and back to the game. "Mets two, Pirates four, last of the fourth. Sit down."

I went to a chair not far from the couch that faced the TV set. Ed Kranepool was at bat. He went to three and two and then grounded out, ending the inning, and a commercial started yapping. As I looked around for the secretary and saw she wasn't there, the sound quit and I turned back to Mrs. Odell. Remote control; she had pushed a button.

"I'll leave the picture on," she said. She sized me up head to foot, taking her time. My pants were pressed. "That was a poor excuse for a letter you sent me. 'The most important fact,' you said, but you didn't say what it is."

"Of course I didn't."

"Why 'of course'?"

The commercial had finished and a Pirate was coming to bat. She left the sound off but sent her eyes back to the game, so I sent mine, too. "I work for Nero Wolfe," I told the Pirate as he swung and missed. "He makes a living solving problems for people, and part of what they pay him pays my salary. It would be pretty dumb for me to tell people for free what he has said about their problems. I wrote that letter only because I hate to see a case bobbled."

"Oh, come off it." Her eyes darted to me and back to the game. "You invited me to reach you and wouldn't put him on when I phoned. How much do you want?"

"You might try a million. No one has ever bid high enough to make it tough for me. But I did invite you to reach me, didn't I? Do you know what I suspect? I'll bet that at the back of my mind, down in the subconscious, there was a sneaking idea that after two weeks and three days of the cops and the DA getting nowhere, you might want to discuss it with Nero Wolfe. Do you know anything about him?

"Personally and definitely, no. I know his reputation, certainly."

One Pirate had watched a third strike go by and another one had popped up to the infield. Now a third one lofted a major-league blooper out to left center and both Cleon Jones and Tommy Agee were on the gallop. It would fall in . . . but it didn't. Jones stretched an arm and one-handed it, and kept it. A good inning for Koosman. As the picture of the commercial started, I turned to the couch. "To be honest," I said, "I may as well admit that that letter *was* dumb. How could you needle the police or the District Attorney about neglecting the most important fact if I didn't tell you what it is? I apologize, and I not only apologize, I pay a forfeit. The most important fact is that your husband entered that room and opened that drawer, and the most important question is, why? Unless and until they have the answer to that the ten best investigators in the world couldn't possibly solve the case. Tell Inspector Cramer that, but don't mention Nero Wolfe. The sound of that name riles him." I stood up. "I realize that it's possible that you know why he entered the room and opened the drawer, and you have told the DA and he's saving it, but from the published accounts I doubt it, and so does Mr. Wolfe. Thank you for letting me see Cleon Jones make that catch."

I turned and was going, but she raised her voice. "Damn it, sit down!"

I did so, and as I sat Jerry Grote lined a double to the right-field corner. Bud Harrelson beat out a bunt and Grote moved to third, and Mrs. Odell pushed her button and the sound came on. More action and two Mets crossed the plate. When Ed Charles made the third out the score was tied, and as the commercial started she pushed the button, looked at me and said, "Call Wolfe and tell him I want to see him. Now." She aimed a finger. "The phone on that desk. How long will it take him?"

"Too long. Forever. You certainly don't know him 'definitely.' He leaves the house only for personal errands no one else can do, never on business. I suppose you'd rather not discuss it on the phone, so you'll have to go to him. The address is on the letterhead. Six o'clock would be a good time, he'll be available then, and the game will be —"

"My god, what a nerve," she said. "You think I would?"

"No, I think you wouldn't. But you said you want to see him, and I —"

"All right, all right. Forget it." She pushed the button. Bob Murphy had replaced Ralph Kiner and he talks louder. She had to raise her voice: "Miss Haber will take you down. She's in the hall."

I got up and went. I hadn't the slightest idea, as I was escorted to the elevator and down, and to the entrance, by Miss Haber, and as I walked to Madison Avenue and turned downtown, headed for a bar where I knew there was a TV, whether or not I had wasted a letterhead and a postage stamp and most of an afternoon. On a bet I would have taken either end. But after all, she had said she wanted to see him, and if I know women one-tenth as well as Wolfe pretends to think I do, she was strongly inclined to get what she wanted. By the time the game ended, which the Mets won 7 to 5, I would no longer have taken either end. Two to one I had hooked her. That was how it looked as I used my key on the door of the old brownstone a little before six o'clock.

Of course I couldn't leave the house that evening. When I'm not there Fritz usually answers the phone, but sometimes Wolfe does, and she might call any minute. She *might*. She didn't. It was also possible that she would tell either Cramer or the DA about it and he would call. He didn't. When I went to bed around midnight the odds were no longer two to one. But there was still an off chance, and when I went to the office after breakfast Sunday morning, I rang Lily Rowan and told her I was stuck for the day and would send the tickets for the ball game by messenger, and I hoped she could find someone who could yell at the umpire as loud as I did. And then, about eight minutes after the messenger had come and taken the tickets, the phone rang, and it was Mrs. Odell in person, not the secretary. She said she wanted to speak with Wolfe and I said no, that he didn't even know I had written her and seen her.

"My god," she said; "you might think he's the President. I want to see him. Bring him."

"I can't and he wouldn't. Honestly, Mrs. Odell, I wish he would. It would do him good to get out more, but not a chance. If there was a way of scoring pigheadedness it would be interesting to match him with you. I think he'd win."

"Of course I'm pigheaded. I always have been."

"I'm perfectly willing to make it 'strong-minded' if you prefer."

Silence. It lasted so long that I thought she had quit without bothering to hang up. Then she said, "I'll be there at six o'clock."

"Today? Sunday?"

"Yes." She hung up.

I took a deep breath and enjoyed it. So far so good, but the highest hurdle was still ahead. The Sunday household routine was different. Theodore didn't come on Sunday and Wolfe's morning with the orchids could be anything from twenty minutes to four hours. Also Fritz might leave for the day right after breakfast, or he might not. That day not, he had said. The question was when to spring it. Going up to the plant rooms with it was of course out of the question; I wasn't welcome there even for a real emergency.

I decided not to decide until he came down and I saw what his mood was like.

When he showed, a little after eleven, he had the Sunday *Times* under one arm and a fourteen-inch raceme of Peristeria elata in the other hand, and his "Good morning" was a greeting, not just a growl. So when the flowers were in the vase and his bulk was satisfactorily arranged in the made-to-order chair he wouldn't swap for its weight in uranium, I spoke.

"Before you get started on the *Review of the Week*, I have an item you won't like. A woman is coming to see you at six o'clock today. Mrs. Peter J. Odell, whose husband opened a desk drawer and died. I had to ignore the rule on consulting you before making an appointment."

He was glaring at me. "I was here. I was available."

"Sure, but it was an emergency." I opened a drawer of my desk and took out a paper. "This is a carbon of a letter I sent her Friday afternoon." I rose, handed it to him, and returned to my chair. "She phoned yesterday morning or her secretary did, and I went to see her yesterday afternoon, at her house on Sixty-third Street. She asked me to phone you to come, which of course wasn't discussable. I told her the only place she could see you was your office. She phoned this morning, an hour ago, and said she would be here at six o'clock."

He had read the letter. He read it again, with his lips pressed tight. He dropped it on his desk and looked at me. Not a glare or a scowl, just a hard, straight look. "I don't believe it," he said. "It would be insufferable, as you well know."

I nodded. "Of course that's the reaction I expected. But she'll be here at six. The emergency I referred to is in the safe. Your checkbook. You have of course noticed that since May first I have been giving you a memo of the condition every week instead of twice a month. Of the hundred and fifty-eight days this year you have worked about ten and I have worked less than twenty, not counting office chores. I happened—"

"Not 'less' than twenty. 'Fewer.' "

"Thank you. I happened to learn that Mrs. Odell's pile goes to eight figures, maybe even nine. The alternatives were (a) quit this job and make her an offer, or (b) get her to make you an offer. I tossed a coin and you won. So I wrote her that letter."

"Now," he said through his teeth with his lips barely moving, "*I* have alternatives."

"Certainly. Fire me, or go to work. If you fire me I won't expect severance pay. I would have to draw the check, and for more than a month every time I have drawn a check I have had to set my jaw. In deciding, please remember that at least twice you have yourself put out a hook when the bank balance got too low for comfort. The last time was when you sent me to see a woman named Fraser. The only difference is that this time I did it without consulting you. I like to earn *part* of my pay."

He cupped his hands over the ends of the chair arms, leaned back, and shut his eyes. But his lips didn't start to work in and out, so he didn't really have a problem; he was just looking at it. He may have thought I was holding my breath, but probably not, because he knows me nearly as well as I know him.

I was about to swivel and resume with my copy of the *Times* when he opened his eyes and straightened up and spoke. "Regarding my remark to you about the most important fact that is not getting the attention it deserves. She will of course want to know what it is, and so do I. Have you a suggestion?"

"Sure. I have already told her, yesterday. It's that Odell entered Browning's room and opened the drawer of his desk that everybody knew had only bourbon in it. Why? That's the most important question. You have only read the newspaper accounts, but I have also discussed it for an hour and a half with Lon Cohen and learned a few things that haven't been printed."

"Confound it." He made a face. "Very well. Talk. From Mr. Cohen, the substance. Your conversation with that woman, verbatim."

I talked.

5

MOST of the people who enter that office for the first time have something eating them, but even so they often notice one or more of the objects in view—the fourteen-by-twenty-six Keraghan rug or the three-foot globe or the floral display in the vase on Wolfe's desk. Mrs. Peter J. Odell didn't. When I escorted her to the office, her eyes fixed on Wolfe and stayed there as she crossed the rug and stopped just short of his desk. Of course he stayed put in his chair, as usual.

"Charlotte Haber is my secretary," she said. "I brought her because I may need her." She went to the red leather chair, sat, and put her handbag on the little stand at her elbow. Meanwhile I had moved up one of the yellow chairs for the secretary. From the look Miss Haber had given me at the door, and the one she was now giving Wolfe, it was a good guess that she would rather have been somewhere else. The crease in her narrow forehead made it even narrower, and the way she was puckering her mouth, which was too small anyway, made it almost invisible.

"I have asked three men about you," Mrs. Odell told Wolfe. "You're high-handed and opinionated, and you charge high fees, but you're dependable."

Wolfe grunted. "You should have inquired further. Competence?"

"Oh, apparently you're smart enough. I'll decide that myself. Your man told me that you said the police are neglecting the most important question, why did my husband go to Browning's room and open that drawer? I want to know why that is so important." She got her bag and opened it and took out a checkfold. "How much for telling me that?"

He shook his head. "I discuss details only with clients and you haven't hired me. But since Mr. Goodwin has presumed to quote me to you — without my prior knowledge — I'll make an exception. On trial for murder, a man may be convicted without proof of motive. Establishment of motive of course helps with a jury, but it is not requisite. But in an *investigation* of a murder, motive is of first importance. The question was first asked in an ancient language many centuries ago: *Cui bono?* Try to learn who put that bomb in that drawer without knowing whom it was intended for is close to hopeless, and to learn whom it was intended for it is essential to know why your husband entered the room and opened the drawer, and who knew he was going to. Actually that's the most important question: Who knew he was going to? Did anybody? If it were my problem I would begin by concentrating on that question to the exclusion of all others. I give you that, madam, with my compliments, since Mr. Goodwin quoted me without bothering to get permission."

She still had the checkfold in her hand. "The police think it was intended for Amory Browning."

"No doubt. A reasonable assumption. But if it was actually intended for your husband, they're wasting their time and they'll get nowhere."

"Why do you think it was intended for my husband?"

"I don't. But I think it might have been — and I repeat, I would want first to learn if anyone knew he was going to enter that room and open that drawer, and if so, who."

She sat and looked at him. Then she turned her head to look at me, and turned it further to look at Charlotte Haber. I don't know if that was any help, but probably she had already made up her mind and didn't even know she was doing it. She opened the checkfold, slid a pen out of its loop, wrote, on both the stub and the check, and tore the check out. "You said I haven't hired you," she said. "Now I have. This twenty thousand dollars is for a retainer. I'm going to tell you something and ask you what to do, with the understanding that it is in confidence and you will never tell anyone about it — under any circumstances."

Wolfe shook his head. "I can't accept it on those terms."

"My god, why not? A lawyer would."

"I am not a member of the bar. What a client tells me is not a privileged communication. Archie. Your notebook."

I got it from a drawer, and a pen.

"One carbon," he said. "I acknowledge receipt of a check for twenty thousand dollars from Mrs. Peter J. Odell as a retainer for my services. Period. I guarantee that any information she gives me will be revealed to no one, comma, either by me or by Archie Goodwin, comma, without her consent, comma, unless circumstances arise that put me or him under legal compulsion to reveal it." He turned to her. "I assure you that we do not invite or welcome legal compulsion. Will that do?"

"I don't — I'll look at it."

I put paper in the typewriter and hit the keys. On the wall back of my desk is a mirror four feet high and six feet wide, and in it I could see that Miss Haber was looking surprised. No female secretary thinks a man can use eight fingers and two thumbs on a typewriter. I rolled it out, kept the carbon, and got up to hand Wolfe the original. He signed it and handed it back, and I took it to Mrs. Odell. She read it, pursed her lips, read it again, folded it and put it in her bag, and handed me the check. I gave it a look and took it to Wolfe, and without even a glance at it he dropped it on his desk.

He looked at the client: "I signed that receipt, madam, but I shall not consider myself definitely committed until I learn what you want me to do. I hope it won't be necessary for me to return your check, but I can if I must. In any case, what you tell me will be held in confidence if possible. What do you want?"

"I want advice. I want to know what *I* can do. I know why my husband went to Amory Browning's room and opened that drawer. So does Miss Haber. That's why she's here. I know the bomb was intended for him, and I know who put it there."

I suppose Wolfe has been surprised by things people have said as often as you or me, but his ego has arranged with him not to show it and he rarely does. But that got him. His eyes stretched wide, as wide as I have ever seen them, then they narrowed at her, half closed, and he cleared his throat.

"Indeed," he said. "Have you told the police?"

"No. I have told no one. No one knows about it except Miss Haber and me. I have hoped the police would get him. Why haven't they found out where and how he got the bomb? My god, are they any good at all? It has been more than two weeks. Now, after what you have said, I have got to do something and I want you to tell me what. How much do you know? Do you know that there was to be a directors' meeting at five o'clock that day to decide who would be the new president of CAN?"

"Yes. And that it would be either your husband or Mr. Browning."

She nodded. "And they were both to be at the meeting, and give their ideas about policy and what they thought should be done, and answer questions, and then leave, and we would discuss it and then vote. Did you know that?"

"No."

"Well, that's how it was. If you have read the papers, you know that Amory Browning kept a certain brand of whisky in that bottom drawer of his desk."

"Yes."

"And that every afternoon around four o'clock he took a drink of it."

"That has been said, yes."

"Well, he did. Every afternoon, between four and five o'clock. Everybody knew it. All right, now I'm telling you what you have guaranteed not to repeat. My husband went to that room and opened that drawer to put something in the whisky. It was my idea. Do you know what LSD is?"

"Yes. Lysergic acid diethylamide."

"My god, you can pronounce it. Well, I got some. You don't need to know how I got it. Miss Haber knows. I got some, it was a powder, and I put it in a little plastic container, and I persuaded my husband to use it. The police know he had it. It was in a pocket of his jacket. You didn't know about *that*."

"No."

"They haven't told about it. I think they haven't told anyone but me, and I told them I knew nothing about it. He was going to put it in the whisky. Almost certainly Browning would take a drink before he went to that meeting at five o'clock. We didn't know what that amount of LSD would do to him — of course we didn't know how full the bottle would be. But there was a good chance it would do enough for him to make a bad impression at that meeting, and it was understood and agreed that we would make a final decision that day. All right, now you know why he went to that room and opened that drawer."

Wolfe nodded. "I probably do. It isn't likely that you would trump up a tale of such an exploit — and the police have the LSD. You said that Miss Haber knows how you got it. Did she also know how you planned to use it?"

"Yes."

"Did anyone else know?"

"Yes. Amory Browning."

Wolfe shook his head. "My credulity will stretch only so far, madam. Obviously you are going to tell me that Mr. Browning murdered your husband."

"That's right. He did." Her head turned. "Charlotte?"

Miss Haber's mouth opened, and closed. She lifted a hand, and dropped it. "Please, Mrs. Odell," she said. "I don't think — You tell him. Please?"

"Well, you're here." Mrs. Odell went back to Wolfe. "There are strong people," she said, "and there are weak people, and Miss Haber is one of the weak ones. She's extremely competent, but weak. She found out for me how to get some LSD, and in fact she got it for me, about a month ago. Then she found out what I was going to do with it by eavesdropping on us — my husband and me. Then she phoned Amory Browning and told him what we were going to do. I didn't know that until three days after my husband died. So she was weak three times — getting the LSD for me without knowing what I wanted it for, and phoning Browning, and telling me. You said the most important question is who knew my husband was going to that room and open that drawer. All right, three people knew: Miss Haber and me, and Amory Browning. And she told Browning four days before it happened, so he had plenty of time to get the bomb."

Wolfe was frowning at her with his chin down. "A remarkable performance," he said. "Extraordinary. You seem not to be aware that —"

She cut in. "I'm not through. About Browning getting the bomb. Do you watch television?"

"Rarely."

"About three months ago, CAN had a one-hour special they called 'Where the Little Bombs Come From.' Did you see it?"

"No."

"Lots of people thought it told too much about what bombs are made of and who makes them, but it really didn't, because they changed all the names and didn't give any addresses. That program was Browning's idea and his staff did all the research, so getting one would have been easy for him. If you mean it would have been remarkable for him to get a bomb in four days and know how to use it, it wouldn't."

Wolfe was still frowning. "I didn't mean that. I meant *your* performance. That is of course one detail to be considered, but before considering details I must know if I'm going to be concerned with them. If I take the job, what do you expect me to do?"

"I expect you to tell *me* what to do, and I suppose help me do it. I want Amory Browning indicted and tried and convicted, but I do *not* want what I have told you to be known. I am not going to sit in a witness chair and tell what my husband and I did and answer questions about it. How many things have *you* done that you wouldn't want everyone to know about?"

"Perhaps a thousand. Adulterating a rival's whisky is not one of them, but tastes and methods differ." Wolfe's head turned. "Miss Haber. Do you corroborate what Mrs. Odell has told me of your share in this affair?"

The secretary swallowed. I had her in profile, but apparently her eyes were straight at him. She said "Yes," but it was barely audible, and she repeated it louder, "Yes, I do."

"You got some LSD at her request?"

"Yes, but I'm not going to tell how I got it."

"I don't need to know, at least not now. And you learned how she was going to use it by overhearing conversations she had with her husband?"

"Yes. I thought I had a right to know. LSD is illegal. It can't be sold legally and you can't even have it in your possession."

"And you decided to tell Mr. Browning about it? Why?"

"Because I was afraid it might kill him. The amount I got and gave Mrs. Odell—it was about four tablespoons—I didn't know what it would do. If the whisky bottle was only half full, or even less, and Mr. Odell put all that LSD in it—from the little I knew I thought it *would* kill him. I would be an accessory to a murder, and anyway I didn't want to help kill a man. It may be what Mrs. Odell said, that I'm one of the weak ones—anyhow, I didn't want to be a murderer."

"How did you communicate with Mr. Browning? Did you write to him?"

"I phoned him. I phoned him Friday evening, from a booth, at his place in the country. I didn't tell him my name. I didn't tell him *any* names. I just told him that Tuesday afternoon someone was going to put a dangerous drug in the whisky in his desk drawer and he had better not drink it. He wanted to ask questions, but I hung up. Of course I supposed he would suspect it would be Mr. Odell, but I certainly didn't suppose he would do what he did."

"Where is his country place?"

"In Connecticut. Westport."

"You say you phoned him Friday evening. Which Friday?"

"The Friday before it happened. Four days before."

"That was May sixteenth."

"Was it?" It took her only a moment, not a long one, to figure it. "That's right, May sixteenth."

"You phoned him at what hour?"

"Around nine o'clock. A little after nine. When I thought he would have finished dinner."

"How sure are you it was Mr. Browning?"

"Oh, *quite* sure. He answered the phone himself, and I know his voice. I have heard him on the phone at least a dozen times, when he has called Mr. Odell at home."

Wolfe regarded her. "And you didn't tell Mrs. Odell you had warned him."

"Of course not."

"But you did tell her, three days after Mr. Odell died. Why?"

"Because — well, I *had* to. I said I didn't want to be a murderer, but I *was* one. If I hadn't made that phone call, Mr. Odell would still be alive, and maybe Mr. Browning would too. The LSD might not have hurt him at all. To go right on being with Mrs. Odell every day — I *had* to tell her."

Wolfe turned to the prospective client. "That was two weeks ago. Why haven't you dismissed her?"

"That's a silly question," Mrs. Odell said. "She might tell anyone. She might tell the police. I'm not hiring you to analyze what Miss Haber has done — or what I have done. I want to know how we can make Browning pay for what *he* did without telling what *we* did."

Wolfe closed his eyes, and the forefinger of his right hand started making little circles on his desk blotter. But he wasn't tackling a tough one; his lips didn't move. So he had made his decision and was merely considering whether he should ask more questions before announcing it. In half a minute he quit making circles, lifted his hand to give his forehead a rub, and swiveled to look at me. If they hadn't been there he would have put it into words: "You got me into this. I concede the desirability of a fee, but you got me into *this*."

Having looked it, long enough to count ten, he swiveled back to her. "Very well. It's an impossible job, but I'll accept the retainer. My fee will be based on effort and risk, not on accomplishment. I'll need facts, many facts, but it's nearly dinner time, and anyway I want them at first hand. Archie, list these names: Mr. Browning. Mr. Abbott. Mr. Falk. Mr. Meer. Mrs. Browning. Miss Lugos. Miss Venner." Back to the client: "Will you have those people here tomorrow evening at nine o'clock?"

She stared at him. "I will not. How can I?"

"I don't know, but it shouldn't be too difficult. They were associates of your husband, who was murdered. They should be willing to help you learn who murdered him, and you are concerned at the lack of progress in the official investigation and have engaged my services. Shouldn't they sacrifice an evening at your request?"

"They might. I don't want to ask them. And I won't."

Wolfe picked up the check and held it out. "Take it. You have wasted your time and mine. You want a miracle, and miracles are not in my repertory. Give me the receipt."

"My god," she said, "you *are* highhanded. What can *they* tell you?"

"I don't know, and I need to know. If there is a fact that will help me do what you want done, I want it. If you think I may inadvertently disclose what you have told me, even a hint of it, if you think me capable of such ineptitude, you were a ninny to come to me at all."

She was chewing her lip. "Is this the only —do you *have* to do this?"

"If I take the job as you defined it, yes."

She looked at me, and saw only an open, intelligent, interested, sympathetic phiz.

"Damn it," she said. "Give me the list."

6

SINCE the state of the bank account had been responsible for the state of my nerves for at least six weeks, it might be supposed that ten o'clock Monday morning would find me at the door of the Continental Bank and Trust Company, waiting for it to open so I could deposit the check, but I wasn't. I knew darned well that Wolfe would not be firmly and finally committed until Mrs. Odell came through, and I couldn't blame him. Of the people on the list I had given her, there wasn't one that he could tell me to go and bring with any right or reason to expect me to fill the order, and if he expected to fill *her* order, he had to get some questions answered, and not just by her and Miss Haber. So it was possible that the twenty grand would have to be returned, and if so, it would be neater to return her check than to deposit it and then have to draw one of Wolfe's.

And at four o'clock Monday afternoon, it became about ten to one that she was going to get her check back. She had done fine with the invitations; she reported by phone that all of them had said yes. The hitch was that when she told me she would come a little early, around half past eight, I had to tell her, as instructed by Wolfe, that he had decided she shouldn't come at all. She wasn't invited and wouldn't be admitted. So she blew her top. I tried to explain why, but she wouldn't listen. She commanded me to get Wolfe to change his mind and ring her, and if she hadn't heard from me by four-thirty, she would tell them not to come. I went to the kitchen to tell Fritz I was going on an errand, ran, not walked, to the garage on Tenth Avenue where the Heron sedan that Wolfe owns and I drive is kept, made it to Sixty-third and Madison in nineteen minutes, probably a record for that time of day, and was inside the Odell mansion at 4:28. If I reported that conversation verbatim you would think I was tooting my horn, so I'll merely say that I sold her. I explained that when Browning told lies, as he surely would, if she was there she would almost certainly horn in, and if she expected Wolfe to get results she would have to let him do it his way. Also, of course, if she told them not to come, the deal was off and she would have to find someone who would do it her way, and obviously she didn't have any or she wouldn't have gone to Wolfe and given him a check for twenty grand. She didn't like it, but she lumped it.

Then, leaving, I got a break. I had had to double-park, on Sixty-third Street, and it was a pleasant surprise to see that no city employe had happened by to put a ticket on the windshield. The return trip took thirty-one minutes. When Wolfe came down at six o'clock and I reported, he didn't even say "Satisfactory." He merely scowled and rang for beer. His outlook was bleak. It was now settled that he was going to have to work, and with an obstreperous female for a client.

They all came. The first to arrive, Sylvia Venner, showed a little before nine, and the last, Kenneth Meer, at 9:08. Cass R. Abbott rated the red leather chair on two counts: he was the president of CAN, and, being close to seventy, he had seniority. So I put him there. For the others I had placed two rows of yellow chairs facing Wolfe's desk. I have a sort of rule that when there is company and one of them is, or is supposed to be, a murderer, the place for him or her is the front row nearest to me, so that was where I put Amory Browning. Next to him was his wife, and then Theodore Falk. In the back row Kenneth Meer was in the middle, with Helen Lugos on his right and Sylvia Venner on his left. The only one I had ever seen before was Kenneth Meer. When I let him in, he had looked me in the eye and asked, "More tricks?" and I said, "No, and we have made no use of that one. If anyone here knows about your bloody hands, he didn't learn it from us."

Since you're meeting them, you should see them. Cass R. Abbott, the president, looked like one. The mop of well-tended white hair, which he had a right to be proud of and probably was, was a good cap for the well-arranged, long, pale face. Amory Browning, who would soon be president if he wasn't otherwise engaged, didn't rate it on looks. If he was fifty-two, which would have been my guess, he had probably been pudgy for about five years, and he would be bald in another five. Theodore Falk, the Wall Street Falk, was about the same age, but he had kept himself lean and limber and had a deep tan. He probably played tennis. You have already seen Kenneth Meer's long, pointed nose and wide, square chin.

As for the females, I would have recognized Sylvia Venner from the dozen or so times I had seen her do "The Big Town," the program Browning had bounced her from. She was easy to look at, especially when whe was using certain muscles to show her dimples, but TV girls, like all actresses, are always working at it and if you get really interested you have to make allowances. I don't want to be unfair to Mrs. Browning merely because our client had her husband tagged for murder, but the truth is she was scrawny. I could give details, but why rub it in? She was about her husband's age, and she was scrawny, and facts are facts. Helen Lugos, Browning's secretary, was the one you would have to see with your own eyes, because she was the kind with whom details like color of eyes and hair, and shape of face, and kind of mouth don't really tell it. She was probably three or four years under thirty, but that was only another unimportant detail. The point was that I had put her in the back row chair the other side of Kenneth Meer because that was where I could see her best and oftenest without turning my head much. I would have liked to put her in the red leather chair where I would have had her full face, but of course that was the president's place. Hers was the kind of face that is different from any two angles.

I had invited orders for liquids, but they had all been declined, and when Kenneth Meer was in and seated, I went to Wolfe's desk and gave the kitchen button three stabs, and in a moment he came, detoured between the red leather chair and the wall to his desk, sat, and sent his eyes around. As I pronounced the seven names, he gave each of them a nod—*his* nod, about an eighth of an inch.

"On behalf of Mrs. Odell," he said, "I thank you for coming. She intended to be here, but she conceded my point that her presence would make our discussion more difficult, both for you and for me. I know, of course, that you have all been questioned at length by officers of the law, and I shall not try to emulate them, either in pertinacity or in scope. I frankly admit that I strongly doubt if I'll get what Mrs. Odell wants. She hired me to learn who killed her husband, and the prospect is forlorn. Apparently no one knows whether his death was premeditated, or fortuitous—except the person who put the bomb in the drawer."

His eyes went right, then left. "What information I have has come from three sources: the newspapers, Mrs. Odell, and four or five journalists who have worked on the case and with whom Mr. Goodwin is on friendly terms. There is no agreement among the opinions they have formed. One of them thinks that Mr. Odell went to that room and opened that drawer, and put the bomb in it, in order to—"

"Oh for god's sake." It was Theodore Falk. "That kind of crap?"

Wolfe nodded. "Certainly. In the effort to solve any complex problem, there are always many apparent absurdities; the job is to find the correct answer and demonstrate that it is *not* absurd. Another of the journalists thinks that Mr. Abbott put the bomb in the drawer because he didn't want Mr. Browning to succeed him as president of CAN. Still another thinks that Mrs. Browning did it, or arranged to have it done, because she didn't want her husband to continue to enjoy the favors of Miss Lugos. He hasn't decided whom it was intended for, Mr. Browning or Miss Lugos. And another thinks that Miss Lugos did it because she did want Mr. Browning to continue to enjoy her favors but he—"

"Tommyrot!" Cass R. Abbott, in the red leather chair, blurted it. "I came because Mrs. Odell asked me to, but not to hear a list of idiotic absurdities. She said you wanted to get some facts from us. What facts?"

Wolfe turned a palm up. "How do I know? All of you have been questioned at length by the police; you have given them thousands of facts, and in assembling, comparing and evaluating a collection of facts they are well practiced and extremely competent. It's possible that from the record of all the questions they have asked, and your answers to them, I might form a surmise or reach a conclusion that they have failed to see, but I doubt it. I confess to you, though I didn't to Mrs. Odell, that I have little hope of getting useful facts from you. What I needed, to begin at all, was to see you and hear you. It seems likely that one of you put the bomb in the drawer. There are other possibilities, but probabilities have precedence. A question, Mr. Abbott: Do you think it likely that the person who put the bomb in the drawer is now in this room?"

"*That's* absurd," Abbott snapped. "I wouldn't answer that and you know it."

"But you *have* answered it. You didn't give me a positive no, and you're a positive man." Wolfe's eyes went right. "Mr. Falk. Do you think it likely?"

"Yes, I do," Falk said, "and I could name names, three of them, but I won't. I have no evidence, but I have an opinion, and that's what you asked for."

"I don't expect names. Mrs. Browning. The same question."

"Don't answer, Phyllis," Browning said. A command.

"Of course not. I wasn't going to." Her voice didn't match her scrawniness; it was a full, rich contralto, with color.

Wolfe asked, "Then you, Mr. Browning? Are you going to answer?"

"Yes. I'll tell you exactly what I have told the police and the District Attorney. I not only have no evidence, I have no basis whatever for an opinion. Not even an opinion as to whether the bomb was intended for me or for Odell. It was my room and my desk, but the fact remains that it was Odell who got it. I'll also tell you that I am not surprised that Mrs. Odell has engaged you, and I don't blame her. After nearly three weeks the official investigation is apparently completely stymied."

Wolfe nodded. "I *may* have better luck. Miss Lugos? The same question."

"The same as Mr. Browning," she said. I acknowledge that her voice wasn't as good as Mrs. Browning's; it was thinner and pitched higher. "I have no idea. None at all." Also she wasn't a good liar. When you have asked about ten thousand people about a million questions you may not be able to spot a lie as well as you think you can, but you're right a lot oftener than you're wrong.

"Mr. Meer?"

Naturally I was wondering about Kenneth Meer. Like everybody who reads about murders in newspapers, I knew that he had been the fourth or fifth person to enter Browning's room after the explosion, so he had seen blood all right, but that alone wouldn't account for the blood-on-his-hands crisis that had sent him to the clinic, unless he had bad kinks in his nervous system, bad enough to keep him from working up to such an important job at CAN and hanging onto it. There was the obvious possibility that he had planted the bomb, but surely not for Browning, and if for Odell, how did he know Odell was going to the room and open the drawer? Of course Mrs. Odell had made the answer to that one easy: Browning had told him. Now, how would he answer Wolfe's question?

He answered it with a declaration which he had had plenty of time to decide on: "I think it extremely likely that the person who put the bomb in the drawer is now in this room, but that's all I can say. I can't give any reason or any name."

"You can't, or you won't?"

"Does it matter? Just make it I don't."

"But I ask you if—no. That will come later, if at all. Miss Venner?"

She wasn't showing the dimples. Instead, she had been squinting at Wolfe, and still was. "I don't get it," she said. "I don't think you are dumb, but *this* is dumb, and I wonder why you're doing it. Even if I thought I could name the person who put the bomb in the drawer, would I tell you with them here? Mr. Abbott is the head of the company that employs me, and Mr. Browning is going to be. I can't, but even if I could . . . I don't get it."

"You haven't listened," Wolfe told her. "I said that I had little hope of getting any useful facts from you, and I could have added that even if I do, you probably won't know it. For instance, the question I ask you now.

About three months ago CAN had a special program called 'Where the Little Bombs Come From.' Did you see it?"

"Yes. Of course."

"Then you know that the preparation for that program required extensive research. There had to be numerous contacts between members of the CAN staff and people who knew about bombs and had had experience with them. Call them the *sources*. Now I ask you regarding three weeks ago — Friday, May sixteenth, to Sunday, May eighteenth — where and how did you spend that weekend? It may help to remember that the Tuesday following, two days later, Mr. Odell died."

"But why do you —" She wasn't squinting; her eyes were wide in a stare. "Oh. You think I went to one of the 'sources' and got a bomb. Well, I didn't."

"I don't 'think' anything. I'm trying to get a start for a thought. I asked where and how you spent that weekend. Have you a reason for not telling me?"

"No. I have no reason for telling you either, but I might as well. I've told the police four or five times. I took a train to Katonah late Friday afternoon and was a house guest of friends — Arthur and Louise Dickinson. They know nothing about bombs. I came back by train Sunday evening."

I had got my notebook and a pen and was using them. Wolfe asked, "Mr. Meer? Have you any objection to telling me how you spent that weekend?"

"Certainly not. I drove to Vermont Friday evening and I hiked about forty miles in the mountains Saturday and Sunday, and drove back Sunday night."

"Alone, or with companions?"

"I was alone. I don't like companions on a hike. Something always happens to them. I helped some with the research for that program, and none of the 'sources' was in Vermont."

"I am hoping that Mr. Browning will tell me about the sources. Later. Miss Lugos?"

Her face was really worth watching. As he pronounced her name, she turned her head for a glance at Browning, her boss. It was less than a quarter-turn, but from my angle it wasn't the same face as when she was looking at Wolfe. Her look at Browning didn't seem to be asking or wanting anything; evidently it was just from habit. She turned back to Wolfe and said, "I stayed in town all that weekend. Friday evening I went to a movie with a friend. Saturday afternoon I did some shopping, and Saturday evening I went to a show with three friends. Sunday I got up late and did things in my apartment. In a file at the office we have a record of all the research for that program, all the people who were contacted, and I didn't see any of them that weekend."

Wolfe's lips were tight. In his house, "contact" is not a verb and never will be, and he means it. He was glad to quit her. "Mr. Falk?"

Falk had been holding himself in, shifting in his chair and crossing and uncrossing his legs. Obviously he thought it was *all* crap. "You said," he said, "that you wouldn't try to emulate the police, but that's what you're doing. But Peter Odell was my best and closest friend, and there may be a chance that you're half as good as you're supposed to be. As for that weekend, I spent it at home — my place on Long Island. We had four house guests—no, five—and none of them was a bomb expert. Do you want their names and addresses?"

"I may, later." As Wolfe's eyes went to Mrs. Browning, her husband spoke: "My wife and I were together that weekend. We spent it on a yacht on the Sound, guests of the man who owns it, James Farquhar, the banker. There were two other guests."

"The whole weekend, Mr. Browning?"

"Yes. From late Friday afternoon to late Sunday afternoon."

I put my eyes on my notebook and kept them there. With all the practice I have had with my face, I should of course always have it under control, but I had got two jolts, not just one. First, was that why Wolfe had started the whole rigmarole about that weekend, to check on Browning, and second, had Browning heard it coming and got set for it, or had he just given a straight answer to a straight question? I don't know how well Wolfe handled *his* face, since my eyes were on my notebook, but otherwise he did fine. There were two or three other questions he must have wanted to ask Browning, but he didn't. He merely remarked that he doubted if Mr. Farquhar or the other guests were in the bomb business and then said, "And you, Mr. Abbott?" and my eyes left the notebook.

"I resent this," Abbott said. "I knew Pete Odell for twenty years and we worked together for ten of them, and I have a warm and deep sympathy for his wife, his widow, but this is ridiculous. I assumed you would have some new angle, some new approach, but all you're doing, you're starting the same old grind. Each of us has spent long hours with the police, answering questions and signing statements, and while we want to oblige Mrs. Odell, naturally we do, I certainly don't think she should expect us to repeat the whole performance with you. Why doesn't she ask the police to let you see their files? In one of them you'll find out how I spent that weekend. I spent it at home, near Tarrytown. There were guests. I played golf all day and bridge at night. But I repeat, this is ridiculous."

A corner of Wolfe's mouth was up. "Then it would be fruitless to continue," he said—not complaining, just stating a fact. He put his hands on the edge of his desk for purchase, pushed his chair back, and rose. "I'll have to contrive a new approach. On behalf of Mrs. Odell, I thank you again for coming. Good evening." He moved, detoured again between the wall and the red leather chair, and, out in the hall, turned left.

"I'll be damned," Theodore Falk said.

I think they all said things, but if any of it was important, that will be a gap in this report. I wasn't listening, as I went through the appropriate motions for godspeeding a flock of guests. I had heard enough, more than enough, for one evening. I didn't even notice who went with whom as they descended the seven steps of the stoops to the sidewalk. Closing the door and sliding the chain-bolt in its slot, I went to the kitchen. Fritz, who had kept handy to fill orders for refreshments if called for, was perched on the stool by the big center table with a magazine, but his eyes weren't on it. They were on Wolfe, who was standing, scowling at a glass of beer in his hand, waiting for the bead to settle to the right level.

"It's going on eleven o'clock," I said. "I would love to start on it right now, but I suppose I can't."

"Of course not," he growled. He drank beer. "Do we need to discuss it?"

"I don't think so." I went and got a bottle of scotch from the cupboard.
There are times when milk will not do. "I have a suggestion. Do you want
it?"

He said yes, and I gave it to him.

7

AT five minutes past eleven Tuesday morning, I was seated in a comfortable chair at the end of a big, expensive desk in a big, expensive room on the
thirtieth floor of a big, expensive building on Broad Street, near Wall, facing
a man whose tan was much deeper than Theodore Falk's — so deep that his
hide might have been bronze.

Getting to him had been simple, but first I had had to confirm that he
existed and owned a yacht. At one minute past nine I had dialed the
number of the magazine *Fore and Aft*; no answer. Modern office hours. Half
an hour later I got them, and was told by a man, after I held the wire while
he looked it up, that a man named James J. Farquhar had a fifty-eight-foot
Derecktor cruiser named *Prospero*. So it was a yacht, not just a rowboat with
a mast or an outboard motor. Next I dialed the number of the Federal
Holding Corporation, and via two women and a man, which was par, got
through to Avery Ballou. He sounded as if he still remembered what Wolfe
and I had done for him three years ago, and still appreciated it. I told him
we needed a little favor and asked if he knew a banker named James
Farquhar.

"Sure," he said. "He's next to the top at Trinity Fiduciary. What has he
done?"

"As far as I know, nothing. It isn't another paternity problem. I want to
ask him a couple of questions about something that he's not involved in —
and he won't be. He's the best bet for a piece of information we need, that's
all. But the sooner we get it, the better, and Mr. Wolfe thought you might be
willing to ring him and tell him that if I phone him for an appointment, it
would be a good idea for him to tell me to come right away and get rid of
me."

He said he would, and ten minutes later his secretary phoned and said
Farquhar was expecting a call from me. She even gave me the phone number, and I dialed it and got *his* secretary.

So at 11:05 there I was, at his desk. I was apologizing. "Mr. Wolfe didn't
want to bother you," I said, "about a matter that you will consider trivial,
but he sort of had to. It's about something that happened more than three
weeks ago — Friday, May sixteenth. A lawyer has a client who is being sued
for damages, fifty thousand dollars, and he has asked Mr. Wolfe to check on
a couple of things. The client's name is O'Neill, Roger O'Neill, and a man
named Walsh claims that around half past eight that evening he was in his
small boat, fishing in the Sound, near Madison, about a mile off shore, and
O'Neill's big cruiser came along fast, doing at least twenty, he says, and hit
his boat right in the middle — cut it right in two. The sun had set but it

wasn't dark yet, and Walsh says he had a light up. He wasn't hurt much, but his twelve-year-old son was; he's still in the hospital."

Farquhar was frowning. "But where do I come in? I have a busy morning."

"I'm keeping it as brief as possible. Walsh says there were witnesses. He says a bigger boat, around seventy feet, was cruising by, about two hundred yards farther out, and there were people on deck who must have seen it happen. He tried to see its name, but it was in the water and the light was dim. He thinks it was *Properoo.*" I spelled it. "We can't find a boat with that name listed anywhere, but your yacht, *Prospero,* comes close to it. Friday, May sixteenth. Three weeks ago last Friday. Were you out on the Sound that day?"

"I'm out *every* Friday. That Friday . . . three weeks . . ." He shut his eyes and tilted his head back. "That was . . . No. . . . Oh, sure." His eyes opened and his head leveled. "I was across the Sound. Nowhere near Madison. Before nine o'clock we anchored in a cove near Stony Brook, on the other shore."

"Then it wasn't you." I stood up. "Have you ever seen a boat named *Properoo?*"

"No."

"If you don't mind — Mr. Wolfe always expects me to get everything. Who was on board with you?"

"My wife, and four guests. Mr. and Mrs. Percy Young, and Mr. and Mrs. Amory Browning. And the crew, two. Really, damn it —"

"Okay. I'm sorry I bothered you for nothing, and Mr. Wolfe will be too. Many thanks."

I went.

In the elevator, going down, a woman moved away from me, clear away. I wasn't bothering to manage my face, and probably its expression indicated that I was all set to choke or shoot somebody. I was. Down in the lobby I went to a phone booth and dialed the number I knew best, and when Fritz answered I said, "Me. I want him."

It took a couple of minutes. It always does; he hates the phone.

"Yes, Archie?"

"I'm in a booth in a building on Broad Street. I have just had a talk with James J. Farquhar. At nine o'clock Friday evening, May sixteenth, he anchored his yacht in a cove on the Long Island shore. The four guests aboard were Mr. and Mrs. Percy Young and Mr. and Mrs. Amory Browning. I'm calling because it's nearly eleven-thirty, and if I proceed as instructed I couldn't have her there in less than an hour, which would be too close to lunch. I suggest that I phone her instead of going to get her, and —"

"No. Come home. I'll telephone her. The number?"

"On my yellow pad in the middle drawer. But wouldn't it —"

"No." He hung up.

So he too was set for murder. He was going to dial it himself. He was going to risk keeping lunch waiting. As I headed for the subway, which would be quicker than scouting for a taxi in that territory, I was trying to remember if any other client, male or female, had ever equaled this, and couldn't name one.

But when I entered the old brownstone, and the office, a few minutes before noon, I saw that he wasn't going to choke her or shoot her. He was going to slice her up. At his desk, with his oilstone and a can of oil on a sheet of paper, he was sharpening his penknife. Though he doesn't use it much, he sharpens it about once a week, but almost never at that time of day. Evidently his subconscious had taken over. I went to my desk and sat, opened a drawer and took out the Marley .38, and asked, "Do I shoot her before you carve her, or after?"

He gave me a look. "How likely is it that Mr. Browning telephoned him last night, or saw him, and arranged it?"

"No. A hundred to one. I took my time with a phony buildup and watched his face. Also at least seven other people would have to be arranged: his wife, the four guests, and the crew. Not a chance. You got Miss Haber?"

"Yes." He looked at the clock. "Thirty-five minutes ago. I made it—"

The doorbell rang. I put the Marley in the drawer and closed it, and went. But in the hall, I saw more than I expected. I stepped back in and asked Wolfe, "Did you invite Mrs. Odell too?"

"No."

"Then she invited herself. She came along. So?"

He shut his eyes, opened them, shut them, opened them. "Very well. You may have to drag her to the front room."

That would have been a pleasure—preferably by the hair with her kicking and screaming. She performed as expected. When I opened the front door, she brushed past me rudely and streaked down the hall, with Miss Haber at her tail, trotting to keep up. Thinking she might actually scratch or bite, I was right behind as she entered the office and opened up, heading for Wolfe's desk. I'm not sure whether the five words she got out were "If you think you can" or "If you think you're going," before Wolfe banged a fist on the desk and bellowed at her:

"Shut up!"

I don't know how he does it. His bellow is a loud explosion, a boom, as a bellow should be, but also it has an edge, it cuts, which doesn't seem possible. She stopped and stood with her mouth open. I was between her and him.

"I told Miss Haber to come," Wolfe said in his iciest tone. "Not you. If you sit and listen, you may stay. If you don't, Mr. Goodwin will remove you—from the room and the house. He would enjoy it. I have something to say to Miss Haber, and I will not tolerate interruption. Well?"

Her mouth was even wider than normal because her teeth were clamped on her lower lip. She moved, not fast, toward the red leather chair, but Wolfe snapped, "No. I want Miss Haber in that chair. Archie?"

I went and brought a yellow chair and put it closer to my desk than his. She gave me a look that I did not deserve, and came and sat. I doubted if Charlotte Haber would make it to the red leather chair without help, so I went and touched her arm, and steered her to it.

Wolfe's eyes at her were only slits. "I told you on the telephone," he said, "that if you were not here by twelve o'clock, I would telephone a policeman, Inspector Cramer of Homicide South, and tell him what you told me Sunday evening about your telephone call to Mr. Browning on May sixteenth.

I'll probably find it necessary to tell him anyway, but I thought it proper to give you a chance to explain. Why did you tell me that lie?"

She was making a fair try at meeting his eyes. She spoke: "It wasn't —" Her tongue got in the way and she stopped and started over: "It wasn't a lie. It was exactly like I told you. If Mr. Browning won't admit it, if he denies —"

"Pfui. I haven't discussed it with Mr. Browning. The conclusive evidence that you couldn't have made that call did not come from him. Even candor may not serve you now, but certainly nothing else will. Unless you tell me what and who induced you to tell me that lie, you're in for it. You'll leave here not with your employer, but with a policeman, probably for detention as a material witness. I will not —"

"You can't!" Mrs. Odell was on the edge of her chair. "You know you can't! You guaranteed in writing!"

"Remove her, Archie," Wolfe said. "If necessary, drag her."

I rose. She tilted her head to focus up at me and said, "You don't dare. Don't dare to touch me."

I said, "I dare easy. I admit I'd rather not, but I have bounced bigger and stronger women than you and have no scars. Look. You tried to steal home and got nailed, and no wonder. You didn't even have sense enough to check where Browning was that Friday night. As for that guarantee in that receipt you got, it says, quote, 'Unless circumstances arise that put me or him under legal compulsion to reveal it.' End quote. Okay, the circumstances are here. The cops have spent a thousand hours trying to find out why your husband went to the room and opened the drawer, and who knew he was going to. Now *I* know. So I'm withholding essential evidence in a murder case, and there's a statute that puts me under legal compulsion to reveal it. Also, I'm not just a law-abiding citizen, I'm a licensed private detective, and I don't want to lose my license and have to start a new career, like panhandling or demonstrating. So even if Mr. Wolfe got big-hearted and decided just to bow out, there would still be me. I feel responsible. I *am* responsible. I started this by writing you that letter. Mr. Wolfe told Miss Haber that unless she comes clean he will open the bag. I may or may not stay with him on the *unless*. I am good and sore, and for a dirty crinkled dollar bill with a corner gone I would go now to the drug store on the corner and ring a police sergeant I know. I also know a man on the *Gazette* who would love to have a hot item for the front page, and I could back it up with an affidavit. And would."

I turned to Wolfe. "If I may offer a suggestion. If you still want her bounced, okay, but from her face I think she has got it down."

I turned back to her. "If you get the idea that you can say it was *all* a lie, that you wanted to fasten it on Browning and made it *all* up, nothing doing. They found the LSD in your husband's pocket and they've got it. You're stuck, absolutely, and if you try to wriggle you'll just make it worse."

She had kept her eyes at me. Now they went to her right, clear around past Wolfe to Miss Haber, and they certainly saw nothing helpful. Below the crease in the narrow forehead, the secretary's eyes weren't aimed anywhere. They could have been seeing her hands clasped on her lap, but probably they weren't seeing anything.

Mrs. Odell aimed hers at Wolfe. "You said you haven't discussed it with Browning. The—the LSD. Who have you discussed it with?"

"Mr. Goodwin. No one else."

"Then how did you—How can you—"

"Mr. Goodwin talked this morning with a man who owns a yacht. At nine o'clock in the evening of Friday, May sixteenth, when he anchored in a cove on the Long Island shore, two of the guests aboard were Mr. and Mrs. Amory Browning. In all my experience with chicanery, madam, I have never encountered a more inept performance. A factor in our animus is probably the insult to our intelligence; you should have known that we would inquire as to Mr. Browning's whereabouts that evening, and therefore *you* should have. By the glance you just gave Miss Haber I suspect that you are contemplating another inanity: saying it was some other evening. Pfui. Don't try it. Look at Miss Haber."

She didn't have to; she already had. And she proceeded to demonstrate that she was by no means a complete fool. She cocked her head at me for a long, steady look, and then cocked it at Wolfe. "I don't believe," she said, "that you have really decided to tell the police about it. If you had, you wouldn't have phoned Miss Haber and—"

"I haven't said I have decided. I said, to Miss Haber, 'Unless you tell me what and who induced you to tell that lie.' "

"*I'll* tell you. *I* induced her."

"When?"

"Three days ago. Saturday evening. And Sunday morning, before I called Goodwin. *What* induced her was money. She needs money. She has a younger brother who has got himself into—but that doesn't matter, what she needs it for. And anyway, I think Browning put that bomb there. I'm *sure* he did. I don't know how he knew Peter was going to open that drawer, but I'm sure he did. Maybe Peter told somebody. You didn't know Peter, you don't know what a wonderful man he was. He married me for my money, but he was a wonderful husband. and Browning killed him, and with all the money I have, now there's only one thing I want to do with it. I don't think the police will ever get him, and you know something they don't know. Can you handle Goodwin?"

"No." He was scowling at her. "No one can 'handle' Mr. Goodwin. But he handles himself reasonably well, and he wouldn't divulge information he got as my agent without my consent. My problem is handling me. Your fatuous attempt to hoodwink me relieves me of my commitment, but I too am a licensed private detective. If Mr. Cramer learns that those seven people were here last evening, as he probably will, and if he comes to see me, as he almost certainly will, I'll be in a pickle. I have many times refused to disclose information on the ground that it was not material, but the fact that your husband went to that room and opened that drawer in order to put LSD in the whisky is manifestly material. Confound it, they even have the LSD—that is, you *say* they have it."

"They do. They showed it to me." She opened her bag and took out the checkfold. "I've made one idiotic mistake with you and I don't intend to make another one. I'm going to give you a check for one hundred thousand dollars, but I have sense enough to know that I have to be careful how I do it. If you think that I think I can pay you and Goodwin for not telling the police about the LSD, I don't. I know I can't. But I do think they will never get Browning, and I think you might. I think the only chance of getting him is if you do it. I don't care what it costs. The hundred thousand dollars is just to start. You may have to give somebody twice that much for something." She slid the pen out and started to write on the check stub.

"No," Wolfe said. "You can't pay me at all on the terms you imply. I certainly would not engage to demonstrate that Mr. Browning killed your husband. I might engage to try to learn *who* killed your husband and to get evidence that would convict him. As for withholding information from the police, that must be left to my discretion. Mr. Goodwin and I are disinclined to share with others information that gives us an advantage."

"It *was* Browning. Why do you think it wasn't?"

"I don't. He is as likely a candidate as anyone — much the most likely if he knew of your husband's intention to drug the whisky." He swiveled to face the red leather chair. "Miss Haber. You didn't tell Mr. Browning about it, but whom did you tell?"

"Nobody." It came out louder than she intended, and she repeated it, lower. "Nobody."

"This is extremely important. I *must* know. This time you are expected to tell me the truth."

"I *am* telling you the truth. I *couldn't* have told anyone because I didn't know myself. I didn't know what the LSD was for until last Saturday evening, three days ago, when Mrs. Odell told me . . . When she asked me . . ."

Wolfe turned to Mrs. Odell with his brow up.

"*I* believe her," she said, and he turned back to the secretary.

"Do you go to church, Miss Haber?"

"Yes, I do. Lutheran. Not every Sunday, but often."

He turned to me. "Bring a Bible."

On the third shelf from the bottom, at the left of the globe, there were nine of them, four in different editions in English and five in foreign languages. I picked the one that looked the part best, in black leather, and crossed to the red leather chair.

"Put your right hand on it," Wolfe told her, "and repeat after me: With my hand on the Holy Bible I swear."

I held it at her level and she put her hand on it, palm down, flat, the fingers spread a little. "With my hand on the Holy Bible I swear."

"That I did not know what Mr. Odell intended to do."

She repeated it.

"With the LSD I had procured for Mrs. Odell."

She repeated it.

"Until Saturday, June seventh."

She repeated it.

Wolfe turned to the client. "You can suspect Mr. Browning only if you assume that he knew what your husband was going to do. Miss Haber didn't. I don't suppose you or your husband told him. Whom did you tell?"

"I didn't tell anybody. Absolutely nobody. So Peter must have. I wouldn't have thought — but he *must* have. Of course there were people who wanted Peter to be the new president, not Browning, and he must have told one of them. For instance, Ted Falk, but Ted wouldn't have told Browning.

I can give you names. Sylvia Venner. Then there's a man in public relations —"

"If you please." He had turned his head to look at the wall clock. "It's my
lunch time. You can make a list of the names, with relevant comments. But
there must be no misunderstanding about what you expect me to do. My
commitment is to try to learn who killed your husband and get evidence
that will convict him. Just that. Is that clearly understood?"

"Yes. But I want to be sure . . . No. I suppose I can't be." She opened the
checkfold. "But if it wasn't Browning . . . Oh, damn it. *God damn it.*" She
wrote the check.

8

AT twenty minutes to seven, Theodore Falk, in the red leather chair with
his legs crossed, told Wolfe, "It would depend on what it was he was going
to do."

In the four and a half hours since lunch, much had been done but
nothing visible had been accomplished. We had discussed the Cramer problem. If and when he came, I could open the door only the two inches the
chain on the bolt allowed and tell him Wolfe wasn't available and there was
no telling when he would be, and I was under instructions to tell nobody
anything whatever. He probably couldn't get a warrant, since all he could
tell a judge was that some of the people involved in a murder case had spent
part of an evening in the house, but if he did, and used it, we would stand
mute — or sit mute. Or I could open the door wide and let him in, and Wolfe
would play it by ear, and we voted for that. There was always a chance that
he would supply one or more useful facts.

We had also decided to spend thirty-one dollars an hour, for as long as
necessary, of the client's money, on Saul Panzer, Fred Durkin, and Orrie
Cather — eight each for Fred and Orrie, and fifteen for Saul. If no one had
known that Odell intended to go to Browning's room, the bomb couldn't
have been intended for him, and it was going to take more doing than
having people come to the old brownstone for some conversation. I had
phoned Saul and Orrie and asked them to come Wednesday at ten o'clock,
and left a message for Fred. And I had phoned Theodore Falk, Odell's best
and closest friend, and told him that Wolfe wanted to have a talk with him,
without an audience, and he said he would come around six o'clock.

By a couple of phone calls — one to a vice-president of our bank and one
to Lon Cohen — I had learned that Falk was way up. He was a senior
member of one of the oldest and solidest investment firms and sat on eight
boards of directors. He had a wife and three grown-up children, and he and
they were also solid socially. Evidently a man the race could be proud of,
and from personal observation the only thing I had against him was his
buttoned-down shirt collar. A man who hates loose flaps so much that he
buttons down his collar should also button down his ears.

He came at 6:34.

Wolfe told him that he needed all the information he could get about Odell. Specifically, he needed the answer to a question: If Odell decided to do something secretly, some shabby deed that would help him and hurt someone else, how likely was it that he would have told anyone? And Falk said, "It would depend on what it was he was going to do. You say 'shabby'?"

Wolfe nodded. "Opprobrious. Mean. Furtive. Knavish. Tricky."

Falk uncrossed his legs, slid his rump clear back in the red leather chair, which is deep, recrossed his legs, and tilted his head back. His eyes went left and then right, in no hurry, apparently comparing the pictures on the wall—one of Socrates, one of Shakespeare, and an unwashed coal miner in oil by Sepeshy. (According to Wolfe, man's three resources: intellect, imagination, and muscle.)

In half a minute Falk's head leveled and his eyes settled on Wolfe. "I don't know about you," he said. "I don't know you well enough. A cousin of mine who is an assistant district attorney says you are sharp and straight. Does he know?"

"Probably not," Wolfe said. "Hearsay."

"You solicited Mrs. Odell."

I cut in. "No," I said. "I did."

Wolfe grunted. "Not material." To Falk: "Mr. Goodwin is my agent, and what he does is on my tally. He knew my bank balance was low. Does your firm solicit?"

Falk laughed, showing his teeth, probably knowing how white they looked with his deep tan. "Of course," he said, "you're not a member of the bar." He lifted a hand to rub his lip with a finger tip. That helped him decide to say something, and he said it. "You know that the police have a vial of LSD that was in Odell's pocket."

"Do I?"

"Certainly. Mrs. Odell has told me that she told you. Has she told you what he was going to do with it?"

"I'm sharp, Mr. Falk."

"So you are. Of course you'll tell her what I say, but she already knows that I think she knew what Pete was going to do with the LSD, though she won't admit it, and no wonder, not even to me."

"And you knew."

"I knew what?"

"What he was going to do with the LSD."

"No, I didn't. I don't know even now, but I can make a damn good guess, and so can the police. So can you, if Mrs. Odell hasn't told you. Going to Browning's room and opening that drawer, with LSD in his pocket? Better than a guess. You would call it shabby and opprobrious for him to dope Browning's whisky? And knavish?"

"Not to judge, merely to describe. Do you disagree?"

"I guess not. Not really. Anyway another good guess is that it was her idea, not his. You can tell her I said that, she already knows it. Of course your question is, did I know about it, did he tell me? He didn't. He wouldn't. If he told anybody it would have been me, but a thing like that he wouldn't even tell me. The reason I'm telling you this, I'm beginning to doubt if the police are going to crack it, and you might. One reason you might, Mrs. Odell will probably tell you things she won't tell them. Another reason is that with people like these, like us, the police have to consider things that you can ignore."

"And you want it cracked."

"Hell yes. Pete Odell was my favorite man."

"If no one knew he was going to open that drawer, he died by inadvertence."

"But whoever planted that bomb killed him." Falk turned a palm up. "Look, why am I here? This will make me an hour late for something. I wanted to know if you were going to waste time on the idea that the bomb was *intended* for Odell. The police still think it could have been and there's not a chance. Damn it, I *knew* him. It just isn't thinkable that he would have told anyone he was going to try to bust Browning by doping his whisky."

"If he had told you, would you have tried to dissuade him?"

Falk shook his head. "I can't even discuss it as a hypothesis. If Pete Odell had told me that, I would just have stared at him. It wouldn't have been him. Not his doing it, his telling me."

"So the bomb was for Browning?"

"Yes. Apparently."

"Not certainly?"

"No. You told us yesterday that the journalists have different ideas, and we have too — I mean the people who are involved. They are all just guessing really — except one of course, the one who did it. My guess is no better than anybody else's."

"And no worse. Your guess?"

Falk's eyes came to me and returned to Wolfe. "This isn't being recorded?"

"Only in our skulls."

"Well — Do you know the name Copes? Dennis Copes?"

"No."

"You know Kenneth Meer. He was here last evening. He's Browning's man Friday, and Copes would like to be. Of course in a setup like CAN, most of them want someone else's job, but the Copes-Meer thing is special. My guess is that Meer had a routine of checking that drawer every afternoon and Copes knew it. Copes did a lot of work on that program about bombs and getting one would have been no problem. That's my best guess partly because I can't quite see anyone going for Browning with a bomb. A dozen people *could* have, but I can't see any of them actually doing it. You said one of the reporters thinks it was Browning's wife, but that's absurd."

"Did Kenneth Meer check the drawer every day?"

"I don't know. I understand he says he didn't."

I could fill three or four pages with the things Theodore Falk didn't know, but they didn't help us, so they wouldn't help you. When I returned to the office after going to the hall to let him out, we didn't discuss him, for two reasons: the look we exchanged showed that we didn't need to, and Fritz came to announce dinner. The look was a question, the same question both ways: How straight was Falk? Did we cross him off or not? The look left it open.

The fact was, Wolfe hadn't really bit into it. It was still just batting practice. He had taken the job and was committed, but there was still the slim chance that something might happen — the cops might get it or the client might quit—so he wouldn't have to sweat and slave. Also in my book there was the idea that I had once mentioned to him, the idea that it took a broil with Inspector Cramer to wind him up. Of course when I had offered it, he had fired me, or I had quit, I forget which. But I hadn't dropped the idea, so when the doorbell rang at 11:10 Wednesday morning and I went to the hall and saw who it was on the stoop through the one-way glass, and stepped back in the office and said "Mr. Fuzz," I didn't mind a bit.

Wolfe made a face, opened his mouth and then clamped his jaw, and in five seconds unclamped it to growl, "Bring him."

9

THAT was a first—the first time Inspector Cramer had ever arrived and been escorted to the office in the middle of a session with the hired hands. And Saul Panzer did something he seldom does—he stunted. He was in the red leather chair, and when I ushered Cramer in I expected to find Saul on his feet, moving up another yellow chair to join Fred and Orrie, but no. He was staying put. Cramer, surprised, stood in the middle of the rug and said, loud, "Oh?" Wolfe, surprised at Saul, put his brows up. I, pretending I wasn't surprised, went to get a yellow chair. And damned if Cramer didn't cross in front of Fred and Orrie to *my* chair, swing it around, and park his big fanny on it. As he sat, Saul, his lips a little tight to keep from grinning, got up and came to take the yellow chair I had brought. That left the red leather chair empty and I went and occupied it, sliding back and crossing my legs to show that I was right at home.

Wolfe didn't merely turn his head left to face me; he swiveled. "Was this performance arranged?" he demanded.

"Not by me," I told him. "This chair was empty, that's all."

"I guess I was just too surprised to move," Saul said. "I didn't know the Inspector was coming."

"Balls," Cramer said. "No one knew I was coming." He focused on Wolfe. "I hope I'm not interrupting anything important."

"I hope you are," Wolfe said, not thorny. "We are discussing the prospect of making an important contribution to the investigation of a murder."

Cramer nodded. "Yeah. I thought you would be."

Actually the discussion had barely begun. Saul Panzer, who looks like a guy who was trying to sell encyclopedias but gave up and quit, and is actually the best operative alive; and big-footed, heavy-set Fred Durkin, who looks as if he wouldn't know what an encyclopedia is but actually bought a Britannica for his kids; and good-looking, six-foot Orrie Cather, who would trade an encyclopedia for a full-length mirror if he didn't already have one, but can handle a tough assignment when he needs to, had come in at ten o'clock, and I had briefed them good. On some jobs they are called in on, some details have to be reserved, but not that one. I had given them the whole picture, and Wolfe, coming down from the plant rooms at eleven o'clock, had just got started.

When Wolfe faced Cramer in my chair with me in the red leather chair, I had his profile from his left instead of his right, and I had to adjust to it. I don't know why it made so much difference, but it did. His chin looked more pointed and his hair thicker. He asked Cramer politely, "You have questions?"

"Nothing specific," Cramer was leaning back, comfortable, also polite. "Don't mind me. Go right ahead." Saul's stunt had cued him.

Wolfe's eyes passed Orrie and Saul to Fred. "I was asking," he said, "if Archie covered the ground to your satisfaction. Do you need more?"

"I hope not." Fred riffled the pages of his notebook. "No room for more."

"What do you suggest?"

That routine was nearly always just talk, but now and then it led to something. "Well," Fred said, "you can't just walk up to the counter at Macy's and say one Number Four gelignite bomb and charge my account and don't bother to wrap it." He looked straight at Cramer. "What the hell."

Wolfe nodded. "No doubt the police have made every effort. Twenty-two days. Three weeks yesterday. You suggest . . . ?"

"I need time to sort it out."

"Yes. Orrie?"

"I need more," Orrie said. "For instance, I need to know if Odell had gloves on. One theory is that he was putting the bomb in the drawer to get Browning, and if so, he would have used gloves if he wasn't a moron. I suggest that you ask Inspector Cramer if he was wearing gloves, and if not, that will narrow it. Also you can ask him about fingerprints."

"Anything else?"

"Maybe. After I know that."

"Saul?"

"I may as well say it," Saul said. "Maybe it wasn't just surprise. I had a suggestion ready and the Inspector coming flipped me. I was going to say that if you asked for a look at the files, both Homicide and the DA, they might want to cooperate. After three weeks they must have quite a stack of stuff that—"

"Shove it," Cramer growled. "Who the hell are you, Panzer? Do you think you're Goodwin?" His eyes stopped at me a second on their way to Wolfe. To Wolfe he said, "It's you. It's always you."

A corner of Wolfe's mouth was up a thirty-second of an inch. For him a broad grin. He asked politely, "Does that mean something?"

"You know damn well—" Cramer bit it off. "Skip it. I don't want to interrupt. I have all day. Go right ahead. I might learn something."

"We haven't even started."

"*That* would be something. How you start."

"Well . . ." Wolfe shut his eyes. In ten seconds he opened them, looked at Saul, then at Fred, and then at Orrie. Then at me. "Get Mr. Abbott."

It didn't seem necessary to pretend I had to look up the number, so instead of going to my desk, where Cramer was, I went around to the other end of Wolfe's desk, reached for his phone, and dialed. It took four minutes to get the president of CAN—first an operator and then his secretary, and I had to say it was urgent. Since it was Wolfe's phone and I didn't go to mine, I heard only him.

"Good morning, Mr. Abbott. . . . Yes, I'm busy too, this won't take long.

You said Monday evening that you have a warm and deep sympathy with Mrs. Odell and you want to oblige her; and this request is from her through me. I have just given three men the known facts about Mr. Odell's death. Their names are Saul Panzer, Fred Durkin, and Orrie Cather. They are experienced and competent. I ask you to give them permission to talk with people who are employed by your company — to move freely about the premises and talk with anyone who is available and willing. Only those who are willing. The police can do that without permission, but these men can't. They need a letter from you, and I want to send them to your office to get it. They will be considerate; they will not impose. They will not ask to talk with anyone who was here Monday evening. If you have a complaint about one of them, he will be withdrawn. May they come now for the letters? . . . No, of course not. No compulsion. . . . No, there will be no difficulty about that. Inspector Cramer is here hearing me, and . . . Yes, Inspector Cramer of Homicide South. He is here in my office. . . . No, there is nothing official about this request. Mr. Cramer came to talk with me and interrupted my talk with these men. He has neither approved this request nor objected to it. . . ."

There was some more, mostly about interrupting people at work. When Wolfe hung up I was back in the red leather chair. He leaned back and sent his eyes to Fred and across Orrie to Saul. To them: "So you are going fishing. First to Mr. Abbott for credentials, and then scatter. As usual, anything whatever may or may not be significant. If any single question has precedence, it is who, if anyone, knew that Mr. Odell was going to that room and open that drawer. If you get no answer to that or any other question, you may at least get hints. Report to Archie daily as usual. I doubt if any bribing will be necessary or desirable, but the available funds are unlimited." He turned to me. "Five hundred?"

I said that should do for a start and went and opened the safe. From the supply in the cash box, always used bills, I got thirty twenties, sixty tens, and sixty fives, and split them three ways. Wolfe was telling them, "You heard me say that you will exclude those who were here Monday evening. Saul, you will try Dennis Copes. The question you want answered, did he know or think he knew that Kenneth Meer habitually inspected that drawer, is of course the one you won't ask. Orrie, you will try Dennis Copes's secretary if he has one. We want that question answered. Fred, you will follow your nose. Smile at people. Your smile is admirably deceptive. All of you, don't push and don't impose. There is no urgency. — Mr. Cramer. Have you a question or a comment before they go?"

Cramer said, "No," louder than necessary, and with the used lettuce, distributed by me while Wolfe was talking, in their wallets, they got up and went. I gave Cramer a deceptive smile and said, "Let's trade," and he rose and crossed to the red leather chair and I took the one I belonged in.

Wolfe swiveled to face him. "Obviously," he said, "you are not in armor. Perhaps you will answer one question. Who told you about my Monday evening visitors?"

"Kenneth Meer. He phoned Lieutenant Rowcliff yesterday morning."

"Indeed."

"Yes." Cramer got a cigar from a pocket, stuck it in his mouth, and clamped his teeth on it. "You have Goodwin report verbatim, so I will.

When Rowcliff told me about Meer's call, he said, 'Of course when they left, that fat son-of-a-bitch leaned back in his goddam tailor-made chair and shut his goddam beady eyes and worked his lips a while, and then he sat up and told that smart-ass Goodwin who the murderer was and told him to have him there at six o'clock when he came down from nursing his goddam orchids. So we'll put a man there to see who comes at six o'clock and then all we'll have to do is dig up the evidence and the motive.' Well, we did put a man there, and he reported that Theodore Falk came at half-past six. I thought it would save time and trouble to come and ask you, at least for the motive. That will help, getting the evidence."

Wolfe shook his head. "This isn't like you. Wasting your breath on clumsy sarcasm. And sitting here hearing me send those men on their errands you said nothing to them, or to me, about interference by private investigators in a murder case. How many times have you threatened to take my license? Are you desperate?"

"Yes."

"Oh." Wolfe's eyes opened wide. He shut them and opened them again. "Shall we have beer?"

"Yes."

Wolfe reached to the button to give Fritz the beer signal. Cramer took the cigar from his mouth, inspected the teeth marks, started it back toward his mouth, changed his mind, and laid it on the little table at his elbow. Fritz came with a bottle and glass on a tray and was told to bring another.

Cramer aimed a frown at me and then switched it to Wolfe. "I didn't come to ask for help. I'm not down that low. But it looks close to impossible. Of course lots of murder cases are impossible and have to be put on the open list, which means they're closed actually, but that won't do when the victim is a Peter Odell. But look at it. How can we get a murderer when we don't know who he wanted to kill? After three weeks we don't even know *that*. Durkin thinks we should have traced the bomb. Nuts. Seventeen people had a hand in getting the dope for that goddam program, and they have named nine sources that were contacted, and God knows how many others there were that they haven't named and won't name. And some of them learned enough to make their own bombs, and who did they tell? Of course we're still on that, but it looks worse now than it did a week ago."

He turned his palms up, the fingers spread. "You told them that the first question is who knew Odell was going to that room and open that drawer. Yeah? Sure. They'll bring you a list of names? Like hell they will. I don't suppose you already know who knew? That you told them that because I was here?"

"Nonsense. If I knew that, I probably wouldn't need those men."

Fritz had come with another bottle and glass, and Wolfe got the opener from the drawer and used it, and I got up and served Cramer. Wolfe poured, and as he waited for the foam to reach the right level, he told Cramer, "Of course you know *why* Odell went there and opened that drawer."

"I do?"

"Certainly. With a powerful drug in his pocket, opening the drawer where Browning kept his whisky? You are not a nincompoop."

"Naturally Mrs. Odell has told you."

"She told me that you showed her the LSD. I don't suppose it was flour or sugar, supplied by you. Why would you? Was it?"

"No." Cramer drank, emptied the glass, put it down on the table, picked up the bottle, and poured. He picked up the cigar, put it in his mouth, and took it out again. He looked at Wolfe, whose head was tilted back to drink, and waited for Wolfe's eyes to meet his.

"Why I came," he said. "Not to ask for help, but I thought it was possible that an exchange might help both of us. We have collected a lot of facts, thousands of facts, some established and some not. Mrs. Odell has certainly told you things that she hasn't told us, and maybe some of the others have too. We might trade. Of course it would hurt. You would be crossing your client, and I would be giving you official information that is supposed to be withheld. You don't want to and neither do I. But I'm making a straight offer on the square. I haven't asked you if this is being recorded."

"It isn't."

"Good." He picked up his glass. "That's why I came."

Wolfe swiveled, not his chair, his head, to look at me. The look said, as plain as words, "I hope you're appreciating this," and my look said, "I am." He turned back to Cramer and said, just stating a fact, "It won't do, Mr. Cramer."

"It won't?"

"No. There is mutual respect between you and me, but not mutual trust. If I gave you every word spoken to me by Mrs. Odell, and by the others, you would think it possible, even probable, that I omitted something. You say you have thousands of facts. If you gave me ten thousand, I would think it likely that you had reserved at least one. You know as well as I do that in the long record of man's make-believe, there is no sillier formula than the old legal phrase, 'the truth, the whole truth, and nothing but the truth.' Pfui."

"So you *would* omit something."

"Perhaps. I could add that if I did give you every word, you would know nothing helpful that you don't know now, but you wouldn't believe me."

"You're damn right I wouldn't." He looked at the glass in his hand and squinted at it as if he wondered how it got there. "Thanks for the beer." He put the glass, not empty, on the table, saw the cigar, and picked it up. I expected him to throw it at my wastebasket and miss as usual, but he stuck it in the beer glass, the chewed end down. He stood up. "I had a question, I had one question, but I'm not going to ask it. By God, you had the nerve — those men — with me sitting here —" He turned and walked out.

I didn't go to see him out, but when I heard the front door open and close, I went to the hall to see that he *was* out. Back in, I went to the safe to enter the outlay in the petty cash book. I don't like to leave things hanging. As I headed for my desk, Wolfe said, "I thought I knew that man. Why did he come?"

"He said he's desperate."

"But he isn't. So healthy an ego isn't capable of despair."

I sat. "He wanted to look at you. Of course he knew you wouldn't play along on his cockeyed offer. He thinks he can tell when you've got a good hand, and maybe he can."

"Do *you* think he can? Can you?"

"I'd better not answer that, not right now. We've got a job on. Am I to just sit here and take calls from the help?"

"No. You are to seduce either Miss Lugos or Miss Venner. Which one?"

I raised one brow. He can't do that. "Why not both?"
We discussed it.

10

WHEN I had a chance, after lunch, I looked up "seduce" in the dictionary.
"1. To persuade (one) as into disobedience, disloyalty, or desertion of a lord
or cause. 2. To lead or draw (one) aside or astray, as into an evil, foolish, or
disastrous course or action from that which is good, wise, etc.; as, to be
seduced into war; to *seduce* one from his duty; to tempt or entice; as, pleasures
that *seduced* her from home. 3. To induce to evil; to corrupt, specif., to induce
to surrender chastity; to debauch."

Even on the 3 I couldn't charge him at some appropriate moment with
having asked me to go too far, since we had no evidence that either of them
had any chastity to surrender.

The best spot in the metropolitan area at four o'clock on a Saturday
afternoon in June is an upper box at Shea Stadium, but I wasn't there that
Saturday. I was sitting in the cockpit of a thirty-foot boat, removing a
flounder the size of my open hand from the hook at the end of Sylvia
Venner's line. The object I enjoy most removing from a hook is a sixteen-
inch rainbow or Dolly Varden or cutthroat, but there aren't any in Long
Island Sound. We had spent a couple of hours trying for stripers or blues
without a bite and had settled for salmon eggs on little hooks. The name of
the boat was *Happygolucky*. I had borrowed it from a man named Sopko,
who had once paid Wolfe $7,372.40, including expenses, for getting his son
out of a deep hole he had stumbled into.

It was from Sylvia Venner herself, on the telephone Wednesday afternoon, that I had learned that she didn't care for baseball, didn't like dancing, had seen all the shows in town, and wouldn't enjoy dining at
Rusterman's because she was on a diet. The idea of a boat had come from
her. She said that she loved catching fish, all except actually touching one,
but the soonest she could make it was Saturday.

In fifty-six hours Saul and Fred and Orrie had produced nothing that
would need help from me during the weekend. Friday evening I assembled
the score for the two and a half days on a page of my notebook and got this:

Number of CAN employes who thought or guessed or hinted
—that Odell was putting the bomb in the drawer to get Browning
                                                                          4

—that Browning planted the bomb to get Odell and somehow got
  Odell to go and open the drawer   *1*
—that Dennis Copes planted it to get Kenneth Meer   *2*
—that no one had planted it; the bomb was a left-over from the
  research for the program and was supposed to be de-activated 2
—that Sylvia Venner had planted it to get Browning   *1*
—that Helen Lugos had planted it to get Kenneth Meer   *2*

—that Kenneth Meer had planted it to get Helen Lugos   1
—that some kind of activist had planted it to get just anybody 3
—that it would never be known who had planted it for whom 8

If you skipped that I don't blame you; I include it only because I didn't
want to waste the time I spent compiling it. It adds up to twenty-four, and
they spoke with a total of about a hundred people, so some seventy or eighty
were keeping their thinking or guessing or hinting to themselves. Wolfe and
I agreed, Friday evening, to ignore the favorite guess. The idea that Odell
had himself supplied the bomb was out. His wife would have known about
it, and she would not have given Wolfe a hundred grand to start digging.
Also why the LSD in his pocket? Because he was on the stuff and had it with
him in case his nerves needed a boost? Cramer and the DA had certainly
included that in their tries and had chucked it. So no. Out. One of the four
who liked it was Dennis Copes, but that didn't prove anything. Saul's
description of Copes was "5 feet 9, 160 pounds, brown hair down to his
collar, sideburns that needed trimming, showy shirt and tie, neat plain gray
Hickey-Freeman suit, soft low-pitched voice, nervous hands." He had chatted with him twice and learned nothing useful. Of course he hadn't asked if
he knew or thought he knew that Kenneth Meer had the habit of checking
on the whisky in the drawer, and though he is as good as Wolfe at the trick of
getting an answer to an unasked question, it hadn't worked with Copes.

Actually nothing worked with anybody. I have just looked over my notes,
and since there is nothing in them that helped us they certainly wouldn't
help you.

At four o'clock Saturday afternoon it looked as if I wasn't going to get
anything helpful from Sylvia Venner either. She had stopped bothering
about the dimples. In blue shorts and a white sleeveless shirt with big blue
plastic buttons she was showing plenty of nice smooth skin with a medium
tan, and her well-arranged face was the kind that looks even better in bright
outdoor light than inside. While we were eating the broiled chicken supplied by Fritz, and yogurt and thin little tasteless crackers supplied by her,
and pickles and raw carrots and celery, and she was drinking something
called Four-Root Juice and I was drinking milk, she had suddenly said, "I
suppose you know what etymology is."

"Hah," I said. "I work for Nero Wolfe."

"Why," she said, "is that relevant?"

"Certainly. He knows more words than Shakespeare knew."

"Oh. I don't really know anything about him except what he does. They
tried to get him on my program once, but he wouldn't, so I didn't have to
research him. Are you up on words too?"

"Not really. Just enough to get along on."

"I think words are fascinating. I was thinking, looking at you while you
were dropping the anchor, take words like 'pecker' and 'prick.' In their
vulgar sense, or maybe I should say their colloquial sense."

Without batting an eye I said, "You mean 'prick' as a noun. Not as a verb."

She nodded. "Yes, a noun. It means 'a pointed instrument.' 'Pecker'
means 'an instrument for pecking,' and 'peck' means 'to strike repeatedly
and often with a pointed instrument.' So the definition of 'pecker' and
'prick' is identical."

"Sure. I've never looked them up, but evidently you have."

"Of course. In Webster and in the OED. There's an OED at the office. Of course the point is that—well, well, there's a pun. 'Point.' The point is that they both begin with *p,* and 'penis' begins with *p.*"

"I'll be damned. It certainly does."

"Yes. I think that may be relevant to that old saying, 'Watch your p's and q's.' *But.* But two other words, 'piss' and 'pee' —*p*-double-*e*—they start with *p* too. What it is, it's male chauvinism."

"I'm not sure I get that."

She sipped Four-Root Juice. "It's obvious. Women urinate too. So they have to call it 'piss' or 'pee' just because 'penis' begins with *p.* What if they called it 'viss' or 'vee,' and they made men call it 'viss' or 'vee' too? Would men like that?"

"Viss," I said. "Vee. I don't. . ." I considered it, sipping milk. "Oh. Vagina."

"Certainly. Virgin too, but that may be just coincidence."

"I admit it's a point. A voint. You may not believe this, but personally I wouldn't object. It even appeals to me. 'Excuse me while I viss.' 'Turn your back while I vee.' I rather like the sound of it."

"I don't believe it, and anyway not many men would. It's male chauvinism. And another point, 'poker' begins with a *p* too. Why didn't they make it 'poker' instead of 'pecker'? Because a poker is three feet long!"

"It is not. I've never seen a poker three feet long. More like two feet. Possibly thirty inches."

"You're just quibbling. Even two feet." She put her open hands out, apparently she thought two feet apart, but it was about twenty-eight inches. She picked up a pickle. Vickle. "So they couldn't very well call it 'poker.' Take another letter, take *f.* 'Female' begins with *f.* What is one of men's favorite four-letter colloquial words that begins with *f*?"

"Offhand I couldn't say. I'd have to think."

"All right, think."

So there I was, on a borrowed boat on Long Island Sound, alone with a Women's Libberette who was majoring in etymology. If you think that in the above exchange she was making a roundabout approach to a pass at me, I appreciate the compliment, but I doubt it. If so, my reaction cooled it. Even in such an ideal situation as a boat with a cabin at anchor in smooth water, I refuse to be seduced by quotations from Webster and the Oxford English Dictionary.

She was not a nitwit. Soon after we got our lines out she said, "What are you waiting for? You haven't asked me a single question about the murder."

"What murder?"

"Oh, come off it. Do you think I think my dimples took you?"

"No. I have never seen better dimples, and there's nothing wrong with other parts of you either, but a newspaperman I know thinks you planted the bomb to get Browning, and I wanted to get a close-up of you. With a good look and some talk with a woman, I can tell if she is a murderer. The way they eat helps too. For instance, do they lick their fingers."

She was frowning at me. "Do you really—no, of course you don't. All right, I'll play. Have you decided about me?"

"Not to cross you off, but ten to one you didn't plant the bomb. But three to one, make it five to one, you have a pretty good idea who did. You've been there four years, you know everybody, and you're smart."

"I am not smart. If I was smart I would have hooked that skunk Browning instead of letting Helen Lugos take him. Do you know who I could love?"

"No, but I'd like to."

"All right, I'll tell you. I could love the man who can prove I'm not dumb. I simply can't persuade myself I'm not dumb. Browning is going to be it, he's going to be the top cock, and where will I be? No, I didn't plant the bomb, but I could have."

"Who did?"

"I don't —*now* what have I done?"

She had snarled her line. Not purposely, to change the subject, because half an hour later, after we had unsnarled her and quit on stripers and were trying for blues, she said, "I've got a pretty good idea who might have. The bomb. But not for any signed statement. They always want signed statements. I'm not *that* dumb."

I made a cast. "Not me. I just want an idea to play with."

"Play? My god, you should have seen that room. Browning's office. When I got there Helen Lugos and Ken Meer were trying to keep people out. Ken's hands were bloody. When I heard what had happened—that was later—my first idea was that Ken had done it."

"How did he know Odell would come and open—"

"Not Odell. Browning. To kill Browning. Of course he—"

"Isn't Meer with Browning? His right hand?"

"Yes, but he hates him. No, that's wrong, it's not hate, it's—what, jealousy? It's worse than jealousy. It kills him that Helen does it with Browning. He got an itch for Helen when she came, two years ago, and he's got it bad. I've seen him look at her with that sick look—you know?"

I nodded. "Male chauvinism upside down."

"What? Oh. It is at that. But I dropped that idea. Ken certainly wants Helen, but he wants to move up even more, and if Browning was president he would be in a very good spot. So I still think he probably planted the bomb, but not for Browning, for Odell. So Odell couldn't be president. He knew Odell was going to come and open that drawer."

"How did he know that?"

"You'll have to ask *him*. I can't wrap it up for you." She had her line in and squared around for another cast.

By the time the slant of the sun and my watch agreed that it was time to head for the marina, I had got all the questions in but had nothing to light a fire with. She doubted if Dennis Copes was involved because he was the hippie type and hippies aren't really headed anywhere, they just key up— according to her, not me. I know a hippie who tried—but he's not in this. She didn't know if Copes knew or thought he knew that Kenneth Meer inspected that drawer every day. She doubted if anybody inspected the drawer besides Browning himself, but if anyone did it was probably Helen Lugos; inspecting drawers is routine for secretaries. She had herself inspected it once, out of curiosity, about three years ago. Yes, it was twelve-year-old Ten-Mile Creek.

The Heron was in the parking lot at the marina and I drove Sylvia—sure, we had been Sylvia and Archie the last three hours — to a human hive in the East Seventies, only a block away from a spot where an FBI man had once insulted me because I was tailing a man he wanted to tail. She didn't invite me up. Wolfe was in the middle of dinner when I got home and he doesn't like to dawdle while I catch up, so I ate in the kitchen, with Fritz.

Later, in the office, when I asked him if he wanted Sylvia Venner verbatim he said yes, omitting only trivia, we had all evening. I asked, including the personal parts, and he said, enough of it to exhibit her. So I had a free hand. Omitting trivia, it took only ten minutes to get us on board the boat and under way, and another five to get us to the spot where we anchored and agreed that the air made us hungry. Of course I enjoyed my description of the picnic lunch in detail, but he didn't. He set his jaw and squinted at me, and did something he seldom does; he used profanity. "Good god," he growled. "Are you — how do you feel?"

"All right now. Of course it was tough, but what the hell, I was working. During the feast she said she supposed I knew what etymology is, and I said hah, I work for Nero Wolfe. She asked if that was relevant and said she didn't know much about him, that they tried to get him on her program but he wouldn't. You remember that."

"Yes."

"She said, quote, 'I think words are fascinating. Take words like "pecker" and "prick." In their vulgar sense, or maybe I should say their colloquial sense.'"

"Me: 'You mean "prick" as a noun, not as a verb.'"

"She: 'Yes, a noun. It means "a pointed instrument." "Pecker" just means "an instrument for pecking," and "peck" means "to strike repeatedly and often with a pointed instrument." So the definition of "pecker" and "prick" is identical.'"

"Me: 'Sure. I've never looked them up, but evidently —'"

His grunt stopped me. He growled. "I said omit trivia."

"This is not trivia. She was leading up to a point, and she made it. The point was that men make women say 'piss' and 'pee' — p-double-e — when they urinate because 'penis' begins with p, and what if they made them say 'viss' and 'vee'? Vagina. And she said it's male chauvinism. Doesn't that exhibit her?"

And once again I got a completely different reaction from the one I expected. I suppose I will never know him as well as I think I do. I did know where he stood on the question of male chauvinism, but I should have considered how he felt about words.

He said, "Indeed."

I said, "Yes indeed. Women's Lib."

He flipped a hand. "That's merely the herd syndrome. Fad. The issue is the influence of male dominance on language. Has that woman made a contribution to the study of linguistics? If so, there should be some indica-tion in the record of matriarchy, but there is no adequate . . ."

Letting it hang, he pushed his chair back, rose, went straight to a spot in the shelves, got a book, and returned. As he sat, my good eyes told me it was *History of Human Marriage* by Westermarck. I had given it a ten-minute try one empty day long ago and decided I could get along without it. As he opened it, I asked, "Shall I tell the squad not to come in the morning because the issue now is a matter of linguistics, or will you need them for research?"

He glared at me, transferred it to the book, tossed it on the desk, and said, "Very well, proceed, but only what is material. No flummery."

So I no longer had a free hand. I reported. When I finished and he asked for comments, as usual, I said, "Nothing to raise my pay. One, I doubt if she is saving anything that would open a crack. Two, it would suit her fine if Browning dropped dead, but if she planted the bomb she wouldn't have risked a whole afternoon with me. She's not that kind. Three, at least we know that Meer had blood on his hands that other people could see, so maybe that helps to explain *him.*"

"Not enough to justify that outrageous meal," he said, and reached for the book.

Fritz had left to spend a night and a day and another night as he saw fit, so before I went upstairs to dress properly for joining Lily Rowan's party at the Flamingo, I brought a bottle of beer to help with the language problem.

11

SINCE Wolfe's nine-to-eleven session in the plant rooms doesn't apply on Sundays, he was in the office when the help came at ten o'clock. That was about the most useless two hours we ever spent with them. Wolfe's idea was to have them talk about everyone they had seen, in the slim hope of our getting at least a glimmer of some kind of a hint.

No. Nothing.

If you are inclined to quit because I seem to be getting nowhere, no wonder. I'm sorry, but in these reports, I don't put in stunts to jazz it up, I just report. Of course I can leave things out, and I do. I'll skip that two-hour Sunday conference, except for one little item. Orrie said that Dennis Copes didn't have a secretary, and the girl in the stenographer pool who often took stuff for him was a stuck-up bitch, and he added, "Of course Archie would have had her holding hands." He can't quite ditch the idea that he should have my job. I admit there is one little detail of detective work that he can do better than I can, but he doesn't know what it is so I won't name it. They were told to go back in the morning and try some more. The theory was that somebody there must know *something,* which seemed reasonable.

The only thing that happened that day worth reporting was that Lily Rowan and I, at Shea Stadium, watched the Mets take the Cardinals, 7 to 3.

At ten o'clock Monday morning I sent a messenger to the CAN building with a white carboard box addressed to Miss Helen Lugos. The box contained a cluster of Broughtonia sanguinea. They had been picked by Wolfe, who won't let even me cut his orchids, but the card in the box had my name. At 11:30 I decided that she must have opened it, phoned, and got a female who said that Miss Lugos was engaged and did I wish to leave a message.

When you get up to vice-president, especially one who will soon be president because the other candidate was murdered, even secretaries are often hard to get. I decided that she might not have seen the box yet and postponed it to after lunch.

It was after four o'clock and Wolfe was up in the plant rooms when I finally got her. She said right off, "Thank you for the beautiful flowers." Neither warm nor cool, just polite.

"You're welcome. I suggested them, Mr. Wolfe picked them, and we both packed them. It's a bribe. Mr. Wolfe thinks I understand women better than he does and wants me to have a talk with you. I don't think this office is the best place for it because that's too much like telling you to come to a—oh, the District Attorney's office. I can come to your place, or we can meet anywhere you say, or we can share a meal in the little pink room at Rusterman's. Perhaps dinner this evening? Wome are supposed to like pink rooms, as of course you know. I'm going on talking to give you time to consider it; I didn't suppose you'd have a yes right at the tip of your tongue."

"I haven't got one anywhere. Thank you, but no."

"Then the pink room is out. Have you a suggestion?"

"I have a question. Has Mrs. Odell asked *you* to talk with me?"

"Mrs. Odell hasn't asked *me* anything. She has hired Nero Wolfe to do a job, and she has asked people at CAN to cooperate, from Mr. Abbott down, as you know. We would like to suit their convenience. In this case, *your* convenience."

"Mrs. Odell didn't hire you, she hired Nero Wolfe."

"I work for him."

"I know you do. And I work for Mr. Browning. When he wants to talk with someone, he doesn't expect them to be willing to talk with me instead. If Mr. Wolfe wants to talk with me, all right, I suppose I'll have to. At his office, of course. When does he want me to come?"

There was no point in prolonging it. I said distinctly, "At six o'clock today. An hour and a half from now."

She said distinctly, "Very well, I'll be there," and hung up.

I went to the kitchen, poured myself a glass of milk, and told Fritz, "I'm done. Washed up. I've lost my touch. I'm a has-been. You knew me when."

He was at the big table doing something to a duckling. "Now, Archie," he said. "He told me about that woman's diet when I took his breakfast up this morning, but you ate a good lunch. What else has happened?"

"Another woman. She spit at me just now. Spat. On the phone."

"Then *she* is washed up, not you. You are looking at the wrong side. Just turn it over, that's all you ever have to do, just turn it over."

"I'll be damned." I stared at him. "You sound like a guru."

There was no telling what would happen if Wolfe came down at six o'clock and found an unexpected female sitting in the red leather chair—or rather, there *was*—so when the glass of milk was down I went up three flights, entered, walked down the aisles between the rainbow benches of the three rooms—cool, medium, and warm—and opened the door of the potting room. He and Theodore were at the long bench, making labels. I stopped halfway across and said, "I'm not breaking a rule. Emergency. We have wasted forty dollars' worth of orchids."

He waited until I stopped to turn his head. "She's not available?"

"Oh, she's available, but not for menials. When she dies — the sooner, the better — and ascends, she won't waste her breath on Saint Peter, she'll speak only to Him, with a capital H. She'll be here at six o'clock to speak to You, with a capital Y. I apologize and will expect a pay cut."

"Pfui. I agree that you have not broken a rule." He made a face. "I'll be prompt."

On the way out I stopped to apologize to the two pots of Broughtonia sanguinea. On the way down, I decided that the milk needed help and went to the kitchen for a tall glass of gin and tonic with a sprig of mint and a dash of lime juice. Also for Fritz. I needed friendly companionship.

I was supposing she would be strictly punctual, maybe even a couple of minutes early, but no. She *was* female. She came at 6:18, in a peach-colored blouse with long sleeves and a brownish skirt, narrow, down to a couple of inches below her knees, and she talked to me. She said, "I'm sorry I'm a little late." Not being in a mood to meet her halfway, I said, "So am I."

Wolfe had not told me how he intended to proceed, though he had come down from the plant rooms on the dot at six o'clock, and though he often asks my advice on how to handle a woman and sometimes even follows it. He soon showed me, and her, that this time he needed no help with his game plan. As she got to the red leather chair, he said, "Good afternoon, Miss Lugos. Thank you for coming," and when she was seated and had her ankles crossed and her skirt tugged, he rose, crossed almost to the door, turned, and said, "I have an errand to do in the kitchen. My agent, Mr. Goodwin, will ask you some questions on behalf of Mrs. Odell."

He went.

"I'm as surprised as you are," I told her, "but it's just like him. No consideration for other people. I think I told you that he thinks I understand women better than he does. He actually believes that. So here we are, in a private detective's office which could be bugged, instead of the pink room at Rusterman's. If you like something wet after a day's work, name it and we may have it."

Her lips were twitching a little. "I ought to get up and go," she said. "But I suppose — that would only —"

"Yes," I agreed, "it would only. Anyway, you've flubbed it. On the phone you stiff-armed me. You put me in my place. But if you really meant it, you would have sent the orchids back, or even brought them. Unless you dropped them in the wastebasket?"

She flushed and her lips tightened. I believe I have mentioned that her face was different from any two angles, and it was different flushed. With most faces that you enjoy looking at, you know exactly why, but not with her kind. Flushed, it was again quite different, and I approved of that too. Then suddenly it became another face entirely. She laughed, with her mouth open and her head back, and I think I grinned with pleasure. I really did.

"All right, Mr. Goodwin," she said, "you win. I *didn't* drop them in the wastebasket. They're in a vase. I almost wish we were at Rusterman's. But as you said, here we are. So ask your questions."

I had erased the grin. "Would you like a drink?"

"No, thank you."

"Then let's see. First, I guess, that evening you heard what those people said, six of them, when Mr. Wolfe asked them where they were that week-end. Were they all telling the truth?"

"I don't know. How could I?"

"You might. Maybe you have heard Browning say something that shows he wasn't on a boat from Friday afternoon to Sunday afternoon, or maybe Kenneth Meer has said something that shows he wasn't hiking in Vermont. From your look I think you think I'm a damn fool to suppose you would tell me things like that. But I'm not. In an investigation like this only a damn fool would expect a full and honest answer to any question he asks anybody, but he asks them. For instance, the question I ask you now. This: Did Dennis Copes know that Kenneth Meer looked in that drawer every day to check on the whisky supply?"

"That's a trick question. It assumes that Kenneth Meer did look in the drawer every day."

"So it does. All right, did he?"

"No. As far as I know, he didn't. Mr. Browning checked on the whisky supply himself."

"Did he buy it himself?"

"He buys it by the case. It's sent to his home and he brings it, two bottles at a time."

"Does Kenneth Meer drink bourbon?"

"I don't think so. He drinks vodka."

"Do you drink bourbon?"

"Very seldom. I don't drink much of anything."

"Did *you* look in the drawer every day to check on the whisky supply?"

"No. Mr. Browning did the looking himself."

"I thought secretaries checked everything."

"Well — that's what you thought."

"You know Dennis Copes."

"Certainly."

"Two people think he might have planted the bomb to get Meer because he wants Meer's job. If so, he might have thought Meer looked in the drawer every day. Have you any idea why he might think that?"

"No. I have no idea why he thinks anything."

"One person thinks that Kenneth Meer planted the bomb to get Browning because you go to bed with him. Have you any idea about that?"

"Yes, I have. It's absurd."

"A newspaperman I know doesn't think it's absurd. Of course it's really three ideas. One, that you are intimate with Browning, two, that Meer knows it and can't stand it, and three, that he planted the bomb. Are they all absurd?"

She wasn't visibly reacting. No flush on her skin, no flash in her eyes. She said, with no change in pitch, "The police have asked me about this. My relations with Mr. Browning are my business and his. Certainly not yours. Women do go to bed with men, so it may not be absurd for people to think I am intimate with Amory Browning, but the idea that Kenneth Meer tried to kill him, *that's* absurd. Kenneth Meer has big ideas about his future. He think he's headed for the top, and he's counting on Amory Browning to help him along."

"But you're there. What if he wants you more than anything else? This *is* my business, Miss Lugos. The police think it's theirs, too, you just said so. It's not absurd to think a man's desire for a woman can be so hot that no other desire counts. There have been cases."

"Kenneth Meer isn't one of them. You don't know him, but I do. How much longer is this going to take?"

"I don't know. It depends. Not as long as it would with Mr. Wolfe. He likes to ask questions that seem to be just to pass the time, but I try to stick to the point. For instance, when Mr. Wolfe asked you that evening if you thought the person who put the bomb in the drawer was here in the room, you said you had no idea, but naturally you would say that, with them here. What would you say now, not for quotation?"

"I would say exactly the same. I have no idea. Mr. Goodwin, I — I'm tired. I'd like some — some whisky?"

"Sure. Scotch, bourbon, rye, Irish. Water, soda, ice."

"Just whisky. Any kind — bourbon. It doesn't matter."

She wasn't tired. The fingers of both hands, in her lap, had been curling and uncurling. She was tight. I mean tense, taut. As I went to the kitchen and put a bottle of bourbon — not Ten-Mile Creek — and a glass and a pitcher of water on a tray, I was trying to decide if it was just the strain of discussing her personal affairs with a mere agent, or something even touchier. I still hadn't decided when I had put the tray on the little table by her chair and was back at my desk. She poured about two fingers, downed it with three swallows, made a face and swallowed nothing a couple of times, poured half a glass of water, and swallowed that.

"I told you —" she began, didn't like how it sounded or felt, and started over. "I told you I don't drink much."

I nodded. "I can bring some milk, but it's an antidote for whisky."

"No, thank you." She swallowed nothing again.

"Okay. You said you have no idea who put the bomb in the drawer."

"Yes, I haven't."

I got my notebook and pen. "For this, since this room is *not* bugged, I'll have to make notes. I have to know where you were every minute of that day, that Tuesday, May 20. It was four weeks ago, four weeks tomorrow, but it shouldn't strain your memory, since the police of course asked you that day or the day after. Anyone going to Browning's room went through your room, so we'll have to do the whole day, from the time you arrived. Around ten o'clock?"

"There was another door to his room."

"But not often used except by him?"

"Not often, but sometimes it was. I'm not going to do this. I don't think you have a right to expect me to."

"I have no *right* to expect anything. But Mr. Wolfe can't do the job Mrs. Odell hired him to do unless he can get answers to the essential questions, and this is certainly one of them. One reason I say that is that Kenneth Meer told a newspaperman that anyone who wanted to know how it happened should concentrate on Helen Lugos. Why did Meer say that?"

"I don't believe it." She was staring at me, which made her face different again. "I don't believe he said that."

"But he did. It's a fact, Miss Lugos."

"To a newspaperman?"

"Yes. I won't tell you his name, but if I have to, I can produce him and he can tell you. He wasn't a stranger to Meer. They were choir boys together at St. Andrew's. When he tried to get Meer to go on, Meer clammed. I'm not assuming that when you tell me how and where you spent that day, I'll know why Meer said that, since you'll tell me exactly what you told the police and evidently it didn't help them any, but I must have it because that's how a detective is supposed to detect. You got to work at ten o'clock?"

She said no, nine-thirty.

Even wth my personal and private shorthand it filled more than four pages of my notebook. The timing was perfect. It was exactly 7:30 when we had her in the file room and the sound and shake of the explosion came, and Fritz stepped in to reach for the doorknob. So it was time to eat. If I am in the office with company, and Wolfe isn't, when dinner's ready, Fritz comes and shuts the office door. That notifies me that food is ready to serve, and also it keeps the sound of voices from annoying Wolfe in the dining room across the hall, if I have to continue the conversation.

That time I didn't have to, and I didn't want to. I wanted to consider a couple of the things she had said without her sitting there with her face, and I wanted my share of the ducklings with mushrooms and wild rice and wine while it was hot from the oven. It's one of the dishes Wolfe and Fritz have made up together, and they call it American duckling on account of the wild rice, and I'm for it.

So I said she was tired, and she said yes, she was, and got up, and I thanked her, and thanked her again as I opened the front door to let her out.

Of course I didn't mention her as I joined Wolfe at the dining table. He had one of the ducklings carved, so that would have been talking business during a meal, which is not done. But when we had finished and moved to the office and Fritz had brought coffee, he showed that the week of marking time was getting on his nerves by demanding, "Well?" before I had lifted my cup.

"No," I said.

"Nothing at all?"

"Nothing for me. For you, I can't say. I never can. You want it verbatim, of course."

"Yes."

I gave it to him, complete, up to the details of her day on Tuesday, May 20. For that I used the notebook. As usual, he just listened; no interruptions, no questions. He is the best listener I know. When I finished, the coffeepot and our cups were empty and Fritz had come for them.

I put the notebook in the drawer. "So for me, nothing. Of course she didn't open the bag and shake it, who does? She knows or suspects something that may or may not be true and might or might not help, and to guess what it is needs a better guesser than me. I don't think she planted the bomb. She wasn't there at her desk in the next room when it went off, which was lucky for her, but she says she often went to the file room for something, nearly always when Browning wasn't in his room. Of course the cops have checked that. Also of course it was a waste of time to have her name the seventeen people she saw go into Browning's room. The bomb wasn't put in the drawer while Browning was there unless he did it himself, and there's another door to his room. As for who entered his room when he wasn't there, there was a total of nearly two hours when *she* wasn't there, according to her. As for her reason that Kenneth Meer wouldn't want to kill Browning, toss a coin. You'd have to use a lie detector on Meer himself."

He grunted. "Miss Venner, and now Miss Lugos."

"Meaning I should have seduced at least one of them. Fire me."

"Pfui. I complain of your conduct only directly, never by innuendo. You offend only deliberately, never by shortcoming. Miss Lugos did not plant the bomb?"

"One will get you ten."

"Does she know who did?"

"No bet. She could think she knows. Or not."

"Confound it." He got up and went to the shelves for a book.

12

SIX days later, at noon Sunday, June 22, the five of us sat in the office and looked at each other. Saul and Fred and Orrie and I looked at Wolfe, and he looked back, his eyes moving, not his head, from me past Orrie and Fred to Saul in the red leather chair.

"No," he said. "This is preposterous. Amphigoric. And insupportable." He looked at me. "How much altogether, including you?"

I shut my eyes and in less than half a minute opened them. "Say three thousand dollars. A little more."

"It will be a deduction on my tax return. Call Mrs. Odell and tell her I am quitting. Draw a check to her for the full amount of the retainer."

Fred and Orrie had to turn their heads to look at me. Saul, in the red leather chair, didn't have to turn his head. I looked at Wolfe, especially the left corner of his mouth, to see how bad it was.

Plenty of things had happened. There had been three thunderstorms in a row Wednesday afternoon. Jill Cather, Orrie's wife, had threatened to walk out on him because he didn't get home until five in the morning Tuesday after taking a CAN female researcher to dinner and a show, though he explained that the meal and the tickets had been paid for by the client. The West Side Highway, northbound, had been closed for repairs all day Friday. Fred Durkin, tailing a CAN male employee Thursday evening, had lost him, and he hates to lose a tail; and on Friday, Elaine, his oldest daughter, had admitted she was smoking grass. Saul Panzer had spent two days and a night at Montauk Point trying to find a bomb maker, and drawn a blank. On Friday the Labor Department announced that the Consumer Price Index had gone up .3 of one percent in May. A busy week.

Personally I had done wonders. I had answered at least a hundred phone calls, including dozens from the three helpers. They were *trying* to help. Also including three from Mrs. Odell. I had discussed the situation for about an hour with a member of the CAN news staff, brought by Orrie. His real reason for coming had been to have a chat with Nero Wolfe. I had spent an evening with Sylvia Venner and a male chauvinist friend of hers, also a

CAN employee, at her apartment. I had washed my hands and face every day. I could go on, but that's enough to show you that I was fully occupied.

Wolfe hadn't been idle either. When Inspector Cramer had rung the doorbell at eleven-thirty Friday morning, he had told me to admit him, and he had held up his end of a twenty-minute conversation. Cramer had no chips on his shoulder. What brought him was the fact that Cass R. Abbott, the president of CAN, had come to see Wolfe the day before, a little after six o'clock, and stayed a full hour. Evidently Cramer had the old brownstone under surveillance, and if so, he positively was desperate in spite of his healthy ego. He probably thought that Abbott's coming indicated that Wolfe had a fire lit, and if so, he wanted to warm his hands. I think when he left, he was satisfied that we were as empty as he was, but with those two you never know.

What Abbott's coming actually indicated was that the strain was getting on his nerves, and for a man so high up that would not do. When he got parked in the red leather chair, he told Wolfe he would like to speak with him confidentially, and when Wolfe said he could, there would be no recording, Abbott looked at me, then back to Wolfe, and said, "Privately."

Wolfe shook his head. "Professionally nothing is reserved between Mr. Goodwin and me. If he leaves the room and you tell me anything relevant to the job we are doing — trying to do — I would tell him, withholding nothing."

"Well." Abbott ran his fingers through his mop of fine, white hair. "I have had a check on you but not on Goodwin. You hold up, but does he?"

"If he doesn't, I don't. What good is a chain with a bad link?"

Abbott nodded. "A good line. Who said it?"

"I did. The thought is not new, no thought is, but said better."

"You use words, don't you?"

"Yes. On occasion, in six languages, which is a mere smattering. I would like to be able to communicate with any man alive. As it is, even you and I find it difficult. Are you sure you can prevent my getting more or less than you want me to from what you tell me or ask me?"

Abbott's raised eyebrows made his long, pale face look even longer. "By god, I can try."

"Go ahead."

"When I say 'confidential,' I mean you will not repeat to Mrs. Odell anything I say about her."

Wolfe nodded. "See? You don't mean that. Of course I would repeat it if it would serve my purpose or her interest to do so. She has hired me. If you mean I am not to tell her your name, I am to give her no hint of who said it, yes — Archie?"

"Right," I said. "Noted and filed."

"Then that's understood," Abbott said. He slid further back in the chair, which is deep. "I have known Mrs. Odell twenty years. I suppose you know she is a large stockholder in the Continental Air Network. I know her very well, and I knew him well — her husband. That's one point. Another point is that I have been president of CAN for nine years, and I'm retiring in a few weeks, and I don't want to leave in an atmosphere of distrust and doubt and suspicion. Not distrust or suspicion of me, not of anyone in particular, it's just in the air. It pervades the whole damn place, the whole organization. To leave when it's like that—it would look like I'm getting out from under."

He hit the chair arm with a fist. *"This goddam murder has got to be cleared up!* You probably wondered why I let you turn those three men loose in my building to go anywhere and see anyone. I did it because the police and the District Attorney were completely stumped, they were getting absolutely nowhere, and I thought you might. One reason I thought you might was that there was a good chance that Mrs. Odell had told you things that she hadn't told them. But that was a week ago, a week yesterday, and where have *you* got to?"

"Here." Wolfe patted his desk blotter. "I'm always here."

"Hell, I know you are. Do you know who put that bomb in the drawer? Have you even got a good guess?"

"Yes. You did. You thought they were going to choose Mr. Browning, and you favored Mr. Odell."

"Sure. All you need is proof. As I thought, you have done no better than the police, and you have had ten days. Last evening I discussed the situation with three of my directors, and as a result I phoned this morning to make this appointment. I am prepared to make a proposal with the backing of my Board. I suppose Mrs. Odell has paid you a retainer. If you will withdraw and return her retainer, we will reimburse you for all expenses you have incurred, and we will engage you to investigate the death of Peter Odell on behalf of the corporation, with a retainer in the same amount as Mrs. Odell's. Or possibly more."

I had of course been looking at him. Now I looked at Wolfe. Since he was facing Abbott, he was in profile to me, but I had enough of his right eye to see what I call his slow-motion take. The eye closed, but so slow I couldn't see the motion of the lid. At least twenty seconds. He certainly wasn't giving Abbott a long wink, so the other eye was collaborating, They stayed shut about another twenty seconds, then opened in one, and he spoke. "It's obvious, of course. It's transparent."

"Transparent? It's direct."

"It is indeed. You have concluded that Mr. Odell himself supplied the bomb, intending it for Mr. Browning, and mishandled it. And that Mrs. Odell hired me, not to discover and disclose the truth, but to impede its disclosure and prevent it if possible. You assume that either she is hood-winking me or she has been candid with me. If the former, you decry my sagacity; if the latter, your proposal invites me to betray a trust. A waste of time, both yours and mine. I would have thought—"

"You're taking it wrong. It's not—you're twisting it. We merely think that if you were acting for the corpor—"

"Nonsense. Don't persist. I am neither a ninny nor a blackguard. Under a strain you and your colleagues have lost your wits. There is the possibility that you want to pay me to contrive some kind of skulduggery for you, but I doubt if you have misjudged me to that extreme. If you have, don't bother. Don't try floundering. Just go."

Abbott did not get up and go. He had to take it that he wasn't going to get what he had come for, but he stuck for another half an hour, trying to find out what we had done or hadn't done and what we expected to do. He found out exactly nothing, and so did Wolfe.

When I went back to the office after letting Abbott out, Wolfe glared at me and muttered, "Part of his proposal is worth considering. Returning the retainer."

He considered it for two days and three nights. In the office at noon Sunday, after another two-hour session with us — as I reported six pages back — he told me to call Mrs. Odell and tell her he was quitting and to draw a check to her for the full amount of the retainer; and Saul and Fred and Orrie looked at me and I looked at Wolfe, especially the left corner of his mouth, to see how bad it was.

It was bad all right, it was final, but I did not reach for the phone. "Okay," I said. "Since I started it, I admit I should be the one to finish it, but not with a phone call. I'd rather finish it the way I started it, face to face with her, and to do it right I should take the check and hand it to her instead of mailing it. No deduction for expenses?"

"No. The full amount. Very well, take it."

If we had been alone I might have tried discussing it, but with them there it was hopeless. Discussion would have to be with her, and then with him maybe. I went and got the checkbook from the safe, filled out the stub, tore the check out, and swung the typewriter around. I type all checks. That was the first one I had ever drawn for an even hundred grand, and with all the 0's it was a nice round figure. I took it to Wolfe and he signed it and handed it back. As I took it, Saul said, "I've asked so many people so many questions the last ten days, it's a habit, and I'd like to ask one more. How much is it?"

Even from Saul that was a mouthful, and my eyes opened at him. But Wolfe merely said, "Show it to him. Them."

I did so, and *their* eyes opened, and Saul said, "For her that's petty cash, she's really loaded. Sometimes you ask us for suggestions, and I'd like to make one. Or just another question. Instead of returning it to her, why not offer it to someone who needs it? A two-column ad in the *Times* and the *Gazette* with a heading like COULD YOU USE A HUNDRED THOUSAND DOLLARS? Then, 'I'll pay that amount in cash to the person who gives me information that will satisfactorily identify the person responsible for the death of Peter Odell by the explosion of a bomb on May twentieth.' Your name at the bottom. Of course the wording would—"

Wolfe's "No" stopped him. He repeated it. "No. I will not make a public appeal for someone to do my job for me."

"You have," Saul said. "You have advertised for help twice that I know of."

"For an answer to a particular question. Specific knowledge on a specified point. Not a frantic squawk to be pulled out of a mudhole. No."

So when they left a few minutes later, they weren't expected back. By noon Monday Fred and Orrie would be on chores for Bascom or some other outfit, and Saul too if he felt like it.

As for me, my chore wouldn't wait — or I didn't want it to. As someone said, probably Shakespeare, "'twere better done," and so forth. Of course a person such as a Mrs. Peter Odell would ordinarily not be in town on a June Sunday, but she would be. She was ignoring weekends, and from a phone call by her Saturday morning she knew there would be a Sunday conference. So I rang her and asked if I could come at five o'clock, because earlier she would probably have the television on and I didn't want to share her attention with Cleon Jones at bat or Tom Seaver on the mound.

Wolfe had gone to the kitchen. For Sunday lunch with Fritz away he usually does something simple like eggs *au beurre noir* and a beet and watercress salad, but that time it was going to be larded shad roe casserole with anchovy butter and parsley and chervil and shallots and marjoram and black pepper and cream and bay leaf and onion and butter. It would take a lot of tasting, and he can taste. I went to the kitchen to tell him Mrs. Odell would see me at five o'clock, and he nodded, and I mounted the two flights to my room.

That was a busy four hours; shaving and changing from the skin out, going down for my third of the shad roe, which we ate in the kitchen, looking at the telecast from Montreal — where the Mets were playing the Expos — on the color set, which, like everything else in my room, was bought and paid for by me, and writing. Not on the typewriter, because when I'm being particular, I do better longhand, and that had to be done right. When I went downstairs a little before four-thirty, the third draft was in my pocket, with the check. Wolfe was up in the plant rooms and I buzzed him on the house phone to tell him I was leaving.

Since parking shouldn't be a problem Sunday afternoon, I went to the garage for the Heron, crossed town on Thirty-fourth, and turned uptown on Park. Driving in midtown Manhattan can still be a pleasure — from two to eight A.M. and a couple of hours on Sunday. There was actually a gap at the curb on Sixty-third Street between Fifth and Madison. The LPS man at the entrance to the stone mansion was not the same one, and this one had better manners; he said thank you when he returned my card case. Inside I was ushered to the elevator by the same woman in a neat gray uniform and was told to push the button with a 4. In the upper hall, the client's voice came through the open door to the big room, "In here!"

She was on the oversized couch, one leg on it straight and the other one dangling over the edge, with sections of the Sunday *Times* scattered around. The television was not on — but of course the game was over. As I crossed to her she said, "You'd better have something. You certainly don't on the telephone."

"We got careless once when our phone was tapped and we're leery. I don't suppose it's tapped now, but once was enough. Yes, I have something." I got the check from my pocket. "I thought I should bring it instead of mailing it."

She took it, frowned at it, frowned at me, again at the check, and back at me. "What's the idea?"

"Mr. Wolfe is bowing out. Quite a bow, since he has spent more than three thousand dollars. Three thousand dollars in twelve days and we haven't got a smell. One reason I'm bringing it instead of mailing it, I wanted to tell you that that's all there is to it, he's simply pulling out. He thinks it shows strength of character to admit he's licked. I can't see it and don't intend to, but I'm not a genius."

She surprised me. Up to that moment she had given me no reason to suppose that the arrangements inside her skull were any better than average, but she had reached a conclusion before I finished. Her eyes showed it, and she said it, with a question: "How much did Browning pay him?"

"Uh-huh," I said, and turned a chair to face her, and sat. "You would, naturally. If I talked for five hours, giving cases, I *might* be able to convince you that he couldn't possibly double-cross a client, on account of his opinion of himself, but I think there's a shorter way. I've told you on the phone about the three men we have called in to help. They were there this morning when he said it was hopeless and he was quitting. When he told me to draw a check to return the retainer, Saul Panzer suggested that instead of returning it, he might put an ad in the *Times* saying that he would pay it to anyone who would give him information that would identify the murderer, and Mr. Wolfe said no, he would not make a frantic squawk to be pulled out of a mudhole. That was—"

"Of course! He *would* say that!"

"Please hold it, I've just started. So I drew the check and he signed it, and I phoned you. But I think I can prove that he didn't sell out, and I want to try. I think I can get him to tear the check up and go on with the job, with your help. May I use your typewriter?"

"What for? I don't believe it."

"You will. You'll have to." I got up and crossed to a desk, the one with a typewriter on an extension. As I pulled the chair out and sat, I asked where I would find paper and she said, "The top drawer, but you're not fooling me," and I said, "Wait and see," and got out paper and a sheet of carbon.

She preferred not to wait. As I got the third draft from my pocket and spread it out on the desk, she kicked the sections of the *Times* aside, left the couch, and came and stood at my elbow, and I hit the keys. I didn't hurry because I wanted it clean. No exing. As I pulled it out, I said, "I had to type it here because he might recognize it from my machine, and this is going to be your idea." I handed her the original and gave the carbon a look:

NERO WOLFE HAS $50,000

in cash, given to him by me. He will pay it, on my behalf, to any person or persons who supply information to him that leads to the conclusive identification of the man or woman who placed a bomb in a drawer of the desk of Amory Browning on Tuesday, May 20th, resulting in the death of my husband.

The information is to be given directly to Nero Wolfe, who will use it on my behalf, and the person or persons supplying it will do so under these conditions:

1. All decisions regarding the significance and value of any item of information will be made solely by Nero Wolfe and will be final.

2. The total amount paid will be $50,000. If more than one person supplies useful information, the determination of their relative value and of the distribution of the $50,000 will be made solely by Nero Wolfe and will be final.

3. Any person who communicates with Nero Wolfe or his agent as a result of this advertisement thereby agrees to the above conditions.

"With your name at the bottom," I said. "A reproduction of your signature, Madeline Odell, like on your check, and below it 'Mrs. Peter J. Odell' in parenthesis, as usual, printed. Now hear this. Of course he'll know I wrote it, but if he thinks I wrote it at home and brought it, he'll balk. No go. As I said, that's why I didn't type it there. It has to be your idea, suggested by you after I told you about his reaction to Saul Panzer's suggestion. He may phone you. If he does, you'll have to do it right. Then of course the question will be, what will happen? I think it will work, and certainly it *may* work. It's ten to one that someone knows something that would crack it open, and fifty grand is a lot of bait."

I was on my feet. "So if you'll sign it, the original, and keep the carbon, and I'll need two samples of your signature on plain paper, one for the *Times* and one for the *Gazette*, to make cuts."

"You're pretty good," she said.

"I try hard. Whence all but me have fled."

"What?"

"The burning deck."

"What burning deck?"

"You don't read the right poems." I swiveled the chair. "Sit here? That pen is stingy, I tried it. Mine's better."

"So is the one on my desk." She moved, went to the other desk, which was bigger, and sat. "I'm not convinced, you know. This could be an act. You can phone to say it didn't work."

"If I do, it won't be an act, it will be because he is pigheaded. I mean strong-minded. It will depend on you if he phones."

"Well." She reached for the pen in an elegant jade stand. "*I* have a suggestion. It shouldn't be fifty thousand. Figures like that, fifty thousand or a hundred thousand, they don't hit. In-between figures are better, like sixty-five thousand or eighty-five."

"Right. Absolutely. Change it. Make it sixty-five. Just draw a line through the fifty thousand."

She tried the pen on a scratch pad. I always do.

13

IT worked.

Driving downtown and across to the garage on Tenth Avenue, I considered the approach. Over the years I suppose I have told Wolfe 10,000 barefaced lies, or, if you prefer in-between figures, make it 8,392, either on personal matters that were none of his business or on business details that couldn't hurt and might help, but I have no desire to break a world record, and anyway the point was to make it stick if possible. I decided on a flank attack and then to play it by ear.

When I entered the office at 6:22, he was at his desk working on the Double-Crostic in the *Times,* and of course I didn't interrupt. I took my jacket off and draped it on the back of my chair, loosened my tie, went to the safe and got the checkbook and took it to my desk, and got interested in the stubs for the month of June. *That* was a flank attack all right. In a few minutes, maybe eight, he looked up and frowned at me and asked, "What's the balance now?"

"It depends," I said. I twisted around to get Exhibit A from my jacket pocket and rose and handed it across. He read it, taking his time, dropped it on the desk, narrowed his eyes at me, and said, "Grrr."

"She changed the fifty to sixty-five herself," I said. "That heading could have been Archie Goodwin has sixty-five thousand instead of Nero Wolfe. She didn't actually suggest it, but she thinks I'm pretty good. She said so. When I told her you were quitting and handed her the check, she said, 'How much did Browning pay him?' I told her that if I talked for five hours I might be able to convince her that you wouldn't double-cross a client, but actually I doubt it. You may not give a damn what she thinks of my employer, but I do. I brought her to you. She said things and I said things, and when it became evident that nothing else would convince her, I went to a typewriter and wrote that. I don't claim the wording is perfect. I am not Norman Mailer."

"Bah. That peacock? That blowhard?"

"All right, make it Hemingway."

"There was a typewriter there?"

"Sure. It was the big room on the fourth floor where apparently she does everything but eat and sleep. As you see, the paper is a twenty-pound bond at least half rag. Yours in only twenty percent rag."

He gave it a look, a good look, and I made a note to pat myself on the back for not doing it on my typewriter. "I admit," I said, "that I didn't try to talk her out of it. I certainly did not. In discussing it I told her that I thought it would work, that it's ten to one that someone knows something that would crack it open, and that fifty grand is a lot of bait. That was before she changed it to sixty-five. This is a long answer to your question, What's the balance? As I said, it depends. I brought the check back, but it would only cost eight cents to mail it. If we do, the balance will be a little under six thousand dollars. There was the June fifteenth income tax payment. I'm not badgering you, I'm just answering your question. But I'll permit myself to mention that this way it would not be a frantic squawk for someone to pull you out of a mudhole. I will also mention that if I phone her that the ad — correction, advertisement — has been placed, she will mail another check. For sixty-five thousand. She would make it a million if it would help. As of now nothing else on earth matters to her."

What he did was typical, absolutely him. He didn't say, "Very well" or "Tear the check up" or even "Confound it." He picked the thing up, read it slowly scowling at it, put it to one side under a paper weight, said "I'm doing some smoked sturgeon Muscovite. Please bring a bottle of Madeira from the cellar," and picked up the Double-Crostic.

14

THE ad was on page 6 of the *Times* Tuesday morning and page 9 of the *Gazette* that afternoon—two columns, bold face, with plenty of space all around—and two more conditions had been added:

> 1. *The $65,000 may all be paid to one person, or it may be divided among two or more people.*
> 2. *The $65,000 or any part of it will be paid only for information, not for a suggestion, conjecture, or theory.*

The other conditions, with only three words changed, followed.

We had discussed a certain probability and decided nothing could be done about it. Would Homicide South see the ad? Sure. Would they keep an eye, several eyes, on our front door to see who came? Sure again. Then what? They would horn in on our investigation of a murder. They would try to get for nothing what our client had offered $65,000 for. They would probably even put a tap on our phone, and the scientists have done such wonders for mankind that you can no longer tell whether your wire has been tapped or not. I admit science works both ways; we intended to record all conversations with callers, either in person or by phone. Also, with the bank balance fat again, we had reserves ready. Saul and Fred and Orrie were back, and at two P.M. Tuesday they were in the front room playing pinochle.

The very first one was wild. There had been four phone calls, but they had all been obvious screwballs. The first one in the flesh rang the doorbell a little before three o'clock. Through the one-way glass panel in the front door, he looked like a screwball too, but I opened the door and he handed me a card—a small blue card with a name on it in fancy dark blue letters: Nasir ibn Bekr. Okay, a foreign screwball, but I let him in. He was slim and wiry, he came about up to my chin, his hair and face and eyes were all very dark, and his nose would have gone with a man twice his size. On that warm June day his jacket was buttoned and the collar of his blue shirt was limp. When I turned after closing the door, he handed me a piece of paper, the ad clipped from the *Times,* and said, "I will see Mr. Nero Wolfe."

"Perhaps," I said. "He's busy. You have information?"

"I am not sure. I may have."

Not a screwball. Screwballs are sure. I asked him to wait, motioning to the bench, took the card to the office and handed it to Wolfe, and was told to bring him, but I didn't have to. He was there, right behind me. The big Keraghan in the office is thick, but there's no rug in the hall; he was the silent type. He should be closer to me than the red leather chair, so I blocked it off and motioned to the yellow one near the corner of my desk. Then I went and closed the door to the hall, for a reason. The arrangement was that when I admitted a visitor and intended to show him to the office, I would notify the trio by tapping on the door to the front room. When I had got the visitor to the office, I would close that door so that they would not be seen as they went down the hall to the alcove at the kitchen end, and they would take a look at the visitor through the peephole that was covered on the office side by a trick picture of a waterfall. They would also listen. As I crossed back to my desk, Nasir ibn Bekr said, "Of course this is being recorded," and I said, "Then I won't have to take notes."

Wolfe said, "The conditions in the advertisement are clear?"

He nodded. "Certainly. Perfectly clear. The information I have, it is my personal knowledge, but its worth is for you to determine. I must ask a question. We find nothing in your record to indicate clearly your position regarding the situation in the Near East. Are you anti-Zionist?"

"No."

He turned to me. "Are you?"

"No. My only objection to Jews is that one of them is as good a poker player as I am. Sometimes a little better."

He nodded. "They have learned how to use guile. They have had to." To Wolfe: "Perhaps you know that there are Arab terrorists — mostly Palestinians — active in this country, mostly in Washington and New York."

"It is said that there are, yes."

"It is not just said. There *are*. I am one." He unbuttoned the top button of his jacket, slipped his hand in, and brought out a small brown envelope. From it he got a folded paper. He rose to hand it to Wolfe, but terrorists are in my department and I moved fast enough to get a hand to it first. As I unfolded it, he sat and said, "That is the names of five men, but I am not sure it is their real names. It is the only names I know for them. We meet every week, once a week, on Sunday afternoon, in an apartment in Jackson Heights. That is the address and telephone number. Armad Qarmat lives there. I do not have addresses for the others. As you see, my name is not there. I have printed them because with names like ours that is better than writing."

I had given it a look and handed it to Wolfe.

"I see you have television," Nasir ibn Bekr said. "Perhaps you saw a program on CAN in May, May seventh, 'Oil and Mecca.' "

Wolfe shook his head. "I turn on the television rarely, only to confirm my opinion of it." Not having been asked, I didn't say that I had seen the "Oil and Mecca" program at Lily Rowan's.

"It was a full hour," the terrorist said. "It was partly a documentary in pictures of the production of oil in Arab countries, but it was also a commentary. It did not say that the existence and welfare of Israel were of more importance to civilization, and of course to democracy, than the Arabian oil, but it strongly implied that. It was definitely anti-Arabian and pro-Israel. That was a Wednesday. The following Sunday we discussed it, and we wrote a letter to CAN demanding a retraction of the lies it told. The next Sunday Armad said there had been no answer to the letter, and he had learned that the man responsible for the program was a vice-president of CAN named Amory Browning. That was Sunday, May eighteenth. We decided that it was an opportunity to take action against the anti-Arabian propaganda in this country."

His head turned to me and back to Wolfe. "I should explain that I became a member of the group only a year ago, not quite a year, and I am not yet completely in their confidence. Especially Armad Qarmat has not fully decided about me, and that is why I said I am not sure, I *may* have information. I do know they had three bombs, I saw them one day. In April. That Sunday, May eighteenth, one of them suggested using one of the bombs at the CAN office, and if possible the office of Amory Browning. There was some discussion, and I saw that Armad Qarmat stopped it on account of me. As I said, he has not fully accepted me. The next Sunday, May twenty-fifth, one of them spoke of the explosion of a bomb in Amory Browning's office, killing Peter Odell, another vice-president, but Armad Qarmat said that should not be discussed. Since then there have been four meetings, four Sundays, and the bomb has not been mentioned."

He tilted his head back and took a couple of breaths, then looked at me and back at Wolfe. "There," he said, "I have told you. This morning I saw your advertisement. Sixty-five thousand dollars is a great deal of money. It will be better if I am frank. At first I thought I would give you more . . . more detail. More that was said, as I am sure it must have been said, when I was not present. But then I saw it would be better to tell you exactly how it was, and that is what I have done. The advertisement does not say you require proof."

He slipped his hand inside his jacket, again produced the brown envelope, and took something from it. "In my position," he said, "I have to consider the possibilities. this is a piece of a dollar bill that I tore in half. If you find that what I have told you is the information you ask for in your advertisement, and if I do not come to claim the sixty-five thousands dollars, it may be because I can't. If I am dead, I can't. In that case someone else will come, and if so he will have the other half of the dollar bill. Will that be satisfactory?" He put the piece of the bill on Wolfe's desk, and I went and got it. It was a ragged tear. I handed it to Wolfe.

He cocked his head at the terrorist. "I suppose," he said, "you speak Arabic."

"Of course."

"Arabic is spoken at your Sunday meetings?"

"Of course."

"Fortunately. For you. Your attempt at speaking English as it would be spoken by a cultured Palestinian is inept. You shouldn't try it. What is your real name?"

He didn't bat an eye. "That wouldn't help you," he said. Then he asked a question. To me the words he used were only sounds, but I knew it was a question by the inflection.

"I did," Wolfe said, "but long ago. Arabic is not one of my languages. I want your name because I may need to ask you something."

Nasir ibn Bekr shook his head. "I have told you all I know that could help. This is a big risk for me, coming to you at all, and I will not add to it. You are right, Arabic is not my native tongue. My native tongue is Spanish. But my Arabic is good; it must be. I will say this, if something happens, if one of them says something that you should know, I will telephone or come." He rose and buttoned the top button of his jacket, looked at me and back at Wolfe, and said, "I must thank you."

"A moment," Wolfe said. "This house is under surveillance. By the police. Mr. Goodwin will show you out—at the rear. There's a passage through to Thirty-fourth Street."

The terrorist shook his head. "That isn't necessary. Thank you again, but I can't be followed. No matter who tries, even in Baghdad or Cairo I can get loose."

He moved, and I went to open the door. It would have been mildly interesting to step out to the stoop and see who came out from where, to tail him, but I didn't want to give anyone the idea that we gave a damn. As I turned from shutting the front door, I called down the hall, "All clear!" and the trio appeared from the alcove and followed me into the office. They lined up at the end of Wolfe's desk.

"Comments," Wolfe said. "Fred?"

"I don't think so," Fred said. "How would he get in Browning's room when no one was there, and why would he pick the bottom drawer?"

"Orrie?"

"The League of Jewish Patriots," Orrie said.

"No," Saul said, "he's not the type. They're all athletes. Of course he's a Jew, but not that kind. I agree with Fred. His reasons, and also the timing. The bomb doesn't have to be connected with the fact that that was the day they were going to decide on the new president, but it's hard to believe that it wasn't."

"But it's only ten to one," I said. "Even if it's twenty to one we have to give it a look."

"Actually," Wolfe said, "he is taking no risk. Even if he knows there is only one chance in a thousand, he is giving himself that chance to fill a purse. — Archie. Type this list of names, adding his name, and the address, and give it to Fred. Fred, you will see if it is worth an effort. Enter that apartment only with all possible precaution; it isn't worth even the slightest hazard. Our usual understanding, of course. Further comments?"

There weren't any. I swung the typewriter around, Fred sat, and Saul and Orrie went to the front room.

That's a sample of what the ad brought us. I don't say typical; it wasn't. Of course if you advertised in those two papers that you had sixty-five grand to hand out, no matter what for, and your name and address were in the phone book, you would know you would get plenty of calls and callers, and the best we could expect was that just one of them would really have something. If what I was after was merely to fill pages, it would be easy to add a dozen or so with the next couple of days, up to 9:42 P.M. Thursday evening. Some of the items might even add to your knowledge of human nature—for instance, the middle-aged man in a spotless white suit and a bushy wig who had had a dream Tuesday night. He came Wednesday afternoon. In the dream a man had opened the bottom drawer of a desk and fastened, with tape, a small plastic box to the partition above the drawer, about nine inches back from the front. A thin copper wire about a foot long protruded from the end of the box. With the drawer open only a couple of inches he had taped the loose end of the wire to the inside of the front of the drawer, and closed it, and departed. If we would show him photographs of the men who had entered or might have entered Amory Browning's room that day, he would tell us which one had put the box in the drawer, and he would so testify under oath. That was what made it really good, that he would testify without even being subpoenaed. Or the female star buff who phoned for an appointment and came Thursday morning—a skinny speci-

men with hollow cheeks and big dream eyes. If we would give her the birth
dates of all the suspects she would supply information that would almost
certainly do the trick.

There were three or four that Saul and Orrie spent some time and effort
on. Fred had made no headway with the Arab terrorists.

To show you how low I was by Thursday evening after dinner, I'll admit
what I was doing. First, what I wasn't doing. I was not at the poker table at
Saul's apartment. I was in no mood for being sociable, and I would probably have drawn to an inside straight. I was at my desk in the office, scowling
at the entries in a little loose-leaf book which I call The Nero Wolfe Backlog.
It contained a list of certain items that were in his safe deposit box at the
Continental Trust Company, and I was considering which one or ones
should be disposed of at the current market price if I was asked for a
suggestion, as I would be soon if we got nothing better than Arab terrorists
and dreamers and star buffs. Wolfe was at his desk with a book of stories by
Turgenev, and that was bad too. When he's low he always picks something
that he has already read more than once.

When the doorbell rang, I glanced at my wrist watch as I rose, as usual.
Sometimes it's needed for the record. Eighteen minutes to ten. I went to the
hall, flipped the switch of the stoop light, took a look, stepped back in the
office, and said, "You'll have to mark your place. It's Dennis Copes."

"You haven't seen Dennis Copes."

"No, but Saul described him."

He shut the book without using the bookmark, and of course no dog ear,
since it was Turgenev. I went and opened the front door, and the visitor said,
"You're Archie Goodwin," and stepped right in as if I wasn't there.

"And you're—" I said.

"Copes. Dennis Copes. Not as famous as you, but I will be. Is your
famous fat boss available?"

I was so damn glad to see him, to see someone who might actually have
something to bite on, that I thought that on him the long hair and two-inch
sideburns looked just fine. And when, in the office, he marched across and
put out a hand, Wolfe took it. He seldom shakes hands with anybody, and
never with strangers. He *was* low. As Copes sat he hitched his pants legs
up—the nervous hands Saul had mentioned.

"That was a good ad," he said. "'Any person who communicates as a
result of this advertisement thereby agrees to the above conditions.' Very
neat. What agency?"

Wolfe frowned. "Agency?"

"Who wrote it?"

"Mr. Goodwin."

"Oh." He looked at me: "Nice going Archie." Back to Wolfe: "That ad
would have made a wonderful five-minute spot—you and Mrs. Odell, you
right here at your desk and her standing with her hand on your shoulder.
You would do most of the talking, with your voice. She would have been
glad to pay for prime time—say ten o'clock. A much bigger audience than
the ad. Didn't you consider it?

"No."

"Too bad. How many nibbles have you had?"

"None."

"*None?* Impossible. All right, you're not telling and why should you? But you can't say it's none of my damn business, because in a way it is. If someone else knows what I know, and if they've already told you, I've missed the bus. Have you—let's see, how shall I put it—has anyone told you anything that makes you want to have a talk with Kenneth Meer or Helen Lugos?"

Wolfe eyed him. "Mr. Copes. Mrs. Odell's advertisement asks for information *to* me, not *from* me. I'll say this: if I had received information that gave me reason to speak with Miss Lugos or Mr. Meer, I would have arranged to see them, and I haven't."

Copes nodded. "Fair enough. Now I have to admit something. I have to admit that I should have told the police what I'm going to tell you. I admit I'm not exactly proud of the reason *why* I didn't tell them. I admit it wasn't because of any love I have for Kenneth Meer or Helen Lugos; it was because it would have put me right in the thick of a damn nasty murder mess. All right, I admit that. With you it's different on two counts. One, you won't handle it like they would. You'll have more consideration for—well, for *me*. Two, if you get what I think you'll get, *I'll* get sixty-five thousand dollars and *can* I use it!"

The fingertips of his right hand were dancing a jig on the chair arm, and he turned the hand over and curled them. "Part of what I'm going to tell you probably won't be news to you. You probably know why Odell went to Browning's room and opened that drawer. Don't you?"

Wolfe grunted. "Do you?"

"Yes. He was going to put LSD in the whisky bottle so Browning would bobble it at the directors' meeting or not even be there. You probably know that, from Mrs. Odell. I'm going to tell you how *I* know it. How I *knew* it. I knew it the day before, that he was going to. I knew it on Monday, May nineteenth."

"Indeed."

"Yes. Of course you know there were two doors to Browning's room—one from the anteroom, Helen Lugos's room, and one from the hall. And here's another thing I have to admit, another reason I haven't told the police: that Monday afternoon I entered Browning's room by the door from the hall when I knew he wasn't there. It was right after lunch, and I—"

"Wasn't that door locked?"

"Not always. When Browning left by that door to go down the hall to the rear, he usually pushed the button on the lock so he could go back in without using his key. I wanted to look at something I knew was on his desk, and I knew he wasn't there, so I tried that door and it opened. I didn't make any noise because I didn't want to be interrupted by Helen Lugos, and the door to her room was half open, and I could hear voices—hers and Kenneth Meer's. Mostly his. I suppose this is being recorded."

"Yes."

"Of course. What isn't?" He took a notebook from his pocket and opened it. "So I'd better read it. The first thing I heard him say—he said, 'No, I'm not going to tell you how I found out. That doesn't matter anyway, I *did* find out. Odell is going to dope that bottle of whisky with LSD tomorrow afternoon, or he thinks he is, and I want to be damn sure you don't open the drawer to take a look at the usual time. Don't open it any time after lunch.

Don't open it at all, don't go near it, because—well, *don't.*' And she said, 'But Ken, you'll have to tell me—Wait. I'd better make sure—' And there was the sound of her pushing her chair back."

The fingertips were at it again, this time on his knee. "So I got out quick. She was probably going to come to make sure there was no one in Browning's room. I hadn't got to the desk, I was only a couple of steps from the door—I had left it open a crack—and I got out fast. I didn't go back to my room because there's another man in it with me and I wanted to be alone, so I went to the men's room and sat on the john to think it over. Of course what I wanted to do, I wanted to tell Browning. Maybe Meer was going to tell him but from what he said it didn't sound like it. But I didn't want to tell Browning I had entered his room by the hall door—of course I didn't. And I didn't know what Meer intended to do. I knew he intended to do something since he had told her not to go near the drawer, but what? What would *you* have thought he intended to do?"

Wolfe shook his head. "I don't know him. You did."

"Sure, I knew him, but not well enough for that. For instance, I thought he might wait until about four o'clock Tuesday and then take the bottle from the drawer and put another bottle in its place, and have the whisky analyzed and have the bottle checked for fingerprints. He knew Browning never took a drink until about half past four or a quarter to five, when the program scripts had all been okayed. I considered all the possibilities, what *I* could do, and the one thing I *had* to do was make sure that Browning didn't drink any doped whisky. So I decided to be there in the room with him Tuesday when he okayed the last script—I usually was—and when he got the bottle out, I would say that there was nothing Odell wouldn't do to get the president's job, and it might be a good idea to open the other bottle. There was always another bottle there, unopened, often two."

"You knew that," Wolfe said.

"Sure, several of us did. Often a couple of us were there when he opened the drawer. One thing I considered: tell Browning that I had heard Meer say that to Helen, but not that I had been in his room. But that would have been very tricky because where was I and where were they? You may know that a lot of people think I want Meer's job."

"That has been said, yes."

"Maybe I do and maybe I don't. I want to get on, sure, who doesn't, but it doesn't have to be *his* job. Anyway, I had to consider that too. Of course if I had known what Meer was going to do, if I had even suspected it, I would have gone straight to Browning and told him just like it was. I didn't and of course I regret it."

"You're assuming that Meer had decided to put a bomb in the drawer?"

"Certainly. My God, don't I have to? *Didn't* I have to?"

"You made that assumption that day—the next day? When you learned what had happened?"

"I certainly did."

"Five weeks ago. Five weeks and two days. What have you done to verify it?"

Copes nodded. "It's easy to ask that. What *could* I have done? Could I ask people if they had seen Meer with a bomb? Could I ask them if they had seen him go into Browning's room? Could I ask Helen Lugos *anything?*

Could I hire a detective? Naturally you're thinking I may have cooked this up. Of course you are. You'd be a damn fool if you didn't. But there's one detail, one fact, that you have to consider. As I said, you probably knew that Odell went there to put LSD in the whisky because Mrs. Odell probably told you, but how did I know? One thing, Odell must have had the LSD with him, but there has been no mention of it. It could be that the police are reserving it, or it could be that he had it in his hand when he opened the drawer and no traces of it have been found, but I doubt that because they are very thorough and very expert on that kind of thing. Probably they're keeping it back. Maybe you know?"

Wolfe skipped it. "That's a detail, yes. Not conclusive, but indicative. You're aware, Mr. Copes, that without support your information is worthless. If I challenge Mr. Meer or Miss Lugos by telling them what you have told me and they say you lie, what then? Have you a suggestion?"

"No. The ad didn't say I have to tell you how to *use* the information. You're Nero Wolfe, the great detective; I'm just a guy who happened to hear something. Of course I realize Browning will have to know I entered his room that way, that will have to come out, maybe even on the witness stand. You've got it now on tape. If it costs me my job I'll need that sixty-five thousand. Should I tell Browning myself? Now?"

"No." Wolfe made it positive. "Tell nobody anything. May I see that notebook?"

"Certainly." He took it from his pocket and got up to hand it over. It was loose-leaf with little rings. Wolfe gave several pages a look and stopped at one.

"Did you write this that day? Monday?"

"No. I wrote it the next day, Tuesday evening, after the—after what happened. But that's exactly what he said. I can swear to it."

"You may have to." Wolfe handed the notebook back to him. "I can't tell you how I'll proceed, Mr. Copes, because I don't know. If I need you, I'll know where to find you." He leaned back, his head against the chair back, and shut his eyes. I honestly don't know if he realizes that that's no way to end a conversation. I do.

15

SAUL and Fred and Orrie and I are still discussing what Wolfe said that Friday morning—or rather, what we *didn't* say.

They came at ten o'clock and I played it back for them twice—the tape of the talk with Dennis Copes—and we considered two angles: one, Was it straight or had he hatched it to get Meer? and two, If it was straight, how were we going to wrap it up? By eleven o'clock, when Wolfe came down from the plant rooms, we hadn't got very far with either one. He told us good morning, put a raceme of Dendrobium chrysotoxum in the vase on his desk, sat and sent his eyes around, and asked, "Have you a program?"

"Sure," I said. "Just what you're expecting, ask you for instructions."

"One thing," Saul said. "He comes first. How good is it?"

"Obviously. On that he said one thing that was strikingly suggestive. Have you considered it?"

We looked at one another. "Well," Saul said, "that line about him being just a guy who happened to hear something. We agree that that sounds good. If he's faking it that's *very* good. A wonderful line."

Wolfe shook his head. "I mean something quite different. One specific thing he said that suggests a possible answer to all questions. You haven't considered it?"

"We considered everything," I said. "What specific thing?"

He shook his head again. "Not now. Even if it means what it *may* mean, we must first decide about him. The detail which — as he said — we have to consider: if he didn't learn about the LSD as he says he did, then how? Of course you have discussed that. And?"

"And nothing," Orrie said. "We've talked with a lot of people these two weeks, and not the slightest hint of the LSD angle from anyone. You told us to keep that good and tight and we did."

I said, "The only mention of it we have heard has been from Mrs. Odell and Falk, and he got it from her. Possibly he also got it from his cousin who is an assistant DA, but he didn't say so. Apparently it *is* tight. Abbott evidently thinks Odell had a bomb in his pocket, not LSD."

Wolfe nodded. "We'll have to explore the possibilities. Orrie. You will try again with the CAN personnel, this time on the one question, could his knowledge of the LSD have come through anyone there? He need not have learned it a month or even a week ago; even yesterday would do. Take care not to divulge it yourself. Fred. Forget the Palestinians. You are on speaking terms with members of the police force. A dozen?"

"Only two in Homicide," Fred said.

"That may be enough. Knowledge of the LSD may not be limited to the Homicide men. The first to arrive at the scene may have found it. You need not take pains to reserve our knowledge of it; Mr. Cramer knows that we know about it. Does one of them know Mr. Copes or anyone connected with him? — Saul. You will try the other possible source, Mrs. Odell and Miss Haber. I doubt if Mrs. Odell has mentioned it to anyone whatever, but Miss Haber procured the LSD for her, and Mr. Copes would have needed to know only that to make a plausible conjecture. Does Mr. Copes know anyone she knows and might have told? Probably you should try from his end, not hers, but that's for you to decide. Have enough cash with you. If there is any urgent need for help, Archie will be here."

Wolfe's eyes went to Fred, to Orrie, and back to Saul. "We want this, messieurs. If you find another probable source for Mr. Copes's knowledge of the LSD, it will be more than satisfactory. Ironically, it will probably get him sixty-five thousand dollars for supplying the required information. I wish you luck."

As Saul stood he said, "I have a question. Might it help if we knew what he said that was strikingly suggestive? Could it hurt?"

"Yes, it could hurt. It could divert your interest. I shouldn't have mentioned it. My tendency to strut. Display, like diffidence, is commendable only when it avails. Ignore it."

Just fine. What else could they do? Not to mention me. So when they were gone, I ignored it. I sat and ignored it while he glanced through the little stack of mail I had put on his desk, and when he looked up I asked, "Do I do anything while I am being here?"

"Yes," he said. "This is Friday."

"Right."

"I would like to see Miss Lugos and Mr. Meer, not together. And not today. It's possible that today or this evening we'll get something. Miss Lugos at eleven o'clock tomorrow and Mr. Meer at three?"

"It's a June weekend and it may take pressure. I'm not objecting, I'm just asking. I would enjoy pressing somebody. Anybody."

"So would I."

I got at the phone and dialed.

16

THAT afternoon Orrie and I had a two-piece argument, first on the phone and then face-to-face. Around three o'clock he called to say he would be working the whole weekend because he was taking a female CAN researcher to Atlantic City. I asked if he wished to leave a message for Jill, his wife, in case she called, and he said she was in Tokyo, which was plausible since she was an airline hostess. I said he would be paid to six P.M. Friday, and he said he would come and discuss it. He came a little after four, knowing that Wolfe would be up in the plant rooms, and said it would be a working weekend and he should also get twenty cents a mile for the use of his car; he might get something useful from her and he was certainly going to try. I said okay, eight hours Saturday and eight Sunday, he couldn't expect to be paid for the time he spent in bed, and he said bed was the best place to get really confidential, and I had to agree. But not eight dollars an hour for fifty-two hours, and not the hotel bill. He said Mrs. Odell had a billion, and I said not more than a hundred million even with inflation, and we should leave her something for groceries. We finally settled on a lump sum to cover everything, $364.00, which was seven dollars an hour. I may as well mention now that the client got exactly nothing for that little expense item.

By eleven o'clock Saturday morning, when Helen Lugos came, Fred had also drawn a blank. He had talked with five city employes he knew, one of them a sergeant in Homicide, and none of them had had any contact with Dennis Copes or had any information about him. He doubted if any of them knew about the LSD, but of course they might be keeping the lid on. He was proceeding.

Saul had collected a bag of facts about Copes — where and how he lived, his habits, his friends, his background, his personal finances — but nothing that gave us any pointers, so they wouldn't give you any either, and I'll skip them. He had found no connection whatever with Mrs. Odell or Charlotte Haber, but was preparing an approach to Charlotte's kid brother, since there had been a hint that it was on account of him that she had known how to get the LSD.

Helen Lugos not only wasn't late this time, she was ten minutes early, so she was stuck with a mere agent again until Wolfe came down from the plant rooms. She wanted to know what was so urgent that she had to change her weekend plans, and I explained that I only obeyed orders.

Wolfe entered, told me good morning first and then her, put the flowers for the day in the vase and arranged them so he would have the best view, swiveled his chair to face her, and sat.

"I don't thank you for coming," he said. "I'm not disposed to thank you for anything. I have reason to believe that you are withholding information that would be of value. Indeed, I think you have lied. Don't bother to deny it. I tell you that only to establish the temper of the conversation. I'll be trying to find support for my opinion. What will you be doing?"

She would be staring. She *was* staring. "I know what I *ought* to be doing," she said. "Leaving. I ought to be on my way out."

"But you're not. You wouldn't, even if I'm wrong, because you want to know why. That's what makes us the unique animal, we want to know why and try to find out. We even try to discover why we want to know why, though of course we never will. It's possible that upon consideration you have concluded, or at least suspected, that you may have made a mistake or two. For instance, nineteen days ago, a Monday evening, I asked you if you thought it likely that the person who put the bomb in the drawer was present in this room and you said you had no idea. 'None at all,' you said. And twelve days ago, again a Monday, when you were alone with Mr. Goodwin and he asked what you would say if he asked that question, you replied that you would say exactly the same, you had no idea. I'll try once more. What would you say now?"

"My god," she said. "How many times . . ."

"What would you say now?"

"The same!"

Wolfe nodded. "You should know, Miss Lugos, that this is being recorded electronically. The recorder is on a closet shelf in the kitchen, so that a man there can change the tape if necessary. I now have a special reason for wanting to learn beyond question the nature of your relations with Kenneth Meer. What you tell me will be tested thoroughly by wide inquiry. So?"

"It has already been tested by the police." Her chin was up and a muscle in the side of her neck was twitching, barely perceptible even by good eyes. "We're not — we're associated in our work because we have to be. Personally we don't — we are not close."

"But he would like to be?"

"He thinks he — yes."

"Do you read books?"

She did what everybody does when asked an unexpected and irrelevant question. Her eyes widened and her lips parted. For two seconds exactly the same as if he had asked her if she ate cats. Then she said, "Why — yes. I read books."

"Do you read much fiction?"

"I read *some*."

"Then you may be aware that most competent storytellers, even lesser ones, have an instinctive knowledge of the possibilities of human conduct. They often present two characters who have a strong mutual attachment in secret but who have other people believing that they are hostile. But not the reverse. Not two who have a mutual animus but have others believing that they like or love each other. Storytellers know it can't be done. So do I. I know I can't learn if you and Mr. Meer are in fact close by asking you questions and watching your face as you answer them, so I won't try. I know it's futile for me to ask you anything at all, but I wanted to see you again and hear you speak, and I would like to ask one specific question, more for what the question will tell you than for what the answer will tell me. Mr. Goodwin got your detailed account of your movements on that Tuesday, May twentieth. I would like one detail of the preceding day, Monday, May nineteenth. In the early afternoon, shortly after lunch, Mr. Meer was with you in your room. Tête-à-tête. What did you talk about? What was said?"

I won't say I actually enjoyed what happened next, but I appreciated being there to see it. Having seen him walk out on people I don't know how many times, say a hundred, it kind of evened up to see him once as the walkee instead of the walker. She didn't glare or clamp her jaw or spit, she just got up and went. I admit he didn't glare or spit either; he just sat and watched her go. I did too until she was out; then I stepped to the hall to see that she shut the front door. When I stepped back in, he was opening the drawer to get the bottle opener—so he had rung for beer.

"Tell me once more," I said, "that I understand women better than you do. It gives me confidence. But don't ask me to prove it. I said two weeks ago that she didn't open the bag and shake it. I also said she didn't plant the bomb, but now I don't know. Did Copes strikingly suggest that she did?"

"Confound Copes," he growled. "And nothing can be expected from Saul or Fred during the weekend."

He picked up the top item on the stack of the morning mail. It was a check from Mrs. Odell for $65,000.

17

KENNETH MEER was early too. When I answered the doorbell a little before three, I saw his car down at the curb, a dark green Jaguar. He had an oversized briefcase, brown leather, under his arm, presumably to save the trouble of locking the car, and when I asked if he wanted to leave it on the hall bench, he said no and took it along to the office. I said before, when I first saw him, that his poorly designed face was tired too young, and now, as he sat in the red leather chair and blinked at Wolfe, his long, pointed nose above his wide square chin looked like an exclamation point with a long line crossing at the bottom instead of a dot.

He kept the briefcase on his lap. "I resent this," he said. He sounded as peevish as he looked. "Why couldn't I come yesterday—last evening? Why today?"

Wolfe nodded. "I owe you an apology, Mr. Meer. You have it. I hoped to have by now definite information on a point I wanted to discuss with you, but it hasn't come. However, since you're here, we may as well consider another point. Your bloody hands. A week after the explosion of that bomb you were in distress, severe enough to take you to that clinic and then to me. Later, when I became professionally involved, the nature of your distress was of course of interest. There were various possibilities: You had yourself put the bomb in the drawer and the burden of guilt was too heavy for you. Or you hadn't, but you knew or suspected who had, and your conscience was galling you; your imagined bloody hands were insisting, *please pass the guilt*. Or merely the event itself had hit you too hard; the sight of the havoc and the actual blood on your hands had put you in shock. Those were all valid guesses, but Mr. Goodwin and I didn't bother to discuss them; we rarely waste time discussing guesses."

"I like that, *please pass the guilt*," Meer said. "I like that."

"So do I. Mr. Goodwin will too. He once said that I ride words bareback. But the devil of it is that after more than three weeks the guesses are still guesses, and it may possibly help to mention them to you. Have you a comment?"

"No."

"None at all?"

"No."

"Does the distress persist? Do you still get up in the middle of the night to wash your hands?"

"No."

"Then something that has been done or said must have removed the pressure, or at least eased it. What? Do you know?"

"No."

Wolfe shook his head. "I can't accept that. This morning I was blunt with Miss Lugos and told her I thought she was lying. Now I think you are. There is another point concerning you that I haven't broached that I'll mention now. Why did you tell a man that anyone who wanted to know how it happened should concentrate on Helen Lugos?"

Meer didn't frown or cock his head or even blink. He merely said, "I didn't."

Wolfe's head turned. "Archie?"

"You said it," I told Meer, "to Pete Damiano. I can't name the day, but it was soon after it happened. About a month ago."

"Oh, him." He grinned, or make it that he probably thought he grinned. "Pete would say anything."

"That's witless," Wolfe said. "You knew it was likely, at least possible, that that would be remembered and you would be asked about it, and you should have had a plausible reply ready. Merely to deny it won't do. It's obvious that you're implicated, either by something you know or something you did, and you should be prepared to deal with contingencies. I am, and I believe one is imminent. I ask you the same question I asked Miss Lugos this morning, in the same terms: In the early afternoon of Monday, May nineteenth, shortly after lunch, you were with Miss Lugos in her room, tête-à-tête. What did you talk about? What was said?"

That got a frown. "You asked her that? What did she say?"

"What did *you* say?"

"Nothing. I don't remember."

"Pfui. I've asked you seven questions and got only no's and nothings. I've apologized to you; now I apologize to myself. Another time, Mr. Meer. Mr. Goodwin will show you out."

I rose, but stood, because Meer thought he was going to say something. His lips parted twice but closed again. He looked up at me, saw only an impassive mug, got up, tucked the briefcase under his arm, and moved. I followed him, but got ahead in the hall, opened the front door, and waited until he was down and at the door of the Jaguar to close it. Back in the office, I asked, "Do we need to discuss any guesses?"

Wolfe grunted. "You might as well have gone before lunch. Shall I apologize to you?"

"No, thanks. The phone number is on your pad, as usual." I went and got my bag from the hall and let myself out, on my way to the garage for the Heron and then to the West Side Highway, headed for Lily Rowan's glade in Westchester. That's what she calls it, The Glade.

18

AMORY BROWNING did something Monday morning that had never been done before. He walked down the aisles of the three plant rooms, clear to the potting room, without seeing an orchid. I didn't actually see him, since he was behind me, but I'm sure he did. With that blaze of color, right and left and overhead, you'd think he would have to be blind. In a way he was.

It was twenty past ten and I had just returned from a walk crosstown to the bank and back, to deposit the check from the client, when the ring of the doorbell took me to the hall, and there was the next president of CAN. When I went and opened the door, he crossed the sill and went on by and headed for the office, and when I got there he was standing at the end of Wolfe's desk.

"Where is he?" he demanded.

"Where he always is at this hour, up on the roof. He'll be down at eleven. You can wait, or maybe I can help."

"Get him down here. Now."

The man at the top speaking, but he didn't look it. I had formerly estimated that he had been pudgy for about five years, but now I would have made it ten.

"It can't be done," I said. "With him a rule is a rule. He's part mule. If it's really urgent he might talk on the phone."

"Get him."

"I'll try." I went to the kitchen, sat at the little table where I eat breakfast, reached for the house phone, and pushed the "P" button.

After a two-minute wait, about par, the usual "Yes?"

"Me in the kitchen. Amory Browning is in the office. I once saw a picture somewhere of a dragon snorting fire. That's him. He ordered me to get you down here now. I told him you might talk on the phone."

Silence for eight seconds, then: "Bring him."

"Okay, but have something ready to throw."

The elevator will take up to 600 pounds, but I thought a little deep breathing would be good for him, so I took him to the stairs, and he surprised me by not stopping to catch up on oxygen at the landings. He wasn't panting even at the top. As I said, he was behind me down the aisles, but when I opened the door to the potting room I let him by. Wolfe, in his long-sleeved, yellow smock, was at the side bench opening a bale of tree fern. He turned part way and said, "You don't like to be interrupted at work. Neither do I."

Browning was standing with his feet apart. "You goddam cheap bully!"

"Not 'cheap.' I haven't earned that reproach. What do you want?"

"Nothing. Calling my secretary a liar. Getting her here on a Saturday morning just to butter your ego by insulting her. I came to tell you that you can tell Mrs. Odell that there will be no more cooperation from anyone at CAN. Tell her if she wants to know why, to call me. Is that plain enough?"

"Yes indeed. Is that what you came for, to tell me that?"

"Yes!"

"Very well, you've told me." Wolfe turned back to the bale of tree fern.

Browning was stuck. Of course with the "Is that plain enough?" he should have whirled and headed for the door. Now what could he do for an exit? He could only just go, and I admit he had sense enough to realize it. He just went, and I followed, and again he didn't see an orchid. I supposed that on the way down the three flights he would decide on an exit line to use on me, but evidently he was too mad to bother, though I passed him down in the hall and opened the door for him. Not a word. I went to the office and sat to ask myself why I had bothered to deposit the check.

And in three minutes the doorbell rang and I went to the hall and there was Saul Panzer.

It's moments like that that make life worth living, seeing Saul there on the stoop. If he had just wanted to make a routine report or ask a question or ask for help, he would have phoned. If he had wanted to consult Wolfe, he would have waited until eleven o'clock. And if he had bad news, he would have let his face show it as I came down the hall. So he had something good. I opened the door wide and said, "My god, are you welcome. How good is it?"

"I guess I'm awful obvious," he said, and stepped in. "I *think* it's satisfactory."

I slammed the door shut. "For a nickel I'd kiss you." I looked at my wrist: 10:47. "You'd rather tell him, but I don't want to wait thirteen minutes. Neither do you or you wouldn't be here yet. We'll go up."

It took us about half as long as it had taken Browning and me. I won't say that we didn't see an orchid as we passed through the rooms, but we didn't stop to admire one. Wolfe, still in the yellow smock, was at the sink washing his hands, and Theodore stood there with a paper towel ready for him. Theodore babies him, which is one of the reasons he is not my favorite fellow being.

Wolfe, turning and seeing Saul, was on as quick as I had been. He said, "Indeed," and ignored the dripping water from his hands. "What?"

"Yes, sir," Saul said. "Once in a while I do something exactly right and am lucky along with it, and that's a pleasure. I would enjoy leading up to it, but it's been a long time since we've brought you anything. Dennis Copes's twin sister, Diana, is the wife of Lieutenant J. M. Rowcliff. They have two children, a boy and a girl. Dennis and Diana see each other quite often — as I said, twins."

Wolfe took the towel from Theodore, patted with it, dropped it in the bin, took another, rubbed with it, missed the bin. It fluttered to the floor and Theodore picked it up. Wolfe flattened his right palm against his left and made slow circles.

"Are Mr. Rowcliff and Mr. Copes on good terms?"

"No. They see each other very seldom. Apparently never would suit them fine."

"Mr. Rowcliff and his wife?"

"Three people say they're happy. I know it's hard to believe that anybody could stand Rowcliff, but off duty he may be different."

"Have you caused a stir?"

"No."

That was Saul. Not "I hope not" or "I don't think so." Just "No."

"More than satisfactory." Wolfe took the smock off and hung it on a wall hook, got his vest and jacket from a hanger, and put them on. He looked at the clock on the bench: two minutes to eleven. "I want a word with Theodore and I'll consider this on the way down. Put a bottle of champagne in the refrigerator, Archie — and Saul, we'll probably need you."

Saul and I went.

I suppose I shouldn't include what happened next; it's just too pat. Who will believe it? But Fred deserves to have it in, and it happened. Saul and I had just got to the office, having stopped at the kitchen on the way, and were discussing how it should be handled, when the doorbell rang and I went. It was Fred. I opened the door, and as he entered he blurted, "Is he down yet?" I said he was on the way and he said, "If I hold it in any longer I'll bust. Copes's twin sister is married to that sonofabitch Rowcliff."

All right, it happened. In nineteen days they had got exactly nothing, and here came two of them, practically simultaneously, with the same beautiful slab of bacon. Saul, who had come to the hall and heard him, said, "So we need *two* bottles of champagne," and went to the kitchen. I was telling Fred that Saul had beat him by just sixteen minutes, when the elevator door opened and Wolfe was there, and when he saw the look on Fred's face, he knew what had happened, so I didn't have to tell him, but I did. He led the way to the office, and Saul came and he and Fred moved yellow chairs up.

Wolfe sat and said, "Get Mr. Cramer."

He has been known to rush it, and it had been a long dry spell. "You once made a remark," I said, "about impetuosity. I could quote it verbatim."

"So could I. If we discussed it all day there would still be only one way to learn if we have it or not. Get him."

"If he's not there do you want Rowcliff?"

"No. Only Mr. Cramer."

I pulled the phone around and dialed, and got first the switchboard, then a sergeant I knew only by name, Molloy, and then Inspector Cramer, and Wolfe took his phone. I stayed on.

Wolfe: "Good morning."

"Is it?"

"I think so. I have a problem. I must discuss a matter with Mr. Rowcliff as soon as possible, and it will go better if you are present. It relates to the death of Peter Odell. Could you come now?"

"No. I'll get Rowcliff on another phone."

"That wouldn't do. I have a tape recording both of you should hear."

"A recording of what?"

"You'll know when you hear it. You won't like it, but it may give you a useful hint. It has given me one."

"I can't—wait. Maybe I can. Hold it."

We held it for about two minutes, and then: "Does it have to be Rowcliff?"

"Yes. That's requisite."

"I never expected to hear this, you wanting to see Rowcliff. We'll leave in about ten minutes."

Click.

We hung up. I asked Wolfe, "The Copes tape?"

He said yes, and I went to the safe for the key to the locked cabinet where we keep various items that would be in the safe if there was room. Wolfe started in on Saul and Fred, asking questions that I thought should have been asked before calling Cramer, but he got nothing that tangled it. Fred had nothing but the bare fact that Copes's sister was Rowcliff's wife. Saul, knowing we would need more, had proceeded to get it, but he hadn't seen Diana herself, only neighbors and a woman who cleaned the Rowcliff apartment once a week, and two men who knew Copes. Almost certainly nothing had got to Rowcliff. However, one problem arose that had to be dealt with; Wolfe rang for beer and had the cap off of the bottle before he remembered that we were probably going to open champagne. He called Fritz in for consultation, and they decided it would be interesting to try eel stewed in stale beer, and Fritz thought he knew where he could get eel the next day. Wolfe told him Saul and Fred would join us for lunch, and it should be a little early if possible—one o'clock.

Lieutenant Rowcliff has it in for all private detectives, but I admit he has a special reason for thinking the world would be better off without me. When he gets hot he stutters, and with me it must be catching, because when he's working on me and I see that he is getting close to that point, *I* start to stutter, especially on words that begin with *g* or *t*. It's a misdemeanor to interfere with a police officer in the performance of his duty, but how could he handle that? Wolfe knows about it, and when the doorbell rang at a quarter to twelve and he told Saul to get it, I believe he actually thought I might greet them with "Gu-gu-gu-good morning."

I was at my desk. Fred was in one of the three yellow chairs facing Wolfe's desk, the one nearest me. Cramer, leading the way, of course went to the red leather chair, and Rowcliff took the yellow one nearest him, which left the middle one for Saul. As Cramer sat, he said, "Make it snappy. Rowcliff has someone waiting. What's this about a recording?"

"I'll have to introduce it," Wolfe said. "You probably know the name, Dennis Copes."

"I've heard it. One of the CAN bunch."

"I know him," Rowcliff said. "He wants Meer's job."

Wolfe nodded. "So it is said. As you know, Mrs. Odell's advertisement appeared last Tuesday, six days ago. Mr. Copes came here Thursday evening and said he had to admit something and that he had information to give me under the conditions stated in the advertisement. He did so. The recording is that conversation.—Archie?"

All I had to do was reach to the far corner of my desk to flip a switch. The playback, which was a honey and had cost $922.50, was on the desk at the back. We knew it was a good tape, since we had listened to it three times.

Copes's voice came. "That was a good ad. 'Any person who communicates as 'a result of this advertisement thereby agrees to the above conditions.' Very neat. What agency?"

"Agency?"

"Who wrote it?"

"Mr. Goodwin."

Naturally I watched their faces. The first few minutes they looked at each other a couple of times, but then their eyes stayed mostly on Wolfe. Then Cramer set his jaw and his face got even redder than usual, and Rowcliff started to lick his lips. It has been said that Rowcliff is handsome, and I'll concede that his six feet of meat is distributed well enough, but his face reminds me of a camel with a built-in sneer. All right, I don't like him, so allow for it. Of course licking his lips didn't improve it any.

It got to the end. Wolfe: "You may have to. I can't tell you how I'll proceed, Mr. Copes, because I don't know. If I need you, I'll know where to find you." I reached to the switch and flipped it.

"By god," Cramer said. He was so mad his voice was weak. "Four days ago. Four whole days. And you even told him not to tell anybody anything. And *now* you get us here and—How in hell you expect—"

"Pfui," Wolfe said. "You're not a witling and you know I'm not. If I had believed he was telling the truth, I might or might not have informed you immediately, but I certainly would not have risked telling him not to. I had good reason to suspect that he wasn't. How could Kenneth Meer possibly have known that Odell intended to put LSD in the whisky? I don't know how much of an effort you have made to learn if anyone knew, and if so who, but I know how much *I* have. I thought it extremely doubtful that Meer could have known. But if he didn't, if Copes was lying, how did Copes know even now? Apparently it had been kept an official secret; it had not been disclosed by you or the District Attorney. And I had to know. I had to know if Copes could possibly have learned about the LSD from any other source. Unless such a source could be found, it would be impossible to challenge his account, and I would have to advise him to tell you without further delay. At ten o'clock Friday morning, five of us gathered here to consider it, and Mr. Panzer, Mr. Durkin, and Mr. Cather were given instructions and proceeded to inquire. The obvious possibil—"

"Three days you kept it. By God, three days and three nights." Cramer's voice was not weak.

"The weekend intervened. Anyway I would have kept it as long as there was any hope of finding a probable source. Three weeks or three months. Fortunately a competent performance by Mr. Panzer—and Mr. Durkin—made it *only* three days. Mr. Panzer brought it a little more than an hour ago, and I telephoned you almost immediately. Copes lied. I know how he learned about the LSD."

Wolfe looked at Rowcliff and back at Cramer. "There are several ways I could do this, and I'm taking the quickest, which should also be the most effective. As you know, a friend of Mr. Goodwin's, Mr. Cohen, is in a position of authority and influence at the *Gazette.*" He turned. "Your notebook, Archie."

With no idea what was coming, I got it, and a pen, and crossed my legs.

"A suggested draft for an article in tomorrow's *Gazette.* 'In an interview yesterday afternoon Nero Wolfe, comma, the private investigator, comma, stated that an attempt has been made by Dennis Copes, comma, an employe of the Continental Air Network, comma, to get the sixty-five thousand dollars offered in a recent advertisement by Mrs. Peter Odell, comma, by fraud. Period.'—No. Instead of 'fraud' make it 'by subreption.' It's more precise and will add to vocabularies. 'Paragraph.'

"'Mr. Wolfe said, comma, quote, "Dennis Copes came to my office last Thursday evening and disclosed that he had knowledge of a certain fact relevant to the explosion of a bomb in the office of a CAN executive on the twentieth of May that caused the death of Peter Odell. Period. It was a fact known to me and to the police but had never been divulged, comma, by them or by me. Period. It was a closely guarded secret. Period. Mr. Copes's explanation of how and where he had learned it made it highly probable that the bomb had been placed in the drawer by another employe of CAN, comma, named by him. Paragraph.

"'Quote. "I had reason to suspect that Mr. Copes's account of how he had learned the fact was false, comma, and I undertook to discover if he might have learned it some other way. Period. This morning I learned that there was indeed another way. Period. Mr. Copes has a twin sister named Diana who is the wife of a police lieutenant named J. M. Rowcliff. Period. I think it highly probable, comma, in fact I am satisfied, comma, that Mr. Rowcliff—'"

"Why, goddam you—" Rowcliff was up and moving.

"Back up!" Cramer snapped.

"Let me finish," Wolfe said.

"*I'll* finish you! You—"

"Can it!" Cramer snapped. "Sit down. Sit down and shut your trap." To Wolfe: "You know damn well you can't do this. We'd tear your guts out. You'd be done."

"I doubt it," Wolfe said. "The spotlight of public interest. I would be a cynosure, a man of mark. And my client's resources are considerable. I would have handled this differently if it were not Mr. Rowcliff. If it were Mr. Stebbins, for instance, I would have asked him to come and I would have told him that I wanted merely his private acknowledgment that he had told his wife about the LSD. That woud have satisifed *me* that Copes had learned of the LSD from his sister, and no further proof would have been required. It would not have been necessary even for you to be told, either by him or by me. But with Mr. Rowcliff that would not have been possible. Would it? You know him. You know his animus against me."

"You could have asked *me* to come. And discuss it."

"Certainly. I have. Here we are."

"Balls. Discuss, my ass. 'In an interview yesterday afternoon Nero Wolfe, the private investigator.' That crap. All right, I'll discuss it with Rowcliff and you'll hear from me later. Probably today."

"No." Emphatic. "That won't do. It's urgent. There's a certain step I intend to take without delay. I'll postpone it only if I must. If you and Mr.

Rowcliff leave without satisfying me, Mr. Goodwin will leave ten minutes later with the suggested draft for that article. It may be possible to get it in the late edition of today's paper. And of course reporters will be wanting to see Mr. and Mrs. Rowcliff—and you, I suppose. This is probably a resort to coercion, but I make no apology; the fact that I have Mr. Rowcliff to deal with makes it imperative. Actually I don't ask much. I require only a statement by him, unequivocal, that he told his wife about the LSD found in Peter Odell's pocket. I don't need an admission by his wife that she told her brother. That is a plausible assumption that for me will suffice."

Wolfe turned to Rowcliff. "You may know—or you may not—that there is an understanding between Mr. Cramer and me which he knows I observe. No conversation in this office with him present is recorded without his express consent. This is not being recorded."

"You goddam ape," Rowcliff said.

Cramer asked him, "Did you hear me tell you to shut your trap?"

No reply.

"Say 'yes, sir,'" Cramer said.

Rowcliff licked his lips. "Yes, sir."

"You're a good cop," Cramer said. "I know what you're good for and what you're not good for. I even agree with your opinion of Wolfe up to a point, but *only* up to a point. That understanding he mentioned, you wouldn't trust him to keep it, but I do. That's a flaw you've got. Anyway the point right now is not our opinion of Wolfe, it's what he wants from you. There are aspects of this that you and I can discuss privately, and we will, but if you *did* tell your wife about the LSD, and you can be damn sure I'm going to *know* if you did, the best thing you can do is to say so here and now. You don't have to tell Wolfe, tell me. Did you?"

"Goddam it, Inspector, I'm not—"

"*Did you?*"

"Yes. I'm not going—"

"Shut up." Cramer turned to Wolfe. "I call that unequivocal, damn you."

"So do I," Wolfe said. "Thank you for coming."

"You can shove your thanks." He stood up. "You said something on the phone about a useful hint. You can shove that too. You and your useful hints." He turned to Rowcliff. "You, move. Move!"

It was an order and Rowcliff obeyed it. Anyone else I could name, I would have felt sorry for him. I knew what he had coming and so did he. Saul followed them to the hall; he had let them in, so he would check them out.

As Saul came back in, Wolfe told me, "Get Mr. Browning."

He was certainly making up for lost time, but it had worked with Cramer and Rowcliff so it might work with the next president of CAN too, whatever it was. I pulled the phone around and dialed, and told the switchboard I wanted to speak to Mr. Browning's secretary. When you ask for secretaries usually you aren't asked who you are, and in a minute I had her.

"Mr. Browning's office."

"Miss Lugos, please."

"This is Miss Lugos."

"This is Archie Goodwin. Mr. Wolfe would like to speak to Mr. Browning."

"Nero Wolfe?"

"Yes."

"What about?"

"I don't know. It must be important, since Mr. Browning called him a cheap bully only a couple of hours ago."

"I'll see. Hold the wire."

Of course she would tell me either that Mr. Browning was not available or to put Mr. Wolfe on. But she didn't. After a wait of only a couple of minutes, his voice: "What do you want?"

I didn't have to answer because Wolfe was on.

"Mr. Browning?"

"Yes."

"Nero Wolfe. I have just spoken at some length with Inspector Cramer of the police. He left my office five minutes ago. This afternoon, not later than four o'clock, I am going to tell him who put a bomb in a drawer of your desk, and I think it fitting and desirable that I tell you first. I would also like to tell Miss Lugos why I told her that she lied. Will you come, with her, at half past two?"

Silence, a long minute, then, "I think *you're* lying."

"No. A lie that would be exposed in three hours? No."

"You know who did that? You know now?"

"Yes."

A shorter silence. "I'll call you back."

He hung up. Of course that meant yes. He wouldn't call Cramer, and even if he did, what would that get him? I looked at Wolfe. Sometimes you can tell pretty well how good his hand is by the way he holds his head, and his mouth. That time I couldn't. No sign. I asked him. "Must we leave the room while you're telling them? We're curious. We'd like to know too."

"You will." He looked at the wall clock. 12:25. "Now. Saul, ask Fritz to bring the champagne."

As Saul left, the doorbell rang, and I went. It was Orrie Cather. I opened the door and said. "Greetings. Go ahead and tell me you know who Dennis Copes's twin sister's husband is."

"Huh?" He stepped in. "I didn't know he had a sister. I got bounced from the CAN building."

"Sure. They knew you like champagne. Go right in."

So Orrie was there for the briefing too.

19

THE vice-president and his secretary came on the dot at half past two. Precisely.

We were well-filled. Inside our bellies were three bottles of Dom Perignon champagne, braised sweetbreads with chicken quenelles (small portions because of the unexpected guests), crab meat omelets (added attraction), celery and mushroom salad, and four kinds of cheese. Inside our skulls were the details of where it stood according to Wolfe and the program for the next hour or two. For where it stood I would have given good odds, say ten to one, and so would the other three. For the program, no bet. It was a typical Wolfe concoction. It assumed —*he* assumed—that if an unexpected snag interfered, he would be able to handle it no matter what it was, and your ego has to be riding high to assume that.

To prepare for it only two props were needed. One was the Copes tape in the playback on my desk. For the other all four of us went to the basement. I could have done it alone, but they wanted to help. In a corner of the big storage room there were two thick, old mattresses, no springs in them, which I had used a few times for targets to get bullets for comparison purposes. We decided the best place for them was under the pool table in the adjoining room, where it had been installed when Wolfe had decided that he needed some violent exercise. Doubled, the mattresses were a tight fit under it.

The three were to be in the front room, but when the doorbell rang Saul went to receive the guests and show them in. They didn't have their war paint on. Browning was not a dragon snorting fire, and Helen Lugos was not set to use her claws on someone who had called her a liar. He sat in the red leather chair and said he had an appointment at a quarter past three, and she sat in a yellow one and said nothing.

"This will take a while," Wolfe told Browning. "Perhaps an hour."

"I can't stay an hour."

"We'll see. I'll make it as brief as possible. First you must hear a recording of a conversation I had recently with a member of your staff, Dennis Copes. Here. He came last Thursday evening. —Archie?"

I flipped the switch, and for the fifth time I heard Copes speak highly of that ad. Another time or two and I would begin to think I had picked the wrong line of work, that by now I could have been a vice-president myself, at one of the big agencies. As I had with Cramer and Rowcliff, I watched their faces. Their reaction was very different from the cops'. They looked at Wolfe hardly at all. Mostly they looked at each other, him with a frown that developed into what you might call a gawk, and her first with her eyes wide and then with her lips parted. Twice she started to say something but realized she had to hold it. When it came to the end and I turned it off, they both started to speak at once, he to her and she to him, but Wolfe stopped them. "Don't," he said, loud enough and decisive enough to stop anybody. "Don't waste your breath and your time and mine. I know he lied. It was all a fabrication. That has been established, with the help of Inspector Cramer. He heard the recording this morning. I should tell you, and I do, that this conversation is not being recorded. I give you that assurance on my word of honor, and those who know me would tell you that I would not tarnish that fine old pledge."

Browning demanded, "If you know he lied why bother us with it? Why do *you* waste our time?"

"I don't. You *had* to hear part of it, and to appreciate that part you needed to hear the whole. I have —"

"What part?"

"You said your time is limited."

"It is."

"Then don't interrupt. I have a good deal to say and I am not garrulous. The kernel of Mr. Copes's fabrication was of course the quotation—what he said he heard Kenneth Meer say." To Helen Lugos: "You say he didn't say that? That that conversation didn't occur?"

"I certainly do. It didn't."

"I believe you. But his invention of it told me something that he did not intend and was not aware of. It told me who put the bomb in the drawer, and I'm going to tell you how and why. As I said, I'll make it brief as possible, but you should know that Kenneth Meer is responsible for my concern in this affair. On May twenty-sixth, a Monday, he went to a clinic, gave a false name, and told a doctor that he needed help; that he got blood on his hands recurrently, frequently, not visible to anyone else. He refused—"

Browning demanded, "A clinic? What clinic?"

"Don't interrupt! To include all details would take all day. I assure you that anything I do include can be verified. He refused to give any information about himself. A friend of that doctor, another doctor, consulted me, and Kenneth Meer, still using an alias, came to see me. He still refused to supply any information about himself, but by a ruse, Mr. Goodwin and I learned who he was, and of course we had seen his name in the published reports of the death of Peter Odell. That led to my being consulted by Mrs. Odell and her hiring me. Naturally—"

"So that's how—"

"Don't interrupt! Naturally I considered the possibility that Meer had supplied the bomb and was racked by his sense of guilt. But surely not intending it for you, and information given me by Mrs. Odell made it extremely unlikely that he could have known that Peter Odell intended to go to your room and open that drawer. I will not elaborate on that. I have included that detail, how I first saw Kenneth Meer, only to explain why he has been of special interest throughout. There has always been for me that special reason to suspect him, but there was no plausible basis for a charge. Or rather, there was, but I hadn't the wit to see it. I admit I should have. Mr. Copes revealed it to me."

He turned a palm up. "If you undertake to invent something you heard another man say and you're not a fool, you make it conform to his character, his knowledge, and his style. And Copes had Kenneth Meer saying to Miss Lugos, 'I want to be damn sure you don't open the drawer to take a look at the usual time.' Would he have had him say that to her, especially the 'usual time,' unless he knew, or thought he knew, that Miss Lugos was in the habit of looking in the drawer every day, and that Meer knew it? When he wanted to make the invented quotation not only conceivable but as credible as possible? He would not. He would have included that 'usual' only if it conformed to his knowledge of the fact. Of course if he knew that Miss Lugos had told the police—and Mr. Goodwin—that she had not habitually opened the drawer every day, it was a blunder to include the 'usual.' It was a blunder even if he didn't know that, because it wasn't necessary, but he included it because he thought it increased the credibility of his lie."

Wolfe looked at Helen Lugos. "So when you told Mr. Goodwin that you did not look in the drawer every day, you lied. And you knew that the bomb, put in the drawer by Kenneth Meer, was intended for you. You had known that from the day it happened. You probably knew it, at least surmised it, the moment you entered the wrecked room."

Browning was on his feet. "Come, Helen," he said. "This is absurd. We're going."

"No." Wolfe said. He turned to me, lifted a hand, and wiggled a finger. I went and opened the connecting door to the front room and stuck my head in and said, "Help." Saul and Fred headed for the other door, to the hall, and Orrie came and joined me. Helen Lugos was up and moving, with Browning behind her, but before they reached the door to the hall Saul and Fred were there, and Helen Lugos stopped. Saul swung the door around, closed it, and he and Fred stood with their backs to it.

"You are *not* going, Mr. Browning," Wolfe said. "Come and sit down." Browning turned. "This *is* absurd. Absolutely ridiculous."

"It is not. I have more to say and I mean you to hear it. You might as well sit."

"No. You'll regret this."

"I doubt it." Wolfe turned. "Your notebook, Archie."

I went to my desk, sat, got notebook and pen, and crossed my legs. A replay, though not quite instant.

Wolfe leaned back. "A suggested draft for an article in tomorrow's *Gazette*. 'Yesterday afternoon Nero Wolfe, comma, the private investigator, comma, told a *Gazette* reporter that he has learned who was responsible for the death by violence of Peter Odell, comma, a vice-president of the Continental Air Network, comma, on May twentieth. Period. Mr. Odell was killed by the explosion of a bomb in the office of Amory Browning, comma, also a vice-president of the Continental Air Network. Paragraph.

"'Mr. Wolfe said, comma, quote, "I have established to my satisfaction that the bomb was put in a drawer of Mr. Browning's desk by Kenneth Meer, comma, Mr. Browning's assistant, dash, the drawer in which Mr. Browning kept a supply of bourbon whisky. Period. Mr. Meer knew that Miss Helen Lugos, comma, Mr. Browning's secretary, comma, was in the habit of opening the drawer every afternoon to see that the whisky was there, comma, and he placed the bomb so it would explode when the drawer was opened. Period. However, comma, Mr. Odell entered the room shortly after three o'clock and opened the drawer, comma, it is not known why. Paragraph.

"'Quote. "In these circumstances, comma, established to my satisfaction, comma, it is not only reasonble, comma, it is unavoidable, comma, to suppose that Miss Lugos has been aware that the bomb must have been put in the drawer by Mr. Meer, comma, and the supposition is supported by the fact that she has consistently denied that she habitually opened the drawer every day to check on the whisky. Period. Also it is reasonable to suppose that Mr. Browning was aware of that too, comma, or at least suspected it. Period. Kenneth Meer knew of the intimate personal relationship that existed between Mr. Browning and Miss Lugos, comma, and was tormented by the knowledge. Period. He was torn by two intense and conflicting desires. Colon. His ardent wish to advance through his association with Mr. Browning, comma, and his concupiscence. Period. It may be assumed —"'"

"This is worse than ridiculous." Browning was standing at the end of Wolfe's desk. "It's idiotic. No newspaper would print it. Any of it."

"Oh, yes. The *Gazette* would, with a guaranty from Mrs. Odell to cover all expenses. Yes, indeed. You're up a stump, Mr. Browning, and so is Miss Lugos. Not only the publicity; you would have to sue for libel, or persuade the District Attorney to charge us with criminal libel. That would be obligatory, and both of you would have to submit to questioning under oath. *That* would be idiotic, for a man in your position."

For the second time that day something happened that was hard to believe. Browning stood with his eyes glued to Wolfe, but probably not really seeing him, his shoulders set, and his chin back. Twenty seconds, half a minute, I don't know; and then he turned right around and looked at Helen Lugos, who had stayed over by the door, an arm's reach from Saul and Orrie. And she said, "Ask him what he wants." It was a suggestion, not a command, but even so, from a secretary to a vice-president soon to be a president? Women's Lib, or what?

Whatever it was, it worked fine. He turned back to Wolfe and asked, "What do you want?"

"I like eyes at a level," Wolfe said. "Please sit down."

Helen Lugos came back to the yellow chair, and sat. At least she left the red leather chair for him, and he took it, or some of it—about the front eight inches of the seat, barely enough to keep his rump on—and asked again, "What do you want?"

"From you, not much," Wolfe said. "I am not Jupiter Fidius. I want only to do the job I was hired to do. I think I know the present state of Kenneth Meer's mind. His mood, his spirit. I think he's pregnable. I want to get him on the telephone, tell him you and Miss Lugos are here, and ask him to join us for a discussion. If he refuses or demurs, I want you to speak to him and tell him to come. I don't know how things stand between you and him; of course during these six weeks you would have liked to turn him out, but didn't dare. Will he come if you tell him to?"

"Yes. Then what?"

"We'll see. One possibility, he may acknowledge that he put the bomb in the drawer, but claim that it was intended for Peter Odell—that he knew that Odell intended to come and open the drawer. There are other possibilities, and it may be that his real motive need not be divulged. That would please you and Miss Lugos, and I have no animus against you, but I make no commitment. This is your one chance to get out of it with minor bruises. I know too much now that the police *should* know."

Would he ask her for another suggestion? No. He looked at her, but only for a second, and then said, "All right. If you think—all right."

Wolfe turned to me: "Get him."

That was one of the possible snags. What if he wasn't there? What if he had got a toothache or twisted an ankle and left for the day? But he hadn't. I got him and Wolfe got on. I stayed on.

"Good afternoon, Mr. Meer. I'm calling from my office, at the suggestion of Mr. Browning. He and Miss Lugos are here. We have talked at some length, and have come to a point where we need your help. Can you come at once?"

"Why—they're there?"

"Yes. Since half past two."

"Mr. Browning told you to call me?"

"Yes. He's right here. Do you want to speak to him?"

"I don't—no. No. All right. I'll leave in five minutes."

He hung up. Wolfe told Browning, "He'll leave in five minutes. You and Miss Lugos may wish to speak privately. This room is soundproofed." He stood. "Would you like something to drink?"

Browning looked at her and she shook her head, and he said, "No." Saul and Fred left by the hall door, closing it after them, and Wolfe and Orrie and I left by the door to the front room. In a moment Saul and Fred joined us. Wolfe said, "I'm going to the kitchen. I'm thirsty. Any questions? Any comments?"

Orrie said, "It's all set. It's up to him."

Wolfe went by the hall door. Fred said, "If anyone wants a bet, I'm giving two to one that he'll have it."

Saul said, "I'd rather have your end."

I said, "I don't want *either* end."

They debated it. At a time like that, it only makes it longer to keep looking at your watch, but that's what I did. 3:22, 3:24, 3:27. At that time of day there should be taxis headed downtown on Ninth Avenue in the Fifties, and it was only nineteen blocks. At half past three I went to the hall, leaving the door open, and stood with my nose against the one-way glass of the front door. Me and my watch. 3:32, 3:34, 3:36. He had been run over by a truck or something. He was on his way to the airport. At 3:37 a taxi rolled up in front and stopped alongside the parked cars, and the door opened, and he climbed out, and he had the briefcase. I called through the open door to the front room, "Okay, he has it!" and they came. Orrie went down the hall to the door to the office and stood. Fred stood at my left by the rack; he would be behind the door when I opened it. Saul stood in the doorway to the front room. Kenneth Meer mounted the stoop with the briefcase tucked under his left arm. He pushed the button, and I counted a slow ten and opened the door, and he stepped in. With the briefcase under his arm, that hand was pressed against his left hip, and his right hand was hanging loose. I don't think I have ever made a faster or surer move. Facing him, I got his two wrists, and I got them good, and Saul, from behind him, got the briefcase. His mouth popped open but no sound came, and he went stiff top to bottom, absolutely stiff. Then he tried to turn around, but I had his wrists, and only his head could turn. Saul had backed away, holding the briefcase against his belly with both hands. I said, "Go ahead and don't drop it," and he started down the hall to the rear, where the stair to the basement was, and at the door to the office Orrie joined him. I let go of Meer's wrists, and he stood, still stiff, and stared down the hall at Saul going. He still hadn't made a sound. Then suddenly he started to slump. He made it over to the bench, flopped down on it, bent over with his face in his hands, and started to shake all over. Still no sound, absolutely none. I told Fred, "Keep him company," and headed for the kitchen.

Wolfe was on his stool at the center table with a beer glass in his hand. "You win," I said. "He had it and we got it."

"Where is he?"

"In the hall."

You wouldn't believe how easy and smooth he can remove his seventh of a ton off of a stool. I followed him down the hall. Meer was still huddled on the bench and still shaking. Wolfe stood and looked down at him for a good ten seconds, told Fred, "Stay here," went back down the hall and opened the office door and entered, and I followed. Browning, in the red leather chair, asked, "Did he come? The doorbell rang five min—"

"Shut up," Wolfe snapped, and crossed to his desk and sat and glared at them. "Yes," he said, "he came. When he came Saturday, day before yesterday, he was in his own car, but he didn't leave his briefcase in it. He kept it with him, and he kept it in his lap as he sat where you are now. When I decided today to ask him to come, later, I thought it likely that he would bring the briefcase, and if so there would be a bomb in it, since he would know you two were here. It was only a conjecture, but well-grounded, and it has been verified. He came, and he had the briefcase, and it is now in my basement under a pile of mattresses. On your way out, you will pass him in the hall—prostrated, wretched, defeated. Pass him, just pass him. He is no longer yours. I am now—"

"But my god, what—"

"*Shut up!* I am now going to call Mr. Cramer and ask him to come and bring with him men who know how to deal with bombs. If you don't want to encounter him, leave at once. Go."

He turned to me. "Get him, Archie."

I swiveled and dialed.

A Family Affair

1

WHEN someone pushes the button at the front door of the old brownstone, bells ring in four places: in the kitchen, in the office, down in Fritz's room, and up in my room. Who answers it depends on the circumstances. If it's ten minutes to one at night and I'm out, no one does unless it won't give up. If it keeps going, say for fifteen minutes, Fritz rolls out, comes up, opens the door the two inches the chain permits, and says nothing doing until morning. If I'm home *I* roll out, open a window and look down to see who it is, and deal with the problem.

It doesn't often ring at that hour, but it did that Monday night — Tuesday morning — late in October. I was home, but not up in bed. I was in the office, having just got in from taking Lily Rowan home after a show and a snack at the Flamingo. I always look in the office to see if Wolfe has written anything on the pad on my desk. That night he hadn't, and I was crossing to the safe to check that it was locked when the bell rang, and I went to the hall and through the one-way glass of the front door saw Pierre Ducos on the stoop.

Pierre had often fed me. He had fed many people, in one of the three rooms upstairs at Rusterman's restaurant. I had never seen him anywhere else — certainly never on that stoop in the middle of the night. I slipped the bolt back, opened the door, and said, "I'm not hungry, but come in."

He crossed the sill and said, "I've got to see Mr. Wolfe."

"At this hour?" I shut the door. "Not unless it's life and death."

"It is."

"Even so." I looked at him. I had never seen him without his uniform. I knew his age, fifty-two, but he looked older in a loose-fitting tan topcoat down to his knees. No hat. He looked as if inside of the topcoat he had shrunk, and his face looked smaller and seamier. "Whose life and death?"

"Mine."

"You can tell me about it." I turned. "Come along."

He followed me to the office. When I offered to take his coat he said he would keep it on, which was sensible, since the heat had been off for two hours, and we had lowered the thermostat four degrees to save oil. I moved up one of the yellow chairs for him and sat at my desk and asked him what it was.

He gestured with both hands. "It's what you said. Life and death. For me. A man is going to kill me."

"That won't do. Good waiters are scarce, and anyway you're not old enough to die. Who is he, and why?"

"You make it a joke. Death is not a joke."

"Sure it is. It's life that's not a joke. Who's going to kill you?"

"I'll tell Mr. Wolfe."

"He's in bed asleep. He sees people only by appointment, but for you he would make an exception. Come at eleven in the morning, or if it's urgent, tell me."

"I —" He looked at me. Since he had seen me at close quarters at least fifty times, maybe a hundred, surely he had me sized up, so he may not have been considering me, but he was deciding something for at least ten seconds. He opened his mouth and shut it, then opened it again to speak. "You see, Mr. Goodwin, I know Mr. Wolfe is the greatest detective in the world. Felix says he is — not only Felix, everybody does. Of course you're a good detective too, everybody knows that too, but when a man is sure he's going to be killed unless he — unless . . ." His hands on his knees were fists, and he opened them, palms up. "I've just got to tell Mr. Wolfe."

"Okay. Eleven o'clock tomorrow morning. What time do you go to work?"

"I won't go tomorrow." He looked at his wristwatch. "Just ten hours. If I could — there on that couch? I won't need covers or anything. I won't disturb anything. I won't make any noise."

So he was really wide open, or thought he was. The couch, in the corner beyond my desk, was perfectly sleepable, as I knew from experience, having spent quite a few nights on it in emergencies, and on the other side of the projecting wall that made the corner was an equipped bathroom. But leaving anyone loose all night in the office, with the ten thousand items in the files and drawers, many of them with no locks, was of course out of the question. There were four alternatives: persuade him to tell me, go up and wake Wolfe, give him a bed, or bounce him. The first might take an hour, and I was tired and sleepy. The second was inadvisable. If I bounced him, and he couldn't come at eleven in the morning because he was dead, the next time Wolfe lunched or dined in the little upstairs room at Rusterman's he would be served by a new waiter, and that would be regrettable. Also, of course, I would be sorry.

I looked at him. Should I frisk him? Was there any chance that he had it in for Wolfe personally for some reason unknown to me, or that he had been hired by one of the thousand or so people who thought it would be a better world with no Nero Wolfe? Of course it was possible, but if so, this complicated stunt wasn't the way to do it. It would have been much simpler and surer for Pierre just to put something in a sauce, in anything, the next time Wolfe went there for a meal. Anyway, not only had Pierre seen me at close quarters; I had seen him.

I said, "My pajamas would be too big for you."

He shook his head. "I'll keep my clothes on. Usually I sleep with nothing on."

"All right, there's plenty of cover on the bed in the South Room. It's two flights up, on the same floor as my room, above Mr. Wolfe's room. I was on my way up when you rang the doorbell." I stood. "Come along."

"But Mr. Goodwin, I don't want—I can just stay here." He stood up.

"No, you can't. Either you go up or you go out."

"I don't want to go out. Sunday night a car tried to run over me. He tried to kill me. I'm *afraid* to go out."

"Then follow me. Maybe when you sleep on it . . ."

I moved, crossed to the door, and he came. I flipped the light switch. I don't dawdle going upstairs, and I had to wait for him at the top of the first flight because he was only halfway up. At the second landing I turned left, swung the door of the South Room open, and turned the light on. I didn't have to check on the bed or towels in the bathroom because I knew everything was in order; all I had to do was turn the radiator on.

"I'm sorry, Mr. Goodwin," he said. "I'm very sorry."

"So am I," I said. "I'm sorry you're in a jam. Stick right here until I tell you I've told Mr. Wolfe about you. That will be around nine o'clock. If you open the door and go into the hall before eight o'clock, it will set off a gong in my room and you'll see me coming with guns in both hands. Security. I should have offered you a shot of something. Whisky? Would it help you go to sleep?"

He said no and he was sorry, and I went, shutting the door. As I entered my room, down the hall, I looked at my watch. Seventeen minutes past one. I wouldn't get my eight hours. When I get in that late I usually set my radio-alarm at nine-thirty, but now that wouldn't do. I would have to be up and dressed and telling Wolfe about the company before he went up to the plant rooms at nine o'clock.

Of course I have figured how many minutes had passed after I entered my room when it happened. Six, possibly seven. I refuse to hurry the night routine. I had got my pajamas from the closet, set the alarm, put things from my pockets on the dresser, turned the bedcovers down, turned the telephone and other two switches on, hung up my jacket and necktie, taken my shoes and socks off, and was unbuckling my belt, when the earthquake came and the house shook. Including the floor I was standing on. I have since tried to decide what the sound was like and couldn't. It wasn't like thunder or any kind of gun or any other sound I had ever heard. It wasn't a thud or a bang or a boom; it was just a loud noise. Of course there were doors and walls between it and me.

I jumped to the door and opened it and turned the hall light on. The door to the South Room was shut. I ran to it and turned the knob. No. He had bolted it. I ran down one flight, saw that the door to Wolfe's room was intact, and went and knocked on it. My usual three, a little spaced. I really did, and his voice came.

"Archie?"

I opened the door and entered and flipped the light switch. I don't know why he looks bigger in those yellow pajamas than in clothes. Not fatter, just bigger. He had pushed back the yellow electric blanket and black sheet and was sitting up.

"Well?" he demanded.

"I don't know," I said, and I hope my voice didn't squeak from the pleasure of seeing him. "I put a man in the South Room. The door's bolted. I'm going to see."

Of the three windows in the south wall, the two end ones are always open at night about five inches, and the middle one is shut and locked and draped. I went and pulled the drape, slid the catch, opened it, and climbed through. The fire escape is only a foot wider than the window. I have tried to remember if my bare feet felt the cold of the iron grating as I went up but can't. Of course they didn't when I got high enough to see that most of the glass in the window was gone. I put my hand in between the jagged edges and slipped the catch and pushed the window up, what was left of it, and stuck my head in.

He was on his back with his head toward me and his feet toward the closet door in the right wall. I shoved some glass slivers off the windowsill, climbed through, saw no pieces of glass on the rug, and crossed to him. He had no face left. I had never seen anything like it. It was about what you would get if you pressed a thick slab of pie dough on a man's face and then squirted blood on the lower half. Of course he was dead, but I was squatting to make sure when something hit the door three hard knocks, and I went and slid the bolt and opened it and there was Wolfe. He keeps one of his canes in the stand in the downstairs hall and the other four on a rack in his room, and he ws gripping the biggest and toughest one with a knob the size of my fist, which he says is Montenegrin applewood.

I said, "You won't need that," and sidestepped to give him room.

He crossed the sill, stood, and sent his eyes around.

I said, "Pierre Ducos, Rusterman's. He came just after I got home and said a man was going to kill him and he had to tell you. I said if it was urgent he could tell me or he could come and tell you at eleven o'clock. He said a car had tried to run him down and—"

"I want no details."

"There aren't any. He wanted to wait for you there on the couch, and of course that wouldn't do, so I brought him up here and told him to stay put and went to my room, and in a few minutes, I felt it and heard it and went. He had bolted the door, and—"

"Is he dead?"

"Yes. The windows blew out, to the outside, so it was a bomb. I'll take a look before I call for help. If you—"

I stopped because he was moving. He crossed to Pierre, bent over and looked. Then he straightened and looked around, at the closet door, which had been standing open and had hit the wall and was split, at the ceiling plaster on the floor, at the table wrong side up and the pieces of the lamp that had been on it, at the chair that had been tossed clear across to the foot of the bed, and so on.

He looked at me and said, "I suppose you had to."

That remark has since been discussed at length, but then I merely said, "Yeah. I'm going to—"

"I know what you're going to do. First put your shoes on. I am going to my room and bolt the door. I will stay there until they have come and gone and I will see no one. Tell Fritz that when he brings my breakfast he will make sure that no one is near. When Theodore comes, tell him not to expect me. Is there anything you *must* say?

"No".

He went, still gripping the Montenegrin applewood by the small end. I didn't hear the elevator, so he took the stairs, which he rarely does. Barefoot.

He had *not* known what I was going to do. He hadn't known that I would go down to the basement, to Fritz's room. First I went and put on socks and shoes and a jacket, then down two flights to the office to turn the thermostat up to 70, and then on down to knock on Fritz's door and call my name, loud. He's a sound sleeper, but in half a minute the door opened. The tail of his white nightshirt flapped in the breeze from the open window. Our pajamas-versus-nightshirt debate will never be settled.

"Sorry to intrude," I said, "but there's a mess. A man came, and I put him in the South Room, and a bomb that he brought along went off and killed him. All the damage is in that room. Mr. Wolfe came up for a look and is now in his room with the door bolted. You may not get much more sleep, because a mob will be coming and there will be noise. When you take his breakfast up—"

"Five minutes," he said. "You'll be in the office?"

"No. Upstairs. South Room. When you take his breakfast, be sure you're alone."

"Four minutes. Do you want me upstairs?"

"No. Down. You can let them in, that'll help. There's no rush. I have a couple of chores before I call them."

"Who do I let in?"

"Anybody. Everybody."

"*Bon Dieu.*"

"I agree." I turned and headed for the stairs and on the way up decided not to get rubber gloves from the office because they would make it take longer.

He was still on the floor, and the first question was what had put him there. I couldn't qualify as an expert on that, but I might get an idea, and I did. Here and there among the pieces of plaster on the floor I found several small objects that hadn't come from the ceiling, which I couldn't name. The biggest one was about half the size of my thumbnail. But I found four that I might name, or thought I might—four little pieces of aluminum. The biggest one was a quarter of an inch wide and neary half an inch long, and EDR was printed on it, dark green. A smaller one had DO printed on it, and another had *du*. One had no printing. I left them there, where I found them. The trouble with removing evidence from the scene of a crime is that someday you might want to produce it and have to tell where you got it.

The second question was what had made me consider rubber gloves: was there anything on him that would supply a name or other fact? I got on my knees beside him and did a thorough job. He still had the topcoat on, but there was nothing in the pockets. In the jacket and pants pockets were most of the usual items—cigarettes, matches, a couple of dollars in change, key ring, handkerchief, penknife, wallet with driving license and credit cards and eighty-four dollars in bills—but nothing that offered any hope of a hint. Of course there were other possibilities, his shoes or something taped to his hide, but that would take time, and I had already stretched it.

I went down to the office, and Fritz was there, fully dressed. I sat at my desk, pulled the phone around, and dialed a number I didn't have to look up.

2

THE attitude of Sergeant Purley Stebbins toward Wolfe and me is yes-and-no, or make it no-but-yes. When he finds us within ten miles of a homicide, he wishes he was on traffic or narcotics, but he knows that something will probably happen that he doesn't want to miss. My attitude toward him is that he could be worse. I could name a few that are.

At 4:52 a.m. he sat on one of the yellow chairs in the office, swallowed a bite he had taken from a tongue sandwich made with Fritz's bread, and said, "You know damn well I have to ask him if Ducos or anyone at the restaurant has ever said anything that could be a lead. Or someone does. Someone will come either at eleven o'clock or six."

I had finished my sandwich. "I doubt if he'll get in," I said. "Certainly not at eleven, and probably not at six. He may not be speaking even to me. A man murdered here in his house, within ten feet of him? You know him, don't you?"

"Do I. So does the inspector. I know you too. If you think you can—"

I slapped my desk with a palm. "Don't start that again. I said in my signed statement that I went over him. There might have been something that I should have included when I phoned. But I took nothing. One thing that's not in my statement: I admit I'm withholding evidence. Knowledge of something that would certainly be used at the trial, if and when."

"Oh. You are. You *are*?"

"I am. Of course you'll send everything you found to the lab, and it won't take them long to get it, maybe a couple of days. But you might like to have the pleasure of supplying it yourself. I know what the bomb was in."

"You do. And didn't put this in your statement."

"It would have taken about a page, and I was tired, and also I prefer to tell you. Have you ever seen a Don Pedro cigar?"

He finished swallowing the last bite of the sandwich, with his eyes glued to me. "No."

"Cramer wouldn't buy them to chew. Ninety cents apiece. Rusterman's has them. They come in aluminum tubes. DON PEDRO is on the tube in capital letters, dark green, and *Honduras* is on it, lower case. In the stuff you collected is a piece of aluminum with DO in caps on it, and one with *du* in lower case, and a bigger one with EDR in caps. So this is what happened.When I left the room, he sat or stood or walked around for a few minutes and decided he might as well undress and go to bed and went and opened the closet door. When you take your coat off to hang it up, do you automatically stick your hands in the pockets? I do. So did he. And in one of them was a Don Pedro cigar aluminum tube, which he recognized. He had no idea how it got there, and he screwed the cap off, holding it fairly close to his face — say ten inches. It was a piece of aluminum that made the gash on his jaw. There's a word for the force that pushed his face in, but I've forgotten it. If you want to include it in your report, you can look it up."

Purley's mouth was shut tight. He didn't open it. His eyes at me were half shut. There was half an inch of milk left in my glass, and I lifted it and drank. "What those pieces of aluminum were —" I said, "I had that figured before I phoned, but the rest of it, where it had been and exactly how it happened — I doped that out later to occupy my mind while I sat around. Also I considered what would have happened if I had frisked him before I took him upstairs. Of course I would have wanted to see what was in the tube. Well. I'm still here. I have explained why I didn't frisk him. Since I left this out of my statement, leaving it for you, you ought to send me a box of candy. I like caramels."

He finally opened his mouth. "I'll send you an orchid. Do you know what would happen if Rowcliff got on this?"

"Certainly. He would send a squad out to dig up where I recently bought a Don Pedro cigar. But you have a brain, which you sometimes use."

"Put *that* in a statement some day. My brain tells me that he might have said something which gave you a hint how the tube got in his pocket, but that's not in your statement."

"I guess I forgot. Nuts."

"Also my brain tells me that the DA will want to know why I didn't bring you down as a material witness. The bomb went off at one-twenty-four, and you were in the room and found him two or three minutes later, and you phoned at two-eleven. Forty-five minutes, and you know what the law says, and you've got a license."

"Must we go back to that again?"

"The DA will want to know why I didn't bring you."

"Sure, and you'll tell him. So will I after I get some sleep. It was obvious that there was no rush. Whatever had killed him, he had brought it himself. It was in the middle of the night. If you had got here in two minutes there wasn't a damn thing you could do that wouldn't wait. You can't do anything now until morning, like finding out where he was and who he saw before he came here. There's nobody at Rusterman's but the night watchman, and he's probably asleep. I have a suggestion. Instead of sending me an orchid, give me permission in writing to break the seal on that room and go in and cover the windows with something. It's not sealed anyway. One of the windows, anyone could come up the fire escape and climb in. I admit there's no hurry about the rest of it, the plaster and the other stuff."

"The plaster is gone." He looked at his watch and got to his feet, gripping the chair arms for leverage, which he seldom does. "By god, you admit something. You're going soft. That window's blocked. You let that seal alone. Someone will come for another look, someone who knows about bombs. Also someone will come to see Wolfe."

"I told you, he probably won't —"

"Yeah. Do you know what I think? I think he made a hole in his ceiling and pushed the bomb through." He headed for the door.

I got up and followed, in no hurry. There was no hurry left in me. There wasn't much of anything left in me. When he was out and the door shut, I went and put the chain bolt on, put out the lights in the office and hall, and went up the two flights to my room, actually leaving the plates and glasses there on my desk, which is hard to believe. Fritz had gone to bed nearly an hour ago, when all the mob had cleared out except Purley, after bringing sandwiches without asking if they were wanted.

Of course I was asleep two minutes after I got flat, and I stayed asleep. I don't brag about my sleeping because I suspect it shows that I'm primitive or vulgar or something, but I admit it. But I also admit I set the alarm for ten o'clock. Anyway I would probably be interrupted before that, although I turned my phone switch off. I left the house phone on.

But I wasn't. When the radio said, "And you'll never regret that you obeyed the impulse and decided to try the only face cream that makes you want to touch your own skin," I reached for it without opening my eyes. I tried to argue that another hour wouldn't hurt, but it didn't work because it came to me that there was a problem that wouldn't wait. Theodore. I opened my eyes, reached for the house phone, and buzzed the kitchen.

In five seconds Fritz's voice came. "Yes."

He claims that he is not copying Wolfe, that Wolfe says "Yes?" and he says "Yes."

I said, "You're up and dressed."

"Yes. I took his breakfast."

"Did he eat?"

"Yes."

"My god, you're short and sweet."

"Not sweet, Archie. Neither is he. Are you?"

"No. I'm neither sweet nor sour. I'm done. How about Theodore?"

"He came and went up. I told him he wouldn't come."

"I'll be down, but don't bother with breakfast. I'll eat the second section of the *Times*. With vinegar."

"It's better with ketchup." He hung up.

But when I finally made it down to the kitchen the stage was set. Tools and cup and saucer and the toaster and butter dish were on the little table, and the *Times* was on the rack, and the griddle was on the range. On the big center table was a plate of slices of homemade scrapple. I got a glass and went to the refrigerator for orange juice, poured some, and took a sip.

"As far as I'm concerned," I said, "you and I are still friends. You're the only friend I've got in the world. Let's go somewhere. Switzerland? That ought to be far enough. Have there been phone calls?"

"There have been rings, four, but I didn't answer. Neither did he." He had turned the heat on under the griddle. "That thing on the door of that room, NEW YORK POLICE DEPARTMENT, how long will it stay?"

I drank orange juice. "That's a good idea," I said. "Forget all the other details, such as headlines like GUEST IN NERO WOLFE'S HOUSE KILLED BY BOMB or ARCHIE GOODWIN OPENS DOOR TO HOMICIDE, and concentrate on that door. Wonderful idea."

He was getting bacon fat on the griddle. I went to my chair at the little table and picked up the *Times*. President Ford wanted us to do something about inflation. Nixon was in shock from the operation. Judge Sirica had told Ehrlichman's lawyer he talked too much. The Arabs had made Arafat it. Items which ordinarily would have had me turning to inside pages, but I had to use will power to finish the first paragraphs. I tried other departments — sports, weather, obituaries, metropolitan briefs — and decided that it's possible to tell your mind what to do only when your mind agrees with you. I was going on from there to decide if that meant anything and if so what, when Fritz came with two slices of scrapple on a plate. As he put it down he made a noise which I'll spell "Tchahh!" I asked him why, and he said he forgot the honey and went and brought it.

As I was buttering the third slice of toast the phone rang. I counted. It rang twelve times and stopped. In a couple of minutes Fritz said, "I never saw you do that before."

"There'll probably be a lot of things you never saw me do before. Did you get the plates and glasses I left in the office?"

"I haven't been to the office."

"Did he mention me when you took his breakfast up or went for the tray?"

"No. He asked me if I had been up during the night. I started to tell him about it, how many of them had come, and he stopped me."

"How did he stop you?"

"By looking at me and then turning his back."

"Was he dressed?"

"Yes. The dark brown with little stripes. Yellow shirt and brown tie."

When I put the empty coffee cup down and went to the office it was ten past eleven. Since he hadn't come down at eleven, he probably wasn't coming. I decided it would be childish not to do the chores, so I dusted the desks, removed yesterday's calendar sheets, changed the water in the vase on Wolfe's desk, took the plates and glasses to the kitchen, and put the chair Purley had sat on where it belonged, and was opening the mail when the house phone buzzed. I got it and said, "I'm in the office."

"Have you eaten?"

"Yes."

"Come up here."

I got the carbon of my statement from the drawer and went. Since I had been summoned, of course I didn't knock on his door. He was seated at the table between the windows, with a book. Either he had finished with his copy of the *Times* or his mind had refused to cooperate, like mine. As I crossed to him he put the book down — *The Palace Guard* by Dan Rather and Gary Gates — and growled, "Good morning."

"Good morning," I snarled.

"Have you been downtown?"

"No. I don't answer the phone."

"Sit down and report."

Of course he had the big chair. I brought the other one over and sat and said, "The best start would be for you to read this copy of the statement I gave Stebbins." I handed it to him. It was four pages. Once through is usually enough for him, but that time he went back to the first two pages — what Pierre and I had said, which I had given verbatim.

He eyed me. "What did you reserve?"

"Of my talk with Pierre, nothing. Every word is there. Of the rest, also nothing, except that you were armed when you came, with that club, and that you told me you supposed I had to. It's all there, what was said and what happened, but I didn't include a guess I made. I saved that for

Stebbins. When I left Pierre there, he felt something in his topcoat pocket and took it out. It was an aluminum tube, the kind Don Pedro cigars come in. When he unscrewed the cap, he was holding it only a few inches from his face. You saw his face. There were pieces of aluminum on the floor, and I recognized the printing on them. Of course they had been collected and Stebbins had seen them. Also of course, they would soon make the same guess, so I thought I might as well give it to Stebbins."

He shook his head, either at Purley or at me, I didn't know which. "What else did you give him?"

"Nothing. There was nothing else to give. Nothing to anybody, including the medical examiner and Lieutenant Burnham, whom you have never met. I didn't count, but Fritz says there were nineteen of them altogether. The door of the South Room is sealed. A bomb specialist is coming to get clues, probably this afternoon."

When he wants to give something a good look and is in the office at his desk, in the one chair that he thoroughly approves, he leans back and shuts his eyes, but the back of that chair isn't the right angle for it, so he just squinted and pulled at his ear lobe. A full two minutes.

"Nothing," he said. "Nothing whatever."

"Right. Because you're the greatest detective in the world. Stebbins doesn't believe it. He thinks he told me something, maybe not a name but something, and I left it out because we want to get him ourselves. Of course we do, at least I do. I might have unscrewed the cap of that tube myself. So I owe him something."

"So do I. In my own house, asleep in my own bed, and that. That— that . . ."

I raised my brows at him. That was a first. The first time in my long experience that he had ever been at a loss for words.

He hit the chair arm with a fist. "So. Call Felix. Tell him we'll be there for lunch." He looked at the wall clock. "In half an hour. If no upstairs room is available, perhaps on the top floor, if that's convenient. Do you know of any source of information about Pierre other than the restaurant?"

I said no, got up, went to the phone on the bedstand, switched it on, and dialed.

3

THE top floor at Rusterman's restaurant was once the living quarters of Marko Vukcic, its owner, who had been Wolfe's boyhood friend in Montenegro and one of the only three men I knew who called him by his first name. For a year or so after Marko's death it had been unoccupied, and then Felix, who had been left a one-third share and ran the restaurant under Wolfe's supervision as trustee, had moved in with his wife and two children. Soon the children had got married and left.

At twenty-five minutes to one, Wolfe and I were seated at a table near a window on that floor which looked down on Madison Avenue. Felix, slim and trim, elegant in blue-black and white for the lunch customers, standing at Wolfe's left and my right, said, "Then the scallops. Fresh from the bay, I never saw finer ones, and the shallots were perfect. They'll be ready in ten minutes."

Wolfe nodded. "And the rice fritters. I'll tell—his name is Philip?"

"Philip Correla. Of course everyone knew Pierre, but Philip knew him best. As I said, I don't think I ever saw Pierre except here. We'll miss him, Mr. Wolfe. He was a good man. It's hard to believe, there in your house." He looked at his watch. "You'll excuse me—I'll send Philip." He went. The early ones would be coming down below.

"Uhuh," I said. "A million people will be saying that, it's hard to believe, there in Nero Wolfe's house. Or some of them will say it's easy to believe. I don't know which is worse."

He glared at me.

Of the seventy-some at Rusterman's altogether, there were few that Wolfe had never seen, only seven or eight who had come since he had bowed out as trustee. When Philip Correla appeared, white apron and cap, he crossed to us and said, "You may remember me, Mr. Wolfe. And Mr. Goodwin."

"Certainly," Wolfe said. "You once disagreed with me about *Rouennaise* sauce."

"Yes, sir. You said no bay leaf."

"I nearly always say no bay leaf. Tradition should be respected but not sanctified. I concede that you make good sauces. Will you sit, please? I prefer eyes at a level."

He waited until Philip had moved a chair to face him and was on it. Then: "I presume Felix told you what I want."

"Yes, sir. To ask me about Pierre. We were friends. *Good* friends. I tell you, I cried. In Italy men cry. I didn't leave Italy until I was twenty-four. I met Pierre in Paris." He looked at me. "It said on the radio you found him." He looked at Wolfe. "In your house. It didn't say why he was at your house or why he got killed."

Wolfe took in a bushel of air through his nose and let it out through his mouth. Felix, and now Philip, and they knew him. "He came to ask me something," he said, "but I was in bed. So I don't know what he wanted to ask, and that's why I need information from you. Since you were his friend, since you wept, it may be assumed that you want the man who killed him exposed and punished. Yes?"

"Of course I do. Have you—do you know who killed him?"

"No. I'm going to find out. I want to tell you something in confidence and ask you some questions. You are to tell no one—*no one*. Can you keep it to yourself?"

"Yes, sir."

"Not many people are sure of themselves. Are you?"

"I'm sure I can keep a secret. I'm sure I can keep this kind of a secret."

"Good. Pierre told Mr. Goodwin that a man was going to kill him, but that's all he told him. Had he told you?"

"That a man was going to kill him? No, sir."

"Had he spoken of any threat, any danger impending?"

"No, sir."

"Had he mentioned any recent event, anything done or said by some-body, that might have suggested a possibility of danger?"

"No, sir."

"But you have seen him and spoken with him recently? Yesterday?"

"Of course. I'm in the kitchen, and he's in front, but we usually eat lunch together in the kitchen. We did yesterday. I didn't see him Sunday; of course, we're not here Sunday."

"When did you hear — learn of his death?"

"The radio this morning. The eight-o'clock news."

"Only five hours ago. You were shocked, and there hasn't been much time. You may recall something he said."

"I don't think I will, Mr. Wolfe. If you mean something about danger, about someone might kill him, I'm sure I won't."

"You can't be sure now. Memory plays tricks. This next question is important. He told Mr. Goodwin a man was going to kill him, so something had happened that put him in fear of his life. When? Just last evening? It would help to know when, so this is important. What was he like yesterday at lunch? Was he completely normal? Was there anything unusual about his mood, his behavior?"

"Yes, sir, there was. I was remembering that when you asked if he said anything about danger. He didn't seem to hear things I said and he didn't talk as much. When I asked him if he would rather eat alone he said he was sorry, that he had got orders mixed at lunch and served people wrong. I thought that explained it. Pierre was a very proud man. He thought a waiter should never make a mistake, and he thought he never did. I don't know, maybe he didn't. You can ask Felix. Pierre often mentioned that when you came you always liked to have him. He was proud of his work."

"Had he actually done that? Got orders mixed?"

"I don't know, but he wouldn't have said that if he hadn't. You can ask Felix."

"Did he mention it again later?"

"No, sir. Of course I didn't."

"Had he been like that Saturday? Distraught?"

"I don't —"Philip frowned. "No, sir, he hadn't."

"I suggest that when opportunity offers you sit and close your eyes and try to recall everything he said yesterday. If you do that, make a real effort, you may surprise yourself. People frequently do. Will you do that?"

"Yes, sir, but not here. I couldn't, here. I will later."

"And tell me or Mr. Goodwin."

"Yes, sir."

"Good. We'll hope to hear from you." Wolfe cocked his head. "Now. Another important question. If he was killed by someone who works here, who was it? Who might have had reason to want him dead? Who feared him or hated him or might have profited by his death?"

Philip was shaking his head. "Nobody. Nobody here. Nobody anywhere."

"Pfui. You can't know that. Obviously you can't, since someone killed him."

He was still shaking his head. "No, sir. I mean, yes, sir. Of course. But I can't believe it. That's what I thought when I heard it — who could have killed him? Why would anybody kill Pierre? He never hurt anybody, he wouldn't. Nobody hated him. Nobody was afraid of him. He was a fine man, an honest man. He wasn't perfect, he had that one fault, he bet too much on horse races, but he knew he did and he tried to stop. He didn't want to talk about it, but sometimes he did. I was his best friend, but he never tried to borrow from me."

"Did he borrow from anyone?"

"I don't think so. I don't think he would. I'm sure he didn't from anybody here. If he had, there would have been talk. You can ask Felix."

Apparently the idea was that Felix knew everything.

"Did he bet large amounts?"

"I don't really know. He didn't like to talk about it. Once he told me he won two hundred and thirty dollars, and another time a hundred and something. I forget exactly, but he never spoke about losing."

"How did he bet? Bookmakers?"

"I think he used to, but I'm not sure. Then OTB. He told me when he started at OTB."

"OTB?"

"Yes, sir. Off-Track Betting."

Wolfe looked at me. I nodded. The things he doesn't know, and he reads newspapers. He went back to Philip. "Of course you saw him elsewhere, not only here. Have you ever been in his home?"

"Yes, sir. Many times. His apartment on West Fifty-fourth Street."

"With his wife?"

"She died eight years ago. With his daughter and his father. His father had a little bistro in Paris, but he sold it and came over to live with Pierre when he was seventy years old. He's nearly eighty now."

Wolfe closed his eyes, opened them, looked at me and then at the wall, but there was no clock. He got the tips of his vest between thumb and finger, both hands, and pulled down. He didn't know he did that, and I never mentioned it. It was a sign that his insides had decided that it was time to eat. He looked at me. "Questions? About betting?"

"Not about the betting. One question." I looked at Philip. "The number on Fifty-fourth Street?"

He nodded. "Three-eighteen. Between Ninth Avenue and Tenth."

"There will probably be more questions," Wolfe said, "but they can wait. You have been helpful, Philip, and I am obliged. You will be here for dinner?"

"Yes, sir, of course. Until ten o'clock."

"Mr. Goodwin may come. Felix knows about lunch for us. Please tell him we are ready."

"Yes, sir." Philip was up. "You will tell me what you find out." He looked at me and back at Wolfe. "I want to know. I want to know everything about it."

Well, well. You might have thought he was Inspector Cramer. Wolfe merely said, "So do I. Tell Felix to send our lunch." And Philip turned and walked out without saying yes, sir, and I said, "The question is, was it you or me? He probably thinks me."

Whenever he eats at Rusterman's, Wolfe has a problem. There's a conflict. On the one hand, Fritz is the best cook in the world, and on the other hand, loyalty to the memory of Marko Vukcic won't admit that there is anything wrong with anything served at that restaurant. So he passed the buck to me. When about a third of his portion of the baked scallops was down, he looked at me and said, "Well?"

"It'll do," I said. "Maybe a little too much nutmeg, of course, that's a matter of taste, and I suspect the lemon juice came out of a bottle. The fritters were probably perfect, but they came in piles and Fritz brings them just three at a time, two to you and one to me. That can't be helped."

"I shouldn't have asked you," he said. "Flummery. Your palate is incapable of judging the lemon juice in a cooked dish."

Of course he was under a strain. Business is never to be mentioned at the table, but since there was no client and no prospect of a fee, this was all in the family and therefore wasn't business, and it was certainly on his mind. Also the waiter wasn't Pierre, whom he would never have again. He was some kind of Hungarian or Pole named Ernest, and he was inclined to tilt things. However, he ate, including the almond parfait, which I had suggested, and had a second cup of coffee. As for conversation, that was no problem. Watergate. He probably knew more about every angle of Watergate than any dozen of his fellow citizens, for instance the first names of Haldeman's grandparents.

He had intended to have another talk with Felix, but as we pushed our chairs back and rose he said, "Can you have the car brought to the side entrance?"

"Now?"

"Yes. We're going to see Pierre's father."

I stared at him. "'We'?"

"Yes. If you brought him to the office we would be interrupted. Since Mr. Cramer and the District Attorney have been unable to find us, there may already be a warrant."

"I could bring him here."

"At nearly eighty, he may not be able to walk. Also the daughter may be there."

"Parking in the fifties is impossible. There may be three or four flights and no elevator."

"We'll see. Can it be brought to the side entrance?"

I said of course and got his coat and hat. It certainly was all in the family. For a client, no matter how urgent or how big a fee, it had never come to this and never would. He took the elevator in the rear and I took the one in front, since I had to tell Otto where to send the car.

The West Fifties are a mixture of everything from the "21" Club to grimy walkups and warehouses, but I knew that block on Fifty-fourth was mostly old brownstones, and there was a parking lot near Tenth Avenue. When we were in and rolling, I suggested going to the garage and leaving the Heron, which Wolfe owns and I drive, and taking a taxi, but he thinks a moving vehicle with anyone but me at the wheel is even a bigger risk and vetoed it. So I crossed to Tenth Avenue and then uptown, and there was space at the parking lot. Only one long block to walk.

Number 318 wasn't too bad. Some of those brownstones had been done over inside, and that one even had wooden paneling in the vestibule, and a house phone. I pushed the fourth button up, which was tagged Ducos, put the receiver to my ear, and in a minute, a female voice said, "Who ees eet?" If it was Pierre's daughter, I thought she should have better manners, but probably she had been given a busy day by a string of city employees and journalists. It was ten minutes past three.

"Nero Wolfe," I told her. "W-O-L-F-E. To see Mr. Ducos. He will probably know the name. And Goodwin, Archie Goodwin. We knew Pierre for years."

"*Parlez-vous français?*" she said.

I knew that much, barely. "Mr. Wolfe does," I said. "Hold it." I turned. "She said parly voo fransay. Here." He took the receiver, and I moved to make room. He didn't have to stoop quite as much as me to get his mouth at the right level. Since what he said was for me only noise, I spent the couple of minutes enjoying the idea of a homicide dick pushing that button and hearing parly voo fransay, and hoping it was Lieutenant Rowcliff. Also a couple of journalists I had met, especially Bill Wengert of the *Times*. When Wolfe hung up the receiver, I put a hand on the inside door and, when the click sounded, pushed it open. And there was a do-it-yourself elevator with the door standing open.

If you speak French and would prefer to have a verbatim report of Wolfe's conversation with Léon Ducos, Pierre's father, I'm sorry I can't deliver. All I got was an idea of how it was going from their tones and looks. I'll report on what I saw. First, at the door of the apartment it wasn't Pierre's daughter. She had said good-by to fifty and maybe even sixty. She was short and dumpy, with a round face and a double chin, and she sported a little white apron, and a little white cap thing on top of her gray hair. Probably she spoke English, at least some, but she didn't look it. She took Wolfe's coat and hat and ushered us to the front room. Ducos was there in a wheelchair by a window. The best way to describe him is just to say that he was shriveled but still tough. He probably weighed thirty pounds less than he had at fifty, but what was left of him was intact, and when I took his offered hand I felt his grip. During the hour and twenty minutes we were there he didn't say a word that I understood. Probably he spoke no English at all, and that was why she had asked if I spoke French.

In twenty minutes, even less, their tone and manner had made it plain that no blood would be shed, and I left my chair, looked around, and crossed to a cabinet with a glass door and shelves in the far corner. Most of the shelves had things like little ivory and china figures and sea shell and a wooden apple, but on one there was a collection of inscribed trophies, silver cups and a medal that might have been gold, and a couple of ribbons. The only word on them that I knew was a name. Léon Ducos. Evidently his bistro had done something that people liked. I sent my eyes around, detecting. You do that in the home of a man who has just been murdered, and, as usual, nothing suggested anything. A framed photograph on a table was probably of Pierre's mother.

The white apron appeared at a door nearby and went and said something to Ducos, and he shook his head, and as she was leaving I asked if I could use the bathroom. She showed me, down the hall, and I went, though I really had nothing much to pass but the time, and on the way back there was an open door and I entered. A good detective doesn't have to be invited. There had been no signs anywhere of a daughter, but that room was full of them. It was here. Everything in it said so, and one of the items tagged her good—the contents of a bookcase over by the wall. There were some novels and nonfiction, some of whose titles I recognized, hard covers, and some paperbacks with French titles, but the interesting shelf was the middle one. There were books by Betty Friedan and Kate Millett and four or five more I had heard of, and three by Simone de Beauvoir in French. Of course one or two of them might be on anybody's shelf, but not a whole library. I took one of them out for a look, and her name, Lucile Ducos, was on the title page, and a second one also, and was reaching for another when a voice came from behind.

"What are you doing?"

The white apron. "Nothing much," I said. "I couldn't join in or even understand them and saw these books as I was passing. Are they yours?"

"No. She wouldn't want a man in here, and she wouldn't want a man handling her books." I won't try to spell her accent.

"I'm sorry. Don't tell her, but of course there'll be fingerprints. I didn't touch anything else."

"Did you say your name's Archie Goodwin?"

"I did. It is."

"I knew about you from him. And the radio today. You're a detective. And a policeman wanted to know if you had been here. He told me to call a number if you came."

"I'll bet he did. Are you going to?"

"I don't know, I'll ask Muhsieuw Ducos." I can't spell Muhsieuw the way she said it.

Evidently she wasn't going to leave me there, so I moved, on past her at the door and back to the front room. They were still jabbering, and I went and stood at another window, looking out at the traffic.

It was a quarter past four when we were back in the Heron and rolling out of the parking lot. To Ninth Avenue and downtown. All Wolfe had said was that Ducos had told him something and we would go home and discuss it. He doesn't talk when he's walking or in the car. At the garage Tom said a dick had come a little before noon to see if the car was there—of course it had been—and another one had come around four o'clock and asked if he knew where I had gone with it. From there around the corner and a half a block on Thirty-fifth Street to the brownstone, more exercise for Wolfe, and I knew why. If I had driven him home and then taken the car to the garage, somebody might be camped on the stoop.

There wasn't. We mounted the seven steps, and I pushed the button and Fritz came, saw us through the one-way glass panel, slid the chain bolt, and opened the door, and we entered. As I hung Wolfe's coat up he asked Fritz, "Did that man come?"

"Yes, sir. Two of them. They're up there now. Several men came, five of them not counting those two. The phone has rung nine times. Since you weren't sure about dinner, I didn't stuff the capon, so it may be a little late. It's nearly five o'clock."

"It could have been later. Please bring beer. Milk, Archie?"

I said no, make it gin and tonic, and we went to the office. The mail was there under a paperweight on his desk, but after he got his bulk properly distributed in the chair that had been made to order for it, he shoved the mail aside, leaned back, and shut his eyes. I expected, I may even have hoped, to see his lips start moving in and out, but they didn't. He just sat. After four minutes of it, maybe five, I said, "I don't want to interrupt, but you might like to know that the daughter, whose name is Lucile, is a Women's Libber. Not just one of the herd, a real one. She has —"

His eyes had opened. "I was resting. And you know I will not tolerate that locution."

"All right, Liberationist. She has three books by Simone de Beauvoir, who you have admitted can write, in French, and a shelf full of others I have heard of, some of which you have started but didn't finish. Also she wouldn't want a man in her room. I'm talking because someone should say something, and apparently you don't want to.

Fritz came with the tray. There's something I don't like about my taking something from a tray held by Fritz, and as he reached Wolfe's desk I went and got my gin and tonic. Wolfe opened the drawer to get the solid gold opener. When he had poured, he spoke.

"Miss Ducos feeds facts to a computer at New York University. She usually gets home about half past five. You will see her."

"She may not speak to men." I settled back in my chair. He was going to talk.

He grunted. "She will about her father. She was attached to him but didn't want to be. Mr. Ducos is perceptive and articulate — that is, he was with me. Pierre told you that I am the greatest detective in the world. He told his father that I am the greatest gourmet in the world. His father told me that was why he had told the police nothing, and wouldn't, but he would tell me. He said that only after he learned that I speak French well. Of course that's absurd, but he doesn't know it. Most of what he told me about his son was irrelevant to our purpose, and I won't report it. Or I will, I should, if you insist."

That sounded better than it actually was. Yes, I usually reported in full to him, frequently verbatim, but that wasn't why he was offering to. It was just that if and when he spotted the man who had killed Pierre before I did, he didn't want me to say sure, his father spoke French.

But I kept the grin inside. "Maybe later," I said. "It can wait. Did he tell you anything relevant?"

"He may have. He knew about Pierre's habit of betting horse races, and they frequently discussed it. He said that Pierre never asked him for money on account of it, but that was a lie. That was one of the few points, very few, about which he was not candid. Also it is one of the points on which you may want a full report later. I mention it now only because it was in a discussion about the betting that Pierre told him about a man giving him a hundred dollars. Last Wednesday morning, six days ago, Pierre told him that one day the preceding week — Mr. Ducos thinks it was Friday but isn't sure — there had been a slip of paper left on a tray with the money by a customer, and later when he went to return it the customer had gone. And the day before, Tuesday — the day before the talk with his father — a man had given him a hundred dollars for the slip of paper."

Wolfe turned a palm up. "That's all. But a hundred dollars for a slip of paper? Even with the soaring inflation, that seems extravagant. And another point. Was the man who gave Pierre that hundred dollars the man who had left the slip of paper on the tray? Of course I tried to get the exact words used by Pierre in the talk with his father, and perhaps I did — the important ones. Mr. Ducos is certain that he did not use the word *rendre*. Return. Give back. If he had been returning the slip to the man who had left it on the tray, a hundred dollars could have been merely exuberant gratitude, but if it was not the same man — I don't need to descant on that."

I nodded. "A dozen possibles. And if it was the same man, why did Pierre wait four days to return it? Or why didn't he just give it to Felix and ask him to mail it to him? I like it. Is that the crop?"

"Yes. Of course other things that Mr. Ducos told me might possibly repay inquiry, but this was much the most likely." He turned his head to look at the clock. "Nearly two hours to dinner. If you go now?"

"I doubt it. Felix, I suppose, and maybe some of the waiters, but Philip is by far the best bet, and you know how it is in the kitchen at this hour, especially for a sauce man. Also I had four hours' sleep and I'm not —"

The doorbell. I went to the hall for a look, stepped back in, and said, "Cramer."

He made a noise. "How the devil — was he across the street?"

"No, but someone was and phoned. Naturally."

"You'll have to stay."

He rarely uses breath to say things that are obvious, but of course that was. I went and slid the bolt and swung the door open.

Inspector Cramer of Homicide South has been known to call me Archie. He has also been known to pretend he doesn't remember my name, and that time maybe he really didn't. He marched on by, to the office door and in, and when I got there he was saying, ". . . and every goddam minute from the time you woke up until now. You *and* Goodwin. And you'll sign it."

Wolfe was shaking his head, tilted back. "Pfui," he said.

"Don't phooey me! Of all the —"

"*Shut up!*"

Cramer gawked. He had heard Wolfe tell a hundred people to shut up, and I had heard him tell a thousand, including me, but never Cramer. He didn't believe it.

"I don't invite you to sit," Wolfe said, "or to remove your coat and hat, because I am going to tell you nothing. No, I retract that. I do tell you that I know nothing about the death of Pierre Ducos except what Mr. Goodwin has told me, and he has told Mr. Stebbins everything he told me. Beyond that I shall tell you absolutely nothing. Of course I had to permit examination of that room by qualified men, and I left instructions to admit them. They are still up there. If we are taken in custody as material witnesses, by either you or the District Attorney, we'll stand mute. Released on bail, we'll stand mute. I am going to learn who killed that man in my house. I doubt if you can and I hope you don't, except from me when I'm ready to tell you."

Wolfe aimed a straight finger at him, up at his face, another first. "If I sound uncivil, I do not apologize. I am in a rage and out of control. Whether you have warrants or not, arrest us now and take us; let's get that over with. I have a job to do." He extended his arms, stretched out, the wrists together for handcuffs. Beautiful. I would have loved to do it too, but that would have been piling it on.

If Cramer had had cuffs in his pocket he might actually have used them, judging from the look on his big red face. Knowing Wolfe as well as he did, what *could* he do? His mouth opened and closed again. He looked at me and back at Wolfe. "Out of control," he growled. "Balls. *You* out of control. I know one thing. I know—"

"Oh! We didn't know you were here, Inspector."

Two men were there at the door, a tall rangy one and a broad bulky one with only one arm. Of course I should have heard them; my ears must have been more eager to hear what Cramer would say than I realized. When he turned to face them they saluted, but he didn't return it.

"It took you long enough," he said.

"Yes, sir. It was a job. We didn't know you were here. We—"

"I came to see why it took so damn long. Did you— No. You can tell me in the car." He was moving. They sidestepped to let him by and followed him out. I stayed put. Experts wouldn't need help opening a door. When the sound came of the front door opening and closing, I went for a look down the hall, came back, and said, "What a break for him. He *couldn't* have left without us. He ought to move them up a peg. Of course it was a break for us too, with you out of control."

"Grrrh," he said. "Sit down."

4

AT ten o'clock that evening I was standing by a reading lamp, flipping through the pages of a book entitled *Les Sauces du Monde*. Going through a room trying to find something doesn't take long if you're after a diamond necklace or an elephant tusk or a gun. But if it's a twenty-dollar bill, anything at all that could be between the pages of a book without bulging it, that takes time if there are books in the room. For the Library of Congress, I would say 2748 years.

Most of the forty-some books on shelves in Pierre Ducos's room were about cooking. What I was after didn't have to be a piece of paper, but that was the most likely, since I wanted something, anything, that could lead to either the man who had left the slip of paper on the tray or the one who had paid a C for it. One item that had seemed possible was a notebook I found in a drawer that had lists of names on several pages, but Lucile Ducos had told me they were the names of men who gave big tips. She said Pierre hadn't been good at remembering names and he had written them down for twenty years.

I hadn't been in her room. When, arriving, I had told her grandfather, with her as interpreter, that I wanted to take a look in Pierre's room, and why, I had got the impression that she didn't like it, but he had got emphatic and it took. I had also got the impression that she was staying with me to see if I took anything and if so what. Getting impressions from her wasn't difficult, beginning with the impression that it didn't matter whether I had two legs or four legs, or whether I wore my face in front or behind. But *she* mattered — I mean to her. Her face, which wasn't bad at all, was well cared for, also her nice brown hair, and the cut and hang of her light-brown dress were just right. It was hard to believe she went to all that trouble just for the mirror.

She was seated in an easy chair the other side of the reading lamp. When I did the last book and put it back on the shelf, I turned to her and said, "I suppose you're right, if he put something somewhere it would be in this room. Have you remembered anything he said?

"No"

"Have you tried to?"

"I told you I knew I couldn't because he hadn't said anything."

Her voice had a little too much nose. I looked down at her. Up to a few inches above her knees, she had good legs. A pity. I decided to try another approach. "You know, Miss Ducos," I said, "I have tried to be polite and sympathetic. I really have. But I wonder why you don't give a damn who killed your father. That doesn't seem very — well, natural."

She nodded. "You would. You think I should be weeping and wailing or maybe doing a Medea. Bullshit. I was a good daughter, good enough. Of course I give a damn who killed him, but I don't think you're going to find out the way you're going at it, all this about a man who gave him some money for a piece of paper. Or if you do, it won't be by nagging me to remember something that didn't happen."

"What would you suggest? How would you do it?"

"I don't know. I'm not a great detective like Nero Wolfe. But you say what killed him was a bomb put in his pocket by someone. Who put it there? I'd find out where he was yesterday and who he saw. That would be the first thing I would do."

I nodded. "Sure. And have your toes tramped on by a few dozen homicide experts who are doing just that. If he can be tagged that way, they'll get him without any help from Nero Wolfe. Of course one person your father saw yesterday was you. I haven't asked you about your relations with him, and I'm not going to, because the cops certainly have. And they're asking around about you. You were at the District Attorney's office five hours, you said, so you know how that is. They know all about people killing their fathers. Also, of course they asked you if there was anyone who might have wanted him dead. What did you say?"

"I said no."

"But someone did want him dead."

She sneered. I admit I didn't like her, but I'm not being unfair. She sneered. "I knew you'd say that," she said. "They did too, and it's not only obvious, it's dumb. Somebody might have thought his coat belonged to someone else."

"Then you think it was just a mistake?"

"I didn't say I *think* it. I said it might have been."

"Didn't your grandfather tell you what Nero Wolfe told him your father told me?"

"No. He never tells me anything. He thinks women haven't any brains. You probably do too."

I wanted to say that I merely thought *some* women were a little shy on brains, present company not excepted, but I skipped it. I said, "Your father told me that a man was going to kill him, so it wasn't a mistake. Also it wasn't you, since you're not a man. So let's get back. Evidently your father didn't agree with your grandfather about women, because your grandfather told Mr. Wolfe that your father often asked your advice about things. That's why I think he might have told you something about a man who gave him a hundred dollars for a slip of paper."

"He never asked my *advice*. He just wanted to see what I would say."

I gave up. I wanted to ask her what the difference was between asking her advice and wanting to see what she would say, just to see what she would say, but we were expecting company at the office at eleven o'clock or soon after and I should be there. So I gave up on her, and I had finished the job on the room, since it wasn't likely that he had pried up a floorboard or taken the back off a picture frame. I will concede that she had fairly good manners. She went to the hall with me and opened the door and told me good night. Apparently Mr. Ducos and the white apron had both gone to bed.

It was ten after eleven when I mounted the stoop of the old brownstone, found the bolt wasn't on so I didn't need help to get in, and went to the office. Wolfe would be deep in either a book or a crossword puzzle, but he wasn't. In one of my desk drawers, I keep street maps of all five New York boroughs, and he had them, with Manhattan spread out covering his desk blotter and then some. To my knowledge it was the first time he had ever given it a look. It might be supposed that I wondered what he was after, but I didn't because I learned long ago that wondering what a genius was after was a waste of time. If it really meant anything, which I doubted, he would tell me when he felt like it. As I swiveled my chair and sat to face him, he started folding it up, his fingers quick and nimble and precise, as they always were. Of course they had a lot of practice up in the plant rooms, from nine to eleven mornings and two to four afternoons, but that day he hadn't been there at all.

As he folded he spoke. "I was calculating distances — the restaurant, and Pierre's home, and here. He arrived here at ten minutes to one. Where had he been? Where had his coat been?"

"I'll have to apologize," I said, "to his daughter. I told her that if that kind of detecting will do it they won't need your help. Does it look that bad?"

"No. As you know, I prefer not to read when I may be interrupted at any moment. What did she tell you?"

"Nothing. It's possible she has nothing to tell, but I don't believe it. She sat for an hour with her eye on me while I went over Pierre's room, to make sure I didn't pinch a pair of socks. She's an anomaly — I *think* that's the word I want. Or make — "

"It isn't. A person can't be an anomaly."

"All right, she's a phony. A woman who has all those books with her name in them wants men to stop making women sex symbols, and if she really wants them to stop she wouldn't keep her skin like that, and her hair, and blow her hard-earned pay on a dress that sets her off. Of course she can't help her legs. She's a phony. Since Pierre said it was a man, I admit she probably didn't put the bomb in his pocket, but I would buy it that he told her about the slip of paper and showed it to her, and she knows who killed him and is going to put the squeeze on him, or try to. And she'll get killed and we'll have that too. I suggest that we put a tail on her. If you have other plans for me, get Fred or Orrie, or maybe even Saul. Do you want it verbatim?"

"Do I need it?"

"No."

"Then just the substance."

I crossed my legs. "First she interpreted for me with her grandfather while I asked permission to take a look at Pierre's room, and the other points you wanted covered. Of course she could have hashed that—with an interpreter you never know for sure. Then she went with me—"

The doorbell rang and I got up and went. We had expected Philip around eleven and Felix a little later, but they were both there. And from the look on their faces, they weren't speaking. They spoke to me as I let them in and took their coats, but apparently not to each other. In the office, when they were seated after being greeted by Wolfe's most exaggerated nod, a full half-inch—of course Felix in the red leather chair near the end of Wolfe's desk—Philip sat stiff with no mouth showing on his dark-skinned square face because his lips were pressed so tight, and Felix didn't really sit, he just got his rump on the edge of the chair and blurted, "I kept Philip there, Mr. Wolfe, because he lied to me. As you know, I—"

"If you please." Of course Felix had often heard that tone when Wolfe had been his boss as trustee. "You're upset. I suppose you've had a hard day; but so have I. I'll have beer. Brandy for you?"

"No, sir. Nothing."

"Philip?"

Philip shook his head. I detoured around him on my way to the kitchen. When I came back, Felix was sitting, not perching, and was talking: ". . . eight of them. They kept coming and going all afternoon and evening. I got their names. It was the worst day we have ever had since the day Mr. Vukcic died. The first two came just at the end of lunch, three o'clock, and it never stopped, right on through dinner. It was terrible. Everybody, even the dishwasher. The main thing with them was the dump room—you know, Mr. Vukcic called it that, so we do—the room in the back where the men leave their things. They took everybody there, one at a time, and asked about Pierre's coat. What is it about Pierre's coat?"

"You'll have to ask them." The foam in the glass had reached the right level, and Wolfe picked it up and drank. "You have me to thank for the day they gave you. Because he was killed here, in my house. But for that it would be mere routine for them. Did they arrest anyone?"

"No, sir. I thought one of them was going to arrest me. He said he knew there was something special between you and Pierre, and Mr. Goodwin too, and he said I must know about it. He told me to get my coat and hat, but then he changed his mind. He was the same with—"

"His name was Rowcliff."

"Yes, sir." Felix nodded. "It may be true that you know everything. Mr. Vukcic told me that you thought you did. That man was the same with Philip because I told him that he was Pierre's best friend." He looked at Philip, not as a friend, and then went back to Wolfe. "Philip may have lied to him, I don't know. I know he lied to me. You remember what Mr. Vukcic told Noel that time when he fired him. He told him it wasn't because he stole a goose, anyone might steal a goose, it was because he lied about it. He said he could keep a good restaurant even if some of them stole things sometimes, but not if anybody lied to him, because he had to know what happened. I always remember that and I will not permit them to lie to me, and they know it. If I don't know what happened, it won't be a good restaurant. So when the last one left, I took Philip upstairs and told him I had to know everything about Pierre that he knew, and he lied. I have learned to tell when one of them is lying. I'm not as good at it as Mr. Vukcic was, but I can nearly always tell. Look at him."

We looked. Philip looked back at Felix and unglued his mouth to say, "I told you I was lying. I admitted it."

"You did not. That's another lie."

Philip looked at Wolfe. "I told him I was leaving something out because I couldn't remember. Isn't that admitting it, Mr. Wolfe?"

"It's a nice point," Wolfe said. "It deserves discussion, but I think not here and now. You were leaving out something that Pierre had done or said?"

"Yes, sir. I admitted I couldn't remember it."

Wolfe grunted. "This afternoon I asked you to try to recall everything he said yesterday, and you said you would but you couldn't do it at the restaurant. Now you admit there was something you can't remember?"

"It wasn't that, Mr. Wolfe. It wasn't what he said yesterday."

"Nonsense. A rigmarole. You're wriggling. Do you want me to form the conjecture that you killed him? Do you or don't you want the murderer exposed and punished? Do you or don't you know something that might help to identify him? You said you wept when you learned he was dead. Did you indeed?"

Philip's mouth was closed, clamped again. His eyes closed. He shook his head several times, slow. He opened his eyes, turned his head to look at Felix, turned it back and on around to look at me, and back again to Wolfe, and spoke. "I want to talk to you alone, Mr. Wolfe."

Wolfe turned to Felix. "The front room, Felix. As you know, it's soundproofed."

"But I want —"

"Confound it, it's past midnight. I'll tell you later, or I won't. Certainly *he* won't. I'm spent, and so are you."

I got up and crossed to open the door to the front room, and Felix came. I stuck my head in to see that the door to the hall was closed, shut that one, and returned to my desk. As I sat, Philip said, "I said alone, Mr. Wolfe. Just you."

"No. If Mr. Goodwin leaves and you tell me anything that suggests action, I'll have the bother of repeating to him."

"Then I must — you must both promise not to tell Felix. Pierre was a proud man, Mr. Wolfe, I told you that. He was proud of his work and he didn't want to be just a good waiter, he wanted to be the *best* waiter. He wanted Mr. Vukcic to think he was the best waiter in the best restaurant in the world, and then he wanted Felix to think that. Maybe he does think that, and that's why you must promise not to tell him. He must not know that Pierre did something that no good waiter would ever do."

"We can't promise not to tell him. We can only promise not to tell him unless we must, unless it becomes impossible to find the murderer and expose him without telling Felix. I can promise that, and do. Archie?"

"Yes, sir," I said firmly. "I promise that. Cross my heart and hope to die. That's American, Philip, you may not know it. It means I would rather die than tell him."

"You have already told us," Wolfe said, "that he told you about getting orders mixed and serving them wrong, so that can't be it."

"No, sir. That was just yesterday. It was something much worse. Something he told me last week, Monday, a week ago yesterday. He told me a man had left a piece of paper on the tray with the money, and he had kept it, a piece of paper with something written on it. He told me he had kept it because the man had gone when he went to return it, and then he didn't give it to Felix to send it to him because what was written on it was a man's name and address and he knew the name and he wondered about it. He said he still had it, the piece of paper. So after you talked to me today, after you told me he said a man was going to kill him, I wondered if it could have been on account of that. I thought it might even have been the man whose name was on the paper. I knew it couldn't have been the man who had left the paper on the tray, because he was dead."

"Dead?"

"Yes, sir."

"How did you know he was dead?"

"It had been on the radio and in the paper. Pierre had told me it was Mr. Bassett who left the paper on the tray. We all knew about Mr. Bassett because he always paid in cash and he was a big tipper. Very big. Once he gave Felix a five-hundred-dollar bill."

I suppose I must have heard that, since I just wrote it, but if I was listening it was only with one ear. Millions of people knew about Harvey H. Bassett, president of NATELEC, National Electronics Industries, not because he was a big tipper but because he had been murdered just four days ago, last Friday night.

Wolfe hadn't batted an eye, but he cleared his throat and swallowed. "Yes," he said, "it certainly couldn't have been Mr. Bassett. But the man whose name was on the slip of paper — what *was* his name? Of course Pierre showed it to you."

"No, sir, he didn't"

"At least he told you, he must have. You said he knew the name and wondered about it. So unquestionably he told you what it was. And you will tell me."

"No, sir. I can't. I don't know."

Wolfe's head turned to me. "Go and tell Felix he may as well leave. Tell him we may be engaged with Philip all night."

I left my chair, but so did Philip. "No, you won't," he said, and he meant it. "I'm going home. This has been the worst day of my whole life, and I'm fifty-four years old. First Pierre dead, and then all day knowing I ought to tell this, first Felix and then you and then the police, and wondering if Archie Goodwin killed him. Now I'm thinking maybe I shouldn't have told you, maybe I should have told the police, but then I think how you were with Mr. Vukcic and when he died. And I know how he was about you. But

I've told you everything — *everything*. I can't tell you any more." He headed for the door.

I looked at Wolfe, but he shook his head, so I merely went to the hall and the front, no hurry. Probably Philip wouldn't let me help him on with his coat — but he did. No good nights. I opened the door, closed it after him, returned to the office, and asked Wolfe, "Do you want Felix?"

"No." He was on his feet. "Of course he can tell us about Bassett, but I'm played out, and so are you. One question: Does Philip know the name on that paper?"

"One will get you ten, no. He told me to my face that I may be a murderer and called me Archie Goodwin. He was unloading."

"Confound it. Tell Felix he'll hear from me tomorrow. Today. Good night." He moved.

5

THE dinner paid for by Harvey H. Bassett in an upstairs room at Ruster-man's Friday evening, October 18, had been stag. The guests:

Albert O. Judd, lawyer
Francis Ackerman, lawyer
Roman Vilar, Vilar Associates, industrial security
Ernest Urquhart, lobbyist
Willard K. Hahn, banker
Benjamin Igoe, electronics engineer

Putting that here, I'm way ahead of myself and of you, but I don't like making lists and I wanted to get it down. Also, when I typed it that Wednesday to put on Wolfe's desk, I looked it over to decide if one of them was a murderer and if so which one, and you may want to play that game too. Not that it had to be one of them. The fact that they had been present when Bassett left the slip of paper among the bills on the tray didn't make them any better candidates than anyone else for who could have been with him in a stolen automobile on West Ninety-third Street around midnight a week later with a gun in his hand, but we had to start somewhere, and at least they had known him. Possibly one of them had given him the slip of paper.

I got to bed Tuesday night at twenty past one, almost exactly twenty-four hours after the bomb had interrupted me before I got my pants off. It was a good bet that I would be interrupted before I got them on again Wednesday morning by an invitation from the DA's office, but I wasn't, so I got my full eight hours, and I needed them, and it was ten minutes to ten when I entered the kitchen, went to the refrigerator for orange juice, told Fritz good morning, and asked if Wolfe had had breakfast, and Fritz said yes, at a quarter past eight as usual.

"Was he dressed?"

"Of course."

"*Not* of course. He was played out, he said so himself. He went up?"

"Of course."

"All right, have it your way. Any word for me?"

"No. I'm played out too, Archie, all day the phone ringing and people coming, and I didn't know where he was."

I went to the little table and sat and reached to the rack for the *Times*. It had made the front page, a two-column lead toward the bottom and continued on page 19, where there were pictures of both of us. Of course I was honored because I had found the body. Also of course I read every word, some of it twice, but none of it was news to me; and my mind kept sliding off. Why the hell hadn't he told Fritz to send me up? I was on my third sausage and second buckwheat cake when the phone rang, and I scowled at it as I reached. Again of course, the DA.

But it wasn't; it was Lon Cohen of the *Gazette*.

"Nero Wolfe's office, Arch—"

"Where in God's name were you all day yesterday, and why aren't you in jail?"

"Look, Lon, I—"

"Will you come here, or must I go there?"

"Right now, neither one, and quit interrupting. I admit I could tell you twenty-seven things that your readers have a right to know, but this is a free country and I want to stay free. The minute I can spill one bean I know where to find you. I'm expecting a call so I'm hanging up." I hung up.

I will never know whether there was something wrong with the buckwheat cakes or with me. If it was the cakes, Fritz *was* played out. I made myself eat the usual four to keep him from asking questions and finding out that he had left something out or put too much of something in.

In the office I pretended it was just another day—dusting, emptying the wastebaskets, changing the water in the vase, opening the mail, and so forth. Then I went to the shelf where we keep the *Times* and the *Gazette* for two weeks, got them for the last four days, and took them to my desk. Of course I had read the accounts of the murder of Harvey H. Bassett, but now it was more than just news. The body had been found in a parked Dodge Coronet on West Ninety-third Street near Riverside Drive late Friday night by a cop on his rounds. Only one bullet, a .38, which had entered at exactly the right spot to go through his pump and keep going, clear through. It had been found stuck in the right front door, so the trigger had been pulled by the driver of the car, unless Bassett had pulled it himself, but by Monday's *Times* that was out. It was murder.

I was on Tuesday's *Gazette* when the sound came of the elevator descending. My watch said 11:01. Right on schedule. I swiveled and as Wolfe entered said brightly, "Good morning. I'm having a look at the reports on Harvey H. Bassett. If you're interested, I'm through with the *Times*."

He put a raceme of orchids which I didn't bother to identify in the vase of his desk, and sat. "You're spleeny. You shouldn't be. After that night and yesterday, you might sleep until noon, and there was no urgency. As for Mr. Bassett, I keep my copies of the *Times* in my room for a month, as you know, and I took—"

The doorbell. I went to the hall for a look and stepped back in. "I don't think you've ever met him. Assistant District Attorney Coggin. Daniel F. Coggin. Friendly type with a knife up his sleeve. Handshaker."

"Bring him," he said, and reached for the pile of mail.

So when I ushered the member of the bar in after giving him as good a hand he gave and taking his coat and hat, Wolfe had a circular in one hand and an unfolded letter in the other, and it wouldn't have been polite to put him to the trouble of putting one of them down, so Coggin didn't. Evidently, though he hadn't met him, he knew about his kinks. He just said heartily, "I don't think I've ever had the pleasaure of meeting you, Mr. Wolfe, so I welcome this opportunity." He sat, in the red leather chair, and sent his eyes around. "Nice room. A *good* room. That's a beautiful rug."

"A gift from the Shah of Iran," Wolfe said.

Coggin must have known it was a barefaced lie, but he said, "I wish he'd give me one. Beautiful." He glanced at his wristwatch. "You're a busy man, and I'll be as brief as possible. The District Attorney is wondering why you and Mr. Goodwin were — well, couldn't be found yesterday, though that isn't how he put it — when you knew you were wanted and needed. And your telephone wasn't answered. Nor your doorbell."

"We had errands to do and did them. No one was here but Mr. Brenner, my cook, and when we are out he prefers not to answer bells."

Coggin smiled. "*He* prefers?"

Wolfe smiled back, but his smile shows only at one corner of his mouth, and it takes good eyes to see it. "Good cooks must be humored, Mr. Coggin."

"I wouldn't know, Mr. Wolfe. I haven't got a cook, can't afford it. Now. If you're wondering why I came instead of sending for you, we discussed it at the office. What you said to Inspector Cramer yesterday. Considering your record and your customary — uh — reactions. It was decided to have your license as a private investigator revoked at once, but I thought that was too drastic and suggested that upon reflection you might have realized that you had been — uh — impetuous. I have in my pocket warrants for your arrest, you and Mr. Goodwin, as material witnesses, but I don't *want* to serve them. I would rather not. I even came alone, I insisted on that. I can understand, I *do* understand, why you reacted as you did to Inspector Cramer, but you and Goodwin can't withhold information regarding the murder of a man in your house — a man you had known for years and had talked with many times. I don't *want* you and Goodwin to lose your licenses. He can take shorthand and he can type. I want to leave here with signed statements."

When Wolfe is facing the red leather chair he has to turn his head a quarter-circle to face me. He turned. "Your notebook, Archie."

I opened a drawer and got it, and a pen. He leaned back, closed his eyes, and spoke.

"When Pierre Ducos died by violence in a room of my house at — The exact time, Archie?"

"One-twenty-four."

"One-twenty-four a.m. on October twenty-ninth, comma, nineteen seventy-four, comma, I knew nothing about him or any of his affairs except that he was an experienced and competent restaurant waiter. Period. Archie Goodwin also knew only that about him, comma, plus what he had learned in a brief conversation with him when he arrived at my house shortly before he died. Period. All of that conversation was given verbatim by Mr. Goodwin in a signed statement given by him to a police officer that night at my house. Period. Therefore all knowledge that could possibly be relevant to the death by violence of Pierre Ducos known to either Mr. Goodwin or me at the moment his body was discovered by Mr. Goodwin has been given to the police. Paragraph.

"Since that moment—dash—the moment that the body was discovered—dash—Mr. Goodwin and I have made various inquiries of various persons for the purpose of learning who was responsible for the death of Pierre Ducos in my house, comma, and we are going to continue such inquiries. Period. We have made them and shall make them not as licensed private investigators, comma, but as private citizens on whose private premises a capital crime has been committed. Period. We believe our right to make such an inquiry cannot be successfully challenged, comma, and if such a challenge is made we will resist it. Period. That right would not be affected by revocation of our licenses as investigators. Paragraph.

"Information obtained by us during our inquiry may be divulged by us, comma, or it may not, comma, either to the police or to the public. Period. The decision regarding disclosure will be solely at our discretion and will. Period. If the issue is raised by our responsibilities as private citizens it will of course be decided by the proper legal procedures. Period. If our licenses have not been revoked our responsibilities as private investigators will not be involved. Period. If they have been revoked those responsibilities will not exist. Paragraph.

"We will continue to cooperate with the police to the extent required by law—dash—for instance, comma, we will permit entry at any reasonable time to the room where the crime occurred. Period. We approve and applaud a vigorous effort by the police to find the culprit and will continue to do so. Period."

He opened his eyes and straightened up. "On my letterhead, single-spaced, wide margins, four carbons. All to be signed by me, and by you if you wish. Give the original to Mr. Coggin. Mail one carbon to Mr. Cramer. Take one to Mr. Cohen and offer it as an item for publication in the *Gazette* tomorrow. If he rejects it, make it a two-column display advertisement in ten-point. Take one to the *Times* and offer it, not as an advertisement. If Mr. Coggin interferes by serving his warrants and arresting us before you get it typed, on being taken into custody I will exercise my right to telephone a lawyer, dictate it to Mr. Parker's secretary, and tell him what to do."

He turned his head the quarter-circle. "If you wish to comment, Mr. Coggin, you'll have to raise your voice. Mr. Goodwin will not use a noiseless typewriter."

Coggin was smiling. "It's not up to your usual standard. A lousy cheap bluff."

"Then call it. I believe that's the idiom for the proper reaction to a cheap bluff." Wolfe turned a palm up. "Surely it's obvious; it was to Mr. Cramer. I do approve and applaud the effort by the police to do their duty under law, but in this case I hope they fail. I invite you to have a look at the room upstairs directly over my bedroom. A man was killed in it as I lay asleep. I intend to find the man who did it and bring him to account, with the help of

Mr. Goodwin, whose self-esteem is as wounded as my own. He took him to that room."

His fingers curled into the palm. "No. Not a bluff. I doubt if I am taking a serious risk, but if so, then I am. The constant petty behests of life permit few opportunities for major satisfactions, and when one is offered it should be seized. You know what I told Mr. Cramer we will do if we are charged and taken so there is no need to repeat it." His head turned. "Type it, Archie."

I swiveled and swung the machine around and got paper and carbons. Much of the room shows in the six-by-four mirror on the wall back of my desk, so I knew I wasn't missing anything while I hit the keys, because Coggin's mouth stayed shut. His eyes were aimed in my direction. The amount of copy was just right, wide-margined, for a nice neat page. I rolled it out, removed the carbon paper, and took it to Wolfe, and he signed all of them, including the one we would keep, and I signed under him without bothering to sit.

And when I handed the original to Coggin he said, "I'll take the carbons too. All of them."

"Sorry," I said, "I only work here and I like the job, so I follow instructions."

"Give them to him," Wolfe said. "You have the notebook."

I handed them over. He put the original with them, jiggled them on the little stand to even the edges, folded them, and stuck them in his inside breast pocket. He smiled at Wolfe. Of course the typing and signing had given him seven minutes to look at all angles. "Probably," he said, "you could name him right now and you only have to collect the pieces." He palmed the chair arms for leverage and got to his feet. "I hope there'll be other warrants, not for material witnesses, and I hope I have it and you get ten years with no parole." He turned and stepped, but halfway to the door he stopped and turned to say over his shoulder, "Don't come, Goodwin. You smell."

When the sound came of the front door closing, I crossed over for a look. He was out. I crossed back and said, "So you didn't give me an errand because you knew one of them would come. Wonderful."

He grunted. "I have told you a dozen times, sarcasm is the most futile of weapons. It doesn't cut, it merely bounces off. Why did he want the carbons?"

"Souvenirs. Autographs. Signed by both of us. Someday they'll be auctioned off at Sotheby's." I looked at my watch. "It's twenty minutes to noon. Things will be all set for lunch and the customers won't start coming until nearly one. Or have you a better place to start than Felix?"

"You know I haven't. We want everything he knows about Mr. Bassett and his guests that evening. Unless — you have slept on it, so I ask again, does Philip know what was on that slip of paper?"

"It's still no. As I said, he was unloading. He thinks the name on it might have been Archie Goodwin. Pierre told him he wondered about it. All right, I probably won't be here for lunch."

"A moment. One detail. If Felix supplies names, even one, and you get to him, it might serve to tell him that Pierre told you that he saw one of them hand Mr. Bassett a slip of paper. It *might*. Consider it."

"Yeah. And Pierre's dead."

I went to the hall and to the rack for my coat. No hat. The thermometer outside said 38, more like December than October, no sun, but I have rules too. No hat before Thanksgiving. Rain or snow is good for hair.

6

WITH Felix it was all negatives, and negatives are no good either to write or to read. Except for preferences and opinions about food and how it should be served, I knew more about Harvey M. Bassett than he did, since I had read the newspapers twice and he may not have read them at all. Television and radio, and his working day was a good twelve hours. On the big question, the names of the guests at the dinner on October 18, nearly two weeks ago, he was a complete blank. He had never seen any of them before or since. All he knew was that it had been stag. Evidently he thought better of me than Philip did; he said he had some fresh pompano up from the Gulf and wanted to feed me, but I declined with thanks.

It was 12:42 when I left by the front door and headed uptown. One of my more useless habits is timing all walks, though it may be helpful only about one time in a hundred. It took nine minutes to the *Gazette* building. Lon Cohen's room, two doors down the hall from the publisher's on the twentieth floor, barely had enough space for a big desk with three phones on it, one chair besides his, and shelves with a few books and a thousand newspapers. It was his lunch hour, so I expected to find him alone, and he was.

"I'll be damned," he said. "You still loose?"

"No." I sat. "I'm a fugitive. I came to bring you a new picture of me. The one you ran Sunday, my nose is crooked. I admit it's no treat, but it's not crooked."

"It should be, after Monday night. Damn it, Archie, I'm an hour behind. I'll get Landry, there's a room down the hall, and—"

"No. Not even what I had for breakfast. As I said on the phone, when I can spill one bean you'll get it." I rose. "Right now we could use a fact or two, but if you're an hour behind—" I was going.

"Sit down. All right, I'll be two hours behind. But I'm not going to starve." He took a healthy bite of a tuna-and-lettuce sandwich on whole wheat.

"Not an hour." I sat. "Maybe only three minutes if you can tell me the names of six men who ate dinner on Harvey H. Bassett at Rusterman's, Friday, October eighteenth."

"What?" He stopped chewing to stare. "Bassett? What has that got to do with a bomb killing a man in Nero Wolfe's house?"

"It's connected, but that's off the record. Right now everything's off the record. Repeat, *everything*. Pierre Ducos was the waiter at that dinner. Do you know who was there?"

"No. I didn't know *he* was there."

"How soon can you find out and keep me out of it?"

"Maybe a day, maybe a week. It might be an hour if we could get to Doh Ray Me."

"Who is Doh Ray Me?"

"His wife. Widow. Of course you don't call her that now, not to her face. She's holed up. She won't see anybody, not even the DA. Her doctor eats and sleeps there. They say. What are you staring for? Is *my* nose crooked?"

"I'll be damned." I stood up. "Of course. Why the hell didn't I remember? I must be in shock. See you tomorrow night — I hope. Forget I was here." I went.

There was no phone booth on that floor, so I went to the elevator. On the way down I pinched my memory. Having met only about a tenth of the characters — poets from Bolivia, pianists from Hungary, girls from Wyoming or Utah — who had been given a hand from Lily Rowan, I had never seen Dora Miller. Arriving in New York from Kansas, she had been advised by an artist's agent to change her name to Doremi, and when nobody had pronounced it right, had changed it again to Doraymee. You would think that a singer with that name would surely go far, but at the time Lily had told me about her she had been doing TV commercials. Though the *Times* may not have mentioned that Mrs. Harvey H. Bassett had once been Doraymee, the *Gazette* must have, and I missed it. Shock.

I entered one of the ten booths on the ground floor, shut the door, and dialed a number, and after eight rings, par for that number, a voice came. "Hello?" She always makes it a question.

"Hello. The top of the afternoon to you."

"Well. I haven't rung your number even once, so you owe me a pat on the head or a pat where you think it would do the most good. Are you alive and well? Are you at home?"

"I'm alive. I'm also ten short blocks from you. Only a ten-minute walk if you feel like company."

"You are not company. As you know, we are still trying to decide what each other is. I speak English. Lunch is nearly ready. Cross on the green."

We hung up. That's one of the many good points: *we* hung up.

Even with another tenant, it would be a pleasure to enter that penthouse on East Sixty-third Street, but of course with another tenant it wouldn't be furnished like that. The only two things that I definitely would scrap are the painting on the living-room wall by de Kooning and the electric fireplace in the spare bedroom. I also like the manners. Lily nearly always opens the door herself, and she doesn't lift a hand when a man takes his coat off in the vestibule. We usually don't kiss for a greeting, but that time she put her hands on my arms and offered, and I accepted. More, I returned the compliment.

She backed up and demanded, "Where were you and what were you doing at half past one Monday night, October twenty-eighth?"

"Try again," I said. "You fumbled it. Tuesday morning, October twenty-ninth. But first I want to confess. I'm here under false pretenses. I came because I need help."

She nodded. "Certainly. I knew that when you said the top of the afternoon to me. You only remind me that I'm Irish when you want something.

So you're in a hurry and we'll go straight to the table. There's enough." She led the way through the living room to the den, where the desk and files and shelves and typewriter stand barely leave room enough for a table that two can eat on. As we sat, Mimi came with a loaded tray.

"Go ahead," Lily said.

I want to like my manners too, so I waited until Mimi had finished serving and gone and we had taken bites of celery. Also, at Lily's table, especially when no guest had been expected, often not even Fritz would have known what was on his plate just by looking at it, so I looked at her with my eyebrows up.

She nodded. "You've never had it. We're trying it and haven't decided. Mushrooms and soy beans and black walnuts and sour cream. Don't tell *him*. If you can't get it down, Mimi will do a quick omelet. Even he admitted she could do an omelet. At the ranch."

I had taken a forkload. It didn't need much chewing, not even the walnuts, because they had been pulverized or something. When it was down I said, "I want to make it perfectly clear that—"

"Don't *do* that! I've told you. Even a joke about him turns my stomach."

"You're too careless with pronouns. Your hims. Your first him's opinion of your second him is about the same as yours. So is mine. As for this mix, I'm like you, I haven't decided. I admit it's different." I loaded a fork.

"I'll just watch your face. Tell me why you came."

I waited until the second forkful was with the first. "As I said, I need help. You once told me about a girl from Kansas named Doraymee. Remember?"

"Of course I do. I saw her yesterday."

"You *saw* her? *Yesterday?* You saw Mrs. Harvey H. Bassett?"

"Yes. You must know about her husband, since you always read about murders. She phoned me yesterday afternoon and said she was—" She stopped with her mouth half open. "What is this? She asked about you, and now you're asking about her. What's going on?"

My mouth was half open too. "I don't believe it. Are you saying that Mrs. Bassett phoned you to ask about me? I don't—"

"I didn't say that. She phoned to ask me to come and hold her hand— that was what she wanted, but she didn't say so. She said she just had to see me, I suppose because of what I had done before, when she couldn't make it in New York and was going back home to get a meal. I hadn't really done much, just paid for her room and board for a year. I hadn't seen her for— oh, three or four years. I went, and we talked for an hour or more, and she asked if I had seen you since her husband died. I thought she was just talking. Also she said she had read some of your books about Nero Wolfe's cases, and that surprised me becaue I knew she never read books. I thought she was just talking to get her mind off of her troubles, but now *you* ask about *her*. So I want to know—" She bit it off and stared at me. "My god, Escamillo, is it possible that I *am* capable of jealousy? Of course, if I could be about anybody, it would be about you, but I have always thought . . . I refuse to believe it."

"Relax." I reached to draw fingertips across the back of her hand. "Probably you have been jealous about me since the day you first caught sight of me and heard my voice, that's only natural, but Doraymee has never seen

me and I have never seen her. Our asking about each other is just a coincidence. Usually I'm suspicious of coincidences, but I love this one. I now tell
you something that is absolutely not for publication. Not yet. There's a
connection between the two murders—Bassett and Pierre Ducos—and it's
possible that Doraymee knows something that will help. A week before he
was killed—Friday evening, October eighteenth—Bassett treated six men
to a meal at Rusterman's, and Nero Wolfe wants to know the names of the
six men, and so do I. Possibly she knows. The name of even one would help.
Lon Cohen of the *Gazette,* whom you have met, says that she has holed up
and won't see anybody. I'm not particular; either you might call her and ask
her to see me, or you might go and ask her for the names, or you might just
ask for them on the phone. As I said, even one of them. That's what I came
for, and I want to thank you for this delicious hash. I also want the recipe for
Fritz." I loaded my fork.

She took a bite of celery and chewed. That's another good point: her face
is just as attractive when she is chewing celery or even a good big bite of
steak. She swallowed. "This is the third time you've asked me to help," she
said. "I didn't mind the other two. In fact I enjoyed it."

I nodded. "And there's no reason not to enjoy this one. I wouldn't ask you
to snoop on a friend, you know that. I assume—we assume—that she would
like to have the man who killed her husband tagged and nailed. So would
we. I admit the one we have *got* to tag is the one who killed Pierre Ducos
there in that house when I was going to bed just thirty feet away, but as I
said, they're connected. I can't guarantee she will never be sorry she told
you these names; when you're investigating a murder you can't guarantee
anything, but you can name the odds. A thousand to one." I loaded my fork.
I *think* that stuff was edible; my mind wasn't on it.

"I'd rather just phone and ask her. What if she says she doesn't know
their names and I think she's lying? I like her, you can't help but like her,
but she's a pretty good liar. I don't want to needle her now. She's low, *very*
low."

"Of course not. Make it simple. Leave me out. Just say somebody told
you she saw Bassett at Rusterman's with five or six men just a week before
he was killed and they didn't look very jolly and she wondered if one of them
killed him. Nuts. Listen to me. Telling *you* how to use your tongue."

"No butter today, thank you. All right. There's lemon-sherry pudding
and I want to enjoy it, so I'll go to the bedroom and get it done." She
pushed her chair back and rose. "Friday, October eighteenth."

"Right."

She went. My watch said 2:21. If she got names, I wouldn't enjoy *my*
lemon-sherry pudding, so it was advisable to get that done, and I pushed
the button and Mimi came. Her eyes went down to my plate and up to me.
"You ate more than half of it, Mr. Goodwin. What do you think?"

"To be honest, Mimi, I don't know. When I've got a job on my mind I
forget to taste. I'll have to come again."

She nodded. "I knew you were working on something, I can tell. Shall I
do an omelet?"

I said no thanks, just the pudding and coffee, and she took my plate. In
four minutes she was back, and I burned my tongue on the coffee because
my stomach sent up word that it wanted help. Of course the pudding was

no stranger. Mimi is good at puddings and parfaits and pastries. Also at coffee.

I was licking my spoon when Lily came, talking as she entered. "Don't get up. I got one name." She sat. "That woman is really low, I don't know why. He was twice her age, at least that, and I supposed she married him just to get in out of the rain. Didn't she?"

"I don't know, I never met her. You got a name?"

"Yes, just one. She said she didn't know who the others were, but one of them was a man she knew." She handed me a paper, light green, a sheet from her 5-by-8 memo pad. "She called him Benny. He's an engineer, with NATELEC, Bassett's company. More coffee?"

"No, thanks. You show promise. We'll raise your pay and—"

"I'll do better as I go along. You skip. You're not yourself when you'd rather be somewhere else." She picked up her spoon.

"I would *not* rather—I don't need to tell you what I'd rather." I stood. "I'll tell you everything someday, and I hope you like it." I skipped.

In the elevator I looked at the slip. Benjamin Igoe. That was all, and I should have asked her how to pronounce it. On the sidewalk I stood for half a minute, then headed west and turned downtown on Madison. I had to decide how to handle it—using my intelligence guided by experience, as Wolfe put it. By Fifty-fifth Street it was decided, but my legs would get me there as soon as a taxi or a bus, so I kept going. It was five past three when the doorman at Rusterman's saluted and opened for me, so the lunch rush would be over and Felix could and would listen.

That was all he had to do, listen, except for pronouncing it. I spelled it, and he thought probably Eego, but I preferred Eyego, and since I had been born in Ohio and he had been born in Vienna, I won. When that was settled and he was thoroughly briefed, I went to the bar and ordered an Irish with water on the side. Even after the coffee my stomach still seemed to think something was needed, and I made it Irish to show Lily there was no hard feeling. Then I went and consulted the phone book for the address of National Electronics Industries. Third Avenue, middle Forties, which was a relief. It might have been Queens. I left by the side door.

They had three floors of one of the newer steel-and-glass hives. The directory on the lobby wall said Research and Development on the eighth, Production on the ninth, and Executive on the tenth. He might be anything from stock clerk to Chairman of the Board, but you might as well start at the top, so I went to the tenth but was told that Mr. Eyego was in Production. So I pronounced it right. On the ninth a woman with a double chin used a kind of intercom that was new to me and then told me down the hall to the last door on the right.

It was a corner room with four windows, so he wasn't a stock clerk, though you might have thought so from his brown overalls with big pockets full of things. He was standing over by a filing cabinet. I had never seen a more worried face. That might have been expected, since the president of his company had died only five days ago, but those brow wrinkles had taken at least five years. So it was a surprise when he said in a good strong baritone, "A message from Nero Wolfe? What the hell. Huh?"

My voice went up a little without being told to. "I said message, but it's really a question. It's a little complicated, so if you can spare a few minutes—"

"I can never spare a few minutes, but my mind needs something to take it off of the goddamn problems. All right, ten minutes." He looked at his watch. "Let's sit down."

There was a big desk near a window, but that was probably where the goddam problems were, and he crossed to a couch over by the far wall. he sat and crossed his legs in spite of the loaded pockets, and I pulled a chair around to face him.

"I'll try to keep it brief, but you'll need a little background. For a couple of years Nero Wolfe was in charge of Rusterman's restaurant as trustee, and a man named Felix Mauer was under him. Now Felix is in charge, but he often asks Nero Wolfe for advice, and Mr. Wolfe and I often eat there. We ate lunch there yesterday, and Felix—"

"Huh. A waiter from that restaurant was killed in Wolfe's house, a bomb, and you found the body. Huh?"

"Right. That's why we were there yesterday, to ask questions. The waiter's name was Pierre Ducos, and he waited on you at dinner in an upstairs room at Rusterman's on Friday, October eighteenth. Twelve days ago. Harvey H. Bassett was the host. You remember it?"

"Of course I remember it. It was the last meal I ever ate with him."

"Do you remember the waiter?"

"I never remember people. I only remember diffractions and emissions."

"Mr. Wolfe and I knew Pierre well, and he knew us. When he came there late Monday night, he told me a man was going to kill him. He also told me about the dinner on October eighteenth, and he told me he saw one of the guests hand Bassett a slip of paper and Bassett put it in his wallet, and that was all. He said he wanted to tell Nero Wolfe the rest of it because he was the greatest detective in the world. I took him upstairs to a bedroom, and apparently you know what happened then, like a couple of million other people. Well, there you are. That dinner had been eleven days ago, and why did he tell me about that and about the slip of paper one of you handed Bassett? That's why I'm here, and it brings me to the question I want to ask: did you hand Bassett a slip of paper, and what was on it?"

"No. Huh."

"Did you see one of the others hand him one?"

"No. Huh." He seemed to be scowling at me, but it could have been just the wrinkles.

"Then I have to ask a favor, or rather Nero Wolfe does. We asked Felix who the guests were at that dinner, and the only one he could name was you. He said someone had told him who you were, Benjamin Igoe, the well-known scientist. I don't know if you like to be called a scientist, but that's what Felix was told."

"I don't believe it. Goddam it, I am *not* well known."

"Maybe you are and don't know it. That's what Felix told me. You can call him and ask him."

"Who told him that?"

"He didn't say. He's there now. Give him a ring." I thought he probably would, there and then. Nine men out of ten would have, or maybe only seven or eight.

But not him. He just said, "Huh. By god, if I'm famous it's about time I found out. I'm sixty-four years old. You want a favor?"

"Nero Wolfe does. I'm just the errand boy. He wants —"

"You're a licensed private investigator. Well known."

"You can't believe what you read in the paper. I am *not* well known." I wanted to say huh but didn't. "Mr. Wolfe wants the names of all the men who were at that dinner, but if you never remember people, of course you can't tell me."

"I remember the *names* of everything, including people." He proved it. "Did Pierre Ducos tell you what we talked about?"

I shook my head. "He only told me what I told you."

"We talked about tape recorders. That's what Harvey had us together for. Did you know Harvey Bassett?"

"No. Of course I had heard of him, he was well known too."

"I knew him all my life, most of it, we were at college together. He was three years older than me. I was a prodigy. Huh. No more. I took physics, and he took business. He made a billion dollars more or less, but up to the day he died he couldn't tell an electron from a kilovolt. Also he was unbalanced. He had obsessions. He had one about Richard Nixon. That was why he had us there. He made the equipment for electronic recording, or rather that was one of the things we made and sold, and he thought Richard Nixon had debased it. Polluted it. He wanted to do something about it but didn't know what. So he had us —"

He bit it off and looked at his watch. "Goddamn it, twelve minutes." He jumped up, more like twenty-four than sixty-four. He moved, but I grabbed his arm and said firmly, "Goddam it, the names."

"Oh. Did I say I would?" He crossed to the desk, sat, got a pad of paper and a pen, and wrote, fast, so fast that I knew it wouldn't be legible. But it was. I had stepped over, and he tore it off and handed it to me, and a glance was enough. All five of them.

"Mr. Wolfe will be grateful," I said, and meant it. "*Damn* grateful. He never leaves his house, and almost certainly he will want to tell you so and have a talk. Is there any chance you would drop in on him, perhaps on your way home?"

"I doubt it. I suppose I might. My kind of work, I never know what I'm going to do. Huh. You get out of here."

Turning, I said, "Huh." I didn't really *say* it, it just came out. And I walked out.

Also I walked the ten blocks down to Thirty-fifth street and across town to the old brownstone. As I mounted the stoop it was half past four and Wolfe would be up in the plant rooms, and I hung up my coat and went to the office, sat, and looked at the list. He had written not only the names, but also what they did. If my time hadn't been up, he might have included ages and addresses. I tossed it on the desk and sat and looked at the picture. It was not an entirely new ballgame. By tossing Richard Nixon into that dinner party he had put a completely new face on it. Knowing Wolfe as I did, that was obvious. It was so obvious that it took me only ten minutes to decide what to do first, and I did it. I got at the phone and dialed a number.

It took more than half an hour to get all three of them. Actually I only got Fred; for Saul and Orrie I had to leave urgent messages. Then I pulled the typewriter around and made five copies of the list of names. I don't have to type it here for you because I already have. Then I typed the conversation with Igoe, verbatim, one carbon. I usually don't read things over, but I did that, and was on the second page when the elevator rattled coming down and clanked at the bottom, and Wolfe came.

He went to his desk and sat and said, "You're back." He rarely says things that are obvious, but he says that fairly often because it's a miracle that I'm not limping or bleeding after spending hours out in the concrete jungle.

"Yes, sir. I'll try to cover it all before dinner. I saw Felix and Lon Cohen and Miss Rowan and Felix again and one of the guests at that dinner named Benjamin Igoe, an electronics engineer with NATELEC, Bassett's company, and you'll want it all, but I prefer to give you the last one first. Igoe. I've typed my talk with him for the record." I swiveled to get it from my desk, swiveled again, and got up and handed it to him.

Three pages. He read the last page twice, looked at me with his eyes half shut, and said, "By God."

I stared at him. I may have gaped. He never says by god, and he said it with a capital G. So I didn't say anything.

He did. "Was he gibbering? Was it flummery?"

"No, sir. It was straight."

"He gave you their names?"

"Right." It was in my hand, the one he had written, not a typed copy, and I passed it to him. He read it twice too. He put it down on his desk and then picked it up for another look. "I am not easily overwhelmed," he said. "If I could have them here now, all of them, I would pretermit dinner. I have occasionally asked you to bring people when I knew no one else could, but this — these six — not even you."

"I agree. So before I typed that conversation I did something. I used the telephone. More than once. And got results. You may have one guess."

He looked at me, straight, then closed his eyes. In about a minute, maybe a little more, he opened them and asked, "When will they come?"

"Nine o'clock. Fred sure, and Saul and Orrie probable. As you know, they like doing errands for you."

"Satisfactory," he said. "I'll taste my dinner. I haven't tasted food for two days."

7

I forget who once called them the Three Musketeers. Saul was in the red leather chair, and Fred and Orrie were in the two yellow ones I had moved up to face Wolfe's desk. Saul had brandy, Orrie had vodka and tonic, Fred had bourbon, I had milk, and Wolfe had beer.

Saul Panzer was two inches shorter, much less presentable with his big ears and unpressed pants, and in some ways smarter than me. Fred Durkin was one inch shorter, two inches broader, heavier-bearded, and in some ways a little more gullible. Orrie Cather was half an inch taller, a lot handsomer, and a little vainer. He was still sure he should have my job and thought it was conceivable that someday he would. He also thought he was twice as attractive to all women under forty, and I guess he was. He could say let's look at the record.

I had been doing most of the talking for more than an hour, and their notebooks were more than half full. I had given them the crop, saving nothing, with a little help from Wolfe in spots, but of course omitting irrelevant items such as the luncheon menu at Lily Rowan's. That had also been skipped when reporting to Wolfe before dinner. His real opinion of her wasn't anything near as low as he liked to pretend it was, but he didn't need another minus for her.

I took a sip of milk and said, "Now questions, I suppose."

"No," Wolfe said. His eyes moved left to right and back, to take them in. "I must first tell you the situation. Archie doesn't need to be told; he was aware of it before I was. What Mr. Igoe told him. He sees me every day, and hears me. He knew that for the first time in my life I had an itch that could not be relieved — that I hankered for something I couldn't get. He knew that I would have given all of my orchids — well, most of them — to have an effective hand in the disclosure of the malfeasance of Richard Nixon. I once dictated to him a letter offering my services to Mr. Jaworski, and he typed it, but it wasn't sent. I tore it up."

He picked up the bottle, decided not to pour, and put it down. "Well. Mr. Nixon is now out, no longer in command of our ship of state, no longer the voice of authority to us and of America to the world, but the record is by no means complete. History will dig at it for a century. It is now possible that I may be able to make a contribution. You heard what Igoe told Archie. Was he merely babbling, Archie?"

"No, sir. It was square."

"So I accept it and I expect you to. I trust Archie's eyes and ears, and I think you do. I am assuming that there was some connection between the name on that slip of paper, if it was a name, and the web of events and circumstances that is called Watergate; and further, that it resulted in the death by violence of Harvey Bassett and Pierre Ducos. Of Pierre, in this house. That's what I expect to establish, with your help. I have no client, so there will be no fee. Your usual rates will be paid, and of course expenses. I instruct you not to stint. It's nearing the end of a good year for me, even this year of a delirious economy, and it won't pinch me."

He sat straighter and palmed the chair arms. "Now. You have always trusted my judgment and followed instructions without question. Now you can't. I don't. On this I can't be sure my intellect will ignore the goad of my emotions. It may already have been gulled. The assumptions I have made — are they witless? I have asked Archie. Saul?"

"For a try, no."

"Fred?"

"No, sir."

"Orrie?"

"I agree with Saul. Good enough to work on."

Wolfe nodded. "I'm not convinced, but in any case I am going to get the

man who killed Pierre—and might have killed Archie. But don't trust me
blindly. If you doubt the soundness of my conclusions or instructions, say
so. I would like to come out of this with my self-esteem intact, and so would
you."

He leaned back. "To the job. If one of those six men is the culprit, he was
with Bassett in an automobile last Friday night, and he had access to
Pierre's coat Monday, day before yesterday, no matter what his motive was.
To that the soundness of my assumptions is immaterial, and my emotions
are not involved. Archie has given you lists of their names and has told you
that five of them are in the Manhattan telephone directory. One of the
lawyers, Mr. Ackerman, is in the Washington directory. Saul, you will start
with the other lawyer, Mr. Judd. What is he? Where was he? Of course you
won't ask *him*. If he learns you are inquiring about him, he may ask you,
and if you need to consult with Archie, he will be here. Better Archie than
me; on this I am suspect. As I said."

"Yes, sir. A question?"

"Yes?"

"You have told us not to follow your instructions without question. Lucile
Ducos, Pierre's daughter. What Igoe said and the names he gave may have
made you forget her." He looked at me. "You think he may have shown her
the slip of paper?"

"*May* have, certainly."

"Could I open her up?"

"Possibly. If anybody could. I doubt it."

Back to Wolfe. "The name may not be one of those six men. It may have
no connection with Watergate or Nixon. That may be why you forgot her. I
could give it a try. Archie looks like a male chauvinist, and I don't."

Wolfe's lips were tight. He had asked for it, but even so it was hard to
take. I am supposed to badger him, that's one of the forty-four things I get
paid for, but not them, not even Saul.

"I'll discuss it with Archie," Wolfe said. "In asking about Mr. Judd, if you
reveal that I sent you, so much the better. He may resent it and want to tell
me so. Fred, you will start with Mr. Vilar. Since he deals with what is
euphemistically called security, you will be familiar with those around him.
My comment to Saul apply to you. Questions?"

"No, sir. Archie will be here?"

"Yes. He will see Mr. Igoe again and bring him if possible, but that will
have to wait. At least he will be here tomorrow. Orrie, I believe you are
known at Rusterman's."

"Well . . ." Orrie let it hang five seconds. "I have been there, sure. With
my wife. Not often; I can't afford it."

"You were there two years ago, when money was taken from one of the
men's lockers and Felix asked me to investigate. I sent you."

"Oh, that, sure."

"So you have seen that room, and many of the men have seen you. Pierre's
coat could have been anywhere that he was that day or evening, but that
room is the most likely. Was a stranger seen there that evening? Go and find
out. Archie will tell Felix to expect you. Don't go until eleven o'clock, and
interfere with the routine as little as possible. Have in mind another possibility, that the bomb was put in the coat by one of them. Archie and I

think it unlikely, but it isn't excluded. You will not mention the slip of paper, you know what we promised Philip. Questions?"

Orrie shook his head. "About that, no. That's simple. And Archie will be here. But I'd like to say — about the ante. Fred has a family and needs it, but my wife has a good job with good pay, and we won't starve for a couple of weeks. Also I've got some feelings about Nixon too. If you pay the expenses, I'd like to donate my time."

"No." Wolfe clipped it. "This is my affair. When Archie said it's all in the family, he meant merely that I have no client. No."

"I live here," I said. "I took him up to that room. It's a family affair." Inside I was grinning. Orrie was so damn obvious. He thought my taking in a man with a bomb was a black mark for me, and offering to donate his time showed that he was fully worthy to step in when I stepped out. I'm not saying he was dumb. He wasn't.

Fred said, "Hell, I wouldn't starve either. I've got two families. I don't live here like Archie, but I like to think this is my *professional* family."

Saul said, "So do I. I raise. I'll pay expenses — mine."

Wolfe said, "Pfui. It's *my* affair. Archie, five hundred to each of them. There may be occasion to buy some facts. Record it as usual; it may be deductible, at least some of it."

I went and opened the safe, got the reserve cash box, and made three piles — ten twenties, twenty tens, and twenty fives, all used bills. When I finished, the members of the family were on their feet, including Wolfe. He had shaken hands with them when they arrived, but they didn't offer now because they knew he didn't like it. They took the bills and went to the hall for their coats.

When I returned to the office after letting them out and sliding the bolt, Wolfe had the list of names and the conversation with Igoe in his hand. Taking them up to bed with him. "Still half an hour to midnight," he said. "I'll sleep, and so will you. Good night."

I returned it and started collecting glasses and bottles.

8

AT a quarter past ten Thursday morning I left the South Room and closed the door, which was no longer honored with the seal of the NYPD. Ralph Kerner, of Town House Services Incorporated, closed his imitation-leather-bound book and said, "I'll try to get the estimate to you by Monday. Tell Mr. Wolfe to expect the worst. That's all we get nowadays, the worst, from all directions."

"Yeah, we expect it and we get it. Isn't there a discount for a room where a man has just been murdered?"

He laughed. Always laugh at a customer's joke, even a bum one. "There certainly ought to be. I'll tell Mr. Ohrbach. So you took him up and left him." He laughed. "Good thing you left."

"It sure was. I may be dumb, but not that dumb."

Following him down the two flights, I would have liked to plant a foot on his fanny and push but controlled it.

The office chores were done, but I had been interrupted on a job of research—a phone call to Nathaniel Parker to ask for a report on the lawyers, Judd and Ackerman, one to our bank for a report on Hahn, the banker, and one to Lon Cohen about Roman Vilar, security, and Ernest Urquhart, lobbyist. I had enough on Igoe unless there were developments. Huh. Also one of the bottom shelves had seven directories, not counting the telephone books for the five boroughs and Westchester and Washington, and I had the *Directory of Directors* open at N to see if any of them were on the NATELEC list when Wolfe came down.

Three days' mail was on his desk, and he went at it. First, as usual, a quick once-through, dropping about half in the wastebasket. Of course I had chucked most of the circulars and other junk. He answers nearly all real letters, especially handwritten ones, because, he once told me, it is a mandate of civility. Also, I said, all he had to do was talk to me and he loved to talk, and he nodded and said that when he had to write them by hand he hadn't answered any. I said then he wasn't civilized, and that started him off on one of his hairsplitting speeches. We answered about twenty letters, three or four from orchid collectors and buffs as usual, with a few interruptions, phone calls from Parker and Lon Cohen and Fred Durkin. When I swiveled to my desk I was surprised to see him go to the shelves for a book—Fitzgerald's translation of the *Iliad*. In the mail there had been an inscribed copy of Herblock's new book, *Special Report,* with about a thousand cartoons of Nixon, but apparently he no longer needed to read or look at pictures about it because he was working on it. So he sat and read about a phony horse instead of a phony statesman.

He tasted his lunch all right. First marrow dumplings, and then sweetbreads poached in white wine, dipped in crumbs and eggs, sautéed, and doused with almonds in brown butter. I had had it at Rusterman's, where they call it *ris de veau amandine,* and Fritz's is always better. I know I haven't got Wolfe's palate. I know it because he has told me.

After lunch you might have thought we were back to normal. Theodore brought down a batch of statistics on germination and performance, and I entered them on the file cards. Week in and week out, that routine, about two per cent of which—the few he sells—applies to income and the rest to outgo, takes, on an average, about a third of my time. Wolfe, after listening to my reports on my morning's research, which contributed absolutely nothing, worked hard at comparing Fitzgerald's *Iliad* with the three other translations he brought over from the shelf. That was risky because they were on a high shelf and he had to use the stool. On the dot at four o'clock he left for the plant rooms. You might have thought we hadn't a care in the world. There hadn't been a peep from the members of the family. Wolfe hadn't even glanced at Herblock's *Special Report.* The only flaw was that when I finished typing the letters my legs and lungs wanted to go for a walk, and Saul and Fred and Orrie didn't have walkie-talkies.

At six o'clock the sound came of the elevator complaining as it started down, but it only lasted four seconds. He had stopped off for a look at the South Room, which he hadn't seen since one-thirty Tuesday morning. It was a good ten minutes before it started again, so he gave the ruins more than a glance. When he came and crossed to his desk and got settled, he said my guess of fifteen hundred dollars was probably too low with the bloated prices of everything from sugar to shingles, and I said I was glad to hear him having fun with words, tossing off an alliteration with two words that weren't spelled the same. He said it had been casual, which was a lie, and started reading and signing the letters. He always reads them, not to catch errors, because he knows there won't be any, but to let me know that if I ever make one it will be spotted.

It was ten minutes to seven and I was sealing the envelopes when the phone rang and I got it.

"Nero Wolfe's residence, Archie Goodwin speaking." Up to six o'clock it's "office." After six, "residence." I don't want people to think my nose is on the grindstone. Most offices close at five.

"May I speak to Mr. Wolfe, please? My name is Roman Vi*lar*. V-I-L-A-R."

I covered the mouthpiece and turned. "Fred has flushed one. Roman Vilar, euphemistic security. He asks permission to speak to Mr. Wolfe, please. Only he makes it Vi-*lar*."

"Indeed." Wolfe reached for his receiver. I kept mine.

"Nero Wolfe speaking."

"This is Roman Vilar, Mr. Wolfe. You have never heard of me, but of course I have heard of you. But that isn't correct—you *have* heard of me, or at least your man Goodwin has. Yesterday, from Benjamin Igoe."

"Yes. Mr. Goodwin has told me."

"Of course. And he told you what Mr. Igoe told him. Of course. And Mr. Igoe has told me what he told Goodwin. I have told others, and they are here with me now in my apartment. Mr. Igoe and four others. May I ask a question?"

"Yes. I may answer it."

"Thank you. Have you told the police or the District Attorney what Mr. Igoe told Goodwin?"

"No."

"Thank you. Do you intend to? No, I withdraw that. I can't expect you to tell me what you intend to do. We have been discussing the situation, and one of us was going to go and discuss it with you, but we decided we would all like to be present. Of course not now—it's your dinnertime, or soon will be. Would nine o'clock be convenient?"

"Here. At my office."

"Certainly."

"You know the address."

"Certainly."

"You said four others. Who are they?"

"You have their names. Mr. Igoe gave them to Goodwin."

"Yes. We'll expect you at nine o'clock."

Wolfe hung up. So did I.

"I want a raise," I said. "Beginning yesterday at four o'clock. I admit it will be more inflation, and President Ford expects us to voluntarily lay off, but as somebody said, a man is worth his hire. It took me just ten minutes to get Igoe to spill that."

" 'The laborer is worthy of his hire.' The Bible. Luke. They offered to work for nothing, all three of them, and you want a raise, and it was you who took him up to bed."

I nodded. "And you said to me with him there on the floor and plaster all around him and on him, 'I suppose you had to.' Someday that will have to be fully discussed, but not now. We're talking just to show how different we are. If we were just ordinary people we would be shaking hands and beaming at each other or dancing a jig. It's your turn."

Fritz entered. To announce a meal he always comes in three steps, never four. But seeing us, when he stopped, what he said was, "Something happened."

Damn it, we were and are different. But Fritz knows us. He ought to.

Before going to the dining room I rang Saul's number, got his answering service, and left a message that I couldn't make it to the weekly poker game and give Lon Cohen my love.

9

THE only visible evidence in the office that we had company was six men on chairs. Since this was a family affair, not business, it could be mentioned at the table, and after the cognac flames on a roast duck Mr. Richards had died, and Wolfe had carved it, and Fritz had brought me mine and taken his, we had discussed the question of setting up a refreshment table and had vetoed it. It would have made them think they were welcome and we wished them well, which would have been only half true. They were welcome, but we did not wish them well—at least not one of them.

To a stranger entering the office it's obvious at a glance that the red leather chair is the place. I had intended to put Benjamin Igoe in it, but a bishop with a splendid mop of white hair and quick gray eyes went to it even before he pronounced his name. Ernest Urquhart, the lobbyist. They all pronounced their names for Wolfe before they sat—the other five on two rows of yellow chairs facing Wolfe's desk, three in front and two back. Like this:

```
WOLFE
                                    URQUHART
        me
        JUDD        ACKERMAN        VILAR
            IGOE             HAHN
```

"I'm not really arrogant or impudent, Mr. Wolfe," Urquhart said. "I took this chair only because these gentlemen decided that, since we are all willing talkers, it would be wise to name a spokesman, and they chose me. Not that their tongues are tied. Two of them are lawyers. I can't say with Sir Thomas More, 'and not a lawyer among them.'"

Not a good start. Wolfe didn't like quoters, and he was down on More because he had smeared Richard III. I was wondering whether Urquhart was a lobbyist because he looked like a tolerant and sympathetic bishop, or looked like that because he was a lobbyist. He had the voice for it, too.

"I have all night," Wolfe said.

"It shouldn't take all night. We certainly hope not. As you must have gathered from what Mr. Vilar said on the phone, we're concerned about what Mr. Igoe told Mr. Goodwin about Mr. Bassett—and what Mr. Goodwin told him. Frankly, we think it was unnecessary and indiscreet, and—"

"Leave that out! Goddam it, I told you." It was Igoe's strong baritone, even stronger.

"That was understood, Ernie." Ackerman. Francis Ackerman, lawyer, Washington. I am not going to drag in Watergate, it certainly doesn't need any dragging in by me, but when they had single-filed in from the stoop he had struck me as a fairly good take-off of John Mitchell, with his saggy jowls and scanty chin. His calling Ackerman "Ernie" showed that he was the kind of Washington lawyer who is on nickname terms with lobbyists. Anyhow, one lobbyist.

Urquhart nodded. Not to Ackerman or Igoe or Wolfe; he just nodded. "That slipped out," he told Wolfe. "Please ignore it. What concerns us is the possible *result* of what Mr. Igoe told Mr. Goodwin. And he gave him our names, and today men have been making inquiries about two of us, and apparently they were sent by you. Were they? Sent by you?"

"Yes," Wolfe said.

"You admit it?"

Wolfe wiggled a finger. That was regression—I just looked it up. He had quit finger-wiggling a couple of years back. "Don't do that," he said. "Calling a statement an admission is one of the oldest and scrubbiest lawyers' tricks, and you're not a lawyer. I state it."

"You'll have to make allowances," Urquhart said. "We are not only concerned, we are disturbed. Apprehensive. Mr. Goodwin told Mr. Igoe that at that dinner at Rusterman's one of us handed Mr. Bassett a slip of paper, and—"

"No."

"No?"

"He told Mr. Igoe that Pierre Ducos had *told him* that he had seen one of you hand Mr. Bassett a slip of paper. Also that that was the one fact that Pierre had mentioned, and that therefore we considered it significant."

"Significant of what?"

"I don't know. That's what I intend to find out. One week after that dinner Mr. Bassett was shot and killed. Ten minutes after Pierre told Mr. Goodwin that he saw one of you hand Mr. Bassett a slip of paper at that dinner—told him that and nothing else—he was killed by a bomb in this house. Mr. Urquhart, did you hand Mr. Bassett a slip of paper at that dinner?"

"No. And I want to make—"

"No is enough." Wolfe's head turned. "Did you, Mr. Judd?"

"No."

"Did you, Mr. Ackerman?"

"No."

"Did you, Mr. Vilar?"

"No. I am —"

"Did you, Mr. Hahn?"

"No."

"You told Mr. Goodwin no, Mr. Igoe. I ask you again. Did you?"

"Huh. No."

Wolfe's head went left and right to take them in. "There you are, gentlemen. Rather, there I am. Either Pierre lied to Mr. Goodwin or one of you lies. I don't think Pierre lied; why would he? Another question: did any of you see one of the others hand Mr. Bassett a slip of paper? I don't need another round of noes; I invite a yes. Any of you?"

No yes. Roman Vilar said, "We can't ask Pierre about it. He's dead." Vilar, euphemistic security, was all points—pointed chin, pointed nose, pointed ears, even pointed shoulders. He was probably the youngest of them—at a guess, early forties. His saying that they couldn't ask Pierre also pointed, for me, to the fact that when Wolfe had told me Wednesday morning what to say to them, or one of them, if I got the chance, I hadn't fully realized how much dust could be kicked up by one little lie. One more mention by anybody that Pierre had told me that he had seen one of them hand Bassett a slip of paper and I would begin to believe it myself.

"Yes," Wolfe said, "Pierre Ducos is dead. I saw him, on his back, with no face. I can't ask him either. If I could, almost certainly you would not be here, not all of you. Only one." He focused on Urquhart. "You said you are concerned not only about what Mr. Goodwin told Mr. Igoe but also about what Mr. Igoe told him. So am I. That's why I am having inquiries made about you—all of you. Mr. Igoe used the term 'obsession.' I don't have obsessions, but I too am attentive to the skulduggery of Richard Nixon and his crew. And the purpose of that gathering, arranged by Mr. Bassett, was to discuss it. Yes?"

"I suppose you might —"

"Hold it, Urquhart. Is this being recorded, Wolfe?"

Albert O. Judd, the other lawyer. He was about the same age as Vilar. He looked like a smoothie, but not the oily kind, and he had paid somebody a good four C's for cutting and fitting his light-gray coat and pants, the kind of fabric that suggests stripes but doesn't actually have any. Marvelous.

Wolfe eyed him. "You must know, Mr. Judd, that that question is cogent only if the one who asks it can rely on the one who answers, and why should you rely on me? It isn't to be expected that I'll say yes, and what good is my no? However, I say it. No." His eyes took them in, from Judd around to Urquhart. "Mr. Vilar asked me on the telephone if I had told the police or the District Attorney what Mr. Igoe told Mr. Goodwin, and I said no. He asked me if I intended to but withdrew the question because he couldn't expect me to answer. But I *will* answer. Again no. At present I intend to tell no one. I do intend to learn who killed Pierre Ducos, and I have reason to surmise that in doing so I'll also learn who killed Harvey Bassett."

He turned a palm up. "Gentlemen. I know why you're here, of course. At present the officers of the law have no reason to assume that any of you were implicated in a homicide. Two homicides. Naturally they have inquired about Mr. Bassett's movements and activities immediately prior to his death, but he was a busy man of affairs, and they probably know nothing of that dinner a week earlier. If they knew what I know, they would not merely assume that one or more of you might be implicated; you would be the main focus of their investigation." He turned to me. "Your notebook, Archie."

I got it, and a pen. He had closed his eyes. He opened them to see that I was equipped, and closed them again. "Not a letterhead, plain paper. Merely a list of questions. How long had you known Mr. Bassett and what were your relations with him? Why were you included in a meeting called by him to discuss Richard Nixon's use or abuse of tape recorders? Did you know that Mr. Bassett felt that Mr. Nixon had debased and polluted tape recorders, comma, and did you agree with him? Have you ever been involved in any activity connected with the phenomena called Watergate, comma, and if so what and how and when? Have you ever had any contact with anyone connected with Watergate? To your knowledge, comma, even hearsay, comma, have any of the other five guests ever been connected in any way with Watergate, comma, and if so who? Where were you and what were you doing last Friday night, comma, October twenty-fifth, comma, from six p.m. to two a.m.? Where were you and what were you doing last Monday, comma, October twenty-eighth, comma, from twelve noon to twelve midnight?"

He opened his eyes. "Six carbons. No, only five, we won't need one. No hurry." He turned to them. "That, gentlemen, is a sample of the questions you are going to be asked. Either by me or by the police. You have a choice. You realize that —"

"This has gone far enough. Too far. Wolfe, I am a senior vice-president of the fourth largest bank in New York. We will pay you one hundred thousand dollars to represent our interests. One half tommorrow in cash, and the remainder guaranteed — probably by us jointly and certainly by me personally. Orally. Not in writing."

Willard K. Hahn's voice was soft and low, but the kind of soft and low you don't have to strain to hear. He was a square. He would have been obviously a square even without his square jaw and square shoulders — the opposite of Vilar with his points.

Wolfe was looking down his nose at him. "Not a good offer, Mr. Hahn. If as payment for services, too much. If as a bribe to muzzle me, not enough."

"It's for services. Too much? *You* saying too much, when you have just said we would be the main focus of a murder investigation? Vilar says you charge the highest fees in New York. If I need something, I buy it and I pay for it. I knew Harvey Bassett for twenty years. He was a good customer of my bank. And he's dead. Ben Igoe says he had an obsession about Richard Nixon and the tapes, and that's true, he did, but that wasn't his only obsession. When I heard of his death, how he died, my first thought was his wife — his obsession about *her*. Have you —"

"Goddam it, Hahn, you would!" Igoe's strong baritone. "You would drag her in!"

"You're damn right I would. *He* would drag her in, he always did, you know that, you ought to. Or he would drag her out." Back to Wolfe. "That slip of paper. If one of us handed him a slip of paper, it wouldn't have been about Nixon and tapes. That was what we were talking about, Nixon and tapes, why hand him a slip of paper, why not just say it? Evidently you think that slip of paper had something to do with his being murdered. If it did, it wasn't about tapes. I know nothing about it, I never heard of it until Ben Igoe told me what Goodwin told him, but when he did I — What did I say, Ben?"

"You said it was probably about Dora. Huh. You would."

"I think," Roman Vilar said, "that we should stick to what brought us here. That list of questions, Mr. Wolfe. You say they'll be asked either by you or by the police. Asked by you now? Here and now?"

"No," Wolfe said. "It would take a night and a day. I didn't invite you to come in a body; you invited yourselves. I intended to see you, but singly, after getting reports from the men I sent to make inquiries. I suggest that—"

"You won't see *me* singly." Ackerman, the Washington lawyer. He sounded like John Mitchell, too — at least the way Mitchell sounded on television. "You won't see me at all. I'm surprised that you don't seem to realize what you're trying to do. You're trying to get us to go along with you on a cover-up, and not a cover-up of a break-in to look at some papers, a cover-up of a murder. You say two murders. Of course I don't want to be involved in a murder investigation, nobody does, but at least I'm not guilty. But the way you're playing it, if I go along with you, I *would* be guilty. A cover-up of a murder. Obstruction of justice. Urquhart asked you if this is being recorded. I hope it is. When I talk to the District Attorney I would enjoy being able to tell him that this is on tape and he can—"

"No," Hahn, the banker, said. You wouldn't think such a low, soft voice could cut in, but it did. "You're not going to talk to the District Attorney or anyone else. I'm not a lawyer, but I don't think we'll be charged with obstruction of justice merely because a private detective told us that a man said something about a slip of paper, and I do *not* want to be involved in a murder investigation. I don't think any of us—"

Two or three voices, not soft and low, stopped him. I could try to sort it out and report it, but I won't because it wouldn't decide anything. Wolfe just sat and took it in. I got his eye and asked a question by pointing to my notebook and then the typewriter, but he shook his head.

But it did decide something. When it became obvious that they were all stringing along with Hahn, and Ackerman was a minority of one, Wolfe stopped the yapping by raising his voice.

"Please! Perhaps I can help. Mr. Ackerman is a member of the bar, and I am not, but his position is not tenable. Probably Watergate has made him excessively sensitive about cover-ups. Four lawyers have been disbarred, and more will be. But you can't be charged with obstruction of justice when all you have is hearsay. Perhaps *I* can be charged, but my taking that risk is of no concern to you. If Mr. Ackerman talks to the District Attorney, I'll be in a pickle, but he'll probably regret it, guilty or not."

He looked at the wall clock. "It's past ten o'clock. As I said, I must see each of you singly. Mr. Ackerman, you may want to get back to Washington. Why not stay now and let the others go?"

"No," Hahn said. "I repeat my offer. One hundred thousand dollars."

That started them off again, all of them but Ackerman and Vilar, and

again I won't try to sort it out. But three of them got to their feet, and soon
Urquhart left the red leather chair and made it four, and I got up and
crossed to the door to the hall. Again there was a clear majority, and when
Vilar and Igoe joined me at the door Wolfe spoke up.

"You will hear from me. All of you. From Mr. Goodwin. He will telephone
and make appointments to suit your convenience — and mine. The best
hours for me are eleven in the morning, six in the afternoon, and nine in the
evening, but for this I would trim. I don't want to protract it, and neither do
you. There will —"

I missed the rest because Igoe had headed for the front and I went to help
with his coat and hat.

When all five of them were out and the door shut, and I returned to the
office, Ackerman was in the red leather chair, leaning back with his legs
crossed. He was big and broad, and the yellow chairs were much smaller. As
I crossed to my desk he was saying, ". . . but you don't know anything
about me except that I look like John N. Mitchell."

He not only admitted it, he even put the N in. I liked that.

"I have been told," Wolfe said, "that you are a reputable and respected
member of the bar."

"Certainly. I haven't been indicted or disbarred. I have had an office in
Washington for twenty-four years. I'm not a criminal lawyer, so I haven't
been invited to act for Dean or Haldeman or Ehrlichman or Colson or
Magruder or Hunt or Segretti. Or even Nixon. Do you actually expect to
put me through that catechism you dictated?"

"Probably not. Why were you included in that gathering?"

"It's complicated. Albert Judd was and is chief counsel for NATELEC.
Five years ago he was acting on a tax matter for them and needed a Washington man and got me. That's how I met Harvey Bassett. Bassett thought
he needed a good lobbyist, and I got Ernest Urquhart, one of the best. I
have know him for years. He disappointed me here tonight. He is usually a
wonderful talker, I *know* that, but I guess this wasn't his pitch. I had never
met the other three — Hahn, the banker, or Vilar, the security man, or Igoe.
I knew Igoe is a vice-president of the corporation."

"Then you know nothing about Hahn's comment about Mrs. Bassett.
And Igoe."

I raised a brow. What did that have to do with Watergate and tapes?

"No. Yes, nothing. I —" He flipped a hand. "Except hearsay."

"Whom did you hear say what?"

I have tried to talk him out of that "whom." Only highbrows and grand-
standers and schoolteachers say "whom," and he knows it. It's the mule in
him.

Ackerman's chin was up. "I'm submitting to this, Wolfe, only because of
them. Especially Urquhart and Judd. Judd called me last night — Igoe had
talked to him — and I took a plane to New York this morning and we had
lunch. He told me things about Bassett that I hadn't known, and one of
them was his — he didn't say 'obsession,' he said 'fix' about his wife. I don't
peddle hearsay; you can ask Judd."

"I shall. Did you know how Bassett felt about Nixon and tapes?"

"Yes. A few months ago he and Judd were in Washington about some
patents — I know something about patents — and we spent a whole evening

on Nixon and tapes. Bassett had the wild idea that Nixon could be sued for damages — ten million dollars — for slandering and defaming manufacturers of electronic recorders by using them for criminal and corrupt purposes. We couldn't talk him out of it. He was a nut. I don't know if he was balmy about his wife, but he was about that. Of course that was a part of how he made it big in business — his drive. He had *that*."

"What was said — decided — about it at that meeting?"

"Nothing was decided. Bassett wanted Vilar to say that it was difficult to persuade corporation executives to contract for security appliances and personnel because they thought Nixon had given electronic equipment a bad name. He wanted Urquhart to say that if you tried to lobby for anybody connected in any way with electronics, no one on the Hill would listen to you. He wanted Igoe to say that men working in electronics — all levels, top to bottom — were quitting and you couldn't get replacements. He wanted Judd and me to say that all of that was actionable and we would act. God only knows what he wanted Hahn to do — maybe lend him a couple of million without interest to back the crusade."

Wolfe was eying him. "And you grown men, presumably sentient, soberly discussed that drivel? Or were you tipsy?"

"No. Judd and I hadn't even had martinis, because we knew Bassett would buy Montrachet and Château Latour. He always did. But you didn't know Harvey Bassett. He could sell ice cubes to an Eskimo. Also, of course, he was a source of our income — for at least two of them a major source — and you don't spit in the eye of the source of your income. You take a bite of roast pheasant and a sip of Latour and pretend to listen hard. Most men do. I do. From what I've heard of you, maybe you don't."

"It's a matter of style. I have mine. I have due regard for my sources of income. Is one — "

"Like me, you have different clients for different cases. Who's your client in this one?"

"I am. Myself. I have had my nose pulled. Spat upon. Pierre Ducos was murdered in a bedroom of my house. The man who did it will pay. Is one — "

"Then why are you withholding evidence from the police?"

"Because it's *my* job. And it may not be evidence; I'm finding out. I start a question the third time: Is one of your clients connected in any way with Watergate?"

"Everyone in Washington is connected in some way with Watergate. That's stretching it, but not much. The members of all those juries have thousands of relatives and friends. No present or former client of mine is or has been actually involved in Watergate. You're supposed to be asking the questions, but I'll ask another one. Do you really believe one of us six men killed Harvey Bassett? Or was implicated in his murder or the other one?"

"Of course I do. I'm paying three men forty dollars an hour to inquire about you. To your knowledge, have any of them been connected in any way with Watergate?"

"To my knowledge, no. If I were Haldeman, I would say not to my recollection, but I'm not Haldeman."

"Where were you and what were you doing last Friday night, October twenty-fifth, from six p.m. to two a.m.?"

"By god, you ask it. I remember *because* that was the night Basssett died. I was at home in Washington. From nine p.m. on I was playing bridge with my wife and two friends until after midnight. I sleep late most Saturdays. At nine o'clock my wife woke me to tell me that Bassett had been murdered. What was the other one? Monday? I was at my office. In Washington. Next question."

Wolfe likes to say that no alibi is impregnable, but I hoped he wouldn't send me to crack that one. Wives and bridge-playing friends can lie, but there was Monday too, and for us that was the one we really wanted.

He looked at the wall clock. Eight minutes past eleven. "I'm short on sleep," he said. "Are you going to see the District Attorney?"

Ackerman shook his head. "You heard what they said, especially Judd. He agrees with you; all we have is hearsay — from you. I'll be short on sleep too. I'd like to make the midnight to Washington."

"Then you'll excuse me." Wolfe pushed his chair back and rose. "I'm going to bed." He headed for the door. Ackerman got up, told me, "He's a goddam freak," and walked out.

10

WHEN Wolfe came down to the office at eleven o'clock Friday morning, Roman Vilar was sitting in the red leather chair.

It had been a busy morning — for me — starting with the routine phone calls from the hired hands. I told them about the party we had had — that nothing had been learned to change the program, they were to carry on, Saul on Judd and Fred on Vilar. Orrie's day at Rusterman's had been a blank; no one had seen a stranger in the dump room Monday, day or night. Having been instructed by Wolfe — summoned on the house phone when I went to the kitchen for breakfast — I sicked Orrie on Benjamin Igoe.

There had been three phone calls. From Lon Cohen to say that they had been sorry not to get my usual contribution at the poker game — which was libel, since I win as often as he does and nearly as often as Saul Panzer — and to ask when I would spill a bean. From Bill Wengert of the *Times* to insinuate that he might let me have a short paragraph on page 84 if I would bring it gift-packaged, addressed to him personally. From Francis Ackerman in his Washington office to say that if Wolfe wanted to see him again, tell him a day in advance, and to warn us that our phone might be tapped or our office bugged. Watergate had certainly got on lawyers' nerves.

Not a peep from Cramer or the DA's office. I had got Roman Vilar the third try, a little before ten, and he said he would have to cancel two appointments to come at eleven, and he would.

I had also done the chores, including drawing a check for three grand for Wolfe to sign because the fifteen hundred had about cleaned out the reserve cash box, and clipping November 1 coupons from some municipal bonds —

in the tidy pile in the upper compartment of the safe with its own lock. I made a face as I clipped, because the rate on those bonds was 5.2 per cent, and high-grade tax-exempt municipals then being issued returned close to 8 per cent. Life is no joke if you're in or above the 50-per-cent bracket, as Wolfe was. Equal to 15 per cent on your money, and you only have to clip coupons—or have Archie Goodwin do it if you're busy nursing orchids.

Roman Vilar was not just a security errand boy. Fred had told me that Vilar Associates was maybe the biggest and best-known outfit in industrial security, and on the phone I had to go through two secretaries to get him. And he didn't start the conversation by inviting questions, far from it. He offered Wolfe a job, and me too.

"Before we get onto Harvey Bassett and your problem," he said, "I'd like to make a suggestion. One of my associates suggested it when I told him I was coming here, and three of us discussed it. We have some good investigators on our staff—two of them are absolutely top drawer—but as my associate said, think what it would mean if we were going after a contract with a big corporation, if we could say that if a really tough situation turned up we would put our best man on it, Nero Wolfe. Think what just the *name* would do. Of course there would be a certain amount of work for you, not too much, we know how you feel about work, but the main thing will be the *name*. I don't have to tell you how famous you are, you know that, and that's not all. There is also Archie Goodwin. We want him too, and the starting figure will be a hundred and twenty thousand for you, ten thousand a month, and thirty-six thousand for Goodwin, three thousand a month. We would prefer a five-year contract, but it could be three years if you prefer that, or even an option to terminate it at the end of a year if you would rather have it that way. Starting the first of the year, two months from now, but of course we could announce it immediately. I can see it, nothing loud or flashy, just a simple one-sentence announcement: 'If a major problem arises, our Nero Wolfe will be available.'"

He was leaning forward in the chair, all his points pointing—chin, nose, ears. "Of course," he said, "I don't expect an immediate answer. You'll want to consider it. You'll want to find out about us. But it's a firm offer. I would sign a contract here and now."

"Yes," Wolfe said, "I'll want to find out about you. Where were you and what were you doing last Friday night, October twenty-fifth, from six p.m. to two a.m.?"

Vilar slid back in the chair. He grinned. "I didn't expect *that*."

Wolfe nodded. "A fair exchange. Near the end of my talk with Mr. Ackerman last evening he asked if I really believe one of you six men killed Harvey Bassett, and I said of course, I am paying three men forty dollars an hour to inquire about you. That isn't ten thousand dollars a month, but it's a thick slice. It shouldn't take a month. You're in the security business. Richard Nixon's main buoy, in his frantic effort to keep himself afloat, was his plea of national security. Have you been involved in any way with any of the phenomena included in the term 'Watergate'?"

"No."

"Have you had any connection with anyone who has been involved?"

"One of the technicians who examined that tape with an eighteen-and-a-half-minute gap has done some work for me. Look, Wolfe. In my business I don't answer questions, I ask them. Forget it. Where I was last Friday night, for instance. Go fly a kite. We should have gone along with Ackerman. I may go to the DA myself. Why don't *you?* Why did you turn Hahn down? What are you trying to sell?"

Wolfe wiggled a finger. Regression again. Watergate had really loosened his hinges. "I'm not selling anything, Mr. Vilar." Vi-*lar*. "I'm buying satisfaction. Harvey Bassett wanted you to say that Richard Nixon had made it harder for you to sell your services. Had he in fact made it easier?"

"Well." Vilar stood up, no rush, taking his time. He looked down at Wolfe. It gives you an edge to look down at a man. "Well," he said, "I'll go to the DA myself."

"I doubt it," Wolfe said. He turned to me. "What odds, Archie?"

I pursed my lips. "Four to one."

Back to Vilar. "I'll make it five to one. A hundred dollars to twenty that you won't."

Vilar turned and marched out. "Marched" is wrong. Marching takes good full steps, and his legs weren't long enough. I followed him out and to the front with the idea of asking for a raise, four grand a month instead of three, but decided it wasn't the right moment. Back in the office I told Wolfe, "Actually it's ten to one. He's the kind that lets out all his sail and then puffs to make his own wind."

His eyes narrowed at me. "Who wrote that? Or said it?"

"I did. I've been looking through that book you just bought, *The Southern Voyages,* by that admiral, and I feel nautical. Is Vilar a murderer?"

"No. Possibly Bassett, but not Pierre. He wouldn't risk getting that bomb. Security. Confound it, I doubt if any of them would; they have all submitted to the constraint of prudence. Do you agree?"

"No. One of them might have known where he could get hold of one without anybody knowing. And Igoe could probably make one himself."

He grunted. "He is of course a menace. There is only one object on earth that frightens me: a physicist working on a new trick. Pfui. Reports?"

"Nothing to start a crack. Orrie didn't get a glimmer at Rusterman's, and I gave him Igoe. Saul, Judd is so solid and upright and well liked that he'll probably get a monument. Fred, everybody has a good word for Vilar, but he suspects that if any of them had had enough to drink it would be a different story. Acker —"

"When they call at one, tell them to come at six."

"I already have. They aren't earning their pay and they know it. Ackerman called from Washington to warn us that we may be phoning or talking on tape. That check on your desk is for the cash box, it's low. The letter from Hewitt about a new orchid was mailed last Saturday. Six days from Long Island to Manhattan. Forty-two miles. I could walk it in one day."

He reached for the pile of mail, glanced through it, and got up and went to the kitchen. Lunch was to be spareribs with a red-wine sauce that used eight herbs and spices, and he wanted to be sure Fritz didn't skimp on the garlic. They disagree about garlic. Montenegro vs. Switzerland.

As a rule I keep personal matters out of these reports, but since you know that I had got to Benjamin Igoe through Lily Rowan, I should mention that I had called her twice to let her know that I had seen him and it had led to developments. That afternoon, after we had disposed of the spareribs and answered the mail and I had been to the bank to cash the check, and Wolfe had gone up for his afternoon session with the orchids, I rang her again, told her that I was still out of jail, and said that I would probably be free to spend the weekend as she had suggested if I would still be welcome.

"I'm pretty sure I could stand you for an hour," she said, "and then we'll see. Anyway I want to look at you. I just got back from lunch with Dora Bassett at her house, and she asked about you again. And she has never seen you. Have you got some kind of draw that doesn't even need wires? Electronic?"

"No. Do me a favor. Don't ever mention electronics in my hearing. I'm sick and tired of electronics. Two favors. Tell me what she asked about me."

"Oh, don't get ideas. Nothing personal. She just asked if I had seen you and had you found out who put the bomb in Pierre's coat, but of course she didn't call him Pierre, she said 'that man' or 'that waiter.' I have a right to call him Pierre. As you know, I think he was the best waiter that ever fed me. He remembered that I like my fork at the right of my plate after just one time."

But she didn't ask what or how or why or when, although she knew we were working on it. Incredible. I'd buy a pedestal and put her on it if I thought she would stay. She would either fall off or climb down, I don't know which.

Again at six o'clock, when Wolfe came down, there was someone in the red leather chair. Saul Panzer, and Fred and Orrie were in two yellow ones. For a change we all had martinis. Fred didn't like the taste of gin but he wanted to be sociable. Wolfe would ring for beer, but he didn't, and that was a bad sign. When he skips beer, have your raincoat and rubbers handy.

He sat and surveyed them. "Nothing?"

They nodded. Saul said, "Never have so many done so little. You and Archie have at least looked at them."

"And seen nothing. Nothing that helps. Now. Weekends are always difficult, and don't try. Archie won't be here. Resume Monday morning. Fred, you will continue with Mr. Vilar. He's uneasy, and you may learn why. Call Archie Monday morning as usual. Orrie. How many of them have you seen?"

"All but three. They weren't there. One busboy saw someone in that room Monday he had never seen before, but he has only been there a week and anyway he's not too bright. Also, most of them were cagey. They knew what I was after, about Pierre, and, like everybody else, they don't want to be dragged in on a murder case. It's just possible that you might get something if you saw all of them yourself, but I doubt it. I could bring them in batches."

Of course he knew Wolfe wouldn't. Neither Saul nor Fred would have said that. Wolfe ignored it. "You may as well continue with Mr. Igoe, but call Archie Monday morning. Saul. You could see Mr. Judd himself. Should you?"

Saul shook his head. "I doubt it. I even doubt if *you* should. I have covered him pretty well. You have seen him, here with the others."

"Yes. I suppose Archie has told you that Mr. Hahn offered to pay me a hundred thousand dollars. I'll have to see him myself. I have seen Mr. Ackerman, and Mr. Urquhart is in Washington. You suggested Wednesday evening that you should see Miss Ducos."

"I said I could give it a try. I said Archie looks like a male chauvinist and I don't."

"Yes. See her. She feeds facts to a computer at New York University. Will she go to work tomorrow, Saturday?"

"Probably not. I'll find out. I'll want to ask Archie about her." Saul turned to me. "Any suggestions?"

"If I were a male chauvinist pig in good standing I'd say you might try raping her. As I said, she has good legs."

"I'd like to have a try at her," Orrie told Wolfe. "And Saul would be better with Igoe. Igoe's very brainy. He's a Ph.D."

We looked at him, surprised. He was good with women all right, we all knew that, but suggesting to Wolfe — to Wolfe, not just to me — to switch an errand from Saul to him, that was a surprise.

Wolfe shook his head. "Saul offered first. Has Archie told you that two of them — Ackerman and Vilar — have threatened to go to the District Attorney? We don't think they will, but they might, and if they do we'll have a problem. Mr. Cramer's attention will be directed at those six men, and he will learn that I have sent you to inquire about them. You will be questioned. You know the stand Archie and I have taken with both Mr. Cramer and the District Attorney. That will be futile unless you take the same stand. Tell them absolutely nothing. Stand mute. You will probably be held as material witnesses, possibly even charged with obstruction of justice. Mr. Parker will of course arrange for your release on bail. It's conceivable that eventually you'll be on trial for a felony and convicted, but I'll do everything in my power to prevent it."

He tightened his lips, then: "I suggest an alternative. Either you stay and take the risk, or you leave the jurisdiction immediately. The country. Either Canada or Mexico. Of course, at my expense. If you go, you shouldn't delay. At once. Tonight."

"I'll stay," Fred said. "I've got an idea about Vilar."

"What the hell," Orrie said. "Of course we stay."

"I won't say that," Saul said, "but I want to say *something*." He said it to Wolfe. "I'm surprised, really surprised, that you thought we might go."

"I didn't," Wolfe said.

Nuts. Saul knew damn well he didn't. They were all just putting on a charade.

11

I admit that, like everybody else, I like to think that I have hunches. For instance, the time that I was in the office of the head of a Wall Street brokerage firm and he brought in four members of his staff, and after talking with them five minutes I thought I knew which one of them had been selling information to another firm, and two weeks later he confessed. Or the time a woman came and asked Wolfe to find out who had taken her emerald and ruby bracelets, and when she left I had told him she had given them to her nephew, and he had taken it on anyhow because he wanted to buy some orchid plants, and had regretted it later when he had to sue to get his fee. By the way, that was one of the reasons he thought I could size up any woman in ten minutes.

But I'm not going to say it was a hunch I had that Saturday morning, because I don't see how it could have been. It might have been just something I had for breakfast, but I don't see how that was possible either, because Fritz had catered it as usual.

Whatever caused it, I had it. When I am dressing and getting packed for a weekend at Lily Rowan's pad in Westchester, which she calls The Glade, I thoroughly approve of the outlook. I enjoy shaving. I think my hair looks fine, and my zipper works like a dream. I'm willing to admit that being away from him for forty-eight hours is a factor—a change is good for you— but also I would breathe some fresh air and so forth.

But not that time. The electric shaver was too noisy. My fingers didn't like the idea of tying shoestrings. The tips of my necktie didn't want to come out even. I could go on, but that's enough to give you the idea. However, I made it. At least I didn't trip going downstairs.

Lily was expecting me out in front with the Heron at eleven o'clock, and it was only ten-twenty-five and there was no hurry, so I put my bag down in the hall, went to the kitchen to tell Fritz I was off, and to the office for a glance around. And as I was trying the knob of the safe, the phone rang. I should have left it to Fritz, but habit is habit, and I went and picked it up. "Nero Wolfe's resid—"

"I want to ask you just one question." Lon Cohen.

"If it can be answered yes or no, shoot."

"It can't. Where and when did you last see Lucile Ducos alive?"

I couldn't sink onto my chair, because it was turned wrong. I kicked it to swivel it and sat on the edge. "I don't believe it. Goddam it, I do *not* believe it."

"Yeah, they always say that. Are your eyes pop—"

"Quit clowning. When?"

"Forty minutes ago. We've just got a flash. On the sidewalk on Fifty-fourth Street a few yards from the house she lived in. Shot somewhere in the middle. Freebling is there, and Bob Adams is on the way. If—"

I hung up.

And my hand started for it to pick it up again. Actually. To pick it up and ring Homicide South to ask questions. Of course I pulled it back and sat and stared at it, first with my jaw set and then with my mouth open. Then I shut my eyes and my mouth. Then I did pick the phone up and dialed a number.

After six rings: "Hello?"

"Me. Good morning, only it isn't. Just as I was leaving, Lon Cohen phoned. There has been another murder, less than an hour ago. Lucile Ducos, Pierre's daughter. I'm stuck. I'm worse than stuck, I'm in up to my neck, and so is Wolfe. I hope you have a nice weekend. We don't say 'I'm sorry,' so I won't say it and neither will you. I'll think of you every hour on the hour. Please think of me."

"I don't ask if I can do anything, because if I could, you would tell me."

"I sure would. I will."

We hung up. I sat another three minutes, and then I got up and went and mounted the three flights to the plant rooms, taking my time. That was the third time, or maybe the fourth, I went down the aisles through those three rooms — the cool, then the moderate, then the warm — without seeing a thing. The benches could have been empty.

In the potting room Theodore was sitting at his little desk, writing on his pad of forms, and Wolfe was standing at the long bench, inspecting something in a big pot — presumably an orchid plant, but at that moment I wouldn't have known an orchid from a ragweed. As I crossed over he turned and scowled at me and said, "I thought you had gone."

"So did I. Lon Cohen phoned. Lucile Ducos was shot and killed about an hour ago on the sidewalk a few steps from her house. That's all Lon knew."

"I don't believe it."

"That's exactly what I said. I didn't either until I sat and went through the multiplication table. I beg your pardon for breaking a rule and interrupting you up here."

"Confound it, go."

I nodded. "Of course. Also of course Stebbins will be there and will take me down. You probably won't see me for —"

"No. Go to the country. Have your weekend. Tell Fritz to put the bolt on and ignore the telephone. I'll call Saul and tell him to call Fred and Orrie."

"Uhuh. You haven't sat and thought. For you two minutes should be enough. If the white apron — the maid — if she hasn't talked, she will. They'll know we were there. They'll know she found me in Lucile's room. They'll know Lucile sat and watched me for an hour while I did Pierre's room. So I know things about her they should know, and what I know, of course you know. If I disappear for the weekend and you bolt the door and don't answer the phone, that will only make it worse. I have phoned Miss Rowan."

Up there, when he sits it's usually on one of the stools at a bench, but there's a chair nearly big enough over in a corner, and he crossed to it. Since he hates to tilt his head to look up at someone standing, I went and got one of the heavy boxes for shipping plants in pots and brought it over and sat.

"It's Saturday," he said.

"Yes, sir. Parker will be somewhere playing golf, and even if I found him, judges won't be available, and Coggin almost certainly has still got those warrants. If you want to sleep in your house tonight, you have got to count ten and consider letting go. Don't scowl at *me*. I'm not trying to sell it, I'm not even suggesting it, I'm just telling you where I was when I finished the multiplication table. It seemed to me that even if we unloaded we could still go right on making inquiries about the commission of a capital crime on our private premises."

He growled, "You *are* trying to sell it."

"I am not. I'm game if you are. It's eleven o'clock, time to go down anyway, so come and sit in that chair and lean back and shut your eyes and work your lips. Cramer may be on his way here now. If not, he soon will be, and he may actually have handcuffs. We have been getting away with murder, and you know it and he knows it. Now three murders, because if the white apron is talking he knows about that dinner and the slip of paper Pierre did not tell me about."

He got up and walked out. Marched out. He always moves as if he weighed a twelfth of a ton instead of a seventh. When the door to the warm room had closed behind him, Theodore said, "It's always bad when you come up here."

I concede that as an orchid man Theodore may be as good as he thinks he is, but as a boon companion—a term I once looked up because Wolfe told me it was trite and shouldn't be used—you can have him. So I didn't bother to answer, and I would have liked to leave the box there for him to put back where it belonged, but that would have been like him, not me, so I didn't. I picked it up and returned it before leaving.

Wolfe had of course taken the elevator. When I entered the office he was standing over by the big globe, slowly turning it. Probably deciding where he wished he was, maybe with me along. I went to my desk and sat and said, "When Saul or Fred or Orrie hears the news he'll probably call, especially Saul. If so, what do I tell him?"

He turned the globe a few inches with his back to me. "To call Monday morning."

"He may be in the can Monday morning."

"Then call when Mr. Parker has got him out."

I got up and marched out. To the stairs and up to my room. One, the desire to kick his ample rump was so strong it was advisable to go where I couldn't see him, and two, what I had put on for a weekend in the country was not right for a weekend where I might spend it. While I got out more appropriate items and stripped, I tried to remember a time when he had been as pigheaded as this and couldn't. Then there must be a reason, and what was it? I was still working on that and putting on one of my oldest jackets when the phone rang and I went and got it.

"Nero Wolfe's—"

"You there, Archie? I thought you were going—"

"So did I. I got a piece of news." Saul Panzer. "Evidently you did too."

"Yes. Just now on the radio. I thought you were gone and he might need something."

"He does. He needs a kick in the ass and I was about to deliver it, so I came upstairs. I asked him what to say if you called, and he said tell you to call Monday morning."

"No."

"Yes."

"My god, doesn't he realize the cat's loose?"

"Certainly. I remarked that if he wanted to sleep here tonight he'd have to unload, and he just scowled at me. What did the radio tell you?"

"Only that she got it and the police are investigating. And that she was the daughter of Pierre Ducos. I called not only to ask if he needed something but also to report. I phoned her this morning at nine o'clock and told her that Nero Wolfe wanted me to see her and ask her a couple of questions. She said go ahead and ask them, and I said not on the phone, and she said to call her around noon. When I called at nine o'clock a woman answered, I suppose the one you call the white apron, and I told her my name and I was working for Nero Wolfe."

"Good. That helps. That makes it even better. You'd better stick a tooth-brush in your pocket."

"And a couple of paperbacks to read. If I'm going to stand mute I'll have plenty of leisure."

"Happy weekend," I said and hung up.

There's a shelf of books in my room, my property, and I went to get one — I don't know why, since I wasn't in a mood for any book I had ever heard of — but realized that Fritz was probably wondering what the hell was going on. So I left, descended the two flights and turned right at the bottom instead of left. In the kitchen Fritz was at the big table doing something to something. Normally I would have noticed what, but not that time. All the walls and doors on that floor are soundproofed, so I don't know why he wasn't surprised to see me. He merely asked, "Something happened?"

I got on a stool. "Yes, and more to come. A woman got killed, and it should mean a change of program, but he's trying to set a new world record for mules. Don't bother about lunch for me, I'll chew nails. I know you have problems with him too, garlic and juniper berries and bay leaf, but —"

The doorbell. I slid off the stool, went to the hall, took one look through the one-way glass panel, and entered the office. Wolfe was at his desk with the middle drawer open, counting beer-bottle caps.

"Sooner even than I expected," I said. "Cramer. Saul called. He phoned Lucile Ducos at nine o'clock this morning. The maid answered and he told her his name and said he was working for you. He told Lucile Ducos he wanted to see her and ask her some questions, and she told him to call her around noon."

The doorbell rang.

He said, "Grrrhh."

"I agree. Do I let Cramer in?"

"Yes."

I went to the front and opened the door, swung it wide, and he stepped in. I stood on the sill and looked out and down. His car was double-parked, with the driver in front at the wheel and one in the back seat I had seen but had never met. When I turned, no Cramer. I shut the door and went to the office. He was standing at the edge of Wolfe's desk, his hat and coat on, talking.

". . . and I may sit down and I may not. I've got a stenographer out in the car. If I bring him in, will you talk?"

"No."

"It's barely possible that I have news for you. Do you know that Pierre Ducos's daughter was shot down in front of her house four hours ago?"

"Yes."

"You do. The old man still won't talk, in *any* language, but a Homicide Bureau man and I have just spent an hour with Marie Garrou, the maid. *Will* you talk?"

"No."

"Goddam it, Wolfe, what's eating you?"

"I told you three days ago that I was outraged and out of control. I am no longer out of control, but I am still outraged. Mr. Cramer, I respect your integrity, your ability, and your understanding. I even trust you up to a point; of course no man has complete trust in another, he merely thinks he has because he needs to and hopes to. And in this matter I trust only myself. As I said, I am outraged."

Cramer turned his head to look at me, but he didn't see me. He turned back to Wolfe and leaned over to flatten his palms on the desk. "I came here with a stenographer," he said, "because I trust you too, up to a point. I want to say something not as Inspector Cramer or Mr. Cramer to a private investigator or Mr. Wolfe, but just as Cramer to Wolfe. Man to man. If you don't let go, you're sunk. Done. Let me bring him in and talk to *me*. *Now*."

Wolfe shook his head. "I appreciate this. I do. But even as Wolfe to Cramer, no."

Cramer straightened up and turned and went.

When the sound came of the front door opening and closing, I didn't even go to the hall for a look. If he had stayed inside, all right, he had. I merely remarked to Wolfe, "About any one little fact, I never know for sure whether you have bothered to know it or not. You may or may not know that the Homicide Bureau is a bunch of cops that don't take orders from Cramer. They're under the DA."

"Yes."

So he might have known it and he might not. "And," I said, "one of them helped him buzz Marie Garrou. I now know her name. And Cramer came straight here because he was sorry for you. That's hard to believe, but he did, and you should send him a Christmas card if you're where you can get one."

He squinted at me. "You changed your clothes."

"Certainly. I like to dress properly. This is my cage outfit. Coop. Hoosegow."

He opened the drawer, slid the bottle caps into it, shut the drawer, pushed his chair back, rose, and headed for the door. I supposed to tell Fritz to hurry lunch, but he turned right, and the elevator door opened and closed. Going up to tell Theodore to come tomorrow, Sunday. But I was wrong again; it went up only one flight. He was going to his room to change to *his* cage outfit, whatever that might be. It was at that point that I quit. The only possible explanation was that he really had a screw loose, and therefore my choice was plain. I could bow out for good, go to Twentieth Street, to either Stebbins or Cramer, and open the bag, or I could stick and take it as it came. Just wait and see.

I don't know, actually, why I stuck. I honestly don't know. Maybe it was just habit, the habit of watching him pull rabbits out of hats. Or maybe it was good old-fashioned loyalty, true-blue Archie Goodwin, hats off everybody. Or maybe it was merely curiosity; what *was* eating him and could he possibly get away with it?

But I know why I did what I did. It wasn't loyalty or curiosity that sent me to the kitchen to get things from the refrigerator—just plain horse sense. It would probably be Coggin, and he would like it even better if we were just sitting down to lunch, and I had had enough of the sandwiches they brought you at the DA's office. As I got out sturgeon and bread and milk and cucumber rings and celery and brandied cherries, Fritz looked but said nothing. He knows it is understood that it's his kitchen, and if I take liberties without asking, it is not the moment for conversation. My copy of the *Times* was still in the rack on the little table, and I opened it to Sports. I felt sporty. I was on the cherries when the sound came of the elevator. When I went to the office Wolfe was at his desk with a crossword puzzle.

I admit I have been working up to a climax, and here it is. Wolfe *had* gone up to change. But he had changed not to his oldest suit but his newest one—a soft light-brown with tiny yellow specks that you could see only under a strong light. He had paid Boynton $345.00 for it only a month ago. The same shirt, yellow of course, but another tie, solid dark-brown silk. I couldn't see his shoes, but he had probably changed them too. As I went to my desk and sat, I was trying to prepare a suitable remark, but it didn't come because I knew I should have just learned something new about him, but what?

"The mail," he said.

I hadn't opened it. I reached to my desk tray, a hollowed-out slab of green marble, for the opener and began to slit, and for the next twenty minutes you might have thought it was just a normal weekday. I had my notebook and Wolfe was starting on the third letter when Fritz came to announce lunch, and Wolfe got up and went without a glance at me. I don't know how he knew I had had mine.

I had typed the two letters and was doing the envelopes when the door-bell rang. My watch said 1:22, and the clock agreed. Evidently Coggin knew that Wolfe's lunch hour was a quarter past one. I got up and went. But it wasn't Coggin. It was a pair I had never seen before, standing stiff-backed shoulder to shoulder, and each one had a folded paper in his hand. When I opened the door, the one on the right said, "Warrants to take Nero Wolfe and Archie Goodwin. You're Goodwin. You're under arrest."

"Well," I said, "come in. While we get our coats on."

They crossed the sill and I shut the door. They were 5 feet 11, 180 pounds, very erect. I say "they" because they were twins, long narrow faces and big ears, but one was white and the other one black. "I've had my lunch," I said, "but Mr. Wolfe has just started his. Could we let him finish? Half an hour?"

"Sure, why not?" White said and started shedding his coat.

"No hurry at all," Black said.

They took their time hanging up their coats. No hats. I showed them the door to the office and entered the dining room. Wolfe was opening his mouth for a forkful of something. "Two from the Homicide Bureau," I said. "With warrants. I'm under arrest. I asked if you could finish your lunch, and they said sure, no hurry."

He nodded. I turned and went, in no hurry, in case he wished to comment, but he didn't. In the office, White was in the red leather chair with Wolfe's copy of the *Times*, and Black was over at the bookshelves looking at titles. I went to my desk, finished the envelopes and put things away, picked up the phone, and dialed a number. Sometimes it takes ten minutes to get Lon Cohen, but that time it took only two.

"So you're still around," he said.

"No. Here's that one little bean I said I would spill. Maybe in time for today. A scoop. Nero Wolfe and Archie Goodwin are under arrest as material witnesses. Just now. We are being taken down."

"Then why are you making phone calls?"

"I don't know. See you in court."

I hung up. Black said, "You're not supposed to do that." He was on a yellow chair with a book.

"Of course not," I said, "and I wonder why. 'No hurry at all.' I'm just curious. Do you feel sorry for me? Or for Nero Wolfe?"

"No. Why the hell should we?"

"Then you don't like the guy who sent you."

"Oh, he'll do. He's not the best but he's not the worst."

"Look," White said, "we know about you. Yeah, you're curious, more ways than one. Just forget it. It's Saturday afternoon, and we're off at four o'clock, and if we don't get there too soon we'll *be* off. So there's no hurry. If you have no objection."

He turned to another page of the *Times*. Black opened his book; I couldn't see the title. I got my nail file from the drawer and attended to a rough spot on my right thumbnail.

It was twenty-five minutes past two when we descended the seven steps of the stoop and climbed into the cars, Wolfe with White and me with Black.

12

"STAND mute" sounds simple, as if all you had to do is keep your mouth shut, but actually it's not simple at all. Assistant District Attorneys have had a lot of practice using words. For instance:

"Why did you compel, physically compel, Lucile Ducos to stay with you in her father's room while you searched the room?"

"In the signed statement you gave Sergeant Stebbins you said you included everything Pierre Ducos said to you. But you left out that he saw one of the men at that dinner hand Bassett a slip of paper. Why did you tell that lie?"

"If Ducos didn't tell you who had been at that dinner meeting, how did you learn about Benjamin Igoe?"

"If Ducos didn't tell you about that dinner meeting, who did?"

"Why did you tell Saul Panzer that Lucile Ducos must be kept from talking?"

"When did you learn that Nero Wolfe had persuaded Léon Ducos not to talk to the police?"

"What did you take from the pockets of Pierre Ducos before you reported your discovery of his body?"

"What did you find concealed in a book in the room of Lucile Ducos?"

That's just a few samples. I haven't included a sample of some asked by an assistant DA I had never seen before, a little squirt with gold-rimmed cheaters, because they were so damn ridiculous you wouldn't believe it — implying that Nero Wolfe had opened up. Implying that Saul and Fred and Orrie had talked, sure, that was routine. But Wolfe — now, really. As for me, I don't suppose I set a record for standing mute, but between three o'clock

Saturday afternoon and eleven-thirty Monday morning I must have been asked at least two thousand questions by three assistant DAs and Joe Murphy, the head of the Homicide Bureau. Most of Murphy's questions had nothing to do with murder. He wanted to know exactly why it had taken so long for Wolfe and me to get our coats on Saturday afternoon, and how the *Gazette* had got the news in time for the late edition that day. It was a pleasure to stand mute to him because I was glad to give Black and White a break, but with the others it wasn't easy and my jaw got tired from clamping it. The trouble was I like to be quick with good answers, and they knew it and did their best to get me started, and two of them were good at it. But mute doesn't mean pick and choose, it means mute, tongue-tied, aphonous, and don't forget it.

Of the lock-ups I have slept in, including White Plains, only thirty miles away, New York is the worst. The worst for everything—food, dirt, smell, companionship, prices of everything from newspapers to another blanket— everything. I hadn't seen Wolfe. I will not report on my feelings about him during that fifty-one hours, except to say that they were mixed. It was harder on him than on me, but he had asked for it. I hadn't used my right to make one phone call to ring Nathaniel Parker because I assumed Wolfe had, and anyway Parker had certainly seen the Sunday *Times,* no matter where he was. But where was he now? "Now" was ten minutes to six Monday afternoon, and I sat on my cot trying to pretend I wasn't stewing. The point was, at least one point, that tomorrow would be Election Day and judges might not be available—another reason to stew; an experienced private detective should know how many judges are available on Election Day, and I didn't. I was thinking that, in addition to everything else, Election Day had to come up and I might not be able to vote for Carey, when footsteps stopped at my door, a key scraped in the lock, the door opened, and a stranger said, "You're wanted downstairs, Goodwin. I guess you'd better take things."

There wasn't much to take. I put what there was in my pockets and walked out. My next-door neighbor on the left said something, but he was always saying something, and I didn't listen. The stranger herded me down the hall to the door at the end with steel bars about the size of my wrist, on which he had to use a key, on through, and across to the elevator. As we waited for it to come, he said, "You're number two hundred and twenty-four."

"Oh? I didn't know I had a number."

"You don't. *My* number. Guys I've had that I seen their pitcher in the paper."

"How many years?"

"Nineteen. Nineteen in January."

"Thanks for telling me. Two hundred and twenty-four. An interesting job you've got."

"*You* call it interesting. It's a job."

The elevator came.

In a big room on the ground floor with ceiling lights that glared, Nathaniel Parker sat on a wooden chair at one end of a big desk. The man behind the desk was in uniform, and another one in uniform stood at the other end. As I crossed over, Parker got up and offered a hand and I took it.

The one standing pointed to a little pile of articles on the desk, handed me a 5-by-8 card, and said, "If it's all there, sign on the dotted line. There's your coat on the chair."

It was all there — knife, key ring, wallet with no money in it because I had it in my pocket. Since I had been standing mute, I made sure the card didn't say anything it shouldn't before I signed. My coat smelled of something, but I smelled even worse, so what the hell. Parker was on his feet, and we walked out. The one behind the desk hadn't said a word. Neither did Parker until we were out on the sidewalk. Then he said, "Taxis are impossible, so I brought my car. It's around the corner."

I said firmly, "Also there's a bar around the corner." My voice sounded funny, probably rusty and needed oil. "I'd like to hear you talk a little, and not while you're driving."

The bar was pretty full, but a couple were just leaving a booth and we grabbed it. Parker ordered vodka on the rocks, and when I said a double bourbon and a large glass of milk he raised his brows.

"Milk for my stomach," I told him, "and bourbon for my nerves. How much this time?"

"Thirty thousand. Thirty for Wolfe and the same for you. Coggin pushed hard for fifty thousand because you're implicated, so he says, and you're standing mute. He said the charge will be changed to conspiracy to obstruct justice, and of course that was a mistake, and Judge Karp called him. You don't go to court with a *threat*."

"Where's Wolfe?"

"At home. I took him an hour ago. I want to know exactly what the situation is."

"It's simple. There have been three murders, and we're standing mute."

"Hell, I know that. That's all I know. I have never known Wolfe like this. He's practically standing mute to *me*. I'm counting on you to tell me exactly where it stands. In confidence. I'm your counsel."

The drinks came, and I took a sip of milk and then one of bourbon, and then two larger sips. "I'll tell you everything I know," I said. "It will take an hour and a half. But I can't tell you why we've dived into a foxhole because I don't know. He's standing mute to me too. We could give them practically everything we've got and still go right on with our knitting — we've done that a thousand times, as you know — but he won't. He told Roman Vilar — you know who he is?"

"Yes. He told me that much."

"He told him he's buying satisfaction. Goody. He'll pay for it with our licenses. Of course —"

"Your licenses have been suspended."

"We won't need them if we're behind bars. Where are Saul and Fred and Orrie?"

"They're behind bars now. I'll get them out tomorrow morning. Judge Karp has said he'll sit. You honestly don't know why Wolfe has holed in?"

"Yes, I don't. You're my lawyer?"

"Of course."

"Then I can give you a privileged communication. Have you got an hour?"

"No, but go ahead."

I took a swallow of bourbon and one of milk. "First a question. If I tell you everything as your client, I'll also be telling you things about your other client that he is *not* telling. What about conflict of interest? Should I get another lawyer?"

"Not unless you want a better one. He knows I'm acting for you. He knows you can tell me anything you want to. If he's willing to risk a conflict of interest, it's up to you. Of course, if you *want* another lawyer—"

"No, thank you. You'll be famous. It's a coincidence—Wolfe will like that. Five men being tried now in Washington for conspiracy to obstruct justice—Haldeman, Ehrlichman, Mitchell, Mardian, and Parkinson. Five being charged here with conspiracy to obstruct justice—Wolfe, Goodwin, Panzer, Durkin, and Cather. That's probably what Wolfe has in mind. I'm glad to be in on it. So here's my privileged communication."

I drank, milk and then bourbon for a change, and proceeded to confide in my lawyer.

An hour and a half later, at five minutes past eight, Parker dropped me off at Thirty-fifth Street and Eighth Avenue. I would stretch my legs for a block and a half. He now had plenty of facts but could offer no suggestion on what to do with them, since I still intended to hang on. It was ten to one that he would have liked to advise me to turn loose but couldn't on account of Wolfe. That looked to me a lot like conflict of interest, but I had learned not to try splitting hairs with a lawyer. They think you're not in their class. Anyway we shook hands before I climbed out.

At the brownstone the chain bolt was on and I had to ring for Fritz. I am not rubbing it in when I say that he pinched his nose when I took my coat off; a super cook has a super sense of smell.

"I don't need to say," he said. "Anyway, here you are, *grâce à Dieu*. You look terrible."

I kept the coat on my arm. "I feel worse. This will have to go to the cleaners, and so will I. In about two hours I'll come down and clean out the refrigerator and shelves for you, and you can start over. He's in the dining room?"

"No, I took up a tray, a plain omelet with five eggs and bread for toast, and coffee. Before that he had me rub lilac vegetal on his back. The paper said you were in jail, all of you. Are you going to tell me anything? He didn't."

"It's like this, Fritz. I know ten thousand details that you don't know, but the one important detail, what's going to happen next—I'm no better off than you are. You tell *me* something. You know him as well as I do, maybe better. What's the French word for crazy? Insane. Batty."

"*Fou. Insensé.*"

"I like *fou*. Is he *fou*?"

"No. He looked me in my eye."

"Okay, then wait and see. Do me a favor. Buzz him on the house phone and tell him I'm home."

"But you'll see him. He'll see you."

"No he won't. I'm not *fou* either. *You'll* see me in two hours." I headed for the stairs.

13

YOU would expect—anyway, I would—that the main assault in the campaign of the media to get the story to the American people would come from the *Gazette*. The *Gazette* was the leader in emphasizing flavor and color in everything from markets to murders, and also there was the habit of my exchanging tits for tats with Lon Cohen. But the worst two were Bill Wengert of the *Times* and Art Hollis of CBS News. Now that the dinner party at Rusterman's was in the picture—nobody knew exactly how—and the murder of Harvey H. Bassett of NATELEC was connected with the other two—nobody knew exactly why—probably the brass at the *Times* was on Wengert's neck. And Hollis, the damn fool, had sold CBS the idea of sending a crew with equipment to Nero Wolfe's office for a twenty-six-minute interview without first arranging to get them in. So for a couple of days a fair amount of my time and energy was devoted to public relations. Omitting the details, I will only remark that it is not a good idea to persuade the *Times* that any future item of news with your name in it will not be fit to print.

The most interesting incident Tuesday morning was my walking to a building on Thirty-fourth Street to enter a booth and push levers on a voting machine. I have never understood why anybody passes up that bargain. It doesn't cost a cent, and for that couple of minutes you're the star of the show, with top billing. It's the only way that really counts for you to say I'm it, I'm the one that decides what's going to happen and who's going to make it happen. It's the only time I really feel important and know I have a right to. Wonderful. Sometimes the feeling lasts all the way home if somebody doesn't bump me.

There was no sight or sound of Wolfe until he came down for lunch. No sound of the elevator, so he didn't go up to the plant rooms. I knew he was alive and breathing, because Fritz told me he cleaned up a normal breakfast, and also, when I returned from voting and a walk around a few blocks, Fritz reported that Parker had phoned and Wolfe had taken it up in his room. And the program for lunch was normal—baked bluefish stuffed with ground shrimp, and endive salad with watercress. When Wolfe came down at a quarter past one he looked in at the office door to tell me good morning, though it wasn't morning, and then crossed to the dining room. I had considered eating in the kitchen but had decided that we would have to be on speaking terms, since we had the same counsel. Also it would have given Fritz one more reason to worry, and he didn't need it.

As I got seated at the table, Wolfe asked if there had been any word from Fred or Orrie, and I said yes, they had called and I had told them to stand by, I would call them as soon as I knew what to say. He didn't mention Saul, so I assumed he had called while I was out, though Fritz hadn't said so. And he didn't mention the call from Parker. So evidently, although we were on speaking terms, the speaking wasn't going to include the matter of our right to life and liberty and the pursuit of happiness. When he had carved the bluefish and Fritz had brought me mine and taken his, he asked me where he should go to vote and I told him. Then he asked how many seats I thought the Democrats would gain in the House and the Senate, and we discussed it in detail. Then he asked if I had split the ticket, and I said yes, I had voted for Carey but not for Clark, and we discussed that.

It was quite a performance. Over the years he had had relapses and grouches, and once or twice he had come close to a tantrum, but this was a new one. Our licenses had been suspended, if we crossed the river to Jersey or drove up to Westport or Danbury we would be locked up without bail, and we had three men out on the same limb with us, but pfui. Skip it. It will all come out in the wash. And Fritz was right, he wasn't *fou*, he had merely decided that, since the situation was absolutely hopeless, he would ignore it. When we left the table at ten minutes past two, I decided to give him twenty-four hours and then issue an ultimatum, if necessary.

Four hours later I wan't so sure. I wasn't sure of anything. When we left the dining room he had neither crossed the hall to the office nor taken the elevator back to his room; he had announced that he was going to go and vote and reached to the rack for the coat he had brought down. Certainly; voting was one of the few personal errands that got him out in any weather. But at a quarter past six he hadn't come back, and that was ridiculous. Four hours. All bets were off. He was in a hospital or the morgue, or in an airplane headed for Montenegro. I was regetting that I hadn't turned on the six-o'clock news and considering whether to start phoning now or wait until after dinner when the doorbell rang and I went to the hall, and there he was. He never carried keys. I went and opened the door and he entered, said, "I decided to do an errand," and unbuttoned his coat.

I said, "Much traffic?"

He said, "Of course. There always is."

As I hung up his coat I decided not to wait until tomorrow for the ultimatum. After dinner in the office, when Fritz had gone with the coffee tray. Wolfe went to the kitchen, and I went up to my room to stand at the window and consider how to word it.

That meal stands out as the one I enjoyed least of all the ones I have had at that table. I really thought it might be the last one, but I used my knife and fork as usual, and chewed and swallowed, and heard what he said about things like the expressions on people's faces as they stood in line in front of the voting booths. When we went to the office and sat and Fritz came with the coffee, I still hadn't decided how to start the ultimatum, but that didn't bother me. I knew from long experience that it would go better if I let it start itself.

There were a couple of swallows left of my second cup when the doorbell rang and I went for a look. It was a gang, and I went part way down the hall to make sure before I returned to the office and said, "It's four of the six. Vilar, Judd, Hahn, and Igoe. No Ackerman or Urquhart."

"None of them telephoned?"

"Yes. None."

"Bring them."

I went. I couldn't tell, as I swung the door open and they entered and got their coats off, what to expect. Evidently they hadn't come merely to deliver an ultimatum, for in the office Judd went to the red leather chair and the others moved up yellow ones. And Judd told Wolfe, "You don't look like you've just spent time in jail."

"I have spent more time in a dirtier jail," Wolfe said. "In Algiers."

"Yes? I have never been in jail. Yet. Two of us wanted to come this morning, but I wanted to get more facts. I haven't got them—not enough. Perhaps you can supply them. I understand that you and Goodwin aren't talking, not at all, and neither are the men you hired, but we are being asked about a slip of paper one of us handed Bassett at that dinner, and there has been another murder, and we are even being asked where we were Saturday morning, when that woman was killed. You said you wouldn't go to the District Attorney, and apparently you haven't. You didn't go, you were taken. We want to know what the hell is going on."

"So do I."

"Goddam it," Igoe blurted, "you'll talk to *us!*"

"I will indeed." Wolfe sent his eyes around. "I'm glad you came, gentlemen. I suppose Mr. Ackerman and Mr. Urquhart didn't want to enter this jurisdiction, and I don't blame them. As for the slip of paper, Lucile Ducos knew about it, but she was killed. Evidently Marie Garrou, the maid, also knew about it, possibly by eavesdropping, and she has talked. So you are being harassed, and that's regrettable. But I don't regret hunting you up and entangling you, because one of you supplied information that I may find useful. Two of you. Mr. Igoe told Mr. Goodwin that Mr. Bassett had obsessions—his word—and Mr. Hahn told me that one of his obsessions, a powerful one, centered on his wife."

When I heard him say that, I knew. It came in a flash, like lightning. It wasn't a guess or a hunch, I *knew.* I'm aware that you probably knew a while back and you're surprised that I didn't, but that doesn't prove that you're smarter than I am. You are just reading about it, and I was in it, right in the middle of it. Also, I may have pointed once or twice, but I'm not going back and make changes. I try to make these reports straight, straight accounts of what happened, and I'm not going to try to get tricky.

I'll try to report the rest of that conversation, but I can't swear to it. I was there and I heard it, but I had a decision to make that couldn't wait until they had gone. Obviously Wolfe was standing mute to me. Why? Damn it, *why?* But that *could* wait, and the decision couldn't. The question was, should I let him know that I now knew the score? And something happened that had happened a thousand times before: I discovered that I was only pretending to try to decide. The decision had already been made by my subconscious—I call it that because I don't know any other name for it. I was not going to let him know that I knew. If that was the way he wanted to play it, all right, it took two to play and we would see who fumbled first.

Meanwhile they were talking, and I have changed my mind. I said I would try to report the rest of that conversation, but I would be faking it. If anyone had said anything that changed the picture or added to it, I would report that, but they didn't. Wolfe tried to get Hahn and Igoe started again on Mrs. Bassett, but no. Evidently they had decided they shouldn't have mentioned her. They had come to find out why Wolfe had dragged them in, and specifically they wanted to know—especially Judd and Vilar—about Pierre Ducos, who had died there in Wolfe's house when no one was there

but us, and about his daughter. At one point I expected Wolfe to walk out
on them, but he stuck and let them talk. He had admitted — stated — that it
was regrettable that they were being harassed and that they had supplied
useful information. Also, of course, they might possibly supply more, but
they didn't. I knew they didn't, now that I had caught up.

It was a little past ten o'clock when I returned to the office after seeing
them out, and I had made another decision. It would be an hour before he
went up to bed, and if he started talking, it would be a job to handle my
voice and my face. So instead of sitting I said, "I can catch the last half-
hour of a hockey game if I hurry. Unless I'm needed?" He said no and
reached for a book, and I went to the hall and reached for my coat. Outside,
the wind was playing around looking for things to slap, and I turned my
collar up, walked to the drugstore at the corner of Eighth Avenue, went in
and to the phone booth, and dialed a number.

"Hello?"

"This is the president of the National League for Prison Reform. When
would it be convenient to give me half an hour to discuss our cause?"

"Have you bathed and shaved?"

"No. I'm Exhibit A."

"All right, come ahead. Use the service entrance."

I got a break. Getting a taxi at that time of night may take anything from
a minute to an hour, and here one came as I reached the curb.

Of course it was also a break that Lily was at home with no company. She
had been at the piano, probably playing Chopin preludes. That isn't just a
guess; I can tell by her eyes and the way she uses her voice. Her voice
sounds as if it would like to sing, but she doesn't know it. She told me to go
to the den and in a couple of minutes came with a tray — a bottle of champagne and two glasses.

"I put it in the freezer when you phoned," she said, "so it should be about
right." She sat. "How bad was it?"

"Not bad at all. I sat on the cot and shut my eyes and pretended I was in
front of the fire at The Glade with you in the kitchen broiling a steak." I
pushed on the cork. "No glass for Mimi?"

"She's gone to a movie. How bad *is* it?"

"I wish I knew. I think we'll come out alive, but don't ask for odds." The
cork came, and I tilted the bottle and poured. The den has a door to the
terrace, and I went and opened it and stood the bottle outside. She said,
"To everybody, starting with us," and we touched glasses and drank.

I sat. "Speaking of odds, if florist shops had been open I would have
brought a thousand red roses. I gave you a thousand to one that Doraymee
wouldn't regret telling you about Benjamin Igoe, and I'm pretty sure it was
a bad bet. So I owe you an apology."

"Why will she regret it?"

"I'll tell you someday, I hope soon. I phoned and asked if I could come
for three reasons. One, I like to look at you. Two, I had to apologize. Three,
I thought you might be willing to answer a question or two about
Doraymee."

"She doesn't like to be called that."

"All right, Dora Bassett."

"What kind of a question? Will she regret it if I answer?"

"She might. It's like this. Her husband was murdered. Your favorite waiter was murdered. His daughter was murdered. It's possible that it would help to find out who did it if you would tell me exactly what Dora Bassett said when she asked you about me. That's the question I want to ask. What did she say?"

"I told you. Didn't I?"

"Just if you had seen me since her husband died. And the second time, had I found out who put the bomb in Pierre's coat."

"Well, that was it."

"Do you remember her exact words?"

"You know darned well I don't. I'm not a tape recorder like you."

"Did she mention Nero Wolfe?"

"I think so. I'm not sure."

"Did she mention anyone else? Saul Panzer or Fred Durkin or Orrie Cather?"

"No. She was asking about you. Listen, Escamillo. I don't like this, and you know it. I told you once I don't like to think of you as a private detective, but I realize I wouldn't like to think of you as a stockbroker or a college professor or a truckdriver or a movie actor. I just like to think of you as Archie Goodwin. I like that a lot, and you know it."

She drank champagne, emptied her glass. I put down my glass, bent down to take her slipper off—blue silk or something with streaks of gold or something—poured a couple of ounces of champagne in it, lifted it to my mouth, and drank.

"That's how I like you," I said. "Hereafter I would leave my license as a detective at home if I had one. It's been suspended."

14

WHEN I went to bed and to sleep Tuesday night, I knew I was going to do something in the morning but didn't know what. I only knew that when Wolfe came down, either from the plant rooms at eleven or later for lunch, I wouldn't be there. When I opened my eyes and rolled out Wednesday morning, I knew exactly where I would be at eleven o'clock and what I would be doing. It's very convenient to have a Chairman of the Board who decides things while you sleep. At eleven o'clock I would be in the bedroom of the late Lucile Ducos, determined to find something. There *had* to be something; otherwise it might take weeks, even months.

I would have liked to go right after breakfast, but it was advisable not to tackle the white apron, now known as Marie Garrou, until she had had time to give Grandpa Ducos his breakfast and get him and his wheelchair to the window in the front room, and at least get a good start on the rest of the daily routine. So as I finished my second cup of coffee I told Fritz I would leave at ten-thirty on a personal errand, and would he please tell Wolfe, who had gone up to the plant rooms, that I wouldn't be there for lunch. He asked if he should answer the phone, and I said sure, we still had our freedom of speech.

The office had been neglected for several days and needed attention. The film of dust on the chairs that hadn't been used. The stack of junk mail that had accumulated. The smell of the water in the vase on Wolfe's desk. And a dozen other details. So I didn't get away at ten-thirty. It was twenty minutes of eleven when I got ten double sawbucks from the cash box, wrote "11/6 AG 200" in the book, and closed the door of the safe. As I turned for a look around to see if I had missed anything, the doorbell rang.

It's true that there had been several pictures of her in the *Gazette* and one in the *Times,* but I assert that I would have known her anyway. It was so fit, so *natural,* for Mrs. Harvey Bassett to show, that when a woman was there on the stoop it had to be her. I had gone two miles at eleven o'clock at night to ask Lily Rowan a question about her, and there she was.

I went and opened the door and said, "Good morning," and she said, "I'm Dora Bassett. You're Archie Goodwin," and walked in and kept going, down the hall.

Any way you look at it, surely I was glad to see her, but I wasn't. For about twelve hours I had known that seeing her would certainly be on the program, but I would choose the time and place. Since Wolfe had gone up to the plant rooms, he would come down at the usual hour, and it was twelve minutes to eleven. If I followed precedent I would either go up there or go and buzz him from the kitchen, but precedent had been ignored for more than a week. So when I entered the office I didn't even glance at her — she was standing in the middle of the room — as I crossed to my desk. I sat and reached for the house phone and pushed the button.

He answered quicker than usual. "Yes?"

"Me. Mrs. Harvey H. Bassett just came. I didn't invite her. Perhaps you did."

"No." Silence. "I'll be down at once."

As I hung up she said, "I didn't come to see Nero Wolfe. I came to see you."

I looked at her. So that was Doraymee. The front of her mink or sable or sea-otter coat — it has got to the point where I can't tell cony from coonskin — was open, showing black silk or polyester. She was small but not tiny. Her face was small too, and if it hadn't been so made up, perhaps for the first time since she had lost her husband, it would probably have been easy to look at.

I stood up. "He's coming down, so you'll see both of us. I'll take your coat?"

"I want to see *you.*" She tried to smile. "I know a lot about you, from your books and from Lily Rowan."

"Then you must have known Mr. Wolfe's schedule, to the office at eleven o'clock. He'll want to meet you, naturally." I moved. "I might as well take your coat."

She looked doubtful, then turned for me to get it. I put it on the couch, and when I turned she was in the red leather chair. As I went to my chair she said, "You're taller than I expected. And more — more — *rougher.* Lily thinks you're graceful."

That simply wasn't so. Lily did *not* think I was graceful. Was she trying to butter me and be subtle about it? I didn't have time to decide how to reply because the elevator had hit the bottom and I had to make sure my face was ready for Wolfe. He was not going to have the satisfaction of knowing I had caught up until I was ready.

He went to his desk and turned the chair so he would be facing her. As he sat she said, louder and stronger than before, "I came to see Archie Goodwin."

He said, just stating a fact, "This is my office, Mrs. Bassett."

"We could go to another room."

I didn't have the slightest idea of his game plan. He might have merely wanted to have a look at her and hear her voice, and intended to get up and go to the kitchen. So I told her, "I work for Mr. Wolfe, Mrs. Bassett." If it sounded sarcastic to him, fine. "I would tell him whatever you said to me. Go ahead."

She looked at me. She had fine brown eyes, really too big for her small face. Her make-up hadn't included phony lashes. "I wanted to ask you about my husband," she said. "From the newspapers and television, they seem to think his death — his — his murder — that the murder of that waiter was connected with it. And then his daughter. And he was murdered here." She looked at Wolfe. "Here in your house."

"He was indeed," he said. "What do you want to ask about your husband?"

"Why, I just —" She cleared her throat. "It has been five days, nearly a week, and the police don't tell me anything. I thought you might. They must think you know because they arrested you because you won't talk. I thought you might tell me . . ." She fluttered a hand. "Tell me what you know."

"Then you've wasted a trip, madam. I spent two days and nights in jail rather than tell the police. I'll tell you one thing I know: the murders of your husband and that waiter *are* connected. And that woman. Of course I could tell you an assortment of lies, but I doubt if it's worth the effort. I'll tell you what I think: I think *you* could tell *me* something. It might help if you knew I wouldn't repeat it to the police. To anyone. I wouldn't. I give you my word, and my word is good."

She regarded him, her eyes straight at him. She opened her mouth and closed it again, tight. She looked at me. "Couldn't we go to another room?"

I stood up. Sometimes you don't have to make a decision, not even your subconscious; it's just there. "Certainly," I said. "My room's upstairs. Just leave your coat here."

I use the elevator about once a month, and never alone. As I took her out to it I wished there had been a mirror there on the wall so I could see Wolfe's face. In the last couple of days I had spent a lot of minutes wondering about him, and now he would spend some wondering about me. As the elevator fought its way up and we went down the hall and entered my room and I shut the door, my mind should have been on her and what line to take, but it wasn't. It was downstairs enjoying Wolfe.

But the line I would take was decided by her, not by me. As I turned from closing the door she put hands on me. First she gripped my arms, then she had her arms around my neck with her face pressed against my middle ribs, her shoulders trembling. Well. With a woman in that position you can't even guess. She may be suggesting that you take her clothes off or she may be grabbing the nearest solid object to keep on her feet. But it seems silly just to let your arms hang, and I had mine around her, patting her back. In a minute I gave her fanny a couple of little pats, which is one way of asking a question. Her hold around my neck didn't tighten, which is one way of answering it.

Her shoulders stopped trembling. I said, "You could have done this downstairs. He would have just got up and walked out. And I could have brought you something from the kitchen. Up here there's nothing to drink but water."

She lifted her head enough to move her lips. "I don't want a drink. I wanted *this*. I want your arms around me."

"You do not. You just want arms around you, not necessarily mine. Not that I mind pinch-hitting. Come and sit down."

Her arms loosened. I patted her back again, then put my hands up and around and got her wrists. She let go and straightened up and even used a hand to brush her hair back from her eyes and adjust the fur thing that perched on it. There were two chairs, a big easy one over by the reading lamp and a small straight one at the little desk. I steered her across to the big one and went and brought the small one.

She had come guessing and she would have to leave guessing. Of course I would have liked to know a lot of things that she knew, and her arms around my neck with her shoulders shaking showed that I could probably pry them out of her, but if I tried to, she would have known how much *I* knew, and that wouldn't do. Not yet. So as I sat I said, "I'm sorry that's all I have for you, Mrs. Bassett, just a pair of arms. If you thought I could tell you something that the police don't know or won't tell, I can't. We aren't talking to the police because we have nothing to say. If you have read some of my books, you must know that Nero Wolfe is one of a kind. I admit I'm a little curious about you. Miss Rowan told me you never read books. Why have you read some of mine?"

From the way her big brown eyes looked at me, you wouldn't have thought she had just had her arms around my neck. Nor from her tone as she asked, "What else did she tell you about me?"

"Nothing much. She just mentioned that she had seen you and you had asked her about me."

"I asked her about you because I knew she knew you and your picture was in the paper."

"Sure. Yours was too. Why did you read some of my books?"

"I didn't. I told her I did because I knew about her and you." She stood up. "I'm sorry I came. I guess I—I just thought . . ." She shook her head. "I don't know what I thought. I don't want—My coat's in there where he is."

I was up. I told her I would get her coat and went and opened the door, and she came. That elevator is one of a kind too; it complains more about going down than about going up. Downstairs, she stayed in the hall when I went into the office for her coat. Wolfe wasn't there; presumably he had gone to the kitchen. I wrote on a sheet of my memo pad:

NW:
I'm taking Mrs. B. home. Probably not back for lunch.
                                                        AG

I put it under a paperweight on his desk, went to the hall with Mrs. Bassett's mink or sable or sea otter and held it for her, put my coat on, and let us out. Her Rolls-Royce was there at the curb, but I didn't go and open the door for her because as we descended to the sidewalk the chauffeur climbed out and had it open by the time she was down. When he got back in and it rolled, I walked to Ninth Avenue and turned uptown.

It was ten minutes past noon when I pushed the button in the vestibule at 318 West Fifty-fourth Street. Three minutes passed with no response, and I shook my head. They might have cleared out. It had been four days since the daughter had been killed; the old man might be in a hospital. They might even have gone back to France. But then her voice came, exactly as before: "Who ees eet?"

"Archie Goodwin, from Nero Wolfe. I don't want to bother Mr. Ducos, and anyway I don't speak French, as you know. I'd like to come up, if you can spare a few minutes."

"What for? I don't know anything."

"Maybe not, but Nero Wolfe and I would appreciate it. Sill voo play."

"You don't speak French."

"I know I don't, but everybody knows those three words, even dummies like me. Please?"

"Well . . . for Nero Wolfe . . ."

The click sounded, and I pushed the door and was in, and the elevator was there with the door open. Upstairs, the door of the apartment was open too and she was there on the sill, white apron and cap exactly as before. She looked even shorter and dumpier, and the crease in the double chin looked deeper. From the way she stood and the expression on her face, it was obvious I wasn't going to be invited in, so I had to try throwing a punch, hoping it would land.

"I suppose I call you Marie," I said.

She nodded. "That's my name." You'll have to supply her accent; I'm not going to try to spell it.

"Well, Marie, you probably prefer straight talk, so I'll just say that I know you heard Miss Ducos and me talk that evening. You must have. You told the police about the slip of paper, and other things. Or you may have heard Mr. Ducos and Nero Wolfe talking. I'm not saying you listened when you shouldn't, I'm just saying that you heard. I don't know if you heard Miss Ducos tell me that you didn't like her. Did you?"

"I don't listen when I shouldn't listen."

"I didn't say you do. But you must know *she* didn't like *you*. A woman knows when another woman doesn't like her."

"She's dead, but it won't hurt her to say I didn't like her. I didn't hate her, I had no reason to hate her. And she's dead. You didn't come just to tell me I didn't like her."

"No. It's warm in here." I took my coat off. "I came because we think there's something here that will help us find the man who killed Pierre. Probably the slip of paper, but it could be something else. That's what I was looking for in Pierre's room. But I didn't find it, and maybe it wasn't there, maybe it was in her room, and of course she knew it was. Maybe it's still there, and that's what I came for, to see if I can find it."

No visible reaction. She just said, "The police looked in her room."

"Of course, naturally they would, but they probably weren't very thorough. Anyway, they didn't find it, so I would like to try. Nero Wolfe could have come to ask Mr. Ducos to let me look, but he didn't want to bother him. You can stay with me to see that I don't do anything I shouldn't do."

She was shaking her head. "No." She repeated it. "No."

There are a thousand ways of saying no and I had heard a lot of them. Sometimes it's more the eyes than the tone of voice that tells you what kind of a no it is. Her little dark eyes, nearly black, were a little too close together, and they blinked a little too often. It was ten to one that I couldn't sell her, but even money, maybe better, that I could buy her. "Look, Marie," I said, "you know a man gave Pierre a hundred dollars for that slip of paper."

"No. A hundred dollars? I don't know that."

"Well, he did. But Pierre might have made a copy of it. And Lucile might have found it and made a copy too." My hand went to my pocket and came out with the little roll I had taken from the cash box. I draped my coat over my arm to have both hands and peeled off five of the ten twenties and returned them to my pocket. "All right," I said, "I'll give *you* a hundred dollars to give me a chance to find Lucile's copy or to find something else that may be in her room. It may take five minutes or it may take five hours. Here, take it."

Her eyes said she would, but her hands didn't move. The white apron had two little pockets, and I folded the bills into a little wad and stuck it in her left pocket, and said, "If you don't want to stay with me, you can search me before I leave."

"Only *her* room," she said."

"Right," I said, and she backed up, and I entered. She turned, and I followed her down the hall to Lucile's room. She entered but went in only a couple of steps, and I crossed to a chair by a window and put my coat on it.

"I'm not going to stay," she said. "I have things to do, and you're Archie Goodwin, and I told you, I know about you and Nero Wolfe from him. Do you want a cup of coffee?"

I said no thanks, and she left.

If it was a slip of paper, the most likely place was the books, but after seeing me doing her father's room she might have put it somewhere else. There was a desk with drawers by the right wall, and I went and opened the top drawer. It was locked, but the key was sticking in the lock, probably left there by a city employee. It held an assortment—several kinds of notepaper and envelopes, stubs of bills, presumably paid bills, pencils and pens, a bunch of snapshots with a rubber band around them. Five minutes was enough for that. The second drawer was full of letters in envelopes addressed to Miss Lucile Ducos, various sizes and shapes and colors. A collection of letters is always a problem. If you don't read them, the feeling that you may have missed a bus nags you, and if you do read them it's a hundred to one that there won't be a damn thing you can use. I was taking one out of the envelope just for a look when a bell rang somewhere, not in that room. Not the telephone, probably the doorbell, and I made a face. It probably wasn't a Homicide man, since the murder was four days old, but it could be, and I cocked my ear and heard Marie's voice, so faint I didn't get the words. The voice stopped, and there were footsteps.

She appeared at the door. "A man down there says his name is Sole Panzaire and Nero Wolfe sent him. He wants to come up."

"Did you tell him I'm here?"

"Yes."

"You told him my name?"

"Yes."

"I guess Nero Wolfe sent him to help me." I got the rest of the bills from my pocket and crossed over to her. "He does that sometimes without telling me." Her apron pocket was empty, and I folded one of the twenties and reached to put it in. "Saul Panzer is a good man, Nero Wolfe trusts him. With him to help, it won't take so long."

"I don't like it."

"We don't like it either, Marie, but we want to find the man that killed Pierre."

She turned and went. I started to follow her, decided not to, went back to the desk, listened for the sound of the elevator, and didn't hear it until it stopped on that floor. I opened the drawer and was taking a letter from an envelope when there were footsteps and then Saul's voice. "Any luck, Archie?"

He would. Saving his surprise until there were no other ears to hear it. "Don't push," I told him. "I just got started." I walked to the door for a look in the hall. Empty. I shut the door. He was putting his coat on the chair with mine. "So that's where he was yesterday afternoon," I said. "He went to see you. I'll try not to get in your way, but I'm not going to leave."

We were face to face, eye to eye. "You're on," he said.

"You're damn right I'm on. I'm on my own."

He laughed. Not with his mouth, no noise; he laughed with his eyes, and by shaking his head. And he didn't stop. "Laugh your goddam head off," I said, "but don't get in *my* way. I'm busy." I went to the desk and reached to the drawer for a letter, and my hand was trembling. Saul's voice came from behind.

"Archie, this is the first time I ever knew you to miss one completely. I supposed you had it figured and was enjoying it. You actually didn't know that he thought you'd kill him? That he thinks he *knows* you would?"

The letter dropped from my hand, and I guess my mouth dropped open as I turned. "Balls," I said.

"But he does. He says you wouldn't do it with a gun or a club, just with your hands. You'd hit him so hard you'd break his neck, or you'd throw him so hard and so far he'd break his neck when he landed. I didn't try to argue him out of it, because he *knew* it."

"I thought he knew me. And you think it's funny."

"I *know* it's funny. He does know you. I thought you knew him. It's just that he wants to kill him himself. So do I. So do you."

"Were you on?"

"Not till he came yesterday, but I should have been. A lot of things — Pierre not telling you, that room at Rusterman's, her asking Lily Rowan about you, him and women, him offering to work for nothing, him wanting to take Lucile Ducos—I certainly should have been on." He tapped his skull with his knuckles. "Empty."

"Mine too, until last night. Have you got anything?"

"Nothing solid. I only started to look yesterday at half past five. I've got an idea how he might have met her. As you know, he often does jobs for Del Bascom, and Bascom took on something for Bassett, for NATELEC, about a year ago. At noon I decided to take a look here, and here you are ahead of me."

"Not much ahead, I just started. Okay. I came for myself, and you came for him. Who's in charge?"

He grinned. "It's a temptation, sure it is, but I'm not like Oscar Wilde, I can resist it. Where do you want me to start?"

I was returning the grin. Saul doesn't often drag in such facts as that he knows about people like Oscar Wilde and I don't. "You might try this desk," I said. "I've only done the top drawer. There's a lot of books, and I'll start on them."

15

TWO hours later, when Marie came, we had covered a lot of ground, at least Saul had, and had found exactly nothing. He had done the desk, chairs, closet, bed, floor, dresser, pictures on the wall, and a stack of magazines, and had really done them. Flipping through the hundred and some books had taken me half an hour, and then I had settled down to it, starting over and turning the pages one by one, making sure not to skip. Saul was having another go at shoes from the closet, examining the insides, when the door opened and Marie was there with a loaded tray. She crossed to the table and put the tray down and said, "I went out for the beer. We only drink mineral water. I hope you like *fromage de cochon*. Monsieur Ducos makes it himself. His chair won't go in the kitchen, and I put things in the hall for him."

I had joined her. "Thank you very much," I said. "I admit I'm hungry. *Thank* you." My hand came out of my pocket, but she showed me a palm. "No," she said, "you are guests"—and walked out.

There was a plate with a dozen slices of something, a long, slender loaf of bread, and the beer. Of course Pierre had told her that Nero Wolfe liked beer, and we were from Nero Wolfe, so she went out for beer. I would remember to tell him. We moved the table over by the bed, and I sat on the bed and Saul on the chair. There was no bread knife. Of course; you yank it off. No butter. The slices, *fromage de cochon*, which I looked up a week later, was head cheese, and I hope Fritz doesn't read this, because I'm going to state a fact: it was better than his. We agreed that it was the best head cheese we had ever tasted, and the bread was good enough to go with it. I told Saul I was glad we were getting something for the six double sawbucks I had given her.

Half an hour later it was looking as though that was all we were going to get. We looked at each other, and Saul said, "I skipped something. I didn't look close enough at the inside of the covers. Did you?" I said maybe not, and we each took a book, he from the top shelf and I from the middle one, and the third book I took, there it was. *The Feminine Mystique* by Betty Friedan. The inside of the back cover was pasted-on paper like all books, but it bulged a little in the middle and at the outside edge the edge of another paper showed, about a sixty-fourth of an inch. I got out my knife and opened the small thin blade. Saul put his book back on the shelf and said, "Easy does it," and I didn't even glance at him, which showed the condition we were in. We never say things like that to each other.

I went easy all right. It took a good five minutes to make sure that it was glued down tight except for a small part in the middle, a rectangle about one inch by an inch and a half, where the little bulge was. Then came the delicate part, getting under to the edge of whatever made the bulge. That took another five minutes, but once I had the edge it was simple. I slit along to the corner, then across the end and down the other side, and across the other end. And there it was. A piece of thin paper glued to the paper that had bulged, with writing on it in ink. I am looking at it right now, and the other day I took a picture of it with my best camera to reproduce here:

Orrie Cather
127 E. 94

I handed it to Saul, and he took a look and handed it back and said, "She wrote it."

"Sure. The one Pierre found on the tray, Orrie gave him a hundred dollars for it. That was four days after the dinner, so Pierre had it four days. I said a week ago that she found it and made a copy of it, and she would try to put the squeeze on him and would get killed. ESP." I got out my card case and slipped the piece of paper in under cellophane.

I stood up. "Have you got a program? I have. I'm not going to report in person. I'm going to the nearest phone booth."

"I don't suppose I could listen in?"

"Sure, why not?"

We took a look around. Everything was in order except the table, which was still by the bed, and we put it back where it belonged. Saul took our coats and the book, and I took the tray. We found Marie in the kitchen, which was about one-fourth the size of Wolfe's. I told her the bread and wonderful head cheese had saved our lives, that we hadn't found what we had hoped to find, and that we were taking just one thing, a book that we wanted to have a good look at because it might tell us something. She wouldn't let me pay for the book, because Miss Ducos was dead and they didn't want it. She declined my offer to let her go through our pockets and came to the door to let us out. All in all, we had got my money's worth.

Out on the sidewalk I told Saul, "I said the nearest phone booth, but if you listen in it will be crowded. How about your place?" He said fine, and that his car was parked in the lot near Tenth Avenue, and we headed west. He doesn't like to talk when he's driving any more than I do, but he'll listen, and I told him about the uninvited guest who had come that morning, and he said he wished he had been there, he would have liked to have a look at her.

We left the car in the garage on Thirty-ninth Street where he keeps it and walked a couple of blocks. He lives alone on the top floor of a remodeled house on Thirty-eighth Street between Lexington and Third. The living room is big, lighted with two floor lamps and two table lamps. One wall had windows, one was solid with books, and the other two had doors to the closet and hall, and pictures, and shelves that were cluttered with everything from chunks of minerals to walrus tusks. In the far corner was a grand piano. The telephone was on a desk between windows. He was the only operative in New York who asked and got twenty dollars an hour that year, and he had uses for it.

When I sat at the desk and started to dial, he left for the bedroom, where there's an extension. It was a quarter past four, so Wolfe would be down from the plant rooms. Fritz might answer, or he might; depended on what he was doing.

"Yes?" Him.

"Me. I have a detailed report. I'm with Saul at his place. I didn't take Mrs. Bassett home. At a quarter past twelve I started to search the room of Lucile Ducos. At half past, Saul came and offered to help me. Marie Garrou brought us a plate of marvelous head cheese, for which I paid her a hundred and twenty dollars. I mention that so you won't have to ask if I have eaten. At half past three we found a slip of paper which Lucile had hidden in a book, on which she had written Orrie's name and address. I knew it was Orrie last night when you mentioned what Hahn and Igoe had said about Bassett's obsession on his wife. Saul says you thought I would kill him — that you *knew* I would. Nuts. You may be a genius, but nuts. I once looked genius up in that book of quotations. Somebody said that all geniuses have got a touch of madness. Apparently yours—"

"Seneca."

"Apparently your touch of madness picks on me. That will have to be discussed someday. Now there is a problem, and finding that slip of paper in one of her books—it was *The Feminine Mystique* by Betty Friedan, and I've got it—that settles it, and Saul won't have to do any more digging. As I said, I'm at his place. Fred will be expecting word from you; he won't be working. We're going to have him come, and we'll decide what to do, us three. I have an idea, but we'll discuss it. As far as I'm concerned, you're out of it. You told us your emotions had taken over on Nixon and Watergate, and they have certainly taken over on this—what you thought you knew about me. So. I won't hang up; I'll listen if you want to talk."

He hung up.

I went to the piano and spread my fingers to hit a chord that shows you've decided something, according to Lily. When I turned, Saul was standing there. He didn't say anything, just stood with his brows raised.

I spoke. "I was just following instructions. He instructed us to ignore his decisions and instructions."

"That's a funny sentence."

"I feel funny."

"So do I. Do you want to call Fred, or shall I?"

I said that since Fred was being invited to his place, I thought he should, and he went to the desk and dialed, and didn't have to wait for an answer. Fred must have been sticking near the phone. He would; he hates unfinished business more than either of us.

Saul hung up. "He's on his way. Half an hour, maybe less. Milk or bourbon or what?"

"Nothing, thanks, not right now. You heard me say I have an idea, but I need to take a good look at it before I share it. It's one hell of a problem. Have you got a script?"

"No. Not even a first draft. I want to give it a look too."

Daylight was about gone, and he went and turned on lights and pulled the window drapes. I went and sat on a chair at the table where we played poker. It was by far the worst mess I had ever looked at. If you went at it from one angle, some other angle tripped you up and you had to go back and start over. For instance, Jill, the airline hostess Orrie had married a few years ago when he had decided to settle down and quit trying to prove that Casanova had been a piker, as Saul had once put it. She still had a strong hold on him, and since she was now going to get a hell of a jolt, no matter how we handled it, why not use her? For another instance, Dora Bassett. I didn't know how she felt, about him now, but we could find out, and maybe we could use *her*. And three or four other angles. With any and all of them, of course the bottom question was could we possibly come out with a whole skin, all four of us? It was only when the doorbell rang and Saul went to let Fred in that I realized that I had just been shadow-boxing. No matter how we played it, one thing *had* to happen, and the surest and quickest way to that had to come first.

Saul, always a good host, had a couple of chairs in place in front of the couch and liquids on the coffee table — Ten Mile bourbon for Fred and me and brandy for him — and we sat and poured, Fred on the couch.

"I said on the phone," Saul told Fred, "that it's a powwow. Actually it's a council of war. Tell him, Archie."

"You tell him. You knew before I did."

"Only because Mr. Wolfe told me. But all right. Fred, Orrie Cather killed all three of them."

Fred nodded. "I know he did."

Saul stared at him and said, "What?" I stared and said, "That's the first time I ever heard you tell a double-breasted lie."

"It's not a lie, Archie. I knew it when he asked Mr. Wolfe to give him Lucile Ducos instead of Saul. Why didn't he know Mr. Wolfe wouldn't? That was crazy. Of course there was another thing too, he knew all about that room at Rusterman's. But it was his asking to take Lucile Ducos. That was absolutely cockeyed. Of course I knew I was wrong because Mr. Wolfe didn't know."

"I pass," Saul said. "I'm with Alice in Wonderland. First Archie follows instructions by ignoring instructions, and now you knew it was Orrie but you knew you were wrong."

"I pass too," I said. "All of you knew before I did. I'm out of my class. You talk, and I'll listen."

"You had a hurdle we didn't have," Saul said. "You knew Orrie wanted your job and thought he might get it. You've always gone easy on him, made allowances for him that Fred or I wouldn't make. It's in your reports. You had blinders that we didn't. *I* should have known. You said you had an idea and wanted to give it a good look, and the blinders are off now. Let's have it."

I took a sip of bourbon and a swallow of water. "I just *thought* I had an idea. I was just slashing around. Actually all I've got is facts. Two facts. One, Orrie has asked for it and has to get it. He has bought it, and it has to be delivered. Two, Nero Wolfe, the great detective, the genius, is hogtied. He can't make a move. If he goes by the book, collects the pieces and hands Cramer the package, he will have to get on the witness stand and answer questions under oath about a man he has used and trusted for years. He wouldn't do that, he would rather spend ten years behind bars than do that. You know damn well he wouldn't, and I'm glad he wouldn't. All of us would have to answer questions in public about a guy we have worked with and played pinochle with."

I swallowed bourbon, too big a swallow, and had to swallow air for a chaser. "I don't think he could stand the sight of Orrie Cather. That's why we had to meet here instead of at the office. An hour ago on the telephone I told him we were going to get Fred and decide what to do, and I asked him if he wanted to talk, and he hung up. If we walked into the office with Orrie, he would walk out. He couldn't take it. So we—"

"I'll tell you something," Fred said. "I don't think I could take it either. If he walked in here right now, I wouldn't walk out, I would kill him. I've got my gun, I always carry a gun at night now, but I wouldn't shoot him, I'd break his neck."

"We would all like to break his neck," Saul said, "but we've got necks too. Of course he has to get it, and it's up to us to deliver it, the question is how." He looked at me. "I thought that was the idea you wanted to look at."

I nodded. "We'll all look at it." I looked at my watch: 5:22. "I suggest that you ring him and invite him to come at nine o'clock. Just for a powwow. Okay, Fred?"

He lifted his glass, looked at it, and put it down. "I guess so. Hell, we have to, don't we?"

Saul got up and went to the desk and picked up the phone.

16

I wouldn't want to go through that again. I don't mean the three hours while we discussed it and decided what to do. The hour after he came, while we did it.

I'm not even sure we would have gone through with it if it hadn't been for the bomb. We felt silly, at least I did, standing there at the door of the apartment while he was on his way up the three flights, standing so he could only see Saul as he approached — Saul in the doorway to greet the arriving guest.

As I think I mentioned, Orrie was half an inch taller than me and fully as broad, without a flabby ounce on him. As he stepped in, we jumped him, Saul from the back and Fred and I from the sides, and pinned him. His reflex, his muscles acting on their own, lasted only half a second. Saul's arm was around his neck, locking him. No one said anything. Saul started to go over him from behind, first his right side and then his left. His topcoat wasn't buttoned. From under his left arm Saul took his gun, which was of course to be expected, and dropped it on the rug. Then from his inside breast pocket Saul's hand came out with something that was not to be expected because Orrie didn't smoke: an aluminum cigar tube. Don Pedro.

Fred said, "Jesus Christ."

As I said, without that I'm not sure we would have gone through with it. Saul made sure the cap was screwed on tight and put it in his own breast pocket and finished the frisking job. Fred and I turned loose and moved back, and Orrie turned and took a step. Going to leave. Actually. Saul was there and kicked the door shut. I said, "Hell, you might have known, Orrie. You *should* have known. Coming here with that in your pocket? What do you take us for?"

Fred said, "*You* said it, Saul. You said we had to jump him. Jesus Christ."

Saul said, "On in, Orrie. It's our deal."

I had never had the idea that Orrie Cather was dumb. He was no Saul Panzer, but he wasn't dumb. But he was dumb then. "What for?" he said. "All right, you've got it." His voice was almost normal, just squeezed a little. "I'm not going to blow. I'm going home."

"Oh, no, you're not," Fred said. "My god, don't you know it's coming and you've got to take it?"

Saul had picked up the gun, an old S & W .38 Orrie had had for years, and stuck it in his pocket. "On in, Orrie. We're going to talk." I took hold of his left arm. He jerked loose and took a step and kept going, to the arch and on into the big room. Saul got ahead of him and led the way across to the couch. The four of us had played pinochle in that room. We had tagged Paul Rago for murder in that room. Orrie took the chair in the middle, with Saul on his left and Fred on his right, and me on the couch. As Saul sat, he said, "Tell him, Archie."

"Fred has already told you," I told Orrie. "You've got to take it. We're not going to turn you in. I don't have to explain why that wouldn't —"

"You don't have to explain anything."

"Then I won't. I'll just tell you what we're going to do. We're going to make it impossible for you to live. I'm going to see Jill tomorrow, or Saul is. You're through with her. You're through with any kind of work, not only in New York. Anywhere in the world. You're through with any kind of contact with people that means anything. You know us and you know Nero Wolfe. We know what it will cost us, Nero Wolfe in money and us in time and effort, but that's what we have to pay for not realizing long ago that someday, somehow, we would be sorry we didn't cross you off. Exactly how —"

"You didn't have any reason to cross me off."

"Certainly we did. For instance, Isabel Kerr. Eight years ago. You got yourself in the can on a murder rap, and it was a job to get you out. And —"

"That was just a bad break. You know damn well it was."

"Skip it. It isn't just a bad break that you have killed three people. It isn't just—"

"You can't prove it. You can't prove a damned thing."

Fred said, "Jesus Christ." I said, "We don't have to prove it. We don't want to prove it. I told you, we're not going to turn you in, we're going to make it impossible for you to live. You've bought it, and we're going to deliver it. Actually, we *could* prove it, but you know what it would mean, especially for Nero Wolfe. We could probably prove the first one, Bassett. As you know, they have got the bullet that killed him, a thirty-eight, and the gun that fired it is probably now in Saul's pocket. And Pierre—"

"That was self-defense, Archie. Bassett was going to ruin me."

"Pierre wasn't going to ruin you."

"Yes, he was. When he learned about Bassett he remembered about me and the slip of paper. I had been damn fool enough to give him a hundred dollars for the slip of paper. He demanded a thousand dollars. A grand. He came that Sunday, two days after Bassett, and asked for a grand. He said that was all he wanted, he wouldn't come back, but you know how that is. You said once that all blackmailers ought to be shot."

"You didn't shoot him. Sunday? The next day or evening you went to that room at Rusterman's and put that thing in his coat pocket. Then his daughter was going to ruin you, and you shot her, and they've got that bullet too. You had another bomb, probably got two for the price of one, but you couldn't use it on her because she knew what had killed her father. And you brought it with you here tonight. I thought Saul did a good job with his voice on the phone, but I suppose after killing three people your nerves are on edge. And we *are* going to ruin you."

Saul got up and left the room. Sometimes a trip to the bathroom can't be postponed. But it wasn't the bathroom; his footsteps on the tiled hall floor went on to the kitchen. Fred rose and stretched his legs and sat down again. Orrie glanced up at him and then sent his eyes back to me. No one spoke. Footsteps again, and Saul was back. Instead of returning to his chair, he joined me and on the couch between us he put what he had gone for: a roll of adhesive tape, a pair of pliers, and a couple of paper towels. He got the Don Pedro cigar tube from his pocket, checked the cap again, gripped it in the middle with the pliers, wiped it good with a paper towel, laid it on the edge of the other paper towel, and rolled the towel around it, tucking in the ends. Then about a yard of adhesive tape, all the way with both ends covered. A very neat wrapping job, with an appreciative audience.

"We'll keep the gun," he said. "As you said, Archie, we're not going to turn him in, but we'll keep it just in case. But he can have this. Right?"

"Sure," I said. "Now that you've gift-wrapped it. Fred?"

"I guess so." Fred nodded. "Okay."

Saul got up and offered it, but Orrie didn't take it. His hands were on his knees, the curled fingers moving in and out a little as if they couldn't decide whether to make fists. He hadn't taken his topcoat off. Saul stepped to him, pulled open his topcoat and jacket, put the tube back where he had found it, in the inside breast pocket, and went to his chair. Orrie's hand went into the pocket and came out again, empty.

"Dora Bassett came to see us this morning," I told Orrie. "I took her up to my room, and we had a talk. I'll see Jill tomorrow, if she's not on a flight."

"I'll go along," Fred said. "I like Jill."

"I'll start with Del Bascom," Saul said. "Then Pete Vawter."

Orrie stood up and said, "I'm going to see Nero Wolfe."

We all stared at him. Fred said, "Jesus Christ." Saul said, "How are you going to get in?" I said, "He won't. Of course not. He's cracked."

Orrie turned and walked out. Saul got up and followed, and I tagged along, and Fred was right behind me. My mind was on a point of etiquette — should you open the door for a departing guest in whose pocket you have just put a bomb that you hope he'll use? Saul didn't; he stayed behind. Orrie not only opened the door, he pulled it shut after him, with us standing there. The spring lock clicked in place, but Saul slid the bolt, which was sensible. Orrie was good with locks, and he just might have ideas. Apparently no one felt like talking; we stood there.

"No bets," I said. "No bets either way."

"Me neither," Saul said. "Not a dime. If it takes a year, it will be a bad year for all of us. And you have a family, Fred."

"Right here and now," Fred said, "I've got me, and I'm empty. I could swallow some of that salami I turned down, if you can spare it."

"*That's* a bet," Saul said and headed for the kitchen.

17

AT a quarter past eleven Thursday morning I pushed the button at the door of the old brownstone for Fritz to come and slide the bolt. Behind my elbows were Saul and Fred. Fred had gone home to his own bed and come back at nine o'clock, but I had slept on the couch in Saul's living room. I hadn't overslept, and neither had Saul; we had turned on the radio at six and seven and eight and nine and ten, so we were well informed on current events. A little after ten I had called the *Gazette* and left word for Lon Cohen that I could be reached at Saul's place until eleven and then at the office. I hadn't called Wolfe. I had told him we were going to decide what to do, and let him think we were spending the night at it. For breakfast Saul and I had had two thick slices of broiled ham, six poached eggs, and about a dozen thin slices of buttered toast sprinkled with chives. Saul grows chives in a sixteen-inch box in his kitchen window.

It wouldn't be accurate reporting to say that Wolfe's mouth dropped open when he saw us walk in, but it might have, though it never had, if he hadn't heard our voices in the hall. What he did do, he put on an act. He finished a paragraph in a book he was reading, took his time inserting the thin strip of gold he used for a bookmark, put the book down, and said, "Good morning."

Saul went to the red leather chair, Fred pulled up a yellow one, and I went to my desk, sat, and said, "I have asked Saul to report. He was the host."

Saul said, "Fred came about an hour after Archie phoned you. I called Orrie and asked him to come at nine o'clock. We decided to try to make him kill himself. When he came we jumped him without warning. He had his gun as usual, and in a pocket of his jacket he had a Don Pedro cigar tube. We went in and sat down and talked for about half an hour. Mostly Archie talked. He told him we were going to make it impossible for him to live. Orrie said Bassett was going to ruin him and Pierre hit him for a thousand dollars. I sealed the cigar tube with adhesive tape and put it back in his pocket, but we kept his gun. He left a little before ten o'clock."

Wolfe said, "Satisfactory," but he said it only with his eyes. His mouth stayed shut tight. He leaned back and closed his eyes and breathed deep. Saul looked at me and was going to say something, but he didn't get it out because he was interrupted by a noise. Two noises. First the ring of the doorbell, and a moment later a shattering crack and clatter, somewhere close. We jumped and ran to the hall, Fred in front because he was closest. But in the hall he stopped and I passed him. As I neared the front door I slowed because the floor was covered with pieces of glass. There was nothing left of the glass panel in the door, three feet by four feet, but some jagged edges. I slid the bolt and opened the door enough to get through and stepped out.

Down on the sidewalk at the foot of the steps was Orrie Cather's topcoat. From up above that's just what it was, his topcoat. I went down the seven steps, and then I could see his face. There was nothing much wrong with his face. He had liked his face too much to hold it the way Pierre had held it. Nine days and ten hours had passed, two hundred and twenty-six hours, since I had stood and looked down at what had been Pierre's face.

I lifted my head, and Saul and Fred were there, one on each side. "Okay," I said, "stand by. I'm going in and ring Lon Cohen. I owe him something."

18

AT half past nine that evening Wolfe and I were leaving the dining room, an hour later than usual, for after-dinner coffee in the office, when the doorbell rang. Wolfe shot a glance at the front door. He didn't stop, but he had seen who it was, because I had stood my ground with Ralph Kerner of Town House Services and insisted that the temporary emergency job on the front door had to include some one-way glass. The bolt was a new one and wasn't well fitted. I slid it and opened up, and Inspector Cramer entered.

He gave me a funny look, as if he wanted to ask me a question but couldn't decide how to put it. Then he looked around, at the marks on the wall and bench and rack, and the floor mat. I said, "The glass. You should have seen it." He said, "Yeah, I bet," and headed down the hall. I followed.

He always goes straight to the red leather chair, but not that time. Three steps in he stopped and sent his eyes around, left to right and then right to left. Then he went to the big globe and turned it, in no hurry, clear around, first to the right and then to the left, while I stood and stared. Then he took off his coat and dropped it on a yellow chair, crossed to the red leather chair, sat, and said, "I've been wanting to do that for years. I don't think I've ever mentioned that it's the biggest and finest globe I ever saw. Also I've never mentioned that this is the best working room I know. The best-looking. I mention it now because I may never see it again."

"Indeed." Wolfe's brows were up. "Are you retiring? You're not old enough."

"No, I'm not retiring. Maybe I should. I'm not old enough, but I'm tired enough. But I'm not. But you are. You could call it retiring."

"Apparently you have been misinformed. Or are you guessing?"

"No, I'm not guessing." Cramer got a cigar from a pocket, not a Don Pedro, stuck it in his mouth and clamped his teeth on it, and took it out again. He hadn't lit one for years. "It's no go, Wolfe. This time you *are* done. Not only the DA, the Commissioner. I think he has even spoken to the Mayor. Is this being recorded?"

"Of course not. My word of honor if you need it."

"I don't." Cramer put the cigar between his teeth, took it out, threw it at my wastebasket, and missed by two feet. "You know," he said, "I don't really know how dumb you think I am. I never have known."

"Pfui. That's flummery. My knowledge of you is not mere surmise. I *know* you. Certainly your mental processes have limits, so have mine, but you are not dumb—your word—at all. If you were dumb, you would have in fact concluded that I am done—again, your word—and you wouldn't have come. You would have abandoned me to the vengeance of the District Attorney—perhaps with a touch of regret that you wouldn't have another chance to come and whirl that globe around."

"Goddam it, I didn't *whirl* it!"

"Spin, rotate, twirl, circumvolute—your choice. So why did you come?"

"*You* tell *me.*"

"I will. Because you suspected that I might not be done, there might be a hole I could wriggle out through, and you wanted to know where and how."

"That would be a wriggle. You wriggle?"

"Confound it, quit scorning my diction. I choose words to serve my purpose. Archie, tell Fritz he may bring the coffee. Three cups. Or would you prefer beer or brandy?"

Cramer said no, he would like coffee, and I went. Tired as I was after a long, hard day, including such items as telling Jill what had happened to Orrie, I didn't drag my feet. I too wanted to know where and how. When I went back in, Wolfe was talking.

". . . but I'm not going to tell you what I intend to do. Actually I don't intend to do anything. I'm going to loaf, drift, for the first time in ten days. Read books, drink beer, discuss food with Fritz, logomachize with Archie. Perhaps chat with you if you have occasion to drop in. I'm loose, Mr. Cramer. I'm at peace."

"Like hell you are. Your licenses have been suspended."

"Not for long, I think. When the coffee comes—"

It came. Fritz was there with the tray. He put it on Wolfe's desk and left. Wolfe poured, and he remembered that Cramer took sugar and cream, though it had been at least three years since he had had coffee with us. I got up and served Cramer and got mine, sat and stirred and took a sip, and crossed my legs, hoping that by bedtime I would be at peace too.

Wolfe took a swallow — he can take coffee hotter than I can — and leaned back. "I told you nine days ago," he said, "Tuesday of last week, that I was going to tell you absolutely nothing. I repeat that. I am going to tell you nothing. But if you care to listen, I'll make a supposition. I'll imagine a situation and describe it. Do you want me to?"

"You can start. I can always interrupt." Cramer took too big a sip of hot coffee. I was afraid he would have to spit it out, but his mouth and jaw worked on it and he got it down.

"A long and elaborate supposition," Wolfe said. "Suppose that five days ago, last Saturday, an accumulation of facts and observations forced me to surmise that a man who had been associated with me for years had committed three murders. The first item of that accumulation had come the morning Pierre Ducos died in my house when Archie — I drop the formality — Archie told me what Pierre had said when he arrived. He refused to give Archie any details; he would tell only me. Perhaps it was my self-esteem that made me give that item too little thought; Pierre said I was the greatest detective in the world. All is vanity."

He drank coffee. "The second item of the accumulation came Wednesday evening, a week ago yesterday, when Orrie Cather offered to donate his services, to take no pay. He made the offer first, before either Saul Panzer or Fred Durkin. That was out of character. For him it was remarkable. Shall I iterate and reiterate that this is merely a series of suppositions?"

"Hell no. You're just imagining it. Sure. Go ahead."

"The third item was an old fact. The best opportunity — the only one I knew of — for someone to put the bomb in Pierre's pocket had been when he was at work and his coat was in his locker at the restaurant. Orrie Cather was familiar with that room; he had once helped with an investigation there, and the lock would have been no problem for him. The fourth item was that Mrs. Harvey Bassett questioned a friend of hers about Archie Goodwin — had she seen him, and had he learned who had killed Pierre Ducos. The fifth item was that Mr. Bassett had an obsession about his wife — information supplied by two of the men who were at that dinner. It was at that point that I first thought it possible that Orrie Cather was somehow involved, for the sixth item was my knowledge of Orrie's contacts with women and his habitual conduct with them."

He emptied his cup and poured, and I took Cramer's cup and mine and got refills.

"As I said," Wolfe resumed, "it's a long and elaborate supposition. The seventh item was another mention of Mrs. Bassett by one of those men. The eighth item was another action out of character by Orrie Cather. With him present, I told Saul Panzer to see Lucile Ducos and try to learn if she knew anything and if so what, and Orrie suggested that he should see her instead of Saul. It was unheard of for him to suggest that he would be better than Saul for anything whatever. And the next day, last Saturday, came the ninth and last item. Lucile Ducos was shot and killed as she left her home that morning. That was conclusive. It pointed up all the other items, brought them into focus. It was no longer a conjecture that Orrie was implicated; it was a conclusion."

It certainly was a conclusion, the way he told it. Lucile had been killed five days ago. I should have known. We all should have known. I said some chapters back that you probably knew, but, as I also said, you were just reading it and we were in the middle of it. It was like getting the idea that a member of your family had committed three murders. A family affair. Would you have known?

Wolfe was going on. "One more supposition. Suppose that yesterday Archie and Saul, having arrived at the same conclusion, went to that apartment on Fifty-fourth Street and searched the room of Lucile Ducos and found something that your men had failed to find. Hidden in a book on her shelves was a slip of paper on which she had written Orrie Cather's name and address. That made it —"

"By God. I want that. You can't —"

"Pfui. This is supposition. That made it unnecessary for them to spend time and energy seeking further support for their conclusion. They went to Saul's apartment, got Fred to join them, discussed the situation, asked Orrie Cather to come, and when he came they told him how it stood and that they intended, with my help, to make it impossible for him to live. Also they took his gun and kept it."

Wolfe drank coffee and leaned back. "Here reality takes over from invention. This you already know. At half past eleven o'clock this morning Orrie Cather rang my doorbell and was hurtled down to the sidewalk, dead. Evidently he had two of those bombs, since Sergeant Stebbins has told me that scraps of aluminum have been found similar to those found ten days ago on the floor of that room upstairs. Also evidently he didn't wait to see if he would be admitted, because he knew he wouldn't be."

He straightened up and emptied his second cup and reached to put it on the tray. "There's more coffee, still hot, if you would like some. I've finished."

Cramer was staring at him. "And you say you're going to loaf. Drift. It's incredible. *You're* incredible. You're at peace. Good God."

Wolfe nodded. "You haven't had time to consider it from either angle. First your angle. Assume that Orrie Cather is alive and this conversation has not taken place. Where would you stand? Not only would you have no evidence against him; you wouldn't even suspect that he was involved." He turned to me. "What odds would you give that he would never suspect it?"

"A hundred to one. At least."

Back to Cramer. "And you should have. The one item of solid evidence, one that would have been persuasive for a jury, was the slip of paper with Orrie's name on it, which Lucile Ducos had hidden in a book. Your men searched her room and didn't find it. Archie and Saul did find it. You don't know now whether it has been destroyed or is there in my safe. With me, and Archie and Saul and Fred and Orrie, standing mute, you would not only have no evidence, you would have no suspicion. Orrie would be in no jeopardy and almost certainly never would be. In time you would add three to your list of unsolved homicides."

Cramer just sat with his jaw clamped. Of course what really hurt was the slip of paper they had missed. If they had found it — No. I prefer not to put in black and white what it would have been like if they had found it.

"Apparently," Wolfe said, "you don't wish to comment. So much for your angle. Now the other angle — the District Attorney. Orrie Cather is *not* alive. Assume that when you leave here you go to the District Attorney — No, it's past ten o'clock. Assume that in the morning you go to him and report this conversation. Even assume that it is being recorded on a contraption on your person —"

"You know damn well it isn't."

"Assume that it is, and you give it to him. With Orrie Cather dead, what can he do? He can't prefer charges against him, even for three murders. He would of course like to get us, all four of us — have our bail rescinded, lock us up, put us on trial, and convict us. Convict us of what? Not of murder; no murder will have been legally established. It can't be legally established without someone to charge and convict. Establish a murder by charging us with complicity, and us standing mute? Pfui. Somehow manage to get a report, even a tape recording, of this conversation, into an action of law? Again pfui. I had merely amused myself by inventing a rigmarole of suppositions. I had cozened you."

He turned a palm up. "Being a resourceful man, he could probably pester us, though I don't know exactly how. He has his position and his staff, the power and prestige of his office, but I have resources too. I have ten million people who like to be informed and diverted, and a comfortable relationship with a popular newspaper. If he chooses to try to get satisfaction, I'll try to make him regret it." He turned to me again. "Archie, what odds that we'll have our licenses back before the end of the year?"

I lifted my shoulders and let them down. "Offhand, I'd say twenty to one."

Back to Cramer. "That will be satisfactory for me. I am already in an uncomfortably high tax bracket for the year and would take no jobs anyway. If you want to ask questions about my elaborate supposition, I may answer them."

"I want to ask one. How did she hide the slip of paper in the book? Put it in between the pages?"

"No. She put it on the inside of the back cover, face down, and pasted a sheet of paper over it."

"What's the title of the book?"

"*The Feminine Mystique,* by Betty Friedan. I read about a third of it."

"Where is it?"

Wolfe flipped a hand. "I suppose it has been destroyed."

"Balls. You wouldn't. Wolfe, I want that book. And the slip of paper."

"Mr. Cramer." Wolfe cocked his head. "You haven't reflected. If you reprimand the men who searched that room for misfeasance, whether or not you show them the slip of paper and the book, where will you be? You'll be committed. You will have to report this entire conversation to the District Attorney, of course telling him that you think it was a collection not of suppositions but of facts. You may decide to report it to him anyway, but I doubt it. As I said, your mental processes have limits, but you are not dumb. You would probably be prodded into a long and difficult investigation the couldn't possibly have an adequate result — for instance, you might discover how Mr. Bassett learned Orrie Cather's name and address, but then what? No matter what you discover, even what solid evidence you get, the dominant fact, that Orrie Cather is dead, will remain."

"And you killed him. Your men killed him on your order."

Wolfe nodded. "I won't challenge your right to put it like that. Of course I would put it differently. I might say that the ultimate responsibility for his death rests with the performance of the genes at the instant of his conception, but that could be construed as a rejection of free will, and I do *not* reject it. If it pleases you to say that I killed him, I won't contend. You have worked hard on it for ten days and should have *some* satisfaction."

"Satisfaction my ass." He stood up. "Yes, ten days. I'll reflect on it all right." He went and got his coat and put it on and came back, to the corner of Wolfe's desk, and said, "I'm going home and try to get some sleep. You probably have never had to try to get some sleep. You probably never will."

He turned, saw the globe, and went and whirled it so hard that it hadn't quite stopped when he was through to the hall. When the sound came of the front door closing, Wolfe said, "Will you bring brandy, Archie? And two glasses. If Fritz is up, bring him and three glasses. We'll try to get some sleep."